THE FOUR ADVENTURES OF
Richard Hannay

JOHN BUCHAN

The Four Adventures of Richard Hannay

THE THIRTY-NINE STEPS
GREENMANTLE · MR. STANDFAST
THE THREE HOSTAGES

with an introduction by Robin W. Winks

DAVID R. GODINE · *Publisher*
BOSTON

This book contains the complete texts of
John Buchan's four Richard Hannay novels:
THE THIRTY-NINE STEPS, GREENMANTLE,
MR. STANDFAST, THE THREE HOSTAGES

First U. S. edition published in 1988 by
DAVID R. GODINE, PUBLISHER
Post Office Box 450
Jaffrey, New Hampshire 03452
www.godine.com

This edition originally published in the U.K. by Hodder and Stoughton

Library of Congress Cataloging-in-Publication Data
Buchan, John, 1875–1940.
The four adventures of Richard Hannay.
Contents: The first adventure of the Thirty-nine steps—
The second adventure of Greenmantle—
The third adventure of Mr. Standfast—[etc.]
1. Hannay, Richard (Fictitious character)—Fiction.
2. Spy stories, English. I. Title
PR6003.U13A6 1988 823'.912 86-45583
ISBN 0-87923-871-2

FOURTH SOFTCOVER PRINTING 2002
Printed in Canada

JOHN BUCHAN: *Stalking the Wilder Game*

John Buchan was already a highly regarded writer when at characteristic speed he wrote the first adventure of Richard Hannay. *The Thirty-Nine Steps*, the book often said to have established the basic formula for the spy (or conspiracy) thriller, was Buchan's twenty-sixth book. There would be five Hannay novels[1] out of well over a hundred books written by John Buchan, and though they would be his most popular work, they were not invariably his best. *Steps* would sell twenty-five thousand copies within six months of publication in 1915 and over a million copies in Buchan's lifetime. Yet none of the Hannay books took Buchan long to write—indeed, no book can have taken him long, for from the publication of his first serious short stories while he was still in his teens until his death at sixty-four, he averaged three books a year—and he tended to be dismissive of his "shockers," calling them "precipitous yarns." He did not really mean this self-deprecation, however, and he was pleased with the praise his Hannays brought him and glad of the pleasure he knew they gave others. Those critics who believed Buchan meant it when he dismissed the Hannay books as tales for boys did not know their man very well. Buchan poured some of his best writing, and a good bit of his most sincere thought, into the four books reprinted here.

In many ways Buchan was the last of the Victorians, though he was still a young man when Queen Victoria died. He believed deeply in the British Empire, in Scotland (and England), in the precepts of his Presbyterian upbringing, and in the energizing power of the democratic intellect. But to each of these threads of common Victorian belief he brought his own rather special view. Readers who are determined to see Buchan as the epitome of conventional imperial, Victorian, and Edwardian views can find evidence of that conventionality in his most popular work, but those who trouble to read him entire will discover an unconventional mind. Though Buchan did believe in hard work—this was Victorian, though also the natural effect of growing up in a Calvinistic household—and in duty, integrity, and courage, Victorian Britain scarcely held a monopoly on these virtues. He was highly productive in part because he had to be (he needed the income his successful books brought in) and in part because the hint of teacher and preacher in him required an outlet. Most of all, however, he wrote because he enjoyed writing, and because putting words on paper helped him to make his thoughts clear to himself as well as to others. When friends and fans wrote to him, as they did in abundance after each of the Hannay books appeared, to wonder at how he could get so much done—for not only were these a small fraction of his total output, his writing as a whole was only one aspect of his total career, and all phases were, generally, going on simultaneously—he invariably replied that the books hardly took any time at all, and no psychic energy, for they were simply so much fun to do.

Perhaps it is because the books were fun—fun to write, fun to read, fun for others to imitate—that Buchan has been taken less seriously as an author than he warrants. He was, after all, a distinguished historian. His life of the Marquis of Montrose, published the year before *The Thirty-Nine Steps*, was widely reviewed as a remarkable work by a mature historian (though there were critics who felt it was partisan), and wanting to get his sums right, Buchan returned to Montrose again in 1928. There were well-received lives of Caesar (in 1932) and Sir Walter Scott (also 1932), of Cromwell (in 1934) and of Augustus (in 1937). There was a great deal of first-rate military history, much of it written more or less at the same time as the Hannay novels, and there was lively and well-informed local history too. His life of Lord Minto, a key figure in the history of the Empire, and especially for Canada and India, which appeared in 1924—the same year as *The Three Hostages*, the last of the Hannay volumes reprinted here—would not be improved upon until archives were opened and scholarship was organized along the assault-team lines of the modern university history department: that is, until the 1960s.

But even were Buchan to be measured solely by his fiction, he would still stand well forward in the ranks of his contemporaries. Too often he is dismissed—for dismissal it is—by being linked with H. Rider Haggard and G. A. Henty on the one hand or with the so-called "Clubland Heroes" (Dornford Yates, Herman Cyril McNeile, who as "Sapper" created Bulldog Drummond, and in lineage thereafter The Saint, Ian Fleming, ad infinitum) on the other. This is not the company he rightfully keeps. His natural forebears are Robert Louis Stevenson and Sir Arthur Conan Doyle, and despite all the action that marks his adventure stories when viewed in short focus, in his treatment of character he has more in common with Anthony Powell and C. P. Snow than with the romantic novelists of empire.

Precisely because he wished to tell a good story—that is, to entertain, an honorable intention—and did so superbly in the language of his day, Buchan often is not read closely enough. All writers create their fictions out of three sources: imagination, experience, and research. Buchan drew on all in equal measure. But he was also an alert, deeply read man of sensitive taste, who understood that he could bring even more pleasure to a wider audience (and, no doubt, to himself) by being mindful of the levels at which all serious fiction speaks. With his second Hannay novel, *Green-mantle*, Buchan is working on three levels at once: the level of the pure adventure yarn, quite suitable to be read aloud to a classroom of thirteen-year-old boys; the tough-minded, adult novel (Stumm, in *Greenmantle*, is pretty obviously homosexual, not a theme to be explored in a "boy's book"); and an intense examination (a bit later we would say a symbolic inquiry) into the nature of good and evil. It seems incredible that anyone could read these books and think them innocent, for all the dirt of human life is here; it is equally incredible that one could read *Mr. Standfast* and not recognize that Buchan has drawn his moral, and ultimately the character of the mature Hannay, directly from John Bunyan's *Pilgrim's Progress*.

Buchan assumed his readers would recognize his title and see the parallels as he developed them; for the few who might not, he closed *Mr. Standfast* with an apposite scene, and a lengthy quotation, from Bunyan's work.

But times change. Buchan's Hannay books were written virtually within the time-frame in which they take place. *Greenmantle*, which closes with a stirring attack by Russian troops on German and Ottoman forces in eastern Turkey, was published in 1916, before Russia had withdrawn from the war. *Mr. Standfast* depicts the battle at Amiens, and turns on the desperate need to get knowledge of the German plans for the second Battle of the Somme into British hands, only months after these events took place. Buchan was writing out of the headlines, and we cannot understand him unless we understand that. He requires the sensitivities of the historically aware, not the contentious appraisal of the fashionable. He did not write for a time when schools no longer taught John Bunyan. Indeed, one wonders what he would make of a Lecturer in English from a University in his own country who could, in 1985, while tracing the ancestry of John Le-Carré's disillusioned, duty-bound George Smiley, note that Smiley uses the nom de plume of Mr. Standfast and direct the allusion to "Buchan's nationalistic spy adventure," apparently unaware that the source is Bunyan.

In any event, Buchan seems not to be much read any longer by those who take themselves very seriously, or, if read, he is misread to prove some point urgent to the present rather than to the world in which Buchan lived. He is accused of being nationalistic, he is linked in any number of histories of the British Empire to a variety of jingoists, he is said to be anti-Semitic (a famous attack, this), a racist, a defender of apartheid—all of those invidious qualities that a defender of the empire surely must display. He was, in fact, none of these in the sense that we mean them today.

These charges against Buchan generally rest on the assumption that Richard Hannay was Buchan's true voice. But then, were this so, Edward Leithen would have to be Buchan's other true voice. No doubt there is some validity in these assumptions: Hannay was the man of action, little given to introspection, intensely loyal to his own ideas of fair play, engaged in a psychological as well as physical journey across a challenging and threatening landscape. Leithen is introduced in *The Power-House*, Buchan's first shocker, and he is the focus of *Sick Heart River* (*Mountain Meadow* in the United States, 1941), Buchan's last such book. (The first Leithen adventure appeared in *Blackwood's* magazine in 1913, though not as a book until 1916, so that *The Thirty-Nine Steps* is often mistakenly identified as Buchan's first thriller.) Leithen is a man of introspection, the man of thought, loyal to his ideas, caught up in a spiritual journey over an equally challenging and threatening landscape of the mind. Certainly Buchan did see himself balanced between the two—the classical mind/body problem—as he wrestled with his own religious convictions and with his physical self which, as he was often ill, made his long, furious walks all the more important to him. But Buchan was far more than Hannay and Leithen, and to extrapolate the fullness of Buchan's beliefs from their remarks is a mistake. In any event, the game falls at the outset, for one may not make a convincing case for describing even Hannay as anti-Semitic, racist, or jingoist.

Let us take these charges as they arise. Of what does Richard Hannay/ John Buchan's anti-Semitism consist? One may read the four novels brought together here and mark the passages that may be construed in this vein. There are, by my count, twenty such passages in over six hundred pages of prose. Each is precisely that, a passage, not a sustained statement. Admirers of Buchan frequently seek to take him off the ugly hook of anti-Semitism by the defense of context, claiming that passing remarks about Jew money-lenders were commonplace in his day, or that had he not made them, his books would have seemed unreal to his audience. Such a defense is unnecessary, however, though a word about context is nonetheless useful.

Words have meaning only in context, and the reader's responsibility is to know the context. Consider this exchange, which takes place in the margins of a book on the shelf of the library at Yale University. The book is on intelligence—spies, if you will—and its use in time of war or the threat of war, a subject John Buchan knew a good bit about, knowledge that he used (especially in terms of what is now called tradecraft) in his Hannay adventures. The book is *Strategic Intelligence for American World Policy*; it is by Sherman Kent, a professional historian who had helped create the Research and Analysis branch of the Office of Strategic Services during World War II. Published in 1949, Kent's book was the first major American contribution to the theory of intelligence, and it is still read for its theoretical analysis as well as an historic document. Kent had written, ". . . [an intelligence staff] is made up of men whose patterns of thought are likely to color their hypotheses and whose colored hypotheses are likely to make one conclusion more attractive than the evidence warrants." In other words, we are all creatures of our times. As an historian Kent was well aware of this, and he also knew that the truism applied to his own work. Then follows the running debate in the margin, penciled in by readers—one need not assume they are students, merely readers given to acting out on a library book—next to the word *men* in the quotation: "What is this asshole's problem?" In bold hand follows a reply, "What's yours?" A third hand takes up the argument: "Seriously, fucking psuedo-feminist. I'm a woman and I understand that this book was written in 1949! Cool out Bitch!" A fourth voice has the last word: "Exactly. Context, ever heard of that?"

What might Buchan have made of this exchange? The words would not have shocked him: he engaged in a considerable correspondence with Ezra Pound when the poet was at his most anarchic (and anti-Semitic), and Pound did not spare the presumably staid and by then very highly placed Buchan his vocabulary, while Buchan replied calmly, chiding Pound toward the end for his bias.[2] Rather, if lines from *The Thirty-Nine Steps* were thrown in his face decades later (indeed, decades after he was dead) as evidence of his anti-Semitism, Buchan too might have muttered something about context. For the lines most often quoted occur very early in the novel, when "an American, from Kentucky," Mr. Frederick Scudder, declares that "the Jew" is behind an international capitalist conspiracy. "The Jew is everywhere," Scudder confides to Richard Hannay, for the Jew has been so persecuted, he was now not far down the backstairs of any movement by which he might get his own back—behind the Germans, the anarchists, even the "elegant young man who talks Eton-and-Harrow English." The real boss, says Scudder, is "a little white-faced Jew in a bath-chair with an eye like a rattlesnake."

Now this is fairly nasty, though unhappily also fairly standard, stuff of its kind, and one might have thought that a reader could see that Scudder is a bit of a conspiracy bug, the kind of man who might be found running around in a small town in Kentucky in a white sheet. True, he is also courageous, but then Buchan never confuses moral evil with physical cowardice, even his worst villains proving to have an abundance of courage: only the reader who believes Buchan was writing for children would conclude that, by giving Scudder some courage and a bit of intelligence on matters about which he is not a crank, Buchan is approving the words he puts into Scudder's mouth. Hannay obviously thinks Scudder a bit odd, reminding him that Scudder's "Jew-anarchists seemed to have got left behind a little," a nice example of Hannay's straightforward use of a crank's argument to parody him. Later Sir Walter Bullivant, clearly the voice of calm reason in *Steps*, dismisses Scudder's judgment and attests to his "odd biases." But no, a reader intent on finding anti-Semitism in Hannay—who, being a white South African, must, after all, be a racist as well—will find it here in words that Hannay clearly disapproves, and will then argue that Buchan believes as Hannay has been said to believe. Buchan may have been anti-Semitic—though I do not believe it, and I have been through his private papers and found nothing to support such a view—but it is not possible to sustain such a charge from passages like this, and the nineteen others like it. One might as well call Buchan anti-American because he makes his principal American figure, John Blenkiron, sound like a grammatical fool. When Hannay returns to Scudder, and finds him dead, and takes Scudder's notebook, he concludes that "the little man had told me a pack of lies. All his yarns about the Balkans and the Jew-Anarchists . . . were eyewash. . . ."

Hannay, and by extension Buchan, are racists, we are told. Again, the evidence is hard to find. True, Hannay not only approves of but has enormous affection for the old Boer Pieter Pienaar, who plays a central rôle in *Greenmantle* and *Mr. Standfast,* and Pienaar may harbor the conventional Boer views of the black African. He refers to them as Kaffirs, now a term of abuse, though not clearly so in 1916, and surely the word an old trekker would use. Once Hannay refers to a "nigger," though again context is all, and the context is an African reminiscence. He is given plenty of other opportunities to use racist language and takes none of them: he had killed a few men himself, he says, in the Matabele War, and we can be certain they were black men, though he simply calls them men. Time and again he praises the courage, resourcefulness, and knowledge of his black trackers in the African veldt, and he is pleased to use, and to credit, the knowledge he gained in Mashonaland, and Damaraland, and amongst the Zulu. Where is the racism in this? Anyone who has read Buchan's work on the South African War, or on Milner and the Kindergarten, or on the Canadian North, will know that he does not condescend to native peoples.

As for the jingoism, unless intending that one's own nation is to win in time of war is jingoistic, there is precious little in these books to sustain such a charge. The enemy often emerges as brave, fully as talented, as committed to victory as is "our side." There is no virulent anti-German hectoring in these or in Buchan's other books. In *Greenmantle,* in the midst of the war, the Kaiser is dealt with quite sympathetically. Partially to keep the press at Nelson's, his publisher, fully employed, Buchan launched a massive project, a twenty-four-volume *History of the War,* to appear in fortnightly parts, each volume fifty thousand words in length, and though the volumes often came out within weeks of the events Buchan described in them, while emotions ran high, he did not lapse into patriotic cant. The series was widely praised for its sense of battle, for its objectivity, and for its evenhandedness, all in terse, cool prose. Bad British leadership was pointed out, good German generalship was praised, no evil empire was adduced. In his politics, as in his fiction, Buchan was scarcely a jingoist. Nor, of course, was Kipling, that other much misquoted (or at least misconstrued) laureate of empire.

To be sure, Buchan was, as we all are, a product of his times. There are attitudes in the Hannay books, attitudes about patriotism, or women, or religion, which are not those generally held today. He is not very adept, by modern standards, at handling romance. Today we would find it hard to credit a Richard Hannay who, when seated next to Hilda von Einem, the stirring, dangerous, and evil figure who lurks behind the Greenmantle, feels uncomfortable because he has never been in a motor-car with a lady before. But a man schooled in the South African bush as Hannay had been, a mining engineer and a military man, might well never have known a woman, in the Biblical or other sense, and ludicrous as one might find the scene were it to occur in 1987, it did not: it takes place in 1916. Some commentators criticize Buchan for not writing as the spy novelist writes today. He was not writing today, and the reader who requires that his adventure must seethe with sex ought, as a general rule, to read very little before, say, the 1930s or even later.

Buchan knew his world extremely well. We can enter that world through the door he holds open to us. There are worlds he did not know, and if they are our destination we must choose another guide. He knew nature, and the smell of Scotland, and the wet-dog odor of a British country house. He knew Whitehall, and Oxford, and publishing. He knew Fleet Street, and journalism broadly, and wartime intelligence. He knew politics, and he knew the empire at first hand. He knew Norway, and the islands, and Canada. He knew the classics, and Calvin, and the law of taxation. This was quite a bit to know, and he brought it all to bear in his writing. Best of all, he worked hard at knowing himself, and that too comes through in the books. But we should not forget that, as much as he enjoyed writing them, he did not earn his main merit-badges in life from his shockers. These came from public service. He became Lord Tweedsmuir, and Governor-General of Canada, and he collected honorary degrees from Harvard and Yale, for reasons that went far beyond Richard Hannay. Yet Hannay reveals these reasons too.

*   *   *   *

John Buchan is the father of the modern spy thriller. This is so even though the Hannay books are not, strictly speaking, about spies at all in the professional sense of the word. They are about penetration of the enemy, about lonely escape and wild journeys, about the thin veneer that stands between civilization and barbarism even in the most elegant drawing-room in London. Buchan wrote the formula, and from the appearance of *The Thirty-Nine Steps* until the rise of the disillusioned spy, of the man who has discovered that there is no moral difference between "us" and "them"— that is, until John LeCarré's third book, in 1963, *The Spy Who Came in From the Cold*—the formula remained tied to Buchan. The formula was not well understood, certainly, for most books that appeared under the confident declaration that they were "in the Buchan mold" bore only surface resemblance to that mold, but it was there, a goal to be attained by the few.

Because Buchan's shockers were seen as formulaic, they tended to be dismissed by "serious" critics, who also dismissed western, detective, mystery, and later science fiction because, it was said, they were written to a formula. Most were and are, it is true, and most are dismissible, unless one is a student of popular culture. But just as a precedent does not truly exist until it is followed—one cannot know that a precedent is a precedent until a second occurrence—the person who invents a formula is not to be blamed when his invention becomes formulaic. It is not, after all, a formula until it is followed by others. One would not charge Whitman with the tawdry on the ground that many a tawdry poet tried to imitate his "barbaric yawp." Buchan wrote the words and set them to his own music.

What is the Buchan formula? *The Thirty-Nine Steps* shows the formula at its most pure, for the subsequent Hannay novels depart in some measure from it. Take an attractive man, not too young—Hannay is thirty-seven in *Steps,* two years younger than Buchan when he began to write the book— and not too old, since he must have the knowledge of maturity and substantial experience on which he will draw while being able to respond to the physical rigors of chase and pursuit. Let the hero, who appears at first to be relatively ordinary, and who thinks of himself as commonplace, be drawn against his best judgment into a mystery he only vaguely comprehends, so that he and the reader may share the growing tension together. Set him a task to perform: to get the secret plans, let us say, from point A to point B, or to bring the news from Ghent to Aix. Place obstacles in his path—the enemy, best left as ill-defined as possible, so that our hero cannot be certain who he might trust. See to it that he cannot turn to established authority for help, indeed that the police, the military, the establishment will be actively working against him.

Then set a clock ticking: the hero must get from point A to point B in a sharply defined time, a time-frame known to both pursuer and pursued. In *Steps* we are informed at the outset that it is May 19; on May 24 the clock starts: Hannay reckons that he must stay on the move for three weeks, the first twenty days in hiding if possible, with a single day then left to complete his task. Be certain that pursuit takes place across a marginally familiar ground, so that the reader may identify with it, though be equally certain that the ground is sufficiently exotic to test the mettle of both sides in the Great Game. The winner will be the person with the resourcefulness to use the environment to his advantage, to go to ground *with* rather than against the landscape. Thus the locale is of the greatest importance, not simply because it may be exotic, or vaguely threatening, but because it is in reality the third player in the game, a great, neutral (and therefore, to the harried, apparently malevolent) landscape. The hero may possess some esoteric knowledge from what proves to be a more unconventional past than we had at first suspected—he will know how to throw a Mashona hunting-knife into the air and catch it between his lips, just so! or how to render an opponent unconscious by pressing precisely here, behind the ear. At stake will be the salvation of the world, or the future of Britain, which for the purposes of fiction is to be seen as much the same thing. The device is then wound up and set in motion.

Buchan's sense of place is acute, and he makes that sense work for his readers in the manner of Conan Doyle. Through landscape Buchan establishes a sense of moral as well as natural order: the forest cover, the streams (always called by their appropriate Scots, or Irish, or Afrikaans word), the mountains and lakes of the country. By establishing the kind of place in which the action will occur, Buchan subtly tells the reader how to react to any disturbance within that place, within its natural order. Just as Doyle's descriptions of the Grimpen Mire and the Devonshire moor in *The Hound of the Baskervilles* establish far more than mere mood, by showing us landscape as moral environment, so does Buchan invest the simple movement of a branch in the wind with a sense of menace. Doyle warned his reader explicitly: "Life has become like that great Grimpen Mire, with little green patches everywhere into which one may sink and with no guide to point the track." Buchan made the same point a bit differently, on this occasion speaking of the streets of London as landscape, in *The Power-House*: "You think that a wall as solid as the earth separates civilization from barbarism. I tell you the division is a thread, a sheet of glass." Thus the environment becomes a series of dramatic contrasts reflecting human nature.

Buchan, and those later writers, all British, who most successfully followed in his footsteps—Geoffrey Household, who at his best is equally good; Michael Gilbert, who is almost always at his best and more creditable since he does not, as Buchan was shamelessly content to do, lean on coincidence to move the plot along; the young Alastair MacLean before he began to repeat himself and to grow sloppy in his research—often add a further turn to the screw. This is the theme of the watcher in the shadows, the sense that yet another party is in the game, another sentient human being who will use the environment even more effectively than the original protagonists, a player whose motives we cannot guess. With (or, in the hands of a truly skillful writer, even without) this dimly seen, portentous figure, the tables may be turned, the hunter becomes the hunted, the reader a virtual participant, the historian himself the object of inquiry.

All of this works at two, often three, levels of awareness at once, quite apart from the possibility of an equal number of levels of meaning. There is the purely visual: one can see the action taking place almost cinematically (one wonders why Steven Spielberg or Peter Weir have not tried, in their very different ways, to make a film of *Greenmantle* or *Mr. Standfast*). Buchan is a master at working this level to great effect, for his lucid stage directions make even the most complex action explicable. (Buchan's description of the Russian capture of Erzerum, at the end of *Greenmantle*, was widely praised by those who had witnessed the event.) There is the purely visceral: the prickling at the back of the scalp, the *frisson* that makes one put another log on the fire, pull the comforter up higher, reach for that glass of single malt. Again, Buchan is supremely good at this, for he is at heart a teller of tales, as his neglected short stories clearly show: the story told around the campfire, the ear alert to whatever it is that can be heard moving just outside the circle of light, the hint of animals on the prowl, of H. P. Lovecraft and even Poe that requires building, and then reducing, tension, so that a novel is in fact a series of discrete episodes, of tales linked by the necessity of movement and by the inexorable ticking of that clock. And then there is the level of intellectual awareness, of a philosophy displayed, a code of ethics demonstrated, of words chosen to just the right effect (or on occasion to poor effect, as changing times render certain images less effective), of a mind at work—the protagonist's, the author's, the reader's.

One other element to be found in Buchan, though generally not essential to the formula, is the presence of a Mr. Big, a super-criminal who seeks to destroy civilization or, through greed, to capture the world's markets, the world's supply of secret weapons, above all the world's attention. The man with the hooded eyes in *Steps* gives way to Hilda von Einem in *Greenmantle*, to the Graf von Schwabing in *Mr. Standfast*, to Medina in *The Three Hostages*. Many espionage thrillers have been written without a Mr. Big; those writers who are otherwise the rightful heirs to the Buchan mantle— Household and Gilbert—almost never use the device. But it is a respectable part of the inheritance, nonetheless, as shown by the almost invariable presence of just such a figure in the highly successful novels of Ian Fleming.

Goldfinger, Dr. No, Blofeld, these men who, in Fleming's fiction, threaten the world, are the lineal descendants of Buchan's own creations.

Buchan wrote five books each about Richard Hannay and Edward Leithen. It is Leithen, a future Solicitor-General, whose first adventure most clearly shows the menace in the urban landscape and introduces a Mr. Big—in this case the cultured and formidable Andrew Lumley, an "honourable and distinguished gentleman, belonging to the best clubs, counting as [his] acquaintances the flower of . . . society." Through Leithen, Buchan is prepared to entertain the notion of conspiracy within, while in Hannay, the conspirators are from outside society. It is Leithen who must run "like a thief in a London thoroughfare on a June afternoon"; it is Leithen who anticipates that other lineage of the precipitous yarn, a lineage best traced by Eric Ambler and Graham Greene. As Buchan's most perceptive commentator, David Daniell, has noted, Leithen acts, when he acts, from "a wise passiveness." Hannay goes out to meet danger, he initiates action; Leithen observes danger and awaits it, he analyzes, he responds. Though both provide us with insights into Buchan's character, neither is Buchan. Rather, the one, Hannay, is immediate, while the other, Leithen, commands a range of distancing techniques that provide perspective; through both— and only through both—we can see Buchan at his narrative best.

One hopes that a volume on Sir Edward Leithen may, for the modern reader, follow this collection of the adventures of Sir Richard Hannay, for only by experiencing the formula through the eyes of both men can we fully understand Buchan's love of the sudden, mysterious place that is linked through history to a distant, non-rational, past. In this way Buchan the historian demonstrates the connectedness of things, the relevance of past to present, glimpsed so clearly in his best short stories. In "The Grove of Ashtaroth," published in 1910, he connects the twentieth century to the ancient conical tower of Zimbabwe, in southern Africa, and in "The Wind in the Portico," one of the stories in *The Runagates Club*, published in 1928 (and incidentally also involving Hannay once more), Buchan ties our century directly to ancient Rome.

What may get between the modern reader and John Buchan today is not his alleged anti-Semitism or racism, which any astute reader can see are not there, but his use of religion. As David Daniell has pointed out in *The Interpreter's House*,[3] the second and third volumes of the Hannay quartet give us vast symbols by which we may plumb Buchan's most closely held beliefs. He is not a racist, and certainly not a snob (despite having been discussed by one critic as one of the "snobbery with violence" school of writers), but he does believe that when a person forgets who he is, loses touch with his roots, becomes a person of mixed faiths (he has nothing at all to say about mixed race)—that is, when he becomes confused—then he may well falter in the battle between a true and a twisted faith. Buchan does not suggest that there is only one true faith; rather, there is a true faith for each individual, and this must be unadulterated. One most follow, follow the gleam, must burn with a hard gem-like flame, but it must be one's own flame, not one toward which the confused turn hypnotically, following the cadence, the gleam, of another. This is the democracy of intellect of which he writes. One may hold to Islam, which Buchan respects, but not to an Islam twisted by politics; the same is true of the Calvinism that Buchan took, at least on the surface, as his own. One must not confuse the surface event with the inner reality. Today this is an exquisitely difficult message for most of the world.

*   *   *   *

John Buchan was serious about his writing, and this is why he enjoyed it so, but we need not be solemn, or solely serious, when we approach him. He meant, above all, to entertain. In September 1924, a preparatory school-master wrote to him to report that he had read *The Thirty-Nine Steps* to his class four times, and one can understand this (try it), for the words roll easily off the tongue, as all that is truly well written must do. Buchan gave his readers the pleasure of sound, creating splashy brooks and the startle of bird-song amidst the mist and fog of Erzerum and the hills of Scotland alike. *Greenmantle* is perhaps Buchan's most fully representative book, for he adds the pleasure of good companionship, Blenkiron and Sandy Arbuthnot becoming as central to Hannay's character as he is himself.* Mary Lamington, who becomes Lady Hannay, plays an important part in both *Mr. Standfast* and *The Three Hostages,* the last especially popular in America and both far more favorably received by women readers than the first two books had been. She, Sandy, and Blenkiron become "friends for life," a reader reports, Buchan's remarkable romances "the anodynes & sedatives of the British Pharmacopea." This is true, and one must not forget the simple pleasure, as Captain William Fisher (later Admiral Sir William Fisher) said to Buchan late in 1916, of being "off with Blenkiron, Sandy and Hannay to discover the meaning of *Kasredin, Cancer, V.I.,*" those three words written as clues by Harry Bullivant in his dying moment. *Greenmantle* was, a friend wrote, a "glorious novel," an experiment in translating the cerebral adventure of a Sherlock Holmes into a yarn suffused with that special quality Robert Louis Stevenson called "the profit of life." "The game is afoot, Watson," becomes the cry that operates at two levels, "Get ready, my lord, it is the hour to ride."[5]

There is also a distinct pleasure in seeing Buchan synthesize both what

---

*An American will find Blenkiron considerably less attractive than Buchan apparently meant him to be, for his confounded duodenal ulcer and his ill-educated and quite inaccurate form of demotic American speech are rather off-putting to the modern reader. It is useful to know that Buchan was suffering from just such an ulcer himself when he wrote of Blenkiron, so that one may have some hint of the exorcism involved. Very seldom do British writers get American speech right, in part because they think it far simpler than it is. Two of Buchan's readers wrote to protest his notion of how Americans spoke, one giving him a good lesson on the proper American use of *got,* which Buchan simply never got right.[4]

he knows and what he believes into his fiction. Throughout the war, as he wrote his twenty-four-volume history, its exceptionally lucid battle passages still as clear an account as we have of some of the most intense confrontations in modern warfare, spinning out well over a million words, he nonetheless held back his most telling phrases and his most heightened sense of scene in order to describe again some of the same battles in his fiction. It is a pleasure to be alert to this intelligent economy of effort, to see Buchan as he sets forth the relatedness of things. It is this sense of connectedness that allows him to get away with his otherwise outrageous use of coincidence, for the coincidence is rendered acceptable at the margin because of the synthesizing that has gone before. This makes it possible for Buchan to delineate character in a phrase, by telling us of the books one finds on a shelf, and of what the narrator thinks of them. There is a good bit of Sir Walter Scott, and a strong application of Jane Austen, both writers Buchan admired, in the way he lets us see behind action to character.

There are, of course, the pleasures that come from trying to outwit the author, for though Buchan did not write mysteries, the books do present their little puzzles. Who goes through Hannay's belongings at Biggleswick (*Mr. Standfast*)? Buchan forgets to tell us. How in fact will a ship standing off shore at Bradgate (in *The Thirty-Nine Steps*) actually spot the thirty-nine steps themselves, as those at watch on the ship must in order to make the correct rendezvous, since the tide will lap on two other sets of steps in the same way (see Chapter X)? And why, given his sterling mental health, does Hannay appear more than once, and especially in *Greenmantle,* to be something of a masochist?

Above all, there is the pleasure of seeing, through Buchan's novels, a life well lived. Buchan was a success by any standard, and this mattered to him. He was not complacent over his success, certainly not smug, and so we can share in that pleasure. He liked his long walks, and rock climbing, and those acts of theater called ceremony supported by traditions that tie the present meaningfully to the past. He was at ease with his mixture of Calvinism and Platonism, at ease with himself, though he never ceased to think of life as a journey in which there was always more to be observed, more to be learned. As his son William remarked, "My father's hands were mainly for writing," and we can be grateful that this teller of tales so chose to employ those hands. We have from him at the very least two convictions that are less simple than they seem: that the amateur, thrown into the right circumstances, can react with imagination and courage in equal measure, to beat the professionals at their own game, and that there is a permanence to violence and crime beneath the surface of the civilized, with which those who live in society must learn to deal.[6] These are in no measure profound thoughts, but they are no less valid for that, and they come directly from Buchan's own experience.

John Buchan was born in Perth, in Scotland, on August 26, 1875, the son of a minister of the Church of Scotland. He attended schools in Kirkcaldy and Glasgow, where his father was minister to the John Knox Free

Church in the Gorbals, in the Glaswegian slums. John Buchan won a bursary to Glasgow University, and went on to Brasenose College, at Oxford, on a classical scholarship. While still a student he published his first books, including *John Burnet of Barns,* obviously the work of a young writer though still quite readable even today. He read for the bar, became a regular contributor to and for a time virtually editor of the *Spectator,* and was a reviewer of manuscripts for the publisher John Lane. At twenty-six Buchan sailed for South Africa as a member on the staff of Lord Milner, the British High Commissioner, whose task it was to work out the practical implications of the treaty that closed the Boer War. Though Buchan had prepared to be a tax lawyer, he joined a publishing house as chief literary advisor, and from that time forward he was both writer and man of affairs and almost never a barrister. In 1910, with the publication of *Prester John,* still one of his best-known (and now least read) titles, in which he told of the great black preacher John Laputa, he joined the ranks of those who might expect to make a living by the skill of their pen alone.

Travel was Buchan's drink, the worldly experience of public affairs his meat. In 1907 he married Susan Grosvenor, an independent-minded grand-daughter of Lord Ebury and, though not wealthy, socially well placed. They honeymooned in the Dolomites and Venice; thereafter they traveled together whenever possible. From 1911 Buchan actively pursued a political career, became a correspondent in France for *The Times* and in 1916 a major in the Intelligence Corps. The following year Buchan was appointed Director of Information and, in the year after, Director of Intelligence in a newly created Ministry of Information. In 1927, amidst the writing of no fewer than five books, he was elected to Parliament as Member for Scottish universities. This was also the period of his most effective writing, for though he did not again create figures so compelling to the public imagination as Hannay and Leithen, he published several of his best books: *Huntingtower, John Macnab* (arguably Buchan at the height of his powers), *Castle Gay, The Blanket of the Dark, The Gap in the Curtain.* In 1933 Buchan was appointed High Commissioner to the General Assembly of the Church of Scotland, and again the next year, and in 1935 he was appointed Governor-General of Canada and, as Baron Tweedsmuir, took up residence in Ottawa.

He was one of the most inspirited, successful Governors-General Canada had known, and yet he continued to write, even returning one last time to Richard Hannay in that story that is missing here, *The Island of Sheep,* published in 1936. On September 9, 1939, as Governor-General, Lord Tweedsmuir signed Canada's declaration of war against Germany, the connectedness of things all too plain, the war he had thought over in 1918 renewed after a little more than two decades of uneasy peace. Two months later he went to New York for medical treatment, not expecting, as some commentators have said, to die, but rather making plans for a biography of the Apostle Paul. Early in February 1940, Buchan was struck down, suffering a cerebral thrombosis, and on February 11 he died. Later that year his autobiography, *Memory Hold-the-Door,* was published. In North America the book was entitled *Pilgrim's Way,* the reference to Bunyan abundantly clear throughout.[7]

In his memoirs Buchan says that his earliest recollections were not of himself, but of his environment. He included all of humanity as part of the environment, of course, never forgetting that people are part of the ecology, and in some measure his principal figures are drawn from his wide circle of friends and acquaintances. The poignancy of *Mr. Standfast,* in particular, arises from the fact that schoolmates, friends from his days at Oxford, colleagues in the military, were dying in France, and no week passed in the last months of the war when Buchan did not have occasion to reflect on death. The Battle of Arras, in the Spring of 1917, brought dreaded news in double measure, for his close friend Tommy Nelson was killed in March, and in April his brother Alastair died of wounds. John and Alastair had kept up a lively correspondence through the early part of the war, seeing it almost in terms of the title of one of John's postwar collections of adventures, a *Book of Escapes and Hurried Journeys,* and John had written to friends with pride about how Alastair had been taken into Winston Churchill's battalion of Royal Scots Fusiliers. After the Spring of 1917 John never wrote of war in the effervescent tones of *Greenmantle.*

That effervescence, so evident in figures like Sandy Arbuthnot, came from the originals on whom Buchan drew, and they too were changed by the long, grotesque war, which cut down the core of British youth in its prime. Sandy had been based on the Honorable Aubrey Herbert, five years Buchan's junior, the second son of the fourth Earl of Carnarvon. Herbert was a fine linguist, a scholar-gypsy who traveled alone in China, the Balkans (it is said that he was twice offered the throne of Albania), and the Middle East. Herbert had taken a first in Modern History at Oxford; nearsighted, he had been unable to get into the army, yet he showed up in the British Expeditionary Force in 1914 apparently by the simple though brash expedient of obtaining the uniform of an officer of the Irish Guards and then mixing with the Guards as they marched from Wellington Barracks to their troopship. Wounded near Mons, Herbert was put into intelligence in the Middle East, where he became expert on the Turks in particular. This happy and dashing young man also "rested in melancholy," however, for he expected to go blind, and did so in 1922, losing his sight as he was addressing Parliament. Hoping to gain his vision back, he had all of his teeth removed, it then being medical opinion that eyes and teeth were intimately related, and from this totally foolish operation he died of blood poisoning.[8]

Hannay himself is usually said to be based on William Edmund Ironside, also five years Buchan's junior, and in time Field Marshal Lord Ironside of Archangel. Buchan met Ironside while working with Lord Milner in South Africa (just as he apparently met the figure who became Pieter Pienaar while in Bulawayo, in Southern Rhodesia). Ironside spoke fourteen languages, and was in particular an adept at the taal of the South African veld. He had been decorated by the Germans when he worked as a spy behind German lines in Southwest Africa, then a German colony, for they had taken him as a Boer. Ironside also was assigned to intelligence, largely in Russia. In 1938 he became the Chief of the Imperial General Staff.[9]

Of course, Buchan also drew, as most writers do, on his reading. He had catholic tastes: Thomas Hardy, D. H. Lawrence (whose "The Rocking-Horse Winner" he thought one of the best short stories ever written), Virginia Woolf, but also E. Phillips Oppenheim (Buchan rather thought Oppenheim had a better claim to being the father of the spy thriller), Agatha Christie, P. G. Wodehouse. In Canada he delved into Canadian literature, and American too, and he especially enjoyed the autobiography of William Lyon "Billy" Phelps, a legendary Yale professor of English who brought literature alive for generations of college undergraduates. (As Buchan wrote to Phelps, he shared all of his prejudices though not all of his enthusiasms. One wishes Buchan had been more explicit.) He enjoyed poetry, and echoes of lines from the great nineteenth-century British poets in particular resonate out from Buchan's books. He never lost his interest in following the oddities of politics and the currents of literature, and he could have been speaking of both when he wrote to Ezra Pound in 1934 that "the world gets more fantastic every day. . . ."[10]

To be sure, Buchan enjoyed his success, and he liked to feel part of large events. During World War I friends and supporters were predicting great things for him, even hinting at a major Cabinet appointment or the prime ministership one day, if he would commit his intellect and his energies more wholeheartedly to politics. He was a product of a Britain in what, with hindsight, we may now see was its golden age, when the British felt that they commanded the world. And they very nearly did so, for the British Empire, of which Buchan was so much a part, though by no means an unthinking supporter, stretched around the globe, encompassing nearly a hundred lands that are now independent nations. Three-quarters of the people of the world lived under the tenuous control of colonial empires, and of these imperial nations, Britain was by far the most extensive. There is no hint of smugness about the empire itself in Buchan's writings, but he could at times be so accepting of British values and so certain of the character of the class from which he had come (less certain of the class into which he had moved, as The Power-House made clear) that he does seem occasionally complacent in his happiness. The empire began to disappear in the trenches in France, for Britain's decline at home began with the First War, even though in extent the empire was actually at its widest sway in the inter-war years. Buchan saw this—no one who was a Director of Information and had access to the facts could fail to be aware of just how devastating a war the British were said to have won had truly been in British society—and the growing strain of melancholy in the inter-war years becomes increasingly apparent with the rise of Hitler's Germany. Buchan did not live to see the empire lost and Britain muddle into even more precipitous decline, but he lived to see the outbreak of the Second

War and to know that, as the New Zealand writer John Mulgan put it, the inter-war years were merely "the bit in between."

Buchan moved at ease in a world that often was all that he has been accused of being. It could be stridently and, more insidiously, almost silently anti-Semitic. Gentlemen in their clubs would speak of "niggers" and "wogs" (and also of "frogs" and "wops") without any sense of their own vulgarity. Britain was, and in fundamental ways may still be, a racist society, and Common Room talk was often entirely too common. But there is no evidence that Buchan ever espoused these views himself. One does not find the term "wog" in Buchan's vocabulary, though it was almost certainly in Ironside's, and though Buchan may not have supported the racism inherent in any system of commands in which race is a factor, he supported those who did. Of course unthinking or hasty readers may, in fact, have taken support for their own anti-Semitism or racism from particular passages in the Hannay novels, for the pace of movement in them is such that a reader accustomed to assuming that the surface is all there is may not have noticed that the epithets were from the mouths of those of whom Hannay disapproved. Buchan was taken to task once by his friend Maurice Headlam for a scene in which the villain spits in the face of the hero; this is, Buchan wrote, "a Kaffir trick." How so, Headlam asked; is this not an attack used by many who are not to be described as "backward"? He then told Buchan of how Irish Unionists at a recent Dublin meeting had been forced to file out between lines of their opponents and were spat upon, man and woman, one and all.[11] Buchan took the point, for he knew that his own subconscious was not invariably free of bias. In 1906 Buchan had written that "truth, virtue, happiness, all the ideals" were best reached through "a clash of opposites," and he did not doubt that each of his contemporaries had those opposites within himself. One must, he said through the words of Sandy, get outside oneself and into the skin of others. This was not alone because impersonation would require it. To be an historian required it. Above all, if one was to know oneself it was required.

It is in this self-questioning, in his break with the conventional values of liberal imperialism, in his insistence that to be whole one must stand back and test one's premises, that Buchan established his position as more than simply another romantic novelist of empire. Buchan was no servant of a rampant capitalism or of an empire bound together by practitioners of the profit motive: such people were "merchants of pessimism," for there must be something more important in life than profit.

In all of this Buchan's true descendant, at least where the Hannay books are concerned, is Graham Greene. Greene was explicit on this, linking his own "entertainments" to his youthful reading of Buchan, attesting to the "remarkable . . . completeness of the world" the Buchan novels describe. Greene's own awareness of the precarious hold civilization has on humankind comes more from Leithen than Hannay, to be sure, and Greene is warm in his praise for the way in which Buchan prepared his readers "for the death that may come to any of us, as it nearly came to Leithen, by the railings of the Park or the doorway of the mews." Both in *Orient Express* (as the book is now known, though in England it was originally published as *Stamboul Train*) and to some extent in *England Made Me*, Greene drew on the Richard Hannay who had given him so much early pleasure, breaking with the Buchan model only a bit in *This Gun for Hire*, about a man "out to revenge himself for all the dirty tricks of life," and yet the story of a hunted man, a man on the run, Buchan with a twist of lemon.[12] Only with *The Quiet American*, in which the man who would do good does evil in the doing of that good, does Greene succeed in throwing off the hand of Buchan, so firmly placed on his shoulders in childhood. Even so, allowing for a model that operates in reverse, there is much in Greene's *The Honourary Consul* or *The Human Factor* to make us think of the world of Hannay and Leithen gone sour.

What Buchan feared most was unreasoning passion. *Prester John* is about the intent to unleash such passions. So too is the last book reprinted here. In *The Three Hostages* Dominick Medina (not, incidentally, a Jew, though some writers have said he was; he is in fact partly Irish, but since Buchan has his share of Irish heroes, he is generally not suspected of being anti-Irish) wants to rule the world. He will betray it from within, for he is part of that clubland that can mask its passions with impeccable manners. From John Laputa in *Prester John* to Dominick Medina there is a direct line, that tensed thin thread that holds civilization in place. The enemy is within. This is no message of cheer, no certitude for "boys' books"; indeed, it prefigures much that we sum up in the phrase "the modern temper." Without nurturing, things fall apart: empires, polities, states. Only nature is permanent—Tweeddale, or the veld, or the Canadian North. And then, with just a hint of a wink, Buchan most likely would have added: and all of humanity is part of nature—human nature—too.[13]

—ROBIN W. WINKS

Acknowledgments:

The bulk of John Buchan's papers are at Queen's University, Kingston, Ontario, and I wish to thank Mr. George F. Henderson of Queen's for making them available to me in microfilm. Substantial files of Buchan letters are to be found in many other places, of course, for he was an indefatigable correspondent, and I have encountered his letters in the Huntington Library in San Marino, California, at the University of California, Los Angeles, in the Bienecke Library at Yale University, and the Liddell Hart Centre for Military Archives at King's College, London. This essay also draws on Buchan letters at the Boston Public Library, the Dartmouth College Library, and in the National Library of Scotland. I wish, too, to thank Janet Adam Smith, whose excellent biography forestalled an early intention on my part to write Buchan's life, and Norman Etherington, of the Department of History, the University of Adelaide, who shares my interest in Buchan and who turned my attention back to him as an undergraduate at Yale. The views, errors, and idiosyncracies of this essay are, however, all my own responsibility.

NOTES

1. There are two other books in which Hannay figures. *The Courts of the Morning*, published in 1929, is Sandy Arbuthnot's story, and Hannay appears only in the introduction. *The Island of Sheep* (published as *The Man from Norlands* in the United States) appeared in 1936, and though Hannay plays a major rôle in it, the book belongs to his son, Peter John. In *The Island of Sheep* we meet a middle-aged Hannay who is worried that he has gone stale, and Buchan uses the novel primarily to give us a strong sense of the passing of a generation, of Hannay as a father, and of family ties. Both books, as well as the few short stories in which Hannay figures, are usually left out of the Hannay canon, and *Courts of the Morning* is seldom included in the "count."

2. This correspondence is in the Ezra Pound Papers in the Bienecke Library at Yale. Anyone interested in Buchan's alleged anti-Semitism would find it instructive reading.

3. David Daniell, *The Interpreter's House: A Critical Assessment of the Work of John Buchan* (London: Nelson, 1975), pp. 137–138.

4. See the Buchan Papers at Queen's University, Kingston, Ontario, especially H. W. Bell to Buchan, May 19, 1919.

5. The quotations in this paragraph come from the Buchan Papers: Esther Carling to Buchan, September 11, 1924, William Fisher to Buchan, October 30 and November 5, 1916, and H. M. B. Reid to Buchan, May 21 and 24, 1916, respectively. Those interested in Buchan's critical reception will find the *John Buchan Journal*, begun in Spring, 1980, and issued by the John Buchan Society (Limpsfield, 16 Ranfurly Road, Bridge of Weir, Renfrewshire, Scotland) quite useful.

6. See William Buchan, *John Buchan: A Memoir* (London: Buchan & Enright, 1982), p. 138.

7. The best biography of John Buchan is by Janet Adam Smith: *John Buchan, A Biography* (London: Rupert Hart-Davis, 1965). In *John Buchan and His World* (New York: Scribner's, 1979), Janet Adam Smith provides a more synoptic view.

8. See Margaret FitzHerbert, *The Man who was Greenmantle: A Biography of Aubrey Herbert* (London: John Murray, 1983).

9. The most succinct statement on Ironside as Hannay appears in William Amos, *The Originals: An A–Z of Fiction's Real-Life Characters* (Boston: Little, Brown, 1985), which is also good on Sandy.

10. Yale University, Bienecke Library: Buchan to Phelps, April 29, 1939, and *ibid.*, the Ezra Pound Papers, Buchan to Pound, February 21, 1934.

11. Buchan Papers: Headlam to Buchan, August 24, 1924. While Headlam was taking Buchan to task, the American adventure-writer Richard Harding Davis was writing to tell him how much he admired all the same work (August 23, 1924).

12. See Graham Greene, *The Lost Childhood and Other Essays* (New York: Viking, 1952), pp. 104–05; *Ways of Escape* (New York: Simon & Schuster, 1980), p. 72; and Marie-Françoise Allain, *The Other Man: Conversations with Graham Greene* (New York: Simon & Schuster, 1983), throughout. The Buchan formula is at work in *The Ministry of Fear*, for further example, and as in much of Greene's fiction, to see the parallels one need only substitute the state, or on occasion the Church and a pursuing God, for Andrew Lumley or the enemy spies in Buchan's novels.

13. Readers who wish to pursue Buchan further should consult the books by David Daniell and Janet Adam Smith, cited above, and Archibald Hanna, Jr., *John Buchan, 1875–1940: A Bibliography* (Hamden, Conn.: Shoe String Press, 1953). Buchan is treated at some length in John G. Cawelti and Bruce A. Rosenberg, *The Spy Story* (Chicago: University of Chicago Press, 1987), and Michael Denning, *Cover Stories: Narrative and Ideology in the British Spy Thriller* (London: Routledge & Kegan Paul, 1987). Reviews and correspondence in the *Times Literary Supplement* (September 11 and 18, October 2 and 23, 1987) continue the debate on Buchan's alleged anti-semitism. Juanita Kruse, *John Buchan and the Idea of Empire*, is forthcoming in 1988 (Lewiston, N.Y.: Edwin Mellen Press).

THE FIRST ADVENTURE

The Thirty-Nine Steps

1 THE MAN WHO DIED

I returned from the City about three o'clock on that May afternoon pretty well disgusted with life. I had been three months in the Old Country, and was fed up with it. If any one had told me a year ago that I would have been feeling like that I should have laughed at him; but there was the fact. The weather made me liverish, the talk of the ordinary Englishman made me sick, I couldn't get enough exercise, and the amusements of London seemed as flat as soda-water that has been standing in the sun. "Richard Hannay," I kept telling myself, "you have got into the wrong ditch, my friend, and you had better climb out."

It made me bite my lips to think of the plans I had been building up those last years in Bulawayo. I had got my pile—not one of the big ones, but good enough for me; and I had figured out all kinds of ways of enjoying myself. My father had brought me out from Scotland at the age of six, and I had never been home since; so England was a sort of Arabian Nights to me, and I counted on stopping there for the rest of my days.

But from the first I was disappointed with it. In about a week I was tired of seeing sights, and in less than a month I had had enough of restaurants and theatres and race-meetings. I had no real pal to go about with, which probably explains things. Plenty of people invited me to their houses, but they didn't seem much interested in me. They would fling me a question or two about South Africa, and then get on to their own affairs. A lot of Imperialist ladies asked me to tea to meet schoolmasters from New Zealand and editors from Vancouver, and that was the dismallest business of all. Here was I, thirty-seven years old, sound in wind and limb, with enough money to have a good time, yawning my head off all day. I had just about settled to clear out and get back to the veld, for I was the best bored man in the United Kingdom.

That afternoon I had been worrying my brokers about investments to give my mind something to work on, and on my way home I turned into my club—rather a pot-house, which took in Colonial members. I had a long drink, and read the evening papers. They were full of the row in the Near East, and there was an article about Karolides, the Greek Premier. I rather fancied the chap. From all accounts he seemed the one big man in the show; and he played a straight game too, which was more than could be said for most of them. I gathered that they hated him pretty blackly in Berlin and Vienna, but that we were going to stick by him, and one paper said that he was the only barrier between Europe and Armageddon. I remember

9

wondering if I could get a job in those parts. It struck me that Albania was the sort of place that might keep a man from yawning.

About six o'clock I went home, dressed, dined at the Café Royal, and turned into a music-hall. It was a silly show, all capering women and monkey-faced men, and I did not stay long. The night was fine and clear as I walked back to the flat I had hired near Portland Place. The crowd surged past me on the pavements, busy and chattering, and I envied the people for having something to do. These shop-girls and clerks and dandies and police-men had some interest in life that kept them going. I gave half a crown to a beggar because I saw him yawn; he was a fellow-sufferer. At Oxford Circus I looked up into the spring sky and I made a vow. I would give the Old Country another day to fit me into something; if nothing happened, I would take the next boat for the Cape.

My flat was the first floor in a new block behind Langham Place. There was a common staircase, with a porter and a liftman at the entrance, but there was no restaurant or anything of that sort, and each flat was quite shut off from the others. I hate servants on the premises, so I had a fellow to look after me who came in by the day. He arrived before eight o'clock every morning and used to depart at seven, for I never dined at home.

I was just fitting my key into the door when I noticed a man at my elbow. I had not seen him approach, and the sudden appearance made me start. He was a slim man, with a short brown beard and small, gimlety blue eyes. I recognized him as the occupant of a flat on the top floor, with whom I had passed the time of day on the stairs.

"Can I speak to you?" he said. "May I come in for a minute?" He was steadying his voice with an effort, and his hand was pawing my arm.

I got my door open and motioned him in. No sooner was he over the threshold than he made a dash for my back room, where I used to smoke and write my letters. Then he bolted back.

"Is the door locked?" he asked feverishly, and he fastened the chain with his own hand.

"I am very sorry," he said humbly. "It's a mighty liberty, but you look the kind of man who would understand. I've had you in my mind all this week when things got troublesome. Say, will you do me a good turn?"

"I'll listen to you," I said. "That's all I'll promise." I was getting worried by the antics of this nervous little chap.

There was a tray of drinks on the table beside him, from which he filled himself a stiff whisky-and-soda. He drank it off in three gulps, and cracked the glass as he set it down.

"Pardon," he said, "I'm a bit rattled to-night. You see, I happen at this moment to be dead."

I sat down in an arm-chair and lit my pipe.

"What does it feel like?" I asked. I was pretty certain that I had to deal with a madman.

A smile flickered over his drawn face. "I'm not mad—yet. Say, sir, I've been watching you, and I reckon you're a cool customer. I reckon, too, you're an honest man, and not afraid of playing a bold hand. I'm going to confide in you. I need help worse than any man ever needed it, and I want to know if I can count you in."

"Get on with your yarn," I said, "and I'll tell you."

He seemed to brace himself for a great effort, and then started on the queerest rigmarole. I didn't get hold of it at first, and I had to stop and ask him questions. But here is the gist of it:—

He was an American, from Kentucky, and after college, being pretty well off, he had started out to see the world. He wrote a bit, and acted as war correspondent for a Chicago paper, and spent a year or two in South-Eastern Europe. I gathered that he was a fine linguist, and had got to know pretty well the society in those parts. He spoke familiarly of many names that I remembered to have seen in the newspapers.

He had played about with politics, he told me, at first for the interest of them, and then because he couldn't help himself. I read him as a sharp, restless fellow, who always wanted to get down to the roots of things. He got a little further down than he wanted.

I am giving you what he told me as well as I could make it out. Away behind all the Governments and the armies there was a big subterranean movement going on, engineered by very dangerous people. He had come on it by accident; it fascinated him; he went further, and then he got caught. I gathered that most of the people in it were the sort of educated anarchists that make revolutions, but that beside them there were financiers who were playing for money. A clever man can make big profits on a falling market, and it suited the book of both classes to set Europe by the ears.

He told me some queer things that explained a lot that had puzzled me—things that happened in the Balkan War, how one state suddenly came out on top, why alliances were made and broken, why certain men disappeared, and where the sinews of war came from. The aim of the whole conspiracy was to get Russia and Germany at loggerheads.

When I asked Why, he said that the anarchist lot thought it would give them their chance. Everything would be in the melting-pot, and they looked to see a new world emerge. The capitalists would rake in the shekels, and make fortunes by buying up wreckage. Capital, he said, had no conscience and no fatherland. Besides, the Jew was behind it, and the Jew hated Russia worse than hell.

"Do you wonder?" he cried. "For three hundred years they have been persecuted, and this is the return match for the *pogroms*. The Jew is everywhere, but you have to go far down the backstairs to find him. Take any big Teutonic business concern. If you have dealings with it the first man you meet is Prince *von und zu* Something, an elegant young man who talks Eton-and-Harrow English. But he cuts no ice. If your business is big, you get behind him and find a prognathous Westphalian with a retreating brow and the manners of a hog. He is the German business man that gives your English papers the shakes. But if you're on the biggest kind of job and are bound to get to the real boss, ten to one you are brought up against a little white-faced

Jew in a bath-chair with an eye like a rattlesnake. Yes, sir, he is the man who is ruling the world just now, and he has his knife in the Empire of the Tsar, because his aunt was outraged and his father flogged in some one-horse location on the Volga."

I could not help saying that his Jew-anarchists seemed to have got left behind a little.

"Yes and no," he said. "They won up to a point, but they struck a bigger thing than money, a thing that couldn't be bought, the old elemental fighting instincts of man. If you're going to be killed you invent some kind of flag and country to fight for, and if you survive you get to love the thing. Those foolish devils of soldiers have found something they care for, and that has upset the pretty plan laid in Berlin and Vienna. But my friends haven't played their last card by a long sight. They've gotten the ace up their sleeves, and unless I can keep alive for a month they are going to play it and win."

"But I thought you were dead," I put in.

"*Mors janua vitae*," he smiled. (I recognized the quotation: it was about all the Latin I knew.) "I'm coming to that, but I've got to put you wise about a lot of things first. If you read your newspaper, I guess you know the name of Constantine Karolides?"

I sat up at that, for I had been reading about him that very afternoon.

"He is the man that has wrecked all their games. He is the one big brain in the whole show, and he happens also to be an honest man. Therefore he has been marked down these twelve months past. I found that out—not that it was difficult, for any fool could guess as much. But I found out the way they were going to get him, and that knowledge was deadly. That's why I have had to decease."

He had another drink, and I mixed it for him myself, for I was getting interested in the beggar.

"They can't get him in his own land, for he has a bodyguard of Epirotes that would skin their grandmothers. But on the 15th day of June he is coming to this city. The British Foreign Office has taken to having international tea-parties, and the biggest of them is due on that date. Now Karolides is reckoned the principal guest, and if my friends have their way he will never return to his admiring countrymen."

"That's simple enough, anyhow," I said. "You can warn him and keep him at home."

"And play their game?" he asked sharply. "If he does not come they win, for he's the only man that can straighten out the tangle. And if his Government are warned he won't come, for he does not know how big the stakes will be on June the 15th."

"What about the British Government?" I said. "They're not going to let their guests be murdered. Tip them the wink, and they'll take extra precautions."

"No good. They might stuff this city with plain-clothes detectives and double the police and Constantine would still be a doomed man. My friends are not playing this game for candy. They want a big occasion for the taking off, with the eyes of all Europe on it. He'll be murdered by an Austrian, and there'll be plenty of evidence to show the connivance of the big folk in Vienna and Berlin. It will all be an infernal lie, of course, but the case will look black enough to the world. I'm not talking hot air, my friend. I happen to know every detail of the hellish contrivance, and I can tell you it will be the most finished piece of blackguardism since the Borgias. But it's not going to come off if there's a certain man who knows the wheels of the business alive right here in London on the 15th day of June. And that man is going to be your servant, Franklin P. Scudder."

I was getting to like the little chap. His jaw had shut like a rat-trap, and there was the fire of battle in his gimlety eyes. If he was spinning me a yarn he could act up to it.

"Where did you find out this story?" I asked.

"I got the first hint in an inn on the Achensee in Tyrol. That set me inquiring, and I collected my other clues in a fur-shop in the Galician quarter of Buda, in a Strangers' Club in Vienna, and in a little bookshop off the Racknitzstrasse in Leipzig. I completed my evidence ten days ago in Paris. I can't tell you the details now, for it's something of a history. When I was quite sure in my own mind I judged it my business to disappear, and I reached this city by a mighty queer circuit. I left Paris a dandified young French-American, and I sailed from Hamburg a Jew diamond merchant. In Norway I was an English student of Ibsen collecting materials for lectures, but when I left Bergen I was a cinema-man with special ski films. And I came here from Leith with a lot of pulp-wood propositions in my pocket to put before the London newspapers. Till yesterday I thought I had muddied my trail some, and was feeling pretty happy. Then . . ."

The recollection seemed to upset him, and he gulped down more whisky.

"Then I saw a man standing in the street outside this block. I used to stay close in my room all day, and only slip out after dark for an hour or two. I watched him for a bit from my window, and I thought I recognized him. . . . He came in and spoke to the porter. . . . When I came back from my walk last night I found a card in my letterbox. It bore the name of the man I want least to meet on God's earth."

I think that the look in my companion's eyes, the sheer naked scare on his face, completed my conviction of his honesty. My own voice sharpened a bit as I asked him what he did next.

"I realized that I was bottled as sure as a pickled herring, and that there was only one way out. I had to die. If my pursuers knew I was dead they would go to sleep again."

"How did you manage it?"

"I told the man that valets me that I was feeling pretty bad, and I got myself to look like death. That wasn't difficult, for I'm no slouch at disguises. Then I got a corpse—you can always get a body in London if you know where to go for it. I fetched it back in a trunk on the top of a four-wheeler, and I had to be assisted upstairs to my room. You see I had to pile up some evidence for the inquest. I went to bed and got my man to mix me a sleeping-draught, and then told him to clear out. He wanted to fetch a doctor, but I swore some, and said I couldn't abide leeches. When I was left alone I started in to fake up that corpse. He was my size, and I judged had perished from too much alcohol, so I put some spirits handy about the place. The jaw was the weak point in the likeness, so I blew it away with a revolver. I daresay there will be somebody to-morrow to swear to having heard a shot, but there are no neighbours on my floor, and I guessed I could risk it. So I left the body in bed dressed up in my pyjamas with a revolver lying on the bed-clothes and a considerable mess around. Then I got into a suit of clothes I had kept waiting for emergencies. I didn't dare to shave for fear of leaving tracks, and besides, it wasn't any kind of use my trying to get into the streets. I had had you in my mind all day, and there seemed nothing to do but to make an appeal to you. I watched from my window till I saw you come home, and then slipped down the stair to meet you. . . . There, sir, I guess you know about as much as me of this business."

He sat blinking like an owl, fluttering with nerves and yet desperately determined. By this time I was pretty well convinced that he was going straight with me. It was the wildest sort of narrative, but I had heard in my time many steep tales which had turned out to be true, and I had made a practice of judging the man rather than the story. If he had wanted to get a location in my flat, and then cut my throat, he would have pitched a milder yarn.

"Hand me your key," I said, "and I'll take a look at the corpse. Excuse my caution, but I'm bound to verify a bit if I can."

He shook his head mournfully. "I reckoned you'd ask for that, but I haven't got it. It's on my chain on the dressing-table. I had to leave it behind, for I couldn't leave any clues to breed suspicions. The gentry who are after me are pretty bright-eyed citizens. You'll have to take me on trust for the night, and to-morrow you'll get proof of the corpse business right enough."

I thought for an instant or two. "Right. I'll trust you for the night. I'll lock you into this room and keep the key. Just one word, Mr. Scudder. I believe you're straight, but if so be you are not I should warn you that I'm a handy man with a gun."

"Sure," he said, jumping up with some briskness. "I haven't the privilege of your name, sir, but let me tell you that you're a white man. I'll thank you to lend me a razor."

I took him into my bedroom and turned him loose. In half an hour's time a figure came out that I scarcely recognized. Only his gimlety hungry eyes were the same. He was shaved clean, his hair was parted in the middle, and he had cut his eyebrows. Further, he carried himself as if he had been drilled, and was the very model, even to the brown complexion, of some British officer who had had a long spell in India. He had a monocle, too, which he stuck in his eye, and every trace of the American had gone out of his speech.

"My hat! Mr. Scudder—" I stammered.

"Not Mr. Scudder," he corrected; "Captain Theophilus Digby, of the 40th Gurkhas, presently home on leave. I'll thank you to remember that, sir."

I made him up a bed in my smoking-room and sought my own couch, more cheerful than I had been for the past month. Things did happen occasionally, even in this God-forgotten metropolis.

I woke next morning to hear my man, Paddock, making the deuce of a row at the smoking-room door. Paddock was a fellow I had done a good turn to out on the Selakwe, and I had inspanned him as my servant as soon as I got to England. He had about as much gift of the gab as a hippopotamus, and was not a great hand at valeting, but I knew I could count on his loyalty.

"Stop that row, Paddock," I said. "There's a friend of mine, Captain—Captain" (I couldn't remember the name) "dossing down in there. Get breakfast for two and then come and speak to me."

I told Paddock a fine story about how my friend was a great swell, with his nerves pretty bad from overwork, who wanted absolute rest and peace. Nobody had got to know he was here, or he would be besieged by communications from the India Office and the Prime Minister and his cure would be ruined. I am bound to say Scudder played up splendidly when he came to breakfast. He fixed Paddock with his eyeglass, just like a British officer, asked him about the Boer War, and slung out at me a lot of stuff about imaginary pals. Paddock couldn't learn to call me "sir," but he "sirred" Scudder as if his life depended on it.

I left him with the newspaper and a box of cigars, and went down to the City till luncheon. When I got back the liftman had an important face.

"Nawsty business 'ere this morning, sir. Gent in No. 15 been and shot 'isself. They've just took 'im to the mortuary. The police are up there now."

I ascended to No. 15, and found a couple of bobbies and an inspector busy making an examination. I asked a few idiotic questions, and they soon kicked me out. Then I found the man that had valeted Scudder, and pumped him, but I could see he suspected nothing. He was a whining fellow with a churchyard face, and half a crown went far to console him.

I attended the inquest next day. A partner of some publishing firm gave evidence that the deceased had brought him wood-pulp propositions, and had been, he believed, an agent of an American business. The jury found it a case of suicide while of unsound mind, and the few effects were handed over to the American Consul to deal with. I gave Scudder a full account of the affair, and it interested him greatly. He said he wished he could have attended the inquest, for he reckoned it would be about as spicy as to read one's own obituary notice.

The first two days he stayed with me in that back room he was very peaceful. He read and smoked a bit, and made a heap of jottings in a note-book, and every night we had a game of chess, at which he beat me hollow. I think he was nursing his nerves back to health, for he had had a pretty trying time. But on the third day I could see he was beginning to get restless. He fixed up a list of the days till June 15th, and ticked each off with a red pencil, making remarks in shorthand against them. I would find him sunk in a brown study, with his sharp eyes abstracted, and after those spells of meditation he was apt to be very despondent.

Then I could see that he began to get edgy again. He listened for little noises, and was always asking me if Paddock could be trusted. Once or twice he got very peevish, and apologized for it. I didn't blame him. I made every allowance, for he had taken on a fairly stiff job.

It was not the safety of his own skin that troubled him, but the success of the scheme he had planned. That little man was clean grit all through, without a soft spot in him. One night he was very solemn.

"Say, Hannay," he said, "I judge I should let you a bit deeper into this business. I should hate to go out without leaving somebody else to put up a fight." And he began to tell me in detail what I had only heard from him vaguely.

I did not give him very close attention. The fact is, I was more interested in his own adventures than in his high politics. I reckoned that Karolides and his affairs were not my business, leaving all that to him. So a lot that he said slipped clean out of my memory. I remember that he was very clear that the danger to Karolides would not begin till he had got to London, and would come from the very highest quarters, where there would be no thought of suspicion. He mentioned the name of a woman—Julia Czechenyi—as having something to do with the danger. She would be the decoy, I gathered, to get Karolides out of the care of his guards. He talked, too, about a Black Stone and a man that lisped in his speech, and he described very particularly somebody that he never referred to without a shudder—an old man with a young voice who could hood his eyes like a hawk.

He spoke a good deal about death, too. He was mortally anxious about winning through with his job, but he didn't care a rush for his life.

"I reckon it's like going to sleep when you are pretty well tired out, and waking to find a summer day with the scent of hay coming in at the window. I used to thank God for such mornings way back in the Blue-Grass country, and I guess I'll thank Him when I wake up on the other side of Jordan."

Next day he was much more cheerful, and read the life of Stonewall Jackson most of the time. I went out to dinner with a mining engineer I had got to see on business, and came back about half-past ten in time for our game of chess before turning in.

I had a cigar in my mouth, I remember, as I pushed open the smoking-room door. The lights were not lit, which struck me as odd. I wondered if Scudder had turned in already.

I snapped the switch, but there was nobody there. Then I saw something in the far corner which made me drop my cigar and fall into a cold sweat.

My guest was lying sprawled on his back. There was a long knife through his heart which skewered him to the floor.

2 THE MILKMAN SETS OUT ON HIS TRAVELS

I sat down in an arm-chair and felt very sick.

That lasted for maybe five minutes, and was succeeded by a fit of the horrors. The poor staring white face on the floor was more than I could bear, and I managed to get a table-cloth and cover it. Then I staggered to a cupboard, found the brandy and swallowed several mouthfuls. I had seen men die violently before; indeed I had killed a few myself in the Matabele War; but this cold-blooded indoor business was different. Still I managed to pull myself together. I looked at my watch, and saw that it was half-past ten.

An idea seized me, and I went over the flat with a small-tooth comb. There was nobody there, nor any trace of anybody, but I shuttered and bolted all the windows and put the chain on the door.

By this time my wits were coming back to me, and I could think again. It took me about an hour to figure the thing out; and I did not hurry, for, unless the murderer came back, I had till about six o'clock in the morning for my cogitations.

I was in the soup—that was pretty clear. Any shadow of a doubt I might have had about the truth of Scudder's tale was now gone. The proof of it was lying under the table-cloth. The men who knew that he knew what he knew had found him, and had taken the best way to make certain of his silence. Yes; but he had been in my rooms four days, and his enemies must have reckoned that he had confided in me. So I would be the next to go. It might be that very night, or next day, or the day after, but my number was up all right.

Then suddenly I thought of another probability. Supposing I went out now and called in the police or went to bed and let Paddock find the body and call them in the morning. What kind of a story was I to tell about Scudder? I had lied to Paddock about him, and the whole thing looked desperately fishy. If I made a clean breast of it and told the police everything he had told me, they would simply laugh at me. The odds were a thousand to one that I would be charged with the murder, and the circumstantial evidence was strong enough to hang me. Few people knew me in England; I had no real pal who could come forward and swear to my character. Perhaps that was what those secret enemies were playing for. They were clever enough for anything, and an English prison was as good a way of getting rid of me till after June 15th as a knife in my chest.

Besides, if I told the whole story, and by any miracle was believed, I should

17

be playing their game. Karolides would stay at home, which was what they wanted. Somehow or other the sight of Scudder's dead face had made me a passionate believer in his scheme. He was gone, but he had taken me into his confidence, and I was pretty well bound to carry on his work.

You may think this ridiculous for a man in danger of his life, but that was the way I looked at it. I am an ordinary sort of fellow, not braver than other people, but I hate to see a good man downed, and that long knife would not be the end of Scudder if I could play the game in his place.

It took me an hour or two to think this out, and by that time I had come to a decision. I must vanish somehow, and keep vanished till the end of the second week in June. Then I must somehow find a way to get in touch with the Government people and tell them what Scudder had told me. I wished to heaven he had told me more, and that I had listened more carefully to the little he had told me. I knew nothing but the barest facts. There was a big risk that, even if I weathered the other dangers, I would not be believed in the end. I must take my chance of that, and hope that something might happen which would confirm my tale in the eyes of the Government.

My first job was to keep going for the next three weeks. It was now the 24th day of May, and that meant twenty days of hiding before I could venture to approach the powers that be. I reckoned that two sets of people would be looking for me—Scudder's enemies to put me out of existence, and the police, who would want me for Scudder's murder. It was going to be a giddy hunt, and it was queer how the prospect comforted me. I had been slack so long that almost any chance of activity was welcome. When I had to sit alone with that corpse and wait on fortune I was no better than a crushed worm, but if my neck's safety was to hang on my own wits I was prepared to be cheerful about it.

My next thought was whether Scudder had any papers about him to give me a better clue to the business. I drew back the table-cloth and searched his pockets, for I had no longer any shrinking from the body. The face was wonderfully calm for a man who had been struck down in a moment. There was nothing in the breast-pocket, and only a few loose coins and a cigar-holder in the waistcoat. The trousers held a little penknife and some silver, and the side-pocket of his jacket contained an old crocodile-skin cigar-case. There was no sign of the little black book in which I had seen him making notes. That had no doubt been taken by his murderer.

But as I looked up from my task I saw that some drawers had been pulled out in the writing-table. Scudder would never have left them in that state, for he was the tidiest of mortals. Someone must have been searching for something—perhaps for the pocket-book.

I went round the flat, and found that everything had been ransacked—the inside of books, drawers, cupboards, boxes, even the pockets of the clothes in my wardrobe, and the sideboard in the dining-room. There was no trace of the book. Most likely the enemy had found it, but they had not found it on Scudder's body.

Then I got out an atlas and looked at a big map of the British Isles. My notion was to get off to some wild district, where my veldcraft would be of some use to me, for I would be like a trapped rat in a city. I considered that Scotland would be best, for my people were Scotch and I could pass any-where as an ordinary Scotsman. I had half an idea at first to be a German tourist, for my father had had German partners, and I had been brought up to speak the tongue pretty fluently, not to mention having put in three years prospecting for copper in German Damaraland. But I calculated that it would be less conspicuous to be a Scot, and less in a line with what the police might know of my past. I fixed on Galloway as the best place to go to. It was the nearest wild part of Scotland, so far as I could figure it out, and from the look of the map was not over thick with population.

A search in Bradshaw informed me that a train left St. Pancras at 7.10, which would land me at any Galloway station in the late afternoon. That was well enough, but a more important matter was how I was to make my way to St. Pancras, for I was pretty certain that Scudder's friends would be watching outside. This puzzled me for a bit; then I had an inspiration, on which I went to bed and slept for two troubled hours.

I got up at four and opened my bedroom shutters. The faint light of a fine summer morning was flooding the skies, and the sparrows had begun to chatter. I had a great revulsion of feeling, and felt a God-forgotten fool. My inclination was to let things slide, and trust to the British police taking a reasonable view of my case. But as I reviewed the situation I could find no arguments to bring against my decision of the previous night, so with a wry mouth I resolved to go on with my plan. I was not feeling in any particular funk; only disinclined to go looking for trouble, if you understand me.

I hunted out a well-used tweed suit, a pair of strong nailed boots, and a flannel shirt with a collar. Into my pockets I stuffed a spare shirt, a cloth cap, some handkerchiefs, and a toothbrush. I had drawn a good sum in gold from the bank two days before, in case Scudder should want money, and I took fifty pounds of it in sovereigns in a belt which I had brought back from Rhodesia. That was about all I wanted. Then I had a bath, and cut my moustache, which was long and drooping, into a short stubby fringe.

Now came the next step. Paddock used to arrive punctually at 7.30 and let himself in with a latch-key. But about twenty minutes to seven, as I knew from bitter experience, the milkman turned up with a great clatter of cans, and deposited my share outside my door. I had seen that milkman sometimes when I had gone out for an early ride. He was a young man about my own height, with an ill-nourished moustache, and he wore a white overall. On him I staked all my chances.

I went into the darkened smoking-room where the rays of morning light were beginning to creep through the shutters. There I breakfasted off a whisky-and-soda and some biscuits from the cupboard. By this time it was getting on for six o'clock. I put a pipe in my pocket and filled my pouch from the tobacco jar on the table by the fireplace.

As I poked into the tobacco my fingers touched something hard, and I drew out Scudder's little black pocket-book. . . .

That seemed to me a good omen. I lifted the cloth from the body, and was amazed at the peace and dignity of the dead face. "Good-bye, old chap," I said: "I am going to do my best for you. Wish me well, wherever you are."

Then I hung about in the hall waiting for the milkman. That was the worst part of the business, for I was fairly choking to get out of doors. Six-thirty passed, then six-forty, but still he did not come. The fool had chosen this day of all days to be late.

At one minute after the quarter to seven I heard the rattle of the cans outside. I opened the front door, and there was my man, singling out my cans from a bunch he carried and whistling through his teeth. He jumped a bit at the sight of me.

"Come in here a moment," I said. "I want a word with you." And I led him into the dining-room.

"I reckon you're a bit of a sportsman," I said, "and I want you to do me a service. Lend me your cap and overall for ten minutes, and here's a sovereign for you."

His eyes opened at the sight of the gold, and he grinned broadly. "Wot's the gyme?" he asked.

"A bet," I said. "I haven't time to explain, but to win it I've got to be a milkman for the next ten minutes. All you've got to do is to stay here till I come back. You'll be a bit late, but nobody will complain, and you'll have that quid for yourself."

"Right-o!" he said cheerily. "I ain't the man to spoil a bit of sport. 'Ere's the rig, guv'nor."

I stuck on his flat blue hat and his white overall, picked up the cans, banged my door, and went whistling downstairs. The porter at the foot told me to shut my jaw, which sounded as if my make-up was adequate.

At first I thought there was nobody in the street. Then I caught sight of a policeman a hundred yards down, and a loafer shuffling past on the other side. Some impulse made me raise my eyes to the house opposite, and there at a first-floor window was a face. As the loafer passed he looked up, and I fancied a signal was exchanged.

I crossed the street, whistling gaily and imitating the jaunty swing of the milkman. Then I took the first side-street, and went up a left-hand turning which led past a bit of vacant ground. There was no one in the little street, so I dropped the milk-cans inside the hoarding and sent the hat and overall after them. I had only just put on my cloth cap when a postman came round the corner. I gave him good-morning and he answered me unsuspiciously. At the moment the clock of a neighbouring church struck the hour of seven.

There was not a second to spare. As soon as I got to Euston Road I took to my heels and ran. The clock at Euston Station showed five minutes past the hour. At St. Pancras I had no time to take a ticket, let alone that I had not settled upon my destination. A porter told me the platform, and as I entered it I saw the train already in motion. Two station officials blocked the way, but I dodged them and clambered into the last carriage.

Three minutes later, as we were roaring through the northern tunnels, an irate guard interviewed me. He wrote out for me a ticket to Newton-Stewart, a name which had suddenly come back to my memory, and he conducted me from the first-class compartment where I had ensconced myself to a third-class smoker, occupied by a sailor and a stout woman with a child. He went off grumbling, and as I mopped my brow I observed to my companions in my broadest Scots that it was a sore job catching trains. I had already entered upon my part.

"The impidence o' that gyaird!" said the lady bitterly. "He needit a Scots tongue to pit him in his place. He was complainin' o' this wean no haein' a ticket and her no fower till August twalmonth, and he was objectin' to this gentleman spittin'."

The sailor morosely agreed, and I started my new life in an atmosphere of protest against authority. I reminded myself that a week ago I had been finding the world dull.

3 THE ADVENTURE OF THE LITERARY INNKEEPER

I had a solemn time travelling north that day. It was fine May weather, with the hawthorn flowering on every hedge, and I asked myself why, when I was still a free man, I had stayed on in London and not got the good of this heavenly country. I didn't dare face the restaurant car, but I got a luncheon-basket at Leeds and shared it with the fat woman. Also I got the morning's papers, with news about starters for the Derby and the beginning of the cricket season, and some paragraphs about how Balkan affairs were settling down and a British squadron was going to Kiel.

When I had done with them I got out Scudder's little black pocket-book and studied it. It was pretty well filled with jottings, chiefly figures, though now and then a name was printed in. For example, I found the words "Hofgaard," "Luneville," and "Avocado" pretty often, and especially the word "Pavia."

Now I was certain that Scudder never did anything without a reason, and I was pretty sure that there was a cipher in all this. That is a subject which has always interested me, and I did a bit at it myself once as intelligence officer at Delagoa Bay during the Boer War. I have a head for things like chess and puzzles, and I used to reckon myself pretty good at finding out ciphers. This one looked like the numerical kind where sets of figures correspond to the letters of the alphabet, but any fairly shrewd man can find the clue to that sort after an hour or two's work, and I didn't think Scudder would have been content with anything so easy. So I fastened on the printed words, for you can make a pretty good numerical cipher if you have a key word which gives you the sequence of the letters.

I tried for hours, but none of the words answered. Then I fell asleep and woke at Dumfries just in time to bundle out and get into the slow Galloway train. There was a man on the platform whose looks I didn't like, but he never glanced at me, and when I caught sight of myself in the mirror of an automatic machine I didn't wonder. With my brown face, my old tweeds, and my slouch, I was the very model of one of the hill farmers who were crowding into the third-class carriages.

I travelled with half a dozen in an atmosphere of shag and clay pipes. They had come from the weekly market, and their mouths were full of prices. I heard accounts of how the lambing had gone up the Cairn and the Deuch and a dozen other mysterious waters. Above half the men had lunched heavily and were highly flavoured with whisky, so they took no notice of me. We rumbled slowly into a land of little wooded glens and then to a great wide moorland place, gleaming with lochs, with high blue hills showing northwards.

About five o'clock the carriage emptied, and I was left alone as I had hoped. I got out at the next station, a little place whose name I scarcely noted, set right in the heart of a bog. It reminded me of one of those forgotten little stations in the Karroo. An old station-master was digging in his garden, and with his spade over his shoulder sauntered to the train, took charge of a parcel, and went back to his potatoes. A child of ten received my ticket, and I emerged on a white road that straggled over the brown moor.

It was a gorgeous spring evening, with every hill showing as clear as a cut amethyst. The air had the queer, rooty smell of bogs, but it was as fresh as mid-ocean, and it had the strangest effect on my spirits. I actually felt light-hearted. I might have been a boy out for a spring holiday tramp, instead of a man of thirty-seven very much wanted by the police. I felt just as I used to feel when I was starting for a big trek on a frosty morning on the high veld. If you believe me, I swung along that road whistling. There was no plan of campaign in my head, only just to go on and on in this blessed, honest-smelling hill country, for every mile put me in better humour with myself.

In a roadside planting I cut a walking-stick of hazel, and presently struck off the highway up a by-path which followed the glen of a brawling stream. I reckoned that I was still far ahead of any pursuit, and for that night might please myself. It was some hours since I had tasted food, and I was getting very hungry when I came to a herd's cottage set in a nook beside a waterfall. A brown-faced woman was standing by the door, and greeted me with the kindly shyness of moorland places. When I asked for a night's lodging she said I was welcome to the "bed in the loft," and very soon she set before me a hearty meal of ham and eggs, scones, and thick sweet milk.

At the darkening her man came in from the hills, a lean giant, who in one step covered as much ground as three paces of ordinary mortals. They asked no questions, for they had the perfect breeding of all dwellers in the wilds, but I could see they set me down as a kind of dealer, and I took some trouble to confirm their view. I spoke a lot about cattle, of which my host knew little, and I picked up from him a good deal about the local Galloway markets, which I tucked away in my memory for future use. At ten I was nodding in my chair, and the "bed in the loft" received a weary man who never opened his eyes till five o'clock set the little homestead agoing once more.

They refused any payment, and by six I had breakfasted and was striding southwards again. My notion was to return to the railway line a station or two farther on than the place where I had alighted yesterday and to double back. I reckoned that that was the safest way, for the police would naturally assume that I was always making farther from London in the direction of some western port. I thought I had a good bit of a start, for, as I reasoned, it would take some hours to fix the blame on me, and several more to identify the fellow who got on board the train at St. Pancras.

It was the same jolly, clear spring weather, and I simply could not contrive to feel careworn. Indeed I was in better spirits than I had been for months. Over a long ridge of moorland I took my road, skirting the side of a high hill which the herd had called Cairnsmore of Fleet. Nesting curlews and plovers were crying everywhere, and the links of green pasture by the streams were dotted with young lambs. All the slackness of the past months was slipping from my bones, and I stepped out like a four-year-old. By-and-by I came to a swell of moorland which dipped to the vale of a little river, and a mile away in the heather I saw the smoke of a train.

The station, when I reached it, proved to be ideal for my purpose. The moor surged up around it and left room only for the single line, the slender siding, a waiting-room, an office, the station-master's cottage, and a tiny yard of gooseberries and sweet-william. There seemed no road to it from anywhere, and to increase the desolation the waves of a tarn lapped on their grey granite beach half a mile away. I waited in the deep heather till I saw the smoke of an east-going train on the horizon. Then I approached the tiny booking-office and took a ticket for Dumfries.

The only occupants of the carriage were an old shepherd and his dog—a wall-eyed brute that I mistrusted. The man was asleep, and on the cushions beside him was that morning's *Scotsman*. Eagerly I seized on it, for I fancied it would tell me something.

There were two columns about the Portland Place Murder, as it was called. My man Paddock had given the alarm and had the milkman arrested. Poor devil, it looked as if the latter had earned his sovereign hardly; but for me he had been cheap at the price, for he seemed to have occupied the police the better part of the day. In the latest news I found a further instalment of the story. The milkman had been released, I read, and the true criminal, about whose identity the police were reticent, was believed to have got away from London by one of the northern lines. There was a short note about me as the owner of the flat. I guessed the police had stuck that in, as a clumsy contrivance to persuade me that I was unsuspected.

There was nothing else in the paper, nothing about foreign politics or Karolides, or the things that had interested Scudder. I laid it down, and found that we were approaching the station at which I had got out yesterday. The potato-digging station-master had been gingered into some activity, for the west-going train was waiting to let us pass, and from it had descended three men who were asking him questions. I supposed that they were the local police, who had been stirred up by Scotland Yard, and had traced me as far as this one-horse siding. Sitting well back in the shadow I watched them carefully. One of them had a book, and took down notes. The old potato-digger seemed to have turned peevish, but the child who had collected my ticket was talking volubly. All the party looked out across the moor where the white road departed. I hoped they were going to take up my tracks there.

As we moved away from that station my companion woke up. He fixed me with a wandering glance, kicked his dog viciously, and inquired where he was. Clearly he was very drunk.

"That's what comes o' bein' a teetotaller," he observed in bitter regret.

I expressed my surprise that in him I should have met a blue-ribbon stalwart.

"Ay, but I'm a strong teetotaller," he said pugnaciously. "I took the pledge last Martinmas, and I havena touched a drop o' whisky sinsyne. No even at Hogmanay, though I was sair temptit."

He swung his heels up on the seat, and burrowed a frowsy head into the cushions.

"And that's a' I get," he moaned. "A heid hetter than hell fire, and twae een lookin' different ways for the Sabbath."

"What did it?" I asked.

"A drink they ca' brandy. Bein' a teetotaller I keepit off the whisky, but I was nip-nippin' a' day at this brandy, and I doubt I'll no be weel for a fortnicht." His voice died away into a stutter, and sleep once more laid its heavy hand on him.

My plan had been to get out at some station down the line, but the train suddenly gave me a better chance, for it came to a standstill at the end of a culvert which spanned a brawling porter-coloured river. I looked out and saw that every carriage window was closed and no human figure appeared in the landscape. So I opened the door, and dropped quickly into the tangle of hazels which edged the line.

It would have been all right but for that infernal dog. Under the impression that I was decamping with its master's belonging, it started to bark, and all but got me by the trousers. This woke up the herd, who stood bawling at the carriage door in the belief that I had committed suicide. I crawled through the thicket, reached the edge of the stream, and in cover of the bushes put a hundred yards or so behind me. Then from my shelter I peered back, and saw the guard and several passengers gathered round the open carriage door and staring in my direction. I could not have made a more public departure if I had left with a bugler and a brass band.

Happily the drunken herd provided a diversion. He and his dog, which was attached by a rope to his waist, suddenly cascaded out of the carriage, landed on their heads on the track, and rolled some way down the bank towards the water. In the rescue which followed the dog bit somebody, for I could hear the sound of hard swearing. Presently they had forgotten me, and when after a quarter of a mile's crawl I ventured to look back, the train had started again and was vanishing in the cutting.

I was in a wide semicircle of moorland, with the brown river as radius, and the high hills forming the northern circumference. There was not a sign or sound of a human being, only the plashing water and the interminable crying of curlews. Yet, oddly enough, for the first time I felt the terror of the hunted on me. It was not the police that I thought of, but the other folk, who knew that I knew Scudder's secret and dared not let me live. I was certain that they would pursue me with a keenness and vigilance unknown to the British law, and that once their grip closed on me I should find no mercy.

I looked back, but there was nothing in the landscape. The sun glinted on the metals of the line and the wet stones in the stream, and you could not have found a more peaceful sight in the world. Nevertheless I started to run. Crouching low in the runnels of the bog, I ran till the sweat blinded my eyes. The mood did not leave me till I had reached the rim of mountain and flung myself panting on a ridge high above the young waters of the brown river.

From my vantage-ground I could scan the whole moor right away to the railway line and to the south of it where green fields took the place of heather. I have eyes like a hawk, but I could see nothing moving in the whole countryside. Then I looked east beyond the ridge and saw a new kind of landscape—shallow green valleys with plentiful fir plantations and the faint lines of dust which spoke of highroads. Last of all I looked into the blue May sky, and there I saw that which set my pulses racing. . . .

Low down in the south a monoplane was climbing into the heavens. I was as certain as if I had been told that that aeroplane was looking for me, and that it did not belong to the police. For an hour or two I watched it from a pit of heather. It flew low along the hilltops, and then in narrow circles over the valley up which I had come. Then it seemed to change its mind, rose to a great height, and flew away back to the south.

I did not like this espionage from the air, and I began to think less well of the countryside I had chosen for a refuge. These heather hills were no sort of cover if my enemies were in the sky, and I must find a different kind of sanctuary. I looked with more satisfaction to the green country beyond the ridge, for there I should find woods and stone houses.

About six in the evening I came out of the moorland to a white ribbon of road which wound up the narrow vale of a lowland stream. As I followed it, fields gave place to bent, the glen became a plateau, and presently I had reached a kind of pass where a solitary house smoked in the twilight. The road swung over a bridge, and leaning on the parapet was a young man.

He was smoking a long clay pipe and studying the water with spectacled eyes. In his left hand was a small book with a finger marking the place. Slowly he repeated—

> "As when a Gryphon through the wilderness
> With wingèd step, o'er hill and moory dale
> Pursues the Arimaspian."

He jumped round as my step rung on the keystone, and I saw a pleasant sunburnt boyish face.

"Good-evening to you," he said gravely. "It's a fine night for the road."

The smell of peat smoke and of some savoury roast floated to me from the house.

"Is that place an inn?" I asked.

"At your service," he said politely. "I am the landlord, sir, and I hope you will stay the night, for to tell you the truth I have had no company for a week."

I pulled myself up on the parapet of the bridge and filled my pipe. I began to detect an ally.

"You're young to be an innkeeper," I said.

"My father died a year ago and left me the business. I live there with my grandmother. It's a slow job for a young man, and it wasn't my choice of profession."

"Which was?"

He actually blushed. "I want to write books," he said.

"And what better chance could you ask?" I cried. "Man, I've often thought that an innkeeper should make the best story-teller in the world."

"Not now," he said eagerly. "Maybe in the old days when you had pilgrims and ballad-makers and highwaymen and mail-coaches on the road. But not now. Nothing comes here but motor-cars full of fat women, who stop for lunch, and a fisherman or two in the spring, and the shooting tenants in August. There is not much material to be got out of that. I want to see life, to travel the world, and write things like Kipling and Conrad. But the most I've done yet is to get some verses printed in *Chambers's Journal*."

I looked at the inn standing golden in the sunset against the brown hills.

"I've knocked a bit about the world, and I wouldn't despise such a hermitage. D'you think that adventure is found only in the tropics or among gentry in red shirts? Maybe you're rubbing shoulders with it at this moment."

"That's what Kipling says," he said, his eyes brightening, and he quoted some verse about "Romance brings up the 9.15."

"Here's a true tale for you then," I cried, "and a month from now you can make a novel out of it."

Sitting on the bridge in the soft May gloaming I pitched him a lovely yarn. It was true in essentials, too, though I altered the minor details. I made out that I was a mining magnate from Kimberley, who had had a lot of trouble with I.D.B. and had shown up a gang. They had pursued me across the ocean, and had killed my best friend, and were now on my tracks.

I told the story well, though I say it who shouldn't. I pictured a flight across the Kalahari to German Africa, the crackling, parching days, the wonderful blue-velvet nights. I described an attack on my life on the voyage home, and I made a really horrid affair of the Portland Place murder. "You're looking for adventure," I cried; "well, you've found it here. The devils are after me, and the police are after them. It's a race that I mean to win."

"By God!" he whispered, drawing his breath in sharply, "it is all pure Rider Haggard and Conan Doyle."

"You believe me," I said gratefully.

"Of course I do," and he held out his hand. "I believe everything out of the common. The only thing to distrust is the normal."

He was very young, but he was the man for my money.

"I think they're off my track for the moment, but I must lie close for a couple of days. Can you take me in?"

He caught my elbow in his eagerness and drew me towards the house. "You can lie as snug here as if you were in a moss-hole. I'll see that nobody blabs, either. And you'll give me some more material about your adventures?"

As I entered the inn porch I heard from far off the beat of an engine. There silhouetted against the dusky West was my friend, the monoplane.

He gave me a room at the back of the house, with a fine outlook over the plateau, and he made me free of his own study, which was stacked with cheap editions of his favourite authors. I never saw the grandmother, so I guessed she was bedridden. An old woman called Margit brought me my meals, and the innkeeper was around me at all hours. I wanted some time to myself, so I invented a job for him. He had a motor-bicycle, and I sent him off next morning for the daily paper, which usually arrived with the post in the late afternoon. I told him to keep his eyes skinned, and make note of any strange figures he saw, keeping a special sharp look-out for motors and aeroplanes. Then I sat down in real earnest to Scudder's note-book.

He came back at midday with the *Scotsman*. There was nothing in it, except some further evidence of Paddock and the milkman, and a repetition of yesterday's statement that the murderer had gone North. But there was a long article, reprinted from the *Times*, about Karolides and the state of affairs in the Balkans, though there was no mention of any visit to England. I got rid of the innkeeper for the afternoon, for I was getting very warm in my search after the cipher.

As I told you, it was a numerical cipher, and by an elaborate system of experiments I had pretty well discovered what were the nulls and stops. The trouble was the key word, and when I thought of the odd million words he might have used I felt pretty hopeless. But about three o'clock I had a sudden inspiration.

The name Julia Czechenyi flashed across my memory. Scudder had said it was the key to the Karolides business, and it occurred to me to try it on his cipher.

It worked. The five letters of "Julia" gave me the position of the vowels. A was J, the tenth letter of the alphabet, and so represented by X in the cipher. E was = XXI, and so on. "Czechenyi" gave me the numerals for the principal consonants. I scribbled that scheme on a bit of paper and sat down to read Scudder's pages.

In half an hour I was reading with a whitish face and fingers that drummed on the table.

I glanced out of the window and saw a big touring car coming up the glen towards the inn. It drew up at the door, and there was the sound of people alighting. There seemed to be two of them, men in aquascutums and tweed caps.

Ten minutes later the innkeeper slipped into the room, his eyes bright with excitement.

"There's two chaps below looking for you," he whispered. "They're in the dining-room having whiskys-and-sodas. They asked about you and said they had hoped to meet you here. Oh! and they described you jolly well, down to your boots and shirt. I told them you had been here last night and had gone off on a motor-bicycle this morning, and one of the chaps swore like a navvy."

I made him tell me what they looked like. One was a dark-eyed thin fellow with bushy eyebrows, the other was always smiling and lisped in his talk. Neither was any kind of foreigner; on this my young friend was positive.

I took a bit of paper and wrote these words in German as if they were part of a letter:—

. . . "Black Stone. Scudder had got on to this, but he could not act for a fortnight. I doubt if I can do any good now, especially as Karolides is uncertain about his plans. But if Mr. T. advises I will do the best I . . ."

I manufactured it rather neatly, so that it looked like a loose page of a private letter.

"Take this down and say it was found in my bedroom, and ask them to return it to me if they overtake me."

Three minutes later I heard the car begin to move, and peeping from behind the curtain caught sight of the two figures. One was slim, the other was sleek; that was the most I could make of my reconnaissance.

The innkeeper appeared in great excitement. "Your paper woke them up," he said gleefully. "The dark fellow went as white as death and cursed like blazes, and the fat one whistled and looked ugly. They paid for their drinks with half a sovereign and wouldn't wait for change."

"Now I'll tell you what I want you to do," I said. "Get on your bicycle and go off to Newton-Stewart to the Chief Constable. Describe the two men, and say you suspect them of having had something to do with the London murder. You can invent reasons. The two will come back, never fear. Not to-night, for they'll follow me forty miles along the road, but first thing to-morrow morning. Tell the police to be here bright and early."

He set off like a docile child, while I worked at Scudder's notes. When he came back we dined together, and in common decency I had to let him pump me. I gave him a lot of stuff about lion hunts and the Matabele War, thinking all the while what tame businesses these were compared to this I was now engaged in. When he went to bed I sat up and finished Scudder. I smoked in a chair till daylight, for I could not sleep.

About eight next morning I witnessed the arrival of two constables and a sergeant. They put their car in a coach-house under the innkeeper's instructions, and entered the house. Twenty minutes later I saw from my window a second car come across the plateau from the opposite direction. It did not come up to the inn, but stopped two hundred yards off in the shelter of a patch of wood. I noticed that its occupants carefully reversed it before leaving it. A minute or two later I heard their steps on the gravel outside the window.

My plan had been to lie hid in my bedroom and see what happened. I had a notion that, if I could bring the police and my other more dangerous pursuers together, something might work out of it to my advantage. But now I had a better idea. I scribbled a line of thanks to my host, opened the window, and dropped quietly into a gooseberry bush. Unobserved I crossed the dyke, crawled down the side of a tributary burn, and won the highroad on the far side of the patch of trees. There stood the car, very spick and span in the morning sunlight, but with the dust on her which told of a long journey. I started her, jumped into the chauffeur's seat, and stole gently out on to the plateau.

Almost at once the road dipped so that I lost sight of the inn, but the wind seemed to bring me the sound of angry voices.

4 THE ADVENTURE OF THE RADICAL CANDIDATE

You may picture me driving that 40 h.p. car for all she was worth over the crisp moor roads on that shining May morning; glancing back at first over my shoulder, and looking anxiously to the next turning; then driving with a vague eye, just wide enough awake to keep on the highway. For I was thinking desperately of what I had found in Scudder's pocket-book.

The little man had told me a pack of lies. All his yarns about the Balkans and the Jew-Anarchists and the Foreign Office Conference were eyewash, and so was Karolides. And yet not quite, as you shall hear. I had staked everything on my belief in his story, and had been let down; here was his book telling me a different tale and instead of being once-bit-twice-shy, I believed it absolutely.

Why, I don't know. It rang desperately true, and the first yarn, if you understand me, had been in a queer way true also in spirit. The 15th day of June was going to be a day of destiny, a bigger destiny than the killing of a Dago. It was so big that I didn't blame Scudder for keeping me out of the game and wanting to play a lone hand. That, I was pretty clear, was his intention. He had told me something which sounded big enough, but the real thing was so immortally big that he, the man who had found it out, wanted it all for himself. I didn't blame him. It was risks after all that he was chiefly greedy about.

The whole story was in the notes—with gaps, you understand, which he would have filled up from his memory. He stuck down his authorities, too, and had an odd trick of giving them all a numerical value and then striking a balance, which stood for the reliability of each stage in the yarn. The four names he had printed were authorities, and there was a man, Ducrosne, who got five out of a possible five; and another fellow, Ammersfoort, who got three. The bare bones of the tale were all that was in the book—these, and one queer phrase which occurred half a dozen times inside brackets. ("Thirty-nine steps") was the phrase; and at its last time of use it ran—("Thirty-nine steps, I counted them—high tide 10.17 p.m."). I could make nothing of that.

The first thing I learned was that it was no question of preventing war. That was coming, as sure as Christmas: had been arranged, said Scudder, ever since February 1912. Karolides was going to be the occasion. He was booked all right, and was to hand in his checks on June 14th, two weeks and four days from that May morning. I gathered from Scudder's notes that nothing on earth could prevent that. His talk of Epirote guards that would skin their own grandmothers was all billy-o.

The second thing was that this war was going to come as a mighty surprise to Britain. Karolides' death would set the Balkans by the ears, and then Vienna would chip in with an ultimatum. Russia wouldn't like that, and there would be high words. But Berlin would play the peacemaker, and pour oil on the waters, till suddenly she would find a good cause for a quarrel, pick it up, and in five hours let fly at us. That was the idea, and a pretty good one too. Honey and fair speeches, and then a stroke in the dark. While we were talking about the goodwill and good intentions of Germany our coast would be silently ringed with mines, and submarines would be waiting for every battleship.

But all this depended upon the third thing, which was due to happen on June 15th. I would never have grasped this if I hadn't once happened to meet a French staff officer, coming back from West Africa, who had told me a lot of things. One was that, in spite of all the nonsense talked in Parliament, there was a real working alliance between France and Britain, and that the two General Staffs met every now and then, and made plans for joint action in case of war. Well, in June a very great swell was coming over from Paris, and he was going to get nothing less than a statement of the disposition of the British Home Fleet on mobilization. At least I gathered it was something like that; anyhow, it was something uncommonly important.

But on the 15th day of June there were to be others in London—others, at whom I could only guess. Scudder was content to call them collectively the "Black Stone." They represented not our Allies, but our deadly foes; and the information, destined for France, was to be diverted to their pockets. And it was to be used, remember—used a week or two later, with great guns and swift torpedoes, suddenly in the darkness of a summer night.

This was the story I had been deciphering in a back room of a country inn, overlooking a cabbage garden. This was the story that hummed in my brain as I swung in the big touring car from glen to glen.

My first impulse had been to write a letter to the Prime Minister, but a little reflection convinced me that it would be useless. Who would believe my tale? I must show a sign, some token in proof, and Heaven knew what that could be. Above all, I must keep going myself, ready to act when things got riper, and that was going to be no light job with the police of the British Isles in full cry after me and the watchers of the Black Stone running silently and swiftly on my trail.

I had no very clear purpose in my journey, but I steered east by the sun, for I remembered from the map that if I went north I would come into a region of coal pits and industrial towns. Presently I was down from the moorlands and traversing the broad haugh of a river. For miles I ran alongside a park wall, and in a break of the trees I saw a great castle. I swung through little old thatched villages, and over peaceful lowland streams, and past gardens blazing with hawthorn and yellow laburnum. The land was so deep in peace that I could scarcely believe that somewhere behind me were those who sought my life; ay, and that in a month's time, unless I had the almightiest of luck, these round country faces would be pinched and staring, and men would be lying dead in English fields.

About midday I entered a long straggling village, and had a mind to stop and eat. Half-way down was the Post Office, and on the steps of it stood the post-mistress and a policeman hard at work conning a telegram. When they saw me they wakened up, and the policeman advanced with raised hand, and cried on me to stop.

I nearly was fool enough to obey. Then it flashed upon me that the wire had to do with me; that my friends at the inn had come to an understanding, and were united in desiring to see more of me, and that it had been easy enough for them to wire the description of me and the car to thirty villages through which I might pass. I released the brakes just in time. As it was, the policeman made a claw at the hood, and only dropped off when he got my left in his eye.

I saw that main roads were no place for me, and turned into the byways. It wasn't an easy job without a map, for there was the risk of getting on to a farm road and ending in a duck pond or a stable-yard, and I couldn't afford that kind of delay. I began to see what an ass I had been to steal the car. The big green brute would be the safest kind of clue to me over the breadth of Scotland. If I left it and took to my feet, it would be discovered in an hour or two and I would get no start in the race.

The immediate thing to do was to get to the loneliest roads. These I soon found when I struck up a tributary of the big river, and got into a glen with steep hills all about me, and a corkscrew road at the end which climbed over a pass. Here I met nobody, but it was taking me too far north, so I slewed east along a bad track and finally struck a big double-line railway. Away below me I saw another broadish valley, and it occurred to me that if I crossed it I might find some remote inn to pass the night. The evening was now drawing in, and I was furiously hungry, for I had eaten nothing since breakfast except a couple of buns I had bought from a baker's cart.

Just then I heard a noise in the sky, and lo and behold there was that infernal aeroplane, flying low, about a dozen miles to the south and rapidly coming towards me.

I had the sense to remember that on a bare moor I was at the aeroplane's mercy, and that my only chance was to get to the leafy cover of the valley. Down the hill I went like blue lightning, screwing my head round, whenever I dared, to watch that damned flying machine. Soon I was on a road between hedges, and dipping to the deep-cut glen of a stream. Then came a bit of thick wood where I slackened speed.

Suddenly on my left I heard the hoot of another car, and realized to my horror that I was almost upon a couple of gateposts through which a private road debouched on the highway. My horn gave an agonized roar, but it was too late. I clapped on my brakes, but my impetus was too great, and there before me a car was sliding athwart my course. In a second there would have been the deuce of a wreck. I did the only thing possible, and ran slap into the hedge on the right, trusting to find something soft beyond.

But there I was mistaken. My car slithered through the hedge like butter, and then gave a sickening plunge forward. I saw what was coming, leapt on the seat and would have jumped out. But a branch of hawthorn got me in the chest, lifted me up and held me, while a ton or two of expensive metal slipped below me, bucked and pitched, and then dropped with an almighty smash fifty feet to the bed of the stream.

Slowly that thorn let me go. I subsided first on the hedge, and then very gently on a bower of nettles. As I scrambled to my feet a hand took me by the arm, and a sympathetic and badly scared voice asked me if I were hurt.

I found myself looking at a tall young man in goggles and a leather ulster, who kept on blessing his soul and whinnying apologies. For myself, once I got my wind back, I was rather glad than otherwise. This was one way of getting rid of the car.

"My blame, sir," I answered him. "It's lucky that I did not add homicide to my follies. That's the end of my Scotch motor tour, but it might have been the end of my life."

He plucked out a watch and studied it. "You're the right sort of fellow," he said. "I can spare a quarter of an hour, and my house is two minutes off. I'll see you clothed and fed and snug in bed. Where's your kit, by the way? Is it in the burn along with the car?"

"It's in my pocket," I said, brandishing a toothbrush. "I'm a colonial and travel light."

"A colonial," he cried. "By Gad, you're the very man I've been praying for. Are you by any blessed chance a Free Trader?"

"I am," said I, without the foggiest notion of what he meant.

He patted my shoulder and hurried me into his car. Three minutes later we drew up before a comfortable-looking shooting-box set among pine trees, and he ushered me indoors. He took me first to a bedroom and flung half a dozen of his suits before me, for my own had been pretty well reduced to rags. I selected a loose blue serge, which of the lot differed most conspicuously from my former garments, and borrowed a linen collar. Then he haled me to the dining-room, where the remnants of a meal stood on the table, and announced that I had just five minutes to feed. "You can take a snack in your pocket, and we'll have supper when we get back. I've got to be at the Masonic Hall at eight o'clock, or my agent will comb my hair."

I had a cup of coffee and some cold ham, while he yarned away on the hearthrug.

"You find me in the deuce of a mess, Mr.—; by-the-by, you haven't told me your name. Twisdon? Any relation of old Tommy Twisdon of the Sixtieth? No? Well, you see I'm Liberal Candidate for this part of the world, and I had a meeting on to-night at Brattleburn—that's my chief town, and an infernal Tory stronghold. I had got the Colonial ex-Premier fellow, Crumpleton, coming to speak for me to-night, and had the thing tremendously billed and the whole place ground-baited. This afternoon I had a wire from the ruffian saying he had got influenza at Blackpool, and here am I left to do the whole thing myself. I had meant to speak for ten minutes and must now go on for forty, and, though I've been racking my brains for three hours to think of something, I simply cannot last the course. Now you've got to be a good chap and help me. You're a Free Trader, and can tell our people what a wash-out Protection is in the Colonies. All you fellows have the gift of the gab—I wish to heaven I had it. I'll be for evermore in your debt."

I had very few notions about Free Trade one way or the other, but I saw no other chance to get what I wanted. My young gentleman was far too absorbed in his own difficulties to think how odd it was to ask a stranger who had just missed death by an ace and had lost a 1,000-guinea car to address a meeting for him on the spur of the moment. But my necessities did not allow me to contemplate oddnesses or to pick and choose my supports.

"All right," I said. "I'm not much good as a speaker, but I'll tell them a bit about Australia."

At my words the cares of the ages slipped from his shoulders, and he was rapturous in his thanks. He lent me a big driving coat—and never troubled to ask why I had started on a motor tour without possessing an ulster—and, as we slipped down the dusty roads, poured into my ears the simple facts of his history. He was an orphan, and his uncle had brought him up—I've forgotten the uncle's name, but he was in the Cabinet, and you can read his speeches in the papers. He had gone round the world after leaving

Cambridge, and then, being short of a job, his uncle had advised politics. I gathered that he had no preference in parties. "Good chaps in both," he said cheerfully, "and plenty of blighters, too. I'm Liberal, because my family have always been Whigs." But if he was lukewarm politically he had strong views on other things. He found out I knew a bit about horses, and jawed away about the Derby entries; and he was full of plans for improving his shooting. Altogether, a very clean, decent, callow young man.

As we passed through a little town two policemen signalled us to stop, and flashed their lanterns on us. "Beg pardon, Sir Harry," said one. "We've got instructions to look out for a cawr, and the description's no unlike yours."

"Right-o," said my host, while I thanked Providence for the devious ways I had been brought to safety. After that he spoke no more, for his mind began to labour heavily with his coming speech. His lips kept muttering, his eye wandered, and I began to prepare myself for a second catastrophe. I tried to think of something to say myself, but my mind was dry as a stone. The next thing I knew we had drawn up outside a door in a street, and were being welcomed by some noisy gentlemen with rosettes.

The hall had about five hundred in it, women mostly, a lot of bald heads, and a dozen or two young men. The chairman, a weaselly minister with a reddish nose, lamented Crumpleton's absence, soliloquized on his influenza, and gave me a certificate as a "trusted leader of Australian thought." There were two policemen at the door, and I hoped they took note of that testimonial. Then Sir Harry started.

I never heard anything like it. He didn't begin to know how to talk. He had about a bushel of notes from which he read, and when he let go of them he fell into one prolonged stutter. Every now and then he remembered a phrase he had learned by heart, straightened his back, and gave it off like Henry Irving, and the next moment he was bent double and crooning over his papers. It was the most appalling rot, too. He talked about the "German menace," and said it was all a Tory invention to cheat the poor of their rights and keep back the great flood of social reform, but that "organized labour" realized this and laughed the Tories to scorn. He was all for reducing our Navy as a proof of our good faith, and then sending Germany an ultimatum telling her to do the same or we would knock her into a cocked hat. He said that, but for the Tories, Germany and Britain would be fellow-workers in peace and reform. I thought of the little black book in my pocket! A giddy lot Scudder's friends cared for peace and reform.

Yet in a queer way I liked the speech. You could see the niceness of the chap shining out behind the muck with which he had been spoonfed. Also it took a load off my mind. I mightn't be much of an orator, but I was a thousand per cent. better than Sir Harry.

I didn't get on so badly when it came to my turn. I simply told them all I could remember about Australia, praying there should be no Australian there—all about its labour party and emigration and universal service. I doubt if I remembered to mention Free Trade, but I said there were no Tories in Australia, only Labour and Liberals. That fetched a cheer, and I woke them up a bit when I started in to tell them the kind of glorious business I thought could be made out of the Empire if we really put our backs into it.

Altogether I fancy I was rather a success. The minister didn't like me, though, and when he proposed a vote of thanks, spoke of Sir Harry's speech as "statesmanlike" and mine as having "the eloquence of an emigration agent."

When we were in the car again my host was in wild spirits at having got his job over. "A ripping speech, Twisdon," he said. "Now, you're coming home with me. I'm all alone, and if you'll stop a day or two I'll show you some very decent fishing."

We had a hot supper—and I wanted it pretty badly—and then drank grog in a big cheery smoking-room with a crackling wood fire. I thought the time had come for me to put my cards on the table. I saw by this man's eye that he was the kind you can trust.

"Listen, Sir Harry," I said. "I've something pretty important to say to you. You're a good fellow, and I'm going to be frank. Where on earth did you get that poisonous rubbish you talked to-night?"

His face fell. "Was it as bad as that?" he asked ruefully. "It did sound rather thin. I got most of it out of the *Progressive Magazine* and pamphlets that agent chap of mine keeps sending me. But you surely don't think Germany would ever go to war with us?"

"Ask that question in six weeks and it won't need an answer," I said. "If you'll give me your attention for half an hour I am going to tell you a story."

I can see yet that bright room with the deers' heads and the old prints on the walls, Sir Harry standing restlessly on the stone curb of the hearth, and myself lying back in an arm-chair, speaking. I seemed to be another person, standing aside and listening to my own voice, and judging carefully the reliability of my tale. It was the first time I had ever told any one the exact truth, so far as I understood it, and it did me no end of good, for it straightened out the thing in my own mind. I blinked no detail. He heard all about Scudder, and the milkman, and the note-book, and my doings in Galloway. Presently he got very excited and walked up and down the hearthrug.

"So you see," I concluded, "you have got here in your house the man that is wanted for the Portland Place murder. Your duty is to send your car for the police and give me up. I don't think I'll get very far. There'll be an accident and I'll have a knife in my ribs an hour or so after arrest. Nevertheless it's your duty, as a law-abiding citizen. Perhaps in a month's time you'll be sorry, but you have no cause to think of that."

He was looking at me with bright steady eyes. "What was your job in Rhodesia, Mr. Hannay?" he asked.

"Mining engineer," I said. "I've made my pile cleanly and I've had a good time in the making of it."

"Not a profession that weakens the nerves, is it?"

I laughed. "Oh, as to that, my nerves are good enough." I took down a hunting-knife from a stand on the wall, and did the old Mashona trick of tossing it and catching it in my lips. That wants a pretty steady heart.

He watched me with a smile. "I don't want proofs. I may be an ass on the platform, but I can size up a man. You're no murderer and you're no fool, and I believe you are speaking the truth. I'm going to back you up. Now, what can I do?"

"First, I want you to write a letter to your uncle. I've got to get in touch with the Government people sometime before the 15th of June."

He pulled his moustache. "That won't help you. This is Foreign Office business, and my uncle would have nothing to do with it. Besides, you'd never convince him. No, I'll go one better. I'll write to the Permanent Secretary at the Foreign Office. He's my godfather, and one of the best going. What do you want?"

He sat down at a table and wrote to my dictation. The gist of it was that if a man called Twisdon (I thought I had better stick to that name) turned up before June 15th he was to entreat him kindly. He said Twisdon would prove his *bona fides* by passing the word "Black Stone" and whistling "Annie Laurie."

"Good," said Sir Harry. "That's the proper style. By the way, you'll find my godfather—his name's Sir Walter Bullivant—down at his country cottage for Whitsuntide. It's close to Artinswell on the Kennet. That's done. Now, what's the next thing?"

"You're about my height. Lend me the oldest tweed suit you've got. Anything will do, so long as the colour is the opposite of the clothes I destroyed this afternoon. Then show me a map of the neighbourhood and explain to me the lie of the land. Lastly, if the police come seeking me, just show them the car in the glen. If the other lot turn up, tell them I caught the south express after your meeting."

He did, or promised to do, all these things. I shaved off the remnants of my moustache, and got inside an ancient suit of what I believe is called heather mixture. The map gave me some notion of my whereabouts, and told me the two things I wanted to know—where the main railway to the south could be joined, and what were the wildest districts near at hand.

At two o'clock he wakened me from my slumbers in the smoking-room arm-chair, and led me blinking into the dark starry night. An old bicycle was found in a tool-shed and handed over to me.

"First turn to the right up by the long fir wood," he enjoined. "By daybreak you'll be well into the hills. Then I should pitch the machine into a bog and take to the moors on foot. You can put in a week among the shepherds, and be as safe as if you were in New Guinea."

I pedalled diligently up the steep roads of hill gravel till the skies grew pale with morning. As the mists cleared before the sun, I found myself in a wide green world with glens falling on every side and a far-away blue horizon. Here, at any rate, I could get early news of my enemies.

5 THE ADVENTURE OF THE SPECTACLED ROADMAN

I sat down on the very crest of the pass and took stock of my position.

Behind me was the road climbing through a long cleft in the hills, which was the upper glen of some notable river. In front was a flat space of maybe a mile, all pitted with bog-holes and rough with tussocks, and then beyond it the road fell steeply down another glen to a plain whose blue dimness melted into the distance. To left and right were round-shouldered green hills as smooth as pancakes, but to the south—that is, the left hand—there was a glimpse of high heathery mountains, which I remembered from the map as the big knot of hill which I had chosen for my sanctuary. I was on the central boss of a huge upland country, and could see everything moving for miles. In the meadows below the road half a mile back a cottage smoked, but it was the only sign of human life. Otherwise there was only the calling of plovers and the tinkling of little streams.

It was now about seven o'clock, and as I waited I heard once again that ominous beat in the air. Then I realized that my vantage-ground might be in reality a trap. There was no cover for a tomtit in those bald green places.

I sat quite still and hopeless while the beat grew louder. Then I saw an aeroplane coming up from the east. It was flying high, but as I looked it dropped several hundred feet and began to circle round the knot of hill in narrowing circles, just as a hawk wheels before it pounces. Now it was flying very low, and now the observer on board caught sight of me. I could see one of the two occupants examining me through glasses.

Suddenly it began to rise in swift whorls, and the next I knew it was speeding eastward again till it became a speck in the blue morning.

That made me do some savage thinking. My enemies had located me, and the next thing would be a cordon round me. I didn't know what force they could command, but I was certain it would be sufficient. The aeroplane had seen my bicycle, and would conclude that I would try to escape by the road. In that case there might be a chance on the moors to the right or left. I wheeled the machine a hundred yards from the highway and plunged it into a moss-hole, where it sank among pond-weed and water-buttercups. Then I climbed to a knoll which gave me a view of the two valleys. Nothing was stirring on the long white ribbon that threaded them.

I have said there was not cover in the whole place to hide a rat. As the day advanced it was flooded with soft fresh light till it had the fragrant sunniness of the South African veld. At other times I would have liked the place, but now it seemed to suffocate me. The free moorlands were prison walls, and the keen hill air was the breath of a dungeon.

I tossed a coin—heads right, tails left—and it fell heads, so I turned to the north. In a little I came to the brow of the ridge which was the containing wall of the pass. I saw the highroad for maybe ten miles, and far down it something that was moving, and that I took to be a motor-car. Beyond the ridge I looked on a rolling green moor, which fell away into wooded glens. Now my life on the veld has given me the eyes of a kite, and I can see things for which most men need a telescope. . . . Away down the slope, a couple of miles away, men were advancing like a row of beaters at a shoot.

I dropped out of sight behind the skyline. That way was shut to me, and I must try the bigger hills to the south beyond the highway. The car I had noticed was getting nearer, but it was still a long way off with some very steep gradients before it. I ran hard, crouching low except in the hollows, and as I ran I kept scanning the brow of the hill before me. Was it imagination, or did I see figures—one, two, perhaps more—moving in a glen beyond the stream?

If you are hemmed in on all sides in a patch of land there is only one chance of escape. You must stay in the patch, and let your enemies search it and not find you. That was good sense, but how on earth was I to escape notice in that table-cloth of a place? I would have buried myself to the neck in mud or lain below water or climbed the tallest tree. But there was not a stick of wood, the bog-holes were little puddles, the stream was a slender trickle. There was nothing but short heather, and bare hill bent, and the white highway.

Then in a tiny bight of road, beside a heap of stones, I found the Roadman.

He had just arrived, and was wearily flinging down his hammer. He looked at me with a fishy eye and yawned.

"Confoond the day I ever left the herdin'!" he said, as if to the world at large. "There I was my ain maister. Now I'm a slave to the Goavernment, tethered to the roadside, wi' sair een, and a back like a suckle."

He took up the hammer, struck a stone, dropped the implement with an oath, and put both hands to his ears. "Mercy on me! My heid's burstin'!" he cried.

He was a wild figure, about my own size but much bent, with a week's beard on his chin, and a pair of big horn spectacles.

"I canna dae't," he cried again. "The Surveyor maun just report me. I'm for my bed."

I asked him what was the trouble, though indeed that was clear enough.

"The trouble is that I'm no sober. Last nicht my dochter Merran was waddit, and they danced till fower in the byre. Me and some ither chiels sat down to the drinkin', and here I am. Peety that I ever lookit on the wine when it was red!"

I agreed with him about bed.

"It's easy speakin," he moaned. "But I got a postcaird yestreen sayin' that the new Road Surveyor would be round the day. He'll come and he'll no find me, or else he'll find me fou, and either way I'm a done man. I'll awa back to my bed and say I'm no weel, but I doot that'll no help me, for they ken my kind o' no-weel-ness."

Then I had an inspiration. "Does the new Surveyor know you?" I asked.

"No him. He's just been a week at the job. He rins about in a wee motor-cawr, and wad speir the inside oot o' a whelk."

"Where's your house?" I asked, and was directed by a wavering finger to the cottage by the stream.

"Well, back to your bed," I said, "and sleep in peace. I'll take on your job for a bit and see the Surveyor."

He stared at me blankly; then, as the notion dawned on his fuddled brain, his face broke into the vacant drunkard's smile.

"You're the billy," he cried. "It'll be easy eneuch managed. I've finished that bing o' stanes, so you needna chap ony mair this forenoon. Just take the barry, and wheel eneuch metal frae yon quarry doon the road to mak anither bing the morn. My name's Alexander Trummle, and I've been seeven year at the trade, and twenty afore that herdin' on Leithen Water. My freens ca' me Ecky, and whiles Specky, for I wear glesses, being weak i' the sicht. Just you speak the Surveyor fair, and ca' him Sir, and he'll be fell pleased. I'll be back or midday."

I borrowed his spectacles and filthy old hat; stripped off coat, waistcoat, and collar, and gave him them to carry home; borrowed, too, the foul stump of a clay pipe as an extra property. He indicated my simple tasks, and without more ado set off at an amble bedwards. Bed may have been his chief object, but I think there was also something left in the foot of a bottle. I prayed that he might be safe under cover before my friends arrived on the scene.

Then I set to work to dress for the part. I opened the collar of my shirt—it was a vulgar blue-and-white check such as ploughmen wear—and revealed a neck as brown as any tinker's. I rolled up my sleeves, and there was a forearm which might have been a blacksmith's, sunburnt and rough with old scars. I got my boots and trouser legs all white from the dust of the road, and hitched up my trousers, tying them with string below the knee. Then I set to work on my face. With a handful of dust I made a watermark round my neck, the place where Mr. Turnbull's Sunday ablutions might be expected to stop. I rubbed a good deal of dirt also into the sunburn of my cheeks. A roadman's eyes would no doubt be a little inflamed, so I contrived to get some dust in both of mine; and by dint of vigorous rubbing produced a bleary effect.

The sandwiches Sir Harry had given me had gone off with my coat, but the roadman's lunch, tied up in a red handkerchief, was at my disposal. I ate with great relish several of the thick slabs of scone and cheese and drank a little of the cold tea. In the handkerchief was a local paper tied with string and addressed to Mr. Turnbull—obviously meant to solace his midday leisure. I did up the bundle again, and put the paper conspicuously beside it.

My boots did not satisfy me, but by dint of kicking among the stones I reduced them to the granite-like surface which marks a roadman's footgear. Then I bit and scraped my finger nails till the edges were all cracked and uneven. The men I was matched against would miss no detail. I broke one of the bootlaces and retied it in a clumsy knot, and loosed the other so that my thick grey socks bulged over the uppers. Still no sign of anything on the road. The motor I had observed half an hour ago must have gone home.

My toilet complete, I took up the barrow and began my journeys to and from the quarry a hundred yards off.

I remember an old scout in Rhodesia, who had done many queer things in his day, once telling me that the secret of playing a part was to think yourself into it. You could never keep it up, he said, unless you could manage to convince yourself that you were *it*. So I shut off all other thoughts and switched them on to the road-mending. I thought of the little white cottage as my home. I recalled the years I had spent herding on Leithen Water, I made my mind dwell lovingly on sleep in a box-bed and a bottle of cheap whisky. Still nothing appeared on that long white road.

Now and then a sheep wandered off the heather to stare at me. A heron flopped down to a pool in the stream and started to fish, taking no more notice of me than if I had been a milestone. On I went, trundling my loads of stone, with the heavy step of the professional. Soon I grew warm, and the dust on my face changed into solid and abiding grit. I was already counting the hours till evening should put a limit to Mr. Turnbull's monotonous toil.

Suddenly a crisp voice spoke from the road, and looking up I saw a little Ford two-seater, and a round-faced young man in a bowler hat.

"Are you Alexander Turnbull?" he asked. "I am the new County Road Surveyor. You live at Blackhopefoot, and have charge of the section from Laidlaw-byres to the Riggs? Good! A fair bit of road, Turnbull, and not badly engineered. A little soft about a mile off, and the edges want cleaning. See you look after that. Good-morning. You'll know me the next time you see me."

Clearly my get-up was good enough for the dreaded Surveyor. I went on with my work, and as the morning grew towards noon I was cheered by a little traffic. A baker's van breasted the hill, and sold me a bag of ginger biscuits which I stowed in my trousers pocket against emergencies. Then a herd passed with sheep, and disturbed me somewhat by asking loudly, "What had become o'Specky?"

"In bed wi' the colic," I replied, and the herd passed on. . . .

Just about midday a big car stole down the hill, glided past and drew up a hundred yards beyond. Its three occupants descended as if to stretch their legs, and sauntered towards me.

Two of the men I had seen before from the window of the Galloway inn— one lean, sharp, and dark, the other comfortable and smiling. The third had the look of a countryman—a vet, perhaps, or a small farmer. He was dressed in ill-cut knickerbockers, and the eye in his head was as bright and wary as a hen's.

"'Morning," said the last. "That's a fine easy job o' yours."

I had not looked up on their approach, and now, when accosted, I slowly and painfully straightened my back, after the manner of roadmen; spat vigorously, after the manner of the low Scot, and regarded them steadily before replying. I confronted three pairs of eyes that missed nothing.

THE SPECTACLED ROADMAN 41

"There's waur jobs and there's better," I said sententiously. "I wad rather hae yours, sittin' a' day on your hinderlands on thae cushions. It's you and your muckle cawrs that wreck my roads! If we a' had oor richts, ye sud be made to mend what ye break."

The bright-eyed man was looking at the newspaper lying beside Turnbull's bundle.

"I see you get your papers in good time," he said.

I glanced at it casually. "Ay, in gude time. Seein' that that paper cam out last Setterday I'm just sax days late."

He picked it up, glanced at the superscription, and laid it down again. One of the others had been looking at my boots, and a word in German called the speaker's attention to them.

"You've fine taste in boots," he said. "These were never made by a country shoemaker."

"They were not," I said readily. "They were made in London. I got them frae the gentleman that was here last year for the shootin'. What was his name now?" And I scratched a forgetful head.

Again the sleek one spoke in German. "Let us get on," he said. "This fellow is all right."

They asked one last question.

"Did you see any one pass early this morning? He might be on a bicycle or he might be on foot."

I very nearly fell into the trap and told a story of a bicyclist hurrying past in the grey dawn. But I had the sense to see my danger. I pretended to consider very deeply.

"I wasna up very early," I said. "Ye see, my dochter was merrit last nicht, and we keepit it up late. I opened the house door about seeven and there was naebody on the road then. Since I cam up here there has just been the baker and the Ruchill herd, besides you gentlemen."

One of them gave me a cigar, which I smelt gingerly and stuck in Turnbull's bundle. They got into their car and were out of sight in three minutes.

My heart leaped with an enormous relief, but I went on wheeling my stones. It was as well, for ten minutes later the car returned, one of the occupants waving a hand to me. Those gentry left nothing to chance.

I finished Turnbull's bread and cheese, and pretty soon I had finished the stones. The next step was what puzzled me. I could not keep up this road-making business for long. A merciful Providence had kept Mr. Turnbull indoors, but if he appeared on the scene there would be trouble. I had a notion that the cordon was still tight round the glen, and that if I walked in any direction I should meet with questioners. But get out I must. No man's nerve could stand more than a day of being spied on.

I stayed at my post till about five o'clock. By that time I had resolved to go down to Turnbull's cottage at nightfall and take my chance of getting over the hills in the darkness. But suddenly a new car came up the road, and slowed down a yard or two from me. A fresh wind had risen, and the occupant wanted to light a cigarette.

It was a touring car, with the tonneau full of an assortment of baggage. One man sat in it, and by an amazing chance I knew him. His name was Marmaduke Jopley, and he was an offence to creation. He was a sort of blood stockbroker, who did his business by toadying eldest sons and rich young peers and foolish old ladies. "Marmie" was a familiar figure, I understood, at balls and polo-weeks and country houses. He was an adroit scandal-monger, and would crawl a mile on his belly to anything that had a title or a million. I had a business introduction to his firm when I came to London, and he was good enough to ask me to dinner at his club. There he showed off at a great rate, and pattered about his duchesses till the snobbery of the creature turned me sick. I asked a man afterwards why nobody kicked him, and was told that Englishmen reverenced the weaker sex.

Anyhow there he was now, nattily dressed, in a fine new car, obviously on his way to visit some of his smart friends. A sudden daftness took me, and in a second I had jumped into the tonneau and had him by the shoulder.

"Hullo, Jopley," I sang out. "Well met, my lad!"

He got a horrid fright. His chin dropped as he stared at me. "Who the devil are you?" he gasped.

"My name's Hannay," I said. "From Rhodesia, you remember."

"Good God, the murderer!" he choked.

"Just so. And there'll be a second murder, my dear, if you don't do as I tell you. Give me that coat of yours. That cap, too."

He did as he was bid, for he was blind with terror. Over my dirty trousers and vulgar shirt I put on his smart driving-coat, which buttoned high at the top and thereby hid the deficiencies of my collar. I stuck the cap on my head, and added his gloves to my get-up. The dusty roadman in a minute was transformed into one of the neatest motorists in Scotland. On Mr. Jopley's head I clapped Turnbull's unspeakable hat, and told him to keep it there.

Then with some difficulty I turned the car. My plan was to go back the road he had come, for the watchers, having seen it before, would probably let it pass unremarked, and Marmie's figure was in no way like mine.

"Now, my child," I said, "sit quite still and be a good boy. I mean you no harm. I'm only borrowing your car for an hour or two. But if you play me any tricks, and above all if you open your mouth, as sure as there's a God above me I'll wring your neck. *Savez?*"

I enjoyed that evening's ride. We ran eight miles down the valley, through a village or two, and I could not help noticing several strange-looking folk lounging by the roadside. These were the watchers who would have had much to say to me if I had come in other garb or company. As it was, they looked incuriously on. One touched his cap in salute, and I responded graciously.

As the dark fell I turned up a side glen which, as I remember from the map, led into an unfrequented corner of the hills. Soon the villages were left behind, then the farms, and then even the wayside cottages. Presently we came to a lonely moor where the night was blackening the sunset gleam in the bog pools. Here we stopped, and I obligingly reversed the car and restored to Mr. Jopley his belongings.

"A thousand thanks," I said. "There's more use in you than I thought. Now be off and find the police."

As I sat on the hillside, watching the tail lights dwindle, I reflected on the various kinds of crime I had now sampled. Contrary to general belief, I was not a murderer, but I had become an unholy liar, a shameless impostor, and a highwayman with a marked taste for expensive motor-cars.

6 THE ADVENTURE OF THE BALD ARCHAEOLOGIST

I spent the night on a shelf of the hillside, in the lee of a boulder where the heather grew long and soft. It was a cold business, for I had neither coat nor waistcoat. These were in Mr. Turnbull's keeping, as was Scudder's little book, my watch and—worst of all—my pipe and tobacco pouch. Only my money accompanied me in my belt, and about half a pound of ginger biscuits in my trousers pocket.

I supped off half those biscuits, and by worming myself deep into the heather got some kind of warmth. My spirits had risen, and I was beginning to enjoy this crazy game of hide-and-seek. So far I had been miraculously lucky. The milkman, the literary innkeeper, Sir Harry, the roadman, and the idiotic Marmie, were all pieces of undeserved good fortune. Somehow the first success gave me a feeling that I was going to pull the thing through.

My chief trouble was that I was desperately hungry. When a Jew shoots himself in the City and there is an inquest, the newspapers usually report that the deceased was "well-nourished." I remember thinking that they would not call me well-nourished if I broke my neck in a bog-hole. I lay and tortured myself—for the ginger biscuits merely emphasized the aching void—with the memory of all the good food I had thought so little of in London. There were Paddock's crisp sausages and fragrant shavings of bacon and shapely poached eggs—how often I had turned up my nose at them! There were the cutlets they did at the club, and a particular ham that stood on the cold table, for which my soul lusted. My thoughts hovered over all varieties of mortal edible, and finally settled on a porter-house steak and a quart of bitter with a welsh rabbit to follow. In longing hopelessly for these dainties I fell asleep.

I woke very cold and stiff about an hour after dawn. It took me a little while to remember where I was, for I had been very weary and had slept heavily. I saw first the pale blue sky through a net of heather, then a big shoulder of hill, and then my own boots placed neatly in a blaeberry bush. I raised myself on my arms and looked down into the valley, and that one look set me lacing up my boots in mad haste.

For there were men below, not more than a quarter of a mile off, spaced out on the hillside like a fan, and beating the heather. Marmie had not been slow in looking for his revenge.

I crawled out of my shelf into the cover of a boulder, and from it gained a shallow trench which slanted up the mountain face. This led me presently into the narrow gully of a burn, by way of which I scrambled to the top of the ridge. From there I looked back, and saw that I was still undiscovered. My pursuers were patiently quartering the hillside and moving upwards.

Keeping behind the skyline I ran for maybe half a mile, till I judged I was above the uppermost end of the glen. Then I showed myself, and was instantly noted by one of the flankers, who passed the word to the others. I heard cries coming up from below, and saw that the line of search had changed its direction. I pretended to retreat over the skyline, but instead went back the way I had come, and in twenty minutes was behind the ridge overlooking my sleeping place. From that viewpoint I had the satisfaction of seeing the pursuit streaming up the hill at the top of the glen on a hopelessly false scent.

I had before me a choice of routes, and I chose a ridge which made an angle with the one I was on, and so would soon put a deep glen between me and my enemies. The exercise had warmed my blood, and I was beginning to enjoy myself amazingly. As I went I breakfasted on the dusty remnants of the ginger biscuits.

I knew very little about the country, and I hadn't a notion what I was going to do. I trusted to the strength of my legs, but I was well aware that those behind me would be familiar with the lie of the land, and that my ignorance would be a heavy handicap. I saw in front of me a sea of hills, rising very high towards the south, but northwards breaking down into broad ridges which separated wide and shallow dales. The ridge I had chosen seemed to sink after a mile or two to a moor which lay like a pocket in the uplands. That seemed as good a direction to take as any other.

My stratagem had given me a fair start—call it twenty minutes—and I had the width of a glen behind me before I saw the first heads of the pursuers. The police had evidently called in local talent to their aid, and the men I could see had the appearance of herds or gamekeepers. They hallooed at the sight of me, and I waved my hand. Two dived into the glen and began to climb my ridge, while the others kept their own side of the hill. I felt as if I were taking part in a schoolboy game of hare and hounds.

But very soon it began to seem less of a game. Those fellows behind me were hefty men on their native heath. Looking back I saw that only three were following direct, and I guessed that the others had fetched a circuit to cut me off. My lack of local knowledge might very well be my undoing, and I resolved to get out of this tangle of glens to the pocket of moor I had seen from the tops. I must so increase my distance as to get clear away from them, and I believed I could do this if I could find the right ground for it. If there had been cover I would have tried a bit of stalking, but on these bare slopes you could see a fly a mile off. My hope must be in the length of my legs and the soundness of my wind, but I needed easier ground for that, for I was not bred a mountaineer. How I longed for a good Afrikander pony!

I put on a great spurt and got off my ridge and down into the moor before any figures appeared on the skyline behind me. I crossed a burn, and came out on a highroad which made a pass between two glens. All in front of me was a big field of heather sloping up to a crest which was crowned with an odd feather of trees. In the dyke by the roadside was a gate, from which a grass-grown track led over the first wave of the moor.

I jumped the dyke and followed it, and after a few hundred yards—as soon as it was out of sight of the highway—the grass stopped and it became a very respectable road, which was evidently kept with some care. Clearly it ran to a house, and I began to think of doing the same. Hitherto my luck had held, and it might be that my best chance would be found in this remote dwelling. Anyhow there were trees there, and that meant cover.

I did not follow the road, but the burnside which flanked it on the right, where the bracken grew deep and the high banks made a tolerable screen. It was well I did so, for no sooner had I gained the hollow than, looking back, I saw the pursuit topping the ridge from which I had descended.

After that I did not look back; I had no time. I ran up the burnside, crawling over the open places, and for a large part wading in the shallow stream. I found a deserted cottage with a row of phantom peat-stacks and an overgrown garden. Then I was among young hay, and very soon had come to the edge of a plantation of wind-blown firs. From there I saw the chimneys of the house smoking a few hundred yards to my left. I forsook the burnside, crossed another dyke, and almost before I knew was on a rough lawn. A glance back told me that I was well out of sight of the pursuit, which had not yet passed the first lift of the moor.

The lawn was a very rough place, cut with a scythe instead of a mower, and planted with beds of scrubby rhododendrons. A brace of black game, which are not usually garden birds, rose at my approach. The house before me was the ordinary moorland farm, with a more pretentious whitewashed wing added. Attached to this wing was a glass veranda, and through the glass I saw the face of an elderly gentleman meekly watching me.

I stalked over the border of coarse hill gravel and entered the open veranda door. Within was a pleasant room, glass on one side, and on the other a mass of books. More books showed in an inner room. On the floor, instead of tables, stood cases such as you see in a museum, filled with coins and queer stone implements.

There was a knee-hole desk in the middle, and seated at it, with some papers and open volumes before him, was the benevolent old gentleman. His face was round and shiny, like Mr. Pickwick's, big glasses were stuck on the end of his nose, and the top of his head was as bright and bare as a glass bottle. He never moved when I entered, but raised his placid eyebrows and waited on me to speak.

It was not an easy job, with about five minutes to spare, to tell a stranger who I was and what I wanted, and to win his aid. I did not attempt it. There was something about the eye of the man before me, something so keen and knowledgeable, that I could not find a word. I simply stared at him and stuttered.

"You seem in a hurry, my friend," he said slowly.

I nodded towards the window. It gave a prospect across the moor through a gap in the plantation, and revealed certain figures half a mile off straggling through the heather.

"Ah, I see," he said, and took up a pair of field-glasses through which he patiently scrutinized the figures.

"A fugitive from justice, eh? Well, we'll go into the matter at our leisure. Meantime I object to my privacy being broken in upon by the clumsy rural policeman. Go into my study, and you will see two doors facing you. Take the one on the left and close it behind you. You will be perfectly safe."

And this extraordinary man took up his pen again.

I did as I was bid, and found myself in a little dark chamber which smelt of chemicals, and was lit only by a tiny window high up in the wall. The door had swung behind me with a click like the door of a safe. Once again I had found an unexpected sanctuary.

All the same I was not comfortable. There was something about the old gentleman which puzzled and rather terrified me. He had been too easy and ready, almost as if he had expected me. And his eyes had been horribly intelligent.

No sound came to me in that dark place. For all I knew the police might be searching the house, and if they did they would want to know what was behind this door. I tried to possess my soul in patience, and to forget how hungry I was.

Then I took a more cheerful view. The old gentleman could scarcely refuse me a meal, and I fell to reconstructing my breakfast. Bacon and eggs would content me, but I wanted the better part of a flitch of bacon and half a hundred eggs. And then, while my mouth was watering in anticipation, there was a click and the door stood open.

I emerged into the sunlight to find the master of the house sitting in a deep arm-chair in the room he called his study, and regarding me with curious eyes.

"Have they gone?" I asked.

"They have gone. I convinced them that you had crossed the hill. I do not choose that the police should come between me and one whom I am delighted to honour. This is a lucky morning for you, Mr. Richard Hannay."

As he spoke his eyelids seemed to tremble and to fall a little over his keen grey eyes. In a flash the phrase of Scudder's came back to me, when he had described the man he most dreaded in the world. He said that he "could hood his eyes like a hawk." Then I saw that I had walked straight into the enemy's headquarters.

My first impulse was to throttle the old ruffian and make for the open air. He seemed to anticipate my intention, for he smiled gently, and nodded to the door behind me. I turned, and saw two men-servants who had me covered with pistols.

He knew my name, but he had never seen me before. And as the reflection darted across my mind I saw a slender chance.

"I don't know what you mean," I said roughly. "And who are you calling Richard Hannay? My name's Ainslie."

"So?" he said, still smiling. "But of course you have others. We won't quarrel about a name."

I was pulling myself together now, and I reflected that my garb, lacking coat and waistcoat and collar, would at any rate not betray me. I put on my surliest face and shrugged my shoulders.

"I suppose you're going to give me up after all, and I call it a damned dirty trick. My God, I wish I had never seen that cursed motor-car! Here's the money and be damned to you," and I flung four sovereigns on the table.

He opened his eyes a little. "Oh no, I shall not give you up. My friends and I will have a little private settlement with you, that is all. You know a little too much, Mr. Hannay. You are a clever actor, but not quite clever enough."

He spoke with assurance, but I could see the dawning of a doubt in his mind.

"Oh, for God's sake stop jawing!" I cried. "Everything's against me. I haven't had a bit of luck since I came on shore at Leith. What's the harm in a poor devil with an empty stomach picking up some money he finds in a bust-up motor-car? That's all I done, and for that I've been chivied for two days by those blasted bobbies over those blasted hills. I tell you I'm fair sick of it. You can do what you like, old boy! Ned Ainslie's got no fight left in him."

I could see that the doubt was gaining.

"Will you oblige me with the story of your recent doings?" he asked.

"I can't, guv'nor," I said in a real beggar's whine. "I've not had a bite to eat for two days. Give me a mouthful of food, and then you'll hear God's truth."

I must have showed my hunger in my face, for he signalled to one of the men in the doorway. A bit of cold pie was brought and a glass of beer, and I wolfed them down like a pig—or rather, like Ned Ainslie, for I was keeping up my character. In the middle of my meal he spoke suddenly to me in German, but I turned on him a face as blank as a stone wall.

Then I told him my story—how I had come off an Archangel ship at Leith a week ago, and was making my way overland to my brother at Wigtown. I had run short of cash—I hinted vaguely at a spree—and I was pretty well on my uppers when I had come on a hole in a hedge, and, looking through, had seen a big motor-car lying in the burn. I had poked about to see what had happened, and had found three sovereigns lying on the seat and one on the floor. There was nobody there or any sign of an owner, so I had pocketed the cash. But somehow the law had got after me. When I had tried to change a sovereign in a baker's shop, the woman had cried on the police, and a little later, when I was washing my face in a burn, I had been nearly gripped, and had only got away by leaving my coat and waistcoat behind me.

"They can have the money back," I cried, "for a fat lot of good it's done me. Those perishers are all down on a poor man. Now, if it had been you, guv'nor, that had found the quids, nobody would have troubled you."

"You're a good liar, Hannay," he said.

I flew into a rage. "Stop fooling, damn you! I tell you my name's Ainslie, and I never heard of any one called Hannay in my born days. I'd sooner have the police than you with your Hannays and your monkey-faced pistol tricks. . . . No, guv'nor, I beg pardon, I don't mean that. I'm much obliged to you for the grub, and I'll thank you to let me go now the coast's clear."

It was obvious that he was badly puzzled. You see he had never seen me, and my appearance must have altered considerably from my photographs, if he had got one of them. I was pretty smart and well dressed in London, and now I was a regular tramp.

"I do not propose to let you go. If you are what you say you are, you will soon have a chance of clearing yourself. If you are what I believe you are, I do not think you will see the light much longer."

He rang a bell, and a third servant appeared from the veranda.

"I want the Lanchester in five minutes," he said. "There will be three to luncheon."

Then he looked steadily at me, and that was the hardest ordeal of all.

There was something weird and devilish in those eyes, cold, malignant, unearthly, and most hellishly clever. They fascinated me like the bright eyes of a snake. I had a strong impulse to throw myself on his mercy and offer to join his side, and if you consider the way I felt about the whole thing you will see that that impulse must have been purely physical, the weakness of a brain mesmerized and mastered by a stronger spirit. But I managed to stick it out and even to grin.

"You'll know me next time, guv'nor," I said.

"Karl," he spoke in German to one of the men in the doorway, "you will put this fellow in the storeroom till I return, and you will be answerable to me for his keeping."

I was marched out of the room with a pistol at each ear.

The storeroom was a damp chamber in what had been the old farmhouse. There was no carpet on the uneven floor, and nothing to sit down on but a school form. It was black as pitch, for the windows were heavily shuttered. I made out by groping that the walls were lined with boxes and barrels and sacks of some heavy stuff. The whole place smelt of mould and disuse. My gaolers turned the key in the door, and I could hear them shifting their feet as they stood on guard outside.

I sat down in that chilly darkness in a very miserable frame of mind. The old boy had gone off in a motor to collect the two ruffians who had interviewed me yesterday. Now, they had seen me as the roadman, and they would remember me, for I was in the same rig. What was a roadman doing twenty miles from his beat, pursued by the police? A question or two would put them on the track. Probably they had seen Mr. Turnbull, probably Marmie too; most likely they could link me up with Sir Harry, and then the whole thing would be crystal clear. What chance had I in this moorland house with three desperadoes and their armed servants?

I began to think wistfully of the police, now plodding over the hills after my wraith. They at any rate were fellow-countrymen and honest men, and their tender mercies would be kinder than these ghoulish aliens. But they wouldn't have listened to me. That old devil with the eyelids had not taken long to get rid of them. I thought he probably had some kind of graft with the constabulary. Most likely he had letters from Cabinet Ministers saying he was to be given every facility for plotting against Britain. That's the sort of owlish way we run our politics in this jolly old country.

The three would be back for lunch, so I hadn't more than a couple of hours to wait. It was simply waiting on destruction, for I could see no way out of this mess. I wished that I had Scudder's courage, for I am free to confess I didn't feel any great fortitude. The only thing that kept me going was that I was pretty furious. It made me boil with rage to think of those three spies getting the pull on me like this. I hoped that at any rate I might be able to twist one of their necks before they downed me.

The more I thought of it the angrier I grew, and I had to get up and move about the room. I tried the shutters, but they were the kind that lock with a key, and I couldn't move them. From the outside came the faint clucking of hens in the warm sun. Then I groped among the sacks and boxes. I couldn't open the latter, and the sacks seemed to be full of things like dog-biscuits that smelt of cinnamon. But, as I circumnavigated the room, I found a handle in the wall which seemed worth investigating.

It was the door of a wall cupboard—what they call a "press" in Scotland,— and it was locked. I shook it, and it seemed rather flimsy. For want of something better to do I put out my strength on that door, getting some purchase on the handle by looping my braces round it. Presently the thing gave with a crash which I thought would bring in my warders to inquire. I waited for a bit, and then started to explore the cupboard shelves.

There was a multitude of queer things there. I found an odd vesta or two in my trouser pockets and struck a light. It went out in a second, but showed me one thing. There was a little stock of electric torches on one shelf. I picked up one, and found it was in working order.

With the torch to help me I investigated further. There were bottles and cases of queer-smelling stuffs, chemicals no doubt for experiments, and there were coils of fine copper wire and yanks and yanks of a thin oiled silk. There was a box of detonators, and a lot of cord for fuses. Then away at the back of a shelf I found a stout brown cardboard box, and inside it a wooden case. I managed to wrench it open, and within lay half a dozen little grey bricks, each a couple of inches square.

I took up one, and found that it crumbled easily in my hand. Then I smelt it and put my tongue to it. After that I sat down to think. I hadn't been a mining engineer for nothing, and I knew lentonite when I saw it.

With one of these bricks I could blow the house to smithereens. I had used the stuff in Rhodesia and knew its power. But the trouble was that my knowledge wasn't exact. I had forgotten the proper charge and the right way of preparing it, and I wasn't sure about the timing. I had only a vague notion, too, as to its power, for though I had used it I had not handled it with my own fingers.

But it was a chance, the only possible chance. It was a mighty risk, but against it was an absolute black certainty. If I used it the odds were, as I reckoned, about five to one in favour of my blowing myself into the tree-tops; but if I didn't I should certainly be occupying a six-foot hole in the garden by the evening. That was the way I had to look at it. The prospect was pretty dark either way, but anyhow there was a chance, both for myself and for my country.

The remembrance of little Scudder decided me. It was about the beastliest moment of my life, for I'm no good at these cold-blooded resolutions. Still I managed to rake up the pluck to set my teeth and choke back the horrid doubts that flooded in on me. I simply shut off my mind and pretended I was doing an experiment as simple as Guy Fawkes fireworks.

I got a detonator, and fixed it to a couple of inches of fuse. Then I took a quarter of a lentonite brick, and buried it near the door below one of the sacks in a crack of the floor, fixing the detonator in it. For all I knew half of those boxes might be dynamite. If the cupboard held such deadly explosives, why not the boxes? In that case there would be a glorious skyward journey for me and the German servants and about an acre of the surrounding country. There was also the risk that the detonation might set off the other bricks in the cupboard, for I had forgotten most that I knew about lentonite. But it didn't do to begin thinking about the possibilities. The odds were horrible, but I had to take them.

I ensconced myself just below the sill of the window, and lit the fuse. Then I waited for a moment or two. There was dead silence—only a shuffle of heavy boots in the passage, and the peaceful cluck of hens from the warm out-of-doors. I commended my soul to my Maker, and wondered where I would be in five seconds. . . .

A great wave of heat seemed to surge upwards from the floor, and hang for a blistering instant in the air. Then the wall opposite me flashed into a golden yellow and dissolved with a rending thunder that hammered my brain into a pulp. Something dropped on me, catching the point of my left shoulder.

And then I think I became unconscious.

My stupor can scarcely have lasted beyond a few seconds. I felt myself being choked by thick yellow fumes, and struggled out of the debris to my feet. Somewhere behind me I felt fresh air. The jambs of the window had fallen, and through the ragged rent the smoke was pouring out to the summer noon. I stepped over the broken lintel, and found myself standing in a yard in a dense and acrid fog. I felt very sick and ill, but I could move my limbs, and I staggered blindly forward away from the house.

A small mill lade ran in a wooden aqueduct at the other side of the yard, and into this I fell. The cool water revived me, and I had just enough wits left to think of escape. I squirmed up the lade among the slippery green slime till I reached the mill wheel. Then I wriggled through the axle hole into the old mill and tumbled on to a bed of chaff. A nail caught the seat of my trousers, and I left a wisp of heather mixture behind me.

The mill had been long out of use. The ladders were rotten with age, and in the loft the rats had gnawed great holes in the floor. Nausea shook me, and a wheel in my head kept turning, while my left shoulder and arm seemed to be stricken with the palsy. I looked out of the window and saw a fog still hanging over the house and smoke escaping from an upper window. Please God I had set the place on fire, for I could hear confused cries coming from the other side.

But I had no time to linger, since this mill was obviously a bad hiding-place. Any one looking for me would naturally follow the lade, and I made certain the search would begin as soon as they found that my body was not in the storeroom. From another window I saw that on the far side of the mill stood an old stone dovecot. If I could get there without leaving tracks I might find a hiding-place, for I argued that my enemies, if they thought I could move, would conclude I had made for open country, and would go seeking me on the moor.

I crawled down the broken ladder, scattering chaff behind me to cover my footsteps. I did the same on the mill floor, and on the threshold where the door hung on broken hinges. Peeping out, I saw that between me and the dovecot was a piece of bare cobbled ground, where no footmarks would show. Also it was mercifully hid by the mill buildings from any view from the house. I slipped across the space, got to the back of the dovecot and prospected a way of ascent.

That was one of the hardest jobs I ever took on. My shoulder and arm ached like hell, and I was so sick and giddy that I was always on the verge of falling. But I managed it somehow. By the use of out-jutting stones and gaps in the masonry and a tough ivy root I got to the top in the end. There was a little parapet behind which I found space to lie down. Then I proceeded to go off into an old-fashioned swoon.

I woke with a burning head and the sun glaring in my face. For a long time I lay motionless, for those horrible fumes seemed to have loosened my joints and dulled my brain. Sounds came to me from the house—men speaking throatily and the throbbing of a stationary car. There was a little gap in the parapet to which I wriggled, and from which I had some sort of prospect of the yard. I saw figures come out—a servant with his head bound up, and then a younger man in knickerbockers. They were looking for something, and moved towards the mill. Then one of them caught sight of the wisp of cloth on the nail, and cried out to the other. They both went back to the house, and brought two more to look at it. I saw the rotund figure of my late captor, and I thought I made out the man with the lisp. I noticed that all had pistols.

For half an hour they ransacked the mill. I could hear them kicking over the barrels and pulling up the rotten planking. Then they came outside, and stood just below the dovecot, arguing fiercely. The servant with the bandage was being soundly rated. I heard them fiddling with the door of the dovecot, and for one horrid moment I fancied they were coming up. Then they thought better of it, and went back to the house.

All that long blistering afternoon I lay baking on the roof-top. Thirst was my chief torment. My tongue was like a stick, and to make it worse I could hear the cool drip of water from the mill lade. I watched the course of the little stream as it came in from the moor, and my fancy followed it to the top of the glen, where it must issue from an icy fountain fringed with ferns and mosses. I would have given a thousand pounds to plunge my face into that.

I had a fine prospect of the whole ring of moorland. I saw the car speed away with two occupants, and a man on a hill pony riding east. I judged they were looking for me, and I wished them joy of their quest.

But I saw something else more interesting. The house stood almost on the summit of a swell of moorland which crowned a sort of plateau, and there was no higher point nearer than the big hills six miles off. The actual summit, as I have mentioned, was a biggish clump of trees—firs mostly, with a few ashes and beeches. On the dovecot I was almost on a level with the tree-tops, and could see what lay beyond. The wood was not solid, but only a ring, and inside was an oval of green turf, for all the world like a big cricket field.

I didn't take long to guess what it was. It was an aerodrome, and a secret one. The place had been most cunningly chosen. For suppose any one were watching an aeroplane descending here, he would think it had gone over the hill beyond the trees. As the place was on the top of a rise in the midst of a big amphitheatre, any observer from any direction would conclude it had passed out of view behind the hill. Only a man very close at hand would realize that the aeroplane had not gone over but had descended in the midst of the wood. An observer with a telescope on one of the higher hills might have discovered the truth, but only herds went there, and herds do not carry spy-glasses. When I looked from the dovecot I could see far away a blue line which I knew was the sea, and I grew furious to think that our enemies had this secret conning-tower to rake our waterways.

Then I reflected that if that aeroplane came back the chances were ten to one that I would be discovered. So through the afternoon I lay and prayed for the coming of darkness, and glad I was when the sun went down over the big western hills and the twilight haze crept over the moor. The aeroplane was late. The gloaming was far advanced when I heard the beat of wings and saw it volplaning downward to its home in the wood. Lights twinkled for a bit and there was much coming and going from the house. Then the dark fell, and silence.

Thank God it was a black night. The moon was well on its last quarter and would not rise till late. My thirst was too great to allow me to tarry, so about nine o'clock, so far as I could judge, I started to descend. It wasn't easy, and half-way down I heard the back door of the house open, and saw the gleam of a lantern against the mill wall. For some agonizing minutes I hung by the ivy and prayed that whoever it was he would not come round by the dovecot. Then the light disappeared, and I dropped as softly as I could on to the hard soil of the yard.

I crawled on my belly in the lee of a stone dyke till I reached the fringe of trees which surrounded the house. If I had known how to do it I would have tried to put that aeroplane out of action, but I realized that any attempt would probably be futile. I was pretty certain that there would be some kind of defence round the house, so I went through the wood on hands and knees, feeling carefully every inch before me. It was as well, for presently I came on a wire about two feet from the ground. If I had tripped over that, it would doubtless have rung some bell in the house and I would have been captured.

A hundred yards farther on I found another wire cunningly placed on the edge of a small stream. Beyond that lay the moor, and in five minutes I was deep in bracken and heather. Soon I was round the shoulder of the rise, in the little glen from which the mill lade flowed. Ten minutes later my face was in the spring, and I was soaking down pints of the blessed water.

But I did not stop till I had put half a dozen miles between me and that accursed dwelling.

7   THE DRY-FLY FISHERMAN

I sat down on a hill-top and took stock of my position. I wasn't feeling very happy, for my natural thankfulness at my escape was clouded by my severe bodily discomfort. Those lentonite fumes had fairly poisoned me, and the baking hours on the dovecot hadn't helped matters. I had a crushing headache, and felt as sick as a cat. Also my shoulder was in a bad way. At first I thought it was only a bruise, but it seemed to be swelling, and I had no use of my left arm.

My plan was to seek Mr. Turnbull's cottage, recover my garments, and especially Scudder's note-book, and then make for the main line and get back to the south. It seemed to me that the sooner I got in touch with the Foreign Office man, Sir Walter Bullivant, the better. I didn't see how I could get more proof than I had got already. He must just take or leave my story, and, anyway, with him I would be in better hands than those devilish Germans. I had begun to feel quite kindly towards the British police.

It was a wonderful starry night, and I had not much difficulty about the road. Sir Harry's map had given me the lie of the land, and all I had to do was to steer a point or two west of south-west to come to the stream where I had met the roadman. In all these travels I never knew the names of the places, but I believe that stream was no less than the upper waters of the river Tweed. I calculated I must be about eighteen miles distant, and that meant I could not get there before morning. So I must lie up a day somewhere, for I was too outrageous a figure to be seen in the sunlight. I had neither coat, waistcoat, collar, nor hat, my trousers were badly torn, and my face and hands were black with the explosion. I daresay I had other beauties, for my eyes felt as if they were furiously bloodshot. Altogether I was no spectacle for God-fearing citizens to see on a highroad.

Very soon after daybreak I made an attempt to clean myself in a hill burn, and then approached a herd's cottage, for I was feeling the need of food. The herd was away from home, and his wife was alone, with no neighbour for five miles. She was a decent old body, and a plucky one, for though she got a fright when she saw me, she had an axe handy, and would have used it on any evil-doer. I told her that I had had a fall—I didn't say how—and she saw by my looks that I was pretty sick. Like a true Samaritan she asked no questions, but gave me a bowl of milk with a dash of whisky in it, and let me sit for a little by her kitchen fire. She would have bathed my shoulder, but it ached so badly that I would not let her touch it.

I don't know what she took me for—a repentant burglar, perhaps; for when I wanted to pay her for the milk and tendered a sovereign, which was the smallest coin I had, she shook her head and said something about "giving it to them that had a right to it." At this I protested so strongly that I think she believed me honest, for she took the money and gave me a warm new plaid for it, and an old hat of her man's. She showed me how to wrap the plaid round my shoulders, and when I left the cottage I was the living image of the kind of Scotsman you see in the illustrations to Burns's poems. But at any rate I was more or less clad.

It was as well, for the weather changed before midday to a thick drizzle of rain. I found shelter below an overhanging rock in the crook of a burn, where a drift of dead brackens made a tolerable bed. There I managed to sleep till nightfall, waking very cramped and wretched, with my shoulder gnawing like a toothache. I ate the oatcake and cheese the old wife had given me, and set out again just before the darkening.

I pass over the miseries of that night among the wet hills. There were no stars to steer by, and I had to do the best I could from my memory of the map. Twice I lost my way, and I had some nasty falls into peat bogs. I had only about ten miles to go as the crow flies, but my mistakes made it nearer twenty. The last bit was completed with set teeth and a very light and dizzy head. But I managed it, and in the early dawn I was knocking at Mr. Turnbull's door. The mist lay close and thick, and from the cottage I could not see the highroad.

Mr. Turnbull himself opened to me—sober and something more than sober. He was primly dressed in an ancient but well-tended suit of black; he had been shaved not later than the night before; he wore a linen collar; and in his left hand he carried a pocket Bible. At first he did not recognize me.

"Whae are ye that comes stravaigin' here on the Sabbath mornin'?" he asked.

I had lost all count of the days. So the Sabbath was the reason for his strange decorum.

My head was swimming so wildly that I could not frame a coherent answer. But he recognized me, and he saw that I was ill.

"Hae ye got my specs?" he asked.

I fetched them out of my trouser pocket and gave him them.

"Ye'll hae come for your jaicket and westcoat," he said. "Come in-bye. Losh, man, ye're terrible dune i' the legs. Haud up till I get ye to a chair."

I perceived I was in for a bout of malaria. I had a good deal of fever in my bones and the wet night had brought it out, while my shoulder and the effects of the fumes combined to make me feel pretty bad. Before I knew, Mr. Turnbull was helping me off with my clothes, and putting me to bed in one of the two cupboards that lined the kitchen walls.

He was a true friend in need, that old roadman. His wife was dead years ago, and since his daughter's marriage he lived alone. For the better part of ten days he did all the rough nursing I needed. I simply wanted to be left in peace while the fever took its course, and when my skin was cool again I found that the bout had more or less cured my shoulder. But it was a baddish go, and though I was out of bed in five days, it took me some time to get my legs again.

He went out each morning, leaving me milk for the day, and locking the door behind him; and came in in the evening to sit silent in the chimney corner. Not a soul came near the place. When I was getting better, he never bothered me with a question. Several times he fetched me a two-days'-old *Scotsman*, and I noticed that the interest in the Portland Place murder seemed to have died down. There was no mention of it, and I could find very little about anything except a thing called the General Assembly—some ecclesiastical spree, I gathered.

One day he produced my belt from a lockfast drawer. "There's a terrible heap o' siller in't," he said. "Ye'd better coont it to see it's a' there."

He never even sought my name. I asked him if anybody had been around making inquiries subsequent to my spell at the roadmaking.

"Ay, there was a man in a motor-cawr. He speired whae had ta'en my place that day, and I let on I thocht him daft. But he keepit on at me, and syne I said he maun be thinkin' o' my gude-brither frae the Cleuch that whiles lent me a haun'. He was a wersh-lookin' sowl, and I couldna understand the half o' his English tongue."

I was getting pretty restless those last days, and as soon as I felt myself fit I decided to be off. That was not till the 12th day of June, and as luck would have it a drover went past that morning taking some cattle to Moffat. He was a man named Hislop, a friend of Turnbull's, and he came in to his breakfast with us and offered to take me with him.

I made Turnbull accept five pounds for my lodging, and a hard job I had of it. There never was a more independent being. He grew positively rude when I pressed him, and shy and red, and took the money at last without a thank you. When I told him how much I owed him, he grunted something about "ae guid turn deservin' anither." You would have thought from our leave-taking that we had parted in disgust.

Hislop was a cheery soul, who chattered all the way over the pass and down the sunny vale of Annan. I talked of Galloway markets and sheep prices, and he made up his mind I was a "pack-shepherd" from those parts—whatever that may be. My plaid and my old hat, as I have said, gave me a fine theatrical Scots look. But driving cattle is a mortally slow job, and we took the better part of the day to cover a dozen miles.

If I had not had such an anxious heart I would have enjoyed that time. It was shining blue weather, with a constantly changing prospect of brown hills and far green meadows, and a continual sound of larks and curlews and falling streams. But I had no mind for the summer, and little for Hislop's conversation, for as the fateful 15th of June drew near I was overweighed with the hopeless difficulties of my enterprise.

I got some dinner in a humble Moffat public-house, and walked the two miles to the junction on the main line. The night express for the south was not due till near midnight, and to fill up the time I went up on the hillside and fell asleep, for the walk had tired me. I all but slept too long, and had to run to the station and catch the train with two minutes to spare. The feel of the hard third-class cushions and the smell of stale tobacco cheered me up wonderfully. At any rate, I felt now that I was getting to grips with my job.

I was decanted at Crewe in the small hours, and had to wait till six to get a train for Birmingham. In the afternoon I got to Reading, and changed into a local train which journeyed into the deeps of Berkshire. Presently I was in a land of lush water-meadows and slow reedy streams. About eight o'clock in the evening, a weary and travel-stained being—a cross between a farm labourer and a vet—with a checked black-and-white plaid over his arm (for I did not dare to wear it south of the Border), descended at the little station of Artinswell. There were several people on the platform, and I thought I had better wait to ask my way till I was clear of the place.

The road led through a wood of great beeches and then into a shallow valley, with the green backs of downs peeping over the distant trees. After Scotland the air smelt heavy and flat, but infinitely sweet, for the chestnuts and lilac bushes were domes of blossom. Presently I came to a bridge, below which a clear slow stream flowed between snowy beds of water-buttercups. A little above it was a mill; and the lasher made a pleasant cool sound in the scented dusk. Somehow the place soothed me and put me at my ease. I fell to whistling as I looked into the green depths, and the tune which came to my lips was "Annie Laurie."

A fisherman came up from the water-side, and as he neared me he too began to whistle. The tune was infectious, for he followed my suit. He was a huge man in untidy old flannels and a wide-brimmed hat, with a canvas bag slung on his shoulder. He nodded to me, and I thought I had never seen a shrewder or better-tempered face. He leaned his delicate ten-foot split-cane rod against the bridge, and looked with me at the water.

"Clear, isn't it?" he said pleasantly. "I back our Kennet any day against the Test. Look at that big fellow. Four pounds if he's an ounce. But the evening rise is over and you can't tempt 'em."

"I don't see him," said I.

"Look! There! A yard from the reeds just above that stickle."

"I've got him now. You might swear he was a black stone."

"So," he said, and whistled another bar of "Annie Laurie."

"Twisdon's the name, isn't it?" he said over his shoulder, his eyes still fixed on the stream.

"No," I said. "I mean to say, Yes." I had forgotten all about my *alias*.

"It's a wise conspirator that knows his own name," he observed, grinning broadly at a moorhen that emerged from the bridge's shadow.

I stood up and looked at him, at the square, cleft jaw and broad, lined brow and the firm folds of cheek, and began to think that here at last was an ally worth having. His whimsical blue eyes seemed to go very deep.

Suddenly he frowned. "I call it disgraceful," he said, raising his voice. "Disgraceful that an able-bodied man like you should dare to beg. You can get a meal from my kitchen, but you'll get no money from me."

A dog-cart was passing, driven by a young man who raised his whip to salute the fisherman. When he had gone, he picked up his rod.

"That's my house," he said, pointing to a white gate a hundred yards on. "Wait five minutes and then go round to the back door." And with that he left me.

I did as I was bidden. I found a pretty cottage with a lawn running down to the stream, and a perfect jungle of guelder-rose and lilac flanking the path. The back door stood open, and a grave butler was awaiting me.

"Come this way, sir," he said, and he led me along a passage and up a back staircase to a pleasant bedroom looking towards the river. There I found a complete outfit laid out for me—dress clothes with all the fixings, a brown flannel suit, shirts, collars, ties, shaving things and hair-brushes, even a pair of patent shoes. "Sir Walter thought as how Mr. Reggie's things would fit you, sir," said the butler. "He keeps some clothes 'ere, for he comes regular on the week-ends. There's a bathroom next door, and I've prepared a 'ot bath. Dinner in 'alf an hour, sir. You'll 'ear the gong."

The grave being withdrew, and I sat down in a chintz-covered easy-chair and gaped. It was like a pantomime to come suddenly out of beggardom into this orderly comfort. Obviously Sir Walter believed in me, though why he did I could not guess. I looked at myself in the mirror and saw a wild, haggard brown fellow, with a fortnight's ragged beard, and dust in ears and eyes, collarless, vulgarly shirted, with shapeless old tweed clothes, and boots that had not been cleaned for the better part of a month. I made a fine tramp and a fair drover; and here I was ushered by a prim butler into this temple of gracious ease. And the best of it was that they did not even know my name.

I resolved not to puzzle my head, but to take the gifts the gods had provided. I shaved and bathed luxuriously, and got into the dress clothes and clean crackling shirt, which fitted me not so badly. By the time I had finished the looking-glass showed a not unpersonable young man.

Sir Walter awaited me in a dusky dining-room where a little round table was lit with silver candles. The sight of him—so respectable and established and secure, the embodiment of law and government and all the conventions—took me aback and made me feel an interloper. He couldn't know the truth about me, or he wouldn't treat me like this. I simply could not accept his hospitality on false pretences.

"I'm more obliged to you than I can say, but I'm bound to make things clear," I said. "I'm an innocent man, but I'm wanted by the police. I've got to tell you this, and I won't be surprised if you kick me out."

He smiled. "That's all right. Don't let that interfere with your appetite. We can talk about these things after dinner."

I never ate a meal with greater relish, for I had had nothing all day but railway sandwiches. Sir Walter did me proud, for we drank a good champagne and had some uncommon fine port afterwards. It made me almost hysterical to be sitting there, waited on by a footman and a sleek butler, and remember that I had been living for three weeks like a brigand, with every man's hand against me. I told Sir Walter about tiger-fish in the Zambesi that bite off your fingers if you give them a chance, and we discussed sport up and down the globe, for he had hunted a bit in his day.

We went to his study for coffee, a jolly room full of books and trophies and untidiness and comfort. I made up my mind that if ever I got rid of this business and had a house of my own I would create just such a room. Then when the coffee-cups were cleared away, and we had got our cigars alight, my host swung his long legs over the side of his chair and bade me get started with my yarn.

"I've obeyed Harry's instructions," he said, "and the bribe he offered me was that you would tell me something to wake me up. I'm ready, Mr. Hannay."

I noticed with a start that he called me by my proper name.

I began at the very beginning. I told of my boredom in London, and the night I had come back to find Scudder gibbering on my doorstep. I told him all Scudder had told me about Karolides and the Foreign Office conference, and that made him purse his lips and grin. Then I got to the murder, and he grew solemn again. He heard all about the milkman and my time in Galloway, and my deciphering Scudder's notes at the inn.

"You've got them here?" he asked sharply, and drew a long breath when I whipped the little book from my pocket.

I said nothing of the contents. Then I described my meeting with Sir Harry, and the speeches at the hall. At that he laughed uproariously.

"Harry talked dashed nonsense, did he? I quite believe it. He's as good a chap as ever breathed, but his idiot of an uncle has stuffed his head with maggots. Go on, Mr. Hannay."

My day as roadman excited him a bit. He made me describe the two fellows in the car very closely, and seemed to be raking back in his memory. He grew merry again when he heard of the fate of that ass Jopley.

But the old man in the moorland house solemnized him. Again I had to describe every detail of his appearance.

"Bland and bald-headed and hooded his eyes like a bird. . . . He sounds a sinister wild-fowl! And you dynamited his hermitage, after he had saved you from the police. Spirited piece of work, that!"

Presently I reached the end of my wanderings. He got up slowly, and looked down at me from the hearthrug.

"You may dismiss the police from your mind," he said. "You're in no danger from the law of this land."

"Great Scot!" I cried. "Have they got the murderer?"

"No. But for the last fortnight they have dropped you from the list of possibles."

"Why?" I asked in amazement.

"Principally because I received a letter from Scudder. I knew something of the man, and he did several jobs for me. He was half crank, half genius, but he was wholly honest. The trouble about him was his partiality for playing a lone hand. That made him pretty well useless in any Secret Service—a pity, for he had uncommon gifts. I think he was the bravest man in the world, for he was always shivering with fright, and yet nothing would choke him off. I had a letter from him on the 31st of May."

"But he had been dead a week by then."

"The letter was written and posted on the 23rd. He evidently did not anticipate an immediate decease. His communications usually took a week to reach me, for they were sent under cover to Spain and then to Newcastle. He had a mania, you know, for concealing his tracks."

"What did he say?" I stammered.

"Nothing. Merely that he was in danger, but had found shelter with a good friend, and that I would hear from him before the 15th of June. He gave me no address, but said he was living near Portland Place. I think his object was to clear you if anything happened. When I got it I went to Scotland Yard, went over the details of the inquest, and concluded that you were the friend. We made inquiries about you, Mr. Hannay, and found you were respectable. I thought I knew the motives for your disappearance—not only the police, the other one too—and when I got Harry's scrawl I guessed at the rest. I have been expecting you any time this past week."

You can imagine what a load this took off my mind. I felt a free man once more, for I was now up against my country's enemies only, and not my country's law.

"Now let us have the little note-book," said Sir Walter.

It took us a good hour to work through it. I explained the cipher, and he was jolly quick at picking it up. He emended my reading of it on several points, but I had been fairly correct on the whole. His face was very grave before he had finished, and he sat silent for a while.

"I don't know what to make of it," he said at last. "He is right about one thing—what is going to happen the day after to-morrow. How the devil can it have got known? That is ugly enough in itself. But all this about war and the Black Stone,—it reads like some wild melodrama. If only I had more confidence in Scudder's judgment. The trouble about him was that he was too romantic. He had the artistic temperament, and wanted a story to be better than God meant it to be. He had a lot of odd biases too. Jews, for example, made him see red. Jews and the high finance.

"The Black Stone," he repeated. "*Der schwarze Stein.* It's like a penny novelette. And all this stuff about Karolides. That is the weak part of the tale, for I happen to know that the virtuous Karolides is likely to outlast us both. There is no State in Europe that wants him gone. Besides, he has just been playing up to Berlin and Vienna and giving my Chief some uneasy moments. No! Scudder has gone off the track there. Frankly, Hannay, I don't believe that part of his story. There's some nasty business afoot, and he found out too much and lost his life over it. But I am ready to take my oath that it is ordinary spy work. A certain great European Power makes a hobby of her spy system, and her methods are not too particular. Since she pays by piecework her blackguards are not likely to stick at a murder or two. They want our naval dispositions for their collection at the Marineamt; but they will be pigeon-holed—nothing more."

Just then the butler entered the room.

"There's a trunk call from London, Sir Walter. It's Mr. 'Eath, and he wants to speak to you personally."

My host went off to the telephone.

He returned in five minutes with a whitish face. "I apologize to the shade of Scudder," he said. "Karolides was shot dead this evening at a few minutes after seven."

8   THE COMING OF THE BLACK STONE

I came down to breakfast next morning, after eight hours of blessed dreamless sleep, to find Sir Walter decoding a telegram in the midst of muffins and marmalade. His fresh rosiness of yesterday seemed a thought tarnished.

"I had a busy hour on the telephone after you went to bed," he said. "I got my Chief to speak to the First Lord and the Secretary for War, and they are bringing Royer over a day sooner. This wire clinches it. He will be in London at five. Odd that the code word for a *Sous-chef d'État Major-Général* should be 'Porker.'"

He directed me to the hot dishes and went on.

"Not that I think it will do much good. If your friends were clever enough to find out the first arrangement, they are clever enough to discover the change. I would give my head to know where the leak is. We believed there were only five men in England who knew about Royer's visit, and you may be certain there were fewer in France, for they manage these things better there."

While I ate he continued to talk, making me to my surprise a present of his full confidence.

"Can the dispositions not be changed?" I asked.

"They could," he said. "But we want to avoid that if possible. They are the result of immense thought, and no alteration would be as good. Besides, on one or two points change is simply impossible. Still, something could be done, I suppose, if it were absolutely necessary. But you see the difficulty, Hannay. Our enemies are not going to be such fools as to pick Royer's pocket or any childish game like that. They know that would mean a row and put us on our guard. Their aim is to get the details without any one of us knowing, so that Royer will go back to Paris in the belief that the whole business is still deadly secret. If they can't do that they fail, for, once we suspect, they know that the whole thing must be altered."

"Then we must stick by the Frenchman's side till he is home again," I said. "If they thought they could get the information in Paris they would try there. It means that they have some deep scheme on foot in London which they reckon is going to win out."

"Royer dines with my Chief, and then comes to my house, where four people will see him—Whittaker from the Admiralty, myself, Sir Arthur Drew, and General Winstanley. The First Lord is ill, and has gone to Sherringham. At my house he will get a certain document from Whittaker, and after that he will be motored to Portsmouth, where a destroyer will take him to Havre. His journey is too important for the ordinary boat-train. He will never be left unattended for a moment till he is safe on French soil. The same with Whittaker till he meets Royer. That is the best we can do, and it's hard to see how there can be any miscarriage. But I don't mind admitting that I'm horribly nervous. This murder of Karolides will play the deuce in the chancelleries of Europe."

After breakfast he asked me if I could drive a car.

"Well, you'll be my chauffeur to-day and wear Hudson's rig. You're about his size. You have a hand in this business and we are taking no risks. There are desperate men against us, who will not respect the country retreat of an overworked official."

When I first came to London I had bought a car and amused myself with running about the south of England, so I knew something of the geography. I took Sir Walter to town by the Bath Road and made good going. It was a soft breathless June morning, with a promise of sultriness later, but it was delicious enough swinging through the little towns with their freshly watered streets, and past the summer gardens of the Thames Valley. I landed Sir Walter at his house in Queen Anne's Gate punctually by half-past eleven. The butler was coming up by train with the luggage.

The first thing he did was to take me round to Scotland Yard. There we saw a prim gentleman, with a clean-shaven, lawyer's face.

"I've brought you the Portland Place murderer," was Sir Walter's introduction.

The reply was a wry smile. "It would have been a welcome present, Bullivant. This, I presume, is Mr. Richard Hannay, who for some days greatly interested my department."

"Mr. Hannay will interest it again. He has much to tell you, but not to-day. For certain grave reasons his tale must wait for twenty-four hours. Then, I can promise you, you will be entertained and possibly edified. I want you to assure Mr. Hannay that he will suffer no further inconvenience."

This assurance was promptly given. "You can take up your life where you left off," I was told. "Your flat, which probably you no longer wish to occupy, is waiting for you, and your man is still there. As you were never publicly accused, we considered that there was no need of a public exculpation. But on that, of course, you must please yourself."

"We may want your assistance later on, Macgillivray," Sir Walter said as we left.

Then he turned me loose.

"Come and see me to-morrow, Hannay. I needn't tell you to keep deadly quiet. If I were you I would go to bed, for you must have considerable arrears of sleep to overtake. You had better lie low, for if one of your Black Stone friends saw you there might be trouble."

I felt curiously at a loose end. At first it was very pleasant to be a free man, able to go where I wanted without fearing anything. I had only been a month under the ban of the law, and it was quite enough for me. I went to the Savoy and ordered very carefully a very good luncheon, and then smoked the best cigar the house could provide. But I was still feeling nervous. When I saw anybody look at me in the lounge, I grew shy, and wondered if they were thinking about the murder.

After that I took a taxi and drove miles away up into North London. I walked back through fields and lines of villas and terraces and then slums and mean streets, and it took me pretty nearly two hours. All the while my restlessness was growing worse. I felt that great things, tremendous things, were happening or about to happen, and I, who was the cog-wheel of the whole business, was out of it. Royer would be landing at Dover, Sir Walter would be making plans with the few people in England who were in the secret, and somewhere in the darkness the Black Stone would be working. I felt the sense of danger and impending calamity, and I had the curious feeling, too, that I alone could avert it, alone could grapple with it. But I was out of the game now. How could it be otherwise? It was not likely that Cabinet Ministers and Admiralty Lords and Generals would admit me to their councils.

I actually began to wish that I could run up against one of my three enemies. That would lead to developments. I felt that I wanted enormously to have a vulgar scrap with those gentry, where I could hit out and flatten something. I was rapidly getting into a very bad temper.

I didn't feel like going back to my flat. That had to be faced some time, but as I still had sufficient money I thought I would put it off till next morning, and go to a hotel for the night.

My irritation lasted through dinner, which I had at a restaurant in Jermyn Street. I was no longer hungry, and let several courses pass untasted. I drank the best part of a bottle of Burgundy, but it did nothing to cheer me. An abominable restlessness had taken possession of me. Here was I, a very ordinary fellow, with no particular brains; and yet I was convinced that somehow I was needed to help this business through—that without me it would all go to blazes. I told myself it was sheer silly conceit, that four or five of the cleverest people living, with all the might of the British Empire at their back, had the job in hand. Yet I couldn't be convinced. It seemed as if a voice kept speaking in my ear, telling me to be up and doing, or I would never sleep again.

The upshot was that about half-past nine I made up my mind to go to Queen Anne's Gate. Very likely I would not be admitted, but it would ease my conscience to try.

I walked down Jermyn Street, and at the corner of Duke Street passed a group of young men. They were in evening dress, had been dining somewhere, and were going on to a music-hall. One of them was Mr. Marmaduke Jopley.

He saw me and stopped short.

"By God, the murderer!" he cried. "Here, you fellows, hold him! That's Hannay, the man who did the Portland Place murder!" He gripped me by the arm, and the others crowded round.

I wasn't looking for any trouble, but my ill-temper made me play the fool. A policeman came up, and I should have told him the truth, and, if he didn't believe it, demanded to be taken to Scotland Yard, or for that matter to the nearest police station. But a delay at that moment seemed to me unendurable, and the sight of Marmie's imbecile face was more than I could bear. I let out with my left, and had the satisfaction of seeing him measure his length in the gutter.

Then began an unholy row. They were all on me at once, and the policeman took me in the rear. I got in one or two good blows, for I think, with fair play, I could have licked the lot of them, but the policeman pinned me behind, and one of them got his fingers on my throat.

Through a black crowd of rage I heard the officer of the law asking what was the matter, and Marmie, between his broken teeth, declaring that I was Hannay the murderer.

"Oh, damn it all," I cried, "make the fellow shut up. I advise you to leave me alone, constable. Scotland Yard knows all about me, and you'll get a proper wigging if you interfere with me."

"You've got to come along of me, young man," said the policeman. "I saw you strike that gentleman crool 'ard. You begun it too, for he wasn't doing nothing. I seen you. Best go quietly or I'll have to fix you up."

Exasperation and an overwhelming sense that at no cost must I delay gave me the strength of a bull elephant. I fairly wrenched the constable off his feet, floored the man who was gripping my collar, and set off at my best pace down Duke Street. I heard a whistle being blown, and the rush of men behind me.

I have a very fair turn of speed, and that night I had wings. In a jiffey I was in Pall Mall and had turned down towards St. James's Park. I dodged the policeman at the Palace gates, dived through a press of carriages at the entrance to the Mall, and was making for the bridge before my pursuers had crossed the roadway. In the open ways of the Park I put on a spurt. Happily there were few people about, and no one tried to stop me. I was staking all on getting to Queen Anne's Gate.

When I entered that quiet thoroughfare it seemed deserted. Sir Walter's house was in the narrow part, and outside it three or four motor-cars were drawn up. I slackened speed some yards off and walked briskly to the door. If the butler refused me admission, or if he even delayed to open the door, I was done.

He didn't delay. I had scarcely rung before the door opened.

"I must see Sir Walter," I panted. "My business is desperately important."

That butler was a great man. Without moving a muscle he held the door open, and then shut it behind me. "Sir Walter is engaged, sir, and I have orders to admit no one. Perhaps you will wait."

The house was of the old-fashioned kind, with a wide hall and rooms on both sides of it. At the far end was an alcove with a telephone and a couple of chairs, and there the butler offered me a seat.

"See here," I whispered. "There's trouble about and I'm in it. But Sir Walter knows, and I'm working for him. If any one comes and asks if I am here, tell him a lie."

He nodded, and presently there was a noise of voices in the street, and a furious ringing at the bell. I never admired a man more than that butler. He opened the door, and with a face like a graven image waited to be questioned. Then he gave them it. He told them whose house it was, and what his orders were, and simply froze them off the doorstep. I could see it all from my alcove, and it was better than any play.

I hadn't waited long till there came another ring at the bell. The butler made no bones about admitting this new visitor.

While he was taking off his coat I saw who it was. You couldn't open a newspaper or a magazine without seeing that face—the grey beard cut like a spade, the firm fighting mouth, the blunt square nose, and the keen blue eyes. I recognized the First Sea Lord, the man, they say, that made the modern British Navy.

He passed my alcove and was ushered into a room at the back of the hall. As the door opened I could hear the sound of low voices. It shut, and I was left alone again.

For twenty minutes I sat there, wondering what I was to do next. I was still perfectly convinced that I was wanted, but when or how I had no notion. I kept looking at my watch, and as the time crept on to half-past ten I began to think that the conference must soon end. In a quarter of an hour Royer should be speeding along the road to Portsmouth. . . .

Then I heard a bell ring, and the butler appeared. The door of the back room opened, and the First Sea Lord came out. He walked past me, and in passing he glanced in my direction, and for a second we looked each other in the face.

Only for a second, but it was enough to make my heart jump. I had never seen the great man before, and he had never seen me. But in that fraction of time something sprang into his eyes, and that something was recognition. You can't mistake it. It is a flicker, a spark of light, a minute shade of difference which means one thing and one thing only. It came involuntarily, for in a moment it died, and he passed on. In a maze of wild fancies I heard the street door close behind him.

I picked up the telephone book and looked up the number of his house. We were connected at once, and I heard a servant's voice.

"Is his Lordship at home?" I asked.

"His Lordship returned half an hour ago," said the voice, "and has gone to bed. He is not very well to-night. Will you leave a message, sir?"

I rung off and almost tumbled into a chair. My part in this business was not yet ended. It had been a close shave, but I had been in time.

Not a moment could be lost, so I marched boldly to the door of that back room and entered without knocking. Five surprised faces looked up from a round table. There was Sir Walter, and Drew the War Minister, whom I knew from his photographs. There was a slim elderly man, who was probably Whittaker, the Admiralty official, and there was General Winstanley, conspicuous from the long scar on his forehead. Lastly, there was a short stout man with an iron-grey moustache and bushy eyebrows, who had been arrested in the middle of a sentence.

Sir Walter's face showed surprise and annoyance.

"This is Mr. Hannay, of whom I have spoken to you," he said apologetically to the company. "I'm afraid, Hannay, this visit is ill-timed."

I was getting back my coolness. "That remains to be seen, sir," I said; "but I think it may be in the nick of time. For God's sake, gentlemen, tell me who went out a minute ago?"

"Lord Alloa," Sir Walter said, reddening with anger.

"It was not," I cried; "it was his living image, but it was not Lord Alloa. It was some one who recognized me, some one I have seen in the last month. He had scarcely left the doorstep when I rang up Lord Alloa's house and was told he had come in half an hour before and had gone to bed."

"Who—who—" someone stammered.

"The Black Stone," I cried, and I sat down in the chair so recently vacated and looked round at five badly scared gentlemen.

9 THE THIRTY-NINE STEPS

"Nonsense!" said the official from the Admiralty.

Sir Walter got up and left the room while we looked blankly at the table. He came back in ten minutes with a long face. "I have spoken to Alloa," he said. "Had him out of bed—very grumpy. He went straight home after Mulross's dinner."

"But it's madness," broke in General Winstanley. "Do you mean to tell me that that man came here and sat beside me for the best part of half an hour and that I didn't detect the imposture? Alloa must be out of his mind."

"Don't you see the cleverness of it?" I said. "You were too interested in other things to have any eyes. You took Lord Alloa for granted. If it had been anybody else you might have looked more closely, but it was natural for him to be here, and that put you all to sleep."

Then the Frenchman spoke, very slowly and in good English.

"The young man is right. His psychology is good. Our enemies have not been foolish!"

He bent his wise brows on the assembly.

"I will tell you something," he said. "It happened many years ago in Senegal. I was quartered in a remote station, and to pass the time used to go fishing for big barbel in the river. A little Arab mare used to carry my luncheon basket—one of the salted dun breed you got at Timbuctoo in the old days. Well, one morning I had good sport, and the mare was unaccountably restless. I could hear her whinnying and squealing and stamping her feet, and I kept soothing her with my voice while my mind was intent on fish. I could see her all the time, as I thought, out of a corner of my eye, tethered to a tree twenty yards away. . . . After a couple of hours I began to think of food. I collected my fish in a tarpaulin bag, and moved down the stream towards the mare, trolling my line. When I got up to her I flung the tarpaulin on her back. . . ."

He paused and looked round.

"It was the smell that gave me warning. I turned my head and found myself looking at a lion three feet off. . . . An old man-eater, that was the terror of the village. . . . What was left of the mare, a mass of blood and bones and hide, was behind him."

"What happened?" I asked. I was enough of a hunter to know a true yarn when I heard it.

"I stuffed my fishing-rod into his jaws, and I had a pistol. Also my servants came presently with rifles. But he left his mark on me." He held up a hand which lacked three fingers.

"Consider," he said. "The mare had been dead more than an hour, and the brute had been patiently watching me ever since. I never saw the kill, for I was accustomed to the mare's fretting, and I never marked her absence, for my consciousness of her was only of something tawny, and the lion filled that part. If I could blunder thus, gentlemen, in a land where men's senses are keen, why should we busy preoccupied urban folk not err also?"

Sir Walter nodded. No one was ready to gainsay him.

"But I don't see," went on Winstanley. "Their object was to get these dispositions without our knowing it. Now it only required one of us to mention to Alloa our meeting to-night for the whole fraud to be exposed."

Sir Walter laughed dryly. "The selection of Alloa shows their acumen. Which of us was likely to speak to him about to-night? Or was he likely to open the subject?"

I remembered the First Sea Lord's reputation for taciturnity and shortness of temper.

"The one thing that puzzles me," said the General, "is what good his visit here would do that spy fellow? He could not carry away several pages of figures and strange names in his head."

"That is not difficult," the Frenchman replied. "A good spy is trained to have a photographic memory. Like your own Macaulay. You noticed he said nothing, but went through these papers again and again. I think we may assume that he has every detail stamped on his mind. When I was younger I could do the same trick."

"Well, I suppose there is nothing for it but to change the plans," said Sir Walter ruefully.

Whittaker was looking very glum. "Did you tell Lord Alloa what has happened?" he asked. "No? Well, I can't speak with absolute assurance, but I'm nearly certain we can't make any serious change unless we alter the geography of England."

"Another thing must be said," it was Royer who spoke. "I talked freely when that man was here. I told something of the military plans of my Government. I was permitted to say so much. But that information would be worth many millions to our enemies. No, my friends, I see no other way. The man who came here and his confederates must be taken, and taken at once."

"Good God," I cried, "and we have not a rag of a clue."

"Besides," said Whittaker, "there is the post. By this time the news will be on its way."

"No," said the Frenchman. "You do not understand the habits of the spy. He receives personally his reward, and he delivers personally his intelligence. We in France know something of the breed. There is still a chance, *mes amis*. These men must cross the sea, and there are ships to be searched and ports to be watched. Believe me, the need is desperate for both France and Britain."

Royer's grave good sense seemed to pull us together. He was the man of action among fumblers. But I saw no hope in any face, and I felt none. Where among the fifty millions of these islands and within a dozen hours were we to lay hands on the three cleverest rogues in Europe?

Then suddenly I had an inspiration.

"Where is Scudder's book?" I cried to Sir Walter. "Quick, man, I remember something in it."

He unlocked the door of a bureau and gave it to me.

I found the place. "*Thirty-nine steps*," I read, and again, "*Thirty-nine steps—I counted them—High tide*, 10.17 p.m."

The Admiralty man was looking at me as if he thought I had gone mad.

"Don't you see it's a clue," I shouted. "Scudder knew where these fellows laired—he knew where they were going to leave the country, though he kept the name to himself. To-morrow was the day, and it was some place where high tide was at 10.17."

"They may have gone to-night," some one said.

"Not they. They have their own snug secret way, and they won't be hurried. I know Germans, and they are mad about working to a plan. Where the devil can I get a book of Tide Tables?"

Whittaker brightened up. "It's a chance," he said. "Let's go over to the Admiralty."

We got into two of the waiting motor-cars—all but Sir Walter, who went off to Scotland Yard—to "mobilize Macgillivray," so he said.

We marched through empty corridors and big bare chambers where the charwomen were busy, till we reached a little room lined with books and maps. A resident clerk was unearthed, who presently fetched from the library the Admiralty Tide Tables. I sat at the desk and the others stood round, for somehow or other I had got charge of this expedition.

It was no good. There were hundreds of entries, and so far as I could see 10.17 might cover fifty places. We had to find some way of narrowing the possibilities.

I took my head in my hands and thought. There must be some way of reading this riddle. What did Scudder mean by steps? I thought of dock steps, but if he had meant that I didn't think he would have mentioned the number. It must be some place where there were several staircases, and one marked out from the others by having thirty-nine steps.

Then I had a sudden thought, and hunted up all the steamer sailings. There was no boat which left for the Continent at 10.17 p.m.

Why was high tide important? If it was a harbour it must be some little place where the tide mattered, or else it was a heavy-draught boat. But there was no regular steamer sailing at that hour, and somehow I didn't think they would travel by a big boat from a regular harbour. So it must be some little harbour where the tide was important, or perhaps no harbour at all.

But if it was a little port I couldn't see what the steps signified. There were no sets of staircases on any harbour that I had ever seen. It must be some place which a particular staircase identified, and where the tide was full at

10.17. On the whole it seemed to me that the place must be a bit of open coast. But the staircases kept puzzling me.

Then I went back to wider considerations. Whereabouts would a man be likely to leave for Germany, a man in a hurry, who wanted a speedy and a secret passage? Not from any of the big harbours. And not from the Channel or the West Coast or Scotland, for, remember, he was starting from London. I measured the distance on the map, and tried to put myself in the enemy's shoes. I should try for Ostend or Antwerp or Rotterdam, and I should sail from somewhere on the East Coast between Cromer and Dover.

All this was very loose guessing, and I don't pretend it was ingenious or scientific. I wasn't any kind of Sherlock Holmes. But I have always fancied I had a kind of instinct about questions like this. I don't know if I can explain myself, but I used to use my brains as far as they went, and after they came to a blank wall I guessed, and I usually found my guesses pretty right.

So I set out all my conclusions on a bit of Admiralty paper. They ran like this:—

FAIRLY CERTAIN

(1) Place where there are several sets of stairs; one that matters distinguished by having thirty-nine steps.

(2) Full tide at 10.17 p.m. Leaving shore only possible at full tide.

(3) Steps not dock steps, and so place probably not harbour.

(4) No regular night steamer at 10.17. Means of transport must be tramp (unlikely), yacht, or fishing-boat.

There my reasoning stopped. I made another list, which I headed "Guessed," but I was just as sure of the one as the other.

GUESSED

(1) Place not harbour but open coast.

(2) Boat small—trawler, yacht, or launch.

(3) Place somewhere on East Coast between Cromer and Dover.

It struck me as odd that I should be sitting at that desk with a Cabinet Minister, a Field-Marshal, two high Government officials, and a French General watching me, while from the scribble of a dead man I was trying to drag a secret which meant life or death for us.

Sir Walter had joined us, and presently Macgillivray arrived. He had sent out instructions to watch the ports and railway stations for the three men whom I had described to Sir Walter. Not that he or anybody else thought that that would do much good.

"Here's the most I can make of it," I said. "We have got to find a place where there are several staircases down to the beach, one of which has thirty-nine steps. I think it's a piece of open coast with biggish cliffs, somewhere between the Wash and the Channel. Also it's a place where full tide is at 10.17 to-morrow night."

Then an idea struck me. "Is there no Inspector of Coastguards or some fellow like that who knows the East Coast?"

Whittaker said there was, and that he lived in Clapham. He went off in a car to fetch him, and the rest of us sat about the little room and talked of anything that came into our heads. I lit a pipe and went over the whole thing again till my brain grew weary.

About one in the morning the coastguard man arrived. He was a fine old fellow, with the look of a naval officer, and was desperately respectful to the company. I left the War Minister to cross-examine him, for I felt he would think it cheek in me to talk.

"We want you to tell us the places you know on the East Coast where there are cliffs, and where several sets of steps run down to the beach."

He thought for a bit. "What kind of steps do you mean, sir? There are plenty of places with roads cut down through the cliffs, and most roads have a step or two in them. Or do you mean regular staircases—all steps, so to speak?"

Sir Arthur looked towards me. "We mean regular staircases," I said.

He reflected a minute or two. "I don't know that I can think of any. Wait a second. There's a place in Norfolk—Brattlesham—beside a golf course, where there are a couple of staircases to let the gentlemen get a lost ball."

"That's not it," I said.

"Then there are plenty of Marine Parades, if that's what you mean. Every seaside resort has them."

I shook my head.

"It's got to be more retired than that," I said.

"Well, gentlemen, I can't think of anywhere else. Of course, there's the Ruff—"

"What's that?" I asked.

"The big chalk headland in Kent, close to Bradgate. It's got a lot of villas on the top, and some of the houses have staircases down to a private beach. It's a very high-toned sort of place, and the residents there like to keep by themselves."

I tore open the Tide Tables and found Bradgate. High tide there was at 10.27 p.m. on the 15th of June.

"We're on the scent at last," I cried excitedly. "How can I find out what is the tide at the Ruff?"

"I can tell you that, sir," said the coastguard man. "I once was lent a house there in this very month, and I used to go out at night to the deep-sea fishing. The tide's ten minutes before Bradgate."

I closed the book and looked round at the company.

"If one of those staircases has thirty-nine steps we have solved the mystery, gentlemen," I said. "I want the loan of your car, Sir Walter, and a map of the roads. If Mr. Macgillivray will spare me ten minutes, I think we can prepare something for to-morrow."

It was ridiculous in me to take charge of the business like this, but they didn't seem to mind, and after all I had been in the show from the start. Besides, I was used to rough jobs, and these eminent gentlemen were too clever not to see it. It was General Royer who gave me my commission. "I for one," he said, "am content to leave the matter in Mr. Hannay's hands."

By half-past three I was tearing past the moonlit hedgerows of Kent, with Macgillivray's best man on the seat beside me.

10   VARIOUS PARTIES CONVERGING
ON THE SEA

A pink and blue June morning found me at Bradgate looking from the Griffin Hotel over a smooth sea to the lightship on the Cock sands which seemed the size of a bell-buoy. A couple of miles farther south and much nearer the shore a small destroyer was anchored. Scaife, Macgillivray's man, who had been in the Navy, knew the boat, and told me her name and her commander's, so I sent off a wire to Sir Walter.

After breakfast Scaife got from a house agent a key for the gates of the staircases on the Ruff. I walked with him along the sands, and sat down in a nook of the cliffs while he investigated the half-dozen of them. I didn't want to be seen, but the place at this hour was quite deserted, and all the time I was on that beach I saw nothing but the seagulls.

It took him more than an hour to do the job, and when I saw him coming towards me, conning a bit of paper, I can tell you my heart was in my mouth. Everything depended, you see, on my guess proving right.

He read aloud the number of steps in the different stairs. "Thirty-four, thirty-five, thirty-nine, forty-two, forty-seven," and "twenty-one" where the cliffs grew lower. I almost got up and shouted.

We hurried back to the town and sent a wire to Macgillivray. I wanted half a dozen men, and I directed them to divide themselves among different specified hotels. Then Scaife set out to prospect the house at the head of the thirty-nine steps.

He came back with news that both puzzled and reassured me. The house was called Trafalgar Lodge, and belonged to an old gentleman called Appleton— a retired stockbroker, the house agent said. Mr. Appleton was there a good deal in the summer time, and was in residence now—had been for the better part of a week. Scaife could pick up very little information about him, except that he was a decent old fellow, who paid his bills regularly, and was always good for a fiver for a local charity. Then Scaife seems to have penetrated to the back door of the house, pretending he was an agent for sewing-machines. Only three servants were kept, a cook, a parlour-maid, and a housemaid, and they were just the sort that you would find in a respectable middle-class household. The cook was not the gossiping kind, and had pretty soon shut the door in his face, but Scaife said he was positive she knew nothing. Next door there was a new house building which would give good cover for observation, and the villa on the other side was to let, and its garden was rough and shrubby.

I borrowed Scaife's telescope, and before lunch went for a walk along the Ruff. I kept well behind the rows of villas, and found a good observation point on the edge of the golf course. There I had a view of the line of turf along the cliff top, with seats placed at intervals, and the little square plots, railed in and planted with bushes, whence the staircases descended to the beach. I saw Trafalgar Lodge very plainly, a red-brick villa with a veranda, a tennis lawn behind, and in front the ordinary seaside flower garden full of marguerites and scraggy geraniums. There was a flagstaff from which an enormous Union Jack hung limply in the still air.

Presently I observed someone leave the house and saunter along the cliff. When I got my glasses on him I saw it was an old man, wearing white flannel trousers, a blue serge jacket, and a straw hat. He carried field-glasses and a newspaper, and sat down on one of the iron seats and began to read. Sometimes he would lay down the paper and turn his glasses on the sea. He looked for a long time at the destroyer. I watched him for half an hour, till he got up and went back to the house for his luncheon, when I returned to the hotel for mine.

I wasn't feeling very confident. This decent commonplace dwelling was not what I had expected. The man might be the bald archaeologist of that horrible moorland farm, or he might not. He was exactly the kind of satisfied old bird you will find in every suburb and every holiday place. If you wanted a type of the perfectly harmless person you would probably pitch on that.

But after lunch, as I sat in the hotel porch, I perked up, for I saw the thing I had hoped for and had dreaded to miss. A yacht came up from the south and dropped anchor pretty well opposite the Ruff. She seemed about a hundred and fifty tons, and I saw she belonged to the Squadron from the white ensign. So Scaife and I went down to the harbour and hired a boatman for an afternoon's fishing.

I spent a warm and peaceful afternoon. We caught between us about twenty pounds of cod and lythe, and out in that dancing blue sea I took a cheerier view of things. Above the white cliffs of the Ruff I saw the green and red of the villas, and especially the great flagstaff of Trafalgar Lodge. About four o'clock, when we had fished enough, I made the boatman row us round the yacht, which lay like a delicate white bird, ready at a moment to flee. Scaife said she must be a fast boat from her build, and that she was pretty heavily engined.

Her name was the *Ariadne*, as I discovered from the cap of one of the men who was polishing brasswork. I spoke to him, and got an answer in the soft dialect of Essex. Another hand that came along passed me the time of day in an unmistakable English tongue. Our boatman had an argument with one of them about the weather, and for a few minutes we lay on our oars close to the starboard bow.

Then the men suddenly disregarded us and bent their heads to their work as an officer came along the deck. He was a pleasant, clean-looking young fellow, and he put a question to us about our fishing in very good English. But there could be no doubt about him. His close-cropped head and the cut of his collar and tie never came out of England.

That did something to reassure me, but as we rowed back to Bradgate my obstinate doubts would not be dismissed. The thing that worried me was the reflection that my enemies knew that I had got my knowledge from Scudder, and it was Scudder who had given me the clue to this place. If they knew that Scudder had this clue, would they not be certain to change their plans? Too much depended on their success for them to take any risks. The whole question was how much they understood about Scudder's knowledge. I had talked confidently last night about Germans always sticking to a scheme, but if they had any suspicions that I was on their track they would be fools not to cover it. I wondered if the man last night had seen that I recognized him. Somehow I did not think he had, and to that I clung. But the whole business had never seemed so difficult as that afternoon when by all calculations I should have been rejoicing in assured success.

In the hotel I met the commander of the destroyer, to whom Scaife introduced me, and with whom I had a few words. Then I thought I would put in an hour or two watching Trafalgar Lodge.

I found a place farther up the hill, in the garden of an empty house. From there I had a full view of the court, on which two figures were having a game of tennis. One was the old man whom I had already seen; the other was a younger fellow, wearing some club colours in the scarf round his middle. They played with tremendous zest, like two city gents who wanted hard exercise to open their pores. You couldn't conceive a more innocent spectacle. They shouted and laughed and stopped for drinks, when a maid brought out two tankards on a salver. I rubbed my eyes and asked myself if I was not the most immortal fool on earth. Mystery and darkness had hung about the men who hunted me over the Scotch moor in aeroplane and motor-car, and notably about that infernal antiquarian. It was easy enough to connect these folk with the knife that pinned Scudder to the floor, and with fell designs on the world's peace. But here were two guileless citizens taking their innocuous exercise, and soon about to go indoors to a humdrum dinner, where they would talk of market prices and the last cricket scores and the gossip of their native Surbiton. I had been making a net to catch vultures and falcons, and lo and behold! two plump thrushes had blundered into it.

Presently a third figure arrived, a young man on a bicycle, with a bag of golf clubs slung on his back. He strolled round to the tennis lawn and was welcomed riotously by the players. Evidently they were chaffing him, and their chaff sounded horribly English. Then the plump man, mopping his brow with a silk handkerchief, announced that he must have a tub. I heard his very words—"I've got into a proper lather," he said. "This will bring down my weight and my handicap, Bob. I'll take you on to-morrow and give you a stroke a hole." You couldn't find anything much more English than that.

They all went into the house, and left me feeling a precious idiot. I had been barking up the wrong tree this time. These men might be acting; but if they were, where was their audience? They didn't know I was sitting thirty yards off in a rhododendron. It was simply impossible to believe that these three hearty fellows were anything but what they seemed—three ordinary, game-playing, suburban Englishmen, wearisome, if you like, but sordidly innocent.

And yet there were three of them; and one was old, and one was plump, and one was lean and dark; and their house chimed in with Scudder's notes; and half a mile off was lying a steam yacht with at least one German officer. I thought of Karolides lying dead and all Europe trembling on the edge of earthquake, and the men I had left behind me in London who were waiting anxiously for the events of the next hours. There was no doubt that hell was afoot somewhere. The Black Stone had won, and if it survived this June night would bank its winnings.

There seemed only one thing to do—go forward as if I had no doubts, and if I was going to make a fool of myself to do it handsomely. Never in my life have I faced a job with greater disinclination. I would rather in my then mind have walked into a den of anarchists, each with his Browning handy, or faced a charging lion with a popgun, than enter that happy home of three cheerful Englishmen and tell them that their game was up. How they would laugh at me!

But suddenly I remembered a thing I heard once in Rhodesia from old Peter Pienaar. I have quoted Peter already in this narrative. He was the best scout I ever knew, and before he had turned respectable he had been pretty often on the windy side of the law, when he had been wanted badly by the authorities. Peter once discussed with me the question of disguises, and he had a theory which struck me at the time. He said, barring absolute certainties like finger-prints, mere physical traits were very little use for identification if the fugitive really knew his business. He laughed at things like dyed hair and false beards and such childish follies. The only thing that mattered was what Peter called "atmosphere."

If a man could get into perfectly different surroundings from those in which he had been first observed, and—this is the important part—really play up to these surroundings and behave as if he had never been out of them, he would puzzle the cleverest detectives on earth. And he used to tell a story of how he once borrowed a black coat and went to church and shared the same hymn-book with the man that was looking for him. If that man had seen him in decent company before he would have recognized him; but he had only seen him snuffing the lights in a public-house with a revolver.

The recollection of Peter's talk gave me the first real comfort I had had that day. Peter had been a wise old bird, and these fellows I was after were about the pick of the aviary. What if they were playing Peter's game? A fool tries to look different: a clever man looks the same and *is* different.

Again, there was that other maxim of Peter's which had helped me when I had been a roadman. "If you are playing a part, you will never keep it up unless you convince yourself that you are *it*." That would explain the game of tennis. Those chaps didn't need to act, they just turned a handle and passed into another life, which came as naturally to them as the first. It sounds a platitude, but Peter used to say that it was the big secret of all the famous criminals.

It was now getting on for eight o'clock, and I went back and saw Scaife to give him his instructions. I arranged with him how to place his men, and then I went for a walk, for I didn't feel up to any dinner. I went round the deserted golf course, to a point on the cliffs farther north beyond the line of the villas. On the little trim newly made roads I met people in flannels coming back from tennis and the beach, and a coastguard from the wireless station, and donkeys and pierrots padding homewards. Out at sea in the blue dusk I saw lights appear on the *Ariadne* and on the destroyer away to the south, and beyond the Cock sands the bigger lights of steamers making for the Thames. The whole scene was so peaceful and ordinary that I got more dashed in spirits every second. It took all my resolution to stroll towards Trafalgar Lodge about half-past nine.

On the way I got a piece of solid comfort from the sight of a greyhound that was swinging along at a nursemaid's heels. He reminded me of a dog I used to have in Rhodesia, and of the time when I took him hunting with me in the Pali hills. We were after rhebok, the dun kind, and I recollected how we had followed one beast, and both he and I had clean lost it. A greyhound works by sight, and my eyes are good enough, but that buck simply leaked out of the landscape. Afterwards I found out how it managed it. Against the grey rock of the kopjes it showed no more than a crow against a thundercloud. It didn't need to run away; all it had to do was to stand still and melt into the background.

Suddenly as these memories chased across my brain I thought of my present case and applied the moral. The Black Stone didn't need to bolt. It was quietly absorbed into the landscape. I was on the right track, and I jammed that down in my mind and vowed never to forget it. The last word was with Peter Pienaar.

Scaife's men would be posted now, but there was no sign of a soul. The house stood as open as a market-place for anybody to observe. A three-foot railing separated it from the cliff road; the windows on the ground floor were all open, and shaded lights and the low sound of voices revealed where the occupants were finishing dinner. Everything was as public and above-board as a charity bazaar. Feeling the greatest fool on earth, I opened the gate and rang the bell.

A man of my sort, who has travelled about the world in rough places, gets on perfectly well with two classes, what you may call the upper and the lower.

He understands them and they understand him. I was at home with herds
and tramps and roadmen, and I was sufficiently at my ease with people like
Sir Walter and the men I had met the night before. I can't explain why, but it
is a fact. But what fellows like me don't understand is the great comfortable,
satisfied middle-class world, the folk that live in villas and suburbs. He
doesn't know how they look at things, he doesn't understand their conventions,
and he is as shy of them as of a black mamba. When a trim parlour-maid
opened the door, I could hardly find my voice.

I asked for Mr. Appleton, and was ushered in. My plan had been to walk
straight into the dining-room, and by a sudden appearance wake in the men
that start of recognition which would confirm my theory. But when I found
myself in that neat hall the place mastered me. There were the golf clubs and
tennis rackets, the straw hats and caps, the rows of gloves, the sheaf of
walking-sticks, which you will find in ten thousand British homes. A stack of
neatly folded coats and waterproofs covered the top of an old oak chest; there
was a grandfather clock ticking; and some polished brass warming-pans on
the walls, and a barometer, and a print of Chiltern winning the St. Leger.
The place was as orthodox as an Anglican Church. When the maid asked me
for my name I gave it automatically, and was shown into the smoking-room,
on the right side of the hall.

That room was even worse. I hadn't time to examine it, but I could see
some framed group photographs above the mantelpiece, and I could have
sworn they were English public school or college. I had only one glance, for I
managed to pull myself together and go after the maid. But I was too late. She
had already entered the dining-room and given my name to her master, and I
had missed the chance of seeing how the three took it.

When I walked into the room the old man at the head of the table had risen
and turned round to meet me. He was in evening dress—a short coat and
black tie, as was the other whom I called in my own mind the plump one.
The third, the dark fellow, wore a blue serge suit and a soft white collar, and
the colours of some club or school.

The old man's manner was perfect. "Mr. Hannay?" he said hesitatingly.
"Did you wish to see me? One moment, you fellows, and I'll rejoin you. We
had better go to the smoking-room."

Though I hadn't an ounce of confidence in me, I forced myself to play the
game. I pulled up a chair and sat down on it.

"I think we have met before," I said, "and I guess you know my business."

The light in the room was dim, but so far as I could see their faces, they
played the part of mystification very well.

"Maybe, maybe," said the old man. "I haven't a very good memory, but
I'm afraid you must tell me your errand, sir, for I really don't know it."

"Well, then," I said, and all the time I seemed to myself to be talking pure
foolishness—"I have come to tell you that the game's up. I have here a
warrant for the arrest of you three gentlemen."

"Arrest," said the old man, and he looked really shocked. "Arrest! Good
God, what for?"

"For the murder of Franklin Scudder in London on the 23rd day of last month."

"I never heard the name before," said the old man in a dazed voice.

One of the others spoke up. "That was the Portland Place murder. I read about it. Good heavens, you must be mad, sir! Where do you come from?"

"Scotland Yard," I said.

After that for a minute there was utter silence. The old man was staring at his plate and fumbling with a nut, the very model of innocent bewilderment.

Then the plump one spoke up. He stammered a little, like a man picking his words.

"Don't get flustered, uncle," he said. "It is all a ridiculous mistake; but these things happen sometimes, and we can easily set it right. It won't be hard to prove our innocence. I can show that I was out of the country on the 23rd of May, and Bob was in a nursing home. You were in London, but you can explain what you were doing."

"Right, Percy! Of course that's easy enough. The 23rd! That was the day after Agatha's wedding. Let me see. What was I doing? I came up in the morning from Woking, and lunched at the club with Charlie Symons. Then —oh yes, I dined with the Fishmongers. I remember, for the punch didn't agree with me, and I was seedy next morning. Hang it all, there's a cigar box I brought back from the dinner." He pointed to an object on the table, and laughed nervously.

"I think, sir," said the young man, addressing me politely, "you will see you are mistaken. We want to assist the law like all Englishmen, and we don't want Scotland Yard to be making fools of themselves. That's so, uncle?"

"Certainly, Bob." The old fellow seemed to be recovering his voice. "Certainly, we'll do anything in our power to assist the authorities. But— but this is a bit too much. I can't get over it."

"How Nellie will chuckle," said the plump man. "She always said that you would die of boredom because nothing ever happened to you. And now you've got it thick and strong," and he began to laugh very pleasantly.

"By Jove, yes. Just think of it! What a story to tell at the club. Really, Mr. Hannay, I suppose I should be angry, to show my innocence, but it's too funny! I almost forgive you the fright you gave me! You looked so glum, I thought I might have been walking in my sleep and killing people."

It couldn't be acting, it was too confoundedly genuine. My heart went into my boots, and my first impulse was to apologize and clear out. But I told myself I must see it through, even though I was to be the laughing-stock of Britain. The light from the dinner-table candlesticks was not very good, and to cover my confusion I got up, walked to the door and switched on the electric light. The sudden glare made them blink, and I stood scanning the three faces.

Well, I made nothing of it. One was old and bald, one was stout, one was dark and thin. There was nothing in their appearance to prevent them being the three who had hunted me in Scotland, but there was nothing to identify them. I simply can't explain why I who, as a roadman, had looked into two pairs of eyes and as Ned Ainslie into another pair, why I, who have a good memory and reasonable powers of observation, could find no satisfaction. They seemed exactly what they professed to be, and I could not have sworn to one of them.

There in that pleasant dining-room, with etchings on the walls, and a picture of an old lady in a bib above the mantelpiece, I could see nothing to connect them with the moorland desperadoes. There was a silver cigarette box beside me, and I saw that it had been won by Percival Appleton, Esq., of the St. Bede's Club, in a golf tournament. I had to keep firm hold of Peter Pienaar to prevent myself bolting out of that house.

"Well," said the old man politely, "are you reassured by your scrutiny, sir?"

I couldn't find a word.

"I hope you'll find it consistent with your duty to drop this ridiculous business. I make no complaint, but you see how annoying it must be to respectable people."

I shook my head.

"O Lord," said the young man. "This is a bit too thick!"

"Do you propose to march us off to the police station?" asked the plump one. "That might be the best way out of it, but I suppose you won't be content with the local branch. I have the right to ask to see your warrant, but I don't wish to cast any aspersions upon you. You are only doing your duty. But you'll admit it's horribly awkward. What do you propose to do?"

There was nothing to do except to call in my men and have them arrested, or to confess my blunder and clear out. I felt mesmerized by the whole place, by the air of obvious innocence—not innocence merely, but frank honest bewilderment and concern in the three faces.

"Oh, Peter Pienaar," I groaned inwardly, and for a moment I was very near damning myself for a fool and asking their pardon.

"Meantime I vote we have a game of bridge," said the plump one. "It will give Mr. Hannay time to think over things, and you know we have been wanting a fourth player. Do you play, sir?"

I accepted as if it had been an ordinary invitation at the club. The whole business had mesmerized me. We went into the smoking-room where a card table was set out, and I was offered things to smoke and drink. I took my place at the table in a kind of dream. The window was open, and the moon was flooding the cliffs and sea with a great tide of yellow light. There was moonshine, too, in my head. The three had recovered their composure, and were talking easily—just the kind of slangy talk you will hear in any golf club-house. I must have cut a rum figure, sitting there knitting my brows, with my eyes wandering.

My partner was the young dark one. I play a fair hand at bridge, but I must have been rank bad that night. They saw that they had got me puzzled, and that put them more than ever at their ease. I kept looking at their faces, but they conveyed nothing to me. It was not that they looked different; they 〈 different. I clung desperately to the words of Peter Pienaar.

Then something awoke me.

The old man laid down his hand to light a cigar. He didn't pick it up at once, but sat back for a moment in his chair, with his fingers tapping on his knees.

It was the movement I remembered when I had stood before him in the moorland farm, with the pistols of his servants behind me.

A little thing, lasting only a second, and the odds were a thousand to one that I might have had my eyes on my cards at the time and missed it. But I didn't, and, in a flash, the air seemed to clear. Some shadow lifted from my brain, and I was looking at the three men with full and absolute recognition.

The clock on the mantelpiece struck ten o'clock.

The three faces seemed to change before my eyes and reveal their secrets. The young one was the murderer. Now I saw cruelty and ruthlessness, where before I had only seen good-humour. His knife, I made certain, had skewered Scudder to the floor. His kind had put the bullet in Karolides.

The plump man's features seemed to dislimn, and form again, as I looked at them. He hadn't a face, only a hundred masks that he could assume when he pleased. That chap must have been a superb actor. Perhaps he had been Lord Alloa of the night before; perhaps not; it didn't matter. I wondered if he was the fellow who had first tracked Scudder, and left his card on him. Scudder had said he lisped, and I could imagine how the adoption of a lisp might add terror.

But the old man was the pick of the lot. He was sheer brain, icy, cool, calculating, as ruthless as a steam hammer. Now that my eyes were opened I wondered where I had seen the benevolence. His jaw was like chilled steel, and his eyes had the inhuman luminosity of a bird's. I went on playing, and every second a greater hate welled up in my heart. It almost choked me, and I couldn't answer when my partner spoke. Only a little longer could I endure their company.

"Whew! Bob! Look at the time," said the old man. "You'd better think about catching your train. Bob's got to go to town to-night," he added, turning to me. The voice rang now as false as hell.

I looked at the clock, and it was nearly half-past ten.

"I am afraid he must put off his journey," I said.

"Oh, damn," said the young man, "I thought you had dropped that rot. I've simply got to go. You can have my address, and I'll give any security you like."

"No," I said, "you must stay."

At that I think they must have realized that the game was desperate. Their only chance had been to convince me that I was playing the fool, and that had failed. But the old man spoke again.

"I'll go bail for my nephew. That ought to content you, Mr. Hannay."

Was it fancy, or did I detect some halt in the smoothness of that voice?

been, for as I glanced at him, his eyelids fell in that fear had stamped on my memory.

..nt the lights were out. A pair of strong arms gripped me round
.., covering the pockets in which a man might be expected to carry a
..l.

"*Schnell, Franz,*" cried a voice, "*das Boot, das Boot!*" As it spoke I saw two of my fellows emerge on the moonlit lawn.

The young dark man leapt for the window, was through it, and over the low fence before a hand could touch him. I grappled the old chap, and the room seemed to fill with figures. I saw the plump one collared, but my eyes were all for the out-of-doors, where Franz sped on over the road towards the railed entrance to the beach stairs. One man followed him, but he had no chance. The gate of the stairs locked behind the fugitive, and I stood staring, with my hands on the old boy's throat, for such a time as a man might take to descend those steps to the sea.

Suddenly my prisoner broke from me and flung himself on the wall. There was a click as if a lever had been pulled. Then came a low rumbling far, far below the ground, and through the window I saw a cloud of chalky dust pouring out of the shaft of the stairway.

Some one switched on the lights.

The old man was looking at me with blazing eyes.

"He is safe," he cried. "You cannot follow in time. . . . He is gone. . . . He has triumphed. . . . *Der schwarze Stein ist in der Siegeskrone.*"

There was more in those eyes than any common triumph. They had been hooded like a bird of prey, and now they flamed with a hawk's pride. A white fanatic heat burned in them, and I realized for the first time the terrible thing I had been up against. This man was more than a spy; in his foul way he had been a patriot.

As the handcuffs clinked on his wrists I said my last word to him.

"I hope Franz will bear his triumph well. I ought to tell you that the *Ariadne* for the last hour has been in our hands."

Seven weeks later, as all the world knows, we went to war. I joined the New Army the first week, and owing to my Matabele experience got a captain's commission straight off. But I had done my best service, I think, before I put on khaki.

THE SECOND ADVENTURE

Greenmantle

11 A MISSION IS PROPOSED

I had just finished breakfast and was filling my pipe when I got Bullivant's telegram. I was at Furling, the big country house in Hampshire where I had come to convalesce after Loos, and Sandy, who was in the same case, was hunting for the marmalade. I flung him the flimsy with the blue strip pasted down on it, and he whistled.

"Hullo, Dick, you've got the battalion. Or maybe it's a staff billet. You'll be a blighted brass-hat, coming it heavy over the hard-working regimental officer. And to think of the language you've wasted on brass-hats in your time!"

I sat and thought for a bit, for that name Bullivant carried me back eighteen months to the hot summer before the war. I had not seen the man since, though I had read about him in the papers. For more than a year I had been a busy battalion officer, with no other thought than to hammer a lot of raw stuff into good soldiers. I had succeeded pretty well, and there was no prouder man on earth than Richard Hannay when he took his Lennox Highlanders over the parapets on that glorious and bloody 25th day of September. Loos was no picnic, and we had had some ugly bits of scrapping before that, but the worst bit of the campaign I had seen was a tea-party to the show* I had been in with Bullivant before the war started.

The sight of his name on a telegram form seemed to change all my outlook on life. I had been hoping for the command of a battalion, and looking forward to being in at the finish with Brother Boche. But this message jerked my thoughts on to a new road. There might be other things in the war than straightforward fighting. Why on earth should the Foreign Office want to see an obscure major of the New Army, and want to see him in double-quick time?

"I'm going up to town by the ten train," I announced; "I'll be back in time for dinner."

"Try my tailor," said Sandy. "He's got a very nice taste in red tabs. You can use my name."

An idea struck me. "You're pretty well all right now. If I wire for you, will you pack your own kit and mine and join me?"

"Right-o! I'll accept a job on your staff if they give you a corps. If so be as you come down to-night, be a good chap and bring a barrel of oysters from Sweeting's."

* Major Hannay's narrative of this affair has been published under the title of *The Thirty-nine Steps*.

83

I travelled up to London in a regular November drizzle, which cleared up about Wimbledon to watery sunshine. I never could stand London during the war. It seemed to have lost its bearings and broken out into all manner of badges and uniforms which did not fit in with my notion of it. One felt the war more in its streets than in the field, or rather one felt the confusion of war without feeling the purpose. I dare say it was all right; but since August 1914 I never spent a day in town without coming home depressed to my boots.

I took a taxi and drove straight to the Foreign Office. Sir Walter did not keep me waiting long. But when his secretary took me to his room I would not have recognized the man I had known eighteen months before.

His big frame seemed to have dropped flesh, and there was a stoop in the square shoulders. His face had lost its rosiness and was red in patches, like that of a man who gets too little fresh air. His hair was much greyer and very thin about the temples, and there were lines of overwork below the eyes. But the eyes were the same as before, keen and kindly and shrewd, and there was no change in the firm set of the jaw.

"We must on no account be disturbed for the next hour," he told his secretary. When the young man had gone he went across to both doors and turned the keys in them.

"Well, Major Hannay," he said, flinging himself into a chair beside the fire. "How do you like soldiering?"

"Right enough," I said, "though this isn't just the kind of war I would have picked myself. It's a comfortless, bloody business. But we've got the measure of the old Boche now, and it's dogged as does it. I count on getting back to the Front in a week or two."

"Will you get the battalion?" he asked. He seemed to have followed my doings pretty closely.

"I believe I've a good chance. I'm not in this show for honour and glory, though. I want to do the best I can, but I wish to Heaven it was over. All I think of is coming out of it with a whole skin."

He laughed. "You do yourself an injustice. What about the forward observation post at the Lone Tree? You forgot about the whole skin then."

I felt myself getting red. "That was all rot," I said, "and I can't think who told you about it. I hated the job, but I had to do it to prevent my subalterns going to glory. They were a lot of fire-eating young lunatics. If I had sent one of them he'd have gone on his knees to Providence and asked for trouble."

Sir Walter was still grinning.

"I'm not questioning your caution. You have the rudiments of it, or our friends of the Black Stone would have gathered you in at our last merry meeting. I would question it as little as your courage. What exercises my mind is whether it is best employed in the trenches."

"Is the War Office dissatisfied with me?" I asked sharply.

"They are profoundly satisfied. They propose to give you command of your battalion. Presently, if you escape a stray bullet, you will no doubt be a Brigadier. It is a wonderful war for youth and brains. But . . . I take it you are in this business to serve your country, Hannay?"

"I reckon I am," I said. "I am certainly not in it for my health."

He looked at my leg where the doctors had dug out the shrapnel fragments, and smiled quizzically. "Pretty fit again?" he asked.

"Tough as a sjambok. I thrive on the racket and eat and sleep like a schoolboy."

He got up and stood with his back to the fire, his eyes staring abstractedly out of the window at the wintry park.

"It is a great game, and you are the man for it, no doubt. But there are others who can play it, for soldiering to-day asks for the average rather than the exception in human nature. It is like a big machine where the parts are standardized. You are fighting, not because you are short of a job, but because you want to help England. How if you could help her better than by commanding a battalion—or a brigade—or, if it comes to that, a division? How if there is a thing which you alone can do? Not some *embusqué* business in an office, but a thing compared to which your fight at Loos was a Sunday-school picnic. You are not afraid of danger? Well, in this job you would not be fighting with an army around you, but alone. You are fond of tackling difficulties? Well, I can give you a task which will try all your powers. Have you anything to say?"

My heart was beginning to thump uncomfortably. Sir Walter was not the man to pitch a case too high.

"I am a soldier," I said, "and under orders."

"True; but what I am about to propose does not come by any conceivable stretch within the scope of a soldier's duties. I shall perfectly understand if you decline. You will be acting as I should act myself—as any sane man would. I would not press you for worlds. If you wish it, I will not even make the proposal, but let you go here and now, and wish you good luck with your battalion. I do not wish to perplex a good soldier with impossible decisions."

This piqued me and put me on my mettle.

"I am not going to run away before the guns fire. Let me hear what you propose."

Sir Walter crossed to a cabinet, unlocked it with a key from his chain, and took a piece of paper from a drawer. It looked like an ordinary half-sheet of notepaper.

"I take it," he said, "that your travels have not extended to the East."

"No," I said, "barring a shooting trip in East Africa."

"Have you by any chance been following the present campaign there?"

"I've read the newspapers pretty regularly since I went to hospital. I've got some pals in the Mesopotamia show, and of course I'm keen to know what is going to happen at Gallipoli and Salonika. I gather that Egypt is pretty safe."

"If you will give me your attention for ten minutes I will supplement your newspaper reading."

Sir Walter lay back in an arm-chair and spoke to the ceiling. It was the best story, the clearest and the fullest, I had ever got of any bit of the war. He told me just how and why and when Turkey had left the rails. I heard about her grievances over our seizure of her ironclads, of the mischief the coming of the

Goeben had wrought, of Enver and his precious Committee and the way they had got a cinch on the old Turk. When he had spoken for a bit, he began to question me.

"You are an intelligent fellow, and you will ask how a Polish adventurer, meaning Enver, and a collection of Jews and gipsies should have got control of a proud race. The ordinary man will tell you that it was German organization backed up with German money and German arms. You will inquire again how, since Turkey is primarily a religious power, Islam has played so small a part in it all. The Sheikh-ul-Islam is neglected, and though the Kaiser proclaims a Holy War and calls himself Hadji Mohammed Guilliamo, and says the Hohenzollerns are descended from the Prophet, that seems to have fallen pretty flat. The ordinary man again will answer that Islam in Turkey is becoming a back number, and that Krupp guns are the new gods. Yet—I don't know. I do not quite believe in Islam becoming a back number.

"Look at it in another way," he went on. "If it were Enver and Germany alone dragging Turkey into a European war for purposes that no Turk cared a rush about, we might expect to find the regular army obedient, and Constantinople. But in the provinces, where Islam is strong, there would be trouble. Many of us counted on that. But we have been disappointed. The Syrian army is as fanatical as the hordes of the Mahdi. The Senussi have taken a hand in the game. The Persian Moslems are threatening trouble. There is a dry wind blowing through the East, and the parched grasses wait the spark. And the wind is blowing towards the Indian border. Whence comes that wind, think you?"

Sir Walter had lowered his voice, and was speaking very slow and distinct. I could hear the rain dripping from the eaves of the window, and far off the hoot of taxis in Whitehall.

"Have you an explanation, Hannay?" he asked again.

"It looks as if Islam had a bigger hand in the thing than we thought," I said. "I fancy religion is the only thing to knit up such a scattered empire."

"You are right," he said. "You must be right. We have laughed at the Holy War, the Jehad that old von der Goltz prophesied. But I believe that stupid old man with the big spectacles was right. There is a Jehad preparing. The question is, How?"

"I'm hanged if I know," I said; "but I'll bet it won't be done by a pack of stout German officers in *pickelhaubes*. I fancy you can't manufacture Holy Wars out of Krupp guns alone and a few staff officers and a battle-cruiser with her boilers burst."

"Agreed. They are not fools, however much we try to persuade ourselves of the contrary. But supposing they had got some tremendous sacred sanction—some holy thing, some book or gospel or some new prophet from the desert, something which would cast over the whole ugly mechanism of German war the glamour of the old torrential raids which crumpled the Byzantine Empire and shook the walls of Vienna? Islam is a fighting creed, and the mullah still stands in the pulpit with the Koran in one hand and a drawn sword in the other. Supposing there is some Ark of the Covenant which will madden the remotest Moslem peasant with dreams of Paradise? What then, my friend?"

"Then there will be hell let loose in those parts pretty soon."

"Hell which may spread. Beyond Persia, remember, lies India."

"You keep to suppositions. How much do you know?" I asked.

"Very little, except the fact. But the fact is beyond dispute. I have reports from agents everywhere—pedlars in South Russia, Afghan horse-dealers, Turcoman merchants, pilgrims on the road to Mecca, sheikhs in North Africa, sailors on the Black Sea coasters, sheep-skinned Mongols, Hindu fakirs, Greek traders in the Gulf, as well as respectable consuls who use ciphers. They tell the same story. The East is waiting for a revelation. It has been promised one. Some star—man, prophecy, or trinket—is coming out of the West. The Germans know, and that is the card with which they are going to astonish the world."

"And the mission you spoke of for me is to go and find out?"

He nodded gravely. "That is the crazy and impossible mission."

"Tell me one thing, Sir Walter," I said. "I know it is the fashion in this country if a man has special knowledge to set him to some job exactly the opposite. I know all about Damaraland, but instead of being put on Botha's staff, as I applied to be, I was kept in Hampshire mud till the campaign in German South-West Africa was over. I know a man who could pass as an Arab, but do you think they would send him to the East? They left him in my battalion—a lucky thing for me, for he saved my life at Loos. I know the fashion, but isn't this just carrying it a bit too far? There must be thousands of men who have spent years in the East and talk any language. They're the fellows for this job. I never saw a Turk in my life except a chap who did wrestling turns in a show at Kimberley. You've picked about the most useless man on earth."

"You've been a mining engineer, Hannay," Sir Walter said. "If you wanted a man to prospect for gold in Barotseland you would of course like to get one who knew the country and the people and the language. But the first thing you would require in him would be that he had a nose for finding gold and knew his business. That is the position now. I believe that you have a nose for finding out what our enemies try to hide. I know that you are brave and cool and resourceful. That is why I tell you the story. Besides . . ."

He unrolled a big map of Europe on the wall.

"I can't tell you where you'll get on the track of the secret, but I can put a limit to the quest. You won't find it east of the Bosphorus—not yet. It is still in Europe. It may be in Constantinople, or in Thrace. It may be farther west. But it is moving eastwards. If you are in time you may cut into its march to Constantinople. That much I can tell you. The secret is known in Germany, too, to those whom it concerns. It is in Europe that the seeker must search—at present."

"Tell me more," I said. "You can give me no details and no instructions. Obviously you can give me no help if I come to grief."

He nodded. "You would be beyond the pale."

"You give me a free hand?"

"Absolutely. You can have what money you like, and you can get what help you like. You can follow any plan you fancy, and go anywhere you think fruitful. We can give no directions."

"One last question. You say it is important. Tell me just how important."

"It is life and death," he said solemnly. "I can put it no higher and no lower. Once we know what is the menace we can meet it. As long as we are in the dark it works unchecked and we may be too late. The war must be won or lost in Europe. Yes; but if the East blazes up, our effort will be distracted from Europe and the great *coup* may fail. The stakes are no less than victory and defeat, Hannay."

I got out of my chair and walked to the window. It was a difficult moment in my life. I was happy in my soldiering; above all, happy in the company of my brother officers. I was asked to go off into the enemy's lands on a quest for which I believed I was manifestly unfitted—a business of lonely days and nights, of nerve-racking strain, of deadly peril shrouding me like a garment. Looking out on the bleak weather I shivered. It was too grim a business, too inhuman for flesh and blood. But Sir Walter had called it a matter of life and death, and I had told him that I was out to serve my country. He could not give me orders, but was I not under orders—higher orders than my Brigadier's? I thought myself incompetent, but cleverer men than me thought me competent, or at least competent enough for a sporting chance. I knew in my soul that if I declined I should never be quite at peace in the world again. And yet Sir Walter had called the scheme madness, and said that he himself would never have accepted.

How does one make a great decision? I swear that when I turned round to speak I meant to refuse. But my answer was Yes, and I had crossed the Rubicon. My voice sounded cracked and far away.

Sir Walter shook hands with me and his eyes blinked a little.

"I may be sending you to your death, Hannay.—Good God, what a damned task-mistress duty is!—If so, I shall be haunted with regrets, but *you* will never repent. Have no fear of that. You have chosen the roughest road, but it goes straight to the hill-tops."

He handed me the half-sheet of notepaper. On it were written three words—"*Kasredin,*" "*cancer,*" and "*v. I.*"

"That is the only clue we possess," he said. "I cannot construe it, but I can tell you the story. We have had our agents working in Persia and Mesopotamia for years—mostly young officers of the Indian Army. They carry their lives in their hand, and now and then one disappears, and the cellars of Bagdad might tell a tale. But they find out many things, and they count the game worth the candle. They have told us of the star rising in the West, but they could give us no details. All but one—the best of them. He had been working between Mosul and the Persian frontier as a muleteer, and had been south into the Bakhtiari hills. He found out something, but his enemies knew that he knew and he was pursued. Three months ago, just before Kut, he staggered into Delamain's camp with ten bullet holes in him and a knife slash on his forehead. He mumbled his name, but beyond that and the fact that there was a Something coming from the West he told them nothing. He died in ten minutes. They found this paper on him, and since he cried out the word 'Kasredin' in his last moments, it must have had something to do with his quest. It is for you to find out if it has any meaning."

I folded it up and placed it in my pocket-book.

"What a great fellow! What was his name?" I asked.

Sir Walter did not answer at once. He was looking out of the window. "His name," he said at last, "was Harry Bullivant. He was my son. God rest his brave soul!"

12 THE GATHERING OF THE MISSIONARIES

I wrote out a wire to Sandy, asking him to come up by the two-fifteen train and meet me at my flat.

"I have chosen my colleague," I said.

"Eddy Arbuthnot's boy? His father was at Harrow with me. I know the fellow—Harry used to bring him down to fish—tallish, with a lean, high-boned face and a pair of brown eyes like a pretty girl's. I know his record too. There's a good deal about him in this office. He rode through Yemen, which no white man ever did before. The Arabs let him pass, for they thought him stark mad and argued that the hand of Allah was heavy enough on him without their efforts. He's blood brother to every kind of Albanian bandit. Also he used to take a hand in Turkish politics, and got a huge reputation. Some Englishman was once complaining to old Mahmoud Shevkat about the scarcity of statesmen in Western Europe, and Mahmoud broke in with, 'Have you not the Honourable Arbuthnot?' You say he's in your battalion. I was wondering what had become of him, for we tried to get hold of him here, but he had left no address. Ludovick Arbuthnot—yes, that's the man. Buried deep in the commissioned ranks of the New Army? Well, we'll get him out pretty quick!"

"I knew he had knocked about the East, but I didn't know he was that kind of swell. Sandy's not the chap to buck about himself."

"He wouldn't," said Sir Walter. "He had always a more than Oriental reticence. I've got another colleague for you, if you like him."

He looked at his watch. "You can get to the Savoy Grill Room in five minutes in a taxi-cab. Go in from the Strand, turn to your left, and you will see in the alcove on the right-hand side a table with one large American gentleman sitting at it. They know him there, so he will have the table to himself. I want you to go and sit down beside him. Say you come from me. His name is Mr. John Scantlebury Blenkiron, now a citizen of Boston, Mass., but born and raised in Indiana. Put this envelope in your pocket, but don't read its contents till you have talked to him. I want you to form your own opinion about Mr. Blenkiron."

I went out of the Foreign Office in as muddled a frame of mind as any diplomatist who ever left its portals. I was most desperately depressed. To begin with, I was in a complete funk. I had always thought I was about as brave as the average man, but there's courage and courage, and mine was certainly not of the impassive kind. Stick me down in a trench, and I could stand being shot at as well as most people, and my blood could get hot if it were given a chance. But I think I had too much imagination. I couldn't shake off the beastly forecasts that kept crowding my mind.

In about a fortnight, I calculated, I would be dead. Shot as a spy—a rotten sort of ending! At the moment I was quite safe, looking for a taxi in the middle of Whitehall, but the sweat broke on my forehead. I felt as I had felt in my adventure before the war. But this was far worse, for it was more cold-blooded and premeditated, and I didn't seem to have even a sporting chance. I watched the figures in khaki passing on the pavement, and thought what a nice safe prospect they had compared to mine. Yes, even if next week they were in the Hohenzollern, or the Hairpin trench at the Quarries, or that ugly angle at Hooge. I wondered why I had not been happier that morning before I got that infernal wire. Suddenly all the trivialities of English life seemed to me inexpressibly dear and terribly far away. I was very angry with Bullivant, till I remembered how fair he had been. My fate was my own choosing.

When I was hunting the Black Stone the interest of the problem had helped to keep me going. But now I could see no problem. My mind had nothing to work on but three words of gibberish on a sheet of paper and a mystery of which Sir Walter had been convinced, but to which he couldn't give a name. It was like a story I had read of St. Theresa setting off at the age of ten with her small brother to convert the Moors. I sat huddled in the taxi with my chin on my breast, wishing that I had lost a leg at Loos and been comfortably tucked away for the rest of the war.

Sure enough I found my man in the Grill Room. There he was, feeding solemnly, with a napkin tucked under his chin. He was a big fellow with a fat, sallow, clean-shaven face. I disregarded the hovering waiter and pulled up a chair beside the American at the little table. He turned on me a pair of full sleepy eyes, like a ruminating ox.

"Mr. Blenkiron?" I asked.

"You have my name, sir," he said. "Mr. John Scantlebury Blenkiron. I would wish you good morning if I saw anything good in this darned British weather."

"I come from Sir Walter Bullivant," I said, speaking low.

"So?" said he. "Sir Walter is a very good friend of mine. Pleased to meet you, Mr.—or I guess it's Colonel—"

"Hannay," I said; "Major Hannay." I was wondering what this sleepy Yankee could do to help me.

"Allow me to offer you luncheon, Major. Here, waiter, bring the *carte*. I regret that I cannot join you in sampling the efforts of the management of this ho-tel. I suffer, sir, from dyspepsia—duo-denal dyspepsia. It gets me two hours after a meal and gives me hell just below the breastbone. So I am obliged to adopt a diet. My nourishment is fish, sir, and boiled milk and a little dry toast. It's a melancholy descent from the days when I could do justice to a lunch at Sherry's and sup off oyster-crabs and devilled bones." He sighed from the depths of his capacious frame.

I ordered an omelette and a chop, and took another look at him. The large eyes seemed to be gazing steadily at me without seeing me. They were as vacant as an abstracted child's; but I had an uncomfortable feeling that they saw more than mine.

"You have been fighting, Major? The Battle of Loos? Well, I guess that must have been some battle. We in America respect the fighting of the British soldier, but we don't quite catch on to the de-vices of the British generals. We opine that there is more bellicosity than science among your highbrows. That is so? My father fought at Chattanooga, but these eyes have seen nothing gorier than a Presidential election. Say, is there any way I could be let in to a scene of real bloodshed?"

His serious tone made me laugh. "There are plenty of your countrymen in the present show," I said. "The French Foreign Legion is full of young Americans, and so is our Army Service Corps. Half the chauffeurs you strike in France seem to come from the States."

He sighed. "I did think of some belligerent stunt a year back. But I reflected that the good God had not given John S. Blenkiron the kind of martial figure that would do credit to the tented field. Also I recollected that we Americans were nootrals—benevolent nootrals—and that it did not become me to be butting into the struggles of the effete monarchies of Europe. So I stopped at home. It was a big renunciation, Major, for I was lying sick during the Philippines business, and I have never seen the lawless passions of men let loose on a battlefield. And, as a stoodent of humanity, I hankered for the experience."

"What have you been doing?" I asked. The calm gentleman had begun to interest me.

"Waal," he said, "I just waited. The Lord has blessed me with money to burn, so I didn't need to go scrambling like a wild cat for war contracts. But I reckoned I would get let into the game somehow, and I was. Being a nootral, I was in an advantageous position to take a hand. I had a pretty hectic time for a while, and then I reckoned I would leave God's country and see what was doing in Europe. I have counted myself out of the bloodshed business, but, as your poet sings, peace has its victories not less renowned than war, and I reckon that means that a nootral can have a share in a scrap as well as a belligerent."

"That's the best kind of neutrality I've ever heard of," I said.

"It's the right kind," he replied solemnly. "Say, Major, what are your lot fighting for? For your own skins and your Empire and the peace of Europe. Waal, those ideals don't concern us one cent. We're not Europeans, and there aren't any German trenches on Long Island yet. You've made the ring in Europe, and if we came butting in it wouldn't be the rules of the game. You wouldn't welcome us, and I guess you'd be right. We're that delicate-minded we can't interfere, and that was what my friend, President Wilson, meant when he opined that America was too proud to fight. So we're nootrals. But likewise we're benevolent nootrals. As I follow events, there's a skunk been let loose in the world, and the odour of it is going to make life none too sweet till it is cleared away. It wasn't us that stirred up that skunk, but we've got to take a hand in disinfecting the planet. See? We can't fight, but, by God! some of us are going to sweat blood to sweep the mess up. Officially we do nothing except give off Notes like a leaky boiler gives off steam. But as individooal citizens we're in it up to the neck. So, in the spirit of Thomas Jefferson and Woodrow Wilson, I'm going to be the nootralist kind of nootral till Kaiser will be sorry he didn't declare war on America at the beginning."

I was completely recovering my temper. This fellow was a perfect jewel, and his spirit put purpose into me.

"I guess you British were the same kind of nootral when your Admiral warned off the German fleet from interfering with Dewey in Manila Bay in '98." Mr. Blenkiron drank up the last drop of his boiled milk, and lit a thin black cigar.

I leaned forward. "Have you talked to Sir Walter?" I asked.

"I have talked to him, and he has given me to understand that there's a deal ahead which you're going to boss. There are no flies on that big man, and if he says it's good business then you can count me in."

"You know that it's uncommonly dangerous?"

"I judged so. But it won't do to begin counting risks. I believe in an all-wise and beneficent Providence, but you have got to trust Him and give Him a chance. What's life anyhow? For me it's living on a strict diet and having frequent pains in my stomach. It isn't such an almighty lot to give up, provided you get a good price on the deal. Besides, how big is the risk? About one o'clock in the morning, when you can't sleep, it will be the size of Mount Everest, but if you run out to meet it, it will be a hillock you can jump over. The grizzly looks very fierce when you're taking your ticket for the Rockies and wondering if you'll come back, but he's just an ordinary bear when you've got the sight of your rifle on him. I won't think about risks till I'm up to my neck in them and don't see the road out."

I scribbled my address on a piece of paper and handed it to the stout philosopher. "Come to dinner to-night at eight," I said.

"I thank you, Major. A little fish, please, plain-boiled, and some hot milk. You will forgive me if I borrow your couch after the meal and spend the evening on my back. That is the advice of my noo doctor."

I got a taxi and drove to my club. On the way I opened the envelope Sir Walter had given me. It contained a number of jottings, the *dossier* of Mr.

Blenkiron. He had done wonders for the Allies in the States. He had nosed out the Dumba plot, and had been instrumental in getting the portfolio of Dr. Albert. Von Papen's spies had tried to murder him, after he had defeated an attempt to blow up one of the big gun factories. Sir Walter had written at the end: "The best man we ever had. Better than Scudder. He would go through hell with a box of bismuth tablets and a pack of Patience cards."

I went into the little back smoking-room, borrowed an atlas from the library, poked up the fire, and sat down to think. Mr. Blenkiron had given me the fillip I needed. My mind was beginning to work now, and was running wide over the whole business. Not that I hoped to find anything by my cogitations. It wasn't thinking in an arm-chair that would solve the mystery. But I was getting a sort of grip on a plan of operations. And to my relief I had stopped thinking about the risks. Blenkiron had shamed me out of that. If a sedentary dyspeptic could show that kind of nerve, I wasn't going to be behind him.

I went back to my flat about five o'clock. My man Paddock had gone to the wars long ago, so I had shifted to one of the new blocks in Park Lane where they provide food and service. I kept the place on to have a home to go to when I got leave. It's a miserable business holidaying in an hotel.

Sandy was devouring tea-cakes with the serious resolution of a convalescent.

"Well, Dick, what's the news? Is it a brass-hat or the boot?"

"Neither," I said. "But you and I are going to disappear from his Majesty's forces. Seconded for special service."

"O my sainted aunt!" said Sandy. "What is it? For Heaven's sake put me out of pain. Have we to tout deputations of suspicious neutrals over munition works or take the shivering journalist in a motor-car where he can imagine he sees a Boche?"

"The news will keep. But I can tell you this much. It's about as safe and easy as to go through the German lines with a walking-stick."

"Come, that's not so dusty," said Sandy, and began cheerfully on the muffins.

I must spare a moment to introduce Sandy to the reader, for he cannot be allowed to slip into this tale by a side-door. If you will consult the Peerage you will find that to Edward Cospatrick, fifteenth Baron Clanroyden, there was born in the year 1882, as his second son, Ludovick Gustavus Arbuthnot, commonly called the Honourable, etc. The said son was educated at Eton and New College, Oxford, was a captain in the Tweeddale Yeomanry, and served for some years as honorary attaché at various embassies. The Peerage will stop short at this point, but that is by no means the end of the story. For the rest you must consult very different authorities. Lean brown men from the ends of the earth may be seen on the London pavements now and then in creased clothes, walking with the light outland step, slinking into clubs as if they could not remember whether or not they belonged to them. From them you may get news of Sandy. Better still, you will hear of him at little forgotten fishing ports where the Albanian mountains dip to the Adriatic. If you struck a Mecca pilgrimage the odds are you would meet a dozen of Sandy's friends in it. In shepherds' huts in the Caucasus you will find bits of his cast-off clothing, for he has a knack of shedding garments as he goes. In the caravanserais of Bokhara and Samarkand he is known, and there are shikaris in the Pamirs who still speak of him round their fires. If you were going to visit Petrograd or Rome or Cairo it would be no use asking him for introductions; if he gave them, they would lead you into strange haunts. But if Fate compelled you to go to Llasa or Yarkand or Seistan he could map out your road for you and pass the word to potent friends. We call ourselves insular, but the truth is that we are the only race on earth that can produce men capable of getting inside the skin of remote peoples. Perhaps the Scots are better than the English, but we're all a thousand per cent. better than anybody else. Sandy was the wandering Scot carried to the pitch of genius. In old days he would have led a crusade or discovered a new road to the Indies. To-day he merely roamed as the spirit moved him, till the war swept him up and dumped him down in my battalion.

I got out Sir Walter's half-sheet of notepaper. It was not the original—naturally he wanted to keep that—but it was a careful tracing. I took it that Harry Bullivant had not written down the words as a memo. for his own use. People who follow his career have good memories. He must have written them in order that, if he perished and his body was found, his friends might get a clue. Wherefore, I argued, the words must be intelligible to somebody or other of our persuasion, and likewise they must be pretty well gibberish to any Turk or German that found them.

The first, "*Kasredin*," I could make nothing of.

I asked Sandy.

"You mean Nasr-ed-din," he said, still munching crumpets.

"What's that?" I asked sharply.

"He's the General believed to be commanding against us in Mesopotamia. I remember him years ago in Aleppo. He talked bad French and drank the sweetest of sweet champagne."

I looked closely at the paper. The "K" was unmistakable.

"Kasredin is nothing. It means in Arabic the House of Faith, and might cover anything from Hagia Sofia to a suburban villa. What's your next puzzle, Dick? Have you entered for a prize competition in a weekly paper?"

"*Cancer*," I read out.

"It is the Latin for a crab. Likewise it is the name of a painful disease. It is also a sign of the Zodiac."

"*v. I*," I read.

"There you have me. It sounds like the number of a motor-car. The police would find out for you. I call this rather a difficult competition. What's the prize?"

I passed him the paper. "Who wrote it? It looks as if he had been in a hurry."

"Harry Bullivant," I said.

Sandy's face grew solemn. "Old Harry. He was at my tutor's. The best fellow God ever made. I saw his name in the casualty list before Kut . . . Harry didn't do things without a purpose. What's the story of this paper?"

"Wait till after dinner," I said. "I'm going to change and have a bath. There's an American coming to dine, and he's part of the business."

Mr. Blenkiron arrived punctual to the minute in a fur coat like a Russian prince's. Now that I saw him on his feet I could judge him better. He had a fat face, but was not too plump in figure, and very muscular wrists showed below his shirtcuffs. I fancied that, if the occasion called, he might be a good man with his hands.

Sandy and I ate a hearty meal, but the American picked at his boiled fish and sipped his milk a drop at a time. When the servant had cleared away, he was as good as his word and laid himself out on my sofa. I offered him a good cigar, but he preferred one of his own lean black abominations. Sandy stretched his length in an easy chair and lit his pipe. "Now for your story, Dick," he said.

I began, as Sir Walter had begun with me, by telling them about the puzzle in the Near East. I pitched a pretty good yarn, for I had been thinking a lot about it, and the mystery of the business had caught my fancy. Sandy got very keen.

"It is possible enough. Indeed, I've been expecting it, though I'm hanged if I can imagine what card the Germans have got up their sleeve. It might be any one of twenty things. Thirty years ago there was a bogus prophecy that played the devil in Yemen. Or it might be a flag such as Ali Wad Helu had, or a jewel like Solomon's necklace in Abyssinia. You never know what will start off a Jehad! But I rather think it's a man."

"Where could he get his purchase?" I asked.

"It's hard to say. If it were merely wild tribesmen like the Bedawin he might have got a reputation as a saint and miracle worker. Or he might be a fellow that preached a pure religion, like the chap that founded the Senussi. But I'm inclined to think he must be something extra special if he can put a spell on the whole Moslem world. The Turk and the Persian wouldn't follow the ordinary new theology game. He must be of the Blood. Your Mahdis and Mullahs and Imams were nobodies, but they had only a local prestige. To capture all Islam—and I gather that is what we fear—the man must be of the Koreish, the tribe of the Prophet himself."

"But how could any impostor prove that? for I suppose he's an impostor."

"He would have to combine a lot of claims. His descent must be pretty good to begin with, and there are families, remember, that claim the Koreish blood. Then he'd have to be rather a wonder on his own account—saintly, eloquent, and that sort of thing. And I expect he'd have to show a sign, though what that could be I haven't a notion."

"You know the East about as well as any living man. Do you think that kind of thing is possible?" I asked.

"Perfectly," said Sandy, with a grave face.

"Well, there's the ground cleared to begin with. Then there's the evidence of pretty well every secret agent we possess. That all seems to prove the fact.

But we have no details and no clues except that bit of paper." I told them the story of it.

Sandy studied it with wrinkled brows. "It beats me. But it may be the key for all that. A clue may be dumb in London and shout aloud at Bagdad."

"That's just the point I was coming to. Sir Walter says this thing is about as important for our cause as big guns. He can't give me orders, but he offers the job of going out to find what the mischief is. Once he knows that, he says he can checkmate it. But it's got to be found out soon, for the mine may be sprung at any moment. I've taken on the job. Will you help?"

Sandy was studying the ceiling.

"I should add that it's about as safe as playing chuck-farthing at the Loos Cross-roads, the day you and I went in. And if we fail nobody can help us."

"Oh, of course, of course," said Sandy in an abstracted voice.

Mr. Blenkiron, having finished his after-dinner recumbency, had sat up and pulled a small table towards him. From his pocket he had taken a pack of Patience cards and had begun to play the game called the Double Napoleon. He seemed to be oblivious of the conversation.

Suddenly I had a feeling that the whole affair was stark lunacy. Here were we three simpletons sitting in a London flat and projecting a mission into the enemy's citadel without an idea what we were to do or how we were to do it. And one of the three was looking at the ceiling and whistling softly through his teeth, and another was playing Patience. The farce of the thing struck me so keenly that I laughed.

Sandy looked at me sharply.

"You feel like that? Same with me. It's idiocy, but all war is idiotic and the most wholehearted idiot is apt to win. We're to go on this mad trail wherever we think we can hit it. Well, I'm with you. But I don't mind admitting that I'm in a blue funk. I had got myself adjusted to the trench business and was quite happy. And now you have hoicked me out, and my feet are cold."

"I don't believe you know what fear is," I said.

"There you're wrong, Dick," he said earnestly. "Every man who isn't a maniac knows fear. I have done some daft things, but I never started on them without wishing they were over. Once I'm in the show I get easier, and by the time I'm coming out I'm sorry to leave it. But at the start my feet are icy."

"Then I take it you're coming?"

"Rather," he said. "You didn't imagine I would go back on you?"

"And you, sir?" I addressed Blenkiron.

His game of Patience seemed to be coming out. He was completing eight little heaps of cards with a contented grunt. As I spoke, he raised his sleepy eyes and nodded.

"Why, yes," he said. "You gentlemen mustn't think that I haven't been following your most engrossing conversation. I guess I haven't missed a syllable. I find that a game of Patience stimulates the digestion after meals and conduces to quiet reflection. John S. Blenkiron is with you all the time."

He shuffled the cards and dealt for a new game.

I don't think I ever expected a refusal, but this ready assent cheered me wonderfully. I couldn't have faced the thing alone.

"Well, that's settled. Now for ways and means. We three have got to put ourselves in the way of finding out Germany's secret, and we have to go where it is known. Somehow or other we have to reach Constantinople, and to beat the biggest area of country we must go by different roads. Sandy, my lad, you've got to get into Turkey. You're the only one of us that knows that engaging people. You can't get in by Europe very easily, so you must try Asia. What about the coast of Asia Minor?"

"It could be done," he said. "You'd better leave that entirely to me. I'll find out the best way. I suppose the Foreign Office will help me to get to the jumping-off place?"

"Remember," I said, "it's no good getting too far east. The secret, so far as concerns us, is still west of Constantinople."

"I see that. I'll blow in on the Bosphorus by a short tack."

"For you, Mr. Blenkiron, I would suggest a straight journey. You're an American, and can travel through Germany direct. But I wonder how far your activities in New York will allow you to pass as a neutral?"

"I have considered that, sir," he said. "I have given some thought to the pecooliar psychology of the great German nation. As I read them they're as cunning as cats, and if you play the feline game they will outwit you every time. Yes, sir, they are no slouches at sleuth-work. If I were to buy a pair of false whiskers and dye my hair and dress like a Baptist parson and go into Germany on the peace racket, I guess they'd be on my trail like a knife, and I should be shot as a spy inside of a week or doing solitary in the Moabit prison. But they lack the larger vision. They can be bluffed, sir. With your approval I shall visit the Fatherland as John S. Blenkiron, once a thorn in the flesh of their brightest boys on the other side. But it will be a different John S. I reckon he will have experienced a change of heart. He will have come to appreciate the great, pure, noble soul of Germany, and he will be sorrowing for his past like a converted gun-man at a camp meeting. He will be a victim of the meanness and perfidy of the British Government. I am going to have a first-class row with your Foreign Office about my passport, and I am going to speak harsh words about them up and down this metropolis. I am going to be shadowed by your sleuths at my port of embarkation, and I guess I shall run up hard against the British Le-gations in Scandinavia. By that time our Teutonic friends will have begun to wonder what has happened to John S., and to think that maybe they have been mistaken in that child. So, when I get to Germany they will be waiting for me with an open mind. Then I judge my conduct will surprise and encourage them. I will confide to them valuable secret information about British preparations, and I will show up the British lion as the meanest kind of cur. You may trust me to make a good impression. After that I'll move eastwards, to see the de-molition of the British Empire in those parts. By the way, where is the rendezvous?"

"This is the 17th day of November. If we can't find out what we want in two months we may chuck the job. On the 17th of January we should forgather in Constantinople. Whoever gets there first waits for the others. If by that date we're not all present, it will be considered that the missing man has got into trouble and must be given up. If ever we get there we'll be coming from different points and in different characters, so we want a rendezvous where all kinds of odd folk assemble. Sandy, you know Constantinople. You fix the meeting-place."

"I've already thought of that," he said, and going to the writing-table he drew a little plan on a sheet of paper. "That lane runs down from the Kurdish Bazaar in Galata to the ferry of Ratchik. Half-way down on the left-hand side is a café kept by a Greek called Kuprasso. Behind the café is a garden, surrounded by high walls which were part of the old Byzantine theatre. At the end of the garden is a shanty called the Garden-house of Suliman the Red. It has been called in its time a dancing-hall and a gambling hell and God knows what else. It's not a place for respectable people, but the ends of the earth converge there and no questions are asked. That's the best spot I can think of for a meeting-place."

The kettle was simmering by the fire, the night was raw, and it seemed the hour for whisky punch. I made a brew for Sandy and myself and boiled some milk for Blenkiron.

"What about language?" I asked. "You're all right, Sandy?"

"I know German fairly well; and I can pass anywhere as a Turk. The first will do for eavesdropping and the second for ordinary business."

"And you?" I asked Blenkiron.

"I was left out at Pentecost," he said. "I regret to confess I have no gift of tongues. But the part I have chosen for myself don't require the polyglot. Never forget I'm plain John S. Blenkiron, a citizen of the great American Republic."

"You haven't told us your own line, Dick," Sandy said.

"I am going to the Bosphorus through Germany, and, not being a neutral, it won't be a very cushioned journey."

Sandy looked grave.

"That's sounds pretty desperate. Is your German good enough?"

"Pretty fair; quite good enough to pass as a native. But officially I shall not understand one word. I shall be a Boer from Western Cape Colony: one of Maritz's old lot who after a bit of trouble has got through Angola and reached Europe. I shall talk Dutch and nothing else. And, my hat! I shall be pretty bitter about the British. There's a powerful lot of good swearwords in the Taal. I shall know all about Africa and be panting to get another whack at the *verdommt rooinek*. With luck they may send me to the Uganda show or to Egypt, and I shall take care to go by Constantinople. If I'm to deal with Mohammedan natives they're bound to show me what hand they hold. At least, that's the way I look at it."

We filled our glasses—two of punch and one of milk—and drank to our next merry meeting. Then Sandy began to laugh, and I joined in. The sense of hopeless folly again descended on me. The best plans we could make were like a few buckets of water to ease the drought of the Sahara or the old lady who would have stopped the Atlantic with a broom. I thought with sympathy of little Saint Theresa.

13   PETER PIENAAR

Our various departures were unassuming all but the American's. Sandy spent a busy fortnight in his subterranean fashion, now in the British Museum, now running about the country to see old exploring companions, now at the War Office, now at the Foreign Office, but mostly in my flat, sunk in an arm-chair and meditating. He left finally on December 1 as a King's Messenger for Cairo. Once there I knew the King's Messenger would disappear, and some queer Oriental ruffian take his place. It would have been impertinence in me to inquire into his plans. He was the real professional, and I was only the dabbler.

Blenkiron was a different matter. Sir Walter told me to look out for squalls, and the twinkle in his eye gave me a notion of what was coming. The first thing the sportsman did was to write a letter to the papers signed with his name. There had been a debate in the House of Commons on foreign policy, and the speech of some idiot there gave him his cue. He declared that he had been heart and soul with the British at the start, but that he was reluctantly compelled to change his views. He said our blockade of Germany had broken all the laws of God and humanity, and he reckoned that Britain was now the worst exponent of Prussianism going. That letter made a fine racket, and the paper that printed it had a row with the Censor.

But that was only the beginning of Mr. Blenkiron's campaign. He got mixed up with some mountebanks called the League of Democrats against Aggression, gentlemen who thought that Germany was all right if we would only keep from hurting her feelings. He addressed a meeting under their auspices, which was broken up by the crowd, but not before John S. had got off his chest a lot of amazing stuff. I wasn't there, but a man who was told me that he never heard such clotted nonsense. He said that Germany was right in wanting the freedom of the seas, and that America would back her up, and that the British Navy was a bigger menace to the peace of the world than the Kaiser's army. He admitted that he had once thought differently, but he was an honest man and not afraid to face facts. The oration closed suddenly, when he got a brussels-sprout in the eye, at which my friend said he swore in a very unpacifist style.

After that he wrote other letters to the press, saying that there was no more liberty of speech in England, and a lot of scallawags backed him up. Some Americans wanted to tar and feather him, and he got kicked out of the Savoy. There was an agitation to get him deported, and questions were asked in Parliament, and the Under-Secretary for Foreign Affairs said his department had the matter in hand. I was beginning to think that Blenkiron was carrying his tomfoolery too far, so I went to see Sir Walter, but he told me to keep my mind easy.

"Our friend's motto is 'Thorough,'" he said, "and he knows very well what he is about. We have officially requested him to leave, and he sails from Newcastle on Monday. He will be shadowed wherever he goes, and we hope to provoke more outbreaks. He is a very capable fellow."

The last I saw of him was on the Saturday afternoon when I met him in St. James's Street and offered to shake hands. He told me that my uniform was a pollution, and made a speech to a small crowd about it. They hissed him and he had to get into a taxi. As he departed there was just the suspicion of a wink in his left eye. On Monday I read that he had gone off, and the papers observed that our shores were well quit of him.

I sailed on December 3 from Liverpool in a boat bound for the Argentine that was due to put in at Lisbon. I had of course to get a Foreign Office passport to leave England, but after that my connection with the Government ceased. All the details of my journey were carefully thought out. Lisbon would be a good jumping-off place, for it was the rendezvous of scallawags from most parts of Africa. My kit was an old Gladstone bag, and my clothes were the relics of my South African wardrobe. I let my beard grow for some days before I sailed, and, since it grows fast, I went on board with the kind of hairy chin you will see on the young Boer. My name was now Brandt, Cornelis Brandt—at least so my passport said, and passports never lie.

There were just two other passengers on that beastly boat, and they never appeared till we were out of the Bay. I was pretty bad myself, but managed to move about all the time, for the frowst in my cabin would have sickened a hippo. The old tub took two days and a night to waddle from Ushant to Finisterre. Then the weather changed and we came out of snow squalls into something very like summer. The hills of Portugal were all blue and yellow like the Kalahari, and before we made the Tagus I was beginning to forget I had ever left Rhodesia. There was a Dutchman among the sailors with whom I used to patter the *taal*, and but for "Good morning" and "Good evening" in broken English to the captain, that was about all the talking I did on the cruise.

We dropped anchor off the quays of Lisbon on a shiny blue morning, pretty near warm enough to wear flannels. I had now got to be very wary. I did not leave the ship with the shore-going boat, but made a leisurely breakfast. Then I strolled on deck, and there, just casting anchor in the middle of the stream, was another ship with the blue and white funnel I knew so well. I calculated that a month before she had been smelling the mangrove swamps of Angola. Nothing could better answer my purpose. I proposed to board her, pretending I was looking for a friend, and come on shore from her, so that any one in Lisbon who chose to be curious would think I had landed straight from Portuguese Africa.

I hailed one of the adjacent ruffians and got into his row-boat, with my kit. We reached the vessel—they called her the *Henry the Navigator*—just as the first shore-boat was leaving. The crowd in it were all Portuguese, which suited my book.

But when I went up the ladder the first man I met was old Peter Pienaar.

Here was a piece of sheer monumental luck. Peter had opened his eyes and his mouth, and had got as far as "*Allemachtig*," when I shut him up.

"Brandt," I said, "Cornelis Brandt. That's my name now, and don't you forget it. Who is the captain here? Is it still old Sloggett?"

"*Ja*," said Peter, pulling himself together. "He was speaking about you yesterday."

This was better and better. I sent Peter below to get hold of Sloggett, and presently I had a few words with that gentleman in his cabin with the door shut.

"You've got to enter my name on the ship's books. I came aboard at Mossamedes. And my name's Cornelis Brandt."

At first Sloggett was for objecting. He said it was a felony. I told him that I dared say it was, but he had got to do it for reasons which I couldn't give, but which were highly creditable to all parties. In the end he agreed and I saw it done. I had a pull on old Sloggett, for I had known him ever since he owned a dissolute tug-boat at Delagoa Bay.

Then Peter and I went ashore and swaggered into Lisbon as if we owned De Beers. We put up at the big hotel opposite the railway station, and looked and behaved like a pair of low-bred South Africans home for a spree. It was a fine bright day, so I hired a motor-car and said I would drive it myself. We asked the name of some beauty spot to visit, and were told Cintra and shown the road to it. I wanted a quiet place to talk, for I had a good deal to say to Peter Pienaar.

I christened that car the Lusitanian Terror, and it was a marvel that we did not smash ourselves up. There was something immortally wrong with its steering-gear. Half a dozen times we slewed across the road, inviting destruction. But we got there in the end, and had luncheon in an hotel opposite the Moorish palace. There we left the car and wandered up the slopes of a hill, where, sitting among scrub very like the veld, I told Peter the situation of affairs.

But first a word must be said about Peter. He was the man that taught me all I ever knew of veldcraft, and a good deal about human nature besides. He was out of the Old Colony—Burgersdorp, I think—but he had come to the Transvaal when the Lydenburg goldfields started. He was prospector, transport rider, and hunter in turns, but principally hunter. In those early days he was none too good a citizen. He was in Swaziland with Bob Macnab, and you know what that means. Then he took to working off bogus gold propositions on Kimberley and Johannesburg magnates, and what he didn't know about salting a mine wasn't knowledge. After that he was in the Kalahari, where he and Scotty Smith were familiar names. An era of comparative respectability dawned for him with the Matabele War, when he did uncommon good scouting and transport work. Cecil Rhodes wanted to establish him on a stock farm down Salisbury way, but Peter was an independent devil and would call no man master. He took to big-game hunting, which was what God intended him for, for he could track a tsessebe in thick bush, and was far the finest shot I have seen in my life. He took parties to the Pungwe flats, and Barotseland, and up to Tanganyika. Then he made a speciality of the Ngami region, where I once hunted with him, and he was with me when I went prospecting in Damaraland.

When the Boer War started, Peter, like many of the very great hunters, took the British side and did most of our intelligence work in the North Transvaal. Beyers would have hanged him if he could have caught him, and there was no love lost between Peter and his own people for many a day. When it was all over and things had calmed down a bit, he settled in Bulawayo and used to go with me when I went on trek. At the time when I left Africa two years before, I had lost sight of him for months, and heard that he was somewhere on the Congo poaching elephants. He had always a great idea of making things hum so loud in Angola that the Union Government would have to step in and annex it. After Rhodes Peter had the biggest notions south of the Line.

He was a man of about five foot ten, very thin and active, and as strong as a buffalo. He had pale blue eyes, a face as gentle as a girl's, and a soft sleepy voice. From his present appearance it looked as if he had been living hard lately. His clothes were of the cut you might expect to get at Lobito Bay, he was as lean as a rake, deeply browned with the sun, and there was a lot of grey in his beard. He was fifty-six years old, and used to be taken for forty. Now he looked about his age.

I first asked him what he had been up to since the war began. He spat, in the Kaffir way he had, and said he had been having hell's time.

"I got hung up on the Kafue," he said. "When I heard from old Letsitela that the white men were fighting I had a bright idea that I might get into German South West from the north. You see I knew that Botha couldn't long keep out of the war. Well, I got into German territory all right, and then a *skellum* of an officer came along, and commandeered all my mules, and wanted to commandeer me with them for his fool army. He was a very ugly man with a yellow face." Peter filled a deep pipe from a kudu-skin pouch.

"Were you commandeered?" I asked.

"No. I shot him—not so as to kill, but to wound badly. It was all right, for he fired first on me. Got me too in the left shoulder. But that was the beginning of bad trouble. I trekked east pretty fast, and got over the border among the Ovamba. I have made many journeys, but that was the worst. Four days I went without water, and six without food. Then by bad luck I fell in with 'Nkitla—you remember, the half-caste chief. He said I owed him money for cattle which I bought when I came there with Carowab. It was a lie, but he held to it, and would give me no transport. So I crossed the

Kalahari on my feet. Ugh, it was as slow as a *vrouw* coming from *nachtmaal*. It took weeks and weeks, and when I came to Lechwe's kraal, I heard that the fighting was over and that Botha had conquered the Germans. That, too, was a lie, but it deceived me, and I went north into Rhodesia, where I learned the truth. But by then I judged the war had gone too far for me to get any profit out of it, so I went into Angola to look for German refugees. By that time I was hating Germans worse than hell."

"But what did you propose to do with them?" I asked.

"I had a notion they would make trouble with the Government in those parts. I don't specially love the Portugoose, but I'm for him against the Germans every day. Well, there was trouble, and I had a merry time for a month or two. But by-and-by it petered out, and I thought I had better clear for Europe, for South Africa was settling down just as the big show was getting really interesting. So here I am, Cornelis, my old friend. If I shave my beard, will they let me join the Flying Corps?"

I looked at Peter sitting there smoking, as imperturbable as if he had been growing mealies in Natal all his life and had run home for a month's holiday with his people in Peckham.

"You're coming with me, my lad," I said. "We're going into Germany."

Peter showed no surprise. "Keep in mind that I don't like the Germans," was all he said. "I'm a quiet Christian man, but I've the devil of a temper."

Then I told him the story of our mission.

"You and I have got to be Maritz's men. We went into Angola, and now we're trekking for the Fatherland to get a bit of our own back from the infernal English. Neither of us knows any German—publicly. We'd better plan out the fighting we were in—Kakamas will do for one, and Schuit Drift. You were a Ngamiland hunter before the war. They won't have your *dossier*, so you can tell any lie you like. I'd better be an educated Afrikander, one of Beyer's bright lads, and a pal of old Hertzog. We can let our imagination loose about that part, but we must stick to the same yarn about the fighting."

"*Ja*, Cornelis," said Peter. (He had called me Cornelis ever since I had told him my new name. He was a wonderful chap for catching on to any game.) "But after we get into Germany, what then? There can't be much difficulty about the beginning. But once we're among the beer-swillers I don't quite see our line. We're to find out about something that's going on in Turkey? When I was a boy the predikant used to preach about Turkey. I wish I was better educated and remembered whereabouts in the map it was."

"You leave that to me," I said; "I'll explain it all to you before we get there. We haven't got much of a spoor, but we'll cast about, and with luck will pick it up. I've seen you do it often enough when we hunted kudu on the Kafue."

Peter nodded. "Do we sit still in a German town?" he asked anxiously. "I shouldn't like that, Cornelis."

"We move gently eastwards to Constantinople," I said.

Peter grinned. "We should cover a lot of new country. You can reckon on me, friend Cornelis. I've always had a hankering to see Europe."

He rose to his feet and stretched his long arms.

"We'd better begin at once. God, I wonder what's happened to old Solly Maritz, with his bottle face? Yon was a fine battle at the drift when I was sitting up to my neck in the Orange praying that Brits' lads would take my head for a stone."

Peter was as thorough a mountebank, when he got started, as Blenkiron himself. All the way back to London he yarned about Maritz and his adventures in German South West till I half believed they were true. He made a very good story of our doings, and by his constant harping on it I pretty soon got it into my memory. That was always Peter's way. He said if you were going to play a part, you must think yourself into it, convince yourself that you were *it*, till you really were it and didn't act but behaved naturally. The two men who had started that morning from the hotel door had been bogus enough, but the two that returned were genuine desperadoes, itching to get a shot at England.

We spent that evening piling up evidence in our favour. Some kind of republic had been started in Portugal, and ordinarily the cafés would have been full of politicians, but the war had quieted all these local squabbles, and the talk was of nothing but what was doing in France and Russia. The place we went to was a big, well-lighted show on a main street, and there were a lot of sharp-eyed fellows wandering about that I guessed were spies and police agents. I knew that Britain was the one country that didn't bother about this kind of game, and that it would be safe enough to let ourselves go.

I talked Portuguese fairly well, and Peter spoke it like a Lourenço Marques bar-keeper, with a lot of Shangaan words to fill up. He started on curaçoa, which I reckoned was a new drink to him, and presently his tongue ran freely. Several neighbours pricked up their ears, and soon we had a small crowd round our table.

We talked to each other of Maritz and our doings. It didn't seem to be a popular subject in that café. One big blue-black fellow said that Maritz was a dirty swine who would soon be hanged. Peter quickly caught his knife wrist with one hand and his throat with the other, and demanded an apology. He got it. The Lisbon *boulevardiers* have not lost any lions.

After that there was a bit of a squash in our corner. Those near us were very quiet and polite, but the outer fringe made remarks. When Peter said that if Portugal, which he admitted he loved, was going to stick to England she was backing the wrong horse, there was a murmur of disapproval. One decent-looking old fellow, who had the air of a ship's captain, flushed all over his honest face, and stood up looking straight at Peter. I saw that we had struck an Englishman, and mentioned it to Peter in Dutch.

Peter played his part perfectly. He suddenly shut up, and, with furtive looks around him, began to jabber to me in a low voice. He was the very picture of the stage conspirator.

The old fellow stood staring at us. "I don't very well understand this damned lingo," he said; "but if so be you dirty Dutchmen are sayin' anything against England, I'll ask you to repeat it. And if so be as you repeats it I'll take either of you on and knock the face off him."

He was a chap after my own heart, but I had to keep the game up. I said in Dutch to Peter that we mustn't get brawling in a public-house. "Remember the big thing," I said darkly. Peter nodded, and the old fellow, after staring at us for a bit, spat scornfully, and walked out.

"The time is coming when the Englander will sing small," I observed to the crowd. We stood drinks to one or two, and then swaggered into the street. At the door a hand touched my arm, and, looking down, I saw a little scrap of a man in a fur coat.

"Will the gentlemen walk a step with me and drink a glass of beer?" he said in very stiff Dutch.

"Who the devil are you?" I asked.

"*Gott strafe England!*" was his answer, and, turning back the lapel of his coat, he showed some kind of ribbon in his buttonhole.

"Amen," said Peter. "Lead on, friend. We don't mind if we do."

He led us to a back street and then up two pairs of stairs to a very snug little flat. The place was filled with fine red lacquer, and I guessed that art-dealing was his nominal business. Portugal, since the republic broke up the convents and sold up the big royalist grandees, was full of bargains in the lacquer and curio line.

He filled us two long tankards of very good Munich beer.

"*Prosit,*" he said, raising his glass. "You are from South Africa. What make you in Europe?"

We both looked sullen and secretive.

"That's our own business," I answered. "You don't expect to buy our confidence with a glass of beer."

"So?" he said. "Then I will put it differently. From your speech in the café I judge you do not love the English."

Peter said something about stamping on their grandmothers, a Kaffir phrase which sounded gruesome in Dutch.

The man laughed. "That is all I want to know. You are on the German side?"

"That remains to be seen," I said. "If they treat me fair I'll fight for them, or for anybody else that makes war on England. England has stolen my country and corrupted my people and made me an exile. We Afrikanders do not forget. We may be slow but we win in the end. We two are men worth a great price. Germany fights England in East Africa. We know the natives as no Englishmen can ever know them. They are too soft and easy and the Kaffirs laugh at them. But we can handle the blacks so that they will fight like devils for fear of us. What is the reward, little man, for our services? I will tell you. There will be no reward. We ask none. We fight for hate of England."

Peter grunted a deep approval.

"That is good talk," said our entertainer, and his close-set eyes flashed. "There is room in Germany for such men as you. Where are you going now, I beg to know?"

"To Holland," I said. "Then maybe we will go to Germany. We are tired with travel and may rest a bit. This war will last long and our chance will come."

"But you may miss your market," he said significantly. "A ship sails to-morrow for Rotterdam. If you take my advice, you will go with her."

This was what I wanted, for if we stayed in Lisbon some real soldier of Maritz might drop in any day and blow the gaff.

"I recommend you to sail in the *Machado*," he repeated. "There is work for you in Germany—oh yes, much work; but if you delay the chance may pass. I will arrange your journey. It is my business to help the allies of my fatherland."

He wrote down our names and an epitome of our doings contributed by Peter, who required two mugs of beer to help him through. He was a Bavarian, it seemed, and we drank to the health of Prince Rupprecht, the same blighter I was trying to do in at Loos. That was an irony which Peter unfortunately could not appreciate. If he could he would have enjoyed it.

The little chap saw us back to our hotel, and was with us next morning after breakfast, bringing the steamer tickets. We got on board about two in the afternoon, but on my advice he did not see us off. I told him that, being British subjects and rebels at that, we did not want to run any risks on board, assuming a British cruiser caught us up and searched us. But Peter took twenty pounds off him for travelling expenses, it being his rule never to miss an opportunity of spoiling the Egyptians.

As we were dropping down the Tagus we passed the old *Henry the Navigator*.

"I met Sloggett in the street this morning," said Peter, "and he told me a little German man had been off in a boat at daybreak looking up the passenger list. Yon was a right notion of yours, Cornelis. I am glad we are going among Germans. They are careful people whom it is a pleasure to meet."

14 ADVENTURES OF TWO DUTCHMEN ON THE LOOSE

The Germans, as Peter said, are a careful people. A man met us on the quay at Rotterdam. I was a bit afraid that something might have turned up in Lisbon to discredit us, and that our little friend might have warned his pals by telegram. But apparently all was serene.

Peter and I had made our plans pretty carefully on the voyage. We had talked nothing but Dutch, and had kept up between ourselves the rôle of Maritz's men, which Peter said was the only way to play a part well. Upon my soul, before we got to Holland I was not very clear in my own mind what my past had been. Indeed the danger was that the other side of my mind, which should be busy with the great problem, would get atrophied, and that I should soon be mentally on a par with the ordinary back-veld desperado. We had agreed that it would be best to get into Germany at once, and when the agent on the quay told us of a train at midday we decided to take it.

I had another fit of cold feet before we got over the frontier. At the station there was a King's Messenger whom I had seen in France, and a war correspondent who had been trotting round our part of the front before Loos. I heard a woman speaking pretty clean-cut English, which amid the hoarse Dutch jabber sounded like a lark among crows. There were copies of the English papers for sale, and English cheap editions. I felt pretty bad about the whole business, and wondered if I should ever see these homely sights again.

But the mood passed when the train started. It was a clear blowing day, and as we crawled through the flat pastures of Holland my time was taken up answering Peter's questions. He had never been in Europe before, and formed a high opinion of the farming. He said he reckoned that such land would carry four sheep a morgen. We were thick in talk when we reached the frontier station and jolted over a canal bridge into Germany.

I had expected a big barricade with barbed wire and entrenchments. But there was nothing to see on the German side but half a dozen sentries in the field-grey I had hunted at Loos. An under-officer, with the black-and-gold button of the Landsturm, hoicked us out of the train, and we were all shepherded in a big bare waiting-room, where a large stove burned. They took us two at a time into an inner room for examination. I had explained to Peter all about this formality, but I was glad we went in together, for they made us strip to the skin, and I had to curse him pretty seriously to make him keep quiet. The men who did the job were fairly civil, but they were mighty thorough. They took down a list of all we had in our pockets and bags, and all the details from the passports the Rotterdam agent had given us.

We were dressing when a man in a lieutenant's uniform came in with a paper in his hand. He was a fresh-faced lad of about twenty, with short-sighted spectacled eyes.

"Herr Brandt," he called out.

I nodded.

"And this is Herr Pienaar?" he asked in Dutch.

He saluted. "Gentlemen, I apologize. I am late because of the slowness of the Herr Commandant's motor-car. Had I been in time you would not have been required to go through this ceremony. We have been advised of your coming, and I am instructed to attend you on your journey. The train for Berlin leaves in half an hour. Pray do me the honour to join me in a bock."

With a feeling of distinction we stalked out of the ordinary ruck of passengers and followed the lieutenant to the station restaurant. He plunged at once into conversation, talking the Dutch of Holland, which Peter, who had forgotten his schooldays, found a bit hard to follow. He was unfit for active service, because of his eyes and a weak heart, but he was a desperate fire-eater in that stuffy restaurant. By his way of it Germany could gobble up the French and the Russians whenever she cared, but she was aiming at getting all the Middle East in her hands first, so that she could come out conqueror with the practical control of half the world.

"Your friends the English," he said, grinning, "will come last. When we have starved them and destroyed their commerce with our under-sea boats we will show them what our navy can do. For a year they have been wasting their time in brag and politics, and we have been building great ships—oh, so many! My cousin at Kiel—" and he looked over his shoulder.

But we never heard about that cousin at Kiel. A short sunburnt man came in and our friend sprang up and saluted, clicking his heels like a pair of tongs.

"These are the South African Dutch, Herr Captain," he said.

The newcomer looked us over with bright intelligent eyes, and started questioning Peter in the *taal*. It was well that we had taken some pains with our story, for this man had been years in German South West, and knew every mile of the borders. Zorn was his name, and both Peter and I thought we remembered hearing him spoken of.

I am thankful to say that we both showed up pretty well. Peter told his story to perfection, not pitching it too high, and asking me now and then for a name or to verify some detail. Captain Zorn looked satisfied.

"You seem the right kind of fellows," he said. "But remember"—and he bent his brows on us—"we do not understand slimness in this land. If you are honest you will be rewarded, but if you dare to play a double game you will be shot like dogs. Your race has produced over many traitors for my taste."

"I ask no reward," I said gruffly. "We are not Germans or Germany's slaves. But so long as she fights against England we will fight for her."

"Bold words," he said; "but you must bow your stiff necks to discipline first. Discipline has been the weak point of you Boers, and you have suffered for it. You are no more a nation. In Germany we put discipline first and last, and therefore we will conquer the world. Off with you now. Your train starts in three minutes. We will see what von Stumm will make of you."

That fellow gave me the best "feel" of any German I had yet met. He was a white man and I could have worked with him. I liked his stiff chin and steady blue eyes.

My chief recollection of our journey to Berlin was its commonplaceness. The spectacled lieutenant fell asleep, and for the most part we had the carriage to ourselves. Now and again a soldier on leave would drop in, most of them tired men with heavy eyes. No wonder, poor devils, for they were coming back from the Yser or the Ypres salient. I would have liked to talk to them, but officially of course I knew no German, and the conversation I overheard did not signify much. It was mostly about regimental details, though one chap, who was in better spirits than the rest, observed that this was the last Christmas of misery, and that next year he would be holidaying at home with full pockets. The others assented, but without much conviction.

The winter day was short, and most of the journey was made in the dark.

I could see from the window the lights of little villages, and now and then the blaze of ironworks and forges. We stopped at a town for dinner, where the platform was crowded with drafts waiting to go westward. We saw no signs of any scarcity of food, such as the English newspapers wrote about. We had an excellent dinner at the station restaurant, which, with a bottle of white wine, cost just three shillings apiece. The bread, to be sure, was poor, but I can put up with the absence of bread if I get a juicy fillet of beef and as good vegetables as you will see in the Savoy.

I was a little afraid of our giving ourselves away in our sleep, but I need have had no fear, for our escort slumbered like a hog with his mouth wide open. As we roared through the darkness I kept pinching myself to make me feel that I was in the enemy's land on a wild mission. The rain came on, and we passed through dripping towns, with the lights shining from the wet streets. As we went eastward the lighting seemed to grow more generous. After the murk of London it was queer to slip through garish stations with a hundred arc lights glowing, and to see long lines of lamps running to the horizon. Peter dropped off early, but I kept awake till midnight, trying to focus thoughts that persistently strayed. Then I too dozed, and did not awake till about five in the morning, when we ran into a great busy terminus as bright as midday. It was the easiest and most unsuspicious journey I ever made.

The lieutenant stretched himself and smoothed his rumpled uniform. We carried our scanty luggage to a *droschke*, for there seemed to be no porters. Our escort gave the address of some hotel, and we rumbled out into brightly lit empty streets.

"A mighty dorp," said Peter. "Of a truth the Germans are a great people."

The lieutenant nodded good-humouredly.

"The greatest people on earth," he said, "as their enemies will soon bear witness."

I would have given a lot for a bath, but I felt that it would be outside my part, and Peter was not of the washing persuasion. But we had a very good breakfast of coffee and eggs, and then the lieutenant started on the telephone. He began by being dictatorial, then he seemed to be switched on to higher authorities, for he grew more polite, and at the end he fairly crawled. He made some arrangements, for he informed us that in the afternoon we would see some fellow whose title he could not translate into Dutch. I judged he was a great swell, for his voice became reverential at the mention of him.

He took us for a walk that morning after Peter and I had attended to our toilets. We were an odd pair of scallawags to look at, but as South African as a wait-a-bit bush. Both of us had ready-made tweed suits, grey flannel shirts with flannel collars, and felt hats with broader brims than they like in Europe. I had strong nailed brown boots, Peter a pair of those mustard-coloured abominations which the Portuguese affect and which made him hobble like a Chinese lady. He had a scarlet satin tie which you could hear a mile off. My beard had grown to quite a respectable length, and I trimmed it like General Smuts'. Peter's was the kind of loose flapping thing the *takhaar* loves, which has scarcely ever been shaved, and is combed once in a blue moon. I must say we made a pretty solid pair. Any South African would have set us down as a Boer from the back-veld who had bought a suit of clothes in the nearest store, and his cousin from some one-horse dorp who had been to school and thought himself the devil of a fellow. We fairly reeked of the subcontinent, as the papers call it.

It was a fine morning after the rain, and we wandered about in the streets for a couple of hours. They were busy enough, and the shops looked rich and bright with their Christmas goods, and one big store where I went to buy a pocket-knife was packed with customers. One didn't see very many young men, and most of the women wore mourning. Uniforms were everywhere, but their wearers generally looked like dug-outs or office fellows. We had a glimpse of the squat building which housed the General Staff and took off our hats to it. Then we stared at the Marineamt, and I wondered what plots were hatching there behind old Tirpitz's whiskers. The capital gave one an impression of ugly cleanness and a sort of dreary effectiveness. And yet I found it depressing—more depressing than London. I don't know how to put it, but the whole big concern seemed to have no soul in it, to be like a big factory instead of a city. You won't make a factory look like a house, though you decorate its front and plant rose bushes all round it. The place depressed and yet cheered me. It somehow made the German people seem smaller.

At three o'clock the lieutenant took us to a plain white building in a side street with sentries at the door. A young Staff officer met us and made us wait for five minutes in an anteroom. Then we were ushered into a big room with a polished floor on which Peter nearly sat down. There was a log fire burning, and seated at a table was a little man in spectacles with his hair brushed back from his brow like a popular violinist. He was the boss, for the lieutenant saluted him and announced our names. Then he disappeared, and the man at the table motioned us to sit down in two chairs before him.

"Herr Brandt and Herr Pienaar?" he asked, looking over his glasses.

But it was the other man that caught my eye. He stood with his back to the fire leaning his elbows on the mantelpiece. He was a perfect mountain of a fellow, six and a half feet if he was an inch, with shoulders on him like a shorthorn bull. He was in uniform, and the black-and-white ribbon of the Iron Cross showed at a buttonhole. His tunic was all wrinkled and strained as if it could scarcely contain his huge chest, and mighty hands were clasped over his stomach. That man must have had the length of reach of a gorilla. He had a great, lazy, smiling face, with a square cleft chin which stuck out beyond the rest. His brow retreated and the stubbly back of his head ran forward to meet it, while his neck below bulged out over his collar. His head was exactly the shape of a pear with the sharp end topmost.

He stared at me with his small bright eyes and I stared back. I had struck something I had been looking for for a long time, and till that moment I wasn't sure that it existed. Here was the German of caricature, the real German, the fellow we were up against. He was as hideous as a hippopotamus, but effective. Every bristle on his odd head was effective.

The man at the table was speaking. I took him to be a civilian official of sorts, pretty high up from his surroundings, perhaps an under-secretary. His Dutch was slow and careful, but good—too good for Peter. He had a paper before him and was asking us questions from it. They did not amount to much, being pretty well a repetition of those Zorn had asked us at the frontier. I answered fluently, for I had all our lies by heart.

Then the man on the hearthrug broke in. "I'll talk to them, Excellency," he said in German. "You are too academic for these outland swine."

He began in the *taal*, with the thick guttural accent that you get in German South West. "You have heard of me," he said. "I am the Colonel von Stumm who fought the Hereros."

Peter pricked up his ears. "*Ja*, Baas, you cut off the chief Baviaan's head and sent it in pickle about the country. I have seen it."

The big man laughed. "You see I am not forgotten," he said to his friend, and then to us: "So I treat my enemies, and so will Germany treat hers. You, too, if you fail me by a fraction of an inch." And he laughed loud again.

There was something horrible in that boisterousness. Peter was watching him from below his eyelids, as I have seen him watch a lion about to charge.

He flung himself on a chair, put his elbows on the table, and thrust his face forward.

"You have come from a damned muddled show. If I had Maritz in my power I would have him flogged at a wagon's end. Fools and pig-dogs, they had the game in their hands and they flung it away. We could have raised a fire that would have burned the English into the sea, and for lack of fuel they let it die down. Then they try to fan it when the ashes are cold."

He rolled a paper pellet and flicked it into the air. "That is what I think of your idiot general," he said, "and of all you Dutch. As slow as a fat *vrouw* and as greedy as an *aasvogel*."

We looked very glum and sullen.

"A pair of dumb dogs," he cried. "A thousand Brandenburgers would have won in a fortnight. Seitz hadn't much to boast of, mostly clerks and farmers and half-castes, and no soldier worth the name to lead them, but it took Botha and Smuts and a dozen generals to hunt him down. But Maritz!" His scorn came like a gust of wind.

"Maritz did all the fighting there was," said Peter sulkily. "At any rate he wasn't afraid of the sight of khaki like your lot."

"Maybe he wasn't," said the giant in a cooing voice; "maybe he had his reasons for that. You Dutchmen have always a feather-bed to fall on. You can always turn traitor. Maritz now calls himself Robinson, and has a pension from his friend Botha."

"That," said Peter, "is a very damned lie."

"I asked for information," said Stumm with a sudden politeness. "But that is all past and done with. Maritz matters no more than your old Cronjes and Krugers. The show is over, and you are looking for safety. For a new master perhaps? But, man, what can you bring? What can you offer? You and your Dutch are lying in the dust with the yoke on your necks. The Pretoria lawyers have talked you round. You see that map," and he pointed to a big one on the wall. "South Africa is coloured green. Not red for the English, or yellow for the Germans. Some day it will be yellow, but for a little it will be green—the colour of neutrals, of nothings, of boys and young ladies and chicken-hearts."

I kept wondering what he was playing at.

Then he fixed his eyes on Peter. "What do you come here for? The game's up in your own country. What can you offer us Germans? If we gave you ten million marks and sent you back you could do nothing. Stir up a village row, perhaps, and shoot a policeman. South Africa is counted out in this war. Botha is a cleverish man and has beaten you calves'-heads of rebels. Can you deny it?"

Peter couldn't. He was terribly honest in some things, and these were for certain his opinions.

"No," he said, "that is true, Baas."

"Then what in God's name can you do?" shouted Stumm.

Peter mumbled some foolishness about nobbling Angola for Germany and starting a revolution among the natives. Stumm flung up his arms and cursed, and the Under-Secretary laughed.

It was high time for me to chip in. I was beginning to see the kind of fellow this Stumm was, and as he talked I thought of my mission, which had got overlaid by my Boer past. It looked as if he might be useful.

"Let me speak," I said. "My friend is a great hunter, but he fights better than he talks. He is no politician. You speak truth. South Africa is a closed door for the present, and the key to it is elsewhere. Here in Europe, and in the East, and in other parts of Africa. We have come to help you to find the key."

Stumm was listening. "Go on, my little Boer. It will be a new thing to hear a *takhaar* on world-politics."

"You are fighting," I said, "in East Africa; and soon you may fight in Egypt. All the east coast north of the Zambesi will be your battle-ground. The English run about the world with little expeditions. I do not know where the places are, though I read of them in the papers. But I know my Africa. You want to beat them here in Europe and on the seas. Therefore, like wise generals, you try to divide them and have them scattered throughout the globe while you stick at home. That is your plan?"

"A second Falkenhayn," said Stumm, laughing.

"Well, England will not let East Africa go. She fears for Egypt and she fears too for India. If you press her there she will send armies and more armies till she is so weak in Europe that a child can crush her. That is England's way. She cares more for her Empire than for what may happen to her allies. So I say press and still press there, destroy the railway to the Lakes, burn her capital, pen up every Englishman in Mombasa island. At this moment it is worth for you a thousand Damaralands."

The man was really interested and the Under-Secretary too pricked up his ears.

"We can keep our territory," said the former; "but as for pressing, how the devil are we to press? The accursed English hold the sea. We cannot ship men or guns there. South are the Portuguese and west the Belgians. You cannot move a mass without a lever."

"The lever is there, ready for you," I said.

"Then for God's sake show it me," he cried.

I looked at the door to see that it was shut, as if what I had to say was very secret.

"You need men, and the men are awaiting. They are black, but they are the stuff of warriors. All round your borders you have the remains of great fighting tribes, the Angoni, the Masai, the Manyumwezi, and above all the Somalis of the north, and the dwellers on the Upper Nile. The British recruit their black regiments there, and so do you. But to get recruits is not enough. You must set whole nations moving, as the Zulu under Tchaka flowed over South Africa."

"It cannot be done," said the Under-Secretary.

"It can be done," I said quietly. "We two are here to do it."

This kind of talk was jolly difficult for me, chiefly because of Stumm's asides in German to the official. I had above all things to get the credit of knowing no German, and, if you understand a language well, it is not very easy when you are interrupted not to show that you know it, either by a direct answer, or by referring to the interruption in what you say next. I had to be always on my guard, and yet it was up to me to be very persuasive and convince these fellows that I would be useful. Somehow or other I had to get into their confidence.

"I have been for years up and down in Africa—Uganda and the Congo and the Upper Nile. I know the ways of the Kaffir as no Englishman does. We Afrikanders see into the black man's heart, and though he may hate us he does our will. You Germans are like the English; you are too big folk to understand plain men. 'Civilize,' you cry. 'Educate,' say the English. The black man obeys and puts away his gods, but he worships them all the time in his soul. We must get his gods on our side, and then he will move mountains.—We must do as John Laputa did with Sheba's necklace."

"That's all in the air," said Stumm, but he did not laugh.

"It is sober common sense," I said. "But you must begin at the right end. First find the race that fears its priests. It is waiting for you—the Mussulmans of Somaliland and the Abyssinian border and the Blue and White Nile. They would be like dried grasses to catch fire if you used the flint and steel of their religion. Look what the English suffered from a crazy Mullah who ruled only a dozen villages. Once get the flames going and they will lick up the pagans of the west and south. That is the way of Africa. How many thousands, think you, were in the Mahdi's army who never heard of the Prophet till they saw the black flags of the Emirs going into battle?"

Stumm was smiling. He turned his face to the official and spoke with his hand over his mouth, but I caught his words. They were: "This is the man for Hilda." The other pursed his lips and looked a little scared.

Stumm rang a bell and the lieutenant came in and clicked his heels. He nodded towards Peter. "Take that man away with you. We have done with him. The other fellow will follow presently."

Peter went out with a puzzled face and Stumm turned to me.

"You are a dreamer, Brandt," he said. "But I do not reject you on that account. Dreams sometimes come true, when an army follows the visionary. But who is going to kindle the flame?"

"You," I said.

"What the devil do you mean?" he asked.

"That is your part. You are the cleverest people in the world. You have already half the Mussulman lands in your power. It is for you to show us how to kindle a holy war, for clearly you have the secret of it. Never fear but we will carry out your order."

"We have no secret," he said shortly, and glanced at the official, who stared out of the window.

I dropped my jaw and looked the picture of disappointment. "I do not believe you," I said slowly. "You play a game with me. I have not come six thousand miles to be made a fool of."

"Discipline, by God," Stumm cried. "This is none of your ragged commandos." In two strides he was above me and had lifted me out of my seat. His great hands clutched my shoulders, and his thumbs gouged my armpits. I felt as if I were in the grip of a big ape. Then very slowly he shook me so that my teeth seemed loosened and my head swam. He let me go and I dropped limply back in the chair.

"Now, go! *Futsack!* And remember that I am your master. I, Ulric von Stumm, who owns you as a Kaffir owns his mongrel. Germany may have some use for you, my friend, when you fear me as you never feared your God."

As I walked dizzily away the big man was smiling in his horrible way, and that little official was blinking and smiling too. I had struck a dashed queer country, so queer that I had had no time to remember that for the first time in my life I had been bullied without hitting back. When I realized it I nearly choked with anger. But I thanked Heaven I had shown no temper, for I remembered my mission. Luck seemed to have brought me into useful company.

15   FURTHER ADVENTURES OF THE SAME

Next morning there was a touch of frost and a nip in the air which stirred my blood and put me in buoyant spirits. I forgot my precarious position and the long road I had still to travel. I came down to breakfast in great form, to find

Peter's even temper badly ruffled. He had remembered Stumm in the night and disliked the memory; this he muttered to me as we rubbed shoulders at the dining-room door. Peter and I got no opportunity for private talk. The lieutenant was with us all the time, and at night we were locked in our rooms. Peter discovered this through trying to get out to find matches, for he had the bad habit of smoking in bed.

Our guide started on the telephone, and announced that we were to be taken to see a prisoners' camp. In the afternoon I was to go somewhere with Stumm, but the morning was for sightseeing. "You will see," he told us, "how merciful is a great people. You will also see some of the hated English in our power. That will delight you. They are the forerunners of all their nation."

We drove in a taxi through the suburbs and then over a stretch of flat market-garden-like country to a low rise of wooded hills. After an hour's ride we entered the gate of what looked like a big reformatory or hospital. I believe it had been a home for destitute children. There were sentries at the gate and massive concentric circles of barbed wire through which we passed under an arch that was let down like a portcullis at nightfall. The lieutenant showed his permit, and we ran the car into a brick-paved yard and marched through a lot more sentries to the office of the commandant.

He was away from home, and we were welcomed by his deputy, a pale young man with a head nearly bald. There were introductions in German which our guide translated into Dutch, and a lot of elegant speeches about how Germany was foremost in humanity as well as martial valour. Then they stood us sandwiches and beer, and we formed a procession for a tour of inspection. There were two doctors, both mild-looking men in spectacles, and a couple of warders—under-officers of the good old burly, bullying sort I knew well. That was the cement which kept the German Army together. Her men were nothing to boast of on the average; no more were the officers, even in crack corps like the Guards and the Brandenburgers; but she seemed to have an inexhaustible supply of hard, competent N.C.O.'s.

We marched round the wash-houses, the recreation-ground, the kitchens, the hospital—with nobody in it save one chap with the "flu." It didn't seem to be badly done. This place was entirely for officers, and I expect it was a show place where American visitors were taken. If half the stories one heard were true there were some pretty ghastly prisons away in South and East Germany.

I didn't half like the business. To be a prisoner has always seemed to me about the worst thing that could happen to a man. The sight of German prisoners used to give me a bad feeling inside, whereas I looked at dead Boches with nothing but satisfaction. Besides, there was the off-chance that I might be recognized. So I kept very much in the shadow whenever we saw anybody in the corridors.

The few we met passed us incuriously. They saluted the deputy-commandant, but scarcely wasted a glance on us. No doubt they thought we were inquisitive Germans come to gloat over them. They looked fairly fit, but a little puffy about the eyes, like men who get too little exercise. They seemed thin, too. I expect the food, for all the commandant's talk, was nothing to boast of. In one room people were writing letters. It was a big place with only a tiny stove to warm it, and the windows were shut, so that the atmosphere was a cold frowst. In another room a fellow was lecturing on something to a dozen hearers and drawing figures on a blackboard. Some were in ordinary khaki, others in any old thing they could pick up, and most wore greatcoats. Your blood gets thin when you have nothing to do but hope against hope and think of your pals and the old days.

I was moving along, listening with half an ear to the lieutenant's prattle and the loud explanations of the deputy-commandant, when I pitchforked into what might have been the end of my business. We were going through a sort of convalescent room, where people were sitting who had been in hospital. It was a big place, a little warmer than the rest of the building, but still abominably fuggy. There were about half a dozen men in the room, reading and playing games. They looked at us with lacklustre eyes for a moment, and then returned to their occupations. Being convalescents I suppose they were not expected to get up and salute.

All but one, who was playing Patience at a little table by which we passed. I was feeling very bad about the thing, for I hated to see these good fellows locked away in this infernal German hole when they might have been giving the Boche his deserts at the Front. The commandant went first with Peter, who had developed a great interest in prisons. Then came our lieutenant with one of the doctors; then a couple of warders; and then the second doctor and myself. I was absent-minded at the moment and was last in the queue.

The Patience player suddenly looked up and I saw his face. I'm hanged if it wasn't Dolly Riddell, who was our brigade machine-gun officer at Loos. I had heard that the Germans had got him when they blew up a mine at the Quarries.

I had to act pretty quick, for his mouth was agape, and I saw he was going to speak. The doctor was a yard ahead of me.

I stumbled and spilt his cards on the floor. Then I kneeled to pick them up and gripped his knee. His head bent to help me and I spoke low in his ear. "I'm Hannay all right. For God's sake don't wink an eye. I'm here on a secret job."

The doctor had turned to see what was the matter. I got a few more words in. "Cheer up, old man. We're winning hands down."

Then I began to talk excited Dutch and finished the collection of the cards. Dolly was playing his part well, smiling as if he were amused by the antics of a monkey. The others were coming back, the deputy-commandant with an angry light in his dull eye. "Speaking to the prisoners is forbidden," he shouted.

I looked blankly at him till the lieutenant translated.

"What kind of fellow is he?" said Dolly in English to the doctor. "He spoils my game and then jabbers High-Dutch at me."

Officially I knew English, and that speech of Dolly's gave me my cue. I pretended to be very angry with the very damned Englishman, and went out of the room close by the deputy-commandant, grumbling like a sick jackal. After that I had to act a bit. The last place we visited was the close-confinement part where prisoners were kept as a punishment for some breach of the rules. They looked cheerless enough, but I pretended to gloat over the sight, and said so to the lieutenant, who passed it on to the others. I have rarely in my life felt such a cad.

On the way home the lieutenant discoursed a lot about prisoners and detention camps, for at one time he had been on duty at Ruhleben. Peter, who had been in quod more than once in his life, was deeply interested and kept on questioning him. Among other things he told us was that they often put bogus prisoners among the rest, who acted as spies. If any plot to escape was hatched these fellows got into it and encouraged it. They never interfered till the attempt was actually made and then they had them on toast. There was nothing the Boche liked so much as an excuse for sending a poor devil to "solitary."

That afternoon Peter and I separated. He was left behind with the lieutenant and I was sent off to the station with my bag in the company of a Landsturm sergeant. Peter was very cross, and I didn't care for the look of things; but I brightened up when I heard I was going somewhere with Stumm. If he wanted to see me again he must think me of some use, and if he was going to use me he was bound to let me into his game. I liked Stumm about as much as a dog likes a scorpion, but I hankered for his society.

At the station platform, where an ornament of the Landsturm saved me all trouble about tickets, I could not see my companion. I stood waiting, while a great crowd, mostly of soldiers, swayed past me and filled all the front carriages. An officer spoke to me gruffly and told me to stand aside behind a wooden rail. I obeyed, and suddenly found Stumm's eyes looking down at me.

"You know German?" he asked sharply.

"A dozen words," I said carelessly. "I've been to Windhuk and learned enough to ask for my dinner. Peter—my friend—speaks it a bit."

"So," said Stumm. "Well, get into the carriage. Not that one! There, thickhead!"

I did as I was bid, he followed, and the door was locked behind us. The precaution was needless, for the sight of Stumm's profile at the platform end would have kept out the most brazen. I wondered if I had woke up his suspicions. I must be on my guard to show no signs of intelligence if he suddenly tried me in German, and that wouldn't be easy, for I knew it as well as I knew Dutch.

We moved into the country, but the windows were blurred with frost, and I saw nothing of the landscape. Stumm was busy with papers and let me alone. I read on a notice that one was forbidden to smoke, so to show my ignorance of German I pulled out my pipe. Stumm raised his head, saw what I was doing, and gruffly bade me put it away, as if he were an old lady that disliked the smell of tobacco.

In half an hour I got very bored, for I had nothing to read and my pipe was *verboten*. People passed now and then in the corridors, but no one offered to enter. No doubt they saw the big figure in uniform and thought he was the deuce of a Staff swell who wanted solitude. I thought of stretching my legs in the corridor, and was just getting up to do it when somebody slid the door back and a big figure blocked the light.

He was wearing a heavy ulster and a green felt hat. He saluted Stumm, who looked up angrily, and smiled pleasantly on us both.

"Say, gentlemen," he said, "have you room in here for a little one? I guess I'm about smoked out of my car by your brave soldiers. I've got a delicate stomach. . . ."

Stumm had risen with a brow of wrath, and looked as if he were going to pitch the intruder off the train. Then he seemed to halt and collect himself, and the other's face broke into a friendly grin.

"Why, it's Colonel Stumm," he cried. (He pronounced it like the first syllable in "stomach.") "Very pleased to meet you again, Colonel. I had the honour of making your acquaintance at our Embassy. I reckon Ambassador Gerard didn't cotton to our conversation that night." And the newcomer plumped himself down in the corner opposite me.

I had been pretty certain I would run across Blenkiron somewhere in Germany, but I didn't think it would be so soon. There he sat staring at me with his full unseeing eyes, rolling out platitudes to Stumm, who was nearly bursting in his effort to keep civil. I looked moody and suspicious, which I took to be the right line.

"Things are getting a bit dead at Salonika," said Mr. Blenkiron by way of a conversational opening.

Stumm pointed to a notice which warned officers to refrain from discussing military operations with mixed company in a railway carriage.

"Sorry," said Blenkiron, "I can't read that tombstone language of yours. But I reckon that that notice to trespassers, whatever it signifies, don't apply to you and me. I take it this gentleman is in your party."

I sat and scowled, fixing the American with suspicious eyes.

"He is a Dutchman," said Stumm; "South African Dutch, and he is not happy, for he doesn't like to hear English spoken."

"We'll shake on that," said Blenkiron cordially. "But who said I spoke English? It's good American. Cheer up, friend, for it isn't the call that makes the big wapiti, as they say out west in my country. I hate John Bull worse than a poison rattle. The Colonel can tell you that."

I dare say he could, but at that moment we slowed down at a station and Stumm got up to leave. "Good day to you, Herr Blenkiron," he cried over his shoulder. "If you consider your comfort, don't talk English to strange travellers. They don't distinguish between the different brands."

I followed him in a hurry, but was recalled by Blenkiron's voice.

"Stay, friend," he shouted, "you've left your grip," and he handed me my bag from the luggage rack. But he showed no sign of recognition, and the last I saw of him was sitting sunk in a corner with his head on his chest as if he were going to sleep. He was a man who kept up his parts well.

There was a motor-car waiting—one of the grey military kind—and we started at a terrific pace over bad forest roads. Stumm had put away his papers in a portfolio, and flung me a few sentences on the journey.

"I haven't made up my mind about you, Brandt," he announced. "You may be a fool or a knave or a good man. If you are a knave, we will shoot you."

"And if I am a fool?" I asked.

"Send you to the Yser or the Dvina. You will be respectable cannon-fodder."

"You cannot do that unless I consent," I said.

"Can't we?" he said, smiling wickedly. "Remember you are a citizen of nowhere. Technically you are a rebel, and the British, if you go to them, will hang you, supposing they have any sense. You are in our power, my friend, to do precisely what we like with you."

He was silent for a second, and then he said meditatively:

"But I don't think you are a fool. You may be a scoundrel. Some kinds of scoundrels are useful enough. Other kinds are strung up with a rope. Of that we shall know more soon."

"And if I am a good man?"

"You will be given a chance to serve Germany, the proudest privilege a mortal can have." The strange man said this with a ringing sincerity in his voice that impressed me.

The car swung out from the trees into a park lined with saplings, and in the twilight I saw before me a biggish house like an overgrown Swiss chalet. There was a kind of archway with a sham portcullis, and a terrace with battlements which looked as if they were made of stucco. We drew up at a Gothic front door where a thin middle-aged man in a shooting jacket was waiting.

As we moved into the lighted hall I got a good look at our host. He was very lean and brown, with the stoop in the shoulder that one gets from being constantly on horseback. He had untidy grizzled hair and a ragged beard, and a pair of pleasant, short-sighted brown eyes.

"Welcome, Herr Colonel," he said. "Is this the friend you spoke of?"

"This is the Dutchman," said Stumm. "His name is Brandt. Brandt, you see before you Herr Gaudian."

I knew the name of course; there weren't many in my profession that didn't. He was one of the biggest railway engineers in the world, the man who had built the Bagdad and Syrian railways, and the new lines in German East. I suppose he was about the greatest living authority on tropical construction. He knew the East and he knew Africa; clearly I had been brought down for him to put me through my paces.

A blonde maid-servant took me to my room, which had a bare polished floor, a stove, and windows that, unlike most of the German kind I had sampled, seemed made to open. When I had washed I descended to the hall which was hung round with trophies of travel, like Dervish jibbahs and Masai shields and one or two good buffalo heads. Presently a bell was rung. Stumm appeared with his host, and we went in to supper.

I was jolly hungry and would have made a good meal if I hadn't constantly had to keep jogging my wits. The other two talked in German, and when a question was put to me Stumm translated. The first thing I had to do was to pretend I didn't know German and looked listlessly round the room while they were talking. The second was to miss not a word, for there lay my chance. The third was to be ready to answer questions at any moment, and to show in the answering that I had not followed the previous conversation. Likewise I must not prove myself a fool in these answers, for I had to convince them that I was useful. It took some doing, and I felt like a witness in the box under a stiff cross-examination, or a man trying to play three games of chess at once.

I heard Stumm telling Gaudian the gist of my plan. The engineer shook his head.

"Too late," he said. "It should have been done at the beginning. We neglected Africa. You know the reason why."

Stumm laughed. "The von Einem! Perhaps, but her charm works well enough."

Gaudian glanced towards me while I was busy with an orange salad. "I have much to tell you of that. But it can wait. Your friend is right in one thing. Uganda is a vital spot for the English, and a blow there will make their whole fabric shiver. But how can we strike? They have still the coast, and our supplies grow daily smaller."

"We can send no reinforcements, but have we used all the local resources? That is what I cannot satisfy myself about. Zimmerman says we have, but Tressler thinks differently, and now we have this fellow coming out of the void with a story which confirms my doubt. He seems to know his job. You try him."

Thereupon Gaudian set about questioning me and his questions were very thorough. I knew just enough and no more to get through, but I think I came out with credit. You see I have a capacious memory, and in my time I had met scores of hunters and pioneers and listened to their yarns, so I could pretend to knowledge of a place even when I hadn't been there. Besides, I had once been on the point of undertaking a job up Tanganyika way, and I had got up that country-side pretty accurately.

"You say that with our help you can make trouble for the British on the three borders?" Gaudian asked at length.

"I can spread the fire if some one else will kindle it," I said.

"But there are thousands of tribes with no affinities."

"They are all African. You can bear me out. All African peoples are alike in one thing—they can go mad, and the madness of one infects the others. The English know this well enough."

"Where would you start the fire?" he asked.

"Where the fuel is driest. Up in the North among the Mussulman peoples. But there you must help me. I know nothing about Islam, and I gather that you do."

"Why?" he asked.

"Because of what you have done already," I answered.

Stumm had translated all this time, and had given the sense of my words very fairly. But with my last answer he took liberties. What he gave was:

"Because the Dutchman thinks that we have some big card in dealing with the Moslem world." Then, lowering his voice and raising his eyebrows, he said some word like "Ühnmantl."

The other looked with a quick glance of apprehension at me. "We had better continue our talk in private, Herr Colonel," he said. "If Herr Brandt will forgive us, we will leave him for a little to entertain himself." He pushed the cigar-box towards me, and the two got up and left the room.

I pulled my chair up to the stove, and would have liked to drop off to sleep. The tension of the talk at supper had made me very tired. I was accepted by these men for exactly what I professed to be. Stumm might suspect me of being a rascal, but it was a Dutch rascal. But all the same I was skating on thin ice. I could not sink myself utterly in the part, for if I did I would get no good out of being there. I had to keep my wits going all the time, and join the appearance and manners of a back-veld Boer with the mentality of a British intelligence officer. Any moment the two parts might clash and I would be faced with the most alert and deadly suspicion.

There would be no mercy from Stumm. That large man was beginning to fascinate me, even though I hated him. Gaudian was clearly a good fellow, a white man and a gentleman. I could have worked with him, for he belonged to my own totem. But the other was an incarnation of all that makes Germany detested, and yet he wasn't altogether the ordinary German, and I couldn't help admiring him. I noticed he neither smoked nor drank. His grossness was apparently not in the way of fleshly appetites. Cruelty, from all I had heard of him in German South West, was his hobby; but there were other things in him, some of them good, and he had that kind of crazy patriotism which becomes a religion. I wondered why he had not some high command in the field, for he had had the name of a good soldier. But probably he was a big man in his own line, whatever it was, for the Under-Secretary fellow had talked small in his presence, and so great a man as Gaudian clearly respected him. There must be no lack of brains inside that funny pyramidal head.

As I sat beside the stove I was casting back to think if I had got the slightest clue to my real job. There seemed to be nothing so far. Stumm had talked of a von Einem woman who was interested in his department, perhaps the same woman as the Hilda he had mentioned the day before to the Under-Secretary. There was not much in that. She was probably some minister's or ambassador's wife who had a finger in high politics. If I could have caught the word Stumm had whispered to Gaudian which made him start and look askance at me! But I had only heard a gurgle of something like "Ühnmantl," which wasn't any German word that I knew.

The heat put me into a half-doze and I began dreamily to wonder what other people were doing. Where had Blenkiron been posting to in that train, and what was he up to at this moment? He had been hobnobbing with ambassadors and swells—I wondered if he had found out anything. What was Peter doing? I fervently hoped he was behaving himself, for I doubted if Peter had really tumbled to the delicacy of our job. Where was Sandy, too? As like as not bucketing in the hold of some Greek coaster in the Ægean.

Then I thought of my battalion somewhere on the line between Hulluch and La Bassée, hammering at the Boche, while I was five hundred miles or so inside the Boche frontier.

It was a comic reflection, so comic that it woke me up. After trying in vain to find a way of stoking that stove, for it was a cold night, I got up and walked about the room. There were portraits of two decent old fellows, probably Gaudian's parents. There were enlarged photographs, too, of engineering works, and a good picture of Bismarck. And close to the stove there was a case of maps mounted on rollers.

I pulled out one at random. It was a geological map of Germany, and with some trouble I found out where I was. I was an enormous distance from my goal, and moreover I was clean off the road to the East. To go there I must first go to Bavaria and then into Austria. I noticed the Danube flowing eastwards and remembered that that was one way to Constantinople.

Then I tried another map. This one covered a big area, all Europe from the Rhine and as far east as Persia. I guessed that it was meant to show the Bagdad railway and the through routes from Germany to Mesopotamia. There were markings on it; and, as I looked closer, I saw that there were dates scribbled in blue pencil, as if to denote the stages of a journey. The dates began in Europe, and continued right on into Asia Minor and then south to Syria.

For a moment my heart jumped, for I thought I had fallen by accident on the clue I wanted. But I never got that map examined. I heard footsteps in the corridor, and very gently I let the map roll up and turned away. When the door opened I was bending over the stove trying to get a light for my pipe.

It was Gaudian, to bid me join him and Stumm in his study.

On our way there he put a kindly hand on my shoulder. I think he thought I was bullied by Stumm and wanted to tell me that he was my friend, and he had no other language than a pat on the back.

The soldier was in his old position with his elbows on the mantelpiece and his formidable great jaw stuck out.

"Listen to me," he said. "Herr Gaudian and I are inclined to make use of you. You may be a charlatan, in which case you will be in the devil of a mess and have yourself to thank for it. If you are a rogue you will have little scope for roguery. We will see to that. If you are a fool, you will yourself suffer for it. But if you are a good man, you will have a fair chance, and if you succeed we will not forget it. To-morrow I go home and you will come with me and get your orders."

I made shift to stand at attention and salute.

Gaudian spoke in a pleasant voice, as if he wanted to atone for Stumm's imperiousness. "We are men who love our Fatherland, Herr Brandt," he said. "You are not of that Fatherland, but at least you hate its enemies. Therefore we are allies, and trust each other like allies. Our victory is ordained by God, and we are none of us more than His instruments."

Stumm translated in a sentence, and his voice was quite solemn. He held up his right hand and so did Gaudian, like a man taking an oath or a parson blessing his congregation.

Then I realized something of the might of Germany. She produced good and bad, cads and gentlemen, but she could put a bit of the fanatic into them all.

16 THE INDISCRETIONS OF THE SAME

I was standing stark naked next morning in that icy bedroom, trying to bathe in about a quart of water, when Stumm entered. He strode up to me and stared me in the face. I was half a head shorter than him to begin with, and a man does not feel his stoutest when he has no clothes, so he had the pull on me every way.

"I have reason to believe that you are a liar," he growled.

I pulled the bed-cover round me, for I was shivering with cold, and the German idea of a towel is a pocket-handkerchief. I own I was in a pretty blue funk.

"A liar!" he repeated. "You and that swine Pienaar."

With my best effort at surliness I asked what we had done.

"You lied, because you said you knew no German. Apparently your friend knows enough to talk treason and blasphemy."

This gave me back some heart.

"I told you I knew a dozen words. But I told you Peter could talk a bit. I told you that yesterday at the station." Fervently I blessed my luck for that casual remark.

He evidently remembered, for his tone became a trifle more civil.

"You are a precious pair. If one of you is a scoundrel, why not the other?"

"I take no responsibility for Peter," I said. I felt I was a cad in saying it, but that was the bargain we had made at the start. "I have known him for years as a great hunter and a brave man. I know he fought well against the English. But more I cannot tell you. You have to judge him for yourself. What has he done?"

I was told, for Stumm had got it that morning on the telephone. While telling it he was kind enough to allow me to put on my trousers.

It was just the sort of thing I might have foreseen. Peter, left alone, had become first bored and then reckless. He had persuaded the lieutenant to take him out to supper at a big Berlin restaurant. There, inspired by the lights and music—novel things for a back-veld hunter—and no doubt bored stiff by his company, he had proceeded to get drunk. That had happened in my experience with Peter about once in every three years, and it always happened for the same reason. Peter, bored and solitary in a town, went on the spree. He had a head like a rock but he got to the required condition by wild mixing. He was quite a gentleman in his cups and not in the least violent, but he was apt to be very free with his tongue. And that was what occurred at the Franciscana.

He had begun by insulting the Emperor, it seemed. He drank his health, but said he reminded him of a wart-hog, and thereby scarified the lieutenant's soul. Then an officer—some tremendous swell—at an adjoining table had objected to his talking so loud, and Peter had replied insolently in respectable German. After that things became mixed. There was some kind of a fight, during which Peter calumniated the German army and all its female ancestry. How he wasn't shot or run through I can't imagine, except that the lieutenant loudly proclaimed that he was a crazy Boer. Anyhow the upshot was that Peter was marched off to gaol, and I was left in a pretty pickle.

"I don't believe a word of it," I said firmly. I had most of my clothes on now and felt more courageous. "It is all a plot to get him into disgrace and draft him off to the Front."

Stumm did not storm as I expected, but smiled.

"That was always his destiny," he said, "ever since I saw him. He was no use to us except as a man with a rifle. Cannon-fodder, nothing else. Do you imagine, you fool, that this great Empire in the thick of a world-war is going to trouble its head to lay snares for an ignorant *takhaar?*"

"I wash my hands of him," I said. "If what you say of his folly is true I have no part in it. But he was my companion and I wish him well. What do you propose to do with him?"

"We will keep him under our eye," he said, with a wicked twist of the mouth. "I have a notion that there is more at the back of this than appears. We will investigate the antecedents of Herr Pienaar. And you, too, my friend. On you also we have our eye."

I did the best thing I could have done, for what with anxiety and disgust I lost my temper.

"Look here, sir," I cried, "I've had about enough of this. I came to Germany abominating the English and burning to strike a blow for you. But you haven't given me much cause to love you. For the last two days I've had nothing from you but suspicion and insult. The only decent man I've met is Herr Gaudian. It's because I believe that there are many in Germany like him that I'm prepared to go on with this business and do the best I can. But, by God, I wouldn't raise my little finger for *your* sake."

He looked at me very steadily for a minute. "That sounds like honesty," he said at last in a civil voice. "You had better come down and get your coffee."

I was safe for the moment but in very low spirits. What on earth would happen to poor old Peter? I could do nothing even if I wanted, and, besides, my first duty was to my mission. I had made this very clear to him at Lisbon and he had agreed, but all the same it was a beastly reflection. Here was that ancient worthy left to the tender mercies of the people he most detested on earth. My only comfort was that they couldn't do very much with him. If they sent him to the Front, which was the worst they could do, he would escape, for I would have backed him to get through any mortal lines. It wasn't much fun for me either. Only when I was to be deprived of it did I realize how much his company had meant to me. I was absolutely alone now, and I didn't like it. I seemed to have about as much chance of joining Blenkiron and Sandy as of flying to the moon.

After breakfast I was told to get ready. When I asked where I was going Stumm advised me to mind my own business, but I remembered that last night he had talked of taking me home with him and giving me my orders. I wondered where his home was.

Gaudian patted me on the back when we started and wrung my hand. He was a capital good fellow, and it made me feel sick that I was humbugging him. We got into the same big grey car, with Stumm's servant sitting beside the chauffeur. It was a morning of hard frost, the bare fields were white with rime, and the fir-trees powdered like a wedding-cake. We took a different road from the night before, and after a run of half a dozen miles came to a little town with a big railway station. It was a junction on some main line, and after five minutes' waiting we found our train.

Once again we were alone in the carriage. Stumm must have had some colossal graft, for the train was crowded.

I had another three hours of complete boredom. I dared not smoke, and could do nothing but stare out of the window. We soon got into a hilly country, where a good deal of snow was lying. It was the 23rd day of December, and even in war time one had a sort of feel of Christmas. You could see girls carrying evergreens, and when we stopped at a station the soldiers on leave had all the air of holiday making. The middle of Germany was a cheerier place than Berlin or the western parts. I liked the look of the old peasants, and the women in their neat Sunday best, but I noticed, too, how pinched they were. Here in the country, where no neutral tourists came, there was not the same stage-management as in the capital.

Stumm made an attempt to talk to me on the journey. I could see his aim. Before this he had cross-examined me, but now he wanted to draw me into ordinary conversation. He had no notion how to do it. He was either peremptory and provocative, like a drill sergeant, or so obviously diplomatic that any fool would have been put on his guard. That is the weakness of the German. He has no gift for laying himself alongside different types of men. He is such a hard-shell being that he cannot put out feelers to his kind. He may have plenty of brains, as Stumm had, but he has the poorest notion of psychology of any of God's creatures. In Germany only the Jew can get outside himself, and that is why, if you look into the matter, you will find that a Jew is at the back of most German enterprises.

After midday we stopped at a station for luncheon. We had a very good meal in the restaurant, and when we were finishing two officers entered. Stumm got up and saluted and went aside to talk to them. Then he came back and made me follow him to a waiting-room, where he told me to stay till he fetched me. I noticed that he called a porter and had the door locked when he went out.

It was a chilly place with no fire, and I kicked my heels there for twenty minutes. I was living by the hour now, and did not trouble to worry about this strange behaviour. There was a volume of time-tables on a shelf, and I turned the pages idly till I struck a big railway map. Then it occurred to me to find out where we were going. I had heard Stumm take my ticket for a place called Schwandorf, and after a lot of searching I found it. It was away south in Bavaria, and so far as I could make out less than fifty miles from the Danube. That cheered me enormously. If Stumm lived there he would most likely start me off on my travels by the railway which I saw running to Vienna and then on to the East. It looked as if I might get to Constantinople after all. But I feared it would be a useless achievement, for what could I do when I got there? I was being hustled out of Germany without picking up the slenderest clue.

The door opened and Stumm entered. He seemed to have got bigger in the interval and to carry his head higher. There was a proud light, too, in his eye.

"Brandt," he said, "you are about to receive the greatest privilege that ever fell to one of your race. His Imperial Majesty is passing through here, and has halted for a few minutes. He has done me the honour to receive me, and when he heard my story he expressed a wish to see you. You will follow me to his presence. Do not be afraid. The All-Highest is merciful and gracious. Answer his questions like a man."

I followed him with a quickened pulse. Here was a bit of luck I had never dreamed of. At the far side of the station a train had drawn up, a train consisting of three big coaches, chocolate-coloured and picked out with gold. On the platform beside it stood a small group of officers, tall men in long grey-blue cloaks. They seemed to be mostly elderly, and one or two of the faces I thought I remembered from photographs in the picture papers.

As we approached they drew apart, and left us face to face with one man. He was a little below middle height, and all muffled in a thick coat with a fur collar. He wore a silver helmet with an eagle atop of it, and kept his left hand resting on his sword. Below the helmet was a face the colour of grey paper, from which shone curious sombre restless eyes with dark pouches beneath them. There was no fear of my mistaking him. These were the features which, since Napoleon, have been best known to the world.

I stood as stiff as a ramrod and saluted. I was perfectly cool and most desperately interested. For such a moment I would have gone through fire and water.

"Majesty, this is the Dutchman I spoke of," I heard Stumm say.

"What language does he speak?" the Emperor asked.

"Dutch," was the reply; "but being a South African he also talks English."

A spasm of pain seemed to flit over the face before me. Then he addressed me in English.

"You have come from a land which will yet be our ally to offer your sword to our service? I accept the gift and hail it as a good omen. I would have given your race its freedom, but there were fools and traitors among you who misjudged me. But that freedom I shall yet give you in spite of yourselves. Are there many like you in your country?"

"There are thousands, sire," I said, lying cheerfully. "I am one of many who think that my race's life lies in your victory. And I think that that victory must be won not in Europe alone. In South Africa for the moment there is no chance, so we look to other parts of the continent. You will win in Europe. You have won in the East, and it now remains to strike the English where they cannot fend the blow. If we take Uganda, Egypt will fall. By your permission I go there to make trouble for your enemies."

A flicker of a smile passed over the worn face. It was the face of one who slept little and whose thoughts rode him like a nightmare.

"That is well," he said. "Some Englishman once said that he would call in the New World to redress the balance of the Old. We Germans will summon the whole earth to suppress the infamies of England. Serve us well, and you will not be forgotten."

Then he suddenly asked: "Did you fight in the last South African War?"

"Yes, sire," I said. "I was in the command of that Smuts who has now been bought by England."

"What were your countrymen's losses?" he asked eagerly.

I did not know, but I hazarded a guess. "In the field some twenty thousand. But many more by sickness and in the accursed prison camps of the English."

Again a spasm of pain crossed his face.

"Twenty thousand," he repeated huskily. "A mere handful. To-day we lose as many in a skirmish in the Polish marshes."

Then he broke out fiercely:

"I did not seek the war. . . . It was forced on me. . . . I laboured for peace. . . . The blood of millions is on the heads of England and Russia, but England most of all. God will yet avenge it. He that takes the sword will perish by the sword. Mine was forced from the scabbard in self-defence, and I am guiltless. Do they know that among your people?"

"All the world knows it, sire," I said.

He gave his hand to Stumm and turned away. The last I saw of him was a figure moving like a sleep-walker, with no spring in his step, amid his tall suite. I felt that I was looking on at a far bigger tragedy than any I had seen in action. Here was one that had loosed Hell, and the furies of Hell had got hold of him. He was no common man, for in his presence I felt an attraction which was not merely the mastery of one used to command. That would not have impressed me, for I had never owned a master. But here was a human being who, unlike Stumm and his kind, had the power of laying himself alongside other men. That was the irony of it. Stumm would not have cared a tinker's curse for all the massacres in history. But this man, the chief of a nation of Stumms, paid the price in war for the gifts that had made him successful in peace. He had imagination and nerves, and the one was white hot and the others were quivering. I would not have been in his shoes for the throne of the Universe. . . .

All afternoon we sped southward, mostly in a country of hills and wooded valleys. Stumm, for him, was very pleasant. His Imperial master must have been gracious to him, and he passed a bit of it on to me. But he was anxious to see that I had got the right impression.

"The All-Highest is merciful, as I told you," he said.

I agreed with him.

"Mercy is the prerogative of kings," he said sententiously, "but for us lesser folks it is a trimming we can well do without."

I nodded my approval.

"I am not merciful," he went on, as if I needed telling that. "If any man stands in my way I trample the life out of him. That is the German fashion. That is what has made us great. We do not make war with lavender gloves and fine phrases, but with hard steel and hard brains. We Germans will cure the green-sickness of the world. The nations rise against us. Pouf! They are soft flesh, and flesh cannot resist iron. The shining ploughshare will cut its way through acres of mud."

I hastened to add that these were also my opinions.

"What the hell do your opinions matter? You are a thick-headed boor of the veld. . . . Not but what," he added, "there is mettle in you slow Dutchmen once we Germans have had the forging of it!"

The winter evening closed in, and I saw that we had come out of the hills and were in a flat country. Sometimes a big sweep of river showed, and, looking out at one station, I saw a funny church with a thing like an onion on the top of its spire. It might almost have been a mosque, judging from the pictures I remembered of mosques. I wished to heaven I had given geography more attention in my time.

Presently we stopped, and Stumm led the way out. The train must have been specially halted for him, for it was a one-horse little place whose name I could not make out. The station-master was waiting, bowing and saluting, and outside was a motor-car with big headlights. Next minute we were sliding through dark woods where the snow lay far deeper than in the north. There was a mild frost in the air, and the tyres slipped and skidded at the corners.

We hadn't far to go. We climbed a little hill and on the top of it stopped at the door of a big black castle. It looked enormous in the winter night, with not a light showing anywhere on its front. The door was opened by an old fellow who took a long time about it and got well cursed for his slowness. Inside the place was very noble and ancient. Stumm switched on the electric light, and there was a great hall with black tarnished portraits of men and women in old-fashioned clothes and mighty horns of deer on the walls.

There seemed to be no superfluity of servants. The old fellow said that food was ready, and without more ado we went into the dining-room— another vast chamber with rough stone walls above the panelling—and found some cold meats on a table beside a big fire. The servant presently brought in a ham omelette, and on that and the cold stuff we dined. I remember there was nothing to drink but water. It puzzled me how Stumm kept his great body going on the very moderate amount of food he ate. He was the type you expect to swill beer by the bucket and put away a pie at a sitting.

When he had finished he rang for the old man and told him that we should be in the study for the rest of the evening. "You can lock up and go to bed when you like," he said, "but see you have coffee ready at seven sharp in the morning."

Ever since I entered that house I had the uncomfortable feeling of being in a prison. Here was I alone in this great place with a fellow who could, and would, wring my neck if he wanted. Berlin and all the rest of it had seemed comparatively open country; I had felt that I could move freely and at the worst make a bolt for it. But here I was trapped, and I had to tell myself every minute that I was there as a friend and colleague. The fact is, I was afraid of Stumm, and I don't mind admitting it. He was a new thing in my experience and I didn't like it. If only he had drunk and guzzled a bit I should have been happier.

We went up a staircase to a room at the end of a long corridor. Stumm locked the door behind him and laid the key on a table. That room took my breath away, it was so unexpected. In place of the grim bareness of downstairs here was a place all luxury and colour and light. It was very large, but low in the ceiling, and the walls were full of little recesses with statues in them. A thick grey carpet of velvet pile covered the floor, and the chairs were low and soft and upholstered like a lady's boudoir. A pleasant fire burned on the hearth and there was a flavour of scent in the air, something like incense or burnt sandalwood. A French clock on the mantelpiece told me that it was ten minutes past eight. Everywhere on little tables and in cabinets was a profusion of nicknacks, and there was some beautiful embroidery framed on screens. At first sight you would have said it was a woman's drawing-room.

But it wasn't. I soon saw the difference. There had never been a woman's hand in that place. It was the room of a man who had a fashion for frippery, who had a perverted taste for soft delicate things. It was the complement to his bluff brutality. I began to see the queer other side to my host, that evil side which gossip had spoken of as not unknown in the German army. The room seemed a horribly unwholesome place, and I was more than ever afraid of Stumm.

The hearthrug was a wonderful old Persian thing, all faint greens and pinks. As he stood on it he looked uncommonly like a bull in a china shop. He seemed to bask in the comfort of it, and sniffed like a satisfied animal. Then he sat down at an escritoire, unlocked a drawer and took out some papers.

"We will now settle your business, friend Brandt," he said. "You will go to Egypt and there take your orders from one whose name and address are in this envelope. This card," and he lifted a square piece of grey pasteboard with a big stamp at the corner and some code words stencilled on it, "will be your passport. You will show it to the man you seek. Keep it jealously, and never use it save under orders or in the last necessity. It is your badge as an accredited agent of the German Crown."

I took the card and the envelope and put them in my pocket-book.

"Where do I go after Egypt?" I asked.

"That remains to be seen. Probably you will go up the Blue Nile. Riza, the man you will meet, will direct you. Egypt is a nest of our agents who work peacefully under the nose of the English Secret Service."

"I am willing," I said. "But how do I reach Egypt?"

"You will travel by Holland and London. Here is your route," and he took a paper from his pocket. "Your passports are ready and will be given you at the frontier."

This was a pretty kettle of fish. I was to be packed off to Cairo by sea, which would take weeks, and God knows how I would get from Egypt to Constantinople. I saw all my plans falling in pieces about my ears, and just when I thought they were shaping nicely.

Stumm must have interpreted the look on my face as fear.

"You have no cause to be afraid," he said. "We have passed the word to the English police to look out for a suspicious South African named Brandt, one of Maritz's rebels. It is not difficult to have that kind of hint conveyed to the proper quarter. But the description will not be yours. Your name will be Van der Linden, a respectable Java merchant going home to his plantations after a visit to his native shores. You had better get your *dossier* by heart, but I guarantee you will be asked no questions. We manage these things well in Germany."

I kept my eyes on the fire, while I did some savage thinking. I knew they would not let me out of their sight till they saw me in Holland, and, once there, there would be no possibility of getting back. When I left this house I would have no chance of giving them the slip. And yet I was well on my way to the East, the Danube could not be fifty miles off, and that way ran the road to Constantinople. It was a fairly desperate position. If I tried to get away Stumm would prevent me, and the odds were that I would go to join Peter in some infernal prison camp.

Those moments were some of the worst I ever spent. I was absolutely and utterly baffled, like a rat in a trap. There seemed nothing for it but to go back to London and tell Sir Walter the game was up. And that was about as bitter as death.

He saw my face and laughed.

"Does your heart fail you, my little Dutchman? You funk the English? I will tell you one thing for your comfort. There is nothing in the world to be feared except me. Fail, and you have cause to shiver. Play me false, and you had far better never have been born."

His ugly sneering face was close above mine. Then he put out his hands and gripped my shoulders as he had done the first afternoon.

I forget if I mentioned that part of the damage I got at Loos was a shrapnel bullet low down at the back of my neck. The wound had healed well enough, but I had pains there on a cold day. His fingers found the place and it hurt like hell.

There is a very narrow line between despair and black rage. I had about given up the game, but the sudden ache of my shoulder gave me purpose again. He must have seen the rage in my eyes, for his own became cruel.

"The weasel would like to bite," he cried. "But the poor weasel has found its master. Stand still, vermin. Smile, look pleasant, or I will make pulp of you. Do you dare to frown at me?"

I shut my teeth and said never a word. I was choking in my throat and could not have uttered a syllable if I had tried.

Then he let me go, grinning like an ape.

I stepped back a pace and gave him my left between the eyes.

For a second he did not realize what had happened, for I don't suppose any one had dared to lift a hand to him since he was a child. He blinked at me mildly. Then his face grew red as fire.

"God in Heaven," he said quietly. "I am going to kill you," and he flung himself on me like a mountain.

I was expecting him and dodged the attack. I was quite calm now, but pretty hopeless. The man had a gorilla's reach and could give me at least a couple of stone. He wasn't soft either, but looked as hard as granite. I was only just from hospital and absurdly out of training. He would certainly kill me if he could, and I saw nothing to prevent him.

My only chance was to keep him from getting to grips, for he could have squeezed in my ribs in two seconds. I fancied I was lighter on my legs than him, and I had a good eye. Black Monty at Kimberley had taught me to fight a bit, but there is no art on earth which can prevent a big man in a narrow space from sooner or later cornering a lesser one. That was the danger.

Backwards and forwards we padded on the soft carpet. He had no notion of guarding himself, and I got in a good few blows. Then I saw a queer thing. Every time I hit him he blinked and seemed to pause. I guessed the reason for that. He had gone through life keeping the crown of the causeway, and nobody had ever stood up to him. He wasn't a coward by a long chalk, but he was a bully, and had never been struck in his life. He was getting struck now in real earnest, and he didn't like it. He had lost his bearings and was growing as mad as a hatter.

I kept half an eye on the clock. I was more hopeful now, and was looking for the right kind of chance. The risk was that I might tire sooner than him and be at his mercy.

Then I learned a truth I have never forgotten. If you are fighting a man who means to kill you, he will be apt to down you unless you mean to kill him too. Stumm did not know any rules to this game, and I forgot to allow for that. Suddenly, when I was watching his eyes, he launched a mighty kick at my stomach. If he had got me, this yarn would have had an abrupt ending. But by the mercy of God I was moving sideways when he let out, and his heavy boot just grazed my left thigh.

It was the place where most of the shrapnel had lodged, and for a second I was sick with pain and stumbled. Then I was on my feet again but with a new feeling in my blood. I had to smash Stumm or never sleep in my bed again.

I got a wonderful power from this new cold rage of mine. I felt I couldn't tire, and I danced round and dotted his face till it was streaming with blood. His bulky padded chest was no good to me, so I couldn't try for the mark.

He began to snort now and his breath came heavily. "You infernal cad," I said in good round English, "I'm going to knock the stuffing out of you," but he didn't know what I was saying.

Then at last he gave me my chance. He half tripped over a little table and his face stuck forward. I got him on the point of the chin, and put every ounce of weight I possessed behind the blow. He crumpled up in a heap and rolled over, upsetting a lamp and knocking a big China jar in two. His head, I remember, lay under the escritoire from which he had taken my passport.

I picked up the key and unlocked the door. In one of the gilded mirrors I smoothed my hair and tidied up my clothes. My anger had completely gone and I had no particular ill-will left against Stumm. He was a man of remarkable qualities, which would have brought him to the highest distinction in the Stone Age. But for all that he and his kind were back numbers.

I stepped out of the room, locked the door behind me, and started out on the second stage of my travels.

17   CHRISTMASTIDE

Everything depended on whether the servant was in the hall. I had put Stumm to sleep for a bit, but I couldn't flatter myself he would long be quiet, and when he came to he would kick the locked door to matchwood. I must get out of the house without a minute's delay, and if the door was shut and the old man gone to bed I was done.

I met him at the foot of the stairs, carrying a candle.

"Your master wants me to send off an important telegram. Where is the nearest office? There's one in the village, isn't there?" I spoke in my best German, the first time I had used the tongue since I crossed the frontier.

"The village is five minutes off at the foot of the avenue," he said. "Will you be long, sir?"

"I'll be back in a quarter of an hour," I said. "Don't lock up till I get in."

I put on my ulster and walked out into a clear starry night. My bag I left lying on a settle in the hall. There was nothing in it to compromise me, but I wished I could have got a toothbrush and some tobacco out of it.

So began one of the craziest escapades you can well imagine. I couldn't stop to think of the future yet, but must take one step at a time. I ran down

the avenue, my feet crackling on the hard snow, planning hard my programme for the next hour.

I found the village—half a dozen houses with one biggish place that looked
like an inn. The moon was rising, and as I approached I saw that it was some
kind of a store. A funny little two-seated car was purring before the door, and
I guessed this was also the telegraph office.

I marched in and told my story to a stout woman with spectacles on her
nose who was talking to a young man.

"It is too late," she shook her head. "The Herr Burgrave knows that well.
There is no connection from here after eight o'clock. If the matter is urgent
you must go to Schwandorf."

"How far is that?" I asked, looking for some excuse to get decently out of
the shop.

"Seven miles," she said; "but here is Franz and the post-wagon. Franz,
you will be glad to give the gentleman a seat beside you."

The sheepish-looking youth muttered something which I took to be assent,
and finished off a glass of beer. From his eyes and manner he looked as if he
were half-drunk.

I thanked the woman, and went out to the car, for I was in a fever to take
advantage of this unexpected bit of luck. I could hear the postmistress
enjoining Franz not to keep the gentleman waiting, and presently he came
out and flopped into the driver's seat. We started in a series of voluptuous
curves, till his eyes got accustomed to the darkness.

At first we made good going along the straight, broad highway lined with
woods on one side and on the other snowy fields melting into haze. Then he
began to talk, and as he talked he slowed down. This by no means suited my
book, and I seriously wondered whether I should pitch him out and take
charge of the thing. He was obviously a weakling left behind in the conscription, and I could have done it with one hand. But by a fortunate chance I left
him alone.

"That is a fine hat of yours, mein Herr," he said. He took off his own blue
peaked cap, the uniform, I suppose, of the driver of the post-wagon, and laid
it on his knee. The night air ruffled a shock of tow-coloured hair.

Then he calmly took my hat and clapped it on his head.

"With this thing I should be a gentleman," he said.

I said nothing, but put on his cap and waited.

"That is a noble overcoat, mein Herr," he went on. "It goes well with the
hat. It is the kind of garment I have always desired to own. In two days it will
be the holy Christmas, when gifts are given. Would that the good God sent
me such a coat as yours!"

"You can try it on to see how it looks," I said good-humouredly.

He stopped the car with a jerk, and pulled off his blue coat. The exchange
was soon effected. He was about my height, and my ulster fitted not so
badly. I put on his overcoat, which had a big collar that buttoned round the
neck.

The idiot preened himself like a girl. Drink and vanity had primed him for any folly. He drove so carelessly for a bit that he nearly put us into a ditch. We passed several cottages and at the last he slowed down.

"A friend of mine lives here," he announced. "Gertrud would like to see me in the fine clothes which the most amiable Herr has given me. Wait for me, I will not be long." And he scrambled out of the car and lurched into the little garden.

I took his place and moved very slowly forward. I heard the door open and the sound of laughing and loud voices. Then it shut, and looking back I saw that my idiot had been absorbed into the dwelling of his Gertrud. I waited no longer, but sent the car forward at its best speed.

Five minutes later the infernal thing began to give trouble—a nut loose in the antiquated steering-gear. I unhooked a lamp, examined it, and put the mischief right, but I was a quarter of an hour doing it. The highway ran now in a thick forest, and I noticed branches going off every now and then to the right. I was just thinking of turning up one of them, for I had no anxiety to visit Schwandorf, when I heard behind me the sound of a great car driven furiously.

I drew in to the right side—thank goodness I remembered the rule of the road—and proceeded decorously, wondering what was going to happen. I could hear the brakes being clapped on and the car slowing down. Suddenly a big grey bonnet slipped past me and as I turned my head I heard a familiar voice.

It was Stumm, looking like something that has been run over. He had his jaw in a sling, so that I wondered if I had broken it, and his eyes were beautifully bunged up. It was that that saved me, that and his raging temper. The collar of the postman's coat was round my chin, hiding my beard, and I had his cap pulled well down on my brow. I remembered what Blenkiron had said—that the only way to deal with the Germans was naked bluff. Mine was naked enough, for it was all that was left to me.

"Where is the man you brought from Andersbach?" he roared, as well as his jaw would allow him.

I pretended to be mortally scared, and spoke in the best imitation I could manage of the postman's high cracked voice.

"He got out a mile back, Herr Burgrave," I quavered. "He was a rude fellow who wanted to go to Schwandorf, and then changed his mind."

"Where, you fool? Say exactly where he got down or I will wring your neck."

"In the wood this side of Gertrud's cottage . . . on the left hand. . . . I left him running among the trees." I put all the terror I knew into my pipe, and it wasn't all acting.

"He means the Heinrichs' cottage, Herr Colonel," said the chauffeur. "This man is courting the daughter."

Stumm gave an order and the great car backed, and, as I looked round, I saw it turning. Then as it gathered speed it shot forward, and presently was lost in the shadows. I had got over the first hurdle.

But there was no time to be lost. Stumm would meet the postman and would be tearing after me any minute. I took the first turning, and bucketed along a narrow woodland road. The hard ground would show very few tracks, I thought, and I hoped the pursuit would think I had gone on to Schwandorf. But it wouldn't do to risk it, and I was determined very soon to get the car off the road, leave it, and take to the forest. I took out my watch and calculated I could give myself ten minutes.

I was very nearly caught. Presently I came on a bit of rough heath, with a slope away from the road and here and there a patch of black which I took to be a sandpit. Opposite one of these I slewed the car to the edge, got out, started it again and saw it pitch head-foremost into the darkness. There was a splash of water and then silence. Craning over I could see nothing but murk and the marks at the lip where the wheels had passed. They would find my tracks in daylight, but scarcely at this time of night.

Then I ran across the road to the forest. I was only just in time, for the echoes of the splash had hardly died away when I heard the sound of another car. I lay flat in a hollow below a tangle of snow-laden brambles and looked between the pine trees at the moonlit road. It was Stumm's car again, and to my consternation it stopped just a little short of the sandpit.

I saw an electric torch flashed, and Stumm himself got out and examined the tracks on the highway. Thank God, they would be still there for him to find, but had he tried half a dozen yards on he would have seen them turn towards the sandpit. If that had happened he would have beaten the adjacent woods and most certainly found me. There was a third man in the car, with my hat and coat on him. That poor devil of a postman had paid dear for his vanity.

They took a long time before they started again, and I was jolly well relieved when they went scouring down the road. I ran deeper into the woods till I found a track which—as I judged from the sky which I saw in a clearing—took me nearly due west. That wasn't the direction I wanted, so I bore off at right angles, and presently struck another road which I crossed in a hurry. After that I got entangled in some confounded kind of enclosure, and had to climb paling after paling of rough stakes plaited with osiers. Then came a rise in the ground and I was on a low hill of pines which seemed to last for miles. All the time I was going at a good pace, and before I stopped to rest I calculated I had put six miles between me and the sandpit.

My mind was getting a little more active now; for the first part of the journey I had simply staggered from impulse to impulse. These impulses had been uncommon lucky, but I couldn't go on like that for ever. *Ek sal 'n plan maak*, says the old Boer when he gets into trouble, and it was up to me now to make a plan.

As soon as I began to think I saw the desperate business I was in for. Here was I, with nothing except what I stood up in—including a coat and cap that weren't mine—alone in mid-winter in the heart of South Germany. There was a man behind me looking for my blood, and soon there would be a hue-and-cry for me up and down the land. I had heard that the German police were pretty efficient, and I couldn't see that I stood the slimmest chance. If they caught me they would shoot me beyond doubt. I asked myself on what charge, and answered, "For knocking about a German officer." They couldn't have me up for espionage, for as far as I knew they had no evidence. I was simply a Dutchman that had got riled and had run amok. But if they cut down a cobbler for laughing at a second lieutenant—which is what happened at Zabern—I calculated that hanging would be too good for a man that had broken a colonel's jaw.

To make things worse my job was not to escape—though that would have been hard enough—but to get to Constantinople, more than a thousand miles off, and I reckoned I couldn't get there as a tramp. I had to be sent there, and now I had flung away my chance. If I had been a Catholic I would have said a prayer to St. Theresa, for she would have understood my troubles.

My mother used to say that when you felt down on your luck it was a good cure to count your mercies. So I set about counting mine. The first was that I was well started on my journey, for I couldn't be above two score miles from the Danube. The second was that I had Stumm's pass. I didn't see how I could use it, but there it was. Lastly, I had plenty of money—fifty-three English sovereigns and the equivalent of three pounds in German paper which I had changed at the Berlin hotel. Also I had squared accounts with old Stumm. That was the biggest mercy of all.

I thought I had better get some sleep, so I found a dryish hole below an oak root and squeezed myself into it. The snow lay deep in these woods and I was sopping wet up to the knees. All the same I managed to sleep for some hours, and got up and shook myself just as the winter's dawn was breaking through the tree-tops. Breakfast was the next thing, and I must find some sort of dwelling.

Almost at once I struck a road, a big highway running north and south. I trotted along in the bitter morning to get my circulation started, and presently I began to feel a little better. In a little I saw a church spire, which meant a village. Stumm wouldn't be likely to have got on my tracks yet, I calculated, but there was always the chance that he had warned all the villages round by telephone and that they might be on the look-out for me. But that risk had to be taken, for I must have food.

It was the day before Christmas, I remembered, and people would be holidaying. The village was quite a big place, but at this hour—just after eight o'clock—there was nobody in the street except a wandering dog. I chose the most unassuming shop I could find, where a little boy was taking down the shutters—one of those general stores where they sell everything. The boy fetched a very old woman who hobbled in from the back, fitting on her spectacles.

"Grüss Gott," she said in a friendly voice, and I took off my cap. I saw from my reflection in a saucepan that I looked moderately respectable in spite of my night in the woods.

I told her a story of how I was walking from Schwandorf to see my mother at an imaginary place called Judenfeld, banking on the ignorance of villagers about any place five miles from their homes. I said my luggage had gone astray, and I hadn't time to wait for it, since my leave was short. The old lady was sympathetic and unsuspecting. She sold me a pound of chocolate, a box of biscuits, the better part of a ham, two tins of sardines, and a rucksack to carry them. I also bought some soap, a comb and a cheap razor, and a small Tourists' Guide, published by a Leipzig firm. As I was leaving I saw what seemed like garments hanging up in the back shop, and turned to have a look at them. They were the kind of thing that Germans wear on their summer walking tours—long shooting capes made of a green stuff they call *loden*. I bought one, and a green felt hat and an alpenstock to keep it company. Then wishing the old woman and her belongings a merry Christmas, I departed and took the shortest cut out of the village. There were one or two people about now, but they did not seem to notice me.

I went into the woods again and walked for two miles till I halted for breakfast. I was not feeling quite so fit, and I did not make much of my provisions, beyond eating a biscuit and some chocolate. I felt very thirsty and longed for hot tea. In an icy pool I washed and with infinite agony shaved my beard. That razor was the worst of its species, and my eyes were running all the time with the pain of the operation. Then I took off the postman's coat and cap, and buried them below some bushes. I was now a clean-shaven German pedestrian with a green cape and hat, and an absurd walking-stick with an iron-shod end—the sort of person who roams in thousands over the Fatherland in summer, but is a rarish bird in mid-winter.

The Tourists' Guide was a fortunate purchase, for it contained a big map of Bavaria which gave me my bearings. I was certainly not forty miles from the Danube—more like twenty. The road through the village I had left would have taken me to it. I had only to walk due south and I would reach it before night. So far as I could make out there were long tongues of forest running down to the river, and I resolved to keep to the woodlands. At the worst I would meet a forester or two, and I had a good enough story for them. On the highroad there might be awkward questions.

When I started out again I felt very stiff and the cold seemed to be growing intense. This puzzled me, for I had not minded it much up to now, and, being warm-blooded by nature, it never used to worry me. A sharp winter night on the high-veld was a long sight chillier than anything I had struck so far in Europe. But now my teeth were chattering and the marrow seemed to be freezing in my bones.

The day had started bright and clear, but a wrack of grey clouds soon covered the sky, and a wind from the east began to whistle. As I stumbled along through the snowy undergrowth I kept longing for bright warm places. I thought of those long days on the veld when the earth was like a great yellow bowl, with white roads running to the horizon and a tiny white farm basking in the heart of it, with its blue dam and patches of bright green lucerne. I thought of those baking days on the east coast when the sea was like mother-of-pearl and the sky one burning turquoise. But most of all I thought of warm scented noons on trek, when one dozed in the shadow of the wagon and sniffed the wood-smoke from the fire where the boys were cooking dinner.

From these pleasant pictures I returned to the beastly present—the thick
snowy woods, the lowering sky, wet clothes, a hunted present, and a dismal
future. I felt miserably depressed, and I couldn't think of any mercies to
count. It struck me that I might be falling sick.

About midday I awoke with a start to the belief that I was being pursued. I
cannot explain how or why the feeling came, except that it is a kind of instinct
that men get who have lived much in wild countries. My senses, which had
been numbed, suddenly grew keen, and my brain began to work double
quick.

I asked myself what I would do if I were Stumm, with hatred in my heart, a
broken jaw to avenge, and pretty well limitless powers. He must have found
the car in the sandpit and seen my tracks in the wood opposite. I didn't know
how good he and his men might be at following a spoor, but I knew that any
ordinary Kaffir could have nosed it out easily. But he didn't need to do that.
This was a civilized country full of roads and railways. I must sometime and
somewhere come out of the woods. He could have all the roads watched, and
the telephone would set every one on my track within a radius of fifty miles.
Besides, he would soon pick up my trail in the village I had visited that
morning. From the map I learned that it was called Greif, and it was likely to
live up to that name and be a hook for me.

Presently I came to a rocky knoll which rose out of the forest. Keeping well
in shelter I climbed to the top and cautiously looked around me. Away to the
east I saw the vale of a river with broad fields and church spires. West and
south the forest rolled unbroken in a wilderness of snowy tree-tops. There
was no sign of life anywhere, not even a bird, but I knew very well that
behind me in the woods were men moving swiftly on my tracks, and that it
was pretty well impossible for me to get away.

There was nothing for it but to go on till I dropped or was taken. I shaped
my course south with a shade of west in it, for the map showed me that in that
direction I would soonest strike the Danube. What I was going to do when I
got there I didn't trouble to think. I had fixed the river as my immediate goal
and the future must take care of itself.

I was now certain that I had fever on me. It was still in my bones, as a
legacy from Africa, and had come out once or twice when I was with the
battalion in Hampshire. The bouts had been short, for I had known of their
coming and dosed myself. But now I had no quinine, and it looked as if I
were in for a heavy go. It made me feel desperately wretched and stupid, and
I all but blundered into capture.

For suddenly I came on a road and was going to cross it blindly, when a
man rode slowly past on a bicycle. Luckily I was in the shade of a clump of
hollies and he was not looking my way, though he was scarcely three yards
off. I crawled forward to reconnoitre. I saw about half a mile of road running
straight through the forest, and every two hundred yards was a bicyclist.
They wore uniform and appeared to be acting as sentries.

This could only have one meaning. Stumm had picketed all the roads and
cut me off in an angle of the woods. There was no chance of getting across

unobserved. As I lay there with my heart sinking, I had the horrible feeling that the pursuit might be following me from behind, and that at any moment I would be enclosed between two fires.

For more than an hour I stayed there with my chin in the snow. I didn't see any way out, and I was feeling so ill that I didn't seem to care. Then my chance came suddenly out of the skies.

The wind rose, and a great gust of snow blew from the east. In five minutes it was so thick that I couldn't see across the road. At first I thought it a new addition to my troubles, and then very slowly I saw the opportunity. I slipped down the bank and made ready to cross.

I almost blundered into one of the bicyclists. He cried out and fell off his machine, but I didn't wait to investigate. A sudden access of strength came to me and I darted into the woods on the farther side. I knew I would be soon swallowed from sight in the drift, and I knew that the falling snow would hide my tracks. So I put my best foot forward.

I must have run miles before the hot fit passed, and I stopped from sheer bodily weakness. There was no sound except the crush of falling snow, the wind seemed to have gone, and the place was very solemn and quiet. But Heavens! how the snow fell! It was partly screened by the branches, but all the same it was piling itself up deep everywhere. My legs seemed made of lead, my head burned, and there were fiery pains over all my body. I stumbled on blindly, without a notion of any direction, determined only to keep going to the last. For I knew that if I once lay down I would never rise again.

When I was a boy I was fond of fairy tales, and most of the stories I remembered had been about great German forests and snow and charcoal burners and woodmen's huts. Once I had longed to see these things, and now I was fairly in the thick of them. There had been wolves, too, and I wondered idly if I should fall in with a pack. I felt myself getting light-headed. I fell repeatedly and laughed sillily every time. Once I dropped into a hole and lay for some time at the bottom giggling. If any one had found me then he would have taken me for a madman.

The twilight of the forest grew dimmer, but I scarcely noticed it. Evening was falling, and soon it would be night, a night without morning for me. My body was going on without the direction of my brain, for my mind was filled with craziness. I was like a drunk man who keeps running, for he knows that if he stops he will fall, and I had a sort of bet with myself not to lie down—not at any rate just yet. If I lay down I should feel the pain in my head worse. Once I had ridden for five days down country with fever on me, and the flat bush trees had seemed to melt into one big mirage and dance quadrilles before my eyes. But then I had more or less kept my wits. Now I was fairly daft, and every minute growing dafter.

Then the trees seemed to stop and I was walking on flat ground. It was a clearing, and before me twinkled a little light. The change restored me to consciousness, and I felt with horrid intensity the fire in my head and bones and the weakness of my limbs. I longed to sleep, and I had a notion that a place to sleep was before me. I moved towards the light and presently saw through a screen of snow the outline of a cottage.

I had no fear, only an intolerable longing to lie down. Very slowly I made my way to the door and knocked. My weakness was so great that I could hardly lift my hand.

There were voices within, and a corner of the curtain was lifted from the window. Then the door opened and a woman stood before me, a woman with a thin kindly face.

"Grüss Gott," she said, while children peeped from behind her skirts.

"Grüss Gott," I replied. I leaned against the doorpost, and speech forsook me.

She saw my condition. "Come in, sir," she said. "You are sick and it is no weather for a sick man."

I stumbled after her and stood dripping in the centre of the little kitchen, while three wondering children stared at me. It was a poor place, scantily furnished, but a good log-fire burned on the hearth. The shock of warmth gave me one of those minutes of self-possession which come sometimes in the middle of a fever.

"I am sick, mother, and I have walked far in the storm and lost my way. I am from Africa, where the climate is hot, and your cold brings me fever. It will pass in a day or two if you can give me a bed."

"You are welcome," she said; "but first I will make you coffee."

I took off my dripping cloak, and crouched close to the hearth. She gave me coffee—poor washy stuff, but blessedly hot. Poverty was spelled large in everything I saw. I felt the tides of fever beginning to overflow my brain again, and I made a great attempt to set my affairs straight before I was overtaken. With difficulty I took out Stumm's pass from my pocket-book.

"That is my warrant," I said. "I am a member of the Imperial Secret Service and for the sake of my work I must move in the dark. If you will permit it, mother, I will sleep till I am better, but no one must know that I am here. If any one comes, you must deny my presence."

She looked at the big seal as if it were a talisman.

"Yes, yes," she said, "you will have the bed in the garret and be left in peace till you are well. We have no neighbours near, and the storm will shut the roads. I will be silent, I and the little ones."

My head was beginning to swim, but I made one more effort.

"There is food in my rucksack—biscuits and ham and chocolate. Pray take it for your use. And here is some money to buy Christmas fare for the little ones." And I gave her some of the German notes.

After that my recollection becomes dim. She helped me up a ladder to the garret, undressed me, and gave me a thick coarse nightgown. I seem to remember that she kissed my hand, and that she was crying. "The good Lord has sent you," she said. "Now the little ones will have their prayers answered and the Christkind will not pass by our door."

18 THE ESSEN BARGES

I lay for four days like a log in that garret bed. The storm died down, the thaw set in, and the snow melted. The children played about the doors and told stories at night round the fire. Stumm's myrmidons no doubt beset every road and troubled the lives of innocent wayfarers. But no one came near the cottage, and the fever worked itself out while I lay in peace.

It was a bad bout, but on the fifth day it left me, and I lay, as weak as a kitten, staring at the rafters and the little skylight. It was a leaky, draughty old place, but the woman of the cottage had heaped deerskins and blankets on my bed and kept me warm. She came in now and then, and once she brought me a brew of some bitter herbs which greatly refreshed me. A little thin porridge was all the food I could eat, and some chocolate made from the slabs in my rucksack.

I lay and dozed through the day, hearing the faint chatter of children below, and getting stronger hourly. Malaria passes as quickly as it comes and leaves a man little the worse, though this was one of the sharpest turns I ever had. As I lay I thought, and my thoughts followed curious lines. One queer thing was that Stumm and his doings seemed to have been shot back into a lumber-room of my brain and the door locked. He didn't seem to be a creature of the living present, but a distant memory on which I could look calmly. I thought a good deal about my battalion and the comedy of my present position. You see I was getting better, for I called it comedy now, not tragedy.

But chiefly I thought of my mission. All that wild day in the snow it had seemed the merest farce. The three words Harry Bullivant had scribbled had danced through my head in a crazy fandango. They were present to me now, but coolly and sanely in all their meagreness.

I remember that I took each one separately and chewed on it for hours. *Kasredin*—there was nothing to be got out of that. *Cancer*—there were too many meanings, all blind. *v. I*—that was the worst gibberish of all.

Before this I had always taken the *I* as the letter of the alphabet. I had thought the *v.* must stand for *von*, and I had considered the German names beginning with I—Ingolstadt, Ingeburg, Ingenohl, and all the rest of them. I had made a list of about seventy at the British Museum before I left London. Now I suddenly found myself taking the *I* as the numeral One. Idly, not thinking what I was doing, I put it into German.

Then I nearly fell out of the bed. *Von Einem*—the name I had heard at Gaudian's house, the name Stumm had spoken behind his hand, the name to which Hilda was probably the prefix. It was a tremendous discovery—the

141

first real bit of light I had found. Harry Bullivant knew that some man or woman called von Einem was at the heart of the mystery. Stumm had spoken of the same personage with respect and in connection with the work I proposed to do in raising the Moslem Africans. If I found von Einem I would be getting very warm. What was the word that Stumm had whispered to Gaudian and scared that worthy? It had sounded like "Ühnmantl." If I could only get that clear, I would solve the riddle.

I think that discovery completed my cure. At any rate on the evening of the fifth day—it was Wednesday, the 29th of December—I was well enough to get up. When the dark had fallen and it was too late to fear a visitor, I came downstairs and, wrapped in my green cape, took a seat by the fire.

As we sat there in the firelight, with the three white-headed children staring at me with saucer eyes, and smiling when I looked their way, the woman talked. Her man had gone to the wars on the Eastern Front, and the last she had heard from him he was in a Polish bog and longing for his dry native woodlands. The reason of the struggle meant little to her. It was an act of God, a thunderbolt out of the sky, which had taken a husband from her, and might soon make her a widow and her children fatherless. She knew nothing of its causes and purposes, and thought of the Russians as a gigantic nation of savages, heathens who had never been converted, and who would eat up German homes if the good Lord and the brave German soldiers did not stop them. I tried hard to find out if she had any notion of affairs in the West, but she hadn't, beyond the fact that there was trouble with the French. I doubt if she knew of England's share in it. She was a decent soul, with no bitterness against anybody, not even the Russians if they would spare her man.

That night I realized the crazy folly of war. When I saw the splintered shell of Ypres and heard hideous tales of German doings, I used to want to see the whole land of the Boche given up to fire and sword. I thought we could never end the war properly without giving the Huns some of their own medicine. But that woodcutter's cottage cured me of such nightmares. I was for punishing the guilty but letting the innocent go free. It was our business to thank God and keep our hands clean from the ugly blunders to which Germany's madness had driven her. What good would it do Christian folk to burn poor little huts like this and leave children's bodies by the wayside? To be able to laugh and to be merciful are the only things that make man better than the beasts.

The place, as I have said, was desperately poor. The woman's face had the skin stretched tight over the bones and that transparency which means under-feeding; I fancied she did not have the liberal allowance that soldiers' wives get in England. The children looked better nourished, but it was by their mother's sacrifice. I did my best to cheer them up. I told them long yarns about Africa and lions and tigers, and I got some pieces of wood and whittled them into toys. I am fairly good with a knife, and I carved very presentable likenesses of a monkey, a springbok, and a rhinoceros. The children went to bed hugging the first toys, I expect, they ever possessed.

It was clear to me that I must leave as soon as possible. I had to get on with my business, and besides, it was not fair to the woman. Any moment I might be found here, and she would get into trouble for harbouring me. I asked her if she knew where the Danube was, and her answer surprised me. "You will reach it in an hour's walk," she said. "The track through the wood runs straight to the ferry."

Next morning after breakfast I took my departure. It was drizzling weather, and I was feeling very lean. Before going I presented my hostess and the children with two sovereigns apiece. "It is English gold," I said, "for I have to travel among our enemies and use our enemies' money. But the gold is good, and if you go to any town they will change it for you. But I advise you to put it in your stocking-foot and use it only if all else fails. You must keep your home going, for some day there will be peace and your man will come back from the wars."

I kissed the children, shook the woman's hand, and went off down the clearing. They had cried "Auf Wiedersehen," but it wasn't likely I would ever see them again.

The snow had all gone, except in patches in the deep hollows. The ground was like a full sponge, and a cold rain drifted in my eyes. After half an hour's steady trudge the trees thinned, and presently I came out on a knuckle of open ground cloaked in dwarf junipers. And there before me lay the plain, and a mile off a broad brimming river.

I sat down and looked dismally at the prospect. The exhilaration of my discovery the day before had gone. I had stumbled on a worthless piece of knowledge, for I could not use it. Hilda von Einem, if such a person existed and possessed the great secret, was probably living in some big house in Berlin, and I was about as likely to get anything out of her as to be asked to dine with the Kaiser. Blenkiron might do something, but where on earth was Blenkiron? I dared say Sir Walter would value the information, but I could not get to Sir Walter. I was to go on to Constantinople, running away from the people who really pulled the ropes. But if I stayed I could do nothing, and I could not stay. I must go on, and I didn't see how I could go on. Every course seemed shut to me, and I was in as pretty a tangle as any man ever stumbled into.

For I was morally certain that Stumm would not let the thing drop. I knew too much, and besides I had outraged his pride. He would beat the countryside till he got me, and he undoubtedly would get me if I waited much longer. But how was I to get over the border? My passport would be no good, for the number of that pass would long ere this have been wired to every police station in Germany, and to produce it would be to ask for trouble. Without it I could not cross the borders by any railway. My studies of the Tourists' Guide had suggested that once I was in Austria I might find things slacker and move about easier. I thought of having a try at the Tyrol and I also thought of Bohemia. But these places were a long way off, and there were several thousand chances each day that I would be caught on the road.

This was Thursday, the 30th of December, the second last day of the year. I was due in Constantinople on the 17th of January. Constantinople! I had thought myself a long way from it in Berlin, but now it seemed as distant as the moon.

But that big sullen river in front of me led to it. And as I looked my attention was caught by a curious sight. On the far eastern horizon, where the water slipped round a corner of hill, there was a long trail of smoke. The streamers thinned out, and seemed to come from some boat well round the corner, but I could see at least two boats in view. Therefore there must be a long train of barges, with a tug in tow.

I looked to the west and saw another such procession coming into sight. First went a big river steamer—it can't have been much less than 1,000 tons—and after came a string of barges. I counted no less than six besides the tug. They were heavily loaded and their draught must have been considerable, but there was plenty of depth in the flooded river.

A moment's reflection told me what I was looking at. Once Sandy, in one of the discussions you have in hospital, had told us just how the Germans munitioned their Balkan campaign. They were pretty certain of dishing Serbia at the first go, and it was up to them to get through guns and shells to the old Turk, who was running pretty short in his first supply. Sandy said that they wanted the railway, but they wanted still more the river, and they could make certain of that in a week. He told us how endless strings of barges, loaded up at the big factories of Westphalia, were moving through the canals from the Rhine or the Elbe to the Danube. Once the first reached Turkey, there would be regular delivery, you see—as quick as the Turks could handle the stuff. And they didn't return empty, Sandy said, but came back full of Turkish cotton and Bulgarian beef and Rumanian corn. I don't know where Sandy got the knowledge, but there was the proof of it before my eyes.

It was a wonderful sight, and I could have gnashed my teeth to see those loads of munitions going snugly off to the enemy. I calculated they would give our poor chaps hell in Gallipoli. And then, as I looked, an idea came into my head, and with it an eighth part of a hope.

There was only one way for me to get out of Germany, and that was to leave in such good company that I would be asked no questions. That was plain enough. If I travelled to Turkey, for instance, in the Kaiser's suite, I would be as safe as the mail; but if I went on my own I was done. I had, so to speak, to get my passport *inside* Germany, to join some caravan which had free marching powers. And there was the kind of caravan before me—the Essen barges.

It sounded lunacy, for I guessed that munitions of war would be as jealously guarded as old Hindenburg's health. All the safer, I replied to myself, once I get there. If you are looking for a deserter you don't seek him at the favourite regimental public-house. If you're after a thief, among the places you'd be apt to leave unsearched would be Scotland Yard.

It was sound reasoning, but how was I to get on board? Probably the beastly things did not stop once in a hundred miles, and Stumm would get me long before I struck a halting-place. And even if I did get a chance like that, how was I to get permission to travel?

One step was clearly indicated—to get down to the river bank at once. So I set off at a sharp walk across squelchy fields, till I struck a road where the ditches had overflowed so as almost to meet in the middle. The place was so bad that I hoped travellers might be few. And as I trudged, my thoughts were busy with my prospects as a stowaway. If I bought food I might get a chance to lie snug on one of the barges. They would not break bulk till they got to their journey's end.

Suddenly I noticed that the steamer, which was now abreast me, began to move towards the shore, and as I came over a low rise I saw on my left a straggling village with a church and a small landing-stage. The houses stood about a quarter of a mile from the stream, and between them was a straight, poplar-fringed road.

Soon there could be no doubt about it. The procession was coming to a stand-still. The big tug nosed her way in and lay up alongside the pier, where in that season of flood there was enough depth of water. She signalled to the barges and they also started to drop anchors, which showed that there must be at least two men aboard each. Some of them dragged a bit and it was rather a cock-eyed train that lay in mid-stream. The tug got out a gangway, and from where I lay I saw half a dozen men leave it, carrying something on their shoulders.

It could be only one thing—a dead body. Some one of the crew must have died, and this halt was to bury him. I watched the procession move towards the village and I reckoned they would take some time there, though they might have wired ahead for a grave to be dug. Anyhow, they would be long enough to give me a chance.

For I had decided upon the brazen course. Blenkiron had said you couldn't cheat the Boche, but you could bluff him. I was going to put up the most monstrous bluff. If the whole countryside was hunting for Richard Hannay, Richard Hannay would walk through as a pal of the hunters. For I remembered the pass Stumm had given me. If that was worth a tinker's curse it should be good enough to impress a ship's captain.

Of course there were a thousand risks. They might have heard of me in the village and told the ship's party the story. For that reason I resolved not to go there but to meet the sailors when they were returning to the boat. Or the captain might have been warned and got the number of my pass, in which case Stumm would have his hands on me pretty soon. Or the captain might be an ignorant fellow who had never seen a Secret Service pass and did not know what it meant, and would refuse me transport by the letter of his instructions. In that case I might wait on another convoy.

I had shaved and made myself a fairly respectable figure before I left the cottage. It was my cue to wait for the men when they left the church, wait on that quarter-mile of straight highway. I judged the captain must be in the party. The village, I was glad to observe, seemed very empty. I have my own notions about the Bavarians as fighting men, but I am bound to say that, judging by my observations, very few of them stayed at home.

That funeral took hours. They must have had to dig the grave, for I waited near the road in a clump of cherry-trees, with my feet in two inches of mud and water, till I felt chilled to the bone. I prayed to God it would not bring back my fever, for I was only one day out of bed. I had very little tobacco left in my pouch, but I stood myself one pipe and I ate one of the three cakes of chocolate I still carried.

At last, well after midday, I could see the ship's party returning. They marched two by two, and I was thankful to see that they had no villagers with them. I walked to the road, turned up it, and met the vanguard, carrying my head as high as I knew how.

"Where's your captain?" I asked, and a man jerked his thumb over his shoulder. The others wore thick jerseys and knitted caps, but there was one man at the rear in uniform.

He was a short, broad man with a weatherbeaten face and an anxious eye.

"May I have a word with you, Herr Captain?" I said, with what I hoped was a judicious blend of authority and conciliation.

He nodded to his companion, who walked on.

"Yes?" he asked rather impatiently.

I proffered him my pass. Thank heaven he had seen the kind of thing before, for his face at once took on that curious look which one person in authority always wears when he is confronted with another. He studied it closely and then raised his eyes.

"Well, sir?" he said. "I observe your credentials. What can I do for you?"

"I take it you are bound for Constantinople?" I asked.

"The boats go as far as Rustchuk," he replied. "There the stuff is transferred to the railway."

"And you reach Rustchuk when?"

"In ten days, bar accidents. Let us say twelve to be safe."

"I want to accompany you," I said. "In my profession, Herr Captain, it is necessary sometimes to make journeys by other than the common route. That is now my desire. I have the right to call upon some other branch of our country's service to help me. Hence my request."

Very plainly he did not like it.

"I must telegraph about it. My instructions are to let no one aboard, not even a man like you. I am sorry, sir, but I must get authority first before I can fall in with your desire. Besides, my boat is ill-found. You had better wait for the next batch and ask Dreyser to take you. I lost Walter to-day. He was ill when he came aboard—a disease of the heart—but he would not be persuaded. And last night he died."

"Was that him you have been burying?" I asked.

"Even so. He was a good man and my wife's cousin, and now I have no engineer. Only a fool of a boy from Hamburg. I have just come from wiring to my owners for a fresh man, but even if he comes by the quickest train he will scarcely overtake us before Vienna or even Buda."

I saw light at last.

"We will go together," I said, "and cancel that wire. For behold, Herr Captain, I am an engineer, and will gladly keep an eye on your boilers till we get to Rustchuk."

He looked at me doubtfully.

"I am speaking truth," I said. "Before the war I was an engineer in Damaraland. Mining was my branch, but I had a good general training, and I know enough to run a river boat. Have no fear. I promise you I will earn my passage."

His face cleared, and he looked what he was, an honest, good-humoured North German seaman.

"Come then in God's name," he cried, "and we will make a bargain. I will let the telegraph sleep. I require authority from the Government to take a passenger, but I need none to engage a new engineer."

He sent one of the hands back to the village to cancel his wire. In ten minutes I found myself on board, and ten minutes later we were out in mid-stream and our tows were lumbering into line. Coffee was being made ready in the cabin, and while I waited for it I picked up the captain's binoculars and scanned the place I had left.

I saw some curious things. On the first road I had struck on leaving the cottage there were men on bicycles moving rapidly. They seemed to wear uniform. On the next parallel road, the one that ran through the village, I could see others. I noticed, too, that several figures appeared to be beating the intervening fields.

Stumm's cordon had got busy at last, and I thanked my stars that not one of the villagers had seen me. I had not got away much too soon, for in another half-hour he would have had me.

19   THE RETURN OF THE STRAGGLER

Before I turned in that evening I had done some good hours' work in the engine-room. The boat was oil-fired, and in very fair order, so my duties did not look as if they would be heavy. There was nobody who could be properly called an engineer; only, besides the furnace-men, a couple of lads from Hamburg who had been a year ago apprentices in a shipbuilding yard. They were civil fellows, both of them consumptive, who did what I told them and said little. By bedtime, if you had seen me in my blue jumpers, a pair of carpet slippers, and a flat cap—all the property of the deceased Walter—you would have sworn I had been bred to the firing of river boats, whereas I had acquired most of my knowledge on one run down the Zambesi, when the proper engineer got drunk and fell overboard among the crocodiles.

The captain—they called him Schenk—was out of his bearings in the job.

He was a Frisian and a first-class deep-water seaman, but, since he knew the Rhine delta, and because the German mercantile marine was laid on the ice till the end of war, they had turned him on to this show. He was bored by the business, and didn't understand it very well. The river charts puzzled him, and though it was pretty plain going for hundreds of miles, yet he was in a perpetual fidget about the pilotage. You could see that he would have been far more in his element smelling his way through the shoals of the Ems mouth, or beating against a north-easter in the shallow Baltic. He had six barges in tow, but the heavy flood of the Danube made it an easy job except when it came to going slow. There were two men on each barge, who came aboard every morning to draw rations. That was a funny business, for we never lay to if we could help it. There was a dinghy belonging to each barge, and the men used to row to the next and get a lift in that barge's dinghy, and so forth. Six men would appear in the dinghy of the barge nearest us and carry off supplies for the rest. The men were mostly Frisians, slow-spoken, sandy-haired lads, very like the breed you strike on the Essex coast.

It was the fact that Schenk was really a deep-water sailor, and so a novice to the job, that made me get on with him. He was a good fellow and quite willing to take a hint, so before I had been twenty-four hours on board he was telling me all his difficulties, and I was doing my best to cheer him. And difficulties came thick, because the next night was New Year's Eve.

I knew that that night was a season of gaiety in Scotland, but Scotland wasn't in it with the Fatherland. Even Schenk, though he was in charge of valuable stores and was voyaging against time, was quite clear that the men must have permission for some kind of beano. Just before darkness we came abreast a fair-sized town, whose name I never discovered, and decided to lie to for the night. The arrangement was that one man should be left on guard in each barge, and the other get four hours' leave ashore. Then he would return and relieve his friend, who should proceed to do the same thing. I foresaw that there would be some fun when the first batch returned, but I did not dare to protest. I was desperately anxious to get past the Austrian frontier, for I had a half-notion we might be searched there, but Schenk took this *Sylvesterabend* business so seriously that I would have risked a row if I had tried to argue.

The upshot was what I expected. We got the first batch aboard about midnight, blind to the world, and the others straggled in at all hours next morning. I stuck to the boat for obvious reasons, but next day it became too serious, and I had to go ashore with the captain to try and round up the stragglers. We got them all in but two, and I am inclined to think these two had never meant to come back. If I had a soft job like a river boat I shouldn't be inclined to run away in the middle of Germany with the certainty that my best fate would be to be scooped up for the trenches, but your Frisian has no more imagination than a haddock. The absentees were both watchmen from the barges, and I fancy the monotony of the life had got on their nerves.

The captain was in a raging temper, for he was short-handed to begin with. He would have started a press-gang, but there was no superfluity of men in that township: nothing but boys and grandfathers. As I was helping to run the trip I was pretty annoyed also, and I sluiced down the drunkards with icy Danube water, using all the worst language I knew in Dutch and German. It was a raw morning, and as we raged through the river-side streets I remember I heard the dry crackle of wild geese going overhead, and wished I could get a shot at them. I told one fellow—he was the most troublesome—that he was a disgrace to a great Empire, and was only fit to fight with the filthy English.

"God in Heaven!" said the captain, "we can delay no longer. We must make shift the best we can. I can spare one man from the deck hands, and you must give up one from the engine-room."

That was arranged, and we were tearing back rather short in the wind when I espied a figure sitting on a bench beside the booking-office on the pier. It was a slim figure, in an old suit of khaki: some cast-off duds which had long lost the semblance of a uniform. It had a gentle face, and was smoking peacefully, looking out upon the river and the boats and us noisy fellows with meek philosophical eyes. If I had seen Lord Kitchener sitting there and looking like nothing on earth I couldn't have been more surprised.

The man stared at me without recognition. He was waiting for his cue.

I spoke rapidly in Sesutu, for I was afraid the captain might know Dutch.

"Where have you come from?" I asked.

"They shut me up in *tronk*," said Peter, "and I ran away. I am tired, Cornelis, and want to continue the journey by boat."

"Remember you have worked for me in Africa," I said. "You are just home from Damaraland. You are a German who has lived thirty years away from home. You can tend a furnace and have worked in mines."

Then I spoke to the captain.

"Here is a fellow who used to be in my employ, Captain Schenk. It's almighty luck we've struck him. He's old, and not very strong in the head, but I'll go bail he's a good worker. He says he'll come with us and I can use him in the engine-room."

"Stand up," said the captain.

Peter stood up, light and slim and wiry as a leopard. A sailor does not judge men by girth and weight.

"He'll do," said Schenk, and the next minute he was readjusting his crews and giving the strayed revellers the rough side of his tongue. As it chanced, I could not keep Peter with me, but had to send him to one of the barges, and I had time for no more than five words with him, when I told him to hold his tongue and live up to his reputation as a half-wit. That accursed *Sylvesterabend* had played havoc with the whole outfit, and the captain and I were weary men before we got things straight.

In one way it turned out well. That afternoon we passed the frontier and I never knew it till I saw a man in a strange uniform come aboard, who copied some figures on a schedule, and brought us a mail. With my dirty face and general air of absorption in duty, I must have been an unsuspicious figure. He took down the names of the men in the barges, and Peter's name was given as it appeared on the ship's roll—Anton Blum.

"You must feel it strange, Herr Brandt," said the captain, "to be scruti-nized by a policeman, you who give orders, I doubt not, to many policemen."

I shrugged my shoulders. "It is my profession. It is my business to go unrecognized often by my own servants." I could see that I was becoming rather a figure in the captain's eyes. He liked the way I kept the men up to their work, for I hadn't been a nigger-driver for nothing.

Late on that Sunday night we passed through a great city which the captain told me was Vienna. It seemed to last for miles and miles, and to be as brightly lit as a circus. After that, we were in big plains and the air grew perishing cold. Peter had come aboard once for his rations, but usually he left it to his partner, for he was lying very low. But one morning—I think it was the 5th of January, when we had passed Buda and were moving through great sodden flats just sprinkled with snow—the captain took it into his head to get me to overhaul the barge loads. Armed with a mighty typewritten list, I made a tour of the barges, beginning with the hindmost. There was a fine old stock of deadly weapons—mostly machine guns and some field-pieces, and enough shells to blow up the Gallipoli peninsula. All kinds of shell were there, from the big 14-inch crumps to rifle grenades and trench mortars. It made me fairly sick to see all these good things preparing for our own fellows, and I wondered whether I would not be doing my best service if I engineered a big explosion. Happily I had the common sense to remember my job and my duty to stick to it.

Peter was in the middle of the convoy, and I found him pretty unhappy, principally through not being allowed to smoke. His companion was an ox-eyed lad, whom I ordered to the look-out while Peter and I went over the lists.

"Cornelis, my old friend," he said, "there are some pretty toys here. With a spanner and a couple of clear hours I could make these Maxims about as deadly as bicycles. What do you say to a try?"

"I've considered that," I said, "but it won't do. We're on a bigger business than wrecking munition convoys. I want to know how you got here."

He smiled with that extraordinary Sunday-school docility of his.

"It was very simple, Cornelis. I was foolish in the café—but they have told you of that. You see I was angry, and did not reflect. They had separated us, and I could see would treat me like dirt. Therefore my bad temper came out, for, as I have told you, I do not like Germans."

Peter gazed lovingly at the little bleak farms which dotted the Hungarian plain.

"All night I lay in *tronk* with no food. In the morning they fed me, and took me hundreds of miles in a train to a place which I think is called Neuburg. It was a great prison, full of English officers. . . . I asked myself many times on the journey what was the reason of this treatment, for I could see no sense in it. If they wanted to punish me for insulting them they had the chance to send me off to the trenches. No one could have objected. If they thought me useless they could have turned me back to Holland. I could not have stopped them. But they treated me as if I were a dangerous man, whereas all their conduct hitherto had shown that they thought me a fool. I could not understand it.

"But I had not been one night in that Neuburg place before I thought of the reason. They wanted to keep me under observation as a check upon you, Cornelis. I figured it out this way. They had given you some very important work which required them to let you into some big secret. So far, good. They evidently thought much of you, even yon Stumm man, though he was as rude as a buffalo. But they did not know you fully, and they wanted a check on you. That check they found in Peter Pienaar. Peter was a fool, and if there was anything to blab, sooner or later Peter would blab it. Then they would stretch out a long arm and nip you short, wherever you were. Therefore they must keep old Peter under their eye."

"That sounds likely enough," I said.

"It was God's truth," said Peter. "And when it was all clear to me I settled that I must escape. Partly because I am a free man and do not like to be in prison, but mostly because I was not sure of myself. Some day my temper would go again, and I might say foolish things for which Cornelis would suffer. So it was very certain that I must escape.

"Now, Cornelis, I noticed pretty soon that there were two kinds among the prisoners. There were the real prisoners, mostly English and French, and there were humbugs. The humbugs were treated apparently like the others, but not really, as I soon perceived. There was one man who passed as an English officer, another as a French Canadian, and the others called themselves Russians. None of the honest men suspected them, but they were there as spies to hatch plots for escape and get the poor devils caught in the act, and to worm out confidences which might be of value. That is the German notion of good business. I am not a British soldier to think all men are gentlemen. I know that amongst men there are desperate *skellums*, so I soon picked up this game. It made me very angry, but it was a good thing for my plan. I made my resolution to escape the day I arrived at Neuburg, and on Christmas Day I had a plan made."

"Peter, you're an old marvel. Do you mean to say you were quite certain of getting away whenever you wanted?"

"Quite certain, Cornelis. You see, I have been wicked in my time, and know something about the inside of prisons. You may build them like great castles, or they may be like a back-veld *tronk*, only mud and corrugated iron, but there is always a key and a man who keeps it, and that man can be bested. I knew I could get away, but I did not think it would be so easy. That was due to the bogus prisoners, my friends the spies.

"I made great pals with them. On Christmas night we were very jolly together. I think I spotted every one of them the first day. I bragged about my past and all I had done, and I told them I was going to escape. They backed me up and promised to help. Next morning I had a plan. In the afternoon, just after dinner, I had to go to the commandant's room. They treated me a little differently from the others, for I was not a prisoner of war, and I went there to be asked questions and to be cursed as a stupid

Dutchman. There was no strict guard kept there, for the place was on the second floor, and distant by many yards from any staircase. In the corridor outside the commandant's room there was a window which had no bars, and four feet from the window the limb of a great tree. A man might reach that limb, and if he were active as a monkey might descend to the ground. Beyond that I knew nothing, but I am a good climber, Cornelis.

"I told the others of my plan. They said it was good, but no one offered to come with me. They were very noble; they declared that the scheme was mine and I should have the fruit of it, for if more than one tried detection was certain. I agreed and thanked them—thanked them with tears in my eyes. Then one of them very secretly produced a map. We planned out my road, for I was going straight to Holland. It was a long road, and I had no money, for they had taken all my sovereigns when I was arrested, but they promised to get up a subscription among themselves to start me. Again I wept tears of gratitude. That was on Sunday, the day after Christmas. I settled to make the attempt on the Wednesday afternoon.

"Now, Cornelis, when the lieutenant took us to see the British prisoners, you remember, he told us many things about the ways of prisons. He told us how they loved to catch a man in the act of escape, so that they could use him harshly with a clear conscience. I thought of that, and calculated that now my friends would have told everything to the commandant, and that they would be waiting to bottle me on the Wednesday. Till then I reckoned I would be slackly guarded, for they would look on me as safe in the net. . . .

"So I went out of the window next day. It was the Monday afternoon. . . ."

"That was a bold stroke," I said admiringly.

"The plan was bold, but it was not skilful," said Peter modestly. "I had no money beyond seven marks, and I had but one stick of chocolate. I had no overcoat, and it was snowing hard. Further, I could not get down the tree, which had a trunk as smooth and branchless as a blue gum. For a little I thought I should be compelled to give in, and I was not happy.

"But I had leisure, for I did not think I would be missed before nightfall, and given time a man can do most things. By and by I found a branch which led beyond the outer wall of the yard and hung above the river. This I followed, and then dropped from it into the stream. It was a drop of some yards, and the water was very swift, so that I nearly drowned. I would rather swim the Limpopo, Cornelis, among all the crocodiles than that icy river. Yet I managed to reach the shore and get my breath lying in the bushes. . . .

"After that it was plain going, though I was very cold. I knew that I would be sought on the northern roads, as I had told my friends, for no one would dream of an ignorant Dutchman going south away from his kinsfolk. But I had learned enough from the map to know that our road lay south-east, and I had marked this big river."

"Did you hope to pick me up?" I asked.

"No, Cornelis. I thought you would be travelling in first-class carriages while I should be plodding on foot. But I was set on getting to the place you spoke of (how do you call it?). Constant Nople, where our big business lay. I thought I might be in time for that."

"You're an old Trojan, Peter," I said; "but go on. How did you get to that landing-stage where I found you?"

"It was a hard journey," he said meditatively. "It was not easy to get beyond the barbed-wire entanglements which surrounded Neuburg—yes, even across the river. But in time I reached the woods and was safe, for I did not think any German could equal me in wild country. The best of them, even their foresters, are but babes in veldcraft compared with such as me. . . . My troubles came only from hunger and cold. Then I met a Peruvian smouse* and sold him my clothes and bought from him these. I did not want to part with my own, which were better, but he gave me ten marks on the deal. After that I went into a village and ate heavily."

"Were you pursued?" I asked.

"I do not think so. They had gone north, as I expected, and were looking for me at the railway stations which my friends had marked for me. I walked happily and put a bold face on it. If I saw a man or woman look at me suspiciously I went up to them at once and talked. I told a sad tale, and all believed it. I was a poor Dutchman travelling home on foot to see a dying mother, and I had been told that by the Danube I should find the main railway to take me to Holland. There were kind people who gave me food, and one woman gave me half a mark, and wished me God speed. . . . Then on the last day of the year I came to the river and found many drunkards."

"Was that when you resolved to get on one of the river boats?"

"*Ja*, Cornelis. As soon as I heard of the boats I saw where my chance lay. But you might have knocked me over with a straw when I saw you come on shore. That was good fortune, my friend. . . . I have been thinking much about the Germans, and I will tell you the truth. It is only boldness that can baffle them. They are a most diligent people. They will think of all likely difficulties, but not of all possible ones. They have not much imagination. They are like steam engines which must keep to prepared tracks. There they will hunt any man down, but let him trek for open country, and they will be at a loss. Therefore boldness, my friend; for ever boldness. Remember as a nation they wear spectacles, which means that they are always peering."

Peter broke off to gloat over the wedges of geese and the strings of wild swans that were always winging across those plains. His tale had bucked me up wonderfully. Our luck had held beyond all belief, and I had a kind of hope in the business now which had been wanting before. That afternoon, too, I got another fillip.

I came on deck for a breath of air and found it pretty cold after the heat of the engine-room. So I called to one of the deck hands to fetch me up my cloak from the cabin—the same I had bought that first morning in the Greif village.

"*Der grüne Mantel?*" the man shouted up, and I cried, Yes. But the words seemed to echo in my ears, and long after he had given me the garment I stood staring abstractedly over the bulwarks.

*Peter meant a Polish-Jew pedlar.

His voice had awakened a chord of memory, or, to be accurate, it had given emphasis to what before had been only blurred and vague. For he had spoken the words which Stumm had uttered behind his hand to Gaudian. I had heard something like *"Ühnmantl,"* and could make nothing of it. Now I was as certain of those words as of my own existence. They had been *"Grüne Mantel." Grüne Mantel,* whatever it might be, was the name which Stumm had not meant me to hear, which was some talisman for the task I had proposed, and which was connected in some way with the mysterious von Einem.

This discovery put me in high fettle. I told myself that, considering the difficulties, I had managed to find out a wonderful amount in a very few days. It only shows what a man can do with the slenderest evidence if he keeps chewing and chewing on it. . . .

Two mornings later we lay alongside the quays at Belgrade, and I took the opportunity of stretching my legs. Peter had come ashore for a smoke, and we wandered among the battered river-side streets, and looked at the broken arches of the great railway bridge which the Germans were working at like beavers. There was a temporary pontoon affair to take the railway across, but I calculated that the main bridge would be ready inside a month. It was a clear, cold, blue day, and as one looked south one saw ridge after ridge of snowy hills. The upper streets of the city were still fairly whole, and there were shops open where food could be got. I remember hearing English spoken, and seeing some Red Cross nurses in the custody of Austrian soldiers coming from the railway station.

It would have done me a lot of good to have had a word with them. I thought of the gallant people whose capital this had been, how three times they had flung the Austrians back over the Danube, and then had only been beaten by the black treachery of their so-called allies. Somehow that morning in Belgrade gave both Peter and me a new purpose in our task. It was our business to put a spoke in the wheel of this monstrous bloody Juggernaut that was crushing out the little heroic nations.

We were just getting ready to cast off when a distinguished party arrived at the quay. There were all kinds of uniforms—German, Austrian, and Bulgarian, and amid them one stout gentleman in a fur coat and a black felt hat. They watched the barges up-anchor, and before we began to jerk into line I could hear their conversation. The fur coat was talking English.

"I reckon that's pretty good noos, General," it said; "if the English have run away from Gallypoly we can use these noo consignments for the bigger game. I guess it won't be long before we see the British lion moving out of Egypt with sore paws."

They all laughed. "The privilege of that spectacle may soon be ours," was the reply.

I did not pay much attention to the talk; indeed I did not realize till weeks later that that was the first tidings of the great evacuation of Cape Helles. What rejoiced me was the sight of Blenkiron, as bland as a barber among those swells. Here were two of the missionaries within reasonable distance of their goal.

20 THE GARDEN-HOUSE OF SULIMAN THE RED

We reached Rustchuk on January 10, but by no means landed on that day. Something had gone wrong with the unloading arrangements, or more likely with the railway behind them, and we were kept swinging all day well out in the turbid river. On the top of this Captain Schenk got an ague, and by that evening was a blue and shivering wreck. He had done me well and I reckoned I would stand by him. So I got his ship's papers and the manifests of cargo, and undertook to see to the transhipment. It wasn't the first time I had tackled that kind of business, and I hadn't much to learn about steam cranes. I told him I was going on to Constantinople and would take Peter with me, and he was agreeable. He would have to wait at Rustchuk to get his return cargo, and could easily inspan a fresh engineer.

I worked about the hardest twenty-four hours of my life getting the stuff ashore. The landing officer was a Bulgarian, quite a competent man if he could have made the railways give him the trucks he needed. There was a collection of hungry German transport officers always putting in their oars, and being infernally insolent to everybody. I took the high and mighty line with them; and, as I had the Bulgarian commandant on my side, after about two hours' blasphemy got them quieted.

But the big trouble came the next morning when I had got nearly all the stuff aboard the trucks.

A young officer in what I took to be a Turkish uniform rode up with an aide-de-camp. I noticed the German guards saluting him, so I judged he was rather a swell. He came up to me and asked me very civilly in German for the way-bills. I gave him them and he looked carefully through them, marking certain items with a blue pencil. Then he coolly handed them to his aide-de-camp and spoke to him in Turkish.

"Look here, I want these back," I said. "I can't do without them, and we've no time to waste."

"Presently," he said, smiling, and went off.

I said nothing, reflecting that the stuff was for the Turks and they naturally had to have some say in its handling. The loading was practically finished when my gentleman returned. He handed me a neatly typed new set of way-bills. One glance at them showed that some of the big items had been left out.

"Here, this won't do," I cried. "Give me back the right set. This thing's no good to me."

For answer he winked gently, smiled like a dusky seraph, and held out his hand. In it I saw a roll of money.

"For yourself," he said. "It is the usual custom."

It was the first time any one had ever tried to bribe me, and it made me boil up like a geyser. I saw his game clearly enough. Turkey would pay for the lot to Germany: probably had already paid the bill; but she would pay double for the things not on the way-bills, and pay to this fellow and his friends. This struck me as rather steep even for Oriental methods of doing business.

"Now look here, sir," I said, "I don't stir from this place till I get the correct way-bills. If you won't give me them, I will have every item out of the trucks and make a new list. But a correct list I have, or the stuff stays here till Doomsday."

He was a slim, foppish fellow, and he looked more puzzled than angry.

"I offer you enough," he said, again stretching out his hand.

At that I fairly roared. "If you try to bribe me, you infernal little haberdasher, I'll have you off that horse and chuck you in the river."

He no longer misunderstood me. He began to curse and threaten, but I cut him short.

"Come along to the commandant, my boy," I said, and I marched away, tearing up his typewritten sheets as I went and strewing them behind me like a paper-chase.

We had a fine old racket in the commandant's office. I said it was my business, as representing the German Government, to see the stuff delivered to the consignee at Constantinople ship-shape and Bristol-fashion. I told him it wasn't my habit to proceed with cooked documents. He couldn't but agree with me, but there was that wrathful Oriental with his face as fixed as a Buddha.

"I am sorry, Rasta Bey," he said; "but this man is in the right."

"I have authority from the Committee to receive the stores," he said sullenly.

"Those are not my instructions," was the answer. "They are consigned to the artillery commandant at Chataldja, General von Oesterzee."

The man shrugged his shoulders. "Very well. I will have a word to say to General von Oesterzee, and many to this fellow who flouts the Committee." And he strode away like an impudent boy.

The harassed commandant grinned. "You've offended his lordship, and he is a bad enemy. All those damned Comitadjis are. You would be well advised not to go to Constantinople."

"And have that blighter in the red hat loot the trucks on the road. No, thank you. I am going to see them safe at Chataldja, or whatever they call the artillery depot."

I said a good deal more, but that is an abbreviated translation of my remarks. My word for "blighter" was *Trottel*, and I used some other expressions which would have ravished my Young Turk friend to hear. Looking back, it seems pretty ridiculous to have made all this fuss about guns which were going to be used against my own people. But I didn't see that at the time. My professional pride was up in arms, and I couldn't bear to have a hand in a crooked deal.

"Well, I advise you to go armed," said the commandant. "You will have a guard for the trucks, of course, and I will pick you good men. They may hold you up all the same. I can't help you once you are past the frontier, but I'll send a wire to Oesterzee and he'll make trouble if anything goes wrong. I still think you would have been wiser to humour Rasta Bey."

As I was leaving he gave me a telegram. "Here's a wire for your Captain Schenk." I slipped the envelope in my pocket and went out.

Schenk was pretty sick, so I left a note for him. At one o'clock I got the train started, with a couple of German Landwehr in each truck and Peter and I in a horse-box. Presently I remembered Schenk's telegram, which still reposed in my pocket. I took it out and opened it, meaning to wire it from the first station we stopped at. But I changed my mind when I read it. It was from some official at Regensburg, asking him to put under arrest and send back by the first boat a man called Brandt, who was believed to have come aboard at Absthafen on the 30th of December.

I whistled and showed it to Peter. The sooner we were at Constantinople the better, and I prayed we would get there before the fellow who sent this wire repeated it and got the commandant to send on the message and have us held up at Chataldja. For my back had got fairly stiffened about these munitions, and I was going to take any risk to see them safely delivered to their proper owner. Peter couldn't understand me at all. He still hankered after a grand destruction of the lot somewhere down the railway. But then, this wasn't the line of Peter's profession, and his pride was not at stake.

We had a mortally slow journey. It was bad enough in Bulgaria, but when we crossed the frontier at a place called Mustafa Pasha we struck the real supineness of the East. Happily I found a German officer there who had some notion of hustling, and, after all, it was his interest to get the stuff moved. It was the morning of the 16th, after Peter and I had been living like pigs on black bread and condemned tinned stuff, that we came in sight of a blue sea on our right hand and knew we couldn't be very far from the end.

It was jolly near the end in another sense. We stopped at a station and were stretching our legs on the platform when I saw a familiar figure approaching. It was Rasta, with half a dozen Turkish gendarmes.

I called to Peter, and we clambered into the truck next our horse-box. I had been half expecting some move like this and had made a plan.

The Turk swaggered up and addressed us. "You can get back to Rustchuk," he said. "I take over from you here. Hand me the papers."

"Is this Chataldja?" I asked innocently.

"It is the end of your affair," he said haughtily. "Quick, or it will be the worse for you."

"Now, look here, my son," I said; "you're a kid and know nothing. I hand over to General von Oesterzee and to no one else."

"You are in Turkey," he cried, "and will obey the Turkish Government."

"I'll obey the Government right enough," I said; "but if you're the Government I could make a better one with a bib and a rattle."

He said something to his men, who unslung their rifles.

"Please don't begin shooting," I said. "There are twelve armed guards on this train who will take their orders from me. Besides, I and my friend can shoot a bit."

"Fool!" he cried, getting very angry. "I can order up a regiment in five minutes."

"Maybe you can," I said; "but observe the situation. I am sitting on enough toluol to blow up this countryside. If you dare to come aboard I will shoot you. If you call in your regiment I will tell you what I'll do. I'll fire this stuff, and I reckon they'll be picking up bits of you and your regiment off the Gallipoli Peninsula."

He had put up a bluff—a poor one—and I had called it. He saw I meant what I said, and became silken.

"Good-bye, sir," he said. "You have had a fair chance and rejected it. We shall meet again soon, and you will be sorry for your insolence."

He strutted away, and it was all I could do to keep from running after him. I wanted to lay him over my knee and spank him.

We got safely to Chataldja, and were received by von Oesterzee like long-lost brothers. He was the regular gunner-officer, not thinking about anything except his guns and shells. I had to wait about three hours while he was checking the stuff with the invoices, and then he gave me a receipt which I still possess. I told him about Rasta, and he agreed that I had done right. It didn't make him as mad as I expected, because, you see, he got his stuff safe in any case. It was only that the wretched Turks had to pay twice for a lot of it.

He gave Peter and me luncheon, and was altogether very civil and inclined to talk about the war. I would have liked to hear what he had to say, for it would have been something to get the inside view of Germany's Eastern campaign, but I did not dare to wait. Any moment there might arrive an incriminating wire from Rustchuk. Finally he lent us a car to take us the few miles to the city.

So it came about that at five minutes past three on the 16th of January, with only the clothes we stood up in, Peter and I entered Constantinople.

I was in considerable spirits, for I had got the final lap successfully over, and I was looking forward madly to meeting my friends; but, all the same, the first sight was a mighty disappointment. I don't quite know what I had expected—a sort of fairyland Eastern city, all white marble and blue water, and stately Turks in surplices, and veiled houris, and roses and nightingales, and some sort of string band discoursing sweet music. I had forgotten that winter is pretty much the same everywhere. It was a drizzling day, with a south-east wind blowing, and the streets were long troughs of mud. The first part I struck looked like a dingy colonial suburb—wooden houses and corrugated-iron roofs, and endless dirty, sallow children. There was a cemetery, I remember, with Turks' caps stuck at the head of each grave. Then we got into narrow steep streets which descended to a kind of big canal. I saw what I took to be mosques and minarets, and they were about as impressive as factory chimneys. By and by we crossed a bridge, and paid a penny for the privilege. If I had known it was the famous Golden Horn I would have looked at it with more interest, but I saw nothing save a lot of moth-eaten barges and some queer little boats like gondolas. Then we came into busier streets, where ramshackle cabs drawn by lean horses spluttered through the mud. I saw one old fellow who looked like my notion of a Turk, but most of the population had the appearance of London old-clothes men. All but the soldiers, Turk and German, who seemed well-set-up fellows.

Peter had padded along at my side like a faithful dog, not saying a word, but clearly not approving of this wet and dirty metropolis.

"Do you know that we are being followed, Cornelis?" he said suddenly, "ever since we came into this evil-smelling dorp."

Peter was infallible in a thing like that. The news scared me badly, for I feared that the telegram had come to Chataldja. Then I thought it couldn't be that, for if von Oesterzee had wanted me he wouldn't have taken the trouble to stalk me. It was more likely my friend Rasta.

I found the ferry of Ratchik by asking a soldier, and a German sailor there told me where the Kurdish Bazaar was. He pointed up a steep street which ran past a high block of warehouses with every window broken. Sandy had said the left-hand side coming down, so it must be the right-hand side going up. We plunged into it, and it was the filthiest place of all. The wind whistled up it and stirred the garbage. It seemed densely inhabited, for at all the doors there were groups of people squatting, with their heads covered, though scarcely a window showed in the blank walls.

The street corkscrewed endlessly. Sometimes it seemed to stop; then it found a hole in the opposing masonry and edged its way in. Often it was almost pitch dark; then would come a greyish twilight where it opened out to the width of a decent lane. To find a house in that murk was no easy job, and by the time we had gone a quarter of a mile I began to fear we had missed it. It was no good asking any of the crowd we met. They didn't look as if they understood any civilized tongue.

At last we stumbled on it—a tumble-down coffee-house, with A. Kuprasso above the door in queer amateur lettering. There was a lamp burning inside, and two or three men smoking at small wooden tables.

We ordered coffee, thick black stuff like treacle, which Peter anathematized. A negro brought it, and I told him in German I wanted to speak to Mr. Kuprasso. He paid no attention, so I shouted louder at him, and the noise brought a man out of the back parts.

He was a fat, oldish fellow with a long nose, very like the Greek traders you see on the Zanzibar coast. I beckoned to him and he waddled forward, smiling oilily. Then I asked him what he would take, and he replied, in very halting German, that he would have a sirop.

"You are Mr. Kuprasso," I said. "I wanted to show this place to my friend. He has heard of your garden-house and the fun there."

"The Signor is mistaken. I have no garden-house."

"Rot," I said; "I've been here before, my boy. I recall your shanty at the back and many merry nights there. What was it you called it? Oh, I remember—the Garden-House of Suliman the Red."

He put his finger to his lip and looked incredibly sly. "The Signor remembers that. But that was in the old happy days before war came. The place is long since shut. The people here are too poor to dance and sing."

"All the same I would like to have another look at it," I said, and I slipped an English sovereign into his hand.

He glanced at it in surprise and his manner changed. "The Signor is a Prince, and I will do his will." He clapped his hands and the negro appeared, and at his nod took his place behind a little side-counter.

"Follow me," he said, and led us through a long, noisome passage, which was pitch dark and very unevenly paved. Then he unlocked a door and with a swirl the wind caught it and blew it back on us.

We were looking into a mean little yard, with on one side a high curving wall, evidently of great age, with bushes growing in the cracks of it. Some scraggy myrtles stood in broken pots, and nettles flourished in a corner. At one end was a wooden building like a dissenting chapel, but painted a dingy scarlet. Its windows and skylights were black with dirt, and its door, tied up with rope, flapped in the wind.

"Behold the Pavilion," Kuprasso said proudly.

"That is the old place," I observed with feeling. "What times I've seen there! Tell me, Mr. Kuprasso, do you ever open it now?"

He put his thick lips to my ear.

"If the Signor will be silent I will tell him. It is sometimes open—not often. Men must amuse themselves, even in war. Some of the German officers come here for their pleasure, and but last week we had the ballet of Mademoiselle Cici. The police approve—but not often, for this is no time for too much gaiety. I will tell you a secret. Tomorrow afternoon there will be dancing—wonderful dancing! Only a few of my patrons know. Who, think you, will be there?"

He bent his head closer and said in a whisper—

"The Compagnie des Heures Roses."

"Oh, indeed," I said with a proper tone of respect, though I hadn't a notion what he meant.

"Will the Signor wish to come?"

"Sure," I said. "Both of us. We're all for the rosy hours."

"Then the fourth hour after midday. Walk straight through the café and one will be there to unlock the door. You are newcomers here? Take the advice of Angelo Kuprasso and avoid the streets after nightfall. Stamboul is no safe place nowadays for quiet men."

I asked him to name an hotel, and he rattled off a list from which I chose one that sounded modest and in keeping with our get-up. It was not far off, only a hundred yards to the right at the top of the hill.

When we left his door the night had begun to drop. We hadn't gone twenty yards before Peter drew very near to me and kept turning his head like a hunted stag.

"We are being followed close, Cornelis," he said calmly.

Another ten yards and we were at a cross-road where a little *place* faced a biggish mosque. I could see in the waning light a crowd of people who seemed to be moving towards us. I heard a high-pitched voice cry out a jabber of excited words, and it seemed to me that I had heard the voice before.

21 THE COMPANIONS OF THE ROSY HOURS

We battled to a corner, where a jut of building stood out into the street. It was our only chance to protect our backs, to stand up with the rib of stone between us. It was only the work of seconds. One instant we were groping our solitary way in the darkness, the next we were pinned against a wall with a throaty mob surging round us.

It took me a moment or two to realize that we were attacked. Every man has one special funk in the back of his head, and mine was to be the quarry of an angry crowd. I hated the thought of it—the mess, the blind struggle, the sense of unleashed passions different from those of any single blackguard. It was a dark world to me, and I don't like darkness. But in my nightmares I had never imagined anything just like this. The narrow, fetid street, with the icy winds fanning the filth, the unknown tongue, the hoarse savage murmur, and my utter ignorance as to what it might all be about, made me cold in the pit of my stomach.

"We've got it in the neck this time, old man," I said to Peter, who had out the pistol the commandant at Rustchuk had given him. These pistols were our only weapons. The crowd saw them and hung back, but if they chose to rush us it wasn't much of a barrier two pistols would make.

Rasta's voice had stopped. He had done his work, and had retired to the background. There were shouts from the crowd—"*Alleman*" and a word "*Khafiyeh*" constantly repeated. I didn't know what it meant at the time, but now I know that they were after us because we were Boches and spies. There was no love lost between the Constantinople scum and their new masters. It seemed an ironical end for Peter and me to be done in because we were Boches. And done in we should be. I had heard of the East as a good place for people to disappear in; there were no inquisitive newspapers or incorruptible police.

I wished to Heaven I had a word of Turkish. But I made my voice heard for a second in a pause of the din, and shouted that we were German sailors who had brought down big guns for Turkey, and were going home next day. I asked them what the devil they thought we had done? I don't know if any fellow there understood German; anyhow, it only brought a pandemonium of cries in which that ominous word *Khafiyeh* was predominant.

Then Peter fired over their heads. He had to, for a chap was pawing at his throat. The answer was a clatter of bullets on the wall above us. It looked as if they meant to take us alive, and that I was very clear should not happen. Better a bloody end in a street scrap than the tender mercies of that bandbox bravo.

I don't quite know what happened next. A press drove down at me and I fired. Some one squealed, and I looked the next moment to be strangled. And then suddenly the scrimmage ceased, and there was a wavering splash of light in that pit of darkness.

I never went through many worse minutes than these. When I had been hunted in the past weeks there had been mystery enough, but no immediate peril to face. When I had been up against a real urgent, physical risk, like Loos, the danger at any rate had been clear. One knew what one was in for. But here was a threat I couldn't put a name to, and it wasn't in the future, but pressing hard at our throats.

And yet I couldn't feel it was quite real. The patter of the pistol bullets against the wall, like so many crackers, the faces felt rather than seen in the dark, the clamour which to me was pure gibberish, had all the madness of a nightmare. Only Peter, cursing steadily in Dutch by my side, was real. And then the light came, and made the scene more eerie!

It came from one or two torches carried by wild fellows with long staves who drove their way into the heart of the mob. The flickering glare ran up the steep walls and made monstrous shadows. The wind swung the flame into long streamers, dying away in a fan of sparks.

And now a new word was heard in the crowd. It was *Chinganeh*, shouted not in anger but in fear.

At first I could not see the newcomers. They were hidden in the deep darkness under their canopy of light, for they were holding their torches high at the full stretch of their arms. They were shouting, too, wild shrill cries ending sometimes in a gush of rapid speech. Their words did not seem to be directed against us, but against the crowd. A sudden hope came to me that for some unknown reason they were on our side.

The press was no longer heavy against us. It was thinning rapidly and I could hear the scuffle as men made off down the side streets. My first notion was that these were the Turkish police. But I changed my mind when the leader came out into a patch of light. He carried no torch, but a long stave with which he belaboured the heads of those who were too tightly packed to flee.

It was the most eldritch apparition you can conceive. A tall man dressed in skins, with bare legs and sandal-shod feet. A wisp of scarlet cloth clung to his shoulders, and, drawn over his head down close to his eyes, was a skull-cap of some kind of pelt with the tail waving behind it. He capered like a wild animal, keeping up a strange high monotone that fairly gave me the creeps.

I was suddenly aware that the crowd had gone. Before us was only this figure and his half-dozen companions, some carrying torches and all wearing clothes of skin. But only the one who seemed to be their leader wore the skull-cap; the rest had bare heads and long tangled hair.

The fellow was shouting gibberish at me. His eyes were glassy, like a man who smokes hemp, and his legs were never still a second. You would think such a figure no better than a mountebank, and yet there was nothing comic in it. Fearful and sinister and uncanny it was; and I wanted to do anything but laugh.

As he shouted he kept pointing with his stave up the street which climbed the hillside.

"He means us to move," said Peter. "For God's sake, let's get away from this witch-doctor."

I couldn't make sense of it, but one thing was clear. These maniacs had delivered us for the moment from Rasta and his friends.

Then I did a dashed silly thing. I pulled out a sovereign and offered it to the leader. I had some kind of notion of showing gratitude, and as I had no words I had to show it by deed.

He brought his stick down on my wrist and sent the coin spinning in the gutter. His eyes blazed, and he made his weapon sing round my head. He cursed me—oh, I could tell cursing well enough, though I didn't follow a word; and he cried to his followers and they cursed me too. I had offered him a mortal insult and stirred up a worse hornets' nest than Rasta's push.

Peter and I, with a common impulse, took to our heels. We were not looking for any trouble with demoniacs. Up the steep narrow lane we ran with that bedlamite crowd at our heels. The torches seemed to have gone out, for the place was black as pitch, and we tumbled over heaps of offal and splashed through running drains. The men were close behind us, and more than once I felt a stick on my shoulder. But fear lent us wings, and suddenly before us was a blaze of light and we saw the debouchment of our street in a main thoroughfare. The others saw it too, for they slackened off. Just before we reached the light we stopped and looked round. There was no sound or sight behind us in the dark lane which dipped to the harbour.

"This is a queer country, Cornelis," said Peter, feeling his limbs for bruises. "Too many things happen in too short a time. I am breathless."

The big street we had struck seemed to run along the crest of the hill. There were lamps in it, and crawling cabs, and quite civilized-looking shops. We soon found the hotel to which Kuprasso had directed us, a big place in a courtyard with a very tumbledown-looking portico, and green sun shutters which rattled drearily in the winter's wind. It proved, as I had feared, to be packed to the door, mostly with German officers. With some trouble I got an interview with the proprietor, the usual Greek, and told him that we had been sent there by Mr. Kuprasso. That didn't affect him in the least, and we would have been shot into the street if I hadn't remembered about Stumm's pass.

So I explained that we had come from Germany with munitions and only wanted rooms for one night. I showed him the pass and blustered a good deal, till he became civil and said he would do the best he could for us.

That best was pretty poor. Peter and I were doubled up in a small room which contained two camp beds and little else, and had broken windows through which the wind whistled. We had a wretched dinner of stringy mutton boiled with vegetables, and a white cheese strong enough to raise the dead. But I got a bottle of whisky, for which I paid a sovereign, and we managed to light the stove in our room, fasten the shutters, and warm our hearts with a brew of toddy. After that we went to bed and slept like logs for twelve hours. On the road from Rustchuk we had had uneasy slumbers.

I woke next morning and, looking out from the broken window, saw that it was snowing. With a lot of trouble I got hold of a servant and made him bring us some of the treacly Turkish coffee. We were both in pretty low spirits. "Europe is a poor cold place," said Peter, "not worth fighting for. There is only one white man's land, and that is South Africa." At the time I heartily agreed with him.

I remember that, sitting on the edge of my bed, I took stock of our position. It was not very cheering. We seemed to have been amassing enemies at a furious pace. First of all there was Rasta, whom I had insulted and who wouldn't forget it in a hurry. He had his crowd of Turkish riff-raff and was bound to get us sooner or later. Then there was the maniac in the skin hat. He didn't like Rasta, and I made a guess that he and his weird friends were of some party hostile to the Young Turks. But, on the other hand, he didn't like us, and there would be bad trouble the next time we met him. Finally, there was Stumm and the German Government. It could only be a matter of hours at the best before he got the Rustchuk authorities on our trail. It would be easy to trace us from Chataldja, and once they had us we were absolutely done. There was a big, black *dossier* against us, which by no conceivable piece of luck could be upset.

It was very clear to me that, unless we could find sanctuary and shed all our various pursuers during this day, we should be done in for good and all. But where on earth were we to find sanctuary? We had neither of us a word of the language, and there was no way I could see of taking on new characters. For that we wanted friends and help, and I could think of none anywhere. Somewhere, to be sure, there was Blenkiron, but how could we get in touch with him? As for Sandy, I had pretty well given him up. I always thought his enterprise the craziest of the lot and bound to fail. He was probably some-where in Asia Minor, and a month or two later would get to Constantinople and hear in some pot-house the yarn of the two wretched Dutchmen who had disappeared so soon from men's sight.

That rendezvous at Kuprasso's was no good. It would have been all right if we had got here unsuspected, and could have gone on quietly frequenting the place till Blenkiron picked us up. But to do that we wanted leisure and secrecy, and here we were with a pack of hounds at our heels. The place was horribly dangerous already. If we showed ourselves there we should be gathered in by Rasta, or by the German military police, or by the madman in the skin cap. It was a stark impossibility to hang about on the off-chance of meeting Blenkiron.

I reflected with some bitterness that this was the 17th day of January, the day of our assignation. I had had high hopes all the way down the Danube of meeting with Blenkiron—for I knew *he* would be in time—of giving him the information I had had the good fortune to collect, of piecing it together with what he had found out, and of getting the whole story which Sir Walter hungered for. After that, I thought it wouldn't be hard to get away by Rumania, and to get home through Russia. I had hoped to be back with my battalion in February, having done as good a bit of work as anybody in the war. As it was, it looked as if my information would die with me, unless I could find Blenkiron before the evening.

I talked the thing over with Peter, and he agreed that we were fairly up against it. We decided to go to Kuprasso's that afternoon, and to trust to luck for the rest. It wouldn't do to wander about the streets, so we sat tight in our room all morning, and swopped old hunting yarns to keep our minds from the beastly present. We got some food at midday—cold mutton and the same cheese, and finished our whisky. Then I paid the bill, for I didn't care to stay there another night. About half-past three we went into the street, without the foggiest notion where we would find our next quarters.

It was snowing heavily, which was a piece of luck for us. Poor old Peter had no greatcoat, so we went into a Jew's shop and bought a ready-made abomination, which looked as if it might have been meant for a parson. It was no good saving my money when the future was so black. The snow made the streets deserted, and we turned down the long lane which led to Ratchik ferry and found it perfectly quiet. I do not think we met a soul till we got to Kuprasso's shop.

We walked straight through the café, which was empty, and down the dark passage, till we were stopped by the garden door. I knocked and it swung open. There was the bleak yard, now puddled with snow, and a blaze of light from the pavilion at the other end. There was a scraping of fiddles, too, and the sound of human talk. We paid the negro at the door, and passed from the bitter afternoon into a garish saloon.

There were forty or fifty people there, drinking coffee and sirops and filling the air with the fumes of latakia. Most of them were Turks in European clothes and the fez, but there were some German officers and what looked like German civilians—Army Service Corps clerks probably, and mechanics from the Arsenal. A woman in cheap finery was tinkling at the piano, and there were several shrill females with the officers. Peter and I sat down modestly in the nearest corner, where old Kuprasso saw us and sent us coffee. A girl who looked like a Jewess came over to us and talked French, but I shook my head and she went off again.

Presently a girl came on the stage and danced, a silly affair, all a clashing

of tambourines and wriggling. I have seen native women do the same thing
better in a Mozambique kraal. Another sang a German song, a simple,
sentimental thing about golden hair and rainbows, and the Germans present
applauded. The place was so tinselly and common that, coming to it from
weeks of rough travelling, it made me impatient. I forgot that, while for the
others it might be a vulgar little dancing-hall, for us it was as perilous as a
brigands' den.

Peter did not share my mood. He was quite interested in it, as he was
interested in everything new. He had a genius for living in the moment.

I remember there was a drop-scene on which was daubed a blue lake with
very green hills in the distance. As the tobacco smoke grew thicker and the
fiddles went on squealing, this tawdry picture began to mesmerize me. I
seemed to be looking out of a window at a lovely summer landscape where
there were no wars or dangers. I seemed to feel the warm sun and to smell the
fragrance of blossom from the islands. And then I became aware that a queer
scent had stolen into the atmosphere.

There were braziers burning at both ends to warm the room, and the thin
smoke from these smelt like incense. Somebody had been putting a powder
in the flames, for suddenly the place became very quiet. The fiddles still
sounded, but far away like an echo. The lights went down, all but a circle on
the stage, and into that circle stepped my enemy of the skin cap.

He had three others with him. I heard a whisper behind me, and the words
were those which Kuprasso had used the day before. These bedlamites were
called the Companions of the Rosy Hours, and Kuprasso had promised great
dancing.

I hoped to goodness they would not see us, for they had fairly given me the
horrors. Peter felt the same, and we both made ourselves very small in that
dark corner. But the newcomers had no eyes for us.

In a twinkling the pavilion changed from a common saloon, which might
have been in Chicago or Paris, to a place of mystery—yes, and of beauty. It
became the Garden-House of Suliman the Red, whoever that sportsman may
have been. Sandy had said that the ends of the earth converged there, and he
had been right. I lost all consciousness of my neighbours—stout German,
frock-coated Turk, frowsy Jewess—and saw only strange figures leaping in a
circle of light, figures that came out of the deepest darkness to make big magic.

The leader flung some stuff into the brazier and a great fan of blue light
flared up. He was weaving circles, and he was singing something shrill and
high, whilst his companions made a chorus with their deep monotone. I can't
tell you what the dance was. I had seen the Russian ballet just before the war,
and one of the men in it reminded me of this man. But the dancing was the
least part of it. It was neither sound nor movement nor scent that wrought the
spell, but something far more potent. In an instant I found myself reft away
from the present with its dull dangers, and looking at a world all young and
fresh and beautiful. The gaudy drop-scene had vanished. It was a window I
was looking from, and I was gazing at the finest landscape on earth, lit by the
pure clean light of morning.

It seemed to be part of the veld, but like no veld I had ever seen. It was wider and wilder and more gracious. Indeed, I was looking at my first youth. I was feeling the kind of immortal light-heartedness which only a boy knows in the dawning of his days. I had no longer any fear of these magic-makers. They were kindly wizards, who had brought me into fairyland.

Then slowly from the silence there distilled drops of music. They came like water falling a long way into a cup, each the essential quality of pure sound. We, with our elaborate harmonies, have forgotten the charm of single notes. The African natives know it, and I remember a learned man once telling me that the Greeks had the same art. Those silver bells broke out of infinite space, so exquisite and perfect that no mortal words could have been fitted to them. That was the music, I expect, that the morning stars made when they sang together.

Slowly, very slowly, it changed. The glow passed from blue to purple, and then to an angry red. Bit by bit the notes spun together till they had made a harmony—a fierce, restless harmony. And I was conscious again of the skin-clad dancers beckoning out of their circle.

There was no mistake about the meaning now. All the daintiness and youth had fled, and passion was beating in the air—terrible, savage passion, which belonged neither to day nor night, life nor death, but to the half-world between them. I suddenly felt the dancers as monstrous, inhuman, devilish. The thick scents that floated from the brazier seemed to have a tang of new-shed blood. Cries broke from the hearers—cries of anger and lust and terror. I heard a woman sob, and Peter, who is as tough as any mortal, took tight hold of my arm.

I now realized that these Companions of the Rosy Hours were the only thing in the world to fear. Rasta and Stumm seemed simpletons by contrast. The window I had been looking out of was changed to a prison wall—I could see the mortar between the massive blocks. In a second these devils would be smelling out their enemies like some foul witch-doctors. I felt the burning eyes of their leader looking for me in the gloom. Peter was praying audibly beside me, and I could have choked him. His infernal chatter would reveal us, for it seemed to me that there was no one in the place except us and the magic-workers.

Then suddenly the spell was broken. The door was flung open and a great gust of icy wind swirled through the hall, driving clouds of ashes from the braziers. I heard loud voices without, and a hubbub began inside. For a moment it was quite dark, and then some one lit one of the flare lamps by the stage. It revealed nothing but the common squalor of a low saloon—white faces, sleepy eyes, and frowsy heads. The drop-scene was there in all its tawdriness.

The Companions of the Rosy Hours had gone. But at the door stood men in uniform. I heard a German a long way off murmur, "Enver's body-guards," and I heard him distinctly; for, though I could not see clearly, my hearing was desperately acute. That is often the way when you suddenly come out of a swoon.

The place emptied like magic. Turk and German tumbled over each other, while Kuprasso wailed and wept. No one seemed to stop them, and then I saw the reason. Those guards had come for us. This must be Stumm at last. The authorities had tracked us down, and it was all up with Peter and me.

A sudden revulsion leaves a man with low vitality. I didn't seem to care greatly. We were done, and there was an end of it. It was Kismet, the act of God, and there was nothing for it but to submit. I hadn't a flicker of a thought of escape or resistance. The game was utterly and absolutely over.

A man who seemed to be a sergeant pointed to us and said something to Kuprasso, who nodded. We got heavily to our feet and stumbled towards them. With one on each side of us we crossed the yard, walked through the dark passage and the empty shop, and out into the snowy street. There was a closed carriage waiting which they motioned us to get into. It looked exactly like the Black Maria.

Both of us sat still, like truant schoolboys, with our hands on our knees. I didn't know where I was going and I didn't care. We seemed to be rumbling up the hill, and then I caught the glare of lighted streets.

"This is the end of it, Peter," I said.

"*Ja*, Cornelis," he replied, and that was all our talk.

By and by—hours later it seemed—we stopped. Some one opened the door and we got out, to find a courtyard with a huge dark building around. The prison, I guessed, and I wondered if they would give us blankets, for it was perishing cold.

We entered a door, and found ourselves in a big stone hall. It was quite warm, which made me more hopeful about our cells. A man in some kind of uniform pointed to the staircase, up which we plodded wearily. My mind was too blank to take clear impressions, or in any way to forecast the future. Another warder met us and took us down a passage till we halted at a door. He stood aside and motioned us to enter.

I guessed that this was the governor's room, and we should be put through our first examination. My head was too stupid to think, and I made up my mind to keep perfectly mum. Yes, even if they tried thumbscrews. I had no kind of a story, but I resolved not to give anything away. As I turned the handle I wondered idly what kind of sallow Turk or bulging-necked German we should find inside.

It was a pleasant room, with a polished wood floor and a big fire burning on the hearth. Beside the fire a man lay on a couch, with a little table drawn up beside him. On that table was a small glass of milk and a number of Patience cards spread in rows.

I stared blankly at the spectacle, till I saw a second figure. It was the man in the skin cap, the leader of the dancing maniacs. Both Peter and I backed sharply at the sight and then stood stock still.

For the dancer crossed the room in two strides and gripped both of my hands.

"Dick, old man," he cried, "I'm most awfully glad to see you again!"

22 FOUR MISSIONARIES SEE LIGHT
IN THEIR MISSION

A spasm of incredulity, a vast relief, and that sharp joy which comes of reaction chased each other across my mind. I had come suddenly out of very black waters into an unbelievable calm. I dropped into the nearest chair and tried to grapple with something far beyond words.

"Sandy," I said, as soon as I got my breath, "you're an incarnate devil. You've given Peter and me the fright of our lives."

"It was the only way, Dick. If I hadn't come mewing like a tom-cat at your heels yesterday, Rasta would have had you long before you got to your hotel. You two have given me a pretty anxious time, and it took some doing to get you safe here. However, that is all over now. Make yourselves at home, my children."

"Over!" I cried incredulously, for my wits were still wool-gathering. "What place is this?"

"You may call it my humble home"—it was Blenkiron's sleek voice that spoke. "We've been preparing for you, Major, but it was only yesterday I heard of your friend."

I introduced Peter.

"Mr. Pienaar," said Blenkiron, "pleased to meet you. Well, as I was observing, you're safe enough here, but you've cut it mighty fine. Officially, a Dutchman called Brandt was to be arrested this afternoon and handed over to the German authorities. When Germany begins to trouble about that Dutchman she will find difficulty in getting the body; but such are the languid ways of an Oriental despotism. Meantime the Dutchman will be no more. He will have ceased upon the midnight without pain, as your poet sings."

"But I don't understand," I stammered. "Who arrested us?"

"My men," said Sandy. "We have a bit of a graft here, and it wasn't difficult to manage it. Old Moellendorff will be nosing after the business to-morrow, but he will find the mystery too deep for him. That is the advantage of a Government run by a pack of adventurers. But, by Jove, Dick, we hadn't any time to spare. If Rasta had got you, or the Germans had had the job of lifting you, your goose would have been jolly well cooked. I had some unquiet hours this morning."

The thing was too deep for me. I looked at Blenkiron, shuffling his Patience cards with his old sleepy smile, and Sandy, dressed like some bandit in melodrama, his lean face as brown as a nut, his bare arms all tattooed with crimson rings, and the fox pelt drawn tight over brow and ears. It was still a nightmare world, but the dream was getting pleasanter. Peter said not a word, but I could see his eyes heavy with his own thoughts.

Blenkiron hove himself from the sofa and waddled to a cupboard.

"You boys must be hungry," he said. "My duo-denum has been giving me hell as usual, and I don't eat no more than a squirrel. But I laid in some stores, for I guessed you would want to stoke up some after your travels."

He brought out a couple of Strassburg pies, a cheese, a cold chicken, a loaf, and three bottles of champagne.

"Fizz," said Sandy rapturously. "And a dry Heidsieck too! We're in luck, Dick, old man."

I never ate a more welcome meal, for we had starved in that dirty hotel. But I had still the old feeling of the hunted, and before I began I asked about the door.

"That's all right," said Sandy. "My fellows are on the stair and at the gate. If the *Metreb* are in possession, you may bet that other people will keep off. Your past is blotted out, clean vanished away, and you begin to-morrow morning with a new sheet. Blenkiron's the man you've got to thank for that. He was pretty certain you'd get here, but he was also certain that you'd arrive in a hurry with a good many inquiries behind you. So he arranged that you should leak away and start fresh."

"Your name is Richard Hanau," Blenkiron said, "born in Cleveland, Ohio, of German parentage on both sides. One of our brightest mining engineers, and the apple of Guggenheim's eye. You arrived this afternoon from Constanza, and I met you at the packet. The clothes for the part are in your bedroom next door. But I guess all that can wait, for I'm anxious to get to business. We're not here on a joy-ride, Major, so I reckon we'll leave out the dime-novel adventures. I'm just dying to hear them, but they'll keep. I want to know how our mootual inquiries have prospered."

He gave Peter and me cigars, and we sat ourselves in arm-chairs in front of the blaze. Sandy squatted cross-legged on the hearthrug and lit a foul old briar pipe, which he extricated from some pouch among his skins. And so began that conversation which had never been out of my thoughts for four hectic weeks.

"If I presume to begin," said Blenkiron, "it's because I reckon my story is the shortest. I have to confess to you, gentlemen, that I have failed."

He drew down the corners of his mouth till he looked a cross between a music-hall comedian and a sick child.

"If you were looking for something in the root of the hedge, you wouldn't want to scour the road in a high-speed automobile. And still less would you want to get a bird's-eye view in an aeroplane. That parable about fits my case. I have been in the clouds and I've been scorching on the pikes, but what I was wanting was in the ditch all the time, and I naturally missed it. . . . I had the wrong stunt, Major. I was too high up and refined. I've been processing through Europe like Barnum's Circus, and living with generals and trans-parencies. Not that I haven't picked up a lot of noos, and got some very interesting sidelights on high politics. But the thing I was after wasn't to be found on my beat, for those that knew it weren't going to tell. In that kind of society they don't get drunk and blab after their tenth cocktail. So I guess I've no contribution to make to quieting Sir Walter Bullivant's mind, except that he's dead right. Yes, sir, he has hit the spot and rung the bell. There is a mighty miracle-working proposition being floated in these parts, but the promoters are keeping it to themselves. They aren't taking in more than they can help on the ground floor."

Blenkiron stopped to light a fresh cigar. He was leaner than when he left London and there were pouches below his eyes. I fancy his journey had not been as fur-lined as he made out.

"I've found out one thing, and that is, that the last dream Germany will part with is the control of the Near East. That is what your statesmen don't figure enough on. She'll give up Belgium and Alsace-Lorraine and Poland, but by God! she'll never give up the road to Mesopotamia till you have her by the throat and make her drop it. Sir Walter is a pretty bright-eyed citizen, and he sees it right enough. If the worst happens, Kaiser will fling overboard a lot of ballast in Europe, and it will look like a big victory for the Allies, but he won't be beaten if he has the road to the East safe. Germany's like a scorpion: her sting's in her tail, and that tail stretches way down into Asia.

"I got that clear, and I also made out that it wasn't going to be dead easy for her to keep that tail healthy. Turkey's a bit of an anxiety, as you'll soon discover. But Germany thinks she can manage it, and I won't say she can't. It depends on the hand she holds, and she reckons it a good one. I tried to find out, but they gave me nothing but eyewash. I had to pretend to be satisfied, for the position of John S. wasn't so strong as to allow him to take liberties. If I asked one of the highbrows, he looked wise and spoke of the might of German arms and German organization and German staff-work. I used to nod my head and get enthusiastic about these stunts, but it was all soft soap. She has a trick in hand—that much I know, but I'm darned if I can put a name to it. I pray to God you boys have been cleverer."

His tone was quite melancholy, and I was mean enough to feel rather glad. He had been the professional with the best chance. It would be a good joke if the amateur succeeded where the expert failed.

I looked at Sandy. He filled his pipe again, and pushed back his skin cap from his brows. What with his long dishevelled hair, his high-boned face, and stained eyebrows he had the appearance of some mad mullah.

"I went straight to Smyrna," he said. "It wasn't difficult, for you see I had laid down a good many lines in former travels. I reached the town as a Greek money-lender from the Fayum, but I had friends there I could count on, and the same evening I was a Turkish gipsy, a member of the most famous fraternity in Western Asia. I had long been a member, and I'm blood-brother of the chief boss, so I stepped into the part ready made. But I found out that the Company of the Rosy Hours was not what I had known it in 1910. Then it had been all for the Young Turks and reform; now it hankered after the old régime and was the last hope of the Orthodox. It had no use for Enver and his friends, and it did not regard with pleasure the *beaux yeux* of the Teuton. It stood for Islam and the old ways, and might be described as a Conservative-Nationalist caucus. But it was uncommon powerful in the provinces, and Enver and Talaat daren't meddle with it. The dangerous thing about it was that it said nothing and apparently did nothing. It just bided its time and took notes.

"You can imagine that this was the very kind of crowd for my purpose. I knew of old its little ways, for with all its orthodoxy it dabbled a good deal in magic, and owed half its power to its atmosphere of the uncanny. The Companions could dance the heart out of the ordinary Turk. You saw a bit of one of our dances this afternoon, Dick—pretty good, wasn't it? They could go anywhere, and no questions asked. They knew what the ordinary man was thinking, for they were the best intelligence department in the Ottoman Empire—far better than Enver's *Khafiyeh*. And they were popular, too, for they had never bowed the knee to the *Nemseh*—the Germans who are squeezing out the life-blood of the Osmanli for their own ends. It would have been as much as the life of the Committee or its German masters was worth to lay a hand on us, for we clung together like leeches and we were not in the habit of sticking at trifles.

"Well, you may imagine it wasn't difficult for me to move where I wanted. My dress and the password franked me anywhere. I travelled from Smyrna by the new railway to Panderma on the Marmora, and got there just before Christmas. That was after Anzac and Suvla had been evacuated, but I could hear the guns going hard at Cape Helles. From Panderma I started to cross to Thrace in a coasting steamer. And there an uncommon funny thing happened—I got torpedoed.

"It must have been about the last effort of a British submarine in those waters. But she got us all right. She gave us ten minutes to take to the boats, and then sent the blighted old packet and a fine cargo of 6-inch shells to the bottom. There weren't many passengers, so it was easy enough to get ashore in the ship's boats. The submarine sat on the surface watching us, as we wailed and howled in the true Oriental way, and I saw the captain quite close in the conning-tower. Who do you think it was? Tommy Elliot, who lives on the other side of the hill from me at home.

"I gave Tommy the surprise of his life. As we bumped past him, I started the 'Flowers of the Forest'—the old version—on the antique stringed instrument I carried, and I sang the words very plain. Tommy's eyes bulged out of his head, and he shouted at me in English to know who the devil I was. I replied in the broadest Scots, which no man in the submarine or in our boat could have understood a word of. 'Maister Tammy,' I cried, 'what for wad ye skail a dacent tinkler lad intil a cauld sea? I'll gie ye your kail through the reek for this ploy the next time I forgaither wi' ye on the tap o' Caerdon.'

"Tommy spotted me in a second. He laughed till he cried, and as we moved off shouted to me in the same language to 'pit a stoot hert tae a stey brae.' I hope to Heaven he had the sense not to tell my father, or the old man will have had a fit. He never much approved of my wanderings, and thought I was safely anchored in the battalion.

"Well, to make a long story short, I got to Constantinople, and pretty soon found touch with Blenkiron. The rest you know. . . . And now for business. I have been fairly lucky—but no more, for I haven't got to the bottom of the thing nor anything like it. But I've solved the first of Harry Bullivant's riddles. I know the meaning of *Kasredin*.

"Sir Walter was right, as Blenkiron has told us. There's a great stirring in Islam, something moving on the face of the waters. They make no secret of it. Those religious revivals come in cycles, and one was due about now. And they are quite clear about the details. A seer has arisen of the blood of the Prophet, who will restore the Khalifate to its old glories and Islam to its old purity. His sayings are everywhere in the Moslem world. All the orthodox believers have them by heart. That is why they are enduring grinding poverty and preposterous taxation and that is why their young men are rolling up to the armies and dying without complaint in Gallipoli and Transcaucasia. They believe they are on the eve of a great deliverance.

"Now the first thing I found out was that the Young Turks had nothing to do with this. They are unpopular and unorthodox and no true Turks. But Germany has. How, I don't know, but I could see quite plainly that in some subtle way Germany was regarded as a collaborator in the movement. It is that belief that is keeping the present régime going. The ordinary Turk loathes the Committee, but he has some queer perverted expectation from Germany. It is not a case of Enver and the rest carrying on their shoulders the unpopular Teuton; it is a case of the Teuton carrying the unpopular Committee. And Germany's graft is just this and nothing more—that she has some hand in the coming of the new deliverer.

"They talk about the thing quite openly. It is called the *Kaába-i-hurriyeh*, the Palladium of Liberty. The prophet himself is known as Zimrud—'the Emerald'—and his four ministers are called also after jewels—Sapphire, Ruby, Pearl, and Topaz. You will hear their names as often in the talk of the towns and villages as you will hear the names of generals in England. But no one knew where Zimrud was or when he would reveal himself, though every week came his messages to the faithful. All that I could learn was that he and his followers were coming from the West.

"You will say, what about *Kasredin*? That puzzled me dreadfully, for no one used the phrase. The Home of the Spirit! It is an obvious cliché, as in England some new sect might call itself the Church of Christ. Only no one seemed to use it.

"But by and by I discovered that there was an inner and an outer circle in this mystery. Every creed has an esoteric side which is kept from the common herd. I struck this side in Constantinople. Now there is a very famous Turkish *shaka* called *Kasredin*, one of those old half-comic miracle-plays with an allegorical meaning which they call *orta oyun*, and which take a week to read. That tale tells of the coming of a prophet, and I found that the select of the faith spoke of the new revelation in terms of it. The curious thing is that in that tale the prophet is aided by one of the few women who play much part in the hagiology of Islam. That is the point of the tale, and it is partly a jest, but mainly a religious mystery. The prophet, too, is not called Emerald."

"I know," I said; "he is called Greenmantle."

Sandy scrambled to his feet, letting his pipe drop in the fireplace.

"Now how on earth did you find out that?" he cried.

Then I told them of Stumm and Gaudian and the whispered words I had not been meant to hear. Blenkiron was giving me the benefit of a steady stare, unusual from one who seemed always to have his eyes abstracted, and Sandy had taken to ranging up and down the room.

"Germany's in the heart of the plan. That is what I always thought. If we're to find the Kaába-i-hurriyeh it is no good fossicking among the Committee or in the Turkish provinces. The secret's in Germany. Dick, you should not have crossed the Danube."

"That's what I half feared," I said. "But, on the other hand, it is obvious that the thing must come east, and sooner rather than later. I take it they can't afford to delay too long before they deliver the goods. If we can stick it out here we must hit the trail. . . . I've got another bit of evidence. I have solved Harry Bullivant's third puzzle."

Sandy's eyes were very bright and I had an audience on wires.

"Did you say that in the tale of *Kasredin* a woman is the ally of the prophet?"

"Yes," said Sandy; "what of that?"

"Only that the same thing is true of Greenmantle. I can give you her name."

I fetched a piece of paper and a pencil from Blenkiron's desk and handed it to Sandy.

"Write down Harry Bullivant's third word."

He promptly wrote down "*v.I.*"

Then I told them of the other name Stumm and Gaudian had spoken. I told of my discovery as I lay in the woodman's cottage.

"The '*I*' is not the letter of the alphabet, but the numeral. The name is von Einem—Hilda von Einem."

"Good old Harry," said Sandy softly. "He was a dashed clever chap. Hilda von Einem! Who and where is she? for if we find her we have done the trick."

Then Blenkiron spoke. "I reckon I can put you wise on that, gentlemen," he said. "I saw her no later than yesterday. She is a lovely lady. She happens also to be the owner of this house."

Both Sandy and I began to laugh. It was too comic to have stumbled across Europe and lighted on the very headquarters of the puzzle we had set out to unriddle.

But Blenkiron did not laugh. At the mention of Hilda von Einem he had suddenly become very solemn, and the sight of his face pulled me up short.

"I don't like it, gentlemen," he said. "I would rather you had mentioned any other name on God's earth. I haven't been long in this city, but I have been long enough to size up the various political bosses. They haven't much to them. I reckon they wouldn't stand up against what we could show them in the U-nited States. But I have met the Frau von Einem, and that lady's a very different proposition. The man that will understand her has got to take a biggish size in hats."

"Who is she?" I asked.

"Why, that is just what I can't tell you. She was a great excavator of Babylonish and Hittite ruins, and she married a diplomat who went to glory three years back. It isn't what she has been, but what she is, and that's a mighty clever woman."

Blenkiron's respect did not depress me. I felt as if at last we had got our job narrowed to a decent compass, for I had hated casting about in the dark. I asked where she lived.

"That I don't know," said Blenkiron. "You won't find people unduly anxious to gratify your natural curiosity about Frau von Einem."

"I can find that out," said Sandy. "That's the advantage of having a push like mine. Meantime, I've got to clear, for my day's work isn't finished. Dick, you and Peter must go to bed at once."

"Why?" I asked in amazement. Sandy spoke like a medical adviser.

"Because I want your clothes—the things you've got on now. I'll take them off with me and you'll never see them again."

"You've a queer taste in souvenirs," I said.

"Say rather the Turkish police. The current in the Bosphorus is pretty strong, and these sad relics of two misguided Dutchmen will be washed up to-morrow about Seraglio Point. In this game you must drop the curtain neat and pat at the end of each scene, if you don't want trouble later with the missing heir and the family lawyer."

23   I MOVE IN GOOD SOCIETY

I walked out of that house next morning with Blenkiron's arm in mine, a different being from the friendless creature who had looked vainly the day before for sanctuary. To begin with, I was splendidly dressed. I had a navy-blue suit with square padded shoulders, a neat black bow-tie, shoes with a hump at the toe, and a brown bowler. Over that I wore a greatcoat lined with wolf fur. I had a smart malacca cane, and one of Blenkiron's cigars in my mouth. Peter had been made to trim his beard, and, dressed in unassuming pepper-and-salt, looked with his docile eyes and quiet voice a very respectable servant. Old Blenkiron had done the job in style, for, if you'll believe it, he had brought the clothes all the way from London. I realized now why he and Sandy had been fossicking in my wardrobe. Peter's suit had been of Sandy's procuring, and it was not the fit of mine. I had no difficulty about the accent. Any man brought up in the colonies can get his tongue round American, and I flattered myself I made a very fair shape at the lingo of the Middle West.

The wind had gone to the south and the snow was melting fast. There was a blue sky above Asia, and away to the north masses of white cloud drifting over the Black Sea. What had seemed the day before the dingiest of cities now took on a strange beauty, the beauty of unexpected horizons and tongues of grey water winding below cypress-studded shores. A man's temper has a lot to do with his appreciation of scenery. I felt a free man once more, and could use my eyes.

That street was a jumble of every nationality on earth. There were Turkish regulars in their queer conical khaki helmets, and wild-looking levies who had no kin with Europe. There were squads of Germans in flat forage caps, staring vacantly at novel sights, and quick to salute an officer on the side-walk. Turks in closed carriages passed, and Turks on good Arab horses, and Turks who looked as if they had come out of the Ark. But it was the rabble that caught the eye—a very wild, pinched, miserable rabble. I never in my life saw such swarms of beggars, and you walked down that street to the accompaniment of entreaties for alms in all the tongues of the Tower of Babel. Blenkiron and I behaved as if we were interested tourists. We would stop and laugh at one fellow and give a penny to a second, passing comments in high-pitched Western voices.

We went into a café and had a cup of coffee. A beggar came in and asked alms. Hitherto Blenkiron's purse had been closed, but now he took out some small nickels and planked five down on the table. The man cried down blessings and picked up three. Blenkiron very swiftly swept the other two into his pocket.

That seemed to me queer, and I remarked that I had never before seen a beggar who gave change. Blenkiron said nothing, and presently we moved on and came to the harbour side.

There were a number of small tugs moored alongside, and one or two bigger craft—fruit boats, I judged, which used to ply in the Ægean. They looked pretty well moth-eaten from disuse. We stopped at one of them and watched a fellow in a blue nightcap splicing ropes. He raised his eyes once and looked at us, and then kept on with his business.

Blenkiron asked him where he came from, but he shook his head, not understanding the tongue. A Turkish policeman came up and stared at us suspiciously, till Blenkiron opened his coat, as if by accident, and displayed a tiny square of ribbon, at which he saluted. Failing to make conversation with the sailor, Blenkiron flung him three of his black cigars. "I guess you can smoke, friend, if you can't talk," he said.

The man grinned and caught the three neatly in the air. Then to my amazement he tossed one of them back.

The donor regarded it quizzically as it lay on the pavement. "That boy's a connoisseur of tobacco," he said. As we moved away I saw the Turkish policeman pick it up and put it inside his cap.

We returned by the long street on the crest of the hill. There was a man selling oranges on a tray, and Blenkiron stopped to look at them. I noticed that the man shuffled fifteen into a cluster. Blenkiron felt the oranges, as if to see that they were sound, and pushed two aside. The man instantly restored them to the group, never raising his eyes.

"This ain't the time of year to buy fruit," said Blenkiron as we passed on. "Those oranges are rotten as medlars."

We were almost on our own doorstep before I guessed the meaning of the business.

"Is your morning's work finished?" I said.

"Our morning's walk?" he asked innocently.

"I said 'work.'"

He smiled blandly. "I reckoned you'd tumble to it. Why, yes, except that I've some figuring still to do. Give me half an hour and I'll be at your service, Major."

That afternoon, after Peter had cooked a wonderfully good luncheon, I had a heart-to-heart talk with Blenkiron.

"My business is to get noos," he said; "and before I start in on a stunt I make considerable preparations. All the time in London when I was yelping at the British Government, I was busy with Sir Walter arranging things ahead. We used to meet in queer places and at all hours of the night. I fixed up a lot of connections in this city before I arrived, and especially a noos service with your Foreign Office by way of Rumania and Russia. In a day or two I guess our friends will know all about our discoveries."

At that I opened my eyes very wide.

"Why, yes. You Britishers haven't any notion how wide-awake your Intelligence Service is. I reckon it's easy the best of all the belligerents. You never talked about it in peace time, and you shunned the theatrical ways of the Teuton. But you had the wires laid good and sure. I calculate there isn't much that happens in any corner of the earth that you don't know within twenty-four hours. I don't say your highbrows use the noos well. I don't take much stock in your political push. They're a lot of silver-tongues, no doubt, but it ain't oratory that is wanted in this racket. The William Jennings Bryan stunt languishes in war time. Politics is like a chicken-coop, and those inside get to behave as if their little run were all the world. But if the politicians make mistakes it isn't from lack of good instruction to guide their steps. If I had a big proposition to handle and could have my pick of helpers I'd plump for the Intelligence Department of the British Admiralty. Yes, sir, I take off my hat to your Government sleuths."

"Did they provide you with ready-made spies here?" I asked in astonishment.

"Why, no," he said. "But they gave me the key, and I could make my own arrangements. In Germany I buried myself deep in the local atmosphere and never peeped out. That was my game, for I was looking for something in Germany itself, and didn't want any foreign cross-bearings. As you know, I failed where you succeeded. But as soon as I crossed the Danube I set about opening up my lines of communication, and I hadn't been two days in this metropolis before I had got my telephone exchange buzzing. Some time I'll explain the thing to you, for it's a pretty little business. I've got the cutest cipher. . . . No, it ain't my invention. It's your Government's. Any one, babe, imbecile, or dotard, can carry my messages—you saw some of them to-day—but it takes some mind to set the piece, and it takes a lot of figuring at my end to work out the results. Some day you shall hear it all, for I guess it would please you."

"How do you use it?" I asked.

"Well, I get early noos of what is going on in this cabbage patch. Likewise I get authentic noos of the rest of Europe, and I can send a message to Mr. X. in Petrograd and Mr. Y. in London, or, if I wish, to Mr. Z. in Noo York. What's the matter with that for a post office? I'm the best-informed man in Constantinople, for old General Liman only hears one side, and mostly lies at that, and Enver prefers not to listen at all. Also, I could give them points on what is happening at their very door, for our friend Sandy is a big boss in the best-run crowd of mountebanks that ever fiddled secrets out of men's hearts. Without their help I wouldn't have cut much ice in this city."

"I want you to tell me one thing, Blenkiron," I said. "I've been playing a part for the past month, and it wears my nerves to tatters. Is this job very tiring, for if it is, I doubt I may buckle up."

He looked thoughtful. "I can't call our business an absolute rest-cure any time. You've got to keep your eyes skinned, and there's always the risk of the little packet of dynamite going off unexpected. But as these things go, I rate this stunt as easy. We've only got to be natural. We wear our natural clothes, and talk English, and sport a Theodore Roosevelt smile, and there isn't any call for theatrical talent. Where I've found the job tight was when I had got to be natural, and my naturalness was the same brand as that of everybody round about, and all the time I had to do unnatural things. It isn't easy to be going down town to business and taking cocktails with Mr. Carl Rosenheim, and next hour being engaged trying to blow Mr. Rosenheim's friends sky high. And it isn't easy to keep up a part which is clean outside your ordinary life. I've never tried that. My line has always been to keep my normal personality. But you have, Major, and I guess you found it wearing."

"Wearing's a mild word," I said. "But I want to know another thing. It seems to me that the line you've picked is as good as could be. But it's a cast-iron line. It commits us pretty deep and it won't be a simple job to drop it."

"Why, that's just the point I was coming to," he said. "I was going to put you wise about that very thing. When I started out I figured on some situation like this. I argued that unless I had a very clear part with a big bluff in it I wouldn't get the confidences which I needed. We've got to be at the heart of the show, taking a real hand and not just looking on. So I settled I would be a big engineer—there was a time when there weren't many bigger in the United States than John S. Blenkiron. I talked large about what might be done in Mesopotamia in the way of washing the British down the river. Well, that talk caught on. They knew of my reputation as an hydraulic expert, and they were tickled to death to rope me in. I told them I wanted a helper, and I told them about my friend Richard Hanau, as good a German as ever supped sauerkraut, who was coming through Russia and Rumania as a benevolent neutral; but when he got to Constantinople would drop his neutrality and double his benevolence. They got reports on you by wire from the States—I arranged that before I left London. So you're going to be welcomed and taken to their bosoms just like John S. was. We've both gotten jobs we can hold down, and now you're in these pretty clothes you're the dead ringer of the brightest kind of American engineer. . . . But we can't go back on our tracks. If we wanted to leave for Constanza next week they'd be very polite, but they'd never let us. We've got to go on with this adventure and nose our way down into Mesopotamia, hoping that our luck will hold. . . . God knows how we will get out of it; but it's no good going out to meet trouble. As I observed before, I believe in an all-wise and beneficent Providence, but you've got to give Him a chance."

I am bound to confess the prospect staggered me. We might be let in for fighting—and worse than fighting—against our own side. I wondered if it wouldn't be better to make a bolt for it, and said so.

He shook his head. "I reckon not. In the first place we haven't finished our inquiries. We've got Greenmantle located right enough, thanks to you, but we still know mighty little about that holy man. In the second place it won't be as bad as you think. This show lacks cohesion, sir. It is not going to last for ever. I calculate that before you and I strike the site of the garden that Adam and Eve frequented there will be a queer turn of affairs. Anyhow, it's good enough to gamble on."

Then he got some sheets of paper and drew me a plan of the dispositions of the Turkish forces. I had no notion he was such a close student of war, for his exposition was as good as a staff lecture. He made out that the situation was none too bright anywhere. The troops released from Gallipoli wanted a lot of refitment, and would be slow in reaching the Transcaucasian frontier, where the Russians were threatening. The Army of Syria was pretty nearly a rabble under the lunatic Djemal. There wasn't the foggiest chance of a serious invasion of Egypt being undertaken. Only in Mesopotamia did things look fairly cheerful, owing to the blunders of British strategy. "And you may take it from me," he said, "that if the old Turk mobilized a total of a million men, he has lost 40 per cent. of them already. And if I'm anything of a prophet he's going pretty soon to lose more."

He tore up the papers and enlarged on politics. "I reckon I've got the measure of the Young Turks and their precious Committee. Those boys aren't any good. Enver's bright enough, and for sure he's got sand. He'll stick out a fight like a Vermont game-chicken, but he lacks the larger vision, sir. He doesn't understand the intricacies of the job no more than a sucking child, so the Germans play with him, till his temper goes and he bucks like a mule. Talaat is a sulky dog who wants to batter mankind with a club. Both these boys would have made good cow-punchers in the old days, and they might have got a living out West as the gunmen of a Labour Union. They're about the class of Jesse James or Bill the Kid, excepting that Enver's college-reared and can patter languages. But they haven't the organizing power to manage the Irish vote in a ward election. Their one notion is to get busy with their firearms, and people are getting tired of the Black Hand stunt. Their hold on the country is just the hold that a man with a Browning has over a crowd with walking-sticks. The cooler heads in the Committee are growing shy of them, and an old fox like Djavid is lying low till his time comes. Now it doesn't want arguing that a gang of that kind has got to hang close together or they may hang separately. They've gotten no grip on the ordinary Turk, barring the fact that they are active and he is sleepy, and that they've got their guns loaded."

"What about the Germans here?" I asked.

Blenkiron laughed. "It is no sort of a happy family. But the Young Turks know that without the German boost they'll be strung up like Haman, and the Germans can't afford to neglect any ally. Consider what would happen if Turkey got sick of the game and made a separate peace. The road would be open for Russia to the Ægean. Ferdy of Bulgaria would take his depreciated goods to the other market, and not waste a day thinking about it. You'd have Rumania coming in on the Allies' side. Things would look pretty black for that control of the Near East on which Germany has banked her winnings. Kaiser says that's got to be prevented at all costs, but how is it going to be done?"

Blenkiron's face had become very solemn again. "It won't be done unless Germany's got a trump card to play. Her game's mighty near bust, but it's still got a chance. And that chance is a woman and an old man. I reckon our landlady has a bigger brain than Enver and Liman. She's the real boss of the show. When I came here I reported to her, and presently you've got to do the same. I am curious as to how she'll strike you, for I'm free to admit that she impressed me considerable."

"It looks as if our job were a long way from the end," I said.

"It's scarcely begun," said Blenkiron.

That talk did a lot to cheer my spirits, for I realized that it was the biggest of big game we were hunting this time. I'm an economical soul, and if I'm going to be hanged I want a good stake for my neck.

Then began some varied experiences. I used to wake up in the morning, wondering where I should be at night, and yet quite pleased at the uncertainty. Greenmantle became a sort of myth with me. Somehow I couldn't fix any idea in my head of what he was like. The nearest I got was a picture of an old man in a turban coming out of a bottle in a cloud of smoke, which I remembered from a child's edition of the *Arabian Nights*. But if he was dim, the lady was dimmer. Sometimes I thought of her as a fat old German crone, sometimes as a harsh-featured woman like a schoolmistress with thin lips and eyeglasses. But I had to fit the East into the picture, so I made her young and gave her a touch of the languid houri in a veil. I was always wanting to pump Blenkiron on the subject, but he shut up like a rat-trap. He was looking for bad trouble in that direction, and was disinclined to speak about it before-hand.

We led a peaceful existence. Our servants were two of Sandy's lot, for Blenkiron had very rightly cleared out the Turkish caretakers, and they worked like beavers under Peter's eye, till I reflected I had never been so well looked after in my life. I walked about the city with Blenkiron, keeping my eyes open, and speaking very civil. The third night we were bidden to dinner at Moellendorff's, so we put on our best clothes and set out in an ancient cab. Blenkiron had fetched a dress-suit of mine, from which my own tailor's label had been cut and a New York one substituted.

General Liman and Metternich the Ambassador had gone up the line to Nish to meet the Kaiser, who was touring in those parts, so Moellendorff was the biggest German in the city. He was a thin, foxy-faced fellow, cleverish but monstrously vain, and he was not very popular either with the Germans or the Turks. He was polite to both of us, but I am bound to say that I got a bad fright when I entered the room, for the first man I saw was Gaudian.

I doubt if he would have recognized me even in the clothes I had worn in Stumm's company, for his eyesight was wretched. As it was, I ran no risk in dress-clothes, with my hair brushed back and a fine American accent. I paid him high compliments as a fellow engineer, and translated part of a very technical conversation between him and Blenkiron. Gaudian was in uniform, and I liked the look of his honest face better than ever.

But the great event was the sight of Enver. He was a slim fellow of Rasta's build, very foppish and precise in his dress, with a smooth oval face like a girl's, and rather fine straight black eyebrows. He spoke perfect German, and had the best kind of manners, neither pert nor overbearing. He had a pleasant trick, too, of appealing all round the table for confirmation, and so bringing everybody into the talk. Not that he spoke a great deal, but all he said was good sense, and he had a smiling way of saying it. Once or twice he ran counter to Moellendorff, and I could see there was no love lost between these two. I didn't think I wanted him as a friend—he was too cold-blooded and artificial; and I was pretty certain that I didn't want those steady black eyes as an enemy. But it was no good denying his quality. The little fellow was all cold courage, like the fine polished blue steel of a sword.

I fancy I was rather a success at that dinner. For one thing I could speak German, and so had a pull on Blenkiron. For another I was in a good temper, and really enjoyed putting my back into my part. They talked very high-flown stuff about what they had done and were going to do, and Enver was great on Gallipoli. I remember he said that he could have destroyed the whole British Army if it hadn't been for somebody's cold feet—at which Moellendorff looked daggers. They were so bitter about Britain and all her works that I gathered they were getting pretty panicky, and that made me as jolly as a sandboy. I'm afraid I was not free from bitterness myself on that subject. I said things about my own country that I sometimes wake in the night and sweat to think of.

Gaudian got on to the use of water power in war, and that gave me a chance.

"In my country," I said, "when we want to get rid of a mountain we wash it away. There's nothing on earth that will stand against water. Now, speaking with all respect, gentlemen, and as an absolute novice in the military art, I sometimes ask why this God-given weapon isn't more used in the present war. I haven't been to any of the fronts, but I've studied them some from maps and the newspapers. Take your German position in Flanders, where you've got the high ground. If I were a British general I reckon I would very soon make it no sort of position."

Moellendorff asked, "How?"

"Why, I'd wash it away. Wash away the fourteen feet of soil down to the stone. There's a heap of coalpits behind the British front where they could generate power, and I judge there's an ample water supply from rivers and canals. I'd guarantee to wash you away in twenty-four hours—yes, in spite of all your big guns. It beats me why the British haven't got on to this notion. They used to have some bright engineers."

Enver was on to the point like a knife, far quicker than Gaudian. He cross-examined me in a way that showed he knew how to approach a technical subject, though he mightn't have much technical knowledge. He was just giving me a sketch of the flooding in Mesopotamia when an aide-de-camp brought in a chit which fetched him to his feet.

"I have gossiped long enough," he said. "My kind host, I must leave you. Gentlemen, all my apologies and farewells."

Before he left he asked my name and wrote it down. "This is an unhealthy city for strangers, Mr. Hanau," he said in very good English. "I have some small power of protecting a friend, and what I have is at your disposal." This with the condescension of a king promising his favour to a subject.

The little fellow amused me tremendously, and rather impressed me too. I said so to Gaudian after he had left, but that decent soul didn't agree.

"I do not love him," he said. "We are allies—yes; but friends—no. He is no true son of Islam, which is a noble faith and despises liars and boasters and betrayers of their salt."

That was the verdict of one honest man on this ruler in Israel. The next night I got another from Blenkiron on a greater than Enver.

He had been out alone and had come back pretty late, with his face grey and drawn with pain. The food we ate—not at all bad of its kind—and the cold east wind played havoc with his dyspepsia. I can see him yet, boiling milk on a spirit lamp, while Peter worked at a Primus stove to get him a hot-water bottle. He was using horrid language about his inside.

"My God, Major, if I were you with a sound stomach I'd fairly conquer the world. As it is, I've got to do my work with half my mind, while the other half is dwelling in my intestines. I'm like the child in the Bible that had a fox gnawing at its vitals."

He got his milk boiling and began to sip it.

"I've been to see our pretty landlady," he said. "She sent for me and I hobbled off with a grip full of plans, for she's mighty set on Mesopotamy."

"Anything about Greenmantle?" I asked eagerly.

"Why, no, but I have reached one conclusion. I opine that the hapless prophet has no sort of time with that lady. I opine that he will soon wish himself in Paradise. For if Almighty God ever created a female devil it's Madame von Einem."

He sipped a little more milk with a grave face.

"That isn't my duo-denal dyspepsia, Major. It's the verdict of a ripe experience, for I have a cool and penetrating judgment, even if I've a deranged stomach. And I give it as my considered conclusion that that woman's mad and bad—but principally bad."

24   THE LADY OF THE MANTILLA

Since that first night I had never clapped eyes on Sandy. He had gone clean out of the world, and Blenkiron and I waited anxiously for a word of news. Our own business was in good trim, for we were presently going east towards Mesopotamia, but unless we learned more about Greenmantle our journey would be a grotesque failure. And learn about Greenmantle we could not, for nobody by word or deed suggested his existence, and it was impossible of course for us to ask questions. Our only hope was Sandy, for what we wanted to know was the prophet's whereabouts and his plans. I suggested to Blenkiron that we might do more to cultivate Frau von Einem, but he shut his jaw like a trap. "There's nothing doing for us in that quarter," he said. "That's the most dangerous woman on earth; and if she got any kind of notion that we were wise about her pet schemes I reckon you and I would very soon be in the Bosphorus."

This was all very well; but what was going to happen if the two of us were bundled off to Bagdad with instructions to wash away the British? Our time was getting pretty short, and I doubted if we could spin out more than three days more in Constantinople. I felt just as I had felt with Stumm the last night when I was about to be packed off to Cairo and saw no way of avoiding it. Even Blenkiron was getting anxious. He played Patience incessantly, and was disinclined to talk. I tried to find out something from the servants, but they either knew nothing or wouldn't speak—the former, I think. I kept my eyes lifting, too, as I walked about the streets, but there was no sign anywhere of the skin coats or the weird stringed instruments. The whole Company of the Rosy Hours seemed to have melted into the air, and I began to wonder if they had ever existed.

Anxiety made me restless, and restlessness made me want exercise. It was no good walking about the city. The weather had become foul again, and I was sick of the smells and the squalor and the flea-bitten crowds. So Blenkiron and I got horses, Turkish cavalry mounts with heads like trees, and went out through the suburbs into the open country.

It was a grey drizzling afternoon, with the beginnings of a sea fog which hid the Asiatic shore of the straits. It wasn't easy to find open ground for a gallop, for there were endless small patches of cultivation and the gardens of country houses. We kept on the high land above the sea, and when we reached a bit of downland came on squads of Turkish soldiers digging trenches. Whenever we let the horses go we had to pull up sharp for a digging party or a stretch of barbed wire. Coils of the beastly thing were lying loose everywhere, and Blenkiron nearly took a nasty toss over one. Then we were always being stopped by sentries and having to show our passes. Still the ride did us good and shook up our livers, and by the time we turned for home I was feeling more like a white man.

We jogged back in the short winter twilight, past the wooded grounds of white villas, held up every few minutes by transport-wagons and companies of soldiers. The rain had come on in real earnest, and it was two very bedraggled horsemen that crawled along the muddy lanes. As we passed one villa, shut in by a high white wall, a pleasant smell of wood-smoke was wafted towards us, which made me sick for the veld. My ear, too, caught the twanging of a zither, which somehow reminded me of the afternoon in Kuprasso's garden-house.

I pulled up and proposed to investigate, but Blenkiron very testily declined.

"Zithers are as common here as fleas," he said. "You don't want to be fossicking around somebody's stables and find a horse-boy entertaining his friends. They don't like visitors in this country; and you'll be asking for trouble if you go inside those walls. I guess it's some old Buzzard's harem." Buzzard was his own private peculiar name for the Turk, for he said he had had as a boy a natural-history book with a picture of a bird called the turkey-buzzard, and couldn't get out of the habit of applying it to the Ottoman people.

I wasn't convinced, so I tried to mark down the place. It seemed to be about three miles out from the city, at the end of a steep lane on the inland side of the hill coming from the Bosphorus. I fancied somebody of distinction lived there, for a little farther on we met a big empty motor-car snorting its way up, and I had a notion that the car belonged to the walled villa.

Next day Blenkiron was in grievous trouble with his dyspepsia. About midday he was compelled to lie down, and having nothing better to do I had out the horses again and took Peter with me. It was funny to see Peter in a Turkish army saddle, riding with the long Boer stirrup and the slouch of the back-veld.

That afternoon was unfortunate from the start. It was not the mist and drizzle of the day before, but a stiff northern gale which blew sheets of rain in our faces and numbed our bridle hands. We took the same road, but pushed

west of the trench-digging parties and got to a shallow valley with a white
village among cypresses. Beyond that there was a very respectable road which
brought us to the top of a crest that in clear weather must have given a fine
prospect. Then we turned our horses, and I shaped our course so as to strike
the top of the long lane that abutted on the town. I wanted to investigate the
white villa.

But we hadn't gone far on our road back before we got into trouble. It
arose out of a sheep-dog, a yellow mongrel brute that came at us like a
thunderbolt. It took a special fancy to Peter, and bit savagely at his horse's
heels and sent it capering off the road. I should have warned him, but I did
not realize what was happening till too late. For Peter, being accustomed to
mongrels in Kaffir kraals, took a summary way with the pest. Since it
despised his whip, he out with his pistol and put a bullet through its head.

The echoes of the shot had scarcely died away when the row began. A big
fellow appeared running towards us, shouting wildly. I guessed he was the
dog's owner, and proposed to pay no attention. But his cries summoned two
other fellows—soldiers by the look of them—who closed in on us, unslinging
their rifles as they ran. My first idea was to show them our heels, but I had no
desire to be shot in the back, and they looked like men who wouldn't stop
short of shooting. So we slowed down and faced them.

They made as savage-looking a trio as you would want to avoid. The
shepherd looked as if he had been dug up, a dirty ruffian with matted hair
and a beard like a bird's nest. The two soldiers stood staring with sullen
faces, fingering their guns, while the other chap raved and stormed and kept
pointing at Peter, whose mild eyes stared unwinkingly at his assailant.

The mischief was that neither of us had a word of Turkish. I tried German,
but it had no effect. We sat looking at them, and they stood storming at us,
and it was fast getting dark. Once I turned my horse round as if to proceed,
and the two soldiers jumped in front of me.

They jabbered among themselves, and then one said very slowly: "He . . .
want . . . pounds," and he held up five fingers. They evidently saw by the cut
of our jib that we weren't Germans.

"I'll be hanged if he gets a penny," I said angrily, and the conversation
languished.

The situation was getting serious, so I spoke a word to Peter. The soldiers
had their rifles loose in their hands, and before they could lift them we had
the pair covered with our pistols.

"If you move," I said, "you are dead." They understood that all right and
stood stock still, while the shepherd stopped his raving and took to muttering
like a gramophone when the record is finished.

"Drop your guns," I said sharply. "Quick, or we shoot."

The tone, if not the words, conveyed my meaning. Still staring at us, they
let the rifles slide to the ground. The next second we had forced our horses on
the top of them, and the three were off like rabbits. I sent a shot over their
heads to encourage them. Peter dismounted and tossed the guns into a bit of
scrub where they would take some finding.

This hold-up had wasted time. By now it was getting very dark, and we hadn't ridden a mile before it was black night. It was an annoying predicament, for I had completely lost my bearings and at the best had only a foggy notion of the lie of the land. The wisest plan seemed to be to try and get to the top of a rise in the hope of seeing the lights of the city, but all the countryside was so pockety that it was hard to strike the right kind of rise.

We had to trust to Peter's instinct. I asked him where our line lay, and he sat very still for a minute sniffing the air. Then he pointed the direction. It wasn't what I would have taken myself, but on a point like that he was pretty near infallible.

Presently we came to a long slope which cheered me. But at the top there was no light visible anywhere—only a black void like the inside of a shell. As I stared into the gloom it seemed to me that there were patches of deeper darkness that might be woods.

"There is a house half-left in front of us," said Peter.

I peered till my eyes ached and saw nothing.

"Well, for Heaven's sake, guide me to it," I said, and with Peter in front we set off down the hill.

It was a wild journey, for darkness clung as close to us as a vest. Twice we stepped into patches of bog, and once my horse saved himself by a hair from going head forward into a gravel pit. We got tangled up in strands of wire, and often found ourselves rubbing our noses against tree trunks. Several times I had to get down and make a gap in barricades of loose stones. But after a ridiculous amount of slipping and stumbling we finally struck what seemed the level of a road, and a piece of special darkness in front which turned out to be a high wall.

I argued that all mortal walls had doors, so we set to groping along it, and presently found a gap. There was an old iron gate on broken hinges, which we easily pushed open, and found ourselves on a back path to some house. It was clearly disused, for masses of rotting leaves covered it, and by the feel of it underfoot it was grass-grown.

We were dismounted now, leading our horses, and after about fifty yards the path ceased and came out on a well-made carriage drive. So, at least, we guessed, for the place was as black as pitch. Evidently the house couldn't be far off, but in which direction I hadn't a notion.

Now I didn't want to be paying calls on any Turk at that time of day. Our job was to find where the road opened into the lane, for after that our way to Constantinople was clear. One side the lane lay, and the other the house, and it didn't seem wise to take the risk of tramping up with horses to the front door. So I told Peter to wait for me at the end of the back-road, while I would prospect a bit. I turned to the right, my intention being if I saw the light of a house to return, and with Peter take the other direction.

I walked like a blind man in that nether pit of darkness. The road seemed well kept, and the soft wet gravel muffled the sounds of my feet. Great trees overhung it, and several times I wandered into dripping bushes. And then I stopped short in my tracks, for I heard the sound of whistling.

It was quite close, about ten yards away. And the strange thing was that it was a tune I knew, about the last tune you would expect to hear in this part of the world. It was the Scots air: "Ca' the yowes to the knowes," which was a favourite of my father's.

The whistler must have felt my presence, for the air suddenly stopped in the middle of a bar. An unbounded curiosity seized me to know who the fellow could be. So I started in and finished his tune myself.

There was silence for a second, and then the unknown began again and stopped. Once more I chipped in and finished it.

Then it seemed to me that he was coming nearer. The air in that dank tunnel was very still, and I thought I heard a light foot. I think I took a step backward. Suddenly there was a flash of an electric torch from a yard off, so quick that I could see nothing of the man who held it.

Then a low voice spoke out of the darkness—a voice I knew well—and, following it, a hand was laid on my arm. "What the devil are you doing here, Dick?" it said, and there was something like consternation in the tone.

I told him in a hectic sentence, for I was beginning to feel badly rattled myself.

"You've never been in greater danger in your life," said the voice. "Great God, man, what brought you wandering here to-day of all days?"

You can imagine that I was pretty scared, for Sandy was the last man to put a case too high. And the next second I felt worse, for he clutched my arm and dragged me in a bound to the side of the road. I could see nothing, but I felt that his head was screwed round, and mine followed suit. And there, a dozen yards off, were the acetylene lights of a big motor-car.

It came along very slowly, purring like a great cat, while we pressed into the bushes. The headlight seemed to spread a fan far to either side, showing the full width of the drive and its borders, and about half the height of the over-arching trees. There was a figure in uniform sitting beside the chauffeur, whom I saw dimly in the reflex glow, but the body of the car was dark.

It crept towards us, passed, and my mind was just getting easy again when it stopped. A switch was snapped within, and the limousine was brightly lit up. Inside I saw a woman's figure.

The servant had got out and opened the door and a voice came from within—a clear soft voice speaking in some tongue I did not understand. Sandy had started forward at the sound of it, and I followed him. It would never do for me to be caught skulking in the bushes.

I was so dazzled by the suddenness of the glare that at first I blinked and saw nothing. Then my eyes cleared and I found myself looking at the inside of a car upholstered in some soft dove-coloured fabric, and beautifully finished off in ivory and silver. The woman who sat in it had a mantilla of black lace over her head and shoulders, and with one slender jewelled hand she kept its folds over the greater part of her face. I saw only a pair of pale grey-blue eyes—these and the slim fingers.

I remember that Sandy was standing very upright with his hands on his hips, by no means like a servant in the presence of his mistress. He was a fine figure of a man at all times, but in those wild clothes, with his head thrown back and his dark brows drawn below his skull-cap, he looked like some savage king out of an older world. He was speaking Turkish, and glancing at me now and then as if angry and perplexed. I took the hint that he was not supposed to know any other tongue, and that he was asking who the devil I might be.

Then they both looked at me, Sandy with the slow unwinking stare of the gipsy, the lady with those curious beautiful pale eyes. They ran over my clothes, my brand-new riding-breeches, my splashed boots, my wide-brimmed hat. I took off the last and made my best bow.

"Madam," I said, "I have to ask pardon for trespassing in your garden. The fact is, I and my servant—he's down the road with the horses and I guess you noticed him—the two of us went for a ride this afternoon, and got good and well lost. We came in by your back gate, and I was prospecting for your front door to find some one to direct us, when I bumped into this brigand-chief who didn't understand my talk. I'm American, and I'm here on a big Government proposition. I hate to trouble you, but if you'd send a man to show us how to strike the city I'd be very much in your debt."

Her eyes never left my face. "Will you come into the car?" she said in English. "At the house I will give you a servant to direct you."

She drew in the skirts of her fur cloak to make room for me, and in my muddy boots and sopping clothes I took the seat she pointed out. She said a word in Turkish to Sandy, switched off the light, and the car moved on.

Women had never come much my way, and I knew about as much of their ways as I knew about the Chinese language. All my life I had lived with men only, and rather a rough crowd at that. When I made my pile and came home I looked to see a little society, but I had first the business of the Black Stone on my hands, and then the war, so my education languished. I had never been in a motor-car with a lady before, and I felt like a fish on a dry sandbank. The soft cushions and the subtle scents filled me with acute uneasiness. I wasn't thinking now about Sandy's grave words, or about Blenkiron's warning, or about my job and the part this woman must play in it. I was thinking only that I felt mortally shy. The darkness made it worse. I was sure that my companion was looking at me all the time and laughing at me for a clown.

The car stopped and a tall servant opened the door. The lady was over the threshold before I was at the step. I followed her heavily, the wet squelching from my field-boots. At that moment I noticed that she was very tall.

She led me through a long corridor to a room where two pillars held lamps in the shape of torches. The place was dark but for their glow, and it was as warm as a hothouse from invisible stoves. I felt soft carpets underfoot, and on the walls hung some tapestry or rug of an amazingly intricate geometrical pattern, but with every strand as rich as jewels. There, between the pillars, she turned and faced me. Her furs were thrown back, and the black mantilla had slipped down to her shoulders.

"I have heard of you," she said. "You are called Richard Hanau, the American. Why have you come to this land?"

"To have a share in the campaign," I said. "I'm an engineer, and I thought I could help out with some business like Mesopotamia."

"You are on Germany's side?" she asked.

"Why, yes," I replied. "We Americans are supposed to be nootrals, and that means we're free to choose any side we fancy. I'm for the Kaiser."

Her cool eyes searched me, but not in suspicion. I could see she wasn't troubling with the question whether I was speaking the truth. She was sizing me up as a man. I cannot describe that calm appraising look. There was no sex in it, nothing even of that implicit sympathy with which one human being explores the existence of another. I was a chattel, a thing infinitely removed from intimacy. Even so I have myself looked at a horse which I thought of buying, scanning his shoulders and hocks and paces. Even so must the old lords of Constantinople have looked at the slaves which the chances of war brought to their markets, assessing their usefulness for some task or other with no thought of a humanity common to purchased and purchaser. And yet—not quite. This woman's eyes were weighing me, not for any special duty, but for my essential qualities. I felt that I was under the scrutiny of one who was a connoisseur in human nature.

I see I have written that I knew nothing about women. But every man has in his bones a consciousness of sex. I was shy and perturbed, but horribly fascinated. This slim woman, poised exquisitely like some statue between the pillared lights, with her fair cloud of hair, her long delicate face, and her pale bright eyes, had the glamour of a wild dream. I hated her instinctively, hated her intensely, but I longed to arouse her interest. To be valued coldly by those eyes was an offence to my manhood, and I felt antagonism rising within me. I am a strong fellow, well set up, and rather above the average height, and my irritation stiffened me from heel to crown. I flung my head back and gave her cool glance for cool glance, pride against pride.

Once, I remember, a doctor on board ship who dabbled in hypnotism told me that I was the most unsympathetic person he had ever struck. He said I was about as good a mesmeric subject as Table Mountain. Suddenly I began to realize that this woman was trying to cast some spell over me. The eyes grew large and luminous, and I was conscious for just an instant of some will battling to subject mine. I was aware, too, in the same moment of a strange scent which recalled that wild hour in Kuprasso's garden-house. It passed quickly, and for a second her eyes dropped. I seemed to read in them failure, and yet a kind of satisfaction too, as if they had found more in me than they expected.

"What life have you led?" the soft voice was saying.

I was able to answer quite naturally, rather to my surprise. "I have been a mining engineer up and down the world."

"You have faced danger many times?"

"I have faced danger."

"You have fought with men in battles?"

"I have fought in battles."

Her bosom rose and fell in a kind of sigh. A smile—a very beautiful thing— flitted over her face. She gave me her hand.

"The horses are at the door now," she said, "and your servant is with them. One of my people will guide you to the city."

She turned away and passed out of the circle of light into the darkness beyond. . . .

Peter and I jogged home in the rain with one of Sandy's skin-clad Companions loping at our side. We did not speak a word, for my thoughts were running like hounds on the track of the past hours. I had seen the mysterious Hilda von Einem, I had spoken to her, I had held her hand. She had insulted me with the subtlest of insults and yet I was not angry. Suddenly the game I was playing became invested with a tremendous solemnity. My old antagonists, Stumm and Rasta and the whole German Empire, seemed to shrink into the background, leaving only the slim woman with her inscrutable smile and devouring eyes. "Mad and bad," Blenkiron had called her, "but principally bad." I did not think they were the proper terms, for they belonged to the narrow world of our common experience. This was something beyond and above it, as a cyclone or an earthquake is outside the decent routine of nature. Mad and bad she might be, but she was also great.

Before we arrived our guide had plucked my knee and spoken some words which he had obviously got by heart. "The Master says," ran the message, "expect him at midnight."

25 AN EMBARRASSED TOILET

I was soaked to the bone, and while Peter set off to look for dinner, I went to my room to change. I had a rub down and then got into pyjamas for some dumb-bell exercise with two chairs, for that long wet ride had stiffened my arm and shoulder muscles. They were a vulgar suit of primitive blue, which Blenkiron had looted from my London wardrobe. As Cornelis Brandt I had sported a flannel night-gown.

My bedroom opened off the sitting-room, and while I was busy with my gymnastics I heard the door open. I thought at first it was Blenkiron, but the briskness of the tread was unlike his measured gait. I had left the light burning there, and the visitor, whoever he was, had made himself at home. I slipped on a green dressing-gown Blenkiron had lent me, and sallied forth to investigate.

My friend Rasta was standing by the table, on which he had laid an envelope. He looked round at my entrance and saluted.

"I come from the Minister of War, sir," he said, "and bring your passports for to-morrow. You will travel by . . ." And then his voice tailed away and his black eyes narrowed to slits. He had seen something which switched him off the metals.

At that moment I saw it too. There was a mirror on the wall behind him, and as I faced him I could not help seeing my reflection. It was the exact image of the engineer on the Danube boat—blue jeans, *loden* cloak, and all. The accursed mischance of my costume had given him the clue to an identity which was otherwise buried deep in the Bosphorus.

I am bound to say for Rasta that he was a man of quick action. In a trice he had whipped round to the other side of the table between me and the door, where he stood regarding me wickedly.

By this time I was at the table and stretched out a hand for the envelope. My one hope was nonchalance.

"Sit down, sir," I said, "and have a drink. It's a filthy night to move about in."

"Thank you, no, Herr Brandt," he said. "You may burn these passports, for they will not be used."

"Whatever's the matter with you?" I cried. "You've mistaken the house, my lad. I'm called Hanau—Richard Hanau—and my partner's Mr. John S. Blenkiron. He'll be here presently. Never knew any one of the name of Brandt, barring a tobacconist in Denver City."

"You have never been to Rustchuk?" he said with a sneer.

"Not that I know of. But, pardon me, sir, if I ask your name and your business here. I'm darned if I'm accustomed to be called by Dutch names or have my word doubted. In my country we consider that impolite as between gentlemen."

I could see that my bluff was having its effect. His stare began to waver, and when he next spoke it was in a more civil tone.

"I will ask pardon if I'm mistaken, sir, but you're the image of a man who a week ago was at Rustchuk, a man much wanted by the Imperial Government."

"A week ago I was tossing in a dirty little hooker coming from Constanza. Unless Rustchuk's in the middle of the Black Sea I've never visited the township. I guess you're barking up the wrong tree. Come to think of it, I was expecting passports. Say, do you come from Enver Damad?"

"I have that honour," he said.

"Well, Enver is a very good friend of mine. He's the brightest citizen I've struck this side of the Atlantic."

The man was calming down, and in another minute his suspicions would have gone. But at that moment, by the crookedest kind of luck, Peter entered with a tray of dishes. He did not notice Rasta, and walked straight to the table and plumped down his burden on it. The Turk had stepped aside at his entrance, and I saw by the look in his eyes that his suspicions had become a certainty. For Peter, stripped to the shirt and trousers, was the identical shabby little companion of the Rustchuk meeting.

I had never doubted Rasta's pluck. He jumped for the door and had a pistol out in a trice pointing at my head.

"*Bonne fortune*," he cried. "Both the birds at one shot." His hand was on the latch, and his mouth was open to cry. I guessed there was an orderly waiting on the stairs.

He had what you call the strategic advantage, for he was at the door, while I was at the other end of the table and Peter at the side of it at least two yards from him. The road was clear before him, and neither of us was armed. I made a despairing step forward, not knowing what I meant to do, for I saw no light. But Peter was before me.

He had never let go of the tray, and now, as a boy skims a stone on a pond, he skimmed it with its contents at Rasta's head. The man was opening the door with one hand while he kept me covered with the other, and he got the contrivance fairly in the face. A pistol shot cracked out, and the bullet went through the tray, but the noise was drowned in the crash of glasses and crockery. The next second Peter had wrenched the pistol from Rasta's hand and had gripped his throat.

A dandified young Turk, brought up in Paris and finished in Berlin, may be as brave as a lion, but he cannot stand in a rough-and-tumble against a back-veld hunter, though more than double his age. There was no need for me to help. Peter had his own way, learned in a wild school, of knocking the sense out of a foe. He gagged him scientifically, and trussed him up with his own belt and two straps from a trunk in my bedroom.

"This man is too dangerous to let go," he said, as if his procedure were the most ordinary thing in the world. "He will be quiet now till we have time to make a plan."

At that moment there came a knocking at the door. That is the sort of thing that happens in melodrama, just when the villain has finished off his job neatly. The correct thing to do is to pale to the teeth, and with a rolling, conscience-stricken eye glare round the horizon. But that was not Peter's way.

"We'd better tidy up if we're to have visitors," he said calmly.

Now there was one of those big oak German cupboards against the wall which must have been brought in in sections, for, complete, it would never have got through the door. It was empty now, but for Blenkiron's hat-box. In it he deposited the unconscious Rasta, and turned the key. "There's enough ventilation through the top," he observed, "to keep the air good." Then he opened the door.

A magnificent kavass in blue and silver stood outside. He saluted and proffered a card on which was written in pencil, "Hilda von Einem."

I would have begged for time to change my clothes, but the lady was behind him. I saw the black mantilla and the rich sable furs. Peter vanished through my bedroom, and I was left to receive my guest in a room littered with broken glass and a senseless man in the cupboard.

There are some situations so crazily extravagant that they key up the spirit to meet them. I was almost laughing when that stately lady stepped over my threshold.

"Madam," I said, with a bow that shamed my old dressing-gown and strident pyjamas, "you find me at a disadvantage. I came home soaking from my ride, and was in the act of changing. My servant has just upset a tray of crockery, and I fear this room's no fit place for a lady. Allow me three minutes to make myself presentable."

She inclined her head gravely and took a seat by the fire. I went into my bedroom, and as I expected found Peter lurking by the other door. In a hectic sentence I bade him get Rasta's orderly out of the place on any pretext, and tell him his master would return later. Then I hurried into decent garments and came out to find my visitor in a brown study.

At the sound of my entrance she started from her dream and stood up on the hearthrug, slipping the long robe of fur from her slim body.

"We are alone?" she said. "We will not be disturbed?"

Then an inspiration came to me. I remembered that Frau von Einem, according to Blenkiron, did not see eye to eye with the Young Turks; and I had a queer instinct that Rasta could not be to her liking. So I spoke the truth.

"I must tell you that there's another guest here to-night. I reckon he's feeling pretty uncomfortable. At present he's trussed up on a shelf in that cupboard."

She did not trouble to look round.

"Is he dead?" she asked calmly.

"By no means," I said, "but he's fixed so he can't speak, and I guess he can't hear much."

"He was the man who brought you this?" she asked, pointing to the envelope on the table which bore the big blue stamp of the Ministry of War.

"The same," I said. "I'm not perfectly sure of his name, but I think they call him Rasta."

Not a flicker of a smile crossed her face, but I had a feeling that the news pleased her.

"Did he thwart you?" she asked.

"Why, yes. He thwarted me some. His head is a bit swelled, and an hour or two on the shelf will do him good."

"He is a powerful man," she said, "a jackal of Enver's. You have made a dangerous enemy."

"I don't value him at two cents," said I, though I thought grimly that as far as I could see the value of him was likely to be about the price of my neck.

"Perhaps you are right," she said with serious eyes. "In these days no enemy is dangerous to a bold man. I have come to-night, Mr. Hanau, to talk business with you, as they say in your country. I have heard well of you, and to-day I have seen you. I may have need of you, and you assuredly will have need of me. . . ."

She broke off, and again her strange potent eyes fell on my face. They were like a burning searchlight which showed up every cranny and crack of the soul. I felt it was going to be horribly difficult to act a part under that compelling gaze. She could not mesmerize me, but she could strip me of my fancy dress and set me naked in the masquerade.

"What came you forth to seek?" she asked. "You are not like the stout American Blenkiron, a lover of shoddy power and a devotee of a feeble science. There is something more than that in your face. You are on our side, but you are not of the Germans with their hankerings for a rococo Empire. You come from America, the land of pious follies, where men worship gold and words. I ask, what come you forth to seek?"

As she spoke I seemed to get a vision of a figure like one of the old gods looking down on human nature from a great height, a figure disdainful and passionless, but with its own magnificence. It kindled my imagination, and I answered with the stuff I had often cogitated when I had tried to explain to myself just how a case could be made out against the Allied cause.

"I will tell you, Madam," I said. "I am a man who has followed a science, but I have followed it in wild places, and I have gone through it and come out at the other side. The world, as I see it, had become too easy and cushioned. Men had forgotten their manhood in soft speech, and imagined that the rules of their smug civilization were the laws of the universe. But that is not the teaching of science, and it is not the teaching of life. We had forgotten the greater virtues, and we were becoming emasculated humbugs whose gods were our own weaknesses. Then came war, and the air was cleared. Germany, in spite of her blunders and her grossness, stood forth as the scourge of cant. She had the courage to cut through the bonds of humbug and to laugh at the fetishes of the herd. Therefore I am on Germany's side. But I came here for another reason. I know nothing of the East, but as I read history it is from the desert that the purification comes. When mankind is smothered with shams and phrases and painted idols a wind blows out of the wilds to cleanse and simplify life. The world needs space and fresh air. The civilization we have boasted of is a toy-shop and a blind alley, and I hanker for open country."

This confounded nonsense was well received. Her pale eyes had the cold light of the fanatic. With her bright hair and the long exquisite oval of her face she looked like some destroying fury of a Norse legend. At that moment I think I first really feared her; before I had half hated and half admired. Thank Heaven, in her absorption she did not notice that I had forgotten the speech of Cleveland, Ohio.

"You are of the Household of Faith," she said. "You will presently learn many things, for the Faith marches to victory. Meantime I have one word for you. You and your companion travel eastward."

"We go to Mesopotamia," I said. "I reckon these are our passports," and I pointed to the envelope.

She picked it up, opened it, and then tore it in pieces and tossed it in the fire.

"The orders are countermanded," she said. "I have need of you and you go with me. Not to the flats of the Tigris, but to the great hills. To-morrow you will receive new passports."

She gave me her hand and turned to go. At the threshold she paused, and looked towards the oak cupboard. "To-morrow I will relieve you of your prisoner. He will be safer in my hands."

She left me in a condition of pretty blank bewilderment. We were to be tied to the chariot-wheels of this fury, and started on an enterprise compared to which fighting against our friends at Kut seemed tame and reasonable. On the other hand, I had been spotted by Rasta, and had got the envoy of the most powerful man in Constantinople locked in a cupboard. At all costs we had to keep Rasta safe, but I was very determined that he should not be handed over to the lady. I was going to be no party to cold-blooded murder, which I judged to be her expedient. It was a pretty kettle of fish, but in the meantime I must have food, for I had eaten nothing for nine hours. So I went in search of Peter.

I had scarcely begun my long-deferred meal when Sandy entered. He was before his time, and he looked as solemn as a sick owl. I seized on him as a drowning man clutches a spar.

He heard my story of Rasta with a lengthening face.

"That's bad," he said. "You say he spotted you, and your subsequent doings of course would not disillusion him. It's an infernal nuisance, but there's only one way out of it. I must put him in the charge of my own people. They will keep him safe and sound till he's wanted. Only he mustn't see me." And he went out in a hurry.

I fetched Rasta from his prison. He had come to his senses by this time, and lay regarding me with stony, malevolent eyes.

"I'm very sorry, sir," I said, "for what has happened. But you left me no alternative. I've got a big job on hand and I can't have it interfered with by you or any one. You're paying the price of a suspicious nature. When you know a little more you'll want to apologize to me. I'm going to see that you are kept quiet and comfortable for a day or two. You've no cause to worry, for you'll suffer no harm. I give you my word of honour as an American citizen."

Two of Sandy's miscreants came in and bore him off, and presently Sandy himself returned. When I asked where he was being taken, Sandy said he didn't know. "They've got their orders, and they'll carry them out to the letter. There's a big unknown area in Constantinople to hide a man, into which the *Khafiyeh* never enter."

Then he flung himself in a chair and lit his old pipe.

"Dick," he said, "this job is getting very difficult and very dark. But my knowledge has grown in the last few days. I've found out the meaning of the second word that Harry Bullivant scribbled."

"*Cancer?*" I asked.

"Yes. It means just what it reads and no more. Greenmantle is dying—has been dying for months. This afternoon they brought a German doctor to see him, and the man gave him a few hours of life. By now he may be dead."

The news was a staggerer. For a moment I thought it cleared up things. "Then that busts the show," I said. "You can't have a crusade without a prophet."

"I wish I thought it did. It's the end of one stage, but the start of a new and blacker one. Do you think that woman will be beaten by such a small thing as the death of her prophet? She'll find a substitute—one of the four Ministers, or some one else. She's a devil incarnate, but she has the soul of a Napoleon. The big danger is only beginning."

Then he told me the story of his recent doings. He had found out the house of Frau von Einem without much trouble, and had performed with his ragamuffins in the servants' quarters. The prophet had a large retinue, and the fame of the minstrels—for the Companions were known far and wide in the land of Islam—came speedily to the ears of the Holy Ones. Sandy, a leader in this most orthodox coterie, was taken into favour and brought to the notice of the four Ministers. He and his half-dozen retainers became inmates of the villa, and Sandy, from his knowledge of Islamic lore and his ostentatious piety, was admitted to the confidence of the household. Frau von Einem welcomed him as an ally, for the Companions had been the most devoted propagandists of the new revelation.

As he described it, it was a stange business. Greenmantle was dying and often in great pain, but he struggled to meet the demands of his protectress. The four Ministers, as Sandy saw them, were unworldly ascetics; the prophet himself was a saint, though a practical saint with some notions of policy; but the controlling brain and will were those of the lady. Sandy seemed to have won his favour, even his affection. He spoke of him with a kind of desperate pity.

"I never saw such a man. He is the greatest gentleman you can picture, with a dignity like a high mountain. He is a dreamer and a poet, too—a genius if I can judge these things. I think I can assess him rightly, for I know something of the soul of the East, but it would be too long a story to tell now. The West knows nothing of the true Oriental. It pictures him as lapped in colour and idleness and luxury and gorgeous dreams. But it is all wrong. The *Kâf* he yearns for is an austere thing. It is the austerity of the East that is its beauty and its terror. . . . It always wants the same things at the back of its head. The Turk and the Arab came out of big spaces, and they have the desire of them in their bones. They settle down and stagnate, and by and by they degenerate into that appalling subtlety which is their ruling passion gone crooked. And then comes a new revelation and a great simplifying. They want to live face to face with God without a screen of ritual and images and priestcraft. They want to prune life of its foolish fringes and get back to the noble bareness of the desert. Remember, it is always the empty desert and the empty sky that cast their spell over them—these, and the hot, strong, antiseptic sunlight which burns up all rot and decay. . . . It isn't inhuman. It's the humanity of one part of the human race. It isn't ours, it isn't as good as ours, but it's jolly good all the same. There are times when it grips me so hard that I'm inclined to forswear the gods of my fathers!

"Well, Greenmantle is the prophet of this great simplicity. He speaks straight to the heart of Islam, and it's an honourable message. But for our sins it's been twisted into part of that damned German propaganda. His unworldliness has been used for a cunning political move, and his creed of space and simplicity for the furtherance of the last word in human degeneracy. My God, Dick, it's like seeing St. Francis run by Messalina."

"The woman has been here to-night," I said. "She asked me what I stood for, and I invented some infernal nonsense which she approved of. But I can see one thing. She and her prophet may run for different stakes, but it's the same course."

Sandy started. "She's been here!" he cried. "Tell me, Dick, what did you think of her?"

"I thought she was about two parts mad, but the third part was uncommon like inspiration."

"That's about right," he said. "I was wrong in comparing her to Messalina. She's something a dashed sight more complicated. She runs the prophet just because she shares his belief. Only what in him is sane and fine, in her is mad and horrible. You see, Germany also wants to simplify life."

"I know," I said. "I told her that an hour ago, when I talked more rot to the second than any mortal man ever achieved. It will come between me and my sleep for the rest of my days."

"Germany's simplicity is that of the neurotic, not the primitive. It is megalomania and egotism and the pride of the man in the Bible that waxed fat and kicked. But the results are the same. She wants to destroy and simplify; but it isn't the simplicity of the ascetic, which is of the spirit, but the simplicity of the madman that grinds down all the contrivances of civilization to a featureless monotony. The prophet wants to save the souls of his people; Germany wants to rule the inanimate corpse of the world. But you can get the same language to cover both. And so you have the partnership of St. Francis and Messalina. Dick, did you ever hear of a thing called the Superman?"

"There was a time when the papers were full of nothing else," I answered. "I gather it was invented by a sportsman called Nietzsche."

"Maybe," said Sandy. "Old Nietzsche has been blamed for a great deal of rubbish he would have died rather than acknowledge. But it's a craze of the new, fatted Germany. It's a fancy type which could never really exist, any more than the Economic Man of the politicians. Mankind has a sense of humour which stops short of the final absurdity. There never has been and there never could be a real Superman. . . . But there might be a Super-woman."

"You'll get into trouble, my lad, if you talk like that," I said.

"It's true all the same. Women have got a perilous logic which we never have, and some of the best of them don't see the joke of life like the ordinary man. They can be far greater than men, for they can go straight to the heart of things. There never was a man so near the divine as Joan of Arc. But I think too they can be more entirely damnable than anything that ever was breeched, for they don't stop still now and then and laugh at themselves. . . . There is no Superman. The poor old donkeys that fancy themselves in the part are either crack-brained professors who couldn't rule a Sunday-school class, or bristling soldiers with pint-pot heads who imagine that the shooting of a Duc d'Enghien made a Napoleon. But there is a Super-woman, and her name's Hilda von Einem."

"I thought our job was nearly over," I groaned, "and now it looks as if it hadn't well started. Bullivant said that all we had to do was to find out the truth."

"Bullivant didn't know. No man knows except you and me. I tell you, the woman has immense power. The Germans have trusted her with their trump card, and she's going to play it for all she is worth. There's no crime that will stand in her way. She has set the ball rolling, and if need be she'll cut all her prophets' throats and run the show herself. . . . I don't know about your job, for honestly I can't quite see what you and Blenkiron are going to do. But I'm very clear about my own duty. She's let me into the business, and I'm going to stick to it in the hope that I'll find a chance of wrecking it. . . . We're moving eastward to-morrow—with a new prophet if the old one is dead."

"Where are you going?" I asked.

"I don't know. But I gather it's a long journey, judging by the preparations. And it must be to a cold country, judging by the clothes provided."

"Well, wherever it is, we're going with you. You haven't heard our end of the yarn. Blenkiron and I have been moving in the best circles as skilled American engineers who are going to play Old Harry with the British on the Tigris. I'm a pal of Enver's now, and he has offered me his protection. The lamented Rasta brought our passports for the journey to Mesopotamia to-morrow, but an hour ago your lady tore them up and put them in the fire. We are going with her, and she vouchsafed the information that it was towards the great hills."

Sandy whistled long and low. "I wonder what the deuce she wants with you? This thing is getting dashed complicated, Dick. . . . Where, more by token, is Blenkiron? He's the fellow to know about high politics."

The missing Blenkiron, as Sandy spoke, entered the room with his slow, quiet step. I could see by his carriage that for once he had no dyspepsia, and by his eyes that he was excited.

"Say, boys," he said, "I've got something pretty considerable in the way of noos. There's been big fighting on the Eastern border, and the Buzzards have taken a bad knock."

His hands were full of papers, from which he selected a map and spread it on the table.

"They keep mum about the thing in this capital, but I've been piecing the story together these last days, and I think I've got it straight. A fortnight ago old man Nicholas descended from his mountains and scuppered his enemies there—at Kuprikeui, where the main road eastward crosses the Araxes. That was only the beginning of the stunt, for he pressed on on a broad front, and the gentleman called Kiamil, who commands in those parts, was not up to the job of holding him. The Buzzards were shepherded in from north and east and south, and now the Muscovite is sitting down outside the forts of Erzerum. I can tell you they're pretty miserable about the situation in the highest quarters. . . . Enver is sweating blood to get fresh divisions to Erzerum from Gally-poly, but it's a long road and it looks as if they would be too late for the fair. . . . You and I, Major, start for Mesopotamy to-morrow, and that's about the meanest bit of bad luck that ever happened to John S. We're missing the chance of seeing the goriest fight of this campaign."

I picked up the map and pocketed it. Maps were my business, and I had been looking for one.

"We're not going to Mesopotamia," I said. "Our orders have been cancelled."

"But I've just seen Enver, and he said he had sent round our passports."

"They're in the fire," I said. "The right ones will come along to-morrow morning."

Sandy broke in, his eyes bright with excitement.

"The great hills! . . . We're going to Erzerum. . . . Don't you see that the Germans are playing their big card? They're sending Greenmantle to the point of danger in the hope that his coming will rally the Turkish defence. Things are beginning to move, Dick, old man. No more kicking the heels for us. We're going to be in it up to the neck, and Heaven help the best man. . . . I must be off now, for I've a lot to do. *Au revoir.* We meet some time soon in the hills."

Blenkiron still looked puzzled, till I told him the story of that night's doings. As he listened, all the satisfaction went out of his face, and that funny, childish air of bewilderment crept in.

"It's not for me to complain, for it's in the straight line of our dooty, but I reckon there's going to be big trouble ahead of this caravan. It's Kismet, and we've got to bow. But I won't pretend that I'm not considerable scared at the prospect."

"Oh, so am I," I said. "The woman frightens me into fits. We're up against it this time all right. All the same I'm glad we're to be let into the real star metropolitan performance. I didn't relish the idea of touring the provinces."

"I guess that's correct. But I could wish that the good God would see fit to take that lovely lady to Himself. She's too much for a quiet man at my time of life. When she invites us to go in on the ground-floor I feel like taking the elevator to the roof-garden."

26   THE BATTERED CARAVANSERAI

Two days later, in the evening, we came to Angora, the first stage in our journey.

The passports had arrived next morning, as Frau von Einem had promised, and with them a plan of our journey. More, one of the Companions, who spoke a little English, was detailed to accompany us—a wise precaution, for no one of us had a word of Turkish. These were the sum of our instructions. I heard nothing more of Sandy or Greenmantle or the lady. We were meant to travel in our own party.

We had the railway to Angora, a very comfortable German *Schlafwagen*, tacked to the end of a troop-train. There wasn't much to be seen of the country, for after we left the Bosphorus we ran into scuds of snow, and except that we seemed to be climbing on to a big plateau I had no notion of the landscape. It was a marvel that we made such good time, for that line was congested beyond anything I have ever seen. The place was crawling with the Gallipoli troops, and every siding was packed with supply trucks. When we stopped—which we did on an average about once an hour—you could see vast camps on both sides of the line, and often we struck regiments on the march along the railway track. They looked a fine, hardy lot of ruffians, but many were deplorably ragged, and I didn't think much of their boots. I wondered how they would do the five hundred miles of road to Erzerum.

Blenkiron played Patience, and Peter and I took a hand at picquet, but mostly we smoked and yarned. Getting away from that infernal city had cheered us up wonderfully. Now we were out on the open road, moving to the sound of the guns. At the worst we should not perish like rats in a sewer. We would be all together, too, and that was a comfort. I think we felt the relief which a man who has been on a lonely outpost feels when he is brought back to his battalion. Besides, the thing had gone clean beyond our power to direct. It was no good planning and scheming, for none of us had a notion what the next step might be. We were fatalists now, believing in Kismet, and that is a comfortable faith.

All but Blenkiron. The coming of Hilda von Einem into the business had put a very ugly complexion on it for him. It was curious to see how she affected the different members of our gang. Peter did not care a rush; man, woman, and hippogriff were the same to him; he met it all as calmly as if he were making plans to round up an old lion in a patch of bush, taking the facts as they came and working at them as if they were a sum in arithmetic. Sandy and I were impressed—it's no good denying it; horribly impressed—but we were too interested to be scared, and we weren't a bit fascinated. We hated her too much for that. But she fairly struck Blenkiron dumb. He said himself it was just like a rattlesnake and a bird.

I made him talk about her, for if he sat and brooded he would get worse. It was a strange thing that this man, the most imperturbable and I think about the most courageous I have ever met, should be paralysed by a slim woman. There was no doubt about it. The thought of her made the future to him as black as a thunder cloud. It took the power out of his joints, and if she was going to be much around, it looked as if Blenkiron might be counted out.

I suggested that he was in love with her, but this he vehemently denied.

"No, sir; I haven't got no sort of affection for the lady. My trouble is that she puts me out of countenance, and I can't fit her in as an antagonist. I guess we Americans haven't got the right poise for dealing with that kind of female. We've exalted our womenfolk into little tin gods, and at the same time left them out of the real business of life. Consequently, when we strike one playing the biggest kind of man's game we can't place her. We aren't used to regarding them as anything except angels and children. I wish I had had you boys' upbringing."

Angora was like my notion of some place such as Amiens in the retreat from Mons. It was one mass of troops and transport—the neck of the bottle, for more arrived every hour, and the only outlet was the single eastern road. The town was pandemonium into which distracted German officers were trying to introduce some order. They didn't worry much about us, for the heart of Anatolia wasn't a likely hunting-ground for suspicious characters. We took our passports to the commandant, who viséd them readily, and told us he'd do his best to get us transport. We spent the night in a sort of hotel, where all four crowded into one little bedroom, and next morning I had my work cut out getting a motor-car. It took four hours, and the use of every great name in the Turkish Empire, to raise a dingy sort of Studebaker, and another two to get the petrol and spare tyres. As for a chauffeur, love or money couldn't find him, and I was compelled to drive the thing myself.

We left just after midday, and swung out into bare bleak downs patched with scrubby woodlands. There was no snow here, but a wind was blowing from the east which searched the marrow. Presently we climbed up into hills, and the road, though not badly engineered to begin with, grew as rough as the channel of a stream. No wonder, for the traffic was like what one saw on that awful stretch between Cassel and Ypres, and there were no gangs of Belgian roadmakers to mend it. We found troops by the thousands striding along with their impassive Turkish faces, ox convoys, mule convoys, wagons drawn by sturdy little Anatolian horses, and, coming in the contrary direction, many shabby Red Crescent cars and wagons of the wounded. We had to crawl for hours on end, till we got past a block. Just before the darkening we seemed to outstrip the first press, and had a clear run for about ten miles over a low pass in the hills. I began to get anxious about the car, for it was a poor one at the best, and the road was guaranteed sooner or later to knock even a Rolls-Royce into scrap iron.

All the same it was glorious to be out in the open again. Peter's face wore a new look, and he sniffed the bitter air like a stag. There floated up from little wayside camps the odour of wood-smoke and dung-fires. That, and the curious acrid winter smell of great wind-blown spaces, will always come to my memory as I think of that day. Every hour brought me peace of mind and resolution. I felt as I had felt when the battalion first marched from Aire towards the firing line, a kind of keying-up and wild expectation. I'm not used to cities, and lounging about Constantinople had slackened my fibre. Now, as the sharp wind buffeted us, I felt braced to any kind of risk. We were on the great road to the east and the border hills, and soon we should stand upon the farthest battle-front of the war. This was no commonplace intelligence job. That was all over, and we were going into the firing line, going to take part in what might be the downfall of our enemies. I didn't reflect that we were among those enemies, and would probably share their downfall if we were not shot earlier. The truth is, I had got out of the way of regarding the thing as a struggle between armies and nations. I hardly bothered to think where my sympathies lay. First and foremost it was a contest between the four of us and a crazy woman, and this personal antagonism made the strife of armies only a dimly felt background.

We slept that night like logs on the floor of a dirty khan, and started next morning in a powder of snow. We were getting very high up now, and it was perishing cold. The Companion—his name sounded like Hussin—had travelled the road before and told me what the places were, but they conveyed nothing to me. All morning we wriggled through a big lot of troops, a brigade at least, who swung along at a great pace with a fine free stride that I don't think I have ever seen bettered. I must say I took a fancy to the Turkish fighting man: I remembered the testimonial our fellows gave him as a clean fighter, and I felt very bitter that Germany should have lugged him into this dirty business. They halted for a meal, and we stopped too and lunched off some brown bread and dried figs and a flask of very sour wine. I had a few words with one of the officers who spoke a little German. He told me they were marching straight for Russia, since there had been a great Turkish victory in the Caucasus. "We have beaten the French and the British, and now it is Russia's turn," he said stolidly, as if repeating a lesson. But he added that he was mortally sick of war.

In the afternoon we cleared the column and had an open road for some hours. The land now had a tilt eastward, as if we were moving towards the valley of a great river. Soon we began to meet little parties of men coming from the east with a new look in their faces. The first lots of wounded had been the ordinary thing you see on every front, and there had been some pretence at organization. But these new lots were very weary and broken; they were often barefoot, and they seemed to have lost their transport and to be starving. You would find a group stretched by the roadside in the last stages of exhaustion. Then would come a party limping along, so tired that they never turned their heads to look at us. Almost all were wounded, some badly, and most were horribly thin. I wondered how my Turkish friend behind would explain the sight to his men, if he believed in a great victory. They had not the air of the backwash of a conquering army.

Even Blenkiron, who was no soldier, noticed it.

"These boys look mighty bad," he observed. "We've got to hustle, Major, if we're going to get seats for the last act."

That was my own feeling. The sight made me mad to get on faster, for I saw that big things were happening in the East. I had reckoned that four days would take us from Angora to Erzerum, but here was the second nearly over and we were not yet a third of the way. I pressed on recklessly, and that hurry was our undoing.

I have said that the Studebaker was a rotten old car. Its steering gear was pretty dicky, and the bad surface and continual hairpin bends of the road didn't improve it. Soon we came into snow lying fairly deep, frozen hard and rutted by the big transport wagons. We bumped and bounced horribly, and

were shaken about like peas in a bladder. I began to be acutely anxious about
the old boneshaker, the more as we seemed a long way short of the village I
had proposed to spend the night in. Twilight was falling and we were still in
an unfeatured waste, crossing the shallow glen of a stream. There was a
bridge at the bottom of a slope—a bridge of logs and earth which had
apparently been freshly strengthened for heavy traffic. As we approached it at
a good pace the car ceased to answer to the wheel.

I struggled desperately to keep it straight, but it swerved to the left and we
plunged over a bank into a marshy hollow. There was a sickening bump as we
struck the lower ground, and the whole party were shot out into the frozen
slush. I don't yet know how I escaped, for the car turned over and by rights I
should have had my back broken. But no one was hurt. Peter was laughing,
and Blenkiron, after shaking the snow out of his hair, joined him. For myself
I was feverishly examining the machine. It was about as ugly as it could be,
for the front axle was broken.

Here was a piece of hopeless bad luck. We were stuck in the middle of Asia
Minor with no means of conveyance, for to get a new axle there was as likely
as to find snowballs on the Congo. It was all but dark and there was no time to
lose. I got out the petrol tins and spare tyres and cached them among some
rocks on the hillside. Then we collected our scanty baggage from the derelict
Studebaker. Our only hope was Hussin. He had got to find us some lodging
for the night, and next day we would have a try for horses or a lift in some
passing wagon. I had no hope of another car. Every automobile in Anatolia
would now be at a premium.

It was so disgusting a mishap that we all took it quietly. It was too bad to be
helped by hard swearing. Hussin and Peter set off on different sides of the
road to prospect for a house, and Blenkiron and I sheltered under the nearest
rock and smoked savagely.

Hussin was the first to strike oil. He came back in twenty minutes with
news of some kind of dwelling a couple of miles up the stream. He went off to
collect Peter, and, humping our baggage, Blenkiron and I plodded up the
waterside. Darkness had fallen thick by this time, and we took some bad
tosses among the bogs. When Hussin and Peter overtook us they found a
better road, and presently we saw a light twinkle in the hollow ahead.

It proved to be a wretched tumble-down farm in a grove of poplars—a
foul-smelling, muddy yard, a two-roomed hovel of a house, and a barn which
was tolerably dry and which we selected for our sleeping place. The owner was
a broken old fellow whose sons were all at the war, and he received us with the
profound calm of one who expects nothing but unpleasantness from life.

By this time we had recovered our tempers, and I was trying hard to put
my new Kismet philosophy into practice. I reckoned that if risks were
foreordained, so were difficulties, and both must be taken as part of the day's
work. With the remains of our provisions and some curdled milk we satisfied
our hunger and curled ourselves up among the pease straw of the barn.
Blenkiron announced with a happy sigh that he had now been for two days
quit of his dyspepsia.

That night, I remember, I had a queer dream. I seemed to be in a wild place among mountains, and I was being hunted, though who was after me I couldn't tell. I remember sweating with fright, for I seemed to be quite alone and the terror that was pursuing me was more than human. The place was horribly quiet and still, and there was deep snow lying everywhere, so that each step I took was heavy as lead. A very ordinary sort of nightmare, you will say. Yes, but there was one strange feature in this one. The night was pitch dark, but ahead of me in the throat of the pass there was one patch of light, and it showed a rum little hill with a rocky top: what we call in South Africa a *castrol* or saucepan. I had a notion that if I could get to that *castrol* I should be safe, and I panted through the drifts towards it with the avenger of blood at my heels. I woke gasping, to find the winter morning struggling through the cracked rafters, and to hear Blenkiron say cheerily that his duodenum had behaved all night like a gentleman. I lay still for a bit trying to fix the dream, but it all dissolved into haze except the picture of the little hill, which was quite clear in every detail. I told myself it was a reminiscence of the veld, some spot down in the Wakkerstroom country, though for the life of me I couldn't place it.

I pass over the next three days, for they were one uninterrupted series of heart-breaks. Hussin and Peter scoured the country for horses, Blenkiron sat in the barn and played Patience, while I haunted the roadside near the bridge in the hope of picking up some kind of conveyance. My task was perfectly futile. The columns passed, casting wondering eyes on the wrecked car among the frozen rushes, but they could offer no help. My friend the Turkish officer promised to wire to Angora from some place or other for a fresh car, but, remembering the state of affairs at Angora, I had no hope from that quarter. Cars passed, plenty of them, packed with staff-officers, Turkish and German, but they were in far too big a hurry even to stop and speak. The only conclusion I reached from my roadside vigil was that things were getting very warm in the neighbourhood of Erzerum. Everybody on that road seemed to be in mad haste either to get there or to get away.

Hussin was the best chance, for, as I have said, the Companions had a very special and peculiar graft throughout the Turkish Empire. But the first day he came back empty-handed. All the horses had been commandeered for the war, he said; and though he was certain that some had been kept back and hidden away, he could not get on their track. The second day he returned with two—miserable screws and deplorably short in the wind from a diet of beans. There was no decent corn or hay left in that countryside. The third day he picked up a nice little Arab stallion: in poor condition, it is true, but perfectly sound. For these beasts we paid good money, for Blenkiron was well supplied and we had no time to spare for the interminable Oriental bargaining.

Hussin said he had cleaned up the countryside, and I believed him. I dared not delay another day, even though it meant leaving him behind. But he had no notion of doing anything of the kind. He was a good runner, he said, and could keep up with such horses as ours for ever. If this was the manner of our progress, I reckoned we would be weeks in getting to Erzerum.

We started at dawn on the morning of the fourth day, after the old farmer had blessed us and sold us some stale rye-bread. Blenkiron bestrode the Arab, being the heaviest, and Peter and I had the screws. My worst forebodings were soon realized, and Hussin, loping along at my side, had an easy job to keep up with us. We were about as slow as an ox-wagon. The brutes were unshod, and with the rough roads I saw that their feet would very soon go to pieces. We jogged along like a tinker's caravan, about five miles to the hour, as feckless a party as ever disgraced a highroad.

The weather was now a cold drizzle, which increased my depression. Cars passed us and disappeared in the mist, going at thirty miles an hour to mock our slowness. None of us spoke, for the futility of the business clogged our spirits. I bit hard on my lip to curb my restlessness, and I think I would have sold my soul there and then for anything that could move fast. I don't know any sorer trial than to be mad for speed and have to crawl at a snail's pace. I was getting ripe for any kind of desperate venture.

About midday we descended on a wide plain full of the marks of rich cultivation. Villages became frequent, and the land was studded with olive groves and scarred with water furrows. From what I remembered of the map I judged that we were coming to that champagne country near Siwas, which is the granary of Turkey, and the home of the true Osmanli stock.

Then at a turning of the road we came to the caravanserai.

It was a dingy, battered place, with the pink plaster falling in patches from its walls. There was a courtyard abutting on the road, and a flat-topped house with a big hole in its side. It was a long way from any battle-ground, and I guessed that some explosion had wrought the damage. Behind it, a few hundred yards off, a detachment of cavalry were encamped beside a stream, with their horses tied up in long lines of pickets.

And by the roadside, quite alone and deserted, stood a large new motor-car.

In all the road before and behind there was no man to be seen except the troops by the stream. The owners, whoever they were, must be inside the caravanserai.

I have said I was in the mood for some desperate deed, and lo and behold, Providence had given me the chance. I coveted that car as I have never coveted anything on earth. At the moment all my plans had narrowed down to a feverish passion to get to the battlefield. We had to find Greenmantle at Erzerum, and once there we should have Hilda von Einem's protection. It was a time of war, and a front of brass was the surest safety. But, indeed, I could not figure out any plan worth speaking of. I saw only one thing—a fast car which might be ours.

I said a word to the others, and we dismounted and tethered our horses at the near end of the courtyard. I heard the low hum of voices from the cavalrymen by the stream, but they were three hundred yards off and could not see us. Peter was sent forward to scout in the courtyard. In the building itself there was but one window looking on the road, and that was in the upper floor. Meantime I crawled along beside the wall to where the car stood, and had a look at it. It was a splendid six-cylinder affair, brand-new, with the tyres little worn. There were seven tins of petrol stacked behind, as well as spare tyres, and, looking in, I saw map-cases and field-glasses strewn on the seats as if the owners had only got out for a minute to stretch their legs.

Peter came back and reported that the courtyard was empty. "There are men in the upper room," he said; "more than one, for I heard their voices. They are moving about restlessly, and may soon be coming out."

I reckoned that there was no time to be lost, so I told the others to slip down the road fifty yards beyond the caravanserai and be ready to climb in as I passed. I had to start the infernal thing, and there might be shooting.

I waited by the car till I saw them reach the right distance. I could hear voices from the second floor of the house and footsteps moving up and down. I was in a fever of anxiety, for any moment a man might come to the window. Then I flung myself on the starting handle and worked like a demon.

The cold made the job difficult, and my heart was in my mouth, for the noise in that quiet place must have woke the dead. Then, by the mercy of Heaven, the engines started, and I sprang to the driving seat, released the clutch, and opened the throttle. The great car shot forward, and I seemed to hear behind me shrill voices. A pistol bullet bored through my hat, and another buried itself in a cushion beside me.

In a second I was clear of the place and the rest of the party were embarking. Blenkiron got on the step and rolled himself like a sack of coals into the tonneau. Peter nipped up beside me, and Hussin scrambled in from the back over the folds of the hood. We had our baggage in our pockets and nothing to carry.

Bullets dropped round us, but did no harm. Then I heard a report at my ear, and out of a corner of my eye saw Peter lower his pistol. Presently we were out of range, and, looking back, I saw three men gesticulating in the middle of the road.

"May the devil fly away with this pistol," said Peter ruefully. "I never could make good shooting with a little gun. Had I had my rifle . . ."

"What did you shoot for?" I asked in amazement. "We've got the fellows' car, and we don't want to do them any harm."

"It would have saved trouble had I had my rifle," said Peter quietly. "The little man you call Rasta was there, and he knew you. I heard him cry your name. He is an angry little man, and I observe that on this road there is a telegraph."

27 TROUBLE BY THE WATERS OF BABYLON

From that moment I date the beginning of my madness. Suddenly I forgot all cares and difficulties of the present and future and became foolishly light-hearted. We were rushing towards the great battle where men were busy at my proper trade. I realized how much I had loathed the lonely days in Germany, and still more the dawdling week in Constantinople. Now I was clear of it all, and bound for the clash of armies. It didn't trouble me that we were on the wrong side of the battle line. I had a sort of instinct that the darker and wilder things grew the better chance for us.

"Seems to me," said Blenkiron, bending over me, "that this joy-ride is going to come to an untimely end pretty soon. Peter's right. That young man will set the telegraph going, and we'll be held up at the next township."

"He's got to get to a telegraphic office first," I answered. "That's where we have the pull on him. He's welcome to the screws we left behind, and if he finds an operator before the evening I'm the worst kind of Dutchman. I'm going to break all the rules and bucket this car for what she's worth. Don't you see that the nearer we get to Erzerum the safer we are?"

"I don't follow," he said slowly. "At Erzerum I reckon they'll be waiting for us with the handcuffs. Why in thunder couldn't those hairy ragamuffins keep the little cuss safe? Your record's a bit too precipitous, Major, for the most innocent-minded military boss."

"Do you remember what you said about the Germans being open to bluff? Well, I'm going to put up the steepest sort of bluff. Of course they'll stop us. Rasta will do his damnedest. But remember that he and his friends are not very popular with the Germans, and Madame von Einem is. We're her protégés, and the bigger the German swell I get before the safer I'll feel. We've got our passports and our orders, and he'll be a bold man that will stop us once we get into the German zone. Therefore I'm going to hurry as fast as God will let me."

It was a ride that deserved to have an epic written about it. The car was good, I handled her well, though I say it who shouldn't. The road in that big central plain was fair, and often I knocked fifty miles an hour out of her. We passed troops by a circuit over the veld, where we took some awful risks, and once we skidded by some transport with our off wheels almost over the lip of a ravine. We went through the narrow streets of Siwas like a fire-engine, while I shouted out in German that we carried despatches for headquarters. We shot out of drizzling rain into brief spells of winter sunshine, and then into a snow blizzard which all but whipped the skin from our faces. And always before us the long road unrolled, with somewhere at the end of it two armies clinched in a death-grapple.

That night we looked for no lodgings. We ate a sort of meal in the car with the hood up, and felt our way on in the darkness, for the headlights were in perfect order. Then we turned off the road for four hours' sleep, and I had a go at the map. Before dawn we started again, and came over a pass into the vale of a big river. The winter dawn showed its gleaming stretches, ice-bound among the sprinkled meadows. I called to Blenkiron:

"I believe that river is the Euphrates," I said.

"So," he said, acutely interested. "Then that's the waters of Babylon. Great snakes, that I should have lived to see the fields where King Nebuchadnezzar grazed! Do you know the name of that big hill, Major?"

"Ararat, as like as not," I cried, and he believed me.

We were among the hills now, great, rocky, black slopes, and, seen through side glens, a hinterland of snowy peaks. I remember I kept looking for the *castrol* I had seen in my dream. The thing had never left off haunting me, and I was pretty clear now that it did not belong to my South African memories. I am not a superstitious man, but the way that little *kranz* clung to my mind made me think it was a warning sent by Providence. I was pretty certain that when I clapped eyes on it I would be in for bad trouble.

All morning we travelled up that broad vale, and just before noon it spread out wider, the road dipped to the water's edge, and I saw before me the white roofs of a town. The snow was deep now, and lay down to the riverside, but the sky had cleared, and against a space of blue heaven some peaks to the south rose glittering like jewels. The arches of a bridge, spanning two forks of the stream, showed in front, and as I slowed down at the bend a sentry's challenge rang out from a block-house. We had reached the fortress of Erzhingian, the headquarters of a Turkish corps and the gate of Armenia.

I showed the man our passports, but he did not salute and let us move on. He called another fellow from the guardhouse, who motioned us to keep pace with him as he stumped down a side lane. At the other end was a big barracks with sentries outside. The man spoke to us in Turkish, which Hussin interpreted. There was somebody in that barracks who wanted badly to see us.

"By the waters of Babylon we sat down and wept," quoted Blenkiron softly. "I fear, Major, we'll soon be remembering Zion."

I tried to persuade myself that this was merely the red tape of a frontier fortress, but I had an instinct that difficulties were in store for us. If Rasta had started wiring I was prepared to put up the brazenest bluff, for we were still eighty miles from Erzerum, and at all costs we were going to be landed there before night.

A fussy staff-officer met us at the door. At the sight of us he cried to a friend to come and look.

"Here are the birds safe. A fat man and two lean ones and a savage who looks like a Kurd. Call the guard and march them off. There's no doubt about their identity."

"Pardon me, sir," I said, "but we have no time to spare and we'd like to be in Erzerum before the dark. I would beg you to get through any formalities as soon as possible. This man," and I pointed to the sentry, "has our passports."

"Compose yourself," he said impudently; "you're not going on just yet, and when you do it won't be in a stolen car." He took the passports and fingered them casually. Then something he saw there made him cock his eyebrows.

"Where did you steal these?" he asked, but with less assurance in his tone.

I spoke very gently. "You seem to be the victim of a mistake, sir. These are our papers. We are under orders to report ourselves at Erzerum without an hour's delay. Whoever hinders us will have to answer to General von Liman. We'll be obliged if you will conduct us at once to the Governor."

"You can't see General Posselt," he said; "this is my business. I have a wire from Siwas that four men stole a car belonging to one of Enver Damad's staff. It describes you all, and says that two of you are notorious spies wanted by the Imperial Government. What have you to say to that?"

"Only that it is rubbish. My good sir, you have seen our passes. Our errand is not to be cried on the housetops, but five minutes with General Posselt will make things clear. You will be exceedingly sorry for it if you delay us another minute."

He was impressed in spite of himself, and after pulling his moustache turned on his heel and left us. Presently he came back and said very gruffly that the Governor would see us. We followed him along a corridor into a big room looking out on the river, where an oldish fellow sat in an arm-chair by a stove, writing letters with a fountain pen.

This was Posselt, who had been Governor of Erzerum till he fell sick and Ahmed Fevzi took his place. He had a peevish mouth and big blue pouches below his eyes. He was supposed to be a good engineer and to have made Erzerum impregnable, but the look in his face gave me the impression that his reputation at the moment was a bit unstable.

The staff-officer spoke to him in an undertone.

"Yes, yes, I know," he said testily. "Are these the men? They look a pretty lot of scoundrels. What's that you say? They deny it. But they've got the car. They can't deny that. Here, you," and he fixed on Blenkiron, "who the devil are you?"

Blenkiron smiled sleepily at him, not understanding one word, and I took up the parable.

"Our passports, sir, give our credentials," I said.

He glanced through them, and his face lengthened.

"They're right enough. But what about this story of stealing a car?"

"It is quite true," I said, "but I would prefer to use a pleasanter word. You will see from our papers that every authority on the road is directed to give us the best transport. Our own car broke down, and after a long delay we got some wretched horses. It is vitally important that we should be in Erzerum without delay, so I took the liberty of appropriating an empty car we found outside an inn. I am sorry for the discomfort of the owners, but our business was too grave to wait."

"But the telegram says you are notorious spies!"

I smiled. "Who sent the telegram?"

"I see no reason why I shouldn't give you his name. It was Rasta Bey. You've picked an awkward fellow to make an enemy of."

I did not smile, but laughed. "Rasta!" I cried. "He's one of Enver's satellites. That explains many things. I should like a word with you alone, sir."

He nodded to the staff-officer, and when he had gone I put on my most Bible face and looked as important as a provincial mayor at a royal visit.

"I can speak freely," I said, "for I am speaking to a soldier of Germany. There is no love lost between Enver and those I serve. I need not tell you that. This Rasta thought he had found a chance of delaying us, so he invents this trash about spies. Those Comitadjis have spies on the brain. . . . Especially he hates Frau von Einem."

He jumped at the name.

"You have orders from her?" he asked, in a respectful tone.

"Why, yes," I answered, "and those orders will not wait."

He got up and walked to a table, whence he turned a puzzled face on me. "I'm torn in two between the Turks and my own countrymen. If I please one I offend the other, and the result is a damnable confusion. You can go on to Erzerum, but I shall send a man with you to see that you report to headquarters there. I'm sorry, gentlemen, but I'm obliged to take no chances in this business. Rasta's got a grievance against you, but you can easily hide behind the lady's skirts. She passed through this town two days ago."

Ten minutes later we were coasting through the slush of the narrow streets with a stolid German lieutenant sitting beside me.

The afternoon was one of those rare days when in the pauses of snow you have a spell of weather as mild as May. I remembered several like it during our winter's training in Hampshire. The road was a fine one, well engineered, and well kept too, considering the amount of traffic. We were little delayed, for it was sufficiently broad to let us pass troops and transport without slackening pace. The fellow at my side was good-humoured enough, but his presence naturally put the lid on our conversation. I didn't want to talk, however. I was trying to piece together a plan, and making very little of it, for I had nothing to go upon. We must find Hilda von Einem and Sandy, and between us we must wreck the Greenmantle business. That done, it didn't matter so much what happened to us. As I reasoned it out, the Turks must be in a bad way, and, unless they got a fillip from Greenmantle, would crumple up before the Russians. In the rout I hoped we might get a chance to change sides. But it was no good looking so far forward; the first thing was to get to Sandy.

Now I was still in the mood of reckless bravado which I had got from bagging the car. I did not realize how thin our story was, and how easily Rasta might have a big graft at headquarters. If I had, I would have shot out the German lieutenant long before we got to Erzerum, and found some way of getting mixed up in the ruck of the population. Hussin could have helped me to that. I was getting so confident since our interview with Posselt that I thought I could bluff the whole outfit.

But my main business that afternoon was pure nonsense. I was trying to find my little hill. At every turn of the road I expected to see the *castrol* before us. You must know that ever since I could stand I have been crazy about high mountains. My father took me to Basutoland when I was a boy, and I reckon I have scrambled over almost every bit of upland south of the Zambesi, from the Hottentots Holland to the Zoutpansberg, and from the ugly yellow kopjes of Damaraland to the noble cliffs of Mont aux Sources. One of the things I had looked forward to in coming home was the chance of climbing the Alps. But now I was among peaks that I fancied were bigger than the Alps, and I could hardly keep my eyes on the road. I was pretty certain that my *castrol* was among them, for that dream had taken an almighty hold on my mind. Funnily enough, I was ceasing to think it a place of evil omen, for one soon forgets the atmosphere of nightmare. But I was convinced that it was a thing I was destined to see, and to see pretty soon.

Darkness fell when we were some miles short of the city, and the last part was difficult driving. On both sides of the road transport and engineers' stores were parked, and some of it strayed into the highway. I noticed lots of small details—machine-gun detachments, signalling parties, squads of stretcher-bearers—which mean the fringe of an army, and as soon as the night began the white fingers of searchlights began to grope in the skies.

And then, above the hum of the roadside, rose the voice of the great guns. The shells were bursting four or five miles away, and the guns must have been as many more distant. But in that upland pocket of plain in the frosty night they sounded most intimately near. They kept up their solemn litany, with a minute's interval between each—no *rafale* which rumbles like a drum, but the steady persistence of artillery exactly ranged on a target. I judged they must be bombarding the outer forts, and once there came a loud explosion and a red glare as if a magazine had suffered.

It was a sound I had not heard for five months, and it fairly crazed me. I remembered how I had first heard it on the ridge before Laventie. Then I had been half afraid, half solemnized, but every nerve had been quickened. Then it had been the new thing in my life that held me breathless with anticipation; now it was the old thing, the thing I had shared with so many good fellows, my proper work, and the only task for a man. At the sound of the guns I felt that I was moving in natural air once more. I felt that I was coming home.

We were stopped at a long line of ramparts, and a German sergeant stared at us till he saw the lieutenant beside me, when he saluted and we passed on. Almost at once we dipped into narrow twisting streets, choked with soldiers, where it was a hard business to steer. There were few lights—only now and then the flare of a torch which showed the grey stone houses, with every window latticed and shuttered. I had put out my headlights and had only side lamps, so we had to pick our way gingerly through the labyrinth. I hoped we would strike Sandy's quarters soon, for we were all pretty empty, and a frost had set in which made our thick coats seem as thin as paper.

The lieutenant did the guiding. We had to present our passports, and I anticipated no more difficulty than in landing from the boat at Boulogne. But I wanted to get it over, for my hunger pinched me and it was fearsome cold. Still the guns went on, like hounds baying before a quarry. The city was out of range, but there were strange lights on the ridge to the east.

At last we reached our goal and marched through a fine old carved archway into a courtyard, and thence into a draughty hall.

"You must see the *Sektionschef*," said our guide.

I looked round to see if we were all there, and noticed that Hussin had disappeared. It did not matter, for he was not on the passports.

We followed as we were directed through an open door. There was a man standing with his back towards us looking at a wall map, a very big man with a neck that bulged over his collar.

I would have known that neck among a million. At the sight of it I made a half turn to bolt back. It was too late, for the door had closed behind us, and there were two armed sentries beside it.

The man slewed round and looked into my eyes. I had a despairing hope that I might bluff it out, for I was in different clothes and had shaved my beard. But you cannot spend ten minutes in a death-grapple without your adversary getting to know you.

He went very pale, then recollected himself and twisted his features into the old grin.

"So," he said, "the little Dutchman! We meet after many days."

It was no good lying or saying anything. I shut my teeth and waited.

"And you, Herr Blenkiron? I never liked the look of you. You babbled too much, like all your damned Americans."

"I guess your personal dislikes haven't got anything to do with the matter," said Blenkiron calmly. "If you're the boss here, I'll thank you to cast your eye over these passports, for we can't stand waiting for ever."

This fairly angered him. "I'll teach you manners," he cried, and took a step forward to reach for Blenkiron's shoulder—the game he had twice played with me.

Blenkiron never took his hands from his coat pockets. "Keep your distance," he drawled in a new voice. "I've got you covered, and I'll make a hole in your bullet head if you lay a hand on me."

With an effort Stumm recovered himself. He rang a bell and fell to smiling. An orderly appeared to whom he spoke in Turkish, and presently a file of soldiers entered the room.

"I'm going to have you disarmed, gentlemen," he said. "We can conduct our conversation more pleasantly without pistols."

It was idle to resist. We surrendered our arms, Peter almost in tears with vexation. Stumm swung his legs over a chair, rested his chin on the back, and looked at me.

"Your game is up, you know," he said. "These fools of Turkish police said the Dutchmen were dead, but I had the happier inspiration. I believed the good God had spared them for me. When I got Rasta's telegram I was certain, for your doings reminded me of a little trick you once played me on the Schwandorf road. But I didn't think to find this plump old partridge," and he smiled at Blenkiron. "Two eminent American engineers and their servant bound for Mesopotamia on business of high Government importance! It was a good lie; but if I had been in Constantinople it would have had a short life. Rasta and his friends are no concern of mine. You can trick them as you please. But you have attempted to win the confidence of a certain lady, and her interests are mine. Likewise you have offended me, and I do not forgive. By God," he cried, his voice growing shrill with passion, "by the time I have done with you your mothers in their graves will weep that they ever bore you!"

It was Blenkiron who spoke. His voice was as level as the chairman's of a bank, and it fell on that turbid atmosphere like acid on grease.

"I don't take no stock in high-falutin. If you're trying to scare me by that dime-novel talk I guess you've hit the wrong man. You're like the sweep that stuck in the chimney, a bit too big for your job. I reckon you've a talent for romance that's just wasted in soldiering. But if you're going to play any ugly games on me I'd like you to know that I'm an American citizen, and pretty well considered in my own country and in yours, and you'll sweat blood for it later. That's a fair warning, Colonel Stumm."

I don't know what Stumm's plans were, but that speech of Blenkiron's put into his mind just the needed amount of uncertainty. You see, he had Peter and me right enough, but he hadn't properly connected Blenkiron with us, and was afraid either to hit out at all three, or to let Blenkiron go. It was lucky for us that the American had cut such a dash in the Fatherland.

"There is no hurry," he said blandly. "We shall have long happy hours together. I'm going to take you all home with me, for I'm a hospitable soul. You will be safer with me than in the town gaol, for it's a trifle draughty. It lets things in, and it might let things out."

Again he gave an order, and we were marched out, each with a soldier at his elbow. The three of us were bundled into the back seat of the car, while two men sat before us with their rifles between their knees, one got up behind on the baggage rack, and one sat beside Stumm's chauffeur. Packed like sardines we moved into the bleak streets, above which the stars twinkled in ribbons of sky.

Hussin had disappeared from the face of the earth, and quite right too. He was a good fellow, but he had no call to mix himself up in our troubles.

28 SPARROWS ON THE HOUSETOPS

"I've often regretted," said Blenkiron, "that miracles have left off happening."

He got no answer, for I was feeling the walls for something in the nature of a window.

"For I reckon," he went on, "that it wants a good old-fashioned copper-bottomed miracle to get us out of this fix. It's plumb against all my principles. I've spent my life using the talents God gave me to keep things from getting to the point of rude violence, and so far I've succeeded. But now you come along, Major, and you hustle a respectable middle-aged citizen into an aboriginal mix-up. It's mighty indelicate. I reckon the next move is up to you, for I'm no good at the house-breaking stunt."

"No more am I," I answered; "but I'm hanged if I'll chuck up the sponge. Sandy's somewhere outside, and he's got a hefty crowd at his heels."

I simply could not feel the despair which by every law of common sense was due to the case. The guns had intoxicated me. I could still hear their deep voices, though yards of wood and stone separated us from the upper air.

What vexed us most was our hunger. Barring a few mouthfuls on the road we had eaten nothing since the morning, and as our diet for the past days had not been generous we had some leeway to make up. Stumm had never looked near us since we were shoved into the car. We had been brought to some kind of house and bundled into a place like a wine-cellar. It was pitch dark, and after feeling round the walls, first on my feet and then on Peter's back, I decided that there were no windows. It must have been lit and ventilated by some lattice in the ceiling. There was not a stick of furniture in the place: nothing but a damp earth floor and bare stone sides. The door was a relic of the Iron Age, and I could hear the paces of a sentry outside it.

When things get to the pass that nothing you can do can better them, the only thing is to live for the moment. All three of us sought in sleep a refuge from our empty stomachs. The floor was the poorest kind of bed, but we rolled up our coats for pillows and made the best of it. Soon I knew by Peter's regular breathing that he was asleep, and I presently followed him. . . .

I was awakened by a pressure below my left ear. I thought it was Peter, for it is the old hunter's trick of waking a man so that he makes no noise. But another voice spoke. It told me that there was no time to lose and to rise and follow, and the voice was the voice of Hussin.

Peter was awake, and we stirred Blenkiron out of heavy slumber. We were bidden take off our boots and hang them by their laces round our necks, as

214

country boys do when they want to go barefoot. Then we tiptoed to the door, which was ajar.

Outside was a passage with a flight of steps at one end which led to the open air. On these steps lay a faint shine of starlight, and by its help I saw a man huddled up at the foot of them. It was our sentry, neatly and scientifically gagged and tied up.

The steps brought us to a little courtyard about which the walls of the houses rose like cliffs. We halted while Hussin listened intently. Apparently the coast was clear, and our guide led us to one side, which was clothed by a stout wooden trellis. Once it may have supported fig trees, but now the plants were dead and only withered tendrils and rotten stumps remained.

It was child's play for Peter and me to go up that trellis, but it was the deuce and all for Blenkiron. He was in poor condition and puffed like a grampus, and he seemed to have no sort of head for heights. But he was as game as a buffalo, and started in gallantly till his arms gave out and he fairly stuck. So Peter and I went up on each side of him, taking an arm apiece, as I had once seen done to a man with vertigo in the Kloof Chimney on Table Mountain. I was mighty thankful when I got him panting on the top and Hussin had shinned up beside us.

We crawled along a broadish wall, with an inch or two of powdery snow on it, and then up a sloping buttress on to the flat roof of the house. It was a miserable business for Blenkiron, who would certainly have fallen if he could have seen what was below him, and Peter and I had to stand to attention all the time. Then began a more difficult job. Hussin pointed out a ledge which took us past a stack of chimneys to another building slightly lower, this being the route he fancied. At that I sat down resolutely and put on my boots, and the others followed. Frost-bitten feet would be a poor asset in this kind of travelling.

It was a bad step for Blenkiron, and we only got him past it by Peter and I spread-eagling ourselves against the wall and passing him in front of us with his face towards us. We had no grip, and if he had stumbled we should all three have been in the courtyard. But we got it over, and dropped as softly as possible on to the roof of the next house. Hussin had his finger to his lips, and I soon saw why. For there was a lighted window in the wall we had descended.

Some imp prompted me to wait behind and explore. The others followed Hussin and were soon at the far end of the roof, where a kind of wooden pavilion broke the line, while I tried to get a look inside. The window was curtained, and had two folding sashes which clasped in the middle. Through a gap in the curtain I saw a little lamp-lit room and a big man sitting at a table littered with papers.

I watched him, fascinated, as he turned to consult some document and made a marking on the map before him. Then he suddenly rose, stretched himself, cast a glance at the window, and went out of the room, making a great clatter in descending the wooden staircase. He left the door ajar and the lamp burning.

I guessed he had gone to have a look at his prisoners, in which case the

show was up. But what filled my mind was an insane desire to get a sight of
his map. It was one of those mad impulses which utterly cloud right reason, a
thing independent of any plan, a crazy leap in the dark. But it was so strong
that I would have pulled that window out by its frame, if need be, to get to
that table.

There was no need, for the flimsy clasp gave at the first pull, and the sashes
swung open. I scrambled in, after listening for steps on the stairs. I crumpled
up the map and stuck it in my pocket, as well as the paper from which I had
seen him copying. Very carefully I removed all marks of my entry, brushed
away the snow from the boards, pulled back the curtain, got out and
refastened the window. Still there was no sound of his return. Then I started
off to catch up the others.

I found them shivering in the roof pavilion. "We've got to move pretty
fast," I said, "for I've just been burgling old Stumm's private cabinet.
Hussin, my lad, d'you hear that? They may be after us any moment, so I pray
Heaven we soon strike better going."

Hussin understood. He led us at a smart pace from one roof to another, for
here they were all of the same height, and only low parapets and screens
divided them. We never saw a soul, for a winter's night is not the time you
choose to saunter on your housetop. I kept my ears open for trouble behind
us, and in about five minutes I heard it. A riot of voices broke out, with one
louder than the rest, and, looking back, I saw lanterns waving. Stumm had
realized his loss and found the tracks of the thief.

Hussin gave one glance behind and then hurried us on at a breakneck pace,
with old Blenkiron gasping and stumbling. The shouts behind us grew
louder, as if some eye quicker than the rest had caught our movement in the
starlit darkness. It was very evident that if they kept up the chase we should
be caught, for Blenkiron was about as useful on a roof as a hippo.

Presently we came to a big drop, with a kind of ladder down it, and at the
foot a shallow ledge running to the left into a pit of darkness. Hussin gripped
my arm and pointed down it. "Follow it," he whispered, "and you will reach
a roof which spans a street. Cross it, and on the other side is a mosque. Turn
to the right there and you will find easy going for fifty metres, well screened
from the higher roofs. For Allah's sake, keep in the shelter of the screen.
Somewhere there I will join you."

He hurried us along the ledge for a bit and then went back, and with snow
from the corners covered up our tracks. After that he went straight on
himself, taking strange short steps like a bird. I saw his game. He wanted to
lead our pursuers after him, and he had to multiply the tracks, and trust to
Stumm's fellows not spotting that they all were made by one man.

But I had quite enough to think of in getting Blenkiron along that ledge.
He was pretty nearly foundered, he was in a sweat of terror, and as a matter
of fact he was taking one of the biggest risks of his life, for we had no rope
and his neck depended on himself. I could hear him invoking some unknown
deity called Holy Mike. But he ventured gallantly, and we got to the roof
which ran across the street. That was easier, though ticklish enough, but it

was no joke skirting the cupola of that infernal mosque. At last we found the parapet and breathed more freely, for we were now under shelter from the direction of danger. I spared a moment to look round, and thirty yards off, across the street, I saw a weird spectacle.

The hunt was proceeding along the roofs parallel to the one we were lodged on. I saw the flicker of the lanterns, waved up and down as the bearers slipped in the snow, and I heard their cries like hounds on a trail. Stumm was not among them: he had not the shape for that sort of business. They passed us and continued to our left, now hid by a jutting chimney, now clear to view against the skyline. The roofs they were on were perhaps six feet higher than ours, so even from our shelter we could mark their course. If Hussin were going to be hunted across Erzerum it was a bad look-out for us, for I hadn't the foggiest notion where we were or where we were going to.

But as we watched we saw something more. The wavering lanterns were now three or four hundred yards away, but on the roofs just opposite us across the street there appeared a man's figure. I thought it was one of the hunters, and we all crouched lower, and then I recognized the lean agility of Hussin. He must have doubled back, keeping in the dusk to the left of the pursuit, and taking big risks in the open places. But there he was now, exactly in front of us, and separated only by the width of the narrow street.

He took a step backward, gathered himself for a spring, and leaped clean over the gap. Like a cat he lighted on the parapet above us, and stumbled forward with the impetus right on our heads.

"We are safe for the moment," he whispered, "but when they miss me they will return. We must make good haste."

The next half-hour was a maze of twists and turns, slipping down icy roofs and climbing icier chimney-stacks. The stir of the city had gone, and from the black streets below came scarcely a sound. But always the great tattoo of guns beat in the east. Gradually we descended to a lower level, till we emerged on the top of a shed in a courtyard. Hussin gave an odd sort of cry, like a demented owl, and something began to stir below us.

It was a big covered wagon, full of bundles of forage, and drawn by four mules. As we descended from the shed into the frozen litter of the yard, a man came out of the shade and spoke low to Hussin. Peter and I lifted Blenkiron into the cart, and scrambled in beside him, and I never felt anything more blessed than the warmth and softness of that place after the frosty roofs. I had forgotten all about my hunger, and only yearned for sleep. Presently the wagon moved out of the coutryard into the dark streets.

Then Blenkiron began to laugh, a deep internal rumble which shook him violently and brought down a heap of forage on his head. I thought it was hysterics, the relief from the tension of the past hour. But it wasn't. His body might be out of training, but there was never anything the matter with his nerves. He was consumed with honest merriment.

"Say, Major," he gasped, "I don't usually cherish dislikes for my fellow-men, but somehow I didn't cotton to Colonel Stumm. But now I almost love him. You hit his jaw very bad in Germany, and now you've annexed his private file, and I guess it's important or he wouldn't have been so mighty set on steeplechasing over those roofs. I haven't done such a thing since I broke into neighbour Brown's woodshed to steal his tame 'possum, and that's forty years back. It's the first piece of genooine amusement I've struck in this game, and I haven't laughed so much since old Jim Hooker told the tale of 'Cousin Sally Dillard' when we were hunting ducks in Michigan and his wife's brother had an apoplexy in the night and died of it."

To the accompaniment of Blenkiron's chuckles I did what Peter had done in the first minute, and fell asleep.

When I awoke it was still dark. The wagon had stopped in a courtyard which seemed to be shaded by great trees. The snow lay deeper here, and by the feel of the air we had left the city and climbed to higher ground. There were big buildings on one side, and on the other what looked like the lift of a hill. No lights were shown, the place was in profound gloom, but I felt the presence near me of others besides Hussin and the driver.

We were hurried, Blenkiron only half awake, into an outbuilding, and then down some steps to a roomy cellar. There Hussin lit a lantern, which showed what had once been a storehouse for fruit. Old husks still strewed the floor and the place smelt of apples. Straw had been piled in corners for beds, and there was a rude table, and a divan of boards covered with sheepskins.

"Where are we?" I asked Hussin.

"In the house of the Master," he said. "You will be safe here, but you must keep still till the Master comes."

"Is the Frankish lady here?" I asked.

Hussin nodded, and from a wallet brought out some food—raisins and cold meat and a loaf of bread. We fell on it like vultures, and as we ate Hussin disappeared. I noticed that he locked the door behind him.

As soon as the meal was ended the others returned to their interrupted sleep. But I was wakeful now and my mind was sharp-set on many things. I got Blenkiron's electric torch and lay down on the divan to study Stumm's map.

The first glance showed me that I had lit on a treasure. It was the staff map of the Erzerum defences, showing the forts and the field trenches, with little notes scribbled in Stumm's neat small handwriting. I got out the big map which I had taken from Blenkiron, and made out the general lie of the land. I saw the horseshoe of Deve Boyun to the east which the Russian guns were battering. Stumm's was just like the kind of squared artillery map we used in France, 1 in 10,000, with spidery red lines showing the trenches, but with the difference that it was the Turkish trenches that were shown in detail and the Russian only roughly indicated. The thing was really a confidential plan of the whole Erzerum *enceinte*, and would be worth untold gold to the enemy. No wonder Stumm had been in a wax at its loss.

The Deve Boyun lines seemed to me monstrously strong, and I remembered the merits of the Turk as a fighter behind strong defences. It looked as if Russia were up against a second Plevna or a new Gallipoli.

Then I took to studying the flanks. South lay the Palantuken range of mountain, with forts defending the passes, where ran the roads to Mush and Lake Van. That side, too, looked pretty strong. North in the valley of the Euphrates I made out two big forts, Tafta and Kara Gubek, defending the road from Olti. On this part of the map Stumm's notes were plentiful, and I gave them all my attention. I remembered Blenkiron's news about the Russians advancing on a broad front, for it was clear that Stumm was taking pains about the flank of the fortress.

Kara Gubek was the point of interest. It stood on a rib of land between two peaks, which from the contour lines rose very steep. So long as it was held it was clear that no invader could move down the Euphrates glen. Stumm had appended a note to the peaks—"*not fortified*"; and about two miles to the north-east there was a red cross and the name "*Prjevalsky.*" I assumed that to be the farthest point yet reached by the right wing of the Russian attack.

Then I turned to the paper from which Stumm had copied the jottings on to his map. It was typewritten, and consisted of notes on different points. One was headed "*Kara Gubek*" and read: "*No time to fortify adjacent peaks. Difficult for enemy to get batteries there, but not impossible. This the real point of danger, for if Prjevalsky wins the peaks Kara Gubek and Tafta must fall, and enemy will be on left rear of Deve Boyun main position.*"

I was soldier enough to see the tremendous importance of this note. On Kara Gubek depended the defence of Erzerum, and it was a broken reed if one knew where the weakness lay. Yet, searching the map again, I could not believe that any mortal commander would see any chance in the adjacent peaks, even if he thought them unfortified. That was information confined to the Turkish and German staffs. But if it could be conveyed to the Grand Duke he would have Erzerum in his power in a day. Otherwise he would go on battering at the Deve Boyun ridge for weeks, and long ere he won it the Gallipoli divisions would arrive, he would be outnumbered by two to one, and his chance would have vanished.

My discovery set me pacing up and down that cellar in a perfect fever of excitement. I longed for wireless, a carrier pigeon, an aeroplane—anything to bridge over that space of half a dozen miles between me and the Russian lines. It was maddening to have stumbled on vital news and to be wholly unable to use it. How could three fugitives in a cellar, with the whole hornet's nest of Turkey and Germany stirred up against them, hope to send this message of life and death?

I went back to the map and examined the nearest Russian positions. They were carefully marked. Prjevalsky in the north, the main force beyond Deve Boyun, and the southern columns up to the passes of the Palantuken but not yet across them. I could not know which was nearest to us till I discovered where we were. And as I thought of this I began to see the rudiments of a desperate plan. It depended on Peter, now slumbering like a tired dog on a couch of straw.

Hussin had locked the door, and I must wait for information till he came back. But suddenly I noticed a trap in the roof, which had evidently been used for raising and lowering the cellar's stores. It looked ill-fitting and might be unbarred, so I pulled the table below it, and found that with a little effort I could raise the flap. I knew I was taking immense risks, but I was so keen on my plan that I disregarded them. After some trouble I got the thing prised open, and catching the edges of the hole with my fingers raised my body and got my knees on the edge.

It was the outbuilding of which our refuge was the cellar, and it was half filled with light. Not a soul was there, and I hunted about till I found what I wanted. This was a ladder leading to a sort of loft, which in turn gave access to the roof. Here I had to be very careful, for I might be overlooked from the high buildings. But by good luck there was a trellis for grape vines across the place, which gave a kind of shelter. Lying flat on my face I stared over a great expanse of country.

Looking north I saw the city in a haze of morning smoke, and, beyond, the plain of the Euphrates and the opening of the glen where the river left the hills. Up there among the snowy heights, were Tafta and Kara Gubek. To the east was the ridge of Deve Boyun, where the mist was breaking before the winter's sun. On the roads up to it I saw transport moving, I saw the circle of the inner forts, but for a moment the guns were silent. South rose a great wall of white mountain, which I took to be the Palantuken. I could see the roads running to the passes, and the smoke of camps and horse-lines right under the cliffs.

I had learned what I needed. We were in the outbuildings of a big country house two or three miles south of the city. The nearest point of the Russian front was somewhere in the foothills of the Palantuken.

As I descended I heard, thin and faint and beautiful, like the cry of a wild bird, the muezzin from the minarets of Erzerum.

When I dropped through the trap the others were awake. Hussin was setting food on the table, and viewing my descent with anxious disapproval.

"It's all right," I said; "I won't do it again, for I've found out all I wanted. Peter, old man, the biggest job of your life is before you!"

29 GREENMANTLE

Peter scarcely looked up from his breakfast.

"I'm willing, Dick," he said. "But you mustn't ask me to be friends with Stumm. He makes my stomach cold, that one."

For the first time he had stopped calling me "Cornelis." The day of make-believe was over for all of us.

"Not to be friends with him," I said, "but to bust him and all his kind."

"Then I'm ready," said Peter cheerfully. "What is it?"

I spread out the maps on the divan. There was no light in the place but Blenkiron's electric torch, for Hussin had put out the lantern. Peter got his nose into the things at once, for his intelligence work in the Boer War had made him handy with maps. It didn't want much telling from me to explain to him the importance of the one I had looted.

"That news is worth many million pounds," said he, wrinkling his brows, and scratching delicately the tip of his left ear. It was a way he had when he was startled.

"How can we get it to our friends?"

Peter cogitated. "There is but one way. A man must take it. Once, I remember, when we fought the Matabele it was necessary to find out whether the chief Makapan was living. Some said he had died, others that he'd gone over the Portuguese border, but I believed he lived. No native could tell us, and since his kraal was well defended no runner could get through. So it was necessary to send a man."

Peter lifted up his head and laughed. "The man found the chief Makapan. He was very much alive and made good shooting with a shotgun. But the man brought the chief Makapan out of his kraal and handed him over to the Mounted Police. You remember Captain Arcoll, Dick—Jim Arcoll? Well, Jim laughed so much that he broke open a wound in his head, and had to have the doctor."

"You were that man, Peter," I said.

"*Ja*, I was the man. There are more ways of getting into kraals than there are ways of keeping people out."

"Will you take this chance?"

"For certain, Dick. I am getting stiff with doing nothing, and if I sit in houses much longer I shall grow old. A man bet me five pounds on the ship that I could not get through a trench line, and if there had been a trench line handy I would have taken him on. I will be very happy, Dick, but I do not say I will succeed. It is new country to me, and I will be hurried, and hurry makes bad stalking."

I showed him what I thought the likeliest place—in the spurs of the Palantuken mountains. Peter's way of doing things was all his own. He scraped earth and plaster out of a corner and sat down to make a little model of the landscape on the table, following the contours of the map. He did it extraordinarily neatly, for, like all great hunters, he was as deft as a weaver-bird. He puzzled over it for a long time, and conned the map till he must have got it by heart. Then he took his field-glasses—a very good single Zeiss which was part of the spoils from Rasta's motor-car—and announced that he was going to follow my example and get on to the housetop. Presently his legs disappeared through the trap, and Blenkiron and I were left to our reflections.

Peter must have found something uncommon interesting, for he stayed on the roof the better part of the day. It was a dull job for us, since there was no light, and Blenkiron had not even the consolation of a game of Patience. But for all that he was in good spirits, for he had had no dyspepsia since we left Constantinople, and announced that he believed he was at last getting even with his darned duodenum. As for me, I was pretty restless, for I could not imagine what was detaining Sandy. I was clear that our presence must have been kept secret from Hilda von Einem, for she was a pal of Stumm's, and he must by now have blown the gaff on Peter and me. How long could this secrecy last, I asked myself. We had now no sort of protection in the whole outfit. Rasta and the Turks wanted our blood; so did Stumm and the Germans; and once the lady found we were deceiving her she would want it most of all. Our only help was Sandy, and he gave no sign of his existence. I began to fear that with him, too, things had miscarried.

And yet I wasn't really depressed, only impatient. I could never again get back to the beastly stagnation of that Constantinople week. The guns kept me cheerful. There was the devil of a bombardment all day, and the thought that our Allies were thundering within half a dozen miles gave me a perfectly groundless hope. If they burst through the defence Hilda von Einem and her prophet and all our enemies would be overwhelmed in the deluge. And that blessed chance depended very much on old Peter, now brooding like a pigeon on the housetops.

It was not till the late afternoon that Hussin appeared again. He took no notice of Peter's absence, but lit a lantern and set it on the table. Then he went to the door and waited. Presently a light step fell on the stairs, and Hussin drew back to let some one enter. He promptly departed and I heard the key turn in the lock behind him.

Sandy stood there, but a new Sandy who made Blenkiron and me jump to our feet. The pelts and skin cap had gone, and he wore instead a long linen tunic clasped at the waist by a broad girdle. A strange green turban adorned his head, and as he pushed it back I saw that his hair had been shaved. He looked like some acolyte—a weary acolyte, for there was no spring in his walk or nerve in his carriage. He dropped numbly on the divan and laid his head in his hands. The lantern showed his haggard eyes with dark lines beneath them.

"Good God, old man, have you been sick?" I cried.

"Not sick," he said hoarsely. "My body is right enough, but the last few days I have been living in hell."

Blenkiron nodded sympathetically. That was how he himself would have described the company of the lady.

I marched across to him and gripped both his wrists.

"Look at me," I said, "straight in the eyes."

His eyes were like a sleep-walker's, unwinking, unseeing. "Great heavens, man, you've been drugged!" I said.

"Drugged," he cried, with a weary laugh. "Yes, I have been drugged, but not by any physic. No one has been doctoring my food. But you can't go through hell without getting your eyes red-hot."

I kept my grip on his wrists. "Take your time, old chap, and tell us about it. Blenkiron and I are here, and old Peter's on the roof not far off. We'll look after you."

"It does me good to hear your voice, Dick," he said. "It reminds me of clean, honest things."

"They'll come back, never fear. We're at the last lap now. One more spurt and it's over. You've got to tell me what the new snag is. Is it that woman?"

He shivered like a frightened colt. "Woman!" he cried. "Does a woman drag a man through the nether pit? She's a she-devil. Oh, it isn't madness that's wrong with her. She's as sane as you and as cool as Blenkiron. Her life is an infernal game of chess, and she plays with souls for pawns. She is evil—evil—evil. . . ." And once more he buried his head in his hands.

It was Blenkiron who brought sense into this hectic atmosphere. His slow, beloved drawl was an antiseptic against nerves.

"Say, boy," he said, "I feel just like you about the lady. But our job is not to investigate her character. Her Maker will do that good and sure some day. We've got to figure how to circumvent her, and for that you've got to tell us what exactly's been occurring since we parted company."

Sandy pulled himself together with a great effort.

"Greenmantle died that night I saw you. We buried him secretly by her order in the garden of the villa. Then came the trouble about his successor. . . . The four Ministers would be no party to a swindle. They were honest men, and vowed that their task now was to make a tomb for their master and pray for the rest of their days at his shrine. They were as immovable as a granite hill, and she knew it. . . . Then they too died."

"Murdered?" I gasped.

"Murdered . . . all four in one morning. I do not know how, but I helped to bury them. Oh, she had Germans and Kurds to do her foul work, but their hands were clean compared to hers. Pity me, Dick, for I have seen honesty and virtue put to the shambles and have abetted the deed when it was done. It will haunt me till my dying day."

I did not stop to console him, for my mind was on fire with his news.

"Then the prophet is gone, and the humbug is over," I cried.

"The prophet still lives. She has found a successor."

He stood up in his linen tunic.

"Why do I wear these clothes? Because I am Greenmantle. I am the Kaába-i-hurriyeh for all Islam. In three days' time I will reveal myself to my people and wear on my breast the green ephod of the prophet."

He broke off with an hysterical laugh.

"Only you see, I won't. I will cut my throat first."

"Cheer up!" said Blenkiron soothingly. "We'll find some prettier way than that."

"There is no way," he said; "no way but death. We're done for, all of us. Hussin got you out of Stumm's clutches, but you're in danger every moment. At the best you have three days, and then you, too, will be dead."

I had no words to reply. This change in the bold and unshakable Sandy took my breath away.

"She made me her accomplice," he went on. "I should have killed her on the graves of those innocent men. But instead I did all she asked, and joined in her game. . . . She was very candid, you know. . . . She cares no more than Enver for the faith of Islam. She can laugh at it. But she has her own dreams, and they consume her as a saint is consumed by his devotion. She has told me them, and if the day in the garden was hell, the days since have been the innermost fires of Tophet. I think—it is horrible to say it—that she has got some kind of crazy liking for me. When we have reclaimed the East I am to be by her side when she rides on her milk-white horse into Jerusalem. . . . And there have been moments—only moments, I swear to God—when I have been fired myself by her madness. . . ."

Sandy's figure seemed to shrink and his voice grew shrill and wild. It was too much for Blenkiron. He indulged in a torrent of blasphemy such as I believe had never before passed his lips.

"I'm blessed if I'll listen to this God-darned stuff. It isn't delicate. You get busy, Major, and pump some sense into your afflicted friend."

I was beginning to see what had happened. Sandy was a man of genius—as much as anybody I ever struck—but he had the defects of such high-strung, fanciful souls. He would take more than mortal risks, and you couldn't scare him by any ordinary terror. But let his old conscience get cross-eyed, let him find himself in some situation which in his eyes involved his honour, and he might go stark crazy. The woman, who roused in me and Blenkiron only hatred, could catch his imagination and stir in him—for the moment only—an unwilling response. And then came bitter and morbid repentance, and the last desperation.

It was no time to mince matters. "Sandy, you old fool," I cried, "be thankful you have friends to keep you from playing the fool. You saved my life at Loos, and I'm jolly well going to get you through this show. I'm bossing the outfit now, and for all your confounded prophetic manners you've got to take your orders from me. You aren't going to reveal yourself to your people, and still less are you going to cut your throat. Greenmantle will avenge the murder of his Ministers, and make that bedlamite woman sorry she was born. We're going to get clear away, and inside of a week we'll be having tea with the Grand Duke Nicholas."

I wasn't bluffing. Puzzled as I was about ways and means I had still the blind belief that we should win out. And as I spoke two legs dangled through the trap and a dusty and blinking Peter descended in our midst.

I took the maps from him and spread them on the table.

"First, you must know that we've had an almighty piece of luck. Last night Hussin took us for a walk over the roofs of Erzerum, and by the blessing of Providence I got into Stumm's room and bagged his staff map. . . . Look there . . . d'you see his notes? That's the danger-point of the whole defence. Once the Russians get that fort, Kara Gubek, they've turned the main position. And it can be got; Stumm knows it can; for these two adjacent hills are not held. . . . It looks a mad enterprise on paper, but Stumm knows that it is possible enough. The question is: Will the Russians guess that? I say no, not unless some one tells them. Therefore, by hook or by crook, we've got to get that information through to them."

Sandy's interest in ordinary things was beginning to flicker up again. He studied the map and began to measure distances.

"Peter's going to have a try for it. He thinks there's a sporting chance of his getting through the lines. If he does—if he gets this map to the Grand Duke's staff—then Stumm's goose is cooked. In three days the Cossacks will be in the streets of Erzerum."

"What are the chances?" Sandy asked.

I glanced at Peter. "We're hard-bitten fellows and can face the truth. I think the chances against success are about five to one."

"Two to one," said Peter modestly. "Not worse than that. I don't think you're fair to me, Dick, my old friend."

I looked at that lean, tight figure and the gentle, resolute face, and I changed my mind. "I'm hanged if I think there are any odds," I said. "With anybody else it would want a miracle, but with Peter I believe the chances are level."

"Two to one," Peter persisted. "If it was evens I wouldn't be interested."

"Let me go," Sandy cried. "I talk the lingo, and can pass as a Turk, and I'm a million times likelier to get through. For God's sake, Dick, let me go."

"Not you. You're wanted here. If you disappear the whole show's busted too soon, and the three of us left behind will be strung up before morning. . . . No, my son. You're going to escape, but it will be in company with Blenkiron and me. We've got to blow the whole Greenmantle business so high that the bits of it will never come to earth again. . . . First, tell me how many of your fellows will stick by you? I mean the Companions."

"The whole half-dozen. They are very worried already about what has happened. She made me sound them in her presence, and they were quite ready to accept me as Greenmantle's successor. But they have their suspicions about what happened at the villa, and they've no love for the woman. . . . They'd follow me through hell if I bade them, but they would rather it was my own show."

"That's all right," I cried. "It is the one thing I've been doubtful about. Now observe this map. Erzerum isn't invested by a long chalk. The Russians are round it in a broad half-moon. That means that all the west, south-west, and north-west is open and undefended by trench lines. There are flanks far away to the north and south in the hills which can be turned, and once we get round a flank there's nothing between us and our friends. . . . I've figured out our road," and I traced it on the map. "If we can make that big circuit to the west and get over that pass unobserved we're bound to strike a Russian column the next day. It'll be a rough road, but I fancy we've all ridden as bad in our time. But one thing we must have, and that's horses. Can we and your six ruffians slip off in the darkness on the best beasts in this township? If you can manage that, we'll do the trick."

Sandy sat down and pondered. Thank Heaven, he was thinking now of action and not of his own conscience.

"It must be done," he said at last, "but it won't be easy. Hussin's a great fellow, but as you know well, Dick, horses right up at the battle-front are not easy to come by. To-morrow I've got some kind of infernal fast to observe, and the next day that woman will be coaching me for my part. We'll have to give Hussin time. . . . I wish to Heaven it could be to-night." He was silent again for a bit, and then he said: "I believe the best time would be the third night, the eve of the Revelation. She's bound to leave me alone that night."

"Right-o," I said. "It won't be much fun sitting waiting in this cold sepulchre; but we must keep our heads and risk nothing by being in a hurry. Besides, if Peter wins through, the Turk will be a busy man by the day after to-morrow."

The key turned in the door and Hussin stole in like a shade. It was the signal for Sandy to leave.

"You fellows have given me a new lease of life," he said. "I've got a plan now, and I can set my teeth and stick it out."

He went up to Peter and gripped his hand. "Good luck. You're the bravest man I've ever met, and I've seen a few." Then he turned abruptly and went out, followed by an exhortation from Blenkiron to "Get busy about the quadrupeds."

Then we set about equipping Peter for his crusade. It was a simple job, for we were not rich in properties. His get-up, with his thick fur-collared greatcoat, was not unlike the ordinary Turkish officer seen in a dim light. But Peter had no intention of passing for a Turk, or indeed of giving anybody the chance of seeing him, and he was more concerned to fit in with the landscape. So he stripped off the greatcoat and pulled a grey sweater of mine over his jacket, and put on his head a woollen helmet of the same colour. He had no need of the map, for he had long since got his route by heart, and what was once fixed in that mind stuck like wax; but I made him take Stumm's plan and paper, hidden below his shirt. The big difficulty, I saw, would be getting to the Russians without being shot, assuming he passed the Turkish trenches. I could only hope that he would strike some one with a smattering of English or German. Twice he ascended to the roof and came back cheerful, for there was promise of wild weather.

Hussin brought in our supper, and Peter made up a parcel of food. Blenkiron and I had both small flasks of brandy, and I gave him mine.

Then he held out his hand quite simply, like a good child who is going off to bed. It was too much for Blenkiron. With large tears rolling down his face he announced that, if we all came through, he was going to fit him into the softest berth that money could buy. I don't think he was understood, for old Peter's eyes had now the far-away absorption of the hunter who has found game. He was thinking only of his job.

Two legs and a pair of very shabby boots vanished through the trap, and suddenly I felt utterly lonely and desperately sad. The guns were beginning to roar again in the east, and in the intervals came the whistle of the rising storm.

30 PETER PIENAAR GOES TO THE WARS

This chapter is the tale that Peter told me—long after, sitting beside a stove in the hotel at Bergen, where we were waiting for our boat.

He climbed on the roof and shinned down the broken bricks of the outer walls. The outbuilding we were lodged in abutted on a road, and was outside the proper *enceinte* of the house. At ordinary times I have no doubt there were sentries, but Sandy and Hussin had probably managed to clear them off this end for a little. Anyhow he saw nobody as he crossed the road and dived into the snowy fields.

He knew very well that he must do the job in the twelve hours of darkness ahead of him. The immediate front of a battle is a bit too public for any one to lie hidden in by day, especially when two or three feet of snow make everything kenspeckle. Now hurry in a job of this kind was abhorrent to Peter's soul, for, like all Boers, his tastes were for slowness and sureness, though he could hustle fast enough when haste was needed. As he pushed through the winter fields he reckoned up the things in his favour, and found the only one the dirty weather. There was a high, gusty wind, blowing scuds of snow but never coming to any great fall. The frost had gone, and the lying snow was as soft as butter. That was all to the good, he thought, for a clear, hard night would have been the devil.

The first bit was through farm lands, which were seamed with little snow-filled water-furrows. Now and then would come a house and a patch of fruit trees, but there was nobody abroad. The roads were crowded enough, but Peter had no use for roads. I can picture him swinging along with his bent back, stopping every now and then to sniff and listen, alert for the foreknowledge of danger. When he chose he could cover country like an antelope.

Soon he struck a big road full of transport. It was the road from Erzerum to the Palantuken pass, and he waited his chance and crossed it. After that the ground grew rough with boulders and patches of thorn-trees, splendid cover where he could move fast without worrying. Then he was pulled up suddenly on the bank of a river. The map had warned him of it, but not that it would be so big.

It was a torrent swollen with melting snow and rains in the hills, and it was running fifty yards wide. Peter thought he could have swum it, but he was very averse to a drenching. "A wet man makes too much noise," he said, and besides, there was the off-chance that the current would be too much for him. So he moved up stream to look for a bridge.

227

In ten minutes he found one, a new-made thing of trestles, broad enough to take transport wagons. It was guarded, for he heard the tramp of a sentry, and as he pulled himself up the bank he observed a couple of long wooden huts, obviously some kind of billets. These were on the near side of the stream, about a dozen yards from the bridge. A door stood open and a light showed in it, and from within came the sound of voices. . . . Peter had a sense of hearing like a wild animal, and he could detect even from the confused gabble that the voices were German.

As he lay and listened some one came over the bridge. It was an officer, for the sentry saluted. The man disappeared in one of the huts. Peter had struck the billets and repairing shop of a squad of German sappers.

He was just going ruefully to retrace his steps and try to find a good place to swim the stream when it struck him that the officer who had passed him wore clothes very like his own. He, too, had had a grey sweater and a Balaclava helmet, for even a German officer ceases to be dressy on a midwinter's night in Anatolia. The idea came to Peter to walk boldly across the bridge and trust to the sentry not seeing the difference.

He slipped round a corner of the hut and marched down the road. The sentry was now at the far end, which was lucky, for if the worst came to the worst he could throttle him. Peter, mimicking the stiff German walk, swung past him, his head down as if to protect him from the wind.

The man saluted. He did more, for he offered conversation. The officer must have been a genial soul. "It's a rough night, Captain," he said. "The wagons are late. Pray God, Michael hasn't got a shell in his lot. They've begun putting over some big ones."

Peter grunted good-night in German and strode on. He was just leaving the road when he heard a great halloo behind him.

The real officer must have appeared on his heels, and the sentry's doubts had been stirred. A whistle was blown, and, looking back, Peter saw lanterns waving in the gale. They were coming out to look for the duplicate.

He stood still for a second, and noticed the lights spreading out south of the road. He was just about to dive off it on the north side when he was aware of a difficulty. On that side a steep bank fell to a ditch, and the bank beyond bounded a big flood. He could see the dull ruffle of the water under the wind.

On the road itself he would soon be caught; south of it the search was beginning; and the ditch itself was no place to hide, for he saw a lantern moving up it. Peter dropped into it all the same and made a plan. The side below the road was a little undercut and very steep. He resolved to plaster himself against it, for he would be hidden from the road, and a searcher in the ditch would not be likely to explore the unbroken sides. It was always a maxim of Peter's that the best hiding-place was the worst, the least obvious to the minds of those who were looking for you.

He waited till the lights both in the road and the ditch came nearer, and then he gripped the edge with his left hand, where some stones gave him purchase, dug the toes of his boots into the wet soil, and stuck like a limpet. It needed some strength to keep the position for long, but the muscles of his arms and legs were like whipcord.

The searcher in the ditch soon grew tired, for the place was very wet, and joined his comrades on the road. They came along, running, flashing the lanterns into the trench, and exploring all the immediate countryside.

Then rose a noise of wheels and horses from the opposite direction. Michael and the delayed wagons were approaching. They dashed up at a great pace, driven wildly, and for one horrid second Peter thought they were going to spill into the ditch at the very spot where he was concealed. The wheels passed so close to the edge that they almost grazed his fingers. Somebody shouted an order, and they pulled up a yard or two nearer the bridge. The others came up and there was a consultation.

Michael swore he had passed no one on the road.

"That fool Hannus has seen a ghost," said the officer testily. "It's too cold for this child's play."

Hannus, almost in tears, repeated his tale. "The man spoke to me in good German," he cried.

"Ghost or no ghost he is safe enough up the road," said the officer. "Kind God, that was a big one!" He stopped and stared at a shell-burst, for the bombardment from the east was growing fiercer.

They stood discussing the fire for a minute and presently moved off. Peter gave them two minutes law and then clambered back to the highway and set off along it at a run. The noise of the shelling and the wind, together with the thick darkness, made it safe to hurry.

He left the road at the first chance and took to the broken country. The ground was now rising towards a spur of the Palantuken, on the far slope of which were the Turkish trenches. The night had begun by being pretty nearly as black as pitch; even the smoke from the shell explosions, which is often visible in darkness, could not be seen. But as the wind blew the snow-clouds athwart the sky patches of stars came out. Peter had a compass, but he didn't need to use it, for he had a kind of "feel" for landscape, a special sense which is born in savages and can only be acquired after long experience by the white man. I believe he could smell where the north lay. He had settled roughly which part of the line he would try, merely because of its nearness to the enemy. But he might see reason to vary this, and as he moved he began to think that the safest place was where the shelling was hottest. He didn't like the notion, but it sounded sense.

Suddenly he began to puzzle over queer things in the ground, and, as he had never seen big guns before, it took him a moment to fix them. Presently one went off at his elbow with a roar like the Last Day. These were the Austrian howitzers—nothing over 8-inch, I fancy, but to Peter they looked like leviathans. Here, too, he saw for the first time a big and quite recent shell-hole, for the Russian guns were searching out the position. He was so interested in it all that he poked his nose where he shouldn't have been, and dropped plump into the pit behind a gun-emplacement.

Gunners all the world over are the same—shy people, who hide themselves in holes and hibernate and mortally dislike being detected.

A gruff voice cried *"Wer da?"* and a heavy hand seized his neck.

Peter was ready with his story. He belonged to Michael's wagon-team and had been left behind. He wanted to be told the way to the sappers' camp. He was very apologetic, not to say obsequious.

"It is one of those Prussian swine from the Marta Bridge," said a gunner. "Land him a kick to teach him sense. Bear to your right, mannikin, and you will find a road. And have a care when you get there, for the Russkoes have it registered."

Peter thanked them and bore off to the right. After that he kept a wary eye on the howitzers, and was thankful when he got out of their area on to the slopes up the hill. Here was the type of country that was familiar to him, and he defied any Turk or Boche to spot him among the scrub and boulders. He was getting on very well, when once more, close to his ear, came a sound like the crack of doom.

It was the field-guns now, and the sound of a field-gun close at hand is bad for the nerves if you aren't expecting it. Peter thought he had been hit, and lay flat for a little to consider. Then he found the right explanation, and crawled forward very warily.

Presently he saw his first Russian shell. It dropped half a dozen yards to his right, making a great hole in the snow and sending up a mass of mixed earth, snow, and broken stones. Peter spat out the dirt and felt very solemn. You must remember that never in his life had he seen big shelling, and was now being landed in the thick of a first-class show without any preparation. He said he felt cold in his stomach, and very wishful to run away, if there had been anywhere to run to. But he kept on to the crest of the ridge, over which a big glow was broadening like a sunrise. He tripped once over a wire, which he took for some kind of snare, and after that went very warily. By and by he got his face between two boulders and looked over into the true battlefield.

He told me it was exactly what the predikant used to say that Hell would be like. About fifty yards down the slope lay the Turkish trenches—they were dark against the snow, and now and then a black figure like a devil showed for an instant and disappeared. The Turks clearly expected an infantry attack, for they were sending up calcium rockets and Véry flares. The Russians were battering their line and spraying all the hinterland, not with shrapnel, but with good, solid high-explosives. The place would be as bright as day for a moment, all smothered in a scurry of smoke and snow and debris, and then a black pall would fall on it, when only the thunder of the guns told of the battle.

Peter felt very sick. He had not believed there could be so much noise in the world, and the drums of his ears were splitting. Now, for a man to whom courage is habitual, the taste of fear—naked utter fear—is a horrible thing. It seems to wash away all his manhood. Peter lay on the crest, watching the shells burst, and confident that any moment he might be a shattered remnant. He lay and reasoned with himself, calling himself every name he could think of, but conscious that nothing would get rid of that lump of ice below his heart.

Then he could stand it no longer. He got up and ran for his life.

But he ran forward.

It was the craziest performance. He went hell-for-leather over a piece of ground which was being watered with H. E., but by the mercy of Heaven nothing hit him. He took some fearsome tosses in shell-holes, but partly erect and partly on all fours he did the fifty yards and tumbled into a Turkish trench right on top of a dead man.

The contact with that body brought him to his senses. That men could die at all seemed a comforting, homely thing after that unnatural pandemonium. The next moment a crump took the parapet of the trench some yards to his left, and he was half buried in an avalanche.

He crawled out of that, pretty badly cut about the head. He was quite cool now and thinking hard about his next step. There were men all around him, sullen dark faces as he saw them when the flares went up. They were manning the parapets and waiting tensely for something else than the shelling. They paid no attention to him, for I fancy in that trench units were pretty well mixed up, and under a bad bombardment no one bothers about his neighbour. He found himself free to move as he pleased. The ground of the trench was littered with empty cartridge-cases, and there were many dead bodies.

The last shell, as I have said, had played havoc with the parapet. In the next spell of darkness Peter crawled through the gap and twisted among some snowy hillocks. He was no longer afraid of shells any more than he was afraid of a veld thunderstorm. But he was wondering very hard how he should ever get to the Russians. The Turks were behind him now, but there was the biggest danger in front.

Then the artillery ceased. It was so sudden that he thought he had gone deaf, and could hardly realize the blessed relief of it. The wind, too, seemed to have fallen, or perhaps he was sheltered by the lee of the hill. There were a lot of dead here also, and that he couldn't understand, for they were new dead. Had the Turks attacked and been driven back? When he had gone about thirty yards he stopped to take his bearings. On the right were the ruins of a large building set on fire by the guns. There was a blur of woods and the debris of walls round it. Away to the left another hill ran out farther to the east, and the place he was in seemed to be a kind of cup between the spurs. Just before him was a little ruined building, with the sky seen through its rafters, for the smouldering ruin on the right gave a certain light. He wondered if the Russian firing-line lay there.

Just then he heard voices—smothered voices—not a yard away and apparently below the ground. He instantly jumped to what this must mean. It was a Turkish trench—a communication trench. Peter didn't know much about modern warfare, but he had read in the papers, or heard from me, enough to make him draw the right moral. The fresh dead pointed to the same conclusion. What he had got through were the Turkish support trenches, not their firing-line. That was still before him.

He didn't despair, for the rebound from panic had made him extra courageous. He crawled forward, an inch at a time, taking no sort of risk, and presently found himself looking at the parados of a trench. Then he lay quiet to think out the next step.

The shelling had stopped, and there was that queer kind of peace which falls sometimes on two armies not a quarter of a mile distant. Peter said he could hear nothing but the far-off sighing of the wind. There seemed to be no movement of any kind in the trench before him, which ran through the ruined building. The light of the burning was dying, and he could just make out the mound of earth a yard in front. He began to feel hungry, and got out his packet of food and had a swig at the brandy flask. That comforted him, and he felt master of his fate again. But the next step was not so easy. He must find out what lay behind that mound of earth.

Suddenly a curious sound fell on his ears. It was so faint that at first he doubted the evidence of his senses. Then as the wind fell it came louder. It was exactly like some hollow piece of metal being struck by a stick, musical and oddly resonant.

He concluded it was the wind blowing a branch of a tree against an old boiler in the ruin before him. The trouble was that now there was scarcely enough wind for that in this sheltered cup.

But as he listened he caught the note again. It was a bell, a fallen bell, and the place before him must have been a chapel. He remembered that an Armenian monastery had been marked on the big map, and he guessed it was the burned building on his right.

The thought of a chapel and a bell gave him the notion of some human agency. And then suddenly the notion was confirmed. The sound was regular and concerted—dot, dash, dot—dash, dot, dot. The branch of a tree and the wind may play strange pranks, but they do not produce the longs and shorts of the Morse code.

This was where Peter's intelligence work in the Boer War helped him. He knew the Morse, he could read it, but he could make nothing of the signalling. It was either in some special code or in a strange language.

He lay still and did some calm thinking. There was a man in front of him, a Turkish soldier, who was in the enemy's pay. Therefore he could fraternize with him, for they were on the same side. But how was he to approach him without getting shot in the process? Again, how could a man send signals to the enemy from a firing-line without being detected? Peter found an answer in the strange configuration of the ground. He had not heard a sound till he was a few yards from the place, and they would be inaudible to men in the reserve trenches and even in the communication trenches. If somebody moving up the latter caught the noise, it would be easy to explain it naturally. But the wind blowing down the cup would carry it far in the enemy's direction.

There remained the risk of being heard by those parallel with the bell in the firing trench. Peter concluded that that trench must be very thinly held, probably only by a few observers, and the nearest might be a dozen yards off. He had read about that being the French fashion under a big bombardment.

The next thing was to find out how to make himself known to this ally. He decided that the only way was to surprise him. He might get shot, but he trusted to his strength and agility against a man who was almost certainly wearied. When he had got him safe, explanations might follow.

Peter was now enjoying himself hugely. If only those infernal guns kept silent he would play out the game in the sober, decorous way he loved. So very delicately he began to wriggle forward to where the sound was.

The night was as black as ink round him, and very quiet, too, except for soughings of the dying gale. The snow had drifted a little in the lee of the ruined walls, and Peter's progress was naturally very slow. He could not afford to dislodge one ounce of snow. Still the tinkling went on, now in greater volume. Peter was in terror lest it should cease before he got his man. Presently his hand clutched at empty space. He was on the lip of the front trench. The sound was now a yard to his right, and with infinite care he shifted his position. Now the bell was just below him, and he felt the big rafter of the woodwork from which it had fallen. He felt something else—a stretch of wire fixed in the ground with the far end hanging in the void. That would be the spy's explanation if any one heard the sound and came seeking the cause.

Somewhere in the darkness before and below him was the man, not a yard off. Peter remained very still, studying the situation. He could not see, but he could feel the presence, and he was trying to decide the relative position of man and bell and their exact distance from him. The thing was not so easy as it looked, for if he jumped for where he believed the figure was, he might miss it and get a bullet in the stomach. A man who played so risky a game was probably handy with his firearms. Besides, if he should hit the bell, he would make a hideous row and alarm the whole front.

Fate suddenly gave him the right chance. The unseen figure stood up and moved a step, till his back was against the parados. He actually brushed against Peter's elbow, who held his breath.

There is a catch that the Kaffirs have which would need several diagrams to explain. It is partly a neck hold, and partly a paralysing backward twist of the right arm, but if it is practised on a man from behind, it locks him as sure as if he were handcuffed. Peter slowly got his body raised and his knees drawn under him, and reached for his prey.

He got him. A head was pulled backward over the edge of the trench, and he felt in the air the motion of the left arm pawing feebly but unable to reach behind.

"Be still," whispered Peter in German; "I mean you no harm. We are friends of the same purpose. Do you speak German?"

"*Nein*," said a muffled voice.

"English?"

"Yes," said the voice.

"Thank God," said Peter. "Then we can understand each other. I've watched your notion of signalling, and a very good one it is. I've got to get through to the Russian lines somehow before morning, and I want you to help me. I'm English—a kind of English—so we're on the same side. If I let go your neck will you be good and talk reasonably?"

The voice assented. Peter let go, and in the same instant slipped to the side. The man wheeled round and flung out an arm but gripped vacancy.

"Steady, friend," said Peter; "you mustn't play tricks with me or I'll be angry."

"Who are you? Who sent you?" asked the puzzled voice.

Peter had a happy thought. "The Companions of the Rosy Hours," he said.

"Then are we friends indeed," said the voice. "Come out of the darkness, friend, and I will do you no harm. I am a good Turk, and I fought beside the English in Kordofan and learned their tongue. I live only to see the ruin of Enver, who has beggared my family and slain my twin brother. Therefore I serve the *Muscov ghiaours*."

"I don't know what the Musky Jaws are, but if you mean the Russians I'm with you. I've got news for them which will make Enver green. The question is, how I'm to get to them, and that is where you shall help me, my friend."

"How?"

"By playing that little tune of yours again. Tell them to expect within the next half-hour a deserter with an important message. Tell them, for God's sake, not to fire at anybody till they've made certain it isn't me."

The man took the blunt end of his bayonet and squatted beside the bell. The first stroke brought out a clear, searching note which floated down the valley. He struck three notes at slow intervals. For all the world, Peter said, he was like a telegraph operator calling up a station.

"Send the message in English," said Peter.

"They may not understand it," said the man.

"Then send it any way you like. I trust you, for we are brothers."

After ten minutes the man ceased and listened. From far away came the sound of a trench-gong, the kind of thing they used on the Western Front to give the gas-alarm.

"They say they will be ready," he said. "I cannot take down messages in the darkness, but they have given me the signal which means 'Consent.' "

"Come, that is pretty good," said Peter. "And now I must be moving. You take a hint from me. When you hear big firing up to the north get ready to beat a quick retreat, for it will be all up with that city of yours. And tell your folk, too, that they're making a bad mistake letting those fool Germans rule their land. Let them hang Enver and his little friends, and we'll all be happy once more."

"May Satan receive his soul!" said the Turk. "There is wire before us, but I will show you a way through. The guns this evening made many rents in it. But haste, for a working party may be here presently to repair it. Remember there is much wire before the other lines."

Peter, with certain directions, found it pretty easy to make his way through the entanglement. There was one bit which scraped a hole in his back, but very soon he had come to the last posts and found himself in open country. The place, he said, was a graveyard of the unburied dead that smelt horribly as he crawled among them. He had no inducements to delay, for he thought he could hear behind him the movement of the Turkish working party, and was in terror that a flare might reveal him and a volley accompany his retreat.

From one shell-hole to another he wormed his way, till he struck an old ruinous communication trench which led in the right direction. The Turks must have been forced back in the past week, and the Russians were now in the evacuated trenches. The thing was half full of water, but it gave Peter a feeling of safety, for it enabled him to get his head below the level of the ground. Then it came to an end, and he found before him a forest of wire.

The Turk in his signal had mentioned half an hour, but Peter thought it was nearer two hours before he got through that noxious entanglement. Shelling had made little difference to it. The uprights were all there, and the barbed strands seemed to touch the ground. Remember, he had no wire-cutter; nothing but his bare hands. Once again fear got hold of him. He felt caught in a net, with monstrous vultures waiting to pounce on him from above. At any moment a flare might go up and a dozen rifles find their mark. He had altogether forgotten about the message which had been sent, for no message could dissuade the ever-present death he felt around him. It was, he said, like following an old lion into bush when there was but one narrow way in and no road out.

The guns began again—the Turkish guns from behind the ridge—and a shell tore up the wire a short way before him. Under cover of the burst he made good a few yards, leaving large portions of his clothing in the strands. Then quite suddenly, when hope had almost died in his heart, he felt the ground rise steeply. He lay very still, a star-rocket from the Turkish side lit up the place, and there in front was a rampart with the points of bayonets showing beyond it. It was the Russian hour for stand-to.

He raised his cramped limbs from the ground and shouted, "Friend! English!"

A face looked down at him, and then the darkness again descended.

"Friend!" he said hoarsely. "English!"

He heard speech behind the parapet. An electric torch was flashed on him for a second. A voice spoke, a friendly voice, and the sound of it seemed to be telling him to come over.

He was now standing up, and as he got his hands on the parapet he seemed to feel bayonets very near him. But the voice that spoke was kindly, so with a heave he scrambled over and flopped into the trench. Once more the electric torch was flashed, and revealed to the eyes of the onlookers an indescribably dirty, lean, middle-aged man with a bloody head, and scarcely a rag of shirt on his back. The said man, seeing friendly faces around him, grinned cheerfully.

"That was a rough trek, friends," he said; "I want to see your general pretty quick, for I've got a present for him."

He was taken to an officer in a dug-out, who addressed him in French, which he did not understand. But the sight of Stumm's plan worked wonders. After that he was fairly bundled down communication trenches and then over swampy fields to a farm among trees. There he found staff officers, who looked at him and looked at his map, and then put him on a horse and hurried him eastwards. At last he came to a big ruined house, and was taken into a room which seemed to be full of maps and generals.

The conclusion must be told in Peter's words.

"There was a big man sitting at a table drinking coffee, and when I saw him my heart jumped out of my skin. For it was the man I hunted with on the Pungwe in '98—him whom the Kaffirs called 'Buck's Horn,' because of his long curled moustaches. He was a prince even then, and now he is a very great general. When I saw him, I ran forward and gripped his hand and cried, '*Hoe gat het, Mynheer?*' and he knew me and shouted in Dutch, 'Damn, if it isn't old Peter Pienaar!' Then he gave me coffee and ham and good bread, and he looked at my map.

" 'What is this?' he cried, growing red in the face.

" 'It is the staff map of one Stumm, a German *skellum* who commands in yon city,' I said.

"He looked at it close and read the markings, and then he read the other paper which you gave me, Dick. And then he flung up his arms and laughed. He took a loaf and tossed it into the air so that it fell on the head of another general. He spoke to them in their own tongue, and they too laughed, and one or two ran out as if on some errand. I have never seen such merrymaking. They were clever men, and knew the worth of what you gave me.

"Then he got to his feet and hugged me, all dirty as I was, and kissed me on both cheeks.

" 'Before God, Peter,' he said, 'you're the mightiest hunter since Nimrod. You've often found me game, but never game so big as this!' "

31 THE LITTLE HILL

It was a wise man who said that the biggest kind of courage was to be able to sit still. I used to feel that when we were getting shelled in the reserve trenches outside Vermelles. I felt it before we went over the parapets at Loos, but I never felt it so much as in the last two days in that cellar. I had simply to set my teeth and take a pull on myself. Peter had gone on a crazy errand which I scarcely believed could come off. There were no signs of Sandy;

somewhere within a hundred yards he was fighting his own battles, and I was tormented by the thought that he might get jumpy again and wreck everything. A strange Companion brought us food, a man who spoke only Turkish and could tell us nothing; Hussin, I judged, was busy about the horses. If I could only have done something to help on matters I could have scotched my anxiety, but there was nothing to be done, nothing but wait and brood. I tell you I began to sympathize with the general behind the lines in a battle, the fellow who makes the plan which others execute. Leading a charge can be nothing like so nerve-shaking a business as sitting in an easy-chair and waiting on the news of it.

It was bitter cold, and we spent most of the day wrapped in our greatcoats and buried deep in the straw. Blenkiron was a marvel. There was no light for him to play Patience by, but he never complained. He slept a lot of the time, and when he was awake talked as cheerily as if he were starting out on a holiday. He had one great comfort—his dyspepsia was gone. He sang hymns constantly to the benign Providence that had squared his duo-denum.

My only occupation was to listen for the guns. The first day after Peter left they were very quiet on the front nearest us, but in the late evening they started a terrific racket. The next day they never stopped from dawn to dusk, so that it reminded me of that tremendous forty-eight hours before Loos. I tried to read into this some proof that Peter had got through, but it would not work. It looked more like the opposite, for this desperate hammering must mean that the frontal assault was still the Russian game.

Two or three times I climbed on the housetop for fresh air. The day was foggy and damp, and I could see very little of the countryside. Transport was still bumping southward along the road to the Palantuken, and the slow wagon loads of wounded returning. One thing I noticed, however. There was a perpetual coming and going between the house and the city. Motors and mounted messengers were constantly arriving and departing, and I concluded that Hilda von Einem was getting ready for her part in the defence of Erzerum.

These ascents were all on the first day after Peter's going. The second day, when I tried the trap, I found it closed and heavily weighted. This must have been done by our friends, and very right too. If the house were becoming a place of public resort, it would never do for me to be journeying roofward.

Late on the second night Hussin reappeared. It was after supper, when Blenkiron had gone peacefully to sleep and I was beginning to count the hours till the morning. I could not close an eye during these days and not much at night.

Hussin did not light a lantern. I heard his key in the lock, and then his light step close to where we lay.

"Are you asleep?" he said, and when I answered he sat down beside me.

"The horses are found," he said, "and the Master bids me tell you that we start in the morning three hours before dawn."

It was welcome news. "Tell me what is happening," I begged; "we have been lying in this tomb for three days and heard nothing."

"The guns are busy," he said. "The Allemans come to this place every hour, I know not for what. Also there has been a great search for you. The searchers have been here, but they were sent away empty. . . . Sleep, my lord, for there is wild work before us."

I did not sleep much, for I was strung too high with expectation, and I envied Blenkiron his now eupeptic slumbers. But for an hour or so I dropped off, and my old nightmare came back. Once again I was in the throat of a pass, hotly pursued, straining for some sanctuary which I knew I must reach. But I was no longer alone. Others were with me: how many I could not tell, for when I tried to see their faces they dissolved in mist. Deep snow was underfoot, a grey sky was over us, black peaks were on all sides, but ahead in the midst of the pass was that curious *castrol* which I had first seen in my dream on the Erzerum road.

I saw it distinct in every detail. It rose to the left of the road through the pass, and above a hollow where great boulders stood out in the snow. Its sides were steep, so that the snow had slipped off in patches, leaving stretches of glistening black shale. The *kranz* at the top did not rise sheer, but sloped at an angle of forty-five, and on the very summit there seemed a hollow, as if the earth within the rock-rim had been beaten by weather into a cup. That is often the way with a South African *castrol*, and I knew it was so with this. We were straining for it, but the snow clogged us, and our enemies were very close behind.

Then I was awakened by a figure at my side. "Get ready, my lord," it said; "it is the hour to ride."

Like sleep-walkers we moved into the sharp air. Hussin led us out of an old postern and then through a place like an orchard to the shelter of some tall evergreen trees. There horses stood, champing quietly from their nose-bags. "Good," I thought; "a feed of oats before a big effort."

There were nine beasts for nine riders. We mounted without a word, and filed through a grove of trees to where a broken paling marked the beginning of cultivated land. There for the matter of twenty minutes Hussin chose to guide us through deep, clogging snow. He wanted to avoid any sound till we were well beyond earshot of the house. Then we struck a by-path which presently merged in a hard highway, running, as I judged, south-west by west. There we delayed no longer, but galloped furiously into the dark.

I had got back all my exhilaration. Indeed I was intoxicated with the movement, and could have laughed out loud and sung. Under the black canopy of the night perils are either forgotten or terribly alive. Mine were forgotten. The darkness I galloped into led me to freedom and friends. Yes, and success, which I had not dared to hope and scarcely even to dream of.

Hussin rode first, with me at his side. I turned my head and saw Blenkiron behind me, evidently mortally unhappy about the pace we set and the mount he sat. He used to say that horse-exercise was good for his liver, but it was a gentle amble and a short gallop that he liked, and not this mad helter-skelter. His thighs were too round to fit saddle leather. We passed a fire in a hollow, the bivouac of some Turkish unit, and all the horses shied violently. I knew by Blenkiron's oaths that he had lost his stirrups and was sitting on his horse's neck.

Beside him rode a tall figure swathed to the eyes in wrappings and wearing round his neck some kind of shawl whose ends floated behind him. Sandy, of course, had no European ulster, for it was months since he had worn proper clothes. I wanted to speak to him, but somehow I did not dare. His stillness forbade me. He was a wonderful fine horseman, with his firm English hunting seat; and it was as well, for he paid no attention to his beast. His head was still full of unquiet thoughts.

Then the air around me began to smell acrid and raw, and I saw that a fog was winding up from the hollows.

"Here's the devil's own luck," I cried to Hussin. "Can you guide us in a mist?"

"I do not know." He shook his head. "I had counted on seeing the shape of the hills."

"We've a map and a compass, anyhow. But these make slow travelling. Pray God it lifts!"

Presently the black vapour changed to grey, and the day broke. It was little comfort. The fog rolled in waves to the horses' ears, and riding at the head of the party I could but dimly see the next rank.

"It is time to leave the road," said Hussin, "or we may meet inquisitive folk."

We struck to the left, over ground which was for all the world like a Scotch moor. There were pools of rain on it, and masses of tangled snow-laden junipers, and long reefs of wet slaty stone. It was bad going, and the fog made it hopeless to steer a good course. I had out the map and the compass, and tried to fix our route so as to round the flank of a spur of the mountains which separated us from the valley we were aiming at.

"There's a stream ahead of us," I said to Hussin. "Is it fordable?"

"It is only a trickle," he said, coughing. "This accursed mist is from Eblis." But I knew long before we reached it that it was no trickle. It was a hill stream coming down in spate, and, as I soon guessed, in a deep ravine. Presently we were at its edge, one long whirl of yeasty falls and brown rapids. We could as soon get horses over it as to the topmost cliffs of the Palantuken. Hussin stared at it in consternation. "May Allah forgive my folly, for I should have known. We must return to the highway and find a bridge. My sorrow, that I should have led my lords so ill."

Back over that moor we went with my spirits badly damped. We had none too long a start, and Hilda von Einem would rouse heaven and earth to catch us up. Hussin was forcing the pace, for his anxiety was as great as mine.

Before we reached the road the mist blew back and revealed a wedge of country right across to the hills beyond the river. It was a clear view, every object standing out wet and sharp in the light of morning. It showed the bridge with horsemen drawn up across it, and it showed, too, cavalry pickets moving along the road.

They saw us at the same instant. A word was passed down the road, a shrill whistle blew, and the pickets put their horses at the bank and started across the moor.

"Did I not say this mist was from Eblis?" growled Hussin, as we swung round and galloped back on our tracks. "These cursed Zaptiehs have seen us, and our road is cut."

I was for trying the stream at all costs, but Hussin pointed out that it would do us no good. The cavalry beyond the bridge were moving up the other bank. "There is a path through the hills that I know, but it must be travelled on foot. If we can increase our lead and the mist cloaks us, there is yet a chance."

It was a weary business plodding up to the skirts of the hills. We had the pursuit behind us now, and that put an edge on every difficulty. There were long banks of broken screes, I remember, where the snow slipped in wreaths from under our feet. Great boulders had to be circumvented, and patches of bog, where the streams from the snows first made contact with the plains, mired us to our girths. Happily the mist was down again, but this, though it hindered the chase, lessened the chances of Hussin finding the path.

He found it nevertheless. There was the gully and the rough mule-track leading upwards. But there also had been a landslip, quite recent from the marks. A large scar of raw earth had broken across the hillside, which with the snow above it looked like a slice cut out of an iced chocolate-cake.

We stared blankly for a second, till we recognized its hopelessness.

"I'm for trying the crags," I said. "Where there once was a way another can be found."

"And be picked off at their leisure by these marksmen," said Hussin grimly. "Look!"

The mist had opened again, and a glance behind showed me the pursuit closing up on us. They were now less than three hundred yards off. We turned our horses and made off eastward along the skirts of the cliffs.

Then Sandy spoke for the first time. "I don't know how you fellows feel, but I'm not going to be taken. There's nothing much to do except to find a good place and put up a fight. We can sell our lives dearly."

"That's about all," said Blenkiron cheerfully. He had suffered such tortures on that gallop that he welcomed any kind of stationary fight.

"Serve out the arms," said Sandy.

The Companions all carried rifles slung across their shoulders. Hussin, from a deep saddle-bag, brought out rifles and bandoliers for the rest of us. As I laid mine across my saddle-bow I saw it was a German Mauser of the latest pattern.

"It's hell-for-leather till we find a place for a stand," said Sandy. "The game's against us this time."

Once more we entered the mist, and presently found better going on a long stretch of even slope. Then came a rise, and on the crest of it I saw the sun. Presently we dipped into bright daylight and looked down on a broad glen, with a road winding up it to a pass in the range. I had expected this. It was one way to the Palantuken pass, some miles south of the house where we had been lodged.

And then, as I looked southward, I saw what I had been watching for for days. A little hill split the valley, and on its top was a *kranz* of rocks. It was the *castrol* of my persistent dream.

On that I promptly took charge. "There's our fort," I cried. "If we once get there we can hold it for a week. Sit down and ride for it."

We bucketed down that hillside like men possessed, even Blenkiron sticking on manfully among the twists and turns and slithers. Presently we were on the road and were racing past marching infantry and gun teams and empty wagons. I noted that most seemed to be moving downward and few going up. Hussin screamed some words in Turkish that secured us a passage, but indeed our crazy speed left them staring. Out of a corner of my eyes I saw that Sandy had flung off most of his wrappings and seemed to be all a dazzle of rich colour. But I had thought for nothing except the little hill, now almost fronting us across the shallow glen.

No horses could breast that steep. We urged them into the hollow, and then hastily dismounted, humped the packs, and began to struggle up the side of the *castrol*. It was strewn with great boulders, which gave a kind of cover that very soon was needed. For, snatching a glance back, I saw that our pursuers were on the road above us and were getting ready to shoot.

At normal times we would have been easy marks, but, fortunately, wisps and streamers of mist now clung about that hollow. The rest could fend for themselves, so I stuck to Blenkiron and dragged him, wholly breathless, by the least exposed route. Bullets spattered now and then against the rocks, and one sang unpleasantly near my head. In this way we covered three-fourths of the distance, and had only the bare dozen yards where the gradient eased off up to the edge of the *kranz*.

Blenkiron got hit in the leg, our only casualty. There was nothing for it but to carry him, so I swung him on my shoulders, and with a bursting heart did that last lap. It was hottish work, and the bullets were pretty thick about us, but we all got safely to the *kranz* and a short scramble took us over the edge. I laid Blenkiron inside the *castrol* and started to prepare our defence.

We had little time to do it. Out of the thin fog figures were coming, crouching in cover. The place we were in was a natural redoubt, except that there were no loopholes or sandbags. We had to show our heads over the rim to shoot, but the danger was lessened by the superb field of fire given by those last dozen yards of glacis. I posted the men and waited, and Blenkiron, with a white face, insisted on taking his share, announcing that he used to be handy with a gun.

I gave the order that no man was to shoot till the enemy had come out of the rocks on to the glacis. The thing ran right round the top, and we had to watch all sides to prevent them getting us in flank or rear. Hussin's rifle cracked out presently from the back, so my precautions had not been needless.

We were all three fair shots, though none of us up to Peter's miraculous standard, and the Companions, too, made good practice. The Mauser was the weapon I knew best, and I didn't miss much. The attackers never had a chance, for their only hope was to rush us by numbers, and, the whole party being not above two dozen, they were far too few. I think we killed three, for their bodies were left lying, and wounded at least six, while the rest fell back towards the road. In a quarter of an hour it was all over.

"They are dogs of Kurds," I heard Hussin say fiercely. "Only a Kurdish *ghiaour* would fire on the livery of the Kaába."

Then I had a good look at Sandy. He had discarded shawls and wrappings and stood up in the strangest costume man ever wore in battle. Somehow he had procured field-boots and an old pair of riding-breeches. Above these, reaching well below his middle, he had a wonderful silken jibbah or ephod of a bright emerald. I call it silk, but it was like no silk I have ever known, so exquisite in the mesh, with such a sheen and depth in it. Some strange pattern was woven on the breast, which in the dim light I could not trace. I'll warrant no rarer or costlier garment was ever exposed to lead on a bleak winter hill.

Sandy seemed unconscious of his garb. His eye, listless no more, scanned the hollow. "That's only the overture," he cried. "The opera will soon begin. We must put a breastwork up in these gaps or they'll pick us off from a thousand yards."

I had meantime roughly dressed Blenkiron's wound with a linen rag which Hussin provided. It was from a ricochet bullet which had chipped into his left shin. Then I took a hand with the others in getting up earthworks to complete the circuit of the defence. It was no easy job, for we wrought only with our knives and had to dig deep down below the snowy gravel. As we worked I took stock of our refuge.

The *castrol* was a rough circle about ten yards in diameter, its interior filled with boulders and loose stones, and its parapet about four feet high. The mist had cleared for a considerable space, and I could see the immediate surroundings. West, beyond the hollow, was the road we had come, where now the remnants of the pursuit were clustered. North, the hill fell steeply to the valley bottom, but to the south, after a dip, there was a ridge which shut the view. East lay another fork of the stream, the chief fork I guessed, and it was evidently followed by the main road to the pass, for I saw it crowded with transport. The two roads seemed to converge somewhere farther south out of my sight.

I guessed we could not be very far from the front, for the noise of guns sounded very near, both the sharp crack of the field-pieces and the deeper boom of the howitzers. More, I could hear the chatter of machine guns, a magpie note among the baying of hounds. I even saw the bursting of Russian shells, evidently trying to reach the main road. One big fellow—an 8-inch—landed not ten yards from a convoy to the east of us, and another in the hollow through which we had come. These were clearly ranging shots, and I wondered if the Russians had observation posts on the heights to mark them. If so, they might soon try a curtain, and we should be very near its edge. It would be an odd irony if we were the target of friendly shells.

"By the Lord Harry," I heard Sandy say, "if we had a brace of machine guns we could hold this place against a division."

"What price shells?" I asked. "If they get a gun up they can blow us to atoms in ten minutes."

"Please God the Russians keep them too busy for that," was his answer.

With anxious eyes I watched our enemies on the road. They seemed to have grown in numbers. They were signalling, too, for a white flag fluttered. Then the mist rolled down on us again, and our prospect was limited to ten yards of vapour.

"Steady," I cried; "they may try to rush us at any moment. Every man keep his eye on the edge of the fog, and shoot at the first sign."

For nearly half an hour by my watch we waited in that queer white world, our eyes smarting with the strain of peering. The sound of the gun seemed to be hushed, and everything grown deathly quiet. Blenkiron's squeal, as he knocked his wounded leg against a rock, made every man start.

Then out of the mist there came a voice.

It was a woman's voice, high, penetrating, and sweet, but it spoke in no tongue I knew. Only Sandy understood. He made a sudden movement as if to defend himself against a blow.

The speaker came into clear sight on the glacis a yard or two away. Mine was the first face she saw.

"I come to offer terms," she said in English. "Will you permit me to enter?"

I could do nothing except take off my cap and say, "Yes, ma'am." Blenkiron, snuggled up against the parapet, was cursing furiously below his breath.

She climbed up the *kranz* and stepped over the edge as lightly as a deer. Her clothes were strange—spurred boots and breeches over which fell a short green kirtle. A little cap skewered with a jewelled pin was on her head, and a cape of some coarse country cloth hung from her shoulders. She had rough gauntlets on her hands, and she carried for weapon a riding-whip. The fog-crystals clung to her hair, I remember, and a silvery film of fog lay on her garments.

I had never before thought of her as beautiful. Strange, uncanny, wonderful, if you like, but the word beauty had too kindly and human a sound for such a face. But as she stood with heightened colour, her eyes like stars, her poise like a wild bird's, I had to confess that she had her own loveliness. She might be a devil, but she was also a queen. I considered that there might be merits in the prospect of riding by her side into Jerusalem.

Sandy stood rigid, his face very grave and set. She held out both hands to him, speaking softly in Turkish. I noticed that the six Companions had disappeared from the *castrol* and were somewhere out of sight on the farther side.

I do not know what she said, but from her tone, and above all from her eyes, I judged that she was pleading—pleading for his return, for his partnership in her great adventure; pleading, for all I knew, for his love.

His expression was like a death-mask, his brows drawn tight in a little frown and his jaw rigid.

"Madam," he said, "I ask you to tell your business quick and to tell it in English. My friends must hear it as well as me."

"Your friends!" she cried. "What has a prince to do with these hirelings? Your slaves, perhaps, but not your friends."

"My friends," Sandy repeated grimly. "You must know, Madam, that I am a British officer."

That was beyond doubt a clean staggering stroke. What she had thought of his origin God knows, but she had never dreamed of this. Her eyes grew larger and more lustrous, her lips parted as if to speak, but her voice failed her. Then by an effort she recovered herself, and out of that strange face went all the glow of youth and ardour. It was again the unholy mask I had first known.

"And these others?" she asked in a level voice.

"One is a brother officer of my regiment. The other is an American friend. But all three of us are on the same errand. We came east to destroy Greenmantle and your devilish ambitions. You have yourself destroyed your prophets, and now it is your turn to fail and disappear. Make no mistake, Madam; that folly is over. I will tear this sacred garment into a thousand pieces and scatter them on the wind. The people wait to-day for the revelation, but none will come. You may kill us if you can, but we have at least crushed a lie and done service to our country."

I would not have taken my eyes from her face for a king's ransom. I have written that she was a queen, and of that there is no manner of doubt. She had the soul of a conqueror, for not a flicker of weakness or disappointment marred her air. Only pride and the stateliest resolution looked out of her eyes.

"I said I came to offer terms. I will still offer them, though they are other than I thought. For the fat American, I will send him home safely to his own country. I do not make war on such as he. He is Germany's foe, not mine. You," she said, turning fiercely on me, "I will hang before dusk."

Never in my life had I been so pleased. I had got my revenge at last. This woman had singled me out above the others as the object of her wrath, and I almost loved her for it.

She turned to Sandy and the fierceness went out of her face.

"You seek truth," she said. "So also do I, and if we use a lie it is only to break down a greater. You are of my household in spirit, and you alone of all men I have seen are fit to ride with me on my mission. Germany may fail, but I shall not fail. I offer you the greatest career that mortal has known. I offer you a task which will need every atom of brain and sinew and courage. Will you refuse that destiny?"

I do not know what effect this vapouring might have had in hot scented rooms, or in the languor of some rich garden; but on that cold hilltop it was as unsubstantial as the mist around us. It sounded not even impressive, only crazy.

"I stay with my friends," said Sandy.

"Then I will offer more. I will save your friends. They, too, shall share in my triumph."

This was too much for Blenkiron. He scrambled to his feet to speak the protest that had been wrung from his soul, forgot his game leg, and rolled back on the ground with a groan.

Then she seemed to make a last appeal. She spoke in Turkish now, and I do not know what she said, but I judged it was the plea of a woman to her lover. Once more she was the proud beauty, but there was a tremor in her pride—I had almost written a tenderness. To listen to her was like horrid treachery, like eavesdropping on something pitiful. I know my cheeks grew scarlet and Blenkiron turned away his head.

Sandy's face did not move. He spoke in English.

"You can offer me nothing that I desire," he said. "I am the servant of my country, and her enemies are mine. I can have neither part nor lot with you. That is my answer, Madam von Einem."

Then her steely restraint broke. It was like a dam giving before a pent-up mass of icy water. She tore off one of her gauntlets and hurled it in his face. Implacable hate looked out of her eyes.

"I have done with you," she cried. "You have scorned me, but you have dug your own grave."

She leaped on the parapet and the next second was on the glacis. Once more the mist had fled, and across the hollow I saw a field-gun in place and men around it who were not Turkish. She waved her hand to them, and hastened down the hillside.

But at that moment I heard the whistle of a long-range Russian shell. Among the boulders there was the dull shock of an explosion and a mushroom of red earth. It all passed in an instant of time: I saw the gunners on the road point their hands and I heard them cry; I heard too a kind of sob from Blenkiron—all this before I realized myself what had happened. The next thing I saw was Sandy, already beyond the glacis, leaping with great bounds down the hill. They were shooting at him, but he heeded them not. For the space of a minute he was out of sight, and his whereabouts was shown only by the patter of bullets.

Then he came back—walking quite slowly up the last slope, and he was carrying something in his arms. The enemy fired no more; they realized what had happened.

He laid his burden down gently in a corner of the *castrol*. The cap had fallen off, and the hair was breaking loose. The face was very white, but there was no wound or bruise on it.

"She was killed at once," I heard him saying. "Her back was broken by a shell-fragment. Dick, we must bury her here. . . . You see, she . . . she liked me. I can make her no return but this."

We set the Companions to guard, and with infinite slowness, using our hands and our knives, we made a shallow grave below the eastern parapet. When it was done we covered her face with the linen cloak which Sandy had worn that morning. He lifted the body and laid it reverently in its place.

"I did not know that anything could be so light," he said.

It wasn't for me to look on at that kind of scene. I went to the parapet with Blenkiron's field-glasses and had a stare at our friends on the road. There was no Turk there, and I guessed why, for it would not be easy to use the men of Islam against the wearer of the green ephod. The enemy were German or Austrian, and they had a field-gun. They seemed to have got it laid on our fort; but they were waiting. As I looked I saw behind them a massive figure I seemed to recognize. Stumm had come to see the destruction of his enemies.

To the east I saw another gun in the fields just below the main road. They had got us on both sides, and there was no way of escape. Hilda von Einem was to have a noble pyre and goodly company for the dark journey.

Dusk was falling now, a clear bright dusk where the stars pricked through a sheen of amethyst. The artillery were busy all around the horizon, and towards the pass on the other road, where Fort Palantuken stood, there was the dust and smoke of a furious bombardment. It seemed to me, too, that the guns on the other fronts had come nearer. Deve Boyun was hidden by a spur of hill, but up in the north white clouds, like the streamers of evening, were hanging over the Euphrates glen. The whole firmament hummed and twanged like a taut string that has been struck. . . .

As I looked, the gun to the west fired—the gun where Stumm was. The shell dropped ten yards to our right. A second later another fell behind us.

Blenkiron had dragged himself to the parapet. I don't suppose he had ever been shelled before, but his face showed curiosity rather than fear.

"Pretty poor shooting, I reckon," he said.

"On the contrary," I said, "they know their business. They're bracketing. . . ."

The words were not out of my mouth when one fell right among us. It struck the far rim of the *castrol*, shattering the rock, but bursting mainly outside. We all ducked, and barring some small scratches no one was a penny the worse. I remember that much of the debris fell on Hilda von Einem's grave.

I pulled Blenkiron over the far parapet, and called on the rest to follow, meaning to take cover on the rough side of the hill. But as we showed ourselves shots rang out from our front, shots fired from a range of a few hundred yards. It was easy to see what had happened. Riflemen had been sent to hold us in rear. They would not assault so long as we remained in the *castrol*, but they would block any attempt to find safety outside it. Stumm and his gun had us at their mercy.

We crouched below the parapet again. "We may as well toss for it," I said. "There's only two ways—to stay here and be shelled or try to break through those fellows behind. Either's pretty unhealthy."

But I knew there was no choice. With Blenkiron crippled we were pinned to the *castrol*. Our numbers were up all right.

32   THE GUNS OF THE NORTH

But no more shells fell.

The night grew dark and showed a field of glittering stars, for the air was sharpening again towards frost. We waited for an hour, crouching just behind the far parapets, but never came that ominous familiar whistle.

Then Sandy rose and stretched himself. "I'm hungry," he said. "Let's have out the food, Hussin. We've eaten nothing since before daybreak. I wonder what is the meaning of this respite?"

I fancied I knew.

"It's Stumm's way," I said. "He wants to torture us. He'll keep us hours on tenterhooks, while he sits over yonder exulting in what he thinks we're enduring. He has just enough imagination for that. . . . He would rush us if he had the men. As it is, he's going to blow us to pieces, but do it slowly and smack his lips over it."

Sandy yawned. "We'll disappoint him, for we won't be worried, old man. We three are beyond that kind of fear."

"Meanwhile we're going to do the best we can," I said. "He's got the exact range for his whizz-bangs. We've got to find a hole somewhere just outside the *castrol*, and some sort of head-cover. We're bound to get damaged whatever happens, but we'll stick it out to the end. When they think they have finished with us and rush the place, there may be one of us alive to put a bullet through old Stumm. What do you say?"

They agreed, and after our meal Sandy and I crawled out to prospect, leaving the others on guard in case there should be an attack. We found a hollow in the glacis a little south of the *castrol*, and, working very quietly, managed to enlarge it and cut a kind of shallow cave in the hill. It would be no use against a direct hit, but it would give some cover from flying fragments. As I read the situation, Stumm could land as many shells as he pleased in the *castrol* and wouldn't bother to attend to the flanks. When the bad shelling began there would be shelter for one or two in the cave.

Our enemies were watchful. The riflemen on the east burnt Véry flares at intervals, and Stumm's lot sent up a great star-rocket. I remember that just before midnight hell broke loose round Fort Palantuken. No more Russian shells came into our hollow, but all the road to the east was under fire, and at the Fort itself there was a shattering explosion and a queer scarlet glow which looked as if a magazine had been hit. For about two hours the firing was intense, and then it died down. But it was towards the north that I kept turning my head. There seemed to be something different in the sound there, something sharper in the report of the guns, as if shells were dropping in a narrow valley whose rock walls doubled the echo. Had the Russians by any blessed chance worked round that flank?

I got Sandy to listen, but he shook his head. "Those guns are a dozen miles off," he said. "They're no nearer than three days ago. But it looks as if the sportsmen on the south might have a chance. When they break through and stream down the valley, they'll be puzzled to account for what remains of us. . . . We're no longer three adventurers in the enemy's country. We're the advance guard of the Allies. Our pals don't know about us, and we're going to be cut off, which has happened to advance guards before now. But all the same, we're in our own battle-line again. Doesn't that cheer you, Dick?"

It cheered me wonderfully, for I knew now what had been the weight on my heart ever since I accepted Sir Walter's mission. It was the loneliness of it. I was fighting far away from my friends, far away from the true fronts of battle. It was a side-show which, whatever its importance, had none of the exhilaration of the main effort. But now we had come back to familiar ground. We were like the Highlanders cut off at Cité St. Auguste on the first day of Loos, or those Scots Guards at Festubert of whom I had heard. Only, the others did not know of it, would never hear of it. If Peter succeeded he might tell the tale, but most likely he was lying dead somewhere in the no-man's-land between the lines. We should never be heard of again any more, but our work remained. Sir Walter would know that, and he would tell our few belongings that we had gone out in our country's service.

We were in the *castrol* again, sitting under the parapets. The same thought must have been in Sandy's mind, for he suddenly laughed.

"It's a queer ending, Dick. We simply vanish into the infinite. If the Russians get through they will never recognize what is left of us among so much of the wreckage of battle. The snow will soon cover us, and when the spring comes there will only be a few bleached bones. Upon my soul it is the kind of death I always wanted." And he quoted softly to himself a verse of an old Scots ballad:

> "Mony's the ane for him maks mane,
> But nane sall ken whar he is gane.
> Ower his white banes, when they are bare,
> The wind sall blaw for evermair."

"But our work lives," I cried, with a sudden great gasp of happiness. "It's the job that matters, not the men that do it. And our job's done. We have won, old chap—won hands down—and there is no going back on that. We have won any way; and if Peter has had a slice of luck, we've scooped the pool. . . . After all, we never expected to come out of this thing with our lives."

Blenkiron, with his leg stuck out stiffly before him, was humming quietly to himself, as he often did when he felt cheerful. He had only one song,

"John Brown's Body"; usually only a line at a time, but now he got as far as a whole verse:

"He captured Harper's Ferry, with his nineteen men so true,
And he frightened old Virginny till she trembled through and through.
They hung him for a traitor, themselves the traitor crew,
  But his soul goes marching on."

"Feeling good?" I asked.

"Fine. I'm about the luckiest man on God's earth, Major. I've always wanted to get into a big show, but I didn't see how it would come the way of a homely citizen like me, living in a steam-warmed house and going down town every morning. I used to envy my old dad that fought at Chattanooga, and never forgot to tell you about it. But I guess Chattanooga was like a scrap in a Bowery bar compared to this. When I meet the old man in Glory he'll have to listen some to me. . . ."

It was just after Blenkiron spoke that we got a reminder of Stumm's presence. The gun was well laid, for a shell plumped on the near edge of the *castrol*. It made an end of one of the Companions who was on guard there, badly wounded another, and a fragment gashed my thigh. We took refuge in the shallow cave, but some wild shooting from the east side brought us back to the parapets, for we feared an attack. None came, nor any more shells, and once again the night was quiet.

I asked Blenkiron if he had any near relatives.

"Why, no, except a sister's son, a college-boy who has no need of his uncle. It's fortunate that we three have no wives. I haven't any regrets, neither, for I've had a mighty deal out of life. I was thinking this morning that it was a pity I was going out when I had just got my duo-denum to listen to reason. But I reckon that's another of my mercies. The good God took away the pain in my stomach so that I might go to Him with a clear head and a thankful heart."

"We're lucky fellows," said Sandy; "we've all had our whack. When I remember the good times I've had I could sing a hymn of praise. We've lived long enough to know ourselves, and to shape ourselves into some kind of decency. But think of those boys who have given their lives freely when they scarcely knew what life meant. They were just at the beginning of the road, and they didn't know what dreary bits lay before them. It was all sunshiny and bright-coloured, and yet they gave it up without a moment's doubt. And think of the men with wives and children and homes that were the biggest things in life to them. For fellows like us to shirk would be black cowardice. It's small credit for us to stick it out. But when those others shut their teeth and went forward, they were blessed heroes. . . ."

After that we fell silent. A man's thoughts at a time like that seem to be double-powered, and the memory becomes very sharp and clear. I don't know what was in the others' minds, but I know what filled my own. . . .

I fancy it isn't the men who get most out of the world and are always buoyant and cheerful that most fear to die. Rather it is the weak-engined souls, who go about with dull eyes, that cling most fiercely to life. They have not the joy of being alive which is a kind of earnest of immortality. . . . I know that my thoughts were chiefly about the jolly things that I had seen and done; not regret, but gratitude. The panorama of blue noons on the veld unrolled itself before me, and hunter's nights in the bush, the taste of food and sleep, the bitter stimulus of dawn, the joy of wild adventure, the voices of old staunch friends. Hitherto the war had seemed to make a break with all that had gone before, but now the war was only part of the picture. I thought of my battalion, and the good fellows there, many of whom had fallen on the Loos parapets. I had never looked to come out of that myself. But I had been spared, and given the chance of a greater business, and I had succeeded. That was the tremendous fact, and my mood was humble gratitude to God, and exultant pride. Death was a small price to pay for it. As Blenkiron would have said, I had got good value in the deal. . . .

The night was getting bitter cold, as happens before dawn. It was frost again, and the sharpness of it woke our hunger. I got out the remnants of the food and wine and we had a last meal. I remember we pledged each other as we drank.

"We have eaten our Passover Feast," said Sandy. "When do you look for the end?"

"After dawn," I said. "Stumm wants daylight to get the full savour of his revenge."

Slowly the sky passed from ebony to grey, and black shapes of hill outlined themselves against it. A wind blew down the valley, bringing the acrid smell of burning, but something too of the freshness of morn. It stirred strange thoughts in me and woke the old morning vigour of the blood which was never to be mine again. For the first time in that long vigil I was torn with regret.

"We must get into the cave before it is full light," I said. "We had better draw lots for the two to go."

The choice fell on one of the Companions and Blenkiron.

"You can count me out," said the latter. "If it's your wish to find a man to be alive when our friends come up to count their spoil, I guess I'm the worst of the lot. I'd prefer, if you don't mind, to stay here. I've made my peace with my Maker, and I'd like to wait quietly on His call. I'll play a game of Patience to pass the time."

He would take no denial, so we drew again, and the lot fell to Sandy.

"If I'm the last to go," he said, "I promise I don't miss. Stumm won't be long in following me."

He shook hands with his cheery smile, and he and the Companion slipped over the parapet in the final shadows before dawn.

Blenkiron spread his Patience cards on a flat rock, and dealt for the Double Napoleon. He was perfectly calm, and hummed to himself his only tune. For myself I was drinking in my last draught of the hill air. My contentment was going. I suddenly felt bitterly loath to die.

Something of the same kind must have passed through Blenkiron's head. He suddenly looked up and asked, "Sister Anne, Sister Anne, do you see anybody coming?"

I stood close to the parapet, watching every detail of the landscape as shown by the revealing daybreak. Up on the shoulders of the Palantuken, snowdrifts lipped over the edges of the cliffs. I wondered when they would come down as avalanches. There was a kind of croft on one hillside, and from a hut the smoke of breakfast was beginning to curl. Stumm's gunners were awake and apparently holding council. Far down on the main road a convoy was moving—I heard the creak of the wheels two miles away, for the air was deathly still.

Then, as if a spring had been loosed, the world suddenly leaped to a hideous life. With a growl the guns opened round all the horizon. They were especially fierce to the south, where a *rafale* beat as I had never heard it before. The one glance I cast behind me showed the gap in the hills choked with fumes and dust.

But my eyes were on the north. From Erzerum city tall tongues of flames leaped from a dozen quarters. Beyond, toward the opening of the Euphrates glen, there was the sharp crack of field-guns. I strained eyes and ears, mad with impatience, and I read the riddle.

"Sandy," I yelled, "Peter has got through. The Russians are round the flank. The town is burning. Glory to God, we've won, we've won!"

And as I spoke the earth seemed to split beside me, and I was flung forward on the gravel which covered Hilda von Einem's grave.

As I picked myself up, and to my amazement found myself uninjured, I saw Blenkiron rubbing the dust out of his eyes and arranging a disordered card. He had stopped humming, and was singing aloud:

> "He captured Harper's Ferry, with his nineteen men so true,
> And he frightened old Virginny . . ."

"Say, Major," he cried, "I believe this game of mine is coming out."

I was now pretty well mad. The thought that old Peter had won, that *we* had won beyond our wildest dreams, that if we died there were those coming who would exact the uttermost vengeance, rode my brain like a fever. I sprang on the parapet and waved my hand to Stumm, shouting defiance. Rifle shots cracked out from behind, and I leaped back just in time for the next shell.

The charge must have been short, for it was a bad miss, landing somewhere on the glacis. The next was better and crashed on the near parapet, carving a great hole in the rocky *kranz*. This time my arm hung limp, broken by a fragment of stone, but I felt no pain. Blenkiron seemed to bear a charmed life, for he was smothered in dust, but unhurt. He blew the dust away from his cards very gingerly and went on playing.

"Sister Anne," he asked, "do you see anybody coming?"

Then came a dud which dropped neatly inside on the soft ground. I was determined to break for the open and chance the rifle fire, for if Stumm went on shooting the *castrol* was certain death. I caught Blenkiron round the middle, scattering his cards to the winds, and jumped over the parapet.

"Don't apologize, Sister Anne," said he. "The game was as good as won. But for God's sake drop me, for if you wave me like the banner of freedom I'll get plugged good and sure."

My one thought was to get cover for the next minutes, for I had an instinct that our vigil was near its end. The defences of Erzerum were crumbling like sand-castles, and it was a proof of the tenseness of my nerves that I seemed to be deaf to the sound. Stumm had seen us cross the parapet, and he started to sprinkle all the surroundings of the *castrol*. Blenkiron and I lay like a working-party caught by machine guns between the lines, taking a pull on ourselves as best we could. Sandy had some kind of cover, but we were on the bare farther slope, and the riflemen on that side might have had us at their mercy.

But no shots came from them. As I looked east, the hillside, which a little before had been held by our enemies, was as empty as the desert. And then I saw on the main road a sight which for a second time made me yell like a maniac. Down that glen came a throng of men and galloping limbers—a crazy, jostling crowd, spreading away beyond the road to the steep slopes, and leaving behind it many black dots to darken the snows. The gates of the South had yielded, and our friends were through them.

At that sight I forgot all about our danger. I didn't give a cent for Stumm's shells. I didn't believe he could hit me. The fate which had mercifully preserved us for the first taste of victory would see us through to the end.

I remember bundling Blenkiron along the hill to find Sandy. But our news was anticipated. For down our own side-glen came the same broken tumult of men. More; for at their backs, far up at the throat of the pass, I saw horsemen—the horsemen of the pursuit. Old Nicholas had flung his cavalry in.

Sandy was on his feet, with his lips set and his eye abstracted. If his face hadn't been burned black by weather it would have been pale as a dishclout. A man like him doesn't make up his mind for death and then be given his life again without being wrenched out of his bearings. I thought he didn't understand what had happened, so I beat him on the shoulders.

"Man, d'you see?" I cried. "The Cossacks! The Cossacks! God! how they're taking that slope! They're into them now. By Heaven, we'll ride with them! We'll get the gun horses!"

A little knoll prevented Stumm and his men from seeing what was happening farther up the glen, till the first wave of the rout was on them. He had gone to bombarding the *castrol* and its environs while the world was cracking over his head. The gun team was in the hollow below the road, and down the hill among the boulders we crawled, Blenkiron as lame as a duck, and me with a limp left arm.

The poor beasts were straining at their pickets and sniffing the morning wind, which brought down the thick fumes of the great bombardment and the indescribable babbling cries of a beaten army. Before we reached them that maddened horde had swept down on them, men panting and gasping in their flight, many of them bloody from wounds, many tottering in the first stages of collapse and death. I saw the horses seized by a dozen hands, and a desperate fight for their possession. But as we halted there our eyes were fixed on the battery on the road above us, for round it was now sweeping the van of the retreat.

I had never seen a rout before, when strong men come to the end of their tether and only their broken shadows stumble towards the refuge they never find. No more had Stumm, poor devil. I had no ill-will left for him, though coming down that hill I was rather hoping that the two of us might have a final scrap. He was a brute and a bully, but, by God! he was a man. I heard his great roar when he saw the tumult, and the next I saw was his monstrous figure working at the gun. He swung it south and turned it on the fugitives.

But he never fired it. The press was on him, and the gun was swept sideways. He stood up, a foot higher than any of them, and he seemed to be trying to check the rush with his pistol. There is power in numbers, even though every unit is broken and fleeing. For a second to that wild crowd Stumm was the enemy, and they had strength enough to crush him. The wave flowed round and then across him. I saw the butt-ends of rifles crash on his head and shoulders, and the next second the stream had passed over his body. . . .

That was God's judgment on the man who had set himself above his kind.

Sandy gripped my shoulder and was shouting in my ear:

"They're coming, Dick. Look at the grey devils! . . . Oh, God be thanked, it's our friends!"

The next minute we were tumbling down the hillside, Blenkiron hopping on one leg between us. I heard dimly Sandy crying, "Oh, well done our side!" and Blenkiron declaiming about Harper's Ferry, but I had no voice at all and no wish to shout. I know that tears were in my eyes, and that if I had been left alone I would have sat down and cried with pure thankfulness. For sweeping down the glen came a cloud of grey cavalry on little wiry horses, a cloud which stayed not for the rear of the fugitives, but swept on like a flight of rainbows, with the steel of their lanceheads glittering in the winter sun. They were riding for Erzerum.

Remember that for three months we had been with the enemy and had never seen the face of an Ally in arms. We had been cut off from the fellowship of a great cause, like a fort surrounded by an army. And now we were delivered, and there fell around us the warm joy of comradeship as well as the exultation of victory.

We flung caution to the winds and went stark mad. Sandy, still in his emerald coat and turban, was scrambling up the farther slope of the hollow, yelling greetings in every language known to man. The leader saw him, with a word checked his men for a moment—it was marvellous to see the horses reined in in such a breakneck ride—and from the squadron half a dozen troopers swung loose and wheeled towards us. Then a man in a grey overcoat and a sheepskin cap was on the ground beside us wringing our hands.

"You are safe, my old friends"—it was Peter's voice that spoke—"I will take you back to our army, and get you breakfast."

"No, by the Lord, you won't," cried Sandy. "We've had the rough end of the job, and now we'll have the fun. Look after Blenkiron and these fellows of mine. I'm going to ride knee by knee with your sportsmen for the city."

Peter spoke a word, and two of the Cossacks dismounted. The next I knew I was mixed up in the cloud of greycoats, galloping down the road up which the morning before we had strained to the *castrol*.

That was the great hour of my life, and to live through it was worth a dozen years of slavery. With a broken left arm I had little hold on my beast, so I trusted my neck to him and let him have his will. Black with dirt and smoke, hatless, with no kind of uniform, I was a wilder figure than any Cossack. I soon was separated from Sandy, who had two hands and a better horse, and seemed resolute to press forward to the very van. That would have been suicide for me, and I had all I could do to keep my place in the bunch I rode with.

But, great God! what an hour it was! There was loose shooting on our flank, but nothing to trouble us, though the gun team of some Austrian howitzer, struggling madly at a bridge, gave us a bit of a tussle. Everything flitted past me like smoke, or like the mad *finale* of a dream just before waking. I knew the living movement under me, and the companionship of men, but all dimly, for at heart I was alone, grappling with the realization of a new world. I felt the shadows of the Palantuken glen fading, and the great burst of light as we emerged on the wider valley. Somewhere before us was a pall of smoke seamed with red flames, and beyond the darkness of still higher hills. All that time I was dreaming, crooning daft catches of song to myself, so happy, so deliriously happy that I dared not try to think. I kept muttering a kind of prayer made up of Bible words to Him who had shown me His goodness in the land of the living.

But as we drew out from the skirts of the hills and began the long slope to the city, I woke to clear consciousness. I felt the smell of sheepskin and lathered horses, and above all the bitter smell of fire. Down in the trough lay Erzerum, now burning in many places, and from the east, past the silent forts, horsemen were closing in on it. I yelled to my comrades that we were nearest, that we would be first in the city, and they nodded happily and shouted their strange war-cries. As we topped the last ridge I saw below me the van of our charge—a dark mass on the snow—while the broken enemy on both sides were flinging away their arms and scattering in the fields.

In the very front, now nearing the city ramparts, was one man. He was like the point of the steel spear soon to be driven home. In the clear morning air I could see that he did not wear the uniform of the invaders. He was turbaned and rode like one possessed, and against the snow I caught the dark sheen of emerald. As he rode it seemed that the fleeing Turks were stricken still, and sank by the roadside with eyes strained after his unheeding figure. . . .

Then I knew that the prophecy had been true, and that their prophet had not failed them. The long-looked for revelation had come. Greenmantle had appeared at last to an awaiting people.

THE THIRD ADVENTURE

Mr. Standfast

33   THE WICKET-GATE

I spent one third of my journey looking out of the window of a first-class carriage, the next in a local motor-car following the course of a trout stream in a shallow valley, and the last tramping over a ridge of down and through great beech woods to my quarters for the night. In the first part I was in an infamous temper; in the second I was worried and mystified; but the cool twilight of the third stage calmed and heartened me, and I reached the gates of Fosse Manor with a mighty appetite and a quiet mind.

As we slipped up the Thames Valley on the smooth Great Western line I had reflected ruefully on the thorns in the path of duty. For more than a year I had never been out of khaki, except the months I spent in hospital. They gave me my battalion before the Somme, and I came out of that weary battle after the first big September fighting with a crack in my head and a D.S.O. I had received a C.B. for the Erzerum business, so what with these and my Matabele and South African medals and the Legion of Honour, I had a chest like the High Priest's breastplate. I rejoined in January, and got a brigade on the eve of Arras. There we had a star turn, and took about as many prisoners as we put infantry over the top. After that we were hauled out for a month, and subsequently planted in a bad bit on the Scarpe with a hint that we would soon be used for a big push. Then suddenly I was ordered home to report to the War Office, and passed on by them to Bullivant and his merry men. So here I was sitting in a railway carriage in a grey tweed suit, with a neat new suit-case on the rack labelled C.B. The initials stood for Cornelius Brand, for that was my name now. And an old boy in the corner was asking me questions and wondering audibly why I wasn't fighting, while a young blood of a second lieutenant with a wound stripe was eyeing me with scorn.

The old chap was one of the cross-examining type, and after he had borrowed my matches he set to work to find out all about me. He was a tremendous fire-eater, and a bit of a pessimist about our slow progress in the west. I told him I came from South Africa and was a mining engineer.

"Been fighting with Botha?" he asked.

"No," I said. "I'm not the fighting kind."

The second lieutenant screwed up his nose.

"Is there no conscription in South Africa?"

"Thank God there isn't," I said, and the old fellow begged permission to tell me a lot of unpalatable things. I knew his kind and didn't give much for it. He was the sort who, if he had been under fifty, would have crawled on his

257

belly to his tribunal to get exempted, but being over the age was able to pose as a patriot. But I didn't like the second lieutenant's grin, for he seemed a good class of lad. I looked steadily out of the window for the rest of the way, and wasn't sorry when I got to my station.

I had had the queerest interview with Bullivant and Macgillivray. They asked me first if I was willing to serve again in the old game and I said I was. I felt as bitter as sin, for I had got fixed in the military groove, and had made good there. Here was I—a brigadier and still under forty, and with another year of the war there was no saying where I might end. I had started out without any ambition, only a great wish to see the business finished. But now I had acquired a professional interest in the thing, I had a nailing good brigade, and I had got the hang of our new kind of war as well as any fellow from Sandhurst and Camberley. They were asking me to scrap all I had learned, and start again in a new job. I had to agree, for discipline's discipline, but I could have knocked their heads together in my vexation.

What was worse, they wouldn't, or couldn't, tell me anything about what they wanted me for. It was the old game of running me in blinkers. They asked me to take it on trust and put myself unreservedly in their hands. I would get my instructions later, they said.

I asked if it was important.

Bullivant narrowed his eyes. "If it weren't, do you suppose we could have wrung an active brigadier out of the War Office? As it was, it was like drawing teeth."

"Is it risky?" was my next question.

"In the long run—damnably," was the answer.

"And you can't tell me anything more?"

"Nothing as yet. You'll get your instructions soon enough. You know both of us, Hannay, and you know we wouldn't waste the time of a good man on folly. We are going to ask you for something which will make a big call on your patriotism. It will be a difficult and arduous task, and it may be a very grim one before you get to the end of it. But we believe you can do it, and that no one else can. . . . You know us pretty well. Will you let us judge for you?"

I looked at Bullivant's shrewd, kind old face and Macgillivray's steady eyes. These men were my friends and wouldn't play with me.

"All right," I said. "I'm willing. What's the first step?"

"Get out of uniform and forget you ever were a soldier. Change your name. Your old one, Cornelius Brandt, will do, but you'd better spell it 'Brand' this time. Remember that you are an engineer just back from South Africa, and that you don't care a rush about the war. You can't understand what all the fools are fighting about, and you think we might have peace at once by a little friendly business talk. You needn't be pro-German—if you like you can be rather severe on the Hun. But you must be in deadly earnest about a speedy peace."

I expect the corners of my mouth fell, for Bullivant burst out laughing.

"Hang it all, man, it's not so difficult. I feel sometimes inclined to argue that way myself, when my dinner doesn't agree with me. It's not so hard as to wander round the Fatherland abusing Britain, which was your last job."

"I'm ready," I said. "But I want to do one errand on my own first. I must see a fellow in my brigade who is in a shell-shock hospital in the Cotswolds. Isham's the name of the place."

The two men exchanged glances. "This looks like fate," said Bullivant. "By all means go to Isham. The place where your work begins is only a couple of miles off. I want you to spend next Thursday night as the guest of two maiden ladies called Wymondham at Fosse Manor. You will go down there as a lone South African visiting a sick friend. They are hospitable souls and entertain many angels unawares."

"And I get my orders there?"

"You get your orders and you are under bond to obey them . . ." And Bullivant and Macgillivray smiled at each other.

I was thinking hard about that odd conversation as the small Ford car, which I had wired for to the inn, carried me away from the suburbs of the county town into a land of rolling hills and green water-meadows. It was a gorgeous afternoon and the blossom of early June was on every tree. But I had no eyes for landscape and the summer, being engaged in reprobating Bullivant and cursing my fantastic fate. I detested my new part and looked forward to naked shame. It was bad enough for any one to have to pose as a pacificist, but for me, as strong as a bull and as sunburnt as a gipsy and not looking my forty years, it was a black disgrace. To go into Germany as an anti-British Afrikander was a stoutish adventure, but to lounge about at home talking rot was a very different-sized job. My stomach rose at the thought of it, and I had pretty well decided to wire to Bullivant and cry off. There are some things that no one has a right to ask of any white man.

When I got to Isham and found poor old Blaikie I didn't feel happier. He had been a friend of mine in Rhodesia, and after the German South-West affair was over had come home to a Fusilier battalion, which was in my brigade at Arras. He had been buried by a big crump just before we got our second objective, and was dug out without a scratch on him, but as daft as a hatter. I had heard he was mending, and had promised his family to look him up the first chance I got. I found him sitting on a garden seat staring steadily before him like a look-out at sea. He knew me all right and cheered up for a second, but very soon he was back staring, and every word he uttered was like the careful speech of a drunken man. A bird flew out of a bush, and I could see him holding himself tight to keep from screaming. The best I could do was to put a hand on his shoulder and stroke him as one strokes a frightened horse. The sight of the price my old friend had paid didn't put me in love with pacificism.

We talked of brother officers and South Africa, for I wanted to keep his thoughts off the war, but he kept edging round to it. "How long will the damned thing last?" he asked.

"Oh, it's practically over," I lied cheerfully. "No more fighting for you and precious little for me. The Boche is done in all right. . . . What you've got to do, my lad, is to sleep fourteen hours in the twenty-four and spend half the rest catching trout. We'll have a shot at the grouse-bird together this autumn, and we'll get some of the old gang to join us."

Someone put a tea-tray on the table beside us, and I looked up to see the very prettiest girl I ever set eyes on. She seemed little more than a child, and before the war would probably have still ranked as a flapper. She wore the neat blue dress and apron of a V.A.D., and her white cap was set on hair like spun gold. She smiled demurely as she arranged the tea-things, and I thought I had never seen eyes at once so merry and so grave. I stared after her as she walked across the lawn, and I remember noticing that she moved with the free grace of an athletic boy.

"Who on earth's that?" I asked Blaikie.

"That? Oh, one of the sisters," he said listlessly. "There are squads of them. I can't tell one from another."

Nothing gave me such an impression of my friend's sickness as the fact that he should have no interest in something so fresh and jolly as that girl. Presently my time was up and I had to go, and as I looked back I saw him sunk in his chair again, his eyes fixed on vacancy, and his hands gripping his knees.

The thought of him depressed me horribly. Here was I condemned to some rotten buffoonery in inglorious safety, while the salt of the earth like Blaikie was paying the ghastliest price. From him my thoughts flew to old Peter Pienaar, and I sat down on a roadside wall and read his last letter. It nearly made me howl.

Peter, you must know, had shaved his beard and joined the Royal Flying Corps the summer before, when we got back from the Greenmantle affair. That was the only kind of reward he wanted, and, though he was absurdly over age, the authorities allowed it. They were wise not to stickle about rules, for Peter's eyesight and nerves were as good as those of any boy of twenty. I knew he would do well, but I was not prepared for his immediate blazing success. He got his pilot's certificate in record time and went out to France; and presently even we foot-sloggers, busy shifting ground before the Somme, began to hear rumours of his doings. He developed a perfect genius for air fighting. There were plenty better trick flyers, and plenty who knew more about the science of the game, but there was no one with quite Peter's genius for an actual scrap. He was as full of dodges a couple of miles up in the sky as he had been among the rocks of the Berg. He apparently knew how to hide in the empty air as cleverly as in the long grass of the Lebombo Flats. Amazing yarns began to circulate among the infantry about this new airman, who could take cover below one plane of an enemy squadron while all the rest were looking for him. I remember talking about him with the South Africans when we were out resting next door to them after the bloody Delville Wood business. The day before we had seen a good battle in the clouds when the Boche plane had crashed, and a Transvaal machine-gun officer brought the report that the British airman had been Pienaar. "Well done, the old *takhaar!*" he cried, and started to yarn about Peter's methods. It appeared that Peter had a theory that every man has a blind spot, and that he knew just how to find that blind spot in the world of air. The best cover, he maintained, was not in cloud or a wisp of fog, but in the unseeing patch in the eye of your enemy. I recognized that talk for the real thing. It was on a par with Peter's doctrine of "atmosphere" and "the double bluff" and all the other principles that his queer old mind had cogitated out of his rackety life.

By the end of August that year Peter's was about the best-known figure in the Flying Corps. If the reports had mentioned names he would have been a national hero, but he was only "Lieutenant Blank," and the newspapers, which expatiated on his deeds, had to praise the service and not the man. That was right enough, for half the magic of our Flying Corps was its freedom from advertisement. But the British Army knew all about him, and the men in the trenches used to discuss him as if he were a crack football player. There was a very big German airman called Lensch, one of the Albatross heroes, who about the end of August claimed to have destroyed thirty-two Allied machines. Peter had then only seventeen planes to his credit, but he was rapidly increasing his score. Lensch was a mighty man of valour and a good sportsman after his fashion. He was amazingly quick at manoeuvring his machine in the actual fight, but Peter was supposed to be better at forcing the kind of fight he wanted. Lensch, if you like, was the tactician, and Peter the strategist. Anyhow the two were out to get each other. There were plenty of fellows who saw the campaign as a struggle not between Hun and Briton, but between Lensch and Pienaar.

The 15th of September came, and I got knocked out and went to hospital. When I was fit to read the papers again and receive letters, I found to my consternation that Peter had been downed. It happened at the end of October when the south-west gales badly handicapped our air work. When our bombing or reconnaissance jobs behind the enemy lines were completed, instead of being able to glide back into safety, we had to fight our way home slowly against a head wind, exposed to Archies and Hun planes. Somewhere east of Bapaume on a return journey Peter fell in with Lensch—at least the German Press gave Lensch the credit. His petrol tank was shot to bits and he was forced to descend in a wood near Morchies. "The celebrated British airman, Pinner," in the words of the German *communiqué*, was made prisoner.

I had no letter from him till the beginning of the New Year, when I was preparing to return to France. It was a very contented letter. He seemed to have been fairly well treated, though he had always a low standard of what he expected from the world in the way of comfort. I inferred that his captors had not identified with the brilliant airman the Dutch miscreant who a year before had broken out of a German gaol. He had discovered the pleasures of reading and had perfected himself in an art which he had once practised indifferently. Somehow or other he had got a *Pilgrim's Progress*, from which he seemed to extract enormous pleasure. And then at the end, quite casually, he mentioned that he had been badly wounded and that his left leg would never be much use again.

After that I got frequent letters, and I wrote to him every week and sent him every kind of parcel I could think of. His letters used to make me both ashamed and happy. I had always banked on old Peter, and here he was behaving like an early Christian martyr—never a word of complaint, and just as cheery as if it were a winter morning on the high veld and we were off to ride down springbok. I knew what the loss of a leg must mean to him, for bodily fitness had always been his pride. The rest of life must have unrolled itself before him very drab and dusty to the grave. But he wrote as if he were on the top of his form and kept commiserating me on the discomforts of my job. The picture of that patient, gentle old fellow, hobbling about his compound and puzzling over his *Pilgrim's Progress*, a cripple for life after five months of blazing glory, would have stiffened the back of a jellyfish.

This last letter was horribly touching, for summer had come and the smell of the woods behind his prison reminded Peter of a place in the Woodbush, and one could read in every sentence the ache of exile. I sat on that stone wall and considered how trifling were the crumpled leaves in my bed of life compared with the thorns Peter and Blaikie had to lie on. I thought of Sandy far off in Mesopotamia, and old Blenkiron groaning with dyspepsia somewhere in America, and I considered that they were the kind of fellows who did their jobs without complaining. The result was that when I got up to go on I had recovered a manlier temper. I wasn't going to shame my friends or pick and choose my duty. I would trust myself to Providence, for, as Blenkiron used to say, Providence was all right if you gave him a chance.

It was not only Peter's letter that steadied and calmed me. Isham stood high up in a fold of the hills away from the main valley and the road I was taking brought me over the ridge and back to the stream-side. I climbed through great beech woods, which seemed in the twilight like some green place far below the sea, and then over a short stretch of hill pasture in the rim of the vale. All about me were little fields enclosed with walls of grey stone and full of dim sheep. Below were dusky woods around what I took to be Fosse Manor, for the great Roman Fosse Way, straight as an arrow, passed over the hills to the south and skirted its grounds. I could see the stream slipping among its water-meadows and could hear the splash of the weir. A tiny village settled in the crook of the hill, and its church tower sounded seven with a curiously sweet chime. Otherwise there was no noise but the twitter of small birds and the night wind in the tops of the beeches.

In that moment I had a kind of revelation. I had a vision of what I had been fighting for, what we all were fighting for. It was peace, deep and holy and ancient, peace older than the oldest wars, peace which would endure when all our swords were hammered into ploughshares. It was more; for in that hour England first took hold of me. Before my country had been South Africa, and when I thought of home it had been the wide sun-steeped spaces of the veld or some scented glen of the Berg. But now I realized that I had a new home. I understood what a precious thing this little England was, how old and kindly and comforting, how wholly worth striving for. The freedom of an acre of her soil was cheaply bought by the blood of the best of us. I knew what it meant to be a poet, though for the life of me I could not have made a line of verse. For in that hour I had a prospect as if from a hilltop which made all the present troubles of the road seem of no account. I saw not only victory after war but a new and happier world after victory, when I should inherit something of this English peace and wrap myself in it till the end of my days.

Very humbly and quietly, like a man walking through a cathedral, I went down the hill to the Manor lodge, and came to a door in an old red-brick façade, smothered in magnolias which smelt like hot lemons in the June dusk. The car from the inn had brought on my baggage, and presently I was dressing in a room which looked out on a water-garden. For the first time for more than a year I put on a starched shirt and a dinner-jacket, and as I dressed I could have sung from pure light-heartedness. I was in for some arduous job, and some time that evening in that place I should get my marching orders. Some one would arrive—perhaps Bullivant—and read me the riddle. But whatever it was, I was ready for it, for my whole being had found a new purpose. Living in the trenches, you are apt to get your horizon narrowed down to the front line of enemy barbed wire on one side and the nearest rest billets on the other. But now I seemed to see beyond the fog to a happy country.

High-pitched voices greeted my ears as I came down the broad staircase, voices which scarcely accorded with the panelled walls and the austere family portraits; and when I found my hostesses in the hall I thought their looks still less in keeping with the house. Both ladies were on the wrong side of forty, but their dress was that of young girls. Miss Doria Wymondham was tall and thin with a mass of nondescript pale hair confined by a black velvet fillet. Miss Claire Wymondham was shorter and plumper and had done her best by ill-applied cosmetics to make herself look like a foreign *demi-mondaine*. They greeted me with the friendly casualness which I had long ago discovered was the right English manner towards your guests; as if they had just strolled in and billeted themselves, and you were quite glad to see them but mustn't be asked to trouble yourself further. The next second they were cooing like pigeons round a picture which a young man was holding up in the lamplight.

He was a tallish, lean fellow of round about thirty years, wearing grey flannels and shoes dusty from the country roads. His thin face was sallow as if from living indoors, and he had rather more hair on his head than most of us. In the glow of the lamp his features were very clear, and I examined them with interest, for, remember, I was expecting a stranger to give me orders. He had a long, rather strong chin and an obstinate mouth with peevish lines about its corners. But the remarkable feature was his eyes. I can best describe them by saying that they looked *hot*—not fierce or angry, but so restless that they seemed to ache physically and to want sponging with cold water.

They finished their talk about the picture—which was couched in a jargon of which I did not understand one word—and Miss Doria turned to me and the young man.

"My cousin Launcelot Wake—Mr. Brand. . . ."

We nodded stiffly, and Mr. Wake's hand went up to smooth his hair in a self-conscious gesture.

"Has Barnard announced dinner? By the way, where is Mary?"

"She came in five minutes ago and I sent her to change," said Miss Claire. "I won't have her spoiling the evening with that horrid uniform. She may masquerade as she likes out-of-doors, but this house is for civilized people."

The butler appeared and mumbled something. "Come along," cried Miss
Doria, "for I'm sure you are starving, Mr. Brand. And Launcelot has
bicycled ten miles."

The dining-room was very unlike the hall. The panelling had been stripped
off, and the walls and ceiling were covered with a dead-black satiny paper on
which hung the most monstrous pictures in large dull-gold frames. I could
only see them dimly, but they seemed to be a mere riot of ugly colour. The
young man nodded towards them. "I see you have got the Dégousses hung at
last," he said.

"How exquisite they are!" cried Miss Claire. "How subtle and candid and
brave! Doria and I warm our souls at their flame."

Some aromatic wood had been burned in the room, and there was a queer
sickly scent about. Everything in that place was strained and uneasy and
abnormal—the candle shades on the table, the mass of faked china fruit in
the centre dish, the gaudy hangings and the nightmarish walls. But the food
was magnificent. It was the best dinner I had eaten since 1914.

"Tell me, Mr. Brand," said Miss Doria, her long white face propped on a
much-beringed hand. "You are one of us? You are in revolt against this crazy
war?"

"Why, yes," I said, remembering my part. "I think a little common sense
would settle it right away."

"With a little common sense it would never have started," said Mr. Wake.

"Launcelot's a C.O., you know," said Miss Doria.

I did not know, for he did not look any kind of soldier. . . . I was just about
to ask him what he commanded, when I remembered that the letters stood
also for "Conscientious Objector," and stopped in time.

At that moment someone slipped into the vacant seat on my right hand. I
turned and saw the V.A.D. girl who had brought tea to Blaikie that afternoon
at the hospital.

"He was exempted by his Department," the lady went on, "for he's a Civil
Servant, and so he never had a chance of testifying in court, but no one has
done better work for our cause. He is on the committee of the L.D.A., and
questions have been asked about him in Parliament."

The man was not quite comfortable at this biography. He glanced nervously
at me and was going to begin some kind of explanation, when Miss Doria cut
him short. "Remember our rule, Launcelot. No turgid war controversy
within these walls."

I agreed with her. The war had seemed closely knit to the summer
landscape for all its peace, and to the noble old chambers of the Manor. But
in that demented modish dining-room it was shriekingly incongruous.

Then they spoke of other things. Mostly of pictures or common friends,
and a little of books. They paid no heed to me, which was fortunate, for I
know nothing about these matters and didn't understand half the language.
But once Miss Doria tried to bring me in. They were talking about some
Russian novel—a name like *Leprous Souls*—and she asked me if I had read it.
By a curious chance I had. It had drifted somehow into our dug-out on the

Scarpe, and after we had all stuck in the second chapter it had disappeared in the mud to which it naturally belonged. The lady praised its "poignancy" and "grave beauty." I assented, and congratulated myself on my second escape—for if the question had been put to me I should have described it as God-forgotten twaddle.

I turned to the girl, who welcomed me with a smile. I had thought her pretty in her V.A.D. dress, but now, in a filmy black gown and with her hair no longer hidden by a cap, she was the most ravishing thing you ever saw. And I observed something else. There was more than good looks in her young face. Her broad, low brow and her laughing eyes were amazingly intelligent. She had an uncanny power of making her eyes go suddenly grave and deep, like a glittering river narrowing into a pool.

"We shall never be introduced," she said, "so let me reveal myself. I'm Mary Lamington and these are my aunts. . . . Did you really like *Leprous Souls*?"

It was easy enough to talk to her. And oddly enough her mere presence took away the oppression I had felt in that room. For she belonged to the out-of-doors and to the old house and to the world at large. She belonged to the war, and to that happier world beyond it—a world which must be won by going through the struggle and not by shirking it, like those two silly ladies.

I could see Wake's eyes often on the girl, while he boomed and oraculated and the Misses Wymondham prattled. Presently the conversation seemed to leave the flowery paths of art and to verge perilously near forbidden topics. He began to abuse our generals in the field. I could not choose but listen. Miss Lamington's brows were slightly bent, as if in disapproval, and my own temper began to rise.

He had every kind of idiotic criticism—incompetence, faint-heartedness, corruption. Where he got the stuff I can't imagine, for the most grousing Tommy, with his leave stopped, never put together such balderdash. Worst of all, he asked me to agree with him.

It took all my sense of discipline. "I don't know much about the subject," I said, "but out in South Africa I did hear that the British leading was the weak point. I expect there's a good deal in what you say."

It may have been fancy, but the girl at my side seemed to whisper, "Well done!"

Wake and I did not remain long behind before joining the ladies. I purposely cut it short, for I was in mortal fear lest I should lose my temper and spoil everything. I stood up with my back against the mantelpiece for as long as a man may smoke a cigarette, and I let him yarn to me, while I looked steadily at his face. By this time I was very clear that Wake was not the fellow to give me my instructions. He wasn't playing a game. He was a perfectly honest crank, but not a fanatic, for he wasn't sure of himself. He had somehow lost his self-respect and was trying to argue himself back into it. He had considerable brains, for the reasons he gave for differing from most of his countrymen were good so far as they went. I shouldn't have cared to take him on in public argument. If you had told me about such a fellow a week before I should have been sick at the thought of him. But now I didn't dislike him. I was bored by him and I was also tremendously sorry for him. You could see he was as restless as a hen.

When we went back to the hall he announced that he must get on the road, and commandeered Miss Lamington to help him find his bicycle. It appeared he was staying at an inn a dozen miles off for a couple of days' fishing, and the news somehow made me like him better. Presently the ladies of the house departed to bed for their beauty sleep, and I was left to my own devices.

For some time I sat smoking in the hall wondering when the messenger would arrive. It was getting late, and there seemed to be no preparation in the house to receive anybody. The butler came in with a tray of drinks and I asked him if he expected another guest that night. "I 'adn't 'eard of it, sir," was his answer. "There 'asn't been a telegram that I know of, and I 'ave received no instructions."

I lit my pipe and sat for twenty minutes reading a weekly paper. Then I got up and looked at the family portraits. The moon coming through the lattice invited me out-of-doors as a cure for my anxiety. It was after eleven o'clock, and I was still without any knowledge of my next step. It is a maddening business to be screwed up for an unpleasant job and to have the wheels of the confounded thing tarry.

Outside the house beyond a flagged terrace the lawn fell away, white in the moonshine, to the edge of the stream, which here had expanded into a miniature lake. By the water's edge was a little formal garden with grey stone parapets which now gleamed like dusky marble. Great wafts of scent rose from it, for the lilacs were scarcely over and the may was in full blossom. Out from the shade of it came suddenly a voice like a nightingale.

It was singing the old song "Cherry Ripe," a common enough thing which I had chiefly known from barrel-organs. But heard in the scented moonlight it seemed to hold all the lingering magic of an elder England and of this hallowed countryside. I stepped inside the garden bounds and saw the head of the girl Mary.

She was conscious of my presence, for she turned towards me.

"I was coming to look for you," she said, "now that the house is quiet. I have something to say to you, General Hannay."

She knew my name, and must be somehow in the business. The thought entranced me.

"Thank God I can speak to you freely," I cried. "Who and what are you—living in that house in that kind of company?"

"My good aunts!" She laughed softly. "They talk a great deal about their souls, but they really mean their nerves. Why, they are what you call my camouflage, and a very good one too."

"And that cadaverous young prig?"

"Poor Launcelot! Yes—camouflage too—perhaps something a little more. You must not judge him too harshly."

"But . . . but—" I did not know how to put it, and stammered in my eagerness. "How can I tell that you are the right person for me to speak to? You see I am under orders, and I have got none about you."

"I will give you proof," she said. "Three days ago Sir Walter Bullivant and Mr. Macgillivray told you to come here to-night and to wait here for further instructions. You met them in the little smoking-room at the back of the Rota Club. You were bidden take the name of Cornelius Brand, and turn yourself from a successful general into a pacificist South African engineer. Is that correct?"

"Perfectly."

"You have been restless all evening looking for the messenger to give you these instructions. Set your mind at ease. No messenger is coming. You will get your orders from me."

"I could not take them from a more welcome source," I said.

"Very prettily put. If you want further credentials I can tell you much about your own doings in the past three years. I can explain to you, who don't need the explanation, every step in the business of the Black Stone. I think I could draw a pretty accurate map of your journey to Erzerum. You have a letter from Peter Pienaar in your pocket—I can tell you its contents. Are you willing to trust me?"

"With all my heart," I said.

"Good. Then my first order will try you pretty hard. For I have no orders to give except to bid you go and steep yourself in a particular kind of life. Your first duty is to get 'atmosphere,' as your friend Peter used to say. Oh, I will tell you where to go and how to behave. But I can't bid you *do* anything, only live idly with open eyes and ears till you have got the 'feel' of the situation."

She stopped and laid a hand on my arm.

"It won't be easy. It would madden me, and it will be a far heavier burden for a man like you. You have got to sink down deep into the life of the half-baked, the people whom this war hasn't touched or has touched in the wrong way, the people who split hairs all day and are engrossed in what you and I would call selfish little fads. Yes. People like my aunts and Launcelot, only for the most part in a different social grade. You won't live in an old manor like this, but among gimcrack little 'arty' houses. You will hear everything you regard as sacred laughed at and condemned, and every kind of nauseous folly acclaimed, and you must hold your tongue and pretend to agree. You will have nothing in the world to do except to let the life soak into you, and, as I have said, keep your eyes and ears open."

"But you must give me some clue as to what I should be looking for?"

"My orders are to give you none. Our chiefs—yours and mine—want you to go where you are going without any kind of *parti pris*. Remember we are still in the intelligence stage of the affair. The time hasn't yet come for a plan of campaign, and still less for action."

"Tell me one thing," I said. "Is it a really big thing we're after?"

"A—really—big—thing," she said slowly and very gravely. "You and I and some hundred others are hunting the most dangerous man in all the world. Till we succeed everything that Britain does is crippled. If we fail or succeed too late the Allies may never win the victory which is their right. I will tell you one thing to cheer you. It is in some sort a race against time, so your purgatory won't endure too long."

I was bound to obey, and she knew it, for she took my willingness for granted.

From a little gold satchel she selected a tiny box, and opening it extracted a thing like a purple wafer with a white St. Andrew's Cross on it. "What kind of watch have you? Ah, a hunter. Paste that inside the lid. Some day you may be called on to show it. . . . One other thing. Buy to-morrow a copy of the *Pilgrim's Progress* and get it by heart. You will receive letters and messages some day and the style of our friends is apt to be reminiscent of John Bunyan. . . . The car will be at the door to-morrow to catch the ten-thirty, and I will give you the address of the rooms that have been taken for you. . . . Beyond that I have nothing to say, except to beg you to play the part well and keep your temper. You behaved very nicely at dinner."

I asked one last question as we said good-night in the hall. "Shall I see you again?"

"Soon, and often," was the answer. "Remember we are colleagues."

I went upstairs feeling extraordinarily comforted. I had a perfectly beastly time ahead of me, but now it was all glorified and coloured with the thought of the girl who had sung "Cherry Ripe" in the garden. I commended the wisdom of that old serpent Bullivant in the choice of his intermediary, for I'm hanged if I would have taken such orders from anyone else.

34   "THE VILLAGE NAMED MORALITY"

Up on the high veld our rivers are apt to be strings of pools linked by muddy trickles—the most stagnant kind of watercourse you would look for in a day's journey. But presently they reach the edge of the plateau and are tossed down into the flats in noble ravines, and roll thereafter in full and sounding currents to the sea. So with the story I am telling. It began in smooth reaches as idle as a mill pond; yet the day soon came when I was in the grip of a torrent, flung breathless from rock to rock by a destiny which I could not control. But for the present I was in a backwater, no less than the Garden City of Biggleswick, where Mr. Cornelius Brand, a South African gentleman visiting England on holiday, lodged in a pair of rooms in the cottage of Mr. Tancred Jimson.

The house—or "home" as they preferred to name it at Biggleswick—was one of some two hundred others which ringed a pleasant Midland common. It was badly built and oddly furnished; the bed was too short, the windows did not fit, the doors did not stay shut; but it was as clean as soap and water and scrubbing could make it. The three-quarters of an acre of garden were mainly devoted to the culture of potatoes, though under the parlour window Mrs. Jimson had a plot of sweet-smelling herbs, and lines of lank sunflowers fringed the path that led to the front door. It was Mrs. Jimson who received me as I descended from the station fly—a large red woman with hair bleached by constant exposure to weather, clad in a gown which, both in shape and material, seemed to have been modelled on a chintz curtain. She was a good kindly soul, and as proud as Punch of her house. "We follow the simple life here, Mr. Brand," she said. "You must take us as you find us." I assured her that I asked for nothing better, and as I unpacked in my fresh little bedroom with a west wind blowing in at the window I considered that I had seen worse quarters.

I had bought in London a considerable number of books, for I thought that, as I would have time on my hands, I might as well do something about my education. They were mostly English classics, whose names I knew but which I had never read, and they were all in a little flat-backed series at a shilling apiece. I arranged them on the top of a chest of drawers, but I kept *Pilgrim's Progress* beside my bed, for that was one of my working tools and I had got to get it by heart. Mrs. Jimson, who came in while I was unpacking, to see if the room was to my liking, approved my taste. At our midday dinner she wanted to discuss books with me, and was so full of her own knowledge that I was able to conceal my ignorance. "We are all labouring to express our personalities," she informed me. "Have you found your medium, Mr. Brand? Is it to be the pen or the pencil? Or perhaps it is music? You have the brow of an artist, the frontal 'bar of Michelangelo,' you remember!"

I told her that I concluded I would try literature, but before writing anything I would read a bit more.

It was a Saturday, so Jimson came back from town in the early afternoon. He was a managing clerk in some shipping office, but you wouldn't have guessed it from his appearance. His city clothes were loose dark-grey flannels, a soft collar, an orange tie, and a soft black hat. His wife went down the road to meet him, and they returned hand-in-hand, swinging their arms like a couple of school children. He had a skimpy red beard streaked with grey, and mild blue eyes behind strong glasses. He was the most friendly creature in the world, full of rapid questions, and eager to make me feel one of the family. Presently he got into a tweed norfolk jacket, and started to cultivate his garden. I took off my coat and lent him a hand, and when he stopped to rest from his labours—which was every five minutes, for he had no kind of physique—he would mop his brow and rub his spectacles and declaim about the good smell of the earth and the joy of getting close to Nature.

Once he looked at my big brown hands and muscular arms with a kind of wistfulness. "You are one of the *doers*, Mr. Brand," he said, "and I could find it in my heart to envy you. You have seen Nature in wild forms in far countries. Some day I hope you will tell us about your life. I must be content with my little corner, but happily there are no territorial limits for the mind. This modest dwelling is a watch-tower from which I look over all the world."

After that he took me for a walk. We met parties of returning tennis players and here and there a golfer. There seemed to be an abundance of young men, mostly rather weedy-looking, but with one or two well-grown ones who should have been fighting. The names of some of them Jimson mentioned with awe. An unwholesome youth was Aronson, the great novelist; a sturdy, bristling fellow with a fierce moustache was Letchford, the celebrated leader writer of the *Critic*. Several were pointed out to me as artists who had gone one better than anybody else, and a vast billowy creature was described as the leader of the new Orientalism in England. I noticed that these people, according to Jimson, were all "great," and that they all dabbled in something "new." There were quantities of young women, too, most of them rather badly dressed and inclining to untidy hair. And there were several decent couples taking the air like householders of an evening all the world over. Most of these last were Jimson's friends, to whom he introduced me. They were his own class—modest folk, who sought for a coloured background to their prosaic city lives and found it in this odd settlement.

At supper I was initiated into the peculiar merits of Biggleswick. "It is one great laboratory of thought," said Mrs. Jimson. "It is glorious to feel that you are living among the eager vital people who are at the head of all the newest movements, and that the intellectual history of England is being made in our studies and gardens. The war to us seems a remote and secondary affair. As someone has said, the great fights of the world are all fought in the mind."

A spasm of pain crossed her husband's face. "I wish I could feel it far away. After all, Ursula, it is the sacrifice of the young that gives people like us leisure and peace to think. Our duty is to do the best which is permitted to us, but that duty is a poor thing compared with what our young soldiers are giving! I may be quite wrong about the war. . . . I know I can't argue with Letchford. But I will not pretend to a superiority I do not feel."

I went to bed feeling that in Jimson I had struck a pretty sound fellow. As I lit the candles on my dressing-table I observed that the stack of silver which I had taken out of my pockets when I washed before supper was top heavy. It had two big coins at the top and sixpences and shillings beneath. Now it is one of my oddities that ever since I was a boy I have arranged my loose coins symmetrically, with the smallest uppermost. That made me observant and led me to notice a second point. The English classics on the top of the chest of drawers were not in the order I had left them. Izaak Walton had got to the left of Sir Thomas Browne, and the poet Burns was wedged disconsolately between two volumes of Hazlitt. Moreover a receipted bill which I had stuck in the *Pilgrim's Progress* to mark my place had been moved. Some one had been going through my belongings.

A moment's reflection convinced me that it couldn't have been Mrs. Jimson. She had no servant and did the housework herself, but my things had been untouched when I left the room before supper, for she had come to tidy up before I had gone downstairs. Some one had been here while we were at supper, and had examined elaborately everything I possessed. Happily I had little luggage, and no papers save the new books and a bill or two in the name of Cornelius Brand. The inquisitor, whoever he was, had found nothing. . . . The incident gave me a good deal of comfort. It had been hard to believe that any mystery could exist in this public place, where people lived brazenly in the open, and wore their hearts on their sleeves and proclaimed their opinions from the roof-tops. Yet mystery there must be, or an inoffensive stranger with a kit-bag would not have received these strange attentions. I made a practice after that of sleeping with my watch below my pillow, for inside the case was Mary Lamington's label.

Now began a period of pleasant idle receptiveness. Once a week it was my custom to go up to London for the day to receive letters and instructions, if any should come. I had moved from my chambers in Park Lane, which I leased under my proper name, to a small flat in Westminster taken in the name of Cornelius Brand. The letters addressed to Park Lane were forwarded to Sir Walter, who sent them round under cover of my new address. For the rest I used to spend my mornings reading in the garden, and I discovered for the first time what a pleasure was to be got from old books. They recalled and amplified that vision I had seen from the Cotswold ridge, the revelation of the priceless heritage which is England. I imbibed a mighty quantity of history, but especially I liked the writers, like Walton, who got at the very heart of the English countryside. Soon, too, I found the *Pilgrim's Progress* not a duty but a delight. I discovered new jewels daily in the honest old story, and my letters to Peter began to be as full of it as Peter's own epistles. I loved, also, the songs of the Elizabethans, for they reminded me of the girl who had sung to me in the June night.

In the afternoons I took my exercise in long tramps along the good dusty English roads. The country fell away from Biggleswick into a plain of wood and pasture-land, with low hills on the horizon. The place was sown with villages, each with its green and pond and ancient church. Most, too, had inns, and there I had many a draught of ale, for the inn at Biggleswick was a reformed place which sold nothing but washy cider. Often, tramping home in the dusk, I was so much in love with the land that I could have sung with the pure joy of it. And in the evening, after a bath, there would be supper, when a rather fagged Jimson struggled between sleep and hunger, and the lady, with an artistic mutch on her untidy head, talked ruthlessly of culture.

Bit by bit I edged my way into local society. The Jimsons were a great help, for they were popular, and had a nodding acquaintance with most of the inhabitants. They regarded me as a meritorious aspirant towards a higher life, and I was paraded before their friends with the suggestion of a vivid, if Philistine, past. If I had any gift for writing, I would make a book about the inhabitants of Biggleswick. About half were respectable citizens who came there for country air and low rates, but even these had a touch of queerness and had picked up the jargon of the place. The younger men were mostly Government clerks or writers or artists. There were a few widows with flocks of daughters, and on the outskirts were several bigger houses—mostly houses which had been there before the garden city was planted. One of them was brand new, a staring villa with sham-antique timbering, stuck on the top of a hill among raw gardens. It belonged to a man called Moxon Ivery, who was a kind of academic pacificist and a great god in the place. Another, a quiet Georgian manor house, was owned by a London publisher, an ardent Liberal whose particular branch of business compelled him to keep in touch with the new movements. I used to see him hurrying to the station swinging a little black bag and returning at night with the fish for dinner.

I soon got to know a surprising lot of people, and they were the rummiest birds you can imagine. For example, there were the Weekeses, three girls who lived with their mother in a house so artistic that you broke your head whichever way you turned in it. The son of the family was a conscientious objector who had refused to do any sort of work whatever, and had got quodded for his pains. They were immensely proud of him and used to relate his sufferings in Dartmoor with a gusto which I thought rather heartless. Art was their great subject, and I am afraid they found me pretty heavy going. It was their fashion never to admire anything that was obviously beautiful, like a sunset or a pretty woman, but to find surprising loveliness in things which I thought hideous. Also they talked a language that was beyond me. This kind of conversation used to happen.—MISS WEEKES: "Don't you admire Ursula Jimson?" SELF: "Rather!" MISS W.: "She is so John-esque in her lines." SELF: "Exactly!" MISS W.: "And Tancred, too—he is so full of *nuances*." SELF: "Rather!" MISS W.: "He suggests one of Dégousse's countrymen." SELF: "Exactly!"

They hadn't much use for books, except some Russian ones, and I acquired merit in their eyes for having read *Leprous Souls*. If you talked to them about that divine countryside, you found they didn't give a rap for it and had never been a mile beyond the village. But they admired greatly the sombre effect of a train going into Marylebone station on a rainy day.

But it was the men who interested me most. Aronson, the novelist, proved on acquaintance the worst kind of blighter. He considered himself a genius whom it was the duty of the country to support, and he sponged on his wretched relatives and any one who would lend him money. He was always babbling about his sins, and pretty squalid they were. I should like to have flung him among a few good old-fashioned full-blooded sinners of my acquaintance; they would have scared him considerably. He told me that he sought "reality" and "life" and "truth," but it was hard to see how he could know much about them, for he spent half the day in bed smoking cheap cigarettes, and the rest sunning himself in the admiration of half-witted girls. The creature was tuberculous in mind and body, and the only novel of his I read pretty well turned my stomach. Mr. Aronson's strong point was jokes about the war. If he heard of any acquaintance who had joined up or was even doing war work his merriment knew no bounds. My fingers used to itch to box the little wretch's ears.

Letchford was a different pair of shoes. He was some kind of a man, to begin with, and had an excellent brain and the worst manners conceivable. He contradicted everything you said, and looked out for an argument as other people look for their dinner. He was a double-engined, high-speed pacificist, because he was the kind of cantankerous fellow who must always be in a minority. If Britain had stood out of the war he would have been a raving militarist, but since she was in it he had got to find reasons why she was wrong. And jolly good reasons they were, too. I couldn't have met his arguments if I had wanted to, so I sat docilely at his feet. The world was all crooked for Letchford, and God had created him with two left hands. But the fellow had merits. He had a couple of jolly children whom he adored, and he would walk miles with me on a Sunday, and spout poetry about the beauty and greatness of England. He was forty-five; if he had been thirty and in my battalion I could have made a soldier out of him.

There were dozens more whose names I have forgotten, but they had one common characteristic. They were puffed up with spiritual pride, and I used to amuse myself with finding their originals in the *Pilgrim's Progress*. When I tried to judge them by the standard of old Peter, they fell woefully short. They shut out the war from their lives, some out of funk, some out of pure levity of mind, and some because they were really convinced that the thing was all wrong. I think I grew rather popular in my rôle of the seeker after truth, the honest colonial who was against the war by instinct and was looking for instruction in the matter. They regarded me as a convert from an alien world of action which they secretly dreaded, though they affected to despise it. Anyhow they talked to me very freely, and before long I had all the pacificist arguments by heart. I made out that there were three schools. One objected to war altogether, and this had few adherents except Aronson and Weekes, C.O., now languishing in Dartmoor. The second thought that the Allies' cause was tainted, and that Britain had contributed as much as Germany to the catastrophe. This included all the adherents of the L.D.A.—or League of Democrats against Aggression,—a very proud body. The third and much the largest, which embraced everybody else, held that we had fought long enough and that the business could now be settled by negotiation, since Germany had learned her lesson. I was myself a modest member of the last school, but I was gradually working my way up to the second, and I hoped with luck to qualify for the first. My acquaintances approved my progress. Letchford said I had a core of fanaticism in my slow nature, and that I would end by waving the red flag.

Spiritual pride and vanity, as I have said, were at the bottom of most of them, and, try as I might, I could find nothing very dangerous in it all. This vexed me, for I began to wonder if the mission which I had embarked on so solemnly were not going to be a fiasco. Sometimes they worried me beyond endurance. When the news of Messines came nobody took the slightest interest, while I was aching to tooth every detail of that great fight. And when they talked on military affairs, as Letchford and others did sometimes, it was difficult to keep from sending them all to the devil, for their amateur cocksureness would have riled Job. One had to batten down the recollection of our fellows out there who were sweating blood to keep these fools snug. Yet I found it impossible to be angry with them for long, they were so babyishly innocent. Indeed, I couldn't help liking them, and finding a sort of quality in them. I had spent three years among soldiers, and the British regular, great fellow that he is, has his faults. His discipline makes him in a funk of red tape and any kind of superior authority. Now these people were quite honest and in a perverted way courageous. Letchford was, at any rate. I could no more have done what he did and got hunted off platforms by the crowd and hooted at by women in the streets than I could have written his leading articles.

All the same I was rather low about my job. Barring the episode of the ransacking of my effects the first night, I had not a suspicion of a clue or a hint of any mystery. The place and the people were as open and bright as a Y.M.C.A. hut. But one day I got a solid wad of comfort. In a corner of Letchford's paper, the *Critic*, I found a letter which was one of the steepest pieces of invective I had ever met with. The writer gave tongue like a beagle pup about the prostitution, as he called it, of American republicanism to the vices of European aristrocracies. He declared that Senator La Follete was a much-misunderstood patriot, seeing that he alone spoke for the toiling millions who had no other friend. He was mad with President Wilson, and he prophesied a great awakening when Uncle Sam got up against John Bull in Europe and found out the kind of standpatter he was. The letter was signed "John S. Blenkiron" and dated "London, July 3rd."

The thought that Blenkiron was in England put a new complexion on my business. I reckoned I would see him soon, for he wasn't the man to stand still in his tracks. He had taken up the rôle he had played before he left in December 1915, and very right too, for not more than half a dozen people knew of the Erzerum affair, and to the British public he was only the man who had been fired out of the Savoy for talking treason. I had felt a bit lonely before, but now somewhere within the four corners of the island the best companion God ever made was writing nonsense with his tongue in his old cheek.

There was an institution in Biggleswick which deserves mention. On the south side of the common, near the station, stood a red-brick building called the Moot Hall, which was a kind of church for the very undevout population. Undevout in the ordinary sense, I mean, for I had already counted twenty-seven varieties of religious conviction, including three Buddhists, a Celestial Hierarch, five Latter-day Saints, and about ten varieties of Mystic whose names I could never remember. The hall had been the gift of the publisher I have spoken of, and twice a week it was used for lectures and debates. The place was managed by a committee and was surprisingly popular, for it gave all the bubbling intellects a chance for airing their views. When you asked where somebody was and were told he was "at Moot," the answer was spoken in the respectful tone in which you would mention a sacrament.

I went there regularly and got my mind broadened to cracking point. We had all the stars of the New Movements. We had Doctor Chirk, who lectured on "God." which, as far as I could make out, was a new name he had invented for himself. There was a woman, a terrible woman, who had come back from Russia with what she called a "message of healing." And to my joy, one night there was a great buck nigger who had a lot to say about "Africa for the Africans." I had a few words with him in Sesutu afterwards, and rather spoiled his visit. Some of the people were extraordinarily good, especially one jolly old fellow who talked about English folk songs and dances, and wanted us to set up a maypole. In the debates which generally followed I began to join, very coyly at first, but presently with some confidence. If my time at Biggleswick did nothing else it taught me to argue on my feet.

The first big effort I made was on a full-dress occasion, when Launcelot Wake came down to speak. Mr. Ivery was in the chair—the first I had seen of him—a plump middle-aged man, with a colourless face and nondescript features. I was not interested in him till he began to talk, and then I sat bolt upright and took notice. For he was the genuine silver-tongue, the sentences flowing from his mouth as smooth as butter and as neatly dove-tailed as a parquet floor. He had a sort of man-of-the-world manner, treating his opponents with condescending geniality, deprecating all passion and exaggeration, and making you feel that his urbane statement must be right, for if he had wanted he could have put the case so much higher. I watched him, fascinated, studying his face carefully; and the thing that struck me was that there was nothing in it—nothing, that is to say, to lay hold on. It was simply nondescript, so almightily commonplace that that very fact made it rather remarkable.

Wake was speaking of the revelations of the Sukhomlinov trial in Russia, which showed that Germany had not been responsible for the war. He was jolly good at the job, and put up as clear an argument as a first-class lawyer. I had been sweating away at the subject and had all the ordinary case at my fingers' ends, so when I got a chance of speaking I gave them a long harangue, with some good quotations I had cribbed out of the *Vossische Zeitung*, which Letchford lent me. I felt it was up to me to be extra violent, for I wanted to establish my character with Wake, seeing that he was a friend of Mary and Mary would know that I was playing the game. I got tremendously applauded, far more than the chief speaker, and after the meeting Wake came up to me with his hot eyes, and wrung my hand. "You're coming on well, Brand," he said, and then he introduced me to Mr. Ivery. "Here's a second and a better Smuts," he said.

Ivery made me walk a bit of the road home with him. "I am struck by your grip on these difficult problems, Mr. Brand," he told me. "There is much I can tell you, and you may be of great value to our cause." He asked me a lot of questions about my past, which I answered with easy mendacity. Before we parted he made me promise to come one night to supper.

Next day I got a glimpse of Mary, and to my vexation she cut me dead. She was walking with a flock of bareheaded girls, all chattering hard, and though she saw me quite plainly she turned away her eyes. I had been waiting for my cue, so I did not lift my hat, but passed on as if we were strangers. I reckoned it was part of the game, but that trifling thing annoyed me, and I spent a morose evening.

The following day I saw her again, this time walking sedately with Mr.

Ivery, and dressed in a very pretty summer gown, and a broad-brimmed straw hat with flowers on it. This time she stopped with a bright smile and held out her hand. "Mr. Brand, isn't it?" she asked with a pretty hesitation. And then, turning to her companion—"This is Mr. Brand. He stayed with us last month in Gloucestershire."

Mr. Ivery announced that he and I were already acquainted. Seen in broad daylight he was a very personable fellow, somewhere between forty-five and fifty, with a middle-aged figure and a curiously young face. I noticed that there were hardly any lines on it, and it was rather that of a very wise child than that of a man. He had a pleasant smile which made his jaw and cheeks expand like india-rubber. "You are coming to sup with me, Mr. Brand," he cried after me. "On Tuesday after Moot. I have already written." He whisked Mary away from me, and I had to content myself with contemplating her figure till it disappeared round a bend of the road.

Next day in London I found a letter from Peter. He had been very solemn of late, and very reminiscent of old days now that he concluded his active life was over. But this time he was in a different mood. "*I think*," he wrote, "*that you and I will meet again soon, my old friend. Do you remember when we went after that big black-maned lion in the Rooirand and couldn't get on his track, and then one morning we both woke up and said we would get him to-day?—and we did, but he very near got you first. I've had a feel these last days that we're both going down into the Valley to meet with Apollyon, and that the devil will give us a bad time, but anyhow we'll be together.*"

I had the same kind of feel myself, though I didn't see how Peter and I were going to meet, unless I went out to the Front again and got put in the bag and sent to the same Boche prison. But I had an instinct that my time in Biggleswick was drawing to a close, and that presently I would be in rougher quarters. I felt quite affectionate towards the place, and took all my favourite walks, and drank my own health in the brew of the village inns, with a consciousness of saying good-bye. Also I made haste to finish my English classics, for I concluded I wouldn't have much time in the future for miscellaneous reading.

The Tuesday came, and in the evening I set out rather late for the Moot Hall, for I had been getting into decent clothes after a long, hot stride. When I reached the place it was pretty well packed, and I could only find a seat on the back benches. There on the platform was Ivery, and beside him sat a figure that thrilled every inch of me with affection and wild anticipation. "I have now the privilege," said the chairman, "of introducing to you the speaker whom we so warmly welcome, our fearless and indefatigable American friend, Mr. Blenkiron."

It was the old Blenkiron, but almightily changed. His stoutness had gone, and he was as lean as Abraham Lincoln. Instead of a puffy face, his cheek-bones and jaw stood out hard and sharp, and in place of his former pasty colour his complexion had the clear glow of health. I saw now that he was a splendid figure of a man, and when he got to his feet every movement had the suppleness of an athlete in training. In that moment I realized that my serious business had now begun. My senses suddenly seemed quicker, my nerves tenser, my brain more active. The big game had started, and he and I were playing it together.

I watched him with strained attention. It was a funny speech, stuffed with extravagance and vehemence, not very well argued and terribly discursive. His main point was that Germany was now in a fine democratic mood and might well be admitted into a brotherly partnership—that indeed she had never been in any other mood, but had been forced into violence by the plots of her enemies. Much of it, I should have thought, was in stark defiance of the Defence of the Realm Acts, but if any wise Scotland Yard officer had listened to it he would probably have considered it harmless because of its contradictions. It was full of a fierce earnestness, and it was full of humour—long-drawn American metaphors at which that most critical audience roared with laughter. But it was not the kind of thing that they were accustomed to and I could fancy what Wake would have said of it. The conviction grew upon me that Blenkiron was deliberately trying to prove himself an honest idiot. If so, it was a huge success. He produced on one the impression of the type of sentimental revolutionary who ruthlessly knifes his opponent and then weeps and prays over his tomb.

Just at the end he seemed to pull himself together and to try a little argument. He made a great point of the Austrian socialists going to Stockholm, going freely and with their Government's assent, from a country which its critics called an autocracy, while the democratic western peoples held back. "I admit I haven't any real water-tight proof," he said, "but I will bet my bottom dollar that the influence which moved the Austrian Government to allow this embassy of freedom was the influence of Germany herself. And that is the land from which the Allied Pharisees draw in their skirts lest their garments be defiled!"

He sat down amid a good deal of applause, for his audience had not been bored, though I could see that some of them thought his praise of Germany a bit steep. It was all right in Biggleswick to prove Britain in the wrong, but it was a slightly different thing to extol the enemy. I was puzzled about this last point, for it was not of a piece with the rest of his discourse, and I was trying to guess at his purpose. The chairman referred to it in his concluding remarks. "I am in a position," he said, "to bear out all that the lecturer has said. I can go farther. I can assure him on the best authority that his surmise is correct, and that Vienna's decision to send delegates to Stockholm was largely dictated by representations from Berlin. I am given to understand that the fact has in the last few days been admitted in the Austrian Press."

A vote of thanks was carried, and then I found myself shaking hands with Ivery, while Blenkiron stood a yard off, talking to one of the Misses Weekes. The next moment I was being introduced. "Mr. Brand, very pleased to meet you," said the voice I knew so well. "Mr. Ivery has been telling me about you, and I guess we've both got something to say to each other. We're both from noo countries, and we've got to teach the old nations a little horse-sense."

Mr. Ivery's car—the only one left in the neighbourhood—carried us to his villa, and presently we were seated in a brightly lit dining-room. It was not a pretty house, but it had the luxury of an expensive hotel, and the supper we had was as good as any London restaurant. Gone were the old days of fish and toast and boiled milk. Blenkiron squared his shoulders and showed himself a noble trenchman.

"A year ago," he told our host, "I was the meanest kind of dyspeptic. I had the love of righteousness in my heart but I had the devil in my stomach. Then I heard stories about the Robson Brothers, the star surgeons way out west in White Springs, Nebraska. They were reckoned the neatest hands in the world at carving up a man and removing devilments from his intestines. Now, sir, I've always fought pretty shy of surgeons, for I considered that our Maker never intended His handiwork to be reconstructed like a bankrupt Dago railway. But by that time I was feeling so almighty wretched that I could have paid a man to put a bullet through my head. 'There's no other way,' I said to myself. 'Either you forget your religion and your miserable cowardice and get cut up, or it's you for the Golden Shore.' So I set my teeth and journeyed to White Springs, and the Brothers had a look at my duodenum. They saw the darned thing wouldn't do, so they side-tracked it and made a noo route for my nootrition traffic. It was the cunningest piece of surgery since the Lord took a rib out of the side of our First Parent. They've got a mighty fine way of charging too, for they take five per cent. of a man's income, and it's all one to them whether he's a Meat King or a clerk on twenty dollars a week. I can tell you I took some trouble to be a very rich man last year."

All through the meal I sat in a kind of stupor. I was trying to assimilate the new Blenkiron, and drinking in the comfort of his heavenly drawl, and I was puzzling my head about Ivery. I had a ridiculous notion that I had seen him before, but, delve as I might into my memory, I couldn't place him. He was the incarnation of the commonplace: a comfortable middle-class sentimentalist, who patronized pacificism out of vanity, but was very careful not to dip his hands too far. He was always damping down Blenkiron's volcanic utterances. "Of course, as you know, the other side have an argument which I find rather hard to meet. . . ." "I can sympathize with patriotism, and even with jingoism, in certain moods, but I always come back to this difficulty. . . ." "Our opponents are not ill-meaning so much as ill-judging,"—these were the sort of sentences he kept throwing in. And he was full of quotations from private conversations he had had with every sort of person—including members of the Government. I remember that he expressed great admiration for Mr. Balfour.

Of all that talk I only recalled one thing clearly, and I recalled it because Blenkiron seemed to collect his wits and try to argue, just as he had done at the end of his lecture. He was speaking about a story he had heard from some one, who had heard it from some one else, that Austria in the last week of July 1914 had accepted Russia's proposal to hold her hand and negotiate, and that the Kaiser had sent a message to the Tsar saying he agreed. According to his story this telegram had been received in Petrograd, and had been re-written like Bismarck's Ems telegram, before it reached the Emperor. He expressed his disbelief in the yarn. "I reckon if it had been true," he said, "we'd have had the right text out long ago. They'd have kept a copy in Berlin. All the same I did hear a sort of rumour that some kind of message of that sort was being published in a German paper."

Mr. Ivery looked wise. "You are right," he said. "I happen to know that it has been published. You will find it in the *Weser Zeitung*."

"You don't say?" he said admiringly. "I wish I could read the old tombstone language. But if I could they wouldn't let me have the papers."

"Oh yes they would." Mr. Ivery laughed pleasantly. "England has still a good share of freedom. Any respectable person can get a permit to import the enemy press. I'm not considered quite respectable, for the authorities have a narrow definition of patriotism, but happily I have respectable friends."

Blenkiron was staying the night, and I took my leave as the clock struck twelve. They both came into the hall to see me off, and as I was helping myself to a drink, and my host was looking for my hat and stick, I suddenly heard Blenkiron's whisper in my ear. "London . . . the day after to-morrow," he said. Then he took a formal farewell. "Mr Brand, it's been an honour for me, as an American citizen, to make your acquaintance, sir. I will consider myself fortunate if we have an early reunion. I am stopping at Claridge's Ho-tel, and I hope to be privileged to receive you there."

35   THE REFLECTIONS OF A CURED DYSPEPTIC

Thirty-five hours later I found myself in my rooms at Westminster. I thought there might be a message for me there, for I didn't propose to go and call openly on Blenkiron at Claridge's till I had his instructions. But there was no message—only a line from Peter, saying he had hopes of being sent to Switzerland. That made me realize that he must be pretty badly broken up.

Presently the telephone bell rang. It was Blenkiron who spoke. "Go down and have a talk with your brokers about the War Loan. Arrive there about twelve o'clock and don't go upstairs till you have met a friend. You'd better have a quick luncheon at your club, and then come to Traill's bookshop in the Haymarket at two. You can get back to Biggleswick by the 5.16."

I did as I was bid, and twenty minutes later, having travelled by Underground, for I couldn't raise a taxi, I approached the block of chambers in Leadenhall Street where dwelt the respected firm who managed my investments. It was still a few minutes before noon, and as I slowed down a familiar figure came out of the bank next door.

Ivery beamed recognition. "Up for the day, Mr. Brand?" he asked.

"I have to see my brokers," I said, "read the South African papers in my club, and get back by the 5.16. Any chance of your company?"

"Why, yes—that's my train. *Au revoir*. We meet at the station." He bustled off, looking very smart with his neat clothes and a rose in his buttonhole.

I lunched impatiently, and at two was turning over some new books in Traill's shop with an eye on the street door behind me. It seemed a public place for an assignation. I had begun to dip into a big illustrated book on flower gardens when an assistant came up. "The manager's compliments, sir, and he thinks there are some old works of travel upstairs that might interest you." I followed him obediently to an upper floor lined with every kind of volume and with tables littered with maps and engravings. "This way, sir," he said and opened a door in the wall concealed by bogus bookbacks. I found myself in a little study, and Blenkiron sitting in an arm-chair smoking.

He got up and seized both my hands. "Why, Dick, this is better than good noos. I've heard all about your exploits since we parted a year ago on the wharf at Liverpool. We've both been busy on our own jobs, and there was no way of keeping you wise about my doings, for after I thought I was cured I got worse than hell inside, and, as I told you, had to get the doctor-men to dig into me. After that I was playing a pretty dark game, and had to get down and out of decent society. But, holy Mike! I'm a new man. I used to do my work with a sick heart and a taste in my mouth like a graveyard, and now I can eat and drink what I like and frolic round like a colt. I wake up every morning whistling and thank the good God that I'm alive. It was a bad day for Kaiser when I got on the cars for White Springs."

"This is a rum place to meet," I said, "and you brought me by a round-about road."

He grinned and offered me a cigar.

"There were reasons. It don't do for you and me to advertise our acquaintance in the street. As for the shop, I've owned it for five years. I've a taste for good reading, though you wouldn't think it, and it tickles me to hand it out across the counter. . . . First, I want to hear about Biggleswick."

"There isn't a great deal to it. A lot of ignorance, a large slice of vanity, and a pinch or two of wrong-headed honesty—these are the ingredients of the pie. Not much real harm in it. There's one or two dirty literary gents who should be in a navvies' battalion, but they're about as dangerous as yellow Kaffir dogs. I've learned a lot and got all the arguments by heart, but you might plant a Biggleswick in every shire and it wouldn't help the Boche. I can see where the danger lies all the same. These fellows talked academic anarchism, but the genuine article is somewhere about, and to find it you've got to look in the big industrial districts. We had faint echoes of it in Biggleswick. I mean that the really dangerous fellows are those who want to close up the war at once and so get on with their blessed class war, which cuts across nationalities. As for being spies and that sort of thing, the Biggleswick lads are too callow."

"Ye-es," said Blenkiron reflectively. "They haven't got as much sense as God gave to geese. You're sure you didn't hit against any heavier metal?"

"Yes. There's a man called Launcelot Wake, who came down to speak once. I had met him before. He has the makings of a fanatic, and he's the more dangerous because you can see his conscience is uneasy. I can fancy him bombing a Prime Minister merely to quiet his own doubts."

"So," he said. "Nobody else?"

I reflected. "There's Mr. Ivery, but you know him better than I. I shouldn't put much on him, but I'm not precisel' certain, for I never had a chance of getting to know him."

"Ivery," said Blenkiron in surprise. "He has a hobby for half-baked youth, just as another rich man might fancy orchids or fast trotters. You sure can place him right enough."

"I dare say. Only I don't know enough to be positive."

He sucked at his cigar for a minute or so. "I guess, Dick, if I told you all I've been doing since I reached these shores you would call me a romancer. I've been away down among the toilers. I did a spell as unskilled dilooted labour in the Barrow shipyards. I was barman in a ho-tel on the Portsmouth Road, and I put in a black month driving a taxicab in the city of London. For a while I was the accredited correspondent of the *Noo York Sentinel*, and used to go with the rest of the bunch to the pow-wows of under-secretaries of State and War Office generals. They censored my stuff so cruel that the paper fired me. Then I went on a walking tour round England and sat for a fortnight in a little farm in Suffolk. By and by I came back to Claridge's and this bookshop, for I had learned most of what I wanted.

"I had learned," he went on, turning his curious, full, ruminating eyes on me, "that the British working-man is about the soundest piece of humanity on God's earth. He grumbles a bit and jibs a bit when he thinks the Government are giving him a crooked deal, but he's got the patience of Job and the sand of a gamecock. And he's got humour too, that tickles me to death. There's not much trouble in that quarter, for it's he and his kind that's beating the Hun. . . . But I picked up a thing or two besides that."

He leaned forward and tapped me on the knee. "I reverence the British Intelligence Service. Flies don't settle on it to any considerable extent. It's got a mighty fine mesh, but there's one hole in that mesh, and it's our job to mend it. There's a high-powered brain in the game against us. I struck it a couple of years ago when I was hunting Dumba and Albert, and I thought it was in Noo York but it wasn't. I struck its working again at home last year and located its head office in Europe. So I tried Switzerland and Holland, but only bits of it were there. The centre of the web where the old spider sits is right here in England, and for six months I've been shadowing that spider. There's a gang to help, a big gang and a clever gang and partly an innocent gang. But there's only one brain, and it's to match that that the Robson Brothers settled my duodenum."

I was listening with quickened pulse, for now at last I was getting to business.

"What is he—international socialist, or anarchist, or what?" I asked.

"Pure-blooded Boche agent, but the biggest-sized brand in the catalogue— bigger than Steinmeier or old Bismarck's Staubier. Thank God I've got him located. . . . I must put you wise about some things."

He lay back in his rubbed leather arm-chair and yarned for twenty minutes. He told me how at the beginning of the war Scotland Yard had had a pretty complete register of enemy spies, and without making any fuss had just tidied them away. After that, the covey having been broken up, it was a question of picking off stray birds. That had taken some doing. There had been all kinds of inflammatory stuff around, Red Masons and international anarchists, and, worst of all, international finance-touts, but they had mostly been ordinary cranks and rogues, the tools of the Boche agents rather than agents themselves. However, by the middle of 1915 most of the stragglers had been gathered in. But there remained loose ends, and towards the close of last year somebody was very busy combining these ends into a net. Funny cases cropped up of the leakage of vital information. They began to be bad about October 1916, when the Hun submarines started on a special racket. The enemy suddenly appeared possessed of a knowledge which we thought to be shared only by half a dozen officers. Blenkiron said he was not surprised at the leakage, for there's always a lot of people who hear things they oughtn't to. What surprised him was that it got so quickly to the enemy.

Then after last February, when the Hun submarines went in for frightfulness on a big scale, the thing grew desperate. Leakages occurred every week, and the business was managed by people who knew their way about, for they avoided all the traps set for them, and when bogus news was released on purpose, they never sent it. A convoy which had been kept a deadly secret would be attacked at the one place where it was helpless. A carefully prepared defensive plan would be checkmated before it could be tried. Blenkiron said that there was no evidence that a single brain was behind it all, for there was no similarity in all the cases, but he had a strong impression all the time that it was the work of one man. We had managed to close some of the bolt-holes, but we couldn't put our hands near the big ones.

"By this time," said he, "I reckoned I was about ready to change my methods. I had been working by what the high-brows call induction, trying to argue up from the deeds to the doer. Now I tried a new lay, which was to calculate down from the doer to the deeds. They call it de-duction. I opined that somewhere in this island was a gentleman whom we will call Mr. X, and that, pursuing the line of business he did, he must have certain characteristics. I considered very carefully just what sort of personage he must be. I had noticed that his device was apparently the Double Bluff. That is to say, when he had two courses open to him, A and B, he pretended he was going to take B, and so got us guessing that he would try A. Then he took B after all. So I reckoned that his camouflage must correspond to this little idiosyncrasy. Being a Boche agent, he wouldn't pretend to be a hearty patriot, an honest old blood-and-bones Tory. That would be only the Single Bluff. I considered that he would be a pacificist, cunning enough just to keep inside the law, but with the eyes of the police on him. He would write books which would not be allowed to be exported. He would get himself disliked in the popular papers, but all the mug-wumps would admire his moral courage. I drew a mighty fine picture to myself of just the man I expected to find. Then I started out to look for him."

Blenkiron's face took on the air of a disappointed child. "It was no good. I kept barking up the wrong tree and wore myself out playing the sleuth on white-souled innocents."

"But you've found him all right," I cried, a sudden suspicion leaping into my brain.

"He's found," he said sadly, "but the credit does not belong to John S. Blenkiron. That child merely muddied the pond. The big fish was left for a young lady to hook."

"I know," I cried excitedly. "Her name is Miss Mary Lamington."

He shook a disapproving head. "You've guessed right, my son, but you've forgotten your manners. This is a rough business and we won't bring in the name of a gently reared and pure-minded young girl. If we speak of her at all we call her by a pet name out of the *Pilgrim's Progress*. . . . Anyhow she hooked the fish, though he isn't landed. D'you see any light?"

"Ivery," I gasped.

"Yes. Ivery. Nothing to look at, you say. A common, middle-aged, pie-faced, golf-playing high-brow, that you wouldn't keep out of a Sunday school. A touch of the drummer, too, to show he has no dealings with your effete aristocracy. A languishing silver-tongue that adores the sound of his own voice. As mild, you'd say, as curds and cream."

Blenkiron got out of his chair and stood above me. "I tell you, Dick, that man makes my spine cold. He hasn't a drop of good red blood in him. The dirtiest *apache* is a Christian gentleman compared to Moxon Ivery. He's as cruel as a snake and as deep as hell. But, by God, he's got a brain below his hat. He's hooked and we're playing him, but Lord knows if he'll ever be landed!"

"Why on earth don't you put him away?" I asked.

"We haven't the proof—legal proof, I mean; though there's buckets of the other kind. I could put up a morally certain case, but he'd beat me in a court of law. And half a hundred sheep would get up in Parliament and bleat about persecution. He has a graft with every collection of cranks in England and with all the geese that cackle about the liberty of the individual when the Boche is ranging about to enslave the world. No, sir, that's too dangerous a game. Besides, I've a better in hand. Moxon Ivery is the best accredited member of this State. His *dossier* is the completest thing outside the Recording Angel's little notebook. We've taken up his references in every corner of the globe, and they're all as right as Morgan's balance sheet. From these it appears he's been a high-toned citizen ever since he was in short clothes. He was raised in Norfolk, and there are people living who remember his father. He was educated at Melton School and his name's in the register. He was in business in Valparaiso, and there's enough evidence to write three volumes of his innocent life there. Then he came home with a modest competence two years before the war, and has been in the public eye ever since. He was Liberal candidate for a London constitooency, and he has decorated the board of every institootion formed for the amelioration of mankind. He's got enough *alibis* to choke a boa constrictor, and they're water-tight and copper-bottomed, and they're mostly damned lies. . . . But you can't beat him at that stunt. The man's the superbest actor that ever walked the earth. You can see it in his face. It isn't a face, it's a mask. He could make himself look like Shakespeare or Julius Cæsar or Billy Sunday or Brigadier-General Richard Hannay if he wanted to. He hasn't got any personality either—he's got fifty, and there's no one he could call his own. I reckon when the devil gets the handling of him at last he'll have to put sand on his claws to keep him from slipping through."

Blenkiron was settled in his chair again, with one leg hoisted over the side.

"We've closed a fair number of his channels in the last few months. No, he don't suspect me. The world knows nothing of its greatest men, and to him I'm only a Yankee peace-crank, who gives big subscriptions to loony societies and will travel a hundred miles to let off steam before any kind of audience. He's been to see me at Claridge's and I've arranged that he shall know all my record. A darned bad record it is too, for two years ago I was violent pro-British before I found salvation and was requested to leave England. When I was home last I was officially anti-war, when I wasn't stretched upon a bed of pain. Mr. Moxon Ivery don't take any stock in John S. Blenkiron as a serious proposition. And while I've been here I've been so low down in the social scale and working in so many devious ways that he can't connect me up. . . . As I was saying, we've cut most of his wires, but the biggest we haven't got at. He's still sending stuff out, and mighty compromising stuff it is. Now listen close, Dick, for we're coming near your own business."

It appeared that Blenkiron had reason to suspect that the channel still open had something to do with the North. He couldn't get closer than that, till he heard from his people that a certain Abel Gresson had turned up in Glasgow from the States. This Gresson he discovered was the same as one Wrankester, who as a leader of the Industrial Workers of the World had been mixed up in some ugly cases of *sabotage* in Colorado. He kept his news to himself, for he didn't want the police to interfere, but he had his own lot get into touch with Gresson and shadow him closely. The man was very discreet but very mysterious, and he would disappear for a week at a time leaving no trace. For some unknown reason—he couldn't explain why—Blenkiron had arrived at the conclusion that Gresson was in touch with Ivery, so he made experiments to prove it.

"I wanted various cross-bearings to make certain, and I got them the night before last. My visit to Biggleswick was good business."

"I don't know what they meant," I said, "but I know where they came in. One was in your speech when you spoke of the Austrian socialists, and Ivery took you up about them. The other was after supper when he quoted the *Weser Zeitung*."

"You're no fool, Dick," he said with his slow smile. "You've hit the mark first shot. You knew me and you could follow my process of thought in those remarks. Ivery, not knowing me so well, and having his head full of just that sort of argument, saw nothing unusual. Those bits of noos were pumped into Gresson that he might pass them. And he did pass them on—to Ivery. They completed my chain."

"But they were commonplace enough things which he might have guessed for himself."

"No, they weren't. They were the nicest tit-bits of political noos which all the cranks have been reaching after."

"Anyhow, they were quotations from German papers. He might have had the papers themselves earlier than you thought."

"Wrong again. The paragraph never appeared in the *Weser Zeitung*. But we faked up a torn bit of that noospaper, and a very pretty bit of forgery it was, and Gresson, who's a kind of a scholar, was allowed to have it. He passed it on, Ivery showed it me two nights ago. Nothing like it ever sullied the columns of Boche journalism. No, it was a perfectly final proof. . . . Now, Dick, it's up to you to get after Gresson."

"Right," I said. "I'm jolly glad I'm to start work again. I'm getting fat from lack of exercise. I suppose you want me to catch Gresson out in some piece of blackguardism and have him and Ivery snugly put away."

"I don't want anything of the kind," he said very slowly and distinctly. "You've got to attend very close to your instructions. I cherish these two beauties as if they were my own white-headed boys. I wouldn't for the world interfere with their comfort and liberty. I want them to go on corresponding with their friends. I want to give them every facility."

He burst out laughing at my mystified face.

"See here, Dick. How do we want to treat the Boche? Why, to fill him up with all the cunningest lies and get him to act on them. Now here is Moxon Ivery, who has always given them good information. They trust him absolutely and we would be fools to spoil their confidence. Only if we can find out Moxon's methods, we can arrange to use them ourselves and send noos in his name which isn't quite so genooine. Every word he dispatches goes straight to the Grand High Secret General Staff, and old Hindenburg and Ludendorff put towels round their heads and cipher it out. We want to encourage them to go on doing it. We'll arrange to send true stuff that don't matter, so as they'll continue to trust him, and a few selected falsehoods that'll matter like hell. It's a game you can't play for ever, but with luck, I propose to play it long enough to confuse Fritz's little plans."

His face became serious and wore the air that our corps commander used to have at the big pow-wow before a push.

"I'm not going to give you instructions, for you're man enough to make your own. But I can give you the general hang of the situation. You tell Ivery you're going north to inquire into industrial disputes at first hand. That will seem to him natural and in line with your recent behaviour. He'll tell his people that you're a guileless colonial who feels disgruntled with Britain, and may come in useful. You'll go to a man of mine in Glasgow, a red-hot agitator who chooses that way of doing his bit for his country. It's a darned hard way and a darned dangerous. Through him you'll get in touch with Gresson, and you'll keep alongside that bright citizen. Find out what he is doing, and get a chance of following him. He must never suspect you, and for that purpose you must be very near the edge of the law yourself. You go up there as an unabashed pacificist and you'll live with folk that will turn your stomach. Maybe you'll have to break some of these two-cent rules the British Government has invented to defend the realm, and it's up to you not to get caught out. . . . Remember, you'll get no help from me. You've got to wise up about Gresson with the whole forces of the British State arrayed officially against you. I guess it's a steep proposition, but you're man enough to make good."

As we shook hands he added a last word. "You must take your own time, but it's not a case for slouching. Every day that passes Ivery is sending out the worst kind of poison. The Boche is blowing up for a big campaign in the field, and a big effort to shake the nerve and confuse the judgment of our civilians. The whole earth's war-weary, and we've about reached the danger point. There's pretty big stakes hang on you, Dick, for things are getting mighty delicate."

I purchased a new novel in the shop and reached St. Pancras in time to have a cup of tea at the buffet. Ivery was at the bookstall buying an evening paper. When we got into the carriage he seized my *Punch* and kept laughing and calling my attention to the pictures. As I looked at him, I thought that he made a perfect picture of the citizen turned countryman going back of an evening to his innocent home. Everything was right—his neat tweeds, his light spats, his spotted neckcloth and his aquascutum.

Not that I dared look at him much. What I had learned made me eager to search his face, but I did not dare show any increased interest. I had always been a little off-hand with him, for I had never much liked him, so I had to keep on the same manner. He was as merry as a grig, full of chat and friendly and amusing. I remember he picked up the book I had brought off that morning to read in the train—the second volume of Hazlitt's *Essays*, the last of my English classics, and discoursed so wisely about books that I wished I had spent more time in his company at Biggleswick. "Hazlitt was the academic Radical of his day," he said. "He is always lashing himself into a state of theoretical fury over abuses he never encountered in person. Men who are up against the real thing save their breath for action."

That gave me my cue to tell him about my journey to the North. I said I had learned a lot in Biggleswick, but I wanted to see industrial life at close quarters. "Otherwise I might become like Hazlitt," I said.

He was very interested and encouraging.

"That's the right way to set about it," he said. "Where were you thinking of going?"

I told him that I had thought of Barrow, but decided to try Glasgow, since the Clyde seemed to be a warm corner.

"Right," he said. "I only wish I was coming with you. It'll take you a little while to understand the language. You'll find a good deal of senseless bellicosity among the workmen, for they've got parrot-cries about the war as they used to have parrot-cries about their labour politics. But there's plenty of shrewd brains and sound hearts too. You must write and tell me your conclusions."

It was a warm evening, and he dozed the last part of the journey. I looked at him and wished I could see into the mind at the back of that mask-like face. I counted for nothing in his eyes, not even enough for him to want to make me a tool, and I was setting out to try to make a tool of him. It sounded a forlorn enterprise. And all the while I was puzzled with a persistent sense of recognition. I told myself it was idiocy, for a man with a face like that must have hints of resemblance to a thousand people. But the idea kept nagging at me till we reached our destination.

As we emerged from the station into the golden evening I saw Mary Lamington again. She was with one of the Weekes girls, and after the Biggleswick fashion was bareheaded, so that the sun glinted from her hair. Ivery swept his hat off and made her a pretty speech, while I faced her steady eyes with the expressionlessness of the stage conspirator.

"A charming child," he observed as we passed on. "Not without a touch of seriousness, too, which may yet be touched to noble issues."

I considered, as I made my way to my final supper with the Jimsons, that the said child was likely to prove a sufficiently serious business for Mr. Moxon Ivery before the game was out.

36   ANDREW AMOS

I took the train three days later from King's Cross to Edinburgh. I went to the Pentland Hotel in Princes Street and left there a suit-case containing some clean linen and a change of clothes. I had been thinking the thing out, and had come to the conclusion that I must have a base somewhere and a fresh outfit. Then, in well-worn tweeds and with no more luggage than a small trench kit-bag, I descended upon the city of Glasgow.

I walked from the station to the address which Blenkiron had given me. It was a hot summer evening, and the streets were filled with bareheaded women and weary-looking artisans. As I made my way down the Dumbarton Road I was amazed at the number of able-bodied fellows about, considering that you couldn't stir a mile on any British front without bumping up against a Glasgow battalion. Then I realized that there were such things as munitions and ships, and I wondered no more.

A stout and dishevelled lady at a close-mouth directed me to Mr. Amos's dwelling. "Twa stairs up. Andra will be in noo, havin' his tea. He's no yin for overtime. He's generally hame on the chap of six." I ascended the stairs with a sinking heart, for like all South Africans I have a horror of dirt. The place was pretty filthy, but at each landing there were two doors with well-polished handles and brass plates. On one I read the name of Andrew Amos.

A man in his shirt-sleeves opened to me, a little man with a collar, and with an unbuttoned waistcoat. That was all I saw of him in the dim light, but he held out a paw like a gorilla's and drew me in.

The sitting-room, which looked over many chimneys to a pale yellow sky against which two factory stalks stood out sharply, gave me light enough to observe him fully. He was about five feet four, broad-shouldered, and with a great towsy head of grizzled hair. He wore spectacles, and his face was like some old-fashioned Scots minister's, for he had heavy eyebrows and whiskers which joined each other under his jaw, while his chin and enormous upper lip were clean-shaven. His eyes were steely grey and very solemn, but full of smouldering energy. His voice was enormous and would have shaken the walls if he had not had the habit of speaking with half-closed lips. He had not a sound tooth in his head.

A saucer full of tea and a plate which had once contained ham and eggs were on the table. He nodded towards them and asked me if I had fed.

"Ye'll no eat onything? Well, some would offer ye a dram, but this house is staunch teetotal. I doot you'll have to try the nearest public if ye're thirsty."

I disclaimed any bodily wants, and produced my pipe, at which he started to fill an old clay. "Mr. Brand's your name?" he asked in his gusty voice. "I was expectin' ye, but Dod! man, ye're late!"

He extricated from his trousers pocket an ancient silver watch, and regarded it with disfavour. "The dashed thing has stoppit. What do ye make the time, Mr. Brand?"

He proceeded to prise open the lid of his watch with the knife he had used to cut his tobacco, and, as he examined the works, he turned the back of the case towards me. On the inside I saw pasted Mary Lamington's purple-and-white wafer.

I held my watch so that he could see the same token. His keen eyes, raised for a second, noted it, and he shut his own with a snap and returned it to his pocket. His manner lost its wariness, and became almost genial.

"Ye've come up to see Glasgow, Mr. Brand? Well, it's a steerin' bit, and there's honest folk bides in it, and some not so honest. They tell me ye're from South Africa. That's a long gait away, but I ken something about South Africa, for I had a cousin's son oot there for his lungs. He was in a shop in Main Street, Bloomfountain. They called him Peter Dobson. Ye would maybe mind of him."

Then he discoursed of the Clyde. He was an in-comer, he told me, from the Borders, his native place being the town of Galashiels, or, as he called it, "Gawly." "I began as a power-loom tuner in Stavert's mill. Then my father dee'd and I took up his trade of jiner. But it's no world nowadays for the sma' independent business, so I cam to the Clyde and learned a shipwright's job. I may say I've become a leader in the trade, for though I'm no an official of the Union, and not likely to be, there's no man's word carries more weight than mine. And the Goavernment kens that, for they've sent me on Commissions up and down the land to look at wuds and report on the nature of the timber. Bribery, they think it is, but Andrew Amos is not to be bribit. He'll have his say about ony Goavernment on earth, and tell them to their face what he thinks of them. Ay, and he'll fight the case of the workin'-man against his oppressor, should it be the Goavernment or the fatted calves they ca' Labour Members. Ye'll have heard tell o' the shop stewards, Mr. Brand?"

I admitted I had, for I had been well coached by Blenkiron in the current history of industrial disputes.

"Well, I'm a shop steward. We represent the rank and file against office-bearers that have lost the confidence o' the workin'-man. But I'm no socialist and I would have ye keep mind of that. I'm yin o' the old Border radicals, and I'm not like to change. I'm for individual liberty and equal rights and chances for all men. I'll no more bow down before a Dagon of a Goavernment official than before the Baal of a feckless Tweedside laird. I've to keep my views to mysel', for thae young lads are all drucken-daft with their wee books about Cawpital and Collectivism and a wheen long senseless words I wouldna fyle my tongue with. Them and their socialism! There's more gumption in a page of John Stuart Mill than in all that foreign trash. But, as I say, I've got to keep a quiet sough, for the world is gettin' socialism now like the measles. It all comes of a defective eddication."

"And what does a Border radical say about the war?" I asked.

He took off his spectacles and cocked his shaggy brows at me. "I'll tell ye, Mr. Brand. All that was bad in all that I've ever wrestled with since I cam to years o' discretion—Tories and lairds and manufacturers and publicans and the Auld Kirk—all that was bad, I say, for there were orra bits of decency, ye'll find in the Germans full measure pressed down and running over. When the war started, I considered the subject calmly for three days, and then I said: 'Andra Amos, ye've found the enemy at last. The ones ye fought before were in a manner o' speakin' just misguided friends. It's either you or the Kaiser this time, my man!'"

His eyes had lost their gravity and had taken on a sombre ferocity. "Ay, and I've not wavered. I got a word early in the business as to the way I could serve my country best. It's not been an easy job, and there's plenty of honest folk the day will give me a bad name. They think I'm stirrin' up the men at home and desertin' the cause o' the lads at the front. Man, I'm keepin' them straight. If I didna fight their battles on a sound economic isshue, they would take the dorts and be at the mercy of the first blagyird that preached revolution. Me and my like are safety-valves, if ye follow me. And dinna you make ony mistake, Mr. Brand. The men that are agitating for a rise in wages are not for peace. They're fighting for the lads overseas as much as for themselves. There's not yin in a thousand that wouldna sweat himself blind to beat the Germans. The Goavernment has made mistakes, and maun be made to pay for them. If it were not so, the men would feel like a moose in a trap, for they would have no way to make their grievance felt. What for should the big man double his profits and the small man be ill set to get his ham and egg on Sabbath mornin'? That's the meaning o' Labour unrest, as they call it, and it's a good thing, says I, for if Labour didna get its leg over the traces now and then, the spunk o' the land would be dead in it, and Hindenburg could squeeze it like a rotten aipple."

I asked if he spoke for the bulk of the men.

"For ninety per cent. in ony ballot. I don't say that there's not plenty of riff-raff—the pint-and-a-dram gentry and the soft-heads that are aye reading bits of newspapers, and muddlin' their wits with foreign whigmaleeries. But the average man on the Clyde, like the average man in ither places, hates just three things, and that's the Germans, the profiteers, as they call them, and the Irish. But he hates the Germans first."

"The Irish!" I exclaimed in astonishment.

"Ay, the Irish," cried the last of the old Border radicals. "Glasgow's stinkin' nowadays with two things, money and Irish. I mind the day when I followed Mr. Gladstone's Home Rule policy, and used to threep about the noble, generous, warm-hearted sister nation held in a foreign bondage. My Goad! I'm not speakin' about Ulster, which is a dour, ill-natured den, but our own folk all the same. But the men that will not do a hand's turn to help the war and take the chance of our necessities to set up a bawbee rebellion are hateful to Goad and man. We treated them like pet lambs and that's the thanks we get. They're coming over here in thousands to tak the jobs of the lads that are doing their duty. I was speakin' last week to a widow woman that keeps a wee dairy down the Dalmarnock Road. She has two sons, and both in the airmy, one in the Cameronians and one a prisoner in Germany. She was telling me that she could not keep goin' any more, lacking the help of the boys, though she had worked her fingers to the bone. 'Surely it's a crool job, Mr. Amos,' she says, 'that the Goavernment should tak baith my laddies, and I'll maybe never see them again, and let the Irish gang free and tak the bread frae our mouth. At the gasworks across the road they took on a hundred Irish last week, and every yin o' them as young and well set up as you would ask to see. And my wee Davie, him that's in Germany, had aye a weak chest, and Jimmy was troubled wi' a bowel complaint. That's surely no justice!' . . ."

He broke off and lit a match by drawing it across the seat of his trousers. "It's time I got the gas lichtit. There's some men coming here at half-ten."

As the gas squealed and flickered in the lighting, he sketched for me the coming guests. "There's Macnab and Niven, two o' my colleagues. And there's Gilkison of the Boiler-fitters, and a lad Wilkie—he's got consumption, and writes wee bits in the papers. And there's a queer chap o' the name o' Tombs—they tell me he comes frae Cambridge and is a kind of a professor there—anyway he's more stuffed wi' havers than an egg wi' meat. He telled me he was here to get at the heart o' the workin'-man, and I said to him that he would hae to look a bit further than the sleeve o' the workin'-man's jaicket. There's no muckle in his head, poor soul. Then there'll be Tam Norie, him that edits our weekly paper—*Justice for All*. Tam's a humorist and great on Robert Burns, but he hasna the balance o' a dwinin' teetotum. . . . Ye'll understand, Mr. Brand, that I keep my mouth shut in such company, and don't express my own views more than is absolutely necessary. I criticize whiles, and that gives me a name for whunstane common sense, but I never let my tongue wag. The feck o' the lads comin' the night are not the real workin'-man—they're just the froth on the pot, but it's the froth that will be useful to you. Remember they've heard tell o' ye already, and ye've some sort o' reputation to keep up."

"Will Mr. Abel Gresson be here?" I asked.

"No," he said. "Not yet. Him and me havena yet got to the point o' payin' visits. But the men that come will be Gresson's friends, and they'll speak of ye to him. It's the best kind of introduction ye could seek."

The knocker sounded, and Mr. Amos hastened to admit the first comers. These were Macnab and Wilkie: the one a decent middle-aged man with a fresh-washed face and a celluloid collar; the other a round-shouldered youth, with lank hair and the large eyes and luminous skin which are the marks of phthisis. "This is Mr. Brand, boys, from South Africa," was Amos's presentation. Presently came Niven, a bearded giant, and Mr. Norie, the editor, a fat dirty fellow smoking a rank cigar. Gilkison of the Boiler-fitters, when he arrived, proved to be a pleasant young man in spectacles who spoke with an educated voice and clearly belonged to a slightly different social scale. Last came Tombs, the Cambridge "professor," a lean youth with a sour mouth and eyes that reminded me of Launcelot Wake.

"Ye'll no be a mawgnate, Mr. Brand, though ye come from South Africa," said Mr. Norie with a great guffaw.

"Not me. I'm a working engineer," I said. "My father was from Scotland, and this is my first visit to my native country, as my friend Mr. Amos was telling you."

The consumptive looked at me suspiciously. "We've got two-three of the comrades here that the cawpitalist Government expelled from the Transvaal. If ye're our way of thinking, ye will maybe ken them."

I said I would be overjoyed to meet them, but that at the time of the outrage in question I had been working on a mine a thousand miles farther north.

Then ensued an hour of extraordinary talk. Tombs in his sing-song namby-pamby University voice was concerned to get information. He asked endless questions, chiefly of Gilkison, who was the only one who really understood his language. I thought I had never seen any one quite so fluent and so futile, and yet there was a kind of feeble violence in him like a demented sheep. He was engaged in venting some private academic spite against society, and I thought that in a revolution he would be the class of lad I would personally conduct to the nearest lamp-post. And all the while Amos and Macnab and Niven carried on their own conversation about the affairs of their society, wholly impervious to the tornado raging around them.

It was Mr. Norie, the editor, who brought me into the discussion.

"Our South African friend is very blate," he said in his boisterous way. "Andra, if this place of yours wasn't so damned teetotal and we had a dram apiece, we might get his tongue loosened. I want to hear what he's got to say about the war. You told me this morning he was sound in the faith."

"I said no such thing," said Mr. Amos. "As ye ken well, Tam Norie, I don't judge soundness on that matter as you judge it. I'm for the war myself, subject to certain conditions that I've often stated. I know nothing of Mr.

Brand's opinions, except that he's a good democrat, which is more than I can say of some o' your friends."

"Hear to Andra," laughed Mr. Norie. "He's thinkin' the inspector in the Socialist State would be a waur kind of awristocrat then the Duke of Buccleugh. Weel, there's maybe something in that. But about the war he's wrong. Ye ken my views, boys. This war was made by the cawpitalists, and it has been fought by the workers, and it's the workers that maun have the ending of it. That day's comin' very near. There are those that want to spin it out till Labour is that weak it can be pit in chains for the rest o' time. That's the manoeuvre we're out to prevent. We've got to beat the Germans, but it's the workers that has the right to judge when the enemy's beaten and not the cawpitalists. What do you say, Mr. Brand?"

Mr. Norie had obviously pinned his colours to the fence, but he gave me the chance I had been looking for. I let them have my views with a vengeance, and these views were that for the sake of democracy the war must be ended. I flatter myself I put my case well, for I had got up every rotten argument and I borrowed largely from Launcelot Wake's armoury. But I didn't put it too well, for I had a very exact notion of the impression I wanted to produce. I must seem to be honest and in earnest, just a bit of a fanatic, but principally a hard-headed business man who knew when the time had come to make a deal. Tombs kept interrupting me with imbecile questions, and I had to sit on him. At the end Mr. Norie hammered with his pipe on the table.

"That'll sort ye, Andra. Ye're entertainin' an angel unawares. What do ye say to that, my man?"

Mr. Amos shook his head. "I'll no deny there's something in it, but I'm not convinced that the Germans have got enough of a wheepin'." Macnab agreed with him; the others were with me. Norie was for getting me to write an article for his paper, and the consumptive wanted me to address a meeting.

"Wull ye say a' that over again the morn's night at our hall in Newmilns Street? We've got a lodge meeting o' the I.W.B., and I'll make them pit ye in the programme." He kept his luminous eyes, like a sick dog's, fixed on me, and I saw that I had made one ally. I told him I had come to Glasgow to learn and not to teach, but I would miss no chance of testifying to my faith.

"Now, boys, I'm for my bed," said Amos, shaking the dottle from his pipe. "Mr. Tombs, I'll conduct ye the morn over the Brigend works, but I've had enough clavers for one evening. I'm a man that wants his eight hours' sleep."

The old fellow saw them to the door, and came back to me with the ghost of a grin in his face.

"A queer crowd, Mr. Brand! Macnab didna like what ye said. He had a laddie killed in Gallypoly, and he's no lookin' for peace this side the grave. He's my best friend in Glasgow. He's an elder in the Gaelic kirk in the Cowcaddens, and I'm what ye call a freethinker, but we're wonderful agreed on the fundamentals. Ye spoke your bit verra well, I must admit. Gresson will hear tell of ye as a promising recruit."

"It's a rotten job," I said.

"Ay, it's a rotten job. I often feel like voamiting over it mysel'. But it's no for us to complain. There's waur jobs oot in France for better men. . . . A word in your ear, Mr. Brand. Could ye not look a bit more sheepish? Ye stare folk ower straight in the een, like a Hieland sergeant-major up at Maryhill Barracks." And he winked slowly and grotesquely with his left eye.

He marched to a cupboard and produced a black bottle and a glass. "I'm blue-ribbon myself, but ye'll be the better of something to tak the taste out of your mouth. There's Loch Katrine water at the pipe there. . . . As I was saying, there's not much ill in that lot. Tombs is a black offence, but a dominie's a dominie all the world over. They may crack about their Industrial Workers and the braw things they're going to do, but there's a wholesome dampness about the tinder on Clydeside. They should try Ireland."

"Supposing," I said, "there was a really clever man who wanted to help the enemy. You think he could do little good by stirring up trouble in the shops here?"

"I'm positive."

"And if he were a shrewd fellow, he'd soon tumble to that?"

"Ay."

"Then if he still stayed on here he would be after bigger game—something really dangerous and damnable?"

Amos drew down his brows and looked me in the face. "I see what ye're ettlin' at. Ay! That would be my conclusion. I came to it weeks syne about the man ye'll maybe meet the morn's night."

Then from below the bed he pulled a box from which he drew a handsome flute. "Ye'll forgive me, Mr. Brand, but I aye like a tune before I go to my bed. Macnab says his prayers, and I have a tune on the flute, and the principle is just the same."

So that singular evening closed with music—very sweet and true renderings of old Border melodies like "My Peggy is a young thing," and "When the kye come hame." I fell asleep with a vision of Amos, his face all puckered up at the mouth and a wandering sentiment in his eye, recapturing in his dingy world the emotions of a boy.

The widow-woman from next door, who acted as a housekeeper, cook, and general factotum to the establishment, brought me shaving water next morning, but I had to go without a bath. When I entered the kitchen I found no one there, but while I consumed the inevitable ham and egg, Amos arrived back for breakfast. He brought with him the morning's paper.

"The *Herald* says there's been a big battle at Eepers," he announced.

I tore open the sheet and read of the great attack of July 31st which was spoiled by the weather. "My God!" I cried. "They've got St. Julien and that dirty Frezenberg ridge . . . and Hooge . . . and Sanctuary Wood. I know every inch of the damned place. . . ."

"Mr. Brand," said a warning voice, "that'll never do. If our friends last night heard ye talk like that ye might as well tak the train back to London. . . . They're speakin' about ye in the yards this morning. Ye'll get a good turn-out at your meeting the night, but they're sayin' that the polis will interfere. That mightna be a bad thing, but I trust ye to show discretion, for ye'll no be muckle use to onybody if they jyle ye in Duke Street. I hear Gresson will be there with a fraternal message from his lunattics in America. . . . I've arranged that ye go down to Tam Norie this forenoon and give him a hand with his bit paper. Tam will tell ye the whole clash o' the West country, and I look to ye to keep him off the drink. He's aye arguin' that writin' and drinkin' gang thegither, and quotin' Robert Burns, but the creature has a wife and five bairns dependin' on him."

I spent a fantastic day. For two hours I sat in Norie's dirty den, while he smoked and orated, and, when he remembered his business, took down in shorthand my impressions of the Labour situation in South Africa for his rag. They were fine breezy impressions, based on the most wholehearted ignorance, and if they ever reached the Rand I wonder what my friends there made of Cornelius Brand, their author. I stood him dinner in an indifferent eating-house in a street off the Broomielaw, and thereafter had a drink with him in a public-house, and was introduced to some of his less reputable friends.

About tea-time I went back to Amos's lodgings, and spent an hour or so writing a long letter to Mr. Ivery. I described to him everybody I had met, I gave highly coloured views of the explosive material on the Clyde, and I deplored the lack of clear-headedness in the progressive forces. I drew an elaborate picture of Amos, and deduced from it that the Radicals were likely to be a bar to true progress. "They have switched their old militancy," I wrote, "on to another track, for with them it is a matter of conscience to be always militant." I finished up with some very crude remarks on economics culled from the table-talk of the egregious Tombs. It was the kind of letter which I hoped would establish my character in his mind as a laborious innocent.

Seven o'clock found me in Newmilns Street, where I was seized upon by Wilkie. He had put on a clean collar for the occasion and had partially washed his thin face. The poor fellow had a cough that shook him like the walls of a power-house when the dynamos are going.

He was very apologetic about Amos. "Andra belongs to a past worrld," he said. "He has a big repittation in his society, and he's a fine fighter, but he has no kind of Vision, if ye understand me. He's an auld Gladstonian, and that's done and damned in Scotland. He's not a modern, Mr. Brand, like you and me. But to-night ye'll meet one or two chaps that'll be worth your while to ken. Ye'll maybe no go quite as far as them, but ye're on the same road. I'm hoping for the day when we'll have oor Councils of Workmen and Soldiers like the Russians all over the land and dictate our terms to the pawrasites in Pawrliament. They tell me, too, the boys in the trenches are comin' round to our side."

We entered the hall by a back door, and in a little waiting-room I was introduced to some of the speakers. They were a scratch lot as seen in that dingy place. The chairman was a shop steward in one of the Societies, a fierce little rat of a man, who spoke with a cockney accent and addressed me as "Comrade." But one of them roused my liveliest interest. I heard the name of Gresson, and turned to find a fellow of about thirty-five, rather sprucely dressed, with a flower in his buttonhole. "Mr. Brand," he said, in a rich American voice which recalled Blenkiron's. "Very pleased to meet you, sir. We have come from remote parts of the globe to be present at this gathering." I noticed that he had reddish hair, and small bright eyes, and a nose with a droop like a Polish Jew's.

As soon as we reached the platform I saw that there was going to be trouble. The hall was packed to the door, and in all the front half there was the kind of audience I expected to see—working-men of the political type who before the war would have thronged to party meetings. But not all the crowd at the back had come to listen. Some were scallawags, some looked like better-class clerks out for a spree, and there was a fair quantity of khaki. There were also one or two gentlemen not strictly sober.

The chairman began by putting his foot in it. He said we were there to-night to protest against the continuation of the war and to form a branch of the new British Council of Workmen and Soldiers. He told them with a fine mixture of metaphors that we had got to take the reins into our own hands, for the men who were running the war had their own axes to grind and were marching to oligarchy through the blood of the workers. He added that we had no quarrel with Germany half as bad as we had with our own capitalists. He looked forward to the day when British soldiers would leap from their trenches and extend the hand of friendship to their German comrades.

"No me!" said a solemn voice. "I'm not seekin' a bullet in my wame,"—at which there was laughter and cat-calls.

Tombs followed and made a worse hash of it. He was determined to speak, as he would have put it, to democracy in its own language, so he said "hell" several times, loudly but without conviction. Presently he slipped into the manner of the lecturer, and the audience grew restless. "I propose to ask myself a question—" he began, and from the back of the hall came—"and a damned sully answer ye'll get." After that there was no more Tombs.

I followed with extreme nervousness, and to my surprise got a fair hearing. I felt as mean as a mangy dog on a cold morning, for I hated to talk rot before soldiers—especially before a couple of Royal Scots Fusiliers, who, for all I knew, might have been in my own brigade. My line was the plain, practical, patriotic man, just come from the colonies, who looked at things with fresh eyes, and called for a new deal. I was very moderate, but to justify my appearance there I had to put in a wild patch or two, and I got these by impassioned attacks on the Ministry of Munitions. I mixed up a little mild praise of the Germans, whom I said I had known all over the world for decent fellows. I received little applause, but no marked dissent, and sat down with deep thankfulness.

The next speaker put the lid on it. I believe he was a noted agitator, who had already been deported. Towards him there was no lukewarmness, for one half of the audience cheered wildly when he rose, and the other half hissed and groaned. He began with whirlwind abuse of the idle rich, then of the middle classes (he called them the "rich man's flunkeys"), and finallly of the Government. All that was fairly well received, for it is the fashion of the Briton to run down every Government and yet to be very averse to parting with it. Then he started on the soldiers and slanged the officers ("gentry pups" was his name for them), and the generals, whom he accused of idleness, of cowardice, and of habitual intoxication. He told us that our own kith and kin were sacrificed in every battle by leaders who had not the guts to share their risks. The Scots Fusiliers looked perturbed, as if they were in doubt of his meaning. Then he put it more plainly. "Will any soldier deny that the men are the barrage to keep the officers' skins whole?"

"That's a bloody lee," said one of the Fusilier Jocks.

The man took no notice of the interruption, being carried away by the torrent of his own rhetoric, but he had not allowed for the persistence of the interrupter. The Jock got slowly to his feet, and announced that he wanted satisfaction. "If ye open your dirty gab to blagyird honest men, I'll come up on the platform and wring your neck."

At that there was a fine old row, some crying out "Order," some "Fair Play," and some applauding. A Canadian at the back of the hall started a song, and there was an ugly press forward. The hall seemed to be moving up from the back, and already men were standing in all the passages and right to the edge of the platform. I did not like the look in the eyes of these newcomers, and among the crowd I saw several who were obviously plain-clothes policemen.

The chairman whispered a word to the speaker, who continued when the noise had temporarily died down. He kept off the army and returned to the Government, and for a little sluiced out pure anarchism. But he got his foot in it again, for he pointed to the Sinn Feiners as examples of manly independence. At that pandemonium broke loose, and he never had another look in. There were several fights going on in the hall between the public and courageous supporters of the orator.

Then Gresson advanced to the edge of the platform in a vain endeavour to retrieve the day. I must say he did it uncommonly well. He was clearly a practised speaker, and for a moment his appeal, "Now, boys, let's cool down a bit and talk sense," had an effect. But the mischief had been done, and the crowd was surging round the lonely redoubt where we sat. Besides, I could see that for all his clever talk the meeting did not like the look of him. He was as mild as a turtle dove, but they wouldn't stand for it. A missile hurtled past my nose, and I saw a rotten cabbage envelop the baldish head of the ex-deportee. Some one reached out a long arm and grabbed a chair, and with it took the legs from Gresson. Then the lights suddenly went out, and we retreated in good order by the platform door with a yelling crowd at our heels.

It was here that the plain-clothes men came in handy. They held the door while the ex-deportee was smuggled out by some side entrance. That class of lad would soon cease to exist but for the protection of the law which he would abolish. The rest of us, having less to fear, were suffered to leak into Newmilns Street. I found myself next to Gresson, and took his arm. There was something hard in his coat pocket.

Unfortunately there was a big lamp at the point where we emerged, and there for our confusion were the Fusilier Jocks. Both were strung to fighting pitch, and were determined to have some one's blood. Of me they took no notice, but Gresson had spoken after their ire had been roused, and was marked out as a victim. With a howl of joy they rushed for him.

I felt his hand steal to his side-pocket. "Let that alone, you fool," I growled in his ear.

"Sure, mister," he said, and the next second we were in the thick of it.

It was like so many street fights I have seen—an immense crowd which surged up around us, and yet left a clear ring. Gresson and I got against the wall on the side-walk, and faced the furious soldiery. My intention was to do as little as possible, but the first minute convinced me that my companion had no idea how to use his fists, and I was mortally afraid that he would get busy with the gun in his pocket. It was that fear that brought me into the scrap. The Jocks were sportsmen every bit of them, and only one advanced to the combat. He hit Gresson a clip on the jaw with his left, and but for the wall would have laid him out. I saw in the lamplight the vicious gleam in the American's eye and the twitch of his hand to his pocket. That decided me to interfere and I got in front of him.

This brought the second Jock into the fray. He was a broad, thickset fellow, of the adorable bandy-legged stocky type that I had seen go through the Railway Triangle at Arras as though it were blotting-paper. He had some notion of fighting, too, and gave me a rough time, for I had to keep edging the other fellow off Gresson.

"Go home, you fool," I shouted. "Let this gentleman alone. I don't want to hurt you."

The only answer was a hook-hit which I just managed to guard, followed by a mighty drive with his right which I dodged so that he braked his knuckles on the wall. I heard a yell of rage, and observed that Gresson seemed to have kicked his assailant on the shin. I began to long for the police.

Then there was that swaying of the crowd which betokens the approach of the forces of law and order. But they were too late to prevent trouble. In self-defence I had to take my Jock seriously, and got in my blow when he had over-reached himself and lost his balance. I never hit any one so unwillingly in my life. He went over like a poled ox, and measured his length on the causeway.

I found myself explaining things politely to the constables. "These men objected to this gentleman's speech at the meeting and I had to interfere to protect him. No, no! I don't want to charge anybody. It was all a misunderstanding." I helped the stricken Jock to rise and offered him ten bob for consolation.

He looked at me sullenly and spat on the ground. "Keep your dirty money," he said. "I'll be even with ye yet, my man—you and that red-headed scab. I'll mind the looks of ye the next time I see ye."

Gresson was wiping the blood from his cheek with a silk handkerchief. "I guess I'm in your debt, Mr. Brand," he said. "You may bet I won't forget it."

★

I returned to an anxious Amos. He heard my story in silence, and his only comment was—"Well done the Fusiliers!"

"It might have been worse, I'll not deny," he went on. "Ye've established some kind of a claim upon Gresson, which may come in handy. . . . Speaking about Gresson, I've news for ye. He's sailing on Friday as purser in the *Tobermory*. The *Tobermory*'s a boat that wanders every month up the West Highlands as far as Stornoway. I've arranged for ye to take a trip on that boat, Mr. Brand."

I nodded. "How did you find out that?" I asked.

"It took some finding," he said drily, "but I've ways and means. Now I'll not trouble ye with advice, for ye ken your job as well as me. But I'm going north myself the morn to look after some of the Ross-shire wuds, and I'll be in the way of getting telegrams at the Kyle. Ye'll keep that in mind. Keep in mind, too, that I'm a great reader of the *Pilgrim's Progress* and that I've a cousin of the name of Ochterlony."

37   VARIOUS DOINGS IN THE WEST

The *Tobermory* was no ship for passengers. Its decks were littered with a hundred oddments, so that a man could barely walk a step without tacking, and my bunk was simply a shelf in the frowsty little saloon, where the odour of ham and eggs hung like a fog. I joined her at Greenock and took a turn on deck with the captain after tea, when he told me the names of the big blue hills to the north. He had a fine old copper-coloured face and side-whiskers like an archbishop, and having spent all his days beating up the western seas, had as many yarns in his head as Peter himself.

"On this boat," he announced, "we don't ken what a day may bring forth. I may pit into Colonsay for twa hours and bide there three days. I get a telegram at Oban and the next thing I'm awa ayont Barra. Sheep's the difficult business. They maun be fetched for the sales, and they're dooms slow to lift. So ye see it's not what ye call a pleasure trip, Maister Brand."

Indeed it wasn't, for the confounded tub wallowed like a fat sow as soon as we rounded a headland and got the weight of the south-western wind. When asked my purpose, I explained that I was a colonial of Scots extraction, who was paying his first visit to his fatherland and wanted to explore the beauties of the West Highlands. I let him gather that I was not rich in the world's goods.

"Ye'll have a passport?" he asked. "They'll no let ye go north o' Fort William without one."

Amos had said nothing about passports, so I looked blank.

"I could keep ye on board for the whole voyage," he went on, "but ye wouldna be permitted to land. If ye're seekin' enjoyment, it would be a poor job sittin' on this deck and admirin' the works o' God and no allowed to step on the pierhead. Ye should have applied to the military gentlemen in Glesca. But ye've plenty o' time to make up your mind afore we get to Oban. We've a heap o' calls to make Mull and Islay way."

The purser came up to inquire about my ticket, and greeted me with a grin.

"Ye're acquaint with Mr. Gresson, then?" said the captain. "Weel, we're a cheery wee ship's company, and that's the great thing on this kind o' job."

I made but a poor supper, for the wind had risen to half a gale, and saw hours of wretchedness approaching. The trouble with me is that I cannot be honestly sick and get it over. Queasiness and headache beset me and there is no refuge but bed. I turned into my bunk, leaving the captain and the mate smoking shag not six feet from my head, and fell into a restless sleep. When I woke the place was empty, and smelt vilely of stale tobacco and cheese. My throbbing brows made sleep impossible, and I tried to ease them by staggering up on deck. I saw a clear windy sky, with every star as bright as a live coal, and a heaving waste of dark waters running to ink-black hills. Then a douche of spray caught me and sent me down the companion to my bunk again, where I lay for hours trying to make a plan of campaign.

I argued that if Amos had wanted me to have a passport he would have provided one, so I needn't bother my head about that. But it was my business to keep alongside Gresson, and if the boat stayed a week in some port and he went off ashore, I must follow him. Having no passport I would have to be always dodging trouble, which would handicap my movements and in all likelihood make me more conspicuous than I wanted. I guessed that Amos had denied me the passport for the very reason that he wanted Gresson to think me harmless. The area of danger would, therefore, be the passport country, somewhere north of Fort William.

But to follow Gresson I must run risks and enter that country. His suspicions, if he had any, would be lulled if I left the boat at Oban, but it was up to me to follow overland to the north and hit the place where the *Tobermory* made a long stay. The confounded tub had no plans; she wandered about the West Highlands looking for sheep and things; and the captain himself could give me no time-table of her voyage. It was incredible that Gresson should take all this trouble if he did not know that at some place—and the right place—he would have time to get a spell ashore. But I could scarcely ask Gresson for that information, though I determined to cast a wary fly over him. I knew roughly the *Tobermory's* course—through the Sound of Islay to Colonsay; then up the east side of Mull to Oban; then through the Sound of Mull to the islands with names like cocktails, Rum and Eigg and Coll; then to Skye; and then for the Outer Hebrides. I thought the last would be the place, and it seemed madness to leave the boat, for the Lord knew how I should get across the Minch. This consideration upset all my plans again, and I fell into a troubled sleep without coming to any conclusion.

Morning found us nosing between Jura and Islay, and about midday we touched at a little port, where we unloaded some cargo and took on a couple of shepherds who were going to Colonsay. The mellow afternoon and the good smell of salt and heather got rid of the dregs of my queasiness, and I spent a profitable hour on the pierhead with a guide-book called *Baddeley's Scotland*, and one of Bartholomew's maps. I was beginning to think that Amos might be able to tell me something, for a talk with the captain had suggested that the *Tobermory* would not dally long in the neighbourhood of Rum and Eigg. The big droving season was scarcely on yet, and sheep for Oban market would be lifted on the return journey. In that case Skye was the first place to watch, and if I could get wind of any cargo waiting there I would be able to make a plan. Amos was somewhere near the Kyle, and that was across the narrows from Skye. Looking at the map it seemed to me, that in spite of being passportless, I might be able somehow to make my way up through Morvern and Arisaig to the latitude of Skye. The difficulty would be to get across the strip of sea, but there must be boats to beg, borrow, or steal.

I was pouring over *Baddeley* when Gresson sat down beside me. He was in good temper, and disposed to talk, and to my surprise his talk was all about the beauties of the countryside. There was a kind of apple-green light over everything; the steep heather hills cut into the sky like purple amethysts, while beyond the straits the western ocean stretched its pale molten gold to the sunset. Gresson waxed lyrical over the scene. "This just about puts me right inside, Mr. Brand. I've got to get away from that little old town pretty frequent or I begin to moult like a canary. A man feels a man when he gets to a place that smells as good as this. Why in hell do we ever get messed up in those stone and lime cages? I reckon some day I'll pull my freight for a clean location and settle down there and make little poems. This place would about content me. And there's a spot out in California in the Coast ranges that I've been keeping my eye on." The odd thing was that I believe he meant it. His ugly face was lit up with a serious delight.

He told me he had taken this voyage before, so I got out *Baddeley* and asked for advice. "I can't spend too much time on holidaying," I told him, "and I want to see all the beauty spots. But the best of them seem to be in the area that this fool British Government won't let you into without a passport. I suppose I shall have to leave you at Oban."

"Too bad," he said sympathetically. "Well, they tell me there's some pretty sights round Oban." And he thumbed the guide-book and began to read about Glencoe.

I said that was not my purpose, and pitched him a yarn about Prince Charlie and how my mother's great-great-grandfather had played some kind of part in that show. I told him I wanted to see the place where the Prince landed and where he left for France. "So far as I can make out that won't take me into the passport country, but I'll have to do a bit of footslogging. Well, I'm used to padding the hoof. I must get the captain to put me off in Morvern and then I can foot it round the top of Lochiel and get back to Oban through Appin. How's that for a holidaying trek?"

He gave the scheme his approval. "But if it was me, Mr. Brand, I would have a shot at puzzling your gallant policemen. You and I don't take much stock in Governments and their two-cent laws, and it would be a good game to see just how far you could get into the forbidden land. A man like you could put up a good bluff on those hayseeds. I don't mind having a bet . . ."

"No," I said, "I'm out for a rest, and not for sport. If there was anything to be gained I'd undertake to bluff my way to the Orkney Islands. But it's a wearing job and I've better things to think about."

"So? Well, enjoy yourself your own way. I'll be sorry when you leave us, for I owe you something for that rough-house, and besides there's darned little company in the old moss-back captain."

That evening Gresson and I swopped yarns after supper to the accompaniment of the "Ma Goad!" and "Is't possible?" of captain and mate. I went to bed after a glass or two of weak grog, and made up for the last night's vigil by falling sound asleep. I had very little kit with me, beyond what I stood up in and could carry in my waterproof pockets, but on Amos's advice I had brought my little nickel-plated revolver. This lived by day in my hip-pocket, and at night I put it behind my pillow. But when I woke next morning to find us casting anchor in a bay below rough low hills, which I knew to be the island of Colonsay, I could find no trace of the revolver. I searched every inch of the bunk and only shook out feathers from the mouldy ticking. I remembered perfectly putting the thing behind my head before I went to sleep, and now it had vanished utterly. Of course I could not advertise my loss, and I didn't greatly mind it, for this was not a job where I could do much shooting. But it made me think a good deal about Mr. Gresson. He simply could not suspect me; if he had bagged my gun, as I was pretty certain he had, it must be because he wanted it for himself and not that he might disarm me. Every way I argued it I reached the same conclusion. In Gresson's eyes I must seem as harmless as a child.

We spent the better part of a day at Colonsay, and Gresson, so far as his duties allowed, stuck to me like a limpet. Before I went ashore I wrote out a telegram for Amos. I devoted a hectic hour to the *Pilgrim's Progress*, but I could not compose any kind of intelligible message with reference to its text. We had all the same edition—the one in the *Golden Treasury* series—so I could have made up a sort of cipher by referring to lines and pages, but that would have taken up a dozen telegraph forms and seemed to me too elaborate for the purpose. So I sent this message:

"*Ochterlony, Post Office, Kyle.*
"*I hope to spend part of holiday near you and to see you if boat's programme permits. Are any good cargoes waiting in your neighbourhood? Reply Post Office, Oban.*"

It was highly important that Gresson should not see this, but it was the deuce of a business to shake him off. I went for a walk in the afternoon along the shore and passed the telegraph office, but the confounded fellow was with me all the time. My only chance was just before we sailed, when he had to go on board to check some cargo. As the telegraph office stood full in view of the ship's deck I did not go near it. But in the back-end of the clachan I found the schoolmaster, and got him to promise to send the wire. I also bought off him a couple of well-worn sevenpenny novels.

The result was that I delayed our departure for ten minutes, and when I came on board faced a wrathful Gresson. "Where the hell have you been?" he asked. "The weather's blowing up dirty and the old man's mad to get off. Didn't you get your legs stretched enough this afternoon?"

I explained humbly that I had been to the schoolmaster to get something to read and produced my dingy red volumes. At that his brow cleared. I could see that his suspicions were set at rest.

We left Colonsay about six in the evening with the sky behind us banking for a storm, and the hills of Jura to starboard an angry purple. Colonsay was too low an island to be any kind of breakwater against a western gale, so the weather was bad from the start. Our course was north by east, and when we had passed the butt-end of the island we nosed about in the trough of big seas, shipping tons of water and rolling like a buffalo. I know as much about boats as about Egyptian hieroglyphics, but even my landsman's eyes could tell that we were in for a rough night. I was determined not to get queasy again, but when I went below the smell of tripe and onions promised to be my undoing; so I dined off a slab of chocolate and a cabin biscuit, put on my waterproof, and resolved to stick it out on deck.

I took up position near the bows, where I was out of reach of the oily steamer smells. It was as fresh as the top of a mountain, but mighty cold and wet, for a gusty drizzle had set in, and I got the spindrift of the big waves. There I balanced myself, as we lurched into the twilight, hanging on with one hand to a rope which descended from the stumpy mast. I noticed that there was only an indifferent rail between me and the edge, but that interested me and helped to keep off sickness. I swung to the movement of the vessel, and though I was mortally cold it was rather pleasant than otherwise. My notion was to get the nausea whipped out of me by the weather, and, when I was properly tired, to go down and turn in.

I stood there till the dark had fallen. By that time I was an automaton, the way a man gets on sentry-go, and I could have easily hung on till morning. My thoughts ranged about the earth, beginning with the business I had set out on and presently—by way of recollections of Blenkiron and Peter— reaching the German forest where, in the Christmas of 1915, I had been nearly done in by fever and old Stumm. I remembered the bitter cold of that wild race, and the way the snow seemed to burn like fire when I stumbled and got my face into it. I reflected that sea-sickness was kitten's play to a good bout of malaria.

The weather was growing worse, and I was getting more than spindrift from the seas. I hooked my arm round the rope, for my fingers were numbing. Then I fell to dreaming again, principally about Fosse Manor and Mary Lamington. This so ravished me that I was as good as asleep.

I was trying to reconstruct the picture as I had last seen her at Biggleswick station. . . .

A heavy body collided with me and shook my arm from the rope. I slithered across the yard of deck, engulfed in a whirl of water. One foot caught a stanchion of the rail, and it gave with me, so that for an instant I was more than half overboard: But my fingers clawed wildly and caught in the links of what must have been the anchor chain. They held, though a ton's weight seemed to be tugging at my feet . . . Then the old tub rolled back, the waters slipped off, and I was sprawling on a wet deck with no breath in me and a gallon of brine in my windpipe.

I heard a voice cry out sharply, and a hand helped me to my feet. It was Gresson, and he seemed excited.

"God, Mr. Brand, that was a close call! I was coming up to find you, when this damned ship took to lying on her side. I guess I must have cannoned into you, and I was calling myself bad names when I saw you rolling into the Atlantic. If I hadn't got a grip on the rope I would have been down beside you. Say, you're not hurt? I reckon you'd better come below and get a glass of rum under your belt. You're about as wet as mother's dishclouts."

There's one advantage about campaigning. You take your luck when it comes and don't worry about what might have been. I didn't think any more of the business, except that it had cured me of wanting to be sea-sick. I went down to the reeking cabin without one qualm in my stomach, and ate a good meal of welsh-rabbit and bottled Bass, with a tot of rum to follow up. Then I shed my wet garments, and slept in my bunk till we anchored off a village in Mull in a clear blue morning.

It took us four days to crawl up that coast and make Oban, for we seemed to be a floating general store for every hamlet in those parts. Gresson made himself very pleasant, as if he wanted to atone for nearly doing me in. We played some poker, and I read the little books I had got in Colonsay, and then rigged up a fishing-line, and caught saithe and lythe and an occasional big haddock. But I found the time pass slowly, and I was glad when about noon one day we came into a bay blocked with islands and saw a clean little town sitting on the hills, and the smoke of a railway engine.

I went ashore and purchased a better brand of hat in a tweed store. Then I made a bee-line for the post office, and asked for telegrams. One was given to me, and as I opened it I saw Gresson at my elbow.

It ran thus:

"Brand, Post Office, Oban. Page 117, paragraph 3. Ochterlony."

I passed it to Gresson with a rueful face.

"There's a piece of foolishness," I said. "I've got a cousin who's a Presbyterian minister up in Ross-shire, and before I knew about this passport humbug I wrote to him and offered to pay him a visit. I told him to wire me here if it was convenient, and the old idiot has sent me the wrong telegram. This was likely as not meant for some brother parson, who's got my message instead."

"What's the guy's name?" Gresson asked curiously, peering at the signature.

"Ochterlony. David Ochterlony. He's a great swell at writing books, but he's no earthly use at handling the telegraph. However, it don't signify, seeing I'm not going near him." I crumpled up the pink form and tossed it on the floor. Gresson and I walked back to the *Tobermory* together.

That afternoon, when I got a chance, I had out my *Pilgrim's Progress*. Page 117, paragraph 3, read:

"Then I saw in my dream, that a little off the road, over against the Silver-mine, stood Demas (gentleman-like) to call to passengers to come and see: who said to Christian and his fellow, Ho, turn aside hither and I will show you a thing."

At tea I led the talk to my own past life. I yarned about my experiences as a mining engineer, and said I could never get out of the trick of looking at country with the eye of the prospector. "For instance," I said, "if this had been Rhodesia, I would have said there was a good chance of copper in these little kopjes above the town. They're not unlike the hills round the Messina mine." I told the captain that after the war I was thinking of turning my attention to the West Highlands and looking out for minerals.

"Ye'll make nothing of it," said the captain. "The costs are ower big, even if ye found the minerals, for ye'd have to import a' your labour. The West Hielandman is no fond o' hard work. Ye ken the psalm o' the crofter?

> " 'O that the peats would cut themselves,
>   The fish chump on the shore,
> And that I in my bed might lie
>   Henceforth for evermore!' "

"Has it ever been tried?" I asked.

"Often. There's marble and slate quarries, and there was word o' coal in Benbecula. And there's the iron-mines at Ranna."

"Where's that?" I asked.

"Up forenent Skye. We call in there, and generally bide a bit. There's a heap of cargo for Ranna, and we usually get a good load back. But as I tell ye, there's few Hielanders working there. Mostly Irish and lads frae Fife and Falkirk way."

I didn't pursue the subject, for I had found Demas's silver-mine. If the *Tobermory* lay at Ranna for a week, Gresson would have time to do his own private business. Ranna would not be the spot, for the island was bare to the world in the middle of a much-frequented channel. But Skye was just across the way, and when I looked in my map at its big, wandering peninsulas I concluded that my guess had been right, and that Skye was the place to make for.

That night I sat on deck with Gresson, and in a wonderful starry silence we watched the lights die out of the houses in the town, and talked of a thousand things. I noticed—what I had had a hint of before—that my companion was no common man. There were moments when he forgot himself and talked like an educated gentleman: then he would remember, and relapse into the lingo of Leadville, Colorado. In my character of the ingenuous inquirer I set him posers about politics and economics, the kind of thing I might have been supposed to pick up from unintelligent browsing among little books. Generally he answered with some slangy catchword, but occasionally he was interested beyond his discretion, and treated me to an harangue like an equal. I discovered another thing, that he had a craze for poetry, and a capacious memory for it. I forget how we drifted into the subject, but I remember he quoted some queer haunting stuff which he said was Swinburne, and verses by people I had heard of from Letchford at Biggleswick. Then he saw by my silence that he had gone too far, and fell back into the jargon of the West. He wanted to know about my plans, and we went down into the cabin and had a look at the map. I explained my route, up Morvern and round the head of Lochiel, and back to Oban by the east side of Lock Linnhe.

"Got you," he said. "You've a hell of a walk before you. That bug never bit me, and I guess I'm not envying you any. And after that, Mr. Brand?"

"Back to Glasgow to do some work for the cause," I said lightly.

"Just so," he said with a grin. "It's a great life if you don't weaken."

We steamed out of the bay next morning at dawn, and about nine o'clock I got on shore at a little place called Lochaline. My kit was all on my person, and my waterproof's pockets were stuffed with chocolates and biscuits I had bought in Oban. The captain was discouraging. "Ye'll get your bellyfull o' Hieland hills, Mr. Brand, afore ye win round the Loch head. Ye'll be wishin' yerself back on the *Tobermory*." But Gresson speeded me joyfully on my way, and said he wished he were coming with me. He even accompanied me the first hundred yards, and waved his hat after me till I was round the turn of the road.

The first stage in that journey was pure delight. I was thankful to be rid of the infernal boat, and the hot summer scents coming down the glen were comforting after the cold, salt smell of the sea. The road lay up the side of a small bay, at the top of which a big white house stood among gardens. Presently I had left the coast and was in a glen where a brown salmon-river swirled through acres of bog-myrtle. It had its source in a loch, from which the mountain rose steeply—a place so glassy in that August forenoon that every scaur and wrinkle of the hillside was faithfully reflected. After that I crossed a low pass to the head of another sea-loch, and, following the map, struck over the shoulder of a great hill and ate my luncheon far up on its side, with a wonderful vista of wood and water below me.

All that morning I was very happy, not thinking about Gresson or Ivery, but getting my mind clear in those wide spaces, and my lungs filled with the brisk hill air. But I noticed one curious thing. On my last visit to Scotland, when I covered more moorland miles a day than any man since Claverhouse, I had been fascinated by the land, and had pleased myself with plans for settling down in it. But now, after three years of war and general racketing, I felt less drawn to that kind of landscape. I wanted something more green and peaceful and habitable, and it was to the Cotswolds that my memory turned with longing.

I puzzled over this till I realized that in all my Cotswold pictures a figure kept going and coming—a young girl with a cloud of gold hair, and the strong, slim grace of a boy, who had sung "Cherry Ripe" in a moonlit garden. Up on that hillside I understood very clearly that I, who had been as careless of women as any monk, had fallen wildly in love with a child of half my age. I was loath to admit it, though for weeks the conclusion had been forcing itself on me. Not that I didn't revel in my madness, but that it seemed too hopeless a business, and I had no use for barren philandering. But, seated on a rock munching chocolate and biscuits, I faced up to the fact and resolved to trust my luck. After all we were comrades in a big job, and it was up to me to be man enough to win her. The thought seemed to brace any courage that was in me. No task seemed too hard, with her approval to gain and her companionship somewhere at the back of it. I sat for a long time in a happy dream, remembering all the glimpses I had had of her, and humming her song to an audience of one blackfaced sheep.

On the highroad half a mile below me, I saw a figure on a bicycle mounting the hill, and then getting off to mop its face at the summit. I turned my Zeiss glasses on to it, and observed that it was a country policeman. It caught sight of me, stared for a bit, tucked its machine into the side of the road, and then very slowly began to climb the hillside. Once it stopped, waved its hand and shouted something which I could not hear. I sat finishing my luncheon, till the features were revealed to me of a fat, oldish man, blowing like a grampus, his cap well on the back of a bald head, and his trousers tied about the shins with string.

There was a spring beside me, and I had out my flask to round off my meal.

"Have a drink," I said.

His eye brightened, and a smile overran his moist face.

"Thank you, sir. It will be very warrm coming up the brae."

"You oughtn't to," I said. "You really oughtn't, you know. Scorching up hills and then doubling up a mountain are not good for your time of life."

He raised the cap of my flask in solemn salutation. "Your very good health." Then he smacked his lips and had several cupfuls of water from the spring.

"You will haf come from Achranich way, maybe?" he said in his soft sing-song, having at last found his breath.

"Just so. Fine weather for the birds, if there was anybody to shoot them."

"Ach, no. There will be few shots fired to-day, for there are no gentlemen left in Morvern. But I was asking you, if you come from Achranich, if you haf seen anybody on the road."

From his pocket he extricated a brown envelope and a bulky telegraph form. "Will you read it, sir, for I haf forgot my spectacles?"

It contained a description of one Brand, a South African and a suspected character, whom the police were warned to stop and return to Oban. The description wasn't bad, but it lacked any one good distinctive detail. Clearly the policeman took me for an innocent pedestrian, probably the guest of some moorland shooting-box, with my brown face and rough tweeds and hobnailed shoes.

I frowned and puzzled a little. "I did see a fellow about three miles back on the hillside. There's a public-house just where the burn comes in, and I think he was making for it. Maybe that was your man. This wire says 'South African'; and now I remember the fellow had the look of a colonial."

The policeman sighed. "No doubt it will be the man. Perhaps he will haf a pistol and will shoot."

"Not him," I laughed. "He looked a mangy sort of chap, and he'll be scared out of his senses at the sight of you. But take my advice and get somebody with you before you tackle him. You're always the better of a witness."

"That is so," he said, brightening. "Ach, these are the bad times! In old days there wass nothing to do but watch the doors at the flowershows and keep the yachts from poaching the sea-trout. But now it is spies, spies, and 'Donald, get out of your bed, and go off twenty mile to find a German.' I wass wishing the war wass by, and the Germans all dead."

"Hear, hear!" I cried, and on the strength of it gave him another dram.

I accompanied him to the road, and saw him mount his bicycle and zigzag like a snipe down the hill towards Achranich. Then I set off briskly northward. It was clear that the faster I moved the better.

As I went I paid disgusted tribute to the efficiency of the Scottish police. I wondered how on earth they had marked me down. Perhaps it was the Glasgow meeting, or perhaps my association with Ivery at Biggleswick. Anyhow there was somebody somewhere mighty quick at compiling a *dossier*. Unless I wanted to be bundled back to Oban I must make good speed to the Arisaig coast.

Presently the road fell to the gleaming sea-loch which lay like the blue blade of a sword among the purple of the hills. At the head there was a tiny clachan, nestled among birches and rowans, where a tawny burn wound to the sea. When I entered the place it was about four o'clock in the afternoon, and peace lay on it like a garment. In the wide, sunny street there was no sign of life, and no sound except of hens clucking and of bees busy among the roses. There was a little grey box of a kirk, and close to the bridge a thatched cottage which bore the sign of a post and telegraph office.

For the past hour I had been considering that I had better prepare for mishaps. If the police of these parts had been warned they might prove too much for me, and Gresson would be allowed to make his journey unwatched. The only thing to do was to send a wire to Amos and leave the matter in his hands. Whether that was possible or not depended upon this remote postal authority.

I entered the little shop, and passed from bright sunshine to a twilight smelling of paraffin and black-striped peppermint balls. An old woman with a mutch sat in an arm-chair behind the counter. She looked up at me over her spectacles and smiled, and I took to her on the instant. She had the kind of old wise face that God loves.

Beside her I noticed a little pile of books, one of which was a Bible. Open on her lap was a paper, the *United Free Church Monthly*. I noticed these details greedily, for I had to make up my mind on the part to play.

"It's a warm day, mistress," I said, my voice falling into the broad Lowland speech, for I had an instinct that she was not of the Highlands.

She laid aside her paper. "It is that, sir. It is grand weather for the hairst, but here that's no till the hinner end o' September, and at the best it's a bit scart o' aits."

"Ay. It's a different thing down Annandale way," I said.

Her face lit up. "Are ye from Dumfries, sir?"

"Not just from Dumfries, but I know the Borders fine."

"Ye'll no beat them," she cried. "Not that this is no a guid place and I've muckle to be thankful for since John Sanderson—that was ma man—brocht me here forty-seeven year syne come Martinmas. But the aulder I get the mair I think o' the bit whaur I was born. It was twae miles from Wamphray on the Lockerbie road, but they tell me the place is noo just a rickle o' stanes."

"I was wondering, mistress, if I could get a cup of tea in the village."

"Ye'll hae a cup wi' me," she said. "It's no often we see onybody frae the Borders hereaways. The kettle's just on the boil."

She gave me tea and scones and butter, and black-currant jam, and treacle biscuits that melted in the mouth. And as we ate we talked of many things—chiefly of the war and of the wickedness of the world.

"There's nae lads left here," she said. "They a' joined the Camerons, and the feck o' them fell at an awfu' place called Lowse. John and me never had no boys, jist the one lassie that's married on Donald Frew, the Strontian carrier. I used to vex mysel' about it, but now I thank the Lord that in His mercy He spared me sorrow. But I wad hae liked to have had one laddie fechtin' for his country. I whiles wish I was a Catholic and could pit up prayers for the sodgers that are deid. It maun be a great consolation."

I whipped out the *Pilgrim's Progress* from my pocket. "That is the grand book for a time like this."

"Fine I ken it," she said. "I got it for a prize in the Sabbath School when I was a lassie."

I turned the pages. I read out a passage or two, and then I seemed struck with a sudden memory.

"This is a telegraph office, mistress. Could I trouble you to send a telegram? You see I've a cousin that's a minister in Ross-shire at the Kyle, and him and me are great correspondents. He was writing about something in the *Pilgrim's Progress*, and I think I'll send him a telegram in answer."

"A letter would be cheaper," she said.

"Ay, but I'm on holiday, and I've no time for writing."

She gave me a form, and I wrote:

"*Ochterlony. Post Office, Kyle.—Demas will be at his mine within the week. Strive with him, lest I faint by the way.*"

"Ye're unco lavish wi' the words, sir," was her only comment.

We parted with regret, and there was nearly a row when I tried to pay for the tea. I was bidden remember her to one Davie Tudhope, farmer in Nether Mirecleuch, the next time I passed by Wamphray.

The village was as quiet when I left it as when I had entered. I took my way up the hill with an easier mind, for I had got off the telegram, and I hoped I had covered my tracks. My friend the postmistress would, if questioned, be unlikely to recognize any South African suspect in the frank and homely traveller who had spoken with her of Annandale and the *Pilgrim's Progress*.

The soft mulberry gloaming of the west coast was beginning to fall on the hills. I hoped to put in a dozen miles before dark to the next village on the map, where I might find quarters. But ere I had gone far I heard the sound of a motor behind me, and a car slipped past bearing three men. The driver favoured me with a sharp glance, and clapped on the brakes. I noted that the two men in the tonneau were carrying sporting rifles.

"Hi, you, sir," he cried. "Come here." The two rifle-bearers—solemn gillies—brought their weapons to attention.

"By God," he said, "it's the man. What's your name? Keep him covered, Angus." The gillies duly covered me, and I did not like the look of their wavering barrels. They were obviously as surprised as myself.

I had about half a second to make my plans. I advanced with a very stiff air, and asked him what the devil he meant. No Lowland Scots for me now. My tone was that of an adjutant of a Guards battalion.

My inquisitor was a tall man in an ulster, with a green felt hat on his small head. He had a lean, well-bred face and very choleric blue eyes. I set him down as a soldier, retired, Highland regiment or cavalry, old style.

He produced a telegraph form, like the policeman.

"Middle height   strongly built   grey tweeds—brown hat—speaks with a colonial accent—much sunburnt. What's your name, sir?"

I did not reply in a colonial accent, but with the *hauteur* of the British officer when stopped by a French sentry. I asked him again what the devil he had to do with my business. This made him angry, and he began to stammer.

"I'll teach you what I have to do with it. I'm a deputy-lieutenant of this county, and I have Admiralty instructions to watch the coast. Damn it, sir, I've a wire here from the Chief Constable describing you. You're Brand, a very dangerous fellow, and we want to know what the devil you're doing here."

As I looked at his wrathful eye and lean head, which could not have held much brains, I saw that I must change my tone. If I irritated him he would get nasty and refuse to listen and hang me up for hours. So my voice became respectful.

"I beg your pardon, sir, but I've not been accustomed to be pulled up suddenly and asked for my credentials. My name is Blaikie—Captain Robert Blaikie, of the Scots Fusiliers. I'm home on three weeks' leave, to get a little peace after Hooge. We were only hauled out five days ago." I hoped my old friend in the shell-shock hospital at Isham would pardon my borrowing his identity.

The man looked puzzled. "How the devil am I to be satisfied about that? Have you any papers to prove it?"

"Why, no. I don't carry passports about with me on a walking tour. But you can wire to the depot, or to my London address."

He pulled at his yellow moustache. "I'm hanged if I know what to do. I want to get home for dinner. I tell you what, sir, I'll take you on with me and put you up for the night. My boy's at home convalescing, and if he says you're *pukka* I'll ask your pardon and give you a dashed good bottle of port. I'll trust him, and I warn you he's a keen hand."

There was nothing to do but consent, and I got in beside him with an uneasy conscience. Supposing the son knew the real Blaikie! I asked the name of the boy's battalion, and was told the 10th Seaforths. That wasn't pleasant hearing, for they had brigaded with us on the Somme. But Colonel Broadbury—for he told me his name—volunteered another piece of news which set my mind at rest. The boy was not yet twenty, and had only been out seven months. At Arras he had got a bit of shrapnel in his thigh, which had played the deuce with the sciatic nerve, and he was still on crutches.

We spun over ridges of moorland, always keeping northward, and brought up at a pleasant whitewashed house close to the sea. Colonel Broadbury ushered me into a hall where a small fire of peats was burning, and on a couch beside it lay a slim, pale-faced young man. He had dropped his policeman's manner, and behaved like a gentleman. "Ted," he said, "I've brought a friend home for the night. I went out to look for a suspect and found a British officer. This is Captain Blaikie, of the Scots Fusiliers."

The boy looked at me pleasantly. "I'm very glad to meet you, sir. You'll excuse me not getting up, but I've got a game leg." He was the copy of his father in features, but dark and sallow where the other was blond. He had just the same narrow head, and stubborn mouth, and honest, quick-tempered eyes. It is the type that makes dashing regimental officers, and earns V.C.'s, and gets done in wholesale. I was never that kind. I belonged to the school of the cunning cowards.

In the half-hour before dinner the last wisp of suspicion fled from my host's mind. For Ted Broadbury and I were immediately deep in "shop." I had met most of his senior officers, and I knew all about their doings at Arras, for his brigade had been across the river on my left. We fought the great fight over again, and yarned about technicalities and slanged the Staff in the way young officers have, the father throwing in questions that showed how mighty proud he was of his son. I had a bath before dinner, and as he led me to the bathroom he apologized very handsomely for his bad manners. "Your coming's been a god-send for Ted. He was moping a bit in this place. And, though I say it that shouldn't, he's a dashed good boy."

I had my promised bottle of port, and after dinner I took on the father at billiards. Then we settled in the smoking-room, and I laid myself out to entertain the pair. The result was that they would have had me stay a week, but I spoke of the shortness of my leave, and said I must get on to the railway and then back to Fort William for my luggage.

So I spent that night between clean sheets, and ate a Christian breakfast, and was given my host's car to set me a bit on the road. I dismissed it after half a dozen miles, and, following the map, struck over the hills to the west. About midday I topped a ridge, and beheld the Sound of Sleat shining beneath me. There were other things in the landscape. In the valley on the right a long goods train was crawling on the Mallaig railway. And across the strip of sea, like some fortress of the old gods, rose the dark bastions and turrets of the hills of Skye.

38 THE SKIRTS OF THE COOLIN

Obviously I must keep away from the railway. If the police were after me in Morvern, that line would be warned, for it was a barrier I must cross if I were to go farther north. I observed from the map that it turned up the coast, and concluded that the place for me to make for was the shore south of that turn, where Heaven might send me some luck in the boat line. For I was pretty certain that every porter and station-master on that tinpot outfit was anxious to make better acquaintance with my humble self.

I lunched off the sandwiches the Broadburys had given me, and in the bright afternoon made my way down the hill, crossed at the foot of a small freshwater lochan, and pursued the issuing stream through midge-infested woods of hazels to its junction with the sea. It was rough going, but very pleasant, and I fell into the same mood of idle contentment that I had enjoyed the previous morning. I never met a soul. Sometimes a roe deer broke out of the covert, or an old black-cock startled me with his scolding. The place was bright with heather, still in its first bloom, and smelt better than the myrrh of Arabia. It was a blessed glen, and I was as happy as a king, till I began to feel the coming of hunger, and reflected that the Lord alone knew when I might get a meal. I had still some chocolate and biscuits, but I wanted something substantial.

The distance was greater than I thought, and it was already twilight when I reached the coast. The shore was open and desolate—great banks of pebbles to which straggled alders and hazels from the hillside scrub. But as I marched northward and turned a little point of land I saw before me in a crook of the bay a smoking cottage. And, plodding along by the water's edge, was the bent figure of a man, laden with nets and lobster pots. Also, beached on the shingle was a boat.

I quickened my pace and overtook the fisherman. He was an old man with a ragged grey beard, and his rig was seaman's boots and a much-darned blue jersey. He was deaf, and did not hear me when I hailed him. When he caught sight of me he never stopped, though he very solemnly returned my good evening. I fell into step with him, and in his silent company reached the cottage.

He halted before the door and unslung his burdens. The place was a two-roomed building with a roof of thatch, and the walls all grown over with a yellow-flowered creeper. When he had straightened his back, he looked seaward and at the sky, as if to prospect the weather. Then he turned on me his gentle, absorbed eyes. "It will haf been a fine day, sir. Wass you seeking the road to anywhere?"

"I was seeking a night's lodging," I said. "I've had a long tramp on the hills, and I'd be glad of a chance of not going farther."

"We will haf no accommodation for a gentleman," he said gravely.

"I can sleep on the floor, if you can give me a blanket and a bite of supper."

"Indeed you will not," and he smiled slowly. "But I will ask the wife. Mary, come here!"

An old woman appeared in answer to his call, a woman whose face was so old that she seemed like his mother. In Highland places one sex ages quicker than the other.

"This gentleman would like to bide the night. I wass telling him that we had a poor small house, but he says he will not be minding it."

She looked at me with the timid politeness that you find only in outland places.

"We can do our best, indeed, sir. The gentleman can have Colin's bed in the loft, but he will haf to be doing with plain food. Supper is ready if you will come in now."

I had a scrub with a piece of yellow soap at an adjacent pool in the burn, and then entered a kitchen blue with peat reek. We had a meal of boiled fish, oatcakes, and skim-milk cheese, with sups of strong tea to wash it down. The old folks had the manners of princes. They pressed food on me and asked me no questions, till for very decency's sake I had to put up a story and give some account of myself.

I found they had a son in the Argylls and a younger boy in the Navy. But they seemed disinclined to talk of them or of the war. By a mere accident I hit on the old man's absorbing interest. He was passionate about the land. He had taken part in long-forgotten agitations, and had suffered eviction in some ancient landlord's quarrel farther north. Presently he was pouring out to me all the woes of the crofter—woes that seemed so antediluvian and forgotten that I listened as one would listen to an old song. "You who come from a new country will not haf heard of these things," he kept telling me, but by that peat fire I made up for my defective education. He told me of evictions in the year One somewhere in Sutherland, and of harsh doings in the Outer Isles. It was far more than a political grievance. It was the lament of the conservative for vanished days and manners. "Over in Skye was the fine land for black cattle, and every man had his bit herd on the hillside. But the lairds said it wass better for sheep, and then they said it wass not good for sheep, so they put it under deer, and now there is no black cattle anywhere in Skye." I tell you it was like sad music on the bagpipes hearing that old fellow. The war and all things modern meant nothing to him; he lived among the tragedies of his youth and his prime.

I'm a Tory myself and a bit of a land reformer, so we agreed well enough. So well, that I got what I wanted without asking for it. I told him I was going to Skye, and he offered to take me over in his boat in the morning. "It will be no trouble. Indeed no. I will be going that way myself to the fishing."

I told him that after the war every acre of British soil would have to be used for the men that had earned the right to it. But that did not comfort him. He was not thinking about the land itself, but about the men who had been driven from it fifty years before. His desire was not for reform, but for restitution, and that was past the power of any Government. I went to bed in the loft in a sad, reflective mood, considering how in speeding our new-fangled plough we must break down a multitude of molehills and how desirable and unreplaceable was the life of the moles.

In brisk, shining weather, with a wind from the south-east, we put off next morning. In front was a brown line of low hills, and behind them, a little to the north, that black toothcomb of mountain which I had seen the day before from the Arisaig ridge.

"That is the Coolin," said the fisherman. "It is a bad place where even the deer cannot go. But all the rest of Skye wass the fine land for black cattle."

As we neared the coast, he pointed out many places. "Look there, sir, in that glen. I haf seen six cot houses smoking there, and now there is not any left. There were three men of my own name had crofts on the *machars* beyond the point, and if you go there you will only find the marks of their bit gardens. You will know the place by the gean trees."

When he put me ashore in a sandy bay between green ridges of bracken, he was still harping upon the past. I got him to take a pound—for the boat and not for the night's hospitality, for he would have beaten me with an oar if I had suggested that. The last I saw of him, as I turned round at the top of the hill, he had still his sail down, and was gazing at the lands which had once been full of human dwellings and now were desolate.

I kept for a while along the ridge, with the Sound of Sleat on my right, and beyond it the high hills of Knoydart and Kintail. I was watching for the *Tobermory*, but saw no sign of her. A steamer put out from Mallaig, and there were several drifters crawling up the channel, and once I saw the white ensign and a destroyer bustled northward, leaving a cloud of black smoke in her wake. Then, after consulting the map, I struck across country, still keeping the higher ground, but, except at odd minutes, being out of sight of the sea. I concluded that my business was to get to the latitude of Ranna without wasting time.

So soon as I changed my course I had the Coolin for company. Mountains have always been a craze of mine, and the blackness and mystery of those grim peaks went to my head. I forgot all about Fosse Manor and the Cotswolds. I forgot, too, what had been my chief feeling since I left Glasgow, the sense of the absurdity of my mission. It had all seemed too far-fetched and whimsical. I was running apparently no great personal risk, and I had always the unpleasing fear that Blenkiron might have been too clever and that the whole thing might be a mare's nest. But that dark mountain mass changed my outlook. I began to have a queer instinct that that was the place, that something might be concealed there, something pretty damnable. I remember I sat on a top for half an hour raking the hills with my glasses. I made out ugly precipices, and glens which lost themselves in primeval blackness. When the sun caught them—for it was a gleamy day—it brought out no colours, only degrees of shade. No mountains I had ever seen—not the Drakensberg or the red kopjes of Damaraland or the cold, white peaks around Erzerum—ever looked so unearthly and uncanny.

Oddly enough, too, the sight of them set me thinking about Ivery. There seemed no link between a smooth, sedentary being, dwelling in villas and lecture-rooms, and that shaggy tangle of precipices. But I felt there was, for I had begun to realize the bigness of my opponent. Blenkiron had said that he spun his web wide. That was intelligible enough among the half-baked youth of Biggleswick, and the pacificist societies, or even the toughs of the Clyde. I could fit him in all right to that picture. But that he should be playing his game among those mysterious crags seemed to make him bigger and more desperate, altogether a different kind of proposition. I didn't exactly dislike the idea, for my objection to my past weeks had been that I was out of my proper job, and this was more my line of country. I always felt that I was a better bandit than a detective. But a sort of awe mingled with my satisfaction. I began to feel about Ivery as I had felt about the three devils of the Black Stone who had hunted me before the war, and as I never felt about any other Hun. The men we fought at the Front and the men I had run across in the Greenmantle business, even old Stumm himself, had been human miscreants. They were formidable enough, but you could gauge and calculate their capacities. But this Ivery was like a poison gas that hung in the air and got into unexpected crannies and that you couldn't fight in an upstanding way. Till then, in spite of Blenkiron's solemnity, I had regarded him simply as a problem. But now he seemed an intimate and omnipresent enemy, intangible, too, as the horror of a haunted house. Up on that sunny hillside, with the sea winds round me and the whaups calling, I got a chill in my spine when I thought of him.

I am ashamed to confess it, but I was also horribly hungry. There was something about the war that made me ravenous, and the less chance of food the worse I felt. If I had been in London with twenty restaurants open to me, I should as likely as not have gone off my feed. That was the cussedness of my stomach. I had still a little chocolate left, and I ate the fisherman's buttered scones for luncheon, but long before the evening my thoughts were dwelling on my empty interior.

I put up that night in a shepherd's cottage miles from anywhere. The man was called Macmorran, and he had come from Galloway when sheep were booming. He was a very good imitation of a savage, a little fellow with red hair and red eyes, who might have been a Pict. He lived with a daughter who had once been in service in Glasgow, a fat young woman with a face entirely covered with freckles and a pout of habitual discontent. No wonder, for that cottage was a pretty mean place. It was so thick with peat reek that throat and eyes were always smarting. It was badly built, and must have leaked like a sieve in a storm. The father was a surly fellow, whose conversation was one long growl at the world, the high prices, the difficulty of moving his sheep, the meanness of his master, and the God-forsaken character of Skye. "Here's me no seen baker's bread for a month, and no company but a wheen ignorant Hielanders that yatter Gawlic. I wish I was back in the Glenkens. And I'd gang the morn if I could get paid what I'm awed."

However, he gave me supper—a braxy ham and oatcake, and I bought the remnants off him for use next day. I did not trust his blankets, so I slept the night by the fire in the ruins of an arm-chair, and woke at dawn with a foul taste in my mouth. A dip in the burn refreshed me, and after a bowl of porridge I took the road again. For I was anxious to get to some hill-top that looked over to Ranna.

Before midday I was close under the eastern side of the Coolin, on a road which was more a rockery than a path. Presently I saw a big house ahead of me that looked like an inn, so I gave it a miss and struck the highway that led to it a little farther north. Then I bore off to the east, and was just beginning to climb a hill which I judged stood between me and the sea, when I heard wheels on the road and looked back.

It was a farmer's gig carrying one man. I was about half a mile off, and something in the cut of his jib seemed familiar. I got my glasses on him and made out a short, stout figure clad in a mackintosh, with a woollen comforter round its throat. As I watched, it made a movement as if to rub its nose on its sleeve. That was the pet trick of one man I knew. Inconspicuously I slipped through the long heather so as to reach the road ahead of the gig. When I rose like a wraith from the wayside the horse started, but not the driver.

"So ye're there," said Amos's voice. "I've news for ye. The *Tobermory* will be in Ranna by now. She passed Broadford two hours syne. When I saw her I yoked this beast and came up on the chance of foregathering with ye."

"How on earth did you know I would be here?" I asked in some surprise.

"Oh, I saw the way your mind was working from your telegram. And says I to mysel'—that man Brand, says I, is not the chiel to be easy stoppit. But I was feared ye might be a day late, so I came up the road to hold the fort. Man, I'm glad to see ye. Ye're younger and soopler than me, and yon Gresson's a stirrin' lad."

"There's one thing you've got to do for me," I said. "I can't go into inns and shops, but I can't do without food. I see from the map there's a town about six miles on. Go there and buy me anything that's tinned—biscuits and tongue and sardines, and a couple of bottles of whisky if you can get them. This may be a long job, so buy plenty."

"Whaur'll I put them?" was his only question.

We fixed on a cache, a hundred yards from the highway, in a place where two ridges of hill enclosed the view so that only a short bit of ground was visible. "I'll get back to the Kyle," he told me, "and a'body there kens Andra

Amos, if ye should find a way of sendin' a message or comin' yourself. Oh, and I've got a word to ye from a lady that we ken of. She says, the sooner ye're back in Vawnity Fair the better she'll be pleased, always provided ye've got over the Hill Difficulty."

A smile screwed up his old face, and he waved his whip in farewell. I interpreted Mary's message as an incitement to speed, but I could not make the pace. That was Gresson's business. I think I was a little nettled, till I cheered myself by another interpretation. She might be anxious for my safety, she might want to see me again, anyhow the mere sending of the message showed I was not forgotten. I was in a pleasant muse as I breasted the hill, keeping discreetly in the cover of the many gullies. At the top I looked down on Ranna and the sea.

There lay the *Tobermory* busy unloading. It would be some time, no doubt, before Gresson could leave. There was no row-boat in the channel yet, and I might have to wait hours. I settled myself snugly between two rocks, where I could not be seen, and where I had a clear view of sea and shore. But presently I found that I wanted some long heather to make a couch, and I emerged to get some. I had not raised my head for a second when I flopped down again. For I had a neighbour on the hill-top.

He was about two hundred yards off, just reaching the crest, and, unlike me, walking quite openly. His eyes were on Ranna, so he did not notice me, but from my cover I scanned every line of him. He looked an ordinary countryman, wearing badly cut, baggy knickerbockers of the kind that gillies affect. He had a face like a Portuguese Jew, but I had seen that type before among people with Highland names; they might be Jews or not, but they could speak Gaelic. Presently he disappeared. He had followed my example and selected a hiding-place.

It was a clear, hot day, but very pleasant in that airy place. Good scents came up from the sea, the heather was warm and fragrant, bees droned about, and stray seagulls swept the ridge with their wings. I took a look now and then towards my neighbour, but he was deep in his hidy-hole. Most of the time I kept my glasses on Ranna, and watched the doings of the *Tobermory*. She was tied up at the jetty, but seemed in no hurry to unload. I watched the captain disembark and walk up to a house on the hillside. Then some idlers sauntered down towards her and stood talking and smoking close to her side. The captain returned, and left again. A man with papers in his hand appeared, and a woman with what looked like a telegram. The mate went ashore in his best clothes. Then at last, after midday, Gresson appeared. He joined the captain at the pier-master's office, and presently emerged on the other side of the jetty where some small boats were beached. A man from the *Tobermory* came in answer to his call, a boat was launched, and began to make its way into the channel. Gresson sat in the stern, placidly eating his luncheon.

I watched every detail of that crossing with some satisfaction that my forecast was turning out right. About half-way across Gresson took the oars, but soon surrendered them to the *Tobermory* man, and lit a pipe. He got out a pair of binoculars and raked my hillside. I tried to see if my neighbour was making any signal, but all was quiet. Presently the boat was hid from me by the bulge of the hill, and I caught the sound of her scraping on the beach.

Gresson was not a hill-walker like my neighbour. It took him the best part of an hour to get to the top, and he reached it at a point not two yards from my hiding-place. I could hear by his labouring breath that he was very blown. He walked straight over the crest till he was out of sight of Ranna, and flung himself on the ground. He was now about fifty yards from me, and I made shift to lessen the distance. There was a grassy trench skirting the north side of the hill, deep and thickly overgrown with heather. I wound my way along it till I was about twelve yards from him, where I stuck, owing to the trench dying away. When I peered out of the cover I saw that the other man had joined him, and that the idiots were engaged in embracing each other.

I dared not move an inch nearer, and as they talked in a low voice I could hear nothing of what they said. Nothing except one phrase, which the strange man repeated twice, very emphatically. "To-morrow night," he said, and I noticed that his voice had not the Highland inflection which I looked for. Gresson nodded and glanced at his watch, and then the two began to move downhill towards the road I had travelled that morning.

I followed as best I could, using a shallow dry watercourse of which sheep had made a track, and which kept me well below the level of the moor. It took me down the hill, but some distance from the line the pair were taking, and I had to reconnoitre frequently to watch their movements. They were still a quarter of a mile or so from the road when they stopped and stared, and I stared with them. On that lonely highway travellers were about as rare as roadmenders, and what caught their eye was a farmer's gig driven by a thickset elderly man with a woollen comforter round his neck.

I had a bad moment, for I reckoned that if Gresson recognized Amos he might take fright. Perhaps the driver of the gig thought the same, for he appeared to be very drunk. He waved his whip, he jiggoted the reins, and he made an effort to sing. He looked towards the figures on the hillside, and cried out something. The gig narrowly missed the ditch, and then to my relief the horse bolted. Swaying like a ship in a gale, the whole outfit lurched out of sight round the corner of hill where lay my cache. If Amos could stop the beast and deliver the goods there, he had put up a masterly bit of buffoonery.

The two men laughed at the performance, and then they parted. Gresson retraced his steps up the hill. The other man—I called him in my mind the Portuguese Jew—started off at a great pace due west, across the road, and over a big patch of bog towards the northern butt of the Coolin. He had some errand which Gresson knew about, and he was in a hurry to perform it. It was clearly my job to get after him.

I had a rotten afternoon. The fellow covered the moorland miles like a deer, and under the hot August sun I toiled on his trail. I had to keep well behind, and as much as possible in cover, in case he looked back; and that meant that when he had passed over a ridge I had to double not to let him get too far ahead, and when we were in an open place I had to make wide circuits to keep hidden. We struck a road which crossed a low pass and skirted the flank of the mountains, and this we followed till we were on the western side and within sight of the sea. It was gorgeous weather, and out on the blue water I saw cool sails moving and little breezes ruffling the calm, while I was glowing like a furnace. Happily I was in fair training, and I needed it. The Portuguese Jew must have done a steady six miles an hour over abominable country.

About five o'clock we came to a point where I dared not follow. The road ran flat by the edge of the sea, so that several miles of it was visible. Moreover, the man had begun to look round every few minutes. He was getting near something, and wanted to be sure that no one was in his neighbourhood. I left the road accordingly, and took to the hillside, which to my undoing was one long cascade of screes and tumbled rocks. I saw him drop over a rise which seemed to mark the rim of a little bay into which descended one of the big corries of the mountains. It must have been a good half-hour later before I at my greater altitude, and with far worse going, reached the same rim. I looked into the glen and my man had disappeared.

He could not have crossed it, for the place was wider than I had thought. A ring of black precipices came down to within half a mile of the shore, and between them was a big stream—long, shallow pools at the sea end and a chain of waterfalls above. He had gone to earth like a badger somewhere, and I dared not move in case he might be watching me from behind a boulder.

But even as I hesitated he appeared again, fording the stream, his face set on the road we had come. Whatever his errand was he had finished it, and was posting back to his master. For a moment I thought I should follow him, but another instinct prevailed. He had not come to this wild place for the scenery. Somewhere down in that glen there was something or somebody that held the key of the mystery. It was my business to stay there till I had unlocked it. Besides, in two hours it would be dark, and I had had enough walking for one day.

I made my way to the stream side and had a long drink. The corrie behind me was lit up with the westering sun, and the bald cliffs were flushed with pink and gold. On each side of the stream was turf like a lawn, perhaps a hundred yards wide, and then a tangle of long heather and boulders right up to the edge of the great rocks. I had never seen a more delectable evening, but I could not enjoy its peace because of my anxiety about the Portuguese Jew. He had not been there more than half an hour, just long enough for a man to travel to the first ridge across the burn and back. Yet he had found time to do his business. He might have left a letter in some prearranged place—in which case I would stay there till the man it was meant for turned up. Or he might have met some one, though I didn't think that possible. As I scanned the acres of rough moor and then looked at the sea lapping delicately on the grey sand I had the feeling that a knotty problem was before me. It was too dark to try to track his steps. That must be left for the morning, and I prayed that there would be no rain in the night.

I ate for supper most of the braxy ham and oatcake I had brought from

Macmorran's cottage. It took some self-denial, for I was ferociously hungry, to save a little for breakfast next morning. Then I pulled heather and bracken and made myself a bed in the shelter of a rock which stood on a knoll above the stream. My bed-chamber was well hidden, but at the same time if anything should appear in the early dawn, it gave me a prospect. With my waterproof I was perfectly warm, and, after smoking two pipes, I fell asleep.

My night's rest was broken. First it was a fox which came and barked in my ear and woke me to a pitch-black night, with scarcely a star showing. The next time it was nothing but a wandering hill-wind, but as I sat up and listened I thought I saw a spark of light near the edge of the sea. It was only for a second, but it disquieted me. I got out and climbed on the top of the rock, but all was still save for the gentle lap of the tide and the croak of some night bird among the crags. The third time I was suddenly wide awake, and without any reason, for I had not been dreaming. Now I have slept hundreds of times alone beside my horse on the veld, and I never knew any cause for such awakenings but the one, and that was the presence near me of some human being. A man who is accustomed to solitude gets this extra sense, which announces like an alarm-clock the approach of one of his kind.

But I could hear nothing. There was a scraping and rustling on the moor, but that was only the wind and the little wild things of the hills. A fox, perhaps, or a blue hare. I convinced my reason, but not my senses, and for long I lay awake with my ears at full cock and every nerve tense. Then I fell asleep, and woke to the first flush of dawn.

The sun was behind the Coolin and the hills were black as ink, but far out in the western seas was a broad band of gold. I got up and went down to the shore. The mouth of the stream was shallow, but as I moved south I came to a place where two small capes enclosed an inlet. It must have been a fault in the volcanic rock, for its depth was portentous. I stripped and dived far into its cold abysses, but I did not reach the bottom. I came to the surface rather breathless, and struck out to sea, where I floated on my back and looked at the great rampart of crag. I saw that the place where I had spent the night was only a little oasis of green at the base of one of the grimmest corries the imagination could picture. It was as desert as Damaraland. I noticed, too, how sharply the cliffs rose from the level. There were chimneys and gullies by which a man might have made his way to the summit, but no one of them could have been scaled except by a mountaineer.

I was feeling better now, with all the frowsiness washed out of me, and I dried myself by racing up and down the heather. Then I noticed something. There were marks of human feet at the top of the deep-water inlet—not mine, for they were on the other side. The short sea-turf was bruised and trampled in several places, and there were broken stems of bracken. I thought that some fisherman had probably landed there to stretch his legs.

But that set me thinking of the Portuguese Jew. After breakfasting on my last morsels of food—a knuckle of braxy and a bit of oatcake—I set about tracking him from the place where we had first entered the glen. To get my bearings, I went back over the road I had come myself, and after a good deal of trouble I found his spoor. It was pretty clear as far as the stream, for he had been walking—or rather running—over ground with many patches of gravel on it. After that it was difficult, and I lost it entirely in the rough heather below the crags. All that I could make out for certain was that he had crossed the stream, and that his business, whatever it was, had been with the few acres of tumbled wilderness below the precipices.

I spent a busy morning there, but found nothing except the skeleton of a sheep picked clean by the ravens. It was a thankless job, and I got very cross over it. I had an ugly feeling that I was on a false scent and wasting my time. I wished to Heaven I had old Peter with me. He could follow spoor like a Bushman, and would have riddled the Portuguese Jew's track out of any jungle on earth. That was a game I had never learned, for in old days I had always left it to my natives. I chucked the attempt, and lay disconsolately on a warm patch of grass and smoked and thought about Peter. But my chief reflections were that I had breakfasted at five, that it was now eleven, that I was intolerably hungry, that there was nothing here to feed a grasshopper, and that I should starve unless I got supplies.

It was a long road to my cache, but there were no two ways of it. My only hope was to sit tight in the glen, and it might involve a wait of days. To wait I must have food, and though it meant relinquishing guard for a matter of six hours, the risk had to be taken. I set off at a brisk pace with a very depressed mind.

From the map it seemed that a short cut lay over a pass in the range. I resolved to take it, and that short cut, like most of its kind, was unblessed by Heaven. I will not dwell upon the discomforts of the journey. I found myself slithering among screes, climbing steep chimneys, and travelling precariously along razor-backs. The shoes were nearly rent from my feet by the infernal rocks, which were all pitted as if by some geological small-pox. When at last I crossed the divide, I had a horrible business getting down from one level to another in a gruesome corrie, where each step was composed of smooth boiler-plates. But at last I was among the bogs on the east side, and came to the place beside the road where I had fixed my cache.

The faithful Amos had not failed me. There were the provisions—a couple of small loaves, a dozen tins, and a bottle of whisky. I made the best pack I could of them in my waterproof, swung it on my stick, and started back, thinking that I must be very like the picture of Christian on the title-page of my *Pilgrim's Progress*.

I was liker Christian before I reached my destination—Christian after he had got up the Hill Difficulty. The morning's walk had been bad, but the afternoon's was worse, for I was in a fever to get back, and, having had enough of the hills, chose the longer route I had followed the previous day. I was mortally afraid of being seen, for I cut a queer figure, so I avoided every stretch of road where I had not a clear view ahead. Many weary detours I made among moss-hags and screes and the stony channels of burns. But I got there at last, and it was almost with a sense of comfort that I flung my pack down beside the stream where I had passed the night.

I ate a good meal, lit my pipe, and fell into the equable mood which follows upon fatigue ended and hunger satisfied. The sun was westering, and its light fell upon the rock-wall above the place where I had abandoned my search for the spoor.

As I gazed at it idly I saw a curious thing.

It seemed to be split in two and a shaft of sunlight came through between. There could be no doubt about it. I saw the end of the shaft on the moor beneath, while all the rest lay in shadow. I rubbed my eyes, and got out my glasses. Then I guessed the explanation. There was a rock tower close against the face of the main precipice, and indistinguishable from it to any one looking direct at the face. Only when the sun fell on it obliquely could it be discovered. And between the tower and the cliff there must be a substantial hollow.

The discovery brought me to my feet, and set me running towards the end of the shaft of sunlight. I left the heather, scrambled up some yards of screes, and had a difficult time on some very smooth slabs, where only the friction of tweed and rough rock gave me a hold. Slowly I worked my way towards the speck of sunlight, till I found a handhold and swung myself into the crack. On one side was the main wall of the hill, on the other a tower some ninety feet high, and between them a long crevice varying in width from three to six feet. Beyond it there showed a small bright patch of sea.

There was more, for at that point where I entered it there was an overhang which made a fine cavern, low at the entrance but a dozen feet high inside, and as dry as tinder. Here, thought I, is the perfect hiding-place. Before going farther I resolved to return for food. It was not very easy descending, and I slipped the last twenty feet, landing on my back in a soft patch of screes. At the burnside I filled my flask from the whisky bottle, and put half a loaf, a tin of sardines, a tin of tongue, and a packet of chocolate in my waterproof pockets. Laden as I was, it took me some time to get up again, but I managed it, and stored my belongings in a corner of the cave. Then I set out to explore the rest of the crack.

It slanted down and then rose again to a small platform. After that it dropped in easy steps to the moor beyond the tower. If the Portuguese Jew had come here, that was the way by which he had reached it, for he would not have had the time to make my ascent. I went very cautiously, for I felt I was on the eve of a big discovery. The platform was partly hidden from my end by a bend in the crack, and it was more or less screened by an outlying bastion of the tower from the other side. Its surface was covered with fine powdery dust, as were the steps beyond it. In some excitement I knelt down and examined it.

Beyond doubt there was spoor here. I knew the Portuguese Jew's footsteps by this time, and I made them out clearly, especially in one corner. But there were other footsteps, quite different. The one showed the tackets of rough country boots, the others were from unnailed soles. Again I longed for Peter to make certain, though I was pretty sure of my conclusions. The man I had followed had come here, and he had not stayed long. Some one else had been here, probably later, for the unnailed shoes overlaid the tackets. The first man might have left a message for the second. Perhaps the second was that human presence of which I had been dimly conscious in the night-time.

I carefully removed all traces of my own footmarks, and went back to my cave. My head was humming with my discovery. I remembered Gresson's words to his friend: "To-morrow night." As I read it, the Portuguese Jew had taken a message from Gresson to some one, and that some one had come from somewhere and picked it up. The message contained an assignation for this very night. I had found a point of observation, for no one was likely to come near my cave, which was reached from the moor by such a toilsome climb. There I should bivouac and see what the darkness brought forth. I remember reflecting on the amazing luck which had so far attended me. As I looked from my refuge at the blue haze of twilight creeping over the waters, I felt my pulses quicken with a wild anticipation.

Then I heard a sound below me, and craned my neck round the edge of the tower. A man was climbing up the rock by the way I had come.

39   I HEAR OF THE WILD BIRDS

I saw an old green felt hat, and below it lean tweed-clad shoulders. Then I saw a knapsack with a stick slung through it, as the owner wriggled his way on to a shelf. Presently he turned his face upward to judge the remaining distance. It was the face of a young man, a face sallow and angular, but now a little flushed with the day's sun and the work of climbing. It was a face that I had first seen at Fosse Manor.

I felt suddenly sick and heartsore. I don't know why, but I had never really associated the intellectuals of Biggleswick with a business like this. None of them but Ivery, and he was different. They had been silly and priggish, but no more—I would have taken my oath on it. Yet here was one of them engaged in black treason against his native land. Something began to beat in my temples when I remembered that Mary and this man had been friends, that he had held her hand, and called her by her Christian name. My first impulse was to wait till he got up, and then pitch him down among the boulders and let his German accomplices puzzle over his broken neck.

With difficulty I kept down that tide of fury. I had my duty to do, and to keep on terms with this man was part of it. I had to convince him that I was an accomplice, and that might not be easy. I leaned over the edge, and, as he got to his feet on the ledge above the boiler-plates, I whistled so that he turned his face to me.

"Hullo, Wake," I said.

He started, stared for a second, and recognized me. He did not seem over-pleased to see me. "Brand!" he cried. "How did you get here?" He swung himself up beside me, straightened his back and unbuckled his knapsack. "I thought this was my own private sanctuary, and that nobody knew it but me. Have you spotted the cave? It's the best bedroom in Skye." His tone was, as usual, rather acid.

That little hammer was beating in my head. I longed to get my hands on his throat and choke the smug treason in him. But I kept my mind fixed on one purpose—to persuade him that I shared his secret and was on his side. His off-hand self-possession seemed only the clever screen of the surprised conspirator who was hunting for a plan.

We entered the cave, and he flung his pack into a corner. "Last time I was here," he said, "I covered the floor with heather. We must get some more if we would sleep soft." In the twilight he was a dim figure, but he seemed a new man from the one I had last seen in the Moot Hall at Biggleswick. There was a wiry vigour in his body and a purpose in his face. What a fool I had been to set him down as no more than a conceited *flâneur*!

He went out to the shelf again and sniffed the fresh evening. There was a wonderful red sky in the west, but in the crevice the shades had fallen, and only the bright patches at either end told of the sunset.

"Wake," I said, "you and I have to understand each other. I'm a friend of Ivery and I know the meaning of this place. I discovered it by accident, but I want you to know that I'm heart and soul with you. You may trust me in to-night's job as if I were Ivery himself. I . . ."

He swung round and looked at me sharply. His eyes were hot again, as I remembered them at our first meeting.

"What do you mean? How much do you know?"

The hammer was going hard in my forehead, and I had to pull myself together to answer.

"I know that at the end of this crack a message was left last night, and that some one came out of the sea and picked it up. That some one is coming again when the darkness falls, and there will be another message."

He had turned his head away. "You are talking nonsense. No submarine could land on this coast."

I could see that he was trying me.

"This morning," I said, "I swam in the deep-water inlet below us. It is the most perfect submarine shelter in Britain."

He still kept his face from me, looking the way he had come. For a moment he was silent, and then he spoke in the bitter, drawling voice which had annoyed me at Fosse Manor.

"How do you reconcile this business with your principles, Mr. Brand? You were always a patriot, I remember, though you didn't see eye to eye with the Government."

It was not quite what I had expected, and I was unready. I stammered in my reply. "It's because I am a patriot that I want peace. I think that . . . I mean . . ."

"Therefore you are willing to help the enemy to win?"

"They have already won. I want that recognized and the end hurried on." I was getting my mind clearer, and continued fluently. "The longer the war lasts, the worse this country is ruined. We must make the people realize the truth, and—"

But he swung round suddenly, his eyes blazing.

"You blackguard!" he cried, "you damnable blackguard!" And he flung himself on me like a wild-cat.

I had got my answer. He did not believe me, he knew me for a spy, and he was determined to do me in. We were beyond finesse now, and back at the old barbaric game. It was his life or mine. The hammer beat furiously in my head as we closed, and a fierce satisfaction rose in my heart.

He never had a chance, for though he was in good trim and had the light, wiry figure of the mountaineer, he hadn't a quarter of my muscular strength. Besides, he was wrongly placed, for he had the outside station. Had he been on the inside he might have toppled me over the edge by his sudden assault. As it was, I grappled him and forced him to the ground, squeezing the breath out of his body in the process. I must have hurt him considerably, but he never gave a cry. With a good deal of trouble I lashed his hands behind his back with the belt of my waterproof, carried him inside the cave and laid him in the dark end of it. Then I tied his feet with the strap of his own knapsack. I would have to gag him, but that could wait.

I had still to contrive a plan of action for the night, for I did not know what part he had been meant to play in it. He might be the messenger instead of the Portuguese Jew, in which case he would have papers about his person. If he knew of the cave, others might have the same knowledge, and I had better shift him before they came. I looked at my wrist-watch, and the luminous dial showed that the hour was half-past nine.

Then I noticed that the bundle in the corner was sobbing.

It was a horrid sound and it worried me. I had a little pocket electric torch and I flashed it on Wake's face. If he was crying, it was with dry eyes.

"What are you going to do with me?" he asked.

"That depends," I said grimly.

"Well, I'm ready. I may be a poor creature, but I'm damned if I'm afraid of you, or anything like you." That was a brave thing to say, for it was a lie; his teeth were chattering.

"I'm ready for a deal," I said.

"You won't get it," was his answer. "Cut my throat if you mean to, but for God's sake don't insult me. . . . I choke when I think about you. You come to us and we welcome you, and receive you in our houses, and tell you our inmost thoughts, and all the time you're a bloody traitor. You want to sell us to Germany. You may win now, but by God! your time will come! That is my last word to you . . . you swine!"

The hammer stopped beating in my head. I saw myself suddenly as a blind, preposterous fool. I strode over to Wake, and he shut his eyes as if he expected a blow. Instead I unbuckled the straps which held his legs and arms.

"Wake, old fellow," I said, "I'm the worst kind of idiot. I'll eat all the dirt you want. I'll give you leave to knock me black and blue, and I won't lift a hand. But not now. Now we've another job on hand. Man, we're on the same side, and I never knew it. It's too bad a case for apologies, but if it's any consolation to you I feel the lowest dog in Europe at this moment."

He was sitting up rubbing his bruised shoulders. "What do you mean?" he asked hoarsely.

"I mean that you and I are allies. My name's not Brand. I'm a soldier—a general, if you want to know. I went to Biggleswick under orders, and I came chasing up here on the same job. Ivery's the biggest German agent in Britain and I'm after him. I've struck his communication lines, and this very night, please God, we'll get the last clue to the riddle. Do you hear? We're in this business together, and you've got to lend a hand."

I told him briefly the story of Gresson, and how I had tracked his man here. As I talked we ate our supper, and I wish I could have watched Wake's face. He asked questions, for he wasn't convinced in a hurry. I think it was my mention of Mary Lamington that did the trick. I don't know why, but that seemed to satisfy him. But he wasn't going to give himself away.

"You may count on me," he said, "for this is black, blackguardly treason. But you know my politics, and I don't change them for this. I'm more against your accursed war than ever, now that I know what war involves."

"Right-o," I said, "I'm a pacificist myself. You won't get any heroics about war from me. I'm all for peace, but we've got to down those devils first."

It wasn't safe for either of us to stick in that cave, so we cleared away the marks of our occupation, and hid our packs in a deep crevice of the rock. Wake announced his intention of climbing the tower, while there was still a faint afterglow of light. "It's broad on the top, and I can keep a watch out to sea if any light shows. I've been up it before. I found the way two years ago. No, I won't fall asleep and tumble off. I slept most of the afternoon on the top of Sgurr Vhiconnich, and I'm wakeful as a bat now."

I watched him shin up the face of the tower, and admired greatly the speed and neatness with which he climbed. Then I followed the crevice southward to the hollow just below the platform where I had found the footmarks. There was a big boulder there, which partly shut off the view of it from the direction of our cave. The place was perfect for my purpose, for between the boulder and the wall of the tower was a narrow gap, through which I could hear all that passed on the platform. I found a stance where I could rest in comfort and keep an eye through the crack on what happened beyond.

There was still a faint light on the platform, but soon that disappeared and black darkness settled down on the hills. It was the dark of the moon, and, as had happened the night before, a thin wrack blew over the sky, hiding the stars. The place was very still, though now and then would come the cry of a bird from the crags that beetled above me, and from the shore the pipe of a tern or oyster-catcher. An owl hooted from somewhere up on the tower. That I reckoned was Wake, so I hooted back and was answered.

I unbuckled my wrist-watch and pocketed it, lest its luminous dial should betray me; and I noticed that the hour was close on eleven. I had already removed my shoes, and my jacket was buttoned at the collar so as to show no shirt. I did not think that the coming visitor would trouble to explore the crevice beyond the platform, but I wanted to be prepared for emergencies.

Then followed an hour of waiting. I felt wonderfully cheered and exhilarated, for Wake had restored my confidence in human nature. In that eerie place we were wrapped round with mystery like a fog. Some unknown figure was coming out of the sea, the emissary of that Power we had been at grips with for three years. It was as if the war had just made contact with our own shores, and never, not even when I was alone in the South German forest, had I felt myself so much the sport of a whimsical fate. I only wished Peter could have been with me. And so my thoughts fled to Peter in his prison camp, and I longed for another sight of my old friend as a girl longs for her lover.

Then I heard the hoot of an owl, and presently the sound of careful steps fell on my ear. I could see nothing, but I guessed it was the Portuguese Jew, for I could hear the grinding of heavily nailed boots on the gritty rock.

The figure was very quiet. It appeared to be sitting down, and then it rose and fumbled with the wall of the tower just beyond the boulder behind which I sheltered. It seemed to move a stone and to replace it. After that came silence, and then once more the hoot of an owl. There were steps on the rock staircase, the steps of a man who did not know the road well and stumbled a little. Also they were the steps of one without nails in his boots.

They reached the platform and some one spoke. It was the Portuguese Jew, and he spoke in good German.

"*Die Vögelein schweigen im Walde,*" he said.

The answer came from a clear authoritative voice.

"*Warte nur, balde ruhest du auch.*"

Clearly some kind of password, for sane men don't talk about little birds in that kind of situation. It sounded to me like indifferent poetry.

Then followed a conversation in low tones, of which I only caught odd phrases. I heard two names—*Chelius* and what sounded like a Dutch word, *Bommaerts.* Then to my joy I caught *Elfenbein,* and when uttered it seemed to be followed by a laugh. I heard too a phrase several times repeated, which seemed to me to be pure gibberish—*Die Stubenvögel verstehen.* It was spoken by the man from the sea. And then the word *Wildvögel.* The pair seemed demented about birds.

For a second an electric torch was flashed in the shelter of the rock, and I could see a tanned, bearded face looking at some papers. The light disappeared, and again the Portuguese Jew was fumbling with the stones at the base of the tower. To my joy he was close to my crack, and I could hear every word. "You cannot come here very often," he said, "and it may be hard to arrange a meeting. See, therefore, the place I have made to put the *Vögelfutter.* When I get a chance I will come here, and you will come also when you are able. Often there will be nothing, but sometimes there will be much."

My luck was clearly in, and my exultation made me careless. A stone, on which a foot rested, slipped, and though I checked myself at once, the confounded thing rolled down into the hollow, making a great clatter. I plastered myself in the embrasure of the rock and waited with a beating heart. The place was pitch dark, but they had an electric torch, and if they once flashed it on me I was gone. I heard them leave the platform and climb down into the hollow. There they stood listening, while I held my breath. Then I heard *"Nix, mein Freund,"* and the two went back, the naval officer's boots slipping on the gravel.

They did not leave the platform together. The man from the sea bade a short farewell to the Portuguese Jew, listening, I thought, impatiently to his final message as if eager to be gone. It was a good half-hour before the latter took himself off, and I heard the sound of his nailed boots die away as he reached the heather of the moor.

I waited a little longer, and then crawled back to the cave. The owl hooted, and presently Wake descended lightly beside me; he must have known every foothold and handhold by heart to do the job in that inky blackness. I remember that he asked no question of me, but he used language rare on the lips of conscientious objectors about the men who had lately been in the crevice. We, who four hours earlier had been at death-grips, now curled up on the hard floor like two tired dogs, and fell sound asleep.

I woke to find Wake in a thundering bad temper. The thing he remembered most about the night before was our scrap and the gross way I had insulted him. I didn't blame him, for if any man had taken me for a German spy I would have been out for his blood, and it was no good explaining that he had given me grounds for suspicion. He was as touchy about his blessed principles as an old maid about her age. I was feeling rather extra buckish myself, and that didn't improve matters. His face was like a gargoyle as we went down to the beach to bathe, so I held my tongue. He was chewing the cud of his wounded pride.

But the salt water cleared out the dregs of his distemper. You couldn't be peevish swimming in that jolly, shining sea. We raced each other away beyond the inlet to the outer water, which a brisk morning breeze was curling. Then back to a promontory of heather, where the first beams of the sun coming over the Coolin dried our skins. He sat hunched up staring at the mountains while I prospected the rocks at the edge. Out in the Minch two destroyers were hurrying southward, and I wondered where in that waste of blue was the craft which had come here in the night watches.

I found the spoor of the man from the sea quite fresh on a patch of gravel above the tide-mark.

"There's our friend of the night," I said.

"I believe the whole thing was a whimsy," said Wake, his eyes on the chimneys of Sgurr Dearg. "They were only two natives—poachers, perhaps, or tinkers."

"They don't speak German in these parts."

"It was Gaelic probably."

"What do you make of this, then!" and I quoted the stuff about birds with which they had greeted each other.

Wake looked interested. "That's *Über allen Gipfeln*. Have you ever read Goethe?"

"Never a word. And what do you make of that?" I pointed to a flat rock below the tide-mark covered with a tangle of seaweed. It was of a softer stone than the hard stuff in the hills, and some heavy body had scraped off half the seaweed and a slice of the side. "That wasn't done yesterday morning, for I had my bath here."

Wake got up and examined the place. He nosed about in the crannies of the rocks lining the inlet, and got into the water again to explore better. When he joined me he was smiling. "I apologize for my scepticism," he said. "There's been some petrol-driven craft here in the night. I can smell it, for I've a nose like a retriever. I dare say you're on the right track. Anyhow, though you seem to know a bit about German, you could scarcely invent immortal poetry."

We took our belongings to a green crook of the burn, and made a very good breakfast. Wake had nothing in his pack but plasmon biscuits and raisins, for that, he said, was his mountaineering provender, but he was not averse to sampling my tinned stuff. He was a different-sized fellow out on the hills from the anaemic intellectual of Biggleswick. He had forgotten his beastly self-consciousness, and spoke of his hobby with a serious passion. It seemed he had scrambled about everywhere in Europe, from the Caucasus to the Pyrenees. I could see he must be good at the job, for he didn't brag of his exploits. It was the mountains that he loved, not wriggling his body up hard places. The Coolin, he said, were his favourites, for on some of them you could get two thousand feet of good rock. We got our glasses on the face of Sgurr Alasdair, and he sketched out for me various ways of getting to its grim summit. The Coolin and the Dolomites for him, for he had grown tired of the Chamonix *aiguilles*. I remember he described with tremendous gusto the joys of early dawn in Tyrol, when you ascended through acres of flowery meadows to a tooth of clean white limestone against a clean blue sky. He spoke, too, of the little wild hills in the Bavarian Wettersteingebirge, and of a guide he had picked up there and trained to the job.

"They called him Sebastian Buchwieser. He was the jolliest boy you ever saw, and as clever on crags as a chamois. He is probably dead by now, dead in a filthy Jäger battalion. That's you and your accursed war."

"Well, we've got to get busy to end it in the right way," I said. "And you've got to help, my lad."

He was a good draughtsman, and with his assistance I drew a rough map of the crevice where we had roosted for the night, giving its bearings carefully in relation to the burn and the sea. Then I wrote down all the details about Gresson and the Portuguese Jew, and described the latter in minute detail. I described, too, most precisely the cache where it had been arranged that the messages should be placed. That finished my stock of paper, and I left the record of the oddments overheard of the conversation for a later time. I put the thing in an old leather cigarette-case I possessed, and handed it to Wake.

"You've got to go straight off to the Kyle and not waste any time on the way. Nobody suspects you, so you can travel any road you please. When you get there you ask for Mr. Andrew Amos, who has some Government job in the neighbourhood. Give him that paper from me. He'll know what to do with it all right. Tell him I'll get somehow to the Kyle before midday the day after to-morrow. I must cover my tracks a bit, so I can't come with you, and I want that thing in his hands just as fast as your legs will take you. If any one tries to steal if from you, for God's sake eat it. You can see for yourself that it's devilish important."

"I shall be back in England in three days," he said. "Any message for your other friends?"

"Forget all about me. You never saw me here. I'm still Brand, the amiable colonial studying social movements. If you meet Ivery, say you heard of me on the Clyde deep in sedition. But if you see Miss Lamington, you can tell her I'm past the Hill Difficulty. I'm coming back as soon as God will let me, and I'm going to drop right into the Biggleswick push. Only this time I'll be a little more advanced in my views. . . . You needn't get cross. I'm not saying anything against your principles. The main point is that we both hate dirty treason."

He put the case in his waistcoat pocket. "I'll go round Garsbheinn," he said, "and over by Camasunary. I'll be at the Kyle long before evening. I meant anyhow to sleep at Broadford tonight. . . . Good-bye, Brand, for I've forgotten your proper name. You're not a bad fellow, but you've landed me in melodrama for the first time in my sober existence. I have a grudge against you for mixing up the Coolin with a shilling shocker. You've spoiled their sanctity."

"You've the wrong notion of romance," I said. "Why, man, last night for an hour you were in the front line—the place where the enemy forces touch our own. You were over the top—you were in No-man's-land."

He laughed. "That is one way to look at it"; and then he stalked off and I watched his lean figure till it was round the turn of the hill.

All that morning I smoked peacefully by the burn, and let my thoughts wander over the whole business. I had got precisely what Blenkiron wanted, a post office for the enemy. It would need careful handling, but I could see the juiciest lies passing that way to the *Grosses Hauptquartier*. Yet I had an ugly feeling at the back of my head that it had been all too easy, and that Ivery was not the man to be duped in this way for long. That set me thinking about the queer talk in the crevice. The poetry stuff I dismissed as the ordinary password, probably changed every time. But who were *Chelius* and *Bommaerts*, and what in the name of goodness were the Wild Birds and the Cage Birds? Twice in the past three years I had had two such riddles to solve—Scudder's scribble in his pocket-book, and Harry Bullivant's three words. I remembered how it had only been by constant chewing at them that I had got a sort of meaning, and I wondered if fate would some day expound this puzzle also.

Meantime I had to get back to London as inconspicuously as I had come. It might take some doing, for the police who had been active in Morvern might be still on the track, and it was essential that I should keep out of trouble and give no hint to Gresson and his friends that I had been so far north. However, that was for Amos to advise me on, and about noon I picked up my waterproof with its bursting pockets and set off on a long detour up the coast. All that blessed day I scarcely met a soul. I passed a distillery which seemed to have quit business, and in the evening came to a little town on the sea where I had a bed and supper in a superior kind of public-house.

Next day I struck southward along the coast, and had two experiences of interest. I had a good look at Ranna, and observed that the *Tobermory* was no longer there. Gresson had only waited to get his job finished; he could probably twist the old captain any way he wanted. The second was that at the door of a village smithy I saw the back of the Portuguese Jew. He was talking Gaelic this time—good Gaelic it sounded, and in that knot of idlers he would have passed for the ordinariest kind of gillie.

He did not see me, and I had no desire to give him the chance, for I had an odd feeling that the day might come when it would be good for us to meet as strangers.

That night I put up boldly in the inn at Broadford, where they fed me nobly on fresh sea-trout and I first tasted an excellent liqueur made of honey and whisky. Next morning I was early afoot, and well before midday was in sight of the narrows of the Kyle, and the two little stone clachans which face each other across the strip of sea.

About two miles from the place at a turn of the road I came upon a farmer's gig, drawn up by the wayside, with the horse cropping the moorland grass. A man sat on the bank smoking, with his left arm hooked in the reins. He was an oldish man, with a short, square figure, and a woollen comforter enveloped his throat.

40 THE ADVENTURES OF A BAGMAN

"Ye're punctual to time, Mr. Brand," said the voice of Amos. "But losh! man, what have ye done to your breeks? And your buits? Ye're no just very respectable in your appearance."

I wasn't. The confounded rocks of the Coolin had left their mark on my shoes, which moreover had not been cleaned for a week, and the same hills had rent my jacket at the shoulders, and torn my trousers above the right knee, and stained every part of my apparel with peat and lichen.

I cast myself on the bank beside Amos and lit my pipe. "Did you get my message?" I asked.

"Ay. It's gone on by a sure hand to the destination we ken of. Ye've managed well, Mr. Brand, but I wish ye were back in London." He sucked at his pipe, and the shaggy brows were pulled so low as to hide the wary eyes. Then he proceeded to think aloud.

"Ye canna go back by Mallaig. I don't just understand why, but they're lookin' for you down that line. It's a vexatious business when your friends, meanin' the polis, are doing their best to upset your plans and you no able to enlighten them. I could send word to the Chief Constable and get ye through to London without a stop like a load of fish from Aiberdeen, but that would be spoilin' the fine character ye've been at such pains to construct. Na, na! Ye maun take the risk and travel by Muirtown without ony creedentials."

"It can't be a very big risk," I interpolated.

"I'm no so sure. Gresson's left the *Tobermory*. He went by here yesterday on the Mallaig boat, and there was a wee blackavised man with him that got out at the Kyle. He's there still, stoppin' at the hotel. They ca' him Linklater, and he travels in whisky. I don't like the looks of him."

"But Gresson does not suspect me?"

"Maybe no. But ye wouldna like him to see ye hereaways. Yon gentry don't leave muckle to chance. Be very certain that every man in Gresson's lot kens all about ye, and has your description down to the mole on your chin."

"Then they've got it wrong," I replied.

"I was speakin' feeguratively," said Amos. "I was considerin' your case the feck of yesterday, and I've brought the best I could do for ye in the gig. I wish ye were more respectable clad, but a good topcoat will hide defeecencies."

From behind the gig's seat he pulled out an ancient Gladstone bag and revealed its contents. There was a bowler of a vulgar and antiquated style; there was a ready-made overcoat of some dark cloth, the kind a clerk wears on the road to the office; there was a pair of detachable celluloid cuffs, and there was a linen collar and dickie. Also there was a small hand-case, such as bagmen carry on their rounds.

"That's your luggage," said Amos with pride. "That wee bag's full of samples. Ye'll mind I took the precaution of measurin' ye in Glasgow, so the things'll fit. Ye've got a new name, Mr. Brand, and I've taken a room for ye in the hotel on the strength of it. Ye're Archibald McCaskie, and ye're travellin' for the firm o' Todd, Sons & Brothers, of Edinburgh. Ye ken the folk? They publish wee releegious books, that ye've been trying to sell for Sabbath-school prizes to the Free Kirk ministers in Skye."

The notion amused Amos, and he relapsed into the sombre chuckle which with him did duty for a laugh.

I put my hat and waterproof in the bag and donned the bowler and the topcoat. They fitted fairly well. Likewise the cuffs and collar, though here I struck a snag, for I had lost my scarf somewhere in the Coolin, and Amos, pelican-like, had to surrender the rusty black tie which adorned his own person. It was a queer rig, and I felt like nothing on earth in it, but Amos was satisfied.

"Mr. McCaskie, sir," he said, "ye're the very model of a publisher's traveller. Ye'd better learn a few biographical details, which ye've maybe forgotten. Ye're an Edinburgh man, but ye were some years in London, which explains the way ye speak. Ye bide at 6 Russell Street, off the Meadows, and ye're an elder in the Nethergate U.F. Kirk. Have ye ony special taste ye would lead the crack on to, if ye're engaged in conversation?"

I suggested the English classics.

"And very suitable. Ye can try poalitics, too. Ye'd better be a Free Trader but convertit by Lloyd George. That's a common case, and ye'll need to be by-ordinar common. . . . If I was you, I would daunder about here for a bit, and no arrive at your hotel till after dark. Then ye can have your supper and gang to bed. The Muirtown train leaves at half-past seven in the morning. . . . Na, ye can't come with me. It wouldna do for us to be seen thegither. If I meet ye in the street I'll never let on I ken ye."

Amos climbed into the gig and jolted off home. I went down to the shore and sat among the rocks, finishing about tea-time the remains of my provisions. In the mellow gloaming I strolled into the clachan and got a boat to put me over to the inn. It proved to be a comfortable place, with a motherly old landlady who showed me to my room and promised ham and eggs and cold salmon for supper. After a good wash, which I needed, and an honest attempt to make my clothes presentable, I descended to the meal in a coffee-room lit by a single paraffin lamp.

The food was excellent, and, as I ate, my spirits rose. In two days I should be back in London beside Blenkiron, and somewhere within a day's journey of Mary. I could picture no scene now without thinking how Mary fitted into it. For her sake I held Biggleswick delectable, because I had seen her there. I wasn't sure if this was love, but it was something I had never dreamed of before, something which I now hugged the thought of. It made the whole earth rosy and golden for me, and life so well worth living that I felt like a miser towards the days to come.

I had about finished supper, when I was joined by another guest. Seen in the light of that infamous lamp, he seemed a smart, alert fellow, with a bushy, black moustache, and black hair parted in the middle. He had fed already and appeared to be hungering for human society.

In three minutes he had told me that he had come down from Portree and was on his way to Leith. A minute later he had whipped out a card on which I read "J. J. Linklater," and in the corner the name of Hatherwick Bros. His accent betrayed that he hailed from the west.

"I've been up among the distilleries," he informed me. "It's a poor business distillin' in these times, wi' the teetotallers yowlin' about the nation's shame and the way to lose the war. I'm a temperate man mysel', but I would think shame to spile decent folks' business. If the Government want to stop the drink, let them buy us out. They've permitted us to invest good money in the trade, and they must see that we get it back. The other way will wreck public credit. That's what I say. Supposin' some Labour Government takes the notion that soap's bad for the nation? Are they goin' to shut up Port Sunlight? Or good clothes? Or lum hats? There's no end to their daftness if they once start on that tack. A lawfu' trade's a lawfu' trade, says I, and it's contrary to public policy to pit it at the mercy of a wheen cranks. D'you no agree, sir? By the way, I havena got your name?"

I told him, and he rambled on.

"We're blenders, and do a very high-class business, mostly foreign. The war's hit us wi' our export trade, of course, but we're no as bad as some. What's your line, Mr. McCaskie?"

When he heard he was keenly interested.

"D'ye say so? Ye're from Todd's! Man, I was in the book business mysel', till I changed it for something a wee bit more lucrative. I was on the road for three years for Andrew Matheson. Ye ken the name—Paternoster Row—I've forgotten the number. I had a kind of ambition to start a booksellin' shop of my own and to make Linklater o' Paisley a big name in the trade. But I got the offer from Hatherwick's, and I was wantin' to get married, so filthy lucre won the day. And I'm no sorry I changed. If it hadna been for this war, I would have been makin' four figures with my salary and commissions. . . . My pipe's out. Have you one of those rare and valuable curiosities called a spunk, Mr. McCaskie?"

He was a merry little grig of a man, and he babbled on, till I announced my intention of going to bed. If this was Amos's bagman, who had been seen in company with Gresson, I understood how idle may be the suspicions of a clever man. He had probably foregathered with Gresson on the Skye boat, and wearied that nocturnal soul with his cackle.

I was up betimes, paid my bill, ate a breakfast of porridge and fresh haddocks, and walked the few hundred yards to the station. It was a warm, thick morning, with no sun visible, and the Skye hills misty to their base. The three coaches on the little train were nearly filled when I had bought my ticket, and I selected a third-class smoking carriage which held four soldiers returning from leave.

The train was already moving when a late passenger hurried along the platform and clambered in beside me. A cheery "Mornin', Mr. McCaskie," revealed my fellow guest at the hotel.

We jolted away from the coast up a broad glen and then on to a wide expanse of bog, with big hills showing towards the north. It was a drowsy day, and in that atmosphere of shag and crowded human humanity I felt my eyes closing. I had a short nap, and woke to find that Mr. Linklater had changed his seat and was now beside me.

"We'll no get a *Scotsman* till Muirtown," he said. "Have ye nothing in your samples ye could give me to read?"

I had forgotten about the samples. I opened the case and found the oddest collection of little books, all in gay bindings. Some were religious, with names like *Dew of Hermon* and *Cool Siloam*; some were innocent narratives, *How Tommy Saved his Pennies*, *A Missionary Child in China*, and *Little Susie and her Uncle.* There was a *Life of David Livingstone*, a child's book on sea-shells, and a richly gilt edition of the poems of one James Montgomery. I offered the selection to Mr. Linklater, who grinned and chose the *Missionary Child.* "It's not the reading I'm accustomed to," he said. "I like the strong meat—Hall Caine and Jack London. By the way, how d'you square this business of yours wi' the booksellers? When I was in Matheson's there would have been trouble if we had dealt direct wi' the public like you."

The confounded fellow started to talk about the details of the book trade, of which I knew nothing. He wanted to know on what terms we sold "juveniles," and what discount we gave the big wholesalers, and what class of book we put out "on sale." I didn't understand a word of his jargon, and I must have given myself away badly, for he asked me questions about firms of which I had never heard, and I had to make some kind of answer. I told myself that the donkey was harmless, and that his opinion of me mattered nothing, but as soon as I decently could I pretended to be absorbed in the *Pilgrim's Progress*, a gaudy copy of which was among the samples. It opened at the episode of Christian and Hopeful in the Enchanted Ground, and in that stuffy carriage I presently followed the example of Heedless and Too-Bold and fell sound asleep.

I was awakened by the train rumbling over the points of a little moorland junction. Sunk in a pleasing lethargy, I sat with my eyes closed, and then covertly took a glance at my companion. He had abandoned the *Missionary Child* and was reading a little dun-coloured book, and marking passages with a pencil. His face was absorbed, and it was a new face, not the vacant, good-humoured look of the garrulous bagman, but something shrewd, purposeful, and formidable. I remained hunched up as if still sleeping, and tried to see what the book was. But my eyes, good as they are, could make out nothing of the text or title, except that I had a very strong impression that the book was not written in the English tongue.

I woke abruptly and leaned over to him. Quick as lightning he slid his pencil up his sleeve and turned on me with a fatuous smile.

"What d'ye make o' this, Mr. McCaskie? It's a wee book I picked up at a roup along with fifty others. I paid five shillings for the lot. It looks like Gairman, but in my young days they didna teach us foreign languages."

I took the thing and turned over the pages, trying to keep any sign of intelligence out of my face. It was German right enough, a little manual of hydrography with no publisher's name on it. It had the look of the kind of textbook a Government department might issue to its officials.

I handed it back. "It's either German or Dutch. I'm not much of a scholar, barring a little French and the Latin I got at Heriot's Hospital. . . . This is an awful slow train, Mr. Linklater."

The soldiers were playing nap, and the bagman proposed a game of cards. I remembered in time that I was an elder in the Nethergate U.F. Church, and refused with some asperity. After that I shut my eyes again, for I wanted to think about this new phenomenon.

The fellow knew German—that was clear. He had also been seen in

Gresson's company. I didn't believe he suspected me, though I suspected him profoundly. It was my business to keep strictly to my part and give him no cause to doubt me. He was clearly practising his own part on me, and I must appear to take him literally on his professions. So, presently, I woke up and engaged him in a disputatious conversation about the morality of selling strong liquors. He responded readily, and put the case for alcohol with much point and vehemence. The discussion interested the soldiers, and one of them, to show he was on Linklater's side, produced a flask and offered him a drink. I concluded by observing morosely that the bagman had been a better man when he peddled books for Alexander Matheson, and that put the closure on the business.

That train was a record. It stopped at every station, and in the afternoon it simply got tired and sat down in the middle of a moor and reflected for an hour. I stuck my head out of the window now and then, and smelt the rooty fragrance of bogs, and when we halted on a bridge I watched the trout in the pools of the brown river. Then I slept and smoked alternately, and began to get furiously hungry.

Once I woke to hear the soldiers discussing the war. There was an argument between a lance-corporal in the Camerons and a sapper private about some trivial incident on the Somme.

"I tell ye, I was there," said the Cameron. "We were relievin' the Black Watch, and Fritz was shellin' the road, and we didna get up to the line till one o'clock in the mornin'. Frae Frickout Circus to the south end o' High Wood is every bit o' five mile."

"Not abune three," said the sapper dogmatically.

"Man, I've trampit it."

"Same here. I took up wire every nicht for a week."

The Cameron looked moodily round the company. "I wish there was anither man here that kent the place. He wad bear me out. These boys are no good, for they didna join till later. I tell ye it's five mile."

"Three," said the sapper.

Tempers were rising, for each of the disputants felt his veracity assailed. It was too hot for a quarrel, and I was so drowsy that I was heedless.

"Shut up, you fools," I said. "The distance is six kilometres, so you're both wrong."

"What's a kilometre, Mr. McCaskie?" Linklater asked blandly.

"Multiply by five and divide by eight and you get the miles."

I was on my guard now, and told a long story of a nephew who had been killed on the Somme, and how I had corresponded with the War Office about his case. "Besides," I said, "I'm a great student o' the newspapers, and I've read all the books about the war. It's a difficult time this for us all, and if you can take a serious interest in the campaign it helps a lot. I mean working out the places on the map and reading Haig's dispatches."

"Just so," he said drily, and I thought he watched me with an odd look in his eyes.

A fresh idea possessed me. This man had been in Gresson's company, he knew German, he was obviously something very different from what he professed to be. What if he were in the employ of our own Secret Service? I had appeared out of the void at the Kyle, and I had made but a poor appearance as a bagman, showing no knowledge of my own trade. I was in an area interdicted to the ordinary public, and he had good reason to keep an eye on my movements. He was going south, and so was I; clearly we must somehow part company.

"We change at Muirtown, don't we?" I asked. "When does the train for the south leave?"

He consulted a pocket time-table. "Ten-thirty-three. There's generally four hours to wait, for we're due in at six-fifteen. But this auld hearse will be lucky if it's in by nine."

His forecast was correct. We rumbled out of the hills into haughlands and caught a glimpse of the North Sea. Then we were hung up while a long goods train passed down the line. It was almost dark when at last we crawled into Muirtown station and disgorged our load of hot and weary soldiery.

I bade an ostentatious farewell to Linklater. "Very pleased to have met you. I'll see you later on the Edinburgh train. I'm for a walk to stretch my legs, and a bite o' supper." I was very determined that the ten-thirty for the south should leave without me.

My notion was to get a bed and a meal in some secluded inn, and walk out next morning and pick up a slow train down the line. Linklater had disappeared towards the guard's van to find his luggage, and the soldiers were sitting on their packs with that air of being utterly and finally lost and neglected which characterizes the British fighting-man on a journey. I gave up my ticket and, since I had come off a northern train, walked unhindered into the town.

It was market night, and the streets were crowded. Bluejackets from the Fleet, country folk in to shop, and every kind of military detail thronged the pavements. Fish hawkers were crying their wares, and there was a tatterdemalion piper making the night hideous at a corner. I took a tortuous route and finally fixed on a modest-looking public-house in a back street. When I inquired for a room I could find no one in authority, but a slatternly girl informed me that there was one vacant bed, and that I could have ham and eggs in the bar. So, after hitting my head violently against a cross-beam, I stumbled down some steps and entered a frowsty little place smelling of spilt beer and stale tobacco.

The promised ham and eggs proved impossible—there were no eggs to be had in Muirtown that night—but I was given cold mutton and a pint of indifferent ale. There was nobody in the place but two farmers drinking hot whisky and water and discussing with sombre interest the rise in the price of feeding-stuffs. I ate my supper, and was just preparing to find the where-abouts of my bedroom when through the street door there entered a dozen soldiers.

In a second the quiet place became a babel. The men were strictly sober, but they were in that temper of friendliness which demands a libation of some kind. One was prepared to stand treat; he was the leader of the lot, and it was to celebrate the end of his leave that he was entertaining his pals. From where I sat I could not see him, but his voice was dominant. "What's your fancy, Jock? Beer for you, Andra? A pint and a dram for me. This is better than vongblong and vongrooge, Davie. Man, when I'm sittin' in those estamints, as they ca' them, I often long for a guid Scots public."

The voice was familiar. I shifted my seat to get a view of the speaker, and then I hastily drew back. It was the Scots Fusilier I had clipped on the jaw in defending Gresson after the Glasgow meeting.

But by a strange fatality he had caught sight of me.

"Whae's that i' the corner?" he cried, leaving the bar to stare at me. Now it is a queer thing, but if you have once fought with a man, though only for a few seconds, you remember his face, and the scrap in Glasgow had been under a lamp. The Jock recognized me well enough.

"By God!" he cried, "if this is no a bit o' luck! Boys, here's the man I feucht wi' in Glesca. Ye mind I telled ye about it. He laid me oot, and it's my turn to do the same wi' him. I had a notion I was gaun to mak' a night o't. There's naebody can hit Geordie Hamilton without Geordie gettin' his ain back some day. Get up, man, for I'm gaun to knock the heid off ye."

I duly got up, and with the best composure I could muster looked him in the face.

"You're mistaken, my friend. I never clapped eyes on you before, and I was never in Glasgow in my life."

"That's a damned lee," said the Fusilier. "Ye're the man, and if ye're no, ye're like enough him to need a hidin'!"

"Confound your nonsense!" I said. "I've no quarrel with you, and I've better things to do than be scrapping with a stranger in a public-house."

"Have ye sae? Well, I'll learn ye better. I'm gaun to hit ye, and then ye'll hae to fecht whether ye want it or no. Tam, haud my jacket, and see that my drink's no skailed."

This was an infernal nuisance, for a row here would bring in the police, and my dubious position would be laid bare. I thought of putting up a fight, for I was certain I could lay out the Jock a second time, but the worst of that was that I did not know where the thing would end. I might have to fight the lot of them, and that meant a noble public shindy. I did my best to speak my opponent fair. I said we were all good friends and offered to stand drinks for the party. But the Fusilier's blood was up and he was spoiling for a row, ably abetted by his comrades. He had his tunic off now, and was stamping in front of me with doubled fists.

I did the best thing I could think of in the circumstances. My seat was close to the steps which led to the other part of the inn. I grabbed my hat, darted up them, and before they realized what I was doing had bolted the door behind me. I could hear pandemonium break loose in the bar.

I slipped down a dark passage to another which ran at right angles to it, and which seemed to connect the street door of the inn itself with the back premises. I could hear voices in the little hall, and that stopped me short.

One of them was Linklater's, but he was not talking as Linklater had talked. He was speaking educated English. I heard another with a Scots accent, which I took to be the landlord's, and a third which sounded like some superior sort of constable's, very prompt and official. I heard one phrase, too, from Linklater—"He calls himself McCaskie." Then they stopped, for the turmoil from the bar had reached the front door. The Fusilier and his friends were looking for me by the other entrance.

The attention of the men in the hall was distracted, and that gave me a chance. There was nothing for it but the back door. I slipped through it into a courtyard and almost tumbled over a tub of water. I planted the thing so that any one coming that way would fall over it. A door led me into an empty stable, and from that into a lane. It was all absurdly easy, but as I started down the lane I heard a mighty row and the sound of angry voices. Some one had gone into the tub and I hoped it was Linklater. I had taken a liking to the Fusilier Jock.

There was the beginning of a moon somewhere, but that lane was very dark. I ran to the left, for on the right it looked like a *cul-de-sac*. This brought me into a quiet road of two-storied cottages which showed at one end the lights of a street. So I took the other way, for I wasn't going to have the whole population of Muirtown on the hue-and-cry after me. I came into a country lane, and I also came into the van of the pursuit, which must have taken a short cut. They shouted when they saw me, but I had a small start, and legged it down that road in the belief that I was making for open country.

That was where I was wrong. The road took me round to the other side of the town, and just when I was beginning to think I had a fair chance I saw before me the lights of a signal-box and a little to the left of it the lights of the station. In half an hour's time the Edinburgh train would be leaving, but I had made that impossible. Behind me I could hear the pursuers, giving tongue like hound puppies, for they had attracted some pretty drunken gentlemen to their party.

I was badly puzzled where to turn, when I noticed outside the station a long line of blurred lights, which could only mean a train with the carriage blinds down. It had an engine attached, and seemed to be waiting for the addition of a couple of trucks to start. It was a wild chance, but the only one I saw. I scrambled across a piece of waste ground, climbed an embankment, and found myself on the metals. I ducked under the couplings and got on the far side of the train, away from the enemy.

Then simultaneously two things happened. I heard the yells of my pursuers a dozen yards off, and the train jolted into motion. I jumped on the footboard, and looked into an open window. The compartment was packed with troops, six a side and two men sitting on the floor, and the door was locked. I dived headforemost through the window and landed on the neck of a weary warrior who had just dropped off to sleep.

While I was falling I made up my mind on my conduct. I must be intoxicated, for I knew the infinite sympathy of the British soldier towards those thus overtaken. They pulled me to my feet, and the man I had descended on rubbed his skull and blasphemously demanded explanations.

"Gen'lmen," I hiccoughed, "I 'pologize. I was late for this bl—blighted train and I mus' be in E'inburgh 'morrow or I'll get the sack. I 'pologize. If I've hurt my friend's head, I'll kiss it, and make it well."

At this there was a great laugh. "Ye'd better accept, Pete," said one. "It's the first time onybody ever offered to kiss your ugly heid."

A man asked me who I was, and I appeared to be searching for a card-case.

"Losht," I groaned. "Losht, and so's my wee bag and I've bashed my po' hat. I'm an awful sight, gen'lmen—an awful warning to be in time for trains. I'm John Johnstone, managing clerk to Messrs. Watters, Brown & Elph'stone, 923 Charl'tte Street, E'inburgh. I've been up north seein' my mamma."

"Ye should be in France," said one man.

"Wisht I was, but they wouldn't let me. 'Mr. Johnstone,' they said, 'ye're no dam good. Ye've var'cose veins and a bad heart,' they said. So I says, 'Good-mornin', gen'lmen. Don't blame me if the country's ru'ned.' That's what I said."

I had by this time occupied the only remaining space left on the floor. With the philosophy of their race the men had accepted my presence, and were turning again to their own talk. The train had got up speed, and as I judged it to be a special of some kind I looked for few stoppings. Moreover it was not a corridor carriage, but one of the old-fashioned kind, so I was safe for a time from the unwelcome attention of conductors. I stretched my legs below the seat, rested my head against the knees of a brawny gunner, and settled down to make the best of it.

My reflections were not pleasant. I had got down too far below the surface, and had the naked feeling you get in a dream when you think you have gone to the theatre in your nightgown. I had had three names in two days, and as many characters. I felt as if I had no home or position anywhere, and was only a stray dog with everybody's hand and foot against me. It was an ugly sensation, and it was not redeemed by any acute fear or any knowledge of being mixed up in some desperate drama. I knew I could easily go on to Edinburgh, and when the police made trouble, as they would, a wire to Scotland Yard would settle matters in a couple of hours. There wasn't a suspicion of bodily danger to restore my dignity. The worst that could happen would be that Ivery would hear of my being befriended by the authorities, and then the part I had settled to play would be impossible. He would certainly hear. I had the greatest respect for his intelligence service.

Yet that was bad enough. So far I had done well. I had put Gresson off the scent. I had found out what Blenkiron wanted to know, and I had only to return unostentatiously to London to have won out on the game. I told myself all that, but it didn't cheer my spirits. I was feeling mean and hunted and very cold about the feet.

But I have a tough knuckle of obstinacy in me which makes me unwilling to give up a thing till I am fairly choked off it. The chances were badly against me. The Scottish police were actively interested in my movements and would be ready to welcome me at my journey's end. I had ruined my hat, and my clothes, as Amos had observed, were not respectable. I had got rid of a four-day's beard the night before, but had cut myself in the process, and what with my weather-beaten face and tangled hair looked liker a tinker than a decent bagman. I thought with longing of my portmanteau in the Pentland Hotel, Edinburgh, and the neat blue serge suit and the clean linen that reposed in it. It was no case for a subtle game, for I held no cards. Still I was determined not to chuck in my hand till I was forced to. If the train stopped anywhere I would get out, and trust to my own wits and the standing luck of the British Army for the rest.

The chance came just after dawn, when we halted at a little junction. I got up yawning and tried to open the door, till I remembered it was locked. Thereupon I stuck my legs out of the window on the side away from the platform, and was immediately seized upon by a sleepy Seaforth, who thought I contemplated suicide.

"Let me go," I said. "I'll be back in a jiffy."

"Let him gang, Jock," said another voice. "Ye ken what a man's like when he's been on the bash. The cauld air'll sober him."

I was released, and after some gymnastics dropped on the metals and made my way round the rear of the train. As I clambered on the platform the train began to move, and a face looked out of one of the back carriages. It was Linklater, and he recognized me. He tried to get out, but the door was promptly slammed to by an indignant porter. I heard him protest, and he kept his head out till the train went round the curve. That cooked my goose all right. He would wire to the police from the next station.

Meantime in that clean, bare, chilly place there was only one traveller. He was a slim young man, with a kit-bag and a gun-case. His clothes were beautiful, a green Homburg hat, a smart green tweed overcoat, and boots as brightly polished as a horse chestnut. I caught his profile as he gave up his ticket, and to my amazement I recognized it.

The station-master looked askance at me as I presented myself, dilapidated and dishevelled, to the official gaze. I tried to speak in a tone of authority.

"Who is the man who has just gone out?"

"Whaur's your ticket?"

"I had no time to get one at Muirtown, and as you see I have left my luggage behind me. Take it out of that pound and I'll come back for the change. I want to know if that was Sir Archibald Roylance."

He looked suspiciously at the note. "I think that's the name. He's a captain up at the Fleein' School. What was ye wantin' with him?"

I charged through the booking-office and found my man about to enter a big grey motor-car.

"Archie," I cried and beat him on the shoulders.

He turned round sharply. "What the devil—! Who are you?" And then recognition crept into his face and he gave a joyous shout. "My holy aunt! The General disguised as Charlie Chaplin! Can I drive you anywhere, sir?"

41   I TAKE THE WINGS OF A DOVE

"Drive me somewhere to breakfast, Archie," I said, "for I'm perishing hungry."

He and I got into the tonneau, and the driver swung us out of the station road up a long incline of hill. Sir Archie had been one of my subalterns in the old Lennox Highlanders, and had left us before the Somme to join the Flying Corps. I had heard that he had got his wings and had done well before Arras, and was now training pilots at home. He had been a light-hearted youth, who had endured a good deal of rough-tonguing from me for his sins of omission. But it was the casual class of lad I was looking for now.

I saw him steal amused glances at my appearance.

"Been seein' a bit of life, sir?" he inquired respectfully.

"I'm being hunted by the police," I said.

"Dirty dogs! But don't worry, sir; we'll get you off all right. I've been in the same fix myself. You can lie snug in my little log hut, for that old image Gibbons won't blab. Or, tell you what, I've got an aunt who lives near here and she's a bit of a sportsman. You can hide in her moated grange till the bobbies get tired."

I think it was Archie's calm acceptance of my position as natural and becoming that restored my good temper. He was far too well bred to ask what crime I had committed, and I didn't propose to enlighten him much. But as we swung up the moorland road I let him know that I was serving the Government, but that it was necessary that I should appear to be unauthenticated and that therefore I must dodge the police. He whistled his appreciation.

"Gad, that's a deep game. Sort of camouflage? Speaking from my own experience it is easy to overdo that kind of stunt. When I was at Misieux the French started out to camouflage the caravans where they keep their pigeons, and they did it so darned well that the poor little birds couldn't hit 'em off, and spent the night out."

We entered the white gates of a big aerodrome, skirted a forest of tents and huts, and drew up at a shanty on the far confines of the place. The hour was half-past four, and the world was still asleep. Archie nodded towards one of the hangars, from the mouth of which projected the propeller end of an aeroplane.

"I'm by way of flyin' that bus down to Farnton to-morrow," he remarked. "It's the new Shark-Gladas. Got a mouth like a tree."

An idea flashed into my mind.

"You're going this morning," I said.

"How did you know?" he exclaimed. "I'm due to go to-day, but the grouse up in Caithness wanted shootin' so badly that I decided to wangle another day's leave. They can't expect a man to start for the south of England when he's just off a frowsy journey."

"All the same you're going to be a stout fellow and start in two hours' time. And you're going to take me with you."

He stared blankly, and then burst into a roar of laughter. "You're the man to go tiger-shootin' with. But what price my commandant? He's not a bad chap, but a trifle shaggy about the fetlocks. He won't appreciate the joke."

"He needn't know. He mustn't know. This is an affair between you and me till it's finished. I promise you I'll make it all square with the Flying Corps. Get me down to Farnton before evening, and you'll have done a good piece of work for the country."

"Right-o! Let's have a tub and bit of breakfast, and then I'm your man. I'll tell them to get the bus ready."

In Archie's bedroom I washed and shaved and borrowed a green tweed cap and a brand-new aquascutum. The latter covered the deficiencies of my raiment, and when I commandeered a pair of gloves I felt almost respectable. Gibbons, who seemed to be a jack-of-all-trades, cooked us some bacon and an omelette, and as he ate Archie yarned. In the battalion his conversation had been mostly of race meetings and the forsaken delights of town, but now he had forgotten all that, and, like every good airman I have ever known, wallowed enthusiastically in "shop." I have a deep respect for the Flying Corps, but it is apt to change its jargon every month, and its conversation is hard for the layman to follow. He was desperately keen about the war, which he saw wholly from the viewpoint of the air. Arras to him was over before the infantry crossed the top, and the tough bit of the Somme was October, not September. He calculated that the big air fighting had not come along yet, and all he hoped for was to be allowed out to France to have his share in it. Like all good airmen, too, he was very modest about himself.

"I've done a bit of steeple-chasin' and huntin' and I've good hands for a horse, so I can handle a bus fairly well. It's all a matter of hands, you know. There ain't half the risk of the infantry down below you, and a million times the fun. Jolly glad I changed, sir."

We talked of Peter, and he put him about top. Voss, he thought, was the only Boche that could compare with him, for he hadn't made up his mind about Lensch. The Frenchman Guynemer he ranked high, but in a different way. I remember he had no respect for Richthofen and his celebrated circus.

At six sharp we were ready to go. A couple of mechanics had got out the machine, and Archie put on his coat and gloves and climbed into the pilot's seat, while I squeezed in behind in the observer's place. The aerodrome was waking up, but I saw no officers about. We were scarcely seated when Gibbons called our attention to a motor-car on the road, and presently we heard a shout and saw men waving in our direction.

"Better get off, my lad," I said. "These look like my friends."

The engine started and the mechanics stood clear. As we taxied over the turf I looked back and saw several figures running in our direction. The next second we had left the bumpy earth for the smooth highroad of the air.

I had flown several dozen times before, generally over the enemy lines when I wanted to see for myself how the land lay. Then we had flown low, and been nicely dusted by the Hun Archies, not to speak of an occasional machine gun. But never till that hour had I realized the joy of a straight flight in a swift plane in perfect weather. Archie didn't lose time. Soon the hangars behind looked like a child's toys, and the world ran away from us till it seemed like a great golden bowl spilling over with the quintessence of light. The air was cold and my hands numbed, but I never felt them. As we throbbed and tore southward, sometimes bumping in eddies, sometimes swimming evenly in a stream of motionless ether, my head and heart grew as light as a boy's. I forgot all about the vexations of my job and saw only its joyful comedy. I didn't think that anything on earth could worry me again. Far to the left was a wedge of silver and beside it a cluster of toy houses. That must be Edinburgh, where reposed my portmanteau, and where a most efficient police force was now inquiring for me. At the thought I laughed so loud that Archie must have heard me. He turned round, saw my grinning face, and grinned back. Then he signalled to me to strap myself in. I obeyed, and he proceeded to practise "stunts"—the loop, the spinning nose-dive, and others I didn't know the names of. It was glorious fun, and he handled his machine as a good rider coaxes a nervous horse over a stiff hurdle. He had that extra something in his blood that makes the pilot.

Presently the chessboard of green and brown had changed to a deep purple with faint silvery lines like veins in a rock. We were crossing the Border hills, the place where I had legged it for weary days when I was mixed up in the Black Stone business. What a marvellous element was this air, which took one far above the fatigues of humanity! Archie had done well to change. Peter had been the wise man. I felt a tremendous pity for my old friend hobbling about a German prison-yard, when he had once flown like a hawk. I reflected that I had wasted my life hitherto. And then I remembered that all this glory had only one use in war, and that was to help the muddy British infantryman to down his Hun opponent. He was the fellow, after all, that decided battles, and the thought comforted me.

A great exhilaration is often the precursor of disaster, and mine was to have a sudden downfall. It was getting on for noon and we were well into England—I guessed from the rivers we had passed that we were somewhere in the north of Yorkshire—when the machine began to make odd sounds, and we bumped in perfectly calm patches of air. We dived and then climbed, but the confounded thing kept sputtering. Archie passed back a slip of paper on which he had scribbled: "Engine conked. Must land at Micklegill. Very sorry." So we dropped to a lower elevation where we could see clearly the houses and roads and the long swelling ridges of a moorland country. I could never have found my way about, but Archie's practised eye knew every landmark. We were trundling along very slowly now, and even I was soon able to pick up the hangars of a big aerodrome.

We made Micklegill, but only by the skin of our teeth. We were so low that the smoky chimneys of the city of Bradfield seven miles to the east were half hidden by a ridge of down. Archie achieved a clever descent in the lee of a belt of firs, and got out full of imprecations against the Gladas engine. "I'll go up to the camp and report," he said, "and send mechanics down to tinker this darned gramophone. You'd better go for a walk, sir. I don't want to answer questions about you till we're ready to start. I reckon it'll be an hour's job."

The cheerfulness I had acquired in the upper air still filled me. I sat down in a ditch, as merry as a sandboy, and lit a pipe. I was possessed by a boyish spirit of casual adventure, and waited on the next turn of fortune's wheel with only a pleasant amusement.

That turn was not long in coming. Archie appeared very breathless.

"Look here, sir, there's the deuce of a row up there. They've been wirin' about you all over the country, and they know you're with me. They've got the police, and they'll have you in five minutes if you don't leg it. I lied like billy-o and said I had never heard of you, but they're comin' to see for themselves. For God's sake get off. . . . You'd better keep in cover down that hollow and round the back of these trees. I'll stay here and try to brazen it out. I'll get strafed to blazes anyhow. . . . I hope you'll get me out of the scrape, sir."

"Don't you worry, my lad," I said. "I'll make it all square when I get back to town. I'll make for Bradfield, for this place is a bit conspicuous. Good-bye, Archie. You're a good chap and I'll see you don't suffer."

I started off down a hollow of the moor, trying to make speed atone for lack of strategy, for it was hard to know how much my pursuers commanded from that higher ground. They must have seen me, for I heard whistles blown and men's cries. I struck a road, crossed it, and passed a ridge from which I had a view of Bradfield six miles off. And as I ran I began to reflect that this kind of chase could not last long. They were bound to round me up in the next half-hour unless I could puzzle them. But in that bare green place there was no cover, and it looked as if my chances were pretty much those of a hare coursed by a good greyhound on a naked moor.

Suddenly from just in front of me came a familiar sound. It was the roar of guns—the slam of field batteries and the boom of small howitzers. I wondered if I had gone off my head. As I plodded on the rattle of machine guns was added, and over the ridge before me I saw the dust and fumes of bursting shells. I concluded that I was not mad, and that therefore the Germans must have landed. I crawled up the last slope, quite forgetting the pursuit behind me.

And then I'm blessed if I did not look down on a veritable battle.

There were two sets of trenches with barbed wire and all the fixings, one set filled with troops and the other empty. On these latter shells were bursting, but there was no sign of life in them. In the other lines there seemed the better part of two brigades, and the front trench was stiff with bayonets. My first thought was that Home Forces had gone dotty, for this kind of show could have no sort of training value. And then I saw other things—cameras and camera men on platforms on the flanks, and men with megaphones behind them on wooden scaffoldings. One of the megaphones was going full blast all the time.

I saw the meaning of the performance at last. Some movie merchant had got a graft with the Government, and troops had been turned out to make a war film. It occurred to me that if I were mixed up in that push I might get the cover I was looking for. I scurried down the hill to the nearest camera man.

As I ran, the first wave of troops went over the top. They did it uncommon well, for they entered into the spirit of the thing, and went over with grim faces and that slow, purposeful lope that I had seen in my own fellows at Arras. Smoke grenades burst among them, and now and then some resourceful mountebank would roll over. Altogether it was about the best show I have ever seen. The cameras clicked, the guns banged, a background of boy scouts applauded, and the dust rose in billows to the sky.

But all the same something was wrong. I could imagine that this kind of business took a good deal of planning from the point of view of the movie merchant, for his purpose was not the same as that of the officer in command. You know how a photographer finicks about and is dissatisfied with a pose that seems all right to his sitter. I should have thought the spectacle enough to get any cinema audience off their feet, but the man on the scaffolding near me judged differently. He made his megaphone boom like the swan-song of a dying buffalo. He wanted to change something and didn't know how to do it. He hopped on one leg; he took the megaphone from his mouth to curse, he waved it like a banner and yelled at some opposite number on the other flank. And then his patience forsook him and he skipped down the ladder, dropping his megaphone, past the camera men, on to the battlefield.

That was his undoing. He got in the way of the second wave and was swallowed up like a leaf in a torrent. For a moment I saw a red face and a loud-checked suit, and the rest was silence. He was carried on over the hill, or rolled into an enemy trench, but anyhow he was lost to my ken.

I bagged his megaphone and hopped up the steps to the platform. At last I saw a chance of first-class cover, for with Archie's coat and cap I made a very good appearance as a movie merchant. Two waves had gone over the top, and the cinema men, working like beavers, had filmed the lot. But there was still a fair amount of troops to play with, and I determined to tangle up that outfit so that the fellows who were after me would have better things to think about.

My advantage was that I knew how to command men. I could see that my opposite number with the megaphone was helpless, for the mistake which had swept my man into a shell-hole had reduced him to impotence. The troops seemed to be mainly in charge of N.C.O.'s (I could imagine that the officers would try to shirk this business), and an N.C.O. is the most literal creature on earth. So with my megaphone I proceeded to change the battle order.

I brought up the third wave to the front trenches. In about three minutes the men had recognized the professional touch and were moving smartly to my orders. They thought it was part of the show, and the obedient cameras clicked at everything that came into their orbit. My aim was to deploy the troops on too narrow a front so that they were bound to fan outward, and I had to be quick about it, for I didn't know when the hapless movie merchant might be retrieved from the battlefield and dispute my authority.

It takes a long time to straighten a thing out, but it does not take long to tangle it, especially when the thing is so delicate a machine as disciplined troops. In about eight minutes I had produced chaos. The flanks spread out, in spite of all the shepherding of the N.C.O.'s, and the fringe engulfed the photographers. The cameras on their little platforms went down like ninepins. It was solemn to see the startled face of a photographer, taken unawares, supplicating the purposeful infantry, before he was swept off his feet into speechlessness.

It was no place for me to linger in, so I chucked away the megaphone and got mixed up with the tail of the third wave. I was swept on and came to anchor in the enemy trenches, where I found, as I expected, my profane and breathless predecessor, the movie merchant. I had nothing to say to him, so I stuck to the trench till it ended against the slope of the hill.

On that flank, delirious with excitement, stood a knot of boy scouts. My business was to get to Bradfield as quick as my legs would take me, and as inconspicuously as the gods would permit. Unhappily I was far too great an object of interest to that nursery of heroes. Every boy scout is an amateur detective and hungry for knowledge. I was followed by several, who plied me with questions, and were told that I was off to Bradfield to hurry up part of the cinema outfit. It sounded lame enough, for that cinema outfit was already past praying for.

We reached the road and against a stone wall stood several bicycles. I selected one and prepared to mount.

"That's Mr. Emmott's machine," said one boy sharply. "He told me to keep an eye on it."

"I must borrow it, sonny," I said. "Mr. Emmott's my very good friend and won't object."

From the place where we stood I overlooked the back of the battlefield, and could see an anxious congress of officers. I could see others, too, whose appearance I did not like. They had not been there when I operated on the megaphone. They must have come downhill from the aerodrome, and in all likelihood were the pursuers I had avoided. The exhilaration which I had won in the air and which had carried me into the tomfoolery of the past half-hour was ebbing. I had the hunted feeling once more, and grew middle-aged and cautious. I had a baddish record for the day, what with getting Archie into a scrape and bursting up an official cinema show—neither consistent with the duties of a brigadier-general. Besides, I had still to get to London.

I had not gone two hundred yards down the road when a boy scout, pedalling furiously, came up abreast of me.

"Colonel Edgeworth wants to see you," he panted. "You're to come back at once."

"Tell him I can't wait now," I said. "I'll pay my respects to him in an hour."

"He said you were to come at once," said the faithful messenger. "He's in an awful temper with you, and he's got bobbies with him."

I put on pace and left the boy behind. I reckoned I had the better part of two miles' start and could beat anything except petrol. But my enemies were bound to have cars, so I had better get off the road as soon as possible. I coasted down a long hill to a bridge which spanned a small discoloured stream that flowed in a wooded glen. There was nobody for the moment on the hill behind me, so I nipped into the covert, shoved the bicycle under the bridge, and hid Archie's aquascutum in a bramble thicket. I was now in my own disreputable duds, and I hoped that the shedding of my most conspicuous garment would puzzle my pursuers if they should catch up with me.

But this I was determined they should not do. I made good going down that stream and out into a lane which led from the downs to the market gardens round the city. I thanked Heaven I had got rid of the aquascutum, for the August afternoon was warm and my pace was not leisurely. When I was in secluded ground I ran, and when any one was in sight I walked smartly.

As I went I reflected that Bradfield would see the end of my adventures. The police knew that I was there, and would watch the stations and hunt me down if I lingered in the place. I knew no one there and had no chance of getting an effective disguise. Indeed, I very soon began to wonder if I should get even as far as the streets. For at the moment when I had got a lift on the back of a fishmonger's cart and was screened by its flapping canvas, two figures passed on motor-bicycles, and one of them was the inquisitive boy scout. The main road from the aerodrome was probably now being patrolled by motor-cars. It looked as if there would be a degrading arrest in one of the suburbs.

The fish-cart, helped by half a crown to the driver, took me past the outlying small-villadom, between long lines of workmen's houses, to narrow cobbled lanes and the purlieus of great factories. As soon as I saw the streets well crowded I got out and walked. In my old clothes I must have appeared like some second-class bookie or seedy horse-coper. The only respectable thing I had about me was my gold watch. I consulted it and found the time half-past five.

I wanted food, and was casting about for an eating-house when I heard the purr of a motor-cycle and across the road saw the intelligent boy scout. He saw me, too, and put on the brake with a sharpness which caused him to skid and all but come to grief under the wheels of a wool-wagon. That gave me time to efface myself by darting up a side street. I had an unpleasant sense that I was about to be trapped, for in a place I knew nothing of I had not a chance to use my wits.

I remember trying feverishly to think, and I suppose that my preoccupation made me careless. I was now in a veritable slum, and when I put my hand to my vest pocket I found that my watch had gone.

That put the top stone on my depression. The reaction from the wild humour of the forenoon had left me very cold about the feet. I was getting into the underworld again, and there was no chance of a second Archie Roylance turning up to rescue me. I remember yet the sour smell of the factories and the mist of smoke in the evening air. It is a smell I have never met since without a sort of dulling of spirit.

Presently I came out into a market-place. Whistles were blowing, and there was a great hurrying of people back from the mills. The crowd gave me a momentary sense of security, and I was just about to inquire my way to the railway station when some one jostled my arm.

A rough-looking fellow in mechanic's clothes was beside me.

"Mate," he whispered, "I've got summat o' yours here." And to my amazement he slipped my watch into my hand.

"It was took by mistake. We're friends o' yours. You're right enough if you do what I tell you. There's a peeler over there got his eye on you. Follow me and I'll get you off."

I didn't much like the man's looks, but I had no choice, and anyhow he had given me back my watch. He sidled into an alley between tall houses and I sidled after him. There he took to his heels, and led me a twisting course through smelly courts into a tanyard and then by a narrow lane to the backquarters of a factory. Twice we doubled back, and once we climbed a wall and followed the bank of a blue-black stream with a filthy scum on it. Then we got into a very mean quarter of the town, and emerged in a dingy garden, strewn with tin cans and broken flower-pots. By a back door we entered one of the cottages and my guide very carefully locked it behind him.

He lit the gas and drew the blinds in a small parlour and looked at me long and quizzically. He spoke now in an educated voice.

"I ask no questions," he said, "but it's my business to put my services at your disposal. You carry the passport."

I stared at him, and he pulled out his watch and showed a white-and-purple cross inside the lid.

"I don't defend all the people we employ," he said, grinning. "Men's morals are not always as good as their patriotism. One of them pinched your watch, and when he saw what was inside it he reported to me. We soon picked up your trail, and observed you were in a bit of trouble. As I say, I ask no questions. What can we do for you?"

"I want to get to London without any questions asked. They're looking for me in my present rig, so I've got to change it."

"That's easy enough," he said. "Make yourself comfortable for a little and I'll fix you up. The night train goes at eleven-thirty. . . . You'll find cigars in the cupboard and there's this week's *Critic* on that table. It's got a good article on Conrad, if you care for such things."

I helped myself to a cigar and spent a profitable half-hour reading about the vices of the British Government. Then my host returned and bade me ascend to his bedroom. "You're Private Henry Tomkins of the 12th Gloucesters, and you'll find your clothes ready for you. I'll send on your present togs if you give me an address."

I did as I was bid, and presently emerged in the uniform of a British private, complete down to the shapeless boots and the dropsical puttees. Then my friend took me in hand and finished the transformation. He started on my hair with scissors and arranged a lock which, when well oiled, curled over my forehead. My hands were hard and rough, and only needed some grubbiness and hacking about the nails to pass muster. With my cap on the side of my head, a pack on my back, a service rifle in my hands, and my pockets bursting with penny picture papers, I was the very model of the British soldier returning from leave. I had also a packet of Woodbine cigarettes and a hunch of bread-and-cheese for the journey. And I had a railway warrant made out in my name for London.

Then my friend gave me supper—bread and cold meat and a bottle of Bass, which I wolfed savagely, for I had had nothing since breakfast. He was a curious fellow, as discreet as a tombstone, very ready to speak about general subjects, but never once coming near the intimate business which had linked him and me and Heaven knew how many others by means of a little purple-and-white cross in a watch-case. I remember we talked about the topics that used to be popular at Biggleswick—the big political things that begin with capital letters. He took Amos's view of the soundness of the British working man, but he said something which made me think. He was convinced that there was a tremendous lot of German spy work about, and that most of the practitioners were innocent. "The ordinary Briton doesn't run to treason, but he's not very bright. A clever man in that kind of game can make better use of a fool than of a rogue."

As he saw me off he gave me a piece of advice. "Get out of these clothes as soon as you reach London. Private Tomkins will frank you out of Bradfield, but it mightn't be a healthy *alias* in the metropolis."

At eleven-thirty I was safe in the train, talking the jargon of the returning soldier with half a dozen of my own type in a smoky third-class carriage. I had been lucky in my escape, for at the station entrance and on the platform I had noticed several men with the look of plain-clothes police. Also—though this may have been my fancy—I thought I caught in the crowd a glimpse of the bagman who had called himself Linklater.

42 THE ADVANTAGES OF AN AIR RAID

The train was abominably late. It was due at eight-twenty-seven, but it was nearly ten when we reached St. Pancras. I had resolved to go straight to my rooms in Westminster, buying on the way a cap and waterproof to conceal my uniform should any one be near my door on my arrival. Then I would ring up

Blenkiron and tell him all my adventures. I breakfasted at a coffee-stall, left my pack and rifle in the cloak-room, and walked out into the clear sunny morning.

I was feeling very pleased with myself. Looking back on my madcap journey, I seemed to have had an amazing run of luck and to be entitled to a little credit too. I told myself that persistence always pays and that nobody is beaten till he is dead. All Blenkiron's instructions had been faithfully carried out. I had found Ivery's post office, I had laid the lines of our own special communications with the enemy, and so far as I could see I had left no clue behind me. Ivery and Gresson took me for a well-meaning nincompoop. It was true that I had aroused profound suspicion in the breasts of the Scottish police. But that mattered nothing, for Cornelius Brand, the suspect, would presently disappear, and there was nothing against that rising soldier, Brigadier-General Richard Hannay, who would soon be on his way to France. After all this piece of service had not been so very unpleasant. I laughed when I remembered my grim forebodings in Gloucestershire. Bullivant had said it would be damnably risky in the long run, but here was the end and I had never been in danger of anything worse than making a fool of myself.

I remember that, as I made my way through Bloomsbury, I was not thinking so much of my triumphant report to Blenkiron as of my speedy return to the Front. Soon I would be with my beloved brigade again. I had missed Messines and the first part of Third Ypres, but the battle was still going on, and I had yet a chance. I might get a division, for there had been talk of that before I left. I knew the Army Commander thought a lot of me. But on the whole I hoped I would be left with the brigade. After all I was an amateur soldier, and I wasn't certain of my powers with a bigger command.

In Charing Cross Road I thought of Mary, and the brigade seemed suddenly less attractive. I hoped the war wouldn't last much longer, though with Russia heading straight for the devil I didn't know how it was going to stop very soon. I was determined to see Mary before I left, and I had a good excuse, for I had taken my orders from her. The prospect entranced me, and I was mooning along in a happy dream, when I collided violently with an agitated citizen.

Then I realized that something very odd was happening.

There was a dull sound like the popping of the corks of flat soda-water bottles. There was a humming, too, from very far up in the skies. People in the street were either staring at the heavens or running wildly for shelter. A motor-bus in front of me emptied its contents in a twinkling; a taxi pulled up with a jar and the driver and fare dived into a second-hand bookshop. It took me a moment or two to realize the meaning of it all, and I had scarcely done this when I got a very practical proof. A hundred yards away a bomb fell on a street island, shivering every window-pane in a wide radius, and sending splinters of stone flying about my head. I did what I had done a hundred times before at the Front, and dropped flat on my face.

The man who says he doesn't mind being bombed or shelled is either a liar or a maniac. This London air raid seemed to me a singularly unpleasant business. I think it was the sight of the decent civilized life around one and the orderly streets, for what was perfectly natural in a rubble-heap like Ypres or Arras seemed an outrage here. I remember once being in billets in a Flanders village where I had the Maire's house and sat in a room upholstered in cut velvet, with wax flowers on the mantelpiece and oil paintings of three generations on the walls. The Boche took it into his head to shell the place with a long-range naval gun, and I simply loathed it. It was horrible to have dust and splinters blow into that smug, homely room, whereas if I had been in a ruined barn I wouldn't have given the thing two thoughts. In the same way bombs dropping in central London seemed a grotesque indecency. I hated to see plump citizens with wild eyes, and nursemaids with scared children, and miserable women scuttling like rabbits in a warren.

The drone grew louder, and, looking up, I could see the enemy planes flying in a beautiful formation, very leisurely as it seemed, with all London at their mercy. Another bomb fell to the right, and presently bits of our own shrapnel were clattering viciously around me. I thought it about time to take cover, and ran shamelessly for the best place I could see, which was a Tube station. Five minutes before the street had been crowded; now I left behind me a desert dotted with one bus and three empty taxicabs.

I found the Tube entrance filled with excited humanity. One stout lady had fainted, and a girl had become hysterical, but on the whole people were behaving well. Oddly enough they did not seem inclined to go down the stairs to the complete security of underground; but preferred rather to collect where they could still get a glimpse of the upper world, as if they were torn between fear of their lives and interest in the spectacle. That crowd gave me a good deal of respect for my countrymen. But several were badly rattled, and one man a little way off, whose back was turned, kept twitching his shoulders as if he had colic.

I watched him curiously, and a movement of the crowd brought his face into profile. Then I gasped with amazement, for I saw that it was Ivery.

And yet it was not Ivery. There were the familiar nondescript features, the blandness, the plumpness, but all, so to speak, in ruins. The man was in a blind funk. His features seemed to be dislimning before my eyes. He was growing sharper, finer, in a way younger, a man without grip on himself, a shapeless creature in process of transformation. He was being reduced to his rudiments. Under the spell of panic he was becoming a new man.

And the crazy thing was that I knew the new man better than the old.

My hands were jammed close to my sides by the crowd; I could scarcely turn my head, and it was not the occasion for one's neighbours to observe one's expression. If it had been, mine must have been a study. My mind was far away from air raids, back in the hot summer weather of 1914. . . . I saw a row of villas perched on a headland above the sea. In the garden of one of them two men were playing tennis, while I was crouching behind an adjacent bush. One of these was a plump young man who wore a coloured scarf round his waist and babbled of golf handicaps. . . . I saw him again in the villa dining-room, wearing a dinner-jacket, and lisping a little. . . . I sat opposite him at bridge. I beheld him collared by two of Macgillivray's men, when his comrade had rushed for the thirty-nine steps that led to the sea. . . . I saw, too, the sitting-room of my old flat in Portland Place and heard little Scudder's quick, anxious voice talking about the three men he feared most on earth, one of whom lisped in his speech. I had thought that all three had long ago been laid under the turf. . . .

He was not looking my way, and I could devour his face in safety. There was no shadow of doubt. I had always put him down as the most amazing actor on earth, for had he not played the part of the First Sea Lord and deluded that officer's daily colleagues? But he could do far more than any human actor, for he could take on a new personality and with it a new appearance, and live steadily in the character as if he had been born in it. . . . My mind was a blank, and I could only make blind gropings at conclusions. . . . How had he escaped the death of a spy and a murderer, for I had last seen him in the hands of justice? . . . Of course he had known me from the first day in Biggleswick. . . . I had thought to play with him, and he had played most cunningly and damnably with me. In that sweating sardine-tin of refugees I shivered in the bitterness of my chagrin.

And then I found his face turned to mine, and I knew that he recognized me.

More, I knew that he knew that I had recognized him—not as Ivery, but as that other man. There came into his eyes a curious look of comprehension, which for a moment overcame his funk.

I had sense enough to see that that put the final lid on it. There was still something doing if he believed that I was blind, but if he once thought that I knew the truth he would be through our meshes and disappear like a fog.

My first thought was to get at him and collar him and summon everybody to help me by denouncing him for what he was. Then I saw that that was impossible. I was a private soldier in a borrowed uniform, and he could easily turn the story against me. I must use surer weapons. I must get to Bullivant and Macgillivray and set their big machine to work. Above all I must get to Blenkiron.

I started to squeeze out of that push, for air raids now seemed far too trival to give a thought to. Moreover the guns had stopped, but so sheeplike is human nature that the crowd still hung together, and it took me a good fifteen minutes to edge my way to the open air. I found that the trouble was over, and the street had resumed its usual appearance. Buses and taxis were running, and voluble knots of people were recounting their experiences. I started off for Blenkiron's bookshop, as the nearest harbour of refuge.

But in Piccadilly Circus I was stopped by a military policeman. He asked my name and battalion, and I gave him them, while his suspicious eye ran over my figure. I had no pack or rifle, and the crush in the Tube station had not improved my appearance. I explained that I was going back to France that evening, and he asked for my warrant. I fancy my preoccupation made me nervous and I lied badly. I said I had left it with my kit in the house of my married sister, but I fumbled in giving the address. I could see that the fellow did not believe a word I said.

Just then up came an A.P.M. He was a pompous dug-out, very splendid in his tabs and probably bucked up at having just been under fire. Anyhow he was out to walk in the strict path of duty.

"Tomkins!" he said. "Tomkins! We've got some fellow of that name on our records. Bring him along, Wilson."

"But, sir," I said, "I must—I simply must meet my friend. It's urgent business, and I assure you I'm all right. If you don't believe me, I'll take a taxi and we'll go down to Scotland Yard and I'll stand by what they say."

His brow grew dark with wrath. "What infernal nonsense is this? Scotland Yard! What the devil has Scotland Yard to do with it? You're an impostor. I can see it in your face. I'll have your depot rung up, and you'll be in gaol in a couple of hours. I know a deserter when I see him. Bring him along, Wilson. You know what to do if he tries to bolt."

I had a momentary thought of breaking away, but decided that the odds were too much against me. Fuming with impatience, I followed the A.P.M. to his office on the first floor in a side street. The precious minutes were slipping past; Ivery, now thoroughly warned, was making good his escape; and I, the sole repository of a deadly secret, was tramping in this absurd procession.

The A.P.M. issued his orders. He gave instructions that my depot should be rung up, and he bade Wilson remove me to what he called the guard-room. He sat down at his desk, and busied himself with a mass of buff dockets.

In desperation I renewed my appeal. "I implore you to telephone to Mr. Macgillivray at Scotland Yard. It's a matter of life and death, sir. You're taking a very big responsibility if you don't."

I had hopelessly offended his brittle dignity. "Any more of your insolence and I'll have you put in irons. I'll attend to you soon enough for your comfort. Get out of this till I send for you."

As I looked at his foolish, irritable face, I realized that I was fairly up against it. Short of assault and battery on everybody, I was bound to submit. I saluted respectfully and was marched away.

The hours I spent in that bare anteroom are like a nightmare in my recollection. A sergeant was busy at a desk with more buff dockets, and an orderly waited on a stool by a telephone. I looked at my watch and observed that it was one o'clock. Soon the slamming of a door announced that the A.P.M. had gone to lunch. I tried conversation with the fat sergeant, but he very soon shut me up. So I sat hunched upon the wooden form and chewed the cud of my vexation.

I thought with bitterness of the satisfaction which had filled me in the morning. I had fancied myself the devil of a fine fellow, and I had been no more than a mountebank. The adventures of the past days seemed merely childish. I had been telling lies and cutting over half Britain, thinking I was playing a deep game, and I had only been behaving like a schoolboy. On such occasions a man is rarely just to himself, and the intensity of my self-abasement would have satisfied my worst enemy. It didn't console me that the futility of it all was not my blame. I was not looking for excuses. It was the facts that cried out against me, and on the facts I had been an idiotic failure.

For of course Ivery had played with me, played with me since the first day at Biggleswick. He had applauded my speeches and flattered me, and advised me to go to the Clyde, laughing at me all the time. Gresson, too, had known. Now I saw it all. He had tried to drown me between Colonsay and Mull. It was Gresson who had set the police on me in Morvern. The bagman Linklater had been one of Gresson's creatures. The only meagre consolation was that the gang had thought me dangerous enough to attempt to murder me, and that they knew nothing about my doings in Skye. Of that I was positive. They had marked me down, but for several days I had slipped clean out of their ken.

As I went over all the incidents, I asked if everything was yet lost. I had failed to hoodwink Ivery, but I had found out his post office, and if he only believed I hadn't recognized him for the miscreant of the Black Stone he would go on in his old ways and play into Blenkiron's hands. Yes, but I had seen him in undress, so to speak, and he knew that I had so seen him. The only thing now was to collar him before he left the country, for there was ample evidence on which to hang him. The law must stretch out its long arm and collect him and Gresson and the Portuguese Jew, try them by court-martial, and put them decently underground.

But he had now had more than an hour's warning, and I was entangled with red tape in this accursed A.P.M.'s office. The thought drove me frantic, and I got up and paced the floor. I saw the orderly with rather a scared face making ready to press the bell, and I noticed that the fat sergeant had gone to lunch.

"Say, mate," I said, "don't you feel inclined to do a poor fellow a good turn? I know I'm for it all right, and I'll take my medicine like a lamb. But I want badly to put a telephone call through."

"It ain't allowed," was the answer. "I'd get 'ell from the old man."

"But he's gone out," I urged. "I don't want you to do anything wrong, mate. I leave you to do the talkin' if you'll only send my message. I'm flush of money, and I don't mind handin' you a quid for the job."

He was a pinched little man with a weak chin, and he obviously wavered.

"'Oo d'ye want to talk to?" he asked.

"Scotland Yard," I said, "the home of the police. Lord bless you, there can't be no harm in that. Ye've only got to ring up Scotland Yard—I'll give you the number—and give the message to Mr. Macgillivray. He's the head bummer of all the bobbies."

"That sounds a bit of all right," he said. "The old man 'e won't be back for 'alf an hour, nor the sergeant neither. Let's see your quid, though."

I laid a pound note on the form beside me. "It's yours, mate, if you get through to Scotland Yard and speak the piece I'm goin' to give you."

He went over to the instrument. "What d'you want to say to the bloke with the long name?"

"Say that Richard Hannay is detained at the A.P.M.'s office in Claxon Street. Say he's got important news—say urgent and secret news—and ask Mr. Macgillivray to do something about it at once."

"But 'Annay ain't the name you gave."

"Lord bless you, no. Did you never hear of a man borrowin' another name? Anyhow that's the one I want you to give."

"But if this Mac man comes round 'ere, they'll know 'e's bin rung up, and I'll 'ave the old man down on me."

It took ten minutes and a second pound note to get him past that hurdle. By and by he screwed up courage and rang up the number. I listened with some nervousness while he gave my message—he had to repeat it twice—and waited eagerly on the next words.

"No, sir," I heard him say, "'e don't want you to come round 'ere. 'E thinks as 'ow—I mean to say, 'e wants—"

I took a long stride and twitched the receiver from him.

"Macgillivray," I said, "is that you? Richard Hannay! For the love of God come round here this instant and deliver me from the clutches of a tomfool A.P.M. I've got the most deadly news. There's not a second to waste. For God's sake come quick!" Then I added: "Just tell your fellows to gather in Ivery at once. You know his lairs."

I hung up the receiver and faced a pale and indignant orderly. "It's all right," I said. "I promise you that you won't get into any trouble on my account. And there's your two quid."

The door in the next room opened and shut. The A.P.M. had returned from lunch. . . .

Ten minutes later the door opened again. I heard Macgillivray's voice, and it was not pitched in dulcet tones. He had run up against minor officialdom and was making hay with it.

I was my own master once more, so I forsook the company of the orderly. I found a most rattled officer trying to save a few rags of his dignity, and the formidable figure of Macgillivray instructing him in manners.

"Glad to see you, Dick," he said. "This is General Hannay, sir. It may comfort you to know that your folly may have made just the difference between your country's victory and defeat. I shall have a word to say to your superiors."

It was hardly fair. I had to put in a word for the old fellow, whose tabs seemed suddenly to have grown dingy.

"It was my blame wearing this kit. We'll call it a misunderstanding and forget it. But I would suggest that civility is not wasted even on a poor devil of a defaulting private soldier."

Once in Macgillivray's car, I poured out my tale. "Tell me it's a nightmare," I cried. "Tell me that the three men we collected on the Ruff were shot long ago."

"Two," he replied, "but one escaped. Heaven knows how he managed it, but he disappeared clean out of the world."

"The plump one who lisped in his speech?"

Macgillivray nodded.

"Well, we're in for it this time. Have you issued instructions?"

"Yes. With luck we shall have our hands on him within an hour. We've our net all round his haunts."

"But two hours' start! It's a big handicap, for you're dealing with a genius."

"Yet I think we can manage it. Where are you bound for?"

I told him my rooms in Westminster and then to my old flat in Park Lane. "The day of disguises is past. In half an hour I'll be Richard Hannay. It'll be a comfort to get into uniform again. Then I'll look up Blenkiron."

He grinned. "I gather you've had a riotous time. We've had a good many anxious messages from the north about a certain Mr. Brand. I couldn't discourage our men, for I fancied it might have spoiled your game. I heard that last night they had lost touch with you in Bradfield, so I rather expected to see you here to-day. Efficient body of men the Scottish police."

"Especially when they have various enthusiastic amateur helpers."

"So?" he said. "Yes, of course. They would have. But I hope presently to congratulate you on the success of your mission."

"I'll bet you a pony you don't," I said.

"I never bet on a professional subject. Why this pessimism?"

"Only that I know our gentleman better than you. I've been twice up against him. He's the kind of wicked that don't cease from troubling till they're stone-dead. And even then I'd want to see the body cremated and take the ashes into mid-ocean and scatter them. I've got a feeling that he's the biggest thing you or I will ever tackle."

43 THE VALLEY OF HUMILIATION

I collected some baggage and a pile of newly arrived letters from my rooms in Westminster and took a taxi to my Park Lane flat. Usually I had gone back to that old place with a great feeling of comfort, like a boy from school who ranges about his room at home and examines his treasures. I used to like to see my hunting trophies on the wall and to sink into my own arm-chair. But now I had no pleasure in the thing. I had a bath, and changed into uniform, and that made me feel in better fighting trim. But I suffered from a heavy conviction of abject failure, and had no share in Macgillivray's optimism. The awe with which the Black Stone gang had filled me three years before had revived a thousandfold. Personal humiliation was the least part of my trouble. What worried me was the sense of being up against something inhumanly formidable and wise and strong. I believe I was willing to own defeat and chuck up the game.

Among the unopened letters was one from Peter, a very bulky one which I sat down to read at leisure. It was a curious epistle, far the longest he had ever written me, and its size made me understand his loneliness. He was still at his German prison camp, but expecting every day to go to Switzerland. He said he could get back to England or South Africa, if he wanted, for they were clear that he could never be a combatant again; but he thought he had better stay in Switzerland, for he would be unhappy in England with all his friends fighting. As usual he made no complaints, and seemed to be very grateful for his small mercies. There was a doctor who was kind to him, and some good fellows among the prisoners.

But Peter's letter was made up chiefly of reflections. He had always been a bit of a philosopher, and now, in his isolation, he had taken to thinking hard, and poured out the results to me on pages of thin paper in his clumsy handwriting. I could read between the lines that he was having a stiff fight with himself. He was trying to keep his courage going in face of the bitterest trial he could be called on to face—a crippled old age. He had always known a good deal about the Bible, and that and the *Pilgrim's Progress* were his chief aids to reflection. Both he took quite literally, as if they were newspaper reports of actual recent events.

He mentioned that after much consideration he had reached the conclusion that the three greatest men he had ever heard of or met were Mr. Valiant-for-Truth, the Apostle Paul, and a certain Billy Strang who had been with him in Mashonaland in '92. Billy I knew all about; he had been Peter's hero and leader till a lion got him in the Blaauwberg. Peter preferred Valiant-for-Truth to Mr. Greatheart, I think because of his superior truculence, for, being very gentle himself, he loved a bold speaker. After that he dropped into a vein of self-examination. He regretted that he fell far short of any of the three. He thought that he might with luck resemble Mr. Standfast, for like him he had not much trouble in keeping wakeful, and was also as "poor as a howlet," and didn't bother about women. He only hoped that he could imitate him in making a good end.

Then followed some remarks of Peter's on courage, which came to me in that London room as if spoken by his living voice. I have never known any one so brave, so brave by instinct, or any one who hated so much to be told so. It was almost the only thing that could make him angry. All his life he had been facing death, and to take risks seemed to him as natural as to get up in the morning and eat his breakfast. But now he had started out to consider the very things which before he had taken for granted, and here is an extract from his conclusions. I paraphrase him, for he was not grammatical.

"It's easy enough to be brave if you're feeling well and have food inside you. And it's not so difficult even if you're short of a meal and seedy, for that makes you inclined to gamble. I mean by being brave playing the game by the right rules without letting it worry you that you may very likely get knocked on the head. It's

the wisest way to save your skin. It doesn't do to think about death if you're facing a charging lion or trying to bluff a lot of savages. If you think about it, you'll get it; if you don't, the odds are you won't. That kind of courage is only good nerves and experience. . . . Most courage is experience. Most people are a little scared at new things. . . .

"You want a bigger heart to face danger which you go out to look for, and which doesn't come to you in the ordinary way of business. Still, that's pretty much the same thing—good nerves and good health, and a natural liking for rows. You see, Dick, in all that game there's a lot of fun. There's excitement and the fun of using your wits and skill, and you know that the bad bits can't last long. When Arcoll sent me to Makapan's kraal I didn't altogether fancy the job, but at the worst it was three parts sport, and I got so excited that I never thought of the risk till it was over.

"But the big courage is the cold-blooded kind, the kind that never lets go even when you're feeling empty inside, and your blood's thin, and there's no kind of fun or profit to be had, and the trouble's not over in an hour or two but lasts for months and years. One of the men here was speaking about that kind, and he called it 'Fortitude.' I reckon fortitude's the biggest thing a man can have—just to go on enduring when there's no guts or heart left in you. Billy had it when he trekked solitary from Garungoze to the Limpopo with fever and a broken arm just to show the Portugooses that he wouldn't be downed by them. But the head man at the job was the Apostle Paul. . . ."

Peter was writing for his own comfort, for fortitude was all that was left to him now. But his words came pretty straight to me, and I read them again and again, for I needed the lesson. Here was I losing heart just because I had failed in the first round and my pride had taken a knock. I felt honestly ashamed of myself, and that made me a far happier man. There could be no question of dropping the business, whatever its difficulties. I had a queer religious feeling that Ivery and I had our fortunes intertwined, and that no will of mine could keep us apart. I had faced him before the war and won; I had faced him again and lost; the third time or the twentieth time we would reach a final decision. The whole business had hitherto appeared to me a trifle unreal, at any rate my own connection with it. I had been docilely obeying orders, but my real self had been standing aside and watching my doings with a certain aloofness. But that hour in the Tube station had brought me into the scrum, and I saw the affair not as Bullivant's or even Blenkiron's, but as my own. Before I had been itching to get back to the Front; now I wanted to get on to Ivery's trail, though it should take me through the nether pit. Peter was right: fortitude was the thing a man must possess if he would save his soul.

The hours passed, and, as I expected, there came no word from Macgillivray. I had some dinner sent up to me at seven o'clock, and about eight I was thinking of looking up Blenkiron. Just then came a telephone call asking me to go round to Sir Walter Bullivant's house in Queen Anne's Gate.

Ten minutes later I was ringing the bell, and the door was opened to me by the same impassive butler who had admitted me on that famous night three years before. Nothing had changed in the pleasant green-panelled hall; the alcove was the same as when I had watched from it the departure of the man who now called himself Ivery; the telephone book lay in the very place from which I had snatched it in order to ring up the First Sea Lord. And in the back room, where that night five anxious officials had conferred, I found Sir Walter and Blenkiron.

Both looked worried, the American feverishly so. He walked up and down the hearthrug, sucking an unlit black cigar.

"Say, Dick," he said, "this is a bad business. It wasn't no fault of yours. You did fine. It was us—me and Sir Walter and Mr. Macgillivray that were the quitters."

"Any news?" I asked.

"So far the cover's drawn blank," Sir Walter replied. "It was the devil's own work that our friend looked your way to-day. You're pretty certain he saw that you recognized him?"

"Absolutely. As sure as that he knew I recognized him in your hall three years ago when he was swaggering as Lord Alloa."

"No," said Blenkiron dolefully, "that little flicker of recognition is just the one thing you can't be wrong about. Land alive! I wish Mr. Macgillivray would come."

The bell rang, and the door opened, but it was not Macgillivray. It was a young girl in a white ball-gown, with a cluster of blue cornflowers at her breast. The sight of her fetched Sir Walter out of his chair so suddenly that he upset his coffee cup.

"Mary, my dear, how did you manage it? I didn't expect you till the late train."

"I was in London, you see, and they telephoned on your telegram. I'm staying with Aunt Doria, and I cut her theatre party. She thinks I'm at the Shandwicks' dance, so I needn't go home till morning. . . . Good evening, General Hannay. You got over the Hill Difficulty."

"The next stage is the Valley of Humiliation," I answered.

"So it would appear," she said gravely, and sat very quietly on the edge of Sir Walter's chair with her small, cool hand upon his.

I had been picturing her in my recollection as very young and glimmering, a dancing, exquisite child. But now I revised that picture. The crystal freshness of morning was still there, but I saw how deep the waters were. It was the clean fineness and strength of her that entranced me. I didn't even think of her as pretty, any more than a man thinks of the good looks of the friend he worships.

We waited, hardly speaking a word, till Macgillivray came. The first sight of his face told his story.

"Gone?" asked Blenkiron sharply. The man's lethargic calm seemed to have wholly deserted him.

"Gone," repeated the newcomer. "We have just tracked him down. Oh, he managed it cleverly. Never a sign of disturbance in any of his lairs. His dinner ordered at Biggleswick and several people invited to stay with him for the week-end—one a member of the Government. Two meetings at which he was to speak arranged for next week. Early this afternoon he flew over to France as a passenger in one of the new planes. He had been mixed up with the Air Board people for months—of course as another man with another face. Miss Lamington discovered that just too late. The bus went out of its course and came down in Normandy. By this time our man's in Paris or beyond it."

Sir Walter took off his big tortoiseshell spectacles and laid them carefully on the table.

"Roll up the map of Europe," he said. "This is our Austerlitz. Mary, my dear, I am feeling very old."

Macgillivray had the sharpened face of a bitterly disappointed man. Blenkiron had got very red, and I could see that he was blaspheming violently under his breath. Mary's eyes were quiet and solemn. She kept on patting Sir Walter's hand. The sense of some great impending disaster hung heavily on me, and to break the spell I asked for details.

"Tell me just the extent of the damage," I asked. "Our neat plan for deceiving the Boche has failed. That is bad. A dangerous spy has got beyond our power. That's worse. Tell me, is there still a worst? What's the limit of mischief he can do?"

Sir Walter had risen and joined Blenkiron on the hearthrug. His brows were furrowed and his mouth hard as if he were suffering pain.

"There is no limit," he said. "None that I can see, except the long-suffering of God. You knew the man as Ivery, and you knew him as that other whom you believed to have been shot one summer morning and decently buried. You feared the second—at least if you didn't, I did—most mortally. You realized that we feared Ivery, and you knew enough about him to see his fiendish cleverness. Well, you have the two men combined in one man. Ivery was the best brain Macgillivray and I ever encountered, the most cunning and patient and long-sighted. Combine him with the other, the chameleon who can blend himself with his environment, and has as many personalities as there are types and traits on the earth. What kind of enemy is that to have to fight?"

"I admit it's a steep proposition. But after all how much ill can he do? There are pretty strict limits to the activity of even the cleverest spy."

"I agree. But this man is not a spy who buys a few wretched subordinates and steals a dozen private letters. He's a genius who has been living as part of our English life. There's nothing he hasn't seen. He's been on terms of intimacy with all kinds of politicians. We know that. He did it as Ivery. They rather liked him, for he was clever and flattered them, and they told him things. But God knows what he saw and heard in his other personalities. For all I know he may have breakfasted at Downing Street with letters of introduction from President Wilson, or visited the Grand Fleet as a distinguished neutral. Then think of the women; how they talk. We're the leakiest society on earth, and we safeguard ourselves by keeping dangerous people out of it. We trust to our outer barrage. But any one who has really slipped inside has a million chances. And this, remember, is one man in ten millions, a man whose brain never sleeps for a moment, who is quick to seize the slightest hint, who can piece a plan together out of a dozen bits of gossip. It's like—it's as if the Chief of the Intelligence Department were suddenly to desert to the enemy. . . . The ordinary spy knows only bits of unconnected facts. This man knows our life and our way of thinking and everything about us."

"Well, but a treatise on English life in time of war won't do much good to the Boche."

Sir Walter shook his head. "Don't you realize the explosive stuff that is lying about? Ivery knows enough to make the next German peace offensive really deadly—not the blundering thing which it has been up to now, but something which gets our weak spots on the raw. He knows enough to wreck our campaign in the field. And the awful thing is that we don't know just what he knows or what he is aiming for. This war's a packet of surprises. Both sides are struggling for the margin, the little fraction of advantage, and between evenly matched enemies it's just the extra atom of foreknowledge that tells."

"Then we've got to push off and get after him," I said cheerfully.

"But what are you going to do?" asked Macgillivray. "If it were merely a question of destroying an organization it might be managed, for an organization presents a big front. But it's a question of destroying this one man, and his front is a razor edge. How are you going to find him? It's like looking for a needle in a haystack, and such a needle! A needle which can become a piece of straw or a tin-tack when it chooses!"

"All the same we've got to do it," I said, remembering old Peter's lesson on fortitude, though I can't say I was feeling very stout-hearted.

Sir Walter flung himself wearily into an arm-chair. "I wish I could be an optimist," he said, "but it looks as if we must own defeat. I've been at this work for twenty years, and, though I've been often beaten, I've always held certain cards in the game. Now I'm hanged if I've any. It looks like a knock-out, Hannay. It's no good deluding ourselves. We're men enough to look facts in the face and tell ourselves the truth. I don't see any way of light in the business. We've missed our shot by a hair's-breadth, and that's the same as missing by miles."

I remember he looked at Mary as if for confirmation, but she did not smile or nod. Her face was very grave and her eyes looked steadily at him. Then they moved and met mine, and they seemed to give me my marching orders.

"Sir Walter," I said, "three years ago you and I sat in this very room. We thought we were done to the world, as we think now. We had just that one miserable little clue to hang on to—a dozen words scribbled in a notebook by a dead man. You thought I was mad when I asked for Scudder's book, but we put our backs into the job and in twenty-four hours we had won out. Remember that then we were fighting against time. Now we have a reasonable amount of leisure. Then we had nothing but a sentence of gibberish. Now we have a great body of knowledge, for Blenkiron has been brooding over Ivery like an old hen, and he knows his ways of working and his breed of confederate. You've got something to work on now. Do you mean to tell me that, when the stakes are so big, you're going to chuck in your hand?"

Macgillivray raised his head. "We know a good deal about Ivery, but Ivery's dead. We know nothing of the man who was gloriously resurrected this evening in Normandy."

"Oh yes, you do. There are many faces to the man, but only one mind, and you know plenty about that mind."

"I wonder," said Sir Walter. "How can you know a mind which has no characteristics except that it is wholly and supremely competent? Mere mental powers won't give us a clue. We want to know the character which is behind all the personalities. Above all we want to know its foibles. If we had only a hint of some weakness we might make a plan."

"Well, let's set down all we know," I cried, for the more I argued the keener I grew. I told them in some detail the story of the night in the Coolin and what I had heard there.

"There's the two names *Chelius* and *Bommaerts*. The man spoke them in the same breath as *Elfenbein*, so they must be associated with Ivery's gang. You've got to get the whole Secret Service of the Allies busy to fit a meaning to these two words. Surely to goodness you'll find something! Remember those names don't belong to the Ivery part, but to the big game behind all the different disguises. . . . Then there's the talk about the Wild Birds and the Cage Birds. I haven't a guess at what it means. But it refers to some infernal gang, and among your piles of records there must be some clue. You set the intelligence of two hemispheres busy on the job. You've got all the machinery, and it's my experience that if even one solitary man keeps chewing on a problem he discovers something."

My enthusiasm was beginning to strike sparks from Macgillivray. He was looking thoughtful now, instead of despondent.

"There might be something in that," he said, "but it's a far-out chance."

"Of course it's a far-out chance, and that's all we're ever going to get from Ivery. But we've taken a bad chance before and won. . . . Then you've all that you know about Ivery here. Go through his *dossier* with a small tooth-comb and I'll bet you find something to work on. Blenkiron, you're a man with a cool head. You admit we've a sporting chance."

"Sure, Dick. He's fixed things so that the lines are across the track, but we'll clear somehow. So far as John S. Blenkiron is concerned he's got just one thing to do in the world, and that's to follow the yellow dog and have him neatly and cleanly tidied up. I've got a stack of personal affronts to settle. I was easy fruit and he hasn't been very respectful. You can count me in, Dick."

"Then we're agreed," I cried. "Well, gentlemen, it's up to you to arrange the first stage. You've some pretty solid staff work to put in before you get on the trail."

"And you?" Sir Walter asked.

"I'm going back to my brigade. I want a rest and a change. Besides, the first stage is office work, and I'm no use for that. But I'll be waiting to be summoned, and I'll come like a shot as soon as you hoick me out. I've got a presentiment about this thing. I know there'll be a finish and that I'll be in at it, and I think it will be a desperate, bloody business too."

I found Mary's eyes fixed upon me, and in them I read the same thought. She had not spoken a word, but had sat on the edge of a chair, swinging a foot idly, one hand playing with an ivory fan. She had given me my old orders and I looked to her for confirmation of the new.

"Miss Lamington, you are the wisest of the lot of us. What do you say?"

She smiled—that shy, companionable smile which I had been picturing to myself through all the wanderings of the past month.

"I think you are right. We've a long way to go yet, for the Valley of Humiliation comes only half-way in the *Pilgrim's Progress*. The next stage was Vanity Fair. I might be of some use there, don't you think?"

I remember the way she laughed and flung back her head like a gallant boy.

"The mistake we've all been making," she said, "is that our methods are too *terre-à-terre*. We've a poet to deal with, a great poet, and we must fling our imaginations forward to catch up with him. His strength is his unexpectedness, you know, and we won't beat him by plodding only. I believe the wildest course is the wisest, for it's the most likely to intersect his. . . . Who's the poet among us?"

"Peter," I said. "But he's pinned down with a game leg in Germany. All the same we must rope him in."

By this time we had all cheered up, for it is wonderful what a tonic there is in a prospect of action. The butler brought in tea, which it was Bullivant's habit to drink after dinner. To me it seemed fantastic to watch a slip of a girl pouring it out for two grizzled and distinguished servants of the State and one battered soldier—as decorous a family party as you would ask to see—and to reflect that all four were engaged in an enterprise where men's lives must be reckoned at less than thistledown.

After that we went upstairs to a noble Georgian drawing-room, and Mary played to us. I don't care two straws for music from an instrument—unless it be the pipes or a regimental band—but I dearly love the human voice. But she would not sing, for singing to her, I fancy, was something that did not come at will, but flowed only like a bird's note, when the mood favoured. I did not want it either. I was content to let "Cherry Ripe" be the one song linked with her in my memory.

It was Macgillivray who brought us back to business.

"I wish to Heaven there was one habit of mind we could definitely attach to him and to no one else." (At this moment "He" had only one meaning for us.)

"You can't do nothing with his mind," Blenkiron drawled. "You can't loose the bands of Orion, as the Bible says, or hold Leviathan with a hook. I reckoned I could and made a mighty close study of his de-vices. But the darned cuss wouldn't stay put. I thought I had tied him down to the double bluff, and he went and played the triple bluff on me. There's nothing doing that line."

A memory of Peter recurred to me.

"What about the 'blind spot'?" I asked, and I told them old Peter's pet theory. "Every man that God made has his weak spot somewhere, some flaw in his character which leaves a dull patch in his brain. We've got to find that out, and I think I've made a beginning."

Macgillivray in a sharp voice asked my meaning.

"He's in a funk . . . of something. Oh, I don't mean he's a coward. A man in his trade wants the nerve of a buffalo. He could give us all points in courage. What I mean is that he's not clean white all through. There are yellow streaks somewhere in him . . . I've given a good deal of thought to this courage business, for I haven't got a great deal of it myself. Not like Peter, I mean. I've got heaps of soft places in me. I'm afraid of being drowned for one thing, or of getting my eyes shot out. Ivery's afraid of bombs—at any rate he's afraid of bombs in a big city. I once read a book which talked about a thing called *agoraphobia*. Perhaps it's that. . . . Now if we know that weak spot it helps us in our work. There are some places he won't go to, and there are some things he can't do—not well, anyway. I reckon that's useful."

"Ye-es," said Macgillivray. "Perhaps. But it's not what you'd call a burning and a shining light."

"There's another chink in his armour," I went on. "There's one person in the world he can never practise his transformations on, and that's me. I shall always know him again, though he appeared as Sir Douglas Haig. I can't explain why, but I've got a feel in my bones about it. I didn't recognize him before, for I thought he was dead, and the nerve in my brain which should have been looking for him wasn't working. But I'm on my guard now, and that nerve's functioning at full power. Whenever and wherever and howsoever we meet again on the face of the earth, it will be 'Dr. Livingstone, I presume,' between him and me."

"That is better," said Macgillivray. "If we have any luck, Hannay, it won't be long till we pull you out of his Majesty's Forces."

Mary got up from the piano and resumed her old perch on the arm of Sir Walter's chair.

"There's another blind spot which you haven't mentioned." It was a cool evening, but I noticed that her cheeks had suddenly flushed.

"Last week Mr. Ivery asked me to marry him," she said.

MR. STANDFAST PART II
44 I BECOME A COMBATANT ONCE MORE

I returned to France on September 13th, and took over my old brigade on the 19th of the same month. We were shoved in at the Polygon Wood on the 26th, and after four days got so badly mauled that we were brought out to refit. On October 7th, very much to my surprise, I was given command of a division, and was on the fringes of the Ypres fighting during the first days of November. From that front we were hurried down to Cambrai in support, but came in only for the last backwash of that singular battle. We held a bit of the St. Quentin sector till just before Christmas, when we had a spell of rest in billets, which endured, so far as I was concerned, till the beginning of January, when I was sent off on the errand which I shall presently relate.

That is a brief summary of my military record in the latter part of 1917. I am not going to enlarge on the fighting. Except for the days at the Polygon Wood it was neither very severe nor very distinguished, and you will find it in the history books. What I have to tell of here is my own personal quest, for all the time I was living with my mind turned two ways. In the morasses of the Haanebeek flats, in the slimy support lines at Zonnebeke, in the tortured uplands about Flesquières, and in many other odd places I kept worrying at my private conundrum. At night I would lie awake thinking of it, and many a toss I took into shell-holes, and many a time I stepped off the duckboards, because my eyes were on a different landscape. Nobody ever chewed a few wretched clues into such a pulp as I did during those bleak months in Flanders and Picardy.

For I had an instinct that the thing was desperately grave, graver even than the battle before me. Russia had gone headlong to the devil, Italy had taken it between the eyes and was still dizzy, and our own prospects were none too bright. The Boche was getting uppish and with some cause, and I foresaw a rocky time ahead till America could line up with us in the field. It was the chance for the Wild Birds, and I used to wake in a sweat to think what devilry Ivery might be engineering. I believe I did my proper job reasonably well, but I put in my most savage thinking over the other. I remember how I used to go over every hour of every day from that June night in the Cotswolds till my last meeting with Bullivant in London, trying to find a new bearing. I should probably have got brain fever, if I hadn't had to spend most of my days and nights fighting a stiffish battle with a very watchful Hun. That kept my mind balanced, and I dare say it gave an edge to it; for during those months I was lucky enough to hit on a better scent than Bullivant and Macgillivray and Blenkiron pulling a thousand wires in their London offices.

I will set down in order of time the various incidents in this private quest of mine. The first was my meeting with Geordie Hamilton. It happened just after I rejoined the brigade, when I went down to have a look at our Scots Fusilier battalion. The old brigade had been roughly handled on July 31st, and had had to get heavy drafts to come anywhere near strength. The Fusiliers especially were almost a new lot, formed by joining our remnants to the remains of a battalion in another division and bringing about a dozen officers from the training unit at home.

I inspected the men, and my eyes caught sight of a familiar face. I asked his name, and the colonel got it from the sergeant-major. It was Lance-Corporal George Hamilton.

Now I wanted a new batman, and I resolved then and there to have my old antagonist. That afternoon he reported to me at brigade headquarters. As I looked at that solid bandy-legged figure, standing as stiff to attention as a tobacconist's sign, his ugly face hewn out of brown oak, his honest, sullen mouth, and his blue eyes staring sternly into vacancy, I knew I had got the man I wanted.

"Hamilton," I said, "you and I have met before."

"Sirr?" came the mystified answer.

"Look at me, man, and tell me if you don't recognize me."

He moved his eyes a fraction, in a respectful glance.

"Sirr, I don't mind of you."

"Well, I'll refresh your memory. Do you remember the hall in Newmilns Street and the meeting there? You had a fight with a man outside, and got knocked down."

He made no answer, but his colour deepened.

"And a fortnight later in a public-house in Muirtown you saw the same man, and gave him the chase of his life."

I could see his mouth set, for visions of the penalties laid down by the King's Regulations for striking an officer must have crossed his mind. But he never budged.

"Look me in the face, man," I said. "Do you remember me now?"

He did as he was bid.

"Sirr, I mind of you."

"Have you nothing more to say?"

He cleared his throat. "Sirr, I did not ken I was hittin' an officer."

"Of course you didn't. You did perfectly right, and if the war was over and we were both free men, I would give you a chance of knocking me down here and now. That's got to wait. When you saw me last I was serving my country, though you didn't know it. We're serving together now, and you must get your revenge out of the Boche. I'm going to make you my servant, for you and I have a pretty close bond between us. What do you say to that?"

This time he looked me full in the face. His troubled eye appraised me and was satisfied. "I'm proud to be servant to ye, sirr," he said. Then out of his chest came a strangled chuckle, and he forgot his discipline. "Losh, but ye're the great lad!" He recovered himself promptly, saluted, and marched off.

★

The second episode befell during our brief rest after the Polygon Wood, when I had ridden down the line one afternoon to see a friend in the Heavy Artillery. I was returning in the drizzle of evening, clanking along the greasy *pavé* between the sad poplars, when I struck a Labour company repairing the ravages of a Boche *strafe* that morning. I wasn't very certain of my road and asked one of the workers. He straightened himself and saluted, and I saw beneath a disreputable cap the features of the man who had been with me in the Coolin crevice.

I spoke a word to his sergeant, who fell him out, and he walked a bit of the way with me.

"Great Scott, Wake, what brought you here?" I asked.

"Same thing as brought you. This rotten war."

I had dismounted and was walking beside him, and I noticed that his lean face had lost its pallor and that his eyes were less hot than they used to be.

"You seem to thrive on it," I said, for I did not know what to say. A sudden shyness possessed me. Wake must have gone through some violent cyclones of feeling before it came to this. He saw what I was thinking, and laughed in his sharp, ironical way.

"Don't flatter yourself you've made a convert. I think as I always thought. But I came to the conclusion that since the fates had made me a Government servant I might as well do my work somewhere less cushioned than a chair in the Home Office. . . . Oh, no, it wasn't a matter of principle. One kind of work's as good as another, and I'm a better clerk than a navvy. With me it was self-indulgence: I wanted fresh air and exercise."

I looked at him—mud to the waist, and his hands all blistered and cut with unaccustomed labour. I could realize what his associates must mean to him, and how he would relish the rough-tonguing of non-coms.

"You're a confounded humbug," I said. "Why on earth didn't you go into an O.T.C. and come out with a commission? They're easy enough to get."

"You mistake my case," he said bitterly. "I experienced no sudden conviction about the justice of the war. I stand where I always stood. I'm a non-combatant, and I wanted a change of civilian work. . . . No, it wasn't any idiotic tribunal sent me here. I came of my own free will, and I'm really rather enjoying myself."

"It's a rough job for a man like you," I said.

"Not so rough as the fellows get in the trenches. I watched a battalion marching back to-day and they looked like ghosts who had been years in muddy graves. White faces and dazed eyes and leaden feet. Mine's a cushy job. I like it best when the weather's foul. It cheats me into thinking I'm doing my duty."

I nodded towards a recent shell-hole. "Much of that sort of thing?"

"Now and then. We had a good dusting this morning. I can't say I liked it at the time, but I like to look back on it. A sort of moral anodyne."

"I wonder what on earth the rest of your lot make of you?"

"They don't make anything. I'm not remarkable for my *bonhomie*. They think I'm a prig—which I am. It doesn't amuse me to talk about beer and women or listen to a gramophone or grouse about my last meal. But I'm quite content, thank you. Sometimes I get a seat in a corner of a Y.M.C.A. hut, and I've a book or two. My chief affliction is the padre. He was at Keble in my time, and, as one of my colleagues puts it, wants to be 'too bloody helpful.' . . . What are you doing, Hannay? I see you're some kind of general. They're pretty thick on the ground here."

"I'm a sort of general. Soldiering in the Salient isn't the softest of jobs, but I don't believe it's as tough as yours is for you. D'you know, Wake, I wish I had you in my brigade. Trained or untrained, you're a dashed stout-hearted fellow."

He laughed with a trifle less acidity than usual. "Almost thou persuadest me to be a combatant. No, thank you. I haven't the courage, and besides there's my jolly old principles. All the same I'd like to be near you. You're a good chap, and I've had the honour to assist in your education. . . . I must be getting back, or the sergeant will think I've bolted."

We shook hands, and the last I saw of him was a figure saluting stiffly in the wet twilight.

The third incident was trivial enough, though momentous in its results. Just before I got the division I had a bout of malaria. We were in support in the Salient, in very uncomfortable trenches behind Wieltje, and I spent three days on my back in a dug-out. Outside was a blizzard of rain, and the water now and then came down the stairs through the gas curtain and stood in pools at my bed foot. It wasn't the merriest place to convalesce in, but I was as hard as nails at the time, and by the third day I was beginning to sit up and be bored.

I read all my English papers twice and a big stack of German ones which I used to have sent up by a friend in the G.H.Q. Intelligence, who knew I liked to follow what the Boche was saying. As I dozed and ruminated in the way a man does after fever, I was struck by the tremendous display of one advertisement in the English press. It was a thing called "Gussiter's Deep-breathing System," which, according to its promoter, was a cure for every ill, mental, moral, or physical, that man can suffer. Politicians, generals, admirals, and music-hall artists all testified to the new life it had opened up for them. I remember wondering what these sportsmen got for their testimonies, and thinking I would write a spoof letter myself to old Gussiter.

Then I picked up the German papers and suddenly my eye caught an advertisement of the same kind in the *Frankfurter Zeitung*. It was not Gussiter this time, but one Weissmann, but his game was identical—"deep breathing." The Hun style was different from the English—all about the Goddess of Health, and the Nymphs of the Mountains, and two quotations from Schiller. But the principle was the same.

That made me ponder a little, and I went carefully through the whole batch. I found the advertisement in the *Frankfurter* and in one or two rather obscure *Volksstimmes* and *Volkszeitungs*. I found it too in *Der Grosse Krieg*, the official German propagandist picture paper. They were the same all but one, and that one had a bold variation, for it contained four of the sentences used in the ordinary English advertisement.

This struck me as fishy, and I started to write a letter to Macgillivray pointing out what seemed to be a case of trading with the enemy, and advising him to get on to Mr. Gussiter's financial backing. I thought he might find a Hun syndicate behind him. And then I had another notion which made me rewrite my letter.

I went through the papers again. The English ones which contained the advertisement were all good, solid, bellicose organs; the kind of thing no censorship would object to leaving the country. I had before me a small sheaf of pacificist prints, and they had not the advertisement. That might be for reasons of circulation, or it might not.

The German papers were either Radical or Socialist publications, just the opposite of the English lot, except the *Grosse Krieg*. Now we have a free press, and Germany has, strictly speaking, none. All her journalistic indiscretions are calculated. Therefore the Boche has no objections to his rags getting to enemy countries. He wants it. He likes to see them quoted in columns headed "Through German Glasses," and made the text of articles showing what a good democrat he is becoming.

As I puzzled over the subject, certain conclusions began to form in my mind. The four identical sentences seemed to hint that "Deep Breathing" had Boche affiliations. Here was a chance of communicating with the enemy which would defy the argus-eyed gentlemen who examine the mails. What was to hinder Mr. A at one end writing an advertisement with a good cipher in it, and the paper containing it getting into Germany by Holland in three days? Herr B at the other end replied in the *Frankfurter*, and a few days later shrewd editors and acute Intelligence officers—and Mr. A—were reading it in London, though only Mr. A knew what it really meant.

It struck me as a bright idea, the sort of simple thing that doesn't occur to clever people, and very rarely to the Boche. I wished I was not in the middle of a battle, for I would have had a try at investigating the cipher myself. I wrote a long letter to Macgillivray putting my case, and then went to sleep. When I awoke I reflected that it was a pretty thin argument, and would have stopped the letter, if it hadn't gone off early by a ration party.

After that things began very slowly to happen. The first was when Hamilton, having gone to Boulogne to fetch some mess-stores, returned with the startling news that he had seen Gresson. He had not heard his name, but described him dramatically to me as the "wee red-heided deevil that kickit Ecky Brockie's knee yon time in Glesca, sirr." I recognized the description.

Gresson, it appeared, was joy-riding. He was with a party of Labour delegates who had been met by two officers and carried off in *chars-à-bancs*. Hamilton reported from inquiries among his friends that this kind of visitor came weekly. I thought it a very sensible notion on the Government's part, but I wondered how Gresson had been selected. I had hoped that Macgillivray had weeks ago made a long arm and quodded him. Perhaps they had too little evidence to hang him, but he was the blackest sort of suspect and should have been interned.

A week later I had occasion to be at G.H.Q. on business connected with my new division. My friends in the Intelligence allowed me to use the direct line to London, and I called up Macgillivray. For ten minutes I had an exciting talk, for I had had no news from that quarter since I left England. I heard that the Portuguese Jew had escaped—had vanished from his native heather when they went to get him. They had identified him as a German professor of Celtic languages, who had held a chair in a Welsh college—a dangerous fellow, for he was an upright, high-minded, raging fanatic. Against Gresson they had no evidence at all, but he was kept under strict observation. When I asked about his crossing to France, Macgillivray replied that that was part of their scheme. I inquired if the visit had given them any clues, but I never got an answer, for the line had to be cleared at that moment for the War Office.

I hunted up the man who had charge of these Labour visits, and made friends with him. Gresson, he said, had been a quiet, well-mannered, and most appreciative guest. He had wept tears on Vimy Ridge, and—strictly against orders—had made a speech to some troops he met on the Arras road about how British Labour was remembering the Army in its prayers and sweating blood to make guns. On the last day he had had a misadventure, for he got very sick on the road—some kidney trouble that couldn't stand the jolting of the car—and had to be left at a village and picked up by the party on its way back. They found him better, but still shaky. I cross-examined the particular officer in charge about that halt, and learned that Gresson had been left alone in a peasant's cottage, for he said he only needed to lie down. The place was the hamlet of Eaucourt Sainte-Anne.

For several weeks that name stuck in my head. It had a pleasant, quaint sound, and I wondered how Gresson had spent his hours there. I hunted it up on the map, and promised myself to have a look at it the next time we came out to rest. And then I forgot about it till I heard the name mentioned again.

On October 23rd I had the bad luck, during a tour of my first-line trenches, to stop a small shell-fragment with my head. It was a close, misty day and I had taken off my tin hat to wipe my brow when the thing happened. I got a long, shallow scalp wound which meant nothing but bled a lot, and, as we were not in for any big move, the M.O. sent me back to a clearing station to have it seen to. I was three days in the place and, being perfectly well, had leisure to look about me and reflect, so that I recall that time as a queer, restful interlude in the infernal racket of war. I remember yet how on my last night there a gale made the lamps swing and flicker, and turned the grey-green canvas walls into a mass of mottled shadows. The floor canvas was muddy from the tramping of many feet bringing in the constant dribble of casualties from the line. In my tent there was no one very bad at the time, except a boy with his shoulder half blown off by a whizz-bang, who lay in a drugged sleep at the far end. The majority were influenza, bronchitis, and trench fever—waiting to be moved to the base, or convalescent and about to return to their units.

A small group of us dined off tinned chicken, stewed fruit, and ration cheese round the smoky stove, where two screens manufactured from packing cases gave some protection against the draughts which swept like young tornadoes down the tent. One man had been reading a book called the *Ghost Stories of an Antiquary*, and the talk turned on the unexplainable things that happen to everybody once or twice in a lifetime. I contributed a yarn about the men who went to look for Kruger's treasure in the bushveld and got scared by a green wildebeeste. It is a good yarn and I'll write it down some day. A tall Highlander, who kept his slippered feet on the top of the stove, and whose costume consisted of a kilt, a British warm, a grey hospital dressing-gown, and four pairs of socks, told the story of the Camerons at First Ypres, and of the Lowland subaltern who knew no Gaelic and suddenly found himself encouraging his men with some ancient Highland rigmarole. The poor chap had a racking bronchial cough, which suggested that his country might well use him on some warmer battle-ground than Flanders. He seemed a bit of a scholar and explained the Cameron business in a lot of long words.

I remember how the talk meandered on as talk does when men are idle and thinking about the next day. I didn't pay much attention, for I was reflecting on a change I meant to make in one of my battalion commands, when a fresh voice broke in. It belonged to a Canadian captain from Winnipeg, a very silent fellow who smoked shag tobacco.

"There's a lot of ghosts in this darned country," he said.

Then he started to tell about what happened to him when his division was last back in rest billets. He had a staff job and put up with the divisional command at an old French château. They had only a little bit of the house; the rest was shut up, but the passages were so tortuous that it was difficult to keep from wandering into the unoccupied part. One night, he said, he woke with a mighty thirst, and since he wasn't going to get cholera by drinking the local water in his bedroom, he started out for the room they messed in to try to pick up a whisky-and-soda. He couldn't find it, though he knew the road like his own name. He admitted he might have taken a wrong turning, but he didn't think so. Anyway he landed in a passage which he had never seen before, and, since he had no candle, he tried to retrace his steps. Again he went wrong, and groped on till he saw a faint light which he thought must be the room of the G.S.O.1., a good friend of his. So he barged in, and found a big, dim salon with two figures in it and a lamp burning between them, and a queer, unpleasant smell about. He took a step forward, and then he saw that the figures had no faces. That fairly loosened his joints with fear, and he gave a cry. One of the two ran towards him, the lamp went out, and the sickly scent caught suddenly at his throat. After that he knew nothing till he woke in his own bed next morning with a splitting headache. He said he got the General's permission and went over all the unoccupied part of the house, but he couldn't find the room. Dust lay thick on everything, and there was no sign of recent human presence.

I give the story as he told it in his drawling voice. "I reckon that was the genuine article in ghosts. You don't believe me and conclude I was drunk? I wasn't. There isn't any drink concocted yet that could lay me out like that. I just struck a crack in the old universe and pushed my head outside. It may happen to you boys any day."

The Highlander began to argue with him, and I lost interest in the talk.

But one phrase brought me to attention. "I'll give you the name of the darned place, and next time you're around you can do a bit of prospecting for yourself. It's called the Château of Eaucourt Sainte-Anne, about seven kilometres from Douvecourt. If I was purchasing real estate in this country I'd give that location a miss . . ."

After that I had a grim month, what with the finish of Third Ypres and the hustle to Cambrai. By the middle of December we had shaken down a bit, but the line my division held was not of our choosing, and we had to keep a wary eye on the Boche doings. It was a weary job, and I had no time to think of anything but the military kind of intelligence—fixing the units against us from prisoners' stories, organizing small raids, and keeping the Royal Flying Corps busy. I was keen about the last, and I made several trips myself over the lines with Archie Roylance, who had got his heart's desire and by good luck belonged to the squadron just behind me. I said as little as possible about this, for G.H.Q. did not encourage divisional generals to practise such methods, though there was one famous army commander who made a hobby of them. It was on one of these trips that an incident occurred which brought my spell of waiting on the bigger game to an end.

One dull December day, just after luncheon, Archie and I set out to reconnoitre. You know the way that fogs in Picardy seem suddenly to reek out of the ground and envelop the slopes like a shawl. That was our luck this time. We had crossed the lines, flying very high, and received the usual salute of Hun Archies. After a mile or two the ground seemed to climb up to us, though we hadn't descended, and presently we were in the heart of a cold, clinging mist. We dived for several thousand feet, but the confounded thing grew thicker and no sort of landmark could be found anywhere. I thought if we went on at this rate we should hit a tree or a church steeple and be easy fruit for the enemy.

The same thought must have been in Archie's mind, for he climbed again. We got into a mortally cold zone, but the air was no clearer. Thereupon he decided to head for home, and passed me word to work out a compass course on the map. That was easier said than done, but I had a rough notion of the rate he had travelled since we had crossed the lines and I knew our original direction, so I did the best I could. On we went for a bit, and then I began to get doubtful. So did Archie. We dropped low down, but we could hear none of the row that's always going on for a mile on each side of the lines. The world was very eerie and deadly still, so still that Archie and I could talk through the speaking-tube.

"We've mislaid this blamed battle," he shouted.

"I think your rotten old compass has soured on us," I replied.

We decided that it wouldn't do to change direction, so we held on the same course. I was getting as nervous as a kitten, chiefly owing to the silence. It's not what you expect in the middle of a battlefield. . . . I looked at the compass carefully and saw that it was really crocked. Archie must have damaged it on a former flight and forgotten to have it changed.

He had a very scared face when I pointed this out.

"Great God!" he croaked—for he had a fearsome cold—"we may be about

Calais or near Paris or miles the wrong side of the Boche line. What the devil are we to do?"

And then to put the lid on it his engine went wrong. It was the same performance as on the Yorkshire moors, and seemed to be a speciality of the Shark-Gladas type. But this time the end came quick. We dived steeply, and I could see by Archie's grip on the stick that he was going to have his work cut out to save our necks. Save them he did, but not by much, for we jolted down on the edge of a ploughed field with a series of bumps that shook the teeth in my head. It was the same dense, dripping fog, and we crawled out of the old bus and bolted for cover like two ferreted rabbits.

Our refuge was the lee of a small copse.

"It's my opinion," said Archie solemnly, "that we're somewhere about Le Cateau. Tim Wilbraham got left there in the Retreat, and it took him nine months to make the Dutch frontier. It's a giddy prospect, sir."

I sallied out to reconnoitre. At the other side of the wood was a highway, and the fog so blanketed sound that I could not hear a man on it till I saw his face. The first one I saw made me lie flat in the covert. . . . For he was a German soldier, field-grey, forage cap, red band and all, and he had a pick on his shoulder.

A second's reflection showed me that this was not final proof. He might be one of our prisoners. But it was no place to take chances. I went back to Archie, and the pair of us crossed the ploughed field and struck the road farther on. There we saw a farmer's cart with a woman and a child in it. They looked French, but melancholy, just what you would expect from the inhabitants of a countryside in enemy occupation.

Then we came to the park wall of a great house, and saw dimly the outlines of a cottage. Here sooner or later we would get proof of our whereabouts, so we lay and shivered among the poplars of the roadside. No one seemed abroad that afternoon. For a quarter of an hour it was as quiet as the grave. Then came a sound of whistling, and muffled steps.

"That's an Englishman," said Archie joyfully. "No Boche could make such a beastly noise."

He was right. The form of an Army Service Corps private emerged from the mist, his cap on the back of his head, his hands in his pockets, and his walk the walk of a free man. I never saw a welcomer sight than that jam merchant.

We stood up and greeted him. "What's this place?" I shouted.

He raised a grubby hand to his forelock.

"Ockott Saint Anny, sir," he said. "Beg pardon, sir, but you ain't hurt, sir?"

Ten minutes later I was having tea in the mess of an M. T. workshop while Archie had gone to the nearest Signals to telephone for a car and give instructions about his precious bus. It was almost dark, but I gulped my tea and hastened out into the thick dusk. For I wanted to have a look at the Château.

I found a big entrance with high stone pillars, but the iron gates were locked and looked as if they had not been opened in the memory of man. Knowing the way of such places, I hunted for the side entrance and found a muddy road which led to the back of the house. The front was evidently towards a kind of park; at the back was a nest of outbuildings and a section of moat which looked very deep and black in the winter twilight. This was crossed by a stone bridge with a door at the end of it.

Clearly the Château was not being used for billets. There was no sign of the British soldier; there was no sign of anything human. I crept through the fog as noiselessly as if I trod on velvet, and I hadn't even the company of my own footsteps. I remembered the Canadian's ghost story, and concluded I would be imagining the same sort of thing if I lived in such a place.

The door was bolted and padlocked. I turned along the side of the moat, hoping to reach the house front, which was probably modern and boasted a civilized entrance. There must be somebody in the place, for one chimney was smoking. Presently the moat petered out, and gave place to a cobbled causeway, but a wall, running at right angles with the house, blocked my way. I had half a mind to go back and hammer at the door, but I reflected that major-generals don't pay visits to deserted châteaux at night without a reasonable errand. I should look a fool in the eyes of some old *concierge*. The daylight was almost gone, and I didn't wish to be groping about the house with a candle.

But I wanted to see what was beyond the wall—one of those whims that beset the soberest men. I rolled a dissolute water-butt to the foot of it, and gingerly balanced myself on its rotten staves. This gave me a grip of the flat brick top, and I pulled myself up.

I looked down on a little courtyard with another wall beyond it, which shut off any view of the park. On the right was the Château, on the left more outbuildings; the whole place was not more than twenty yards each way. I was just about to retire the road I had come, for in spite of my fur coat it was uncommon chilly on that perch, when I heard a key turn in the door in the Château wall beneath me.

A lantern made a blur of light in the misty darkness. I saw that the bearer was a woman, an oldish woman, round-shouldered like most French peasants. In one hand she carried a leather bag, and she moved so silently that she must have worn rubber boots. The light was held level with her head and illumined her face. It was the evillest thing I have ever beheld, for a horrible scar had puckered the skin of the forehead and drawn up the eyebrows so that it looked like some diabolical Chinese mask.

Slowly she padded across the yard, carrying the bag as gingerly as if it had been an infant. She stopped at the door of one of the outhouses and set down the lantern and her burden on the ground. From her apron she drew something which looked like a gas-mask, and put it over her head. She also put on a pair of long gauntlets. Then she unlocked the door, picked up the lantern and went in. I heard the key turn behind her.

Crouching on that wall, I felt a very ugly tremor run down my spine. I had a glimpse of what the Canadian's ghost might have been. That hag, hooded like some venomous snake, was too much for my stomach. I dropped off the wall and ran—yes, ran till I reached the highroad and saw the cheery headlights of a transport wagon, and heard the honest speech of the British soldier. That restored me to my senses, and made me feel every kind of a fool.

As I drove back to the line with Archie, I was black ashamed of my funk. I told myself that I had seen only an old countrywoman going to feed her hens. I convinced my reason, but I did not convince the whole of me. An insensate dread of the place hung around me, and I could only retrieve my self-respect by resolving to return and explore every nook of it.

45   THE ADVENTURE OF
THE PICARDY CHÂTEAU

I looked up Eaucourt Sainte-Anne on the map, and the more I studied its position the less I liked it. It was the knot from which sprang all the main routes to our Picardy front. If the Boche ever broke us, it was the place for which old Hindenburg would make. At all hours troops and transport trains were moving through that insignificant hamlet. Eminent generals and their staffs passed daily within sight of the Château. It was a convenient halting-place for battalions coming back to rest. Supposing, I argued, our enemies wanted a key-spot for some assault upon the *moral* or the discipline or the health of the British Army, they couldn't find a better than Eaucourt Sainte-Anne. It was the ideal centre of espionage. But when I guardedly sounded my friends of the Intelligence they didn't seem to be worrying about it.

From them I got a chit to the local French authorities, and, as soon as we came out of the line towards the end of December, I made straight for the country town of Douvecourt. By a bit of luck our divisional quarters were almost next door. I interviewed a tremendous swell in a black uniform and black kid gloves, who received me affably and put his archives and registers at my disposal. By this time I talked French fairly well, having a natural turn for languages, but half the rapid speech of the *sous-préfet* was lost on me. By and by he left me with the papers and a clerk, and I proceeded to grub up the history of the Château.

It had belonged since long before Agincourt to the noble house of the D'Eaucourts, now represented by an ancient Marquise who dwelt at Biarritz. She had never lived in the place, which a dozen years before had been falling to ruins, when a rich American leased it and partially restored it. He had soon got sick of it—his daughter had married a blackguard French cavalry officer with whom he quarrelled, said the clerk—and since then there had been several tenants. I wondered why a house so unattractive should have let so readily, but the clerk explained that the cause was the partridge shooting. It was about the best in France, and in 1912 had shown the record bag.

The list of the tenants was before me. There was a second American, an Englishman called Halford, a Paris Jew-banker, and an Egyptian prince. But the space for 1913 was blank, and I asked the clerk about it. He told me that it had been taken by a woollen manufacturer from Lille, but he had never shot the partridges, though he had spent occasional nights in the house. He had a five years' lease, and was still paying rent to the Marquise. I asked the name, but the clerk had forgotten. "It will be written there," he said.

"But no," I said. "Somebody must have been asleep over this register. There's nothing after 1912."

He examined the page and blinked his eyes. "Some one indeed must have slept. No doubt it was young Louis who is now with the guns in Champagne. But the name will be on the Commissary's list. It is, as I remember, a sort of Flemish."

He nobbled off and returned in five minutes.

"Bommaerts," he said, "Jacques Bommaerts. A young man with no wife but with money—*Dieu de Dieu*, what oceans of it!"

That clerk got twenty-five francs, and he was cheap at the price. I went back to my division with a sense of awe on me. It was a marvellous fate that had brought me by odd routes to this out-of-the-way corner. First, the accident of Hamilton's seeing Gresson; then the night in the clearing station; last the mishap of Archie's plane getting lost in the fog. I had three grounds of suspicion—Gresson's sudden illness, the Canadian's ghost, and that horrid old woman in the dusk. And now I had one tremendous fact. The place was leased by a man called Bommaerts, and that was one of the two names I had heard whispered in that far-away cleft in the Coolin by the stranger from the sea.

A sensible man would have gone off to the *contre-espionage* people and told them his story. I couldn't do this; I felt that it was my own private find and I was going to do the prospecting myself. Every moment of leisure I had I was puzzling over the thing. I rode round by the Château one frosty morning and examined all the entrances. The main one was the grand avenue with the locked gates. That led straight to the front of the house where the terrace was—or you might call it the back, for the main door was on the other side. Anyhow the drive came up to the edge of the terrace and then split into two, one branch going to the stables by way of the outbuildings where I had seen the old woman, the other circling round the house, skirting the moat, and joining the back road just before the bridge. If I had gone to the right instead of the left that first evening with Archie, I should have circumnavigated the place without any trouble.

Seen in the fresh morning light the house looked commonplace enough. Part of it was old as Noah, but most was newish and jerry-built, the kind of flat-chested, thin French château, all front and no depth, and full of draughts and smoky chimneys. I might have gone in and ransacked the place, but I knew I should find nothing. It was borne in on me that it was only when evening fell that that house was interesting, and that I must come, like Nicodemus, by night. Besides I had a private account to settle with my conscience. I had funked the place in the foggy twilight, and it does not do to let a matter like that slide. A man's courage is like a horse that refuses a fence; you have got to take him by the head and cram him at it again. If you don't, he will funk worse next time. I hadn't enough courage to be able to take chances with it, and, though I was afraid of many things, the thing I feared most mortally was being afraid.

I did not get a chance till Christmas Eve. The day before there had been a fall of snow, but the frost set in and the afternoon ended in a green sunset, with the earth crisp and crackling like a shark's skin. I dined early, and took with me Geordie Hamilton, who added to his many accomplishments that of driving a car. He was the only man in the B.E.F. who guessed anything of the game I was after, and I knew that he was as discreet as a tombstone. I put on my oldest trench cap, slacks, and a pair of scaife-soled boots, that I used to change into in the evening. I had a useful little electric torch, which lived in my pocket, and from which a cord led to a small bulb of light that worked with a switch and could be hung on my belt. That left my arms free in case of emergencies. Likewise I strapped on my pistol.

There was little traffic in the hamlet of Eaucourt Sainte-Anne that night. Few cars were on the road, and the M.T. detachment, judging from the din, seemed to be busy on a private spree. It was about nine o'clock when we turned into the side road, and at the entrance to it I saw a solid figure in khaki mounting guard beside two bicycles. Something in the man's gesture, as he saluted, struck me as familiar, but I had no time to hunt for casual memories. I left the car just short of the bridge, and took the road which would bring me to the terraced front of the house.

Once I turned the corner of the Château and saw the long ghostly façade white in the moonlight, I felt less confident. The eeriness of the place smote me. In that still snowy world it loomed up immense and mysterious with its rows of shuttered windows, each with that air which empty houses have of concealing some wild story. I longed to have old Peter with me, for he was the man for this kind of escapade. I had heard that he had been removed to Switzerland, and I pictured him now in some mountain village where the snow lay deep. I would have given anything to have had Peter with a whole leg by my side.

I stepped on the terrace and listened. There was not a sound in the world, not even the distant rumble of a cart. The pile towered above me like a mausoleum, and I reflected that it must take some nerve to burgle an empty house. It would be good enough fun to break into a bustling dwelling and pinch the plate when the folk were at dinner, but to burgle emptiness and silence meant a fight with the terrors in a man's soul. It was worse in my case, for I wasn't cheered with prospects of loot. I wanted to get inside chiefly to soothe my conscience.

I hadn't much doubt I would find a way, for three years of war and the frequent presence of untidy headquarters staffs have loosened the joints of most Picardy houses. There's generally a window that doesn't latch or a door that doesn't bar. But I tried window after window on the terrace without result. The heavy green sun-shutters were down over each, and when I broke the hinges of one there was a long bar within to hold it firm. I was beginning to think of shinning up a rain-pipe and trying the second floor, when a shutter I had laid hold on swung back in my hand. It had been left unfastened, and, kicking the snow from my boots, I entered a room.

A gleam of moonlight followed me, and I saw I was in a big salon with a polished wood floor and dark lumps of furniture swathed in sheets. I clicked the bulb at my belt, and the little circle of light showed a place which had not been dwelt in for years. At the far end was another door, and as I tiptoed towards it something caught my eye on the parquet. It was a piece of fresh snow like that which clumps on the heel of a boot. I had not brought it there. Some other visitor had passed this way, and not long before me.

Very gently I opened the door and slipped in. In front of me was a pile of furniture which made a kind of screen, and behind that I halted and listened. There was somebody in the room. I heard the sound of human breathing and of soft movements. The man, whoever he was, was at the far end from me, and though there was a dim glow of moon through a broken shutter I could see nothing of what he was after. I was beginning to enjoy myself now. I knew of his presence and he did not know of mine, and that is the sport of stalking.

An unwary movement of my hand caused the screen to creak. Instantly the movements ceased and there was utter silence. I held my breath, and after a second or two the tiny sounds began again. I had a feeling, though my eyes could not assure me, that the man before me was at work, and was using a very small shaded torch. There was just the faintest moving shimmer on the wall beyond, though that might come from the crack of moonlight.

Apparently he was reassured, for his movements became more distinct. There was a jar as if a table had been pushed back. Once more there was silence, and I heard only the intake of breath. I have very quick ears, and to me it sounded as if the man were rattled. The breathing was quick and anxious.

Suddenly it changed and became the ghost of a whistle—the kind of sound one makes with the lips and teeth without ever letting the tune break out clear. We all do it when we are preoccupied with something—shaving, or writing letters, or reading the newspaper. But I did not think my man was preoccupied. He was whistling to quiet fluttering nerves.

Then I caught the air. It was "Cherry Ripe."

In a moment, from being hugely at my ease, I became the nervous one. I had been playing peep-bo with the unseen, and the tables were turned. My heart beat against my ribs like a hammer. I shuffled my feet, and again there fell the tense silence.

"Mary," I said—and the word seemed to explode like a bomb in the stillness—"Mary! It's me—Dick Hannay."

There was no answer but a sob and the sound of a timid step.

I took four paces into the darkness and caught in my arms a trembling girl. . . .

Often in the last months I had pictured the kind of scene which would be the culminating point of my life. When our work was over and war had been

forgotten, somewhere—perhaps in a green Cotswold meadow or in a room of
an old manor—I would talk with Mary. By that time we should know each
other well and I would have lost my shyness. I would try to tell her that I
loved her, but whenever I thought of what I should say my heart sank, for
I knew I would make a fool of myself. You can't live my kind of life for
forty years wholly among men and be of any use at pretty speeches to women.
I knew I should stutter and blunder, and I used despairingly to invent
impossible situations where I might make my love plain to her without words
by some piece of melodramatic sacrifice.

But the kind Fates had saved me the trouble. Without a syllable save
Christian names stammered in that eerie darkness we had come to complete
understanding. The fairies had been at work unseen, and the thoughts of
each of us had been moving towards the other, till love had germinated like a
seed in the dark. As I held her in my arms I stroked her hair and murmured
things which seemed to spring out of some ancestral memory. Certainly my
tongue had never used them before, nor my mind imagined them. . . . By and
by she slipped her arms round my neck and with a half sob strained towards
me. She was still trembling.

"Dick," she said, and to hear that name on her lips was the sweetest thing I
had ever known. "Dick, is it really you? Tell me I'm not dreaming."

"It's me, sure enough, Mary dear. And now I have found you I will never
let you go again. But, my precious child, how on earth did you get here?"

She disengaged herself and let her little electric torch wander over my
rough habiliments.

"You look a tremendous warrior, Dick. I have never seen you like this before.
I was in Doubting Castle and very much afraid of Giant Despair, till you came."

"I think I call it the Interpreter's House," I said.

"It's the house of somebody we both know," she went on. "He calls himself
Bommaerts here. That was one of the two names, you remember. I have seen
him since in Paris. Oh, it is a long story and you shall hear it all soon. I knew
he came here sometimes, so I came here too. I have been nursing for the last
fortnight at the Douvecourt Hospital only four miles away."

"But what brought you alone at night?"

"Madness, I think. Vanity, too. You see I had found out a good deal, and
I wanted to find out the one vital thing which has puzzled Mr. Blenkiron. I
told myself it was foolish, but I couldn't keep away. And then my courage
broke down, and before you came I would have screamed at the sound of a
mouse. If I hadn't whistled I would have cried."

"But why alone and at this hour?"

"I couldn't get off in the day. And it was safest to come alone. You see he is in
love with me, and when he heard I was coming to Douvecourt forgot his caution
and proposed to meet me here. He said he was going on a long journey and
wanted to say good-bye. If he had found me alone—well, he would have said
good-bye. If there had been any one with me, he would have suspected, and he
mustn't suspect *me*. Mr. Blenkiron says that would be fatal to his great plan.
He believes I am like my aunts, and that I think him an apostle of peace working

by his own methods against the stupidity and wickedness of all the Governments. He talks more bitterly about Germany than about England. He has told me how he has to disguise himself and play many parts on his mission, and of course I have applauded him. Oh, I have had a difficult autumn."

"Mary," I cried, "tell me you hate him."

"No," she said quietly, "I do not hate him. I am keeping that for later. I fear him desperately. Some day when we have broken him utterly I will hate him, and drive all likeness of him out of my memory like an unclean thing. But till then I won't waste energy on hate. We want to hoard every atom of our strength for the work of beating him."

She had won back her composure, and I turned on my light to look at her. She was in nurse's outdoor uniform, and I thought her eyes seemed tired. The priceless gift that had suddenly come to me had driven out all recollection of my own errand. I thought of Ivery only as a would-be lover of Mary, and forgot the manufacturer from Lille who had rented this house for the partridge shooting.

"And you, Dick," she asked: "is it part of a general's duties to pay visits at night to empty houses?"

"I came to look for traces of M. Bommaerts. I, too, got on his track from another angle, but that story must wait."

"You observe that he has been here to-day?"

She pointed to some cigarette ash spilled on the table edge, and a space on its surface cleared from dust. "In a place like this the dust would settle again in a few hours, and that is quite clean. I should say he has been here just after luncheon."

"Great Scott!" I cried, "what a close shave! I'm in the mood at this moment to shoot him at sight. You say you saw him in Paris and knew his lair. Surely you had a good enough case to have him collared."

She shook her head. "Mr. Blenkiron—he's in Paris too—wouldn't hear of it. He hasn't just figured the thing out yet, he says. We've identified one of your names, but we're still in doubt about Chelius."

"Ah, Chelius! Yes, I see. We must get the whole business complete before we strike. Has old Blenkiron had any luck?"

"Your guess about the 'Deep-breathing' advertisement was very clever, Dick. It was true, and it may give us Chelius. I must leave Mr. Blenkiron to tell you how. But the trouble is this. We know something of the doings of some one who may be Chelius, but we can't link them with Ivery. We know that Ivery is Bommaerts, and our hope is to link Bommaerts with Chelius. That's why I came here. I was trying to burgle this escritoire in an amateur way. It's a bad piece of fake Empire and deserves smashing."

I could see that Mary was eager to get my mind back to business, and with some difficulty I clambered down from the exultant heights. The intoxication of the thing was on me—the winter night, the circle of light in that dreary room, the sudden coming together of two souls from the ends of the earth, the realization of my wildest hopes, the gilding and glorifying of all the future. But she had always twice as much wisdom as me, and we were in the midst of a campaign which had no use for day-dreaming. I turned my attention to the desk.

It was a flat table with drawers, and at the back a half-circle of more drawers with a central cupboard. I tilted it up and most of the drawers slid out, empty of anything but dust. I forced two open with my knife and they held empty cigar boxes. Only the cupboard remained, and that appeared to be locked. I wedged a key from my pocket into its keyhole, but the thing would not budge.

"It's no good," I said. "He wouldn't leave anything he valued in a place like this. That sort of fellow doesn't take risks. If he wanted to hide something there are a hundred holes in this château which would puzzle the best detective."

"Can't you open it?" she asked. "I've a fancy about that table. He was sitting here this afternoon and he may be coming back."

I solved the problem by turning up the escritoire and putting my knee through the cupboard door. Out of it tumbled a little dark-green attaché case.

"This is getting solemn," said Mary. "Is it locked?"

It was, but I took my knife and cut the lock out and spilled the contents on the table. There were some papers, a newspaper or two, and a small bag tied with black cord. The last I opened, while Mary looked over my shoulder. It contained a fine yellowish powder.

"Stand back," I said harshly. "For God's sake, stand back and don't breathe."

With trembling hands I tied up the bag again, rolled it in a newspaper, and stuffed it into my pocket. For I remembered a day near Péronne when a Boche plane had come over in the night and had dropped little bags like this. Happily they were all collected, and the men who found them were wise and took them off to the nearest laboratory. They proved to be full of anthrax germs. . . .

I remembered how Eaucourt Sainte-Anne stood at the junction of a dozen roads where all day long troops passed to and from the lines. From such a vantage ground an enemy could wreck the health of an army. . . .

I remembered the woman I had seen in the courtyard of this house in the foggy dusk, and I knew now why she had worn a gas-mask.

This discovery gave me a horrid shock. I was brought down with a crash from my high sentiment to something earthy and devilish. I was fairly well used to Boche filthiness, but this seemed too grim a piece of the utterly damnable. I wanted to have Ivery by the throat and force the stuff into his body, and watch him decay slowly into the horror he had contrived for honest men.

"Let's get out of this infernal place," I said.

But Mary was not listening. She had picked up one of the newspapers and was gloating over it. I looked and saw that it was open at an advertisement of Weissmann's "Deep-breathing" system.

"Oh, look, Dick," she cried breathlessly.

The column of type had little dots made by a red pencil below certain words.

"It's it," she whispered, "it's the cipher—I'm almost sure it's the cipher!"

"Well, he'd be likely to know it if any one did."

"But don't you see it's the cipher which Chelius uses—the man in Switzerland? Oh, I can't explain now, for it's very long, but I think—I think—I have found out what we have all been wanting. Chelius . . ."

"Whisht!" I said. "What's that?"

There was a queer sound from the out-of-doors as if a sudden wind had risen in the still night.

"It's only a car on the main road," said Mary.

"How did you get in?" I asked.

"By the broken window in the next room. I cycled out here one morning and walked round the place and found the broken catch."

"Perhaps it is left open on purpose. That may be the way M. Bommaerts visits his country home. . . . Let's get off, Mary, for this place has a curse on it. It deserves fire from heaven."

I slipped the contents of the attaché case into my pockets. "I'm going to drive you back," I said. "I've got a car out there."

"Then you must take my bicycle and my servant too. He's an old friend of yours—one Andrew Amos."

"Now how on earth did Andrew get over here?"

"He's one of us," said Mary, laughing at my surprise. "A most useful member of our party, at present disguised as an *infirmier* in Lady Manorwater's hospital at Douvecourt. He is learning French, and . . ."

"Hush!" I whispered. "There's some one in the next room."

I swept her behind a stack of furniture, with my eye glued on a crack of light below the door. The handle turned and the shadows raced before a big electric lamp of the kind they have in stables. I could not see the bearer, but I guessed it was the old woman.

There was a man behind her. A brisk step sounded on the parquet, and a figure brushed past her. It wore the horizon-blue of a French officer, very smart, with those French riding-boots that show the shape of the leg, and a handsome fur-lined pelisse. I would have called him a young man, not more than thirty-five. The face was brown and clean-shaven, the eyes bright and masterful . . . Yet he did not deceive me. I had not boasted idly to Sir Walter when I said that there was one man alive who could never again be mistaken by me.

I had my hand on my pistol, as I motioned Mary farther back into the shadows. For a second I was about to shoot. I had a perfect mark and could have put a bullet through his brain with utter certitude. I think if I had been alone I might have fired. Perhaps not. Anyhow now I could not do it. It seemed like potting at a sitting rabbit. I was obliged, though he was my worst enemy, to give him a chance, while all the while my sober senses kept calling me a fool.

I stepped into the light.

"Hullo, Mr. Ivery," I said. "This is an odd place to meet again!"

In his amazement he fell back a step, while his hungry eyes took in my face. There was no mistake about the recognition. I saw something I had seen once before in him, and that was fear. Out went the light and he sprang for the door.

I fired in the dark, but the shot must have been too high. In the same instant I heard him slip on the smooth parquet and the tinkle of glass as the broken window swung open. Hastily I reflected that his car must be at the moat end of the terrace, and that therefore to reach it he must pass outside this very room. Seizing the damaged escritoire, I used it as a ram, and charged the window nearest me. The panes and shutters went with a crash, for I had driven the thing out of its rotten frame. The next second I was on the moonlit snow.

I got a shot at him as he went over the terrace, and again I went wide. I never was at my best with a pistol. Still I reckoned I had got him, for the car which was waiting below must come back by the moat to reach the highroad. But I had forgotten the great closed park gates. Somehow or other they must have been opened, for as soon as the car started, it headed straight for the grand avenue. I tried a couple of long-range shots after it, and one must have damaged either Ivery or his chauffeur, for there came back a cry of pain.

I turned in deep chagrin to find Mary beside me. She was bubbling with laughter.

"Were you ever a cinema actor, Dick? The last two minutes have been a really high-class performance. 'Featuring Mary Lamington.' How does the jargon go?"

"I could have got him when he first entered," I said ruefully.

"I know," she said in a graver tone. "Only of course you couldn't. . . . Besides, Mr. Blenkiron doesn't want it—yet."

She put her hand on my arm. "Don't worry about it. It wasn't written it should happen that way. It would have been too easy. We have a long road to travel yet before we clip the wings of the Wild Birds."

"Look," I cried. "The fire from heaven!"

Red tongues of flame were shooting up from the outbuildings at the farther end, the place where I had first seen the woman. Some agreed plan must have been acted on, and Ivery was destroying all traces of his infamous yellow powder. Even now the *concierge* with her odds and ends of belongings would be slipping out to some refuge in the village.

In the still dry night the flames rose, for the place must have been made ready for a rapid burning. As I hurried Mary round the moat I could see that part of the main building had caught fire. The hamlet was awakened, and before we reached the corner of the highroad sleepy British soldiers were hurrying towards the scene, and the Town Major was mustering the fire brigade. I knew that Ivery had laid his plans well, and that they hadn't a chance—that long before dawn the Château of Eaucourt Sainte-Anne would be a heap of ashes, and that in a day or two the lawyers of the aged Marquise at Biarritz would be wrangling with the insurance company.

At the corner stood Amos beside two bicycles, solid as a graven image. He recognized me with a gap-toothed grin.

"It's a cauld night, General, but the home fires keep burnin'. I havena seen such a cheery lowe since Dickson's mill at Gawly."

We packed, bicycles and all, into my car with Amos wedged in the narrow seat beside Hamilton. Recognizing a fellow countryman, he gave thanks for the lift in the broadest Doric. "For," said he, "I'm not what you would call a practised hand wi' a velocipede, and my feet are dinnled wi' standin' in the snaw."

As for me, the miles to Douvecourt passed as in a blissful moment of time. I wrapped Mary in a fur rug, and after that we did not speak a word. I had come suddenly into a great possession and was dazed with the joy of it.

46 MR. BLENKIRON DISCOURSES ON LOVE AND WAR

Three days later I got my orders to report at Paris for special service. They came none too soon, for I chafed at each hour's delay. Every thought in my head was directed to the game which we were playing against Ivery. He was the big enemy, compared to whom the ordinary Boche in the trenches was innocent and friendly. I had almost lost interest in my division, for I knew that for me the real battle-front was not in Picardy, and that my job was not so easy as holding a length of line. Also I longed to be at the same work as Mary.

I remember waking up in billets the morning after the night at the Château with the feeling that I had become extraordinarily rich. I felt very humble, too, and very kindly towards all the world—even to the Boche, though I can't say I had ever hated him very wildly. You find hate more among journalists and politicians at home than among fighting men. I wanted to be quiet and alone to think, and since that was impossible I went about my work in a happy abstraction. I tried not to look ahead, but only to live in the present, for I knew that a war was on, and that there was desperate and dangerous business before me, and that my hopes hung on a slender thread. Yet for all that I had sometimes to let my fancies go free, and revel in delicious dreams.

But there was one thought that always brought me back to hard ground, and that was Ivery. I do not think I hated anybody in the world but him. It was his relation to Mary that stung me. He had the insolence with all his toad-like past to make love to that clean and radiant girl. I felt that he and I stood as mortal antagonists, and the thought pleased me, for it helped me to put some honest detestation into my job. Also I was going to win. Twice I had failed, but the third time I should succeed. It had been like ranging shots for a gun—first short, second over, and I vowed that the third should be dead on the mark.

I was summoned to G.H.Q., where I had half an hour's talk with the greatest British commander. I can see yet his patient, kindly face and that steady eye which no vicissitude of fortune could perturb. He took the biggest view, for he was statesman as well as soldier, and knew that the whole world was one battlefield and every man and woman among the combatant nations was in the battle-line. So contradictory is human nature that talk made me wish for a moment to stay where I was. I wanted to go on serving under that man. I realized suddenly how much I loved my work, and when I got back to my quarters that night and saw my men swinging in from a route march I could have howled like a dog at leaving them. Though I say it who shouldn't, there wasn't a better division in the Army.

One morning a few days later I picked up Mary in Amiens. I always liked the place, for after the dirt of the Somme it was a comfort to go there for a bath and a square meal, and it had the noblest church that the hand of man ever built for God. It was a clear morning when we started from the boulevard beside the railway station; and the air smelt of washed streets and fresh coffee, and women were going marketing and the little trams ran clanking by, just as in any other city far from the sound of guns. There was very little khaki or horizon-blue about, and I remember thinking how completely Amiens had got out of the war zone. Two months later it was a different story.

To the end I shall count that day as one of the happiest in my life. Spring was in the air, though the trees and fields had still their winter colouring. A thousand good fresh scents came out of the earth, and the larks were busy over the new furrows. I remember that we ran up a little glen, where a stream spread into pools among sallows, and the roadside trees were heavy with mistletoe. On the tableland beyond the Somme valley the sun shone like April. At Beauvais we lunched badly in an inn—badly as to food, but there was an excellent burgundy at two francs a bottle. Then we slipped down through little flat chested townships to the Seine, and in the late afternoon passed through St. Germain forest. The wide green spaces among the trees set my fancy dwelling on that divine English countryside where Mary and I would one day make our home. She had been in high spirits all the journey, but when I spoke of the Cotswolds her face grew grave.

"Don't let us speak of it, Dick," she said. "It's too happy a thing and I feel as if it would wither if we touched it. I don't let myself think of peace and home, for it makes me too homesick. . . . I think we shall get there some day, you and I . . . but it's a long road to the Delectable Mountains, and Faithful, you know, has to die first. . . . There is a price to be paid."

The words sobered me.

"Who is our Faithful?" I asked.

"I don't know. But he was the best of the Pilgrims."

Then, as if a veil had lifted, her mood changed, and when we came through the suburbs of Paris and swung down the Champs-Elysées she was in a holiday humour. The lights were twinkling in the blue January dusk, and the warm breath of the city came to greet us. I knew little of the place, for I had visited it once only on a four days' Paris leave, but it had seemd to me then the most habitable of cities, and now, coming from the battlefield with Mary by my side, it was the happy ending of a dream.

I left her at her cousin's house near the Rue St. Honoré, and deposited myself, according to instructions, at the Hôtel Louis Quinze. There I wallowed in a hot bath, and got into the civilian clothes which had been sent on from London. They made me feel that this time I had taken leave of my division for good and all.

Blenkiron had a private room, where we were to dine; and a more wonderful litter of books and cigar boxes I have never seen, for he hadn't a notion of tidiness. I could hear him grunting at his toilet in the adjacent bedroom, and I noticed that the table was laid for three. I went downstairs to get a paper, and on the way ran into Launcelot Wake.

He was no longer a private in a Labour battalion. Evening clothes showed beneath his overcoat.

"Hullo, Wake, are you in this push too?"

"I suppose so," he said, and his manner was not cordial. "Anyhow I was ordered down here. My business is to do as I am told."

"Coming to dine?" I asked.

"No. I'm dining with some friends at the Crillon."

Then he looked me in the face, and his eyes were hot as I first remembered them. "I hear I've to congratulate you, Hannay," and he held out a limp hand.

I never felt more antagonism in a human being.

"You don't like it?" I said, for I guessed what he meant.

"How on earth can I like it?" he cried angrily. "Good Lord, man, you'll murder her soul. You an ordinary, stupid, successful fellow, and she—she's the most precious thing God ever made. You can never understand a fraction of her preciousness, but you'll clip her wings all right. She can never fly now. . . ."

He poured out this hysterical stuff to me at the foot of the staircase within hearing of an elderly French widow, with a poodle. I had no impulse to be angry, for I was far too happy.

"Don't, Wake," I said. "We're all too close together to quarrel. I'm not fit to black Mary's shoes. You can't put me too low or her too high. But I've at least the sense to know it. You couldn't want me to be humbler than I feel."

He shrugged his shoulders, as he went out to the street. "Your infernal magnanimity would break any man's temper. . . ."

I went upstairs to find Blenkiron, washed and shaven, admiring a pair of bright patent-leather shoes.

"Why, Dick, I've been wearying bad to see you. I was nervous you would be blown to glory, for I've been reading awful things about your battles in the noospapers. The war correspondents worry me so I can't take breakfast."

He mixed cocktails and clinked his glass on mine. "Here's to the young lady. I was trying to write her a pretty little sonnet, but the darned rhymes wouldn't fit. I've gotten a heap of things to say to you when we've finished dinner."

Mary came in, her cheeks bright from the weather, and Blenkiron promptly fell abashed. But she had a way to meet his shyness, for, when he began an embarrassed speech of good wishes, she put her arms round his neck and kissed him. Oddly enough, that set him completely at his ease.

It was pleasant to eat off linen and china again, pleasant to see old

Blenkiron's benignant face and the way he tucked into his food, but it was delicious for me to sit at a meal with Mary across the table. It made me feel that she was really mine, and not a pixie that would vanish at a word. To Blenkiron she bore herself like an affectionate but mischievous daughter, while the desperately refined manners that afflicted him whenever women were concerned mellowed into something liker his everyday self. They did most of the talking, and I remember he fetched from some mysterious hiding place a great box of chocolates, which you could no longer buy in Paris, and the two ate them like spoiled children. I didn't want to talk, for it was pure happiness for me to look on. I loved to watch her, when the servants had gone, with her elbows on the table like a schoolboy, her crisp gold hair a little crumpled, cracking walnuts with gusto, like some child who has been allowed down from the nursery for dessert and means to make the most of it.

With his first cigar Blenkiron got to business.

"You want to know about the staff work we've been busy on at home. Well, it's finished now, thanks to you, Dick. We weren't getting on very fast till you took to peroosing the press on your sick-bed and dropped us that hint about the 'Deep-breathing' ads."

"Then there was something in it?" I asked.

"There was black hell in it. There wasn't any Gussiter, but there was a mighty fine little syndicate of crooks with old man Gresson at the back of them. First thing, I started out to get the cipher. It took some looking for, but there's no cipher on earth can't be got hold of somehow if you know it's there, and in this case we were helped a lot by the return messages in the German papers. . . . It was bad stuff when we read it, and explained the darned leakages in important noon wu'vu bvvn up against. At first I figured to keep the thing going and turn Gussiter into a corporation, with John S. Blenkiron as president. But it wouldn't do, for at first hint of tampering with their communications the whole bunch got skeery and sent out S.O.S. signals. So we tenderly plucked the flowers."

"Gresson, too?" I asked.

He nodded. "I guess your seafaring companion's now under the sod. We had collected enough evidence to hang him ten times over. . . . But that was the least of it. For your little old cipher, Dick, gave us a line on Ivery."

I asked how, and Blenkiron told me the story. He had about a dozen cross-bearings proving that the organization of the "Deep-breathing" game had its headquarters in Switzerland. He suspected Ivery from the first, but the man had vanished out of his ken, so he started working from the other end, and instead of trying to deduce the Swiss business from Ivery, he tried to deduce Ivery from the Swiss business. He went to Berne and made a conspicuous public fool of himself for several weeks. He called himself an agent of the American propaganda there, and took some advertising space in the press and put in spread-eagle announcements of his mission, with the result that the Swiss Government threatened to turn him out of the country if he tampered that amount with their neutrality. He also wrote a lot of rot in the Geneva newspapers, which he paid to have printed, explaining how he was a pacificist, and was going to convert Germany to peace by "inspirational advertisement of pure-minded war aims." All this was in keeping with his English reputation, and he wanted to make himself a bait for Ivery.

But Ivery did not rise to the fly, and though he had a dozen agents working for him on the quiet he could never hear of the name Chelius. That was, he reckoned, a very private and particular name among the Wild Birds. However, he got to know a good deal about the Swiss end of the "Deep-breathing" business. That took some doing and cost a lot of money. His best people were a girl who posed as a *mannequin* in a milliner's shop in Lyons and a *concierge* in a big hotel at St. Moritz. His most important discovery was that there was a second cipher in the return messages sent from Switzerland, different from the one that the Gussiter lot used in England. He got this cipher, but though he could read it he couldn't make anything out of it. He concluded that it was a very secret means of communication between the inner circle of the Wild Birds, and that Ivery must be at the back of it. . . . But he was still a long way from finding out anything that mattered.

Then the whole situation changed, for Mary got in touch with Ivery. I must say she behaved like a shameless minx, for she kept on writing to him to an address he had once given her in Paris, and suddenly she got an answer. She was in Paris herself, helping to run one of the railway canteens, and staying with her French cousins the de Mezières. One day he came to see her. That showed the boldness of the man, and his cleverness, for the whole secret police of France were after him and they never got within sight or sound. Yet here he was coming openly in the afternoon to have tea with an English girl. It showed another thing, which made me blaspheme. A man so resolute and single-hearted in his job must have been pretty badly in love to take a risk like that.

He came, and he called himself the Capitaine Bommaerts, with a transport job on the staff of the French G.Q.G. He was on the staff right enough too. Mary said that when she heard that name she nearly fell down. He was quite frank with her, and she with him. They were both peacemakers, ready to break the laws of any land for the sake of a great ideal. Goodness knows what stuff they talked together. Mary said she would blush to think of it till her dying day, and I gathered that on her side it was a mixture of Launcelot Wake at his most pedantic and schoolgirl silliness.

He came again, and they met often, unbeknown to the decorous Madame de Mezières. They walked together in the Bois de Boulogne, and once, with a beating heart, she motored with him to Auteuil for luncheon. He spoke of his house in Picardy, and there were moments, I gathered, when he became the declared lover, to be rebuffed with a hoydenish shyness. Presently the pace became too hot, and after some anguished arguments with Bullivant on the long-distance telephone she went off to Douvecourt to Lady Manorwater's hospital. She went there to escape from him, but mainly, I think, to have a look—trembling in every limb, mind you—at the Château of Eaucourt Sainte-Anne.

I had only to think of Mary to know just what Joan of Arc was. No man ever born could have done that kind of thing. It wasn't recklessness. It was sheer calculating courage.

Then Blenkiron took up the tale. The newspaper we found that Christmas Eve in the Château was of tremendous importance, for Bommaerts had pricked out in the advertisement the very special second cipher of the Wild Birds. That proved that Ivery was at the back of the Swiss business. But Blenkiron made doubly sure.

"I considered the time had come," he said, "to pay high for valuable noos, so I sold the enemy a very pretty de-vice. If you ever gave your mind to ciphers and illicit correspondence, Dick, you would know that the one kind of document you can't write on in any invisible ink is a coated paper, the kind they use in the weeklies to print photographs of leading actresses and the stately homes of England. Anything wet that touches it corrugates the surface a trifle, and you can tell with a microscope if some one's been playing with it. Well, we had the good fortune to discover just how to get over that little difficulty—how to write on glazed paper with a liquid so as the cutest analyst couldn't spot it, and likewise how to detect the writing. I decided to sacrifice that invention, casting my bread upon the waters and looking for a good-sized bakery in return. . . . I had it sold to the enemy. The job wanted delicate handling, but the tenth man from me—he was an Austrian Jew—did the deal and scooped fifty thousand dollars out of it. Then I lay low to watch how my friend would use the de-vice, and I didn't wait long."

He took from his pocket a folded sheet of L'Illustration. Over a photogravure plate ran some words in a large sprawling hand, as if written with a brush.

"That page when I got it yesterday," he said, "was an unassuming picture of General Pétain presenting military medals. There wasn't a scratch or a ripple on its surface. But I got busy with it, and see there!"

He pointed out two names. The writing was a set of key-words we did not know, but two names stood out which I knew too well.

They were "Bommaerts" and "Chelius."

"My God!" I cried, "that's uncanny. It only shows that if you chew long enough. . . ."

"Dick," said Mary, "you mustn't say that again. At the best it's an ugly metaphor, and you're making it a platitude."

"Who is Ivery anyhow?" I asked. "Do we know more about him than we knew in the summer? Mary, what did Bommaerts pretend to be?"

"An Englishman." Mary spoke in the most matter-of-fact tone, as if it were a perfectly usual thing to be made love to by a spy, and that rather soothed my annoyance. "When he asked me to marry him he proposed to take me to a country house in Devonshire. I rather think, too, he had a place in Scotland. But of course he's a German."

"Ye-es," said Blenkiron slowly, "I've got on to his record, and it isn't a pretty story. It's taken some working out, but I've got all the links tested now. . . . He's a Boche and a large-sized nobleman in his own state. Did you ever hear of the Graf von Schwabing?"

I shook my head.

"I think I have heard Uncle Charlie speak of him," said Mary, wrinkling her brows. "He used to hunt with the Pytchley."

"That's the man. But he hasn't troubled the Pytchley for the last eight years. There was a time when he was the last thing in smartness in the German court—officer in the Guards, ancient family, rich, darned clever—all the fixings. Kaiser liked him, and it's easy to see why. I guess a man who had as many personalities as the Graf was amusing after-dinner company. Specially among Germans, who in my experience don't excel in the lighter vein. Anyway, he was William's white-headed boy, and there wasn't a mother with a daughter who wasn't out gunning for Otto von Schwabing. He was about as popular in London and Noo York—and in Paris, too. Ask Sir Walter about him, Dick. He says he had twice the brains of Kuhlmann, and better manners than the Austrian fellow he used to yarn about. . . . Well, one day there came an almighty court scandal, and the bottom dropped out of the Graf's world. It was a pretty beastly story, and I don't gather that Schwabing was as deep in it as some others. But the trouble was that those others had to be shielded at all costs, and Schwabing was made the scapegoat. His name came out in the papers and he had to go. . . ."

"What was the case called?" I asked.

Blenkiron mentioned a name, and I knew why the name Schwabing was familiar. I had read the story long ago in Rhodesia.

"It was some smash," Blenkiron went on. "He was drummed out of the Guards, out of the clubs, out of the country. . . . Now, how would you have felt, Dick, if you had been the Graf? Your life and work and happiness crossed out, and all to save a mangy princeling. 'Bitter as hell,' you say? Hungering for a chance to put it across the lot that had outed you? You wouldn't rest till you had William sobbing on his knees asking your pardon, and you not thinking of granting it? That's the way you'd feel, but that wasn't the Graf's way, and what's more it isn't the German way. He went into exile hating humanity, and with a heart all poison and snakes, but itching to get back. And I'll tell you why. It's because his kind of German hasn't got any other home on this earth. Oh yes, I know there's stacks of good old Teutons come and squat in our little country and turn into fine Americans. You can do a lot with them if you catch them young and teach them the Declaration of Independence and make them study our Sunday papers. But you can't deny there's something comic in the rough about all Germans, before you've civilized them. They're a pecooliar people, a darned pecooliar people, else they wouldn't staff all the menial and indecent occupations on the globe. But that pecooliarity, which is only skin-deep in the working Boche, is in the bone of the grandee. Your German aristocracy can't consort on terms of equality with any other Upper Ten. They swagger and bluff about the world, but they know very well that the world's sniggering at them. They're like a boss from Salt Creek Gully who's made his pile and bought a dress suit and dropped into a Newport evening party. They don't know where to put their hands or how to keep their feet still. . . . Your copper-bottomed English nobleman has got to keep jogging himself to treat them as equals instead of sending them down to the servants' hall. Their fine fixings are just the high light that reveals the everlasting jay. They can't be gentlemen, because they aren't sure of themselves. The world laughs at them, and they know it and it riles them like hell. . . . That's why when a Graf is booted out of the Fatherland, he's got to creep back somehow or be a wandering Jew for the rest of time."

Blenkiron lit another cigar and fixed me with his steady, ruminating eye.

"For eight years the man has slaved, body and soul, for the men who degraded him. He's earned his restoration and I dare say he's got it in his pocket. If merit was rewarded he should be covered with Iron Crosses and Red Eagles. . . . He had a pretty good hand to start out with. He knew other countries and he was a dandy at languages. More, he had an uncommon gift for living a part. That is real genius, Dick, however much it gets up against us. Best of all he had a first-class outfit of brains. I can't say I ever struck a better, and I've come across some bright citizens in my time. . . . And now he's going to win out, unless we get mighty busy."

There was a knock at the door and the solid figure of Andrew Amos revealed itself.

"It's time ye was home, Miss Mary. It chappit half-eleven as I came up the stairs. It's comin' on to rain, so I've brought an umbrelly."

"One word," I said. "How old is the man?"

"Just gone thirty-six," Blenkiron replied.

I turned to Mary, who nodded. "Younger than you, Dick," she said wickedly as she got into her big Jaeger coat.

"I'm going to see you home," I said.

"Not allowed. You've had quite enough of my society for one day. Andrew's on escort duty to-night."

Blenkiron looked after her as the door closed.

"I reckon you've got the best girl in the world."

"Ivery thinks the same," I said grimly, for my detestation of the man who had made love to Mary fairly choked me.

"You can see why. Here's this degenerate coming out of his rotten class, all pampered and petted and satiated with the easy pleasures of life. He has seen nothing of women except the bad kind and the overfed specimens of his own country. I hate being impolite about females, but I've always considered the German variety uncommon like cows. He has had desperate years of intrigue and danger, and consorting with every kind of scallawag. Remember, he's a big man and a poet, with a brain and an imagination that takes every grade without changing gears. Suddenly he meets something that is as fresh and lovely as a spring flower, and has wits too, and the steeliest courage, and yet is all youth and gaiety. It's a new experience for him, a kind of revelation, and he's big enough to value her as she should be valued. . . . No, Dick, I can understand you getting cross, but I reckon it an item to the man's credit."

"It's his blind spot all the same," I said.

"His blind spot," Blenkiron repeated solemnly, "and, please God, we're going to remember that."

Next morning in miserable sloppy weather Blenkiron carted me about Paris. We climbed five sets of stairs to a flat away up in Montmartre, where I was talked to by a fat man with spectacles and a slow voice and told various things that deeply concerned me. Then I went to a room in the Boulevard St. Germain, with a little cabinet opening off it, where I was shown papers and maps and some figures on a sheet of paper that made me open my eyes. We lunched in a modest café tucked away behind the Palais Royal, and our companions were two Alsatians who spoke German better than a Boche and had no names—only numbers. In the afternoon I went to a low building beside the Invalides and saw many generals, including more than one whose features were familiar in two hemispheres. I told them everything about myself, and I was examined like a convict, and all particulars about my appearance and manner of speech written down in a book. That was to prepare the way for me, in case of need, among the vast army of those who work underground and know their chief but do not know each other.

The rain cleared before night, and Blenkiron and I walked back to the hotel through that lemon-coloured dusk that you get in a French winter. We passed a company of American soldiers, and Blenkiron had to stop and stare. I could see that he was stiff with pride, though he wouldn't show it.

"What d'you think of that bunch?" he asked.

"First-rate stuff," I said.

"The men are all right," he drawled critically. "But some of the officer-boys are a bit puffy. They want fining down."

"They'll get it soon enough, honest fellows. You don't keep your weight long in this war."

"Say, Dick," he said shyly, "what do you truly think of our Americans? You've seen a lot of them, and I'd value your views." His tone was that of a bashful author asking for an opinion on his first book.

"I'll tell you what I think. You're constructing a great middle-class army, and that's the most formidable fighting machine on earth. This kind of war doesn't want the Berserker so much as the quiet fellow with a trained mind and a lot to fight for. The American ranks are filled with all sorts, from cow-punchers to college boys, but mostly with decent lads that have good prospects in life before them and are fighting because they feel they're bound to, not because they like it. It was the same stock that pulled through in your Civil War. We have a middle-class division, too—Scottish Territorials, mostly clerks and shopmen and engineers and farmers' sons. When I first struck them my only crab was that the officers weren't much better than the men. It's still true, but the men are super-excellent, and consequently so are the officers. That division gets top marks in the Boche calendar for sheer fighting devilment. . . . And, please God, that's what your American army's going to do. You can wash out the old idea of a regiment of scallawags commanded by dukes. That was right enough, maybe, in the days when you hurrooshed into battle waving a banner, but it don't do with high-explosives and a couple of million men on each side and a battle-front of five hundred miles. The hero of this war is the plain man out of the middle classes, who wants to get back to his home and is going to use all the brains and grit he possesses to finish the job soon."

"That sounds about right," said Blenkiron reflectively. "It pleases me some, for you've maybe guessed that I respect the British Army quite a little. Which part of it do you put top?"

"All of it's good. The French are keen judges and they give front place to the Scots and the Australians. For myself I think the backbone of the Army is the old-fashioned English county regiments that hardly ever get into the papers. . . . Though I don't know, if I had to pick, but I'd take the South Africans. There's only a brigade of them, but they're hell's delight in a battle. But then you'll say I'm prejudiced."

"Well," drawled Blenkiron, "you're a mighty Empire anyhow. I've sojourned up and down it, and I can't guess how the old-time highbrows in your little island came to put it together. But I'll let you into a secret, Dick. I read this morning in a noospaper that there was a natural affinity between Americans and the men of the British Dominions. Take it from me, there isn't—at least not with this American. I don't understand them one little bit. When I see your lean, tall Australians with the sun at the back of their eyes, I'm looking at men from another planet. Outside you and Peter, I never got to fathom a South African. The Canadians live over the fence from us, but you mix up a Canuck with a Yank in your remarks and you'll get a bat in the eye. . . . But most of us Americans have gotten a grip on your Old Country. You'll find us mighty respectful to other parts of your Empire, but we say anything we dam' well please about England. You see, we know her that well and like her that well, we can be free with her.

"It's like," he concluded as we reached the hotel, "it's like a lot of boys that are getting on in the world and are a bit jealous and stand-offish with each other. But they're all at home with the old man who used to warm them up with a hickory cane, even though sometimes in their hearts they call him a standpatter."

That night at dinner we talked solid business—Blenkiron and I and a young French colonel from the 111me Section at G.Q.G. Blenkiron, I remember, got very hurt about being called a business man by the Frenchman, who thought he was paying him a compliment.

"Cut it out," he said. "It is a word that's gone bad with me. There's just two kind of men, those who've gotten sense and those who haven't. A big percentage of us Americans make our living by trading, but we don't think because a man's in business or even because he's made big money that he's any natural good at every job. We've made a college professor our President, and do what he tells us like little boys, though he don't earn more than some of us pay our works manager. You English have gotten business men on the brain, and think a fellow's a dandy at handling your Government if he happens to have made a pile by some flat-catching ramp on your Stock Exchange. It makes me tired. You're about the best business nation on earth, but for God's sake don't begin to talk about it or you'll lose your power. And don't go confusing real business with the ordinary gift of raking in the dollars. Any man with sense could make money if he wanted to, but he mayn't want. He may prefer the fun of the job and let other people do the looting. I reckon the biggest business on the globe to-day is the work behind your lines and the way you feed and supply and transport your army. It beats the Steel Corporation and the Standard Oil to a frazzle. But the man at the head of it all don't earn more than a thousand dollars a month. . . . Your nation's getting to worship Mammon, Dick. Cut it out. There's just the one difference in humanity—sense or no sense, and most likely you won't find any more sense in the man that makes a billion selling bonds than in his brother Tim that lives in a shack and sells corn-cobs. I'm not speaking out of sinful jealousy, for there was a day when I was reckoned a railroad king, and I quit with a bigger pile than kings usually retire on. But I haven't the sense of old Peter, who never even had a bank account. . . . And it's sense that wins in this war."

The colonel, who spoke good English, asked a question about a speech which some politician had made.

"There isn't all the sense I'd like to see at the top," said Blenkiron. "They're fine at smooth words. That wouldn't matter, but they're thinking smooth thoughts. What d'you make of the situation, Dick?"

"I think it's the worst since First Ypres," I said. "Everybody's cock-a-whoop, but God knows why."

"God knows why," Blenkiron repeated. "I reckon it's a simple calculation, and you can't deny it any more than a mathematical law. Russia is counted out. The Boche won't get food from her for a good many months, but he can get more men, and he's got them. He's fighting only on one front, and he's been able to bring troops and guns west so he's as strong as the Allies now on paper. And he's stronger in reality. He's got better railways behind him, and he's fighting on inside lines and can concentrate fast against any bit of our front. I'm no soldier, but that's so, Dick?"

The Frenchman smiled and shook his head. "All the same they will not pass. They could not when they were two to one in 1914, and they will not now. If we Allies could not break through in the last year when we had many more men, how will the Germans succeed now with only equal numbers?"

Blenkiron did not look convinced. "That's what they all say. I talked to a general last week about the coming offensive, and he said he was praying for it to hurry up, for he reckoned Fritz would get the fright of his life. It's a good spirit, maybe, but I don't think it's sound on the facts. We've got two mighty great armies of fine fighting-men, but, because we've two commands, we're bound to move ragged like a peal of bells. The Hun's got one army and forty years of stiff tradition, and, what's more, he's going all out this time. He's going to smash our front before America lines up, or perish in the attempt. . . . Why do you suppose all the peace racket in Germany has died down, and the very men that were talking democracy in the summer are now hot for fighting to a finish? I'll tell you. It's because old Ludendorff has promised them complete victory this spring if they spend enough men, and the Boche is a good gambler and is out to risk it. We're not up against a local attack this time. We're standing up to a great nation going bald-headed for victory or destruction. If we're broken, then America's got to fight a new campaign by herself when she's ready and the Boche has time to make Russia his feeding-ground and diddle our blockade. That puts another five years on to the war, maybe another ten. Are we free and independent peoples going to endure that much? . . . I tell you we're tossing to quit before Easter."

He turned towards me, and I nodded assent.

"That's more or less my view," I said. "We ought to hold, but it'll be by our teeth and nails. For the next six months we'll be fighting without any margin."

"But, my friends, you put it too gravely," cried the Frenchman. "We may lose a mile or two of ground—yes. But serious danger is not possible. They had better chances at Verdun and they failed. Why should they succeed now?"

"Because they are staking everything," Blenkiron replied. "It is the last desperate struggle of a wounded beast, and in these struggles sometimes the hunter perishes. Dick's right. We've got a wasting margin and every extra ounce of weight's going to tell. The battle's in the field, and it's also in every corner of every Allied land. That's why within the next two months we've got to get even with the Wild Birds."

The French colonel—his name was de Vallière—smiled at the name, and Blenkiron answered my unspoken question.

"I'm going to satisfy some of your curiosity, Dick, for I've put together considerable noos of the menagerie. Germany has a good army of spies outside her borders. We shoot a batch now and then, but the others go on working like beavers and they do a mighty deal of harm. They're beautifully organized, but they don't draw on such good human material as we, and I reckon they don't pay in results more than ten cents on a dollar of trouble. But there they are. They're the intelligence officers and their business is just to forward noos. They're the birds in the cage, the—what is it your friend called them?"

"*Die Stubenvögel*," I said.

"Yes, but all the birds aren't caged. There's a few outside the bars and they don't collect noos. They *do* things. If there's anything desperate they're put on the job, and they've got power to act without waiting on instructions from home. I've investigated till my brain's tired and I haven't made out more than half a dozen who I can say for certain are in the business. There's your pal, the Portuguese Jew, Dick. Another's a woman in Genoa, a princess of some sort married to a Greek financier. One's the editor of a pro-Ally up-country paper in the Argentine. One passes as a Baptist minister in Colorado. One was a police spy in the Tsar's Government and is now a red-hot revolutionary in the Caucasus. And the biggest, of course, is Moxon Ivery, who in happier times was the Graf von Schwabing. There aren't above a hundred people in the world know of their existence, and these hundred call them the Wild Birds."

"Do they work together?" I asked.

"Yes. They each get their own jobs to do, but they're apt to flock together for a big piece of devilment. There were four of them in France a year ago before the battle of the Aisne, and they pretty near rotted the French army. That's so, colonel?"

The soldier nodded grimly. "They seduced our weary troops and they bought many politicians. Almost they succeeded, but not quite. The nation is sane again, and is judging and shooting the accomplices at its leisure. But the principals we have never caught."

"You hear that, Dick," said Blenkiron. "You're satisfied this isn't a whimsey of a melodramatic old Yank? I'll tell you more. You know how Ivery worked the submarine business from England. Also, it was the Wild Birds that wrecked Russia. It was Ivery that paid the Bolshevists to sedooce the Army, and the Bolshevists took his money for their own purpose, thinking they were playing a deep game, when all the time he was grinning like Satan, for they were playing his. It was Ivery or some other of the bunch that doped the brigades that broke at Caporetto. If I started in to tell you the history of their doings you wouldn't go to bed, and if you did you wouldn't sleep. . . . There's just this to it. Every finished subtle devilry that the Boche has wrought among the Allies since August 1914 has been the work of the Wild Birds and more or less organized by Ivery. They're worth half a dozen army corps to Ludendorff. They're the mightiest poison merchants the world ever saw, and they've the nerve of hell . . ."

"I don't know," I interrupted. "Ivery's got his soft spot. I saw him in the Tube station."

"Maybe, but he's got the kind of nerve that's wanted. And now I rather fancy he's whistling in his flock."

Blenkiron consulted a notebook. "Pavia—that's the Argentine man— started last month for Europe. He transhipped from a coasting steamer in the West Indies and we've temporarily lost track of him, but he has left his hunting-ground. What do you reckon that means?

"It means," Blenkiron continued solemnly, "that Ivery thinks the game's nearly over. The play's working up for a big climax. . . . And that climax is going to be damnation for the Allies, unless we get a move on."

"Right," I said. "That's what I'm here for. What's the move?"

"The Wild Birds mustn't ever go home, and the man they call Ivery or Bommaerts or Chelius has to decease. It's a cold-blooded proposition, but it's him or the world that's got to break. But before he quits this earth we're bound to get wise about some of his plans, and that means that we can't just shoot a pistol at his face. Also we've got to find him first. We reckon he's in Switzerland, but that is a state with quite a lot of diversified scenery to lose a man in. . . . Still I guess we'll find him. But it's the kind of business to plan out as carefully as a battle. I'm going back to Berne on my old stunt to boss the show, and I'm giving the orders. You're an obedient child, Dick, so I don't reckon on any trouble that way."

Then Blenkiron did an ominous thing. He pulled up a little table and started to lay out Patience cards. Since his duodenum was cured he seemed to have dropped that habit, and from his resuming it I gathered that his mind was uneasy. I can see that scene as if it were yesterday—the French colonel in an arm-chair smoking a cigarette in a long amber holder, and Blenkiron sitting primly on the edge of a yellow silk ottoman, dealing his cards and looking guiltily towards me.

"You'll have Peter for company," he said. "Peter's a sad man, but he has a great heart, and he's been mighty useful to me already. They're going to move him to England very soon. The authorities are afraid of him, for he's apt to talk wild, his health having made him peevish about the British. But there's a deal of red tape in the world, and the orders for his repatriation are slow in coming." The speaker winked very slowly and deliberately with his left eye.

I asked if I was to be with Peter, much cheered at the prospect.

"Why, yes. You and Peter are the collateral in the deal. But the big game's not with you."

I had a presentiment of something coming, something anxious and unpleasant.

"Is Mary in it?" I asked.

He nodded and seemed to pull himself together for an explanation.

"See here, Dick. Our main job is to get Ivery back to Allied soil where we can handle him. And there's just the one magnet that can fetch him back. You aren't going to deny that."

I felt my face getting very red, and that ugly hammer began beating in my forehead. Two grave, patient eyes met my glare.

"I'm damned if I'll allow it!" I cried. "I've some right to a say in the thing. I won't have Mary made a decoy. It's too infernally degrading."

"It isn't pretty, but war isn't pretty, and nothing we do is pretty. I'd have blushed like a rose when I was young and innocent to imagine the things I've put my hand to in the last three years. But have you any other way, Dick? I'm not proud, and I'll scrap the plan if you can show me another. . . . Night after night I've hammered the thing out, and I can't hit on a better. . . . Heigh-ho, Dick, this isn't like you," and he grinned ruefully. "You're making yourself a fine argument in favour of celibacy—in time of war, anyhow. What is it the poet sings?—

> 'White hands cling to the bridle rein,
> Slipping the spur from the booted heel.' "

I was as angry as sin, but I felt all the time I had no case. Blenkiron stopped his game of Patience, sending the cards flying over the carpet, and straddled on the hearthrug.

"You're never going to be a piker. What's dooty, if you won't carry it to the other side of hell? What's the use of yapping about your country if you're going to keep anything back when she calls for it? What's the good of meaning to win the war if you don't put every cent you've got on your stake? You'll make me think you're like the jacks in your English novels that chuck in their hand and say it's up to God, and call that 'seeing it through.' . . . No, Dick, that kind of dooty don't deserve a blessing. You dursn't keep back anything if you want to save your soul.

"Besides," he went on, "what a girl it is! She can't scare and she can't soil. She's white-hot youth and innocence, and she'd take no more harm than clean steel from a muck-heap."

I knew I was badly in the wrong, but my pride was all raw.

"I'm not going to agree till I've talked to Mary."

"But Miss Mary has consented," he said gently "She made the plan."

Next day, in clear blue weather that might have been May, I drove Mary down to Fontainebleau. We lunched in the inn by the bridge and walked in to the forest. I hadn't slept much, for I was tortured by what I thought was anxiety for her, but which was in truth jealousy of Ivery. I don't think that I would have minded her risking her life, for that was part of the game we were both in, but I jibbed at the notion of Ivery coming near her again. I told myself it was honourable pride, but I knew deep down in me that it was jealousy.

I asked her if she had accepted Blenkiron's plan, and she turned mischievous eyes on me.

"I knew I should have a scene with you, Dick. I told Mr. Blenkiron so. . . . Of course I agreed. I'm not even very much afraid of it. I'm a member of the team, you know, and I must play up to my form. I can't do a man's work, so all the more reason why I should tackle the thing I can do."

"But," I stammered, "it's such a . . . such a degrading business for a child like you. I can't bear . . . It makes me hot to think of it."

Her reply was merry laughter.

"You're an old Ottoman, Dick. You haven't doubled Cape Turk yet, and I don't believe you're round Seraglio Point. Why, women aren't the brittle things men used to think them. They never were, and the war has made them like whipcord. Bless you, my dear, we're the tougher sex now. We've had to wait and endure, and we've been so beaten on the anvil of patience that we've lost all our megrims."

She put her hands on my shoulders and looked me in the eyes.

"Look at me, Dick, look at your someday-to-be espoused saint. I'm nineteen years of age next August. Before the war I should have only just put my hair up. I should have been the kind of shivering debutante who blushes when she's spoken to, and oh! I should have thought such silly, silly things about life. . . . Well, in the last two years I've been close to it, and to death. I've nursed the dying. I've seen souls in agony and in triumph. England has allowed me to serve her as she allows her sons. Oh, I'm a robust young woman now, and indeed I think women were always robuster than men. . . . Dick, dear Dick, we're lovers, but we're comrades too—always comrades, and comrades trust each other."

I hadn't anything to say, except contrition, for I had had my lesson. I had been slipping away in my thoughts from the gravity of our task, and Mary had brought me back to it. I remember that as we walked through the woodland we came to a place where there were no signs of war. Elsewhere there were men busy felling trees, and anti-aircraft guns, and an occasional transport wagon, but here there was only a shallow grassy vale, and in the distance, bloomed over like a plum in the evening haze, the roofs of an old dwelling-house among gardens.

Mary clung to my arm as we drank in the peace of it.

"That's what lies for us at the end of the road, Dick," she said softly.

And then, as she looked, I felt her body shiver. She returned to the strange fancy she had had in the St. Germain woods three days before.

"Somewhere it's waiting for us and we shall certainly find it. . . . But first we must go through the Valley of the Shadow. . . . And there is the sacrifice to be made . . . the best of us."

47 ST. ANTON

Ten days later the porter Joseph Zimmer of Arosa, clad in the tough and shape-less trousers of his class, but sporting an old velveteen shooting-coat bequeathed to him by a former German master—speaking the guttural tongue of the Grisons, and with all his belongings in one massive rucksack, came out of the little station of St. Anton and blinked in the frosty sunshine. He looked down upon the old village beside its ice-bound lake, but his business was with the new village of hotels and villas which had sprung up in the last ten years south of the station. He made some halting inquiries of the station people, and a cab-driver outside finally directed him to the place he sought—the cottage of the Widow Summermatter, where resided an English *interné*, one Peter Pienaar.

The porter Joseph Zimmer had had a long and roundabout journey. A fortnight before he had worn the uniform of a British major-general. As such he had been the inmate of an expensive Paris hotel, till one morning, in grey tweed clothes and with a limp, he had taken the Paris-Mediterranean Express with a ticket for an officers' convalescent home at Cannes. Thereafter he had declined in the social scale. At Dijon he had been still an Englishman, but at Pontarlier he had become an American bagman of Swiss parentage, returning to wind up his father's estate. At Berne he limped unobtrusively, and at Zurich, in a little back-street hotel, he became frankly the peasant. For he met a friend there from whom he acquired clothes with that odd rank smell, far stronger than Harris tweed, which marks the raiment of most Swiss guides and all Swiss porters. He also acquired a new name and an old aunt, who a little later received him with open arms and explained to her friends that he was her brother's son from Arosa who three winters ago had hurt his leg wood-cutting and had been discharged from the levy.

A kindly Swiss gentleman, as it chanced, had heard of the deserving Joseph, and interested himself to find him employment. The said philanthropist made a hobby of the French and British prisoners returned from Germany, and had in mind an officer, a crabbed South African with a bad leg, who needed a servant. He was, it seemed, an ill-tempered old fellow who had to be billeted alone, and since he could speak German he would be happier with a Swiss native. Joseph haggled somewhat over the wages, but on his aunt's advice he accepted the job, and, with a very complete set of papers and a store of ready-made reminiscences (it took him some time to swot up the names of the peaks and passes he had traversed), set out for St. Anton, having dispatched beforehand a monstrously ill-spelt letter announcing his coming. He could barely read and write, but he was good at maps, which he had studied carefully, and he noticed with satis-faction that the valley of St. Anton gave easy access to Italy.

As he journeyed south the reflections of that porter would have surprised his fellow travellers in the stuffy third-class carriage. He was thinking of a conversation he had had some days before in a café at Dijon with a young Englishman bound for Modane. . . .

We had bumped up against each other by chance in that strange flitting when we all went to different places at different times, asking nothing of each other's business. Wake had greeted me rather shamefacedly and had proposed dinner together.

I am not good at receiving apologies, and Wake's embarrassed me more than they embarrassed him. "I'm a bit of a cad sometimes," he said. "You know I'm a better fellow than I sounded that night, Hannay."

I mumbled something about not talking rot—the conventional phrase. What worried me was that the man was suffering. You could see it in his eyes. But that evening I got nearer Wake than ever before, and he and I became true friends, for he laid bare his soul before me. That was his trouble, that he could lay bare his soul, for ordinary healthy folk don't analyse their feelings. Wake did, and I think it brought him relief.

"Don't think I was ever your rival. I would no more have proposed to Mary than I would have married one of her aunts. She was so sure of herself, so happy in her single-heartedness that she terrified me. My type of man is not meant for marriage, for women must be in the centre of life, and we must always be standing aside and looking on. It was a damnable thing to be born left-handed."

"The trouble about you, my dear chap," I said, "is that you're too hard to please."

"That's one way of putting it. I should put it more harshly. I hate more than I love. All we humanitarians and pacificists have hatred as our mainspring. Odd, isn't it, for people who preach brotherly love? But it's the truth. We're full of hate towards everything that doesn't square in with our ideas, everything that jars on our ladylike nerves. Fellows like you are so in love with their cause that they've no time or inclination to detest what thwarts them. We've no cause—only negatives, and that means hatred, and self-torture, and a beastly jaundice of soul."

Then I knew that Wake's fault was not spiritual pride, as I had diagnosed it at Biggleswick. The man was abased with humility.

"I see more than other people see," he went on, "and I feel more. That's the curse on me. You're a happy man and you get things done, because you only see one side of a case, one thing at a time. How would you like it if a thousand strings were always tugging at you, if you saw that every course meant the sacrifice of lovely and desirable things, or even the shattering of what you know to be unreplaceable? I'm the kind of stuff poets are made of, but I haven't the poet's gift, so I stagger about the world left-handed and game-legged. . . . Take the war. For me to fight would be worse than for another man to run away. From the bottom of my heart I believe that it needn't have happened, and that all war is a blistering iniquity. And yet belief has got very little to do with virtue. I'm not as good a man as you,

Hannay, who have never thought out anything in your life. My time in the Labour battalion taught me something. I knew that with all my fine aspirations I wasn't as true a man as fellows whose talk was silly oaths and who didn't care a tinker's curse about their soul."

I remember that I looked at him with a sudden understanding. "I think I know you. You're the sort of chap who won't fight for his country because he can't be sure that she's altogether in the right. But he'd cheerfully die for her, right or wrong."

His face relaxed in a slow smile. "Queer that you should say that. I think it's pretty near the truth. Men like me aren't afraid to die, but they haven't quite the courage to live. Every man should be happy in a service, like you, where he obeys orders. I couldn't get on in any service. I lack the bump of veneration. I can't swallow things merely because I'm told to. My sort are always talking about 'service,' but we haven't the temperament to serve. I'd give all I have to be an ordinary cog in the wheel, instead of a confounded outsider who finds fault with the machinery. . . . Take a great violent high-handed fellow like you. You can sink yourself till you become only a name and a number. I couldn't if I tried. I'm not sure if I want to, either. I cling to the odds and ends that are my own."

"I wish I had had you in my battalion a year ago," I said.

"No, you don't. I'd only have been a nuisance. I've been a Fabian since Oxford, but you're a better socialist than me. I'm a rancid individualist."

"But you must be feeling better about the war?" I asked.

"Not a bit of it. I'm still lusting for the heads of the politicians that made it and continue it. But I want to help my country. Honestly, Hannay, I love the old place. More, I think, than I love myself, and that's saying a devilish lot Short of fighting—which would be the sin against the Holy Spirit for me—I'll do my damnedest. But you'll remember I'm not used to team work. If I'm a jealous player, beat me over the head."

His voice was almost wistful, and I liked him enormously.

"Blenkiron will see to that," I said. "We're going to break you to harness, Wake, and then you'll be a happy man. You keep your mind on the game and forget about yourself. That's the cure for jibbers."

As I journeyed to St. Anton I thought a lot about that talk. He was quite right about Mary, who would never have married him. A man with such an angular soul couldn't fit into another's. And then I thought that the chief thing about Mary was just her serene certainty. Her eyes had that settled happy look that I remembered to have seen only in one other human face, and that was Peter's. . . . But I wondered if Peter's eyes were still the same.

I found the cottage, a little wooden thing which had been left perched on its knoll when the big hotels grew up around it. It had a fence in front, but behind it was open to the hillside. At the gate stood a bent old woman with a face like a pippin. My make-up must have been good, for she accepted me before I introduced myself.

"God be thanked you are come," she cried. "The poor lieutenant needed a man to keep him company. He sleeps now, as he does always in the afternoon,

for his leg wearies him in the night. . . . But he is brave, like a soldier. . . .
Come, I will show you the house, for you two will be alone now."

Stepping softly she led me indoors, pointing with a warning finger to the
little bedroom where Peter slept. I found a kitchen with a big stove and a
rough floor of planking, on which lay some badly cured skins. Off it was a
sort of pantry with a bed for me. She showed me the pots and pans for
cooking and the stores she had laid in, and where to find water and fuel. "I
will do the marketing daily," she said, "and if you need me, my dwelling is
half a mile up the road beyond the new church. God be with you, young man,
and be kind to that wounded one."

When the Widow Summermatter had departed I sat down in Peter's
arm-chair and took stock of the place. It was quiet and simple and homely,
and through the window came the gleam of snow on the diamond hills. On
the table beside the stove were Peter's cherished belongings—his buck-skin
pouch and the pipe which Jannie Grobelaar had carved for him in St. Helena,
an aluminium field match-box I had given him, a cheap large-print Bible such
as padres present to well-disposed privates, and an old battered *Pilgrim's
Progress* with gaudy pictures. The illustration at which I opened showed
Faithful going up to Heaven from the fire of Vanity Fair like a woodcock
that has just been flushed. Everything in the room was exquisitely neat, and
I knew that that was Peter and not the Widow Summermatter. On a peg
behind the door hung his much-mended coat, and sticking out of a pocket I
recognized a sheaf of my own letters. In one corner stood something which
I had forgotten about—an invalid chair.

The sight of Peter's plain little oddments made me feel solemn. I wondered if
his eyes would be like Mary's now, for I could not conceive what life would be
for him as a cripple. Very gently I opened the bedroom door and slipped inside.

He was lying on a camp bedstead with one of those striped Swiss blankets
pulled up round his ears, and he was asleep. It was the old Peter beyond
doubt. He had the hunter's gift of breathing evenly through his nose, and the
white scar on the deep brown of his forehead was what I had always remembered. The only change since I last saw him was that he had let his beard
grow again, and it was grey.

As I looked at him the remembrance of all we had been through together
flooded back upon me, and I could have cried with joy at being beside him.
Women, bless their hearts! can never know what long comradeship means to
men; it is something not in their lives, something that belongs only to that
wild, undomesticated world which we forswear when we find our mates.
Even Mary understood only a bit of it. I had just won her love, which was the
greatest thing that ever came my way, but if she had entered at that moment I
would scarcely have turned my head. I was back again in the old life and was
not thinking of the new.

Suddenly I saw that Peter was awake, and was looking at me.

"Dick," he said in a whisper, "Dick, my old friend."

The blanket was tossed off, and his long, lean arms were stretched out to
me. I gripped his hands, and for a little we did not speak. Then I saw how

woefully he had changed. His left leg had shrunk, and from the knee down was like a pipe stem. His face, when awake, showed the lines of hard suffering, and he seemed shorter by half a foot. But his eyes were still like Mary's. Indeed they seemed to be more patient and peaceful than in the days when he sat beside me on the buck-wagon and peered over the hunting-veld.

I picked him up—he was no heavier than Mary—and carried him to his chair beside the stove. Then I boiled water and made tea, as we had so often done together.

"Peter, old man," I said, "we're on trek again, and this is a very snug little *rondavel*. We've had many good yarns, but this is going to be the best. First of all, how about your health?"

"Good. I'm a strong man again, but slow like a hippo cow. I have been lonely sometimes, but that is all by now. Tell me of the big battles."

But I was hungry for news of him, and kept him to his own case. He had no complaint of his treatment except that he did not like Germans. The doctors at the hospital had been clever, he said, and had done their best for him, but nerves and sinews and small bones had been so wrecked that they could not mend his leg, and Peter had all the Boer's dislike of amputation. One doctor had been in Damaraland and talked to him of those baked sunny spaces and made him homesick. But he returned always to his dislike of Germans. He had seen them herding our soldiers like brute-beasts, and the commandant had a face like Stumm and a chin that stuck out and wanted hitting. He made an exception for the great airman Lensch, who had downed him.

"He's a white man, that one," he said. "He came to see me in hospital and told me a lot of things. I think he made them treat me well. He is a big man, Dick, who would make two of me, and he has a round, merry face and pale eyes like Frickie Celliers who could put a bullet through a pauw's head at two hundred yards. He said he was sorry I was lame, for he hoped to have more fights with me. Some woman that tells fortunes had said that I would be the end of him, but he reckoned she had got the thing the wrong way on. I hope he will come through this war, for he is a good man, though a German. . . . But the others! They are like the fool in the Bible, fat and ugly in good fortune and proud and vicious when their luck goes. They are not a people to be happy with."

Then he told me that to keep up his spirits he had amused himself with playing a game. He had prided himself on being a Boer, and spoken coldly of the British. He had also, I gathered, imparted many things calculated to deceive. So he left Germany with good marks, and in Switzerland had held himself aloof from the other British wounded, on the advice of Blenkiron, who had met him as soon as he crossed the frontier. I gathered it was Blenkiron who had had him sent to St. Anton, and in his time there, as a disgruntled Boer, he had mixed a good deal with Germans. They had pumped him about our air service, and Peter had told them many ingenious lies and heard curious things in return.

"They are working hard, Dick," he said. "Never forget that. The German is a stout enemy, and when we beat him with a machine he sweats till he has invented a new one. They have great pilots, but never so many good ones as we, and I do not think in ordinary fighting they can ever beat us. But you must watch Lensch, for I fear him. He has a new machine, I hear, with great engines and a short wingspread, but the wings so cambered that he can climb fast. That will be a surprise to spring upon us. You will say that we'll soon better it. So we shall, but if it was used at a time when we were pushing hard it might make the little difference that loses battles."

"You mean," I said, "that if we had a great attack ready and had driven all the Boche planes back from our front, Lensch and his circus might get over in spite of us and blow the gaff?"

"Yes," he said solemnly. "Or, if we were attacked, and had a weak spot, Lensch might show the Germans where to get through. I do not think we are going to attack for a long time; but I am pretty sure that Germany is going to fling every man against us. That is the talk of my friends, and it is not bluff."

That night I cooked our modest dinner, and we smoked our pipes with the stove door open and the good smell of wood-smoke in our nostrils. I told him of all my doings and of the Wild Birds and Ivery and the job we were engaged on. Blenkiron's instructions were that we two should live humbly and keep our eyes and ears open, for we were outside suspicion—the cantankerous lame Boer and his loutish servant from Arosa. Somewhere in the place was a rendezvous of our enemies, and thither came Chelius on his dark errands.

Peter nodded his head sagely. "I think I have guessed the place. The daughter of the old woman used to pull my chair sometimes down to the village, and I have sat in cheap inns and talked to servants. There is a fresh-water pan there, but it is all covered with snow now, and beside it there is a big house that they call the Pink Chalet. I do not know much about it, except that rich folk live in it, but I know the other houses and they are harmless. Also the big hotels, which are too cold and public for strangers to meet in."

I put Peter to bed, and it was a joy to me to look after him, to give him his tonic and prepare the hot-water bottle that comforted his neuralgia. His behaviour was like a docile child's, and he never lapsed from his sunny temper, though I could see how his leg gave him hell. They had tried massage for it and given it up, and there was nothing for him but to endure till nature and his tough constitution deadened the tortured nerves again. I shifted my bed out of the pantry and slept in the room with him, and when I woke in the night, as one does the first time in a strange place, I could tell by his breathing that he was wakeful and suffering.

Next day a bath-chair containing a grizzled cripple and pushed by a limping peasant might have been seen descending the long hill to the village. It was clear frosty weather which made the cheeks tingle, and I felt so full of beans that it was hard to remember my game leg. The valley was shut in on the east by a great mass of rocks and glaciers, belonging to a mountain whose top could not be seen. But on the south, above the snowy fir woods, there was a most delicate lace-like peak with a point like a needle. I looked at it with interest, for beyond it lay the valley which led to the Staub Pass, and beyond that was Italy—and Mary.

The old village of St. Anton had one long, narrow street which bent at

right angles to a bridge which spanned the river flowing from the lake.
Thence the road climbed steeply, but at the other end of the street it ran
on the level by the water's edge, lined with gimcrack boarding-houses, now
shuttered to the world, and a few villas in patches of garden. At the far end,
just before it plunged into a pine wood, a promontory jutted into the lake,
leaving a broad space between the road and the water. Here were the grounds
of a more considerable dwelling—snow-covered laurels and rhododendrons
with one or two bigger trees—and just on the water-edge stood the house
itself, called the Pink Chalet.

I wheeled Peter past the entrance on the crackling snow of the highway.
Seen through the gaps of the trees the front looked new, but the back part
seemed to be of some age, for I could see high walls, broken by few windows,
hanging over the water. The place was no more a chalet than a donjon, but I
suppose the name was given in honour of a wooden gallery above the front
door. The whole thing was washed in an ugly pink. There were outhouses—
garage or stables among the trees—and at the entrance there were fairly
recent tracks of an automobile.

On our way back we had some very bad beer in a café and made friends
with the woman who kept it. Peter had to tell her his story, and I trotted out
my aunt in Zurich, and in the end we heard her grievances. She was a true
Swiss, angry at all the belligerents who had spoiled her livelihood, hating
Germany most but also fearing her most. Coffee, tea, fuel, bread, even milk
and cheese, were hard to get and cost a ransom. It would take the land years
to recover, and there would be no more tourists, for there was little money
left in the world. I dropped a question about the Pink Chalet, and was told
that it belonged to one Schweigler, a professor of Berne, an old man who
came sometimes for a few days in the summer. It was often let, but not now.
Asked if it was occupied, she remarked that some friends of the Schweiglers—
rich people from Basle—had been there for the winter. "They come and go
in great cars," she said bitterly, "and they bring their food from the cities.
They spend no money in this poor place."

Presently Peter and I fell into a routine of life, as if we had always kept
house together. In the morning he went abroad in his chair, in the afternoon I
would hobble about on my own errands. We sank into the background and
took its colour, and a less conspicuous pair never faced the eye of suspicion.
Once a week a young Swiss officer, whose business it was to look after British
wounded, paid us a hurried visit. I used to get letters from my aunt in
Zurich, sometimes with the post-mark of Arosa, and now and then these
letters would contain curiously worded advice or instructions from him
whom my aunt called "the kind patron." Generally I was told to be patient.
Sometimes I had word about the health of "my little cousin across the
mountains." Once I was bidden expect a friend of the patron's, the wise
doctor of whom he had often spoken, but though after that I shadowed the
Pink Chalet for two days no doctor appeared.

My investigations were a barren business. I used to go down to the village in the afternoon and sit in an out-of-the-way café, talking slow German with peasants and hotel porters, but there was little to learn. I knew all there was to hear about the Pink Chalet, and that was nothing. A young man who ski-ed stayed for three nights and spent his days on the alps above the fir woods. A party of four, including two women, was reported to have been there for a night—all ramifications of the rich family of Basle. I studied the house from the lake, which should have been nicely swept into ice-rinks, but from lack of visitors was a heap of blown snow. The high old walls of the back part were built straight from the water's edge. I remember I tried a short cut through the grounds to the highroad and was given "Good afternoon" by a smiling German manservant. One way and another I gathered there were a good many serving-men about the place—too many for the infrequent guests. But beyond this I discovered nothing.

Not that I was bored, for I had always Peter to turn to. He was thinking a lot about South Africa, and the thing he liked best was to go over with me every detail of our old expeditions. They belonged to a life which he could think about without pain, whereas the war was too near and bitter for him. He liked to hobble out-of-doors after the darkness came and look at his old friends, the stars. He called them by the words they use on the veld, and the first star of morning he called the *voorlooper*—the little boy who inspans the oxen—a name I had not heard for twenty years. Many a great yarn we spun in the long evenings, but I always went to bed with a sore heart. The longing in his eyes was too urgent, longing not for old days or far countries, but for the health and strength which had once been his pride.

One night I told him about Mary.

"She will be a happy *mysie*," he said, "but you will need to be very clever with her, for women are queer cattle and you and I don't know their ways. They tell me English women do not cook and make clothes like our *vrouws*, so what will she find to do? I doubt an idle woman will be like a mealie-fed horse."

It was no good explaining to him the kind of girl Mary was, for that was a world entirely beyond his ken. But I could see that he felt lonelier than ever at my news. So I told him of the house I meant to have in England when the war was over—an old house in a green hilly country, with fields that would carry four head of cattle to the *morgen* and furrows of clear water, and orchards of plums and apples. "And you will stay with us all the time," I said. "You will have your own rooms and your own boy to look after you, and you will help me to farm, and we will catch fish together, and shoot the wild ducks when they come up from the pans in the evening. I have found a better countryside than the Houtbosch, where you and I planned to have a farm. It is a blessed and happy place, England."

He shook his head. "You are a kind man, Dick, but your pretty *mysie* won't want an ugly old fellow like me hobbling about her house. . . . I do not think I will go back to Africa, for I should be sad there in the sun. I will find a little place in England, and some day I will visit you, old friend."

That night his stoicism seemed for the first time to fail him. He was silent for a long time and went early to bed, where I can vouch for it he did not sleep. But he must have thought a lot in the night time, for in the morning he had got himself in hand and was as cheerful as a sandboy.

I watched his philosophy with amazement. It was far beyond anything I could have compassed myself. He was so frail and so poor, for he had never had anything in the world but his bodily fitness, and he had lost that now. And remember he had lost it after some months of glittering happiness, for in the air he had found the element for which he had been born. Sometimes he dropped a hint of those days when he lived in the clouds and invented a new kind of battle, and his voice always grew hoarse. I could see that he ached with longing for their return. And yet he never had a word of complaint. That was the ritual he had set himself, his point of honour, and he faced the future with the same kind of courage as that with which he had tackled a wild beast or Lensch himself. Only it needed a far bigger brand of fortitude.

Another thing was that he had found religion. I doubt if that is the right way to put it, for he had always had it. Men who live in the wilds know they are in the hands of God. But his old kind had been a tattered thing, more like heathen superstition, though it had always kept him humble. But now he had taken to reading the Bible and to thinking in his lonely nights, and he had got a creed of his own. I dare say it was crude enough, I am sure it was unorthodox; but if the proof of religion is that it gives a man a prop in bad days, then Peter's was the real thing. He used to ferret about in the Bible and the *Pilgrim's Progress*—they were both equally inspired in his eyes—and find texts which he interpreted in his own way to meet his case. He took every-thing quite literally. What happened three thousand years ago in Palestine might, for all he minded, have been going on next door. I used to chaff him and tell him that he was like the Kaiser, very good at fitting the Bible to his purpose, but his sincerity was so complete that he only smiled. I remember one night, when he had been thinking about his flying days, he found a passage in Thessalonians about the dead rising to meet their Lord in the air, and that cheered him a lot. Peter, I could see, had the notion that his time here wouldn't be very long, and he liked to think that when he got his release he would find once more the old rapture.

Once, when I said something about his patience, he said he had got to try to live up to Mr. Standfast. He had fixed on that character to follow, though he would have preferred Mr. Valiant-for-Truth if he had thought himself good enough. He used to talk about Mr. Standfast in his queer way as if he were a friend of us both, like Blenkiron. . . . I tell you I was humbled out of all my pride by the sight of Peter, so uncomplaining and gentle and wise. The Almighty Himself couldn't have made a prig out of him, and he never would have thought of preaching. Only once did he give me advice. I had always a liking for short cuts, and I was getting a bit restive under the long inaction. One day when I expressed my feelings on the matter, Peter upped and read from the *Pilgrim's Progress*: "Some also have wished that the next way to their Father's house were here, that they might be troubled no more with either hills or mountains to go over, but the Way is the Way, and there is an end."

All the same when we got into March and nothing happened I grew pretty anxious. Blenkiron had said we were fighting against time, and here were the weeks slipping away. His letters came occasionally, always in the shape of communications from my aunt. One told me that I would soon be out of a job, for Peter's repatriation was just about through, and he might get his movement order any day. Another spoke of my little cousin over the hills, and said that she hoped soon to be going to a place called Santa Chiara in the Val Saluzzana. I got out the map in a hurry and measured the distance from there to St. Anton and pored over the two roads thither—the short one by the Staub Pass and the long one by the Marjolana. These letters made me think that things were nearing a climax, but still no instructions came. I had nothing to report in my own messages, I had discovered nothing in the Pink Chalet but idle servants. I was not even sure if the Pink Chalet were not a harmless villa, and I hadn't come within a thousand miles of finding Chelius. All my desire to imitate Peter's stoicism didn't prevent me from getting occasionally rattled and despondent.

The one thing I could do was to keep fit, for I had a notion I might soon want all my bodily strength. I had to keep up my pretence of lameness in the daytime, so I used to take my exercise at night. I would sleep in the after-noon, when Peter had his siesta, and then about ten in the evening, after putting him to bed, I would slip out-of-doors and go for a four or five hours' tramp. Wonderful were those midnight wanderings. I pushed up through the snow-laden pines to the ridges where the snow lay in great wreaths and scallops, till I stood on a crest with a frozen world at my feet and above me a host of glittering stars. Once on a night of full moon I reached the glacier at the valley head, scrambled up the moraine to where the ice began, and peered fearfully into the spectral crevasses. At such hours I had the earth to myself, for there was not a sound except the slipping of a burden of snow from the trees or the crack and rustle which reminded me that a glacier was a moving river. The war seemed very far away, and I felt the littleness of our human struggles, till I thought of Peter turning from side to side to find ease in the cottage far below me. Then I realized that the spirit of man was the greatest thing in this spacious world. . . . I would get back about three or four, have a bath in the water which had been warming in my absence, and creep into bed, almost ashamed of having two sound legs, when a better man a yard away had but one.

Oddly enough at these hours there seemed more life in the Pink Chalet than by day. Once, tramping across the lake long after midnight, I saw lights in the lake-front in windows which for ordinary were blank and shuttered. Several times I cut across the grounds when the moon was dark. On one such occasion a great car with no lights swept up the drive, and I heard low voices at the door. Another time a man ran hastily past me, and entered the house by a little door on the eastern side, which I had not before noticed. . . . Slowly the conviction began to grow on me that we were not wrong in marking down this place, that things went on within it which it deeply concerned us to discover. But I was puzzled to think of a way. I might butt inside, but for all I knew it would be upsetting Blenkiron's plans, for he had given me no instructions about housebreaking. All this unsettled me worse than ever. I began to lie awake planning some means of entrance . . . I would be a peasant from the next valley who had twisted his ankle. . . . I would go seeking an imaginary cousin among the servants. . . . I would start a fire in the place and have the doors flung open to zealous neighbours. . . .

And then suddenly I got instructions in a letter from Blenkiron.

It came inside a parcel of warm socks that arrived from my kind aunt. But the letter for me was not from her. It was in Blenkiron's large sprawling hand and the style of it was all his own. He told me that he had about finished his job. He had got his line on Chelius, who was the bird he expected, and that bird would soon wing its way southward across the mountains for the reason I knew of.

"We've got an almighty move on," he wrote, "and please God you're going to hustle some in the next week. It's going better than I ever hoped." But something was still to be done. He had struck a countryman, one Clarence Donne, a journalist of Kansas City, whom he had taken into the business. Him he described as a "crackerjack" and commended to my esteem. He was coming to St. Anton, for there was a game afoot at the Pink Chalet, which he would give me news of. I was to meet him next evening at nine-fifteen at the little door in the east end of the house. "For the love of Mike, Dick," he concluded, "be on time and do everything Clarence tells you as if he was me. It's a mighty complex affair, but you and he have sand enough to pull it through. Don't worry about your little cousin. She's safe and out of the job now."

My first feeling was one of immense relief, especially at the last words. I read the letter a dozen times to make sure I had its meaning. A flash of suspicion crossed my mind that it might be a fake, principally because there was no mention of Peter, who had figured large in the other missives. But why should Peter be mentioned when he wasn't on in this piece? The signature convinced me. Ordinarily Blenkiron signed himself in full with a fine commercial flourish. But when I was at the Front he had got into the habit of making a kind of hieroglyphic of his surname to me and sticking J. S. after it in a bracket. That was how this letter was signed, and it was sure proof it was all right.

I spent that day and the next in wild spirits. Peter spotted what was on, though I did not tell him for fear of making him envious. I had to be extra kind to him, for I could see that he ached to have a hand in the business. Indeed he asked shyly if I couldn't fit him in, and I had to lie about it and say it was only another of my aimless circumnavigations of the Pink Chalet.

"Try and find something where I can help," he pleaded. "I'm pretty strong still, though I'm lame, and I can shoot a bit."

I declared that he would be used in time, that Blenkiron had promised he would be used, but for the life of me I couldn't see how.

At nine o'clock on the evening appointed I was on the lake opposite the house, close in under the shore, making my way to the rendezvous. It was a coal-black night, for though the air was clear the stars were shining with little light, and the moon had not yet risen. With a premonition that I might be long away from food, I had brought some slabs of chocolate, and my pistol and torch were in my pocket. It was bitter cold, but I had ceased to mind weather, and I wore my one suit and no overcoat.

The house was like a tomb for silence. There was no crack of light anywhere, and none of those smells of smoke and food which proclaim habitation. It was an eerie job scrambling up the steep bank east of the place, to where the flat of the garden started, in a darkness so great that I had to grope my way like a blind man.

I found the little door by feeling along the edge of the building. Then I stepped into an adjacent clump of laurels to wait on my companion. He was there before me.

"Say," I heard a rich Middle West voice whisper, "are you Joseph Zimmer? I'm not shouting any names, but I guess you're the guy I was told to meet here."

"Mr. Donne?" I whispered back.

"The same," he replied. "Shake."

I gripped a gloved and mittened hand which drew me towards the door.

48   I LIE ON A HARD BED

The journalist from Kansas City was a man of action. He wasted no words in introducing himself or unfolding his plan of campaign. "You've got to follow me, mister, and not deviate one inch from my tracks. The explaining part will come later. There's big business in this shack to-night." He unlocked the little door with scarcely a sound, slid the crust of snow from his boots, and preceded me into a passage as black as a cellar. The door swung smoothly behind us, and after the sharp out-of-doors the air smelt stuffy as the inside of a safe.

A hand reached back to make sure that I followed. We appeared to be in a flagged passage under the main level of the house. My hob-nailed boots slipped on the floor, and I steadied myself on the wall, which seemed to be of undressed stone. Mr. Donne moved softly and assuredly, for he was better shod for the job than I, and his guiding hand came back constantly to make sure of my whereabouts.

I remember that I felt just as I had felt when on that August night I had explored the crevice on the Coolin—the same sense that something queer was going to happen, the same recklessness and contentment. Moving a foot at a time with immense care, we came to a right-hand turning. Two shallow steps led us to another passage, and then my groping hands struck a blind wall. The American was beside me, and his mouth was close to my ear.

"Got to crawl now," he whispered. "You lead, mister, while I shed this coat of mine. Eight feet on your stomach and then upright."

I wriggled through a low tunnel, broad enough to take three men abreast, but not two feet high. Half-way through I felt suffocated, for I never liked holes, and I had a momentary anxiety as to what we were after in this cellar pilgrimage. Presently I smelt free air and got on to my knees.

"Right, mister?" came a whisper from behind. My companion seemed to be waiting till I was through before he followed.

"Right," I answered, and very carefully rose to my feet.

Then something happened behind me. There was a jar and a bump as if the roof of the tunnel had subsided. I turned sharply and groped at the mouth. I stuck my leg down and found a block.

"Donne," I said, as loud as I dared, "are you hurt? Where are you?"

But no answer came.

Even then I thought only of an accident. Something had miscarried, and I was cut off in the cellars of an unfriendly house away from the man who knew the road and had a plan in his head. I was not so much frightened as exasperated. I turned from the tunnel mouth and groped into the darkness before me. I might as well prospect the kind of prison into which I had blundered.

I took three steps—no more. My feet seemed suddenly to go from me and fly upward. So sudden was it that I fell heavy and dead like a log, and my head struck the floor with a crash that for a moment knocked me senseless. I was dimly conscious of something falling on me and of an intolerable pressure on my chest. I struggled for breath, and found my arms and legs pinned and my whole body in a kind of wooden vice. I was sick with the concussion, and could do nothing but gasp and choke down my nausea. The cut in the back of my head was bleeding freely and that helped to clear my wits, but I lay for a minute or two incapable of thought. I shut my eyes tight, as a man does when he is fighting with a swoon.

When I opened them there was light. It came from the left side of the room, the broad glare of a strong electric torch. I watched it stupidly, but it gave me the fillip needed to pick up the threads. I remembered the tunnel now and the Kansas journalist. Then behind the light I saw a face which pulled my flickering senses out of the mire.

I saw the heavy ulster and the cap, which I had realized, though I had not seen, outside in the dark laurels. They belonged to the journalist, Clarence Donne, the trusted emissary of Blenkiron. But I saw his face now, and it was that face which I had boasted to Bullivant I could never mistake again upon earth. I did not mistake it now, and I remember I had a faint satisfaction that I had made good my word. I had not mistaken it, for I had not had the chance to look at it till this moment. I saw with acid clearness the common denominator of all its disguises—the young man who lisped in the seaside villa, the stout philanthropist of Biggleswick, the pulpy panic-stricken creature of the Tube station, the trim French staff officer of the Picardy château. . . . I saw more, for I saw it beyond the need of disguise. I was looking at von Schwabing, the exile, who had done more for Germany than any army commander. . . . Mary's words came back to me—"the most dangerous man in the world." . . . I was not afraid, or broken-hearted at failure, or angry—not yet, for I was too dazed and awestruck. I looked at him as one might look at some cataclysm of nature which had destroyed a continent.

The face was smiling.

"I am happy to offer you hospitality at last," it said.

I pulled my wits farther out of the mud to attend to him. The cross-bar on my chest pressed less hard and I breathed better. But when I tried to speak, the words would not come.

"We are old friends," he went on. "We have known each other quite intimately for four years, which is a long time in war. I have been interested in you, for you have a kind of crude intelligence, and you have compelled me to take you seriously. If you were cleverer you would appreciate the compliment. But you were fool enough to think you could beat me, and for that you must be punished. Oh no, don't flatter yourself you were ever dangerous. You were only troublesome and presumptuous, like a mosquito one flicks off one's sleeve."

He was leaning against the side of a heavy closed door. He lit a cigar from a little gold tinder box and regarded me with amused eyes.

"You will have time for reflection, so I propose to enlighten you a little. You are an observer of small things. So? Did you ever see a cat with a mouse? The mouse runs about and hides and manoeuvres and thinks it is playing its own game. But at any moment the cat can stretch out its paw and put an end to it. You are the mouse, my poor General—for I believe you are one of those funny amateurs that the English call generals. At any moment during the last nine months I could have put an end to you with a nod."

My nausea had stopped and I could understand what he said, though I had still no power to reply.

"Let me explain," he went on. "I watched with amusement your gambols at Biggleswick. My eyes followed you when you went to the Clyde and in your stupid twistings in Scotland. I gave you rope, because you were futile, and I had graver things to attend to. I allowed you to amuse yourself at your British Front with childish investigations and to play the fool in Paris. I have followed every step of your course in Switzerland, and I have helped your idiotic Yankee friend to plot against myself. While you thought you were drawing your net around me, I was drawing mine around you. I assure you, it has been a charming relaxation from serious business."

I knew the man was lying. Some part was true, for he had clearly fooled Blenkiron; but I remembered the hurried flight from Biggleswick and Eaucourt Sainte-Anne when the game was certainly against him. He had me at his mercy, and was wreaking his vanity on me. That made him smaller in my eyes, and my first awe began to pass.

"I never cherish rancour, you know," he said. "In my business it is silly to be angry, for it wastes energy. But I do not tolerate insolence, my dear General. And my country has the habit of doing justice on her enemies. It may interest you to know that the end is not far off. Germany has faced a jealous world in arms and she is about to be justified of her great courage. She has broken up bit by bit the clumsy organization of her opponents. Where is Russia to-day, the steam-roller that was to crush us? Where is the poor dupe

Rumania? Where is the strength of Italy, who was once to do wonders for what she called Liberty? Broken, all of them. I have played my part in that work, and now the need is past. My country with free hands is about to turn upon your armed rabble in the West and drive it into the Atlantic. Then we shall deal with the ragged remains of France and the handful of noisy Americans. By midsummer there will be peace dictated by triumphant Germany."

"By God, there won't!" I had found my voice at last.

"By God, there will!" he said pleasantly. "It is what you call a mathematical certainty. You will no doubt die bravely, like the savage tribes that your Empire used to conquer. But we have the greater discipline and the stronger spirit and the bigger brain. Stupidity is always punished in the end, and you are a stupid race. Do not think that your kinsmen across the Atlantic will save you. They are a commercial people and by no means sure of themselves. When they have blustered a little they will see reason and find some means of saving their face. Their comic President will make a speech or two and write us a solemn Note, and we will reply with the serious rhetoric which he loves, and then we shall kiss and be friends. You know in your heart that it will be so."

A great apathy seemed to settle on me. This bragging did not make me angry, and I had no longer any wish to contradict him. It may have been the result of the fall, but my mind had stopped working. I heard his voice as one listens casually to the ticking of a clock.

"I will tell you more," he was saying. "This is the evening of the 18th day of March. Your generals in France expect an attack, but they are not sure where it will come. Some think it may be in Champagne or on the Aisne, some at Ypres, some at St. Quentin. Well, my dear General, you alone will I take into our confidence. On the morning of the 21st, three days from now, we attack the right wing of the British Army. In two days we shall be in Amiens. On the third we shall have driven a wedge as far as the sea. Then in a week or so we shall have rolled up your army from the right, and presently we shall be in Boulogne and Calais. After that Paris falls, and then Peace."

I made no answer. The word "Amiens" recalled Mary, and I was trying to remember the day in January when she and I had motored south from that pleasant city.

"Why do I tell you these things? Your intelligence, for you are not altogether foolish, will have supplied the answer. It is because your life is over. As your Shakespeare says, the rest is silence. . . . No, I am not going to kill you. That would be crude, and I hate crudities. I am going now on a little journey, and when I return in twenty-four hours' time you will be my companion. You are going to visit Germany, my dear General."

That woke me to attention, and he noticed it, for he went on with gusto.

"You have heard of the Untergrundbahn? No? And you boast of an Intelligence service! Yet your ignorance is shared by the whole of your General Staff. It is a little organization of my own. By it we can take unwilling and dangerous people inside our frontier to be dealt with as we please. Some have gone from England and many from France. Officially I believe they are recorded as 'missing,' but they did not go astray on any battlefield. They have been gathered from their homes or from hotels or offices or even the busy streets. I will not conceal from you that the service of our Underground Railway is a little irregular from England and France. But from Switzerland it is smooth as a trunk line. There are unwatched spots on the frontier, and we have our agents among the frontier guards, and we have no difficulty about passes. It is a pretty device, and you will soon be privileged to observe its working. . . . In Germany I cannot promise you comfort, but I do not think your life will be dull."

As he spoke these words, his urbane smile changed to a grin of impish malevolence. Even through my torpor I felt the venom and I shivered.

"When I return I shall have another companion." His voice was honeyed again. "There is a certain pretty lady who was to be the bait to entice me into Italy. It is so? Well, I have fallen to the bait. I have arranged that she shall meet me this very night at a mountain inn on the Italian side. I have arranged, too, that she shall be alone. She is an innocent child, and I do not think that she has been more than a tool in the clumsy hands of your friends. She will come with me when I ask her, and we shall be a merry party in the Underground Express."

My apathy vanished, and every nerve in me was alive at the words.

"You cur!" I cried. "She loathes the sight of you. She wouldn't touch you with the end of a barge pole."

He flicked the ash from his cigar. "I think you are mistaken. I am very persuasive, and I do not like to use compulsion with a woman. But, willing or not, she will come with me. I have worked hard and I am entitled to my pleasure, and I have set my heart on that little lady."

There was something in his tone, gross, leering, assured, half contemptuous, that made my blood boil. He had fairly got me on the raw, and the hammer beat violently in my forehead. I could have wept with sheer rage, and it took all my fortitude to keep my mouth shut. But I was determined not to add to his triumph.

He looked at his watch. "Time passes," he said. "I must depart to my charming assignation. I will give your remembrances to the lady. Forgive me for making no arrangements for your comfort till I return. Your constitution is so sound that it will not suffer from a day's fasting. To set your mind at rest I may tell you that escape is impossible. This mechanism has been proved too often, and if you did break loose from it, my servants would deal with you. But I must speak a word of caution. If you tamper with it or struggle too much it will act in a curious way. The floor beneath you covers a shaft which runs to the lake below. Set a certain spring at work and you may find yourself shot down into the water far below the ice, where your body will rot till the spring. . . . That, of course, is an alternative open to you, if you do not care to wait for my return."

He lit a fresh cigar, waved his hand, and vanished through the doorway. As it shut behind him, the sound of his footsteps instantly died away. The walls must have been as thick as a prison's.

★

I suppose I was what people in books call "stunned." The illumination during the past few minutes had been so dazzling that my brain could not master it. I remember very clearly that I did not think about the ghastly failure of our scheme, or the German plans which had been insolently unfolded to me as to one dead to the world. I saw a single picture—an inn in a snowy valley (I saw it as a small place like Peter's cottage), a solitary girl, that smiling devil who had left me, and then the unknown terror of the Underground Railway. I think my courage went for a bit, and I cried with feebleness and rage. The hammer in my forehead had stopped, for it only beat when I was angry in action. Now that I lay trapped, the manhood had slipped out of my joints, and if Ivery had still been in the doorway, I think I would have whined for mercy. I would have offered him all the knowledge I had in the world if he had promised to leave Mary alone.

Happily he wasn't there, and there was no witness of my cowardice. Happily, too, it is just as difficult to be a coward for long as to be a hero. It was Blenkiron's phrase about Mary that pulled me together—"She can't scare and she can't soil." No, by heavens, she couldn't. I could trust my lady far better than I could trust myself. I was still sick with anxiety, but I was getting a pull on myself. I was done in, but Ivery would get no triumph out of me. Either I would go under the ice, or I would find a chance of putting a bullet through my head before I crossed the frontier. If I could do nothing else, I could perish decently. . . . And then I laughed, and I knew I was past the worst. What made me laugh was the thought of Peter. I had been pitying him an hour ago for having only one leg, but now he was abroad in the living, breathing world with years before him, and I lay in the depths, limbless and lifeless, with my number up.

I began to muse on the cold water under the ice where I could go if I wanted. I did not think that I would take that road, for a man's chances are not gone till he is stone dead, but I was glad the way existed. . . . And then I looked at the wall in front of me, and, very far up, I saw a small square window.

The stars had been clouded when I entered that accursed house, but the mist must have cleared. I saw my old friend Orion, the hunter's star, looking through the bars. And that suddenly made me think.

Peter and I had watched them by night, and I knew the place of all the chief constellations in relation to the St. Anton valley. I believed that I was in a room on the lake side of the Pink Chalet: I must be, if Ivery had spoken the truth. But if so, I could not conceivably see Orion from its window. . . . There was no other possible conclusion. I must be in a room on the east side of the house, and Ivery had been lying. He had already lied in his boasting of how he had outwitted me in England and at the Front. He might be lying about Mary. . . . No, I dismissed that hope. Those words of his had rung true enough.

I thought for a minute and concluded that he had lied to terrorize me and keep me quiet; therefore this infernal contraption had probably its weak point. I reflected, too, that I was pretty strong, far stronger probably than Ivery imagined, for he had never seen me stripped. Since the place was pitch dark I could not guess how the thing worked, but I could feel the cross-bars rigid on my chest and legs and the side-bars which pinned my arms to my sides. . . . I drew a long breath and tried to force my elbows apart. Nothing moved, nor could I raise the bars on my legs the smallest fraction.

Again I tried, and again. The side-bar on my right seemed to be less rigid than the others. I managed to get my right hand raised above the level of my thigh, and then with a struggle I got a grip with it on the cross-bar, which gave me a small leverage. With a mighty effort I drove my right elbow and shoulder against the side-bar. It seemed to give slightly. . . . I summoned all my strength and tried again. There was a crack and then a splintering, the massive bar shuffled limply back, and my right arm was free to move laterally, though the cross-bar prevented me from raising it.

With some difficulty I got at my coat pocket where reposed my electric torch and my pistol. With immense labour and no little pain I pulled the former out and switched it on by drawing the catch against the cross-bar. Then I saw my prison house.

It was a little square chamber, very high, with on my left the massive door by which Ivery had departed. The dark baulks of my rack were plain, and I could roughly make out how the thing had been managed. Some spring had tilted up the flooring, and dropped the framework from its place in the right-hand wall. It was clamped, I observed, by an arrangement in the floor just in front of the door. If I could get rid of that catch it would be easy to free myself, for to a man of my strength the weight would not be impossibly heavy.

My fortitude had come back to me, and I was living only in the moment, choking down any hope of escape. My first job was to destroy the catch that clamped down the rack, and for that my only weapon was my pistol. I managed to get the little electric torch jammed in the corner of the cross-bar, where it lit up the floor towards the door. Then it was hell's own business extricating the pistol from my pocket. Wrist and fingers were always cramping, and I was in terror that I might drop it where I could not retrieve it.

I forced myself to think out calmly the question of the clamp, for a pistol bullet is a small thing, and I could not afford to miss. I reasoned it out from my knowledge of mechanics, and came to the conclusion that the centre of gravity was a certain bright spot of metal which I could just see under the cross-bars. It was bright and so must have been recently repaired, and that was another reason for thinking it important. The question was how to hit it, for I could not get the pistol in line with my eye. Let any one try that kind of shooting, with a bent arm over a bar, when you are lying flat and looking at the mark from under the bar, and he will understand its difficulties. I had six shots in my revolver, and I must fire two or three ranging shots in any case. I must not exhaust all my cartridges, for I must have a bullet left for any servant who came to pry, and I wanted one in reserve for myself. But I did not think shots would be heard outside the room; the walls were too thick.

I held my wrist rigid above the cross-bar and fired. The bullet was an inch to the right of the piece of bright steel. Moving a fraction, I fired again. It had grazed it on the left. With aching eyes glued on the mark, I tried a third time. I saw something leap apart, and suddenly the whole framework under which I lay felt loose and mobile. . . . I was very cool, and restored the pistol to my pocket and took the torch in my hand before I moved. . . . Fortune had been kind, for I was free. I turned on my face, humped my back, and without much trouble crawled out from under the contraption.

I did not allow myself to think of ultimate escape, for that would only flurry me, and one step at a time was enough. I remember that I dusted my clothes and found that the cut in the back of my head had stopped bleeding. I retrieved my hat, which had rolled into a corner when I fell. . . . Then I turned my attention to the next step.

The tunnel was impossible, and the only way was the door. If I had stopped to think I would have known that the chances against my getting out of such a house were a thousand to one. The pistol shots had been muffled by the cavernous walls, but the place, as I knew, was full of servants, and, even if I passed the immediate door, I would be collared in some passage. But I had myself so well in hand that I tackled the door as if I had been prospecting to sink a new shaft in Rhodesia.

It had no handle nor, so far as I could see, a keyhole. . . . But I noticed, as I turned my torch on the ground, that from the clamp which I had shattered a brass rod sunk in the floor led to one of the doorposts. Obviously the thing worked by a spring and was connected with the mechanism of the rack.

A wild thought entered my mind and brought me to my feet. I pushed the door and it swung slowly open. The bullet which freed me had released the spring which controlled it.

Then for the first time, against all my maxims of discretion, I began to hope. I took off my hat and felt my forehead burning, so that I rested it for a moment on the cool wall. . . . Perhaps my luck still held. With a rush came thoughts of Mary and Blenkiron and Peter and everything we had laboured for, and I was mad to win.

I had no notion of the interior of the house or where lay the main door to the outer world. My torch showed me a long passage with something like a door at the far end, but I clicked it off, for I did not dare to use it now. The place was deadly quiet. As I listened I seemed to hear a door open far away, and then silence fell again.

I groped my way down the passage till I had my hands on the far door. I hoped it might open on the hall, where I could escape by a window or a balcony, for I judged the outer door would be locked. I listened, and there came no sound from within. It was no use lingering, so very stealthily I turned the handle and opened it a crack.

It creaked and I waited with beating heart on discovery, for inside I saw the glow of light. But there was no movement, so it must be empty. I poked my head in and then followed with my body.

It was a large room, with logs roaring in a stove, and the floor thick with rugs. It was lined with books, and on a table in the centre a reading-lamp was burning. Several dispatch boxes stood on the table, and there was a little pile of papers. A man had been here a minute before, for a half-smoked cigar was alight on the edge of the inkstand.

At that moment I recovered complete use of my wits and all my self-possession. More, there returned to me some of the old devil-may-careness which before had served me well. Ivery had gone, but this was his sanctum. Just as on the roofs of Erzerum I had burned to get at Stumm's papers, so now it was borne in on me that at all costs I must look at that pile.

I advanced to the table and picked up the top-most paper. It was a little typewritten blue slip with the lettering in italics, and in a corner a curious, involved stamp in red ink. On it I read:

"*Die Wildvögel müssen heimkehren.*"

At the same moment I heard steps, and the door opened on the far side. I stepped back towards the stove, and fingered the pistol in my pocket.

A man entered, a man with a scholar's stoop, an unkempt beard, and large sleepy dark eyes. At the sight of me he pulled up and his whole body grew taut. It was the Portuguese Jew, whose back I had last seen at the smithy door in Skye, and who by the mercy of God had never seen my face.

I stopped fingering the pistol, for I had an inspiration. Before he could utter a word I got in first.

"*Die Vögelein schweigen im Walde,*" I said.

His face broke into a pleasant smile, and he replied:

"*Warte nur, balde ruhest du auch.*

"Ach," he said in German, holding out his hand, "you have come this way, when we thought you would go by Modane. I welcome you, for I know your exploits. You are Conradi, who did so nobly in Italy?"

I bowed. "Yes, I am Conradi," I said.

49   THE COL OF THE SWALLOWS

He pointed to the slip on the table.

"You have seen the orders?"

I nodded.

"The long day's work is over. You must rejoice, for your part has been the hardest, I think. Some day you will tell me about it?"

The man's face was honest and kindly, rather like that of the engineer Gaudian, whom two years before I had met in Germany. But his eyes fascinated me, for they were the eyes of the dreamer and fanatic, who would not desist from his quest while life lasted. I thought that Ivery had chosen well in his colleague.

"My task is not done yet," I said. "I came here to see Chelius."

"He will be back to-morrow evening."

"Too late. I must see him at once. He has gone to Italy, and I must overtake him."

"You know your duty best," he said gravely.

"But you must help me. I must catch him at Santa Chiara, for it is a business of life and death. Is there a car to be had?"

"There is mine. But there is no chauffeur. Chelius took him."

"I can drive myself, and I know the road. But I have no pass to cross the frontier."

"That is easily supplied," he said, smiling.

In one bookcase there was a shelf of dummy books. He unlocked this and revealed a small cupboard, whence he took a tin dispatch box. From some papers he selected one, which seemed to be already signed.

"Name?" he asked.

"Call me Hans Gruber of Brieg," I said. "I travel to pick up my master, who is in the timber trade."

"And your return?"

"I will come back by my old road," I said mysteriously; and if he knew what I meant it was more than I did myself.

He completed the paper and handed it to me. "This will take you through the frontier posts. And now for the car. The servants will be in bed, for they have been preparing for a long journey, but I will myself show it to you. There is enough petrol on board to take you to Rome."

He led me through the hall, unlocked the front door, and we crossed the snowy lawn to the garage. The place was empty but for a great car, which bore the marks of having come from the muddy lowlands. To my joy I now that it was a Daimler, a type with which I was familiar. I lit the lamps, started the engine, and ran it out to the road.

"You will want an overcoat," he said.

"I never wear them."

"Food?"

"I have some chocolate. I will breakfast at Santa Chiara."

"Well, God go with you!"

A minute later I was tearing along the lakeside towards St. Anton village.

I stopped at the cottage on the hill. Peter was not yet in bed. I found him sitting by the fire, trying to read, but I saw by his face that he had been waiting anxiously on my coming.

"We're in the soup, old man," I said as I shut the door. In a dozen sentences I told him of the night's doings, of Ivery's plan, and my desperate errand.

"You wanted a share," I cried. "Well, everything depends on you now. I'm off after Ivery, and God knows what will happen. Meantime, you have got to get on to Blenkiron, and tell him what I've told you. He must get the news through to G.H.Q. somehow. He must trap the Wild Birds before they go. I don't know how, but he must. Tell him it's all up to him and you, for I'm out of it. I must save Mary, and if God's willing I'll settle with Ivery. But the big job is for Blenkiron—and you. Somehow he has made a bad break, and the enemy has got ahead of him. He must sweat blood to make up. . . . My God, Peter, it's the solemnest moment of our lives. I don't see any light, but we mustn't miss any chance. I'm leaving it all to you."

I spoke like a man in a fever, for after what I had been through I wasn't quite sane. My coolness in the Pink Chalet had given place to a crazy restlessness. I can see Peter yet, standing in the ring of lamplight, supporting himself by a chair back, wrinkling his brows and, as he always did in moments of excitement, scratching gently the tip of his left ear. His face was happy.

"Never fear, Dick," he said. "It will all come right. *Ons sal 'n plan maak.*"

And then, still possessed with a demon of disquiet, I was on the road again, heading for the pass that led to Italy.

The mist had gone from the sky, and the stars were shining brightly. The moon, now at the end of its first quarter, was setting in a gap of the mountains, as I climbed the low col from the St. Anton valley to the greater Staubthal. There was frost, and the hard snow crackled under my wheels, but there was also that feel in the air which preludes storm. I wondered if I should run into snow in the high hills. The whole land was deep in peace. There was not a light in the hamlets I passed through, nor a soul on the highway.

In the Staubthal I joined the main road and swung to the left up the narrowing bed of the valley. The road was in noble condition, and the car was running finely, as I mounted through forests of snowy pines to a land where the mountains crept close together, and the highway coiled round the angles of great crags or skirted perilously some profound gorge, with only a line of wooden posts to defend it from the void. In places the snow stood in walls on either side, where the road was kept open by man's labour. In other parts it lay thin, and in the dim light one might have fancied that one was running through open meadowland.

Slowly my head was getting clearer, and I was able to look round my problem. I banished from my mind the situation I had left behind me. Blenkiron must cope with that as best he could. It lay with him to deal with the Wild Birds, my job was with Ivery alone. Some time in the early morning he would reach Santa Chiara, and there he would find Mary. Beyond that my imagination could forecast nothing. She would be alone—I could trust his cleverness for that; he would try to force her to come with him, or he might persuade her with some lying story. Well, please God, I should come in for the tail end of the interview, and at the thought I cursed the steep gradients I was climbing, and longed for some magic to lift the Daimler beyond the summit and set it racing down the slopes towards Italy.

I think it was about half-past three when I saw the lights of the frontier post. The air seemed milder than in the valleys, and there was a soft scurry of snow on my right cheek. A couple of sleepy Swiss sentries with their rifles in their hands stumbled out as I drew up.

They took my pass into the hut and gave me an anxious quarter of an hour while they examined it. The performance was repeated fifty yards on at the Italian post, where to my alarm the sentries were inclined to conversation.

I played the part of the sulky servant, answering in monosyllables and pretending to immense stupidity."

"You are only just in time, friend," said one in German. "The weather grows bad, and soon the pass will close. Ugh, it is as cold as last winter on the Tonale. You remember, Giuseppe?"

But in the end they let me move on. For a little I felt my way gingerly, for on the summit the road had many twists and the snow was confusing to the eyes. Presently came a sharp drop and I let the Daimler go. It grew colder, and I shivered a little: the snow became a wet white fog around the glowing arc of the headlights; and always the road fell, now in long curves, now in steep short dips, till I was aware of a glen opening towards the south. From long living in the wilds I have a kind of sense for landscape without the testimony of the eyes, and I knew where the ravine narrowed or widened though it was black darkness.

In spite of my restlessness I had to go slowly, for after the first rush downhill I realized that, unless I was careful, I might wreck the car and spoil everything. The surface of the road on the southern slope of the mountains was a thousand per cent. worse than that on the other. I skidded and side-slipped, and once grazed the edge of the gorge. It was far more maddening than the climb up, for then it had been a straightforward grind with the Daimler doing its utmost, whereas now I had to hold her back because of my own lack of skill. I reckon that time crawling down from the summit of the Staub some of the weariest hours I ever spent.

Quite suddenly I ran out of the ill weather into a different climate. The sky was clear above me, and I saw that dawn was very near. The first pine woods were beginning, and at last came a straight slope where I could let the car out, I began to recover my spirits, which had been very dashed, and to reckon the distance I had still to travel. . . . And then, without warning, a new world sprang up around me. Out of the blue dusk white shapes rose like ghosts, peaks and needles and domes of ice, their bases fading mistily into shadow, but the tops kindling till they glowed like jewels. I had never seen such a sight, and the wonder of it for a moment drove anxiety from my heart. More, it gave me an earnest of victory. I was in clear air once more, and surely in this diamond ether the foul things, which loved the dark, must be worsted. . . .

And then I saw, a mile ahead, the little square red-roofed building which I knew to be the inn of Santa Chiara.

It was here that misfortune met me. I had grown careless now, and looked rather at the house than the road. At one point the hillside had slipped down—it must have been recent, for the road was well kept—and I did not notice the landslide till I was on it. I slewed to the right, took too wide a curve, and before I knew the car was over the far edge. I slapped on the brakes, but to avoid turning turtle I had to leave the road altogether. I slithered down a steep bank into a meadow, where for my sins I ran into a fallen tree trunk with a jar that shook me out of my seat and nearly broke my arm. Before I examined the car I knew what had happened. The front axle was bent, and the off front wheel badly buckled.

I had no time to curse my stupidity. I clambered back to the road and set off running down it at my best speed. I was mortally stiff, for Ivery's rack was not good for the joints, but I realized it only as a drag on my pace, not as an affliction in itself. My whole mind was set on the house before me and what might be happening there.

There was a man at the door of the inn, who, when he caught a sight of my figure, began to move to meet me. I saw that it was Launcelot Wake, and the sight gave me hope.

But his face frightened me. It was drawn and haggard like one who never sleeps, and his eyes were hot coals.

"Hannay," he cried, "for God's sake what does it mean?"

"Where is Mary?" I gasped, and I remember I clutched at the lapel of his coat.

He pulled me to the low stone wall by the roadside.

"I don't know," he said hoarsely. "We got your orders to come here this morning. We were at Chiavagno, where Blenkiron told us to wait. But last night Mary disappeared. . . . I found she had hired a carriage and come on ahead. I followed at once, and reached here an hour ago to find her gone. . . . The woman who keeps the place is away and there are only two old servants left. They tell me that Mary came here late, and that very early in the morning a closed car came over the Staub with a man in it. They say he asked to see the young lady, and that they talked together for some time, and that then she went off with him in the car down the valley. . . . I must have passed it on my way up. . . . There's been some black devilment that I can't follow. Who was the man? Who was the man?"

He looked as if he wanted to throttle me.

"I can tell you that," I said. "It was Ivery."

He stared for a second as if he didn't understand. Then he leaped to his feet and cursed like a trooper. "You've botched it, as I knew you would. I knew no good would come of your infernal subleties." And he consigned me and Blenkiron and the British Army and Ivery and everybody else to the devil.

I was past being angry. "Sit down, man," I said, "and listen to me." I told him of what had happened at the Pink Chalet. He heard me out with his head in his hands. The thing was too bad for cursing.

"The Underground Railway!" he groaned. "The thought of it drives me mad. Why are you so calm, Hannay? She's in the hands of the cleverest devil in the world, and you take it quietly. You should be a raving lunatic."

"I would be if it were any use, but I did all my raving last night in that den of Ivery's. We've got to pull ourselves together, Wake. First of all, I trust Mary to the other side of eternity. She went with him of her own free will. I don't know why, but she must have had a reason, and be sure it was a good one, for she's far cleverer than you or me. . . . We've got to follow her somehow. Ivery's bound for Germany, but his route is by the Pink Chalet, for he hopes to pick me up there. He went down the valley; therefore he is going to Switzerland by the Marjolana. That is a long circuit, and will take him most of the day. Why he chose that way I don't know, but there it is. We've got to get back by the Staub."

"How did you come?" he asked.

"That's our damnable luck. I came in a first-class six-cylinder Daimler, which is now lying a wreck in a meadow a mile up the road. We've got to foot it."

"We can't do it. It would take too long. Besides, there's the frontier to pass."

I remembered ruefully that I might have got a return passport from the Portuguese Jew, if I had thought of anything at the time beyond getting to Santa Chiara.

"Then we must make a circuit by the hillside and dodge the guards. It's no use making difficulties, Wake. We're fairly up against it, but we've got to go on trying till we drop. Otherwise I'll take your advice and go mad."

"And supposing you get back to St. Anton, you'll find the house shut up and the travellers gone hours before the Underground Railway."

"Very likely. But, man, there's always the glimmering of a chance. It's no good chucking in your hand till the game's out."

"Drop your proverbial philosophy, Mr. Martin Tupper, and look up there."

He had one foot on the wall and was staring at a cleft in the snow-line across the valley. The shoulder of a high peak dropped sharply to a kind of nick and rose again in a long graceful curve of snow. All below the nick was still in deep shadow, but from the configuration of the slopes I judged that a tributary glacier ran from it to the main glacier at the river head.

"That's the Colle delle Rondini," he said, "the Col of the Swallows. It leads straight to the Staubthal near Grünewald. On a good day I have done it in seven hours, but it's not a pass for wintertime. It has been done of course, but not often. . . . . Yet, if the weather held, it might go even now, and that would bring us to St. Anton by the evening. I wonder"—and he looked me over with an appraising eye—"I wonder if you're up to it."

My stiffness had gone and I burned to set my restlessness to physical toil.

"If you can do it, I can," I said.

"No. There you're wrong. You're a hefty fellow, but you're no mountaineer, and the ice of the Colle delle Rondini needs knowledge. It would be insane to risk it with a novice, if there were any other way. But I'm damned if I see any, and I'm going to chance it. We can get a rope and axes in the inn. Are you game?"

"Right you are. Seven hours, you say. We've got to do it in six."

"You will be humbler when you get on the ice," he said grimly. "We'd better breakfast, for the Lord knows when we shall see food again."

We left the inn at five minutes to nine, with the sky cloudless and a stiff wind from the north-west, which we felt even in the deep-cut valley. Wake walked with a long, slow stride that tried my patience. I wanted to hustle, but he bade me keep in step. "You take your orders from me, for I've been at this job before. Discipline in the ranks, remember."

We crossed the river gorge by a plank bridge, and worked our way up the right bank, past the moraine, to the snout of the glacier. It was bad going, for the snow concealed the boulders, and I often floundered in holes. Wake never relaxed his stride, but now and then he stopped to sniff the air.

I observed that the weather looked good, and he differed. "It's too clear. There'll be a full-blown gale on the Col, and most likely snow in the afternoon." He pointed to a fat yellow cloud that was beginning to bulge over the nearest peak. After that I thought he lengthened his stride.

"Lucky I had these boots resoled and nailed at Chiavagno," was the only other remark he made till we had passed the *seracs* of the main glacier and turned up the lesser ice-stream from the Colle delle Rondini.

By half-past ten we were near its head, and I could see clearly the ribbon of pure ice between black crags too steep for snow to lie on, which was the means of ascent to the Col. The sky had clouded over, and ugly streamers floated on the high slopes. We tied on the rope at the foot of the *bergschrund*, which was easy to pass because of the winter's snow. Wake led, of course, and presently we came on to the icefall.

In my time I had done a lot of scrambling on rocks and used to promise myself a season in the Alps to test myself on the big peaks. If I ever go it will be to climb the honest rock towers around Chamounix, for I won't have anything to do with snow mountains. That day on the Colle delle Rondini fairly sickened me of ice. I dare say I might have liked it if I had done it in a holiday mood, at leisure and in good spirits. But to crawl up that couloir with a sick heart and a desperate impulse to hurry was the worst sort of nightmare. The place was as steep as a wall, of smooth black ice that seemed hard as granite. Wake did the step-cutting, and I admired him enormously. He did not seem to use much force, but every step was hewn cleanly the right size, and they were spaced the right distance. In this job he was the true professional. I was thankful Blenkiron was not with us, for the thing would have given a squirrel vertigo. The chips of ice slithered between my legs and I could watch them till they brought up just above the *bergschrund*.

The ice was in shadow and it was bitterly cold. As we crawled up I had not the exercise of using the axe to warm me, and I got very numb standing on one leg waiting for the next step. Worse still, my legs began to cramp. I was in good condition, but that time under Ivery's rack had played the mischief with my limbs. Muscles got out of place in my calves and stood in aching lumps, till I almost squealed with the pain of it. I was mortally afraid I should slip, and every time I moved I called out to Wake to warn him. He saw what was happening, and got the pick of his axe fixed in the ice before I was allowed to stir. He spoke often to cheer me up, and his voice had none of its harshness. He was like some ill-tempered generals I have known, very gentle in a battle.

At the end the snow began to fall, a soft powder like the over-spill of a storm raging beyond the crest. It was just after that that Wake cried out that in five minutes we would be at the summit. He consulted his wrist-watch. "Jolly good time, too. Only twenty-five minutes behind my best. It's not one o'clock."

The next I knew I was lying flat on a pad of snow easing my cramped legs, while Wake shouted in my ear that we were in for something bad. I was aware of a driving blizzard, but I had no thought of anything but the blessed relief from pain. I lay for some minutes on my back with my legs stiff in the air and the toes turned inwards, while my muscles fell into their proper place.

It was certainly no spot to linger in. We looked down into a trough of driving mist, which sometimes swirled aside and showed a knuckle of black rock far below. We ate some chocolate, while Wake shouted in my ear that now we had less step-cutting. He did his best to cheer me, but he could not hide his anxiety. Our faces were frosted over like a wedding cake and the sting of the wind was like a whiplash on our eyelids.

The first part was easy, down a slope of firm snow where steps were not needed. Then came ice again, and we had to cut into it below the fresh surface snow. This was so laborious that Wake took to the rocks on the right side of the couloir, where there was some shelter from the main force of the blast. I found it easier, for I knew something about rocks, but it was difficult enough with every handhold and foothold glazed. Presently we were driven back again to the ice, and painfully cut our way through a throat of the ravine where the sides narrowed. There the wind was terrible, for the narrows made a kind of funnel, and we descended, plastered against the wall, and scarcely able to breathe, while the tornado plucked at our bodies as if it would whisk us like wisps of grass into the abyss.

After that the gorge widened and we had an easier slope, till suddenly we found ourselves perched on a great tongue of rock round which the snow blew like the froth in a whirlpool. As we stopped for breath, Wake shouted in my ear that this was the Black Stone.

"The what?" I yelled.

"The Schwarzstein. The Swiss call the pass the Schwarzsteinthor. You can see it from Grünewald."

I suppose every man has a tinge of superstition in him. To hear that name in that ferocious place gave me a sudden access of confidence. I vowed to see all my doings as part of a great predestined plan. Surely it was not for nothing that the words which had been the key of my first adventure in the long tussle should appear in this last phase. I felt new strength in my legs and more vigour in my lungs. "A good omen," I shouted. "Wake, old man, we're going to win out."

"The worst is still to come," he said.

He was right. To get down that tongue of rock to the lower snows of the couloir was a job that fairly brought us to the end of our tether. I can feel yet the sour, bleak smell of wet rock and ice and the hard nerve pain that racked my forehead. The Kaffirs used to say that there were devils in the high berg, and this place was assuredly given over to the powers of the air who had no thought of human life. I seemed to be in the world which had endured from eternity before man was dreamed of. There was no mercy in it, and the elements were pitting their immortal strength against two pigmies who had profaned their sanctuary. I yearned for warmth, for the glow of a fire, for a tree or blade of grass or anything which meant the sheltered homeliness of mortality. I knew then what the Greeks meant by panic, for I was scared by the apathy of nature. But the terror gave me a kind of comfort too. Ivery and his doings seemed less formidable. Let me but get out of this cold hell and I could meet him with a new confidence.

Wake led, for he knew the road and the road wanted knowing. Otherwise he should have been last on the rope, for that is the place of the better man in a descent. I had some horrible moments following on when the rope grew taut, for I had no help from it. We zigzagged down the rock, sometimes driven to the ice of the adjacent couloirs, sometimes on the outer ridge of the Black Stone, sometimes wriggling down little cracks and over evil boiler-plates. The snow did not lie on it, but the rock crackled with thin ice or oozed ice water. Often it was only by the grace of God that I did not fall headlong, and pull Wake out of his hold to the *bergschrund* far below. I slipped more than once, but always by a miracle recovered myself. To make things worse, Wake was tiring. I could feel him drag on the rope, and his movements had not the precision they had had in the morning. He was the mountaineer, and I the novice. If he gave out, we should never reach the valley.

The fellow was clear grit all through. When we reached the foot of the tooth and sat huddled up with our faces away from the wind, I saw that he was on the edge of fainting. What that effort must have cost him in the way of resolution you may guess, but he did not fail till the worst was past. His lips were colourless, and he was choking with the nausea of fatigue. I found a flask of brandy in his pocket, and a mouthful revived him.

"I'm all out," he said. "The road's easier now, and I can direct you about the rest. . . . You'd better leave me. I'll only be a drag. I'll come on when I feel better."

"No, you don't, you old fool. You've got me over that infernal iceberg, and I'm going to see you home."

I rubbed his arms and legs and made him swallow some chocolate. But when he got on his feet he was as doddery as an old man. Happily we had an easy course down a snow gradient, which we glissaded in very unorthodox style. The swift motion freshened him up a little, and he was able to put on the brake with his axe to prevent us cascading into the *bergschrund*. We crossed it by a snow bridge and started out on the *seracs* of the Schwarzstein glacier.

I am no mountaineer—not of the snow and ice kind, anyway—but I have a big share of physical strength and I wanted it all now. For those *seracs* were an invention of the devil. To traverse that labyrinth in a blinding snowstorm, with a fainting companion who was too weak to jump the narrowest crevasse, and who hung on the rope like lead when there was occasion to use it, was more than I could manage. Besides, every step that brought us nearer to the valley now increased my eagerness to hurry, and wandering in that maze of clotted ice was like the nightmare when you stand on the rails with the express coming and are too weak to climb on the platform. As soon as possible I left the glacier for the hillside, and though that was laborious enough in all conscience, yet it enabled me to steer a straight course. Wake never spoke a word. When I looked at him his face was ashen under a gale which should have made his cheeks glow, and he kept his eyes half closed. He was staggering on at the very limits of his endurance. . . . . .

By and by we were on the moraine, and after splashing through a dozen little glacier streams came on a track which led up the hillside. Wake nodded feebly when I asked if this was right. Then to my joy I saw a gnarled pine. I untied the rope and Wake dropped like a log on the ground. "Leave me," he groaned, "I'm fairly done. I'll come on . . . later." And he shut his eyes. My watch told me that it was after five o'clock.

"Get on my back," I said. "I won't part from you till I've found a cottage. You're a hero. You've brought me over those damned mountains in a blizzard, and that's what no other man in England would have done. Get up."

He obeyed, for he was too far gone to argue. I tied his wrists together with a handkerchief below my chin, for I wanted my arms to hold up his legs. The rope and axes I left in a cache beneath the pine tree. Then I started trotting down the track for the nearest dwelling.

My strength felt inexhaustible and the quick-silver in my bones drove me forward. The snow was still falling, but the wind was dying down, and after the inferno of the pass it was like summer. The road wound over the shale of the hillside and then into what in spring must have been upland meadows. Then it ran among trees, and far below me on the right I could hear the glacier river churning in its gorge. Soon little empty huts appeared, and rough enclosed paddocks, and presently I came out on a shelf above the stream and smelt the wood-smoke of a human habitation.

I found a middle-aged peasant in the cottage, a guide by profession in summer and a woodcutter in winter.

"I have brought my Herr from Santa Chiara," I said, "over the Schwarz-steinthor. He is very weary and must sleep."

I decanted Wake into a chair, and his head nodded on his chest. But his colour was better.

"You and your Herr are fools," said the man gruffly, but not unkindly. "He must sleep or he will have a fever. The Schwarzsteinthor in this devil's weather! Is he English?"

"Yes," I said, "like all madmen. But he's a good Herr, and a brave mountaineer."

We stripped Wake of his Red Cross uniform, now a collection of sopping rags, and got him between blankets with a huge earthenware bottle of hot water at his feet. The woodcutter's wife boiled milk, and this, with a little brandy added, we made him drink. I was quite easy in my mind about him, for I had seen this condition before. In the morning he would be as stiff as a poker, but recovered.

"Now I'm off for St. Anton," I said. "I must get there to-night."

"You are the hardy one," the man laughed. "I will show you the quick road to Grünewald, where is the railway. With good fortune you may get the last train."

I gave him fifty francs on my Herr's behalf, learned his directions for the road, and set off after a draught of goat's milk, munching my last slab of chocolate. I was still strung up to a mechanical activity, and I ran every inch of the three miles to the Staubthal without consciousness of fatigue. I was twenty minutes too soon for the train, and, as I sat on a bench on the platform, my energy suddenly ebbed away. That is what happens after a great exertion. I longed to sleep, and when the train arrived I crawled into a carriage like a man with a stroke. There seemed to be no force left in my limbs. I realized that I was leg-weary, which is a thing you see sometimes with horses, but not often with men.

All the journey I lay like a log in a kind of coma, and it was with difficulty that I recognized my destination, and stumbled out of the train. But I had no sooner emerged from the station of St. Anton than I got my second wind. Much snow had fallen since yesterday, but it had stopped now, the sky was clear, and the moon was riding. The sight of the familiar place brought back all my anxieties. The day on the Col of the Swallows was wiped out of my memory, and I saw only the inn at Santa Chiara, and heard Wake's hoarse voice speaking of Mary. The lights were twinkling from the village below, and on the right I saw the clump of trees which held the Pink Chalet.

I took a short cut across the fields, avoiding the little town. I ran hard, stumbling often, for though I had got my mental energy back my legs were still precarious. The station clock had told me that it was nearly half-past nine.

Soon I was on the highroad, and then at the Chalet gates. I heard as in a dream what seemed to be three shrill blasts on a whistle. Then a big closed car passed me, making for St. Anton. For a second I would have hailed it, but it was past me and away. But I had a conviction that my business lay in the house, for I thought Ivery was there, and Ivery was what mattered.

I marched up the drive with no sort of plan in my head, only a blind rushing on fate. I remembered dimly that I had still three cartridges in my revolver.

The front door stood open and I entered and tiptoed down the passage to the room where I had found the Portuguese Jew. No one hindered me, but it was not for lack of servants. I had the impression that there were people near me in the darkness, and I thought I heard German softly spoken. There was some one ahead of me, perhaps the speakers, for I could hear careful footsteps. It was very dark, but a ray of light came from below the door of the room. Then behind me I heard the hall door clang, and the noise of a key turned in its lock. I had walked straight into a trap and all retreat was cut off.

My mind was beginning to work more clearly, though my purpose was still vague. I wanted to get at Ivery, and I believed that he was somewhere in front of me. And then I thought of the door which led from the chamber where I had been imprisoned. If I could enter that way I would have the advantage of surprise.

I groped on the right-hand side of the passage and found a handle. It opened upon what seemed to be a dining-room, for there was a faint smell of food. Again I had the impression of people near who for some unknown reason did not molest me. At the far end I found another door, which led to a second room, which I guessed to be adjacent to the library. Beyond again must lie the passage from the chamber with the rack. The whole place was as quiet as a shell.

I had guessed right. I was standing in the passage where I had stood the night before. In front of me was the library, and there was the same chink of light showing. Very softly I turned the handle and opened it a crack. . . .

The first thing that caught my eye was the profile of Ivery. He was looking towards the writing-table, where some one was sitting.

50 THE UNDERGROUND RAILWAY

This is the story which I heard later from Mary. . . .

She was at Milan with the new Anglo-American hospital when she got Blenkiron's letter. Santa Chiara had always been the place agreed upon, and this message mentioned specifically Santa Chiara, and fixed a date for her presence there. She was a little puzzled by it, for she had not yet had a word from Ivery, to whom she had written twice by the roundabout address in France which Bommaerts had given her. She did not believe that he would come to Italy in the ordinary course of things, and she wondered at Blenkiron's certainty about the date.

The following morning came a letter from Ivery in which he ardently pressed for a meeting. It was the first of several, full of strange talk of some approaching crisis, in which the forebodings of the prophet were mingled with the solicitude of a lover. "The storm is about to break," he wrote, "and I cannot think only of my own fate. I have something to tell you which vitally concerns yourself. You say you are in Lombardy. The Chiavagno valley is within easy reach, and at its head is the Inn of Santa Chiara, to which I come on the morning of March 19th. Meet me there even if only for half an hour, I implore you. We have already shared hopes and confidences, and I would now share with you a knowledge which I alone in Europe possess. You have the heart of a lion, my lady, worthy of what I can bring you."

Wake was summoned from the Croce Rossa unit with which he was working at Vicenza, and the plan arranged by Blenkiron was faithfully carried out. Four officers of Alpini, in the rough dress of peasants of the hills, met them in Chiavagno on the morning of the 18th. It was arranged that the hostess of Santa Chiara should go on a visit to her sister's son, leaving the inn, now in the shuttered quiet of wintertime, under the charge of two ancient servants. The hour of Ivery's coming on the 19th had been fixed by him for noon, and that morning Mary would drive up the valley, while Wake and the Alpini went inconspicuously by other routes so as to be in station around the place before midday.

But on the evening of the 18th at the Hotel of the Four Kings in Chiavagno Mary received another message. It was from me and told her that I was crossing the Staub at midnight and would be at the inn before dawn. It begged her to meet me there, to meet me alone without the others, because I had that to say to her which must be said before Ivery's coming. I have seen the letter. It was written in a hand which I could not have distinguished from my own scrawl. It was not exactly what I would myself have written, but there were phrases in it which to Mary's mind could have come only from me. Oh, I admit it was cunningly done, especially the love-making, which was just the kind of stammering thing which I would have achieved if I had tried to put my feelings on paper.

Anyhow, Mary had no doubt of its genuineness. She slipped off after dinner, hired a carriage with two broken-winded screws and set off up the valley. She left a line for Wake telling him to follow according to the plan—a line which he never got, for his anxiety when he found she had gone drove him to immediate pursuit.

At about two in the morning of the 19th after a slow and icy journey she arrived at the inn, knocked up the aged servants, made herself a cup of chocolate out of her tea-basket, and sat down to wait on my coming.

She has described to me that time of waiting. A home-made candle in a tall earthenware candlestick lit up the little *salle-à-manger*, which was the one room in use. The world was very quiet, the snow muffled the roads and it was cold with the penetrating chill of the small hours of a March night. Always, she has told me, will the taste of chocolate and the smell of burning tallow bring back to her that strange place and the flutter of the heart with which she waited. For she was on the eve of the crisis of all our labours, she was very young, and youth has a quick fancy which will not be checked. Moreover, it was I who was coming, and save for the scrawl of the night before, we had had no communication for many weeks. . . . She tried to distract her mind by repeating poetry, and the thing that came into her head was Keats's "Nightingale," an odd poem for the time and place.

There was a long wicker chair among the furnishings of the room, and she lay down on it with her fur cloak muffled around her. There were sounds of movement in the inn. The old woman who had let her in, with the scent for intrigue of her kind, had brightened when she heard that another guest was coming. Beautiful women do not travel at midnight for nothing. She also was awake and expectant.

Then quite suddenly came the sound of a car slowing down outside. She sprang to her feet in a tremor of excitement. It was like the Picardy château again—the dim room and a friend coming out of the night. She heard the front door open and a step in the little hall. . . .

She was looking at Ivery. He slipped his driving-coat off as he entered, and bowed gravely. He was wearing a green hunting suit which in the dusk seemed like khaki, and, as he was about my own height, for a second she was misled. Then she saw his face and her heart stopped.

"You!" she cried. She had sunk back again on the wicker chair.

"I have come as I promised," he said, "but a little earlier. You will forgive me my eagerness to be with you."

She did not heed his words, for her mind was feverishly busy. My letter had been a fraud and this man had discovered our plans. She was alone with him, for it would be hours before her friends came from Chiavagno. He had the game in his hands, and of all our confederacy she alone remained to confront him. Mary's courage was pretty near perfect, and for the moment she did not think of herself or her own fate. That came later. She was possessed with poignant disappointment at our failure. All our efforts had gone to the winds, and the enemy had won with contemptuous ease. Her nervousness disappeared before the intense regret, and her brain set coolly and busily to work.

It was a new Ivery who confronted her, a man with vigour and purpose in every line of him and the quiet confidence of power. He spoke with a serious courtesy.

"The time for make-believe is past," he was saying. "We have fenced with each other. I have told you only half the truth, and you have always kept me at arm's length. But you knew in your heart, my dearest lady, that there must be the full truth between us some day, and that day has come. I have often told you that I love you. I do not come now to repeat that declaration. I come to ask you to entrust yourself to me, to join your fate to mine, for I can promise you the happiness which you deserve."

He pulled up a chair and sat beside her. I cannot put down all that he said, for Mary, once she grasped the drift of it, was busy with her own thoughts and did not listen. But I gather from her that he was very candid and seemed to grow as he spoke in mental and moral stature. He told her who he was and what his work had been. He claimed the same purpose as hers, a hatred of war and a passion to rebuild the world into decency. But now he drew a different moral. He was a German: it was through Germany alone that peace and regeneration could come. His country was purged from her faults, and the marvellous German discipline was about to prove itself in the eyes of gods and men. He told her what he had told me in the room at the Pink Chalet, but with another colouring. Germany was not vengeful or vainglorious, only patient and merciful. God was about to give her the power to decide the world's fate, and it was for him and his kind to see that that decision was beneficent. The greater task of his people was only now beginning.

That was the gist of his talk. She appeared to listen, but her mind was far away. She must delay him for two hours, three hours, four hours. If not, she must keep beside him. She was the only one of our company left in touch with the enemy. . . .

"I go to Germany now," he was saying. "I want you to come with me—to be my wife."

He waited for an answer, and got it in the form of a startled question.

"To Germany? How?"

"It is easy," he said, smiling. "The car which is waiting outside is the first stage of a system of travel which we have perfected." Then he told her about the Underground Railway—not as he had told it to me, to scare, but as a proof of power and forethought.

His manner was perfect. He was respectful, devoted, thoughtful in all things. He was the suppliant, not the master. He offered her power and pride, a dazzling career, for he had deserved well of his country, the devotion of the faithful lover. He would take her to his mother's house, where she would be welcomed like a princess. I have no doubt he was sincere, for he had many moods, and the libertine whom he had revealed to me at the Pink

Chalet had given place to the honourable gentleman. He could play all parts well because he could believe in himself in them all.

Then he spoke of danger, not so as to slight her courage, but to emphasize his own thoughtfulness. The world in which she had lived was crumbling, and he alone could offer a refuge. She felt the steel gauntlet through the texture of the velvet glove.

All the while she had been furiously thinking, with her chin in her hand in the old way. . . . She might refuse to go. He could compel her, no doubt, for there was no help to be got from the old servants. But it might be difficult to carry an unwilling woman over the first stages of the Underground Railway. There might be chances. . . . Supposing he accepted her refusal and left her. Then indeed he would be gone for ever and our game would have closed with a fiasco. The great antagonist of England would go home rejoicing, taking his sheaves with him.

At this time she had no personal fear of him. So curious a thing is the human heart that her main preoccupation was with our mission, not with her own fate. To fail utterly seemed too bitter. Supposing she went with him. They had still to get out of Italy and cross Switzerland. If she were with him she would be an emissary of the Allies in the enemy's camp. She asked herself what could she do, and told herself "Nothing." She felt like a small bird in a very large trap, and her chief sensation was that of her own powerlessness. But she had learned Blenkiron's gospel and knew that Heaven sends amazing chances to the bold. And, even as she made her decision, she was aware of a dark shadow lurking at the back of her mind, the shadow of the fear which she knew was awaiting her. For she was going into the unknown with a man whom she hated, a man who claimed to be her lover.

It was the bravest thing I have ever heard of, and I have lived my life among brave men.

"I will come with you," she said. "But you mustn't speak to me, please. I am tired and troubled and I want peace to think."

As she rose weakness came over her and she swayed till his arm caught her. "I wish I could let you rest for a little," he said tenderly, "but time presses. The car runs smoothly and you can sleep there."

He summoned one of the servants, to whom he handed Mary. "We leave in ten minutes," he said, and he went out to see to the car.

Mary's first act in the bedroom to which she was taken was to bathe her eyes and brush her hair. She felt dimly that she must keep her head clear. Her second was to scribble a note to Wake, telling him what had happened and to give it to the servant with a tip. "The gentleman will come in the morning," she said. "You must give it him at once, for it concerns the fate of your country." The woman grinned and promised. It was not the first time she had done errands for pretty ladies.

Ivery settled her in the great closed car with much solicitude, and made her comfortable with rugs. Then he went back to the inn for a second and she saw a light move in the *salle-à-manger*. He returned and spoke to the driver in German, taking his seat beside him.

But first he handed Mary her note to Wake. "I think you left this behind you," he said. He had not opened it.

Alone in the car Mary slept. She saw the figures of Ivery and the chauffeur in the front seat dark against the headlights, and then they dislimned into dreams. She had undergone a greater strain than she knew, and was sunk in the heavy sleep of weary nerves.

When she woke it was daylight. They were still in Italy, as her first glance told her, so they could not have taken the Staub route. They seemed to be among the foothills, for there was little snow, but now and then up tributary valleys she had glimpses of the high peaks. She tried hard to think what it could mean, and then remembered the Marjolana. Wake had laboured to instruct her in the topography of the Alps, and she had grasped the fact of the two open passes. But the Marjolana meant a big circuit, and they would not be in Switzerland till the evening. They would arrive in the dark, and pass out of it in the dark, and there would be no chance of succour. She felt very lonely and very weak.

Throughout the morning her fear grew. The more hopeless her chance of defeating Ivery became the more insistently the dark shadow crept over her mind. She tried to steady herself by watching the show from the windows. The car swung through little villages, past vineyards and pine woods and the blue lakes, and over the gorges of mountain streams. There seemed to be no trouble about passports. The sentries at the controls waved a reassuring hand when they were shown some card which the chauffeur held between his teeth. In one place there was a longish halt, and she could hear Ivery talking Italian with two officers of Bersaglieri, to whom he gave cigars. They were fresh-faced, upstanding boys, and for a second she had an idea of flinging open the door and appealing to them to save her. But that would have been futile, for Ivery was clearly amply certificated. She wondered what part he was now playing.

The Marjolana route had been chosen for a purpose. In one town Ivery met and talked to a civilian official, and more than once the car slowed down and some one appeared from the wayside to speak a word and vanish. She was assisting at the last gathering up of the threads of a great plan, before the Wild Birds returned to their nest. Mostly these conferences seemed to be in Italian, but once or twice she gathered from the movement of the lips that German was spoken and that this rough peasant or that black-hatted bourgeois was not of Italian blood.

Early in the morning, soon after she awoke, Ivery had stopped the car and offered her a well-provided luncheon basket. She could eat nothing, and watched him breakfast off sandwiches beside the driver. In the afternoon he asked her permission to sit with her. The car drew up in a lonely place, and a tea-basket was produced by the chauffeur. Ivery made tea, for she seemed too listless to move, and she drank a cup with him. After that he remained beside her.

"In half an hour we shall be out of Italy," he said. The car was running up a long valley to the curious hollow between snow saddles which is the crest of the Marjolana. He showed her the place on a road map. As the altitude increased and the air grew colder he wrapped the rugs closer around her and apologized for the absence of a foot-warmer. "In a little," he said, "we shall be in a land where your slightest wish will be law."

She dozed again and so missed the frontier post. When she woke the car was slipping down the long curves of the Weiss valley, before it narrows to the gorge through which it debouches on Grünewald.

"We are in Switzerland now," she heard his voice say. It may have been fancy, but it seemed to her that there was a new note in it. He spoke to her with the assurance of possession. They were outside the country of the Allies, and in a land where his web was thickly spread.

"Where do we stop to-night?" she asked timidly.

"I fear we cannot stop. To-night also you must put up with the car. I have a little errand to do on the way, which will delay us for a few minutes, and then we press on. To-morrow, my fairest one, fatigue will be ended."

There was no mistake now about the note of possession in his voice. Mary's heart began to beat fast and wild. The trap had closed down on her, and she saw the folly of her courage. It had delivered her bound and gagged into the hands of one whom she loathed more deeply every moment, whose proximity was less welcome than a snake's. She had to bite hard on her lip to keep from screaming.

The weather had changed, and it was snowing hard, the same storm that had greeted us on the Col of the Swallows. The pace was slower now, and Ivery grew restless. He looked frequently at his watch, and snatched the speaking-tube to talk to the driver. Mary caught the word "St. Anton."

"Do we go by St. Anton?" she found voice to ask.

"Yes," he said shortly.

The word gave her the faintest glimmering of hope, for she knew that Peter and I had lived at St. Anton. She tried to look out of the blurred windows, but could see nothing except that the twilight was falling. She begged for the road map, and saw that so far as she could make out they were still on the broad Grünewald valley, and that to reach St. Anton they had to cross the low pass from the Staubthal. The snow was still drifting thick and the car crawled.

Then she felt the rise as they mounted to the pass. Here the going was bad, very different from the dry frost in which I had covered the same road the night before. Moreover, there seemed to be curious obstacles. Some careless wood cart had dropped logs on the highway, and more than once both Ivery and the chauffeur had to get out to shift them. In one place there had been a small landslide which left little room to pass, and Mary had to descend and cross on foot while the driver took the car over alone. Ivery's temper seemed to be souring. To the girl's relief he resumed the outside seat, where he was engaged in constant argument with the chauffeur.

At the head of the pass stands an inn, the comfortable hostelry of Herr Kronig, well known to all who clamber among the lesser peaks of the Staubthal. There in the middle of the way stood a man with a lantern.

"The road is blocked by a snowfall," he cried. "They are clearing it now. It will be ready in half an hour's time."

Ivery sprang from his seat and darted into the hotel. His business was to speed up the clearing party, and Herr Kronig himself accompanied him to the scene of the catastrophe. Mary sat still, for she had suddenly become possessed of an idea. She drove it from her as foolishness, but it kept returning. Why had those tree trunks been spilt on the road? Why had an easy pass after a moderate snowfall been suddenly closed?

A man came out of the inn-yard and spoke to the chauffeur. It seemed to be an offer of refreshment, for the latter left his seat and disappeared inside. He was away for some time and returned shivering and grumbling at the weather, with the collar of his greatcoat turned up around his ears. A lantern had been hung in the porch, and as he passed Mary saw the man. She had been watching the back of his head idly during the long drive, and had observed that it was of the round bullet type, with no nape to the neck, which is common in the Fatherland. Now she could not see his neck for the coat collar, but she could have sworn that the head was a different shape. The man seemed to suffer acutely from the cold, for he buttoned the collar round his chin and pulled his cap far over his brows.

Ivery came back, followed by a dragging line of men with spades and lanterns. He flung himself into the front seat and nodded to the driver to start. The man had his engine going already so as to lose no time. He bumped over the rough debris of the snowfall and then fairly let the car hum. Ivery was anxious for speed, but he did not want his neck broken, and he yelled out to take care. The driver nodded and slowed down, but presently he had got up speed again.

If Ivery was restless, Mary was worse. She seemed suddenly to have come on the traces of her friends. In the St. Anton valley the snow had stopped, and she let down the window for air, for she was choking with suspense. The car rushed past the station, down the hill by Peter's cottage, through the village, and along the lake shore to the Pink Chalet.

Ivery halted it at the gate. "See that you fill up with petrol," he told the man. "Bid Gustav get the Daimler and be ready to follow in half an hour."

He spoke to Mary through the open window.

"I will keep you only a very little time. I think you had better wait in the car, for it will be more comfortable than a dismantled house. A servant will bring you food and more rugs for the night journey."

Then he vanished up the dark avenue.

Mary's first thought was to slip out and get back to the village, and there to find some one who knew me or could take her where Peter lived. But the driver would prevent her, for he had been left behind on guard. She looked anxiously at his back, for he alone stood between her and liberty.

That gentleman seemed to be intent on his own business. As soon as Ivery's footsteps had grown faint, he had backed the car into the entrance, and turned it so that it faced towards St. Anton. Then very slowly it began to move.

At the same moment a whistle was blown shrilly three times. The door on the right hand opened and some one who had been waiting in the shadows climbed painfully in. Mary saw that it was a little man, and that he was a cripple. She reached a hand to help him, and he fell on to the cushions beside her. The car was gathering speed.

Before she realized what was happening the newcomer had taken her hand and was patting it.

About two minutes later I was entering the gate of the Pink Chalet.

51   THE CAGE OF THE WILD BIRDS

"Why, Mr. Ivery, come right in," said the voice at the table.

There was a screen before me, stretching from the fireplace to keep off the draught from the door by which I had entered. It stood higher than my head, but there were cracks in it through which I could watch the room. I found a little table on which I could lean my back, for I was dropping with fatigue.

Blenkiron sat at the writing-table and in front of him were little rows of Patience cards. Wood ashes still smouldered in the stove, and a lamp stood at his right elbow which lit up the two figures. The bookshelves and the cabinets were in twilight.

"I've been hoping to see you for quite a time." Blenkiron was busy arranging the little heaps of cards, and his face was wreathed in hospitable smiles. I remember wondering why he should play the host to the true master of the house.

Ivery stood erect before him. He was rather a splendid figure now that he had sloughed all disguises and was on the threshold of his triumph. Even through the fog in which my brain worked it was forced upon me that here was a man born to play a big part. He had a jowl like a Roman king on a coin, and scornful eyes that were used to mastery. He was younger than I, confound him, and now he looked it.

He kept his eyes on the speaker, while a smile played round his mouth, a very ugly smile.

"So," he said, "we have caught the old crow too. I had scarcely hoped for such good fortune, and, to speak the truth, I had not concerned myself much about you. But now we shall add you to the bag. And what a bag of vermin to lay out on the lawn!" He flung back his head and laughed.

"Mr. Ivery—" Blenkiron began, but was cut short.

"Drop that name. All that is past, thank God! I am the Graf von Schwabing, an officer of the Imperial Guard. I am not the least of the weapons that Germany has used to break her enemies. . . ."

"You don't say," drawled Blenkiron, still fiddling with his Patience cards.

The man's moment had come, and he was minded not to miss a jot of his triumph. His figure seemed to expand, his eye kindled, his voice rang with pride. It was melodrama of the best kind, and he fairly rolled it round his tongue. I don't think I grudged it him, for I was fingering something in my pocket. He had won all right, but he wouldn't enjoy his victory long, for soon I would shoot him. I had my eye on the very spot above his right ear where I meant to put my bullet. . . . For I was very clear that to kill him was the only way to protect Mary. I feared the whole seventy millions of Germany less than this man. That was the single idea that remained firm against the immense fatigue that pressed down on me.

"I have little time to waste on you," said he who had been called Ivery. "But I will spare a moment to tell you a few truths. Your childish game never had a chance. I played with you in England and I have played with you ever since. You have never made a move but I have quietly countered it. Why, man, you gave me your confidence. The American Mr. Donne . . ."

"What about Clarence?" asked Blenkiron. His face seemed a study in pure bewilderment.

"I was that interesting journalist."

"Now to think of that!" said Blenkiron in a sad, gentle voice. "I thought I was safe with Clarence. Why, he brought me a letter from old Joe Hooper and he knew all the boys down Emporia way."

Ivery laughed. "You have never done me justice, I fear; but I think you will do it now. Your gang is helpless in my hands. General Hannay . . ." And I wish I could give you a notion of the scorn with which he pronounced the word "General."

"Yes—Dick?" said Blenkiron intently.

"He has been my prisoner for twenty-four hours. And the pretty Miss Mary, too. You are all going with me in a little to my own country. You will not guess how. We call it the Underground Railway, and you will have the privilege of studying its working. . . . I had not troubled much about you, for I had no special dislike of you. You are only a blundering fool, what you call in your country easy fruit."

"I thank you, Graf," Blenkiron said solemnly.

"But since you are here you will join the others. . . . One last word. To beat inepts such as you is nothing. There is a far greater thing. My country has conquered. You and your friends will be dragged at the chariot wheels of a triumph such as Rome never saw. Does that penetrate your thick skull? Germany has won, and in two days the whole round earth will be stricken dumb by her greatness."

As I watched Blenkiron a grey shadow of hopelessness seemed to settle on his face. His big body drooped in his chair, his eyes fell, and his left hand shuffled limply among his Patience cards. I could not get my mind to work, but I puzzled miserably over his amazing blunders. He had walked blindly into the pit his enemies had digged for him. Peter must have failed to get my message to him, and he knew nothing of last night's work or my mad journey to Italy. We had all bungled, the whole wretched bunch of us, Peter and Blenkiron and myself. . . . I had a feeling at the back of my head that there was something in it all that I couldn't understand, that the catastrophe could not be quite as simple as it seemed. But I had no power to think, with the insolent figure of Ivery dominating the room. . . . Thank God I had a bullet waiting for him. That was the one fixed point in the chaos of my mind. For the first time in my life I was resolute on killing one particular man, and the purpose gave me a horrid comfort.

Suddenly Ivery's voice rang out sharp. "Take your hand out of your pocket. You fool, you are covered from three points in the walls. A movement and my men will make a sieve of you. Others before you have sat in that chair, and I am used to take precautions. Quick. Both hands on the table."

There was no mistake about Blenkiron's defeat. He was down and out, and I was left with the only card. He leaned wearily on his arms with the palms of his hands spread out.

"I reckon you've gotten a strong hand, Graf," he said, and his voice was flat with despair.

"I hold a royal straight flush," was the answer.

And then suddenly came a change. Blenkiron raised his head, and his sleepy, ruminating eyes looked straight at Ivery.

"I call you," he said.

I didn't believe my ears. Nor did Ivery.

"The hour for bluff is past," he said.

"Nevertheless I call you."

At that moment I felt some one squeeze through the door behind me and take his place at my side. The light was so dim that I saw only a short, square figure, but a familiar voice whispered in my ear, "It's me—Andra Amos. Man, this is a great ploy. I'm here to see the end o't."

No prisoner waiting on the finding of the jury, no commander expecting news of a great battle, ever hung in more desperate suspense than I did during the next seconds. I had forgotten my fatigue; my back no longer needed support. I kept my eyes glued to the crack in the screen, and my ears drank in greedily every syllable.

Blenkiron was now sitting bolt upright with his chin in his hands. There was no shadow of melancholy in his lean face.

"I say I call you, Herr Graf von Schwabing. I'm going to put you wise about some little things. You don't carry arms, so I needn't warn you against monkeying with a gun. You're right in saying that there are three places in these walls from which you can shoot. Well, for your information I may tell you that there's guns in all three, but they're covering you at this moment. So you'd better be good."

Ivery stood to attention like a ramrod. "Karl!" he cried. "Gustav!"

As if by magic, figures stood on either side of him, like warders by a criminal. They were not the sleek German footmen whom I had seen at the Chalet. One I did not recognize. The other was my servant, Geordie Hamilton.

He gave them one glance, looked round like a hunted animal, and then steadied himself. The man had his own kind of courage.

"I've gotten something to say to you," Blenkiron drawled. "It's been a tough fight, but I reckon the hot end of the poker is with you. I compliment you on Clarence Donne. You fooled me fine over that business, and it was only by the mercy of God you didn't win out. You see, there was just the one of us who was liable to recognize you whatever way you twisted your face, and that was Dick Hannay. I give you good marks for Clarence. . . . For the rest, I had you beaten flat."

He looked steadily at him. "You don't believe it. Well, I'll give you proof. I've been watching your Underground Railway for quite a time. I've had my men on the job, and I reckon most of the lines are now closed for repairs. All but the trunk line into France. That I'm keeping open, for soon there's going to be some traffic on it."

At that I saw Ivery's eyelids quiver. For all his self-command he was wilting.

"I admit we cut it mighty fine, along of your fooling me about Clarence. But you struck a bad snag in General Hannay, Graf. Your heart-to-heart talk with him was poor business. You reckoned you had him safe, but that was too big a risk to take with a man like Dick, unless you saw him cold before you left. . . . He got away from this place, and early this morning I knew all he knew. After that it was easy. I got the telegram you had sent this morning in the name of Clarence Donne and it made me laugh. Before midday I had this whole outfit under my hand. Your servants have gone by the Underground Railway—to France. Ehrlich—well, I'm sorry about Ehrlich."

I knew now the name of the Portuguese Jew.

"He wasn't a bad sort of man," Blenkiron said regretfully, "and he was plumb honest. I couldn't get him to listen to reason, and he would play with firearms. So I had to shoot."

"Dead?" asked Ivery sharply.

"Ye-es. I don't miss, and it was him or me. He's under the ice now—where you wanted to send Dick Hannay. He wasn't your kind, Graf, and I guess he has some chance of getting into Heaven. If I weren't a hard-shell Presbyterian I'd say a prayer for his soul."

I looked at Ivery only. His face had gone very pale, and his eyes were wandering. I am certain his brain was working at lightning speed, but he was a rat in a steel trap and the springs held him. If ever I saw a man going through hell it was now. His pasteboard castle had crumbled about his ears and he was giddy with the fall of it. The man was made of pride, and every proud nerve of him was caught on the raw.

"So much for ordinary business," said Blenkiron. "There's the matter of a certain lady. You haven't behaved over-nice about her, Graf, but I'm not going to blame you. You maybe heard a whistle blow when you were coming in here? No! Why, it sounded like Gabriel's trump. Peter must have put some lung power into it. Well, that was the signal that Miss Mary was safe in your car . . . but in our charge. D'you comprehend?"

He did. The ghost of a flush appeared in his cheeks.

"You ask about General Hannay? I'm not just exactly sure where Dick is at this moment, but I opine he's in Italy."

I kicked aside the screen, thereby causing Amos almost to fall on his face.
"I'm back," I said, and pulled up an arm-chair and dropped into it.

I think the sight of me was the last straw for Ivery. I was a wild enough
figure, grey with weariness, soaked, dirty, with the clothes of the porter
Joseph Zimmer in rags from the sharp rocks of the Schwarzsteinthor. As his
eyes caught mine they wavered, and I saw terror in them. He knew he was in
the presence of a mortal enemy.

"Why, Dick," said Blenkiron with a beaming face, "this is mighty oppor-
tune. How in creation did you get here?"

"I walked," I said. I did not want to have to speak, for I was too tired. I
wanted to watch Ivery's face.

Blenkiron gathered up his Patience cards, slipped them into a little leather
case and put it in his pocket.

"I've one thing more to tell you. The Wild Birds have been summoned home,
but they won't ever make it. We've gathered them in—Pavia, and Hofgaard,
and Conradi. Ehrlich is dead. And you are going to join the rest in our cage."

As I looked at my friend, his figure seemed to gain in presence. He sat
square in his chair with a face like a hanging judge, and his eyes, sleepy no
more, held Ivery as in a vice. He had dropped, too, his drawl and the idioms
of his ordinary speech, and his voice came out hard and massive like the clash
of granite blocks.

"You're at the bar now, Graf von Schwabing. For years you've done your
best against the decencies of life. You have deserved well of your own
country, I don't doubt it. But what has your country deserved of the world?
One day soon Germany has to do some heavy paying, and you are the first
instalment."

"I appeal to the Swiss law. I stand on Swiss soil, and I demand that I be
surrendered to the Swiss authorities." Ivery spoke with dry lips and the sweat
was on his brow.

"Oh, no, no," said Blenkiron soothingly. "The Swiss are a nice people,
and I would hate to add to the worries of a poor little neutral state. . . . All
along both sides have been outside the law in this game, and that's going to
continue. We've abode by the rules, and so must you. . . . For years you've
murdered and kidnapped and seduced the weak and ignorant, but we're not
going to judge your morals. We leave that to the Almighty when you get
across Jordan. We're going to wash our hands of you as soon as we can.
You'll travel to France by the Underground Railway and there be handed
over to the French Government. From what I know they've enough against
you to shoot you every hour of the day for a twelve-month."

I think he had expected to be condemned by us there and then and sent to
join Ehrlich beneath the ice. Anyhow, there came a flicker of hope into his
eyes. I dare say he saw some way to dodge the French authorities if he once
got a chance to use his miraculous wits. Anyhow, he bowed with something
very like self-possession, and asked permission to smoke. As I have said, the
man had his own courage.

"Blenkiron," I cried, "we're going to do nothing of the kind."

He inclined his head gravely towards me. "What's your notion, Dick?"

"We've got to make the punishment fit the crime," I said. I was so tired that I had to form my sentences laboriously, as if I were speaking a half-understood foreign tongue.

"Meaning?"

"I mean that if you hand him over to the French he'll either twist out of their hands somehow or get decently shot, which is far too good for him. This man and his kind have sent millions of honest folk to their graves. He has sat spinning his web like a great spider, and for every thread there has been an ocean of blood spilled. It's his sort that made the war, not the brave, stupid fighting Boche. It's his sort that's responsible for all the clotted beastliness. . . . And he's never been in sight of a shell. I'm for putting him in the front line. No, I don't mean any Uriah the Hittite business. I want him to have a sporting chance, just what other men have. But, by God, he's going to learn what is the upshot of the strings he's been pulling so merrily. . . . He told me in two days' time Germany would smash our armies to hell. He boasted that he would be mostly responsible for it. Well, let him be there to see the smashing."

"I reckon that's just," said Blenkiron.

Ivery's eyes were on me now, fascinated and terrified like those of a bird before a rattlesnake. I saw again the shapeless features of the man in the Tube station, the residuum of shrinking mortality behind his disguises. He seemed to be slipping something from his pocket towards his mouth, but Geordie Hamilton caught his wrist.

"Wad ye offer?" said the scandalized voice of my servant. "Sirr, the prisoner would appear to be trying to puishon hisself. Wull I search him?"

After that he stood with wull airm in the grip of a warder.

"Mr. Ivery," I said, "last night, when I was in your power, you indulged your vanity by gloating over me. I expected it, for your class does not breed gentlemen. We treat our prisoners differently, but it is fair that you should know your fate. You are going into France, and I will see that you are taken to the British Front. There with my old division you will learn something of the meaning of war. Understand that by no conceivable chance can you escape. Men will be detailed to watch you day and night and to see that you undergo the full rigour of the battlefield. You will have the same experience as other people, no more, no less. I believe in a righteous God, and I know that sooner or later you will find death—death at the hands of your own people—an honourable death which is far beyond your deserts. But before it comes you will have understood the hell to which you have condemned honest men."

In moments of great fatigue, as in moments of great crisis, the mind takes charge, and may run on a track independent of the will. It was not myself that spoke, but an impersonal voice which I did not know, a voice in whose tones rang a strange authority. Ivery recognized the icy finality of it, and his body seemed to wilt and droop. Only the hold of the warders kept him from falling.

I, too, was about the end of my endurance. I felt dimly that the room had emptied except for Blenkiron and Amos, and that the former was trying to make me drink brandy from the cup of a flask. I struggled to my feet with the intention of going to Mary, but my legs would not carry me. . . . I heard as in a dream Amos giving thanks to an Omnipotence in whom he officially disbelieved. "What's that the auld man in the Bible said? 'Now let Thou Thy servant depart in peace.' That's the way I'm feelin' mysel'." And then slumber came on me like an armed man, and in the chair by the dying wood ash I slept off the ache of my limbs, the tension of my nerves, and the confusion of my brain.

52 THE STORM BREAKS IN THE WEST

The following evening—it was the 20th day of March—I started for France after the dark fell. I drove Ivery's big closed car, and within sat its owner, bound and gagged, as others had sat before him on the same errand. Geordie Hamilton and Amos were his companions. From what Blenkiron had himself discovered and from the papers seized in the Pink Chalet I had full details of the road and its mysterious stages. It was like the journey of a mad dream. In a back street of a little town I would exchange passwords with a nameless figure and be given instructions. At a wayside inn at an appointed hour a voice speaking thick German would advise that this bridge or that railway crossing had been cleared. At a hamlet among pine woods an unknown man would clamber up beside me and take me past a sentry post. Smooth as clockwork was the machine, till in the dawn of a spring morning I found myself dropping into a broad valley through little orchards just beginning to blossom, and knew that I was in France. After that, Blenkiron's own arrangements began, and soon I was drinking coffee with a young lieutenant of Chasseurs, and had taken the gag from Ivery's mouth. The bluecoats looked curiously at the man in the green ulster whose face was the colour of clay and who lit cigarette from cigarette with a shaky hand.

The lieutenant rang up a General of Division who knew all about us. At his headquarters I explained my purpose, and he telegraphed to an Army Headquarters for a permission which was granted. It was not for nothing that in January I had seen certain great personages in Paris, and that Blenkiron had wired ahead of me to prepare the way. Here I handed over Ivery and his guard, for I wanted them to proceed to Amiens under French supervision, well knowing that the men of that great army are not used to let slip what they once hold.

It was a morning of clear spring sunlight when we breakfasted in that little red-roofed town among vineyards with a shining river looping at our feet. The General of Division was an Algerian veteran with a brush of grizzled hair, whose eye kept wandering to a map on the wall where pins and stretched thread made a spider's web.

"Any news from the north?" I asked.

"Not yet," he said. "But the attack comes soon. It will be against our army in Champagne." With a lean finger he pointed out the enemy dispositions.

"Why not against the British?" I asked. With a knife and fork I made a right angle and put a salt dish in the centre. "That is the German concentration. They can so mass that we do not know which side of the angle they will strike till the blow falls."

"It is true," he replied. "But consider. For the enemy to attack towards the Somme would be to fight over many miles of an old battle-ground where all is still desert and every yard of which you British know. In Champagne at a bound he might enter unbroken country. It is a long and difficult road to Amiens, but not so long to Châlons. Such is the view of Pétain. Does it convince you?"

"The reasoning is good. Nevertheless he will strike at Amiens, and I think he will begin to-day."

He laughed and shrugged his shoulders. "*Nous verrons.* You are obstinate, my general, like all your excellent countrymen."

But as I left his headquarters an aide-de-camp handed him a message on a pink slip. He read it, and turned to me with a grave face.

"You have a *flair*, my friend. I am glad we did not wager. This morning at dawn there is great fighting around St. Quentin. Be comforted, for they will not pass. Your Maréchal will hold them."

That was the first news I had of the battle.

At Dijon according to plan I met the others. I only just caught the Paris train, and Blenkiron's great wrists lugged me into the carriage when it was well in motion. There sat Peter, a docile figure in a carefully patched old R.F.C. uniform. Wake was reading a pile of French papers, and in a corner Mary, with her feet up on the seat, was sound asleep.

We did not talk much, for the life of the past days had been so hectic that we had no wish to recall it. Blenkiron's face wore an air of satisfaction, and as he looked out at the sunny spring landscape he hummed his only tune. Even Wake had lost his restlessness. He had on a pair of big tortoiseshell reading glasses, and when he looked up from his newspaper and caught my eye he smiled. Mary slept like a child, delicately flushed, her breath scarcely stirring the collar of the greatcoat which was folded across her throat. I remember looking with a kind of awe at the curve of her young face and the long lashes that lay so softly on her cheek, and wondering how I had borne the anxiety of the last months. Wake raised his head from his reading, glanced at Mary and then at me, and his eyes were kind, almost affectionate. He seemed to have won peace of mind among the hills.

Only Peter was out of the picture. He was a strange disconsolate figure, as he shifted about to ease his leg, or gazed incuriously from the window. He had shaved his beard again, but it did not make him younger, for his face was too lined and his eyes too old to change. When I spoke to him he looked towards Mary and held up a warning finger.

"I go back to England," he whispered. "Your little *mysie* is going to take care of me till I am settled. We spoke of it yesterday at my cottage. I will find a lodging and be patient till the war is over. And you, Dick?"

"Oh, I rejoin my division. Thank God, this job is over. I have an easy mind now, and can turn my attention to straightforward soldiering. I don't mind telling you that I'll be glad to think that you and Mary and Blenkiron are safe at home. What about you, Wake?"

"I go back to my Labour battalion," he said cheerfully. "Like you, I have an easier mind."

I shook my head. "We'll see about that. I don't like such sinful waste. We've had a bit of campaigning together, and I know your quality."

"The battalion's quite good enough for me," and he relapsed into a day-old *Temps*.

Mary had suddenly woke, and was sitting upright, with her fists in her eyes like a small child. Her hand flew to her hair, and her eyes ran over us as if to see that we were all there. As she counted the four of us she seemed relieved.

"I reckon you feel refreshed, Miss Mary," said Blenkiron. "It's good to think that now we can sleep in peace, all of us. Pretty soon you'll be in England and spring will be beginning, and please God it'll be the start of a better world. Our work's over, anyhow."

"I wonder," said the girl gravely. "I don't think there's any discharge in this war. Dick, have you news of the battle? This was the day."

"It's begun," I said, and told them the little I had learned from the French general. "I've made a reputation as a prophet, for he thought the attack was coming in Champagne. It's St. Quentin right enough, but I don't know what has happened. We'll hear in Paris."

Mary had woke with a startled air as if she remembered her old instinct that our work would not be finished without a sacrifice, and that sacrifice the best of us. The notion kept recurring to me with an uneasy insistence. But soon she appeared to forget her anxiety. That afternoon as we journeyed through the pleasant land of France she was in holiday mood, and she forced all our spirits up to her level. It was calm, bright weather, the long curves of ploughland were beginning to quicken into green, the catkins made a blue mist on the willows by the watercourses, and in the orchards by the red-roofed hamlets the blossom was breaking. In such a scene it was hard to keep the mind sober and grey, and the pall of war slid from us. Mary cosseted and fussed over Peter like an elder sister over a delicate little boy. She made him stretch his bad leg full length on the seat, and when she made tea for the party of us it was a protesting Peter who had the last sugar biscuit. Indeed, we were almost a merry company, for Blenkiron told stories of old hunting and engineering days in the West, and Peter and I were driven to cap them, and Mary asked provocative questions, and Wake listened with amused interest. It was well that we had the carriage to ourselves, for no queerer rigs were ever assembled. Mary, as always, was neat and workmanlike in her dress; Blenkiron was magnificent in a suit of russet tweed with a pale-blue shirt and collar, and well-polished brown shoes; but Peter and Wake were in uniforms which had seen far better days, and I wore still the boots and the shapeless and ragged clothes of Joseph Zimmer, the porter from Arosa.

We appeared to forget the war, but we didn't, for it was in the background of all our minds. Somewhere in the north there was raging a desperate fight, and its issue was the true test of our success or failure. Mary showed it by bidding me ask for news at every stopping-place. I asked gendarmes and *permissionnaires*, but I learned nothing. Nobody had even heard of the battle. The upshot was that for the last hour we all fell silent, and when we reached Paris about seven o'clock my first errand was to the bookstall.

I bought a batch of evening papers, which we tried to read in the taxis that carried us to our hotel. Sure enough there was the announcement in big headlines. The enemy had attacked in great strength from south of Arras to the Oise; but everywhere he had been repulsed and held in our battle-zone. The leading articles were confident, the notes by the various military critics were almost braggart. At last the Germans had been driven to an offensive, and the Allies would have the opportunity they had longed for of proving their superior fighting strength. It was, said one and all, the opening of the last phase of the war.

I confess that as I read my heart sank. If the civilians were so over-confident, might not the generals have fallen into the same trap? Blenkiron alone was unperturbed. Mary said nothing, but she sat with her chin in her hands, which with her was a sure sign of deep preoccupation.

Next morning the papers could tell us little more. The main attack had been on both sides of St. Quentin, and though the British had given ground it was only the outpost lines that had gone. The mist had favoured the enemy, and his bombardment had been terrific, especially the gas shells. Every journal added the old, old comment—that he had paid heavily for his temerity, with losses far exceeding those of the defence.

Wake appeared at breakfast in his private's uniform. He wanted to get his railway warrant and be off at once, but when I heard that Amiens was his destination I ordered him to stay and travel with me in the afternoon. I was in the uniform myself now and had taken charge of the outfit. I arranged that Blenkiron, Mary, and Peter should go on to Boulogne and sleep the night there, while Wake and I would be dropped at Amiens to await instructions.

I spent a busy morning. Once again I visited with Blenkiron the little cabinet in the Boulevard St. Germain, and told in every detail our work of the past two months. Once again I sat in the low building beside the Invalides and talked to staff officers. But some of the men I had seen on the first visit were not there. The chiefs of the French Army had gone north.

We arranged for the handling of the Wild Birds, now safely in France, and sanction was given to the course I had proposed to adopt with Ivery. He and his guard were on their way to Amiens, and I would meet them there on the morrow. The great men were very complimentary to us, so complimentary that my knowledge of grammatical French ebbed away and I could only stutter in reply. That telegram sent by Blenkiron on the night of the 18th, from the information given me in the Pink Chalet, had done wonders in clearing up the situation.

But when I asked them about the battle they could tell me little. It was a very serious attack in tremendous force, but the British line was strong and the reserves were believed to be sufficient. Pétain and Foch had gone north to consult with Haig. The situation in Champagne was still obscure, but some French reserves were already moving thence to the Somme sector. One thing they did show me, the British dispositions. As I looked at the plan I saw that my old division was in the thick of the fighting.

"Where do you go now?" I was asked.

"To Amiens, and then, please God, to the battle-front," I said.

"Good fortune to you. You do not give body or mind much rest, my General."

After that I went to the Mission Anglaise, but they had nothing beyond Haig's *communiqué* and a telephone message from G.H.Q. that the critical sector was likely to be that between St. Quentin and the Oise. The northern pillar of our defence, south of Arras, which they had been nervous about, had stood like a rock. That pleased me, for my old battalion of the Lennox Highlanders was there.

Crossing the Place de la Concorde, we fell in with a British staff officer of my acquaintance, who was just starting to motor back to G.H.Q. from Paris leave. He had a longer face than the people at the Invalides.

"I don't like it, I tell you," he said. "It's this mist that worries me. I went down the whole line from Arras to the Oise ten days ago. It was beautifully sited, the cleverest thing you ever saw. The outpost line was mostly a chain of blobs—redoubts, you know, with machine guns—so arranged as to bring flanking fire to bear on the advancing enemy. But mist would play the devil with that scheme, for the enemy would be past the place for flanking fire before we knew it. . . . Oh, I know we had good warning, and had the battle-zone manned in time, but the outpost line was meant to hold out long enough to get everything behind in apple-pie order, and I can't see but how big chunks of it must have gone in the first rush. . . . Mind you, we've banked everything on that battle-zone. It's damned good, but if it's gone—" He flung up his hands.

"Have we good reserves?" I asked.

He shrugged his shoulders.

"Have we positions prepared behind the battle-zone?"

"I didn't notice any," he said drily, and was off before I could get more out of him.

"You look rattled, Dick," said Blenkiron as we walked to the hotel.

"I seem to have got the needle. It's silly, but I feel worse about this show than I've ever felt since the war started. Look at this city here. The papers take it easily and the people are walking about as if nothing was happening. Even the soldiers aren't worried. You may call me a fool to take it so hard, but I've a sense in my bones that we're in for the bloodiest and darkest fight of our lives, and that soon Paris will be hearing the Boche guns as she did in 1914."

"You're a cheerful old Jeremiah. Well, I'm glad Miss Mary's going to be in England soon. Seems to me she's right and that this game of ours isn't quite played out yet. I'm envying you some, for there's a place waiting for you in the fighting line."

"You've got to get home and keep people's heads straight there. That's the weak link in our chain and there's a mighty lot of work before you."

"Maybe," he said abstractedly, with his eye on the top of the Vendôme column.

The train that afternoon was packed with officers recalled from leave, and it took all the combined purchase of Blenkiron and myself to get a carriage reserved for our little party. At the last moment I opened the door to admit a warm and agitated captain of the R.F.C. in whom I recognized my friend and benefactor, Archie Roylance.

"Just when I was gettin' nice and clean and comfy a wire comes tellin' me to bundle back, all along of a new battle. It's a cruel war, sir." The afflicted young man mopped his forehead, grinned cheerfully at Blenkiron, glanced critically at Peter, then caught sight of Mary and grew at once acutely conscious of his appearance. He smoothed his hair, adjusted his tie, and became desperately sedate.

I introduced him to Peter and he promptly forgot Mary's existence. If Peter had had any vanity in him it would have been flattered by the frank interest and admiration in the boy's eyes.

"I'm tremendously glad to see you safe back, sir. I've always hoped I might have a chance of meetin' you. We want you badly now on the Front. Lensch is gettin' a bit uppish."

Then his eye fell on Peter's withered leg and he saw that he had blundered. He blushed scarlet and looked his apologies. But they weren't needed, for it cheered Peter to meet some one who talked of the possibility of his fighting again. Soon the two were deep in technicalities, the appalling technicalities of the airman. It was no good listening to their talk, for you could make nothing of it, but it was bracing up Peter like wine. Archie gave him a minute description of Lensch's latest doings and his new methods. He, too, had heard the rumour that Peter had mentioned to me at St. Anton, of a new Boche plane, with mighty engines and stumpy wings cunningly cambered, which was a devil to climb; but no specimens had yet appeared over the line. They talked of Ball, and Rhys Davids, and Bishop, and McCudden, and all the heroes who had won their spurs since the Somme, and of the new British makes, most of which Peter had never seen and had to have explained to him.

Outside a haze had drawn over the meadows with the twilight. I pointed it out to Blenkiron.

"There's the fog that's doing us in. This March weather is just like October, mist morning and evening. I wish to Heaven we could have some good old drenching spring rains."

Archie was discoursing of the Shark-Gladas machine.

"I've always stuck to it, for it's a marvel in its way, but it has my heart fairly broke. The General here knows its little tricks. Don't you, sir? Whenever things get really excitin' the engine's apt to quit work and take a rest."

"The whole make should be publicly burned," I said, with gloomy recollections.

"I wouldn't go so far, sir. The old Gladas has surprisin' merits. On her day there's nothing like her for pace and climbing-power, and she steers as sweet as a racin' cutter. The trouble about her is she's too complicated. She's like some breeds of car—you want to be a mechanical genius to understand her. . . . If they'd only get her a little simpler and safer, there wouldn't be her match in the field. I'm about the only man that has patience with her and knows her merits, but she's often been nearly the death of me. All the same, if I were in for a big fight against some fellow like Lensch, where it was neck or nothing, I'm hanged if I wouldn't pick the Gladas."

Archie laughed apologetically. "The subject is banned for me in our mess. I'm the old thing's only champion, and she's like a mare I used to hunt that loved me so much she was always tryin' to chew the arm off me. But I wish I could get her a fair trial from one of the big pilots. I'm only in the second class myself after all."

We were running north of St. Just when above the rattle of the train rose a curious dull sound. It came from the east, and was like the low growl of a veld thunderstorm, or a steady roll of muffled drums.

"Hark to the guns!" cried Archie. "My aunt, there's a tidy bombardment goin' on somewhere."

I had been listening on and off to guns for three years. I had been present at the big preparations before Loos and the Somme and Arras, and I had come to accept the racket of artillery as something natural and inevitable like rain or sunshine. But this sound chilled me with its eeriness, I don't know why. Perhaps it was its unexpectedness, for I was sure that the guns had not been heard in this area since before the Marne. The noise must be travelling down the Oise valley, and I judged there was big fighting somewhere about Chauny or La Fère. That meant that the enemy was pressing hard on a huge front, for here was clearly a great effort on his extreme left wing. Unless it was our counter-attack. But somehow I didn't think so.

I let down the window and stuck my head into the night. The fog had crept to the edge of the track, a gossamer mist through which houses and trees and cattle could be seen dim in the moonlight. The noise continued—not a mutter, but a steady rumbling flow as solid as the blare of a trumpet. Presently, as we drew nearer Amiens, we left it behind us, for in all the Somme valley there is some curious configuration which blankets sound. The country folk call it the "Silent Land," and during the first phase of the Somme battle a man in Amiens could not hear the guns twenty miles off at Albert.

As I sat down again I found that the company had fallen silent, even the garrulous Archie. Mary's eyes met mine, and in the indifferent light of the French railway carriage I could see excitement in them—I knew it was excitement, not fear. She had never heard the noise of a great barrage before. Blenkiron was restless, and Peter was sunk in his own thoughts. I was growing very depressed, for in a little I would have to part from my best friends and the girl I loved. But with the depression was mixed an odd expectation which was almost pleasant. The guns had brought back my profession to me; I was moving towards their thunder, and God only knew the end of it. The happy dream I had dreamed of the Cotswolds and a home with Mary beside me seemed suddenly to have fallen away to an infinite distance. I felt once again that I was on the razor-edge of life.

The last part of the journey I was casting back to rake up my knowledge of the countryside. I saw again the stricken belt from Serre to Combles where we had fought in the summer of '16. I had not been present in the advance of the following spring, but I had been at Cambrai and I knew all the down country from Lagnicourt to St. Quentin. I shut my eyes and tried to picture it, and to see the roads running up to the line, and wondered just at what points the big pressure had come. They had told me in Paris that the British were as far south as the Oise, so the bombardment we had heard must be directed to our address. With Passchendaele and Cambrai in my mind, and some notion of the difficulties we had always had in getting drafts, I was puzzled to think where we could have found the troops to man the new front. We must be unholily thin on that long line. And against that awesome bombardment! And the masses and the new tactics that Ivery had bragged of!

When we ran into the dingy cavern which is Amiens station, I seemed to note a new excitement. I felt it in the air rather than deduced it from any special incidents, except that the platform was very crowded with civilians, most of them with an extra amount of baggage. I wondered if the place had been bombed the night before.

"We won't say good-bye yet," I told the others. "The train doesn't leave for half an hour. I'm off to try and get news."

Accompanied by Archie, I hunted out an R.T.O. of my acquaintance. To my questions he responded cheerfully.

"Oh, we're doing famously, sir. I heard this afternoon from a man in Operations that G.H.Q. was perfectly satisfied. We've killed a lot of Huns and only lost a few kilometres of ground. . . . You're going to your division? Well, it's up Péronne way, or was last night. Cheyne and Dunthorne came back from leave and tried to steal a car to get up to it. . . . Oh, I'm having the deuce of a time. These blighted civilians have got the wind up, and a lot are trying to clear out. The idiots say the Huns will be in Amiens in a week. What's the phrase? 'Pourvu que les civils tiennent.' 'Fraid I must push on, sir."

I sent Archie back with these scraps of news and was about to make a rush for the house of one of the Press officers, who would, I thought, be in the way of knowing things, when at the station entrance I ran across Laidlaw. He had been B.G.G.S. in the corps to which my old brigade belonged, and was now on the staff of some army. He was striding towards a car when I grabbed his arm, and he turned on me a very sick face.

"Good Lord, Hannay! Where did you spring from? The news, you say?" He sank his voice, and drew me into a quiet corner. "The news is hellish."

"They told me we were holding," I observed.

"Holding be damned! The Boche is clean through on a broad front. He broke us to-day at Maissemy and Essigny. Yes, the battle-zone. He's flinging in division after division like the blows of a hammer. What else could you expect?" And he clutched my arm fiercely. "How in God's name could eleven divisions hold a front of forty miles? And against four to one in numbers? It isn't war, it's naked lunacy."

I knew the worst now, and it didn't shock me, for I had known it was coming. Laidlaw's nerves were pretty bad, for his face was pale and his eyes bright like a man with a fever.

"Reserves!" and he laughed bitterly. "We had three infantry divisions and two cavalry. They're into the mill long ago. The French are coming up on our right, but they've the devil of a way to go. That's what I'm down here about. And we're getting help from Horne and Plumer. But all that takes days, and meantime we're walking back like we did at Mons. And at this time of day, too. . . . Oh yes, the whole line's retreating. Parts of it were pretty comfortable, but they had to get back or be put in the bag. I wish to Heaven I knew where our right divisions have got to. For all I know they're at Compiègne by now. The Boche was over the canal this morning, and by this time most likely he's across the Somme."

At that I exclaimed, "D'you mean to tell me we're going to lose Péronne?"

"Péronne!" he cried. "We'll be lucky not to lose Amiens! . . . And on top of it all I've got some kind of blasted fever. I'll be raving in an hour."

He was rushing off, but I held him.

"What about my old lot?" I asked.

"Oh, damned good, but they're shot all to bits. Every division did well. It's a marvel they weren't all scuppered, and it'll be a flaming miracle if they find a line they can stand on. Westwater's got a leg smashed. He was brought down this evening, and you'll find him in the hospital. Fraser's killed and Lefroy's a prisoner—at least, that was my last news. I don't know who's got the brigades, but Masterton's carrying on with the division. . . . You'd better get up the line as fast as you can and take over from him. See the Army Commander. He'll be in Amiens to-morrow morning for a pow-wow."

Laidlaw lay wearily back in his car and disappeared into the night, while I hurried to the train.

The others had descended to the platform and were grouped round Archie, who was discoursing optimistic nonsense. I got them into the carriage and shut the door.

"It's pretty bad," I said. "The Front's pierced in several places and we're back to the Upper Somme. I'm afraid it isn't going to stop there. I'm off up the line as soon as I can get my orders. Wake, you'll come with me, for every man will be wanted. Blenkiron, you'll see Mary and Peter safe to England. We're just in time, for to-morrow it mightn't be easy to get out of Amiens."

I can see yet the anxious faces in that ill-lit compartment. We said good-bye after the British style without much to-do. I remember that old Peter gripped my hand as if he would never release it, and that Mary's face had grown very pale. If I had delayed another second I should have howled, for Mary's lips were trembling and Peter had eyes like a wounded stag. "God bless you," I said hoarsely, and as I went off I heard Peter's voice, a little cracked, saying "God bless you, my old friend."

I spent some weary hours looking for Westwater. He was not in the big clearing station, but I ran him to earth at last in the new hospital which had just been got going in the Ursuline convent. He was the most sterling little man, in ordinary life rather dry and dogmatic, with a trick of taking you up sharply which didn't make him popular. Now he was lying very stiff and quiet in the hospital bed, and his blue eyes were solemn and pathetic like a sick dog's.

"There's nothing much wrong with me," he said, in reply to my question. "A shell dropped beside me and damaged my foot. They say they'll have to cut it off. . . . I've an easier mind now you're here, Hannay. Of course you'll take over from Masterton. He's a good man but not quite up to this job. Poor Fraser—you've heard about Fraser. He was done in at the very start. Yes, a shell. And Lefroy. If he's alive and not too badly smashed the Hun has got a troublesome prisoner."

He was too sick to talk, but he wouldn't let me go.

"The division was all right. Don't you believe any one who says we didn't fight like heroes. Our outpost line held up the Hun for six hours, and only about a dozen men came back. We could have stuck it out in the battle-zone if both flanks hadn't been turned. They got through Crabbe's left and came down the Verey ravine, and a big wave rushed Shropshire Wood. . . . We fought it out yard by yard and didn't budge till we saw the Plessis dump blazing in our rear. Then it was about time to go. . . . We haven't many battalion commanders left. Watson, Endicot, Crawshay . . ." He stammered out a list of gallant fellows who had gone.

"Get back double quick, Hannay. They want you. I'm not happy about Masterton. He's too young for the job." And then a nurse drove me out, and I left him speaking in the strange forced voice of great weakness.

At the foot of the staircase stood Mary.

"I saw you go in," she said, "so I waited for you."

"Oh, my dear," I cried, "you should have been in Boulogne by now. What madness brought you here?"

"They know me here and they've taken me on. You couldn't expect me to stay behind. You said yourself everybody was wanted, and I'm in a Service like you. Please don't be angry, Dick."

I wasn't angry, I wasn't even extra anxious. The whole thing seemed to have been planned by fate since the creation of the world. The game we had been engaged in wasn't finished and it was right that we should play it out altogether. With that feeling came a conviction, too, of ultimate victory. Somehow or some time we should get to the end of our pilgrimage. But I remembered Mary's forebodings about the sacrifice required. *The best of us.* That ruled me out, but what about her?

I caught her to my arms. "Good-bye, my very dearest. Don't worry about me, for mine's a soft job and I can look after my skin. But oh! take care of yourself, for you are all the world to me."

She kissed me gravely like a wise child.

"I am not afraid for you," she said. "You are going to stand in the breach, and I know—I know you will win. Remember that there is some one here whose heart is so full of pride of her man that it hasn't any room for fear."

As I went out of the convent door I felt that once again I had been given my orders.

It did not surprise me that, when I sought out my room on an upper floor of the Hôtel de France, I found Blenkiron in the corridor. He was in the best of spirits.

"You can't keep me out of the show, Dick," he said, "so you needn't start arguing. Why, this is the one original chance of a lifetime for John S. Blenkiron. Our little fight at Erzerum was only a side-show, but this is a real high-class Armageddon. I guess I'll find a way to make myself useful."

I had no doubt he would, and I was glad he had stayed behind. But I felt it was hard on Peter to have the job of returning to England alone at such a time, like useless flotsam washed up by a flood.

"You needn't worry," said Blenkiron. "Peter's not making England this trip. To the best of my knowledge he has beat it out of this township by the eastern postern. He had some talk with Sir Archibald Roylance, and presently other gentlemen of the Royal Flying Corps appeared, and the upshot was that Sir Archibald hitched on to Peter's grip and departed without saying farewell. My notion is that he's gone to have a few words with his old friends at some flying station. Or he might have the idea of going back to England by aeroplane, and so having one last flutter before he folds his wings. Anyhow, Peter looked a mighty happy man. The last I saw of him he was smoking his pipe with a batch of young lads in a Flying Corps wagon and heading straight for Germany."

53 HOW AN EXILE RETURNED TO HIS OWN PEOPLE

Next morning I found the Army Commander on his way to Doullens.

"Take over the division!" he said. "Certainly. I'm afraid there isn't much left of it. I'll tell Carr to get through to the Corps Headquarters, when he can find them. You'll have to nurse the remnants, for they can't be pulled out yet—not for a day or two. Bless me, Hannay, there are parts of our line which we're holding with a man and a boy. You've got so stick it out till the French take over. We're not hanging on by our eyelids—it's our eyelashes now."

"What about positions to fall back on, sir?" I asked.

"We're doing our best, but we haven't enough men to prepare them." He plucked open a map. "There we're digging a line—and there. If we can hold that bit for two days we shall have a fair line resting on the river. But we mayn't have time."

Then I told him about Blenkiron, whom of course he had heard of. "He was one of the biggest engineers in the States, and he's got a nailing fine eye for country. He'll make good somehow if you let him help in the job."

"The very fellow," he said, and he wrote an order. "Take this to Jacks and he'll fix up a temporary commission. Your man can find a uniform somewhere in Amiens."

After that I went to the detail camp and found that Ivery had duly arrived.

"The prisoner has given no trouble, sirr," Hamilton reported. "But he's a wee thing peevish. They're saying that the Gairmans is gettin' on fine, and I was tellin' him that he should be proud of his ain folk. But he wasn't verra weel pleased."

Three days had wrought a transformation in Ivery. That face, once so cool and capable, was now sharpened like a hunted beast's. His imagination was preying on him and I could picture its torture. He, who had been always at the top directing the machine, was now only a cog in it. He had never in his life been anything but powerful; now he was impotent. He was in a hard, unfamiliar world, in the grip of something which he feared and didn't understand, in the charge of men who were in no way amenable to his persuasiveness. It was like a proud and bullying manager suddenly forced to labour in a squad of navvies, and worse, for there was the gnawing physical fear of what was coming.

He made an appeal to me.

"Do the English torture their prisoners?" he asked, "You have beaten me. I own it, and I plead for mercy. I will go on my knees if you like. I am not afraid of death—in my own way."

"Few people are afraid of death—in their own way."

"Why do you degrade me? I am a gentleman."

"Not as we define the thing," I said.

His jaw dropped. "What are you going to do with me?" he quavered.

"You have been a soldier," I said. "You are going to see a little fighting—from the ranks. There will be no brutality, you will be armed if you want to defend yourself, you will have the same chance of survival as the men around you. You may have heard that your countrymen are doing well. It is even possible that they may win the battle. What was your forecast to me? Amiens in two days, Abbeville in three. Well, you are a little behind schedule time, but still you are prospering. You told me that you were the chief architect of all this, and you are going to be given the chance of seeing it, perhaps of sharing in it—from the other side. Does it not appeal to your sense of justice?"

He groaned and turned away. I had no more pity for him than I would have had for a black mamba that had killed my friend and was now caught in a cleft tree. Nor, oddly enough, had Wake. If we had shot Ivery outright at St. Anton, I am certain that Wake would have called us murderers. Now he was

· in complete agreement. His passionate hatred of war made him rejoice that a chief contriver of war should be made to share in its terrors.

"He tried to talk me over this morning," he told me. "Claimed he was on my side, and said the kind of thing I used to say last year. It made me rather ashamed of some of my past performances to hear that scoundrel imitating them. . . . By the way, Hannay, what are you going to do with *me*?"

"You're coming on my staff. You're a stout fellow and I can't do without you."

"Remember I won't fight."

"You won't be asked to. We're trying to stem the tide which wants to roll to the sea. You know how the Boche behaves in occupied country, and Mary's in Amiens."

At that news he shut his lips.

"Still—" he began.

"Still," I said, "I don't ask you to forfeit one of your blessed principles. You needn't fire a shot. But I want a man to carry orders for me, for we haven't a line any more, only a lot of blobs like quicksilver. I want a clever man for the job and a brave one, and I know that you're not afraid."

"No," he said, "I don't think I am—much. Well, I'm content!"

I started Blenkiron off in a car for Corps Headquarters, and in the afternoon took the road myself. I knew every inch of the country—the lift of the hill east of Amiens, the Roman highway that ran straight as an arrow to St. Quentin, the marshy lagoons of the Somme, and that broad strip of land wasted by battle between Dompierre and Péronne. I had come to Amiens through it in January, for I had been up to the line before I left for Paris, and then it had been a peaceful place, with peasants tilling their fields and new buildings going up on the old battlefield, and carpenters busy at cottage roofs, and scarcely a transport wagon on the road to remind one of war. Now the main route was choked like the Albert road when the Somme battle first began—troops going up and troops coming down, the latter in the last stages of weariness; a ceaseless traffic of ambulances one way and ammunition wagons the other; busy staff cars trying to worm a way through the mass; strings of gun horses, oddments of cavalry, and here and there blue French uniforms. All that I had seen before; but one thing was new to me. Little country carts with sad-faced women and mystified children in them and piles of household plenishing were creeping westward, or stood waiting at village doors. Beside these tramped old men and boys, mostly in their Sunday best as if they were going to church. I had never seen the sight before, for I had never seen the British Army falling back. The dam which held up the waters had broken and the dwellers in the valleys were trying to save their pitiful treasures. And over everything, horse and man, cart and wheelbarrow, road and tillage, lay the white March dust, the sky was blue as June, small birds were busy in the copses, and in the corners of abandoned gardens I had a glimpse of the first violets.

Presently as we topped a rise we came within full noise of the guns. That, too, was new to me, for it was not an ordinary bombardment. There was a special quality in the sound, something ragged, straggling, intermittent, which I had never heard before. It was the sign of open warfare and a moving battle.

At Péronne, from which the newly returned inhabitants had a second time fled, the battle seemed to be at the doors. There I had news of my division. It was farther south towards St. Christ. We groped our way among bad roads to where its headquarters were believed to be, while the voice of the guns grew louder. They turned out to be those of another division, which was busy getting ready to cross the river. Then the dark fell, and while aeroplanes flew west into the sunset there was a redder sunset in the east, where the unceasing flashes of gun-fire were pale against the angry glow of burning dumps. The sight of the bonnet badge of a Scots Fusilier made me halt, and the man turned out to belong to my division. Half an hour later I was taking over from the much-relieved Masterton in the ruins of what had once been a sugar-beet factory.

There to my surprise I found Lefroy. The Boche had held him prisoner for precisely eight hours. During that time he had been so interested in watching the way the enemy handled an attack that he had forgotten the miseries of his position. He described with blasphemous admiration the endless wheel by which supplies and reserve troops moved up, the silence, the smoothness, the perfect discipline. Then he had realized that he was a captive, and unwounded, and had gone mad. Being a heavy-weight boxer of note, he had sent his two guards spinning into a ditch, dodged the ensuing shots, and found shelter in the lee of a blazing ammunition dump where his pursuers hesitated to follow. Then he had spent an anxious hour trying to get through an outpost line, which he thought was Boche. Only by overhearing an exchange of oaths in the accents of Dundee did he realize that it was our own. . . . It was a comfort to have Lefroy back, for he was both stout hearted and resourceful. But I found that I had a division only on paper. It was about the strength of a brigade, the brigades battalions, and the battalions companies.

This is not the place to write the story of the week that followed. I could not write it even if I wanted to, for I don't know it. There was a plan somewhere, which you will find in the history books, but with me it was blank chaos. Orders came, but long before they arrived the situation had changed, and I could no more obey them than fly to the moon. Often I had lost touch with the divisions on both flanks. Intelligence arrived erratically out of the void, and for the most part we worried along without it. I heard we were under the French—first it was said to be Foch, and then Fayolle, whom I had met in Paris. But the higher command seemed a million miles away, and we were left to use our mother wits. My problem was to give ground as slowly as possible, and at the same time not to delay too long, for retreat we must, with the Boche sending in brand-new divisions each morning. It was a kind of war worlds distant from the old trench battles, and since I had been taught no other I had to invent rules as I went along. Looking back, it seems a miracle that any of us came out of it. Only the grace of God and the uncommon toughness of the British soldier bluffed the Hun and prevented him pouring through the breach to Abbeville and the sea. We were no better

than a mosquito curtain stuck in a doorway to stop the advance of an angry
bull.

The Army Commander was right; we were hanging on with our eyelashes.

We must have been easily the weakest part of the whole front, for we were
holding a line which was never less than two miles and was often, as I judged,
nearer five, and there was nothing in reserve to us except some oddments of
cavalry who chased about the whole battlefield under vague orders. Mercifully
for us the Boche blundered. Perhaps he did not know our condition, for our
airmen were magnificent, and you never saw a Boche plane over our line by
day, though they bombed us merrily by night. If he had called our bluff we
should have been done, but he put his main strength to the north and the
south of us. North he pressed hard on the Third Army, but he got well
hammered by the Guards north of Bapaume and he could make no headway
at Arras. South he drove at the Paris railway and down the Oise valley, but
there Pétain's reserves had arrived, and the French made a noble stand.

Not that he didn't fight hard in the centre where we were, but he hadn't his
best troops, and after we got west of the bend of the Somme he was
outrunning his heavy guns. Still, it was a desperate enough business, for our
flanks were all the time falling back, and we had to conform to movements we
could only guess at. After all, we were on the direct route to Amiens, and it
was up to us to yield slowly so as to give Haig and Pétain time to get up
supports. I was a miser about every yard of ground, for every yard and every
minute was precious. We alone stood between the enemy and the city, and in
the city was Mary.

If you ask me about our plans I can't tell you. I had a new one every hour. I
got instructions from the Corps, but, as I have said, they were usually out of
date before they arrived, and most of my tactics I had to invent myself. I had
a plain task, and to fulfil it I had to use what methods the Almighty allowed
me. I hardly slept, I ate little, I was on the move day and night, but I never
felt so strong in my life. It seemed as if I couldn't tire, and, oddly enough, I
was happy. If a man's whole being is focused on one aim, he has no time to
worry. . . . I remember we were all very gentle and soft-spoken those days.
Lefroy, whose tongue was famous for its edge, now cooed like a dove. The
troops were on their uppers, but as steady as rocks. We were against the end
of the world, and that stiffens a man. . . .

Day after day saw the same performance. I held my wavering front with an
outpost line which delayed each new attack till I could take its bearings. I had
special companies for counter-attack at selected points, when I wanted time
to retire the rest of the division. I think we must have fought more than a
dozen of such little battles. We lost men all the time, but the enemy made no
big scoop, though he was always on the edge of one. Looking back, it seems
like a succession of miracles. Often I was in one end of a village when the
Boche was in the other. Our batteries were always on the move, and the work
of the gunners was past praising. Sometimes we faced east, sometimes north,
and once at a most critical moment due south, for our front waved and blew
like a flag at a mast head. . . . Thank God, the enemy was getting away from

his big engine, and his ordinary troops were fagged and poor in quality. It was when his fresh shock battalions came on that I held my breath. . . . He had a heathenish amount of machine guns and he used them beautifully. Oh, I take off my hat to the Boche performance. He was doing what we had tried to do at the Somme and the Aisne and Ypres, and he was more or less succeeding. And the reason was that he was going bald-headed for victory.

The men, as I have said, were wonderfully steady and patient under the fiercest trial that soldiers can endure. I had all kinds in the division—old army, new army, Territorials—and you couldn't pick and choose between them. They fought like Trojans, and, dirty, weary, and hungry, found still some salt of humour in their sufferings. It was a proof of the rock-bottom sanity of human nature. But we had one man with us who was hardly sane. . . .

In the hustle of those days I now and then caught sight of Ivery. I had to be everywhere at all hours, and often visited that remnant of Scots Fusiliers into which the subtlest brain in Europe had been drafted. He and his keepers were never on outpost duty or in any counter-attack. They were part of the mass whose only business was to retire discreetly. This was child's play to Hamilton, who had been out since Mons; and Amos, after taking a day to get used to it, wrapped himself in his grim philosophy and rather enjoyed it. You couldn't surprise Amos any more than a Turk. But the man with them, whom they never left—that was another matter.

"For the first wee bit," Hamilton reported, "we thocht he was gaun daft. Every shell that came near he jumped like a young horse. And the gas! We had to tie on his mask for him, for his hands were fushionless. There was whiles when he wadna be hindered from standin' up and talkin' to hisself, though the bullets was spittin'. He was what ye call de-moralized. . . . Syne he got as though he didna hear or see onything. He did what we tell't him, and when we let him be he sat down and grat. He's aye greetin'. . . . Queer thing, sirr, but the Gairmans canna hit him. I'm aye shakin' bullets out o' my claes, and I've got a hole in my shouther, and Andra took a bash on his tin hat that wad hae felled onybody that hadna a heid like a stot. But, sirr, the prisoner taks no scaith. Our boys are feared of him. There was an Irishman says to me that he had the evil eye, and ye can see for yerself that he's no canny."

I saw that his skin had become like parchment and that his eyes were glassy. I don't think he recognized me.

"Does he take his meals?" I asked.

"He doesna eat muckle. But he has an unco thirst. Ye canna keep him off the men's water-bottles."

He was learning very fast the meaning of that war he had so confidently played with. I believe I am a merciful man, but as I looked at him I felt no vestige of pity. He was dreeing the weird he had prepared for others. I thought of Scudder, of the thousand friends I had lost, of the great seas of blood and the mountains of sorrow this man and his like had made for the world. Out of the corner of my eye I could see the long ridges above Combles and Longueval which the salt of the earth had fallen to win, and which were again under the hoof of the Boche. I thought of the distracted city behind us and what it meant to me, and the weak, the pitifully weak screen which was all its defence. I thought of the foul deeds which had made the German name to stink by land and sea, foulness of which he was the arch-begetter. And then I was amazed at our forbearance. He would go mad, and madness for him was more decent than sanity.

I had another man who wasn't what you might call normal, and that was Wake. He was the opposite of shell-shocked, if you understand me. He had never been properly under fire before, but he didn't give a straw for it. I had known the same thing with other men, and they generally ended by crumpling up, for it isn't natural that five or six feet of human flesh shouldn't be afraid of what can torture and destroy it. The natural thing is to be always a little scared, like me, but by an effort of the will and attention to work to contrive to forget it. But Wake apparently never gave it a thought. He wasn't foolhardy, only indifferent. He used to go about with a smile on his face, a smile of contentment. Even the horrors—and we had plenty of them—didn't affect him. His eyes, which used to be hot, had now a curious open innocence like Peter's. I would have been happier if he had been a little rattled.

One night, after we had had a bad day of anxiety, I talked to him as we smoked in what had once been a French dug-out. He was an extra right arm to me, and I told him so. "This must be a queer experience for you," I said.

"Yes," he replied, "it is very wonderful. I did not think a man could go through it and keep his reason. But I know many things I did not know before. I know that the soul can be reborn without leaving the body."

I stared at him, and he went on without looking at me.

"You're not a classical scholar, Hannay? There was a strange cult in the ancient world, the worship of *Magna Mater*—the Great Mother. To enter into her mysteries the votary passed through a bath of blood. . . . I think I am passing through that bath. I think that like the initiate I shall be *renatus in aeternum*—reborn into the eternal."

I advised him to have a drink, for that talk frightened me. It looked as if he were becoming what the Scots call "fey." Lefroy noticed the same thing, and was always speaking to me about it. He was as brave as a bull himself, and with very much the same kind of courage; but Wake's gallantry perturbed him. "I can't make the chap out," he told me. "He behaves as if his mind was too full of better things to give a damn for Boche guns. He doesn't take foolish risks—I don't mean that, but he behaves as if risks didn't signify. It's positively eerie to see him making notes with a steady hand when shells are dropping like hailstones and we're all thinking every minute's our last. You've got to be careful with him, sir. He's a long sight too valuable for us to spare."

Lefroy was right about that, for I don't know what I should have done without him. The worst part of our job was to keep touch with our flanks, and that was what I used Wake for. He covered country like a moss-trooper, sometimes on a rusty bicycle, oftener on foot, and you couldn't tire him. I wonder what other divisions thought of the grimy private who was our chief means of communication. He knew nothing of military affairs before, but he got the hang of this rough-and-tumble fighting as if he had been born for it.

He never fired a shot; he carried no arms; the only weapons he used were his brains. And they were the best conceivable. I never met a staff officer who was so quick at getting a point or at sizing up a situation. He had put his back into the business, and first-class talent is not common anywhere. One day a G.S.O.1 from a neighbouring division came to see me.

"Where on earth did you pick up that man Wake?" he asked.

"He's a conscientious objector and a non-combatant," I said.

"Then I wish to Heaven we had a few more conscientious objectors in this show. He's the only fellow who seems to know anything about this blessed battle My general's sending you a chit about him."

"No need," I said, laughing. "I know his value. He's an old friend of mine."

I used Wake as my link with Corps Headquarters, and especially with Blenkiron. For about the sixth day of the show I was beginning to get rather desperate. This kind of thing couldn't go on for ever. We were miles back now, behind the old line of '17, and, as we rested one flank on the river, the immediate situation was a little easier. But I had lost a lot of men, and those that were left were blind with fatigue. The big bulges of the enemy to north and south had added to the length of the total front, and I found I had to fan out my thin ranks. The Boche was still pressing on, though his impetus was slacker. If he knew how little there was to stop him in my section he might make a push which would carry him to Amiens. Only the magnificent work of our airmen had prevented him getting that knowledge, but we couldn't keep the secrecy up for ever. Some day an enemy plane would get over, and it only needed the drive of a fresh storm-battalion or two to scatter us. I wanted a good prepared position, with sound trenches and decent wiring Above all I wanted reserves—reserves. The word was on my lips all day and it haunted my dreams. I was told that the French were to relieve us, but when—when? My reports to Corps Headquarters were one long wail for more troops. I knew there was a position prepared behind us, but I needed men to hold it.

Wake brought in a message from Blenkiron. "We're waiting for you, Dick," he wrote, "and we've gotten quite a nice little home ready for you. This old man hasn't hustled so hard since he struck copper in Montana in '92. We've dug three lines of trenches and made a heap of pretty redoubts, and I guess they're well laid out, for the Army staff has supervised them and they're no slouches at this brand of engineering. You would have laughed to see the labour we employed. We had all breeds of Dago and Chinaman, and some of your own South African blacks, and they got so busy on the job they forgot about bedtime. I used to be reckoned a bit of a slave driver, but my special talents weren't needed with this push. I'm going to put a lot of money into foreign missions henceforward."

I wrote back: "Your trenches are no good without men. For God's sake get something that can hold a rifle. My lot are done to the world."

Then I left Lefroy with the division and went down on the back of an ambulance to see for myself. I found Blenkiron, some of the Army engineers, and a staff officer from Corps Headquarters, and I found Archie Roylance.

They had dug a mighty good line and wired it nobly. It ran from the river
to the wood of La Bruyère on the little hill above the Ablain stream. It was
desperately long, but I saw at once it couldn't well be shorter, for the division
on the south of us had its hands full with the fringe of the big thrust against
the French.

"It's no good blinking the facts," I told them. "I haven't a thousand men,
and what I have are at the end of their tether. If you put 'em in these trenches
they'll go to sleep on their feet. When can the French take over?"

I was told that it had been arranged for next morning, but that it had now
been put off twenty-four hours. It was only a temporary measure, pending
the arrival of British divisions from the north.

Archie looked grave. "The Boche is pushin' up new troops in this sector.
We got the news before I left squadron headquarters. It looks as if it would be
a near thing, sir."

"It won't be a near thing. It's an absolute black certainty. My fellows can't
carry on as they are another day. Great God, they've had a fortnight in hell!
Find me more men or we buckle up at the next push." My temper was
coming very near its limits.

"We've raked the country with a small toothcomb, sir," said one of the
staff officers. "And we've raised a scratch pack. Best part of two thousand.
Good men, but most of them know nothing about infantry fighting. We've
put them into platoons, and done our best to give them some kind of training.
There's one thing may cheer you. We've plenty of machine guns. There's a
machine-gun school near by, and we got all the men who were taking the
course and all the plant."

I don't suppose there was ever such a force put into the field before. It was
a wilder medley than Moussy's camp followers at First Ypres. There was
every kind of detail in the shape of men returning from leave, representing
most of the regiments in the army. There were the men from the machine-
gun school. There were Corps troops—sappers and A.S.C., and a handful of
Corps cavalry. Above all, there was a batch of American engineers, fathered
by Blenkiron. I inspected them where they were drilling and liked the look
of them "Forty-eight hours," I said to myself. "With luck we may just pull
it off."

Then I borrowed a bicycle and went back to the division. But before I left I
had a word with Archie. "This is one big game of bluff, and it's you fellows
alone that enable us to play it. Tell your people that everything depends on
them. They mustn't stint the planes in this sector, for if the Boche once
suspicions how little he's got before him the game's up. He's not a fool and he
knows that this is the short road to Amiens, but he imagines we're holding it
in strength. If we keep up the fiction for another two days the thing's done.
You say he's pushing up troops?"

"Yes, and he's sendin' forward his tanks."

"Well, that'll take time. He's slower now than a week ago, and he's got a
deuce of a country to march over. There's still an outside chance we may win
through. You go home and tell the R.F.C. what I've told you."

He nodded. "By the way, sir, Pienaar's with the squadron. He would like to come up and see you."

"Archie," I said solemnly, "be a good chap and do me a favour. If I think Peter's anywhere near the line I'll go off my head with worry. This is no place for a man with a bad leg. He should have been in England days ago. Can't you get him off—to Amiens, anyhow?"

"We scarcely like to. You see, we're all desperately sorry for him, his fun gone and his career over and all that. He likes bein' with us and listenin' to our yarns. He has been up once or twice too. The Shark-Gladas. He swears it's a great make, and certainly he knows how to handle the little devil."

"Then for Heaven's sake don't let him do it again. I look to you, Archie, remember. Promise."

"Funny thing, but he's always worryin' about you. He has a map on which he marks every day the changes in the position, and he'd hobble a mile to pump any of our fellows who have been up your way."

That night under cover of darkness I drew back the division to the new prepared lines. We got away easily, for the enemy was busy with his own affairs. I suspected a relief by fresh troops.

There was no time to lose, and I can tell you I toiled to get things straight before dawn. I would have liked to send my own fellows back to rest, but I couldn't spare them yet. I wanted them to stiffen the fresh lot, for they were the veterans. The new position was arranged on the same principles as the old front which had been broken on March 21st. There was our forward zone, consisting of an outpost line and redoubts, very cleverly sited, and a line of resistance. Well behind it were the trenches which formed the battle-zone. Both zones were heavily wired, and we had plenty of machine guns; I wish I could say we had plenty of men who knew how to use them. The outposts were merely to give the alarm and fall back to the line of resistance which was to hold out to the last. In the forward zone I put the freshest of my own men, the units being brought up to something like strength by the details returning from leave that the Corps had commandeered. With them I put the American engineers, partly in the redoubts and partly in companies for counter-attack. Blenkiron had reported that they could shoot like Dan'l Boone, and were simply spoiling for a fight. The rest of the force was in the battle-zone, which was our last hope. If that went the Boche had a clear walk to Amiens. Some additional field batteries had been brought up to support our very weak divisional artillery. The front was so long that I had to put all three of my emaciated brigades in the line, so I had nothing to speak of in reserve. It was a most almighty gamble.

We had found a shelter just in time. At 6.30 next day—for a change it was a clear morning with clouds beginning to bank up from the west—the Boche let us know he was alive. He gave us a good drenching with gas shells which didn't do much harm, and then messed up our forward zone with his trench mortars. At 7.20 his men began to come on, first little bunches with machine guns and then the infantry in waves. It was clear they were first troops, and we learned afterwards from prisoners that they were Bavarians—6th or 7th, I forget which, but the division that hung us up at Monchy. At the same time there was the sound of a tremendous bombardment across the river. It looked as if the main battle had swung from Albert and Montdidier to a direct push for Amiens.

I have often tried to write down the events of that day. I tried it in my report to the Corps; I tried it in my own diary; I tried it because Mary wanted it; but I have never been able to make any story that hung together. Perhaps I was too tired for my mind to retain clear impressions, though at the time I was not conscious of special fatigue. More likely it is because the fight itself was so confused, for nothing happened according to the books and the orderly soul of the Boche must have been scarified. . . .

At first it went as I expected. The outpost line was pushed in, but the fire from the redoubts broke up the advance, and enabled the line of resistance in the forward zone to give a good account of itself. There was a check, and then another big wave, assisted by a barrage from field-guns brought far forward. This time the line of resistance gave at several points, and Lefroy flung in the Americans in a counter-attack. That was a mighty performance. The engineers, yelling like dervishes, went at it with the bayonet, and those that preferred swung their rifles as clubs. It was terribly costly fighting and all wrong, but it succeeded. They cleared the Boche out of a ruined farm he had rushed, and a little wood, and re-established our front. Blenkiron, who saw it all, for he went with them and got the tip of an ear picked off by a machine-gun bullet, hadn't any words wherewith to speak of it. "And I once said those boys looked puffy," he moaned.

The next phase, which came about midday, was the tanks. I had never seen the German variety, but had heard that it was speedier and heavier than ours, but unwieldy. We did not see much of their speed, but we found out all about their clumsiness. Had the things been properly handled they should have gone through us like rotten wood. But the whole outfit was bungled. It looked good enough country for the use of them, but the men who made our position had had an eye to this possibility. The great monsters, mounting a field-gun besides other contrivances, wanted something like a highroad to be happy in. They were useless over anything like difficult ground. The ones that came down the main road got on well enough at the start, but Blenkiron very sensibly had mined the highway, and we blew a hole like a diamond pit. One lay helpless at the foot of it, and we took the crew prisoner; another stuck its nose over and remained there till our field-guns got the range and knocked it silly. As for the rest—there is a marshy lagoon called the Patte d'Oei beside the farm of Gavrelle, which runs all the way north to the river, though in most places it only seems like a soft patch in the meadows. This the tanks had to cross to reach our line, and they never made it. Most got bogged, and made pretty targets for our gunners; one or two returned; and one, the Americans, creeping forward under cover of a little stream, blew up with a time fuse.

By the middle of the afternoon I was feeling happier. I knew the big attack was still to come, but I had my forward zone intact, and I hoped for the best. I remember I was talking to Wake, who had been going between the two zones, when I got the first warning of a new and unexpected peril. A dud shell plumped down a few yards from me.

"Those fools across the river are firing short and badly off the straight," I said.

Wake examined the shell. "No, it's a German one," he said.

Then came others, and there could be no mistake about the direction— followed by a burst of machine-gun fire from the same quarter. We ran in cover to a point from which we could see the north bank of the river, and I got my glass on it. There was a lift of land from behind which the fire was coming. We looked at each other, and the same conviction stood in both faces. The Boche had pushed down the northern bank, and we were no longer in line with our neighbours. The enemy was in a situation to catch us with his fire on our flank and left rear. We couldn't retire to conform, for to retire meant giving up our prepared position.

It was the last straw to all our anxieties, and for a moment I was at the end of my wits. I turned to Wake, and his calm eyes pulled me together.

"If they can't retake that ground, we're fairly carted," I said.

"We are. Therefore they must retake it."

"I must get on to Mitchinson." But as I spoke I realized the futility of a telephone message to a man who was pretty hard up against it himself. Only an urgent personal appeal could effect anything. . . . I must go myself. . . . No, that was impossible. I must send Lefroy. . . . But he couldn't be spared. And all my staff officers were up to their necks in the battle. Besides, none of them knew the position as I knew it. . . . And how to get there? It was a long way round by the bridge at Loisy.

Suddenly I was aware of Wake's voice. "You had better send me," he was saying. "There's only one way—to swim the river a little lower down."

"That's too damnably dangerous. I won't send any man to certain death."

"But I volunteer," he said. "That, I believe, is always allowed in war."

"But you'll be killed before you can cross."

"Send a man with me to watch. If I get over, you may be sure I'll get to General Mitchinson. If not, send somebody else by Loisy. There's desperate need for hurry, and you see yourself it's the only way."

The time was past for argument. I scribbled a line to Mitchinson as his credentials. No more was needed, for Wake knew the position as well as I did. I sent an orderly to accompany him to his starting-place on the bank.

"Good-bye," he said, as we shook hands. "You'll see, I'll come back all right." His face, I remember, looked singularly happy.

Five minutes later the Boche guns opened for the final attack.

I believe I kept a cool head; at least so Lefroy and the others reported. They said I went about all afternoon grinning as if I liked it, and that I never raised my voice once. (It's rather a fault of mine that I bellow in a scrap.) But I know I was feeling anything but calm, for the problem was ghastly. It all depended on Wake and Mitchinson. The flanking fire was so bad that I had to give up the left of the forward zone, which caught it fairly, and retire the men there to the battle-zone. The latter was better protected, for between it and the river was a small wood, and the bank rose into a bluff which sloped inwards towards us. This withdrawal meant a switch, and a switch isn't a pretty thing when it has to be improvised in the middle of a battle.

The Boche had counted on that flanking fire. His plan was to break our two wings—the old Boche plan which crops up in every fight. He left our centre at first pretty well alone, and thrust along the river bank and at the wood of La Bruyère, where we linked up with the division on our right. Lefroy was in the first area, and Masterton in the second, and for three hours it was as desperate a business as I have ever faced. . . . The improvised switch went, and more and more of the forward zone disappeared. It was a hot, clear spring afternoon, and in that open fighting the enemy came on like troops at manoeuvres. On the left they got into the battle-zone, and I can see yet Lefroy's great figure leading a counter-attack in person, his face all puddled with blood from a scalp wound. . . .

I would have given my soul to be in two places at once, but I had to risk our left and keep close to Masterton, who needed me most. The wood of La Bruyère was the maddest sight. Again and again the Boche was almost through it. You never knew where he was, and most of the fighting there was duels between machine-gun parties. Some of the enemy got round behind us, and only a fine performance of a company of Cheshires saved a complete break through.

As for Lefroy, I don't know how he stuck it out, and he doesn't know himself, for he was galled all the time by that accursed flanking fire. I got a note about half-past four saying that Wake had crossed the river, but it was some weary hours after that before the fire slackened. I tore back and forward between my wings, and every time I went north I expected to find that Lefroy had broken. But by some miracle he held. The Boches were in his battle-zone time and again, but he always flung them out. I have a recollection of Blenkiron, stark mad, encouraging his Americans with strange tongues. Once as I passed him I saw that he had his left arm tied up. His blackened face grinned at me. "This bit of landscape's mighty unsafe for democracy," he croaked. "For the love of Mike get your guns on to those devils across the river. They're plaguing my boys too bad."

It was about seven o'clock, I think, when the flanking fire slacked off, but it was not because of our divisional guns. There was a short and very furious burst of artillery fire on the north bank, and I knew it was British. Then things began to happen. One of our planes—they had been marvels all day, swinging down like hawks for machine-gun bouts with the Boche infantry— reported that Mitchinson was attacking hard and getting on well. That eased my mind, and I started off for Masterton, who was in greater straits than ever, for the enemy seemed to be weakening on the river bank and putting his main strength in against our right. . . . But my G.S.O.2 stopped me on the road. "Wake," he said. "He wants to see you."

"Not now," I cried.

"He can't live many minutes."

I turned and followed him to the ruinous cowshed which was my divisional headquarters. Wake, as I heard later, had swum the river opposite to Mitchinson's right, and reached the other shore safely, though the current was whipped with bullets. But he had scarcely landed before he was badly hit by shrapnel in the groin. Walking at first with support and then carried on a stretcher, he managed to struggle on to the divisional headquarters, where he gave my message and explained the situation. He would not let his wound be looked to till his job was done. Mitchinson told me afterwards that with a face grey from pain he drew for him a sketch of our position and told him exactly how near we were to our end. . . . After that he asked to be sent back to me, and they got him down to Loisy in a crowded ambulance, and then up to us in a returning empty. The M.O. who looked at his wound saw that the thing was hopeless, and did not expect him to live beyond Loisy. He was bleeding internally, and no surgeon on earth could have saved him.

When he reached us he was almost pulseless, but he recovered for a moment and asked for me.

I found him, with blue lips and a face drained of blood, lying on my camp bed. His voice was very small and far away.

"How goes it?" he asked.

"Please God, we'll pull through . . . thanks to you, old man."

"Good," he said, and his eyes shut.

He opened them once again.

"Funny thing life. A year ago I was preaching peace. . . . I'm still preaching it. . . . I'm not sorry."

I held his hand till two minutes later he died.

In the press of a fight one scarcely realizes death, even the death of a friend. It was up to me to make good my assurance to Wake, and presently I was off to Masterton. There in that shambles of La Bruyère, while the light faded, there was a desperate and most bloody struggle. It was the last lap of the contest. Twelve hours now, I kept telling myself, and the French will be here, and we'll have done our task. Alas! how many of us would go back to rest? . . . Hardly able to totter, our counter-attacking companies went in again. They had gone far beyond the limits of mortal endurance, but the human spirit can defy all natural laws. The balance trembled, hung, and then dropped the right way. The enemy impetus weakened, stopped, and the ebb began.

I wanted to complete the job. Our artillery put up a sharp barrage, and the little I had left comparatively fresh I sent in for a counter-stroke. Most of the men were untrained, but there was that in our ranks which dispensed with training, and we had caught the enemy at the moment of lowest vitality. We pushed him out of La Bruyère, we pushed him back to our old forward zone, we pushed him out of that zone to the position from which he had begun the day.

But there was no rest for the weary. We had lost at least a third of our strength, and we had to man the same long line. We consolidated it as best we could, started to replace the wiring that had been destroyed, found touch with the division on our right, and established outposts. Then, after a conference with my brigadiers, I went back to my headquarters, too tired to feel either satisfaction or anxiety. In eight hours the French would be here. The words made a kind of litany in my ears.

In the cowshed where Wake had lain, two figures awaited me. The talc-enclosed candle revealed Hamilton and Amos, dirty beyond words, smoke-blackened, blood-stained, and intricately bandaged. They stood stiffly to attention.

"Sirr, the prisoner," said Hamilton. "I have to report that the prisoner is deid."

I stared at them, for I had forgotten Ivery. He seemed a creature of a world that had passed away.

"Sirr, it was like this. Ever sin' this mornin' the prisoner seemed to wake up. Ye'll mind that he was in a kind of dwam all week. But he got some new notion in his heid, and when the battle began he exheebited signs of restless-ness. Whiles he wad lie doun in the trench, and whiles he was wantin' back to the dug-out. Accordin' to instructions I provided him wi' a rifle, but he didna seem to ken how to handle it. It was your orders, sirr, that he was to have means to defend hisself if the enemy cam on, so Amos gie'd him a trench knife. But verra soon he looked as if he was ettlin' to cut his throat, so I deprived him of it."

Hamilton stopped for breath. He spoke as if he were reciting a lesson, with no stops between his sentences.

"I jaloused, sirr, that he wadna last oot the day, and Amos here was of the same opinion. The end cam at twenty minutes past three—I ken the time, for I had just compared my watch with Amos. Ye'll mind that the Gairmans were beginnin' a big attack. We were in the front trench of what they ca' the battle-zone, and Amos and me was keepin' oor eyes on the enemy, who could be obsairved dribblin' ower the open. Just then the prisoner catches sight of the enemy and jumps up on the top. Amos tried to hold him, but he kickit him in the face. The next we kenned he was runnin' verra fast towards the enemy, holdin' his hands ower his heid and cryin' out loud in a foreign langwidge."

"It was German," said the scholarly Amos through his broken teeth.

"It was Gairman," continued Hamilton. "It seemed as if he was appealin' to the enemy to help him. But they paid no attention, and he cam under the fire of their machine guns. We watched him spin round like a teetotum and kenned that he was bye with it."

"You are sure he was killed?" I asked.

"Yes, sirr. When we counter-attacked we fund his body."

There is a grave close by the farm of Gavrelle, and a wooden cross at its head bears the name of the Graf von Schwabing and the date of his death. The Germans took Gavrelle a little later. I am glad to think that they read that inscription.

54 THE SUMMONS COMES FOR MR. STANDFAST

I slept for one and three-quarter hours that night, and when I awoke I seemed to emerge from deeps of slumber which had lasted for days. That happens sometimes after heavy fatigue and great mental strain. Even a short sleep sets up a barrier between past and present which has to be elaborately broken down before you can link on with what has happened before. As my wits groped at the job some drops of rain splashed on my face through the broken roof. That hurried me out-of-doors. It was just after dawn and the sky was piled with thick clouds, while a wet wind blew up from the south-west. The long-prayed-for break in the weather seemed to have come at last. A deluge of rain was what I wanted, something to soak the earth and turn the roads into watercourses and clog the enemy transport, something above all to blind the enemy's eyes. . . . For I remembered what a preposterous bluff it all had been, and what a piteous broken handful stood between the Germans and their goal. If they knew, if only they knew, they would brush us aside like flies.

As I shaved I looked back on the events of yesterday as on something that had happened long ago. I seemed to judge them impersonally, and I concluded that it had been a pretty good fight. A scratch force, half of it dog-tired and half of it untrained, had held up at least a couple of fresh divisions. . . . But we couldn't do it again, and there were still some hours before us of desperate peril. When had the Corps said that the French would arrive? . . . I was on the point of shouting for Hamilton to get Wake to ring up Corps Headquarters, when I remembered that Wake was dead. I had liked him and greatly admired him, but the recollection gave me scarcely a pang. We were all dying, and he had only gone on a stage ahead.

There was no morning *strafe*, such as had been our usual fortune in the past week. I went out-of-doors and found a noiseless world under the lowering sky. The rain had stopped falling, the wind of dawn had lessened, and I feared that the storm would be delayed. I wanted it at once to help us through the next hours of tension. Was it in six hours that the French were coming? No, it must be four. It couldn't be more than four, unless somebody had made an infernal muddle. I wondered why everything was so quiet. It would be breakfast time on both sides, but there seemed no stir of man's presence in that ugly strip half a mile off. Only far back in the German hinterland I seemed to hear the rumour of traffic.

An unslept and unshaven figure stood beside me which revealed itself as Archie Roylance.

"Been up all night," he said cheerfully, lighting a cigarette. "No, I haven't

467

had breakfast. The skipper thought we'd better get another anti-aircraft battery up this way, and I was superintendin' the job. He's afraid of the Hun gettin' over your lines and spying out the nakedness of the land. For, you know, we're uncommon naked, sir. Also," and Archie's face became grave, "the Hun's pourin' divisions down on this sector. As I judge, he's blowin' up for a thunderin' big drive on both sides of the river. Our lads yesterday said all the country back of Péronne was lousy with new troops. And he's gettin' his big guns forward, too. You haven't been troubled with them yet, but he has got the roads mended and the devil of a lot of new light railways, and any moment we'll have the five-point-nines sayin' Good-mornin' . . . Pray Heaven you get relieved in time, sir. I take it there's not much risk of another push this mornin'?"

"I don't think so. The Boche took a nasty knock yesterday, and he must fancy we're pretty strong after that counter-attack. I don't think he'll strike till he can work both sides of the river, and that'll take time to prepare. That's what his fresh divisions are for. . . . But remember, he can attack now, if he likes. If he knew how weak we were he's strong enough to send us all to glory in the next three hours. It's just that knowledge that you fellows have got to prevent his getting. If a single Hun plane crosses our lines and returns, we're wholly and utterly done. You've given us splendid help since the show began, Archie. For God's sake keep it up to the finish and put every machine you can spare in this sector."

"We're doin' our best," he said. "We got some more fightin' scouts down from the north, and we're keepin' our eyes skinned. But you know as well as I do, sir, that it's never an ab-so-lute certainty. If the Hun sent over a squadron we might beat 'em all down but one, and that one might do the trick. It's a matter of luck. The Hun's got the wind up all right in the air just now, and I don't blame the poor devil. But I'm inclined to think we haven't had the pick of his push here. Jennings says he's doin' good work in Flanders, and they reckon there's the deuce of a thrust comin' there pretty soon. I think we can manage the kind of footler he's been sendin' over here lately, but if Lensch or some lad like that were to choose to turn up I wouldn't say what might happen. The air's a big lottery," and Archie turned a dirty face skyward where two of our planes were moving very high towards the east.

The mention of Lensch brought Peter to my mind, and I asked if he had gone back.

"He won't go," said Archie, "and we haven't the heart to make him. He's very happy, and plays about with the Gladas single-seater. He's always speakin' about you, sir, and it'd break his heart if we shifted him."

I asked about his health, and was told that he didn't seem to have much pain.

"But he's a bit queer," and Archie shook a sage head. "One of the reasons why he won't budge is because he says God has some work for him to do. He's quite serious about it, and ever since he got the notion he has perked up amazin'. He's always askin' about Lensch, too—not vindictive-like, you understand, but quite friendly. Seems to take a sort of proprietary interest in him. I told him Lensch had had a far longer spell of first-class fightin' than anybody else and was bound by the law of averages to be downed soon, and he was quite sad about it."

I had no time to worry about Peter. Archie and I swallowed breakfast and I had a pow-wow with my brigadiers. By this time I had got through to Corps H.Q. and got news of the French. It was worse than I expected. General Péguy would arrive about ten o'clock, but his men couldn't take over till well after midday. The Corps gave me their whereabouts, and I found it on the map. They had a long way to cover yet, and then there would be the slow business of relieving. I looked at my watch. There were still six hours before us when the Boche might knock us to blazes, six hours of maddening anxiety. . . . Lefroy announced that all was quiet on the front, and that the new wiring at the Bois de la Bruyère had been completed. Patrols had reported that during the night a fresh German division seemed to have relieved one of those we had punished so stoutly yesterday. I asked him if he could stick it out against another attack. "No," he said without hesitation. "We're too few and too shaky on our pins to stand any more. I've only a man to every three yards." That impressed me, for Lefroy was usually the most devil-may-care optimist.

"Curse it, there's the sun," I heard Archie cry. It was true, for the clouds were rolling back and the centre of the heavens was a patch of blue. The storm was coming—I could smell it in the air—but probably it wouldn't break till the evening. Where, I wondered, would we be by that time?

It was now nine o'clock, and I was keeping tight hold on myself, for I saw that I was going to have hell for the next hours. I am a pretty stolid fellow in some ways, but I have always found patience and standing still the most difficult job to tackle, and my nerves were all tattered from the long strain of the retreat. I went up to the line and saw the battalion commanders. Everything was unwholesomely quiet there. Then I came back to my headquarters to study the reports that were coming in from the air patrols. They all said the same thing—abnormal activity in the German back areas. Things seemed shaping for a new 21st of March, and, if our luck were out, my poor little remnant would have to take the shock. I telephoned to the Corps and found them as nervous as myself. I gave them the details of my strength and heard an agonized whistle at the other end of the line. I was rather glad I had companions in the same purgatory.

I found I couldn't sit still. If there had been any work to do I would have buried myself in it, but there was none. Only this fearsome job of waiting. I hardly ever feel cold, but now my blood seemed to be getting thin, and I astonished my staff by putting on a British warm and buttoning up the collar. Round that derelict farm I ranged like a hungry wolf, cold at the feet, queasy in the stomach, and mortally edgy in the mind.

Then suddenly the cloud lifted from me, and the blood seemed to run naturally in my veins. I experienced the change of mood which a man feels sometimes when his whole being is fined down and clarified by long endurance. The fight of yesterday revealed itself as something rather splendid.

What risks we had run and how gallantly we had met them! My heart warmed as I thought of that old division of mine, those ragged veterans that were never beaten as long as breath was left them. And the Americans and the boys from the machine-gun school and all the oddments we had commandeered! And old Blenkiron raging like a good-tempered lion! It was against reason that such fortitude shouldn't win out. We had snarled round and bitten the Boche so badly that he wanted no more for a little. He would come again, but presently we should be relieved and the gallant bluecoats, fresh as paint and burning for revenge, would be there to worry him.

I had no new facts on which to base my optimism, only a changed point of view. And with it came a recollection of other things. Wake's death had left me numb before, but now the thought of it gave me a sharp pang. He was the first of our little confederacy to go. But what an ending he had made, and how happy he had been in that mad time when he had come down from his pedestal and become one of the crowd! He had found himself at the last, and who could grudge him such happiness? If the best were to be taken, he would be chosen first, for he was a big man, before whom I uncovered my head. The thought of him made me very humble. I had never had his troubles to face, but he had come clean through them, and reached a courage which was for ever beyond me. He was the Faithful among us pilgrims, who had finished his journey before the rest. Mary had foreseen it. "There is a price to be paid," she had said—"the best of us."

And at the thought of Mary a flight of warm and happy hopes seemed to settle on my mind. I was looking again beyond the war to that peace which she and I would some day inherit. I had a vision of a green English landscape, with its far-flung scents of wood and meadow and garden. . . . And that face of all my dreams, with the eyes so childlike and brave and honest, as if they, too, saw beyond the dark to a radiant country. A line of an old song, which had been a favourite of my father's, sang itself in my ears:

> "There's an eye that ever weeps and a fair face will be fain
> When I ride through Annan Water wi' my bonny bands again!"

We were standing by the crumbling rails of what had once been the farm sheepfold. I looked at Archie and he smiled back at me, for he saw that my face had changed. Then he turned his eyes to the billowing clouds.

I felt my arm clutched.

"Look there!" said a fierce voice, and his glasses were turned upwards.

I looked, and far up in the sky saw a thing like a wedge of wild geese flying towards us from the enemy's country. I made out the small dots which composed it, and my glasses told me they were planes. But only Archie's practised eye knew that they were enemy.

"Boche?" I asked.

"Boche," he said. "My God, we're for it now."

My heart had sunk like a stone, but I was fairly cool. I looked at my watch and saw that it was ten minutes to eleven.

"How many?"

"Five," said Archie. "Or there may be six—no, only five."

"Listen!" I said. "Get on to your headquarters. Tell them that it's all up with us if a single plane gets back. Let them get well over the line, the deeper in the better, and tell them to send up every machine they possess and down them all. Tell them it's life or death. Not one single plane goes back. Quick!"

Archie disappeared, and as he went our anti-aircraft guns broke out. The formation above opened and zigzagged, but they were too high to be in much danger. But they were not too high to see that which we must keep hidden or perish.

The roar of our batteries died down as the invaders passed westwards. As I watched their progress they seemed to be dropping lower. Then they rose again and a bank of cloud concealed them.

I had a horrid certainty that they must beat us, that some at any rate would get back. They had seen our thin lines and the roads behind us empty of supports. They would see, as they advanced, the blue columns of the French coming up from the south-west, and they would return and tell the enemy that a blow now would open the road to Amiens and the sea. He had plenty of strength for it, and presently he would have overwhelming strength. It only needed a spear-point to burst the jerry-built dam and let the flood through. . . . They would return in twenty minutes, and by noon we would be broken. Unless—unless the miracle of miracles happened, and they never returned.

Archie reported that his skipper would do his damnedest and that our machines were now going up. "We've a chance, sir," he said, "a good sportin' chance." It was a new Archie, with a hard voice, a lean face, and very old eyes.

Behind the jagged walls of the farm buildings was a knoll which had once formed part of the highroad. I went up there alone, for I didn't want anybody near me. I wanted a view-point, and I wanted quiet, for I had a grim time before me. From that knoll I had a big prospect of country. I looked east to our lines on which an occasional shell was falling, and where I could hear the chatter of machine guns. West there was peace, for the woods closed down on the landscape. Up to the north, I remember, there was a big glare as from a burning dump, and heavy guns seemed to be at work in the Ancre valley. Down in the south there was the dull murmur of a great battle. But just around me, in the gap, the deadliest place of all, there was an odd quiet. I could pick out clearly the different sounds. Somebody down at the farm had made a joke and there was a short burst of laughter. I envied the humorist his composure. There was a clatter and jingle from a battery changing position. On the road a tractor was jolting along—I could hear its driver shout and the screech of its unoiled axle.

My eyes were glued to my glasses, but they shook in my hands so that I could scarcely see. I bit my lip to steady myself, but they still wavered. From time to time I glanced at my wrist-watch. Eight minutes gone—ten—seventeen. If only the planes would come into sight! Even the certainty of failure would be better than this harrowing doubt. They should be back by now unless they had swung north across the salient, or unless the miracle of miracles—

Then came the distant yapping of an anti-aircraft gun, caught up the next second by others, while smoke patches studded the distant blue of the sky. The clouds were banking in mid-heaven, but to the west there was a big clear space now woolly with shrapnel bursts. I counted them mechanically—one—three—five—nine—with despair beginning to take the place of my anxiety. My hands were steady now, and through the glasses I saw the enemy.

Five attenuated shapes rode high above the bombardment, now sharp against the blue, now lost in a film of vapour. They were coming back, serenely, contemptuously, having seen all they wanted.

The quiet had gone now and the din was monstrous. Anti-aircraft guns, singly and in groups, were firing from every side. As I watched it seemed a futile waste of ammunition. The enemy didn't give a tinker's curse for it. . . . But surely there was one down. I could only count four now. No, there was the fifth coming out of a cloud. In ten minutes they would be all over the line. I fairly stamped in my vexation. Those guns were no more use than a sick headache. Oh, where in God's name were our own planes?

At that moment they came, streaking down into sight, four fighting scouts with the sun glinting on their wings and burnishing their metal cowls. I saw clearly the rings of red, white, and blue. Before their downward drive the enemy instantly spread out.

I was watching with bare eyes now, and I wanted companionship, for the time of waiting was over. Automatically I must have run down the knoll, for the next instant I knew I was staring at the heavens with Archie by my side. The combatants seemed to couple instinctively. Diving, wheeling, climbing, a pair would drop out of the mêlée or disappear behind a cloud. Even at that height I could hear the methodical rat-tat-tat of the machine guns. Then there was a sudden flare and wisp of smoke. A plane sank, turning and twisting, to earth.

"Hun!" said Archie, who had his glasses on it.

Almost immediately another followed. This time the pilot recovered himself while still a thousand feet from the ground, and started gliding for the enemy lines. Then he wavered, plunged sickeningly, and fell headlong into the wood behind La Bruyère.

Farther east, almost over the front trenches, a two-seater Albatross and a British pilot were having a desperate tussle. The bombardment had stopped, and from where we stood every movement could be followed. First one, then another, climbed uppermost, and dived back, swooped out and wheeled in again, so that the two planes seemed to clear each other only by inches. Then it looked as if they closed and interlocked. I expected to see both go crashing, when suddenly the wings of one seemed to shrivel up, and the machine dropped like a stone.

"Hun," said Archie. "That makes three. Oh, good lads! Good lads!"

Then I saw something which took away my breath. Sloping down in wide circles came a German machine, and, following, a little behind and a little above, a British. It was the first surrender in mid-air I had seen. In my amazement I watched the couple right down to the ground, till the enemy landed in a big meadow across the highroad and our own man in a field nearer the river.

When I looked back into the sky, it was bare. North, south, east, and west, there was not a sign of aircraft, British or German.

A violent trembling took me. Archie was sweeping the heavens with his glasses and muttering to himself. Where was the fifth man? He must have fought his way through, and it was too late.

But was it? From the toe of a great rolling cloud bank a flame shot earthwards, followed by a V-shaped trail of smoke. British or Boche? British or Boche? I didn't wait long for an answer. For, riding over the far end of the cloud, came two of our fighting scouts.

I tried to be cool, and snapped my glasses into their case, though the reaction made me want to shout. Archie turned to me with a nervous smile and a quivering mouth. "I think we have won on the post," he said.

He reached out a hand for mine, his eyes still on the sky, and I was grasping it when it was torn away. He was staring upwards with a white face. We were looking at a sixth enemy plane.

It had been behind the others and much lower, and was making straight at a great speed for the east. The glasses showed me a different type of machine—a big machine with short wings, which looked menacing as a hawk in a covey of grouse. It was under the cloud bank, and above, satisfied, easing down after their fight, and unwitting of this enemy, rode the two British craft.

A neighbouring anti-aircraft gun broke out into a sudden burst, and I thanked Heaven for its inspiration. Curious as to this new development, the two British turned, caught sight of the Boche and dived for him.

What happened in the next minutes I cannot tell. The three seemed to be mixed up in a dog-fight, so that I could not distinguish friend from foe. My hands no longer trembled; I was too desperate. The patter of machine guns came down to us, and then one of the three broke clear and began to climb. The others strained to follow, but in a second he had risen beyond their fire, for he had easily the pace of them. Was it the Hun?

Archie's dry lips were talking.

"It's Lensch," he said.

"How d'you know?" I gasped angrily.

"Can't mistake him. Look at the way he slipped out as he banked. That's his patent trick."

In that agonizing moment hope died in me. I was perfectly calm now, for the time for anxiety had gone. Farther and farther drifted the British pilots behind, while Lensch in the completeness of his triumph looped more than once as if to cry an insulting farewell. In less than three minutes he would be safe inside his own lines, and he carried the knowledge which for us was death.

Some one was bawling in my ear, and pointing upward. It was Archie and his face was wild. I looked and gasped—seized my glasses and looked again.

A second before Lensch had been alone; now there were two machines.

I heard Archie's voice. "My God, it's the Gladas—the little Gladas." His fingers were digging into my arm and his face was against my shoulder. And then his excitement sobered into an awe which choked his speech, as he stammered, "It's old—"

But I did not need him to tell me the name, for I had divined it when I first saw the new plane drop from the clouds. I had that queer sense that comes sometimes to a man that a friend is present when he cannot see him. Somewhere up in the void two heroes were fighting their last battle—and one of them had a crippled leg.

I had never any doubt about the result. Lensch was not aware of his opponent till he was almost upon him, and I wonder if by any freak of instinct he recognized his greatest antagonist. He never fired a shot, nor did Peter. . . . I saw the German twist and side-slip as if to baffle the fate descending upon him. I saw Peter veer over vertically and I knew that the end had come. He was there to make certain of victory and he took the only way. . . . The machines closed, there was a crash which I felt though I could not hear it, and next second both were hurtling down, over and over, to the earth.

They fell in the river just short of the enemy lines, but I did not see them, for my eyes were blinded and I was on my knees.

After that it was all a dream. I found myself being embraced by a French General of Division, and saw the first companies of the cheerful bluecoats for whom I had longed. With them came the rain, and it was under a weeping April sky that early in the night I marched what was left of my division away from the battlefield. The enemy guns were starting to speak behind us, but I did not heed them. I knew that now there were warders at the gate, and I believed that by the grace of God that gate was barred for ever.

They took Peter from the wreckage with scarcely a scar except his twisted leg. Death had smoothed out some of the age in him, and left his face much as I remembered it long ago in the Mashonaland hills. In his pocket was his old battered *Pilgrim's Progress*. It lies before me as I write, and beside it—for I was his only legatee—the little case which came to him weeks later, containing the highest honour that can be bestowed upon a soldier of Britain.

It was from the *Pilgrim's Progress* that I read next morning, when in the lee of an apple orchard Mary and Blenkiron and I stood in the soft spring rain beside his grave. And what I read was the tale of the end, not of Mr. Standfast whom he had singled out for his counterpart, but of Mr. Valiant-for-Truth whom he had not hoped to emulate. I set down the words as a salute and a farewell:

"Then said he, 'I am going to my Father's; and though with great difficulty I am got hither, yet now I do not repent me of all the trouble I have been at to arrive where I am. My sword I give to him that shall succeed me in my pilgrimage, and my courage and skill to him that can get it. My marks and scars I carry with me, to be a witness for me that I have fought His battles who now will be my rewarder.'

"So he passed over, and all the trumpets sounded for him on the other side."

THE FOURTH ADVENTURE

The Three Hostages

55 DR. GREENSLADE THEORIZES

That evening, I remember, as I came up through the Mill Meadow, I was feeling peculiarly happy and contented. It was still mid-March, one of those spring days when noon is like May, and only the cold pearly haze at sunset warns a man that he is not done with winter. The season was absurdly early, for the blackthorn was in flower and the hedge roots were full of primroses. The partridges were paired, the rooks were well on with their nests, and the meadows were full of shimmering grey flocks of fieldfares on their way north. I put up half a dozen snipe on the boggy edge of the stream, and in the bracken in Sturn Wood I thought I saw a woodcock, and hoped that the birds might nest with us this year, as they used to do long ago. It was jolly to see the world coming to life again, and to remember that this patch of England was my own, and all these wild things, so to speak, members of my little household.

As I say, I was in a very contented mood, for I had found something I had longed for all my days. I had bought Fosse Manor just after the War as a wedding present for Mary, and for two and a half years we had been settled there. My son, Peter John, was rising fifteen months, a thoughtful infant, as healthy as a young colt and as comic as a terrier puppy. Even Mary's anxious eye could scarcely detect in him any symptoms of decline. But the place wanted a lot of looking to, for it had run wild during the War, and the woods had to be thinned, gates and fences repaired, new drains laid, a ram put in to supplement the wells, a heap of thatching to be done, and the garden borders to be brought back to cultivation. I had got through the worst of it, and as I came out of the Home Wood on to the lower lawns and saw the old stone gables that the monks had built, I felt that I was anchored at last in the pleasantest kind of harbour.

There was a pile of letters on the table in the hall, but I let them be, for I was not in the mood for any communication with the outer world. As I was having a hot bath Mary kept giving me the news through her bedroom door. Peter John had been raising Cain over a new tooth; the new shorthorn cow was drying off; old George Whaddon had got his granddaughter back from service; there was a new brood of runner-ducks; there was a missel-thrush building in the box hedge by the lake. A chronicle of small beer, you will say, but I was by a long chalk more interested in it than in what might be happening in Parliament or Russia or the Hindu Kush. The fact is I was becoming such a mossback that I had almost stopped reading the papers. Many a day *The Times* would remain unopened, for Mary never looked at anything but the first page to see who was dead or married. Not that I didn't read a lot, for I used to spend my evenings digging into county history and learning all I could about the old fellows who had been my predecessors. I liked to think that I lived in a place that had been continuously inhabited for a thousand years. Cavalier and Roundhead had fought over the countryside, and I was becoming a considerable authority on their tiny battles. That was about the only interest I had left in soldiering.

As we went downstairs, I remember we stopped to look out of the long staircase window which showed a segment of lawn, a corner of the lake, and through a gap in the woods a vista of green downland. Mary squeezed my arm. "What a blessed country," she said. "Dick, did you ever dream of such peace? We're lucky, lucky people."

Then suddenly her face changed in that way she has and grew very grave. I felt a little shiver run along her arm.

"It's too good and beloved to last," she whispered. "Sometimes I am afraid."

"Nonsense," I laughed. "What's going to upset it? I don't believe in being afraid of happiness." I knew very well, of course, that Mary couldn't be afraid of anything.

She laughed too. "All the same I've got what the Greeks called *aidos*. You don't know what that means, you old savage. It means that you must walk humbly and delicately to propitiate the Fates. I wish I knew how."

She walked too delicately, for she missed the last step, and our descent ended in an undignified shuffle right into the arms of Dr. Greenslade.

Paddock—I had got Paddock back after the War and he was now my butler—was helping the doctor out of his ulster, and I saw by the satisfied look on the latter's face that he was through with his day's work and meant to stay to dinner. Here I had better introduce Tom Greenslade, for of all my recent acquaintances he was the one I had most taken to. He was a long lean fellow with a stoop in his back from bending over the handles of motor-bicycles, with reddish hair, and the greeny-blue eyes and freckled skin that often accompany that kind of hair. From his high cheek-bones and his colouring you would have set him down as a Scotsman, but, as a matter of fact, he came from Devonshire—Exmoor, I think, though he had been so much about the world that he had almost forgotten where he was raised. I have travelled a bit, but nothing to Greenslade. He had started as a doctor in a whaling ship. Then he had been in the South African War, and afterwards a temporary magistrate up Lydenburg way. He soon tired of that, and was for a long spell in Uganda and German East, where he became rather a swell on tropical diseases, and nearly perished through experimenting on himself with fancy inoculations. Then he was in South America, where he had a good practice in Valparaiso, and then in the Malay States, where he made a bit of money in the rubber boom. There was a gap of three years after that when he was wandering about Central Asia, partly with a fellow called Duckett exploring Northern Mongolia, and partly in Chinese Tibet hunting for new flowers, for he was mad about botany. He came home in the summer of 1914, meaning to do some laboratory research, but the War swept him up and he went to France as M.O. of a territorial battalion. He got wounded, of course, and after a spell in hospital went out to Mesopotamia, where he stayed till the Christmas of 1918, sweating hard at his job, but managing to tumble into a lot of varied adventures, for he was at Baku with Dunsterville and got as far as Tashkend, where the Bolsheviks shut him up for a fortnight in a bath-house. During the War he had every kind of sickness, for he missed no experience, but nothing seemed to damage permanently his whipcord physique. He told me that his heart and lungs and blood pressure were as good as a lad's of twenty-one, though by this time he was on the wrong side of forty.

But when the War was over he hankered for a quiet life, so he bought a practice in the deepest and greenest corner of England. He said his motive was the same as that which in the rackety Middle Ages made men retire into monasteries: he wanted quiet and leisure to consider his soul. Quiet he may have found, but uncommon little leisure, for I never heard of a country doctor that toiled at his job as he did. He would pay three visits a day to a panel patient, which shows the kind of fellow he was; and he would be out in the small hours at the birth of a gipsy child under a hedge. He was a first-class man in his profession, and kept abreast of it, but doctoring was only one of a thousand interests. I never met a chap with such an insatiable curiosity about everything in heaven and earth. He lived in two rooms in a farmhouse some four miles from us, and I daresay he had several thousand books about him. All day, and often half the night, he would scour the country in his little run-about car, and yet, when he would drop in to see me and have a drink after maybe twenty visits, he was as full of beans as if he had just got out of bed. Nothing came amiss to him in talk—birds, beasts, flowers, books, politics, religion—everything in the world except himself. He was the best sort of company, for behind all his quick keen and cleverness you felt that he was solid bar-gold. But for him I should have taken root in the soil and put out shoots, for I have a fine natural talent for vegetating. Mary strongly approved of him and Peter John adored him.

He was in tremendous spirits that evening, and for once in a way gave us reminiscences of his past. He told us about the people he badly wanted to see again: an Irish Spaniard up in the north of the Argentine who had for cattle-men a most murderous brand of native from the mountains, whom he used to keep in good humour by arranging fights every Sunday, he himself taking on the survivor with his fists and always knocking him out; a Scotch trader from Hankow who had turned Buddhist priest and intoned his prayers with a strong Glasgow accent; and most of all a Malay pirate, who, he said, was a sort of St. Francis with beasts, though a perfect Nero with his fellow-men. That took him to Central Asia, and he observed that if ever he left England again he would make for those parts, since they were the refuge of all the superior rascality of creation. He had a notion that something very odd might happen there in the long run. "Think of it!" he cried. "All the places with names like spells—Bokhara, Samarkand—run by seedy little gangs of communist Jews. It won't go on for ever. Some day a new Genghis Khan or a Timour will be thrown up out of the maelstrom. Europe is confused enough, but Asia is ancient Chaos."

After dinner we sat round the fire in the library, which I had modelled on Sir Walter Bullivant's room in his place on the Kennet, as I had promised myself seven years ago. I had meant it for my own room where I could write and read and smoke, but Mary would not allow it. She had a jolly panelled sitting-room of her own upstairs, which she rarely entered; but though I chased her away, she was like a hen in a garden and always came back, so that presently she had staked out a claim on the other side of my writing-table. I have the old hunter's notion of order, but it was useless to strive with Mary, so now my desk was littered with her letters and needlework, and Peter John's toys and picture-books were stacked in the cabinet where I kept my fly-books, and Peter John himself used to make a kraal every morning inside an upturned stool on the hearth-rug.

It was a cold night and very pleasant by the fireside, where some scented logs from an old pear-tree were burning. The doctor picked up a detective novel I had been reading, and glanced at the title page.

"I can read most things," he said, "but it beats me how you waste time over such stuff. These shockers are too easy, Dick. You could invent better ones for yourself."

"Not I. I call that a dashed ingenious yarn. I can't think how the fellow does it."

"Quite simple. The author writes the story inductively, and the reader follows it deductively. Do you see what I mean?"

"Not a bit," I replied.

"Look here. I want to write a shocker, so I begin by fixing on one or two facts which have no sort of obvious connection."

"For example?"

"Well, imagine anything you like. Let us take three things a long way apart—" He paused for a second to consider—"say, an old blind woman spinning in the Western Highlands, a barn in a Norwegian *saeter*, and a little curiosity shop in North London kept by a Jew with a dyed beard. Not much connection between the three? You invent a connection—simple enough if you have any imagination, and you weave all three into the yarn. The reader, who knows nothing about the three at the start, is puzzled and intrigued, and, if the story is well arranged, finally satisfied. He is pleased with the ingenuity of the solution, for he doesn't realize that the author fixed upon the solution first, and then invented a problem to suit it."

"I see," I said. "You've gone and taken the gilt off my favourite light reading. I won't be able any more to marvel at the writer's cleverness."

"I've another objection to the stuff—it's not ingenious enough, or rather it doesn't take account of the infernal complexity of life. It might have been all right twenty years ago, when most people argued and behaved fairly logically. But they don't nowadays. Have you ever realized, Dick, the amount of stark craziness that the War has left in the world?"

Mary, who was sitting sewing under a lamp, raised her head and laughed.

Greenslade's face had become serious. "I can speak about it frankly here, for you two are almost the only completely sane people I know. Well, as a pathologist, I'm fairly staggered. I hardly meet a soul who hasn't got some slight kink in his brain as a consequence of the last seven years. With most people it's rather a pleasant kink—they're less settled in their grooves, and they see the comic side of things quicker, and are readier for adventure. But with some it's *pukka* madness, and that means crime. Now, how are you going to write detective stories about that kind of world on the old lines? You can take nothing for granted, as you once could, and your argus-eyed, lightning-brained expert has nothing solid with which to build his foundations."

I observed that the poor old War seemed to be getting blamed for a good deal that I was taught in my childhood was due to original sin.

"Oh, I'm not questioning your Calvinism. Original sin is always there, but the meaning of civilization was that we had got it battened down under hatches, whereas now it's getting its head up. But it isn't only sin. It's a dislocation of the mechanism of human reasoning, a general loosening of screws. Oddly enough, in spite of parrot talk about shell-shock, the men who fought suffer less from it on the whole than other people. The classes that shirked the War are the worst—you see it in Ireland. Every doctor nowadays has got to be a bit of a mental pathologist. As I say, you can hardly take anything for granted, and if you want detective stories that are not childish fantasy, you'll have to invent a new kind. Better try your hand, Dick."

"Not I. I'm a lover of sober facts."

"But, hang it, man, the facts are no longer sober. I could tell you—" He paused and I was expecting a yarn, but he changed his mind.

"Take all this chatter about psycho-analysis. There's nothing very new in the doctrine, but people are beginning to work it out into details, and making considerable asses of themselves in the process. It's an awful thing when a scientific truth becomes the quarry of the half-baked. But, as I say, the fact of the subconscious self is as certain as the existence of lungs and arteries."

"I don't believe that Dick has any subconscious self," said Mary.

"Oh yes, he has. Only, people who have led his kind of life have their ordinary self so well managed and disciplined—their wits so much about them, as the phrase goes—that the subconscious rarely gets a show. But I bet if Dick took to thinking about his soul, which he never does, he would find some queer corners. Take my own case." He turned towards me so that I had a full view of his candid eyes and hungry cheek-bones which looked prodigious in the firelight. "I belong more or less to the same totem as you, but I've long been aware that I possessed a most curious kind of subconsciousness. I've a good memory and fair powers of observation, but they're nothing to those of my subconscious self. Take any daily incident. I see and hear, say, about a twentieth part of the details and remember about a hundredth part—that is, assuming that there is nothing special to stimulate my interest. But my subconscious self sees and hears practically everything, and remembers most of it. Only I can't use the memory, for I don't know that I've got it, and can't call it into being when I wish. But every now and then something happens to turn on the tap of the subconscious, and a thin trickle comes through. I find myself sometimes remembering names I was never aware of having heard, and little incidents and details I had never consciously noticed. Imagination, you will say; but it isn't, for everything that that inner memory provides is exactly true. I've tested it. If I could only find some way of tapping it at will, I should be an uncommonly efficient fellow. Incidentally I should become the first scientist of the age, for the trouble with investigation and experiment is that the ordinary brain does not observe sufficiently keenly or remember the data sufficiently accurately."

"That's interesting," I said. "I'm not at all certain I haven't noticed the same thing in myself. But what has that to do with the madness that you say is infecting the world?"

"Simply this. The barriers between the conscious and the subconscious have always been pretty stiff in the average man. But now with the general loosening of screws they are growing shaky and the two worlds are getting mixed. It is like two separate tanks of fluid where the containing wall has worn into holes, and one is percolating into the other. The result is confusion, and, if the fluids are of a certain character, explosions. That is why I say that you can't any longer take the clear psychology of most civilized human beings for granted. Something is welling up from primeval deeps to muddy it."

"I don't object to that," I said. "We've overdone civilization, and personally I'm all for a little barbarism. I want a simpler world."

"Then you won't get it," said Greenslade. He had become very serious now, and was looking towards Mary as he talked. "The civilized is far simpler than the primeval. All history has been an effort to make definitions, clear rules of thought, clear rules of conduct, solid sanctions, by which we can conduct our life. These are the work of the conscious self. The subconscious is an elementary and lawless thing. If it intrudes on life two results must follow. There will be a weakening of the power of reasoning, which, after all, is the thing that brings men nearest to the Almighty. And there will be a failure of nerve."

I got up to get a light, for I was beginning to feel depressed by the doctor's diagnosis of our times. I don't know whether he was altogether serious, for he presently started on fishing, which was one of his many hobbies. There was very fair dry-fly fishing to be had in our little river, but I had taken a deer-forest with Archie Roylance for the season, and Greenslade was coming up with me to try his hand at salmon. There had been no sea-trout the year before in the West Highlands, and we fell to discussing the cause. He was ready with a dozen theories, and we forgot about the psychology of mankind in investigating the uncanny psychology of fish. After that Mary sang to us, for I considered any evening a failure without that, and at half-past ten the doctor got into his old ulster and departed.

As I smoked my last pipe I found my thoughts going over Greenslade's talk. I had found a snug harbour, but how yeasty the waters seemed to be outside the bar and how erratic the tides! I wondered if it wasn't shirking to be so comfortable in a comfortless world. Then I reflected that I was owed a little peace, for I had had a roughish life. But Mary's words kept coming back to me about "walking delicately". I considered that my present conduct filled that bill, for I was mighty thankful for my mercies and in no way inclined to tempt Providence by complacency.

Going up to bed, I noticed my neglected letters on the hall table. I turned them over and saw that they were mostly bills and receipts or tradesmen's circulars. But there was one addressed in a handwriting that I knew, and as I looked at it I experienced a sudden sinking of the heart. It was from Lord Artinswell—Sir Walter Bullivant, as was—who had now retired from the Foreign Office, and was living at his place on the Kennet. He and I occasionally corresponded about farming and fishing, but I had a premonition that this was something different. I waited for a second or two before I opened it.

"MY DEAR DICK,

"This note is in the nature of a warning. In the next day or two you will be asked, nay pressed, to undertake a troublesome piece of business. I am not responsible for the request, but I know of it. If you consent, it will mean the end for a time of your happy vegetable life. I don't want to influence you one way or another; I only give you notice of what is coming in order that you may adjust your mind and not be taken by surprise. My love to Mary and the son.

"Yours ever,

"A."

That was all. I had lost my trepidation and felt very angry. Why couldn't the fools let me alone? As I went upstairs I vowed that not all the cajolery in the world would make me budge an inch from the path I had set myself. I had done enough for the public service and other people's interests, and it was jolly well time that I should be allowed to attend to my own.

56 I HEAR OF THE THREE HOSTAGES

There is an odour about a country house which I love better than any scent in the world. Mary used to say it was a mixture of lamp and dog and wood-smoke, but at Fosse, where there was electric light and no dogs indoors, I fancy it was wood-smoke, tobacco, the old walls, and wafts of the country coming in at the windows. I liked it best in the morning, when there was a touch in it of breakfast cooking, and I used to stand at the top of the staircase and sniff it as I went to my bath. But on the morning I write of I could take no pleasure in it; indeed, it seemed to tantalize me with a vision of country peace which had somehow got broken. I couldn't get that confounded letter out of my head. When I read it I had torn it up in disgust, but I found myself going down in my dressing-gown, to the surprise of a housemaid, piecing together the fragments from the waste-paper basket, and reading it again. This time I flung the bits into the new-kindled fire.

I was perfectly resolved that I would have nothing to do with Bullivant or any of his designs, but all the same I could not recapture the serenity which yesterday had clothed me like a garment. I was down to breakfast before Mary, and had finished before she appeared. Then I lit my pipe and started on my usual tour of my domain, but nothing seemed quite the same. It was a soft, fresh morning with no frost, and the scillas along the edge of the lake were like bits of summer sky. The moor-hens were building, and the first daffodils were out in the rough grass below the clump of Scotch firs, and old George Whaddon was nailing up rabbit wire and whistling through his two remaining teeth, and generally the world was as clear and jolly as spring could make it. But I didn't feel any more that it was really mine, only that I was looking on at a pretty picture. Something had happened to jar the harmony between it and my mind, and I cursed Bullivant and his intrusions.

I returned by the front of the house, and there at the door, to my surprise, stood a big touring Rolls-Royce. Paddock met me in the hall and handed me a card, on which I read the name of Mr. Julius Victor.

I knew it, of course, for the name of one of the richest men in the world—the American banker who had done a lot of Britain's financial business in the War, and was in Europe now at some international conference. I remembered that Blenkiron, who didn't like his race, had once described him to me as "the whitest Jew since the Apostle Paul".

In the library I found a tall man standing by the window looking out at our view. He turned as I entered, and I saw a thin face with a neatly trimmed grey beard, and the most worried eyes I have ever seen in a human countenance. Everything about him was spruce and dapper—his beautifully cut grey suit, his black tie and pink pearl pin, his blue-and-white linen, his exquisitely polished shoes. But the eyes were so wild and anxious that he looked dishevelled.

"General," he said, and took a step towards me.

We shook hands and I made him sit down.

"I have dropped the 'General', if you don't mind," I said. "What I want to know is, have you had breakfast?"

He shook his head. "I had a cup of coffee on the road. I do not eat in the morning."

"Where have you come from, sir?" I asked.

"From London."

Well, London is seventy-six miles from us, so he must have started early. I looked curiously at him, and he got out of his chair and began to stride about.

"Sir Richard," he said, in a low, pleasant voice which I could imagine convincing any man he tried it on, "you are a soldier and a man of the world and will pardon my unconventionality. My business is too urgent to waste time on apologies. I have heard of you from common friends as a man of exceptional resource and courage. I have been told in confidence something of your record. I have come to implore your help in a desperate emergency."

I passed him a box of cigars, and he took one and lit it carefully. I could see his long slim fingers trembling as he held the match.

"You may have heard of me," he went on. "I am a very rich man, and my wealth has given me power, so that Governments honour me with their confidence. I am concerned in various important affairs, and it would be false modesty to deny that my word is weightier than that of many Prime Ministers. I am labouring, Sir Richard, to secure peace in the world, and consequently I have enemies, all those who would perpetuate anarchy and war. My life has been more than once attempted, but that is nothing. I am well guarded. I am not, I think, more of a coward than other men, and I am prepared to take my chance. But now I have been attacked by a subtler weapon, and I confess I have no defence. I had a son, who died ten years ago at college. My only other child is my daughter, Adela, a girl of nineteen. She came to Europe just before Christmas, for she was to be married in Paris in April. A fortnight ago she was hunting with friends in Northamptonshire—the place is called Rushford Court. On the morning of the 8th of March she went for a walk to Rushford village to send a telegram, and was last seen passing through the lodge gates at twenty minutes past eleven. She has not been seen since."

"Good God!" I exclaimed, and rose from my chair. Mr. Victor was looking out of the window, so I walked to the other end of the room and fiddled with the books on a shelf. There was silence for a second or two, till I broke it.

"Do you suppose it is loss of memory?" I asked.

"No," he said. "It is not loss of memory. I know—we have proof—that she has been kidnapped by those whom I call my enemies. She is being held as a hostage."

"You know she is alive?"

He nodded, for his voice was choking again. "There is evidence which points to a very deep and devilish plot. It may be revenge, but I think it more likely to be policy. Her captors hold her as security for their own fate."

"Has Scotland Yard done nothing?"

"Everything that man could do, but the darkness only grows thicker."

"Surely it has not been in the papers. I don't read them carefully, but I could scarcely miss a thing like that."

"It has been kept out of the papers—for a reason which you will be told."

"Mr. Victor," I said, "I'm most deeply sorry for you. Like you, I've just the one child, and if anything of that kind happened to him I should go mad. But I shouldn't take too gloomy a view. Miss Adela will turn up all right, and none the worse, though you may have to pay through the nose for it. I expect it's ordinary blackmail and ransom."

"No," he said very quietly. "It is not blackmail, and if it were, I would not pay the ransom demanded. Believe me, Sir Richard, it is a very desperate affair. More, far more, is involved than the fate of one young girl. I am not going to touch on that side, for the full story will be told you later by one better equipped to tell it. But the hostage is my daughter, my only child. I have come to beg your assistance in the search for her."

"But I'm no good at looking for things," I stammered. "I'm most awfully sorry for you, but I don't see how I can help. If Scotland Yard is at a loss, it's not likely that an utter novice like me would succeed."

"But you have a different kind of imagination and a rarer kind of courage. I know what you have done before, Sir Richard. I tell you you are my last hope."

I sat down heavily and groaned. "I can't begin to explain to you the bottomless futility of your idea. It is quite true that in the War I had some queer jobs and was lucky enough to bring some of them off. But, don't you see, I was a soldier then, under orders, and it didn't greatly signify whether I lost my life from a crump in the trenches or from a private bullet on the backstairs. I was in the mood for any risk, and my wits were strung up and unnaturally keen. But that's all done with. I'm in a different mood now and my mind is weedy and grass-grown. I've settled so deep into the country that I'm just an ordinary hay-seed farmer. If I took a hand—which I certainly won't—I'd only spoil the game."

Mr. Victor stood looking at me intently. I thought for a moment he was going to offer me money, and rather hoped he would, for that would have stiffened me like a ramrod, though it would have spoiled the good notion I had of him. The thought may have crossed his mind, but he was clever enough to reject it.

"I don't agree with a word you say about yourself, and I'm accustomed to size up men. I appeal to you as a Christian gentleman to help me to recover my child. I am not going to press that appeal, for I have already taken up enough of your time. My London address is on my card. Good-bye, Sir Richard, and believe me, I am very grateful to you for receiving me so kindly."

In five minutes he and his Rolls-Royce had gone, and I was left in a miserable mood of shamefaced exasperation. I realized how Mr. Julius Victor had made his fame. He knew how to handle men, for if he had gone on pleading he would only have riled me, whereas he had somehow managed to leave it all to my honour, and thoroughly unsettle my mind.

I went for a short walk, cursing the world at large, sometimes feeling horribly sorry for that unfortunate father, sometimes getting angry because he had tried to mix me up in his affairs. Of course I would not touch the thing; I couldn't; it was manifestly impossible; I had neither the capacity nor the inclination. I was not a professional rescuer of distressed ladies whom I did not know from Eve.

A man, I told myself, must confine his duties to his own circle of friends, except when his country has need of him. I was over forty, and had a wife and a young son to think of; besides, I had chosen a retired life, and had the right to have my choice respected. But I can't pretend that I was comfortable. A hideous muddy wave from the outer world had come to disturb my little sheltered pool. I found Mary and Peter John feeding the swans, and couldn't bear to stop and play with them. The gardeners were digging in sulphates about the fig trees on the south wall, and wanted directions about the young chestnuts in the nursery; the keeper was lying in wait for me in the stable-yard for instructions about a new batch of pheasants' eggs, and the groom wanted me to look at the hocks of Mary's cob. But I simply couldn't talk to any of them. These were the things I loved, but for a moment the gilt was off them, and I would let them wait till I felt better. In a very bad temper I returned to the library.

I hadn't been there two minutes when I heard the sound of a car on the gravel. "Let 'em all come," I groaned, and I wasn't surprised when Paddock entered, followed by the spare figure and smooth keen face of Macgillivray.

I don't think I offered to shake hands. We were pretty good friends, but at that moment there was no one in the world I wanted less to see.

"Well, you old nuisance," I cried, "you're the second visitor from town I've had this morning. There'll be a shortage of petrol soon."

"Have you had a letter from Lord Artinswell?" he asked.

"I have, worse luck," I said.

"Then you know what I've come about. But that can keep till after luncheon. Hurry it up, Dick, like a good fellow, for I'm as hungry as a famished kestrel."

He looked rather like one, with his sharp nose and lean head. It was impossible to be cross for long with Macgillivray, so we went out to look for Mary. "I may as well tell you," I told him, "that you've come on a fool's errand. I'm not going to be jockeyed by you or any one into making an ass of myself. Anyhow, don't mention the thing to Mary. I don't want her to be worried by your nonsense."

So at luncheon we talked about Fosse and the Cotswolds, and about the deer-forest I had taken— Machray they called it—and about Sir Archibald Roylance, my co-tenant, who had just had another try at breaking his neck in a steeplechase. Macgillivray was by way of being a great stalker and could tell me a lot about Machray. The crab of the place was its neighbours, it seemed; for Haripol on the south was too steep for the lessee, a middle-aged manufacturer, to do justice to it, and the huge forest of Glenaicill on the east was too big for any single tenant to shoot, and the Machray end of it was nearly thirty miles by road from the lodge. The result was, said Macgillivray, that Machray was surrounded by unauthorized sanctuaries, which made the deer easy to shift. He said the best time was early in the season when the stags were on the upper ground, for it seemed that Machray had uncommonly fine high pastures. . . . Mary was in good spirits, for somebody had been complimentary about Peter John, and she was satisfied for the moment that he wasn't going to be cut off by an early consumption. She was full of housekeeping questions about Machray, and revealed such spacious plans that Macgillivray said that he thought he would pay us a visit, for it looked as if he wouldn't be poisoned, as he usually was in Scotch shooting-lodges. It was a talk I should have enjoyed if there had not been that uneasy morning behind me and that interview I had still to get over.

There was a shower after luncheon, so he and I settled ourselves in the library. "I must leave at 3.30," he said, "so I have got just a little more than an hour to tell you my business in."

"Is is worth while starting?" I asked. "I want to make it quite plain that under no circumstances am I open to any offer to take on any business of any kind. I'm having a rest and a holiday. I stay here for the summer and then I go to Machray."

"There's nothing to prevent your going to Machray in August," he said, opening his eyes. "The work I am going to suggest to you must be finished long before then."

I suppose that surprised me, for I did not stop him as I had meant to. I let him go on, and before I knew I found myself getting interested. I have a boy's weakness for a yarn, and Macgillivray knew this and played on it.

He began by saying very much what Dr. Greenslade had said the night before. A large part of the world had gone mad, and that involved the growth of inexplicable and unpredictable crime. All the old sanctities had become weakened, and men had grown too well accustomed to death and pain. This meant that the criminal had far greater resources at his command, and, if he were an able man, could mobilize a vast amount of utter recklessness and depraved ingenuity. The moral imbecile, he said, had been more or less a sport before the War; now he was a terribly common product, and throve in batches and battalions. Cruel, humourless, hard, utterly wanting in sense of proportion, but often full of a perverted poetry and drunk with rhetoric—a hideous untamable breed had been engendered. You found it among the young Bolshevik Jews, among the young entry of the wilder communist sects, and very notably among the sullen murderous hobbledehoys in Ireland.

"Poor devils," Macgillivray repeated. "It is for their Maker to judge them, but we who are trying to patch up civilization have to see that they are cleared out of the world. Don't imagine that they are devotees of any movement, good or bad. They are what I have called them, moral imbeciles, who can be swept into any movement by those who understand them. They are the neophytes and hierophants of crime, and it is as criminals that I have to do with them. Well, all this desperate degenerate stuff is being used by a few clever men who are not degenerates or anything of the sort, but only evil. There has never been such a chance for a rogue since the world began."

Then he told me certain facts, which must remain unpublished, at any rate during our lifetimes. The main point was that there were sinister brains at work to organize for their own purposes the perilous stuff lying about. All the contemporary anarchisms, he said, were interconnected, and out of the misery of decent folks and the agony of the wretched tools certain smug *entrepreneurs* were profiting. He and his men, and indeed the whole police force of civilization— he mentioned especially the Americans—had been on the trail of one of the worst of these combines, and by a series of fortunate chances had got their hand on it. Now at any moment they could stretch out that hand and gather it in.

But there was one difficulty. I learned from him that this particular combine was not aware of the danger in which it stood, but that it realized that it must stand in some danger, so it had taken precautions. Since Christmas it had acquired hostages.

Here I interrupted, for I felt rather incredulous about the whole business.

"I think since the War we're all too ready to jump at grandiose explanations of simple things. I'll want a good deal of convincing before I believe in your international clearing-house for crime."

"I guarantee the convincing," he said gravely. "You shall see all our evidence, and, unless you have changed since I first knew you, your conclusion won't differ from mine. But let us come to the hostages."

"One I know about," I put in. "I had Mr. Julius Victor here after breakfast."
Macgillivray exclaimed. "Poor soul! What did you say to him?"

"Deepest sympathy, but nothing doing."

"And he took that answer?"

"I won't say he took it. But he went away. What about the others?"

"There are two more. One is a young man, the heir to a considerable estate, who was last seen by his friends in Oxford on the 17th day of February, just before dinner. He was an undergraduate of Christ Church, and was living out of college in rooms in the High. He had tea at the Gridiron and went to his rooms to dress, for he was dining that night with the Halcyon Club. A servant passed him on the stairs of his lodgings, going up to his bedroom. He apparently did not come down, and since that day has not been seen. You may have heard his name—Lord Mercot."

I started. I had indeed heard the name, and knew the boy a little, having met him occasionally at our local steeplechases. He was the grandson and heir of the old Duke of Alcester, the most respected of the older statesmen of England.

"They have picked their bag carefully," I said. "What is the third case?"

"The cruellest of all. You know Sir Arthur Warcliff. He is a widower—lost his wife just before the War, and he has an only child, a little boy about ten years old. The child—David is his name —was the apple of his eye, and was at a preparatory school near Rye. The father took a house in the neighbourhood to be near him, and the boy used to be allowed to come home for luncheon every Sunday. One Sunday he came to luncheon as usual, and started back in the pony-trap. The boy was very keen about birds, and used to leave the trap and walk the last half-mile by a short cut across the marshes. Well, he left the groom at the usual gate, and, like Miss Victor and Lord Mercot, walked into black mystery."

This story really did horrify me. I remembered Sir Arthur Warcliff—the kind, worn face of the great soldier and administrator, and I could imagine his grief and anxiety. I knew what I should have felt if it had been Peter John. A much-travelled young woman and an athletic young man were defenceful creatures compared to a poor little round-headed boy of ten. But I still felt the whole affair too fantastic for real tragedy.

"But what right have you to connect the three cases?" I asked. "Three people disappear within a few weeks of each other in widely separated parts of England. Miss Victor may have been kidnapped for ransom, Lord Mercot may have lost his memory, and David Warcliff may have been stolen by tramps. Why should they be all part of one scheme? Why, for that matter, should any one of them have been the work of your criminal combine? Have you any evidence for the hostage theory?"

"Yes." Macgillivray took a moment or two to answer. "There is first the general probability. If a band of rascals wanted three hostages they could hardly find three better—the daughter of the richest man in the world, the heir of our greatest dukedom, the only child of a national hero. There is also direct evidence." Again he hesitated.

"Do you mean to say that Scotland Yard has not a single clue to any one of these cases?"

"We have followed up a hundred clues, but they have all ended in dead walls. Every detail, I assure you, has been gone through with a fine comb. No, my dear Dick, the trouble is not that we're specially stupid on this side, but that there is some superlative cunning on the other. That is why I want *you*. You have a kind of knack of stumbling on truths which no amount of ordinary reasoning can get at. I have fifty men working day and night, and we have mercifully kept all the cases out of the papers, so that we are not hampered by the amateur. But so far it is a blank. Are you going to help?"

"No, I'm not. But supposing I were, I don't see that you've a scrap of proof that the three cases are connected, or that any one of them is due to the criminal gang that you say you've got your hand on. You've only given me presumptions, and precious thin at that. Where's your direct evidence?"

Macgillivray looked a little embarrassed. "I've started you at the wrong end," he said. "I should have made you understand how big and desperate the thing is that we're out against, and then you'd have been in a more receptive mood for the rest of the story. You know as well as I do that cold blood is not always the most useful accompaniment in assessing evidence. I said I had direct evidence of connection, and so I have, and the proof to my mind is certain."

"Well, let's see it."

"It's a poem. On Wednesday of last week, two days after David Warcliff disappeared, Mr. Julius Victor, the Duke of Alcester, and Sir Arthur Warcliff received copies of it by the first post. They were typed on bits of flimsy paper, the envelopes had the addresses typed, and they had been posted in the West Central district of London the afternoon before."

He handed me a copy, and this was what I read:

> "Seek where under midnight's sun
> Laggard crops are hardly won;—
> Where the sower casts his seed in
> Furrows of the fields of Eden;—
> Where beside the sacred tree
> Spins the seer who cannot see."

I burst out laughing, for I could not help it—the whole thing was too preposterous. These six lines of indifferent doggerel seemed to me to put the coping-stone of nonsense on the business. But I checked myself when I saw Macgillivray's face. There was a slight flush of annoyance on his cheek, but for the rest it was grave, composed, and in deadly earnest. Now Macgillivray was not a fool, and I was bound to respect his beliefs. So I pulled myself together and tried to take things seriously.

"That's proof that the three cases are linked together," I said. "So much I grant you. But where's the proof that they are the work of the great criminal combine that you say you have got your hand on?"

Macgillivray rose and walked restlessly about the room. "The evidence is mainly presumptive, but to my mind it is certain presumption. You know as well as I do, Dick, that a case may be final and yet very difficult to set out as a series of facts. My view on the matter is made up of a large number of tiny indications and cross-bearings, and I am prepared to bet that if you put your mind honestly to the business you will take the same view. But I'll give you this much by way of direct proof—in hunting the big show we had several communications of the same nature as this doggerel, and utterly unlike anything else I ever struck in criminology. There's one of the miscreants who amuses himself with sending useless clues to his adversaries. It shows how secure the gang thinks itself."

"Well, you've got that gang anyhow. I don't quite see why the hostages should trouble you. You'll gather them in when you gather in the malefactors."

"I wonder. Remember we are dealing with moral imbeciles. When they find themselves cornered they won't play for safety. They'll use their hostages, and when we refuse to bargain they'll take their last revenge on them."

I suppose I stared unbelievingly, for he went on. "Yes. They'll murder them in cold blood—three innocent people—and then swing themselves with a lighter mind. I know the type. They've done it before." He mentioned one or two recent instances.

"Good God!" I cried. "It's a horrible thought! The only thing for you is to go canny, and not strike till you have got the victims out of their clutches."

"We can't," he said solemnly. "That is precisely the tragedy of the business. We must strike early in June. I won't trouble you with the reasons, but, believe me, they are final. There is just a chance of a settlement in Ireland, and there are certain events of the first importance impending in Italy and America, and all depend upon the activities of the gang being at an end by midsummer. Do you grasp that? By midsummer we must stretch out our hand. By midsummer, unless they are released, the three hostages will be doomed. It is a ghastly dilemma, but in the public interest there is only one way out. I ought to say that Victor and the Duke and Warcliff are aware of this fact, and accept the situation. They are big men, and will do their duty even if it breaks their hearts."

There was silence for a minute or two, for I did not know what to say. The whole story seemed to me incredible, and yet I could not doubt a syllable of it when I looked at Macgillivray's earnest face. I felt the horror of the business none the less because it seemed also partly unreal; it had the fantastic grimness of a nightmare. But most of all I realized that I was utterly incompetent to help, and as I understood that I could honestly base my refusal on incapacity and not on disinclination I began to feel more comfortable.

"Well," said Macgillivray, after a pause, "are you going to help us?"

"There's nothing doing with that Sunday-paper anagram you showed me.

That's the sort of riddle that's not meant to be guessed. I suppose you are going to try to work up from the information you have about the combine towards a clue to the hostages."

He nodded.

"Now look here," I said; "you've got fifty of the quickest brains in Britain working at the job. They've found out enough to put a lasso round the enemy which you can draw tight whenever you like. They're trained to the work and I'm not. What on earth would be the use of an amateur like me butting in? I wouldn't be half as good as any one of the fifty. I'm not an expert, I'm not quick-witted, I'm a slow, patient fellow, and this job, as you admit, is one that has to be done against time. If you think it over, you'll see that it's sheer nonsense, my dear chap."

"You've succeeded before with worse material."

"That was pure luck, and it was in the War when, as I tell you, my mind was morbidly active. Besides, anything I did then I did in the field, and what you want me to do now is office work. You know I'm no good at office work—Blenkiron always said so, and Bullivant never used me on it. It isn't because I don't want to help, but because I can't."

"I believe you can. And the thing is so grave that I daren't leave any chance unexplored. Won't you come?"

"No. Because I could do nothing."

"Because you haven't a mind for it."

"Because I haven't the right kind of mind for it."

He looked at his watch and got up, smiling rather ruefully.

"I've had my say, and now you know what I want of you. I'm not going to take your answer as final. Think over what I've said, and let me hear from you within the next day or two."

But I had lost all my doubts, for it was very clear to me that on every ground I was doing the right thing.

"Don't delude yourself with thinking that I'll change my mind," I said, as I saw him into his car. "Honestly, old fellow, if I could be an atom of use I'd join you, but for your own sake you've got to count me out this time."

Then I went for a walk, feeling pretty cheerful. I settled the question of the pheasants' eggs with the keeper, and went down to the stream to see if there was any hatch of fly. It had cleared up to a fine evening, and I thanked my stars that I was out of a troublesome business with an easy conscience, and could enjoy my peaceful life again. I say "with an easy conscience", for though there were little dregs of disquiet still lurking about the bottom of my mind, I had only to review the facts squarely to approve my decision. I put the whole thing out of my thoughts and came back with a fine appetite for tea.

There was a stranger in the drawing-room with Mary, a slim, oldish man, very straight and erect, with one of those faces on which life has written so much that to look at them is like reading a good book. At first I didn't recognize him when he rose to greet me, but the smile that wrinkled the corners of his eyes and the slow deep voice brought back the two occasions in the past when I had run across Sir Arthur Warcliff. . . . My heart sank as I shook hands, the more as I saw how solemn was Mary's face. She had been hearing the story which I hoped she would never hear.

I thought it best to be very frank with him. "I can guess your errand, Sir Arthur," I said, "and I'm extremely sorry that you should have come this long journey to no purpose." Then I told him of the visits of Mr. Julius Victor and Macgillivray, and what they had said, and what had been my answer. I think I made it as clear as day that I could do nothing, and he seemed to assent. Mary, I remember, never lifted her eyes.

Sir Arthur had also looked at the ground while I was speaking, and now he turned his wise old face to me, and I saw what ravages his new anxiety had made in it. He could not have been much over sixty and he looked a hundred.

"I do not dispute your decision, Sir Richard," he said. "I know that you would have helped me if it had been possible. But I confess I am sorely disappointed, for you were my last hope. You see—you see—I had nothing left in the world but Davie. If he had died I think I could have borne it, but to know nothing about him and to imagine terrible things is almost too much for my fortitude."

I have never been through a more painful experience. To hear a voice falter that had been used to command, to see tears in the steadfastest eyes that ever looked on the world, made me want to howl like a dog. I would have given a thousand pounds to be able to bolt into the library and lock the door.

Mary appeared to me to be behaving very oddly. She seemed to have the deliberate purpose of probing the wound, for she encouraged Sir Arthur to speak of his boy. He showed us a miniature he carried with him—an extraordinarily handsome child with wide grey eyes and his head most nobly set upon his shoulders. A grave little boy, with the look of utter trust which belongs to children who have never in their lives been unfairly treated. Mary said something about the gentleness of the face.

"Yes, Davie was very gentle," his father said. "I think he was the gentlest thing I have ever known. That little boy was the very flower of courtesy. But he was curiously stoical, too. When he was distressed, he only shut his lips tight, and never cried. I used often to feel rebuked by him."

And then he told us about Davie's performances at school, where he was not distinguished, except as showing a certain talent for cricket. "I am very much afraid of precocity," Sir Arthur said, with the ghost of a smile. "But he was always educating himself in the right way, learning to observe and think." It seemed that the boy was a desperately keen naturalist, and would be out at all hours watching wild things. He was a great fisherman too, and had killed a lot of trout with the fly on hill burns in Galloway. And as the father spoke I suddenly began to realize the little chap, and to think that he was just the kind of boy I wanted Peter John to be. I liked the stories of his love of nature and trout streams. It came on me like a thunderclap that if I were in his father's place I should certainly go mad, and I was amazed at the old man's courage.

"I think he had a kind of genius for animals," Sir Arthur said. "He knew the habits of birds by instinct, and used to talk of them as other people talk of their friends. He and I were great cronies, and he would tell me long stories in his little quiet voice of birds and beasts he had seen on his walks. He had odd names for them too. . . ."

The thing was almost too pitiful to endure. I felt as if I had known the child all my life, I could see him playing, I could hear his voice, and as for Mary she was unashamedly weeping.

Sir Arthur's eyes were dry now, and there was no catch in his voice as he spoke. But suddenly a sharper flash of realization came on him and his words became a strained cry: "Where is he now? What are they doing to him? O God! My beloved little man—my gentle little Davie!"

That fairly finished me. Mary's arm was round the old man's neck, and I saw that he was trying to pull himself together, but I didn't see anything clearly. I only know that I was marching about the room, scarcely noticing that our guest was leaving. I remember shaking hands with him, and hearing him say that it had done him good to talk to us. It was Mary who escorted him to the car, and when she returned it was to find me blaspheming like a Turk at the window. I had flung the thing open, for I felt suffocated, though the evening was cool. The mixture of anger and disgust and pity in my heart nearly choked me.

"Why the devil can't I be left alone?" I cried. "I don't ask for much—only a little peace. Why in Heaven's name should I be dragged into other people's business? Why on earth—"

Mary was standing at my elbow, her face rather white and tear-stained.

"Of course you are going to help," she said.

Her words made clear to me the decision which I must have taken a quarter of an hour before, and all the passion went out of me like wind out of a pricked bladder.

"Of course," I answered. "By the way, I had better telegraph to Macgillivray. And Warcliff too. What's his address?"

"You needn't bother about Sir Arthur," said Mary. "Before you came in—when he told me the story—I said he could count on you. Oh, Dick, think if it had been Peter John!"

57 RESEARCHES IN THE SUBCONSCIOUS

I went to bed in the perfect certainty that I wouldn't sleep. That happened to me about once a year, when my mind was excited or angry, and I knew no way of dodging it. There was a fine moon, and the windows were sheets of opal cut by the dark jade limbs of trees; light winds were stirring the creepers; owls hooted like sentries exchanging passwords, and sometimes a rook would talk in its dreams; the little odd squeaks and rumbles of wild life came faintly from the woods; while I lay staring at the ceiling with my thoughts running round about in a futile circus. Mary's even breathing tantalized me, for I never knew any one with her perfect gift for slumber. I used to say that if her pedigree could be properly traced it would be found that she descended direct from one of the Seven Sleepers of Ephesus who married one of the Foolish Virgins.

What kept me wakeful was principally the thought of that poor little boy, David Warcliff. I was sorry for Miss Victor and Lord Mercot, and desperately sorry for the parents of all three, but what I could not stand was the notion of the innocent little chap, who loved birds and fishing and the open air, hidden away in some stuffy den by the worst kind of blackguards. The thing preyed on me till I got to think it had happened to us and that Peter John was missing. I rose and prowled about the windows, looking out at the quiet night, and wondering how the same world could contain so much trouble and so much peace.

I laved my face with cold water and lay down again. It was no good letting my thoughts race, so I tried to fix them on one point in the hope that I would get drowsy. I endeavoured to recapitulate the evidence which Macgillivray had recited, but only made foolishness of it, for I simply could not concentrate. I saw always the face of a small boy who bit his lips to keep himself from tears, and another perfectly hideous face that kept turning into one of the lead figures in the rose garden. A ridiculous rhyme, too, ran in my head—something about the "midnight sun" and the "fields of Eden". By-and-by I got it straightened out into the anagram business Macgillivray had mentioned. I have a fly-paper memory for verse when there is no reason why I should remember it, and I found I could repeat the six lines of the doggerel.

After that I found the lines mixing themselves up, and suggesting all kinds of odd pictures to my brain. I took to paraphrasing them—"Under the midnight sun, where harvests are poor"—that was Scandinavia anyhow, or maybe Iceland or Greenland or Labrador. Who on earth was the sower who sowed in the fields of Eden? Adam, perhaps, or Abel, who was the first farmer? Or an angel in heaven? More like an angel, I thought, for the line sounded like a hymn. Anyhow it was infernal nonsense.

The last two lines took to escaping me, and that made me force my mind out of the irritable confusion in which it was bogged. Ah! I had them again:

"Where beside the sacred tree
Spins the seer who cannot see."

The sacred tree was probably Yggdrasil and the spinner one of the Norns. I had once taken an interest in Norse mythology, but I couldn't remember whether one of the Norns was blind. A blind woman spinning. Now where had I heard something like that? Heard it quite recently, too?

The discomfort of wakefulness is that you are not fully awake. But now I was suddenly in full possession of my senses, and worrying at that balderdash like a dog at a bone. I had been quite convinced that there was a clue in it, but that it would be impossible to hit on the clue. But now I had a ray of hope, for I seemed to feel a very faint and vague flavour of reminiscence.

Scandinavian harvests, the fields of Eden, the blind spinner—oh, it was maddening, for every time I repeated them the sense of having recently met with something similar grew stronger. The North—Norway—surely I had it there! Norway—what was there about Norway?—Salmon, elk, reindeer, midnight sun, *saeters*—the last cried out to me. And the blind old woman that spun!

I had it. These were two of the three facts which Dr. Greenslade had suggested the night before as a foundation for his imaginary "shocker". What was the third? A curiosity shop in North London kept by a Jew with a dyed beard. That had no obvious connection with a sower in the fields of Eden. But at any rate he had got two of them identical with the doggerel. . . . It was a clue. It must be a clue. Greenslade had somewhere and somehow heard the jingle or the substance of it, and it had sunk into the subconscious memory he had spoken of, without his being aware of it. Well, I had to dig it out. If I could discover where and how he had heard the thing, I had struck a trail.

When I had reached this conclusion, I felt curiously easier in my mind, and almost at once fell asleep. I awoke to a gorgeous spring morning, and ran down to the lake for my bath. I felt that I wanted all the freshening and screwing up I could get, and when I dressed after an icy plunge I was ready for all comers.

Mary was down in time for breakfast, and busy with her letters. She spoke little, and seemed to be waiting for me to begin; but I didn't want to raise the matter which was uppermost in our minds till I saw my way clearer, so I said I was going to take two days to think things over. It was Wednesday, so I wired to Macgillivray to expect me in London on Friday morning, and I scribbled a line to Mr. Julius Victor. By half-past nine I was on the road making for Greenslade's lodgings.

I caught him in the act of starting on his rounds, and made him sit down and listen to me. I had to give him the gist of Macgillivray's story, with extracts from those of Victor and Sir Arthur. Before I was half-way through he had flung off his overcoat, and before I had finished he had lit a pipe, which was a breach of his ritual not to smoke before the evening. When I stopped he had that wildish look in his light eyes which you see in a cairn terrier's when he is digging out a badger.

"You've taken on this job?" he asked brusquely.

I nodded.

"Well, I shouldn't have had much respect for you if you had refused. How can I help? Count on me, if I'm any use. Good God! I never heard a more damnable story."

"Have you got hold of the rhyme?" I repeated it, and he said it after me.

"Now, you remember the talk we had after dinner the night before last. You showed me how a 'shocker' was written, and you took at random three facts as the foundation. They were, you remember, a blind old woman spinning in the Western Highlands, a *saeter* in Norway, and a curiosity shop in North London, kept by a Jew with a dyed beard. Well, two of your facts are in that six-line jingle I have quoted to you."

"That is an odd coincidence. But is it anything more?"

"I believe that it is. I don't hold with coincidences. There's generally some explanation which we're not clever enough to get at. Your inventions were so odd that I can't think they were mere inventions. You must have heard them somehow and somewhere. You know what you said about your subconscious memory. They're somewhere in it, and, if you can remember just how they got there, you'll give me the clue I want. That six-line rhyme was sent in by people who were so confident that they didn't mind giving their enemies a clue—only it was a clue which they knew could never be discovered. Macgillivray and his fellows can make nothing of it—never will. But if I can start from the other end I'll get it on their rear. Do you see what I mean? I'm going to make you somehow or other dig it out."

He shook his head. "It can't be done, Dick. Admitting your premise—that I heard the nonsense and didn't invent it—the subconscious can't be handled like a business proposition. I remember unconsciously and I can't recall consciously. . . . But I don't admit your premise. I think the whole thing is common coincidence."

"I don't," I said stubbornly, "and even if I did I'm bound to assume the contrary, for it's the only card I possess. You've got to sit down, old chap, and do your damnedest to remember. You've been in every kind of odd show, and my belief is that you *heard* that nonsense. Dig it out of your memory and we've a chance to win. Otherwise, I see nothing but tragedy."

He got up and put on his overcoat. "I've got a long round of visits which will take me all day. Of course I'll try, but I warn you that I haven't the ghost of a hope. These things don't come by care and searching. I'd better sleep at the Manor to-night. How long can you give me?"

"Two days—I go up to town on Friday morning. Yes, you must take up your quarters with us. Mary insists on it."

There was a crying of young lambs from the meadow, and through the open window came the sound of the farm carts jolting from the stack-yard into the lane. Greenslade screwed up his face and laughed.

"A nasty breach in your country peace, Dick. You know I'm with you if there's any trouble going. Let's get the thing clear, for there's a lot of researching ahead of me. My three were an old blind woman spinning in the Western Highlands—Western Highlands, was it?—a *saeter* barn, and a Jew curiosity shop. The other three were a blind spinner under a sacred tree, a *saeter* of sorts, and a sower in the fields of Eden—Lord, such rot! Two pairs seem to coincide, the other pair looks hopeless. Well, here goes for fortune! I'm going to break my rule and take my pipe with me, for this business demands tobacco."

I spent a busy day writing letters and making arrangements about the Manor, for it looked as if I might be little at home for the next month. Oddly enough, I felt no restlessness or any particular anxiety. That would come later; for the moment I seemed to be waiting on Providence in the person of Tom Greenslade. I was trusting my instinct which told me that in those random words of his there was more than coincidence, and that with luck I might get from them a line on our problem.

Greenslade turned up about seven in the evening, rather glum and preoccupied. At dinner he ate nothing, and when we sat afterwards in the library he seemed to be chiefly interested in reading the advertisements in *The Times*. When I asked "What luck?" he turned on me a disconsolate face.

"It is the most futile job I ever took on," he groaned. "So far it's an absolute blank, and anyhow I've been taking the wrong line. I've been trying to *think* myself into recollection, and, as I said, this thing comes not by searching, nor yet by prayer and fasting. It occurred to me that I might get at something by following up the differences between the three pairs. It's a familiar method of inductive logic, for differences are often more suggestive than resemblances. So I worried away at the 'sacred tree' as contrasted with the 'Western Highlands' and the 'fields of Eden' as set against the curiosity shop. No earthly good. I gave myself a headache, and I daresay I've poisoned half my patients. It's no use, Dick, but I'll peg away for the rest of the prescribed two days. I'm letting my mind lie fallow now and trusting to inspiration. I've got two faint glimmerings of notions. First, I don't believe I said 'Western Highlands'."

"I'm positive those were your words. What did you say, then?"

"Hanged if I know, but I'm pretty certain it wasn't that. I can't explain properly, but you get an atmosphere about certain things in your mind, and that phrase somehow jars with the atmosphere. Different key. Wrong tone. Second, I've got a hazy intuition that the thing, if it is really in my memory, is somehow mixed up with a hymn tune. I don't know what tune, and the whole impression is as vague as smoke, but I tell it you for what it is worth. If I could get the right tune, I might remember something."

"You've stopped thinking?"

"Utterly. I'm an Æolian harp to be played on by any wandering wind. You see, if I did hear these three things there is no conscious rational clue to it. They were never part of my workaday mind. The only chance is that some material phenomenon may come along and link itself with them and so rebuild the scene where I heard them. A scent would be best, but a tune might do. Our one hope—and it's about as strong as a single thread of gossamer on the grass—is that that tune may drift into my head. You see the point, Dick? Thought won't do, for the problem doesn't concern the mind, but some tiny physical sensation of nose, ear, or eye might press the button. Now, it may be hallucination, but I've a feeling that the three facts I thought I invented were in some infinitely recondite way connected with a hymn tune."

He went to bed early, while I sat up till nearly midnight writing letters. As I went upstairs, I had a strong sense of futility and discouragement. It seemed the merest trifling to be groping among these spectral unrealities, while tragedy, as big and indisputable as a mountain, was overhanging us. I had to remind myself how often the trivial was the vital before I got rid of the prick in my conscience. I was tired and sleepy, and as I forced myself to think of the immediate problem, the six lines of the jingle were all blurred. While I undressed I tried to repeat them, but could not get the fourth to scan. It came out as "fields of Erin", and after that "the green fields of Erin". Then it became "the green fields of Eden".

I found myself humming a tune.

It was an old hymn which the Salvation Army used to play in the Cape Town streets when I was a schoolboy. I hadn't heard it or thought of it for thirty years. But I remembered the tune very clearly, a pretty, catchy thing like an early Victorian drawing-room ballad, and I remembered the words of the chorus—

> "On the other side of Jordan
> In the green fields of Eden,
> Where the Tree of Life is blooming,
>   There is rest for you."

I marched off to Greenslade's room and found him lying wide awake staring at the ceiling, with the lamp by his bedside lit. I must have broken in on some train of thought, for he looked at me crossly.

"I've got your tune," I said, and I whistled it, and then quoted what words I remembered.

"Tune be blowed," he said. "I never heard it before." But he hummed it after me, and made me repeat the words several times.

"No good, I'm afraid. It doesn't seem to hank on to anything. Lord, this is a fool's game. I'm off to sleep."

But three minutes later came a knock at my dressing-room door, and Greenslade entered. I saw by his eyes that he was excited.

"It's the tune all right. I can't explain why, but those three blessed facts of mine fit into it like prawns in an aspic. I'm feeling my way towards the light now. I thought I'd just tell you, for you may sleep better for hearing it."

I slept like a log, and went down to breakfast feeling more cheerful than I had felt for several days. But the doctor seemed to have had a poor night. His eyes looked gummy and heavy, and he had ruffled his hair out of all hope of order. I knew that trick of his; when his hair began to stick up at the back he was out of sorts either in mind or body. I noticed that he had got himself up in knickerbockers and thick shoes.

After breakfast he showed no inclination to smoke. "I feel as if I were going to be beaten on the post," he groaned. "I'm a complete convert to your view, Dick. I *heard* my three facts and didn't invent them. What's more, my three are definitely linked with the three in those miscreants' doggerel. That tune proves it, for it talks about the 'fields of Eden', and yet is identified in my memory with my three which didn't mention Eden. That's a tremendous point, and proves we're on the right road. But I'm hanged if I can get a step farther. Wherever I heard the facts I heard the tune, but I'm no nearer finding out that place. I've got one bearing, and I need a second to give me the point of intersection I want, and how the deuce I'm to get it I don't know."

Greenslade was now keener even than I was on the chase, and indeed his lean anxious face was uncommonly like an old hound's. I asked him what he was going to do.

"At ten o'clock precisely I start on a walk—right round the head of the Windrush änd home by the Forest. It's going to be a thirty-mile stride at a steady four and a half miles an hour, which, with half an hour for lunch, will get me back here before six. I'm going to drug my body and mind into apathy by hard exercise. Then I shall have a hot bath and a good dinner, and after that, when I'm properly fallow, I may get the revelation. The mistake I made yesterday was in trying to *think*."

It was a gleamy, blustering March morning, the very weather for a walk, and I would have liked to accompany him. As it was I watched his long legs striding up the field we call Big Pasture, and then gave up the day to the job of putting Loch Leven fry into one of the ponds—a task so supremely muddy and wet that I had very little leisure to think of other things. In the afternoon I rode over to the market town to see my builder, and got back only just before dinner to learn that Greenslade had returned. He was now wallowing in a hot bath, according to his programme.

At dinner he seemed to be in better spirits. The wind had heightened his colour, and given him a ferocious appetite, and the 1906 Clicquot, which I regard as the proper drink after a hard day, gave him the stimulus he needed. He talked as he had talked three nights ago, before this business got us in its clutches. Mary disappeared after dinner, and we sat ourselves in big chairs before the library fire, like two drowsy men who have had a busy day in the open air. I thought I had better say nothing till he chose to speak.

He was silent for a long time, and then he laughed, not very mirthfully.

"I'm as far off it as ever. All day I've been letting my mind wander and measuring off miles with my two legs like a pair of compasses. But nothing has come to me. No word yet of that confounded cross-bearing I need. I might have heard that tune in any one of a thousand parts of the globe. You see, my rackety life is a disadvantage—I've had too many different sorts of experience. If I'd been a curate all my days in one village it would have been easier."

I waited, and he went on, speaking not to me but to the fire.

"I've got an impression so strong that it amounts to certainty that I never heard the words 'Western Highlands'. It was something like it, but not that."

"Western Islands," I suggested.

"What could they be?"

"I think I've heard the phrase used about the islands off the west coast of Ireland. Does that help you?"

He shook his head. "No good. I've never been in Ireland."

After that he was silent again, staring at the fire, while I smoked opposite him, feeling pretty blank and dispirited. I realized that I had banked more than I knew on this line of inquiry which seemed to be coming to nothing. . . .

Then suddenly there happened one of those trivial things which look like accidents, but I believe are part of the reasoned government of the universe.

I leaned forward to knock out the ashes of my pipe against the stone edge of the hearth. I hammered harder than I intended, and the pipe, which was an old one, broke off at the bowl. I exclaimed irritably, for I hate to lose an old pipe, and then pulled up sharp at the sight of Greenslade.

He was staring open-mouthed at the fragments in my hand, and his eyes were those of a man whose thoughts are far away. He held up one hand, while I froze into silence. Then the tension relaxed, and he dropped back into his chair with a sigh.

"The cross-bearing!" he said. "I've got it. . . . Medina."

Then he laughed at my puzzled face.

"I'm not mad, Dick. I once talked to a man, and as we talked he broke the bowl of his pipe as you have just done. He was the man who hummed the hymn tune, and though I haven't the remotest recollection of what he said, I am as certain as that I am alive that he gave me the three facts which sunk into the abyss of my subconscious memory. Wait a minute. Yes. I see it as plain as I see you. He broke his pipe just as you have done, and some time or other he hummed that tune."

"Who was he?" I asked, but Greenslade disregarded the question. He was telling his story in his own way, with his eyes still abstracted as if he were looking down a long corridor of memory.

"I was staying at the Bull at Hanham—shooting wildfowl on the sea marshes. I had the place to myself, for it wasn't weather for a country pub, but late one night a car broke down outside, and the owner and his chauffeur had to put up at the Bull. Oddly enough I knew the man. He had been at one of the big shoots at Rousham Thorpe and was on his way back to London. We had a lot to say to each other and sat up into the small hours. We talked about sport, and the upper glens of the Yarkand River, where I first met him. I remember quite a lot of our talk, but not the three facts or the tune, which made no appeal to my conscious memory. Only, of course, they must have been there."

"When did this happen?"

"Early last December, the time we had the black frost. You remember, Dick, how I took a week's holiday and went down to Norfolk after duck."

"You haven't told me the man's name."

"I have. Medina."

"Who on earth is Medina?"

"O Lord! Dick. You're overdoing the rustic. You've heard of Dominick Medina."

I had, of course, when he mentioned the Christian name. You couldn't open a paper without seeing something about Dominick Medina, but whether he was a poet or a politician or an actor-manager I hadn't troubled to inquire. There was a pile of picture-papers on a side-table, and I fetched them and began to turn them over. Very soon I found what I wanted. It was a photograph of a group at a country-house party for some steeplechase, the usual "reading-from-left-to-right" business, and there between a Duchess and a foreign Princess was Mr. Dominick Medina. The poverty of the photograph could not conceal the extraordinary good looks of the man. He had the kind of head I fancy Byron had, and I seemed to discern, too, a fine, clean, athletic figure.

"If you had happened to look at that rag you might have short-circuited your inquiry."

He shook his head. "No. It doesn't happen that way. I had to get your broken pipe and the tune, or I would have been stuck."

"Then I suppose I have to get in touch with this chap and find where he picked up the three facts and the tune. But how if he turns out to be like you, another babbler from the subconscious?"

"That is the risk you run, of course. He may be able to help you, or more likely he may prove only another dead wall."

I felt suddenly an acute sense of the difficulty of the job I had taken on, and something very near hopelessness.

"Tell me about this Medina. Is he a decent fellow?"

"I suppose so. Yes, I should think so. But he moves in higher circles than I'm accustomed to, so I can't judge. But I'll tell you what he is beyond doubt—he's rather a great man. Hang it, Dick, you must have heard of him. He's one of the finest shots living, and he's done some tall things in the exploration way, and he was the devil of a fellow as a partisan leader in South Russia. Also—though it may not interest you—he's an uncommon fine poet."

"I suppose he's some sort of a Dago."

"Not a bit of it. Old Spanish family settled here for three centuries. One of them rode with Rupert. Hold on! I rather believe I've heard that his people live in Ireland, or did live, till life there became impossible."

"What age?"

"Youngish. Not more than thirty-five. Oh! and the handsomest thing in mankind since the Greeks."

"I'm not a flapper," I said impatiently. "Good looks in a man are no sort of recommendation to me. I shall probably take a dislike to his face."

"You won't. From what I know of him and you you'll fall under his charm at first sight. I never heard of a man that didn't. He has a curious musical voice and eyes that warm you—glow like sunlight. Not that I know him well, but I own I found him extraordinarily attractive. And you see from the papers what the world thinks of him."

"All the same I'm not much nearer my goal. I've got to find out where he heard those three blessed facts and that idiotic tune. He'll probably send me to blazes, and, even if he's civil, he'll very likely be helpless."

"Your chance is that he's a really clever man, not an old blunderer like me. You'll get the help of a first-class mind, and that means a lot. Shall I write you a line of introduction?"

He sat down at my desk and wrote. "I'm saying nothing about your errand —simply that I'd like you to know each other—common interest in sport and travel—that sort of thing. You're going to be in London, so I had better give your address as your Club."

Next morning Greenslade went back to his duties and I caught the early train to town. I was not very happy about Mr. Dominick Medina, for I didn't seem able to get hold of him. *Who's Who* only gave his age, his residence— Hill Street—his clubs, and the fact that he was M.P. for a South London division. Mary had never met him, for he had appeared in London after she had stopped going about, but she remembered that her Wymondham aunts raved about him, and she had read somewhere an article on his poetry. As I sat in the express, I tried to reconstruct what kind of fellow he must be—a mixture of Byron and Sir Richard Burton and the young political highbrow. The picture wouldn't compose, for I saw only a figure like a waxwork, with a cooing voice and a shopwalker's suavity. Also his name kept confusing me, for I mixed him up with an old ruffian of a Portuguese I once knew at Beira.

I was walking down St James's Street on my way to Whitehall, pretty much occupied with my own thoughts, when I was brought up by a hand placed flat on my chest, and lo and behold! it was Sandy Arbuthnot.

58   I MAKE THE ACQUAINTANCE OF A POPULAR MAN

You may imagine how glad I was to see old Sandy again, for I had not set eyes on him since 1916. He had been an Intelligence Officer with Maude, and then something at Simla, and after the War had had an administrative job in Mesopotamia, or as they call it nowadays, Iraq. He had written to me from all kinds of queer places, but he never appeared to be coming home, and, what with my marriage and my settling in the country, we seemed to be fixed in ruts that were not likely to intersect. I had seen his elder brother's death in the papers, so he was now Master of Clanroyden and heir to the family estates, but I didn't imagine that that would make a Scotch laird of him. I never saw a fellow less changed by five years of toil and travel. He was desperately slight and tanned—he had always been that—but the contours of his face were still soft like a girl's and his brown eyes were merry as ever.

We stood and stared at each other.

"Dick, old man," he cried, "I'm home for good. Yes—honour bright. For months and months, if not years and years. I've got so much to say to you I don't know where to begin. But I can't wait now. I'm off to Scotland to see my father. He's my chief concern now, for he's getting very frail. But I'll be back in three days. Let's dine together on Tuesday."

We were standing at the door of a club—his and mine—and a porter was stowing his baggage into a taxi. Before I could properly realize that it was Sandy, he was waving his hand from the taxi window and disappearing up the street.

The sight of him cheered me immensely, and I went on along Pall Mall in a good temper. To have Sandy back in England and at call made me feel somehow more substantial, like a commander who knows his reserves are near. When I entered Macgillivray's room I was smiling, and the sight of me woke an answering smile on his anxious face. "Good man!" he said. "You look like business. You're to put yourself at my disposal while I give you your bearings."

He got out his papers and expounded the whole affair. It was a very queer story, yet the more I looked into it the thinner my scepticism grew. I am not going to write it all down, for it is not yet time; it would give away certain methods which have not yet exhausted their usefulness; but before I had gone very far, I took off my hat to these same methods, for they showed amazing patience and ingenuity. It was an odd set of links that made up the chain. There was an importer of Barcelona nuts with a modest office near Tower Hill. There was a copper company, purporting to operate in Spain, whose shares were not quoted on the Stock Exchange, but which had a fine office in London Wall, where you could get the best luncheon in the City. There was a respectable accountant in Glasgow, and a French count, who was also some kind of Highland laird and a great supporter of the White Rose League. There was a country gentleman living in Shropshire, who had bought his place after the War and was a keen rider to hounds and a very popular figure in the county. There was a little office not far from Fleet Street, which professed to be the English agency of an American religious magazine; and there was a certain publicist, who was always appealing in the newspapers for help for the distressed populations of Central Europe. I remembered his appeals well, for I had myself twice sent him small subscriptions. The way Macgillivray had worked out the connection between these gentry filled me with awe.

Then he showed me specimens of their work. It was sheer unmitigated crime, a sort of selling a bear on a huge scale in a sinking world. The aim of the gang was money, and already they had made scandalous profits. Partly their business was mere conscienceless profiteering well inside the bounds of the law, such as gambling in falling exchanges and using every kind of brazen and subtle trick to make their gamble a certainty. Partly it was common fraud of the largest size. But there were darker sides—murder when the victim ran athwart their schemes, strikes engineered when a wrecked industry some-where or other in the world showed symptoms of reviving, shoddy little outbursts in shoddy little countries which increased the tangle. These fellows were wreckers on the grand scale, merchants of pessimism, giving society another kick downhill whenever it had a chance of finding its balance, and then pocketing their profits.

There motive, as I have said, was gain, but that was not the motive of the people they worked through. Their cleverness lay in the fact that they used the fanatics, the moral imbeciles as Macgillivray called them, whose key was a wild hatred of something or other, or a reasoned belief in anarchy. Behind the smug exploiters lay the whole dreary wastes of half-baked craziness. Macgillivray gave me examples of how they used these tools, the fellows who had no thought of profit, and were ready to sacrifice everything, including their lives, for a mad ideal. It was a masterpiece of cold-blooded, devilish ingenuity. Hideous, and yet comic too; for the spectacle of these feverish cranks toiling to create a new heaven and a new earth and thinking themselves the leaders of mankind, when they were dancing like puppets at the will of a few scoundrels engaged in the most ancient of pursuits, was an irony to make the gods laugh.

I asked who was their leader.

Macgillivray said he wasn't certain. No one of the gang seemed to have more authority than the others, and their activities were beautifully specialized. But he agreed that there was probably one master mind, and said grimly that he would know more about that when they were rounded up. "The dock will settle that question."

"How much do they suspect?" I asked.

"Not much. A little, or they would not have taken hostages. But not much, for we have been very careful to make no sign. Only, since we became cognizant of the affair, we have managed very quietly to put a spoke in the wheels of some of their worst enterprises, though I am positive they have no suspicion of it. Also we have put the brake on their propaganda side. They are masters of propaganda, you know. Dick, have you ever considered what a diabolical weapon that can be   using all the channels of modern publicity to poison and warp men's minds? It is the most dangerous thing on earth. You can use it cleanly—as I think on the whole we did in the War—but you can also use it to establish the most damnable lies. Happily in the long run it defeats itself, but only after it has sown the world with mischief. Look at the Irish! They are the cleverest propagandists extant, and managed to persuade most people that they were a brave, generous, humorous, talented, warm-hearted race, cruelly yoked to a dull mercantile England, when God knows they were exactly the opposite."

Macgillivray, I may remark, is an Ulsterman, and has his prejudices.

"About the gang—I suppose they're all pretty respectable to outward view?"

"Highly respectable," he said. "I met one of them at dinner the other night at ——'s"—he mentioned the name of a member of the Government. "Before Christmas I was at a cover shoot in Suffolk, and one of the worst had the stand next me—an uncommonly agreeable fellow."

Then we sat down to business. Macgillivray's idea was that I should study the details of the thing and then get alongside some of the people. He thought I might begin with the Shropshire squire. He fancied that I might stumble on something which would give me a line on the hostages, for he stuck to his absurd notion that I had a special *flair* which the amateur sometimes possessed and the professional lacked. I agreed that that was the best plan, and arranged to spend Sunday in his room going over the secret *dossiers*. I was beginning to get keen about the thing, for Macgillivray had a knack of making whatever he handled as interesting as a game.

I had meant to tell him about my experiments with Greenslade; but after what he had shown me I felt that that story was absurdly thin and unpromising. But as I was leaving, I asked him casually if he knew Mr. Dominick Medina.

He smiled. "Why do you ask? He's scarcely your line of country."

"I don't know. I've heard a lot about him, and I thought I would rather like to meet him."

"I barely know him, but I must confess that the few times I've met him I was enormously attracted. He's the handsomest being alive."

"So I'm told, and it's the only thing that puts me off."

"It wouldn't if you saw him. He's not in the least the ordinary matinée idol. He is the only fellow I ever heard of who was adored by women and also liked by men. He's a first-class sportsman and said to be the best shot in England after His Majesty. He's a coming man in politics, too, and a most finished speaker. I once heard him, and, though I take very little stock in oratory, he almost had me on my feet. He has knocked a bit about the world, and he is also a very pretty poet, though that wouldn't interest you."

"I don't know why you say that," I protested. "I'm getting rather good at poetry."

"Oh, I know. Scott and Macaulay and Tennyson. But that is not Medina's line. He is a deity of *les jeunes* and a hardy innovator. Jolly good, too. The man's a fine classical scholar."

"Well, I hope to meet him soon, and I'll let you know my impression."

I had posted my letter to Medina, enclosing Greenslade's introduction, on my way from the station, and next morning I found a very civil reply from him at my Club. Greenslade had talked of our common interest in big-game shooting, and he professed to know all about me, and to be anxious to make my acquaintance. He was out of town unfortunately for the week-end, he said, but he suggested that I should lunch with him on the Monday. He named a Club, a small, select, old-fashioned one of which most of the members were hunting squires.

I looked forward to meeting him with a quite inexplicable interest, and on Sunday, when I was worrying through papers in Macgillivray's room, I had him at the back of my mind. I had made a picture of something between a Ouida guardsman and the Apollo Belvedere and rigged it out in the smartest clothes. But when I gave my name to the porter at the Club door, and a young man who was warming his hands at the hall fire came forward to meet me, I had to wipe that picture clean off my mind.

He was about my own height, just under six feet, and at first sight rather slightly built, but a hefty enough fellow to eyes which knew where to look for the points of a man's strength. Still he appeared slim, and therefore young, and you could see from the way he stood and walked that he was as light on his feet as a rope-dancer. There is a horrible word in the newspapers, "well-groomed", applied to men by lady journalists, which always makes me think of a glossy horse on which a stableboy has been busy with the brush and curry-comb. I had thought of him as "well-groomed", but there was nothing glossy about his appearance. He wore a rather old well-cut brown tweed suit, with a soft shirt and collar, and a russet tie that matched his complexion. His get-up was exactly that of a country squire who has come up to town for a day at Tattersall's.

I find it difficult to describe my first impression of his face, for my memory is all overlaid with other impressions acquired when I looked at it in very different circumstances. But my chief feeling, I remember, was that it was singularly pleasant. It was very English, and yet not quite English; the colouring was a little warmer than sun or weather would give, and there was a kind of silken graciousness about it not commonly found in our countrymen. It was beautifully cut, every feature regular, and yet there was a touch of ruggedness that saved it from conventionality. I was puzzled about this, till I saw that it came from two things, the hair and the eyes. The hair was a dark brown, brushed in a wave above the forehead, so that the face with its strong fine chin made an almost perfect square. But the eyes were the thing. They were of a startling blue, not the pale blue which is common enough and belongs to our Norse ancestry, but a deep dark blue, like the colour of a sapphire. Indeed if you think of a sapphire with the brilliance of a diamond, you get a pretty fair notion of those eyes. They would have made a plain-headed woman lovely, and in a man's face, which had not a touch of the feminine, they were startling. Startling—I stick to that word—but also entrancing.

He greeted me as if he had been living for this hour, and also with a touch of the deference due to a stranger.

"This is delightful, Sir Richard. It was very good of you to come. We've got a table to ourselves by the fire. I hope you're hungry. I've had a devilish cold journey this morning and I want my luncheon."

I was hungry enough, and I never ate a better meal. He gave me Burgundy on account of the bite in the weather, and afterwards I had a glass of the Bristol Cream for which the Club was famous; but he drank water himself. There were four other people in the room, all of whom he appeared to call by their Christian names, and these lantern-jawed hunting fellows seemed to cheer up at the sight of him. But they didn't come and stand beside him and talk, which is apt to happen to your popular man. There was that about Medina which was at once friendly and aloof, the air of a simple but tremendous distinction.

I remember we began by talking about rifles. I had done a good deal of shikar in my time, and I could see that this man had had a wide experience and had the love of the thing in his bones. He never bragged, but by little dropped remarks showed what a swell he was. We talked of a new .240 bore which had remarkable stopping power, and I said I had never used it on anything more formidable than a Scotch stag. "It would have been a godsend to me in the old days on the Pungwe where I had to lug about a .500 express that broke my back."

He grinned ruefully. "The old days!" he said. "We've all had 'em, and we're all sick to get 'em back. Sometimes I'm tempted to kick over the traces and be off to the wilds again. I'm too young to settle down. And you, Sir Richard—you must feel the same. Do you never regret that that beastly old War is over?"

"I can't say I do. I'm a middle-aged man now and soon I'll be stiff in the joints. I've settled down in the Cotswolds, and though I hope to get a lot of sport before I die I'm not looking for any more wars. I'm positive the Almighty meant me for a farmer."

He laughed. "I wish I knew what He meant me for. It looks like some sort of politician."

"Oh, you!" I said. "You're the fellow with twenty talents. I've only got the one, and I'm jolly well going to bury it in the soil."

I kept wondering how much help I would get out of him. I liked him enormously, but somehow I didn't yet see his cleverness. He was just an ordinary good fellow of my own totem—just such another as Tom Greenslade. It was a dark day, and the firelight silhouetted his profile, and as I stole glances at it I was struck by the shape of his head. The way he brushed his hair front and back made it look square, but I saw that it was really round, the roundest head I have ever seen except in a Kaffir. He was evidently conscious of it and didn't like it, so took some pains to conceal it.

All through luncheon I was watching him covertly, and I could see that he was also taking stock of me. Very friendly these blue eyes were, but very shrewd. He suddenly looked me straight in the face.

"You won't vegetate," he said. "You needn't deceive yourself. You haven't got the kind of mouth for a rustic. What is it to be? Politics? Business? Travel? You're well off?"

"Yes. For my simple tastes I'm rather rich. But I haven't the ambition of a maggot."

"No. You haven't." He looked at me steadily. "If you don't mind my saying it, you have too little vanity. Oh, I'm quick at detecting vanity, and anyhow it's a thing that defies concealment. But I imagine—indeed I know— that you can work like a beaver, and that your loyalty is not the kind that cracks. You won't be able to help yourself, Sir Richard. You'll be caught up in some machine. Look at me. I swore two years ago never to have a groove, and I'm in a deep one already. England is made up of grooves, and the only plan is to select a good one."

"I suppose yours is politics," I said.

"I suppose it is. A dingy game as it's played at present, but there are possibilities. There is a mighty Tory revival in sight, and it will want leading. The newly enfranchised classes, especially the women, will bring it about. The suffragists didn't know what a tremendous force of conservatism they were releasing when they won the vote for their sex. I should like to talk to you about these things some day."

In the smoking-room we got back to sport, and he told me the story of how he met Greenslade in Central Asia. I was beginning to realize that the man's reputation was justified, for there was a curious mastery about his talk, a careless power as if everything came easily to him and was just taken in his stride. I had meant to open up the business which had made me seek his acquaintance, but I did not feel the atmosphere quite right for it. I did not know him well enough yet, and I felt that if I once started on those ridiculous three facts, which were all I had, I must make a clean breast of the whole thing and take him fully into my confidence. I thought the time was scarcely ripe for that, especially as we would meet again.

"Are you by any chance free on Thursday?" he asked as we parted. "I would like to take you to dine at the Thursday Club. You're sure to know some of the fellows, and it's a pleasant way of spending an evening. That's capital! Eight o'clock on Thursday. Short coat and black tie."

As I walked away, I made up my mind that I had found the right kind of man to help me. I liked him, and the more I thought of him the more the impression deepened of a big reservoir of power behind his easy grace. I was completely fascinated, and the proof of it was that I went off to the nearest bookseller's and bought his two slim volumes of poems. I cared far more about poetry than Macgillivray imagined—Mary had done a lot to educate me—but I hadn't been very fortunate in my experiments with the new people. But I understood Medina's verses well enough. They were very simple, with a delicious subtle tune in them, and they were desperately sad. Again and again came the note of regret and transience and disillusioned fortitude. As I read them that evening I wondered how a man, who had apparently such zest for life and got so much out of the world, should be so lonely at heart. It might be a pose, but there was nothing of the conventional despair of the callow poet. This was the work of one as wise as Ulysses and as far-wandering. I didn't see how he could want to write anything but the truth. A pose is a consequence of vanity, and I was pretty clear that Medina was not vain.

Next morning I found his cadences still running in my head and I could not keep my thoughts off him. He fascinated me as a man is fascinated by a pretty woman. I was glad to think that he had taken a liking for me, for he had done far more than Greenslade's casual introduction demanded. He had made a plan for us to meet again, and he had spoken not as an acquaintance but as a friend. Very soon I decided that I would get Macgillivray's permission and take him wholly into our confidence. It was no good keeping a man like that at arm's length and asking him to solve puzzles presented as meaninglessly as an acrostic in a newspaper. He must be told all or nothing, and I was certain that if he were told all he would be a very tower of strength to me. The more I thought of him the more I was convinced of his exceptional brains.

I lunched with Mr. Julius Victor in Carlton House Terrace. He was carrying on his ordinary life, and when he greeted me he never referred to the business which had linked us together. Or rather he only said one word. "I knew I could count on you," he said. "I think I told you that my daughter was engaged to be married this spring. Well, her fiancé has come over from France and will be staying for an indefinite time with me. He can probably do nothing to assist you, but he is here at your call if you want him. He is the Marquis de la Tour du Pin."

I didn't quite catch the name, and, as it was a biggish party, we had sat down to luncheon before I realized who the desolated lover was. It was my ancient friend Turpin, who had been liaison officer with my old division. I had known that he was some kind of grandee, but as everybody went by nicknames I had become used to think of him as Turpin, a version of his title invented, I think, by Archie Roylance. There he was sitting opposite me, a very handsome pallid young man, dressed with that excessive correctness found only among Frenchmen who get their clothes in England. He had been a tremendous swashbuckler when he was with the division, unbridled in speech, volcanic in action, but always with a sad gentleness in his air. He raised his heavy-lidded eyes and looked at me, and then, with a word of apology to his host, marched round the table and embraced me.

I felt every kind of a fool, but I was mighty glad all the same to see Turpin. He had been a good pal of mine, and the fact that he had been going to marry Miss Victor seemed to bring my new job in line with other parts of my life. But I had no further speech with him, for I had conversational women on both sides of me, and in the few minutes while the men were left alone at table I fell into talk with an elderly man on my right, who proved to be a member of the Cabinet. I found that out by a lucky accident, for I was lamentably ill-informed about the government of our country.

I asked him about Medina, and he brightened up at once.

"Can you place him?" he asked. "I can't. I like to classify my fellow-men, but he is a new specimen. He is as exotic as the young Disraeli and as English as the late Duke of Devonshire. The point is, has he a policy, something he wants to achieve, and has he the power of attaching a party to him? If he has these two things, there is no doubt about his future. Honestly, I'm not quite certain. He has very great talents, and I believe if he wanted he would be in the front rank as a public speaker. He has the ear of the House, too, though he doesn't often address it. But I am never sure how much he cares about the whole business, and England, you know, demands wholeheartedness in her public men. She will follow blindly the second-rate if he is in earnest, and reject the first-rate if he is not."

I said something about Medina's view of a great Tory revival, based upon the women. My neighbour grinned.

"I daresay he's right, and I daresay he could whistle women any way he pleased. It's extraordinary the charm he has for them. That handsome face of his and that melodious voice would enslave anything female from a charwoman to a Cambridge intellectual. Half his power of course comes from the fact that they have no charm for *him*. He's as aloof as Sir Galahad from any interest in the sex. Did you ever hear his name coupled with a young woman's? He goes everywhere and they would give their heads for him, and all the while he is as insensitive as a nice Eton boy whose only thought is of getting into the Eleven. You know him?"

I told him, very slightly.

"Same with me. I've only a nodding acquaintance, but one can't help feeling the man everywhere and being acutely interested. It's lucky he's a sound fellow. If he were a rogue he could play the devil with our easy-going society."

That night Sandy and I dined together. He had come back from Scotland in good spirits, for his father's health was improving, and when Sandy was in good spirits it was like being on the Downs in a south-west wind. We had so much to tell each other that we let our food grow cold. He had to hear all about Mary and Peter John, and what I knew of Blenkiron and a dozen other old comrades, and I had to get a sketch—the merest sketch—of his doings since the Armistice in the East. Sandy for some reason was at the moment disinclined to speak of his past, but he was as ready as an undergraduate to talk of his future. He meant to stay at home now, for a long spell at any rate; and the question was how he should fill up his time. "Country life's no good," he said. "I must find a profession or I'll get into trouble."

I suggested politics, and he rather liked the notion.

"I might be bored in Parliament," he reflected, "but I should love the rough-and-tumble of an election. I only once took part in one, and I discovered surprising gifts as a demagogue, and made a speech in our little town which is still talked about. The chief row was about Irish Home Rule, and I thought I'd better have a whack at the Pope. Has it ever struck you, Dick, that ecclesiastical language has a most sinister sound? I knew some of the words, though not their meaning, but I knew that my audience would be just as ignorant. So I had a magnificent peroration. 'Will you, men of Kilclavers,' I asked, 'endure to see a chasuble set up in your market-place? Will you have your daughters sold into simony? Will you have celibacy practised in the public streets?' Gad, I had them all on their feet bellowing 'Never!' "

He also rather fancied business. He had a notion of taking up civil aviation, and running a special service for transporting pilgrims from all over the Moslem world to Mecca. He reckoned the present average cost to the pilgrim at not less than £30, and believed that he could do it for an average of £15 and show a handsome profit. Blenkiron, he thought, might be interested in the scheme and put up some of the capital.

But later, in a corner of the upstairs smoking-room, Sandy was serious enough when I began to tell him the job I was on, for I didn't need Macgillivray's permission to make a confidant of him. He listened in silence while I gave him the main lines of the business that I had gathered from Macgillivray's papers, and he made no comment when I came to the story of the three hostages. But, when I explained my disinclination to stir out of my country rut, he began to laugh.

"It's a queer thing how people like us get a sudden passion for cosiness. I feel it myself coming over me. What stirred you up in the end? The little boy?"

Then very lamely and shyly I began on the rhymes and Greenslade's memory. That interested him acutely. "Just the sort of sensible-nonsensical notion you'd have, Dick. Go on. I'm thrilled."

But when I came to Medina he exclaimed sharply.

"You've met him?"

"Yesterday at luncheon."

"You haven't told him anything?"

"No. But I'm going to."

Sandy had been deep in an armchair with his legs over the side, but now he got up and stood with his arms on the mantelpiece looking into the fire.

"I'm going to take him into my full confidence," I said, "when I've spoken to Macgillivray."

"Macgillivray will no doubt agree?"

"And you? Have you ever met him?"

"Never. But of course I've heard of him. Indeed I don't mind telling you that one of my chief reasons for coming home was a wish to see Medina."

"You'll like him tremendously. I never met such a man."

"So everyone says." He turned his face and I could see that it had fallen into that portentous gravity which was one of Sandy's moods, the complement to his ordinary insouciance. "When are you going to see him again?"

"I'm dining with him the day after to-morrow at a thing called the Thursday Club."

"Oh, he belongs to that, does he? So do I. I think I'll give myself the pleasure of dining also."

I asked about the Club, and he told me that it had been started after the War by some of the people who had had queer jobs and wanted to keep together. It was very small, only twenty members. There were Collatt, one of the Q-boat V.C.'s, and Pugh of the Indian Secret Service, and the Duke of Burminster, and Sir Arthur Warcliff, and several soldiers all more or less well known. "They elected me in 1919," said Sandy, "but of course I've never been to a dinner. I say, Dick, Medina must have a pretty strong pull here to be a member of the Thursday. Though I says it as shouldn't, it's a show most people would give their right hand to be in."

He sat down again and appeared to reflect, with his chin on his hand.

"You're under the spell, I suppose," he said.

"Utterly. I'll tell you how he strikes me. Your ordinary very clever man is apt to be a bit bloodless and priggish, while your ordinary sportsman and good fellow is inclined to be a bit narrow. Medina seems to me to combine all the virtues and none of the faults of both kinds. Anybody can see he's a sportsman, and you've only to ask the swells to discover how high they put his brains."

"He sounds rather too good to be true." I seemed to detect a touch of acidity in his voice. "Dick," he said, looking very serious, "I want you to promise to go slow in this business—I mean about telling Medina."

"Why?" I asked. "Have you anything against him?"

"No—o—o," he said. "I haven't anything against him. But he's just a little incredible, and I would like to know more about him. I had a friend who knew him. I've no right to say this, and I haven't any evidence, but I've a sort of feeling that Medina didn't do him any good."

"What was his name?" I asked, and was told "Lavater"; and when I inquired what had become of him Sandy didn't know. He had lost sight of him for two years.

At that I laughed heartily, for I could see what was the matter. Sandy was jealous of this man who was putting a spell on everybody. He wanted his old friends to himself. When I taxed him with it he grinned and didn't deny it.

59   THE THURSDAY CLUB

We met in a room on the second floor of a little restaurant in Mervyn Street, a pleasant room, panelled in white, with big fires burning at each end. The Club had its own cook and butler, and I swear a better dinner was never produced in London, starting with preposterously early plovers' eggs and finishing with fruit from Burminster's houses. There were a dozen present including myself, and of these, besides my host, I knew only Burminster and Sandy. Collatt was there, and Pugh, and a wizened little man who had just returned from bird-hunting at the mouth of the Mackenzie. There was Palliser-Yeates, the banker, who didn't look thirty, and Fulleylove, the Arabian traveller, who was really thirty and looked fifty. I was specially interested in Nightingale, a slim peering fellow with double glasses, who had gone back to Greek manuscripts and his Cambridge fellowship after captaining a Bedouin tribe. Leithen was there, too, the Attorney-General, who had been a private in the Guards at the start of the War and had finished up a G.S.O.1, a toughly built man with a pale face and very keen quizzical eyes. I should think there must have been more varied and solid brains in that dozen than you would find in an average Parliament.

Sandy was the last to arrive, and was greeted with a roar of joy. Everybody seemed to want to wring his hand and beat him on the back. He knew them all except Medina, and I was curious to see their meeting. Burminster did the introducing, and Sandy for a moment looked shy. "I've been looking forward to this for years," Medina said, and Sandy, after one glance at him, grinned sheepishly and stammered something polite.

Burminster was chairman for the evening, a plump, jolly little man, who had been a pal of Archie Roylance in the Air Force. The talk to begin with was nothing out of the common. It started with horses and the spring handicaps, and then got on to spring salmon fishing, for one man had been on the Helmsdale, another on the Naver, and two on the Tay. The fashion of the Club was to have the conversation general, and there was very little talking in groups. I was next to Medina, between him and the Duke, and Sandy was at the other end of the oval table. He had not much to say, and more than once I caught his eyes watching Medina.

Then by-and-by, as was bound to happen, reminiscences began. Collatt made me laugh with a story of how the Admiralty had a notion that sea-lions might be useful to detect submarines. A number were collected, and trained to swim after submarines to which fish were attached as bait, the idea being that they would come to associate the smell of submarines with food, and go after a stranger. The thing shipwrecked on the artistic temperament. The beasts all came from the music-halls and had names like Flossie and Cissie, so they couldn't be got to realize that there was a war on, and were always going ashore without leave.

That story started the ball rolling, and by the time we had reached the port the talk was like what you used to find in the smoking-room of an East African coastal steamer, only a million times better. Everybody present had done and seen amazing things, and moreover they had the brains and knowledge to orientate their experiences. It was no question of a string of yarns, but rather of the best kind of give-and-take conversation, when a man would buttress an argument by an apt recollection. I especially admired Medina. He talked little, but he made others talk, and his keen interest seemed to wake the best in everybody. I noticed that, as at our luncheon three days before, he drank only water.

We talked, I remember, about the people who had gone missing, and whether any were likely still to turn up. Sandy told us about three British officers who had been in prison in Turkestan since the summer of '18 and had only just started home. He had met one of them at Marseilles, and thought there might be others tucked away in those parts. Then some one spoke of how it was possible to drop off the globe for a bit and miss all that was happening. I said I had met an old prospector in Barberton in 1920 who had come down from Portuguese territory, and when I asked him what he had been doing in the War, he said, "What war?" Pugh said a fellow had just turned up in Hong Kong who had been a captive of Chinese pirates for eight years and had never heard a word of our four years' struggle, till he said something about the Kaiser to the skipper of the boat that picked him up.

Then Sandy, as the newcomer, wanted news about Europe. I remember that Leithen gave him his views on the *malaise* that France was suffering from, and that Palliser-Yeates, who looked exactly like a Rugby three-quarter back, enlightened him—and incidentally myself—on the matter of German reparations. Sandy was furious about the muddle in the Near East and the mishandling of Turkey. His view was that we were doing our best to hammer a much-divided Orient into a hostile unanimity.

"Lord!" he cried, "how I loathe our new manners in foreign policy. The old English way was to regard all foreigners as slightly childish and rather idiotic, and ourselves as the only grown-ups in a kindergarten world. That meant that we had a cool detached view and did even-handed unsympathetic justice. But now we have got into the nursery ourselves and are bear-fighting

on the floor. We take violent sides, and make pets, and of course if you are
-*phil* something or other you have got to be -*phobe* something else. It is all
wrong. We are becoming Balkanized."

We would have drifted into politics if Pugh had not asked him his opinion
of Gandhi. That led him into an exposition of the meaning of the fanatic, a
subject on which he was well qualified to speak, for he had consorted with
most varieties.

"He is always in the technical sense mad—that is, his mind is tilted from
its balance, and since we live by balance he is a wrecker, a crowbar in the
machinery. His power comes from the appeal he makes to the imperfectly
balanced, and as these are never the majority his appeal is limited. But there
is one kind of fanatic whose strength comes from balance, from a lunatic
balance. You cannot say that there is any one thing abnormal about him, for
he is all abnormal. He is as balanced as you or me, but, so to speak, in a
fourth-dimensional world. That kind of man has no logical gaps in his creed.
Within his insane postulates he is brilliantly sane. Take Lenin for instance.
That's the kind of fanatic I'm afraid of."

Leithen asked how such a man got his influence. "You say that there is no
crazy spot in him which appeals to a crazy spot in other people."

"He appeals to the normal," said Sandy solemnly, "to the perfectly sane.
He offers reason, not visions—in any case his visions are reasonable. In
ordinary times he will not be heard, because, as I say, his world is not our
world. But let there come a time of great suffering or discontent, when the
mind of the ordinary man is in desperation, and the rational fanatic will come
by his own. When he appeals to the sane and the sane respond, revolutions
begin."

Pugh nodded his head, as if he agreed. "Your fanatic of course must be a
man of genius."

"Of course. And genius of that kind is happily rare. When it exists, its
possessor is the modern wizard. The old necromancer fiddled away with
cabalistic signs and crude chemicals and got nowhere; the true wizard is the
man who works by spirit on spirit. We are only beginning to realize the
strange crannies of the human soul. The real magician, if he turned up
to-day, wouldn't bother about drugs and dopes. He would dabble in far more
deadly methods, the compulsion of a fiery nature over the limp things that
men call their minds."

He turned to Pugh. "You remember the man we used to call Ram Dass in
the War—I never knew his right name?"

"Rather," said Pugh. "The fellow who worked for us in San Francisco. He
used to get big sums from the agitators and pay them into the British
Exchequer, less his commission of ten per cent."

"Stout fellow!" Durminster exclaimed approvingly.

"Well, Ram Dass used to discourse to me on this subject. He was as wise as
a serpent and as loyal as a dog, and he saw a lot of things coming that we are
just beginning to realize. He said that the great offensives of the future would
be psychological, and he thought the Governments should get busy about

it and prepare their defence. What a jolly sight it would be—all the high officials sitting down to little primers! But there was sense in what he said. He considered that the most deadly weapon in the world was the power of mass-persuasion, and he wanted to meet it at the source, by getting at the mass-persuader. His view was that every spell-binder had got something like Samson's hair which was the key of his strength, and that if this were tampered with he could be made innocuous. He would have had us make pets of the prophets and invite them to Government House. You remember the winter of 1917 when the Bolsheviks were making trouble in Afghanistan and their stuff was filtering through into India. Well, Ram Dass claimed the credit of stopping that game by his psychological dodges."

He looked across suddenly at Medina. "You know the Frontier. Did you ever come across the *guru* that lived at the foot of the Shansi pass as you go over to Kaikand?"

Medina shook his head. "I never travelled that way. Why?"

Sandy seemed disappointed. "Ram Dass used to speak of him. I hoped you might have met him."

The Club madeira was being passed round, and there was a little silence while we sipped it. It was certainly a marvellous wine, and I noticed with pain Medina's abstinence.

"You really are missing a lot, you know," Burminster boomed in his jolly voice, and for a second all the company looked Medina's way.

He smiled and lifted his glass of water.

"*Sit vini abstemius qui hermeneuma tentat aut hominum petit dominatum,*" he said.

Nightingale translated. "Meaning that you must be pussyfoot if you would be a big man."

There was a chorus of protests, and Medina again lifted his glass.

"I'm only joking. I haven't a scrap of policy or principle in the matter. I don't happen to like the stuff—that's all."

I fancy that the only two scholars among us were Nightingale and Sandy. I looked at the latter and was surprised by the change in his face. It had awakened to the most eager interest. His eyes, which had been staring at Medina, suddenly met mine, and I read in them not only interest but disquiet.

Burminster was delivering a spirited defence of Bacchus, and the rest joined in, but Sandy took the other side.

"There's a good deal in that Latin tag," he said. "There are places in the world where total abstinence is reckoned a privilege. Did you ever come across the Ulai tribe up the Karakoram way?" He was addressing Medina. "No? Well, the next time you meet a man in the Guides ask him about them, for they're a curiosity. They're Mohammedan and so should by rights be abstainers, but they're a drunken set of sweeps and the most priest-ridden community on earth. Drinking is not only a habit among them, it's an obligation, and their weekly *tamasha* would make Falstaff take the pledge. But their priests—they're a kind of theocracy—are strict teetotal. It's their privilege and the secret of their power. When one of them has to be degraded he is filled compulsorily full of wine. That's your—how does the thing go?—your '*hominum dominatus*'."

From that moment I found the evening go less pleasantly. Medina was as genial as ever, but something seemed to have affected Sandy's temper and he became positively grumpy. Now and then he contradicted a man too sharply for good manners, but for the most part he was silent, smoking his pipe and answering his neighbours in monosyllables. About eleven I began to feel it was time to leave, and Medina was of the same opinion. He asked me to walk with him, and I gladly accepted, for I did not feel inclined to go to bed.

As I was putting on my coat, Sandy came up. "Come to the Club, Dick," he said. "I want to talk to you." His manner was so peremptory that I opened my eyes.

"Sorry," I said. "I've promised to walk home with Medina."

"Oh, damn Medina!" he said. "Do as I ask or you'll be sorry for it."

I wasn't feeling very pleased with Sandy, especially as Medina was near enough to hear what he said. So I told him rather coldly that I didn't intend to go back on my arrangement. He turned and marched out, cannoning at the doorway into Burminster, to whom he did not apologize. That nobleman rubbed his shoulder ruefully. "Old Sandy hasn't got used to his corn yet," he laughed. "Looks as if the madeira had touched up his liver."

It was a fine still March night with a good moon, and as we walked along Piccadilly I was feeling cheerful. The good dinner I had eaten and the good wine I had drunk played their part in this mood, and there was also the satisfaction of having dined with good fellows and having been admitted into pretty select company. I felt my liking for Medina enormously increase, and I had the unworthy sense of superiority which a man gets from seeing an old friend whom he greatly admires behave rather badly. I was considering what had ailed Sandy when Medina raised the subject.

"A wonderful fellow Arbuthnot," he said. "I have wanted to meet him for years, and he is certainly up to my expectations. But he has been quite long enough abroad. A mind as keen as his, if it doesn't have the company of its equals, is in danger of getting viewy. What he said to-night was amazingly interesting, but I thought it a little fantastic."

I agreed, but the hint of criticism was enough to revive my loyalty. "All the same there's usually something in his most extravagant theories. I've seen him right when all the sober knowledgeable people were wrong."

"That I can well believe," he said. "You know him well?"

"Pretty well. We've been in some queer places together."

The memory of those queer places came back to me as we walked across Berkeley Square. The West End of London at night always affected me with a sense of the immense solidity of our civilization. These great houses, lit and shuttered and secure, seemed the extreme opposite of the world of half-lights and perils in which I had sometimes journeyed. I thought of them as I thought of Fosse Manor, as sanctuaries of peace. But to-night I felt differently towards them. I wondered what was going on at the back of those heavy doors. Might not terror and mystery lurk behind that barricade as well as in tent and slum? I suddenly had a picture of a plump face all screwed up with fright muffled beneath the bed-clothes.

I had imagined that Medina lived in chambers or a flat, but we stopped before a substantial house in Hill Street.

"You're coming in? The night's young and there's time for a pipe."

I had no wish to go to bed, so I followed him as he opened the front door with a latch-key. He switched on a light, which lit the first landing of the staircase but left the hall in dusk. It seemed to be a fine place full of cabinets, the gilding of which flickered dimly. We ascended thickly carpeted stairs, and on the landing he switched off the first light and switched on another which lit a further flight. I had the sensation of mounting to a great height in a queer shadowy world.

"This is a big house for a bachelor," I observed.

"I've a lot of stuff, books and pictures and things, and I like it round me."

He opened a door and ushered me into an enormous room, which must have occupied the whole space on that floor. It was oblong, with deep bays at each end, and it was lined from floor to ceiling with books. Books, too, were piled on the tables, and sprawled on a big flat couch which was drawn up before the fire. It wasn't an ordinary gentleman's library, provided by the bookseller at so much a yard. It was the working collection of a scholar, and the books had that used look which makes them the finest tapestry for a room. The place was lit with lights on small tables, and on a big desk under a reading-lamp were masses of papers and various volumes with paper slips in them. It was workshop as well as library.

A servant entered, unsummoned, and put a tray of drinks on a side-table. He was dressed like an ordinary butler, but I guessed that he had not spent much of his life in service. The heavy jowl, the small eyes, the hair cut straight round the nape of the neck, the swollen muscles about the shoulder and upper arm told me the profession he had once followed. The man had been in the ring, and not so very long ago. I wondered at Medina's choice, for a pug is not the kind of servant I would choose myself.

"Nothing more, Odell," said Medina. "You can go to bed. I will let Sir Richard out."

He placed me in a long armchair, and held the siphon while I mixed myself a very weak whisky-and-soda. Then he sat opposite me across the hearth-rug in a tall old-fashioned chair which he pulled forward from his writing-table. The servant in leaving had turned out all the lights except one at his right hand, which vividly lit up his face, and which, since the fire had burned low, made the only bright patch in the room.

I stretched my legs comfortably and puffed at my pipe, wondering how I would have the energy to get up and go home. The long dim shelves, where creamy vellum and morocco ran out of the dusk into darkness, had an odd effect on me. I was visited again by the fancies which had occupied me coming through Berkeley Square. I was inside one of those massive sheltered houses, and lo and behold! it was as mysterious as the aisles of a forest.

Books—books—old books full of forgotten knowledge! I was certain that if I had the scholarship to search the grave rows I would find out wonderful things.

I was thirsty, so I drank off my whisky-and-soda, and was just adding a little more soda-water from the siphon at my elbow, when I looked towards Medina. There was that in his appearance which made me move my glass so that a thin stream of liquid fell on my sleeve. The patch was still damp next morning.

His face, brilliantly lit up by the lamp, seemed to be also lit from within. It was not his eyes or any one feature that enthralled me, for I did not notice any details. Only the odd lighting seemed to detach his head from its environment so that it hung in the air like a planet in the sky, full of intense brilliance and power.

It is not very easy to write down what happened. For twelve hours afterwards I remembered nothing—only that I had been very sleepy, and must have been poor company and had soon got up to go. . . . But that was not the real story: it was what the man had willed that I should remember, and because my own will was not really mastered I remembered other things in spite of him; remembered them hazily, like a drunkard's dream.

The head seemed to swim in the centre of pale converging lines. These must have been the bookshelves, which in that part of the room were full of works bound in old vellum. My eyes were held by two violet pin-points of light which were so bright that they hurt me. I tried to shift my gaze, but I could only do that by screwing round my head towards the dying fire. The movement demanded a great effort, for every muscle in my body seemed drugged with lethargy.

As soon as I looked away from the light I regained some possession of my wits. I felt that I must be in for some sickness, and had a moment of bad fright. It seemed to be my business to keep my eyes on the shadows in the hearth, for where darkness was there I found some comfort. I was afraid of the light before me as a child of a bogy. I thought that if I said something I should feel better, but I didn't seem to have the energy to get a word out. Curiously enough, I felt no fear of Medina; he didn't seem to be in the business; it was that disembodied light that scared me.

Then I heard a voice speaking, but still I didn't think of Medina. "Hannay," it said. "You are Richard Hannay?"

Against my will I slewed my eyes round, and there hung that intolerable light burning into my eyeballs and my soul. I found my voice now, for it seemed to be screwed out of me, and I said "Yes" like an automaton.

I felt my wits and my senses slipping away under that glare. But my main discomfort was physical, the flaming control of the floating brightness—not face, or eyes, but a dreadful overmastering aura. I thought—if at that moment you could call any process of my mind thought—that if I could only link it on to some material thing I should find relief. With a desperate effort I seemed to make out the line of a man's shoulder and the back of a chair. Let me repeat that I never thought of Medina, for he had been wiped clean out of my world.

"You are Richard Hannay," said the voice. "Repeat, 'I am Richard Hannay'."

The words came out of my mouth involuntarily. I was concentrating all my wits on the comforting outline of the chair-back, which was beginning to be less hazy.

The voice spoke again.

"But till this moment you have been nothing. There was no Richard Hannay before. Now, when I bid you, you begin your life. You remember nothing. You have no past."

"I remember nothing," said my voice, but as I spoke I knew I lied and that knowledge was my salvation.

I have been told more than once by doctors who dabbled in the business that I was the most hopeless subject for hypnotism that they ever struck. One of them once said that I was about as unsympathetic as Table Mountain. I must suppose that the intractable bedrock of commonplaceness in me now met the something which was striving to master me and repelled it. I felt abominably helpless, my voice was not my own, my eyes were tortured and aching, but I had recovered my mind.

I seemed to be repeating a lesson at some one's dictation. I said I was Richard Hannay, who had just come from South Africa on his first visit to England. I knew no one in London, and had no friends. Had I heard of a Colonel Arbuthnot? I had not. Or the Thursday Club? I had not. Or the War? Yes, but I had been in Angola most of the time and had never fought. I had money? Yes, a fair amount, which was in such-and-such a bank and such-and-such investments. . . . I went on repeating the stuff as glibly as a parrot, but all the while I knew I lied. Something deep down in me was insisting that I was Sir Richard Hannay, K.C.B., who had commanded a division in France, and was the squire of Fosse Manor, the husband of Mary, and the father of Peter John.

Then the voice seemed to give orders. I was to do this and that, and I repeated them docilely. I was no longer in the least scared. Some one or something was trying to play monkey-tricks with my mind, but I was master of that, though my voice seemed to belong to an alien gramophone, and my limbs were stupidly weak. I wanted above all things to be allowed to sleep. . . .

I think I must have slept for a little, for my last recollection of that queer sederunt is that the unbearable light had gone, and the ordinary lamps of the room were switched on. Medina was standing by the dead fire, and another man beside him—a slim man with a bent back and a lean grey face. The second man was only there for a moment, but he looked at me closely and I thought Medina spoke to him and laughed. . . . Then I was being helped by Medina into my coat, and conducted downstairs. There were two bright lights in the street which made me want to lie down on the kerb and sleep. . . .

I woke about ten o'clock next morning in my bedroom at the Club, feeling like nothing on earth. I had a bad headache, my eyes seemed to be backed with white fire, and my legs were full of weak pains as if I had influenza. It took me several minutes to realize where I was, and when I wondered what had brought me to such a state I could remember nothing. Only a preposterous litany ran in my brain—the name "Dr. Newhover", and an address in Wimpole Street. I concluded glumly that that for a man in my condition was a useful recollection, but where I had got it I hadn't an idea.

The events of the night before were perfectly clear. I recalled every detail of the Thursday Club dinner, Sandy's brusqueness, my walk back with Medina, my admiration of his great library. I remembered that I had been drowsy there and thought that I had probably bored him. But I was utterly at a loss to account for my wretched condition. It could not have been the dinner; or the wine, for I had not drunk much, and in any case I have a head like cast iron; or the weak whisky-and-soda in Medina's house. I staggered to my feet and looked at my tongue in the glass. It was all right, so there could be nothing the matter with my digestion.

You are to understand that the account I have just written was pieced together as events came back to me, and that at 10 a.m. the next morning I remembered nothing of it—nothing but the incidents up to my sitting down in Medina's library, and the name and address of a doctor I have never heard of. I concluded that I must have got some infernal germ, probably botulism, and was in for a bad illness. I wondered dismally what kind of fool I had made of myself before Medina, and still more dismally what was going to happen to me. I decided to wire for Mary when I had seen a doctor, and to get as soon as possible into a nursing home. I had never had an illness in my life, except malaria, and I was as nervous as a cat.

But after I had had a cup of tea I felt a little better, and inclined to get up. A cold bath relieved my headache, and I was able to shave and dress. It was while I was shaving that I observed the first thing which made me puzzle about the events of the previous evening. The valet who attended to me had put out the contents of my pockets on the dressing-table—my keys, watch, loose silver, notecase, and my pipe and pouch. Now I carry my pipe in a little leather case, and being very punctilious in my habits, I invariably put it back in the case when it is empty. But the case was not there, though I remembered laying it on the table beside me in Medina's room, and moreover the pipe was still half full of unsmoked tobacco. I rang for the man, and learned that he had found the pipe in the pocket of my dinner jacket, but no case. He was positive, for he knew my ways and had been surprised to find my pipe so untidily pocketed.

I had a light breakfast in the coffee-room, and as I ate it I kept wondering as to what exactly I had been doing the night before. Odd little details were coming back to me; in particular, a recollection of some great effort which had taken all the strength out of me. Could I have been drugged? Not the Thursday Club madeira. Medina's whisky-and-soda? The idea was nonsense; in any case a drugged man does not have a clean tongue the next morning.

I interviewed the night porter, for I thought he might have something to tell me.

"Did you notice what hour I came home last night?" I asked.

"It was this morning, Sir Richard," the man replied, with the suspicion of a grin. "About half-past three it would be, or twenty minutes to four."

"God bless my soul!" I exclaimed. "I had no notion it was so late. I sat up talking with a friend."

"You must have been asleep in the car, Sir Richard, for the chauffeur had to wake you, and you were that drowsy I thought I'd better take you upstairs myself. The bedrooms on the top floor is not that easy found."

"I didn't drop a pipe-case?" I asked.

"No, sir." The man's discreet face revealed that he thought I had been dining too well but was not inclined to blame me for it.

By luncheon-time I had decided that I was not going to be ill, for there was no longer anything the matter with my body except a certain stiffness in the joints and the ghost of a headache behind my eyes. But my mind was in a precious confusion. I had stayed in Medina's room till after three, and had not been conscious of anything that happened there after, say, half-past eleven. I had left finally in such a state that I had forgotten my pipe-case, and had arrived at the Club in somebody's car—probably Medina's—so sleepy that I had to be escorted upstairs and had awoke so ill that I thought I had botulism. What in Heaven's name had happened?

I fancy that the fact that I had resisted the influence brought to bear on me with my *mind*, though tongue and limbs had been helpless, enabled me to remember what the wielder of the influence had meant to be forgotten. At any rate bits of that strange scene began to come back. I remembered the uncanny brightness—remembered it not with fear but with acute indignation. I vaguely recalled that I had repeated nonsense to somebody's dictation, but what it was I could not yet remember. The more I thought of it the angrier I grew. Medina must have been responsible, though to connect him with it seemed ridiculous when I thought of what I had seen of him. Had he been making me the subject of some scientific experiment? If so, it was infernal impertinence. Anyhow it had failed—that was a salve to my pride— for I had kept my head through it. The doctor had been right who had compared me with Table Mountain.

I had got thus far in my reflections, when I recollected that which put a different complexion on the business. Suddenly I remembered the circumstances in which I had made Medina's acquaintance. From him Tom Greenslade had heard the three facts which fitted in with the jingle which was the key to the mystery that I was sworn to unravel. Hitherto I had never thought of this dazzling figure except as an ally. Was it possible that he might be an enemy? The turn-about was too violent for my mind to achieve it in one movement. I swore to myself that Medina was straight, that it was sheer mania to believe that a gentleman and a sportsman could ever come within hailing distance of the hideous underworld which Macgillivray had revealed to me. . . . But Sandy had not quite taken to him. . . . I thanked my stars that anyhow I had said nothing to him about my job. I did not really believe that there was any doubt about him, but I realized that I must walk very carefully.

And then another idea came to me. Hypnotism had been tried on me, and it had failed. But those who tried it must believe from my behaviour that it had succeeded. If so, somehow and somewhere they would act on that belief. It was my business to encourage it. I was sure enough of myself to think, that now I was forewarned, no further hypnotic experiments could seriously affect me. But let them show their game, let me pretend to be helpless wax in their hands. Who "they" were I had still to find out.

I had a great desire to get hold of Sandy and talk it over, but though I rung up several of his lairs I could not find him. Then I decided to see Dr. Newhover, for I was certain that that name had come to me out of the medley of last night. So I telephoned and made an appointment with him for that afternoon, and four o'clock saw me starting out to walk to Wimpole Street.

60   THE HOUSE IN GOSPEL OAK

It was a dry March afternoon, with one of those fantastic winds which seem to change their direction hourly, and contrive to be in a man's face at every street corner. The dust was swirling in the gutters, and the scent of hyacinth and narcissus from the flower-shops was mingled with that bleak sandy smell which is London's foretaste of spring. As I crossed Oxford Street, I remember thinking what an odd pointless business I had drifted into. I saw nothing for it but to continue drifting and see what happened. I was on my way to visit a doctor of whom I knew nothing, about some ailment which I was not conscious of possessing. I didn't even trouble to make a plan, being content to let chance have the guiding of me.

The house was one of those solid dreary erections which have usually the names of half a dozen doctors on their front doors. But in this case there was only one—Dr. M. Newhover. The parlour-maid took me into the usual drab waiting-room furnished with Royal Academy engravings, fumed oak, and an assortment of belated picture-papers, and almost at once she returned and ushered me into the consulting-room. This again was of the most ordinary kind—glazed bookcases, wash-hand basin in a corner, roll-top desk, a table with a medical journal or two and some leather cases. And Dr. Newhover at first sight seemed nothing out of the common. He was a youngish man, with high cheek-bones, a high forehead, and a quantity of blond hair brushed straight back from it. He wore a *pince-nez*, and when he removed it showed pale prominent blue eyes. From his look I should have said that his father had called himself Neuhofer.

He greeted me with a manner which seemed to me to be at once patronizing and dictatorial. I wondered if he was some tremendous swell in his profession, of whom I ought to have heard. "Well, Mr. Hannay, what can I do for you?" he said. I noticed that he called me "Mr." though I had given "Sir Richard" both on the telephone and to the parlour-maid. It occurred to me that someone had already been speaking of me to him, and that he had got the name wrong in his memory.

I thought I had better expound the alarming symptoms with which I had awakened that morning.

"I don't know what's gone wrong with me," I said. "I've a pain behind my eyeballs, and my whole head seems muddled up. I feel drowsy and slack, and I've got a weakness in my legs and back like a man who has just had 'flu."

He made me sit down and proceeded to catechize me about my health. I said it had been good enough, but I mentioned my old malaria and several concussions, and I pretended to be pretty nervous about my condition. Then he went through the whole bag of tricks—sounding me with a stethoscope, testing my blood pressure, and hitting me hard below the knee to see if I reacted. I had to play up to my part, but upon my soul I came near to reacting too vigorously to some of his questions and boxing his ears. Always he kept up that odd, intimate, domineering, rather offensive manner.

He made me lie down on a couch while he fingered the muscles of my neck and shoulder and seemed to be shampooing my head with his long chilly hands. I was by this time feeling rather extra well, but I managed to invent little tendernesses here and there and a lot of alarming mental aberrations. I wondered if he were not getting suspicious, for he asked abruptly: "Have you had these symptoms long?" so I thought it better to return to the truth, and told him "only since this morning".

At last he bade me get up, took off the tortoiseshell spectacles he had been wearing and resumed his *pince-nez*, and while I was buttoning my collar seemed to be sunk in reflection. He made me sit in the patient's chair, and stood up and looked down at me with a magisterial air that made me want to laugh.

"You are suffering," he said, "from a somewhat abnormal form of a common enough complaint. Just as the effects of a concussion are often manifest only some days after the blow, so the results of nervous strain may take a long time to develop. I have no doubt that in spite of your good health you have during recent years been working your mind and body at an undue pressure, and now this morning quite suddenly you reap the fruits. I don't want to frighten you, Mr. Hannay, but neurosis is so mysterious a disease in its working that we must take it seriously, especially at its first manifestations. There are one or two points in your case which I am not happy about. There is, for example, a certain congestion—or what seems to me a congestion—in the nerve centres of the neck and head. That may be induced by the accidents—concussion and the like—which you have told me of, or it may not. The true cure must, of course, take time, and rest and change of scene are obligatory. You are fond of sport? A fisherman?"

I told him I was.

"Well, a little later I may prescribe a salmon river in Norway. The remoteness of the life from ordinary existence and the contemplation of swift running water have had wonderful results with some of my patients. But Norway is not possible till May, and in the meantime I am going to order you specific treatment. Yes. I mean massage, but by no means ordinary massage. That science is still in its infancy, and its practitioners are only fumbling at the doorway. But now and then we find a person, man or woman, with a kind of extra sense for disentangling and smoothing out muscular and nervous abnormalities. I am going to send you to such a one. The address may surprise you, but you are a man of the world enough to know that medical skill is not confined to the area between Oxford Street and the Marylebone Road." He took off his glasses, and smiled.

Then he wrote something on a slip of paper and handed it to me. I read "Madame Breda, 4 Palmyra Square, N.W."

"Right!" I said. "Much obliged to you. I hope Madame Breda will cure this infernal headache. When can I see her?"

"I can promise you she will cure the headache. She is a Swedish lady who has lived in London since the War, and is so much an enthusiast in her art that she will only now and then take a private patient. For the most part she gives her skill free to the children's hospitals. But she will not refuse me. As for beginning, I should lose no time for the sake of your own comfort. What about to-morrow morning?"

"Why not to-night? I have nothing to do, and I want to be quit of my headache before bedtime. Why shouldn't I go on there now?"

"No reason in the world. But I must make an appointment. Madame is on the telephone. Excuse me a moment."

He left the room, and returned in a few minutes to say that he had made an appointment for seven o'clock. "It is an outlandish place to get to, but most taxi-drivers know it. If your man doesn't, tell him to drive to Gospel Oak, and then any policeman will direct you."

I had my cheque-book with me, but he didn't want his fee, saying that he was not done with me. I was to come back in a week and report progress. As I left I had a strong impression of a hand as cold as a snake, pale bulging eyes, and cheek-bones like a caricature of a Scotsman. An odd but rather impressive figure was Dr. Newhover. He didn't look a fool, and if I hadn't known the uncommon toughness of my constitution I might have been unsettled by his forebodings.

I walked down to Oxford Street and had tea in a tea-shop. As I sat among the chattering typists and shop-boys I kept wondering whether I was not wasting my time and behaving like a jackass. Here was I, as fit as a hunter, consulting specialists and visiting unknown masseuses in North London, and all with no clear purpose. In less than twenty-four hours I had tumbled into a perfectly crazy world, and for a second I had a horrid doubt whether the craziness was not inside my mind. Had something given in my brain last night in Medina's room, so that now I was what people call "wanting"? I went over the sequence of events again, and was reassured by remembering that in it all I had kept my head. I had not got to the stage of making theories; I was still only waiting on developments, and I couldn't see any other way before me. I must, of course, get hold of Sandy; but first let me see what this massage business meant. It might all be perfectly square; I might have remembered Dr. Newhover's name by a queer trick of memory—heard it, perhaps, from some friend—and that remarkable practitioner might be quite honest. But then I remembered the man's manner—it was quite clear that he knew something of me, that some one had told him to expect me. Then it occurred to me that I might be doing a rash thing in going off to an unknown house in a seedy suburb. So I went into a public telephone-booth, rang up the Club, and told the porter that, if Colonel Arbuthnot called, I was at 4 Palmyra Square, N.W.— I made him write down the address—and would be back before ten o'clock.

I was rather short on exercise, so I decided to walk, since I had plenty of time. Strangely enough, the road was pretty much that which I had taken on that June day of 1914 when I had been waiting on Bullivant and the Black Stone gentry, and had walked clean out of London to pass the time.* Then, I remembered, I had been thrilling with wild anticipation, but now I was an older and much wiser man, and though I was sufficiently puzzled I could curb my restlessness with philosophy. I went up Portland Place, past the Regent's Park, till I left the houses of the well-to-do behind me, and got into that belt of mean streets which is the glacis of the northern heights. Various policemen directed me, and I enjoyed the walk as if I had been exploring, for London is always to me an undiscovered country. I passed yards which not so long ago had been patches of market-garden, and terraces, sometime pretentious, and now sinking into slums; for London is like the tropical bush—if you don't exercise constant care the jungle, in the shape of the slums, will break in. The streets were full of clerks and shop-girls waiting for buses, and workmen from the St. Pancras and Clerkenwell factories going home. The wind was rising, and in the untidy alleys was stirring up a noisome dust; but as the ground rose it blew cleaner and seemed to bring from Kentish fields and the Channel the tonic freshness of spring. I stopped for a little and watched behind me the plain of lights, which was London, quivering in the dark-blue windy dusk.

It was almost dark when at last, after several false casts, I came into Palmyra Square. It was a square only in name, for one side was filled with a warehouse of sorts, and another straggled away in nests of small brick houses. One side was a terrace of artisans' dwellings, quite new, each with a tiny bow-window and names like "Chatsworth" and "Kitchener Villa". The fourth side, facing south, had once had a certain dignity, and the builder who had designed the place seventy years ago had thought, no doubt, that he was creating a desirable residential quarter. There the houses stood apart, each in a patch of garden, which may at one time have had lawns and flowers. Now these gardens were mere dusty yards, the refuge of tin cans and bits of paper, and only a blackened elm, an ill-grown privet hedge, and some stunted lilacs

* See *The Thirty-nine Steps*.

told of the more cheerful past. On one house was the brass plate of a doctor, on another that of a teacher of music; several advertised lodgings to let; the steps were untidy, the gates askew on their hinges, and over everything was written the dreary legend of a shabby gentility on the very brink of squalor.

No. 4 was smarter than the others, and its front door had been newly painted a vivid green. I rang the bell, which was an electric one, and the door was opened by a maid who looked sufficiently respectable. When I entered I saw that the house was on a more generous scale than I had thought, and had once, no doubt, been the home of some comfortable citizen. The hall was not the tank-like thing of the small London dwelling, and the room into which I was ushered, though small, was well furnished and had an electric fire in the grate. It seemed to be a kind of business room, for there was a telephone, a big safe, and on the shelves a line of lettered boxes for papers. I began to think that Madame Breda, whoever she might be, must be running a pretty prosperous show on ordinary business lines.

I was presently led by the maid to a room on the other side of the hall, where I was greeted by a smiling lady. Madame was a plump person in the early forties, with dark hair and a high colour, who spoke English almost without an accent.

"Dr. Newhover has sent you. So? He has told me. Will you please go in there and take off your coat and waistcoat? Your collar, too, please."

I did as I was bid, and in a little curtained cubicle divested myself of these garments and returned in my shirt sleeves. The room was a very pleasant one, with folding doors at one end, furnished like an ordinary drawing-room, with flowers in pots, and books, and what looked like good eighteenth-century prints. Any suspicion I may have had of the *bona fides* of the concern received a rude shock. Madame had slipped over her black dress a white linen overall, such as surgeons wear, and she had as her attendant a thin, odd-looking little girl, who also wore an overall, and whose short hair was crowned with a small white cap.

"This is Gerda," Madame said. "Gerda helps me. She is very clever." She smiled on Gerda, and Gerda smiled back, a limp little contortion of a perfectly expressionless face.

Madame made me lie down on a couch. "You have a headache?"

I mendaciously said that I had.

"That I can soon cure. But there are other troubles? So? These I must explore. But first I will take away the pain."

I felt her light firm fingers playing about my temples and the base of my skull and my neck muscles. A very pleasant sensation it was, and I am certain that if I had been suffering from the worst headache in the world it would have been spirited away. As it was, being in excellent health, I felt soothed and freshened.

"So," she said, beaming down on me. "You are better? You are so beeg that it is not easy to be well all over at once. Now, I must look into more difficult things. You are not happy in your nerves—not altogether. Ah! these nerves! We do not quite know what they are, except that they are what you call the devil. You are very wakeful now. Is it not so? Well, I must put you to sleep. That is necessary, if you are willing."

"Right-o," I answered; but inwardly I said to myself, "No, my woman, I bet you don't." I was curious to see if, now that I was forewarned, I could resist any hypnotic business, as I believed I could.

I imagined that she would try to master me with her eyes, which were certainly remarkable orbs. But her procedure was the very opposite, for the small girl brought some things on a tray, and I saw that they were bandages. First of all, with a fine cambric handkerchief, she swathed my eyes, and then tied above it another of some heavy opaque material. They were loosely bound, so that I scarcely felt them, but I was left in the thickest darkness. I noticed that she took special pains so to adjust them that they should not cover my ears.

"You are not wakeful," I heard her voice say; "I think you are sleepy. You will sleep now."

I felt her fingers stray over my face, and the sensation was different, for whereas, when she had treated my headache, they had set up a delicious cool tingling of the skin, now they seemed to induce wave upon wave of an equally pleasant languor. She pressed my forehead, and my senses seemed to be focused there and to be lulled by that presence. All the while she was cooing to me in a voice which was like the drowsy swell of the sea. If I had wanted to go to sleep I could have dropped off easily, but, as I didn't want to, I had no difficulty in resisting the gentle coercion. That, I fancy, is my position about hypnotism. I am no kind of use under compulsion, and for the thing to affect me it has to have the backing of my own will. Anyhow I could appreciate the pleasantness of it and yet disregard it. But it was my business to be a good subject, so I pretended to drift away into slumber. I made my breath come slowly and softly, and let my body relax into impassivity.

Presently she appeared to be satisfied. She said a word to the child, whose feet I could hear cross the room. There was a sound of opening doors—my ears, remember, were free of the bandages and my hearing is acute—and then it seemed to me that the couch on which I lay began slowly to move. I had a moment of alarm and nearly gave away the show by jerking up my head. The couch seemed to travel very smoothly on rails, and I was conscious that I had passed through the folding doors and was now in another room. Then the movement stopped, and I realized that I was in an entirely different atmosphere. I realized, too, that a new figure had come on the scene.

There was no word spoken, but I had the queer inexplicable consciousness of human presences which is independent of sight and hearing. I have said that the atmosphere of the place had changed. There was a scent in the air which anywhere else I would have sworn was due to peat smoke, and mixed with it another intangible savour which I could not put a name to, but which did not seem to belong to London at all, or to any dwelling, but to some wild out-of-doors. . . . And then I was aware of noiseless fingers pressing my temples.

They were not the plump capable hands of Madame Breda. Nay, they were as fine and tenuous as a wandering wind, but behind their airy lightness was a hint of steel, as if they could choke as well as caress. I lay supine, trying to keep my breathing regular, since I was supposed to be asleep, but I felt an odd excitement rising in my heart. And then it quieted, for the fingers seemed to be smoothing it away. . . . A voice was speaking in a tongue of which I knew not a word, not speaking to me, but repeating, as it were, a private incantation. And the touch and voice combined to bring me nearer to losing my wits than even on the night before, nearer than I have ever been in all my days.

The experience was so novel and overpowering that I find it hard to give even a rough impression of it. Let me put it this way. A man at my time of life sees old age not so very far distant, and the nearer he draws to the end of his journey the more ardently he longs for his receding youth. I do not mean that, if some fairy granted him the gift, he would go back to boyhood; few of us would choose such a return; but he clothes all his youth in a happy radiance and aches to recapture the freshness and wonder with which he then looked on life. He treasures, like a mooning girl, stray sounds and scents and corners of landscape, which for a moment push the door ajar. . . . As I lay blindfolded on that couch I felt mysterious hands and voices plucking on my behalf at the barrier of the years and breaking it down. I was escaping into a delectable country, the Country of the Young, and I welcomed the escape. Had I been hypnotized, I should beyond doubt have moved like a sheep whithersoever this shepherd willed.

But I was awake, and, though on the very edge of surrender, I managed to struggle above the tides. Perhaps to my waking self the compulsion was too obvious and aroused a faint antagonism. Anyhow I had already begun a conscious resistance when the crooning voice spoke in English.

"You are Richard Hannay," it said. "You have been asleep, but I have wakened you. You are happy in the world in which you have wakened?"

My freedom was now complete, for I had begun to laugh, silently, far down at the bottom of my heart. I remembered last night, and the performance in Medina's house which had all day been growing clearer in my memory. I saw it as farce, and this as farce, and at the coming of humour the spell died. But it was up to me to make some kind of an answer, if I wanted to keep up the hoax, so I did my best to screw out an eerie sleep-walker's voice.

"I am happy," I said, and my pipe sounded like the twittering of sheeted ghosts.

"You wish to wake often in this world?"

I signified by a croak that I did.

"But to wake you must first sleep, and I alone can make you sleep and wake. I exact a price, Richard Hannay. Will you pay my price?"

I was puzzled about the voice. It had not the rich foreign tones of Madame Breda, but it had a very notable accent, which I could not place. At one moment it seemed to have a lilt which you find in Western Ross, but there were cadences in it which were not Highland. Also, its *timbre* was curious— very light and thin like a child's. Was it possible that the queer little girl I had seen was the sibyl? No, I decided; the hands had not been a child's hands.

"I will pay the price," I said, which seemed to be the answer required of me.

"Then you are my servant when I summon you. Now, sleep again."

I had never felt less like being any one's servant. The hands fluttered again around my temples, but they had no more effect on me than the buzzing of flies. I had an insane desire to laugh, which I repressed by thinking of the idiotic pointlessness of my recent doings. . . . I felt my couch slide backwards and heard the folding doors open again and close. Then I felt my bandages being deftly undone, and I lay with the light on my closed eyelids, trying to look like a sleeping warrior on a tomb. Some one was pressing below my left ear, and I recognized the old hunter's method of bringing a man back gently from sleep to consciousness, so I set about the job of making a workmanlike awaking. I hope I succeeded. Anyhow I must have looked dazed enough, for the lamps hurt my eyes after the muffled darkness.

I was back in the first room, with only Madame beside me. She beamed on me with the friendliest eyes, and helped me on with my coat and collar. "I have had you under close observation," she said, "for sleep often reveals where the ragged ends of the nerves lie. I have made certain deductions, which I will report to Dr. Newhover. . . . No, there is no fee. Dr. Newhover will make arrangements." She bade me good-bye in the best professional manner, and I descended the steps into Palmyra Square as if I had been spending a commonplace hour having my back massaged for lumbago.

Once in the open air I felt abominably tired and very hungry. By good luck I hadn't gone far when I picked up a taxi and told it to drive to the Club. I looked at my watch and saw that it was later than I thought—close on ten o'clock. I had been several hours in the house, and small wonder I was weary.

I found Sandy wandering restlessly about the hall. "Thank God," he said when he saw me. "Where the devil have you been, Dick? The porter gave me a crazy address in North London. You look as if you wanted a drink."

"I feel as if I wanted food," I said. "I have a lot to tell you, but I must eat first. I've had no dinner."

Sandy sat opposite me while I fed, and forbore to ask questions.

"What put you in such a bad humour last night?" I asked.

He looked very solemn. "Lord knows. No, that's not true. I know well enough. I didn't take to Medina."

"Now I wonder why?"

"I wonder too. But I'm just like a dog: I take a dislike to certain people at first sight, and the queer thing is that my instinct isn't often wrong."

"Well, you're pretty well alone in your opinion. What sets you against him? He is well-mannered, modest, a good sportsman, and you can see he's as clever as they make."

"Maybe. But I've got a notion that the man is one vast lie. However, let's put it that I reserve my opinion. I have various inquiries to make."

We found the little back smoking-room on the first floor empty, and when I had lit my pipe and got well into an armchair, Sandy drew up another at my elbow. "Now, Dick," he said.

"First," I said, "it may interest you to learn that Medina dabbles in hypnotism."

"I know that," he said, "from his talk last night."

"How on earth—?"

"Oh, from a casual quotation he used. It's a longish story, which I'll tell you later. Go on."

I began from the break-up of the Thursday Club dinner, and told him all I could remember of my hours in Medina's house. As a story it met with an immense success. Sandy was so interested that he couldn't sit in his chair, but must get up and stand on the hearth-rug before me. I told him that I had wakened up feeling uncommonly ill, with a blank mind except for the address of a doctor-man in Wimpole Street, and how during the day recollection had gradually come back to me. He questioned me like a cross-examining counsel.

"Bright light—ordinary hypnotic property. Face, which seemed detached —that's a common enough thing in Indian magic. You say you must have been asleep, but were also in a sense awake and could hear and answer questions, and that you felt a kind of antagonism all the time which kept your will alive. You're probably about the toughest hypnotic proposition in the world, Dick, and you can thank God for that. Now, what were the questions? A summons to forget your past and begin as a new creature, subject to the authority of a master. You assented, making private reservations of which the hypnotist knew nothing. If you had not kept your head and made those reservations, you would have remembered nothing at all of last night, but there would have been a subconscious bond over your will. As it is, you're perfectly free; only the man who tried to monkey with you doesn't know that. Therefore you begin by being one up in the game. You know where you are and he doesn't know where he is."

"What do you suppose Medina meant by it? It was infernal impertinence anyhow. But was it Medina? I seem to remember another man in the room before I left."

"Describe him."

"I've only a vague picture—a sad grey-faced fellow."

"Well, assume for the present that the experimenter was Medina. There's such a thing, remember, as spiriting away a man's recollection of his past, and starting him out as a waif in a new world. I've heard in the East of such performances, and of course it means that the memory-less being is at the mercy of the man who has stolen his memory. That is probably not the intention in your case. They wanted only to establish a subconscious control. But it couldn't be done at once with a fellow of your antecedents, so they organized a process. They suggested to you in your trance a doctor's name, and the next stage was his business. You woke feeling very seedy and remembering a doctor's address, and they argued that you would think that you had been advised about the fellow and make a bee-line for him. Remember, they would assume that you had no recollection of anything else from the night's doings. Now go ahead and tell me about the chirurgeon. Did you go to see him?"

I continued my story, and at the Wimpole Street episode Sandy laughed long and loud.

"Another point up in the game. You say you think the leech had been advised of your coming and not by you? By the way, he seems to have talked fairly good sense, but I'd as soon vet a hippopotamus for nerves as you." He wrote down Dr. Newhover's address in his pocket-book. "*Continuez.* You then proceeded, I take it, to 4 Palmyra Square."

At the next stage in my narrative he did not laugh. I daresay I told it better than I have written it down here, for I was fresh from the experience, and I could see that he was a good deal impressed.

"A Swedish masseuse and an odd-looking little girl. She puts you to sleep, or thinks she has, and then, when your eyes are bandaged, some one else nearly charms the soul out of you. That sounds big magic. I see the general lines of it, but it is big magic, and I didn't know that it was practised on these shores. Dick, this is getting horribly interesting. You kept wide awake—you are an old buffalo, you know—but you gave the impression of absolute surrender. Good for you—you are now three points ahead in the game."

"Well, but what is the game? I'm hopelessly puzzled."

"So am I, but we must work on assumptions. Let us suppose Medina is responsible. He may be only trying to find out the extent of his powers, and selects you as the most difficult subject to be found. You may be sure he knows all about your record. He may be only a vain man experimenting."

"In which case," I said, "I propose to punch his head."

"In which case, as you justly observe, you will give yourself the pleasure of punching his head. But suppose that he has got a far deeper purpose, something really dark and damnable. If by his hypnotic power he could make a tool of you, consider what an asset he would have found. A man of your ability and force. I have always said, you remember, that you had a fine natural talent for crime."

"I tell you, Sandy, that's nonsense. It's impossible that there's anything wrong—badly wrong—with Medina."

"Improbable, but not impossible. We're taking no chances. And if he were a scoundrel, think what a power he might be with all his talents and charm and popularity."

Sandy flung himself into a chair and appeared to be meditating. Once or twice he broke silence.

"I wonder what Dr. Newhover meant by talking of a salmon river in Norway. Why not golf at North Berwick?"

And again:

"You say there was a scent like peat in the room? Peat! You are certain?"

Finally he got up. "To-morrow," he said, "I think I will have a look round the house in Gospel Oak. Gospel Oak, by the way, is a funny name, isn't it? You say it has electric light. I will visit it as a man from the corporation to see about the meter. Oh, that can easily be managed. Macgillivray will pass the word for me."

The mention of Macgillivray brought me to attention. "Look here," I said, "I'm simply wasting my time. I got in touch with Medina in order to ask his help, and now I've been landed in a set of preposterous experiences which have nothing to do with my job. I must see Macgillivray to-morrow about getting alongside his Shropshire squire. For the present there can be nothing doing with Medina."

"Shropshire squire be hanged! You're an old ass, Dick. For the present there's everything doing with Medina. You wanted his help. Why? Because he was the next stage in the clue to that nonsensical rhyme. Well, you've discovered that there may be odd things about him. You can't get his help, but you may get something more. You may get the secret itself. Instead of having to burrow into his memory, as you did with Greenslade, you may find it sticking out of his life."

"Do you really believe that?" I asked in some bewilderment.

"I believe nothing as yet. But it is far the most promising line. He thinks that from what happened last night *plus* what happened two hours ago you are under his influence, an acolyte, possibly a tool. It may be all quite straight, or it may be most damnably crooked. You have got to find out. You must keep close to him, and foster his illusions, and play up to him for all you're worth. He is bound to show his hand. You needn't take any steps on your own account. He'll give you the lead all right."

I can't say I liked the prospect, for I have no love for play-acting, but I am bound to admit that Sandy talked sense. I asked him about himself, for I counted on his backing more than I could say.

"I propose to resume my travels," he said. "I wish to pursue my studies in the Bibliothèque Nationale of France."

"But I thought you were with me in this show."

"So I am. I go abroad on your business, as I shall explain to you some day. Also I want to see the man whom we used to call Ram Dass. I believe him to be in Munich at this moment. The day after to-morrow you will read in *The Times* that Colonel the Master of Clanroyden has gone abroad for an indefinite time on private business."

"How long will you be away?" I groaned.

"A week perhaps, or a fortnight—or more. And when I come back it may not be as Sandy Arbuthnot."

61 SOME EXPERIENCES OF A DISCIPLE

I didn't see Sandy again, for he took the night train for Paris next evening, and I had to go down to Oxford that day to appear as a witness in a running-down case. But I found a note for me at the Club when I got back the following morning. It contained nothing except these words: *"Coverts drawn blank, no third person in house."* I had not really hoped for anything from Sandy's expedition to Palmyra Square, and thought no more about it.

He didn't return in a week, nor yet in a fortnight, and, realizing that I had only a little more than two months to do my job in, I grew very impatient. But my time was pretty well filled with Medina, as you shall hear.

While I was reading Sandy's note Turpin turned up and begged me to come for a drive in his new Delage and talk to him. The Marquis de la Tour du Pin, was, if possible, more pallid than before, his eyelids heavier, and his gentleness more silken. He drove me miles into the country, away through Windsor Forest, and as we raced at sixty miles an hour he uncovered his soul. He was going mad, it seemed; was, indeed, already mad, and only a slender and doubtless ill-founded confidence in me prevented him shooting himself. He was convinced that Adela Victor was dead, and that no trace of her would ever be found. "These policemen of yours—bah!" he moaned. "Only in England can people vanish." He concluded, however, that he would stay alive till he had avenged her, for he believed that a good God would some day deliver her murderer into his hands. I was desperately sorry for him, for behind his light gasconading manner there were marks of acute suffering, and indeed in his case I think I should have gone crazy. He asked me for hope, and I gave him it, and told him what I did not believe—that I saw light in the business, and had every confidence that we would restore him his sweetheart safe and sound. At that he cheered up and wanted to embrace me, thereby jolly nearly sending the Delage into a ditch and us both into eternity. He was burning for something to do, and wanted me to promise that as soon as possible I would inspan him into my team. That made me feel guilty, for I knew I had no team, and nothing you could call a clue; so I talked hastily about Miss Victor, lest he should ask me more.

I had her portrait drawn for me in lyric prose. She was slight, it seemed, middling tall, could ride like Diana and dance like the nymphs. Her colouring and hair were those of a brunette, but her eyes were a deep grey, and she had the soft voice which commonly goes with such eyes. Turpin, of course, put all this more poetically, relapsing frequently into French. He told me all kinds of things about her—how she was crazy about dogs, and didn't fear anything in the world, and walked with a throw-out, and lisped delightfully when she was excited. Altogether at the end of it I felt I had a pretty good notion of Miss Victor, especially as I had studied about fifty photographs of her in Macgillivray's room.

As we were nearing home again it occurred to me to ask him if he knew Medina. He said no, but that he was dining at the Victors' that evening—a small dinner-party, mostly political. "He is wonderful, that Mr. Victor. He will not change his life, and his friends think Adela is in New York, for a farewell visit. He is like the Spartan boy with the fox."

"Tell Mr. Victor, with my compliments," I said, "that I would like to dine there to-night. I have a standing invitation. Eight-fifteen, isn't it?"

It turned out to be a very small and select party—the Foreign Secretary,

Medina, Palliser-Yeates, the Duke of Alcester, Lord Sunningdale the ex-Lord Chancellor, Levasseur the French Minister, besides Turpin and myself. There were no women present. The behaviour of the Duke and Mr. Victor was a lesson in fortitude, and you would never have guessed that these two men were living with a nightmare. It was not a talkative assembly, though Sunningdale had a good deal to say to the table about a new book that a German had written on the mathematical conception of infinity, a subject which even his brilliant exposition could not make clear to my thick wits. The Foreign Secretary and Levasseur had a *tête-à-tête*, with Turpin as a hanger-on, and the rest of us would have been as dull as sticks if it had not been for Medina. I had a good chance of observing his quality, and I must say I was astonished at his skill. It was he who by the right kind of question turned Sunningdale's discourse on infinity, which would otherwise have been a pedantic monologue, into good conversation. We got on to politics afterwards, and Medina, who had just come from the House, was asked what was happening.

"They had just finished the usual *plat du jour*, the suspension of a couple of Labour mountebanks," he said.

This roused Sunningdale, who rather affected the Labour party, and I was amused to see how Medina handled the ex-Chancellor. He held him in good-humoured argument, never forsaking his own position, but shedding about the whole subject an atmosphere of witty and tolerant understanding. I felt that he knew more about the business than Sunningdale, that he knew so much he could afford to give his adversary rope. Moreover, he never forgot that he was at a dinner-table, the pitch and key of his talk were exactly right, and he managed to bring every one into it.

To me he was extraordinarily kind. Indeed he treated me like a very ancient friend, bantering and affectionate and yet respectful, and he forced me to take a full share in the conversation. Under his stimulus, I became quite intelligent, and amazed Turpin, who had never credited me with any talents except for fighting. But I had not forgotten what I was there for, and if I had been inclined to, there were the figures of Victor and the Duke to remind me. I watched the two, the one thin, grey-bearded, rather like an admiral with his vigilant dark eyes, the other heavy-jowled, rubicund, crowned with fine silver hair; in both I saw shadows of pain stealing back to the corners of lip and eye, whenever the face was in repose. And Medina— the very *beau idéal* of a courteous, kindly, open-air Englishman. I noted how in his clothes he avoided any touch of overdressing, no fancifully cut waist-coat or too-smartly-tied tie. In manner and presence he was the perfection of un-self-conscious good breeding. It was my business to play up to him, and I let my devotion be pretty evident. The old Duke, whom I now met for the first time, patted my shoulder as we left the dining-room. "I am glad to see that you and Medina are friends, Sir Richard. Thank God that we have a man like him among the young entry. They ought to give him office at once, you know, get him inside the shafts of the coach. Otherwise he'll find something more interesting to do than politics."

By tacit consent we left the house together, and I walked the streets by his side, as I had done three nights before. What a change, I reflected, in my point of view! Then I had been blind, now I was acutely watchful. He slipped an arm into mine as we entered Pall Mall, but its pressure did not seem so much friendly as possessive.

"You are staying at your Club?" he said. "Why not take up your quarters with me, while you are in town? There's ample room in Hill Street."

The suggestion put me into a fright. To stay with him at present would wreck all my schemes; but, supposing he insisted, could I refuse, if it was my rôle to appear to be under his domination? Happily he did not insist. I made a lot of excuses—plans unsettled, constantly running down to the country, and so on.

"All right. But some day I may make the offer again, and then I'll take no refusal."

They were just the kind of words a friend might have used, but somehow, though the tone was all right, they slightly grated on me.

"How are you?" he asked. "Most people who have led your life find the English spring trying. You don't look quite as fit as when I first saw you."

"No. I've been rather seedy this past week—headachy, loss of memory, stuffed-up brain and that sort of thing. I expect it's the spring fret. I've seen a doctor and he doesn't worry about it."

"Who's your man?"

"A chap Newhover in Wimpole Street."

He nodded. "I've heard of him. They tell me he's good."

"He has ordered me massage," I said boldly. "That cures the headaches anyway."

"I'm glad to hear it."

Then he suddenly released my arm.

"I see Arbuthnot has gone abroad."

There was a coldness in his voice to which I hastened to respond.

"So I saw in the papers," I said carelessly. "He's a hopeless fellow. A pity, for he's able enough; but he won't stay put, and that makes him pretty useless."

"Do you care much for Arbuthnot?"

"I used to," I replied shamelessly. "But till the other day I hadn't seen him for years, and I must say he has grown very queer. Didn't you think he behaved oddly at the Thursday dinner?"

He shrugged his shoulders. "I wasn't much taken by him. He's too infernally un-English. I don't know how he got it, but there seems to be a touch of the shrill Levantine in him. Compare him with those fellows to-night. Even the Frenchmen—even Victor, though he's an American and a Jew—are more our own way of thinking."

We were at the Club door, and as I stopped he looked me full in the face.

"If I were you I wouldn't have much to do with Arbuthnot," he said, and in his tone was a command. I grinned sheepishly, but my fingers itched for his ears.

I went to bed fuming. This new possessory attitude, this hint of nigger-driving, had suddenly made me hate Medina. I had been unable to set down the hypnotist business clearly to his account, and, even if I had been certain, I was inclined to think it only the impertinent liberty of a faddist—a thing which I hotly resented but which did not arouse my serious dislike. But now—to feel that he claimed me as his man, because he thought, no doubt, that he had established some unholy power over me—that fairly broke my temper. And his abuse of Sandy put the lid on it—abuse to which I had been shamefully compelled to assent. Levantine, by gad! I swore that Sandy and I would make him swallow that word before he was much older. I couldn't sleep for thinking about it. By this time I was perfectly willing to believe that Medina was up to any infamy, and I was resolved that in him and him alone lay the key to the riddle of the three hostages. But all the time I was miserably conscious that if I suggested such an idea to any one except Sandy I should be set down as a lunatic. I could see that the man's repute was as solidly planted as the British Constitution.

Next morning I went to see Macgillivray. I explained that I had not been idle, that I had been pursuing lines of my own, which I thought more hopeful than his suggestion of getting alongside the Shropshire squire. I said I had nothing as yet to report, and that I didn't propose to give him the faintest notion of what I was after till I had secured some results. But I wanted his help, and I wanted his very best men.

"Glad to see you've got busy, Dick," he said. "I await your commands."

"I want a house watched. No. 4 Palmyra Square, up in North London. So far as I know it is occupied by a woman, who purports to be a Swedish masseuse, and calls herself Madame Breda, one or more maids, and an odd-looking little girl. I want you to have a close record kept of the people who go there, and I want especially to know who exactly are the inmates of the house and who are the most frequent visitors. It must be done very cautiously, for the people must have no suspicion that they are being spied on."

He wrote down the details.

"Also I want you to find out the antecedents of Medina's butler."

He whistled. "Medina. Dominick Medina, you mean?"

"Yes. Oh, I'm not suspecting *him*." We both laughed, as if at a good joke. "But I should like to hear something about his butler, for reasons which I'm not yet prepared to give you. He answers to the name of Odell, and has the appearance of an inferior prize-fighter. Find out all you can about his past, and it mightn't be a bad plan to have him shadowed. You know Medina's house in Hill Street. But for Heaven's sake, let it be done tactfully."

"I'll see to that for my own sake. I don't want head-lines in the evening papers—'House of Member of Parliament Watched. Another Police Muddle'."

"Also, could you put together all you can get about Medina? It might give me a line on Odell."

"Dick," he said solemnly, "are you growing fantastic?"

"Not a bit of it. You don't imagine I'm ass enough to think there's anything shady about Medina. He and I have become bosom friends, and I like him enormously. Everybody swears by him, and so do I. But I have my doubts about Mr. Odell, and I would like to know just how and where Medina picked him up. He's not the ordinary stamp of butler." It seemed to me very important to let no one but Sandy into the Medina business at present, for our chance lay in his complete confidence that all men thought well of him.

"Right," said Macgillivray. "It shall be done. Go your own way, Dick. I won't attempt to dictate to you. But remember that the thing is desperately serious, and that the days are slipping past. We're in April now, and you have only till midsummer to save three innocent lives."

I left his office feeling very solemn, for I had suddenly a consciousness of the shortness of time and the magnitude of the job which I had not yet properly begun. I cudgelled my brains to think of my next step. In a few days I should again visit Dr. Newhover, but there was not likely to be much assistance there. He might send me back to Palmyra Square, or I might try to make an appointment with Madame Breda myself, inventing some new ailment; but I would only find the same old business, which would get me no further forward. As I viewed it, the Newhover and Palmyra Square episodes had been used only to test my submission to Medina's influence, and it was to Medina that I must look for further light. It was a maddening job to sit and wait and tick off the precious days on the calendar, and I longed to consult with Sandy. I took to going down to Fosse for the day, for the sight of Mary and Peter John somehow quieted my mind and fixed my resolution. It was a positive relief when at the end of the week Medina rang me up and asked me to luncheon.

We lunched at his house, which, seen on a bright April day, was a wonderful treasury of beautiful things. It was not the kind of house I fancied myself, being too full of museum pieces, and all the furniture strictly correct according to period. I like rooms in which there is a pleasant jumble of things, and which look as if homely people had lived in them for generations. The dining-room was panelled in white, with a Vandyck above the mantel-piece and a set of gorgeous eighteenth-century prints on the walls. At the excellent meal Medina as usual drank water, while I obediently sampled an old hock, an older port, and a most prehistoric brandy. Odell was in attendance, and I had a good look at him— his oddly shaped head, his flat sallow face, the bunches of black eyebrow above his beady eyes. I calculated that if I saw him again I would not fail to recognize him. We never went near the library on the upper floor, but sat after luncheon in a little smoking-room at the back of the hall, which held my host's rods and guns in glass cabinets, and one or two fine heads of deer and ibex.

I had made up my mind, as I walked to Hill Street, that I was going to convince Medina once and for all of the abjectness of my surrender. He should have proof that I was clay in his hands, for only that way would he fully reveal himself. I detested the job, and as I walked through the pleasant crisp noon-tide I reflected with bitterness that I might have been fishing for salmon in Scotland, or, better still, cantering with Mary over the Cotswold downs.

All through luncheon I kept my eyes fixed on him like a dog's on his master. Several times I wondered if I were not overdoing it, but he seemed to accept my homage as quite natural. I had thought when I first met him that the man had no vanity; now I saw that he had mountains of it, that he was all vanity, and that his public modesty was only a cloak to set off his immense private conceit. He unbent himself, his whole mind was in undress, and behind the veneer of good-fellowship I seemed to see a very cold arrogant soul. Nothing worse, though that was bad enough. He was too proud to boast in words, but his whole attitude was one long brag. He was cynical about everything, except, as I suspected, his private self-worship. The thing would have been monstrously indecent, if it had not been done with such consummate skill. Indeed I found my part easy to play, for I was deeply impressed and had no difficulty in showing it.

The odd thing was that he talked a good deal about myself. He seemed to take pains to rout out the codes and standards, the points of honour and points of conduct, which somebody like me was likely to revere, and to break them down with his cynicism. I felt that I was looking on at an attempt, which the Devil is believed to specialize in, to make evil good and good evil. . . . Of course I assented gladly. Never had master a more ready disciple. . . . He broke down, too, my modest ambitions. A country life, a wife and family —he showed that they were too trivial for more than a passing thought. He flattered me grossly, and I drank it all in with a silly face. I was fit for bigger things, to which he would show me the way. He sketched some of the things— very flattering they were and quite respectable, but somehow they seemed out of the picture when compared to his previous talk. He was clearly initiating me step by step into something for which I was not yet fully ready. . . . I wished Sandy could have seen me sitting in Medina's armchair, smoking one of his cigars, and agreeing to everything he said like a schoolgirl who wants to keep on the good side of her schoolmistress. And yet I didn't find it difficult, for the man's talk was masterly and in its way convincing, and, while my mind repudiated it, it was easy for my tongue to assent. He was in a prodigious good-humour, and he was kindly, as a keeper is kind to a well-broken dog.

On the doorstep I stammered my thanks. "I wish I could tell you what knowing you means to me. It's—it's far the biggest thing in my life. What I mean to say is—" the familiar patois of the tongue-tied British soldier.

He looked at me with those amazing eyes of his, no kindness in them, only patronage and proprietorship. I think he was satisfied that he had got some one who would serve him body and soul.

I, too, was satisfied, and walked away feeling more cheerful than I had done for days. Surely things would begin to move now, I thought. At the Club, too, I got encouragement in the shape of a letter from Sandy. It bore a French postmark which I could not decipher, and it was the merest scribble, but it greatly heartened me.

"*I have made progress,*" it ran, "*but I have still a lot to do and we can't talk to each other yet awhile. But I shall have to send you letters occasionally, which you must burn on receipt. I shall sign them with some letter of the Greek alphabet—no, you wouldn't recognize that—with the names of recent Derby winners. Keep our affair secret as the grave—don't let in a soul, not even Mac. And for God's sake stick close to M. and serve him like a slave.*"

There wasn't much in it, but it was hopeful, though the old ruffian didn't seem in a hurry to come home. I wondered what on earth he had found out—something solid, I judged, for he didn't talk lightly of making progress.

That evening I had nothing to do, and after dinner I felt too restless to sit down to a pipe and book. There was no one in the Club I wanted to talk to, so I sallied forth to another pot-house to which I belonged, where there was a chance of finding some of the younger and cheerier generation. Sure enough the first man I saw there was Archie Roylance, who greeted me with a whoop and announced that he was in town for a couple of days to see his doctor. He had had a bad fall steeplechasing earlier in the year, when he had all but broken his neck, but he declared that he was perfectly fit again except for some stiffness in his shoulder muscles. He was as lame as a duck from his flying smash just before the Armistice, but all the same he got about at a surprising pace. Indeed, out of cussedness he walked more than he used to do in the old days, and had taken to deer-stalking with enthusiasm. I think I have mentioned that he was my partner in the tenancy of Machray forest.

I proposed that we should go to a music-hall or cut into the second act of some play, but Archie had another idea. One of his fads was to be an amateur of dancing, though he had never been a great performer before his smash and would never dance again. He said he wanted to see the latest fashions, and suggested that we should go for an hour to a small (and he added, select) club somewhere in Marylebone, of which he believed he was a member. It bore an evil reputation, he said, for there was a good deal of high play, and the licensing laws were not regarded, but it was the place to see the best dancing. I made no objection, so we strolled up Regent Street in that season of comparative peace when busy people have gone home and the idle are still shut up in theatres and restaurants.

It was a divine April night, and I observed that I wished I were in a better place to enjoy spring weather. "I've just come from a Scotch moor," said Archie. "Lord! the curlews are makin' a joyful noise. That is the bird for my money. Come back with me, Dick, on Friday and I'll teach you a lot of things. You're a wise man, but you might be a better naturalist."

I thought how much I would have given to be able to accept, as the light wind blew down Langham Place. Then I wished that this job would take me out of town into fresh air, where I could get some exercise. The result was that I was in a baddish temper when we reached our destination, which was in one of the streets near Fitzroy Square. The place proved to be about as hard to get into as the Vatican. It took a long harangue and a tip from Archie to persuade the doorkeeper that we were of the right brand of disreputability to be admitted. Finally we found ourselves in a room with sham Chinese decorations, very garishly lit, with about twenty couples dancing, and about twenty more sitting drinking at little tables.

We paid five shillings apiece for a liqueur, found a table and took notice of the show. It seemed to me a wholly rotten and funereal business. A nigger band, looking like monkeys in uniform, pounded out some kind of barbarous jingle, and sad-faced marionettes moved to it. There was no gaiety or devil in that dancing, only a kind of bored perfection. Thin young men with rabbit

heads and hair brushed straight back from their brows, who I suppose were
professional dancing partners, held close to their breasts women of every
shape and age, but all alike in having dead eyes and masks for faces, and the
macabre procession moved like automata to the niggers' rhythm. I daresay it
was all very wonderful, but I was not built by Providence to appreciate it.

"I can't stand much more of this," I told Archie.

"It's no great shakes. But there are one or two high-class performers. Look
at that girl dancing with the young Jew—the one in green."

I looked and saw a slim girl, very young apparently, who might have been
pretty but for the way her face was loaded with paint and the preposterous
style in which her hair was dressed. Little though I know of dancing, I could
see that she was a mistress of the art, for every motion was a delight to watch,
and she made poetry out of that hideous ragtime. But her face shocked me. It
was *blind*, if you understand me, as expressionless as a mummy, a kind of
awful death-in-life. I wondered what kind of experience that poor soul had
gone through to give her the stare of a sleep-walker.

As my eyes passed from her they fell on another figure that seemed
familiar. I saw that it was Odell the butler, splendidly got up for his night out in
dress clothes, white waistcoat, and diamond studs. There was no mistaking the
pugilistic air of the fellow, now I saw him out of service; I had seen a dozen such
behind the bars of sporting public-houses. He could not see me, but I had a fair
view of him, and I observed that he also was watching the girl in green.

"Do you know who she is?" I asked.

"Some professional. Gad, she can dance, but the poor child looks as if she
found it a hard life. I'd rather like to talk to her."

But the music had stopped, and I could see that Odell had made a sign to
the dancer. She came up to him as obediently as a dog, he said something to
another man with him, a man with a black beard, and the three passed out at
the farther door. A moment later I caught a glimpse of her with a cloak round
her shoulders passing the door by which we had entered.

Archie laughed. "That big brute is probably her husband. I bet she earns
the living of both by dancing at these places, and gets beaten every night. I
would say my prayers before taking on that fellow in a scrap."

62   THE BLIND SPINNER

I look back upon those days of waiting as among the beastliest of my life. I
had the clearest conviction now that Medina was the key of the whole puzzle,
but as yet I had found out nothing worth mentioning, and I had to wait

like the sick folk by the pool of Bethesda till something troubled the waters. The only thing that comforted me was the fine old-fashioned dislike to the man which now possessed me. I couldn't pretend to understand more than a fragment of him, but what I understood I detested. I had been annnexed by him as a slave, and every drop of free blood in my veins was in revolt; but I was also resolved to be the most docile slave that ever kissed the ground before a tyrant. Some day my revenge would come, and I promised myself that it would be complete. Meantime I thanked Heaven that he had that blind spot of vanity which would prevent him seeing the cracks in my camouflage.

For the better part of a week we were very little separate. I lunched with him two days out of three, and we motored more than once down to Brighton for fresh air. He took me to a dinner he gave at the House of Commons to a Canadian statesman who was over on a visit, and he made me accompany him to a very smart dance at Lady Amysfort's, and he got me invited to a week-end party at Wirlesdon because he was going there. I went through the whole programme dutifully and not unpleasurably. I must say he treated me admirably in the presence of other people—with a jolly affectionate friendliness, constantly asking for my opinion, and deferring to me and making me talk, so that the few people I met whom I had known before wondered what had come over me. Mary had a letter from a cousin of hers, who reported that I seemed to have got into society and to be making a big success of it—a letter she forwarded to me with a pencilled note of congratulation at the end. On these occasions I didn't find my task difficult, for I fell unconsciously under the man's spell and could easily play up to him. . . . But when we were alone his manner changed. Iron crept into his voice, and, though he was pleasant enough, he took a devil of a lot for granted, and the note of authority grew more habitual. After such occasions I used to go home grinding my teeth. I never had a worse job than to submit voluntarily to that insolent protection.

Repeatedly in my bedroom at the Club I tried to put together the meagre handful of ascertained facts, but they were like a lot of remnants of different jig-saw puzzles and nothing fitted in to anything else. Macgillivray reported that so far he had drawn a blank in the case of Odell; and that the watchers at Palmyra Square had noted very few visitors except tradesmen and organ-grinders. Nothing resembling a gentleman had been seen to enter or leave, so it appeared that my estimate of Madame Breda's flourishing business was wrong. A woman frequently went out and returned, never walking but always in a taxi or a motor-car—probably the same woman, but so hooded and wrapped up as to make details difficult to be clear about. There were a host of little notes—coal or firewood had been delivered one day; twice the wrapped-up lady had gone out in the evening, to come back in a couple of hours, but mostly she made her visits abroad in daylight; the household woke late and retired to bed early; once or twice a sound like weeping had been heard, but it might have been the cat. Altogether it was a poor report, and I concluded that I was either barking up the wrong tree, or that Macgillivray's agents were a pretty useless crowd.

For the rest, what had I? A clear and well-founded suspicion of Medina.

But of what? Only that he was behaving towards me in a way that I resented, that he dabbled in an ugly brand of hypnotism, and that the more I saw of him the less I liked him. I knew that his public repute was false, but I had no worse crime to accuse him of than vanity. He had a butler who had been a prize-fighter, and who had a taste for night clubs. I remember I wrote all this down, and sat staring blankly at it, feeling how trivial it was. Then I wrote down the six-line jingle and stared at that too, and I thought of the girl, and the young man, and the small boy who liked birds and fishing. I hadn't a scrap of evidence to link up Medina with that business, except that Tom Greenslade believed that he had got from him the three facts which appeared more or less in the rhyme; but Tom might be mistaken, or Medina might have learned them in some perfectly innocent way. I hadn't enough evidence to swing a cat on. But yet—the more I thought of Medina the more dark and subtle his figure loomed in my mind. I had a conviction, on which I would have staked my life, that if I stuck to him I would worry out some vital and damning truth; so, with no very lively or cheerful hope, but with complete certainty, I resolved for the hundredth time to let logic go and back my fancy.

As in duty bound I paid another visit to Dr. Newhover. He received me casually, and appeared to have forgotten about my case till he looked up his diary.

"Ah yes, you saw Madame Breda," he said. "I have her report. Your headaches are cured but you are still a little shaky? Yes, please. Take off your coat and waistcoat."

He vetted me very thoroughly, and then sat down in his desk-chair and tapped his eyeglasses on his knee.

"You are better, much better, but you are not cured. That will take time and care, and lies, of course, in your own hands. You are leading a quiet life? Half town, half country—it is probably the best plan. Well, I don't think you can improve on that."

"You said something about fishing in Norway when I was here last."

"No, on the whole I don't recommend it. Your case is slightly different from what I at first supposed."

"You are a fisherman yourself?" I said.

He admitted that he was, and for a minute or two spoke more like a human being. He always used a two-piece Castle-Connell rod, though he granted it was a cumbrous thing to travel with. For flies he swore by Harlows—certainly the best people for Norwegian flies. He thought that there was a greater difference between Norwegian rivers than most people imagined, and Harlows understood that.

He concluded by giving me some simple instructions about diet and exercise.

"If my headaches return, shall I go back to Madame Breda?" I asked.

He shook his head. "Your headaches won't return."

I paid him his fee, and, as I was leaving, I asked if he wanted to see me again.

"I don't think it necessary. At any rate not till the autumn. I may have to be out of London myself a good deal this summer. Of course if you should find the *malaise* recurring, which I do not anticipate, you must come and see me. If I am out of town, you can see my colleague." He scribbled a name and address on a sheet of paper.

I left the house feeling considerably puzzled. Dr. Newhover, who on my first visit had made a great to-do about my health, seemed now to want to be quit of me. His manner was exactly that of a busy doctor dealing with a *malade imaginaire*. The odd thing was that I was really beginning to feel rather seedy, a punishment for my former pretence. It may have been the reaction of my mental worry, but I had the sort of indefinite out-of-sorts feeling which I believe precedes an attack of influenza. Only I had hitherto been immune from influenza.

That night I had another of Sandy's communications, a typed half-sheet with a Paris postmark.

"Keep close to M.," it ran. *"Do everything he wants. Make it clear that you have broken for ever with me. This is desperately important."*

It was signed "Buchan", a horse which Sandy seemed to think had been a Derby winner. He knew no more about racing than I knew of Chinese.

Next morning I woke with a bad taste in my mouth and a feeling that I had probably a bout of malaria due me. Now I had had no malaria since the autumn of '17, and I didn't like the prospect of the revisitation. However, as the day wore on, I felt better, and by midday I concluded I was not going to be ill. But all the same I was as jumpy as a cat in a thunderstorm. I had the odd sense of anticipation which I used to have before a battle, a lurking excitement by no means pleasant—not exactly apprehension, but first cousin to it. It made me want to see Medina, as if there was something between him and me that I ought to get over.

All afternoon this dentist-anteroom atmosphere hung about me, and I was almost relieved when about five o'clock I got a telephone message from Hill Street asking me to come there at six. I went round to the Bath Club and had a swim and a shampoo, and then started for the house. On the way there I had tremors in my legs and a coldness in the pit of the stomach which brought back my childish toothaches. Yes, that was it. I felt exactly like a small boy setting off with dreadful anticipation to have a tooth drawn, and not all my self-contempt could cure me of my funk. The house when I reached it seemed larger and lonelier than ever, and the April evening had darkened down to a scurry of chill dusty winds under a sky full of cloud.

Odell opened the door to me, and took me to the back of the hall, where I found a lift which I had not known existed. We went up to the top of the house, and I realized that I was about to enter again the library where before I had so strangely spent the midnight hours.

The curtains were drawn, shutting out the bleak spring twilight, and the room was warmed by, and had for its only light, a great fire of logs. I smelt more than wood-smoke; there was peat burning among the oak billets. The scent recalled, not the hundred times when I had sniffed peat-reek in happy places, but the flavour of the room in Palmyra Square when I had lain with bandaged eyes and felt light fingers touch my face. I had suddenly a sense that I had taken a long stride forward, that something fateful was about to happen, and my nervousness dropped from me like a cloak.

Medina was standing before the hearth, but his was not the figure that took my eyes. There was another person in the room, a woman. She sat in the high-backed chair which he had used on the former night, and she sat in it as if it were a throne. The firelight lit her face, and I saw that it was very old, waxen with age, though the glow made the wax rosy. Her dress was straight and black like a gaberdine, and she had thick folds of lace at her wrists and neck. Wonderful hair, masses of it, was piled on her head and it was snow-white and fine as silk. Her hands were laid on the arms of the chair, and hands more delicate and shapely I have never seen, though they had also the suggestion of a furious power, like the talons of a bird of prey.

But it was the face that took away my breath. I have always been a great admirer of the beauty of old age, especially in women, but this was a beauty of which I had never dreamed. It was a long face, and the features were large, though exquisitely cut and perfectly proportioned. Usually in an old face there is a certain loosening of muscles or blurring of contours, which detracts from sheer beauty but gives another kind of charm. But in this face there was no blurring or loosening; the mouth was as firm, the curve of the chin as rounded, the arch of the eyes as triumphant as in some proud young girl.

And then I saw that the eyes which were looking at the fire were the most remarkable things of all. Even in that half-light I could see that they were brightly, vividly blue. There was no film or blearing to mar their glory. But I saw also that they were sightless. How I knew it I do not know, for there was no physical sign of it, but my conviction was instantaneous and complete. These starlike things were turned inward. In most blind people the eyes are like marbles, dead windows in an empty house; but—how shall I describe it?—these were blinds drawn in a room which was full of light and move-ment, stage curtains behind which some great drama was always set. Blind though they were, they seemed to radiate an ardent vitality, to glow and flash like the soul within.

I realized that it was the most wonderful face of a woman I had ever looked on. And I realized in the same moment that I hated it, that the beauty of it was devilish, and the soul within was on fire with all the hatred of Hell.

"Hannay," I heard Medina's voice, "I have brought you here because I wish to present you to my mother."

I behaved just like somebody in a play. I advanced to her chair, lifted one of the hands, and put it to my lips. That seemed to me the right thing to do. The face turned towards me and broke into a smile, the kind of smile you may see on the marble of a Greek goddess.

The woman spoke to Medina in a tongue which was strange to me, and he replied. There seemed to be many questions and answers, but I did not trouble to try to catch a word I knew. I was occupied with the voice. I recognized in it those soft tones which had crooned over me as I lay in the room in Palmyra Square. I had discovered who had been the third person in that scene.

Then it spoke to me in English, with that odd lilting accent I had tried in vain to trace.

"You are a friend of Dominick, and I am glad to meet you, Sir Richard Hannay. My son has told me about you. Will you bring a chair and sit close to me?"

I pulled up a long low armchair, so long and low that the sitter was compelled almost to recline. My head was on a level with the hand which lay on the arm of her chair. Suddenly I felt that hand laid on my head, and I recognized her now by touch as well as voice.

"I am blind, Sir Richard," she said, "so I cannot see my son's friends. But I long to know how they look, and I have but one sense which can instruct me. Will you permit me to pass my hands over your face?"

"You may do what you please, Madame," I said. "I would to God I could give you eyes."

"That is a pretty speech," she said. "You might be one of my own people." And I felt the light fingers straying over my brow.

I was so placed that I was looking into the red heart of the fire, the one patch of bright light in the curtained room. I knew what I was in for, and, remembering past experience, I averted my eyes to the dark folios on the lowest shelves beyond the hearth. The fingers seemed to play a gentle tattoo on my temples, and then drew long soft strokes across my eyebrows. I felt a pleasant languor beginning to creep down my neck and spine, but I was fully prepared, and without much trouble resisted it. Indeed my mind was briskly busy, for I was planning how best to play my game. I let my head recline more and more upon the cushioned back of my chair, and I let my eyelids droop.

The gentle fingers were very thorough, and I had let myself sink back beyond their reach before they ceased.

"You are asleep," the voice said. "Now wake."

I was puzzled to know how to stage-manage that wakening, but she saved me the trouble. Her voice suddenly hissed like a snake's. "Stand up!" it said. "Quick—on your life."

I scrambled to my feet with extreme energy, and stood staring at the fire, wondering what to do next.

"Look at your master," came the voice again, peremptory as a drill-sergeant's.

That gave me my cue. I knew where Medina was standing, and, in the words of the Bible, my eyes regarded him as a handmaiden regards her mistress. I stood before him, dumb and dazed and obedient.

"Down," he cried. "Down, on all-fours."

I did as I was bid, thankful that my job was proving so easy.

"Go to the door—no, on all-fours—open it twice, shut it twice, and bring me the paper-knife from the far table in your mouth."

I obeyed, and a queer sight I must have presented prancing across the room, a perfectly sane man behaving like a lunatic.

I brought the paper-knife, and remained dog-wise. "Get up," he said, and I got up.

I heard the woman's voice say triumphantly, "He is well broken," and Medina laughed.

"There is yet the last test," he said. "I may as well put him through it now. If it fails, it means only that he needs more schooling. He cannot remember, for his mind is now in my keeping. There is no danger."

He walked up to me, and gave me a smart slap in the face.

I accepted it with Christian meekness. I wasn't even angry. In fact, I would have turned the other cheek in the Scriptural fashion, if it hadn't occurred to me that it might be over-acting.

Then he spat in my face.

That, I admit, tried me pretty high. It was such a filthy Kaffir trick that I had some trouble in taking it resignedly. But I managed it. I kept my eyes on the ground, and didn't even get out my handkerchief to wipe my cheek till he had turned away.

"Well broken to heel," I heard him say. "It is strange how easily these flat tough English natures succumb to the stronger spirit. I have got a useful weapon in him, mother mine."

They paid no more attention to me than if I had been a piece of furniture, which, indeed, in their eyes I was. I was asleep, or rather awake in a phantasmal world, and I could not return to my normal life till they bade me. I could know nothing—so they thought—and remember nothing, except what they willed. Medina sat in my chair, and the woman had her hand on his head, and they talked as if they were alone in the desert. And all the while I was standing sheepishly on the rug, not daring to move, scarcely to breathe, lest I should give the show away.

They made a pretty picture—"The Prodigal's Return" or "The Old Folks at Home", by Simpkins, R.A., Royal Academy, 1887. No, by Heaven, there was no suggestion of that. It was a marvellous and tragic scene that I regarded. The fitful light of the fire showed figures of an antique beauty and dignity. The regal profile of the woman, her superb pose, and the soft eerie music of her voice were a world removed from vulgarity, and so was the lithe vigour and the proud face of the man. They were more like a king and queen in exile, decreeing the sea of blood which was to wash them back again. I realized for the first time that Medina might be damnable, but was also great. Yes, the man who had spat on me like a stable-boy had also something of the prince. I realized another thing. The woman's touch had flattened down the hair above his forehead, which he brushed square, and his head, outlined in the firelight against the white cushion, was as round as a football. I had suspected this when I first saw him, and now I was certain. What did a head like that portend? I had a vague remembrance that I had heard somewhere that it meant madness—at any rate degeneracy.

They talked rapidly and unceasingly, but the confounded thing was that I could hear very little of it. They spoke in low tones, and I was three yards off and daren't for my life move an inch nearer. Also they spoke for the most part in a language of which I did not know a word—it may have been Choctaw, but was probably Erse. If I had only comprehended that tongue I might there and then have learned all I wanted to know. But sometimes Medina talked English, though it seemed to me that the woman always tried to bring him back to the other speech. All I heard were broken sentences that horribly tantalized me.

My brain was cool and very busy. This woman was the Blind Spinner of the rhymes. No doubt of it. I could see her spinning beside a peat fire, nursing ancient hate and madness, and crooning forgotten poetry. *"Beside the Sacred Tree."* Yggdrasil be hanged! I had it, it was Gospel Oak. Lord, what a fool I had been not to guess it before! The satisfaction of having got one of the three conundrums dead right made me want to shout. These two harpies held the key to the whole riddle, and I had only to keep up my present character to solve it. They thought they were dealing with a hypnotized fool, and instead they had a peculiarly wide-awake, if rather slow and elderly, Englishman. I wished to Heaven I knew what they were saying. Sluicing out malice about my country, no doubt, or planning the ruin of our civilization for the sake of a neurotic dream.

Medina said something impatiently about "danger", as if his purpose were to reassure. Then I caught nothing for several minutes, till he laughed and repeated the word *"secundus"*. Now I was looking for three people, and if there was a *"secundus"* there must have been a *"primus"*, and possibly a *"tertius"*.

"He is the least easy to handle," he said. "And it is quite necessary that Jason should come home. I have decided that the doctor must go out. It won't be for long—only till midsummer."

The date interested me acutely. So did what followed, for he went on:

"By midsummer they liquidate and disband. There is no fear that it won't succeed. We have the whip hand, remember. Trust me, all will go smoothly, and then we begin a new life. . . ."

I thought she sighed, and for the first time she spoke in English:

"I fear sometimes that you are forgetting your own land, Dominick."

He put up an arm and drew her head to his.

"Never, mother mine. It is our strength that we can seem to forget and still remember."

I was finding my stand on that hearth-rug extraordinarily trying. You see I had to keep perfectly rigid, for every now and then Medina would look towards me, and I knew that the woman had an ear like a hound. But my knees were beginning to shake with fatigue and my head to grow giddy, and I feared that, like the soldiers who stand guard round a royal bier, I might suddenly collapse. I did my best to struggle against the growing weakness, and hoped to forget it by concentrating all my attention on the fragments of talk.

"I have news for you," Medina was saying. "Kharama is in Europe and proposes to come to England."

"You will see him?" I thought her voice had a trace of alarm in it.

"Most certainly. I would rather see him than any living man."

"Dominick, be careful. I would rather you confined yourself to our old knowledge. I fear these new things from the East."

He laughed. "They are as old as ours—older. And all knowledge is one. I have already drunk of his learning, and I must have the whole cup."

That was the last I heard, for at that moment I made my exit from the scene in a way which I could not have bettered by much cogitation. My legs suddenly gave under me, the room swam round, and I collapsed on the floor in a dead faint. I must have fallen heavily, for I knocked a leg off one of the little tables.

When I came to—which I suppose was a minute or two later—Odell was bathing my face, and Medina with a grave and concerned air was standing by with a brandy decanter.

"My dear fellow, you gave me a bad fright," he said, and his manner was that of the considerate friend. "You're not feeling ill?"

"I haven't been quite fit all day, and I suppose the hot room knocked me out. I say, I'm most awfully sorry for playing the fool like this. I've damaged your furniture, I'm afraid. I hope I didn't scare the lady."

"What lady?"

"Your mother."

He looked at me with a perfectly blank face, and I saw I had made a mistake.

"I beg your pardon—I'm still giddy. I've been dreaming."

He gave me a glass of brandy and tucked me into a taxi. Long before I got to the Club I was feeling all right, but my mind was in a fine turmoil. I had stumbled at last upon not one clue but many, and though they were confused enough, I hoped with luck to follow them out. I could hardly eat any dinner that night, and my brain was too unsettled to do any serious thinking. So I took a taxi up to Gospel Oak, and, bidding it wait for me, had another look at Palmyra Square. The place seemed to have been dead and decaying for centuries seen in that windy moonless dark, and No. 4 was a shuttered tomb. I opened the gate and, after making sure that the coast was clear, stole round to the back-door where tradesmen called. There were some dilapidated outhouses, and the back garden, with rank grasses and obscene clothes-posts, looked like nothing so much as a neglected graveyard. In that house was the terrible blind Fate that span. As I listened, I heard from somewhere inside the sound of slow heart-broken sobs. I wondered if they came from the queer-looking little girl.

63   I AM INTRODUCED TO STRONG MAGIC

The first thing I did when I got up next morning was to pay a visit to Harlows, the fishing-tackle people. They knew me well enough, for I used to buy my rods there, and one of the assistants had been down to Fosse to teach

Mary how to use a light split-cane. With him I embarked on a long talk about Norwegian rivers and their peculiarities, and very soon got his views on the best flies. I asked which river was considered to be the earliest, and was told in an ordinary season the Nirdal and the Skarso. Then I asked if he knew my friend Dr. Newhover. "He was in here yesterday afternoon," I was told. "He is going to the Skarso this year, and hopes to be on the water in the last week of April. Rather too soon in our opinion, though salmon have been caught in it as early as April 17th. By the end of the first week of May it should be all right." I asked a good deal more about the Skarso, and was told that it was best fished from Merdal at the head of the Merdalfjord. There were only about three miles of fishable water before the big foss, but every yard of it was good. I told him I had hoped to get a beat on the Leardal for June, but had had to give up the notion this year and intended to confine myself to Scotland. I bought a new reel, a quantity of sea-trout flies, and a little book about Norwegian fishing.

Then I went on to see Macgillivray, with whom I had made an appointment by telephone.

"I've come to ask your help," I told him. "I'm beginning to get a move on, but it's ticklish business, and I must walk very warily. First of all, I want you to find out the movements of a certain Dr. Newhover of Wimpole Street. He is going to Norway some time in the next fortnight, to the Skarso to fish, and his jumping-off place will be Stavanger. Find out by which boat he takes a passage, and book me a berth in it also. I'd better have my old name, Cornelius Brand."

"You're not thinking of leaving England just now?" he asked reproachfully.

"I don't know. I may have to go or I may not, but in any case I won't be long away. Anyhow, find out about Dr. Newhover. Now for the more serious business. Just about when have you settled to round up the gang?"

"For the reasons I gave you it must be before midsummer. It is an infernally complicated job and we must work to a time-table. I had fixed provisionally the 20th of June."

"I think you'd better choose an earlier date."

"Why?"

"Because the gang are planning themselves to liquidate by midsummer, and, if you don't hurry, you may draw the net tight and find nothing in it."

"Now how on earth did you find that out?" he asked, and his usually impassive face was vivid with excitement.

"I can't tell you. I found it out in the process of hunting for the hostages, and I give you my word it's correct."

"But you must tell me more. If you have fresh lines on what you call my 'gang', it may be desperately important for me to know."

"I haven't. I've just the one fact, which I have given you. Honestly, old man, I can't tell you anything more till I tell you everything. Believe me, I'm working hard."

I had thought the thing out, and had resolved to keep the Medina business to myself and Sandy. Our one chance with him was that he should be utterly unsuspecting, and even so wary a fellow as Macgillivray might, if he were told, create just that faint breath of suspicion that would ruin all.

He grunted, as if he were not satisfied. "I suppose you must have it your own way. Very well, we'll fix the 10th of June for *Der Tag*. You realize, of course, that the round-up of all must be simultaneous—that's why it takes such a lot of *bandobast*. By the way, you've got the same problem with the hostages. You can't release one without the others, or the show is given away—not your show only, but mine. You realize that?"

"I do," I said, "and I realize that the moving forward of your date narrows my time down to less than two months. If I succeed, I must wait till the very eve of your move. Not earlier, I suppose, than June 9th? Assume I only find one of the three? I wait till June 9th before getting him out of their clutches. Then you strike, and what happens to the other two?"

He shrugged his shoulders. "The worst, I fear. You see, Dick, the gang I mean to crush and the people who hold the hostages are allied, but I take it they are different sets. I may land every member of my gang, and yet not come within speaking distance of the other lot. I don't know, but I'm pretty certain that even if we found the second lot we'd never be able to prove complicity between the two. The first are devilish deep fellows, but the second are great artists."

"All the same," I said, "I'm in hopes of finding at least one of the hostages, and that means some knowledge of the kidnappers."

"I must not ask, but I'd give my head to know how and where you're working. More power to you! But I wonder if you'll ever get near the real prime fountain of iniquity."

"I wonder," I said, and took my leave.

I had been playing with sickness, and now it looked as if I was going to be punished by getting the real thing. For all the rest of that day I felt cheap, and in the evening I was positive I had a temperature. I thought I might have 'flu, so I went round after dinner to see a doctor whom I had known in France. He refused to admit the temperature. "What sort of life have you been leading these last weeks?" he asked; and when I told him that I had been hanging round London waiting for some tiresome business developments, he said that that was the whole trouble. "You're accustomed to an active life in fresh air and you've been stuffing in town, feeding too well and getting no exercise. Go home to-morrow and you'll be as right as a trivet."

"It would rather suit me to be sick for a spell—say a week."

He looked puzzled and then laughed.

"Oh, if you like I'll give you a chit to say you must go back to the country at once or I won't answer for the consequences."

"I'd like that, but not just yet. I'll ring you up when I want it. Meantime I can take it that there's nothing wrong with me?"

"Nothing that a game of squash and a little Eno won't cure."

"Well, when you send me that chit, say I've got to have a quiet week in bed at home—no visitors—regular rest cure."

"Right," he said. "It's a prescription that every son of Adam might follow with advantage four times a year."

When I got back to the Club I found Medina waiting for me. It was the first time he had visited me there, and I pretended to be delighted to see him—almost embarrassed with delight—and took him to the back smoking-room where I had talked with Sandy. I told him that I was out of sorts, and he was very sympathetic. Then, with a recollection of Sandy's last letter, I started out to blaspheme my gods. He commented on the snugness and seclusion of the little room, which for the moment we had to ourselves.

"It wasn't very peaceful when I was last in it," I said. "I had a row here with that lunatic Arbuthnot, before he went abroad."

He looked up at the name.

"You mean you quarrelled. I thought you were old friends."

"Once we were. Now I never want to see the fellow again." I thought I might as well do the job thoroughly, though the words stuck in my throat.

He seemed pleased.

"I told you," he said, "that he didn't attract me."

"Attract!" I cried. "The man has gone entirely to the devil. He has forgotten his manners, his breeding, and everything he once possessed. He has lived so long among cringing Orientals that his head is swollen like a pumpkin. He wanted to dictate to me, and I said I would see him farther—and—oh well, we had the usual row. He's gone back to the East, which is the only place for him, and—no! I never want to clap eyes on him again."

There was a purr of satisfaction in his voice, for he believed, as I meant him to, that his influence over me had been strong enough to shatter an ancient friendship. "I am sure you are wise. I have lived in the East and know something of its ways. There is the road of knowledge and the road of illusion, and Arbuthnot has chosen the second. . . . We are friends, Hannay, and I have much to tell you some day—perhaps very soon. I have made a position for myself in the world, but the figure which the world sees is only a little part of me. The only power is knowledge, and I have attained to a knowledge compared with which Arbuthnot's is the merest smattering."

I noticed that he had dropped the easy, well-bred, deprecating manner which I had first noted in him. He spoke to me now magisterially, arrogantly, almost pompously.

"There has never been a true marriage of East and West," he went on. "To-day we incline to put a false interpretation on the word Power. We think of it in material terms like money, or the control of great patches of inanimate nature. But it still means, as it has always meant, the control of human souls, and to him who acquires that everything else is added. How does such control arise? Partly by knowledge of the intricacies of men's hearts, which is a very different thing from the stock platitudes of the professional psychologists. Partly by that natural dominion of spirit which comes from the possession of certain human qualities in a higher degree than other men. The East has the secret knowledge, but, though it can lay down the practice, it cannot provide the practitioners. The West has the tools, but not the science of their use.

There has never, as I have said, been a true marriage of East and West, but when there is, its seed will rule the world."

I was drinking this in with both ears, and murmuring my assent. Now at last I was to be given his confidence, and I prayed that he might be inspired to go on. But he seemed to hesitate, till a glance at my respectful face reassured him.

"The day after to-morrow a man will be in London, a man from the East, who is a great master of this knowledge. I shall see him, and you will accompany me. You will understand little, for you are only at the beginning, but you will be in the presence of wisdom."

I murmured that I should feel honoured.

"You will hold yourself free for all that day. The time will probably be the evening."

After that he left with the most perfunctory good-bye. I congratulated myself on having attained to just the kind of position I wanted—that of a disciple whose subjection was so much taken for granted that he was treated like a piece of furniture. From his own point of view Medina was justified; he must have thought the subconscious control so strong, after all the tests I had been through, that my soul was like putty in his hands.

Next day I went down to Fosse and told Mary to expect me back very soon for a day or two. She had never plagued me with questions, but something in my face must have told her that I was hunting a trail, for she asked me for news and looked as if she meant to have it. I admitted that I had found out something, and said I would tell her everything when I next came back. That would only have been prudent, for Mary was a genius at keeping secrets, and I wanted some repository of my knowledge in case I got knocked on the head.

When I returned to town I found another note from Sandy, also from France, signed "Alan Breck"—Sandy was terribly out with his Derby winners. It was simply two lines imploring me again to make Medina believe I had broken with him, and that he had gone east of Suez for good.

There was also a line from Macgillivray, saying that Dr. Newhover had taken a passage on the *Gudrun*, leaving Hull at 6.30 p.m. on the 21st, and that a passage had been booked for C. Brand, Esqre., by the same boat. That decided me, so I wrote to my own doctor, asking for the chit he had promised, to be dated the 19th. I was busy with a plan, for it seemed to me that it was my duty to follow up the one trail which presented itself, though it meant letting the rest of the business sleep. I longed more than I could say for a talk with Sandy, who was now playing the fool in France and sending me imbecile notes. I also rang up Archie Roylance, and found to my delight that he had not left town, for I ran him to ground at the Travellers', and fixed a meeting for next morning.

"Archie," I said, when we met, "I want to ask a great favour from you. Are you doing anything special in the next fortnight?"

He admitted that he had thought of getting back to Scotland to watch a pair of nesting greenshanks.

"Let the greenshanks alone, like a good fellow. I've probably got to go to

Norway on the 21st, and I shall want to get home in the deuce of a hurry. The steamer's far too slow."

"Destroyer," he suggested.

"Hang it, this is not the War. Talk sense. I want an aeroplane, and I want you to fetch me."

Archie whistled long and loud.

"You're a surprisin' old bird, Dick. It's no joke being a pal of yours. . . . I daresay I could raise a bus all right. But you've got to chance the weather. And my recollection of Norway is that it's not very well provided with landin' places. What part do you favour?"

I told him the mouth of the Merdalfjord.

"Lord! I've been there," he said. "It's all as steep as the side of a house."

"Yes, but I've been studying the map, and there are some eligible little islands off the mouth, which look flattish from the contouring. I'm desperately serious, old man. I'm engaged on a job where failure means the loss of innocent lives. I'll tell you all about it soon, but meantime you must take my word for it."

I managed to get Archie suitably impressed, and even to interest him in the adventure, for he was never the man to lag behind in anything that included risk and wanted daring. He promised to see Hansen, who had been in his squadron and was believed to have flown many times across the North Sea. As I left him I could see that he was really enormously cheered by the prospect, for if he couldn't watch his blessed birds, the next best thing was to have a chance of breaking his neck.

I had expected to be bidden by Medina to meet his necromancer in some den in the East End or some Bloomsbury lodging-house. Judge of my surprise, then, when I was summoned to Claridge's for nine-thirty that evening. When I got to the hotel it was difficult to believe that a place so bright and commonplace could hold any mystery. There was the usual dancing going on, and squads of people who had dined well were sitting around watching. Medina was standing by a fireplace talking to a man who wore a long row of miniature medals and a star, and whom I recognized as Tom Machin, who had commanded a cavalry brigade in France. Medina nodded casually to me, and Tom, whom I had not seen for years, made a great fuss.

"Regimental dinner," he explained. "Came out for a moment to give instructions about my car. Been telling Medina here of the dirty trick the Government have played on my old crowd. I say it's up to the few sahibs like him in that damned monkey-house at Westminster to make a row about it. You back me up, Hannay. What I say is . . ." and so on with all the eternal iteration of "abso-lutely" and "If you follow me" and "You see what I mean" of the incoherent British regular.

Medina gently disengaged himself. "'Sorry, Tom, but I must be off now. You're dining with Burminster on Thursday, aren't you? We'll talk about that business then. I agree it's an infernal shame."

He signed to me and we went together to the lift. On the first floor, where the main suites are, a turbaned Indian waited for us in the corridor. He led us into a little anteroom, and then disappeared through big folding-doors. I wondered what kind of swell this Oriental necromancer must be who could take rooms like these, for the last time I had been in them was when they were occupied by a Crown Prince who wanted to talk to me about a certain little problem in Anatolia.

"You are about to see Kharama," Medina whispered, and there was an odd exaltation in his voice. "You do not know his name, but there are millions in the East who reverence it like that of a god. I last saw him in a hut in the wildest pass in the Karakoram, and now he is in this gilded hotel with the dance-music of the West jigging below. It is a parable of the unity of all Power."

The door was opened, and the servant beckoned us to enter. It was a large room furnished with the usual indifferent copies of French furniture—very hot and scented, just the kind of place where international financiers make their deals over liqueur brandy and big cigars, or intinerant stars of the cinema world receive their friends. Bright, hard, and glossy, you would have said that no vulgarer environment could be found. . . . And yet after the first glance I did not feel its commonness, for it was filled with the personality of the man who sat on a couch at the far end. I realized that here was one who carried with him his own prepotent atmosphere, and who could transform his surroundings, whether it was a Pamir hut or a London restaurant.

To my surprise he was quite young. His hair was hidden by a great turban, but the face was smooth and hairless, and the figure, so far as I could judge, had not lost the grace of youth. I had imagined some one immensely venerable and old with a beard to his girdle, or, alternately, an obese babu with a soft face like a eunuch. I had forgotten that this man was of the hills. To my amazement he wore ordinary evening dress, well-cut, too, I thought, and over it a fine silk dressing-gown. He had his feet tucked up on the couch, but he did not sit cross-legged. At our entrance he slightly inclined his head, while we both bowed. Medina addressed him in some Indian tongue, and he replied, and his voice was like the purr of a big cat.

He motioned us to sit down, looking not so much at us as through us, and while Medina spoke I kept my eyes on his face. It was the thin, high-boned, high-bred face of the hillman; not the Mongolian type, but that other which is like an Arab, the kind of thing you can see in Pathan troops. And yet, though it was as hard as flint and as fierce as Satan, there was a horrid feline softness in it, like that of a man who would never need to strike a blow in anger, since he could win his way otherwise. The brow was straight and heavy, such as I had always associated with mathematical talent, and broader than is common with Orientals. The eyes I could not see, for he kept them half shut, but there was something uncanny in the way they were chased in his head, with an odd slant, the opposite from what you see in the Chinaman. His mouth had a lift at each corner as if he were perpetually sneering, and yet there was a hint of humour in the face, though it was as grave as a stone statue.

I have rarely seen a human being at once so handsome and so repulsive, but both beauty and horror were merged in the impression of ruthless power. I had been sceptical enough about this Eastern image, as I had been sceptical about Medina's arts, because they had failed with me. But as I looked on that dark countenance I had a vision of a world of terrible knowledge, a hideousness like an evil smell, but a power like a blasting wind or a pestilence. . . . Somehow Sandy's talk at the Thursday Club dinner came back to me, about the real danger to the world lying in the constraint of spirit over spirit. This swarthy brute was the priest of that obscene domination, and I had an insane desire there and then to hammer him into pulp.

He was looking at me, and seemed to be asking a question to which Medina replied. I fancy he was told that I was a *chela*, or whatever was the right name, a well-broken and submissive disciple.

Then to my surprise he spoke in English—good English, with the *chi-chi* accent of the Indian.

"You have followed far in the path of knowledge, brother. I did not think a son of the West could have travelled so far and so soon. You have won two of the three keys to Mastery, if you can make a man forget his past, and begin life anew subject to your will. But what of the third key?"

I thought Medina's voice had a tinge of disappointment. "It is the third key which I look for, master. What good is it to wipe out the past and establish my control if it is only temporary? I want the third key, to lock the door, so that I have my prisoner safe for ever. Is there such a key?"

"The key is there, but to find it is not easy. All control tends to grow weak and may be broken by an accident, except in the case of young children, and some women, and those of feeble mind."

"That I know," said Medina almost pettishly. "But I do not want to make disciples only of babes, idiots, and women."

"Only some women, I said. Among our women perhaps all, but among Western women, who are hard as men, only the softer and feebler."

"That is my trouble. I wish to control for ever, and to control without constant watching on my part. I have a busy life and time is precious. Tell me, master, is there a way?"

I listened to this conversation with feelings of genuine horror. Now I saw Medina's plans, and I realized that he and he alone was at the bottom of the kidnapping. I realized, too, how he had dealt with the three hostages, and how he proposed to deal. Compared to him a murderer was innocent, for a murderer only took life, while he took the soul. I hated him and that dark scoundrel more intensely than I think I have ever hated man; indeed it was only by a great effort that I checked myself from clutching the two by the throat. The three stories, which had been half forgotten and overlaid by my recent experiences, returned sharp and clear to my memory. I saw again Victor's haggard face, I heard Sir Arthur Warcliff's voice break; and my wrath rose and choked me. This stealing of souls was the worst infamy ever devised by devils among mankind. I must have showed my emotion, but happily the two had no eyes for me.

"There is a way, a sure way," the Indian was saying, and a wicked half-smile flitted over his face. "But it is a way which, though possible in my own country, may be difficult in yours. I am given to understand that your police are troublesome, and you have a public repute which it is necessary to cherish. There is another way which is slower, but which is also sure, if it is boldly entered upon."

The sage seemed to open his half-shut eyes, and I thought I saw the opaque brightness which comes from drug-taking.

"Him whom you would make your slave," he said, "you first strip of memory, and then attune to your own will. To keep him attuned you must be with him often and reinforce the control. But this is burdensome, and if the slave be kept apart and seen rarely the influence will ebb—except, as I have said, in the case of a young child. There is a way to rivet the bondage, and it is this. Take him or her whom you govern into the same life as they have been accustomed to live before, and there, among familiar things, assert your control. Your influence will thus acquire the sanction of familiarity—for though the conscious memory has gone, the unconscious remains—and presently will be a second nature."

"I see," said Medina abstractedly. "I had already guessed as much. Tell me, master, can the dominion, once it is established, be shaken off?"

"It cannot, save by the will of him who exercises it. Only the master can release."

After that they spoke again in the foreign tongue of I know not what devilry. It seemed to me that the sage was beginning to tire of the interview, for he rang a bell and when the servant appeared gave him some rapid instructions. Medina rose, and kissed the hand which was held out to him, and I, of course, followed suit.

"You stay here long, master?" he asked.

"Two days. Then I have business in Paris and elsewhere. But I return in May, when I will summon you again. Prosper, brother. The God of wisdom befriend you."

We went downstairs to the dancing and the supper parties. The regimental dinner was breaking up, and Tom Machin was holding forth in the hall to a knot of be-medalled friends. I had to say something to Medina to round off the evening, and the contrast of the two scenes seemed to give me a cue. As we were putting on our coats I observed that it was like coming from light to darkness. He approved. "Like falling from a real world into shadows," he said.

He evidently wished to follow his own thoughts, for he did not ask me to walk home with him. I, too, had a lot to think about. When I got back to the Club I found a note signed "Spion Kop", and with an English postmark. *"Meet me,"* it said, *"on the 21st for breakfast at the inn called 'The Silent Woman' on the Fosse Way as you go over from Colne to Windrush. I have a lot to tell you."*

I thanked Heaven that Sandy was home again, though he chose fantastic spots for his assignations. I, too, had something to say to him. For that evening had given me an insight into Medina's mind, and, what was more, the glimmerings of a plan of my own.

64 CONFIDENCES AT A WAYSIDE INN

My first impulse was to go to Macgillivray about this Kharama fellow, who I was certain was up to mischief. I suspected him of some kind of political intrigue; otherwise what was he doing touring the capitals of Europe and putting up at expensive hotels? But on second thoughts I resolved to let the police alone. I could not explain about Kharama without bringing in Medina, and I was determined to do nothing which would stir a breath of suspicion against him. But I got the chit from my doctor, recommending a week's rest, and I went round to see Medina on the morning of the 19th. I told him I had been feeling pretty cheap for some days, and that my doctor ordered me to go home and go to bed. He didn't look pleased, so I showed him the doctor's letter, and made a poor mouth, as if I hated the business, but was torn between my inclinations and my duty. I think he liked my producing that chit, like a second-lieutenant asking for leave; anyhow he made the best of it, and was quite sympathetic. "I'm sorry you're going out of town," he said, "for I want you badly. But it's as well to get quite fit, and to lie up for a week ought to put you all right. When am I to expect you back?" I told him that without fail I would be in London on the 29th. "I'm going to disappear into a monastery," I said. "Write no letters, receive none, not at home to visitors, only sleep and eat. I can promise you that my wife will watch me like a dragon."

Then I hunted up Archie Roylance, whom I found on the very top of his form. He had seen Hansen, and discovered that on the island of Flacksholm, just off the mouth of the Merdalfjord, there was good landing. It was a big flattish island with a loch in the centre, and entirely uninhabited except for a farm at the south end. Archie had got a machine, a Sopwith, which he said he could trust, and I arranged with him to be at Flacksholm not later than the 27th, and to camp there as best he could. He was to keep watch by day for a motor-boat from the Merdalfjord, and at night if he saw a green light he was to make for it. I told him to take ample supplies, and he replied that he wasn't such a fool as to neglect the commissariat. He said he had been to Fortnum and Mason and was going to load up with liqueurs and *delicatessen*. "Take all the clothes you've got, Dick," he added. "It will be perishing cold in those parts at this time of year." He arranged, too, to cable through Hansen for a motor-launch to be ready at Stavanger for a Mr. Brand who was due by the Hull steamer on the morning of the 23rd. If I had to change my plans I was to wire him at once.

That evening I went down to Fosse a little easier in my mind. It was a blessed relief to get out of London and smell clean air, and to reflect that for a week at any rate I should be engaged in a more congenial job than loafing about town. I found Peter John in the best of health and the Manor garden a glory of spring flowers.

I told Mary that I was ordered by my doctor to go to bed for a week and take a rest cure.

"Dick," she asked anxiously, "you're not ill, are you?"

"Not a bit, only a trifle stale. But officially I'm to be in bed for a week and not a blessed soul is to be allowed to come near me. Tell the servants, please, and get the cook on to invalid dishes. I'll take Paddock into my confidence, and he'll keep up a show of waiting on me."

"A show?"

"Yes; for, you see, I'm going to put in a week in Norway—that is, unless Sandy has anything to say against it."

"But I thought Colonel Arbuthnot was still abroad?"

"So he is—officially. But I'm going to breakfast with him the day after to-morrow at 'The Silent Woman'—you remember, the inn we used to have supper at last summer when I was fishing the Colne."

"Dick," she said solemnly, "isn't it time you told me a little more about what you're doing?"

"I think it is," I agreed, and that night after dinner I told her everything.

She asked a great many questions, searching questions, for Mary's brain was about twice as good as mine. Then she sat pondering for a long time with her chin on her hand.

"I wish I had met Mr. Medina," she said at last. "Aunt Claire and Aunt Doria know him . . . I am afraid of him, terribly afraid, and I think I should be less afraid if I could just see him once. It is horrible, Dick, and you are fighting with such strange weapons. Your only advantage is that you're such a gnarled piece of oak. I wish I could help. It's dreadful to have to wait here and be tortured by anxiety for you, and to be thinking all the time of those poor people. I can't get the little boy out of my head. I often wake in a terror, and have to go up to the night-nursery to hug Peter John. Nanny must think I'm mad. . . . I suppose you're right to go to Norway?"

"I see no other way. We have a clue to the whereabouts of one of the hostages—I haven't a notion which. I must act on that, and besides, if I find one it may give me a line on the others."

"There will still be two lost," she said, "and the time grows fearfully short. You are only one man. Can you not get helpers? Mr. Macgillivray?"

"No. He has his own job, and to let him into mine would wreck both."

"Well, Colonel Arbuthnot? What is he doing?"

"Oh, Sandy's busy enough, and, thank God! he's back in England. I'll know more about his game when I see him, but you may be sure it's a deep one. While I'm away Sandy will be working all the time."

"Do you know, I have never met him. Couldn't I see him some time when you're away? It would be a great comfort to me. And, Dick, can't I help somehow? We've always shared everything, even before we were married, and you know I'm dependable."

"Indeed I do, my darling," I said. "But I can't see how you can help—yet. If I could, I would inspan you straight off, for I would rather have you with me than a regiment."

"It's the poor little boy. I could endure the rest, but the thought of him makes me crazy. Have you seen Sir Arthur?"

"No, I have avoided him. I can stand the sight of Victor and the Duke, but I swear I shall never look Sir Arthur in the face unless I can hand him over his son."

Then Mary got up and stood over me like a delivering angel.

"It is going to be done," she cried. "Dick, you must never give up. I believe in my heart we shall win. We must win or I shall never be able to kiss Peter John again with a quiet mind. Oh, I wish—I wish I could do something!"

I don't think Mary slept that night, and next morning she was rather pale and her eyes had that funny long-sighted look that they had had when I said good-bye to her at Amiens in March '18, before going up to the line.

I spent a blissful day with her and Peter John wandering round our little estate. It was one of those April days which seem to have been borrowed from late May, when you have the warmth of summer joined with the austerity and fresh colouring of spring. The riot of daffodils under the trees was something to thank God for, the banks of the little lake were one cascade of grape hyacinths, blue and white, and every dell in the woods was bright with primroses. We occupied the morning deepening the pools in a tiny stream which was to be one of the spawning-grounds for the new trout in the lake, and Peter John showed conspicuous talent as a hydraulic engineer. His nurse, who was a middle-aged Scotswoman from the Cheviots, finally carried him off for his morning rest, and, when he had gone, Mary desisted from her watery excavations and sat down on a bank of periwinkles.

"What do you really think of Nanny?" she asked.

"About as good as they make," I replied.

"That's what I think too. You know, Dick, I feel I'm far too fussy about Peter John. I give hours of my time to him, and it's quite unnecessary. Nanny can do everything better than I can. I scarcely dare let him out of my sight, and yet I'm certain that I could safely leave him for weeks with Nanny and Paddock—and Dr. Greenslade within call."

"Of course you could," I agreed, "but you'd miss him, as I do, for he's jolly good company."

"Yes, he's jolly good company, the dear fellow," she said.

In the afternoon we went for a canter on the downs, and I came back feeling as fit as a race-horse and keyed up for anything. But that evening, as we walked in the garden before dinner, I had another fit of longing to be free of the business, and to return to my quiet life. I realized that I had buried my heart in my pleasant acres, and the thought of how much I loved them made me almost timid. I think Mary understood what I was feeling, for she insisted on talking about David Warcliff, and before I went to bed had worked me into that honest indignation which is the best stiffener of resolution. She went over my plans with me very carefully. On the 28th, if I could manage it, I was to come home, but if I was short of time I was to send her a wire and go straight to London. The pretence of my being in bed was to be religiously kept up. For safety's sake I was to sign every wire with the name of Cornelius.

Very early next morning, long before any one was stirring, I started the big Vauxhall with Paddock's assistance, and, accompanied by a very modest kit, crept down the avenue. Paddock, who could drive a car, was to return to the house about ten o'clock, and explain to my chauffeur that by my orders he had taken the Vauxhall over to Oxford as a loan for a week to a friend of mine. I drove fast out of the silent hill roads and on to the great Roman way which lay like a strap across the highlands. It was not much after six o'clock when I reached "The Silent Woman", which sat like an observation post on a ridge of down, at a junction of four roads. Smoke was going up from its chimneys, so I judged that Sandy had ordered early breakfast. Presently, as I was garaging the car in an outhouse, Sandy appeared in flannel bags and a tweed jacket, looking as fresh as paint and uncommonly sunburnt.

"I hope you're hungry," he said. "Capital fellow the landlord! He knows what a man's appetite is. I ordered eggs, kidneys, sausages and cold ham, and he seemed to expect it. Yes. These are my headquarters for the present, though Advanced G.H.Q. is elsewhere. By-the-bye, Dick, just for an extra precaution, my name's Thomson—Alexander Thomson—and I'm a dramatic critic taking a belated Easter holiday."

The breakfast was as good as Sandy had promised, and what with the run in the fresh air and the sight of him opposite me I began to feel light-hearted.

"I got your letters," I said; "but, I say, your knowledge of Derby winners is pretty rocky. I thought that was the kind of information no gentleman was without."

"I'm the exception. Did you act on them?"

"I told Medina I had broken with you for good, and never wanted to see your face again. But why did you make such a point of it?"

"Simply because I wanted to be rid of his attentions, and I reckoned that if he thought we had quarrelled and that I had gone off for good, he might let me alone. You see he has been trying hard to murder me."

"Good Lord!" I exclaimed. "When?"

"Four times," said Sandy calmly, counting on his fingers. "Once before I left London. Oh, I can tell you I had an exciting departure. Three times in Paris, the last time only four days ago. I fancy he's off my trail now, for he really thinks I sailed from Marseilles the day before yesterday."

"But why on earth?"

"Well, I made some ill-advised remarks at the Thursday Club dinner. He believes that I'm the only man alive who might uncover him, and he won't sleep peacefully till he knows that I am out of Europe and is convinced that I suspect nothing. I sent you those letters because I wanted to be let alone, seeing I had a lot to do, and nothing wastes time like dodging assassins. But my chief reason was to protect *you*. You mayn't know it, Dick, but you've been walking for three weeks on the edge of a precipice with one foot nearly over. You've been in the most hideous danger, and I was never more relieved in my life than when I saw your solemn old face this morning. You were only safe when he regarded our friendship as broken and me out of the way and you his blind and devoted slave."

"I'm that all right," I said. "There's been nothing like it since Uncle Tom's Cabin."

"Good. That's the great thing, for it gives us a post in the enemy's citadel. But we're only at the beginning of a tremendous fight, and there's no saying how it will go. Have you sized up Medina?"

"Only a little bit. Have you?"

"I'm on the road. He's the most complex thing I've ever struck. But now we've got to pool our knowledge. Shall I start?"

"Yes. Begin at the Thursday dinner. What started you off then? I could see that something he said intrigued you."

"I must begin before that. You see, I'd heard a good deal about Medina up and down the world, and couldn't for the life of me place him. Everybody swore by him, but I had always a queer feeling about the man. I told you about Lavater. Well, I had nothing to go upon there except the notion that his influence upon my friend had been bad. So I began making inquiries, and, as you know, I've more facilities than most people for finding things out. I was curious to know what he had been doing during the War. The ordinary story was that he had been for the first two years pretty well lost in Central Asia, where he had gone on a scientific expedition, and that after that he had been with the Russians, and had finished up by doing great work with Denikin. I went into that story and discovered that he had been in Central Asia all right, but had never been near any fighting front, and had never been within a thousand miles of Denikin. That's what I meant when I told you that I believed the man was one vast lie."

"He made everybody believe it."

"That's the point. He made the whole world believe what he wanted. Therefore he must be something quite out of the common—a propagandist of genius. That was my first conclusion. But how did he work? He must have a wonderful organization, but he must have something more—the kind of personality which can diffuse itself like an atmosphere, and which, like an electric current, is not weakened by distance. He must also have unique hypnotic powers. I had made a study of that in the East, and had discovered how little we know here about the compulsion of spirit by spirit. That, I have always believed, is to-day, and ever has been, the true magic. You remember I said something about that at the Thursday dinner?"

I nodded. "I suppose you did it to try him?"

"Yes. It wasn't very wise, for I might easily have frightened him. But I was luckier than I deserved, and I drew from him a tremendous confession."

"The Latin quotation?"

"The Latin quotation. *Sit vini abstemius qui hermeneuma tentat aut hominum petit dominatum.* I nearly had a fit when I heard it. Listen, Dick. I've always had a craze for recondite subjects, and when I was at Oxford I wasted my time on them when I should have been working for my schools. I only got a third in Greats, but I acquired a lot of unusual information. One of my subjects was Michael Scott. Yes—the wizard, only he wasn't a wizard, but a very patient and original thinker. He was a Borderer like me, and I started out to write a life of him. I kept up the study, and when I was at the Paris Embassy I spent my leisure tracking him through the libraries of Europe. Most of his works were published in the fifteenth and sixteenth centuries, and mighty dull they are, but there are some still in manuscript, and I had always the hope of discovering more, for I was positive that the real Michael Scott was something far bigger than the translator and commentator whom we know. I believed that he taught the mad Emperor Ferdinand some queer things, and that the centre of his teaching was just how one human soul could control another. Well, as it turned out, I was right. I found some leaves of manuscript in the Bibliothèque Nationale, which I was certain were to be attributed to Michael. One of his best-known works, you remember, is the *Physionomia*, but that is only a version of Aristotle. This, too, was part of a *Physionomia*, and a very different thing from the other, for it purported to give the essence of the *Secreta Secretorum*—it would take too long to explain about that—and the teaching of the Therapeutae, with Michael's own comments. It is a manual of the arts of spiritual control—oh, amazingly up-to-date, I assure you, and a long way ahead of our foolish psycho-analysts. Well, that quotation of Medina's comes from that fragment—the rare word 'hermeneuma' caught my attention as soon as he uttered it. That proved that Medina was a student of Michael Scott, and showed me what was the bent of his mind."

"Well, he gave himself away then, and you didn't."

"Oh yes, I did. You remember I asked him if he knew the *guru* who lived at the foot of the Shansi pass as you go over to Kaikand? That was a bad blunder, and it is on account of that question that he has been trying to remove me from the earth. For it was from that *guru* that he learned most of his art."

"Was the *guru's* name Kharama?" I asked.

Sandy stared as if he had seen a ghost.

"Now how on earth do you know that?"

"Simply because I spent an hour with him and Medina a few nights ago."

"The devil you did! Kharama in London! Lord, Dick, this is an awesome business. Quick, tell me every single thing that passed."

I told him as well as I remembered, and he seemed to forget his alarm and to be well satisfied. "This is tremendously important. You see the point of Medina's talk? He wants to rivet his control over those three unfortunate devils, and to do that he is advised to assert it in some environment similar to that of their past lives. That gives us a chance to get on their track. And the control can only be released by him who first imposed it! I happened to know that, but I was not sure that Medina knew it. It is highly important to have found this out."

"Finish your story," I begged him. "I want to know what you have been doing abroad."

"I continued my studies in the Bibliothèque Nationale, and I found that, as I suspected, Medina, or somebody like him, had got on to the Michael Scott MS. and had had a transcript made of it. I pushed my researches further, for Michael wasn't the only pebble on the beach, though he was the biggest. Lord, Dick, it's a queer business in a problem like ours to have to dig for help in the débris of the Middle Ages. I found out something—not much, but something."

"And then?"

"Oh, all the time I was making inquiries about Medina's past—not very fruitful—I've told you most of the results. Then I went to see Ram Dass—you remember my speaking about him. I thought he was in Munich, but I found him in Westphalia, keeping an eye on the German industrials. Don't go to Germany for a holiday, Dick; it's a sad country and a comfortless. I had to see Ram Dass, for he happens to be the brother of Kharama."

"What size of a fellow is Kharama?" I asked.

Sandy's reply was: "For knowledge of the theory unequalled, but only a second-class practitioner"—exactly what Medina had said.

"Ram Dass told me most of what I wanted to know. But he isn't aware that his brother is in Europe. I rather fancy he thinks he is dead. . . . That's all I need tell you now. Fire away, Dick, and give me an exact account of your own doings."

I explained as best I could the gradual change in Medina's manner from friendship to proprietorship. I told how he had begun to talk freely to me, as if I were a disciple, and I described that extraordinary evening in Hill Street when I had met his mother.

"His mother!" Sandy exclaimed, and made me go over every incident several times—the slap in the face, the spitting, my ultimate fainting. He seemed to enjoy it immensely. "Good business," he said. "You never did a better day's work, old man."

"I have found the Blind Spinner at any rate," I said.

"Yes. I had half guessed it. I didn't mention it, but when I got into the house in Gospel Oak as the electric-light man, I found a spinning-wheel in the back room, and they had been burning peat on the hearth. Well, that's Number One."

"I think I am on my way to find Number Two," I said, and I told him of the talk I had overheard between the two about *secundus* and sending "the doctor" somewhere, and of how I had discovered that Dr. Newhover was starting this very day for the Skarso. "It's the first clear clue," I said, "and I think I ought to follow it up."

"Yes. What do you propose to do?"

"I am travelling this evening on the *Gudrun*, and I'm going to trail the fellow till I find out his game. I'm bound to act upon what little information we've got."

"I agree. But this means a long absence from London, and *secundus* is only one of three."

"Just a week," I said. "I've got sick leave from Medina for a week, and I'm supposed to be having a rest cure at Fosse, with Mary warding off visitors. I've arranged with Archie Roylance to pick me up in an aeroplane about the 28th and bring me back. It doesn't allow me much time, but an active man can do the deuce of a lot in a week."

"Bravo!" he cried. "That's your old moss-trooping self!"

"Do you approve?"

"Entirely. And, whatever happens, you present yourself to Medina on the 29th? That leaves us about six weeks for the rest of the job."

"More like five," I said gloomily, and I told him how I had learnt that the gang proposed to liquidate by midsummer, and that Macgillivray had therefore moved the date when he would take action ten days forward. "You see how we are placed. He must collect all the gang at the same moment, and we must release all three hostages, if we can, at the same time. The releasing mustn't be done too soon or it will warn the gang. Therefore if Macgillivray strikes on the 10th of June, we must be ready to strike not earlier than the 9th, and, of course, not later."

"I see," he said, and was silent for a little. "Have you anything more to tell me?"

I ransacked my memory and remembered about Odell. He wrote down the name of the dancing club where I had seen that unprepossessing butler. I mentioned that I had asked Macgillivray to get on to his *dossier*.

"You haven't told Macgillivray too much?" he inquired anxiously, and seemed relieved when I replied that I had never mentioned the Medina business.

"Well, here's the position," he said at last. "You go off for a week hunting Number Two. We are pretty certain that we have got Number One. Number Three—that nonsense about the fields of Eden and the Jew with a dyed beard in a curiosity shop in Marylebone—still eludes us. And of course we have as yet no word of any of the three hostages. There's a terrible lot still to do. How do you picture the thing, Dick? Do you think of the three, the girl, the young man, and the boy, shut up somewhere and guarded by Medina's minions? Do you imagine that if we find their places of concealment we shall have done the job?"

"That was my idea."

He shook his head. "It is far subtler than that. Did no one ever tell you that the best way of hiding a person is to strip him of his memory? Why is it that when a man loses his memory he is so hard to find? You see it constantly in the newspapers. Even a well-known figure if he loses his memory and wanders away is only discovered by accident. The reason is that the human personality is identified far less by appearance than by its habits and mind. Loss of memory means the loss of all true marks of identification, and the physical look alters to correspond. Medina has stolen these three poor souls' memories and set them adrift like waifs. David Warcliff may at this moment be playing in a London gutter along with a dozen guttersnipes, and his own father could scarcely pick him out from the rest. Mercot may be a dock labourer or a deck hand, whom you wouldn't recognize if you met him, though you had sat opposite him in a college hall every night for a year. And Miss Victor may be in a gaiety chorus or a milliner's assistant or a girl in a dancing saloon. . . . Wait a minute. You saw Odell at a dance-club? There may be something in that." I could see his eyes abstracted in thought.

"There's another thing I forgot to mention," I said. "Miss Victor's fiancé is over here, staying in Carlton House Terrace. He is old Turpin, who used to be with the division—the Marquis de la Tour du Pin."

Sandy wrote the name down. "Her fiancé. He may come in useful. What sort of fellow?"

"Brave as a lion, but he'll want watching, for he's a bit of a gascon."

We went out after breakfast and sat in an arbour looking down a shallow side-valley to the upper streams of the Windrush. The sounds of morning were beginning to rise from the little village far away in the bottom—the jolt of a wagon, the "clink-clenk" from the smithy, the babble of children at play. In a fortnight the may-fly would be here, and every laburnum and guelder rose in bloom. Sandy, who had been away from England for years, did not speak for a long time, but drank in the sweet-scented peace of it. "Poor devil," he said at last, "he has nothing like this to love. He can only hate."

I asked whom he was talking about, and he said "Medina."

"I'm trying to understand him. You can't fight a man unless you understand him, and in a way sympathize with him."

"Well, I can't say I sympathize with him, and I most certainly don't understand him."

"Do you remember once telling me that he had no vanity? You were badly out there. He has a vanity which amounts to delirium.

"This is how I read him," he went on. "To begin with, there's a far-away streak of the Latin in him, but he is mainly Irish, and that never makes a good cross. He's the *déraciné* Irish, such as you find in America. I take it that he imbibed from that terrible old woman—I've never met her, but I see her plainly and I know that she is terrible—he imbibed that venomous hatred of imaginary things—an imaginary England, an imaginary civilization, which they call love of country. There is no love in it. They think there is, and sentimentalize about an old simplicity, and spinning-wheels and turf fires and an uncouth language, but it's all hollow. There's plenty of decent plain folk in Ireland, but his kind of *déraciné* is a ghastly throw-back to something you find in the dawn of history, hollow and cruel like the fantastic gods of their own myths. Well, you start with this ingrained hate."

"I agree about the old lady. She looked like Lady Macbeth."

"But hate soon becomes conceit. If you hate, you despise, and when you despise you esteem inordinately the self which despises. This is how I look at it, but remember, I'm still in the dark and only feeling my way to an understanding. I see Medina growing up—I don't know in what environment—conscious of great talents and immense good looks, flattered by those around him till he thinks himself a god. His hatred does not die, but it is transformed into a colossal egotism and vanity, which, of course, is a form of hate. He discovers quite early that he has this remarkable hypnotic power—Oh, you may laugh at it, because you happen to be immune from it, but it is a big thing in the world for all that. He discovers another thing—that he has an extraordinary gift of attracting people and making them believe in him. Some of the worst scoundrels in history have had it. Now, remember his vanity. It makes him want to play the biggest game. He does not want to be a king among pariahs; he wants to be the ruler of what is most strange to him, what he hates and in an unwilling bitter way admires. So he aims at conquering the very heart, the very soundest part of our society. Above all, he wants to be admired by men and admitted into the innermost circle."

"He has succeeded all right," I said.

"He has succeeded, and that is the greatest possible tribute to his huge cleverness. Everything about him is dead right—clothes, manner, modesty, accomplishments. He has made himself an excellent sportsman. Do you know why he shoots so well, Dick? By faith—or fatalism, if you like. His vanity doesn't allow him to believe that he could miss. . . . But he governs himself strictly. In his life he is practically an ascetic, and though he is adored by women he doesn't care a straw for them. There are no lusts of the flesh in that kind of character. He has one absorbing passion which subdues all others—what our friend Michael Scott called 'hominum dominatus'."

"I see that. But how do you explain the other side?"

"It is all the ancestral hate. First of all, of course, he has got to have money, so he gets it in the way Macgillivray knows about. Second, he wants to build up a regiment of faithful slaves. That's where you come in, Dick. There is always that inhuman hate at the back of his egotism. He wants to conquer in order to destroy, for destruction is the finest meat for his vanity. You'll find the same thing in the lives of Eastern tyrants, for when a man aspires to be like God he becomes an incarnate devil."

"It is a tough proposition," I observed dismally.

"It would be an impossible proposition, but for one thing. He is always in danger of giving himself away out of sheer arrogance. Did you ever read the old Irish folk-lore? Very beautiful it is, but there is always something fantastic and silly which mars the finest stories. They lack the grave good-sense which you find in the Norse sagas and, of course, in the Greek. Well, he has this freakish element in his blood. That is why he sent out that rhyme about the three hostages, which by an amazing concatenation of chances put you on to his trail. Our hope is—and, mind you, I think it is a slender hope—that his vanity may urge him to further indiscretions."

"I don't know how you feel about it," I said, "but I've got a pretty healthy hatred for that lad. I'm longing for a quiet life, but I swear I won't settle down again till I've got even with him."

"You never will," said Sandy solemnly. "Don't let's flatter ourselves that you and I are going to down Medina. We are not. A very wise man once said to me that in this life you could often get success, if you didn't want victory. In this case we're out for success only. We want to release the hostages. Victory we can never hope for. Why, man, supposing we succeed fully, we'll never be able to connect Medina with the thing. His tools are faithful, because he has stolen their souls and they work blindly under him. Supposing Macgillivray rounds up all the big gang and puts the halter round their necks. There will be none of them to turn King's evidence and give Medina away. Why? Because none of them *know* anything against him. They're his unconscious agents, and very likely most have never seen him. And you may be pretty sure that his banking accounts are too skilfully arranged to show anything."

"All the same," I said stubbornly, "I have a notion that I'll be able to put a spoke in his wheel."

"Oh, I daresay we can sow suspicion, but I believe he'll be too strong for us. He'll advance in his glorious career, and may become Prime Minister—or Viceroy of India—what a chance the second would be for him!—and publish exquisite little poetry books, as finished and melancholy as *The Shropshire Lad*. Pessimism, you know, is often a form of vanity."

At midday it was time for me to be off, if I was to be at Hull by six o'clock. I asked Sandy what he proposed to do next, and he said he was undecided. "My position," he said, "badly cramps my form. It would be ruination if Medina knew I was in England—ruination for both you and me. Mr. Alexander Thomson must lie very low. I must somehow get in touch with Macgillivray to hear if he has anything about Odell. I rather fancy Odell. But there will probably be nothing doing till you come back, and I think I'll have a little fishing."

"Suppose I want to get hold of you?"

"Suppose nothing of the kind. You mustn't make any move in my direction. That's our only safety. If I want you I'll come to you."

As I was starting he said suddenly: "I've never met your wife, Dick. What about my going over to Fosse and introducing myself?"

"The very thing," I cried. "She is longing to meet you. But remember that I'm supposed to be lying sick upstairs."

As I looked back he was waving his hand, and his face wore its familiar elfish smile.

65   HOW A GERMAN ENGINEER FOUND STRANGE FISHING

I got to Hull about six o'clock, having left my car at the garage in York, and finished the journey by train. I had my kit in a small suit-case and rucksack, and I waited on the quay till I saw Dr. Newhover arrive with a lot of luggage and a big rod-box. When I reckoned he would be in his cabin arranging his belongings, I went on board myself, and went straight to my own cabin, which was a comfortable two-berthed one well forward. There I had sandwiches brought me, and settled myself to doze and read for thirty-six hours.

All that night and all next day it blew fairly hard, and I remained quietly in my bunk, trying to read Boswell's *Life of Johnson*, and thanking my stars that I hadn't lived a thousand years earlier and been a Viking. I didn't see myself ploughing those short steep seas in an open galley. I woke on the morning of the 23rd to find the uneasy motion at an end, and, looking out of my port-hole, saw a space of green sunlit water, a rocky beach, and the white and red of a little town. The *Gudrun* waited about an hour at Stavanger, so I gave Dr. Newhover time to get on shore, before I had a hurried breakfast in the saloon and followed him. I saw him go off with two men, and get on board a motor-launch which was lying beside one of the jetties. The coast was now clear, so I went into the town, found the agents to whom Archie Roylance had cabled, and learned that my own motor-launch was ready and waiting in the inner harbour where the fishing-boats lie. A clerk took me down there, and introduced me to Johan, my skipper, a big, cheerful, bearded Norwegian, who had a smattering of English. I bought a quantity of provisions, and by ten o'clock we were on the move. I asked Johan about the route to Merdal, and he pointed out a moving speck a couple of miles ahead of us. "That is Kristian Egge's boat," he said. "He carries an English fisherman to Merdal, and we follow." I got my glasses on the craft, and made out Newhover smoking in the stern.

It was a gorgeous day, with that funny northern light which makes noon seem like early morning. I enjoyed every hour of it, partly because I had now a definite job before me, and partly because I was in the open air to which I properly belonged. I got no end of amusement watching the wild life—the cormorants and eider-duck on the little islands, and the seals, with heads as round as Medina's, that slipped off the skerries at our approach. The air was chilly and fresh, but when we turned the corner of the Merdalfjord out of the sea-wind and the sun climbed the sky it was as warm as June. A big flat island we passed, all short turf and rocky outcrops, was pointed out to me by Johan as Flacksholm. Soon we were shaping due east in an inlet which was surrounded by dark steep hills, with the snow lying in the gullies. I had Boswell with me in two volumes; the first I had read in the steamer, and the second I was now starting on, when it fell overboard, through my getting up in a hurry to look at a flock of duck. So I presented the odd volume to Johan, and surrendered myself to tobacco and meditation.

In the afternoon the inlet narrowed to a fjord, and the walls of hill grew steeper. They were noble mountains, cut sharp like the edge of the Drakensberg, and crowned with a line of snow, so that they looked like a sugar-coated cake that had been sliced. Streams came out of the upper snow-wreaths and hurled themselves down the steeps—above a shimmering veil of mist, and below a torrent of green water tumbling over pebbles to the sea. The landscape and the weather lulled me into a delectable peace which refused to be disturbed by any "looking before or after", as some poet says. Newhover was ahead of me—we never lost track of his launch—and it was my business to see what he was up to and to keep myself out of his sight. The ways and means of it I left to fortune to provide.

By-and-by the light grew dimmer, and the fjord grew narrower, so that dusk fell on us, though, looking back down the inlet, we could see a bright twilight. I assumed that Newhover would go on to Merdal and the fjord's head, where the Skarso entered the sea, and had decided to stop at Hauge, a village two miles short of it, on the south shore. We came to Hauge about half-past eight, in a wonderful purple dusk, for the place lay right under the shadow of a great cliff. I gave Johan full instructions; he was to wait for me and expect me when I turned up, and to provision himself from the village. On no account must he come up to Merdal, or go out of sight or hail of the boat. He seemed to relish the prospect of a few days' idleness, for he landed me at a wooden jetty in great good-humour, and wished me sport. What he thought I was after I cannot imagine, for I departed with a rucksack on my back and a stout stick in my hand, which scarcely suggested the chase.

I was in good spirits myself as I stretched my legs on the road which led from Hauge to Merdal. The upper fjord lay black on my left hand, the mountains rose black on my right, but though I walked in darkness I could see twilight ahead of me, where the hills fell back from the Skarso valley, that wonderful apple-green twilight which even in spring is all the northern night. I had never seen it before, and I suppose something in my blood answered to the place—for my father used to say that the Hannays came originally from Norse stock. There was a jolly crying of birds from the waters, ducks and geese and oyster-catchers and sandpipers, and now and then would come a great splash as if a salmon were jumping in the brackish tides on his way to the Skarso. I was thinking longingly of my rods left behind, when on turning a corner the lights of Merdal showed ahead, and it seemed to me that I had better be thinking of my next step.

I knew no Norwegian, but I counted on finding natives who could speak English, seeing so many of them have been in England or America. Newhover, I assumed, would go to the one hotel, and it was for me to find lodgings elsewhere. I began to think this spying business might be more difficult than I had thought, for if he saw me he would recognize me, and that must not happen. I was ready, of course, with a story of a walking tour, but he would be certain to suspect, and certain to let Medina know. . . . Well, a lodging for the night was my first business, and I must start inquiries. Presently I came to the little pier of Merdal, which was short of the village itself. There were several men sitting smoking on barrels and coils of rope, and one who stood at the end looking out to where Kristian Egge's boat, which had brought Newhover, lay moored. I turned down the road to it, for it seemed a place to gather information.

I said good-evening to the men, and was just about to ask them for advice about quarters, when the man who had been looking out to sea turned round at the sound of my voice. He seemed an oldish fellow, with rather a stoop in his back, wearing an ancient shooting-jacket. The light was bad, but there was something in the cut of his jib that struck me as familiar, though I couldn't put a name to it.

I spoke to the Norwegians in English, but it was obvious that I had hit on a bunch of indifferent linguists. They shook their heads, and one pointed to the village, as if to tell me that I would be better understood there. Then the man in the shooting-jacket spoke.

"Perhaps I can help," he said. "There is a good inn in Merdal, which at this season is not full."

He spoke excellent English, but it was obvious that he wasn't an Englishman. There was an unmistakable emphasis of the gutturals.

"I doubt the inn may be too good for my purse," I said. "I am on a walking tour and must lodge cheaply."

He laughed pleasantly. "There may be accommodation elsewhere. Peter Bojer may have a spare bed. I am going that way, sir, and can direct you."

He had turned towards me, and his figure caught the beam of the riding-light of the motor-launch. I saw a thin sunburnt face with a very pleasant expression, and an untidy grizzled beard. Then I knew him, and I could have shouted with amazement at the chance which had brought us two together again.

We walked side by side up the jetty road and on to the highway.

"I think," I said, "that we have met before, Herr Gaudian."

He stopped short. "That is my name—but I do not—I do not think——"

"Do you remember a certain Dutchman called Cornelius Brandt, whom you entertained at your country house one night in December '15?"

He looked searchingly in my face.

"I remember," he said. "I also remember a Mr. Richard Hanau, one of Guggenheim's engineers, with whom I talked at Constantinople."

"The same," I said. For a moment I was not clear how he was going to take the revelation, but his next action reassured me, and I saw that I had not been wrong in my estimate of the one German I have ever whole-heartedly liked. He began to laugh, a friendly, tolerant laugh.

"*Kritzi Turken!*" he cried. "It is indeed romantic. I have often wondered whether I should see or hear of you again, and behold! you step out of the darkness on a Norwegian fjord."

"You bear no malice?" I said. "I served my country as you served yours. I played fair, as you played fair."

"Malice!" he cried. "But we are gentlemen; also we are not children. I rejoice to see that you have survived the War. I have always wished you well, for you are a very bold and brave man."

"Not a bit of it," I said—"only lucky."

"By what name shall I call you now—Brandt or Hanau?"

"My name is Richard Hannay, but for the present I am calling myself Cornelius Brand—for a reason which I am going to tell you." I had suddenly made up my mind to take Gaudian into my full confidence. He seemed to have been sent by Providence for that purpose, and I was not going to let such a chance slip

But at my words he stopped short.

"Mr. Hannay," he said, "I do not want your confidence. You are still engaged, I take it, in your country's service? I do not question your motive, but remember I am a German, and I cannot be party to the pursuit of one of my countrymen, however base I may think him."

I could only stare. "But I am not in my country's service," I stammered. "I left it at the Armistice, and I'm a farmer now."

"Do English farmers travel in Norway under false names?"

"That's a private business which I want to explain to you. I assure you there is no German in it. I want to keep an eye on the doings of a fashionable English doctor."

"I must believe you," he said, after a pause. "But two hours ago a man arrived in a launch you see anchored out there. He is a fisherman, and is now at the inn. That man is known to me—too well known. He is a German, who during the War served Germany in secret ways, in America and elsewhere. I did not love him, and I think he did my country grievous ill, but that is a matter for us Germans to settle, and not for foreigners."

"I know your man as Dr. Newhover of Wimpole Street."

"So?" he said. "He has taken again his father's name, which was Neuhofer. We knew him as Kristoffer. What do you want with him?"

"Nothing that any honest German wouldn't approve," and there and then I gave him a sketch of the Medina business. He exclaimed in horror.

"Mr. Hannay," he said hesitatingly, "you are being honest with me?"

"I swear by all that's holy I am telling you the plain truth, and the full truth. Newhover may have done anything you jolly well like in the War. That's all washed out. I'm after him to get a line on a foul business which is English in origin. I want to put a spoke in the wheel of English criminals, and to save innocent lives. Besides, Newhover is only a subordinate. I don't propose to raise a finger against him, only to find out what he is doing."

He held out his hand. "I believe you," he said, "and if I can I will help you."

He conducted me through the long street of the village, past the inn, where I supposed Newhover was now going to bed, and out on to the road which ran up the Skarso valley. We came in sight of the river, a mighty current full of melted snow, sweeping in noble curves through the meadowland in that uncanny dusk. It appeared that he lodged with Peter Bojer, who had a spare bed, and when we reached the cottage, which stood a hundred yards from the highway on the very brink of the stream, Peter was willing to let me have it. His wife gave us supper—an omelette, smoked salmon, and some excellent Norwegian beer—and after it I got out my map and had a survey of the neighbourhood.

Gaudian gave me a grisly picture of the condition of his own country. It seemed that the downfall of the old régime had carried with it the decent wise men like himself, who had opposed its follies, but had lined up with it on patriotic grounds when the War began. He said that Germany was no place for a moderate man, and that the power lay with the bloated industrials, who were piling up fortunes abroad while they were wrecking their country at home. The only opposition, he said, came from the communists, who were half-witted, and the monarchists, who wanted the impossible. "Reason is not listened to, and I fear there is no salvation till my poor people have passed through the last extremity. You foreign Powers have hastened our destruction, when you had it in your hands to save us. I think you have meant well, but you have been blind, for you have not supported our moderate men and have by your harshness played the game of the wreckers among us."

It appeared that he was very poor now, like all the professional classes. I thought it odd that this man, who had a world-wide reputation as an engineer, couldn't earn a big income in any country he chose. Then I saw that it was because he had lost the wish to make money. He had seen too deep into the vanity of human wishes to have any ambition left. He was unmarried, with no near relations, and he found his pleasure in living simply in remote country places and watching flowers and beasts. He was a keen fisherman, but couldn't afford a good beat, so he leased a few hundred yards from a farmer, who had not enough water to get a proper rent for it, and he did a lot of trout fishing in the tarns high up in the hills and in the Skarso above the foss. As he sat facing me beyond the stove, with his kind sad brown eyes and his rugged face, I thought how like he was to a Scottish moorland shepherd. I had liked him when I first saw him in Stumm's company, but now I liked him so much that because of him I was prepared to think better of the whole German race.

I asked him if he had heard of any other Englishman in the valley—any one of the name of Jason, for instance. He said no; he had been there for three weeks, but the fishing did not begin for another fortnight, and foreign visitors had not yet arrived. Then I asked him about the *saeter* farms, and he said that few of these were open yet, since the high pastures were not ready. One or two on the lower altitudes might be already inhabited, but not many, though the winter had been a mild one and the spring had come early. "Look at the Skarso," he said. "Usually in April it is quite low, for the snowfields have not begun to melt. But to-day it is as brimming as if it were the middle of May."

He went over the map with me—an inch-to-a-mile one I had got in London—and showed me the lie of the land. The *saeters* were mostly farther up the river, reached by paths up the tributary glens. There was a good road running the length of the valley, but no side roads to connect with the parallel glens, the Uradal and the Bremendal. I found indeed one track marked on the map, which led to the Uradal by a place called Snaasen. "Yes," said Gaudian, "that is the only thing in the way of what you soldiers would call lateral communications. I've walked it, and I'm sorry for the man who tries the road in bad weather. You can see the beginning of the track from this house; it climbs up beside the torrent just across the valley. Snaasen is more or less inhabited all the year round, and I suppose you would call it a kind of *saeter*. It is a sort of shelter hut for travellers taking that road, and in summer it is a paradise for flowers. You would be surprised at the way the natives can cross the hills even in winter. Snaasen belongs to the big farm two miles up-stream, which carries with it the best beat on the Skarso. Also there is said to be first-class ryper-shooting later in the year, and an occasional bear. By the way, I rather fancy some one told me that the whole thing was owned by, or had been leased to, an Englishman. . . . You are rich, you see, and you do not leave much in Norway for poor people."

I slept like a log on a bed quite as hard as a log, and woke to a brilliant blue morning, with the birds in the pine-woods fairly riotous, and snipe drumming in the boggy meadows, and the Skarso coming down like a sea. I could see the water almost up to the pathway of a long wooden bridge that led to the big farm Gaudian had spoken of. I got my glass on the torrent opposite, and saw the track to Snaasen winding up beside it till it was lost in a fold of the ravine. Above it I scanned the crown of the ridge, which was there much lower than on the sides of the fjord. There was no snow to be seen, and I knew by a sort of instinct that if I got up there I should find a broad tableland of squelching pastures with old snowdrifts in the hollows and tracts of scrubby dwarf birch.

While I was waiting for breakfast I heard a noise from the highroad and saw a couple of the little conveyances they call *stolkjaeres* passing. My glass showed me Dr. Newhover in the first and a quantity of luggage in the second. They took the road across the wooden bridge to the big farm, and I could see the splash of their wheels at the far end of it, where the river was over the road. So Dr. Newhover, or some friend of his, was the lessee of this famous fishing which carried with it the shooting on the uplands behind it. I rather thought I should spend the day finding out more about Snaasen, and I counted myself lucky to have got quarters in such an excellent observation-post as Peter Bojer's cottage.

I wouldn't go near the track to Snaasen till I saw what Newhover did, so Gaudian and I sat patiently at Peter Bojer's window. About ten o'clock a couple of ponies laden with kit in charge of a tow-headed boy appeared at the foot of the track and slowly climbed up the ravine. An hour later came Dr. Newhover, in a suit that looked like khaki, and wearing a long mackintosh cape. He strode out well and breasted the steep path like a mountaineer. I wanted to go off myself in pursuit of him, keeping well behind, but Gaudian very sensibly pointed out how sparse the cover was, and that if he saw a man on that lonely road he would certainly want to know all about him.

We sat out-of-doors after luncheon in a pleasant glare of sun, and by-and-by were rewarded by the sight of the pack-ponies returning, laden with a different size and shape of kit. They did not stop at the big farm, but crossed the wooden bridge and took the highroad for Merdal. I concluded that this was the baggage of the man whom Newhover had replaced, and that he was returning to Stavanger in Kristian Egge's boat. About tea-time the man himself appeared—Jason, or whatever his name was. I saw two figures come down the ravine by the Snaasen road, and stop at the foot and exchange farewells. One of them turned to go back, and I saw that this was Newhover, climbing with great strides like a man accustomed to hills. The other crossed the bridge, and passed within hail of us—a foppish young man, my glass told me, wearing smart riding-breeches, and with an aquascutum slung over his shoulder.

I was very satisfied with what I had learned. I had seen Newhover relieve his predecessor, just as Medina had planned, and I knew where he was lodged. Whatever his secret was it was hidden in Snaasen, and to Snaasen I would presently go. Gaudian advised me to wait till after supper, when there would be light enough to find the way and not too much to betray us. So we both lay down and slept for four hours, and took the road about ten-thirty as fresh as yearlings.

It was a noble night, windless and mild, and, though darkness lurked in the thickets and folds of hill, the sky was filled with a translucent amethyst glow. I felt as if I were out on some sporting expedition, and enjoyed every moment of the walk with that strung-up expectant enjoyment which one gets in any form of chase. The torrent made wild music on our left hand, grumbling in pits and shooting over ledges with a sound like a snowslip. There was every kind of bird about, but I had to guess at them by their sounds and size, for there was no colour in that shadowy world.

By-and-by we reached the top and had a light cold wind in our faces blowing from the snowy mountains to the north. The place seemed a huge broken tableland, and every hollow glistened as if filled with snow or water. There were big dark shapes ahead of us which I took to be the hills beyond the Uradal. Here it was not so easy to follow the track, which twined about in order to avoid the boggy patches, and Gaudian and I frequently strayed from it and took tosses over snags of juniper. Once I was up against an iron pole, and to my surprise saw wires above. Gaudian nodded. "Snaasen is on the telephone," he said.

I had hoped to see some light in the house, so as to tell it from a distance. But we did not realize its presence till we were close upon it, standing a little back from the path, as dark as a tombstone. The inhabitants must have gone early to bed, for there was no sign of life within. It was a two-storied erection of wood, stoutly built, with broad eaves to the roof. Adjacent there stood a big barn or hayshed, and behind it some other outbuildings which might have been byres or dairies. We walked stealthily round the place, and were amazed at its utter stillness. There was no sound of an animal moving in the steading, and when a brace of mallards flew overhead we started at the noise like burglars at the creaking of a board.

Short of burglary there was nothing further to be done, so we took the road home and scrambled at a great pace down the ravine, for it was chilly on the tableland. Before we went to bed we had settled that next day Gaudian should go up to Snaasen like an ordinary tourist and make some excuse to get inside, while I would take a long tramp over the plateau, keeping well away from the house, in case there might be something ado in that barren region.

Next morning saw the same cloudless weather, and we started off about ten o'clock. I had a glorious but perfectly futile day. I went up the Skarso to well above the foss, and then climbed the north wall of the valley by a gully choked with brushwood, which gave out long before the top and left me to finish my ascent by way of some very loose screes and unpleasant boiler-plates. I reached the plateau much farther to the east, where it was at a greater altitude, so that I looked down upon the depression where ran the track to Uradal. I struck due north among boggy meadows and the remains of old snowdrifts, through whose fringes flowers were showing, till I was almost on the edge of Uradal, and looked away beyond it to a fine cluster of rock peaks streaked and patched with ice. The Uradal glen was so deep cut that I could not see into it, so I moved west and struck the Merdal track well to the north of Snaasen. After that I fetched a circuit behind Snaasen, and had a good view of the house from the distance of about half a mile. Two of its chimneys were smoking, and there were sounds of farm work from the yard. There was no sign of live stock, but it looked as if some one was repairing the sheds against the summer season. I waited for more than an hour, but I saw no human being, so I turned homeward, and made a careful descent by the ravine, reconnoitring every corner in case I should run into Newhover.

I found that Gaudian had returned before me. When I asked him what luck he had had he shook his head.

"I played the part of a weary traveller, and asked for milk. An ugly woman gave me beer. She said she had no milk, till the cattle came up from the valleys. She would not talk and she was deaf. She said an English Herr had the ryper-shooting, but lived at Tryssil. That is the name of the big farm by the Skarso. She would tell me no more, and I saw no other person. But I observed that Snaasen is larger than I thought. There are rooms built out at the back, which we thought were barns. There is ample space there for a man to be concealed."

I asked him if he had any plan, and he said he thought of going boldly up next day and asking for Newhover, whom he could say he had seen passing Peter Bojer's cottage. He disliked the man, but had never openly quarrelled with him. I approved of that, but in the meantime I resolved to do something on my own account that night. I was getting anxious, for I felt that my time was growing desperately short; it was now the 25th of April and I was due back in London on the 29th, and, if I failed to turn up, Medina would make inquiries at Fosse Manor and suspect. I had made up my mind to go alone that night to Snaasen and do a little pacific burgling.

I set out about eleven, and I put my pistol in my pocket, as well as my flask and sandwiches and electric torch, for it occurred to me that anything might happen. I made good going across the bridge and up the first part of the track, for I wanted to have as much time as possible for my job. My haste was nearly my undoing, for, instead of reconnoitring and keeping my ears open, I strode up the hill as if I had been walking to make a record. It was by the mercy of Heaven that I was at a point where an outjutting boulder made a sharp corner when I was suddenly aware that some one was coming down the road. I flattened myself into the shadow, and saw Newhover.

He did not see or hear me, for he, too, was preoccupied. He was descending at a good pace, and he must have started in a hurry, for he had no hat. His longish blond locks were all touzled, and his face seemed sharper than usual with anxiety.

I wondered what on earth had happened, and my first notion was to follow him downhill. And then it occurred to me that his absence gave me a sovereign chance at Snaasen. But if the household was astir there might be other travellers on the road, and it behoved me to go warily. Now, near the top of the ravine, just under the edge of the tableland, there was a considerable patch of wood—birches, juniper, and wind-blown pines—for there the torrent flowed in a kind of cup, after tumbling off the plateau and before hurling itself down to the valley. Here it was possible to find an alternative road to the path, so I dived in among the matted whortleberries and moss-covered boulders.

I had not gone ten yards before I realized that there was somebody or something else in the thicket. There was a sound of plunging ahead of me, then the crack of a rotten log, then the noise of a falling stone. It might be a beast, but it struck me that no wild thing would move so awkwardly. Only human boots made that kind of clumsy slipping.

If this was somebody from Snaasen, what was he doing off the track? Could he be watching me? Well, I proposed to do a little stalking on my own account. I got down on all-fours and crawled in cover in the direction of the sound. It was very dark there, but I could see a faint light where the scrub thinned round the stream.

Soon I was at the edge of the yeasty water. The sounds had stopped, but suddenly they began again a little farther up, and there was a scuffle as if part of the bank had given way. The man, whoever he was, seemed to be trying to cross. That would be a dangerous thing to do, for the torrent was wide and very strong. I crawled a yard or two up-stream, and then in an open patch saw what was happening.

A fallen pine made a crazy bridge to a great rock, from which the rest of the current might conceivably be leaped. A man was kneeling on the trunk and beginning to move along it. . . . But as I looked the rotten thing gave way, and the next I saw he was struggling in the foam. It was all the matter of a fraction of a second, and before I knew I was leaning over the brink and clutching at an arm. I gripped it, braced one leg against a rock, and hauled the owner close into the edge out of the main current. He seemed to have taken no hurt, for he found a foothold, and scarcely needed my help to scramble up beside me.

Then to my surprise he went for me tooth and nail. It was like the assault of a wild beast, and its suddenness rolled me on my back. I felt hands on my throat, and grew angry, caught the wrists and wrenched them away. I flung a leg over his back and got uppermost, and after that he was at my mercy. He seemed to realize it, too, for he lay quite quiet and did not struggle.

"What the devil do you mean?" I said angrily. "You'd have been drowned but for me, and then you try to throttle me."

I got out my torch and had a look at him. It was the figure of a slight young man, dressed in rough homespun such as Norwegian farm lads wear. His face was sallow and pinched, and decorated with the most preposterous wispish beard, and his hair was cut roughly as if with garden shears. The eyes that looked up at me were as scared and wild as a deer's.

"What the devil do you mean?" I repeated, and then to my surprise he replied in English.

"Let me up," he said, "I'm too tired to fight. I'll go back with you."

Light broke in on me.

"Don't you worry, old chap," I said soothingly. "You're going back with me, but not to that infernal *saeter*. We've met before, you know. You're Lord Mercot, and I saw you ride Red Prince last year at the 'House' Grind."

He was sitting up, staring at me like a ghost.

"Who are you? Oh, for God's sake, who are you?"

"Hannay's my name. I live at Fosse Manor in the Cotswolds. You once came to dine with us before the Heythrop Ball."

"Hannay!" He repeated stumblingly—"I remember—I think— remember—remember Lady Hannay. Yes—and Fosse. It's on the road between——"

He scrambled to his feet.

"Oh, sir, get me away. He's after me—the new devil with the long face, the man who first brought me here. I don't know what has happened to me, but I've been mad a long time, and I've only got sane in the last days. Then I remembered—and I ran away. But they're after me. Oh, quick, quick! Let's hide."

"See here, my lad," I said, and I took out my pistol. "The first man that lays a hand on you I shoot, and I don't miss. You're as safe now as if you were at home. But this is no place to talk, and I've the devil of a lot to tell you. I'm going to take you down with me to my lodging in the valley. But they're hunting you, so we've got to go cannily. Are you fit to walk? Well, do exactly as I tell you, and in an hour you'll be having a long drink and looking up time-tables."

I consider that journey back a creditable piece of piloting. The poor boy was underfed and shaking with excitement, but he stepped out gallantly, and obeyed me like a lamb. We kept off the track so as to muffle our steps in grass, and took every corner like scouts in a reconnaissance. We met Newhover coming back, but we heard him a long way off, and were in good cover when he passed. He was hurrying as furiously as ever, and I could hear his laboured breathing. After that we had a safe road over the meadow, but we crossed the bridge most circumspectly, making sure that there was no one in the landscape. About half-past one I pushed open Gaudian's bedroom window, woke him, and begged him to forage for food and drink.

"Did you get into Snaasen?" he asked sleepily.

"No, but I've found what we've been looking for. One of the three hostages is at this moment sitting on your cabin-box."

66 I RETURN TO SERVITUDE

We fed Mercot with tinned meats and biscuits and bottled beer, and he ate like a famished schoolboy. The odd thing was that his terror had suddenly left him. I suppose the sight of me, which had linked him up definitely with his past, had made him feel a waif no more, and, once he was quite certain who he was, his natural courage returned. He got great comfort from looking at Gaudian, and indeed I could not imagine a better sedative than a sight of that kind, wise old face. I lent him pyjamas, rubbed him down to prevent a chill from his ducking, put him in my bed, and had the satisfaction of seeing him slip off at once into deep slumber.

Next morning Gaudian and I interviewed Peter Bojer and explained that a young English friend of ours had had an accident while on a walking tour, and might be with us for a day or two. It was not likely that Newhover would advertise his loss, and in any case Peter was no gossip, and Gaudian, who had known him for years, let him see that we wanted the fact of a guest being with us kept as quiet as possible. The boy slept till nearly midday, while I kept a watch on the road. Newhover appeared early, and went down to Merdal village, where he spent the better part of the forenoon. He was probably making inquiries, but they were bound in his own interest to be discreet ones. Then he returned to Tryssil, and later I saw a dejected figure tramping up the Snaasen track. He may have thought that the body of the fugitive was in some pool of the torrent or being swirled down by the Skarso to the sea, and I imagined that that scarcely fitted in with his instructions.

When Mercot awoke at last and had his breakfast he looked a different lad. His eyes had lost their fright, and though he stuttered badly and seemed to have some trouble in collecting his wits, he had obviously taken hold of himself. His great desire was to get clean, and that took some doing, for he could not have had a bath for weeks. Then he wanted to borrow my razor and shave his beard, but I managed to prevent him in time, for I had been thinking the thing out, and I saw that that would never do. So far as I could see, he had recovered his memory, but there were still gaps in it; that is to say, he remembered all his past perfectly well till he left Oxford on February 17th, and he remembered the events of the last few days, but between the two points he was still hazy.

On returning to his rooms that February evening he had found a note about a horse he was trying to buy, an urgent note asking him to come round at once to certain stables. He had just time for this before dressing for dinner, so he dashed out of the house—meeting nobody, as it chanced, on the stairs, and, as the night was foggy, being seen by no one in the streets. After that his memory was a blank. He had wakened in a room in London, which he thought was a nursing home, and had seen a doctor—I could picture that doctor—and had gone to sleep again. After that his recollection was like a black night studded with little points of light which were physical sensations. He remembered being very cold and sometimes very tired, he recollected the smell of paraffin, and of mouldy hay, and of a treacly drink which made him sick. He remembered faces, too, a cross old woman who cursed him, a man who seemed to be always laughing, and whose laugh he feared more than curses. . . .

I suppose that Medina's spell must have been wearing thin during these last days, and that the keeper, Jason, or whoever he was, could not revive it. For Mercot had begun to see Jason no longer as a terror but as an offence—an underbred young bounder whom he detested. And with this clearing of the foreground came a lightening of the background. He saw pictures of his life at Alcester, at first as purely objective things, but soon as in some way connected with himself. Then longing started, passionate longing for something which he knew was his own. . . . It was a short step from that to the realization that he was Lord Mercot, though he happened to be clad like a tramp and was as dirty as a stoker. And then he proceeded to certain halting deductions. Something bad had happened to him: he was in a foreign land—which land he didn't know: he was being ill-treated and kept prisoner; he must escape and get back to his old happy world. He thought of escape quite blindly, without any plan; if only he could get away from that accursed *saeter*, he would remember better, things would happen to him, things would come back to him.

Then Jason went and Newhover came, and Newhover drove him half crazy with fear, for the doctor's face was in some extraordinary way mixed up with his confused memory of the gaps between the old world and the new. He was mad to escape now, but rather to escape from Newhover than to reach anywhere. He watched for his chance, and found it about eight o'clock the evening before, when the others in the house were at supper. Some instinct had led him towards Merdal. He had heard footsteps behind him and had taken to the thicket. . . . I appeared, an enemy as he thought, and he had despairingly flung himself on me. Then I had spoken his name, and that fixed the wavering panorama of his memory. He "came to himself" literally, and was now once more the undergraduate of Christ Church, rather shell-shocked and jumpy, but quite sane.

The question which worried me was whether the cure was complete, whether Newhover could act as Medina's deputy and resurrect the spell. I did not believe that he could, but I wasn't certain. Anyhow it had to be risked.

Mercot repeated his request for the loan of my razor. He was smoking a Turkish cigarette as if every whiff took him nearer Elysium. Badly shorn, ill-clad, and bearded as he was, he had still the ghost of the air of the well-to-do, sporting young man. He wanted to know when the steamer sailed, but there seemed no panic now in his impatience.

"Look here," I said. "I don't think you can start just yet. There's a lot I want to tell you now you're able to hear it."

I gave him a rough summary of Macgillivray's story, and the tale of the three hostages. I think he found it comforting to know that there were others in the same hole as himself. "By Jove!" he said, "what a damnable business! And I'm the only one you've got on the track of. No word of the girl and the little boy?"

"No word!"

"Poor devils," he said, but I do not think he really took in the situation.

"So you see how we are placed. Macgillivray's round-up is fixed for the 10th of June. We daren't release the hostages till the 9th, for otherwise the gang would suspect. They have everything ready, as I've told you, for their own liquidation. Also, we can't release one without the others, unless by the 9th of June we have given up hope of the others. Do you see what I mean?"

He didn't. "All I want is to get home in double-quick time," he said.

"I don't wonder. But you must see that that is impossible, unless we chuck in our hand."

He stared at me, and I saw fright beginning to return to his eyes.

"Do you mean that you want me to go back to that bloody place?"

"That's what I mean. If you think it out, you'll see it's the only way. We must do nothing to spoil the chances of the other two. You're a gentleman, and are bound to play the game."

"But I can't," he cried. "Oh, my God, you can't ask me to." There were tears in his voice, and his eyes were wild.

"It's a good deal to ask, but I know you will do it. There's not a scrap of danger now, for you have got back your memory, and you know where you are. It's up to you to play a game with your gaoler. He is the dupe now. You fill the part of the half-witted farm-boy and laugh at him all the time in your sleeve. Herr Gaudian will be waiting down here to keep an eye on you, and when the time is ripe—and it won't be more than five weeks—I give you full permission to do anything you like with Dr. Newhover."

"I can't, I can't," he wailed, and his jaw dropped like a scared child's.

Then Gaudian spoke. "I think we had better leave the subject for the present. Lord Mercot will do precisely what he thinks right. You have sprung the thing on him too suddenly. I think it might be a good plan if you went for a walk, Hannay. Try the south side of the foss—there's some very pretty scrambling to be had there."

He spoke to me at the door. "The poor boy is all in pieces. You cannot ask him for a difficult decision when his nerves are still raw. Will you leave him with me? I have had some experience in dealing with such cases."

When I got back for supper, after a climb which exercised every muscle in my body, I found Gaudian teaching Mercot a new Patience game. We spent a very pleasant evening, and I noticed that Gaudian led the talk to matters in which the boy could share, and made him speak of himself. We heard about his racing ambitions, his desire to ride in the Grand National, his hopes for his polo game. It appeared that he was destined for the Guards, but he was to be allowed a year's travel when he left the 'Varsity, and we planned out an itinerary for him. Gaudian, who had been almost everywhere in the world, told him of places in Asia where no tourist had ever been and where incredible sport was to be had in virgin forest, and I pitched him some yarns about those few districts of Africa which are still unspoiled. He got very keen, for he had a bit of the explorer in him, and asked modestly if we thought he could pull off certain plans we had suggested. We told him there was no doubt about it. "It's not as tough a proposition as riding in the National," I said.

When we had put him to bed, Gaudian smiled as if well pleased. "He has begun to get back his confidence," he said.

He slept for twelve hours, and when he woke I had gone out, for I thought it better to leave him in Gaudian's hands. I had to settle the business that day, for it was now the 27th. I walked down the fjord to Hauge, and told Johan to be ready to start next morning. I asked him about the weather, which was still cloudless, and he stared at the sky and sniffed, and thought it would hold for a day or two. "But rain is coming," he added, "and wind. The noise of the foss is too loud."

When I returned Gaudian met me at the door. "The boy has recovered," he said. "He will speak to you himself. He is a brave boy and will do a hard task well."

It was a rather shy and self-conscious Mercot that greeted me.

"I'm afraid I behaved rather badly yesterday, sir. I was feeling a bit rattled, and I'm ashamed of myself, for I've always rather fancied my nerve."

"My dear chap," I said, "you've been through enough to crack the nerve of a buffalo."

"I want to say that of course I'll do what you want. I must play the game by the others. That poor little boy! And I remember Miss Victor quite well—I once stayed in the same house with her. I'll go back to the *saeter* when you give the word. Indeed, I'm rather looking forward to it. I promise to play the half-wit so that Dr. Newhover will think me safe in the bag. All I ask is that you let me have my innings with him when the time comes. I've a biggish score to settle."

"Indeed I promise that. Look here, Mercot, if you don't mind my saying it, I think you're behaving uncommonly well. You're a gallant fellow."

"Oh, that's all right," he said, blushing. "When do you want me to start? If it's possible, I'd like another night in a decent bed."

"You shall have it. Early to-morrow morning we'll accompany you to the prison door. You've got to gibber when you see Newhover, and pretend not to be able to give any account of your doings. I leave you to put up a camouflage. The next five weeks will be infernally dull for you, but you must just shut your teeth and stick it out. Remember, Gaudian will be down here all the time and in touch with your friends, and when the day comes you will take your instructions from him. And, by the way, I'm going to leave you my pistol. I suppose you can keep it concealed, for Newhover is not likely to search your pockets. Don't use it, of course, but it may be a comfort to you to know that you have it."

He took it gladly. "Don't be afraid I'll use it. What I'm keeping for Newhover is the best hiding man ever had. He's a bit above my weight, but I don't mind that."

Very early next morning we woke Mercot, and, while the sky was turning from sapphire to turquoise, took our way through the hazy meadows and up the Snaasen track. We left it at the summit, and fetched a circuit round by the back of the *saeter*, but first we made Mercot roll in the thicket till he had a very grubby face and plenty of twigs and dust in his untidy hair. Then the two of us shook hands with him, found a lair in a patch of juniper, and watched him go forward.

A forlorn figure he looked in that cold half-light as he approached the *saeter* door. But he was acting his part splendidly, for he stumbled with fatigue, dropped heavily against the door, and beat on it feebly. It seemed a long time till it opened, and then he appeared to shrink back in terror. The old woman cried out shrilly to summon some one from within, and presently Newhover came out in a dressing-gown. He caught Mercot by the shoulder, and shook him, and that valiant soul behaved exactly like a lunatic, shielding his head and squealing like a rabbit. Finally we saw him dragged indoors. . . . It was horrible to leave him like that, but I comforted myself with the thought of what Newhover would be like in five weeks' time.

We raced back to Peter Bojer's, and after a hasty breakfast started off for Hauge. I settled with Gaudian that he was to report any developments to me by cable, and I was to do the same to him. When the day of release was fixed, he was to go boldly up to Snaasen and deal with the doctor as he liked, making sure that he could not communicate with Medina for a day or two. A motor-launch would be waiting at Merdal to take the two to Stavanger, for I wanted him to see Mercot on board the English steamer. I arranged, too, that he should be supplied with adequate funds, for Mercot had not a penny.

We pushed off at once, for I had to be at Flacksholm in good time, and as the morning advanced I did not feel so sure of the weather. What wind we had had these last days had been mild breezes from the west, but now it seemed to be shifting more to the north, and increasing in vehemence. Down in that deep-cut fjord it was calm enough, but up on the crest of the tableland on the northern shore I could see that it was blowing hard, for my glass showed me little *tourmentes* of snow. Also it had suddenly got much colder. I made Johan force the pace, and early in the afternoon we were out of the shelter of the rock walls in the inlet into which the fjord broadened. Here it was blowing fairly hard, and there was a stiff sea running. Flying squalls of rain beat down on us from the north, and for five minutes or so would shut out the view. It was a regular gusty April day, such as you find in spring salmon-fishing in Scotland, and had my job been merely to catch the boat at Stavanger I should not have minded it at all. But there was no time for the boat, for in little more than twenty-four hours I had to meet Medina. I wondered if Archie Roylance had turned up. I wondered still more how an aeroplane was to make the return journey over these stormy leagues of sea.

Presently the low green lines of Flacksholm showed through the spray, and when Johan began to shape his course to the south-west for Stavanger, I bade him go straight forward and land me on the island. I told him I had a friend who was camping there, and that we were to be picked up in a day or two by an English yacht. Johan obviously thought me mad, but he did as he was told. "There will be no one on the island yet," he said. "The farmer from Rosmaer does not come till June, when the haymaking begins. The winter pasture is poor and sour." That was all to the good, for I did not want any spectator of our madness.

As we drew nearer I could see no sign of life on the low shore, except an infinity of eider-ducks, and a fine osprey which sat on a pointed rock like a heraldic griffin. I was watching the bird, for I had only seen an osprey twice before, when Johan steered me into a creek, where there was deep water alongside a flat reef. This, he told me, was the ordinary landing-place from the mainland. I flung my suit-case and rucksack on shore, said good-bye to Johan and tipped him well, and watched the little boat ploughing south till it was hidden by a squall. Then, feeling every kind of a fool, I seized my baggage and proceeded, like Robinson Crusoe, into the interior.

It was raining steadily, a fine thin rain, and every now and then a squall would burst on me and ruffle the sea. Jolly weather for flying, I reflected, especially for flying over some hundreds of miles of ocean! . . . I found the farm, a few rough wooden buildings and a thing like a stone cattlepen, but there was no sign of human life there. Then I got out my map, and concluded that I had better make for the centre of the island, where there seemed to be some flat ground at one end of the loch. I was feeling utterly depressed, walking like a bagman with my kit in my hand in an uninhabited Norwegian isle, and due in London the next evening. London seemed about as inaccessible in the time as the moon.

When I got to the rim of the central hollow there was a brief clearing of the weather, and I looked down on a little grey tarn set in very green meadows. In the meadows at the north end I saw to my joy what looked like an aeroplane picketed down, and a thing like a small tent near it. Also I could see smoke curling up from a group of boulders adjoining. The gallant Archie had arrived, and my spirits lightened. I made good going down the hill, and, as I shouted, a figure like an Arctic explorer crawled out of the tent.

"Hullo, Dick," it cried. "Any luck?"

"Plenty," I said. "And you?"

"Famous. Got here last night after a clinkin' journey, with the bus behavin' like a lamb. Had an interestin' evenin' with the birds—Lord! such a happy huntin'-ground for 'em. I've been doin' sentry-go on the tops all mornin' lookin' for you, but the weather got dirty, so I returned to the wigwam. Lunch is nearly ready."

"What about the weather?" I asked anxiously.

"*Pas si bête*," he said, sniffing. "The wind is pretty sure to go down at sunset. D'you mind a night journey?"

Archie's imperturbable good-humour cheered me enormously. I must say he was a born campaigner, for he had made himself very snug, and gave me as good a meal as I have ever eaten—a hot stew of tinned stuff and curry, a plum-pudding, and an assortment of what he called *delicatessen*. To keep out the cold we drank benedictine in horn mugs. He could talk about nothing but his blessed birds, and announced that he meant to come back to Flacksholm and camp for a week. He had seen a special variety—some kind of phalarope— that fairly ravished his heart. When I asked questions about the journey ahead of us, he scarcely deigned to answer, so busy he was with speculations on the feathered fauna of Norway.

"Archie," I said, "are you sure you can get me across the North Sea?"

"I won't say 'sure'. There's always a lottery in this game, but with any luck we ought to manage it. The wind will die down, and besides it's a ground wind, and may be quiet enough a few hundred feet up. We'll have to shape a compass course anyhow, so that darkness won't worry us."

"What about the machine?" I asked. I don't know why, but I felt horribly nervous.

"A beauty. But of course you never know. If we were driven much out of a straight course, our petrol might run short."

"What would that mean?"

"Forced landin'."

"But supposing we hadn't reached land?"

"Oh, then we'd be for it," said Archie cheerfully. He added, as if to console me: "We might be picked up by a passin' steamer or a fishin' smack. I've known fellows that had that luck."

"What are the chances of our getting over safely?"

"Evens. Never better or worse than evens in this flyin' business. But it will be all right. Dash it all, a woodcock makes the trip constantly in one flight."

After that I asked no more questions, for I knew I could not get him past the woodcock. I was not feeling happy, but Archie's calm put me to shame. We had a very good tea, and then, sure enough, the wind began to die down, and the clouds opened to show clear sky. It grew perishing cold, and I was glad of every stitch of clothing, and envied Archie his heavy skin coat. We were all ready about nine, and in a dead calm cast loose, taxied over a stretch of turf, rose above the loch so as to clear the hill, and turned our faces to the west, which was like a shell of gold closing down upon the molten gold of the sea.

Luck was with us that night, and all my qualms were belied. Apart from the cold, which was savage, I enjoyed every moment of the trip, till in the early dawn we saw a crawling black line beneath us which was the coast of Aberdeen. We filled up with petrol at a place in Kincardine, and had an enormous breakfast at the local hotel. Everything went smoothly, and it was still early in the day when I found we were crossing the Cheviots. We landed at York about noon, and, while Archie caught the London train, I got my car from the garage and started for Oxford. But first I wired to Mary asking her to wire to Medina in my name that I would reach London by the 7.15. I had a pleasant run south, left the car at Oxford, and duly emerged on the platform at Paddington to find Medina waiting for me.

His manner was almost tender.

"My dear fellow, I do hope you are better?"

"Perfectly fit again, thank you. Ready for anything."

"You look more sunburnt than when you left town."

"It's the wonderful weather we've had. I've been lying basking on the veranda."

67   I VISIT THE FIELDS OF EDEN

There was a change in Medina. I noticed it the following day when I lunched with him, and very particularly at the next dinner of the Thursday Club, to which I went as his guest. It was a small change, which nobody else would have remarked, but to me, who was watching him like a lynx, it was clear enough. His ease of manner towards the world was a little less perfect, and when we were alone he was more silent than before. I did not think that he had begun to suspect any danger to his plans, but the day for their consummation was approaching, and even his cold assurance may have been flawed by little quivers of nervousness. As I saw it, once the big liquidation took place and he realized the assets which were to be the foundation of his main career, it mattered little what became of the hostages. He might let them go; they would wander back to their old world unable to give any account of their absence, and, if the story got out, there would be articles in the medical journals about these unprecedented cases of lost memory. So far I was certain that they had taken no lasting harm. But if the liquidation failed, God knew what their fate would be. They would never be seen again, for if his possession of them failed to avert disaster to his plans, he would play for safety, and, above all, for revenge. Revenge to a mind like his would be a consuming passion.

The fact that I had solved one conundrum and laid my hand on one of the hostages put me in a perfect fever of restlessness. Our time was very short, and there were still two poor souls hidden in his black underworld. It was the little boy I thought most of, and perhaps my preoccupation with him made me stupid about other things. My thoughts were always on the Blind Spinner, and there I could not advance one single inch. Macgillivray's watchers had nothing to report. It was no use my paying another visit to Madame Breda, and going through the same rigmarole. I could only stick to Medina and pray for luck. I had resolved that if he asked me again to take up my quarters with him in Hill Street I would accept, though it might be hideously awkward in a score of ways.

I longed for Sandy, but no word came from him, and I had his strict injunctions not to try to reach him. The only friend I saw in those early days of May was Archie Roylance, who seemed to have forgotten his Scotch greenshanks and settled down in London for the season. He started playing polo, which was not a safe game for a man with a crocked leg, and he opened his house in Grosvenor Street and roosted in a corner of it. He knew I was busy in a big game, and he was mad to be given a share in it, but I had to be very careful with Archie. He was the best fellow alive, but discretion had never been his strong point. So I refused to tell him anything at present, and I warned Turpin, who was an ancient friend of his, to do the same. The three of us dined together one night, and poor old Turpin was rallied by Archie on his glumness.

"You're a doleful bird, you know," he told him. "I heard somewhere you were goin' to be married, and I expect that's the cause. What do you call it—*ranger* yourself? Cheer up, my son. It can't be as bad as it sounds. Look at Dick there."

I switched him on to other subjects, and we got his opinion on the modern stage. Archie had been doing a course of plays, and had very strong views on the drama. Something had got to happen, he said, or he fell asleep in the first act, and something very rarely happened, so he was left to slumber peacefully till he was awakened and turned out by the attendants. He liked plays with shooting in them, and knockabout farce—anything indeed with a noise in it. But he had struck a vein of serious drama which he had found soporific. One piece in especial, which showed the difficulties of a lady of fifty who fell in love with her stepson, he seriously reprobated.

"Rotten," he complained. "What did it matter to any one what the old cat did? But I assure you, everybody round me was gloatin' over it. A fellow said to me it was a masterpiece of tragic irony. What's irony, Dick? I thought it was the tone your commandin' officer adopted, when you made an ass of yourself, and he showed it by complimentin' you on your intelligence. . . . Oh, by the way, you remember the girl in green we saw at that dancin' place? Well, I saw her at the show—at least, I'm pretty sure it was she—in a box with the black-bearded fellow. She didn't seem to be takin' much of it in. Wonder who she is and what she was doin' there? Russian, d'you think? I believe the silly play was translated from the Russian. I want to see that girl dance again."

The next week was absolutely blank, except for my own perpetual worrying. Medina kept me close to him, and I had to relinquish any idea of going down to Fosse for an occasional night. I longed badly for the place and for a sight of Peter John, and Mary's letters didn't comfort me, for they were getting scrappier and scrappier. My hope was that Medina would act on Kharama's advice, and in order to establish his power over his victims, bring them into the open and exercise it in the environment to which they had been accustomed. That wouldn't help me with the little boy, but it might give me a line on Miss Victor. I rather hoped that at some ball I would see him insisting on some strange woman dancing with him, or telling her to go home, or something, and then I would have cause to suspect. But no such luck. He never spoke to a woman in my presence who wasn't somebody perfectly well known. I began to think that he had rejected the Indian's advice as too dangerous.

Kharama, more by token, was back in town, and Medina took me to see him again. The fellow had left Claridge's and was living in a little house in Eaton Place, and away from the glitter of a big hotel he looked even more sinister and damnable. We went there one evening after dinner, and found him squatting on the usual couch in a room lit by one lamp and fairly stinking with odd scents. He seemed to have shed his occidental dress, for he wore flowing robes, and I could see his beastly bare feet under the skirts of them, when he moved to rearrange a curtain.

They took no more notice of me than if I had been a grandfather's clock, and to my disgust they conducted the whole conversation in some Eastern tongue. I gathered nothing from it, except a deduction as to Medina's state of mind. There was an unmistakable hint of nervousness in his voice. He seemed to be asking urgent questions, and the Indian was replying calmly and soothingly. By-and-by Medina's voice became quieter, and suddenly I realized that the two were speaking of me. Kharama's heavy eyes were raised for a second in my direction, and Medina turned ever so little towards me. The Indian asked some question about me, and Medina replied carelessly with a shrug of his shoulders and a slight laugh. The laugh rasped my temper. He was evidently saying that I was packed up and sealed and safe on the shelf.

That visit didn't make me feel happier, and next day, when I had a holiday from Medina's company, I had nothing better to do than to wander about London and think dismal thoughts. Yet, as luck would have it, that aimless walk had its consequences. It was a Sunday, and on the edge of Battersea Park I encountered a forlorn little company of Salvationists conducting a service in the rain. I stopped to listen—I always do—for I am the eternal average man who is bound to halt at every street show, whether it be a motor accident or a Punch and Judy. I listened to the tail-end of an address from a fat man who looked like a reformed publican, and a few words from an earnest lady in spectacles. Then they sang a hymn to a trombone accompaniment, and lo and behold, it was my old friend, which I had last whistled in Tom Greenslade's bedroom at Fosse. "There is rest for the weary," they sang:

> "On the other side of Jordan,
> In the green fields of Eden,
> Where the Tree of Life is blooming,
> There is rest for you."

I joined heartily in the singing, and contributed two half-crowns to the collecting box, for somehow the thing seemed to be a good omen.

I had been rather neglecting that item in the puzzle, and that evening and during the night I kept turning it over till my brain was nearly addled.

"Where the sower casts his seed in
Furrows of the fields of Eden."

That was the version in the rhyme, and in Tom Greenslade's recollection the equivalent was a curiosity shop in North London kept by a Jew with a dyed beard. Surely the two must correspond, though I couldn't just see how. The other two items had panned out so well that it was reasonable to suppose that the third might do the same. I could see no light, and I finally dropped off to sleep with that blessed "fields of Eden" twittering about my head.

I awoke with the same obsession, but other phrases had added themselves to it. One was the "playing-fields of Eton", about which some fellow had said something, and for a moment I wondered if I hadn't got hold of the right trail. Eton was a school for which Peter John's name was down, and therefore it had to do with boys, and might have to do with David Warcliff. But after breakfast I gave up that line, for it led nowhere. The word was "Eden", to rhyme with "seed in". There were other fields haunting me—names like Tothill Fields and Bunhill Fields. These were places in London, and that was what I wanted. The Directory showed no name like that of "Fields of Eden", but was it not possible that there had once in old days been a place called by that odd title?

I spent the morning in the Club library, which was a very good one, reading up Old London. I read all about Vauxhall Gardens and Ranelagh and Cremorne, and a dozen other ancient haunts of pleasure, but I found nothing to my purpose. Then I remembered that Bullivant—Lord Artinswell—had had for one of his hobbies the study of bygone London, so I telephoned to him and invited myself to lunch.

He was very pleased to see me, and it somehow comforted me to find myself again in the house in Queen Anne's Gate where I had spent some of the most critical moments of my life.

"You've taken on the work I wrote to you about," he said. "I knew you would. How are you getting on?"

"So-so. It's a big job, and there's very little time. I want to ask you a question. You're an authority on Old London. Tell me, did you ever come across in your researches the name of the 'Fields of Eden'?"

He shook his head. "Not that I remember. What part of London?"

"I fancy it would be somewhere north of Oxford Street."

He considered. "No. What is your idea? A name of some private gardens or place of amusement?"

"Yes. Just like Cremorne or Vauxhall."

"I don't think so, but we'll look it up. I've a good collection of old maps and plans, and some antique directories."

So after luncheon we repaired to his library and set to work. The maps showed nothing, nor did the books at first. We were searching too far back, in the seventeenth and early eighteenth centuries when you went fox-hunting in what is now Regent's Park and Tyburn gallows stood near the Marble Arch. Then, by sheer luck, I tried a cast nearer our own time, and found a ribald work belonging to about the date of the American War, which purported to be a countryman's guide to the amusements of town. There were all sorts of information about "Cider Cellars" and "Groves of Harmony", which must have been pretty low pubs, and places in the suburbs for cock-fighting and dog-fighting. I turned up the index, and there to my joy I saw the word "Eden".

I read the passage aloud, and I believe my hands were shaking. The place was, as I hoped, north of Oxford Street in what we now call Marylebone. "The Fields of Eden," said the book, "were opened by Mr. Askew as a summer resort for the gentlemen and sportsmen of the capital. There of a fine afternoon may be seen Lord A—— and the Duke of B—— roving among the shady, if miniature groves, not unaccompanied by the fair nymphs of the garden, while from adjacent arbours comes the cheerful tinkle of glasses and the merry clatter of dice, and the harmonious strains of Signora F——'s Italian choir." There was a good deal more of it, but I stopped reading. There was a plan of London in the book, and from it I was able to plot out the boundaries of that doubtful paradise.

Then I got a modern map, and fixed the location on it. The place had been quite small, only a few acres, and to-day it was covered by the block defined by Wellesley Street, Apwith Lane, Little Fardell Street, and the mews behind Royston Square. I wrote this down in my note-book and took my leave.

"You look pleased, Dick. Have you found what you want? Curious that I never heard the name, but it seems to have belonged to the dullest part of London at the dullest period of its history." Lord Artinswell, I could see, was a little nettled, for your antiquary hates to be caught out in his own subject.

I spent the rest of the afternoon making a very thorough examination of a not very interesting neighbourhood. What I wanted was a curiosity shop, and at first I thought I was going to fail. Apwith Lane was a kind of slum, with no shops but a disreputable foreign chemist's and a small dirty confectioner's, round the door of which dirty little children played. The inhabitants seemed to be chiefly foreigners. The mews at the back of Royston Square were, of course, useless; it was long since any dweller in that square had kept a carriage, and they seemed to be occupied chiefly by the motor-vans of a steam laundry and the lorries of a coal merchant. Wellesley Street, at least the part of it in my area, was entirely filled with the show-rooms of various American automobile companies. Little Fardell Street was a curious place. It had one old building which may have been there when the Fields of Eden flourished, and which now seemed to be a furniture repository of a sort, with most of the windows shuttered. The other houses were perhaps forty years old, most of them the offices of small wholesale businesses, such as you find in back streets in the City. There was one big French baker's shop at the corner, a picture-framer's, a watchmaker's, and a small and obviously decaying optician's. I walked down the place twice, and my heart sank, for I could see nothing in the least resembling an antique-shop.

I patrolled the street once more, and then I observed that the old dwelling, which looked like a furniture depository, was also some kind of shop. Through a dirty lower window I caught a glimpse of what seemed to be Persian rugs and the bland face of a soap-stone idol. The door had the air of never having been used, but I tried it and it opened, tinkling a bell in the back premises. I found myself in a small dusty place, littered up like a lumber-room with boxes and carpets and rugs and bric-à-brac. Most of the things were clearly antiques, though to my inexpert eye they didn't look worth much. The Turcoman rugs, especially, were the kind of thing you can buy anywhere in the Levant by the dozen.

A dishevelled Jewess confronted me, wearing sham diamond ear-rings.

"I'm interested in antiques," I said pleasantly, taking off my hat to her. "May I look round?"

"We do not sell to private customers," she said. "Only to the trade."

"I'm sorry to hear that. But may I look round? If I fancied something, I daresay I could get some dealer I know to offer for it."

She made no answer, but fingered her ear-rings with her plump grubby hands.

I turned over some of the rugs and carpets, and my first impression was confirmed. They were mostly trash, and a lacquer cabinet I uncovered was a shameless fake.

"I like that," I said, pointing to a piece of Persian embroidery. "Can't you put a price on it for me?"

"We only sell to the trade," she repeated, as if it were a litany. Her beady eyes, which never left my face, were entirely without expression.

"I expect you have a lot of things upstairs," I said. "Do you think I might have a look at them? I'm only in London for the day, and I might see something I badly wanted. I quite understand that you are wholesale people, but I can arrange any purchase through a dealer. You see, I'm furnishing a country house."

For the first time her face showed a certain life. She shook her head vigorously. "We have no more stock at present. We do not keep a large stock. Things come in and go out every day. We only sell to the trade."

"Well, I'm sorry to have taken up your time. Good-afternoon." As I left the shop, I felt that I had made an important discovery. The business was bogus. There was very little that any dealer would touch, and the profits from all the trade done would not keep the proprietor in Virginian cigarettes.

I paid another visit to the neighbourhood after dinner. The only sign of life was in the slums of Apwith Lane, where frowsy women were chattering on the kerb. Wellesley Street was shuttered and silent from end to end. So was Little Fardell Street. Not a soul was about in it, not a ray of light was seen at any window; in the midst of the din of London it made a little enclave like a graveyard. I stopped at the curiosity shop, and saw that the windows were heavily shuttered and that the flimsy old door was secured by a strong outer frame of iron which fitted into a groove at the edge of the pavement and carried a stout lock. The shutters on the ground-floor windows were substantial things, preposterously substantial for so worthless a show. As I looked at them I had a strong feeling that the house behind that palisade was not as dead as it looked, that somewhere inside it there was life, and that in the night things happened there which it concerned me tremendously to know.

Next morning I went to see Macgillivray.

"Can you lend me a first-class burglar?" I asked. "Only for one night. Some fellow who won't ask any questions and will hold his tongue."

"I've given up being surprised when you're about," he said. "No. We don't keep tame burglars here, but I can find you a man who knows rather more about the art than any professional. Why?"

"Simply because I want to get inside a certain house to-night, and I see no chance of doing it except by breaking my way in. I suppose you could so arrange it that the neighbouring policemen would not interfere. In fact, I want them to help to keep the coast clear."

I went into details with him, and showed him the lie of the land. He suggested trying the back of the house, but I had reconnoitred that side and seen that it was impossible, for the building seemed to join on with the houses in the street behind. In fact, there was no back door. The whole architecture was extremely odd, and I had a notion that the entrance in Little Fardell Street might itself be a back door. I told Macgillivray that I wanted an expert who could let me in by one of the ground-floor windows, and replace everything so that there should be no trace next morning. He rang a bell and asked for Mr. Abel to be sent for. Mr. Abel was summoned, and presently appeared, a small wizened man, like a country tradesman. Macgillivray explained what was required of him, and Mr. Abel nodded. It was a job which offered no difficulties, he said, to an experienced man. He would suggest that he investigated the place immediately after closing time, and began work about ten o'clock. If I arrived at 10.30, he promised to have a means of entrance prepared. He inquired as to who were the constables at the nearest points, and asked that certain special ones should be put on duty, with whom he could arrange matters. I never saw any one approach what seemed to me to be a delicate job with such businesslike assurance.

"Do you want any one to accompany you inside?" Macgillivray asked.

I said no. I thought I had better explore the place alone, but I wanted somebody within call in case there was trouble, and of course if I didn't come back, say within two hours, he had better come and look for me.

"We may have to arrest you as a housebreaker," he said. "How are you going to explain your presence if there's nothing wrong indoors and you disturb the sleep of a respectable caretaker?"

"I must take my chance," I said. I didn't feel nervous about that point. The place would either be empty, or occupied by those who would not invite the aid of the police.

After dinner I changed into an old tweed suit and rubber-soled shoes, and as I sat in the taxi I began to think that I had entered too lightly on the evening's business. How was that little man Abel to prepare an entrance without alarming the neighbourhood, even with the connivance of the police;

and if I found anybody inside, what on earth was I to say? There was no possible story to account for a clandestine entry into somebody else's house, and I had suddenly a vision of the ear-ringed Jewess screeching in the night and my departure for the cells in the midst of a crowd of hooligans from Apworth Lane. Even if I found something very shady indoors, it would only be shady to my own mind in connection with my own problem, and would be all right in the eyes of the law. I was not likely to hit on anything patently criminal, and, even if I did, how was I to explain my presence there? I suffered from a bad attack of cold feet, and would have chucked the business there and then but for that queer feeling at the back of my head that it was my duty to risk it—that if I turned back I should be missing something of tremendous importance. But I can tell you I was feeling far from happy when I dismissed the taxi at the corner of Royston Square, and turned into Little Fardell Street.

It was a dark cloudy evening, threatening rain, and the place was none too brilliantly lit. But to my disgust I saw opposite the door of the curiosity shop a brazier of hot coals and the absurd little shelter which means that part of the street is up. There was the usual roped-in enclosure, decorated with red lamps, a head of débris, and a hole where some of the setts had been lifted. Here was bad luck with a vengeance, that the Borough Council should have chosen this place and moment of all others for investigating the drains. And yet I had a kind of shamefaced feeling of relief, for this put the lid on my enterprise. I wondered why Macgillivray had not contrived the thing better.

I found I had done him an injustice. It was the decorous face of Mr. Abel which regarded me out of the dingy pent-house.

"This seemed to me the best plan, sir," he said respectfully, "It enables me to wait for you here without exciting curiosity. I've seen the men on point duty, and it is all right in that quarter. This street is quiet enough, and taxis don't use it as a short cut. You'll find the door open. The windows might have been difficult, but I had a look at the door first, and that big iron frame is a piece of bluff. The bolt of the lock runs into the side-bar of the frame, but the frame itself is secured to the wall by another much smaller lock, which you can only detect by looking closely. I have opened that for you—quite easily done."

"But the other door—the shop door—that rings a bell inside."

"I found it unlocked," he said, with the ghost of a grin. "Whoever uses this place after closing hours doesn't want to make much noise. The bell is disconnected. You have only to push it open and walk in."

Events were forcing me against all my inclinations to go forward.

"If any one enters when I am inside? . . ." I began.

"You will hear the sound and must take measures accordingly. On the whole, sir, I am inclined to think that there's something wrong with the place. You are armed? No. That is as well. Your position is unauthorized, as one would say, and arms might be compromising."

"If you hear me cry?"

"I will come to your help. If you do not return within—shall we say?—two hours, I will make an entrance along with the nearest constable. The unlocked door will give us a pretext."

"And if I come out in a hurry?"

"I have thought of that. If you have a fair start there is room for you to hide here," and he jerked his thumb towards the pent-house. "If you are hard-pressed I will manage to impede the pursuit."

The little man's calm matter-of-factness put me on my mettle. I made sure that the street was empty, opened the iron frame, and pushed through the shop door, closing it softly behind me.

The shop was as dark as the inside of a nut, not a crack of light coming through the closely shuttered windows. I felt very eerie, as I tiptoed cautiously among the rugs and tables. I listened, but there was no sound of any kind either from within or without, so I switched on my electric torch and waited breathlessly. Still no sound or movement. The conviction grew upon me that the house was uninhabited, and with a little more confidence I started out to explore.

The place did not extend far to the back, as I had believed. Very soon I came upon a dead wall against which every kind of litter was stacked, and that way progress was stopped. The door by which the Jewess had entered lay to the right, and that led me into a little place like a kitchen, with a sink, a cupboard or two, a gas-fire, and in the corner a bed—the kind of lair which a caretaker occupies in a house to let. I made out a window rather high up in the wall, but I could discover no other entrance save that by which I had come. So I returned to the shop and tried the passage to the left.

Here at first I found nothing but locked doors, obviously cupboards. But there was one open, and my torch showed me that it contained a very steep flight of stairs—the kind of thing that in old houses leads to the attics. I tried the boards, for I feared that they would creak, and I discovered that all the treads had been renewed. I can't say I liked diving into that box, but there was nothing else for it unless I were to give up.

At the top I found a door, and I was just about to try to open it when I heard steps on the other side.

I stood rigid in that narrow place, wondering what was to happen next. The man—it was a man's foot—came up to the door and to my consternation turned the handle. Had he opened it I would have been discovered, for he had a light, and Lord knows what mix-up would have followed. But he didn't; he tried the handle and then turned a key in the lock. After that I heard him move away.

This was fairly discouraging, for it appeared that I was now shut off from the rest of the house. When I had waited for a minute or two for the coast to clear, I too tried the handle, expecting to find it fast. To my surprise the door opened; the man had not locked but unlocked it. This could mean only one of two things. Either he intended himself to go out by this way later, or he expected some one and wanted to let him in.

From that moment I recovered my composure. My interest was excited, there was a game to play and something to be done. I looked round the passage in which I found myself and saw the explanation of the architecture which had puzzled me. The old building in Little Fardell Street was the merest slip, only a room thick, and it was plastered against a much more substantial and much newer structure in which I now found myself. The passage was high and broad, and heavily carpeted, and I saw electric fittings at each end. This alarmed me, for if any one came along and switched on the light, there was not cover to hide a cockroach. I considered that the boldest plan would be the safest, so I tiptoed to the end, and saw another passage equally bare going off at right angles. This was no good, so I brazenly assaulted the door of the nearest room. Thank Heaven! it was empty, so I could have a reconnoitring base.

It was a bedroom, well furnished in the Waring and Gillow style, and to my horror I observed that it was a woman's bedroom. It was a woman's dressing-table I saw, with big hair-brushes and oddments of scents and powders. There was a wardrobe with the door ajar full of hanging dresses. The occupant had been there quite lately, for wraps had been flung on the bed and a pair of slippers lay by the dressing-table, as if they had been kicked off hurriedly.

The place put me into the most abject fright. I seemed to have burgled a respectable flat and landed in a lady's bedroom, and I looked forward to some appalling scandal which would never be hushed up. Little Abel roosting in his pent-house seemed a haven of refuge separated from me by leagues of obstacles. I reckoned I had better get back to him as soon as possible, and I was just starting, when that happened which made me stop short. I had left the room door ajar when I entered, and of course I had switched off my torch after my first look round. I had been in utter darkness, but now I saw a light in the passage.

It might be the confounded woman who owned the bedroom, and my heart went into my boots. Then I saw that the passage lights had not been turned on, and that whoever was there had a torch like me. The footsteps were coming by the road I had come myself. Could it be the man for whom the staircase door had been unlocked?

It was a man all right, and whatever his errand, it was not with my room. I watched him through the crack left by the door, and saw his figure pass. It was some one in a hurry who walked swiftly and quietly, and, beyond the fact that he wore a dark coat with the collar turned up and a black soft hat, I could make out nothing. The figure went down the corridor and at the end seemed to hesitate. Then it turned into a room on the left and disappeared.

There was nothing to do but wait, and happily I had not to wait long, for I was becoming pretty nervous. The figure reappeared, carrying something in its hand, and as it came towards me I had a glimpse of its face. I recognized it at once as that of the grey melancholy man whom I had seen the first night in Medina's house, when I was coming out of my stupor. For some reason or another that face had become stamped on my memory, and I had been waiting to see it again. It was sad, forlorn, and yet in a curious way pleasant; anyhow there was nothing repellent in it. But he came from Medina, and at that thought every scrap of hesitation and funk fled from me. I had been right in my instinct; this place was Medina's, it was the Fields of Eden of the rhyme. A second ago I had felt a futile blunderer; now I was triumphant.

He passed my door and turned down the passage which ran at right angles. I stepped after him and saw the light halt at the staircase door, and then disappear. My first impulse was to follow, tackle him in the shop, and get the truth out of him, but I at once discarded that notion, which would have given the whole show away. My business was to make further discoveries. I must visit the room which had been the object of his visit.

I was thankful to be out of that bedroom. In the passage I listened, but could hear no sound anywhere. There was indeed a sound in the air, but it appeared to come from the outer world, a sound like an organ or an orchestra a long way off. I concluded that there must be a church somewhere near where the choir-boys were practising.

The room I entered was a very queer place. It looked partly like a museum, partly like an office, and partly like a library. The curiosity shop had been full of rubbish, but I could see at a glance that there was no rubbish here. There were some fine Italian plaques—I knew something about these, for Mary collected them—and a set of green Chinese jars which looked the real thing. Also, there was a picture which seemed good enough to be a Hobbema. For the rest there were several safes of a most substantial make; but there were no papers lying about, and every drawer of a big writing-table was locked. I had not the wherewithal to burgle the safes and the table, even if I had wanted to. I was certain that most valuable information lurked somewhere in that place, but I did not see how I could get at it.

I was just about to leave, when I realized that the sound of music which I had heard in the passage was much louder here. It was no choir-boys' practising, but strictly secular music, apparently fiddles and drums, and the rhythm suggested a dance. Could this odd building abut on a dance-hall? I looked at my watch and saw that it was scarcely eleven, and that I had only been some twenty minutes indoors. I was now in a mood of almost foolhardy confidence, so I determined to do a little more research.

The music seemed to come from somewhere to the left. The windows of the room, so far as I could judge, must look into Wellesley Street, which showed me how I had misjudged that thoroughfare. There might be a dancing-hall tucked in among the automobile shops. Anyhow, I wanted to see what lay beyond this room, for there must be an entrance to it other than by the curiosity shop. Sure enough I found a door between two bookcases covered with a heavy *portière* and emerged into still another passage.

Here the music sounded louder, and I seemed to be in a place like those warrens behind the stage in a theatre, where rooms are of all kinds of shapes and sizes. The door at the end was locked, and another door which I opened gave on a flight of wooden steps. I did not want to descend just yet, so I tried another door, and then shut it softly. For the room it opened upon was lighted, and I had the impression of human beings not very far off. Also the music, as I opened the door, came out in a great swelling volume of sound.

I stood for a moment hesitating, and then I opened that door again. For I had a notion that the light within did not come from anything in the room. I found myself in a little empty chamber, dusty and cheerless, like one of those cubby-holes you see in the Strand, where the big plate-glass front window reaches higher than the shop, and there is a space between the ceiling and the next floor. All one side was of glass, in which a casement was half open, and through the glass came the glare of a hundred lights from somewhere beyond. Very gingerly I moved forward, till I could look down on what was happening below.

For the last few seconds I think I had known what I was going to see. It was the dancing club which I had visited some weeks before with Archie Roylance. There were the sham Chinese decorations, the blaze of lights, the nigger band, the whole garish spectacle. Only the place was far more crowded than on my previous visit. The babble of laughter and talk which rose from it added a further discord to the ugly music, but there was a fierce raucous gaiety about it all, an overpowering sense of something which might be vulgar, but was also alive and ardent. Round the skirts of the hall was the usual *rastaqouère* crowd of men and women drinking liqueurs and champagne, and mixed with fat Jews and blue-black dagos the flushed faces of boys from barracks or college who imagined they were seeing life. I thought for a moment that I saw Archie, but it was only one of Archie's kind, whose lean red visage made a queer contrast with the dead white of the woman he sat by.

The dancing was madder and livelier than on the last occasion. There was more vigour in the marionettes, and I was bound to confess that they knew their trade, little as I valued it. All the couples were expert, and when now and then a bungler barged in he did not stay long. I saw no sign of the girl in green whom Archie had admired, but there were plenty like her. It was the men I most disliked, pallid skeletons or puffy Latins, whose clothes fitted them too well, and who were sometimes as heavily made-up as the women.

One especially I singled out for violent disapproval. He was a tall young man, with a waist like a wasp, a white face, and hollow drugged eyes. His lips were red like a chorus girl's, and I would have sworn that his cheeks were rouged. Anyhow, he was a loathsome sight. But, ye gods! he could dance. There was no sign of animation in him, so that he might have been a corpse, galvanized by some infernal power and compelled to move through an everlasting dance of death. I noticed that his heavy eyelids were never raised.

Suddenly I got a bad shock. For I realized that this mannequin was no other than my ancient friend, the Marquis de la Tour du Pin.

I hadn't recovered from that when I got a worse. He was dancing with a woman whose hair seemed too bright to be natural. At first I could not see her face clearly, for it was flattened against his chest, but she seemed to be hideously and sparsely dressed. She too knew how to dance, and the slim grace of her body was conspicuous even in her vulgar clothes. Then she turned her face to me, and I could see the vivid lips and the weary old pink and white enamel of her class. Pretty too. . . .

And then I had a shock which nearly sent me through the window. For in this painted dancer I recognized the wife of my bosom and the mother of Peter John.

68   SIR ARCHIBALD ROYLANCE PUTS HIS FOOT IN IT

Three minutes later I was back in the curiosity shop. I switched off my light, and very gently opened the street door. There was a sound of footsteps on the pavement, so I drew back till they had passed. Then I emerged into the quiet street, with Abel's little brazier glowing in front of me, and Abel's little sharp face poked out of his pent-house.

"All right, sir?" he asked cheerfully.

"All right," I said. "I have found what I wanted."

"There was a party turned up not long after you had gone in. Lucky I had locked the door after you. He wasn't inside more than five minutes. A party with a black top-coat turned up at the collar—respectable party he looked—oldish—might have been a curate. Funny thing, sir, but I guessed correctly when you were coming back, and had the door unlocked ready for you. . . . If you've done with me I'll clear up."

"Can you manage alone?" I asked. "There's a good deal to tidy up."

He winked solemnly. "In an hour there won't be a sign of anything. I have my little ways of doing things. Good-night, sir, and thank you." He was like a boots seeing a guest off from an hotel.

I found that the time was just after half-past eleven, so I walked to Tottenham Court Road and picked up a taxi, telling the man to drive to Great Charles Street in Westminster. Mary was in London, and I must see her at once. She had chosen to take a hand in the game, probably at Sandy's instigation, and I must find out what exactly she was doing. The business was difficult enough already with Sandy following his own trail and me forbidden to get into touch with him, but if Mary was also on the job it would be naked chaos unless I knew her plans. I own I felt miserably nervous. There was nobody in the world whose wisdom I put higher than hers, and I would have trusted her to the other side of Tophet, but I hated to think of a woman mixed up in something so ugly and perilous. She was far too young and lovely to be safe on the back-stairs. And yet I remembered that she had been in uglier affairs before this, and I recalled old Blenkiron's words: "She can't scare and she can't soil." And then I began to get a sort of comfort from the feeling that she was along with me in the game; it made me feel less lonely.

But it was pretty rough luck on Peter John. Anyhow, I must see her, and I argued that she would probably be staying with her Wymondham aunts, and that in any case I could get news of her there.

The Misses Wymondham were silly ladies, but their butler would have made Montmartre respectable. He and I had always got on well, and I think the only thing that consoled him when Fosse was sold was that Mary and I were to have it. The house in Great Charles Street was one of those tremendously artistic new dwellings with which the intellectual plutocracy have adorned the Westminster slums.

"Is her ladyship home yet?" I asked.

"No, Sir Richard, but she said she wouldn't be late. I expect her any moment."

"Then I think I'll come in and wait. How are you, Barnard? Found your city legs yet?"

"I am improving, Sir Richard, I thank you. Very pleased to have Miss Mary here, if I may take the liberty of so speaking of her. Miss Claire is in Paris still, and Miss Wymondham is dancing to-night, and won't be back till very late. How are things at Fosse, sir, if I may make so bold? And how is the young gentleman? Miss Mary has shown me his photograph. A very handsome young gentleman, sir, and favours yourself."

"Nonsense, Barnard. He's the living image of his mother. Get me a drink, like a good fellow. A tankard of beer, if you have it, for I've a throat like a grindstone."

I drank the beer and waited in a little room which would have been charming but for the garish colour scheme which Mary's aunts had on the brain. I was feeling quite cheerful again, for Peter John's photograph was on the mantelpiece, and I reckoned that any minute Mary might be at the doorway.

She came in just before midnight. I heard her speak to Barnard in the hall, and then her quick step outside the door. She was preposterously dressed, but she must have done something to her face in the taxi, for the paint was mostly rubbed from it, leaving it very pale.

"Oh, Dick, my darling," she cried, tearing off her cloak and running to my arms. "I never expected you. There's nothing wrong at home?"

"Not that I know of, except that it's deserted. Mary, what on earth brought you here?"

"You're not angry, Dick?"

"Not a bit—only curious."

"How did you know I was here?"

"Guessed. I thought it the likeliest covert to draw. You see I've been watching you dancing to-night. Look here, my dear, if you put so much paint and powder on your face and jam it so close to old Turpin's chest, it won't be easy for the poor fellow to keep his shirt-front clean."

"You—watched—me—dancing! Were you in that place?"

"Well, I wouldn't say in it. But I had a prospect of the show from the gallery. And it struck me that the sooner we met and had a talk the better."

"The gallery! Were you in the house? I don't understand."

"No more do I. I burgled a certain house in a back street for very particular reasons of my own. In the process I may mention that I got one of the worst frights of my life. After various adventures I came to a place where I heard the dickens of a row, which I made out to be dance music. Eventually I found a dirty little room with a window, and to my surprise looked down on a dancing-hall. I knew it, for I had once been there with Archie Roylance. That was queer enough, but imagine my surprise when I saw my wedded wife, raddled like a geisha, dancing with an old friend who seemed to have got himself up to imitate a waxwork."

She seemed scarcely to be listening. "But in the house! Did you see no one?"

"I saw one man and I heard another. The fellow I saw was a man I once met in the small hours with Medina."

"But the other? You didn't see him? You didn't hear him go out?"

"No." I was puzzled at her excitement. "Why are you so keen about the other?"

"Because I think—I'm sure—it was Sandy—Colonel Arbuthnot."

This was altogether beyond me. "Impossible!" I cried. "The place is a lair of Medina's. The man I saw was Medina's servant or satellite. Do you mean to say that Sandy has been exploring that house?"

She nodded. "You see, it is the Fields of Eden."

"Oh, I know. I found that out for myself. Do you tell me that Sandy discovered it too?"

"Yes. That is why I was there. That is why I have been living a perfectly loathsome life and am now dressed like a chorus girl."

"Mary," I said solemnly, "my fine brain won't support any more violent shocks. Will you please to sit down beside me, and give me the plain tale of all you have been doing since I said good-bye to you at Fosse?"

"First," she said, "I had a visit from a dramatic critic on holiday, Mr. Alexander Thomson. He said he knew you and that you had suggested that he should call. He came three times to Fosse, but only once to the house. Twice I met him in the woods. He told me a good many things, and one was that he couldn't succeed and you couldn't succeed, unless I helped. He thought that if a woman was lost only a woman could find her. In the end he persuaded me. You said yourself, Dick, that Nanny was quite competent to take charge of Peter John, with Dr. Greenslade so close at hand. And I hear from her every day, and he is very well and happy."

"You came to London. But when?"

"The day you came back from Norway."

"But I've been having letters regularly from you since then."

"That is my little arrangement with Paddock. I took him into my confidence. I send him the letters in batches and he posts one daily."

"Then you've been here more than a fortnight. Have you seen Sandy?"

"Twice. He has arranged my life for me, and has introduced me to my dancing partner, the Marquis de la Tour du Pin, whom you call Turpin. I think I have had the most horrible, the most wearing time that any woman ever had. I have moved in raffish circles, and have had to be the most raffish of the lot. Do you know, Dick, I believe I'm really a good actress! I have acquired a metallic voice, and a high silly laugh, and hard eyes, and when I lie in bed at night I blush all over for my shamelessness. I know you hate it, but you can't hate it more than I do. But it had to be done. I couldn't be a 'piker', as Mr. Blenkiron used to say."

"Any luck?"

"Oh yes," she said wearily. "I have found Miss Victor. It wasn't very difficult, really. When I had made friends with the funny people that frequent these places it wasn't hard to see who was different from the others. They're all mannequins, but the one I was looking for was bound to be the most mannequinish of the lot. I wanted some one without mind or soul, and I found her. Besides, I had a clue to start with. Odell, you know."

"It was the green girl?"

She nodded. "I couldn't be certain, of course, till I had her lover to help me. He is a good man, your French Marquis. He has played his part splendidly. You see, it would never do to try to *awake* Adela Victor now. We couldn't count on her being able to keep up appearances without arousing suspicion till the day of release arrived. But something had to be done, and that is my business especially. I have made friends with her, and I talk to her and I have attached her to me just a little, like a dog. That will give me the chance to do the rest quickly when the moment comes. You cannot bring back a vanished soul all at once unless you have laid some foundation. We have to be very, very careful, for she is keenly watched, but I think—yes, I am sure—it is going well."

"Oh, bravo!" I cried. "That makes Number Two. I may tell you that I have got Number One." I gave her a short account of my doings in Norway. "Two of the poor devils will get out of the cage, anyhow. I wonder if it wouldn't be possible to pass the word to Victor and the Duke. It would relieve their anxiety."

"I thought of that," she replied, "but Colonel Arbuthnot says No, on no account. He says it might ruin everything. He takes a very solemn view of the affair, you know. And so do I. I have seen Mr. Medina."

"Where?" I asked, in astonishment.

"I got Aunt Doria to take me to a party where he was to be present. Don't be worried. I wasn't introduced to him, and he never heard my name. But I watched him, and knowing what I did I was more afraid than I have ever been in my life. He is extraordinarily attractive—no, not attractive—seductive, and he is as cold and hard as chilled steel. You know these impressions I get of people which I can't explain—you say they are always right. Well, I felt him almost superhuman. He exhales ease and power like a god, but it is a god from a lost world. I can see that, like a god too, it is souls that he covets. Ordinary human badness seems decent in comparison with that Lucifer's pride of his. I think if I ever could commit murder it would be his life I would take. I should feel like Charlotte Corday. Oh, I'm dismally afraid of him."

"I'm not," I said stoutly, "and I see him at closer quarters than most people." The measure of success we had attained was beginning to make me confident.

"Colonel Arbuthnot is afraid for you," she said. "The two times I have seen him in London he kept harping on the need of your keeping very near to him. I think he meant me to warn you. He says that when you are fighting a man with a long-range weapon the only chance is to hug him. Dick, didn't you tell me that Mr. Medina suggested that you should stay in his house? I have been thinking a lot about that, and I believe it would be the safest plan. Once he saw you secure in his pocket he might forget about you."

"It would be most infernally awkward, for I should have no freedom of movement. But all the same I believe you are right. Things may grow very hectic as we get near the day."

"Besides, you might find out something about Number Three. It is the little boy that breaks my heart. The others might escape on their own account—some day; but unless we find *him* he is lost for ever. And Colonel Arbuthnot says that, even if we found him, it might be hard to restore the child's mind. Unless—unless——"

Mary's face had become grim, if one could use the word of a thing so soft and gentle. Her hands were tightly clasped, and her eyes had a strained, far-away look.

"I am going to find him," she cried. "Listen, Dick. That man despises women and rules them out of his life, except in so far as he can make tools of them. But there is one woman who is going to stop at nothing to beat him. . . . When I think of that little David I grow mad and desperate. I am afraid of myself. Have you no hope to give me?"

"I haven't the shadow of a clue," I said dolefully. "Has Sandy none?"

She shook her head. "He is so small, the little fellow, and so easy to hide."

"If I were in Central Africa, I would get Medina by the throat, and peg him down and torture him till he disgorged."

Again she shook her head. "Those methods are useless here. He would laugh at you, for he isn't a coward—at least, I think not. Besides, he is certain to be magnificently guarded. And for the rest, he has the entrenchments of his reputation and popularity, and a quicker brain than any of us. He can put a spell of blindness on the world—on all men and nearly all women."

The arrival of Miss Wymondham made me get up to leave. She was still the same odd-looking creature, with a mass of tow-coloured hair piled above her long white face. She had been dancing somewhere, and looked at once dog-tired and excited. "Mary has been having such a good time," she told me. "Even I can scarcely keep pace with her ardent youth. Can't you persuade her to do her hair differently? The present arrangement is so *démodé*, and puts her whole figure out of drawing. Nancy Travers was speaking about it only to-night. Properly turned out, she said, Mary would be the most ravishing thing in London. By the way, I saw your friend Sir Archie Roylance at the Parminters'. He is lunching here on Thursday. Will you come, Richard?"

I told her that my plans were vague and that I thought I might be out of town. But I arranged with Mary before I left to keep me informed at the Club of any news that came from Sandy. As I walked back I was infected by her distress over little David Warcliff. That was the most grievous business of all, and I saw no light in it, for though everything else happened according to plan, we should never be able to bring Medina to book. The more I thought of it the more hopeless our case against him seemed to be. We might free the hostages, but we could never prove that he had had anything to do with them. I could give damning evidence, to be sure, but who would take my word against his? And I had no one to confirm me. Supposing I indicted him for kidnapping, and told the story of what I knew about the Blind Spinner and Newhover and Odell? He and the world would simply laugh at me, and I should probably have to pay heavy damages for libel. None of his satellites, I was certain, would ever give him away; they couldn't, even if they wanted to, for they didn't know anything. No, Sandy was right. We might have a measure of success, but there would be no victory. And yet only victory would give us full success, for only to get him on his knees, gibbering with terror, would restore the poor little boy. I strode through the empty streets with a sort of hopeless fury in my heart.

One thing puzzled me. What was Sandy doing in that house behind the curiosity shop, if indeed it was Sandy? Whoever had been there had been in league with the sad grey man whom I watched from behind the bedroom door. Now the man was part of Medina's entourage: I had no doubt about the accuracy of my recollection. Had Sandy dealings with some one inside the enemy's citadel? I didn't see how that was possible, for he had told me he was in deadly danger from Medina, and that his only chance was to make him believe that he was out of Europe. . . . As I went to bed, one thing was very clear in my mind. If Medina asked me to stay with him, I would accept. It would probably be safer, though I wasn't so much concerned about that, and it would possibly be more fruitful. I might find out something about the grey man.

Next day I went to see Medina, for I wanted him to believe that I couldn't keep away from him. He was in tremendous spirits about something or other, and announced that he was going off to the country for a couple of days. He made me stay to luncheon, when I had another look at Odell, who seemed to be getting fat. "Your wind, my lad," I said to myself, "can't be as good as it should be. You wouldn't have my money in a scrap." I hoped that Medina was going to have a holiday, for he had been doing a good deal lately in the way of speaking, but he said, "No such luck." He was going down to the country on business—an estate of which he was a trustee wanted looking into. I asked in what part of England, and he said Shropshire. He liked that neighbourhood, and had an idea of buying a place there when he had more leisure.

Somehow that led me to speak of his poetry. He was surprised to learn that I had been studying the little books, and I could see took it as a proof of my devotion. I made a few fulsome observations on their merits, and said that even an ignorant fellow like me could see how dashed good they were. I also remarked that they seemed to me a trifle melancholy.

"Melancholy!" he said. "It's a foolish world, Hannay, and a wise man must have his moods of contempt. Victory loses some of its salt when it is won over fools."

And then he said what I had been waiting for. "I told you weeks ago that I wanted you to take up your quarters with me. Well, I repeat the offer and will take no refusal."

"It is most awfully kind of you," I stammered. "But wouldn't I be in the way?"

"Not in the least. You see the house—it's as large as a barracks. I'll be back from Shropshire by Friday, and I expect you to move in here on Friday evening. We might dine together."

I was content, for it gave me a day or two to look about me. Medina went off that afternoon, and I spent a restless evening. I wanted to be with Mary, but it seemed to me that the less I saw her the better. She was going her own way, and if I showed myself in her neighbourhood it might ruin all. Next day was no better; I actually longed for Medina to return so that I might feel I was doing something, for there was nothing I could turn my hand to, and when I was idle the thought of David Warcliff was always present to torment me. I went out to Hampton Court and had a long row on the river; then I dined at the Club and sat in the little back smoking-room, avoiding any one I knew, and trying to read a book of travels in Arabia. I fell asleep in my chair, and, waking about half-past eleven, was staggering off to bed, when a servant came to tell me that I was wanted on the telephone.

It was Mary; she was speaking from Great Charles Steeet and her voice was sharp with alarm.

"There's been an awful mishap, Dick," she said breathlessly. "Are you alone? You're sure there's no one there? . . . Archie Roylance has made a dreadful mess of things. . . . He came to that dancing-place to-night, and Adela Victor was there, and Odell with her. Archie had seen her before, you know, and apparently was much attracted. No! He didn't recognize me, for when I saw him I kept out of range. But of course he recognized the Marquis. He danced with Adela, and I suppose he talked nonsense to her—anyhow, he made himself conspicuous. The result was that Odell proposed to take her away—I suppose he was suspicious of anybody of Archie's world—and, well, there was a row. The place was very empty—only about a dozen, and mostly a rather bad lot. Archie asked what right he had to carry off the girl, and lost his temper, and the manager was called in—the man with the black beard. He backed up Odell, and then Archie did a very silly thing. He said he was Sir Archibald Roylance, and wasn't going to be dictated to by any Jew, and, worse, he said his friend was the Marquis de la Tour du Pin, and that between them they would burst up this show, and that he wouldn't have a poor girl ordered about by a third-rate American bully. . . . I don't know what happened afterwards. The women were hustled out, and I had to go with the rest. . . . But, Dick, it's bad trouble. I'm not afraid so much for

Archie, though he has probably had a bad mauling, but for the Marquis. They're sure to know who he is and all about him and remember his connection with Adela. They're almost sure to make certain in some horrible way that he can't endanger them again."

"Lord," I groaned, "what a catastrophe! And what on earth can I do? I daren't take any part!"

"No," came a hesitating voice. "I suppose not. But you can warn the Marquis—if nothing has happened to him already."

"Precious poor chance. These fellows don't waste time. But go to bed and sleep, my dear. I'll do my best."

My best at that time of night was pretty feeble. I rang up Victor's house and found, as I expected, that Turpin had not returned. Then I rang up Archie's house in Grosvenor Street and got the same answer about him. It was no good my going off to the back streets of Marylebone, so I went to bed and spent a wretched night.

Very early next morning I was in Grosvenor Street, and there I had news. Archie's man had just had a telephone message from a hospital to say that his master had had an accident, and would he come round and bring clothes. He packed a bag, and he and I drove there at once and found the miserable Archie in bed, the victim officially of a motor accident. He did not seem to be very bad, but it was a rueful face, much battered about the eyes and bandaged as to the jaw, which was turned on me when the nurse left us.

"You remember what I said about the pug with the diamond studs," he whistled, through damaged teeth. "Well, I took him on last night and got tidily laid out. I'm not up to professional standards, and my game leg made me slow."

"You've put your foot into it most nobly," I said. "What do you mean by brawling in a dance-club? You've embarrassed me horribly in the job I'm on."

"But how?" he asked, and but for the bandages his jaw would have dropped.

"Never mind how at present. I want to know exactly what happened. It's more important than you think."

He told me the same story that I had heard from Mary, but much garlanded with objurgations. He denied that he had dined too well—"nothing but a small whisky-and-soda and one glass of port". He had been looking for the girl in green for some time, and, having found her, was not going to miss the chance of making her acquaintance. "A melancholy little being with nothin' to say for herself. She's had hard usage from some swine—you could see it by her eyes—and I expect the pug's the villain. Anyway, I wasn't goin' to stand his orderin' her about like a slave. So I told him so, and a fellow with a black beard chipped in and they began to hustle me. Then I did a dam' silly thing. I tried to solemnize 'em by saying who I was, and old Turpin was there, so I dragged his name in. Dashed caddish thing to do, but I thought a marquis would put the wind up that crowd."

"Did he join in?"

"I don't know—I rather fancy he got scragged at the start. Anyhow, I found myself facin' the pug, seein' bright red, and inclined to fight a dozen. I didn't last for more than one round—my game leg cramped me, I suppose. I got in one or two on his ugly face, and then I suppose I took a knock-out. After that I don't remember anything till I woke up in this bed feelin' as if I had been through a mangle. The people here say I was brought in by two bobbies and a fellow with a motor-car, who said I had walked slap into his bonnet at a street corner and hurt my face. He was very concerned about me, but omitted to leave his name and address. Very thoughtful of the sweeps to make sure there would be no scandal. . . . I say, Dick, you don't suppose this will get into the newspapers? I don't want to be placarded as havin' been in such a vulgar shindy just as I'm thinkin' of goin' in for Parliament."

"I don't think there's the remotest chance of your hearing another word about it, unless you talk too much yourself. Look here, Archie, you've got to promise me never to go near that place again, and never on any account whatever to go hunting for that girl in green. I'll tell you my reasons some day, but you can take it that they're good ones. Another thing. You've got to keep out of Turpin's way. I only hope you haven't done him irreparable damage because of your idiocy last night."

Archie was desperately penitent. "I know I behaved like a cad. I'll go and grovel to old Turpin as soon as they let me up. But he's all right—sure to be. He wasn't lookin' for a fight like me. I expect he only got shoved into the street and couldn't get back again."

I did not share Archie's optimism, and very soon my fear was a certainty. I went straight from the hospital to Carlton House Terrace, and found Mr. Victor at breakfast. I learned that the Marquis de la Tour du Pin had been dining out on the previous evening and had not returned.

69 HOW A FRENCH NOBLEMAN DISCOVERED FEAR

I have twice heard from Turpin the story I am going to set down—once before he understood much of it, a second time when he had got some enlightenment—but I doubt whether to his dying day he will ever be perfectly clear about what happened to him.

I have not had time to introduce Turpin properly, and in any case I am not sure that the job is not beyond me. My liking for the French is profound, but I believe there is no race on earth which the average Briton is less qualified to comprehend. For myself, I could far more easily get inside the skin of a Boche. I knew he was as full of courage as a Berserker, pretty mad, but with that queer core of prudence which your Latin possesses and which in the long run makes his madness less dangerous than an Englishman's. He was high-strung, excitable, imaginative, and, I should have said, in a general way very sensitive to influences such as Medina wielded. But he was forewarned. Mary had told him the main lines of the business, and he was playing the part she had set him as dutifully as a good child. I had not done justice to his power of self-control. He saw his sweetheart leading that blind, unearthly life, and it must have been torture to him to do nothing except look on. But he never attempted to wake her memory, but waited obediently till Mary gave orders, and played the part to perfection of the ordinary half-witted dancing mounte-bank.

When the row with Archie started, and the scurry began, he had the sense to see that he must keep out of it. Then he heard Archie speak his real name, and saw the mischief involved in that, for nobody knew him except Mary, and he had passed as a Monsieur Claud Simond from Buenos Aires. When he saw his friend stand up to the bruiser, he started off instinctively to his help, but stopped in time and turned to the door. The man with the black beard was looking at him, but said nothing.

There seemed to be a good deal of racket at the foot of the stairs. One of the girls caught his arm. "No good that way," she whispered. "It's a raid all right. There's another way out. You don't want your name in to-morrow's papers."

He followed her into a little side passage, which was almost empty and very dark, and there he lost her. He was just starting to prospect, when he saw a little dago whom he recognized as one of the bar-tenders. "Up the stairs, monsieur," the man said. "Then first to the left and down again. You come out in the yard of the Apollo Garage. Quick, monsieur, or *les flics* will be here."

Turpin sped up the steep wooden stairs, and found himself in another passage fairly well lit, with a door at each end. He took the one to the left, and dashed through, wondering how he was to recover his hat and coat, and also what had become of Mary. The door opened easily enough, and in his haste he took two steps forward. It swung behind him, so that he was in complete darkness, and he turned back to open it again to give him light. But it would not open. With the shutting of that door he walked clean out of the world.

At first he was angry, and presently, when he realized his situation, a little alarmed. The place seemed to be small, it was utterly dark, and as stuffy as the inside of a safe. His chief thought at the moment was that it would never do for him to be caught in a raid on a dance-club, for his true name might come out and the harm which Archie's foolish tongue had wrought might be thereby aggravated. But soon he saw that he had stepped out of one kind of danger into what was probably a worse. He was locked in an infernal cupboard in a house which he knew to have the most unholy connections.

He started to grope around, and found that the place was larger than he thought. The walls were bare, the floor seemed to be of naked boards, and there was not a stick of furniture anywhere, nor, so far as he could see, any window. He could not discover the door he had entered by, which on the inside must have been finished dead level with the walls. Presently he found that his breathing was difficult, and that almost put him in a panic, for the dread of suffocation had always been for him the private funk from which the bravest man is not free. To breathe was like having his face tightly jammed against a pillow. He made an effort and controlled himself, for he realized that if he let himself become hysterical he would only suffocate the faster. . . .

Then he declares that he felt a hand pressing on his mouth. . . . It must have been imagination, for he admits that the place was empty; but all the same the hand came again and again—a large soft hand smelling of roses. His nerves began to scream, and his legs to give under him. The roses came down on him in a cloud, and that horrible flabby hand, as big as a hill, seemed to smother him. He tried to move, to get away from it, and before he knew he found himself on his knees. He struggled to get up, but the hand was on him, flattening him out, and that intolerable sweet sickly odour swathed him in its nauseous folds. . . . And then he lost consciousness. . . .

How long he was senseless he doesn't know, but he thinks it must have been a good many hours. When he came to he was no longer in the cupboard. He was lying on what seemed to be a couch in a room which felt spacious, for he could breathe freely, but it was still as black as the nether pit. He had a blinding headache, and felt rather sick and as silly as an owl. He couldn't remember how he had come there, but as his hand fell on his shirt-front, and he realized that he was in dress clothes, he recollected Archie's cry. That was the last clear thing in his head, but it steadied him, for it reminded him how grave was his danger. He has told me that at first he was half stifled with panic, for he was feeling abominably weak; but he had just enough reason left in him to let him take a pull on his nerves. "You must be a man," he repeated to himself. "Even if you have stumbled into hell, you must be a man."

Then a voice spoke out of the darkness, and at the sound of it most of his fright disappeared. It was no voice that he knew, but a pleasant voice, and it spoke to him in French. Not ordinary French, you understand, but the French of his native valley in the South, with the soft slurring patois of his home. It seemed to drive away his headache and nausea, and to soothe every jangled nerve, but it made him weaker. Of that he has no doubt. This friendly voice was making him a child again.

His memory of what it said is hopelessly vague. He thinks that it reminded him of the life of his boyhood—the old château high in a fold of the limestone hills, the feathery chestnuts in the valley bottom, the clear pools where the big trout lived, the snowy winters when the wolves came out of the forests to the farmyard doors, the hot summers when the roads were blinding white and the turf on the downs grew as yellow as corn. The memory of it was all jumbled, and whatever the voice said its effect was more like music than spoken words. It smoothed out the creases in his soul, but it stole also the manhood from him. He was becoming limp and docile and passive like a weak child.

The voice stopped and he felt a powerful inclination to sleep. Then suddenly, between sleeping and waking, he became aware of a light, a star which glowed ahead of him in the darkness. It waxed and then waned, and held his eyes like a vice. At the back of his head he knew that there was some devilry in the business, that it was something which he ought to resist, but for the life of him he could not remember why.

The light broadened till it was like the circle which a magic-lantern makes on a screen. Into the air there crept a strange scent—not the sickly smell of roses, but a hard pungent smell which tantalized him with its familiarity. Where had he met it before? . . . Slowly out of it there seemed to shape a whole world of memories.

Now Turpin before the War had put in some years' service in Africa with the Armée Coloniale as a lieutenant of Spahis, and had gone with various engineering and military expeditions south of the Algerian frontier into the desert. He used to rave to me about the glories of those lost days, that first youth of a man which does not return. . . . This smell was the desert, that unforgettable, untamable thing which stretches from the Mediterranean to the Central African forests, the place where, in the days when it was sea, Ulysses wandered, and where the magic of Circe and Calypso, for all the world knows, may still linger.

In the moon of light a face appeared, a face so strongly lit up that every grim and subtle line of it was magnified. It was an Eastern face, a lean high-boned Arab face, with the eyes set in a strange slant. He had never seen it before, but he had met something like it when he had dabbled in the crude magic of the sands, the bubbling pot, and the green herb fire. At first it was only a face, half averted, and then it seemed to move so that the eyes appeared, like lights suddenly turned on at night as one looks from without at a dark house.

He felt in every bone a thing he had almost forgotten, the spell and the terror of the desert. It was a cruel and inhuman face, hiding God knows what of ancient horror and sin, but wise as the Sphinx and eternal as the rocks. As he stared at it the eyes seemed to master and envelop him, and, as he put it, suck the soul out of him.

You see he had never been told about Kharama. That was the one mistake Mary made, and a very natural one, for it was not likely that he and the Indian would forgather. So he had nothing in his poor muddled head to help him to combat this mastering presence. He didn't try. He said he felt himself sinking into a delicious lethargy, like the coma which overtakes a man who is being frozen to death.

I could get very little out of Turpin about what happened next. The face spoke to him, but whether in French or some African tongue he didn't know—French, he thought—certainly not English. I gather that, while the eyes and the features were to the last degree awe-inspiring, the voice was, if anything, friendly. It told him that he was in instant danger, and that the only hope lay in utter impassivity. If he attempted to exercise his own will he was doomed, and there was sufficient indication of what that doom meant to shake his lethargy into spasms of childish fear. "Your body is too feeble to move," said the voice, "for God has laid His hand on it." Sure enough. Turpin realized that he hadn't the strength of a kitten. "You have surrendered your will to God till He restores it to you." That also was true, for Turpin knew he could not summon the energy to brush his hair, unless he was ordered to. "You will be safe," said the voice, "so long as you sleep. You will sleep till I bid you awake."

Sleep he probably did, for once again came a big gap in his consciousness. . . . The next he knew he was being jolted in something that ran on wheels, and he suddenly rolled over on his side, as the vehicle took a sharp turn. This time it didn't take him quite so long to wake up. He found he was in a big motor-car, with his overcoat on, and his hat on the seat beside him. He was stretched out almost at full length, and comfortably propped up with cushions. All this he realized fairly soon, but it was some time before he could gather up the past, and then it was all blurred and sketchy. . . . What he remembered most clearly was the warning that he was in grave peril and was only safe while he did nothing. That was burned in on his mind, and the lesson was pointed by the complete powerlessness of his limbs. He could hardly turn over from his side to his back, and he knew that if he attempted to stand he would fall down in a heap. He shut his eyes and tried to think.

Bit by bit the past pieced itself together. He remembered Archie's cry— and things before that—Mary—the girl in green. Very soon the truth smote him in the face. He had been kidnapped like the rest, and had had the same tricks played on him. . . . But they had only affected his body. As he realized this tremendous fact Turpin swelled with pride. Some devilry had stolen his physical strength, but his soul was his own still, his memory and his will. A sort of miasma of past fear still clung about him, like the after-taste of influenza, but this only served to make him angry. He was most certainly not going to be beaten. The swine had miscalculated this time; they might have a cripple on their hands, but it would be a very watchful, wary, and determined cripple, quick to seize the first chance to be even with them. His anger made his spirits rise. All his life he had been a man of tropical loves and tempestuous hates. He had loathed the Boche, and freemasons, and communists, and the deputies of his own land, and ever since Adela's disappearance he had nursed a fury against a person or persons unknown: and now every detestation of which he was capable had been focused against those who were responsible for this night's work. The fools! They thought they had got a trussed sheep, when all the time it was a lame tiger.

The blinds of the car were down, but by small painful movements he managed to make out that there was a man in the front seat beside the chauffeur. By-and-by he got a corner of the right-hand blind raised, and saw that it was night-time and that they were moving through broad streets that looked like a suburb. From the beat of the engine he gathered that the car was a Rolls-Royce, but not, he thought, one of the latest models. Presently the motion became less regular, and he realized that the suburban streets were giving place to country roads. His many expeditions in his Delage had taught him a good deal about the ways out of London, but, try as he might, he could not pick up any familiar landmark. The young moon had set, so he assumed that it was near midnight; it was a fine, clear night, not very dark, as he picked up an occasional inn and church, but they never seemed to pass through any village. Probably the driver was taking the less frequented roads—a view he was confirmed in by the frequent right-angled turns and the many patches of indifferent surface.

Very soon he found his efforts at reconnaissance so painful that he gave them up, and contented himself with planning his policy. Of course he must play the part of the witless sheep. That duty, he thought, presented no difficulties, for he rather fancied himself as an actor. The trouble was his bodily condition. He did not believe that a constitution as good as his could have taken any permanent damage from the night's work. . . . The night's! He must have been away for more than one night, for the row with Archie had taken place very near twelve o'clock. This must be the midnight following. He wondered what Mr. Victor was thinking about it—and Mary—and Hannay. The miserable Hannay had now four lost ones to look for instead of three!. . . . Anyhow, the devils had got an ugly prisoner in him. His body must soon be all right, unless, of course, they took steps to keep it all wrong. At that thought Turpin's jaw set. The rôle of the docile sheep might be difficult to keep up very long.

The next he knew the car had turned in at a gate and was following a dark tree-lined avenue. In another minute it had stopped before the door of a house, and he was being lifted out by the chauffeur and the man from the front seat, and carried into a hall. But first a dark bandana was tied over his eyes, and, as he could do nothing with his arms or legs, he had to submit. He felt himself carried up a short staircase, and then along a corridor into a bedroom, where a lamp was lit. Hands undressed him—his eyes still bandaged—and equipped him with pyjamas which were not his own, and were at once too roomy and too short. Then food was brought, and an English voice observed that he had better have some supper before going to sleep. The bandage was taken off, and he saw two male backs disappearing through the door.

Up till now he had felt no hunger or thirst, but the sight of food made him realize that he was as empty as a drum. By twisting his head he could see it all laid out on the table beside his bed—a good meal it looked—cold ham and galantine, an omelette, a salad, cheese, and a small decanter of red wine. His soul longed for it, but what about his feeble limbs? Was this some new torture of Tantalus?

Desire grew, and like an automaton he moved to it. He felt all numbed, with needles and pins everywhere, but surely he was less feeble than he had been in the car. First he managed to get his right arm extended, and by flexing the elbow and wrist a certain life seemed to creep back. Then he did the same thing with his right leg, and presently found that he could wriggle by inches to the edge of the bed. He was soon out of breath, but there could be no doubt about it—he was getting stronger. A sudden access of thirst enabled him to grasp the decanter, and, after some trouble with the stopper, to draw it to his lips. Spilling a good deal, he succeeded in getting a mouthful. "Larose," he murmured, "and a good vintage. It would have been better if it had been cognac."

But the wine put new life into him. He found he could use both arms, and he began wolfishly on the omelette, making a rather messy job of it. By this time he was feeling a remarkably vigorous convalescent, and he continued with the cold meat, till the cramp in his left shoulder forced him to lie back on the pillow. It soon passed, and he was able in fair comfort to finish the meal down to the last lettuce leaf of the salad and the last drop of claret. The Turpin who reclined again on the bed was to all intents the same vigorous young man who the night before had stumbled through that fateful door into the darkness. But it was a Turpin with a profoundly mystified mind.

He would have liked to smoke, but his cigarettes were in the pocket of his dress coat, which had been removed. So he started to do for his legs what he had already achieved for his arms, and with the same happy results. It occurred to him that, while he was alone, he had better discover whether or not he could stand. He made the effort, rolled out of bed on to the floor, hit the little table with his head and set the dishes rattling.

But after a few scrambles he got to his feet and managed to shuffle round the room. The mischief was leaving his body—so much was plain—and but for a natural stiffness in the joints he felt as well as ever. But what it all meant he hadn't a notion. He was inclined to the belief that somehow he had scored off his enemies, and was a tougher proposition than they had bargained for. They had assuredly done no harm to his mind with their witchcraft, and it looked as if they had also failed with his body. The thought emboldened him. The house seemed quiet: why should he not do a little exploration?

He cautiously opened the door, finding it, somewhat to his surprise, unlocked. The passage was lit by a hanging oil-lamp, carpeted with an old-fashioned drugget, and its walls decorated with a set of flower pictures. Turpin came to the conclusion that rarely in his life had he been in a dwelling which seemed more innocent and home-like. He considered himself sensitive to the *nuances* of the sinister in an atmosphere, and there was nothing of that sort in this. He took a step or two down the passage, and then halted, for he thought he heard a sound. Yes, there could be no doubt of it. It was water gushing from a tap. Some one in the establishment was about to have a bath.

Then he slipped back to his room just in time. The some one was approaching with light feet and a rustle of draperies. He had his door shut when the steps passed, and then opened it and stuck his head out. He saw a pink dressing-gown, and above it a slender neck and masses of dark hair. It was the figure which he of all men was likely to know best.

It seemed that the place for him was bed, so he got between the sheets again and tried to think. Adela Victor was here; therefore he was in the hands of her captors, and made a fourth in their bag. But what insanity had prompted these wary criminals to bring the two of them to the same prison? Were they so utterly secure, so confident of their power, that they took this crazy risk? The insolence of it made him furious. In the name of every saint he swore that he would make them regret it. He would free the lady and himself, though he had to burn down the house and wring the neck of every inmate. And then he remembered the delicacy of the business, and the need of exact timing, if the other two hostages were not to be lost, and at the thought he groaned.

There was a tap at the door, and a man entered to clear away the supper table. He seemed an ordinary English valet, with his stiff collar and decent black coat and smug, expressionless face.

"Beg pardon, my lord," he said, "at what hour would you like your shavin' water? Seein' it's been a late night, I make so bold as to suggest ten o'clock."

Turpin assented, and the servant had hardly gone when another visitor appeared. It was a slim pale man, whom he was not conscious of having seen before, a man with grey hair and a melancholy droop of the head. He stood at the foot of the bed, gazing upon the prostrate Turpin, and his look was friendly. Then he addressed him in French of the most Saxon type.

"Êtes-vous comfortable, monsieur? C'est bien. Soyez tranquille. Nous sommes vos amis. Bon soir."

70 OUR TIME IS NARROWED

I lunched that day with Mary—alone, for her aunts were both in Paris—and it would have been hard to find in the confines of the British islands a more dejected pair. Mary, who had always a singular placid gentleness, showed her discomposure only by her pallor. As for me I was as restless as a bantam.

"I wish I had never touched the thing," I cried. "I have done more harm than good."

"You have found Lord Mercot," she protested.

"Yes, and lost Turpin. The brutes are still three up on us. We thought we had found two, and now we have lost Miss Victor again. And Turpin! They'll find him an ugly customer, and probably take strong measures with him. They'll stick to him and the girl and the little boy now like wax; for last night's performance is bound to make them suspicious."

"I wonder," said Mary, always an optimist. "You see, Sir Archie only dragged him in because of his rank. It looked odd his being in Adela's company, but then all the times he has seen her he never spoke a word to her. They must have noticed that. I'm anxious about Sir Archie. He ought to leave London."

"Confound him! He's going to, as soon as he gets out of hospital, which will probably be this afternoon. I insisted on it, but he meant to in any case.

He's heard an authentic report of a green sandpiper nesting somewhere. It would be a good thing if Archie would stick to birds. He has no head for anything else. . . . And now we've got to start again at the beginning."

"Not quite the beginning," she interposed.

"Dashed near it. They won't bring Miss Victor into that kind of world again and all your work goes for nothing, my dear. It's uncommon bad luck that you didn't begin to wake her up, for then she might have done something on her own account. But she's still a dummy, and tucked away, you may be sure, in some place where we can never reach her. And we have little more than three weeks left."

"It is bad luck," Mary agreed. "But, Dick, I've a feeling that I haven't lost Adela Victor. I believe that somehow or other we'll soon get in touch with her again. You remember how children when they lose a ball sometimes send another one after it in the hope that one will find the other. Well, we've sent the Marquis after Adela, and I've a notion we may find them both together. We always did that as children." . . . She paused at the word "children" and I saw pain in her eyes. "Oh, Dick, the little boy! We're no nearer him, and he's far the most tragic of all."

The whole business looked so black, that I had no word of comfort to give her.

"And to put the lid on it," I groaned, "I've got to settle down in Medina's house this evening. I hate the idea like poison."

"It's the safest way," she said.

"Yes, but it puts me out of action. He'll watch me like a lynx, and I won't be able to take a single step on my own—simply sit there and eat and drink and play up to his vanity. Great Scott, I swear I'll have a row with him and break his head."

"Dick, you're not going to—how do you say it?—chuck in your hand? Everything depends on you. You're our scout in the enemy's headquarters. Your life depends on your playing the game. Colonel Arbuthnot said so. And you may find out something tremendous. It will be horrible for you, but it isn't for long, and it's the only way."

That was Mary all over. She was trembling with anxiety for me, but she was such a thorough sportsman that she wouldn't take any soft option.

"You may hear something about David Warcliff," she added.

"I hope to God I do. Don't worry, darling. I'll stick it out. But, look here, we must make a plan. I shall be more or less shut off from the world, and I must have a line of communication open. You can't telephone to me at that house, and I daren't ring you up from there. The only chance is the Club. If you have any message, ring up the head porter and make him write it down. I'll arrange that he keeps it quiet, and I'll pick up the messages when I get the chance. And I'll ring you up occasionally to give you the news. But I must be jolly careful, for, likely as not, Medina will keep an eye on me even there. You're in touch with Macgillivray?"

She nodded.

"And with Sandy?"

"Yes, but it takes some time—a day at least. We can't correspond direct."

"Well, there's the lay-out. I'm a prisoner—with qualifications. You and I can keep up some sort of communication. As you say, there's only about another three weeks."

"It would be nothing if only we had some hope."

"That's life, my dear. We've got to go on to the finish anyhow, trusting that luck will turn in the last ten minutes."

I arrived in Hill Street after tea and found Medina in the back smoking-room, writing letters.

"Good man, Hannay," he said; "make yourself comfortable. There are cigars on that table."

"Had a satisfactory time in Shropshire?" I asked.

"Rotten. I motored back this morning, starting very early. Some tiresome business here wanted my attention. I'm sorry, but I'll be out to dinner to-night. The same thing always happens when I want to see my friends—a hideous rush of work."

He was very hospitable, but his manner had not the ease it used to have. He seemed on the edge about something, and rather preoccupied. I guessed it was the affair of Archie Roylance and Turpin.

I dined alone and sat after dinner in the smoking-room, for Odell never suggested the library, though I would have given a lot to fossick about that place. I fell asleep over the *Field* and was wakened about eleven by Medina. He looked almost tired, a rare thing for him; also his voice was curiously hard. He made some trivial remark about the weather, and a row in the Cabinet which was going on. Then he said suddenly—

"Have you seen Arbuthnot lately?"

"No," I replied, with real surprise in my tone. "How could I? He has gone back to the East."

"So I thought. But I have been told that he has been seen again in England."

For a second I had a horrid fear that he had got on the track of my meeting with Sandy at the Cotswold inn and his visit to Fosse. His next words reassured me.

"Yes. In London. Within the last few days."

It was easy enough for me to show astonishment. "What a crazy fellow he is! He can't stay put for a week together. All I can say is that I hope he won't come my way. I've no particular wish to see him again."

Medina said no more. He accompanied me to my bedroom, asked if I had everything I wanted, bade me good-night, and left me.

Now began one of the strangest weeks in my life. Looking back, it has still the inconsequence of a nightmare, but one or two episodes stand out like reefs in a tide-race. When I woke the first morning under Medina's roof I believed that somehow or other he had come to suspect me. I soon saw that that was nonsense, that he regarded me as a pure chattel; but I saw, too, that a most active suspicion of something had been awakened in his mind. Probably Archie's fiasco, together with the news of Sandy, had done it, and perhaps there was in it something of the natural anxiety of a man nearing the end of a difficult course. Anyhow, I concluded that this tension of mind on his part was bound to make things more difficult for me. Without suspecting me, he kept me perpetually under his eye. He gave me orders as if I were a child, or rather he made suggestions, which in my character of worshipping disciple I had to treat as orders.

He was furiously busy night and day, and yet he left me no time to myself. He wanted to know everything I did, and I had to give an honest account of my doings, for I had a feeling that he had ways of finding out the truth. One lie discovered would, I knew, wreck my business utterly, for if I were under his power, as he believed I was, it would be impossible for me to lie to him. Consequently I dared not pay many visits to the Club, for he would want to know what I did there. I was on such desperately thin ice that I thought it best to stay most of my time in Hill Street, unless he asked me to accompany him. I consulted Mary about this, and she agreed that it was the wise course.

Apart from a flock of maids, there was no other servant in the house but Odell. Twice I met the grey, sad-faced man on the stairs, the man I had seen on my first visit, and had watched a week before in the house behind the curiosity shop. I asked who he was, and was told a private secretary who helped Medina in his political work. I gathered that he did not live regularly in the house, but only came there when his services were required.

Now Mary had said that the other man that evening in Little Fardell Street had been Sandy. If she was right, this fellow might be a friend, and I wondered if I could get in touch with him. The first time I encountered him he never raised his eyes. The second time I forced him by some question to look at me, and he turned on me a perfectly dead expressionless face like a codfish. I concluded that Mary had been in error, for this was the genuine satellite, every feature of whose character had been steam-rollered out of existence by Medina's will.

I was seeing Medina now at very close quarters, and in complete undress, and the impression he had made on me at our first meeting—which had been all overlaid by subsequent happenings—grew as vivid again as daylight. The "good fellow", of course, had gone; I saw behind all his perfection of manner to the naked ribs of his soul. He would talk to me late at night in that awful library, till I felt that he and the room were one presence, and that all the diabolic lore of the ages had been absorbed by this one mortal. You must understand that there was nothing wrong in the ordinary sense with anything he said. If there had been a phonograph recording his talk it could have been turned on with perfect safety in a girls' school. . . . He never spoke foully, or brutally. I don't believe he had a shadow of those faults of the flesh which we mean when we use the word "vice". But I swear that the most wretched libertine before the bar of the Almighty would have shown a clean sheet compared to his.

I know no word to describe how he impressed me except "wickedness". He seemed to annihilate the world of ordinary moral standards, all the little rags of honest impulse and stumbling kindness with which we try to shelter

ourselves from the winds of space. His consuming egotism made life a bare
cosmos in which his spirit scorched like a flame. I have met bad men in my
day, fellows who ought to have been quietly and summarily put out of
existence, but if I had had the trying of them I would have found bits of
submerged decency and stunted remnants of good feeling. At any rate they
were human, and their beastliness was a degeneration of humanity, not its flat
opposite. Medina made an atmosphere which was like a cold bright air in
which nothing can live. He was utterly and consumedly wicked, with no
standard which could be remotely related to ordinary life. That is why, I
suppose, mankind has had to invent the notion of devils. He seemed to be
always lifting the corner of a curtain and giving me peeps into a hoary
mystery of iniquity older than the stars. . . . I suppose that some one who had
never felt his hypnotic power would have noticed very little in his talk except
its audacious cleverness, and that some one wholly under his dominion would
have been less impressed than me, because he would have forgotten his own
standards, and been unable to make the comparison. I was just in the right
position to understand and tremble. . . . Oh, I can tell you, I used to go to
bed solemnized, frightened half out of my wits, and yet in a violent revulsion,
and hating him like hell. I was pretty clear that he was mad, for madness means
just this dislocation of the modes of thought which mortals have agreed upon
is necessary to keep the world together. His head used to seem as round as a
bullet, like nothing you find even in the skulls of cave-men, and his eyes to
have a blue light in them like the sunrise of death in an arctic waste.

One day I had a very narrow escape. I went to the Club, to see if there was
anything from Mary, and received instead a long cable from Gaudian in
Norway. I had just opened it, when I found Medina at my elbow. He had
seen me enter, and followed me in order that we should walk home together.

Now I had arranged a simple code with Gaudian for his cables, and by the
mercy of Heaven that honest fellow had taken special precautions, and got
some friend to send this message from Christiania. Had it borne the Merdal
stamp, it would have been all up with me.

The only course was the bold one, though I pursued it with a quaking
heart.

"Hullo," I cried, "here's a cable from a pal of mine in Norway. Did I tell
you I had been trying to get a beat on the Leardal for July? I had almost
forgotten about the thing. I started inquiring in March, and here's my first
news."

I handed him the two sheets and he glanced at the place of dispatch.

"Code," he said. "Do you want to work it out now?"

"If you don't mind waiting a few seconds. It's a simple code of my own
invention, and I ought to be able to decipher it pretty fast."

We sat down at one of the tables in the hall, and I took up a pen and a sheet
of notepaper. As I think I have mentioned before, I am rather a swell at
codes, and this one in particular I could read without much difficulty. I jotted
down some letters and numbers, and then wrote out a version, which I
handed to Medina. This was what he read:

"Upper beat Leardal available from the first of month. Rent two hundred and fifty with option of August at one hundred more. No limit to rods. Boat on each pool. Tidal waters can also be got for sea trout by arrangement. If you accept please cable word 'Yes'. You should arrive not later than June 29th. Bring plenty of bottled prawns. Motor-boat can be had from Bergen. Andersen, Grand Hotel, Christiania."

But all the time I was scribbling this nonsense I was reading the code correctly and getting the message by heart. Here is what Gaudian really sent:

"Our friend has quarrelled with keeper and beaten him soundly. I have taken charge at farm and frightened latter into docility. He will remain prisoner in charge of ally of mine till I give the word to release. Meantime, think it safer to bring friend to England and start on Monday. Will wire address in Scotland and wait your instructions. No danger of keeper sending message. Do not be anxious, all is well."

Having got that clear in my head, I tore the cable into small pieces and flung them into the waste-paper basket.

"Well, are you going?" Medina asked.

"Not I. I'm off salmon-fishing for the present." I took a cable form from the table, and wrote: "Sorry, must cancel Leardal plan," signed it "Hannay", addressed to "Andersen, Grand Hotel, Christiania", and gave it to the porter to send off. I wonder what happened to that telegram. It is probably still stuck up on the hotel board, awaiting the arrival of the mythical Andersen.

On our way back to Hill Street Medina put his arm in mine, and was very friendly. "I hope to get a holiday," he said, "perhaps just after the beginning of June. Only a day or two off now. I may go abroad for a little. I would like you to come with me."

That puzzled me a lot. Medina could not possibly leave town before the great liquidation, and there could be no motive in his trying to mislead me on such a point, seeing that I was living in his house. I wondered if something had happened to make him change the date. It was of the first importance that I should find this out, and I did my best to draw him about his plans. But I could get nothing out of him except that he hoped for an early holiday, and "early" might apply to the middle of June as well as to the beginning, for it was now the 27th of May.

Next afternoon at tea-time to my surprise Odell appeared in the smoking-room, followed by the long lean figure of Tom Greensdale. I never saw anybody with greater pleasure, but I didn't dare to talk to him alone. "Is your master upstairs?" I asked the butler. "Will you tell him that Dr. Greenslade is here? He is an old friend of his."

We had rather less than two minutes before Medina appeared. "I come from your wife," Greensdale whispered. "She has told me all about the business, and she thought this was the safest plan. I was to tell you that she has news of Miss Victor and the Marquis. They are safe enough. Any word of the little boy?"

He raised his voice as Medina entered. "My dear fellow, this is a great pleasure. I had to be in London for a consultation, and I thought I would look up Hannay. I hardly hoped to have the luck to catch a busy man like you."

Medina was very gracious—no, that is not the word, for there was nothing patronizing in his manner. He asked in the most friendly way about Greenslade's practice, and how he liked English country life after his many wanderings. He spoke with an air of regret of the great valleys of loess and the windy Central Asian tablelands where they had first forgathered. Odell brought in tea, and we made as pleasant a trio of friends as you could find in London. I asked a few casual questions about Fosse, and then I mentioned Peter John. Here Greenslade had an inspiration; he told me afterwards that he thought it might be a good thing to open a channel for further communications.

"I think he's all right," he said slowly. "He's been having occasional stomach-aches, but I expect that is only the result of hot weather and the first asparagus. Lady Hannay is a little anxious—you know what she is, and all mothers to-day keep thinking about appendicitis. So I'm keeping my eye on the little man. You needn't worry, Dick."

I take credit to myself for having divined the doctor's intention. I behaved as if I scarcely heard him, and as if Fosse Manor and my family were things infinitely remote. Indeed, I switched off the conversation to where Medina had last left it, and I behaved towards Tom Greenslade as if his presence rather bored me, and I had very little to say to him. When he got up to go, it was Medina who accompanied him to the front door. All this was a heavy strain upon my self-command, for I would have given anything for a long talk with him—though I had the sense not to believe his news about Peter John.

"Not a bad fellow, that doctor of yours," Medina observed on his return.

"No," I said carelessly. "Rather a dull dog all the same, with his country gossip. But I wish him well, for it is to him that I owe your friendship."

I must count that episode one of my lucky moments, for it seemed to give Medina some special satisfaction. "Why do you make this your only sitting-room?" he asked. "The library is at your disposal, and it is pleasanter in summer than any other part of the house."

"I thought I might be disturbing your work," I said humbly.

"Not a bit of it. Besides, I've nearly finished my work. After to-night I can slack off, and presently I'll be an idle man."

"And then the holiday?"

"Then the holiday." He smiled in a pleasant boyish way, which was one of his prettiest tricks.

"How soon will that be?"

"If all goes well, very soon. Probably after the 2nd of June. By the way, the Thursday Club dines on the 1st. I want you to be my guest again."

Here was more food for thought. The conviction grew upon me that he and his friends had put forward the date of liquidation; they must have suspected something—probably from Sandy's presence in England—and were taking no risks. I smoked that evening till my tongue was sore, and went to bed in a fever of excitement. The urgency of the matter fairly screamed in my ears, for

Macgillivray must know the truth at once, and so must Mary. Mercot was safe, and there was a chance apparently of Turpin and Miss Victor, which must be acted upon instantly if the main date were changed. Of the little boy I had given up all hope. . . . But how to find the truth! I felt like a man in a bad dream who is standing on the line with an express train approaching, and does not know how to climb back on to the platform.

Next morning Medina never left me. He took me in his car to the City, and I waited while he did his business, and then to call in Carlton House Terrace a few doors from the Victors' house. I believe it was the residence of the man who led his party in the Lords. After luncheon he solemnly installed me in the library. "You're not much of a reader, and in any case you would probably find my books dull. But there are excellent armchairs to doze in."

Then he went out and I heard the wheels of his car move away. I felt a kind of awe creeping over me when I found myself left alone in the uncannny place, which I knew to be the devil's kitchen for all his schemes. There was a telephone on his writing-table, the only one I had seen in the house, though there was no doubt one in the butler's pantry. I turned up the telephone book and found a number given, but it was not the one on the receiver. This must be a private telephone, by means of which he could ring up anybody he wanted, but of which only his special friends knew the number. There was nothing else in the room to interest me, except the lines and lines of books, for his table was as bare as a bank manager's.

I tried the books, but most of them were a long sight too learned for me. Most were old, and many were in Latin, and some were evidently treasures, for I would take one down and find it a leather box, with inside it a slim battered volume wrapped in wash-leather. But I found in one corner a great array of works of travel, so I selected one of Aurel Stein's books and settled down in an armchair with it. I tried to fix my attention, but found it impossible. The sentences would not make sense to my restless mind, and I could not follow the maps. So I got up again, replaced the work on its shelf, and began to wander about. It was a dull, close day, and out in the street a watercart was sprinkling the dust and children were going park-wards with their nurses. . . . I simply could not account for my disquiet, but I was like a fine lady with the vapours. I felt that somewhere in that room there was something that it concerned me deeply to know.

I drifted toward the bare writing-table. There was nothing on it but a massive silver inkstand in the shape of an owl, a silver tray of pens and oddments, a leather case of notepaper and a big blotting-book. I would never have made a good thief, for I felt both nervous and ashamed as, after listening for steps, I tried the drawers.

They were all locked—all, that is, except a shallow one at the top, which looked as if it were meant to contain one of those big engagement tablets which busy men affect. There was no tablet there, but there were two sheets of paper.

Both had been torn from a loose-leaf diary, and both covered the same dates—the fortnight between Monday the 29th of May, and Sunday the 11th of June. In the first the space for the days was filled with entries in Medina's neat writing, entries in some sort of shorthand. These entries were close and thick up to and including Friday the 2nd of June; after that there was nothing. The second sheet of paper was just the opposite. The spaces were virgin up to and including the 2nd of June; after that, on till the 11th, they were filled with notes.

As I stared at these two sheets, some happy instinct made me divine their meaning. The first sheet contained the steps that Medina would take up to the day of liquidation, which was clearly the 2nd of June. After that, if all went well, came peace and leisure. But if it didn't go well, the second sheet contained his plans—plans I have no doubt for using the hostages, for wringing safety out of certain great men's fears. . . . My interpretation was confirmed by a small jotting in long hand on the first sheet in the space for 2nd June. It was the two words. *"Dies irae"*, which my Latin was just good enough to construe.

I had lost all my tremors now, but I was a thousandfold more restless. I must get word to Macgillivray at once—no, that was too dangerous—to Mary. I glanced at the telephone and resolved to trust my luck.

I got through to the Wymondhams' house without difficulty. Barnard the butler answered, and informed me that Mary was at home. Then after a few seconds I heard her voice.

"Mary," I said, "the day is changed to the 2nd of June. You understand— warn everybody. . . . I can't think why you are worrying about that child."

For I was conscious that Medina was entering the room. I managed with my knee to close the shallow drawer with the two sheets in it, and I nodded and smiled to him, putting my hand over the receiver,

"Forgive me using your telephone. Fact is, my wife's in London, and she sent me round a note here asking me to ring her up. She's got the boy on her mind."

I put the tube to my ear again. Mary's voice sounded sharp and high-pitched.

"Are you there? I'm in Mr. Medina's library, and I can't disturb him talking through this machine. There's no cause to worry about Peter John. Greenslade is usually fussy enough, and if he's calm there's no reason why you shouldn't be. But if you want another opinion, why not get it? We may as well get the thing straightened out now, for I may be going abroad early in June. . . . Yes, some time after the 2nd."

Thank God Mary was quick-witted.

"The 2nd is very near. Why do you make such sudden plans, Dick? I can't go home without seeing you. I think I'll come straight to Hill Street."

"All right," I said, "do as you please." I rang off and looked at Medina with a wry smile. "What fussers women are! Do you mind if my wife comes round here? She won't be content till she has seen me. She has come up with a crazy notion of taking down a surgeon to give an opinion on the child's appendix. Tommy rot! But that's a woman's way."

He clearly suspected nothing. "Certainly let Lady Hannay come here.

We'll give her tea. I'm sorry that the drawing-room is out of commission just now. She might have liked to see my miniatures."

Mary appeared in ten minutes, and most nobly she acted her part. It was the very model of a distraught silly mother who bustled into the room. Her eyes looked as if she had been crying, and she had managed to disarrange her hat and untidy her hair.

"Oh, I've been so worried," she wailed, after she had murmured apologies to Medina. "He really has had a bad tummy pain, and nurse thought last night that he was feverish. I've seen Mr. Dobson-Wray, and he can come down by the 4.45. . . . He's such a precious little boy, Mr. Medina, that I feel we must take every precaution with him. If Mr. Dobson-Wray says it is all right, I promise not to fuss any more. I think a second opinion would please Dr. Greenslade, for he too looked rather anxious. . . . Oh no, thank you so much, but I can't stay for tea. I have a taxi waiting, and I might miss my train. I'm going to pick up Mr. Dobson-Wray in Wimpole Street."

She departed in the same tornado in which she had come, just stopping to set her hat straight at one of the mirrors in the hall.

"Of course I'll wire when the surgeon has seen him. And, Dick, you'll come down at once if there's anything wrong, and bring nurses. Poor, poor little darling! . . . Did you say after the 2nd of June, Dick? I do hope you'll be able to get off. You need a holiday away from your tiresome family. . . . Good-bye, Mr. Medina. It was so kind of you to be patient with a silly mother. Look after Dick and don't let him worry."

I had preserved admirably the aloof air of the bored and slightly ashamed husband. But now I realized that Mary was not babbling at large, but was saying something which I was meant to take in.

"Poor, poor little darling!" she crooned, as she got into the taxi. "I do pray he'll be all right—I *think* he may, Dick. . . . I hope, oh, I hope . . . to put your mind at ease . . . before the 2nd of June."

As I turned back to Medina I had a notion that the poor little darling was no longer Peter John.

71   THE DISTRICT-VISITOR IN PALMYRA SQUARE

During the last fortnight a new figure had begun to appear in Palmyra Square. I do not know if Macgillivray's watchers reported its presence, for I saw none of their reports, but they must have been cognizant of it, unless they spent all their time in the nearest public-house. It was a district-visitor of the familiar type—a woman approaching middle age, presumably a spinster, who wore a plain black dress and, though the weather was warm, a cheap fur round her neck, and carried a rather old black silk satchel. Her figure was good, and had still a suggestion of youth, but her hair, which was dressed very flat and tight and coiled behind in an unfashionable bun, seemed—the little that was seen of it—to be sprinkled with grey. She was dowdy, and yet not altogether dowdy, for there was a certain faded elegance in her air, and an observer might have noted that she walked well. Besides the black satchel she carried usually a sheaf of papers, and invariably and in all weathers a cheap badly rolled umbrella.

She visited at the doctor's house with the brass plate, and the music-teacher's, and at the various lodging-houses. She was attached, it appeared, to the big church of St. Jude's a quarter of a mile off, which had just got a new and energetic vicar. She was full of enthusiasm for her vicar, praised his earnestness and his eloquence, and dwelt especially, after the way of the elderly maiden ladies, on the charm of his youth. She was also very ready to speak of herself, and eager to explain that her work was voluntary—she was a gentle-woman of modest but independent means, and had rooms in Hampstead, and her father had been a clergyman at Eastbourne. Very full of her family she was to those who would hear her. There was a gentle simplicity about her manners, and an absence of all patronage, which attracted people and made them willing to listen to her when they would have shut the door on another, for the inhabitants of Palmyra Square are not a courteous or patient or religious folk.

Her aim was to enlist the overworked general servants of the Square in some of the organizations of St. Jude's. There were all kinds of activities in that enlightened church—choral societies, and mothers' meetings, and country holiday clubs, and others for adult education. She would hand out sheaves of literature about the Girls' Friendly Society, and the Mothers' Union, and such-like, and try to secure a promise of attendance at some of the St. Jude's functions. I do not think she had much success at the doctor's and the music-teacher's, though she regularly distributed her literature there. The wretched little maids were too down-trodden and harassed to do more than listen dully on the doorstep and say "Yes'm". Nor was she allowed to see the mistresses, except one of the lodging-house keepers, who was a Primitive Methodist and considered St. Jude's a device of Satan. But she had better fortune with the maid at No. 4.

The girl belonged to a village in Kent, and the district-visitor, it seemed, had been asked to look her up by the rector of her old parish. She was a large flat-faced young woman, slow of speech, heavy of movement, and suspicious of nature. At first she greeted the district-visitor coldly, but thawed at the mention of familiar names and accepted a copy of the St. Jude's Magazine. Two days later, when on her afternoon out, she met the district-visitor and consented to walk a little way with her. Now the girl's hobby was dress, and her taste was better than most of her class and aspired to higher things. She had a new hat which her companion admired, but she confessed that she was not quite satisfied with it. The district-visitor revealed a knowledge of fashions which one would have scarcely augured from her own sombre clothes. She pointed out where the trimming was wrong, and might easily be improved, and the girl—her name was Elsie Outhwaite—agreed. "I could put it right for you in ten minutes," she was told. "Perhaps you would let me come and see you when you have a spare half-hour, and we could do it together. I'm rather clever at hats, and used to help my sisters."

The ice was broken and the aloof Miss Outhwaite became confidential. She liked her place, had no cause to complain, received good wages, and, above all, was not fussed. "I minds my own business, and Madame minds 'ers," she said. Madame was a foreigner, and had her queer ways, but had also her good points. She did not interfere unnecessarily, and was not mean. There were handsome presents at Christmas, and every now and then the house would be shut up, and Miss Outhwaite returned to Kent on generous board wages. It was not a hard billet, though, of course, there were a lot of visitors, Madame's clients. "She's a massoose, you know, but very respectable." When asked if there were no other inmates of the house she became reticent. "Not what you would call reg'lar part of the family," she admitted. "There's an old lady, Madame's aunt, that stops with us a bit, but I don't see much of 'er. Madame attends to 'er 'erself, and she 'as her private room. And, of course, there's . . ." Miss Outhwaite seemed suddenly to recollect something, and changed the subject.

The district-visitor professed a desire to make Madame's acquaintance, but was not encouraged. "She's not the sort for the likes of you. She don't 'old with churches and God and such-like—I've 'eard 'er say so. You won't be getting 'er near St. Jude's, miss."

"But if she is so clever and nice I would like to meet her. She could advise me about some of the difficult questions in this big parish. Perhaps she would help with our Country Holidays."

Miss Outhwaite primmed her lips and didn't think so. "You've got to be ill and nervy for Madame to have an interest in you. I'll take in your name if you like, but I expect Madame won't be at 'ome to you."

It was eventually arranged that the district-visitor should call at No. 4 the following afternoon and bring the materials for the reconstructed hat. She duly presented herself, but was warned away by a flustered Miss Outhwaite. "We're that busy to-day I 'aven't a minute to myself." Sunday was suggested, but it appeared that that was the day when the district-visitor was fully occupied, so a provisional appointment was made for the next Tuesday evening.

This time all went well. Madame was out, and the district-visitor spent a profitable hour in Miss Outhwaite's room. Her nimble fingers soon turned the hat, purchased in Queen's Crescent for ten and sixpence, into a distant imitation of a costlier mode. She displayed an innocent interest in the household, and asked many questions which Miss Outhwaite, now in the best of tempers, answered readily. She was told of Madame's habits, her very occasional shortness of temper, her love of every tongue but English. "The worst of them furriners," said Miss Outhwaite, "is that you can't never be sure what they thinks of you. Half the time I'm with Madame and her aunt they're talking some 'eathen language."

As she departed the district-visitor was given a sketch of the topography of the house, about which she showed an unexpected curiosity. Before she left there was a slight *contretemps*. Madame's latch-key was heard in the door and Miss Outhwaite had a moment of panic. "Here, miss, I'll let you out through the kitchen," she whispered. But her visitor showed no embarrassment. "I'd like to meet Madame Breda," she declared. "This is a good chance."

Madame's plump dark face showed surprise, and possibly annoyance, as she observed the two. Miss Outhwaite hastened to explain the situation with a speed which revealed nervousness. "This is a lady from St. Jude's, Madame," she said. "She comes 'ere districk-visiting, and she knows the folks in Radhurst, where I comes from, so I made bold to ask her in."

"I am very glad to meet you, Madame Breda," said the district-visitor. "I hope you don't mind my calling on Elsie Outhwaite. I want her to help in our Girls' Friendly Society work."

"You have been here before, I think," was the reply in a sufficiently civil tone. "I have seen you in the Square sometimes. There is no objection on my part to Outhwaite's attending your meetings, but I warn you that she has very little free time." The woman was a foreigner, no doubt, but on this occasion her English showed little trace of accent.

"That is very good of you. I should have asked your permission first, but you were unfortunately not at home when I called, and Elsie and I made friends by accident. I hope you will let me come again."

As the visitor descended the steps and passed through the bright green gate into the gathering dusk of the Square, Madame Breda watched her contemplatively from one of the windows.

The lady came again four days later—it must, I think, have been the 29th of May. Miss Outhwaite, when she opened the door, looked flustered. "I can't talk to you to-night, miss. Madame's orders is that when you next came you was to be shown in to her room."

"How very kind of her!" said the lady. "I should greatly enjoy a talk with her. And, Elsie—I've got such a nice present for you—a hat which a friend gave me and which is too young—really too young—for me to wear. I'm going to give it you, if you'll accept it. I'll bring it in a day or two."

The district-visitor was shown into the large room on the right-hand side of the hall where Madame received her patients. There was no one there except a queer-looking little girl in a linen smock, who beckoned her to follow to the folding-doors which divided the apartment from the other at the back. The lady did a strange thing, for she picked up the little girl, held her a second in her arms, and kissed her—after the emotional habit of the childless. Then she passed through the folding-doors.

It was an odd apartment in which she found herself—much larger than could have been guessed from the look of the house, and, though the night was warm, there was a fire lit, a smouldering fire which gave off a fine blue smoke. Madame Breda was there, dressed in a low-cut gown as if she had been dining out, and looking handsome and dark and very foreign in the light of the shaded lamps. In an armchair by the hearth sat a wonderful old lady, with a thing like a mantilla over her snow-white hair. It was a room so unlike anything in her narrow experience that the newcomer stood hesitating as the folding-doors shut behind her.

"Oh, Madame Breda, it is so very kind of you to see me," she faltered.

"I do not know your name," Madame said, and then she did a curious thing, for she lifted a lamp and held it in the visitor's face, scrutinizing every line of her shabby figure.

"Clarke—Agnes Clarke. I am the eldest of three sisters—the other two are married—you may have heard of my father—he wrote some beautiful hymns, and edited—"

"How old are you?" Madame broke in, still holding up the lamp.

The district-visitor gave a small, nervous laugh. "Oh, I am not so very old—just over forty—well, to be quite truthful, nearly forty-seven. I feel so young sometimes that I cannot believe it, and then—at other times—when I am tired—I feel a hundred. Alas! I have many useless years behind me. But then we all have, don't you think? The great thing is to be resolved to make the most of every hour that remains to us. Mr. Empson at St. Jude's preached such a beautiful sermon last Sunday about that. He said we must give every unforgiving minute its sixty seconds' worth of distance run—I think he was quoting poetry. It is terrible to think of unforgiving minutes."

Madame did not appear to be listening. She said something to the older lady in a foreign tongue.

"May I sit down, please?" the visitor asked. "I have been walking a good deal to-day."

Madame waved her away from the chair she seemed about to take. "You will sit there, if you please," she said, pointing to a low couch beside the old woman.

The visitor was obviously embarrassed. She sat down on the edge of the couch, a faded, nervous figure compared to the two masterful personages, and her fingers played uneasily with the handle of her satchel.

"Why do you come to this house?" Madame asked, and her tone was almost menacing. "We have nothing to do with your church."

"Oh, but you live in the parish, and it's such a large and difficult parish, and we want help from every one. You cannot imagine how horrible some of the slums are—what bitter poverty in these bad times—and the worn-out mothers and the poor little neglected children. We are trying to make it a brighter place."

"Do you want money?"

"We always want money." The district-visitor's face wore an ingratiating smile. "But we want chiefly personal service. Mr. Empson always says that one little bit of personal service is better than a large subscription—better for the souls of the giver and the receiver."

"What do you expect to get from Outhwaite?"

"She is a young girl from a country village and alone in London. She is a good girl, I think, and I want to give her friends and innocent amusement. And I want her to help too in our work."

The visitor started, for she found the hand of the old woman on her arm. The long fingers were running down it and pressing it. Hitherto the owner of the hand had not spoken, but now she said—

"This is the arm of a young woman. She has lied about her age. No woman of forty-seven ever had such an arm."

The soft passage of the fingers had suddenly become a grip of steel, and the visitor cried out.

"Oh, please, please, you are hurting me. . . . I do not tell lies. I am proud of my figure—just a little. It is like my mother's, and she was so pretty. But oh! I am not young, I wish I was. I'm afraid I'm quite old when you see me by daylight."

The grip had relaxed, and the visitor moved along the couch to be out of its reach. She had begun to cry in a helpless, silly way, as if she were frightened. The two other women spoke to each other in a strange tongue, and then Madame said—

"I will not have you come here. I will not have you meddle with my servants. I do not care a fig for your church. If you come here again you will repent it."

Her tone was harsh, and the visitor looked as if her tears would begin again. Her discomposure had deprived her of the faded grace which had been in her air before, and she was now a pathetic and flimsy creature, like some elderly governess pleading against dismissal.

"You are cruel," she sighed. "I am so sorry if I have done anything wrong, but I meant it for the best. I thought that you might help me, for Elsie said you were clever and kind. Won't you think of poor Elsie? She is so young and far from her people. Mayn't she come to St. Jude's sometimes?"

"Outhwaite has her duties at home, and so I daresay have you, if truth was spoken. Bah! I have no patience with restless English old maids. They say an Englishman's house is his castle, and yet there is a plague of barren virgins always buzzing round in the name of religion and philanthropy. Listen to me. I will not have you in this house. I will not have you talking to Outhwaite. I will not have an idle woman spying on my private affairs."

The visitor dabbed her eyes with a wisp of handkerchief. The old woman had stretched out her hand again and would have laid it on her breast, but she had started up violently. She seemed to be in a mood between distress and fear. She swallowed hard before her voice came, and then it quavered.

"I think I had better go. You have wounded me very deeply. I know I'm not clever, but I try so hard . . . and . . . and—it pains me to be misunderstood. I am afraid I have been tactless, so please forgive me. . . . I won't come again. . . . I'll pray that your hearts may some day be softened."

She seemed to make an effort to regain composure, and with a final dab at her eyes smiled shakily at the unrelenting Madame, who had touched an electric bell. She closed the folding-doors gently behind her, like a repentant child who has been sent to bed. The front room was in darkness, but there was a light in the hall, where Miss Outhwaite waited to show her out.

At the front door the district-visitor had recovered herself.

"Elsie," she whispered, "Madame Breda does not want me to come again. But I must give you the hat I promised you. I'll have it ready by Thursday night. I'm afraid I may be rather late—after eleven perhaps—but don't go to bed till I come. I'll go round to the back door. It's such a smart, pretty hat. I know you'll love it."

Once in the Square she looked sharply about her, cast a glance back at No. 4, and then walked away briskly. There was a man lounging at the corner to whom she spoke; he nodded and touched his hat, and a big motor-car, which had been waiting in the shadows on the other side, drew up at the kerb. It seemed a strange conveyance for the district-visitor, but she entered it as if she were used to it, and when it moved off it was not in the direction of her rooms in Hampstead.

72 THE NIGHT OF THE FIRST OF JUNE

The last two days of May were spent by me in the most miserable restlessness and despondency. I was cut off from all communications with my friends, and I did not see how I could reopen them. For Medina, after his late furious busyness, seemed to have leisure again, and he simply never let me out of his sight. I daresay I might have managed a visit to the Club and a telephone message to Mary, but I durst not venture it, for I realized as I had never done before how delicate was the ground I walked on and how one false step on my part might blow everything sky-high. It would have mattered less if I had been hopeful of success, but a mood of black pessimism had seized me. I could count on Mary passing on my news to Macgillivray and on Macgillivray's taking the necessary steps to hasten the rounding-up; by the 2nd of June Mercot would be restored to his friends, and Miss Victor too, if Mary had got on her track again. But who was arranging all that? Was Mary alone in the business, and where was Sandy? Mercot and Gaudian would be arriving in Scotland, and telegraphing to me any moment, and I could not answer them. I had the maddening feeling that everything was on a knife edge, that the chances of a blunder were infinite, and that I could do nothing. To crown all, I was tortured by the thought of David Warcliff. I had come to the conclusion that Mary's farewell words at Hill Street had meant nothing: indeed, I couldn't see how she could have found out anything about the little boy, for as yet we had never hit on the faintest clue, and the thought of him made success with the other two seem no better than failure. Likewise I was paying the penalty for the assurance about Medina which I had rashly expressed to Mary. I felt the terror of the man in a new way; he seemed to me impregnable beyond the hope of assault; and while I detested him I also shuddered at him—a novel experience, for hitherto I had always found that hatred drove out fear.

He was abominable during those two days—abominable, but also wonderful. He seemed to love the sight of me, as if I were a visible and intimate proof of his power, and he treated me as an Oriental tyrant might treat a favourite slave. He unbent to me as a relief to his long spiritual tension, and let me see the innermost dreams of his heart. I realized with a shudder that he thought me a part of that hideous world he had created, and—I think for the first time in the business—I knew fear on my own account. If he dreamed I could fail him he would become a ravening beast. . . . I remember that he talked a good deal of politics, but, ye gods! what a change from the respectable conservative views which he had once treated me to—a Tory revival owing to the women and that sort of thing! He declared that behind all the world's creeds— Christianity, Buddhism, Islam, and the rest—lay an ancient devil-worship, and that it was raising its head again. Bolshevism, he said, was a form of it, and he attributed the success of Bolshevism in Asia to a revival of what he called Shamanism—I think that was the word. By his way of it the War had cracked the veneer everywhere, and the real stuff was showing through. He rejoiced in the prospect, because the old faiths were not ethical codes but mysteries of the spirit, and they gave a chance for men who had found the ancient magic. I think he wanted to win everything that civilization would give him, and then wreck it, for his hatred of Britain was only a part of his hatred of all that most men hold in love and repute. The common anarchist was a fool to him, for the cities and temples of the whole earth were not sufficient sacrifice to appease his vanity. I knew now what a Goth and a Hun meant, and what had been the temper of scourges like Attila and Timour. . . . Mad, you will say. Yes, mad beyond doubt, but it was the most convincing kind of madness. I had to fight hard, by keeping my mind firm on my job, to prevent my nerve giving.

I went to bed on the last night of May in something very near despair, comforting myself, I remember, by what I had said to Mary, that one must go on to the finish and trust to luck changing in the last ten minutes. I woke to a gorgeous morning, and when I came down to breakfast I was in a shade better spirits. Medina proposed a run out into the country and a walk on some high ground. "It will give us an appetite for the Thursday dinner," he said. Then he went upstairs to telephone, and I was in the smoking-room filling my pipe when suddenly Greenslade was shown in.

I didn't listen to what he had to say, but seized a sheet of paper and scribbled a note: "Take this to the head porter at the Club and he will give you any telegram there is for me. If there is one from Gaudian, as there must be, wire him to start at once and go straight to Julius Victor. Then wire the Duke to meet him there. Do you understand? Now, what have you to tell me?"

"Only that your wife says things are going pretty well. You must turn up to-night at ten-thirty at the Fields of Eden. Also somehow you must get a latch-key for this house, and see that the door is not chained."

"Nothing more?"

"Nothing more."

"And Peter John?"

Greenslade was enlarging on Peter John's case when Medina entered. "I came round to tell Sir Richard that it was all a false alarm. Only the spring fret. The surgeon was rather cross at being taken so far on a fool's errand. Lady Hannay thought he had better hear it from me personally, for then he could start on his holiday with an easy mind."

I was so short with him that Medina must have seen how far my thoughts were from my family. As we motored along the road to Tring I talked of the approaching holiday, like a toadying schoolboy who has been asked to stay for a cricket week with some senior. Medina said he had not fixed the place, but it must be somewhere south in the sun—Algiers, perhaps, and the fringes of the desert, or, better still, some remote Mediterranean spot where we could have both sunlight and blue sea. He talked of the sun like a fire-worshipper. He wanted to steep his limbs in it, and wash his soul in light, and swim in wide warm waters. He rhapsodized like a poet, but what struck me about his rhapsodies was how little sensuous they were. The man's body was the most obedient satellite of his mind, and I don't believe he had any weakness of the flesh. What he wanted was a bath of radiance for his spirit.

We walked all day on the hills around Ivinghoe, and had a late lunch in the village inn. He spoke very little, but strode over the thymy downs with his eyes abstracted. Once, as we sat on the summit, he seemed to sigh, and his face for a moment was very grave.

"What is the highest pleasure?" he asked suddenly. "Attainment? . . . No. Renunciation."

"So I've heard the parsons say," I observed.

He did not heed me. "To win everything that mankind has ever striven for, and then to cast it aside. To be Emperor of the Earth and then to slip out of the ken of mankind and take up the sandals and begging-bowl. The man who can do that has conquered the world—he is not a king but a god. Only he must be a king first to achieve it."

I cannot hope to reproduce the atmosphere of that scene, the bare top of the hill in the blue summer weather, and that man, nearing, as he thought, the summit of success, and suddenly questioning all mortal codes of value. In all my dealings with Medina I was so obsessed by the sense of my inferiority to him, that I was like a cab horse compared to an Arab stallion, and now I felt it like a blow in the face. That was the kind of thing Napoleon might have said—and done—had his schemes not gone astray. I knew I was contending with a devil, but I knew also that it was a great devil.

We returned to town just in time to dress for dinner, and all my nervousness revived a hundredfold. This was the night of crisis, and I loathed having to screw myself up to emergencies late in the day. Such things should take place in the early morning. It was like going over the top in France; I didn't mind it so much when it happened during a drizzling dawn, when one was anyhow depressed and only half-awake, but I abominated an attack in the cold-blooded daylight, or in the dusk when one wanted to relax.

That evening I shaved, I remember, very carefully, as if I were decking myself out for a sacrifice. I wondered what would be my feelings when I next shaved. I wondered what Mary and Sandy were doing. . . .

What Mary and Sandy were doing at that precise moment I do not know, but I can now unfold certain contemporary happenings, which were then hid from me. . . . Mercot and Gaudian were having a late tea in the Midland express, having nearly broken their necks in a furious motor race to catch the train at Hawick. The former was clean and shaven, his hair nicely cut, and his clothes a fairly well-fitting ready-made suit of flannels. He was deeply sunburnt, immensely excited, and constantly breaking in on Gaudian's study of the works of Sir Walter Scott.

"Newhover is to be let loose to-day. What do you suppose he'll do?" he asked.

"Nothing—yet awhile," was the answer. "I said certain things to him. He cannot openly go back to Germany and I do not think he dare come to England. He fears the vengeance of his employer. He will disappear for a little, and then emerge in some new crime with a new name and a changed face. He is the eternal scoundrel."

The young man's face lighted up pleasantly.

"If I live to be a hundred," he said, "I can't enjoy anything half as much as that clip I gave him on the jaw."

In a room in a country house on the Middlesex and Bucks borders Turpin was talking to a girl. He was in evening dress, a very point-device young man, and she was wearing a wonderful gown, grass-green in colour and fantastically cut. Her face was heavily made up, and her scarlet lips and stained eyebrows stood out weirdly against the dead white of her skin. But it was a different face from that which I first saw in the dancing-hall. Life had come back to it, the eyes were no longer dull like pebbles, but were again the windows of a soul. There was still fear in those eyes and bewilderment, but they were human again, and shone at this moment with a wild affection.

"I am terrified," she said. "I have to go to that awful place with that awful man. Please, Antoine, please, do not leave me. You have brought me out of a grave, and you cannot let me slip back again."

He held her close to him and stroked her hair.

"I think it is—how do you say it?—the last lap. My very dear one, we cannot fail our friends. I follow you soon. The grey man—I do not know his name—he told me so, and he is a friend. A car is ordered for me half an hour after you drive off with that Odell."

"But what does it mean?" she asked.

"I do not know, but I think—I am sure—it is the work of our friends. Consider, my little one. I am brought to the house where you are, but those who have charge of you do not know I am here. When Odell comes I am warned and locked in my room. I am not allowed out of it. I have no exercise except sparring with that solemn English valet. He indeed has been most amiable, and has allowed me to keep myself in form. He boxes well, too, but I have studied under our own Jules, and he is no match for me. But when the coast is clear I am permitted to see you, and I have waked you from sleep, my princess. Therefore so far it is good. As to what will happen to-night I do not know, but I fancy it is the end of our troubles. The grey man has told me as much. If you go back to that dance place, I think I follow you, and then we shall see something. Have no fear, little one. You go back as a prisoner no more, but as an actress to play a part, and I know you will play the part well. You will not permit the man Odell to suspect. Presently I come, and I think there will be an *éclaircissement*—also, please God, a reckoning."

The wooden-faced valet entered and signed to the young man, who kissed the girl and followed him. A few minutes later Turpin was in his own room, with the door locked behind him. Then came a sound of the wheels of a car outside, and he listened with a smile on his face. As he stood before the glass putting the finishing touches to his smooth hair he was still smiling—an ominous smile.

Other things, which I did not know about, were happening that evening. From a certain modest office near Tower Hill a gentleman emerged to seek his rooms in Mayfair. His car was waiting for him at the street corner, but to his surprise as he got into it some one entered also from the other side, and the address to which the car ultimately drove was not Clarges Street. The office, too, which he had left locked and bolted, was presently open, and men were busy there till far into the night—men who did not belong to his staff. An eminent publicist, who was the special patron of the distressed populations of Central Europe, was starting out to dine at his club, when he was unaccountably delayed, and had to postpone his dinner. The Spanish copper company in London Wall had been doing little business of late, except to give luncheons to numerous gentlemen, but that night its rooms were lit, and people who did not look like city clerks were investigating its documents. In Paris a certain French count of royalist proclivities, who had a box that night for the opera and was giving a little dinner beforehand, did not keep his appointment, to the discomfiture of his guests, and a telephone message to his rooms near the Champs-Elysées elicited no reply. There was a gruff fellow at the other end who discouraged conversation. A worthy Glasgow accountant, an elder of the kirk and a prospective candidate for Parliament, did not return that evening to his family, and the police, when appealed to, gave curious answers. The office, just off Fleet Street, of the *Christian Advocate* of Milwaukee, a paper which cannot have had much of a circulation in England, was filled about six o'clock with silent, preoccupied people, and the manager, surprised and rather wild of eye, was taken off in a taxi by two large gentlemen who had not had previously the honour of his acquaintance. Odd things seemed to be happening up and down the whole world. More than one ship did not sail at the appointed hour because of the interest of certain people in the passenger lists; a meeting of decorous bankers in Genoa was unexpectedly interrupted by the police; offices of the utmost respectability were occupied and examined by the blundering minions of the law; several fashionable actresses did not appear to gladden their admirers, and more than one pretty dancer was absent from the scene of her usual triumphs; a Senator in Western America, a high official in Rome, and four deputies in France found their movements restricted, and a Prince of the Church, after receiving a telephone message, fell to his prayers. A mining magnate in Westphalia, visiting Antwerp on business, found that he was not permitted to catch the train he had settled on. Five men, all highly placed, and one woman, for no cause apparent to their relatives, chose to rid themselves of life between the hours of six and seven. There was an unpleasant occurrence in a town on the Loire, where an Englishman, motoring to the south of France—a typical English squire, well known in hunting circles in Shropshire—was visited at his hotel by two ordinary Frenchmen, whose conversation seemed unpalatable to him. He was passing something from his waistcoat pocket to his mouth, when they had the audacity to lay violent hands on him, and to slip something over his wrists.

It was a heavenly clear evening when Medina and I set out to walk the half-mile to Mervyn Street. I had been so cloistered and harassed during the past weeks that I had missed the coming of summer. Suddenly the world seemed to have lighted up, and the streets were filled with that intricate odour of flowers, scent, hot wood pavements, and asphalt, which is the summer smell of London. Cars were waiting at house-doors, and women in pretty clothes getting into them; men were walking dinner-wards, with some of whom we exchanged greetings; the whole earth seemed full of laughter and happy movement. And it was shut off from me. I seemed to be living on the other side of a veil from this cheerful world, and I could see nothing but a lonely old man with a tragic face waiting for a lost boy. There was one moment at the corner of Berkeley Square when I accidentally jostled Medina, and had to clench my hands and bite my lips to keep myself from throttling him there and then.

The dining-room in Mervyn Street looked west, and the evening light strove with the candles on the table, and made a fairy-like scene of the flowers and silver. It was a full meeting—thirteen, I think—and the divine weather seemed to have put everybody in the best of spirits. I had almost forgotten Medina's repute with the ordinary man, and was staggered anew at the signs of his popularity. He was in the chair that evening, and a better chairman of such a dinner I have never seen. He had the right word for everybody, and we sat down to table like a party of undergraduates celebrating a successful cricket-match.

I was on the chairman's right hand, next to Burminster, with Palliser-Yeates opposite me. At first the talk was chiefly about the Derby and Ascot entries, about which Medina proved uncommonly well posted. He had a lot of inside knowledge from the Chilton stables, and showed himself a keen critic of form; also he was a perfect pundit about the pedigree of racehorses, and made Burminster, who fancied himself in the same line, gape with admiration. I suppose a brain like his could get up any subject at lightning speed, and he thought this kind of knowledge useful to him, for I don't believe he cared more for a horse than for a cat.

Once, during the Somme battle, I went to dine at a French château behind the lines, as the guest of the only son of the house. It was an ancient place with fishponds and terraces, and there were only two people in it, an old Comtesse and a girl of fifteen called Simone. At dinner, I remember, a decrepit butler filled for me five glasses of different clarets, till I found the one I preferred. Afterwards I walked in the garden with Simone in a wonderful yellow twilight, watching the fat carp in the ponds, and hearing the grumbling of the distant guns. I felt in that hour the poignant contrast of youth and innocence and peace with that hideous world of battle a dozen miles off. To-night I had the same feeling—the jolly party of clean, hard, decent fellows, and the abominable hinterland of mystery and crime of which the man at the head of the table was the master. I must have been poor company, but happily everybody was talkative, and I did my best to grin at Burminster's fooling.

Presently the talk drifted away from sport. Palliser-Yeates was speaking, and his fresh, boyish colour contrasted oddly with his wise eyes and grave voice.

"I can't make out what is happening," he said, in reply to a remark of Leithen's. "The City has suddenly become jumpy, and there's no reason in the facts that I can see for it. There's been a good deal of realization of stocks, chiefly by foreign holders, but there are a dozen explanations of that. No, there's a kind of *malaise* about, and it's unpleasantly like what I remember in June 1914. I was in Whittingtons' then, and we suddenly found the foundations beginning to crumble—oh yes, before the Sarajevo murders. You remember Charlie Esmond's smash—well, that was largely due to the spasm of insecurity that shook the world. People now and then get a feeling in their bones that something bad is going to happen. And probably they are right, and it has begun to happen."

"Good Lord!" said Leithen. "I don't like this. Is it another war?"

Palliser-Yeates did not answer at once. "It looks like it. I admit it's almost unthinkable, but, then, all wars are really unthinkable, till you're in the middle of them."

"Nonsense!" Medina cried. "There's no nation on the globe fit to go to war, except half-civilized races with whom it is the normal condition. You forget how much we know since 1914. You couldn't get even France to fight without provoking a revolution—a middle-class revolution, the kind that succeeds."

Burminster looked relieved. "The next war," he said, "will be a dashed unpleasant affair. So far as I can see there will be very few soldiers killed, but an enormous number of civilians. The safest place will be the front. There will be such a rush to get into the army that we'll have to have conscription to make people remain in civil life. The *embusqués* will be the regulars.''

As he spoke some one entered the room, and to my amazement I saw that it was Sandy.

He was looking extraordinarily fit and as brown as a berry. He murmured an apology to the chairman for being late, patted the bald patch on Burminster's head, and took a seat at the other end of the table. "I'll cut in where you've got to," he told the waiters. "No—don't bother about fish. I want some English roast beef and a tankard of beer."

There was a chorus of questions.

"Just arrived an hour ago. I've been in the East—Egypt and Palestine. Flew most of the way back."

He nodded to me, and smiled at Medina and raised his tankard to him.

I was not in a good position for watching Medina's face, but so far as I could see it was unchanged. He hated Sandy, but he didn't fear him now, when his plans had practically come to fruition. Indeed, he was very gracious to him, and asked in his most genial tones what he had been after.

"Civil aviation," said Sandy. "I'm going to collar the pilgrim traffic to the Holy Places. You've been in Mecca?" he asked Pugh, who nodded. "You remember the *hamelidari* crowd who used to organize the transport from Mespot. Well, I'm a *hamelidari* on a big scale. I am prepared to bring the rank of *hadji* within reach of the poorest and feeblest. I'm going to be the great benefactor of the democracy of Islam, by means of a fleet of patched-up 'planes and a few kindred spirits that know the East. I'll let you fellows in on the ground floor when I float my company. John"—he addressed Palliser-Yeates—"I look to you to manage the flotation."

Sandy was obviously ragging, and no one took him seriously. He sat there with his merry brown face, looking absurdly young and girlish, so that the most suspicious could have seen nothing more in him than the ordinary mad Englishman who lived for adventure and novelty. Me he never addressed, and I was glad of it, for I was utterly at sea. What did he mean by turning up now? What part was he to play in the events of the night? I could not have controlled the anxiety in my voice if I had been forced to speak to him.

A servant brought Medina a note, which he opened at leisure and read. "No answer," he said, and stuffed it into his pocket. I had a momentary dread that he might have got news of Macgillivray's round-up, but his manner reassured me.

There were people there who wanted to turn Sandy to other subjects, especially Fulleylove and the young Cambridge don, Nightingale. They wanted to know about South Arabia, of which at the time the world was talking. Some fellow—I forget his name—was trying to raise an expedition to explore it.

"It's the last geographical secret left unriddled," he said, and now he spoke seriously. "Well, perhaps not quite the last. I'm told there's still something to be done with the southern tributaries of the Amazon. Mornington, you know, believes there's a chance of finding some of the Inca people still dwelling in the unexplored upper glens. But all the rest have gone. Since the beginning of the century we've made a clean sweep of the jolly old mysteries that made the world worth living in. We have been to both the Poles and to Lhasa, and to the Mountains of the Moon. We haven't got to the top of Everest yet, but we know what it is like. Mecca and Medina are as stale as Bournemouth. We know that there's nothing very stupendous in the Brahmaputra gorges. There's little left for a man's imagination to play with, and our children will grow up in a dull, shrunken world. Except, of course, the Great Southern Desert of Arabia."

"Do you think it can be crossed?" Nightingale asked.

"It's hard to say, and the man who tried it would take almighty risks. I don't fancy myself pinning my life to milk camels. They're chancy brutes."

"I don't believe there's anything there," said Fulleylove, "except eight hundred miles of soft sand."

"I'm not so sure. I've heard strange stories. There was a man I met once in Oman, who went west from the Manah oasis . . ."

He stopped to taste the Club madeira, then set down the glass and looked at his watch.

"Great Scott!" he said. "I must be off. I'm sorry, Mr President, but I felt I must see you all again. You don't mind my butting in?"

He was half-way to the door, when Burminster asked where he was going.

"To seek the straw in some sequestered grange. . . . Meaning the ten-thirty from King's Cross. I'm off to Scotland to see my father. Remember, I'm the last prop of an ancient house. Good-bye, all of you. I'll tell you about my schemes at the next dinner."

As the door closed on him I had a sense of the blackest depression and loneliness. He was my one great ally, and he came and disappeared like a ship in the night, without a word to me. I felt like a blind bat, and I must have showed my feeling in my face, for Medina saw it and put it down, I daresay, to my dislike of Sandy. He asked Palliser-Yeates to take his place. "It's not the Scotch express, like Arbuthnot, but I'm off for a holiday very soon, and I have an appointment I must keep." That was all to the good, for I had been wondering how I was to make an excuse for my visit to the Fields of Eden. He asked me when I would be back, and I said listlessly within the next hour. He nodded. "I'll be home by then, and can let you in if Odell has gone to bed." Then with a little chaff of Burminster he left, so much at ease that I was positive he had had no bad news. I waited for five minutes and followed suit. The time was a quarter past ten.

At the entrance to the club in Wellesley Street I expected to have some difficulty, but the man in the box at the head of the stairs, after a sharp glance at me, let me pass. He was not the fellow who had been there on my visit with Archie Roylance, and yet I had a queer sense of having seen his face before. I stepped into the dancing-room with its heavy flavour of scent and its infernal din of mountebank music, sat down at a side-table and ordered a liqueur.

There was a difference in the place, but at first I could not put my finger on it. Everything seemed the same; the only face I knew was Miss Victor's, and that had the same mask-like pallor; she was dancing with a boy who seemed to be trying to talk to her and getting few replies. Odell I did not see, nor the Jew with the beard. I observed with interest the little casement above from which I had looked when I burgled the curiosity shop. There were fewer people to-night, but apparently the same class.

No, not quite the same class. The women were the same, but the men were different. They were older and more—how shall I put it?—responsible-looking, and had not the air of the professional dancing partner or the young man on the spree. They were heavier footed, too, though good enough performers. Somehow I got the notion that most of them were not habitués of this kind of place and were here with a purpose.

As soon as this idea dawned on me I began to notice other things. There were fewer foreign waiters, and their number was steadily decreasing. Drinks would be ordered and would be long in coming; a servant, once he left the hall, seemed to be unaccountably detained. And then I observed another thing. There was a face looking down from the casement above; I could see it like a shadow behind the dirty glass.

Presently Odell appeared, a resplendent figure in evening dress, with a diamond solitaire in his shirt and a red silk handkerchief in his left sleeve. He looked massive and formidable, but puffier than ever, and his small pig's eyes were very bright. I fancied he had been having a glass or two, just enough to excite him. He swaggered about among the small tables, turning now and then to stare at the girl in green, and then went out again. I looked at my watch, and saw that it was a quarter to eleven.

When I lifted my head Mary had arrived. No more paint and powder and bizarre clothes. She was wearing a pale blue gown she had worn at our Hunt Ball in March, and her hair was dressed in the simple way I loved, which showed all the lights and shadows in the gold. She came in like a young queen, cast a swift glance round the room, and then, shading her eyes with her hand, looked up towards the casement. It must have been a signal, for I saw a hand wave.

As she stood there, very still and poised like a runner, the music stopped suddenly. The few men who were still dancing spoke to their partners and moved towards the door. I observed the bearded Jew hurry in and look round. A man touched him on the arm and drew him away, and that was the last I saw of him.

Suddenly Odell reappeared. He must have had some warning which required instant action. I shall never know what it was, but it may have announced the round-up, and the course to be followed towards the hostages. He signed peremptorily to Miss Victor and went forward as if to take her arm. "You gotta come along," I heard, when my eyes were occupied with a new figure.

Turpin was there, a pale taut young man with his brows knit, as I remembered them in tight corners in France. The green girl had darted to Mary's side, and Turpin strode up to her.

"Adela, my dear," he said, "I think it is time for you to be going home."

The next I saw was Miss Victor's hand clutching his arm and Odell advancing with a flush on his sallow face.

"You letta go that goil," he was saying. "You got no business with her. She's my goil."

Turpin was smiling. "I think not, my friend." He disengaged Adela's arm and put her behind him, and with a swift step struck Odell a resounding smack on the cheek with the flat of his hand.

The man seemed to swell with fury. "Hell!" he cried, with a torrent of Bowery oaths. "My smart guy, I've got it in my mitt for you. You for the sleep pill."

I would have given a fortune to be in Turpin's place, for I felt that a scrap was what I needed to knit up my ragged nerves. But I couldn't chip in, for this was clearly his special quarrel, and very soon I saw that he was not likely to need my help.

Smiling wickedly, he moved round the pug, who had his fists up. "*Fiche-moi la paix*," he crooned. "My friend, I am going to massacre you."

I stepped towards Mary, for I wanted to get the women outside, but she was busy attending to Miss Victor, whom the strain of the evening had left on the verge of swooning. So I only saw bits of the fight. Turpin kept Odell at long range, for in-fighting would have been fatal, and he tired him with his lightning movements, till the professional's bad training told and his wind went. When the Frenchman saw his opponent puffing and his cheeks mottling he started to sail in. That part I witnessed, and I hope that Mary and Miss Victor did not understand old Turpin's language, for he spoke gently to himself the whole time, and it was the quintessence of all the esoteric abuse that the French *poilu* accumulated during the four years of war. His tremendous reach gave him an advantage, he was as light on his legs as a fencer, and his arms seemed to shoot out with the force of a steam-hammer. I realized what I had never known before, that his slimness was deceptive, and that stripped he would be a fine figure of sinew and bone. Also I understood that a big fellow, however formidable, if he is untrained and a little drunk, will go down before speed and quick wits and the deftness of youth.

They fought for just over six minutes. Turpin's deadliest blows were on Odell's body, but the knock-out came with one on the point of the chin. The big man crumpled up in a heap, and the back of his head banged on the floor. Turpin wrapped a wisp of a handkerchief round his knuckles, which had suffered from Odell's solitaire, and looked about him.

"What is to become of this offal?" he asked.

One of the dancers replied. "We will look after him, sir. The whole house is in our hands. This man is wanted on a good many grounds."

I walked up to the prostrate Odell, and took the latch-key from his waistcoat pocket. Turpin and Adela had gone, and Mary stood watching me. I observed that she was very pale.

"I am going to Hill Street," I said.

"I will come later," was her answer. "I hope in less than an hour. The key will let you in. There will be people there to keep the door open for me."

Her face had the alert and absorbed look that old Peter Pienaar's used to have when he was after game. There was no other word spoken between us. She entered a big saloon-car which was waiting in the street below, and I walked to Royston Square to find a taxi. It was not yet eleven o'clock.

73 THE NIGHT OF THE FIRST OF JUNE—LATER

A little after eleven that night a late walker in Palmyra Square would have seen a phemonenon rare in the dingy neighbourhood. A large motor-car drew up at the gate of No. 7, where dwelt the teacher of music, who had long retired to rest. A woman descended, wearing a dark cloak and carrying a parcel, and stood for a second looking across the road to where the lean elms in the centre of the Square made a patch of shade. She seemed to find there what she expected, for she hastened to the gate of No. 4. She did not approach the front door, but ran down the path to the back where the tradesmen called, and as soon as she was out of sight several figures emerged from the shadow and moved towards the gate.

Miss Outhwaite opened to her tap. "My, but you're late, miss," she whispered, as the woman brushed past her into the dim kitchen. Then she gasped, for some transformation had taken place in the district-visitor. It was no longer a faded spinster that she saw, but a dazzling lady, gorgeously dressed as it seemed to her, and of a remarkable beauty.

"I've brought your hat, Elsie," she said. "It's rather a nice one, and I think you'll like it. Now go at once and open the front door."

"But Madame . . ." the girl gasped.

"Never mind Madame. You are done with Madame. To-morrow you will come and see me at this address," and she gave her a slip of paper. "I will see that you do not suffer. Now hurry, my dear."

The girl seemed mesmerized, and turned to obey. The district-visitor followed her, but did not wait in the hall. Instead she ran lightly up the stairs, guiding herself by a small electric torch, and when the front door was open and four silent figures had entered she was nowhere to be seen.

For the next quarter of an hour an inquisitive passer-by would have noted lights spring out and then die away in more than one room of No. 4. He might have also heard the sound of low, excited speech. At the end of that space of time he would have seen the district-visitor descend the steps and enter the car, which had moved up to the gate. She was carrying something in her arms.

Within, in a back room, a furious woman was struggling with a telephone, from which she got no answer, since the line had been cut. And an old woman sat in a chair by the hearth, raving and muttering, with a face like death.

When I got to Hill Street, I waited till the taxi had driven off before I entered. There was a man standing in the porch of the house opposite, and as I waited another passed me, who nodded. "Good evening, Sir Richard," he said, and though I did not recognize him I knew where he came from. My spirits were at their lowest ebb, and not even the sight of these arrangements could revive them. For I knew that, though we had succeeded with Miss Victor and Mercot, we had failed with the case which mattered most. I was going to try to scare Medina or to buy him, and I felt that both purposes were futile, for the awe of him was still like a black fog on my soul.

I let myself in with Odell's latch-key and left the heavy door ajar. Then I switched on the staircase lights and mounted to the library. I left the lights burning behind me, for they would be needed by those who followed.

Medina was standing by the fireplace, in which logs had been laid ready for a match. As usual, he had only the one lamp lit, that on his writing-table. He had a slip of paper in his hand, one of the two which had lain in the top drawer, as I saw by the dates and the ruled lines. I fancy he had been attempting in vain to ring up Palmyra Square. Some acute suspicion had been aroused in him, and he had been trying to take action. His air of leisure was the kind which is hastily assumed; a minute before I was convinced that he had been furiously busy.

There was surprise in his face when he saw me.

"Hullo!" he said, "how did you get in? I didn't hear you ring. I told Odell to go to bed."

I was feeling so weak and listless that I wanted to sit down, so I dropped into a chair out of the circle of the lamp.

"Yes," I said. "Odell's in bed all right. I let myself in with his key. I've just seen that Bowery tough put to sleep with a crack on the chin from Turpin. You know—the Marquis de la Tour du Pin."

I had a good strategic position, for I could see his face clearly and he could only see the outline of mine.

"What on earth are you talking about?" he said.

"Odell has been knocked out. You see, Turpin has taken Miss Victor back to her father." I looked at my watch. "And by this time Lord Mercot should be in London—unless the Scotch express is late."

A great tide of disillusion must have swept over his mind, but his face gave no sign of it. It had grown stern, but as composed as a judge's.

"You're behaving as if you were mad. What has come over you? I know nothing of Lord Mercot—you mean the Alcester boy? Or Miss Victor."

"Oh yes, you do," I said wearily. I did not know where to begin, for I wanted to get him at once to the real business. "It's a long story. Do you want me to tell it when you know it all already?" I believe I yawned, and I felt so tired I could hardly put the sentences together.

"I insist that you explain this nonsense," was his reply. One thing he must have realized by now, that he had no power over me, for his jaw was set and his eyes stern, as if he were regarding not a satellite, but an enemy and an equal.

"Well, you and your friends for your own purposes took three hostages, and I have made it my business to free them. I let you believe that your tomfoolery had mastered me—your performance in this room and Newhover and Madame Breda and the old blind lady and all the rest of it. When you thought I was drugged and demented I was specially wide awake. I had to abuse your hospitality—rather a dirty game, you may say, but then I was dealing with a scoundrel. I went to Norway when you thought I was in bed at Fosse, and I found Mercot, and I expect at this moment Newhover is feeling rather cheap. . . . Miss Victor, too. She wasn't very difficult, once we hit on the Fields of Eden. You're a very clever man, Mr. Medina, but you oughtn't to circulate doggerel verses. Take my advice and stick to good poetry."

By this time the situation must have been clear to him, but there was not a quiver in that set hard face. I take off my hat to the best actor I have ever met—the best but one, the German count who lies buried at the farm of Gavrelle.

"You've gone off your head," he said, and his quiet considerate voice belied his eyes.

"Oh no! I rather wish I had. I hate to think that there can be so base a thing in the world as you. A man with the brains of a god and living only to glut his rotten vanity! You should be scotched like a snake."

For a moment I had a blessed thought that he was about to go for me, for I would have welcomed a scrap like nothing else on earth. There may have been a flicker of passion, but it was quickly suppressed. His eyes had become grave and reproachful.

"I have been kind to you," he said, "and have treated you as a friend. This is my reward. The most charitable explanation is that your wits are unhinged. But you had better leave this house."

"Not before you hear me out. I have something to propose, Mr. Medina. You have still a third hostage in your hands. We are perfectly aware of the syndicate you have been working with—the Barcelona nut business, and the Jacobite count, and your friend the Shropshire master-of-hounds. Scotland Yard has had its hand over the lot for months, and to-night the hand will be closed. That shop is shut for good. Now listen to me, for I have a proposal to make. You have the ambition of the Devil, and have already made for yourself a great name. I will do nothing to smirch that name. I will swear a solemn oath to hold my tongue. I will go away from England, if you like. I will bury the memory of the past months, and my knowledge will never be used to put a spoke in your wheel. Also, since your syndicate is burst up, you will want money. Well, I will give you one hundred thousand pounds. And in return for my silence and my cash I ask you to restore to me David Warcliff, safe and sane. Sane, I say, for whatever you have made of the poor little chap you have got to unmake it."

I had made up my mind about this offer as I came along in the taxi. It was a big sum, but I had more money than I needed, and Blenkiron, who had millions, would lend a hand.

His face showed no response, no interest, only the same stern melancholy regard.

"Poor devil!" he said. "You're madder than I thought."

My lassitude was disappearing, and I began to get angry.

"If you do not agree," I said, "I will blacken your reputation throughout the civilized world. What use will England have for a kidnapper and a blackmailer and—a—a—bogus magician?"

But as I spoke I knew that my threats were foolish. He smiled, a wise, pitying smile, which made me shiver with wrath.

"No, it is you who will appear as the blackmailer," he said softly. "Consider. You are making the most outrageous charges. I don't quite follow your meaning, but clearly they are outrageous—and what evidence have you to support them? Your own dreams. Who will believe you? I have had the good fortune to make many friends, and they are loyal friends." There was a gentle regret in his voice. "Your story will be laughed to scorn. Of course people will be sorry for you, for you are popular in a way. They will say that a meritorious soldier, more notable perhaps for courage than for brains, has gone crazy, and they will comment on the long-drawn-out effects of the War. I must of course protect myself. If you blackguard me I will prosecute you for slander and get your mental condition examined."

It was only too true. I had no evidence except my own word. I knew that it would be impossible to link up Medina with the doings of the syndicate—he was too clever for that. His blind mother would die on the rack before she spoke, and his tools could not give him away, because they were tools and knew nothing. The world would laugh at me if I opened my mouth. At that moment I think I had my first full realization of Medina's quality. Here was a man who had just learned that his pet schemes were shattered, who had had his vanity wounded to the quick by the revelation of how I had fooled him, and yet he could play what was left of the game with coolness and precision. I had struck the largest size of opponent.

"What about the hundred thousand pounds, then?" I asked. "That is my offer for David Warcliff."

"You are very good," he said mockingly. "I might feel insulted, if I did not know you were a lunatic."

I sat there staring at the figure in the glow of the one lamp, which seemed to wax more formidable as I looked, and a thousandfold more sinister. I saw the hideous roundness of his head, the mercilessness of his eyes, so that I wondered how I had ever thought him handsome. But now that most of his game was spoiled he only seemed the greater, the more assured. Were there no gaps in his defences? He had kinks in him—witness the silly rhyme which had given me the first clue. . . . Was there no weakness in that panoply which I could use? Physical fear—physical pain—could anything be done with that?

I got to my feet with a blind notion of closing with him. He divined my intention, for he showed something in his hand which gleamed dully. "Take care," he said. "I can defend myself against any maniac."

"Put it away," I said hopelessly. "You're safe enough from me. My God, I hope that somewhere there is a hell." I felt as feeble as a babe, and all the while the thought of the little boy was driving me mad.

Suddenly I saw Medina's eyes look over my shoulder. Some one had come into the room, and I turned and found Kharama.

He was in evening dress, wearing a turban, and in the dusk his dark malign face seemed an embodied sneer at my helplessness. I did not see how Medina took his arrival, for all at once something seemed to give in my head. For the Indian I felt now none of the awe which I had for the other, only a flaming, overpowering hate. That this foul thing out of the East should pursue his devilries unchecked seemed to me beyond bearing. I forgot Medina's pistol and everything else, and went for him like a wild beast.

He dodged me, and, before I knew, had pulled off his turban, and tossed it in my face.

"Don't be an old ass, Dick," he said.

Panting with fury, I stopped short and stared. The voice was Sandy's, and so was the figure. . . . And the face, too, when I came to look into it. He had done something with the corners of his eyebrows and tinted the lids with kohl, but the eyes, which I had never before seen properly opened, were those of my friend.

"What an artist the world has lost in me!" he laughed, and tried to tidy his disordered hair.

Then he nodded to Medina "We meet again sooner than we expected. I missed my train, and came to look for Dick. . . . Lay down that pistol, please. I happen to be armed too, you see. It's no case for shooting anyhow. Do you mind if I smoke?"

He flung himself into an armchair and lit a cigarette. Once more I was conscious of my surroundings, for hitherto for all I knew I might have been arguing in a desert. My eyes had cleared and my brain was beginning to work again. I saw the great room with its tiers of books, some glimmering, some dusky; Sandy taking his ease in his chair and gazing placidly up into Medina's face; Medina with his jaw set but his eyes troubled—yes, for the first time I saw flickers of perplexity in those eyes.

"Dick, I suppose, has been reasoning with you," Sandy said mildly. "And you have told him that he was a madman? Quite right. He is. You have pointed out to him that his story rests on his unsupported evidence, which no one will believe, for I admit it is an incredible tale. You have warned him that if he opens his mouth you will have him shut up as a lunatic. Is that correct, Dick?

"Well," he continued, looking blandly at Medina, "that was a natural view for you to take. Only, of course, you made one small error. His evidence will not be unsupported."

Medina laughed, but there was no ease in his laugh. "Who are the other lunatics?"

"Myself for one. You have interested me for quite a long time, Mr. Medina. I will confess that one of my reasons for coming home in March was to have the privilege of your acquaintance. I have taken a good deal of pains about it. I have followed your own line of studies—indeed, if the present situation weren't so hectic, I should like to exchange notes with you as a fellow-inquirer. I have traced your career in Central Asia and elsewhere with some precision. I think I know more about you than anybody else in the world."

Medina made no answer. The tables were turning, and his eyes were chained to the slight figure in the armchair.

"All this is very interesting," Sandy went on, "but it is not quite germane to the subject before us. Kharama, whom we both remember in his pride, unfortunately died last year. It was kept very secret for obvious reasons—the goodwill of his business was very valuable and depended upon him being alive—and I only heard of it by a lucky accident. So I took the liberty of borrowing his name, Mr. Medina. As Kharama I was honoured with your confidence. Rather a cad's trick, you will say, and I agree, but in an affair like this one has no choice of weapons. . . . You did more than confide in me. You trusted me with Miss Victor and the Marquis de la Tour du Pin, when it was important that they should be in safe keeping. . . . I have a good deal of evidence to support Dick."

"Moonshine!" said Medina. "Two lunacies do not make sense. I deny every detail of your rubbish."

"Out of the mouth of two or three witnesses," said Sandy pleasantly. "There is still a third . . . Lavater," he cried, "come in; we're ready for you."

There entered the grey melancholy man, whom I had seen on my first visit here, and in the house behind Little Fardell Street. I noticed that he walked straight to Sandy's chair, and did not look at Medina.

"Lavater you know already, I think. He used to be a friend of mine, and lately we have resumed the friendship. He was your disciple for some time, but has now relinquished that honour. Lavater will be able to tell the world a good deal about you."

Medina's face had become like a mask, and the colour had gone out of it. He may have been a volcano within, but outside he was cold ice. His voice, acid and sneering, came out like drops of chilly water.

"Three lunatics," he said. "I deny every word you say. No one will believe you. It is a conspiracy of madmen."

"Let's talk business anyhow," said Sandy. "The case against you is proven to the hilt, but let us see how the world will regard it. The strong point on your side is that people don't like to confess they have been fools. You have been a very popular man, Mr. Medina, and your many friends will be loath to believe that you are a scoundrel. You've the hedge of your reputation to protect you. Again, our story is so monstrous that the ordinary Englishman may call it unbelievable, for we are not an imaginative nation. Again, we can get no help from the principal sufferers. Miss Victor and Lord Mercot can tell an ugly story of kidnapping, which may get a life-sentence for Odell, and for Newhover if he is caught, but which does not implicate you. That will be a stumbling-block to most juries, who are not as familiar with occult science as you and I. . . . These are your strong points. But consider what we can bring on the other side. You are a propagandist of genius, as I once told Dick, and I can explain just how you have fooled the world—your exploits with Denikin and such-like. Then the three of us can tell a damning story, and tell it from close quarters. It may sound wild, but Dick has some reputation for good sense, and a good many people think that I am not altogether a fool. Finally, we have on our side Scotland Yard, which is now gathering in your associates, and we have behind us Julius Victor, who is not without influence. . . . I do not say we can send you to prison, though I think it likely, but we can throw such suspicion on you that for the rest of your days you will be a marked man. You will recognize that for you that means utter failure, for to succeed you must swim in the glory of popular confidence."

I could see that Medina was shaken at last. "You may damage me with your lies," he said slowly, "but I will be even with you. You will find me hard to beat."

"I don't doubt it," was Sandy's answer. "I and my friends do not want victory, we want success. We want David Warcliff."

There was no answer, and Sandy went on.

"We make you a proposal. The three of us will keep what we know to ourselves. We will pledge ourselves never to breathe a word of it—if you like we will sign a document to say that we acknowledge our mistake. So far as we are concerned you may go on and become Prime Minister of Britain or Archbishop of Canterbury, or anything you jolly well like. We don't exactly love you, but we will not interfere with the adoration of others. I'll take myself off again to the East with Lavater, and Dick will bury himself in Oxfordshire mud. And in return we ask that you hand over to us David Warcliff in his right mind."

There was no answer.

Then Sandy made a mistake in tactics. "I believe you are attached to your mother," he said. "If you accept our offer she will be safe from annoyance. Otherwise—well, she is an important witness."

The man's pride was stung to the quick. His mother must have been for him an inner sanctuary, a thing apart from and holier than his fiercest ambitions, the very core and shrine of his monstrous vanity. That she should be used as a bargaining counter stirred something deep and primeval in him, something—let me say it—higher and better than I had imagined. A new and a human fury burned the mask off him like tissue paper.

"You fools!" he cried, and his voice was harsh with rage. "You perfect fools! You will sweat blood for that insult."

"It's a fair offer," said Sandy, never moving a muscle. "Do I understand that you refuse?"

Medina stood on the hearth-rug like an animal at bay, and upon my soul I couldn't but admire him. The flame in his face would have scorched most people into abject fear.

"Go to hell, the pack of you! Out of this house! You will never hear a word from me till you are bleating for mercy. Get out . . ."

His eyes must have been dimmed by his rage, for he did not see Mary enter. She had advanced right up to Sandy's chair before even I noticed her. She was carrying something in her arms, something which she held close as a mother holds a child.

It was the queer little girl from the house in Palmyra Square. Her hair had grown longer and fell in wisps over her brow and her pale tear-stained cheeks. A most piteous little object she was, with dull blind eyes, which seemed to struggle with perpetual terror. She still wore the absurd linen smock, her skinny little legs and arms were bare, and her thin fingers clutched at Mary's gown.

Then Medina saw her, and Sandy ceased to exist for him. He stared for a second uncomprehendingly, till the passion in his face turned to alarm. "What have you done with her?" he barked, and flung himself forward.

I thought he was going to attack Mary, so I tripped him up. He sprawled on the floor, and since he seemed to have lost all command of himself I reckoned that I had better keep him there. I looked towards Mary, who nodded. "Please tie him up," she said, and passed me the turban cloth of the late Kharama.

He fought like a tiger, but Lavater and I with a little help from Sandy managed to truss him fairly tight, supplementing the turban with one of the curtain cords. We laid him in an armchair.

"What have you done with her?" he kept on, screwing his head round to look at Mary.

I could not understand his maniacal concern for the little girl, till Mary answered, and I saw what he meant by "her".

"No one has touched your mother. She is in the house in Palmyra Square."

Then Mary laid the child down very gently in the chair where Sandy had been sitting, and stood erect before Medina.

"I want you to bring back this little boy's mind," she said.

I suppose I should have been astonished, but I wasn't—at least, not at her words, though I had not had an inkling beforehand of the truth. All the astonishment I was capable of was reserved for Mary. She stood there looking down on the bound man, her face very pale, her eyes quite gentle, her lips parted as if in expectation. And there was something about her so formidable, so implacable, that the other three of us fell into the background. Her presence dominated everything, and the very grace of her body and the mild sadness of her eyes seemed to make her the more terrifying. I know now how Joan of Arc must have looked when she led her troops into battle.

"Do you hear me?" she repeated. "You took away his soul and you can give it back again. That is all I ask of you."

He choked before he replied. "What boy? I tell you I know nothing. You are all mad."

"I mean David Warcliff. The others are free now, and he must be free to-night. Free, and in his right mind, as when you carried him off. Surely you understand."

There was no answer.

"That is all I ask. It is such a little thing. Then we will go away."

I broke in. "Our offer holds. Do as she asks, and we will never open our mouths about to-night's work."

He was not listening to me, nor was she. It was a duel between the two of them, and as she looked at him, his face seemed to grow more dogged and stone-like. If ever he had felt hatred it was for this woman, for it was a conflict between two opposite poles of life, two worlds eternally at war.

"I tell you I know nothing of the brat . . ."

She stopped him with lifted hand. "Oh, do not let us waste time, please. It is far too late for arguing. If you do what I ask we will go away, and you will never be troubled with us again. I promise—we all promise. If you do not, of course we must ruin you."

I think it was the confidence in her tone which stung him.

"I refuse," he almost screamed. "I do not know what you mean . . . I defy you. . . . You can proclaim your lies to the world. . . . You will not crush me. I am too strong for you."

There was no mistaking the finality of that defiance. I thought it put the lid on everything. We could blast the fellow's reputation, no doubt, and win victory; but we had failed, for we were left with that poor little mindless waif.

Mary's face did not change.

"If you refuse, I must try another way"; her voice was as gentle as a mother's. "I must give David Warcliff back to his father. . . . Dick"—she turned to me—"will you light the fire?"

I obeyed, not knowing what she meant, and in a minute the dry fagots were roaring up the chimney, lighting up our five faces and the mazed child in the chair.

"You have destroyed a soul," she said, "and you refuse to repair the wrong. I am going to destroy your body, and nothing will ever repair it."

Then I saw her meaning, and both Sandy and I cried out. Neither of us had led the kind of life which makes a man squeamish, but this was too much for us. But our protests died half-born, after one glance at Mary's face. She was my own wedded wife, but in that moment I could no more have opposed her than could the poor bemused child. Her spirit seemed to transcend us all and radiate an inexorable command. She stood easily and gracefully, a figure of motherhood and pity rather than of awe. But all the same I did not recognize her; it was a stranger that stood there, a stern goddess that wielded the lightnings. Beyond doubt she meant every word she said, and her quiet voice seemed to deliver judgment as aloof and impersonal as Fate. I could see creeping over Medina's sullenness the shadow of terror.

"You are a desperate man," she was saying. "But I am far more desperate. There is nothing on earth that can stand between me and the saving of this child. You know that, don't you? A body for a soul—a soul for a body—which shall it be?"

The light was reflected from the steel fire-irons, and Medina saw it and shivered.

"You may live a long time, but you will have to live in seclusion. No woman will ever cast eyes on you except to shudder. People will point at you and say 'There goes the man who was maimed by a woman—because of the soul of a child.' You will carry your story written on your face for the world to read and laugh and revile."

She had got at the central nerve of his vanity, for I think that he was ambitious less of achievement than of the personal glory that attends it. I dared not look at her, but I could look at him, and I saw all the passions of hell chase each other over his face. He tried to speak, but only choked. He seemed to bend his whole soul to look at her, and to shiver at what he saw.

She turned her head to glance at the clock on the mantelpiece.

"You must decide before the quarter strikes," she said. "After that there will be no place for repentance. A body for a soul—a soul for a body."

Then from her black silk reticule she took a little oddly shaped green bottle. She held it in her hands as if it had been a jewel, and I gulped in horror.

"This is the elixir of death—of death in life, Mr. Medina. It makes comeliness a mockery. It will burn flesh and bone into shapes of hideousness, but it does not kill. Oh no—it does not kill. A body for a soul—a soul for a body."

It was that, I think, which finished him. The threefold chime which announced the quarter had begun when out of his dry throat came a sound like a clucking hen's. "I agree," a voice croaked, seeming to come from without, so queer and far away it was.

"Thank you," she said, as if some one had opened a door for her. "Dick, will you please make Mr. Medina more comfortable. . . ."

The fire was not replenished, so the quick-burning fagots soon died down. Again the room was shadowy, except for the single lamp that glowed behind Medina's head.

I cannot describe that last scene, for I do not think my sight was clear, and I know that my head was spinning. The child sat on Mary's lap, with its eyes held by the glow of light. "You are Gerda. . . . you are sleepy . . . now you sleep"—I did not heed the patter, for I was trying to think of homely things which would keep my wits anchored. I thought chiefly of Peter John.

Sandy was crouched on a stool by the hearth. I noticed that he had his hands on his knees, and that from one of them protruded something round and dark, like the point of a pistol barrel. He was taking no chances, but the thing was folly, for we were in the presence of far more potent weapons. Never since the world began was there a scene of such utter humiliation. I shivered at the indecency of it. Medina performed his sinister ritual, but on us spectators it had no more effect than a charade. Mary especially sat watching it with the detachment with which one watches a kindergarten play. The man had suddenly become a mountebank under those fearless eyes.

The voices droned on, the man asking questions, the child answering in a weak unnatural voice. "You are David Warcliff . . . you lost your way coming from school . . . you have been ill and have forgotten. . . . You are better now . . . you remember Haverham and the redshanks down by the river. . . . You are sleepy . . . I think you would like to sleep again."

Medina spoke. "You can wake him now. Do it carefully."

I got up and switched on the rest of the lights. The child was peacefully asleep in Mary's arms, and she bent and kissed him. "Speak to him, Dick," she said.

"Davie," I said loudly. "Davie, it's about time for us to get home."

He opened his eyes and sat up. When he found himself on Mary's knee, he began to clamber down. He was not accustomed to a woman's lap, and felt a little ashamed.

"Davie," I repeated. "Your father will be getting tired waiting for us. Don't you think we should go home?"

"Yes, sir," he said, and put his hand in mine.

To my dying day I shall not forget my last sight of that library—the blazing lights which made the books, which I had never seen before except in shadow, gleam like a silk tapestry, the wood-fire dying on the hearth, and the man sunk in the chair. It may sound odd after all that had happened, but my chief feeling was pity. Yes, pity! He seemed the loneliest thing on God's earth. You see he had never had any friends except himself, and his ambitions had made a barrier between him and all humanity. Now that they were gone he was stripped naked, and left cold and shivering in the wilderness of his broken dreams.

Mary leaned back in the car

"I hope I'm not going to faint," she said. "Give me the green bottle, please."

"For Heaven's sake!" I cried.

"Silly!" she said. "It's only eau-de-cologne."

She laughed, and the laugh seemed to restore her a little, though she still looked deadly pale. She fumbled in her reticule, and drew out a robust pair of scissors.

"I'm going to cut Davie's hair. I can't change his clothes, but at any rate I can make his head like a boy's again, so that his father won't be shocked."

"Does he know we are coming?"

"Yes. I telephoned to him after dinner, but of course I said nothing about Davie."

She clipped assiduously, and by the time we came to the Pimlico square where Sir Arthur Warcliff lived she had got rid of the long locks, and the head was now that of a pallid and thin but wonderfully composed little boy. "Am I going back to Dad?" he asked, and seemed content.

I refused to go in—I was not fit for any more shocks—so I sat in the car while Mary and David entered the little house. In about three minutes Mary returned. She was crying, and yet smiling too.

"I made Davie wait in the hall, and went into Sir Arthur's study alone. He looked ill—and oh, so old and worn. I said: 'I have brought Davie. Never mind his clothes. He's all right!' Then I fetched him in. Oh, Dick, it was a miracle. That old darling seemed to come back to life. . . . The two didn't run into each other's arms . . . they shook hands . . . and the little boy bowed his head and Sir Arthur kissed the top of it, and said 'Dear Mouse-head, you've come back to me.' . . . And then I slipped away."

74 MACHRAY

A week later, after much consultation with Sandy, I wrote Medina a letter. The papers said he had gone abroad for a short rest, and I could imagine the kind of mental purgatory he was enduring in some Mediterranean bay. We had made up our mind to be content with success. Victory meant a long campaign in the courts and the press, in which no doubt we should have won, but for which I at any rate had no stomach. The whole business was a nightmare which I longed to shut the door on; we had drawn his fangs, and for all I cared he might go on with his politics and dazzle the world with his gifts, provided he kept his hands out of crime. I wrote and told him that; told him that the three people who knew everything would hold their tongues, but that they reserved the right to speak if he ever showed any sign of running crooked. I had no reply and did not expect one. I had lost all my hate for the man, and so strangely are we made, what I mostly felt was compassion. We are all, even the best of us, egotists and self-deceivers, and without a little comfortable make-believe to clothe us we should freeze in the outer winds. I shuddered when I thought of the poor devil with his palace of cards about his ears and his naked soul. I felt that further triumph would be an offence against humanity.

He must have got my message, for in July he was back at his work, and made a speech at a big political demonstration which was highly commended in the papers. Whether he went about in society I do not know, for Sandy was in Scotland and I was at Fosse, and not inclined to leave it. . . . Meantime Macgillivray's business was going on, and the press was full of strange cases, which no one seemed to think of connecting. I gathered from Macgillivray that though the syndicate was smashed to little bits he had failed to make the complete bag of malefactors that he had hoped. In England there were three big financial exposures followed by long sentences; in Paris there was a first-rate political scandal and a crop of convictions; a labour agitator and a copper magnate in the Middle West went to gaol for life, and there was the famous rounding-up of the murder gang in Turin. But Macgillivray and his colleagues, like me, had success rather than victory; indeed in this world I don't think you can get both at once—you must make your choice.

We saw Mercot at the "House" Ball at Oxford none the worse for his adventures, but rather the better, for he was a man now and not a light-witted boy. Early in July Mary and I went to Paris for Adela Victor's wedding, the most gorgeous show I have ever witnessed, when I had the privilege of kissing the bride and being kissed by the bridegroom. Sir Arthur Warcliff brought David to pay us a visit at Fosse, where the boy fished from dawn to dusk, and began to get some flesh on his bones. Archie Roylance arrived, and the pair took such a fancy to each other that the three of them went off to Norway to have a look at the birds on Flacksholm.

I was busy during those weeks making up arrears of time at Fosse, for my long absence had put out the whole summer programme. One day, as I was down in the Home Meadow, planning a new outlet for one of the ponds, Sandy turned up, announcing that he must have a talk with me and could only spare twenty minutes.

"When does your tenancy of Machray begin?" he asked.

"I have got it now—ever since April. The sea-trout come early there."

"And you can go up whenever you like?"

"Yes. We propose starting about the 5th of August."

"Take my advice and start at once," he said.

I asked why, though I guessed his reason.

"Because I'm not very happy about you here. You've insulted to the marrrow the vainest and one of the cleverest men in the world. Don't imagine he'll take it lying down. You may be sure he is spending sleepless nights planning how he is to get even with you. It's you he is chiefly thinking about. Me he regards as a rival in the same line of business—he'd love to break me, but he'll trust to luck for the chance turning up. Lavater has been his slave and has escaped—but at any rate he once acknowledged his power. *You* have fooled him from start to finish and left his vanity one raw throbbing sore. He won't be at ease till he has had his revenge on you—on you and your wife."

"Peter John!" I exclaimed.

He shook his head. "No, I don't think so. He won't try that line again—at any rate not yet awhile. But he would be much happier, Dick if you were dead."

The thought had been in my mind for weeks, and had made me pretty uncomfortable. It is not pleasant to walk in peril of your life, and move about in constant expectation of your decease. I had considered the thing very carefully, and had come to the conclusion that I could do nothing but try to forget the risk. If I ever allowed myself to think about it, my whole existence would be poisoned. It was a most unpleasant affair, but after all the world is full of hazards. I told Sandy that.

"I'm quite aware of the danger," I said. "I always reckoned that as part of the price I had to pay for succeeding. But I'm hanged if I'm going to allow the fellow to score off me to the extent of disarranging my life."

"You've plenty of fortitude, old fellow," said Sandy, "but you owe a duty to your family and your friends. Of course you might get police protection from Macgillivray, but that would be an infernal nuisance for you, and, besides, what kind of police protection would avail against an enemy as subtle as Medina? . . . No, I want you to go away. I want you to go to Machray now, and stay there till the end of October."

"What good would that do? He can follow me there, if he wants to, and anyhow the whole thing would begin again when I came back."

"I'm not so sure," he said. "In three months' time his wounded vanity may have healed. It's no part of his general game to have a vendetta with you, and only a passion of injured pride would drive him to it. Presently that must die down, and he will see his real interest. Then as for Machray—why, a Scotch deer-forest is the best sanctuary on earth. Nobody can come up that long glen without your hearing about it, and nobody can move on the hills without half a dozen argus-eyed stalkers and gillies following him. They're the right sort of police protection. I want you for all our sakes to go to Machray at once."

"It looks like funking," I objected.

"Don't be an old ass. Is there any man alive, who is not a raving maniac, likely to doubt your courage? You know perfectly well that it is sometimes a brave man's duty to run away."

I thought for a bit. "I don't think he'll hire ruffians to murder me," I said.

"Why?"

"Because he challenged me to a duel. Proposed a place in the Pyrenees and offered to let me choose both seconds."

"What did you reply?"

"I wired, 'Try not to be a fool.' It looks as if he wanted to keep the job of doing me in for himself."

"Very likely, and that doesn't mend matters. I'd rather face half a dozen cut-throats than Medina. What you tell me strengthens my argument."

I was bound to admit that Sandy talked sense, and after he had gone I thought the matter out and decided to take his advice. Somehow the fact that he should have put my suspicions into words made them more formidable, and I knew again the odious feeling of the hunted. It was hardly fear, for I think that, if necessary, I could have stayed on at Fosse and gone about my business with a stiff lip. But all the peace of the place had been spoiled. If a bullet might at any moment come from a covert—that was the crude way I envisaged the risk—then good-bye to the charm of my summer meadows.

The upshot was that I warned Tom Greenslade to be ready to take his holiday, and by the 20th of July he and I and Mary and Peter John were settled in a little whitewashed lodge tucked into the fold of a birch-clad hill, and looking alternately at a shrunken river and a cloudless sky, while we prayed for rain.

Machray in calm weather is the most solitary place on earth, lonelier and quieter even than a Boer farm lost in some hollow of the veld. The mountains rise so sheer and high that it seems that only a bird could escape, and the road from the sea-loch ten miles away is only a strip of heather-grown sand which looks as if it would end a mile off at the feet of each steep hill-shoulder. But when the gales come, and the rain is lashing the roof, and the river swirls at the garden-edge, and the birches and rowans are tossing, then a thousand voices talk, and one lives in a world so loud that one's ears are deafened and one's voice acquires a sharp pitch of protest from shouting against the storm.

We had a few gales, and the last week of July was a very fair imitation of the Tropics. The hills were cloaked in a heat haze, the Aicill river was a chain of translucent pools with a few reddening salmon below the ledges, the burns were thin trickles, the sun drew hot scents out of the heather and bog-myrtle, and movement was a weariness to man and beast. That was for the daytime; but every evening about five o'clock there would come a light wind from the west, which scattered the haze, and left a land swimming in cool amber light. Then Mary and Tom Greenslade and I would take to the hills, and return well on for midnight to a vast and shameless supper. Sometimes in the hot noontides I went alone, with old Angus the head stalker, and long before the season began I had got a pretty close knowledge of the forest.

The reader must bear with me while I explain the lie of the land. The twenty thousand acres of Machray extend on both sides of the Aicill glen, but principally to the south. West lies the Machray sea-loch, where the hills are low and green and mostly sheep-ground. East, up to the riverhead, is Glenaicill Forest, the lodge of which is beyond the watershed on the shore of another sea-loch, and on our side of the divide there is only a stalker's cottage. Glenaicill is an enormous place, far too big to be a single forest. It had been leased for years by Lord Glenfinnan, an uncle of Archie Roylance, but he was a frail old gentleman of over seventy who could only get a stag when they came down to the low ground in October. The result was that the place was ridiculously undershot, and all the western end, which adjoined Machray, was virtually a sanctuary. It was a confounded nuisance, for it made it impossible to stalk our northern beat except in a south-west wind, unless you wanted to shift the deer on to Glenaicill, and that beat had all our best grazing and seemed to attract all our best heads.

Haripol Forest to the south was not so large, but I should think it was the roughest ground in Scotland. Machray had good beats south of the Aicill right up to the watershed, and two noble corries, the Corrie-na-Sidhe and the Corrie Easain. Beyond the watershed was the glen of the Reascuill, both sides of which were Haripol ground. The Machray heights were all over the 3,000 feet, but rounded and fairly easy going, but the Haripol peaks beyond the stream were desperate rock mountains—Stob Ban, Stob Coire Easain, Sgurr Mor—comprising some of the most difficult climbing in the British Isles. The biggest and hardest top of all was at the head of the Reascuill—Sgurr Dearg, with its two pinnacle ridges, its three prongs, and the awesome precipice of its eastern face. Machray marched with Haripol on its summit, but it wasn't often that any of our stalkers went that way. All that upper part of the Reascuill was a series of cliffs and chasms, and the red deer—who is no rock-climber—rarely ventured there. For the rest these four southern beats of ours were as delightful hunting-ground as I have ever seen, and the ladies could follow a good deal of the stalking by means of a big telescope in the library window of the Lodge. Machray was a young man's forest, for the hills rose steep almost from the sea-level, and you might have to go up and down 3,000 feet several times a day. But Haripol—at least the north and east parts of it—was fit only for athletes, and it seemed to be its fate to fall to tenants who were utterly incapable of doing it justice. In recent years it had been leased successively to an elderly distiller, a young racing ne'er-do-weel who drank, and a plump American railway king. It was now in the hands of a certain middle-aged Midland manufacturer, Lord Claybody, who had won an easy fortune and an easier peerage during the War. "Ach, he will be killed," Angus said. "He will never get up a hundred feet of Haripol without being killed." So I found myself, to my disgust, afflicted with another unauthorized sanctuary.

Angus was very solemn about it. He was a lean anxious man, just over fifty, with a face not unlike a stag's, amazingly fast on the hills, a finished cragsman, and with all the Highlander's subtle courtesy. Kennedy, the second stalker, was of Lowland stock; his father had come to the North from Galloway in the days of the boom in sheep, and had remained as a keeper when sheep prices fell. He was a sturdy young fellow, apt to suffer on steep slopes on a warm day, but strong as an ox and with a better head than Angus for thinking out problems of weather and wind. Though he had the Gaelic, he was a true Lowlander, plain-spoken and imperturbable. It was a contrast of new and old, for Kennedy had served in the War, and learned many things beyond the other's ken. He knew, for example, how to direct your eye to the point he wanted, and would give intelligent directions like a battery observer, whereas with Angus it was always "D'ye see yon stone? Ay, but d'ye see another stone?"—and so forth. Kennedy, when we sat down to rest, would smoke a cigarette in a holder, while Angus lit the dottle in a foul old pipe.

In the first fortnight of August we had alternate days of rain, real drenching torrents, and the Aicill rose and let the fish up from the sea. There were few sea-trout that year, but there was a glorious run of salmon. Greenslade killed his first, and by the end of a week had a bag of twelve, while Mary, with the luck which seems to attend casual lady anglers, had four in one day to her own rod. Those were pleasant days, though there were mild damp afternoons when the midges were worse than tropical mosquitoes. I liked it best when a breeze rose and the sun was hot and we had all our meals by the waterside. Once at luncheon we took with us an iron pot, made a fire, and boiled a fresh-killed salmon "in his broo"—a device I recommend to any one who wants the full flavour of that noble fish.

Archie Roylance arrived on August 16th, full of the lust of hunting. He reported that they had seen nothing remarkable in the way of birds at Flacksholm, but that David Warcliff had had great sport with the sea-trout. "There's a good boy for you," he declared. "First-class little sportsman, and to see him and his father together made me want to get wedded straight off. I thought him a bit hipped at Fosse, but the North Sea put him right, and I left him as jolly as a grig. By the way, what was the matter with him in the summer? I gathered that he had been seedy or something, and the old man can't let him out of his sight. . . . Let's get in Angus, and talk deer."

Angus was ready to talk deer till all hours. I had fixed the 21st for the start of the season, though the beasts were in such forward condition that we might have begun four days earlier. Angus reported that he had already seen several stags clear of velvet. But he was inclined to be doleful about our neighbours.

"My uncle Alexander is past prayin' for," said Archie. "He lives for that forest of his, and he won't have me there early in the season, for he says I have no judgment about beasts and won't listen to the stalkers. In October, you see, he has me under his own eye. He refuses to let a stag be killed unless it's a hummel or a diseased ancient. Result is, the place is crawlin' with fine stags that have begun to go back and won't perish till they're fairly moulderin'. Poor notion of a stud has my uncle Alexander. . . . What about Haripol? Who has it this year?"

When he heard he exclaimed delightedly. "I know old Claybody. Rather a good old fellow in his way, and uncommon free-handed. Rum old bird, too! He once introduced his son to me as 'The Honourable Johnson Claybody'. Fairly wallows in his peerage. You know he wanted to take the title of Lord Oxford, because he had a boy goin' up to Magdalen, but even the Heralds' College jibbed at that. But he'll never get up those Haripol hills. He's a little fat puffin' old man. I'm not very spry on my legs now, but compared to Claybody I'm a gazelle."

"He'll maybe have veesitors," said Angus.

"You bet he will. He'll have the Lodge stuffed with young men, for there are various Honourable Claybody daughters. Don't fancy they'll be much good on the hill, though."

"They will not be good, Sir Archibald," said the melancholy Angus, "There will have been some of them on the hill already. They will be no better than towrists."

"Towrists", I should explain, were the poison in Angus's cup. By that name he meant people who trespassed on a deer-forest during, or shortly before, the stalking season, and had not the good manners to give him notice and ask his consent. He distinguished them sharply from what he called "muntaneers", a class which he respected, for they were modest and civil folk who came usually with ropes and ice axes early in the spring, and were accustomed to feast off Angus's ham and eggs and thaw their frozen limbs by Angus's fire. If they came at other seasons it was after discussing their routes with Angus. They went where no deer could travel, and spent their time, as he said, "shamming themselves into shimneys". But the "towrist" was blatant and foolish and abundantly discourteous. He tramped, generally in a noisy party, over deer-ground, and, if remonstrated with, became truculent. A single member of the species could wreck the stalking on a beat for several days. "The next I see on Machray," said Angus, "I will be rolling down a big stone on him." Some of the Haripol guests, it appeared, were of this malign breed, and had been wandering thoughtlessly over the forest, thereby wrecking their own sport—and mine.

"They will have Alan Macnicol's heart broke," he concluded. "And Alan was saying to me that they was afful bad shots. They was shooting at a big stone and missing it. And they will have little ponies to ride on up to the tops, for the creatures is no use at walking. I hope they will fall down and break their necks."

"They can't all be bad shots," said Archie. "By the way, Dick, I forgot to tell you. You know Medina, Dominick Medina? You once told me you knew him. Well, I met him on the steamer, and he said he was going to put in a week with old Claybody."

That piece of news took the light out of the day for me. If Medina was at Haripol it was most certainly with a purpose. I had thought little about the matter since I arrived at Machray, for the place had an atmosphere of impregnable seclusion, and I seemed to have shut a door on my recent life. I had fallen into a mood of content and whole-hearted absorption in the ritual of wild sport. But now my comfort vanished. I looked up at the grim wall of hills towards Haripol and wondered what mischief was hatching behind it.

I warned Angus and Kennedy and the gillies to keep a good look-out for trespassers. Whenever one was seen, they were to get their glasses on him and follow him and report his appearance and doings to me. Then I went out alone to shoot a brace of grouse for the pot, and considered the whole matter very carefully. I had an instinct that Medina had come to these parts to have a reckoning with me, and I was determined not to shirk it. I could not go on living under such a menace; I must face it and reach a settlement. To Mary, of course, I would say nothing, and I saw no use in telling either Archie or Greenslade. It was, metaphorically, and perhaps literally, my own funeral. But next morning I did not go fishing. Instead, I stayed at home and wrote out a full account of the whole affair up to Medina's appearance at Haripol, and I set down baldly what I believed to be his purpose. This was in case I went out one day and did not return. When I finished it, I put the document in my dispatch-box, and felt easier, as a man feels when he has made a will. I only hoped the time of waiting would not be prolonged.

The 21st was a glorious blue day, with a morning haze which promised heat. What wind there was came from the south-east, so I sent Archie out on the Corrie Easain beat, and went myself, with one gillie, to Clach Glas, which is the western peak on the north bank of the Aicill. I made a practice of doing my own stalking, and by this time I knew the ground well enough to do it safely. I saw two shootable stags, and managed to get within range of one of them, but spared him for the good of the forest, as he was a young beast whose head would improve. I had a happy and peaceful day, and found to my relief that I wasn't worrying about the future. The clear air and the great spaces seemed to have given me the placid fatalism of an Arab.

When I returned I was greeted by Mary with the news that Archie had got a stag, and that she had followed most of his stalk through the big telescope. Archie himself arrived just before dinner, very cheerful and loquacious. He found that his game leg made him slow, but he declared that he was not in the least tired. At dinner we had to listen to every detail of his day, and we had a sweep on the beast's weight, which Mary won. Afterwards in the smoking-room he told me more.

"Those infernal tailors from Haripol were out to-day. Pretty wild shots they must be. When we were lunchin' a spent bullet whistled over our heads—a long way off, to be sure, but I call it uncommon bad form. You should have heard Angus curse in Gaelic. Look here, Dick, I've a good mind to drop a line to old Claybody and ask him to caution his people. The odds are a million to one, of course, against their doin' any harm, but there's always that millionth chance. I had a feelin' to-day as if the War had started over again."

I replied that if anything of the sort happened a second time I would certainly protest, but I pretended to make light of it, as a thing only possible with that particular brand of wind. But I realized now what Medina's plans were. He had been tramping about Haripol, getting a notion of the lie of the land, and I knew that he had a big-game hunter's quick eye for country. He had fostered the legend of wild shooting among the Haripol guests, and probably he made himself the wildest of the lot. The bullet which sang over Archie's head was a proof, but he waited on the chance of a bullet which would not miss. If a tragedy happened, every one would believe it was a pure accident, there would be heart-broken apologies, and, though Sandy and one or two others would guess the truth, nothing could be proved, and in any case it wouldn't help *me*. . . . Of course I could stalk only on the north beats of Machray, but the idea no sooner occurred to me than I dismissed it. I must end this hideous suspense. I must accept Medina's challenge and somehow or other reach a settlement.

When Angus came in for orders, I told him that I was going stalking on the Corrie-na-Sidhe beat the day after to-morrow, and I asked him to send word privately to Alan Macnicol at Haripol.

"It will be no use, sir," he groaned. "The veesitors will no heed Alan."

But I told him to send word nevertheless. I wanted to give Medina the chance he sought. It was my business to draw his fire.

Next day we slacked and fished. In the afternoon I went a little way up the hill called Clach Glas, from which I could get a view of the ground on the south side of the Aicill. It was a clear quiet day, with the wind steady in the south-east, and promising to continue there. The great green hollow of Corrie-na-Sidhe was clear in every detail; much of it looked like a tennis-court, but I knew that what seemed smooth sward was really matted blaeber-ries and hidden boulders, and that the darker patches were breast-high bracken and heather. Corrie Easain I could not see, for it was hidden by the long spur of Bheinn Fhada, over which peeped the cloven summit of Sgurr Dearg. I searched all the ground with my glasses, and picked up several lots of hinds, and a few young stags, but there was no sign of human activity. There seemed to be a rifle out, however, on Glenaicill Forest, for I heard two far-away shots towards the north-east. I lay a long time amid the fern, with bees humming around me and pipits calling, and an occasional buzzard or peregrine hovering in the blue, thinking precisely the same thoughts that I used to have in France the day before a big action. It was not exactly nervousness that I felt, but a sense that the foundations of everything had got loose, and that the world had become so insecure that I had better draw down the blinds on hoping and planning and everything, and become a log. I was very clear in my mind that next day was going to bring the crisis.

Of course I didn't want Mary to suspect, but I forgot to caution Archie, and that night at dinner, as ill-luck would have it, he mentioned that Medina was at Haripol. I could see her eyes grow troubled, for I expect she had been having the same anxiety as myself those past weeks, and had been too proud to declare it. As we were going to bed she asked me point-blank what it meant. "Nothing in the world," I said. "He is a great stalker and a friend of the Claybodys. I don't suppose he has the remotest idea that I am here. Anyhow that affair is all over. He is not going to cross our path if he can help it. The one wish in his heart is to avoid us."

She appeared to be satisfied, but I don't know how much she slept that night. I never woke till six o'clock, but when I opened my eyes I felt too big a load on my heart to let me stay in bed, so I went down to the Garden Pool and had a swim. That invigorated me, and indeed it was not easy to be depressed in that gorgeous morning, with the streamers of mist still clinging to the high tops, and the whole glen a harmony of singing birds and tumbling waters. I noticed that the wind, what there was of it, seemed to have shifted more to the east—a very good quarter for the Corrie-na-Sidhe beat.

Angus and Kennedy were waiting outside the smoking-room, and even the pessimism of the head stalker was mellowed by the weather. "I think," he said slowly, "we will be getting a sta-ag. There was a big beast on Bheinn Fhada yesterday—Kennedy seen him—a great beast he was—maybe nineteen stone, but Kennedy never right seen his head. . . . We'd better be moving on, sir."

Mary whispered in my ear. "There's no danger, Dick? You're sure?" I have never heard her voice more troubled.

"Not a scrap," I laughed. "It's an easy day and I ought to be back for tea. You'll be able to follow me all the time through the big telescope."

We started at nine. As I left, I had a picture of Greenslade sitting on a garden-seat busy with fly-casts, and Archie smoking his pipe and reading a three-days-old *Times*, and Peter John going off with his nurse, and Mary looking after me with a curious, tense gaze. Behind, the smoke of the chimneys was rising straight into the still air, and the finches were twittering among the Prince Charlie roses. The sight gave me a pang. I might never enter my little kingdom again. Neither wife nor friends could help me: it was my own problem, which I must face alone.

We crossed the bridge, and began to plod upwards through a wood of hazels. In such a fashion I entered upon the strangest day of my life.

75 HOW I STALKED WILDER GAME THAN DEER

I

9 A.M. TO 2.15 P.M.

Obviously I could make no plan, and I had no clear idea in my head as to what kind of settlement I wanted with Medina. I was certain that I should find him somewhere on the hill, and that, if he got a chance, he would try to kill me. The odds were, of course, against his succeeding straight off, but escape was not what I sought—I must get rid of this menace for ever. I don't think that I wanted to kill him, but indeed I never tried to analyse my feelings. I was obeying a blind instinct, and letting myself drift on the tides of fate.

Corrie-na-Sidhe is an upper corrie, separated from the Aicill valley by a curtain of rock and scree which I daresay was once the moraine of a glacier and down which the Alt-na-Sidhe tumbled in a fine chain of cascades. So steep is its fall that no fish can ascend it, so that, while at the foot it is full of sizable trout, in the corrie itself it holds nothing, as Greenslade reported, but little dark fingerlings. It was very warm as we mounted the chaos of slabs and boulders, where a very sketchy and winding track had been cut for bringing down the deer. Only the toughest kind of pony could make that ascent. Though the day was young the heat was already great, and the glen behind us swam in a glassy sheen. Kennedy, as usual, mopped his brow and grunted, but the lean Angus strode ahead as if he were on the flat.

At the edge of the corrie we halted for a spy. Deep hollows have a trick of drawing the wind, and such faint currents of air as I could detect seemed to be coming on our left rear from the north-east. Angus was positive, however, that though the south had gone out of the wind, it was pretty well due east, with no north in it, and maintained that when we were farther up the corrie we would have it fair on our left cheek. We were not long in finding beasts. There was a big drove of hinds on the right bank of the burn, and another lot, with a few small stags, on the left bank, well up on the face of Bheinn Fhada. But there was nothing shootable there.

"The big stags will be all on the high tops," said Angus. "We must be getting up to the burnhead."

It was easier said than done, for there were the hinds to be circumvented, so we had to make a long circuit far up the hill called Clonlet, which is the westernmost of the Machray tops south of the Aicill. It was rough going, for

659

we mounted to about the 3,000 feet level, and traversed the hillside just under the upper scarp of rock. Presently we were looking down upon the cup which was the head of the corrie, and over the col could see the peak of Stob Coire Easain and the ridge of Stob Ban, both on Haripol and beyond the Reascuill. We had another spy, and made out two small lots of stags on the other side of the Alt-na-Sidhe. They were too far off to get a proper view of them, but one or two looked good beasts, and I decided to get nearer.

We had to make a cautious descent of the hillside in case of deer lying in pockets, for the place was seamed with gullies. Before we were half-way down I got my telescope on one of the lots, and picked out a big stag with a poor head, which clearly wanted shooting. Angus agreed, and we started down a sheltering ravine to get to the burnside. The sight of a quarry made me forget everything else, and for the next hour and a half I hadn't a thought in the world except how to get within range of that beast. One stalk is very much like another, and I am not going to describe this. The only trouble came from a small stag in our rear, which had come over Clonlet and got the scent of our track on the hill-face. This unsettled him and he went off at a great pace towards the top of the burn. I thought at first that the brute would go up to Bheinn Fhada and carry off our lot with him, but he came to a halt, changed his mind, and made for the Haripol march and the col.

After that it was plain sailing. We crawled up the right bank of the Alt-na-Sidhe, which was first-class cover, and then turned up a tributary gully which came down from Bheinn Fhada. Indeed the whole business was too simple to be of much interest to any one except the man with the rifle. When I judged I was about the latitude of my stag, I crept out of the burn and reached a hillock from which I had a good view of him. The head, as I suspected, was poor—only nine points, though the horns were of the rough, thick, old Highland type—but the body was heavy, and he was clearly a back-going beast. After a wait of some twenty minutes he got up and gave me a chance at about two hundreds yards, and I dropped him dead with a shot in the neck, which was the only part of him clear.

It was for me the first stag of the season, and it is always a pleasant moment when the tension relaxes and you light your pipe and look around you. As soon as the gralloch was over I proposed lunch, and we found for the purpose a little nook by a spring. We were within a few hundred yards of the Haripol march, which there does not run along the watershed but crosses the corrie about half a mile below the col. In the old days of sheep there had been a fence, the decaying posts of which could be observed a little way off on a knoll. Between the fence and the col lay some very rough ground, where the Alt-na-Sidhe had its source, ground so broken that it was impossible, without going a good way up the hill, to see from it the watershed ridge.

I finished Mary's stuffed scones and ginger biscuits, and had a drink of whisky and spring water, while Angus and Kennedy ate their lunch a few yards off in the heather. I was just lighting my pipe, when a sound made me pause with the match in my hand. A rifle bullet sang over my head. It was not very near—fifty feet or so above me, and a little to the left.

"The tamned towrists!" I heard Angus exclaim.

I knew it was Medina as certainly as if I had seen him. He was somewhere in the rough ground between the Haripol march and the col—probably close to the col, for the sound of the report seemed to come from a good way off. He could not have been aiming at me, for I was perfectly covered, but he must have seen me when I stalked the stag. He had decided that his chance was not yet come, and the shot was camouflage—to keep up the reputation of Haripol for wild shooting.

"It would be the staggie that went over the march," grunted Angus. "The towrists—to be shooting at yon wee beast!"

I had suddenly made up my mind. I would give Medina the opportunity he sought. I would go and look for him.

I got up and stretched my legs. "I'm going to try a stalk on my own," I told Angus. "I'll go over to Corrie Easain. You had better pull this beast down to the burnside, and then fetch the pony. You might send Hughie and the other pony up Glenaicill to the Mad Burn. If I get a stag I'll gralloch him and get him down somehow to the burn, so tell Hughie to look out for my signal. I'll wave a white handkerchief. The wind is backing round to the north, Angus. It should be all right for Corrie Easain, if I take it from the south."

"It would be better for Sgurr Dearg," said Angus, "but that's ower far. Have you the cartridges, sir?"

"Plenty," I said, patting a side pocket. "Give me that spare rope, Kennedy. I'll want it for hauling down my stag if I get one."

I put my little .240 into its cover, nodded to the men, and turned down the gully to the main burn. I wasn't going to appear on the bare hillside so long as it was possible for Medina to have a shot at me. But soon a ridge shut off the view from the Haripol ground, and I then took a slant up the face of Bheinn Fhada.

Mary had spent most of the morning at the big telescope in the library window. She saw us reach the rim of the corrie and lost us when we moved up the side of Clonlet. We came into view again far up the corrie, and she saw the stalk and the death of the stag. Then she went to luncheon, but hastened back in the middle of it in time to see me scrambling alone among the screes of Bheinn Fhada. At first she was reassured because she thought I was coming home. But when she realized that I was mounting higher and was making for Corrie Easain her heart sank, and, when I had gone out of view, she could do nothing but range miserably about the garden.

II

2.15 P.M. TO ABOUT 5 P.M.

It was very hot on Bheinn Fhada, for I was out of the wind, but when I reached the ridge and looked down on Corrie Easain I found a fair breeze, which had certainly more north than east in it. There was not a cloud in the sky, and every top for miles round stood out clear, except the Haripol peaks,

which were shut off by the highest part of the ridge I stood on. Corrie Easain
lay far below—not a broad cup like Corrie-na-Sidhe, but a deep gash in
the hills, inclined at such an angle that the stream in it was nothing but
white water. We called it the Mad Burn—its Gaelic name, I think, was the
Alt-a-mhuillin—and half-way up and just opposite me a tributary, the Red
Burn, came down from the cliffs of Sgurr Dearg. I could see the northern
peak of that mountain, a beautiful cone of rock, rising like the Matterhorn
from its glacis of scree.

I argued that Medina would have seen me going up Bheinn Fhada and
would assume that I was bound for Corrie Easain. He would re-cross the col
and make for the Haripol side of the *beallach* which led from that corrie to the
Reascuill. Now I wanted to keep the higher ground, where I could follow his
movements, so it was my aim to get to the watershed ridge looking down on
Haripol before he did. The wind was a nuisance, for it was blowing from me
and would move any deer towards him, thereby giving him a clue to my
whereabouts. So I thought that if I could once locate him, I must try to get
the lee side of him. At that time I think I had a vague notion of driving him
towards Machray.

I moved at my best pace along the east face of Bheinn Fhada towards the
beallach—which was a deep rift in the grey rock-curtain through which deer
could pass. My only feeling was excitement, such as I had never known
before in any stalk. I slipped and sprawled among the slabs, slithered over the
screes, had one or two awkward traverses round the butt-end of cliffs, but in
about twenty minutes I was at the point where the *massif* of Bheinn Fhada
joined the watershed ridge. The easy way was now to get on to the ridge, but
I dared not appear on the skyline, so I made a troublesome journey along the
near side of the ridge-wall, sometimes out on the face of sheer precipices, but
more often involved in a chaos of loose boulders which were the débris of the
upper rocks. I was forced pretty far down, and eventually struck the *beallach*
path about five hundred feet below the summit.

At the crest I found I had no view of the Reascuill valley—only a narrow
corrie blocked by a shoulder of hill and the bald top of Stob Coire Easain
beyond. A prospect I must have, so I turned east along the watershed ridge in
the direction of Sgurr Dearg. I was by this time very warm, for I had come at
a brisk pace; I had a rifle to carry, and had Angus's rope round my shoulders
like a Swiss guide; I was wearing an old grey suit, which, with bluish
stockings, made me pretty well invisible on that hillside. Presently as I
mounted the ridge, keeping of course under the skyline, I came to a place
where a lift of rock enabled me to clear the spur and command a mile or so of
the Reascuill.

The place was on the skyline, bare and exposed, and I crawled to the edge
where I could get a view. Below me, after a few hundred yards of rocks
and scree, I saw a long tract of bracken and deep heather sweeping down to
the stream. Medina, I made sure, was somewhere thereabouts, watching the
ridge. I calculated that, with his re-crossing of the col at the head of Corrie-
na-Sidhe and his working round the south end of Bheinn Fhada, he could not

have had the time to get to the *beallach*, or near the *beallach*, before me, and must still be on the lower ground. Indeed I hoped to catch sight of him, for, while I was assured he was pursuing me, he could not know that I was after him, and might be off his guard.

But there was no sign of life in that sunny stretch of green and purple, broken by the grey of boulders. I searched it with my glass and could see no movement except pipits, and a curlew by a patch of bog. Then it occurred to me to show myself. He must be made to know that I had accepted his challenge.

I stood up straight on the edge of the steep, and decided to remain standing till I had counted fifty. It was an insane thing to do, I daresay, but I was determined to force the pace. . . . I had got to forty-one without anything happening. Then a sudden instinct made me crouch and step aside. That movement was my salvation. There was a sound like a twanged fiddle-string, and a bullet passed over my left shoulder. I felt the wind of it on my cheek.

The next second I was on my back wriggling below the skyline. Once there I got to my feet and ran—up the ridge on my left to get a view from higher ground. The shot, so far as I could judge, had come from well below and a little to the east of where I had been standing. I found another knuckle of rock, and crept to the edge of it, so that I looked from between two boulders into the glen.

The place was still utterly quiet. My enemy was hidden there, probably not half a mile off, but there was nothing to reveal his presence. The light wind stirred the bog cotton, a merlin sailed across to Stob Coire Easain, a raven croaked in the crags, but these were the only sounds. There was not even a sign of deer.

My glass showed that half-way down an old ewe was feeding—one of those melancholy beasts which stray into a forest from adjacent sheep-ground, and lead a precarious life among the rocks, lean and matted and wild, till some gillie cuts their throats. They are far sharper-eyed and quicker of hearing than a stag, and an unmitigated curse to the stalker. The brute was feeding on a patch of turf near a big stretch of bracken, and suddenly I saw her raise her head and stare. It was the first time I had ever felt well disposed towards a sheep.

She was curious about something in a shallow gully which flanked the brackens, and so was I. I kept my glass glued on her, and saw her toss her disreputable head, stamp her foot, and then heard her whistle through her nose. This was a snag Medina could not have reckoned with. He was clearly in that gully, working his way upwards in its cover, unwitting that the ewe was giving him away. I argued that he must want to reach the high ground as soon as possible. He had seen me on the ridge, and must naturally conclude that I had beaten a retreat. My first business, therefore, was to reassure him.

I got my rifle out of its cover, which I stuffed into my pocket. There was a little patch of gravel just on the lip of the gully, and I calculated that he would emerge beside it, under the shade of a blaeberry-covered stone. I guessed right. . . . I saw first an arm and then a shoulder part the rushes, and presently a face which peered uphill. My glass showed me that the face was Medina's, very red, and dirty from contact with the peaty soil. He slowly reached for his glass, and began to scan the heights.

I don't know what my purpose was at this time, if indeed I had any purpose. I didn't exactly mean to kill him, I think, though I felt it might come to that. Vaguely I wanted to put him out of action, to put the fear of God into him, and make him come to terms. Of further consequences I never thought. But now I had one clear intention—to make him understand that I accepted his challenge.

I put a bullet neatly into the centre of the patch of gravel, and then got my glass on it. He knew the game all right. In a second, like a weasel, he was back in the gully.

I reckoned that now I had my chance. Along the ridge I went, mounting fast, and keeping always below the skyline. I wanted to get to the lee side of him and so be able to stalk him up-wind, and I thought that I had an opportunity now to turn the head of the Reascuill by one of the steep corries which descend from Sgurr Dearg. Looking back, it all seems very confused and amateurish, for what could I hope to do, even if I had the lee side, beyond killing or wounding him? and I had a chance of that as long as I had the upper ground. But in the excitement of the chase the mind does not take long views, and I was enthralled by the crazy sport of the thing. I did not feel any fear, because I was not worrying about consequences.

Soon I came to the higher part of the ridge and saw frowning above me the great rock face of Sgurr Dearg. I saw, too, a thing I had forgotten. There was no way up that mountain direct from the ridge, for the tower rose as perpendicular as a house-wall. To surmount it a man must traverse on one side or the other—on the Machray side by a scree slope, or on the Haripol side by a deep gully which formed the top of the corrie into which I was now looking. Across that corrie was the first of the great buttresses which Sgurr Dearg sends down to the Reascuill. It was the famous Pinnacle Ridge (as mountaineers called it); I had climbed it three weeks before and found it pretty stiff; but then I had kept the ridge all the way from the valley bottom, and I did not see any practicable road up the corrie face of it, which seemed nothing but slabs and rotten rocks, while the few chimneys had ugly overhangs.

I lay flat and reconnoitred. What was Medina likely to do? After my shot he could not follow up the ridge—the cover was too poor on the upper slopes. I reasoned that he would keep on in the broken ground up the glen till he reached this corrie, and try to find a road to the high ground either by the corrie itself or by one of the spurs. In that case it was my business to wait for him. But first I thought I had better put a fresh clip in my magazine, for the shot I had fired had been the last cartridge in the old clip.

It was now that I made an appalling discovery. I had felt my pockets and told Angus that I had plenty of cartridges. So I had, but they didn't fit. . . . I remembered that two days before I had lent Archie my .240 and had been shooting with a Mannlicher. What I had in my pocket were Mannlicher clips left over from that day. . . . I might chuck my rifle away, for it was no more use than a poker.

At first I was stunned by the fatality. Here was I, engaged in a duel on a wild mountain with one of the best shots in the world, and I had lost my gun! The sensible course would have been to go home. There was plenty of time for that, and long before Medina reached the ridge I could be in cover in the gorge of the Mad Burn. But that way out of it never occurred to me. I had chosen to set the course, and the game must be played out here and now. But I confess I was pretty well in despair and could see no plan. I think I had a faint hope of protracting the thing till dark and then trusting to my hill-craft to get even with him, but I had an unpleasant feeling that he was not likely to oblige me with so long a delay.

I forced myself to think, and decided that Medina would either come up the corrie or take the steep spur which formed the right-hand side of it and ran down to the Reascuill. The second route would give him cover, but also render him liable to a surprise at close quarters if I divined his intention, for I might suddenly confront him four yards off at the top of one of the pitches. He would therefore prefer the corrie, which was magnificently broken up with rocks, and seamed with ravines, and at the same time gave a clear view of all the higher ground.

With my face in a clump of louse-wort I raked the place with my glass; and to my delight saw deer feeding about half-way down in the right-hand corner. Medina could not ascend the corrie without disturbing these deer—a batch of some thirty hinds, with five small and two fairish stags among them. Therefore I was protected from that side, and had only the ridge to watch.

But as I lay there I thought of another plan. Medina, I was pretty certain, would try the corrie first, and would not see the deer till he was well inside it, for they were on a kind of platform which hid them from below. Opposite me across the narrow corrie rose the great black wall of the Pinnacle Ridge, with the wind blowing from me towards it. I remembered a trick which Angus had taught me—how a stalker might have his wind carried against the face of an opposite mountain and then, so to speak, reflected from it and brought back to his own side, so that the deer below him would get it and move away from it up *towards him*. If I let my scent be carried to the Pinnacle Ridge and diverted back, it would move the deer on the platform up the corrie towards me. It would be a faint wind, so they would move slowly away from it—no doubt towards a gap under the tower of Sgurr Dearg which led to the little corrie at the head of the Red Burn. We never stalked that corrie, because it was impossible to get a stag out of it without cutting him up, so the place was a kind of sanctuary to which disturbed deer would naturally resort.

I stood on the skyline, being confident that Medina could not yet be within sight, and let the wind, which was now stronger and nearly due north, ruffle my hair. I did this for about five minutes, and then lay down to watch the result, with my glass on the deer. Presently I saw them become restless, first the hinds and then the small stags lifting their heads and looking towards the Pinnacle Ridge. Soon a little fellow trotted a few yards uphill; then a couple of hinds moved after him; and then by a sudden and simultaneous impulse the whole party began to drift up the corrie. It was a quiet steady advance; they were not scared, only a little doubtful. I saw with satisfaction that their objective seemed to be the gap which led over to the Red Burn.

Medina must see this and would assume that wherever I was I was not ahead of the deer. He might look for me on the other side, but more likely would follow the beasts so as to get the high ground. Once there he could see my movements, whether I was on the slopes of the Pinnacle Ridge or down on the Machray side. He would consider, no doubt, that his marksmanship was so infinitely better than mine that he had only to pick me out from the landscape to make an end of the business.

What I exactly intended I do not know. I had a fleeting notion of lying hidden and surprising him, but the chances against that were about a million to one, and, even if I got him at close quarters, he was armed and I was not. I moved a little to the right so as to keep my wind from the deer, and waited with a chill beginning to creep over my spirit. . . . My watch told me it was five o'clock. Mary and Peter John would be having tea among the Prince Charlie roses, and Greenslade and Archie coming up from the river. It would be heavenly at Machray now among greenery and the cool airs of evening. Up here there was loveliness enough from the stars of butterwort and grass of Parnassus by the well-heads to the solemn tops of Sgurr Dearg, the colour of stormy waves against a faint turquoise sky. But I knew now that the beauty of earth depends on the eye of the beholder, for suddenly the clean airy world around me had grown leaden and stifling.

III

5 P.M. TO ABOUT 7.30 P.M.

It was a good hour before he came. I had guessed rightly, and he had made the deduction I hoped for. He was following the deer towards the gap, assuming that I was on the Machray side. I was in a rushy hollow at a junction of the main ridge and the spur I have mentioned, and I could see him clearly as, with immense circumspection and the use of every scrap of cover, he made his way up the corrie. Once he was over the watershed, I would command him from the higher ground and have the wind to my vantage. I had some hope now, for I ought to be able to keep him on the hill till the light failed, when my superior local knowledge would come to my aid. He must be growing tired, I reflected, for he had had far more ground to cover. For myself, I felt that I could go on for ever.

That might have been the course of events but for a second sheep. Sgurr Dearg had always been noted for possessing a few sheep even on its high rocks—infernal tattered outlaws, strays originally from some decent flock, but now to all intents a new species, unclassified by science. How they lived and bred I knew not, but there was a legend of many a good stalk ruined by their diabolical cunning. I heard something between a snort and a whistle behind me, and, screwing my head round, saw one of these confounded animals poised on a rock and looking in my direction. It could see me perfectly, too, for on that side I had no cover.

I lay like a mouse watching Medina. He was about half a mile off, almost on the top of the corrie, and he had halted for a rest and a spy. I prayed fervently that he would not see the sheep.

He heard it. The brute started its whistling and coughing, and a novice could have seen that it suspected something, and knew where that something was. I observed him get his glass on my lair, though from the place where he was he could see nothing but rushes. Then he seemed to make up his mind and suddenly disappeared from view.

I knew what he was after. He had dropped into a scaur, which would take him to the skyline and enable him to come down on me from above, while he himself would be safe from my observation.

There was nothing to do but to clear out. The spur dropping to the Reascuill seemed to give me the best chance, so I started off, crouching and crawling, to get round the nose of it and on to the steep glen-ward face. It was a miserable job till I had turned the corner, for I expected every moment a bullet in my back. Nothing happened, however, and soon I was slithering down awesome slabs on to insecure ledges of heather. I am a fairly experienced mountaineer, and a lover of rock, but I dislike vegetation mixed up with a climb, and I had too much of it now. There was, perhaps, a thousand feet of that spur, and I think I must hold the speed record for its descent. Scratched, bruised, and breathless, I came to anchor on a bed of screes, with the infant Reascuill tumbling below me, and beyond it, a quarter of a mile off, the black cliffs of the Pinnacle Ridge.

But what was my next step to be? The position was reversed. Medina was above me with a rifle, and my own weapon was useless. He must find out the road I had taken and would be after me like a flame. . . . It was no good going down the glen; in the open ground he would get the chance of twenty shots. It was no good sticking to the spur or the adjacent ridge, for the cover was bad. I could not hide for long in the corrie. . . . Then I looked towards the Pinnacle Ridge and considered that, once I got into those dark couloirs, I might be safe. The Psalmist had turned to the hills for his help—I had better look to the rocks.

I had a quarter of a mile of open to cross, and a good deal more if I was to reach the ridge at a point easy of ascent. There were chimneys in front of me, deep black gashes, but my recollection of them was that they had looked horribly difficult, and had been plentifully supplied with overhangs. Supposing I got into one of them and stuck. Media would have me safe enough. . . . But I couldn't wait to think. With an ugly cold feeling in my inside I got into the ravine of the burn, and had a long drink from a pool. Then I started downstream, keeping close to the right-hand bank, which mercifully was high and dotted with rowan saplings. And as I went I was always turning my head to see behind and above me what I feared.

I think Medina, who of course did not know about my rifle, may have suspected a trap, for he came on slowly, and when I caught sight of him it was not on the spur I had descended, but farther up the corrie. Two things I now realized. One was that I could not make the easy end of the Pinnacle Ridge without exposing myself on some particularly bare ground. The other was that to my left in the Ridge was a deep gully which looked unclimbable. Moreover, the foot of that gully was not a hundred yards from the burn, and the mouth was so deep that a man would find shelter as soon as he entered it.

For the moment I could not see Medina, and I don't think he had yet caught sight of me. There was a trickle of water coming down from the gully to the burn, and that gave me an apology for cover. I ground my nose into the flower-moss and let the water trickle down my neck, as I squirmed my way up, praying hard that my enemy's eyes might be sealed.

I think I had got about half-way, when a turn gave me a view of the corrie, and there was Medina halted and looking towards me. By the mercy of Providence my boots were out of sight, and my head a little lower than my shoulders, so that I suppose among the sand and gravel and rushes I must have been hard to detect. Had he used his telescope I think he must have spotted me, though I am not certain. I saw him staring. I saw him half-raise his rifle to his shoulder, while I heard my heart thump. Then he lowered his weapon, and moved out of sight.

Two minutes later I was inside the gully.

The place ran in like a cave with a sandy floor, and then came a steep pitch of rock, while the sides narrowed into a chimney. This was not very difficult. I swung myself up into the second storey, and found that the cleft was so deep that the black wall was about three yards from the opening, so that I climbed in almost complete darkness and in perfect safety from view. This went on for about fifty feet, and then, after a rather awkward chockstone, I came to a fork. The branch on the left looked hopeless, while that on the right seemed to offer some chances. But I stopped to consider, for I remembered something.

I remembered that this was the chimney which I had prospected three weeks before when I climbed the Pinnacle Ridge. I had prospected it from above, and had come to the conclusion that, while the left fork *might* be climbed, the right was impossible or nearly so, for, modestly as it began, it ran out into a fearsome crack on the face of the cliff, and did not become a chimney again till after a hundred feet of unclimbable rotten granite.

So I tried the left fork, which looked horribly unpromising. The first trouble was a chockstone, which I managed to climb round, and then the confounded thing widened and became perpendicular. I remembered that I had believed a way could be found by taking to the right-hand face, and in the excitement of the climb I forgot all precautions. It simply did not occur to me that this face route might bring me in sight of eyes which at all costs I must avoid.

It was not an easy business, for there was an extreme poverty of decent holds. But I have done worse pitches in my time, and had I not had a rifle to carry (I had no sling), might have thought less of it. Very soon I was past the worst, and saw my way to returning to the chimney, which had once more become reasonable. I stopped for a second to prospect the route, with my foot on a sound ledge, my right elbow crooked round a jag of rock, and my left hand, which held the rifle, stretched out so that my fingers could test the soundness of a certain handhold.

Suddenly I felt the power go out of those fingers. The stone seemed to crumble and splinters flew into my eye. There was a crashing of echoes, which drowned the noise of my rifle as it clattered down the precipice. I remember looking at my hand spread-eagled against the rock, and wondering why it looked so strange.

The light was just beginning to fail, so it must have been about half-past seven.

IV

7.30 P.M. AND ONWARDS

Had anything of the sort happened to me during an ordinary climb I should beyond doubt have lost my footing with the shock and fallen. But, being pursued, I suppose my nerves were keyed to a perpetual expectancy, and I did not slip. The fear of a second bullet saved my life. In a trice I was back in the chimney, and the second bullet spent itself harmlessly on the granite.

Mercifully it was now easier going—honest knee-and-back work, which I could manage in spite of my shattered fingers. I climbed feverishly with a cold sweat on my brow, but every muscle was in order, and I knew I would make no mistake. The chimney was deep, and a ledge of rock hid me from the enemy below. . . . Presently I squeezed through a gap, swung myself up with my right hand and my knees to a shelf, and saw that the difficulties were over. A shallow gully, filled with screes, led up to the crest of the ridge. It was the place from which I had looked down three weeks before.

I examined my left hand, which was in a horrid mess. The top of my thumb was blown off, and the two top joints of my middle and third fingers were smashed to pulp. I felt no pain in them, though they were dripping blood, but I had a queer numbness in my left shoulder. I managed to bind the hand up in a handkerchief, where it made a gory bundle. Then I tried to collect my wits.

Medina was coming up the chimney after me. He knew I had no rifle. He was, as I had heard, an expert cragsman, and he was the younger man by at least ten years. My first thought was to make for the upper part of the Pinnacle Ridge, and try to hide or to elude him somehow till the darkness. But he could follow me in the transparent northern night, and I must soon weaken from loss of blood. I could not hope to put sufficient distance between us for safety, and he had his deadly rifle. Somewhere in the night or in the dawning he would get me. No, I must stay and fight it out.

Could I hold the chimney? I had no weapon but stones, but I might be able to prevent a man ascending by those intricate rocks. In the chimney, at any rate, there was cover, and he could not use his rifle. . . . But would he try the chimney? Why should he not go round by the lower slopes of the Pinnacle Ridge and come on me from above?

It was the dread of his bullets that decided me. My one passionate longing was for cover. I might get him in a place where his rifle was useless and I had a chance to use my greater muscular strength. I did not care what happened to me provided I got my hands on him. Behind all my fear and confusion and pain there was now a cold fury of rage.

So I slipped back into the chimney and descended it to where it turned slightly to the left past a nose of rock. Here I had cover, and could peer down into the darkening deeps of the great couloir.

A purple haze filled the corrie, and the Machray tops were like dull amethysts. The sky was a cloudy blue sprinkled with stars, and mingled with the last flush of sunset was the first tide of the afterglow. . . . At first all was quiet in the gully. I heard a faint trickle of stones which are always falling in such a place, and once the croak of a hungry raven. . . . Was my enemy there? Did he know of the easier route up the Pinnacle Ridge? Would he not assume that if I could climb the cleft he could follow, and would he feel any dread of a man with no gun and a shattered hand?

Then from far below came a sound I recognized—iron hobnails on rock. I began to collect loose stones, and made a little pile of such ammunition beside me. . . . I realized that Medina had begun the ascent of the lower pitches. Every breach in the stillness was perfectly clear—the steady scraping in the chimney, the fall of a fragment of rock as he surmounted the lower chockstone, the scraping again as he was forced out on to the containing wall. The light must have been poor, but the road was plain. Of course I saw nothing of him, for a bulge prevented me, but my ears told me the story. Then there was silence. I realized that he had come to the place where the chimney forked.

I had my stones ready, for I hoped to get him when he was driven out on the face at the overhang, the spot where I had been when he fired.

The sounds began again, and I waited in a desperate choking calm. In a minute or two would come the crisis. I remember that the afterglow was on the Machray tops and made a pale light in the corrie below. In the cleft there was still a kind of dim twilight. Any moment I expected to see a dark thing in movement fifty feet below, which would be Medina's head.

But it did not come. The noise of scraped rock still continued, but it seemed to draw no nearer. Then I realized that I had misjudged the situation. Medina had taken the right-hand fork. He was bound to, unless he had made, like me, an earlier reconnaissance. My route in the half-light must have looked starkly impossible.

The odds were now on my side. No man in the fast-gathering darkness could hope to climb the cliff face and rejoin that chimney after its interruption. He would go on till he stuck—and then it would not be too easy to get back. I reascended my own cleft, for I had a notion that I might traverse across the space between the two forks, and find a vantage point for a view.

Very slowly and painfully, for my left arm was beginning to burn like fire and my left shoulder and neck to feel strangely paralysed, I wriggled across the steep face till I found a sort of *gendarme* of rock, beyond which the cliff fell smoothly to the lip of the other fork. The great gully below was now a pit of darkness but the afterglow still lingered on this upper section, and I saw clearly where Medina's chimney lay, where it narrowed and where it ran out. I fixed myself so as to prevent myself falling, for I feared I was becoming light-headed. Then I remembered Angus's rope, got it unrolled, took a coil round my waist, and made a hitch over the *gendarme*.

There was a smothered cry from below, and suddenly came the ring of metal on stone, and then a clatter of something falling. I knew what it meant. Medina's rifle had gone the way of mine and lay now among the boulders at the chimney foot. At last we stood on equal terms, and, befogged as my mind was, I saw that nothing now could stand between us and a settlement.

It seemed to me that I saw something moving in the half-light. If it was Medina, he had left the chimney and was trying the face. That way I knew there was no hope. He would be forced back, and surely would soon realize the folly of it and descend. Now that his rifle had gone my hatred had ebbed. I seemed only to be watching a fellow-mountaineer in a quandary.

He could not have been forty feet from me, for I heard his quick breathing. He was striving hard for holds, and the rock must have been rotten, for there was a continuous dropping of fragments, and once a considerable boulder hurtled down the couloir.

"Go back, man," I cried instinctively. "Back to the chimney. You can't get farther that way."

I suppose he heard me, for he made a more violent effort, and I thought I could see him sprawl at a foothold which he missed, and then swing out on his hands. He was evidently weakening, for I heard a sob of weariness. If he could not regain the chimney, there was three hundred feet of a fall to the boulders at the foot.

"Medina," I yelled. "I've got a rope. I'm going to send it down to you. Get your arm in the loop."

I made a noose at the end with my teeth and my right hand, working with a maniac's fury.

"I'll fling it straight out," I cried. "Catch it when it falls to you."

My cast was good enough, but he let it pass, and the rope dangled down into the abyss.

"Oh, damn it, man," I roared, "you can trust me. We'll have it out when I get you safe. You'll break your neck if you hang there."

Again I threw, and suddenly the rope tightened. He believed my word, and I think that was the greatest compliment ever paid me in all my days.

"Now you're held," I cried. "I've got a belay here. Try and climb back into the chimney."

He understood and began to move. But his arms and legs must have been numb with fatigue, for suddenly that happened which I had feared. There was a wild slipping and plunging, and then he swung out limply, missing the chimney, right on to the smooth wall of the cliff.

There was nothing for it but to haul him back. I knew Angus's ropes too well to have any confidence in them, and I had only the one good hand. The rope ran through a groove of stone which I had covered with my coat, and I hoped to work it even with a single arm by moving slowly upwards.

"I'll pull you up," I yelled, "but for God's sake give me some help. Don't hang on the rope more than you need."

My loop was a large one, and I think he had got both arms through it. He was a monstrous weight, limp and dead as a sack, for though I could feel him scraping and kicking at the cliff face, the rock was too smooth for fissures. I held the rope with my feet planted against boulders, and wrought till my muscles cracked. Inch by inch I was drawing him in, till I realized the danger.

The rope was grating on the sharp brink beyond the chimney and might at any moment be cut by a knife-edge.

"Medina"—my voice must have been like a wild animal's scream—"this is too dangerous. I'm going to let you down a bit so that you can traverse. There's a sort of ledge down there. For Heaven's sake go canny with this rope."

I slipped the belay from the *gendarme*, and hideously difficult it was. Then I moved farther down to a little platform nearer the chimney. This gave me about six extra yards.

"Now," I cried, when I had let him slip down, "a little to your left. Do you feel the ledge?"

He had found some sort of foothold, and for a moment there was a relaxation of the strain. The rope swayed to my right towards the chimney. I began to see a glimmer of hope.

"Cheer up," I cried. "Once in the chimney you're safe. Sing out when you reach it."

The answer out of the darkness was a sob. I think giddiness must have overtaken him, or that atrophy of muscle which is the peril of rock-climbing. Suddenly the rope scorched my fingers and a shock came on my middle which dragged me to the very edge of the abyss.

I still believed that I could have saved him if I had had the use of both my hands, for I could have guided the rope away from that fatal knife-edge. I knew it was hopeless, but I put every ounce of strength and will into the effort to swing it with its burden into the chimney. He gave me no help, for I think—I hope—that he was unconscious. Next second the strands had parted, and I fell back with a sound in my ears which I pray God I may never hear again—the sound of a body rebounding dully from crag to crag, and then a long soft rumbling of screes like a snowslip.

I managed to crawl the few yards to the anchorage of the *gendarme* before my senses departed. There in the morning Mary and Angus found me.